THE BLACK LIZARD
BIG
BOOK OF
BLACK
MASK
STORIES

ALSO EDITED BY OTTO PENZLER

THE BLACK LIZARD BIG BOOK OF BLACK MASK STORIES

Edited and with a foreword by

OTTO PENZLER

Introduction by

KEITH ALAN DEUTSCH

VINTAGE CRIME/BLACK LIZARD
Vintage Books
A Division of Random House, Inc.
New York

A VINTAGE CRIME/BLACK LIZARD ORIGINAL,
SEPTEMBER 2010

Library of Congress Cataloging-in-Publication Data
The Black Lizard big book of Black Mask stories / edited and with a foreword
by Otto Penzler ; introduction by Keith Alan Deutsch.
p.   cm.— (A Vintage crime/Black Lizard original)
ISBN 978-0-307-45543-7
1. Noir fiction, American.   2. Detective and mystery stories, American.
3. American fiction—20th century.   I. Penzler, Otto.   II. Black mask; a magazine.
PS648.N64B57 2010
813.'087208—dc22
2010024508

Book design by Christopher M. Zucker

Printed in the United States of America
10 9 8 7 6 5 4 3 2 1

For Michael Connelly
Whose generous friendship
can never be repaid

CONTENTS

CONTENTS

FOREWORD

THIS IS NOT THE FIRST anthology to be devoted entirely to the mystery fiction contained in the pages of *Black Mask* magazine, but I am confident that I will be accused of neither hyperbole nor immodesty when I state unequivocally that it is the biggest and most comprehensive. Indeed, apart from *The Black Lizard Big Book of Pulps,* published by Vintage in 2007 and to which this volume is a sequel of sorts, *The Black Lizard Big Book of* Black Mask *Stories* is the biggest and most comprehensive collection of pulp crime fiction ever published.

The first anthology of *Black Mask* stories, *The Hard-Boiled Omnibus* (New York: Simon & Schuster, 1946), was compiled and edited by the legendary editor Joseph T. Shaw, who was more responsible than anyone else for the elevation of the magazine to the stature it achieved during his tenure and which it still enjoys today, all these years after it ceased publication. Had he done nothing more than write to Dashiell Hammett to encourage him to produce a detective story for the magazine, Shaw would still have gone down in the history of the American mystery story as one of its handful of most significant and influential figures. This groundbreaking book was subtitled "Early Stories from *Black Mask*" and contained fifteen stories by many of the stalwarts who regularly contributed to the magazine, eleven of whom are also in these pages, though not with the same stories. While the remaining four authors had some historical interest, the fact that they have gone on to be largely forgotten

today is not pure happenstance. Few readers of this current volume will lament the absence of J. J. des Ormeaux, Reuben Jennings Shay, and Ed Lybeck; the fourth, the excellent Roger Torrey, failed to be included only because I reluctantly had to accept the fact that even the thickest book in the store has a finite number of pages. Perhaps it is a greater surprise to note the absence in Shaw's compilation of some of *Black Mask*'s most beloved authors, including Erle Stanley Gardner, Carroll John Daly, Frederick Nebel, and Cornell Woolrich.

A quarter of a century after the magazine went out of business, Herbert Ruhm edited a paperback original, *The Hard-Boiled Detective* (New York: Vintage, 1977), that contained fourteen stories. Again, most of those authors are represented on the pages of this book, with only three failing to make the cut: William Brandon, Paul W. Fairman, and Curt Hamlin. Strangely, the greatest of all suspense writers, Cornell Woolrich, was also omitted from this otherwise exemplary anthology, as were Horace McCoy (absent from Shaw as well) and Raoul Whitfield (represented twice in Shaw's book, the only author so honored, both under his own name and as Ramon Decolta).

Seven years later, William F. Nolan, a pulp fiction expert and a talented writer of stories and novels in his own right, compiled *The Black Mask Boys* (New York: William Morrow, 1984). Subtitled *Masters in the Hard-Boiled School of Detective Fiction,* this handsome volume contained a mere eight stories but managed to nail most of the big names (Chandler, Daly, Gardner, Hammett, McCoy, Nebel, Whitfield), all of whom are included in the present volume. As is Woolrich, who once again was omitted from the otherwise stellar lineup.

The biggest names in the crime fiction pulp world were all published by *Black Mask,* and it should be noted that they didn't become names because of expensive advertising campaigns or because of the excesses of their private lives. They achieved it the old-fashioned way—by putting to work the genius with which they were blessed, producing much of the greatest hard-boiled fiction ever written.

If you are an aficionado of this type of literature, as most serious readers of fiction are, you will have noticed that so many stories, even by the best pulp writers, are virtually impossible to find. Copies of the original *Black Mask* magazines turn up in used bookstores and on eBay from time to time, with the early issues commanding prices in the hundreds of dollars. They are so rare that only two (and a rumored third) complete collections of *Black Mask* exist; one is at the Library of Congress and the other is in the hands of a private collector. The Special Collections department of UCLA has a superb collection and the good people who are involved in its day-to-day activities, notably Octavio Olvera, have been enormously helpful and generous in making these elusive stories available, and my sincere thanks go out to them. Likewise, Clark W. Evans and Margaret Kieckhefer at the Library of Congress have disproved the notion that all government agencies are inefficient and unfriendly. Thanks to them for filling gaps with copies of some of the most impossibly rare issues.

Finally, a note of appreciation to Keith Alan Deutsch, who wrote the introduction to this monumental collection and who owns the *Black Mask* magazine name and a huge percentage of the material that appeared in it. It should be self-evident that this collection would have been impossible without his encouragement and cooperation, but, beyond the obvious, he has been unfailingly honorable and courteous in all the dealings I've had with him, making the compilation of this wonderful addition to the literature of vintage crime fiction a delightful experience, rather than an onerous chore.

—OTTO PENZLER

INTRODUCTION

Keith Alan Deutsch

THIS PANORAMIC COLLECTION OF stories and novels from *Black Mask* magazine (1920 to 1951) is the most comprehensive presentation of the hard-boiled tradition of writing ever published from this great magazine. I believe this is a significant publishing event because *Black Mask* introduced the hard-boiled detective, and a new style of narration, to American literature.

In many ways, *Black Mask* took the nineteenth-century American Western tale of outlaws and vigilante justice from its home on the range in dime novels, and transplanted that mythic tale to the crooked streets of America's emerging twentieth-century cities. It introduced a new landscape for both American adventures of justice and also a new kind of narration told with the vernacular language of the streets, and featuring new urban villains, and urban (if not always urbane) heroes for the mystery story.

The first hard-boiled detectives were men of the city, all: Carroll John Daly's Three Gun Terry and Race Williams appeared primarily on the wild streets of New York, talking wise and walking that eternal tough-guy-detective line between the law and the outlaw. The first great detective narrator of the new hard-boiled fiction, Dashiell Hammett's professional lawman, the Continental Op (the first Op tale is included in this collection), operated famously in San Francisco, as did Hammett's iconic detective, Sam Spade.

Surprisingly, soon after the publication of *The Maltese Falcon*, Gertrude Stein declared Hammett, not Hemingway, the originator of the modern American, declarative, narrative sentence.

Arguably the greatest stylist of the hard-boiled genre, Raymond Chandler, observed such a fully realized and corrupting Los Angeles landscape in his poetic vision of the *Black Mask* detective tale that his writing has become the literary standard for all twentieth-century narratives of that city, or of any other American city.

All of this said, I do not mean to imply that the hard-boiled *Black Mask* detective always operated in a big city.

Race Williams's first appearance in the magazine in 1923, "Knights of the Open Palm," took place in a Southern, rural setting, and featured the KKK for *Black Mask*'s all-KKK issue (!). In 1925, Hammett's San Francisco Op headed out to Arizona for what was billed by *Black Mask* editors as "a Western detective novelette" in the story "Corkscrew." This tale, by the way, might be considered a warm-up for what I consider to be the Op's finest novel, *Red Harvest*, a kind of Western-town gang showdown that inspired Akira Kurosawa's film *Yojimbo* and the Sergio Leone Man with No Name series of Western films.

In this regard, it should be noted that through the 1920s and 1930s *Black Mask* continued to feature Western adventure tales, often mixed with hard-boiled detective elements, notably in Erle Stanley Gardner's seven Black Barr bandit stories, Nels Leroy Jorgensen's thirty-two (!) gambling Black Burton tales, and in Horace

McCoy's thirteen Jerry Frost of the Texas Air Rangers border mysteries.

Also of note for his decidedly screwball Southern gothic tales of logical detection is Merle Constiner's Memphis-based Luther McGavock, whose eleven oddball adventures all take place in the most rural of settings, and are often filled with local country vernacular and regional folkways.

The new urban mythology of the hard-boiled American hero, with his streetwise language and tough and often dark vision of a corrupt society, immediately influenced the popular American entertainments of radio and silent film. As early as the October 1922 issue of *Black Mask*, the incipient playwright Robert E. Sherwood began a movie review column, "Film Thrillers."

After 1926, when Joseph Shaw took over editing chores, he regularly pitched and sold stories and plots from his favorite contributors for screen adaptation to the emerging Warner Bros. studio.

Both the hard-boiled and the noir genres invented in *Black Mask* by writers who wrote for the magazine and later wrote for radio and film in the 1930s and 1940s, and finally for television in the 1950s, still inform many of the genres that dominate entertainment in all our modern, digital media, from computer games to global film franchises.

Every period from the magazine's influential history is represented in this definitive anthology. All but a few historically significant stories of the more than fifty tales in the collection have never been reprinted before.

One story, "Luck," by Lester Dent, is an unpublished discovery of some note: a completely rewritten version of Dent's often anthologized and much praised classic tale "Sail," which is introduced for the first time in this volume thanks to the help of Will Murray and Dent's estate.

Also newsworthy is the first book publication of two major *Black Mask* novels in their original serialized format with Arthur Rodman Bowker's magnificent illustrated headings, and all the original editorial comments to each segment.

The iconic *The Maltese Falcon* by Dashiell Hammett and the long-lost *Rainbow Murders* by Raoul Whitfield are alone worth the price of admission to this generous collection.

Included also are many of the most popular series characters that were featured over the years: Sam Spade, the Continental Op, Race Williams, Mike Shayne, Flashgun Casey, Bill Lennox (Hollywood Troubleshooter), Oliver Quade (the Human Encyclopedia), Ed Jenkins (the Phantom Crook), Jo Gar (the Little Island Detective), Jerry Frost of the Texas Air Rangers, Kennedy and MacBride of Richmond City, and Raymond Chandler's precursor to Philip Marlowe.

Also in the lineup, most for the first time in any book, are less well-known recurring characters who in their time were an important mainstay of the magazine's identity, and who still retain their original charm: *Black Mask*'s first series character, Ray Cummings's "honest" underworld rogue Timothy McGuirk, who starred in fourteen tales from 1922 to 1926; the first of D. L. Champion's twenty-six funny tales starring Rex Sackler; Dale Clark's house dick O'Hanna appeared in twenty-eight stories; the first of Julius Long's seventeen Ben Corbett tales; one of seven Cellini Smith mysteries by Robert Reeves (typically titled "Blood, Sweat and Biers" by Ken S. White, *Black Mask*'s editor in the 1940s); one of nine "Special Squad" stories by Stewart Sterling that each feature an expert division of the New York Police Department; and one of Theodore A. Tinsley's twenty-five tales starring the wisecracking newspaper columnist Jerry Tracy.

These series characters provided continuity to the run of the magazine issues, and helped maintain reader interest. When featured on the cover, Race Williams, Ed Jenkins, or the Continental Op could increase newsstand sales by ten percent or more.

Speaking of popularity, it should be noted that *Black Mask* quite early on developed a deserved reputation for attracting the most distinguished and respected thinkers and writers among its readership.

As I have already said, Gertrude Stein loved hard-boiled detective fiction, "and how it moves along and Dashiell Hammett was all that and more." Other intellectuals living in France praised Hammett for his moral ambiguity and how all the characters try to deceive one another, including those siren women, but Stein went further and called this Hammett kind of detective story "the only really modern novel form."

Similarly, Ludwig Wittgenstein, the great twentieth-century Cambridge University philosopher, loved hard-boiled detective stories, but, unlike Gertrude Stein, he favored *Black Mask*'s inimitably wry Norbert Davis, with whom he tried to correspond unsuccessfully. Wittgenstein raved to friends about Davis's first novel, *Mouse in the Mountain* (1943). He said hard-boiled detective stories were like "fresh air" compared to "stuffy" English mystery tales. When these hard-boiled detective stories became hard to get during World War II, he wrote: "If the United States won't give us detective mags, we can't give them philosophy, and America will be the loser in the end."

No less a critic than Raymond Chandler also favored Norbert Davis's *Black Mask* fiction. He even studied Davis's early stories while practicing to write his own first detective tale. Despite Davis's penchant for humor, Chandler considered Davis's work to be "noteworthy and characteristic of the most vigorous days" of *Black Mask*.

Even before Hammett's first novels were published as books in 1929, and certainly by the time *The Maltese Falcon* ran in the magazine in 1929 and 1930, *Black Mask* was being read and discussed by notable readers around the world.

In an interview with editor Joseph Shaw in *Author & Composer* magazine in August 1932, Ed Bodin (a pulp fiction agent of the time) mentions that *Black Mask* is read in the White House.

By February of 1934, in *Writer's Review*, in an article called "Are Pulp Readers Kid-Minded?" Joseph Shaw is quoted as "receiving letters from the most intelligent people in the country," and reporting "President Roosevelt, J. P. Morgan and Herbert Hoover read *Black Mask* for relaxation."

In Philadelphia, as a graduate student on a tour of their late residence (now a museum), I discovered that Philip Rosenbach and his younger brother Dr. A. S. W. Rosenbach, the preeminent dealers of rare books, manuscripts, and decorative arts during the first half of the twentieth century, were, from early in its run, *Black Mask* subscribers and collectors.

More than any other pulp fiction magazine, *Black Mask* was recognized for the quality and for the cultural significance of its writing. With the growing literary reputations of Hammett and Chandler, now generally accepted as major American writers of the twentieth century, *Black Mask*'s cultural significance continues to grow.

A PERSONAL HISTORY OF *BLACK MASK* MAGAZINE

Over the years since I first edited and produced the last newsstand issue of *Black Mask* magazine in 1974, I have been asked many times to tell how I acquired the rights to this famous magazine. Because the history of *Black Mask* is intimately entangled in the history of fiction magazines in America, I will tell my personal history of *Black Mask* against an idiosyncratic history of American magazine publishing.

The first great magazine person I met was Adrian Lopez. He was my publisher for *Black Mask*, and I remember with great fondness the hours I spent at his side listening to stories about magazine history. Starting in the 1940s, Adrian published magazines for over sixty years, including *Sir, True, Laff, Real Crime, Surfing,* and *Lady's Circle*. He had been a newspaper reporter and a pulp fiction author in the 1930s. He told me he had written for *Black Mask, Dime Detective, Argosy,* and many other pulps, but I have been able to confirm that he wrote under his own name only for *Gangster Stories*.

One of the first lessons of pulp magazine publishing is that much information has been left off the magazines' mastheads and contents pages. One of the most perplexing problems facing a pulp fiction historian is the endless and confusing array of pseudonyms and house names behind which authors hide.

As a matter of fact, both Dashiell Hammett and Erle Stanley Gardner made their first appearances in *Black Mask* in the early 1920s under pseudonyms Peter Collinson and Charles M. Green, respectively. In the early 1930s, Raoul Whitfield often appeared twice in a single issue of *Black Mask*, once under his own name and once as Ramon Decolta, under which all his famous Jo Gar stories appeared. Many pulps had house names that were used by any writer as needed whenever he had already contributed a story to an issue. But not *Black Mask*. Very few writers appeared twice in one issue of *Black Mask* under any name. An exception I discovered is the tale "Long Live the Dead," by Allen Beck. It was actually written by Hugh B. Cave, but "Smoke Gets in Your Eyes," which is included in this collection, also appeared in that same December 1938 issue of *Black Mask*, and the editors gave Hugh a pen name for that one issue. Even E. R. Hagemann, who compiled the meticulous index of record *A Comprehensive Index to* Black Mask, *1920–1951* (Popular Press, Bowling Green, Ohio, 1981), missed that pseudonym.

Few writers kept records of all their pen names, which makes setting the record straight difficult. Prentice Winchell, who wrote famously for *Black Mask* as Stewart Sterling, was kind enough to send me a long list of his pen names in the early 1970s. Hugh B. Cave kept meticulous records, and I have published a partial bibliography of his writings and pseudonyms in *Long Live the Dead* (Crippen & Landru, Norfolk, Virginia, 2000). But this kind of magazine detective work is always hit-and-miss.

I was lucky exploring and detecting the past of magazine publishing, and especially the history of *Black Mask*. When I suggested to Adrian Lopez that we bring back *Black Mask* in 1973, he was excited. Not only did he like the idea; he knew the man who could help us. His good friend David Geller had acquired Popular Publications, Inc., then the current owner of *Black Mask*, and forty or so other pulp magazines. None were being published. World War II and the rise of paperback books had killed them all.

That David Geller, who was a magazine advertising man and never a magazine editor or publisher, ended up as the proprietor of a treasure chest of famous pulp fiction titles, and hundreds of thousands of intellectual property rights in stories and art in which he had little interest, reveals something about the power and the vulnerability of advertising in the cultural history of twentieth-century magazine publishing.

As Adrian Lopez explained it to me, people like Geller placed direct-mail-order advertisements in magazines, and these direct-mail pitches were often more successful commercial enterprises than publishing the magazines themselves. Geller was one of the best advertising placement men, representing himself and other advertisers, and, as magazines began to fail, he found it profitable to take them over from desperate publishers in order to maintain these publications just for the advertising revenue. Magazines that were losing money on subscriptions and newsstand sales could still be profitable. David Geller Associates is still a major player in direct-response magazine advertising and today represents a monthly marketplace of over 200 million readers.

And so, with Geller's backing, I soon found myself at the editorial offices of Popular Publications, seeking magazine mysteries deep in the complete run of the original bound publisher's volumes of *Black Mask*. When I visited Popular in 1973, it had been reduced from one of the greatest pulp fiction houses of all time to primarily the publisher of *Argosy*, then a large-circulation general-interest magazine that featured factual articles and popular fiction starring famous characters like James Bond, Shane, and Captain Horatio Hornblower.

Argosy had been the very first pulp fiction magazine, started in the 1890s by Frank A. Munsey, whose company went on to produce myriad classic pulp fiction magazines. In 1942, Popular Publications, under the guidance of its founder, Henry Steeger, acquired all the Frank

A. Munsey Co. pulp titles. Two years earlier, Steeger had acquired *Black Mask*, which he considered the jewel of the pulps, from *Black Mask*'s original publisher, Pro-Distributors Publishing Company, Inc.

The name of *Black Mask*'s original publisher is significant, and has been overlooked by many historians. In the first decades of the twentieth century, as pulp fiction and slick magazines became designed commodities sold in the national marketplace as impulse items, the national distribution network grew in importance. Like newspaper distribution on a local city scale, magazine distribution was a tough business on a regional and national scale, and winning good display space could be a battle.

Much has been made of H. L. Mencken's role as the originating publisher of *Black Mask*. Despite his assertions of original ownership, nowhere on any masthead does Mr. Mencken's name appear, nor does his alleged initiating partner George Jean Nathan's. Although *Black Mask*'s address in the first issue is given as 25 West 45th Street in New York, the same as *Smart Set,* which was edited by Mencken and Nathan, *Smart Set* was published and owned by Eltinge F. "Pop" Warner and Eugene F. Crowe. "Pop" Warner also owned Pro-Distributors Publishing Company.

I could never find a chain of title that indicated that ownership in *Black Mask,* or Pro-Distributors, went back to Mencken. That doesn't mean I do not find his statements credible. In fact, given his stated distaste for the early issues, and the rather lackluster editing done by F. M. Osborne, a woman also on the staff of *Smart Set,* I believe Mencken did help start up *Black Mask.* What is certain is that Pro-Distributors Publishing Company, Inc., was the publisher of record from 1920 until 1940, when Henry Steeger acquired *Black Mask* for Popular Publications.

Eltinge "Pop" Warner, who is usually overlooked by commentators, must be given some credit for the success of *Black Mask.* Warner acquired *Field & Stream* magazine from its founders in 1906 and ran that publication so successfully that it is now one of the oldest continuously published magazines in America, and still going strong with an estimated 10 million circulation! Warner had a sure hand as a publisher.

As an aspiring publisher myself, I took about three months to study *Black Mask* in preparation for assembling my first issue. The formative issues of the magazine, from 1922 to 1924, after George W. Sutton Jr. took over as editor, with H. C. North as assistant editor, contain letters by Dashiell Hammett describing his life and professional experiences, and his struggles to improve his writing. There is a vibrant dialogue between editors, readers, and writers of the new fiction. And once the original illustrated headings and illustrated capital initials by that genius of dry brush Arthur Rodman Bowker were added to the mix, the magazine soared.

I was struck by the power of these illustrations, and also by the dynamic way in which these original early editors introduced the stories in their headings and in editorial comments, and in response to letters written by the contributors. Sutton and North, and later Phil Cody, were interesting and intelligent editors, setting trends before the advent of the more famous Joseph Shaw.

Popular Publications was a valuable place for me to study, filled with thousands of issues of perfectly maintained pulp magazine issues of every genre imaginable. I became interested in the magazine publishing context in which *Black Mask* hit its stride in the late 1920s and through the 1930s. I also studied the bound volumes through the 1940s, when Popular Publications took over *Black Mask.*

I discovered that Henry Steeger, once Popular's creative publisher, now had a small office in the Graybar Building near Grand Central Station. When I told Mr. Steeger I was preparing to edit and produce a new newsstand issue of *Black Mask,* he invited me over to talk and we became great magazine friends. Steeger had two brilliant ideas that contributed greatly to Popular's success: First, inspired by the Grand Guignol theater, which he had seen in France, Steeger created *Dime Mystery*, a new kind of pulp that, along with its later companion titles *Horror Stories* and *Terror Tales*, started the "Shudder Pulp" publishing phenomenon. Second, Steeger understood the essential marketing psychology that gave birth to the pulp fiction magazine: that readers wanted exciting entertainment reading *value*, and so Steeger decided to title most of his fiction genre magazines with a value reminder, using "Dime" in his titles: *Dime Detective, Dime Adventure, Dime Western,* and so on. He told me that his appeal to value was one of his great strategies, and led to his extraordinary publishing success. In fact, Steeger's *Dime Detective* became *Black Mask*'s only true rival in the hard-boiled detective field.

Steeger was a brilliant editor. He explained how he raised his rates to attract writers who had long been associated with *Black Mask* to his magazines, especially *Dime Detective*. After the firing of Joseph Shaw from *Black Mask* in 1936, Steeger was able to attract even more famous *Black Mask* writers to his magazines. Raymond Chandler was probably his greatest catch. But Steeger also started increasing the number of series characters in *Dime Detective* so writers would have a steady venue to place heroes in the magazine who became familiar. And Steeger demanded that these new characters be exclusive to *Dime Detective*. Once he acquired *Black Mask* in 1940, he could use all his techniques on both of his hard-boiled magazines.

Like Munsey, Steeger was a magazine genius in his own right. In 1943, one year after he acquired *Argosy* from Munsey, Steeger changed the publication to a slick magazine. As an editor and a publisher, Steeger had innovative vision. He saw that the pulp market was fading in the 1940s. By the beginning of the 1950s, when *Black Mask* and most pulps had stopped publishing, Steeger had evolved *Argosy* into one of the largest-circulation general-interest magazines in the country. He was now making a fortune on advertising—something a slick could do more easily than a rough paper pulp. By the early

1950s, a single color page of advertising sold for over $5,000 in *Argosy*. And so when David Geller became interested in *Argosy* as a major advertising medium for both direct response and display advertising, Steeger sold all of his interest in Popular.

In the early 1970s, when I interviewed Steeger, I noted that general interest magazines were fading. Under David Geller's editors, *Argosy* was losing its luster, it seemed to me. Steeger remained confident, and told me that if he were editing it he could attract a massive circulation again.

At some point in my *Black Mask* preparations, I remembered that I had seen *Black Mask* on the masthead of *Ellery Queen's Mystery Magazine*, a publication started by one-half of the Ellery Queen writing team, Fred Dannay. *EQMM* was started in the 1940s as the pulps were fading. Carefully and beautifully edited, it was a success and continues to this day. Dannay had been a friend of Dashiell Hammett during the 1940s and 1950s and kept Hammett's *Black Mask* stories in print in a series of paperback books and in *EQMM*. Always an excellent historian of mystery and detective fiction, Dannay saw a need to keep the hard-boiled tradition alive in the more sedate pages of his magazine and decided to include *Black Mask* on his masthead, maintaining in a modest way the title and the goodwill, and also giving him a department to feature tougher, darker stories by writers like Hammett and Cornell Woolrich.

I made contact with Joel Davis, the publisher of *EQMM*, and also the son of the founder of the famous magazine publishing house Ziff-Davis. He said I needed the permission of Fred Dannay, with whom I had a number of pleasant conversations, and I negotiated the purchase of the name and goodwill of *Black Mask* magazine, which Dannay had acquired from Steeger in the early 1950s.

During this time of preparation, I had been talking to the great literary agencies that had been around during the pulp days. I spoke with Carl Brandt of Brandt & Brandt, and Lurton

Blassingame, both of whom had represented *Black Mask* contributors in the 1930s. I spent a day in Rafael DeSoto's studio interviewing a man I consider the greatest *Black Mask* cover artist of the late 1930s and 1940s. DeSoto spoke widely about other pulp cover artists, interior illustrators, editors, and publishers at many of the great pulp magazine houses. I spoke to writers, too, like Curt Siodmak, who serialized his novel *Donovan's Brain* for *Black Mask* in 1942. Curt had also scripted noir and horror films that made a lasting impact on popular entertainment, like Val Lewton's *I Walked with a Zombie* and Universal's *The Wolf Man*.

Word about my project got around. Lillian Hellman, Hammett's executrix, made contact with me through Don Congdon, an influential agent. Hellman allowed me to reprint a Hammett Continental Op story in return for certain research I had done in the *Black Mask* stacks. Helga Greene, Raymond Chandler's executrix, asked me to share my Raymond Chandler letters and information with Frank MacShane, a professor at Columbia who was writing an authorized critical biography of Chandler. Steven Marcus, another professor at Columbia, got in touch with me through Hellman. He was writing an introduction and editing a new collection of Hammett stories from *Black Mask*. It turned out that neither Marcus nor MacShane knew each other or their work on *Black Mask* fiction. I introduced them and we all met for a talk at Columbia.

I became friends with Prudence Whitfield and bought a few of her husband's stories for the magazine from her. In time she told me wonderful stories about how Hammett, evidently her lover, had written lines in Hellman's plays. Hammett and Raoul Whitfield had been friends since the early 1920s, and, when Prudence came along and married Raoul, she became one of the "hard-drinking boys." She loaned me about ten unpublished Whitfield stories to read, but asked me not to copy them, and I didn't.

Adrian Lopez decided not to continue publishing *Black Mask*, even though I had produced a second issue ready to go to press. The first issue had done well on the stands, and even garnered a spread in the *Philadelphia Inquirer* under the headline: "*Black Mask* Returns to the Newsstand." The reasons for abandoning the project are complex and no longer important. After my one issue came out, I received queries from many writers as well as Hollywood people. I continued working on *Black Mask*. I had a number of telephone conversations with James M. Cain, who wanted me to make it clear that he was not a hard-boiled writer and did not want to be lumped in with Hammett and the *Black Mask* boys. He considered his major theme one of sexual passion driving and corrupting behavior between a man and a woman in a doomed relationship.

In the late 1970s, when the Filipacchi Group (now Hachette Filipacchi Media) came to the United States from France to produce a doomed new edition of *Look* magazine, they bought Popular Publications from David Geller in order to acquire *Argosy*. Through mutual acquaintances in publishing, I met their international attorney, Didier Guérin, and after a number of talks, he made it clear that they wanted to sell a few of Popular's publications, like *Camera 35*, which was still making money, and *Railroad* magazine, which had been the first special-interest pulp magazine started by Munsey in the 1880s. Amazingly, it was still making money. They did not know what to do with the pulps. So we made a deal. They agreed that despite my ownership of the name *Black Mask* through purchase from *EQMM*, they would transfer all interest, title, and goodwill in *Black Mask*, and all the copyrights to all the fiction and all the art, to me. They also transferred certain intellectual property rights to all the original Popular Publications pulps Henry Steeger had originated, as well as all the Munsey pulps Steeger had purchased in the 1940s. This acquisition included some Street and Smith pulps Popular acquired in 1949. In exchange I gave service and other considerations to the Filipacchi Group, which had assumed the name Popular Publications International when it purchased David Geller's holdings. I also helped them sell *Railroad* magazine in return for my Popular intellectual property rights.

Since those days, I have licensed many stories from *Black Mask* for book publication. I initiated a *Black Mask* Web site, blackmaskmagazine.com, in 2000. In 2007, I licensed back to *EQMM*, now published by Dell, the right to run a *Black Mask* department. Christmas 2008 saw the first CD issue of *Black Mask Audio Magazine*, full-cast dramatizations with sound effects and music of classic *Black Mask* tales produced with Blackstone Audio. Included will be a full-length performance of *The Maltese Falcon* authorized by Dashiell Hammett's estate.

For readers interested in how the stage was set for the appearance of *Black Mask* magazine in 1920, here are a number of observations and facts about fiction magazines in America that may put my personal history in perspective.

Prior to the Civil War, magazines, like newspapers (which also published fiction), were local affairs primarily associated with cities. For example, all of the magazines that published Edgar Allan Poe's fiction during the 1830s and 1840s were sold through subscription lists and published for readers near cities like Baltimore, New York, and Philadelphia. At most, such publications had no more than three thousand subscribers.

Even Charles Dickens, whose novels were serialized in magazines and who became the first popular fiction sensation in America in the 1840s, reached only a small segment of the American population.

It was not until the American Civil War that literacy in the United States blossomed to numbers that would support a true mass market for magazine fiction. But it was the dime novel (five- and ten-cent weekly libraries of rough-paper books), and not magazines, that first found a regional, and then a national, audience for fiction during the last half of the nineteenth century.

Although it is primarily the American West that provides the mythology for most dime-novel fiction, the second-favorite theme of these first mass-market American fiction publications was crime and detection in the great cities, particularly New York. These two major themes of nineteenth-century dime-novel fiction, those that feature the American cowboy hero of the bright plains, or those that feature the American detective hero of the dark cities, became the two great streams of popular fiction and popular culture in twentieth-century America.

The longest-running American detective hero, Street and Smith's Nick Carter, got his start in an 1886 dime novel that was so popular the character was featured in a weekly dime-novel series, the *Nick Carter Library*. In 1915, it became Street and Smith's first mystery pulp, *Detective Story Magazine*. Similarly, in 1919, the dime-novel series starring the iconic hero Buffalo Bill, the *New Buffalo Bill Weekly*, became Street and Smith's first Western pulp, *Western Story Magazine*.

But it was not Street and Smith that killed the dime novel. It was a genius of American magazine publishing, Frank Andrew Munsey (1854–1925), who invented the American pulp fiction magazine and ended the reign of the crudely designed dime novel. In 1896, Munsey's *Argosy* magazine became the first true pulp, switching to an all-fiction format of 192 pages on seven-by-ten-inch untrimmed paper. With a cover price of less than half (ten cents) of more exclusive (twenty-five-cent) slick-paper magazines, circulation grew like a revelation, and by 1903 *Argosy* sold half a million copies per month.

Munsey was the first to take the new high-speed printing presses to print on inexpensive pulp paper to produce large runs of genre-fiction magazines at discounted cover prices that attracted a large working-class readership that could not afford and was not interested in the content of more expensive slick-paper magazines. Munsey also saw that large circulation could attract advertising as a major source of publishing income. The *Argosy* for December

1907 provides a wonderful history of the magazine, and of Munsey's publishing struggles, "told" by Munsey.

Modern magazines, both pulps and slicks, arose at the turn of the twentieth century as a handmaiden to technological advances in printing and marketing. Magazines could be produced as designed objects with color covers, line drawings, and half-tone images to create a graphic editorial environment to sell their content. They also became a powerful emotional and visual marketing environment to sell new brand-name products.

Along with other mass-market consumer products emerging at the beginning of the twentieth century, new national methods of distribution were developed for the widely popular pulp fiction magazines. Although subscriptions were still important, pulp magazines became impulse items, bargains of inexpensive entertainment with brightly painted, four-color covers beckoning readers at newsstands, drugstores, and other outlets all across America.

Munsey's innovation became an entire pulp magazine industry and made many publishing fortunes. Munsey established the practice of closing magazines, or changing their content, as soon as they became unprofitable. He would quickly start new ones in their place. At first his pulps like *Argosy* and *All-Story* magazine featured all types of fiction. But in 1906 he began publishing *Railroad Man's Magazine,* the first special genre pulp magazine, which featured only railroad stories. Eventually his company, and those that followed his example, produced detective, Western, love, adventure, horror, and special-interest fiction pulps of every stripe imaginable. Whatever genre sold was imitated. Pulp readers wanted escapist entertainment that was simple, fast reading, exciting, and graphically illustrated. In time there were over three hundred different shifting pulp fiction titles of all genres.

Of all the pulp fiction magazine titles collected by the Library of Congress from all issues on copyright deposit, only three titles were considered such "extremely rare and valuable" contributions to the history of American culture that they were transferred to special holding facilities in the Rare Books and Special Collections Division of the Library of Congress: *Amazing Stories, Black Mask* magazine, and *Weird Tales.*

This distinguished collection of novels, novellas, and short fiction from *Black Mask* is the best book presentation of America's most universally acclaimed pulp fiction magazine. That means many, many hours of exceptional entertainment. Enjoy!

—KEITH ALAN DEUTSCH
Roxbury, Vermont

THE BLACK LIZARD
BIG
BOOK OF
BLACK
MASK
STORIES

Come and Get It
Erle Stanley Gardner

ERLE STANLEY GARDNER (1889–1970) was born in Malden, Massachusetts, and studied law on his own; he never got a degree, but passed the bar exam in 1911, practicing law for about a decade. He made little money, so he started to write fiction, selling his first mystery to a pulp magazine in 1923. The rest, as many have said, is history. For the next decade, he published approximately 1.2 million words a year, the equivalent of a full-length novel every three weeks. It was not until 1933, however, that he wrote his first novel, *The Case of the Velvet Claws,* which introduced his incorruptible lawyer, Perry Mason, who went on to become the bestselling mystery character in American literature, with 300 million copies sold of eighty-two novels (though Mickey Spillane's Mike Hammer outsold him on a per-book basis). While just about all mystery readers have read at least one Perry Mason novel, just as they've seen at least one episode of *Perry Mason,* the television series that starred Raymond Burr for nine hugely successful years, only the most dedicated fans have seen the six motion pictures in which Mason is far more sophisticated and smooth than in the early novels, which are fairly hard-boiled. Matinee idol Warren William played Mason in *The Case of the Howling Dog* (1934), *The Case of the Curious Bride* (1935), *The Case of the Lucky Legs* (1935), and *The Case of the Velvet Claws* (1936). Ricardo Cortez starred in *The Case of the Black Cat* (1936), and Donald Woods in *The Case of the Stuttering Bishop* (1937).

"Come and Get It" stars Gardner's major pulp character, Ed Jenkins; it ran in April 1927.

Come and Get It

Erle Stanley Gardner

Ed Jenkins was warned by a crook he had once be-friended to be on his guard against a "girl with a mole," that she would lead him into deadly peril. This crook was shot the instant he left Ed's apartment. Seemingly by accident, Ed soon meets the girl with the mole. She takes him to the mysterious head of a newly organized crime trust. Ed is given a "job" to do, threatened with death if he refuses and is offered as a reward certain blackmailing papers that have been held over the head of Helen Chadwick, the one girl in his whole career for whom he seriously cares. Ed is double-crossed. He strikes back. A murder is framed against him and an ambush set wherein he is to be shot with all the evidence of guilt upon him. He narrowly escapes, and now the duel to the death is on between the "Phantom Crook" and the icy-eyed leader of the crime ring. This series of three completed episodes is the most thrilling work the popular Mr. Gardner has yet produced.

I GAZED INTO THE black muzzle of the forty-four "Squint" Dugan was holding to my face, and secretly gave him credit for being much more clever than I had anticipated. I had hardly expected to be discovered in my hiding place, least of all by Squint Dugan.

I watched the slight trembling of his hands, and listened to the yammering of his threats. Dugan is of the type that does not kill in cold blood, but has to bolster his nerves with dope, arouse his rage by a recital of his wrongs. Gradually, bit by bit, he was working up his nerve to tighten his trigger finger.

"Damn yuh, Ed Jenkins! Don't think I ain't wise to the guy that hijacked that cargo. Fifty thousand berries it was, and you lifted it, slick and clean! Just because you worked one of those Phantom Crook stunts don't mean that I ain't hep to yuh. I got the goods on yuh, an' I'm collectin' right now. I ain't alone in this thing, either; not by a hell of a lot, I ain't. There's men back of me who'll see me through, back me to the limit. . . ."

He blustered on, and I yawned.

That yawn laid the foundation for a little scheme I had in mind. Crooks of the Dugan type really have an inferiority complex. That's what makes 'em bluster so much. They're tryin' to make the other man give in, tryin' to sell themselves on the idea that they're as good as the other bird.

"Rather chilly this evening," I remarked casually, after that yawn had had a chance to soak in, and got up, calmly turned my back on the blustering crook and stirred up the fire with the poker. Apparently I didn't know he was alive.

That got him. His voice lost the blah-blah tone, and rose to almost a scream.

"Damn yuh! Can't yuh understand I'm croakin' yuh? I'm just tellin' yuh what for. I'm puttin' out your light, yuh hi-jackin' double-crossin' dude crook. You'll never see the sun rise again. . . ."

I had been holding a chunk of firewood poised over the top of the wood stove, and, without warning, I tossed it at him—not in a hurry, just easily, smoothly.

If he'd had any guts he'd have stood his ground and fired, but he didn't have the nerve. He quailed a bit before his muscles tightened his trigger finger, and that quailing was what I had counted on.

A knowledge of fencing is a fine thing, particularly for a crook, and I'd hooked the toe of that poker through the guard of his gun and jerked it out of his hand before his wrist had dropped from the blow I struck first.

"Now I'll talk," I said, as he cowered in the corner before the light that was in my eyes.

"You don't need to tell me there's been a crime trust organized. I know it. I bargained with the very head of that trust to receive certain papers in return for services rendered, and he held out on me. I can't locate him, but I do know certain members of the gang, and I'm declaring war.

"You got hi-jacked out of fifty thousand dollars' worth of hooch, and the reason you couldn't get any trace of it afterward was because it was dumped in the bay. I didn't want the hooch. I just wanted to attract somebody's attention.

"Now you go back to the man that sent you and tell him to tell the man higher up to tell the man who is at the head of this crime trust that Ed Jenkins, the Phantom Crook, is on the warpath, that until I get those papers they can't operate. I'll spoil every scheme they hatch up, ball up everything they try to pull; and if anyone harms a hair of the head of Helen Chadwick in the meantime, I'll forget my rule of never packing a gun, and start on the warpath and murder the outfit.

"Now get going!"

It was tall talk, but it was the kind of talk that gets through with men like Dugan. Those crooks had never seen me really in action, but they had heard tales from the East. A man can't be known as the Phantom Crook in a dozen states, because he can slip through the fingers of the police at will, without having something on the ball.

Squint Dugan knew that I meant what I said. He took the opportunity to go, and he didn't stand on the order of his going. I knew that my message would reach the chief of that gang, would come to the ears of the man who was so careful to keep his identity a secret from all save his most trusted lieutenants. Also I knew that I had been careless, that I had slipped in allowing them to get a line on my apartment, and that I would have to get another hideout, and be more careful when I did it.

Before Dugan was down the stairs I was working on a new disguise, planning a new place to conceal myself. It was to be a war to the bitter end, with no quarter given nor asked, and I knew it and the other side knew it. Also, I had won the first round, taken the first trick.

My disguise I slipped in a handbag—a white beard, slouch hat, shabby coat. I took a heavy cane and locked the apartment. It was a cheap joint in a poor district, and the rent was paid. I wouldn't be back.

Before I put on the disguise I took a cab to Moe Silverstein's. Moe knew every crook in the game, never forgot a face or a gem and was the smoothest double-crosser in the business.

He looked up as I entered his room on the third floor of a smelly tenement. As soon as he saw me he began to rub his hands smoothly together, as though he were washing them in oil. He was fat, flabby, bald, and he stunk of garlic. His eyes were a liquid, limpid brown, wide, innocent, hurt. He had the stare of a dying deer and a heart of concrete.

"Mine friend, ah, yes, mine friend. It is so, mine friend, Ed Jenkins, the super-crook, the one who makes the police get gray hairs, and you have something for me, friend Jenkins? Some trinket? Some bauble? Yes?"

I drew up a chair and leaned forward, over the table, my face close to Moe's, so close I could smell the gagging odor of the garlic, could see the little muscles that tightened about his eyes.

"A new crook, Moe—a girl with a mole on her left hand. She goes by the name of Maude Enders. Where can I find her?"

His eyes stayed wide, but it took a tightening of the muscles to do it. His hands stopped in their perpetual rubbing.

"For why?"

"Do you know the Weasel?"

His hands began to rub again.

"The Weasel is dead, and I remember no dead crooks. I can make no money from them. It is only the live ones who can make money for Moe Silverstein."

I nodded.

"Yes, I know all of that; but the Weasel was at my apartment just before he was killed. He came to warn me of this girl with the mole, to tell me that she would trap me; and then he was killed with the words scarcely cold on his lips—killed by crooks who had followed him in a closed car."

Again he raised his shoulders, ducked his neck and spread his palms.

"But he is dead."

"Exactly, and the woman with the mole got acquainted with me, and through her I met the man who poses as the head of the new crime trust, the new mastermind of the tenderloin. He is fat with skin that does not move and has eyes that are like chunks of ice. I want to locate the woman with the mole, and, through her, her master."

Moe stopped all motion. He became a frozen chunk of caution, poised, tense, thinking, pulled out from behind his mask.

"Why?"

"Because this man has some papers I want, papers he held out on me. I want to warn him that unless I get those papers he will die."

Actually he shrunk away from me, drew back from the table.

"I know nothing of what you speak. There is no girl with a mole in the game. This talk of a new crime trust is police propaganda for more men. You are crazy, Ed—and soon you will be dead, and then I will have to forget you, to lose another fine prospect. You could deliver much to me if you wanted to work, Ed, but you just hang out on the fringes and meddle. . . . I do not know of the people you mention, and soon you will be forgotten. Good-bye."

As I went out of the door his hands had resumed their rubbing, but his eyes had slipped; they were two narrow slits through which there came stabbing gleams of cold light. I was satisfied.

I went down the steps, doubled back, slipped down the corridor, and hid in a closet, a tight, dark, nasty-smelling closet, and waited.

An hour passed, and then there came the sound of quick, positive steps, steps that pounded down the hall with a banging of the heels, steps that paused before Moe's door.

Again I peeked.

This would probably be my man. He was broad-shouldered, red-faced, aggressive. A young fellow with lots of pep, quick, positive motions, an outthrust chin, coal-black eyes, latest model clothes and dark, bushy eyebrows. His hands were small, slight, dark, jeweled. His face was scraped, massaged, pink. There was a swagger about him, a bearing.

He vanished within the door, and Moe did not throw him out. There was the soft slur of Moe's voice, the harsh bass of the visitor's tones, and I slipped down the hall, down the stairs and out.

The sheik came out in about half an hour, looked cautiously around him, walked a block, rounded a corner and doubled abruptly back, crossed the street, waited a few minutes, and then went on about his business with no further worry about his back-track.

I followed him to the Brookfield Apartments, waited half an hour, picked him up again and followed him to the Mintner Arms, an exclusive bachelor apartment house where only men of the highest references were admitted.

Three hours later I figured he was bedded for the night, and went to a cheap hotel, adjusted my disguise in the washroom and got a room. At daylight I was back on the job in front of the Mintner Arms. My man came out at eight and went into a barber shop and got the works. At nine-thirty he took his complexion out into the open air and headed for the fashionable jewelry district.

I was at the counter in Redfern's Jewel Shoppe looking at the most expensive stones in the case when he made his spiel to old man Redfern. Five caustic comments on stones handed me had ensured the respectful silence of the clerk who was showing me the stones, and I got most of the spiel.

The sheik introduced himself as Carl Schwartz, held out his hand, grasped Redfern's and worked his arm up and down like a pump

handle, reeling out his talk in the meantime. It sounded good.

He was the representative, the special solicitor, of the Down Town Merchants' Exhibit, and they were putting on a great jewel exhibit. All of the leading stores were to be represented. Space was to be sold by the foot, the exhibitors furnishing their own clerks and their own guards. Ten policemen would be in constant charge of the crowd. Admission would be by invitation only. The Exhibit would arrange to have the invitations given to the most influential and wealthy society leaders. The Exhibit would furnish music, a free talk each day by an expert on the intrinsic value of gems, the best mountings, the methods of judging stones, the appropriate gems for each occasion, and give photographic lectures on the latest mountings from Europe. The Exhibit would furnish an armored car to take the gems and the guards from each store to the place of exhibit. The Exhibit would also furnish daily flowers for decorative purposes.

After that he let go of Redfern's hand and produced a diagram of floor space. He was a glib talker, a convincing salesman, and Redfern was falling. The jewel business was pretty quiet, and an exhibit like that would go over big, provided they could get the society women to come, and bring their check books with them.

"Now, Mr. Redfern, I don't want you to say no right now, and I don't want you to say yes. I want you to think it over, to study the diagram, to look up my references. Then, *if* I can convince you that we will absolutely have the cream of the cream there on the opening day; *if* I can get one of the society leaders to act as hostess on the opening days; *if* I can convince you that your exhibit will sell over twenty thousand dollars gross the first day, *then* will you sign up? The space runs from one hundred dollars a day to three hundred, depending on location. The first day we'll have the society leaders. We'll get a big write-up. The next day we'll let down the bars a bit, and finally we'll let in the New-Rich, the splurgers, the spenders, who'll come to get in on the social advertising, to get their pictures in the paper, and they'll buy. That'll be understood before they get the invitations."

Redfern placed a fatherly hand on the boy's shoulder.

"It can't be done, but have a cigar. Come into my private office. What are you doing for lunch? Let's look at that space chart again. . . ."

They moved off, and I waited five minutes and then got in an argument with the clerk, and stumped out of the door, pounding my cane, working my beard, a picture of white-haired indignation—one of the old boys who knew what he didn't want and wasn't going to be Smart-Alecked into buying it.

I had food for thought.

They would make money out of the exhibit alone, perhaps ten thousand dollars—perhaps not. But did they intend to make money out of the exhibit? Did they intend to get the cream of all the jewels in the city under one roof, a roof which had been especially prepared to receive them, and then make a grand haul which would take the best of every jewelry store in the city?

It would be a wonderful thing, a supercrime, and if that *was* the game there were brains and money back of it. But how could they swing it? Each store would furnish its own guard. There would be an armored truck to transport the exhibits. There would be special policemen on duty. The insurance companies would be on the job. There would be a dead-line for crooks established. There would be watchmen, spectators, guards, police, and the exhibit would be in the crowded downtown section.

Carl Schwartz made three calls that day.

The evening papers featured the new jewelry exhibit, mentioned the prominence of the social leaders who would conduct the opening, hinted that invitations were confined to those whose standing was beyond question, and that others of the outer shell were bidding high for invitations. It was a good bit of publicity.

That evening I tailed Schwartz. He was a cinch after one got to know his habits. Always at the start he took great precautions to see that he wasn't followed, and then, when he had con-vinced himself there was no one on his wind, he went simply about his business without so much as a glance at his backtrail.

At eleven he was at The Purple Cow, a cabaret and night club of the wilder sort, and there he was joined by the girl I had lost, the girl I knew as Maude Enders, the girl with the mole on her left hand. That was the break I had been looking for.

By that time I was willing to hazard a bet that the girl was living at the Brookfield Apartments. If Schwartz was in touch with her every night that would explain his visit to the Brookfield the night before.

I knew this girl as a member of the gang of Icy-Eyes, the master crook. I knew that she was a close worker, an inner lieutenant, and somewhere along the line she would report to the man himself. Was Schwartz a crook? Going to Moe Silverstein's would indicate that he was. Perhaps he was merely being played by the girl with the mole. Icy-Eyes had the girl with the mole under his thumb. There was the matter of that murder I had stumbled on. . . . Perhaps Maude Enders hadn't killed that man, but the simple facts of the case would look pretty black before a jury, and Icy-Eyes had those facts, had planted witnesses who would see and hear. Maude Enders would do as he said or . . .

I knew the girl had the eye of a hawk when it came to penetrating disguises, and I had enough of a lead for one night. I sauntered back to my hotel without hanging around The Purple Cow.

At the hotel I got a shock. The police were on my trail. I knew it even before I got in the lobby. There were too many people hanging around the front of the hotel. There was the car with the red spot-light on the right-hand side. I ducked in an alley and slipped off my disguise. I had another concealed in a little bag under my left armpit, a disguise that was good enough to fool the police.

I slipped into the lobby and listened. There was no doubt of it. The clerk was explaining volubly as he took back my room key. I got a glimpse of the number as it was hung back on the board.

"He'll probably be in any time now," said the clerk.

The flat foot who was holding him under the hypnotic stare of the police department's best glare shifted his cigar and tried to look tough.

"Give me the office when he shows up. We've a straight tip on this thing."

I sauntered over and sat in the lobby behind a palm tree and did some thinking. I hadn't been followed when I came to the hotel. My disguise would fool the police. Somewhere I had slipped. Probably there had been someone watching Schwartz, and that someone had picked me up as I took a hand in the game. After all, I was playing against a big combination, a clever combination, and they were pretty keen to have me out of the way. The police in California had nothing on me, but with my record they didn't need much. Just the faintest bit of circumstantial evidence, and they'd have me before a jury, and the jury would take one look at my past record, and the verdict would be in inside of ten minutes.

I went out, took off my disguise so that I was myself once more, and set my feet toward the Brookfield Apartments. I was just a little hot under the collar. I'd respected my immunity in California, and hadn't gone after other people's property. As a result the California police, the California crooks didn't know the real Ed Jenkins. I'd only bestirred myself when there was something in the wind, when someone had tried to frame something on me, and then, nine times out of ten, I'd handled the thing so smoothly, and kept in the background so entirely that the crook who had got his didn't know that the peculiar coincidences which had betrayed him were really engineered by the man he was trying to frame.

It wasn't difficult to get the girl with the mole located. It took ten dollars and five minutes. That mole on her left hand was a big help. She had come in alone fifteen minutes ago.

I went to her apartment, and selected a pass key before the door. It was probably a little ungentlemanly to walk into a girl's apartment that way, particularly when she might be retiring, but I couldn't very well stand in the hall and carry on a conversation through the closed door, telling the whole world the message I was going to deliver to that girl.

The second key did the trick, the lock slipped back and I was inside. The room I entered was illuminated by a silk-shaded reading lamp, furnished after the manner of furnished apartments, and filled with the odor of some subtle perfume. There was no one in the room, but there came the sound of rustling garments from a little dressing closet that opened off of the back end.

I walked in toward the light.

"Come in, Ed Jenkins, draw up a chair. I'll be with you as soon as I have my kimono on."

It was the voice of the girl with the mole, and she was in the dressing closet. She couldn't see me. How did she know who I was? It was too many for me. This gang was more confoundedly clever than I'd given it credit for, but I wouldn't show surprise.

"Take your time," I said. "You got my card?"

If she was going to act smart I'd pretend I'd sent up a card and see what that got me.

It got me a laugh, a low, rippling, throaty laugh.

"No, Ed, I didn't; but after I saw you at The Purple Cow this evening, and after you had to fit two keys to the door in order to get it open, I didn't need any card. In fact I rather expected you. The others thought you'd spend the night in jail, but I knew you better."

With that she walked out, a rose-colored kimono clinging to her youthful form, one bare arm outstretched and her soft, white hand held gracefully out.

I took the hand and raised it to my lips.

"Why the sudden deference?" she asked.

"Merely a recognition of your cleverness," I answered. "You know, Maude, I should hate to have to kill you—after all."

"Yes," she rippled, "I should hate to have you."

I bowed. "About the murder of R. C. Rupert. I happened to stumble across some witnesses, some witnesses who saw a girl with a mole running frantically down the stairs just about the time of the killing. They claim they could identify the woman if they should see her again."

Her hand went to her throat, her face white.

"Ed," she gasped, "Ed . . . It wasn't you! You didn't do that job?"

There was such genuine emotion, such horror in her tone, that I was puzzled. My whole plan of action began to dissolve into nothing.

"*I* kill him?" I said. "I never saw the man in my life. I had thought *you* killed him."

She shook her head, her eyes wide.

"I came into the apartment just after he had been struck down. In fact the blow was delivered just as I stepped inside the door. It was dark, and by the time I found a light I saw what had happened, and then I knew I had walked into a trap. For once I lost my head and dashed down the stairs, and there was that man and woman coming up, and then I knew, knew that they were there to see me as I burst from the apartment, knew that some people wanted to hold a murder charge over my head—and now when you sought to use that club I thought that it was you."

I looked her over narrowly. She was one woman I couldn't read. She might have been telling the truth, but a jury wouldn't believe her. I wasn't sure that I believed her. I had followed her that night, and she had left my apartment, gone to this flat, entered the door, and then there had been a blow and a gasping cry, the sound of a fall, and she had come tearing out. R. C. Rupert had been stabbed, and he hadn't so much as raised a hand to protect himself. There was no sign of a struggle, just the man, the knife and the blood.

And while I studied her, she studied me, studied me in just the same way, searchingly, wonderingly, seeking to penetrate to my thoughts. It was masterly acting.

I waved my hand.

"We'll forget about that, only I know where those witnesses are. It is only incidental, anyway.

"You were with me when I was taken to the head of your gang. In fact you took me there, and you saw him hand me an envelope containing papers, papers which were to be my reward for opening a safe. There were two papers missing from that collection. I played fair and earned the papers, and I got shortchanged. I want you to do this for me. Get me into the hangout of this crook who is the head of the crime trust. Let me talk with him."

She looked at me narrowly.

"Ed, I believe you'd kill him."

I looked her squarely in the eyes.

"I'll kill him if he so much as tries to use those papers."

She laughed, a rippling laugh of good-natured amusement.

"What a wonderful actor you are, Ed! You know you wouldn't, know you couldn't, and yet you almost look as though you would. The head of that crime trust, as you call it, is too well protected, protected by money, position, power, pull, and by the fact that no one knows him. In all the underworld there are only two people who can get to that man at will."

"And you are one?"

"Yes, Ed. I am one."

"And you'll take me?"

She laughed again and shook her head.

"Certainly not. You don't want me to. You're really just running a big bluff, trying to frighten that man from using those papers. Listen, Ed, it can't be done. He knows no fear—knows no mercy. He is planning to use those papers and use them he will. He can afford to ignore you because you are helpless, but you mustn't make any trouble or you will go out—like a candle."

I thought for a bit. She was lying to me, stringing me along. The man did fear me, or he wouldn't have put the police on my trail, wouldn't have sent Squint Dugan with a gun to get revenge. It hadn't been Dugan who had located my apartment. It had been a far shrewder man than the loud-mouthed killer. Why should the girl lie to me, why taunt me with my help-lessness? When a woman taunts a man with being helpless she usually gets him into a condition of blind rage. Did she want to get me so worked up that I would kill old Icy-Eyes, would shoot him down as soon as I came face to face with him? Did she plan to do that and thereby remove the man who held a murder charge over her head?

I could not tell. Women are peculiar; and she had known I was coming, had planned her story, had donned an elaborate negligee, and was sitting there beneath the silk-shaded lamp, her rose-colored kimono drawn apart, revealing a glimpse of lace, an expanse of gleaming silk hose, and was laughing at me, her bare arm toying about beneath the gleaming light, her red lips parted in a smile as she taunted me with my inability to accomplish anything definite.

I arose and bowed. Again I took her hand and raised it to my lips.

"What for this time?" she asked.

"Respect again, m'lady. You seek to have me remove a man you fear. You are clever, and I salute you for your cleverness."

Her face fell.

"Ed, *you* are clever—clever as hell."

I shrugged my shoulders.

"That is something I won't argue about; I admit it. When a woman pays me compliments I admit them and become twice as cautious as before. Here is something you can do, though. Tell this icy-eyed master crook of yours that until he has returned those papers to me his life is not safe. More, you can tell him that he can't pull a single crime of any magnitude and get away with it.

"I shall be watching the underworld, and I will balk him in any crime he tries to pull off if it's worthwhile, and if it's a small, petty crime I'll just dump enough monkey-wrenches into the machinery to throw out a gear here and there. Tell him that."

There was a strange light in her eyes, an inscrutable light.

"You mean that, Ed?"

I nodded.

For a long minute she studied my face.

"If that's the case, leave by the back entrance.

There is a car parked in front with gunmen in it. You are to be killed as you step on the sidewalk."

I could feel my face redden.

"You said I was clever," I told her, "and yet you think you have to warn me of *that*! Bah! As soon as you said that you'd rather expected me, that the 'others' had thought I'd spend the night in jail, but that you knew me better, you gave me my cue to vanish by the rear door. That showed that you had told the others about recognizing me at The Purple Cow, showed that I had been discussed, and that you had said I would probably come to call on you.

"The others thought I would spend the night in jail because they had located my hotel. When they realized that I was on guard, that I knew of their plans, knew that the police had visited my room, then they knew you were right, and they would have a closed car waiting. I appreciate the warning, but don't again tell me of the obvious."

With that I bowed my good-nights and left her, and as I stepped out into the corridor there was a gleam of admiration in her eyes as she stood there, her kimono forgotten, falling from her, her hand outstretched, her lips parted, her eyes warm with emotion. And yet she was cold. There was nothing of physical charm about her despite her wonderful figure, her flashing arms, her heaving breast, her shapely stockings. She was a girl with brains, and she admired but one thing in life—brains. There was no sex appeal about her. She was merely a reasoning machine. Her body was merely the vehicle for her brain— and she was most damnably clever.

At that I didn't take the back entrance. I went up to the top floor, and then out on to the roof. It was cold and there were wisps of fog drifting in from the ocean, leaving globules of moisture on the stucco coping of the roof. Yet I could see the street clearly. It was as she had said. There was a machine parked there, a closed car with motor running, curtains drawn.

I crossed the roof and looked down into the alley. There, beneath my very eyes, crouched in the shadow of a fence, was another man waiting, tense, expectant. Did she know he was there?

Had she warned me of the obvious peril at the front door to send me to my death at the back? I had no means of knowing, but this much I did know: I had saved my life by coming to the roof.

I stepped back to the front of the roof and watched the machine.

The fog thickened until it became a white pall. Lights from the windows of the apartments below sent out golden paths of light into the swirling moisture. The sound of the running motor was queerly muffled.

A curtain was raised. Out into the fog there shone a path of yellow light. The curtain was lowered and the light blotted out. Three times this was repeated. The light shone from the window of Maude Enders' apartment. Probably a signal to let the watchers below know that I had left. If that was so she had delayed giving it, delayed nearly ten minutes. Was she on the square after all—this girl with the mole on her left hand?

Another ten minutes passed. There came the sound of a slamming door as someone got out of the machine below, clicked across the cement sidewalk, pounded up the steps, and entered the apartment house. Five minutes later and he was back out and into the machine. There came the acceleration of the motor as the car moved away, swinging slowly down the street, around the corner, and in front of the alley.

I tiptoed around the coping, following the course of the machine, watching it as it stopped at the alley.

A man got out and walked up the alley, whistling a soft signal. The man who was crouched behind the fence answered it, and then the two moved together, joined in a whispered conference, and then both got into the machine. Once more there came the sound of the motor accelerating, and then the car whined down the block, turned into the main boulevard and was lost in the traffic.

I got back to the trap door and went down the steep steps, back down the floors until I came once more to the apartment of Maude Enders.

This time I knew the right key, and I turned the lock noiselessly.

She was sitting in her chair, her chin cupped in her hands, her luminous eyes staring out into space.

"Ed!" she exclaimed as the light fell on me.

I bowed.

"Just a final good-night, and a reminder that you mustn't forget to tell old Icy-Eyes what I said."

"Ed," she pleaded, her voice suddenly soft. "Ed, I swear I didn't know there was a watcher in the alley, didn't suspect it until after the man came up to see why you hadn't come out; and I delayed the signal for ten minutes, Ed. Honest I did!"

I grinned at her.

"Don't waste any time worrying about me, sister," I told her. "No apologies necessary. I saw your delayed signal and I just dropped in on the road out to say thanks."

Her eyes were wide this time.

"Ed, you *are* clever! . . . I can put you up here if you can stay, Ed. The streets are unsafe, and every hotel is watched."

I bowed my thanks.

"I have work to do, Maude. Thanks all the same, but the streets are never unsafe for the Phantom Crook. Good night."

Perhaps I was showing off a little, but half the pleasure of doing something clever is to have an appreciative audience, and this girl with the mole on her left hand knew clever work when she saw it. Then again, I wanted to satisfy myself that she had been on the square with that tip to pass out by the rear door.

There was a telephone in the lobby, and I phoned for a cab, and didn't step out of the front door until the cab was at the curb. It took me three cabs and half an hour to get to the place I wanted to go, the house of Helen Chadwick. I hoped I'd find her up. It was the second time I'd been there, once just before our engagement had been announced.

Helen Chadwick and her mother were of the upper, upper crust. They were in the middle of the social-elect. Helen's father had been unfortunate before he died. It was worry that killed him. Crooks held evidences of his indiscretion, and they had threatened Helen once or twice with exposure of their knowledge. It wasn't that Helen cared for herself, but there was the memory of her father, and the failing health of her mother to be considered.

Once they had forced Helen to pass me off as her husband-to-be, and we had spent a weekend at the country home of Mr. and Mrs. Loring Kemper, the leaders of the socially elect. I had got her out of that scrape safely, and when I broke the engagement with a smile, there had been tears in the girl's eyes. I had told her that I would come to her if danger threatened again. . . .

I half expected the house would be dark, but it was lit up like a church. There was a late dance going on, and shiny cars were parked all around the block, cars that had chauffeurs hunched behind the wheels, dozing, nodding, shivering.

I paid off the taxi, and skipped up the steps.

A butler answered my ring.

"Miss Chadwick," I told him crisply.

He gave me a fishy eye.

"Your card?"

"Tell her Mr. Jenkins is here, and I'll step in while you're telling her."

He gave ground doubtfully, but give it he did, and I walked on into a reception room. From the other side of the house there came shrill bursts of laughter, gruff voices, the blare of an orchestra, the tinkle of dishes.

Twenty seconds and the man was back.

"Not at home, sir. Step this way, sir."

He bowed me to the door.

As he held the front door open I took him by the collar and swung him around.

"You didn't deliver my message. Why?"

His fishy eyes glinted a cold, hostile glare of scornful enmity.

"Miss Chadwick is never at home to crooks. I recognized you from your published pictures."

I nodded.

"I was afraid so. I recognized you from having seen you with Squint Dugan. Published pictures—hell! You know me because you're a crook. On your way."

A push sent him out on the moist porch, a kick sent him the rest of the way down the stairs, the momentum skidded him across the wet sidewalk and into the gutter. Across the street a chauffeur voiced his approval by a short blast of the horn. In the darkness someone snickered. The butler got up and tried to scrape off the muddy water with the palm of his hand. His livery was a mess, and his face was smeared.

"You needn't come back," I told him. "Your references will be forwarded to you care of the warden at the Wisconsin penitentiary at Waupin. I believe you're wanted there, and I intend to see that you get there."

"What is all this?"

The remark came in a cool, impersonal voice, the sort of a voice one uses to peddlers and office boys.

I carefully closed the door and sprung the night latch. Then I turned to face the owner of that voice. She was gowned in the latest style, her bare arms and throat contrasting against the dark of her gown, her hair framing the soft curve of her oval cheek. There was a patch of rouge high on her cheeks; her lips were vivid crimson. She was a flapper, and yet there was a something else, a something of poise, of more mature responsibility about her than when I had last seen her.

"Ed!" she breathed. . . . "Ed Jenkins!"

I grinned at her. I didn't want any dramatics.

"H'lo, Helen. I just fired your butler. He was a crook, an ex-con, and he was spying on you."

There were tears in her eyes, and her face had gone white beneath the rouge, but she twisted her mouth into a smile.

"Just when I had been hoping, praying that I could get in touch with you."

I nodded.

"More trouble over those papers of your father's?"

There was no need for an answer.

"Listen, Helen. I have got all of those papers

except two. There's no need of going into details. I wasn't going to bother you by reporting, but was just going to trace those documents through the underworld, get 'em and destroy 'em. Two got away, and I had an idea you'd be bothered, so I looked you up."

"Come on in here, Ed," she said, and gave me her hand, leading the way into a small room which opened off the rear hall. "This is filled with wraps, but we can talk here for a minute. . . . Oh, how I hoped I'd see you again, Ed."

I patted her shoulder reassuringly, and she cuddled into the hollow of my arm with a little snuggly motion, as natural as though we'd been engaged for years.

"Ed, there's a man by the name of Schwartz who holds one of those papers. He showed it to me, and it's genuine, all right. He insists that I must use my influence to see that a jewelry exhibit given by the Down Town Merchants' Exhibit is a success. He wants me to have Mrs. Kemper act as hostess and sponsor for the exhibit. Otherwise he threatens to use the paper against me, and expose Father, blacken his memory, give the story to the newspapers and all the rest."

I did some rapid thinking.

"When do you get this paper?"

"As soon as Mrs. Kemper announces that she will act as hostess."

"And will she?"

A voice from the doorway answered.

"She'll do anything for Helen Chadwick. Ed, how are you? It's a pleasure to greet you once more."

I turned and looked into the smiling eyes of Edith Jewett Kemper, leader of the social world, head of the four hundred.

There was a certain wistful sadness in her face as she gave me her hand.

"Ed, you never took advantage of my invitation to come to my house for a visit. There are lots of people who would have given much for such an invitation. I like you, and my husband likes you—and Helen likes you."

I bowed again.

"Thanks. I appreciate it, but to have a crook spending the week at your house might not appear to the best of advantage in the social columns of some of the papers."

She shrugged her bare shoulders.

"The papers be damned. I have my standing sufficiently assured to do as I please."

The conversation was getting a little too personal for me. Those were my friends, and yet they didn't understand how impossible it was to maintain a friendship with a crook. I knew their sincerity, appreciated their interest, but I was a crook, a crook who was known from coast to coast. Ed Jenkins, the Phantom Crook, could have nothing in common with people such as these. The memory of a pleasant week-end, the haunting recollection of those soft eyes of Helen Chadwick's, and a sense of gratitude—those were the ties that bound me to a world that was another existence from my own life, an environment foreign to me, a something separate and apart.

"How did you know I was here?"

She grinned at that.

"I happened to be standing near the front windows, and saw the butler as he went out—down and out. I fancied that would mean Ed Jenkins was calling, and I took the liberty of intruding long enough to say that I don't like to be snubbed. You're not using me right, Ed; and then there's Helen."

I nodded.

"Yes, there's Helen," I said. "It would be a fine endorsement for her future if the papers should learn that the Edward Gordon Jenkins who was with her for a visit at the house of the Kempers was none other than Ed Jenkins, the Phantom Crook. It would surely look well in print!"

Her eyes were soft, dreamy.

"There are things more important than reputation. One should not sacrifice all life for the sake of conventions, for social standing. Social position is merely a bauble, Ed, a pretty, glittering trinket that's as cold as ice."

I could feel the clinging girl press her face against my shoulder. The party was due to get all weeps if I didn't strut my stuff and make a get-away.

"I've been thinking it over, and I want you to act as hostess for the jewel exhibit. See that Helen gets the paper, and then I'll get in touch with you later. In the meantime, I'm on my way. There's work to be done before sunrise."

I gently broke away and started for the door.

Helen stood there, motionless. Mrs. Kemper made as though she would detain me, then thought better of it.

"So long, Ed," called Helen, in a gay voice.

"Be good," I told her.

Mrs. Kemper said nothing, but her eyes were moist, and, as I rounded the corner into the hallway, I saw the two women go into a clinch.

That was over.

The cold fog of the night felt cool and welcome on my face. I was commencing to know the truth. That sense of fierce protection which had come over me as I held Helen to me, that swift pounding of the pulse when I had first heard her voice . . . I put those thoughts behind me, firmly, resolutely. I was a crook. The girl was a thoroughbred. I shook myself out of my daze. There was work to be done, a necessity that I keep my wits clear. Through the foggy night there were crooks peering at the streets, closed cars circling about, cars that were filled with armed men. All crookdom was looking for Ed Jenkins. I had warned the head of the new-formed crime trust. Too much was at stake to take chances. War had been declared and no quarter would be asked or given. Single-handed, my wits were pitted against those of an organized underworld, and the safety and happiness of a girl who had shown friendship for Ed Jenkins was at stake.

The fog cleared my brain, and I began to think, to put together the pieces of the puzzle that had been placed in my hands. There would be a few thousand profit to be made from the jewelry exhibit, but the crook who had engineered that game would not be content with a paltry few thousand. It was intended to loot the exhibit, but how?

Then there was the girl with the mole. She had given her signal ten minutes after I had departed, and then, when the man had gone to her apartment, he had called off his gang without any delay. Without enough delay. Was it possible they suspected this girl with the mole of double-crossing them as far as I was concerned?

I swung down the street until I came to an all-night drug store, summoned a taxi, and took another look at the apartment house where Maude Enders lived. One look was enough. There was a light in the girl's apartment, and a closed car before the door.

She had been summoned, this girl of mystery, this perfectly formed woman who was absolutely unconscious of any charm, who dwelt in a mental world, who thought swiftly and cleverly.

I spoke to the taxi driver and had him drive me around the block, stop at an alley and turn out the lights. From the alley I could see the light in the girl's apartment.

Three minutes and the light snapped out.

The girl with the mole came out of the front door, leaning on the arm of a man who was bundled up in a heavy overcoat, and entered the car. I didn't have to be a prophet to know that the girl was being taken to account, that she was a prisoner right then—a prisoner of the man on whose arm she was leaning, that she was being summoned to the headquarters of the crime trust.

I had almost overlooked that bet. A moment or two more and it would have been too late. I had intended to look up this Schwartz and have it out with him, but this was a better lead. It might result in almost anything.

The closed car moved off and I followed, followed in a way that made it virtually impossible to detect the car in which I was traveling, and in which a twenty-dollar bill had placed me in the driver's seat with the uniformed chauffeur as a passenger.

I cut across in back of the car, swung around a block, headed behind it again, ran a block ahead and let it pass, followed for a ways, ducked through alleys, always watching the tail-light wherever possible, detouring where I was fairly sure of my ground—and then I lost it.

The car had turned off, where? I swung around the four sides of the block, saw a tail-light down a side street, swept past and knew that I had located my quarry.

It was a flat in the better residential district, and the front was black, gloomy, respectable as became a flat-building at that hour of the night. I left the car a block away and began to cross back-yards. Somewhere a dog barked, but he was chained. Exclusive residential districts do not cater to tenants with dogs. Rapidly I adjusted the white whiskers, the steel-rimmed glasses, the wig, the touch of complexion paste which was a part of my disguise as an old man, a pasty-faced, white-haired old blusterer. It had been a good disguise, but the agents of the crime trust had penetrated it. I wore it so that they wouldn't think I knew they had discovered the secret of that disguise. I would let them think Ed Jenkins was a bit of a fool . . . until it suited my purpose to let them think otherwise.

A man guarded the back of the flat, a man who took his job none too seriously. I stooped and filled the little leather pouch—which I always carried as a pocketbook—with fine sand from the back of the yard, a sandy loam which packed hard and fast, and made a formidable weapon out of my purse.

Ten minutes of careful stalking, fifteen, and then he saw me. His hand raced to his hip, there was a swish through the air, and then he went bye-bye, without a sound, the skin hardly bruised.

I stepped over him and took one of the back windows. The kitchen was deserted. A long hall-way showed a faint light. A man sat with his back to the wall, a gun in either hand, nodding, breathing heavily, regularly. I stepped past him and paused before a door from which came the sound of voices.

Without knocking I opened the door and stepped into the room. It was furnished as an office, and a huge desk occupied the center of the floor. Upon this desk was a small, portable read-ing lamp, and the circle of its rays showed the white face of the woman with the mole, the thin, rat-like features of the man who had accompa-nied her, and whom I recognized as one of the most prominent of the criminal lawyers in the city, and showed, also, the huge bulk of the man who was sitting behind that desk.

It was that man in whom I was interested.

He was big, flabby, his skin dead white, his lips fat and spongy, and his face hung in folds about his chin, but there was a soft sheen to the skin, a smoothness of texture. His eyes caught the reflection of the reading lamp and seemed to shoot it forth in a glittering collection of icy rays. There was never so cold and remorseless an expression upon the face of any living mortal I had seen as was contained in the eyes of this heavy man behind the desk.

He was speaking, and he finished his talk before he shifted his glance toward the door. His voice was soft, gentle, an even monotone, and there was no expression in it. It was his eyes which gave the expression, a cold, deadly inten-sity of purpose.

"Yet you delayed the signal. In some manner he escaped, and he left by neither the front nor the rear."

The girl chose her words carefully, and there was a slight break in her voice, the faintest inkling of hysterical panic which she was fight-ing to control.

"Perhaps . . . perhaps he was . . . hiding on an upper floor."

"Not unless he had been warned," came the colorless tones of the man's voice. "And if he was warned, who warned him?"

The slight noise I had made in opening the door had been overlooked. Temporarily it had slipped the mind of this man with the eyes of ice. So en-grossed was he in probing the mind of the girl that he had forgotten to raise his eyes. Had he done so he would probably have taken me for one of his guards. The light threw a sharp glare on the desk, but the rest of the room was in gloom.

I advanced to the table.

The girl was weakening. I could see her head

droop slightly. What her face told I knew not, but that sag of her head and neck told me much.

With an effort, scowling his impatience, the man with the eyes of ice tore his gaze from the girl and raised his glance.

"Well?" he said, and his tone was as colorless as ever, notwithstanding the impatience which gleamed from his eyes.

"Well," I answered, "very well, thank you. In fact I am quite well, and I dropped in to say good evening."

I was watching him like a hawk, looking for that telltale start, that swift tightening of his facial muscles which would show that I had jarred his self-control; but there was nothing. His face remained as passive as though it had been so much pink putty. His eyes were so hard and flinty one would have expected no change there. His voice remained well modulated.

"Ah, yes, Mr. Jenkins, himself. Come in and draw up a chair, Jenkins. We were discussing you."

I walked on in, my eyes on his hands. The rat-faced criminal lawyer had plunged his hand into a side pocket of his coat, but I had no fear of him. He wouldn't have the nerve to shoot until the last minute, and I didn't intend to let them get the lead. I was going to play my own cards for a while.

"I dropped in to tell you that you're all wrong. I waited outside this girl's apartment for a second, just to see if there was to be any telephoning or signaling, and I heard the curtain roller go up and down three times. That meant a machine in front, and a machine in front probably meant a guard in the rear. That's all there was to that.

"However, I wanted to get in touch with you, and when I saw you were going to have this girl down here so you could throw a scare into her, I decided to trail along and have a little conversation on my own hook."

The big man at the desk brushed his hand slightly as though he was waving the girl with the mole entirely to one side, and his eyes never left my face.

"Jenkins, I offered you once before, and I offer you again, a place with me, a place where you can make much money, have men beneath you to do the dangerous work, and can really find some market for the brains you have."

I nodded easily.

"Just after you made that offer before you double-crossed me by holding out some papers on me."

This time there was just the faintest flicker of expression in the gray-blue eyes. It was a slight twinkle of appreciation. He had a sense of humor, this man with the dead-white skin and the ice-cold eyes.

"You should talk of a double-cross. You slipped something over on us that time that was so fast no one ever caught it. It happened that I made a price for certain things in that case, the opening of a safe, let us say. The rest of it was up to the others. How you slipped it over on them I don't know. The lawyer swore he destroyed the will with his own hands and that he watched you to see there could be no substitution, and yet . . ."

I broke in.

"Never mind all that. You double-crossed me at the start by holding out two papers on me. What came afterward was my method of registering disapproval. Now I want those papers and I want them right now, or I'll register a hell of a lot more disapproval, and you'll find yourself sitting in the gutter."

The eyes were cold and hard again.

"Jenkins, I deliver those papers when and how I choose. However, you will throw in with me before you leave this room or you'll leave it feet first."

I hitched my chair closer and let my own eyes bore into his.

"Either you give up those papers or else you will suffer some very great inconvenience."

I could see his fingers gripping the edge of the desk, gripping until the nails were white, but, aside from that, there was no sign of emotion.

"Jenkins," he said in his quiet, well-modulated voice, "you interfered a few days ago and cost me a rake-off on fifty thousand dollars. I can't allow you to be in a position to do it again. I have given you your chance. . . ."

I didn't let him finish. I had played my cards, had given him warning, had let him know that I could find him, could walk into his den at will. The next trick would have been his and I would have lost my lead—my lead and my life.

I swung my wrist and the leather bag filled with packed, sandy loam crashed down upon the desk light. The bulb crashed and the room was in darkness.

I jumped back toward the door, but didn't make the mistake of opening it. The hall was lighted, and I would have been filled with lead before I had got over the threshold. However, I'd counted on that sleepy gunfighter who was supposed to be on guard, and I'd counted on the lawyer.

I figured right both times.

The lawyer fired at the chair in which I had been sitting, fired three times. Then there was sudden silence.

"Fool!" exclaimed the man with the eyes of ice.

There came running steps, and the door crashed open. The man with the two guns had burst into the room ready to go into action, and encountered a wall of inky darkness. The momentum of his rush carried him well past the sill, and I was standing by the door, ready, waiting, planning on just such a move.

As the man plunged in I gave him a quick thrust from behind, pushed him farther into the room, and, shielded behind his stumbling body, I darted through the door and down the hall. The lawyer fired again. The mere fact that he might kill his own guard meant nothing to him. He was desperate. What the bullet struck I didn't find out. I was on my way. It didn't strike me. It would have taken sheer luck for that bullet to have stopped me as I darted around that doorway with the stumbling guard blocking the view.

The man in the back was still asleep when I went past. I had handed him a pretty solid tap, and I figured he would be good for an hour or more. The dog barked again, but that was all. If the pistol shots had been heard in the neighborhood they had probably been taken for the backfires of an automobile exhaust, for the windows were all dark.

I chuckled to myself as I gained the street. The fat bird with the ice-cold eyes would have to change his headquarters again. Beyond doubt I was annoying him greatly. Also I had this to remember. He appreciated his danger now. It was either he or I. The city was too small for the both of us. One or the other was doomed.

However, there was one thing in my favor. He had gone too far with his jewel exhibit to back down now and that gave me a trail that might be followed.

My first problem was a place to hide out. Every rooming house, every hotel would be watched. Through some means he had set the police on my trail, that my California immunity meant nothing. If he could keep me in jail until after the looting of the jewel exhibit he would be satisfied. However, I didn't intend to have either the police or the crooks get on my trail. I had money, and one can do much with money.

I purchased a furnished house from a real estate agency, a bungalow out of the way in a quiet neighborhood.

The police and the crooks expected me to try some disguise, to go to a hotel or rooming house; but they hardly expected I would go and buy myself a little bungalow in the respectable residential district. That slipped one over on them, and disposed of that part of the problem.

Shadowing Schwartz was different. They had tipped him off, and he was one cagey bird. I didn't try to keep him in sight all the time, but tried to cut in on him at certain hours, particularly before he started his jewelry store canvass in the mornings, and after he had knocked off at night.

The more I saw of that jewelry exhibit the more puzzled I became. The newspapers started to play it up big. Day after day they featured the show, mentioned the social distinction of the persons who had received invitations to the opening, wrote of the manner in which Edith Jewett Kemper would be gowned, and handed out a blah-blah of the usual slush.

I sat snugly ensconced in the little bungalow and read the papers, read the frothings of the society editors concerning the importance of the coming show, and took my hat off to the man with the ice-cold eyes.

One thing puzzled me. The newspapers featured the elements of protection which the exhibit was taking to safeguard their patrons from loss, and it was good.

At night the gems were to be parked in a big safe which had been loaned from one of the prominent safe companies as an advertisement. This safe would be set in the *middle* of the floor, and at least five men would be constantly on duty watching the safe.

If the safe had been placed in one end of the room, so that only its doors were visible to the watchers, that would have been one thing. Putting it in the *middle* of the floor was another. I'm a handy man with boxes myself, but if there was any way of crashing into that lead-box with all those precautions, then I sure was a back number. I couldn't figure one out, and that's where I shine, figuring out ways of springing boxes that are seemingly impossible.

Schwartz was a hard baby to handle, and I didn't get the line on him I wanted until the day before the exhibit was to open. That afternoon he slipped out to a downtown garage and inspected an armored truck. This truck was plastered with a sign that was painted on cloth and hung clean across both sides, JEWEL EXHIBIT ARMORED TRUCK. It was the real thing, too, that truck. Steel sides, bulletproof glass, railroad iron bumpers protecting it on all four sides, protected radiator and hood and solid rubber tires. It would take a stick of dynamite to faze that truck.

I didn't dare stick around Schwartz or the garage. Just a quick once-over and I was on my way, stepping on the gas of a car I rented by the week. Automobile shadowing was all I dared to do with the whole gang laying for me, and

watching Schwartz in the hope that they'd get track of me through him.

Time was getting short and I was stumped. I could tell that there was something big in the wind, but I couldn't tell what. The head of that organization wasn't going to monkey with any small stuff. The eight or ten thousand dollars that might be made from the exhibit wouldn't prove interesting. What they intended to do was to get the cream of all the fancy jewelry in the city gathered in one place so they could make a regular haul. An organization the size of that wasn't interested in small profits.

I went back to my bungalow and sat down at the table to do some figuring. For once in my life I was worried. I was going up against a game I couldn't fathom. The other man was holding all the cards, and he was holding 'em close to his vest. My only hope of dominating him was to bust up this proposed gem robbery; and my only hope of being able to live or to get the papers for Helen was in dominating that man with the icy eyes.

I sat and thought, a pencil in my hand tracing aimless lines along a sheet of paper which I had spread before me, and then, suddenly, the answer came to me, came in a flash, and made me want to kick myself all up and down the main street of the city. It was so absurdly simple that there was nothing to it.

When a magician walks down through the audience, borrows a watch from the man in the center aisle, and then turns his back to walk up to the stage, he has an interval of several seconds during which his hands are concealed from the audience. He can switch that watch a hundred times over, and yet, when he appears on the stage, facing the audience, waving a gold watch in his hand and asking the spectators to keep their eyes fastened upon it, no one thinks of questioning the fact that it is the original watch he is holding; no one wonders if perhaps he has not already performed the trick, if the substitution has not already taken place.

It was the same way with the jewelry exhibit. The precautions for taking care of the gems after they had arrived were featured so elaborately that one always thought of the possibility of a robbery taking place then and at no other time. There was a two-fold reason for that. One reason was that it would tend to make the jewelry stores send but one clerk to act both as clerk and guard, and the other, and main reason, was that no one would pay too much attention to the armored truck that was going to take the jewels there. The words "armored truck" had a potent significance, a lulling sense of absolute security. An "armored truck" was like a bank vault. The very words suggested probity, safety, integrity, and yet, after all, an armored truck was merely an inanimate something. It was the driver of the armored truck who had the power of directing the car as an agency either for good or evil.

Even as the details of the scheme were formulating themselves in my mind I was working on a counter scheme, and busying myself with proper preparations. A suit of overalls and jumper from under the seat of my car, a little grease smeared over my bare arms, a derby hat stuck on my head at an angle, and I was ready. A couple of good cigars also came into the picture.

Thirty minutes later and I was at the garage where the armored bus was stored.

"Howdy," I told the night man.

He was a sleepy-eyed, loose-lipped, single-cylinder sort of a bird, and he squinted a suspicious eye at me. I fished out a cigar, handed it to him, took another for myself and squatted beside him while I tendered a match.

We smoked in silence for a minute or two, and then a man came in for his car and the night man had to do ten minutes' work moving and shifting. By the time he came back he looked on me as an old acquaintance.

"Mechanic?" he asked sociably.

I nodded and jerked my head toward the armored truck.

"Yep, that's my baby. I'm the bird that the agency sends out to go over this elephant every ten days and see that it's in runnin' order. I understand it's goin' out tomorrow, and I've been a little slack lately."

The suspicious look came into his eyes again.

"Orders is not to let nobody get near that bus."

I nodded and blew a smoke ring.

"Sure, they have to be careful. There's a guy named Schwartz that's got it rented and you can let him get into it or drive it out, but don't you let nobody else get near it, not unless he's got a written order from Schwartz—or from me."

That registered. He looked me over again with a new respect. I said nothing further but smoked on in silence. Another man came in after a car, and the night man started moving and shuffling the stored cars about. That was my cue! I parked my stub on the bench and sauntered over to the armored bus.

Schwartz had the key to the thing and it was locked tight as a drum, and that bothered me. I had been hoping against hope that it would be open. As it was, I melted around behind it and plastered myself between the rear of the car and the wall of the garage. The gas tank was protected by a sheet of armor, but the cap was in plain sight, and so was the gauge. The tank was full of gasoline. All set, ready to go.

All in all it didn't look like an easy job, and I had a hunch the guy that was acting as night man, car mover and watchman all combined would be curious enough to come over to see what I was doing. It was going to require quick thinking, and quick action. Somehow or other I had to get that car fixed so it would only run about a certain distance.

A little faucet-like arrangement at the bottom of the gas tank proved the best bet. It was the faucet which turned on an emergency gas tank when the big tank ran out. I had a kit of tools with me, and I set to work.

In ten minutes I had short-circuited the emergency gas tank, and had inserted a tight-fitting length of copper tube in the gasoline line to the carburetor. This tube was carefully measured and stuck up to within half an inch of the top of the gasoline level in the main tank. I figured out the approximate gas consumption of the mill, and was willing to bet that bus would run just about three miles and then stop. When that pipe was pulled out it would start going again, but until that was done the armored bus would be anchored. It wasn't as smooth a job as I'd have done if the bus hadn't been locked up, but I fancied it would do. The fact that the sign advertising the car as that of the jewelry exhibit was printed on cloth was a big clue. I fancied I knew what was going to happen all right, and if I was right there was going to be a little surprise party the next day.

Next I went and purchased a siren, one of the kind that are limited by law to the use of police and fire cars. I installed this on my rented car myself, and was ready to go.

Sometime after midnight I woke up with an uneasy feeling that everything wasn't just as it should be. The house was dark and still, a clock ticking away the seconds in the living room, a gentle night breeze coming in through the open window and swaying the white lace curtains. At first I thought that it must have been one of those curtains which had brushed across my face, and had awakened me with that strange feeling that danger was present.

I looked out of the window, feeling the cool breeze on my face. The yard showed faintly in the weird light of a distant street lamp. The stars were blazing steadily overhead. The gray shapes of other houses loomed like intangible shadows . . . and then came the sound again.

It was a faint scraping noise, a gritting, cutting sound which meant much to my trained ears. Someone was cutting a hole in one of the glass windows of the adjoining room, with a diamond glass cutter.

Hurriedly, noiselessly, I arose, got into my clothes, arranged the pillows in the bed so that they represented a sleeping form, and slipped into the closet. There was a shelf in that closet, just over the door, and I climbed up on it silently, swiftly. I was unarmed, but I really needed no weapon. Above that shelf was a small trap door which led into the space between the ceilings and the roof. If necessary I could get through there; but I wanted to see what was in the wind. On that shelf I could stoop and peer into the bedroom. If anyone should enter the closet I could drop on his shoulders as a cougar drops from a tree upon a passing deer.

Silence for a few minutes, then the soft sound of a sash being gently raised. Again there was a period of silence; then I could hear the bedroom door softly creak. Perhaps it was swaying in the wind which came through the window, perhaps not.

Suddenly there was a spurt of flame, a swift hissing noise, another and another . . . shots from a pistol equipped with a silencer.

Again silence, a whisper, the beam of a flashlight shooting swiftly over the bed. "Did yuh get him?"

"Deader'n a herring," came the whispered answer.

The men turned and ran swiftly from the house, making more noise than when they had entered, yet making no sound which would have been so audible as to have attracted attention from without. There came the sound of a starting motor, the spurt of an engine, and a machine slipped smoothly down the pavement.

I climbed down from the shelf and pulled out the pillows from beneath the bedclothes. The upper pillow had three holes in it and feathers were wadded and scattered all over the sheets. Whoever had fired that gun was a good shot, one of the sort who can shoot in the half-light by the feel of the gun and be sure of his mark, who can group three bullets within a circle of three inches in a pillow.

I sighed, climbed into bed and went back to sleep.

This man with the icy eyes certainly was a smooth customer. Of course, I'd had to play into his hands by keeping an eye on this fellow Schwartz. That had given him a lead all the time, but, at that, he was clever.

In the morning I took a look around and found the circle of glass that had been cut from the upper pane so that the window lock could be sprung, and I smashed the glass into a series of jagged fragments so that it would appear the break had been accidental. There was no need to advertise my private affairs to the neighborhood.

I shaved, breakfasted, got out my car with the siren all attached and in perfect working order, and rolled slowly down the street in the line of traffic of early workers. A block from Redfern's I picked my parking place and slipped to the curb. I had come early to get the car located just right, and I stuck there behind the wheel to see that no one interfered with a quick getaway.

About eight o'clock the armored truck, with its painted cloth signs on the sides, showed up and backed to Redfern's curb. Close behind the truck was a high-powered car driven by a man in uniform.

A crowd collected, and I was close enough to the outskirts of the crowd to see what was taking place, and to hear what was said. Schwartz was in charge of things, and he was the typical sales-man. He greeted old man Redfern as though it was a family reunion after a ten years' absence, and worked his arm up and down with rhythmic regularity.

The jewels were brought out and placed in the truck, and Schwartz explained its bomb-proof features to Redfern the while.

"I'm driving the truck myself, and there's a machine full of guards coming right behind. I guess that'll ensure us safety all right. And you've seen the precautions we've taken down at the place. Say, Redfern, why don't you come yourself? The armored truck is full, but there's lots of room in the open car in back. You see, I've got a girl to check up the list of exhibits, and an armed guard with me in the truck. I'm relying on the jewelry stores to furnish the guards for the open car. Stick a gun in your pocket and get in next to the officer there in the car."

Redfern didn't need much urging. He blinked, smiled, patted Schwartz on the back and climbed into the open car. The truck started off, the open car came along behind, and the offi-cer who was driving signaled for open traffic signs from the cops at the intersections. The procession was started.

Ten calls were made, ten loads taken on, five guards crowded into the open machine. Five of the stores didn't think it was necessary to add a guard to the collection. They were satisfied with old man Redfern's respectable face. He was known all up and down the street, was old Red-fern, a shrewd, canny old bird with a long head and a tight purse.

The truck headed toward the exhibit place and I settled down behind my wheel. This was going to be good. I hoped I hadn't missed any bets or bungled any guesses, and I was gambling strong that I hadn't.

All of a sudden there was a whir of a rapidly driven motor. A long, gray roadster shot past me as smoothly and swiftly as a trout skimming through a still pool, and then there was a crash. The roadster had tried to cut in on the open car back of the armored truck, had locked wheels, battered in the front of the open car, skidded to the curb, crashed into a parked car, sprinkled broken glass all over the sidewalk, chased a cou-ple of pedestrians up lamp posts, spilled the cop out onto the curb, scattered the guards about a bit, and the armored truck went gaily on its way, seemingly oblivious of what had happened to the car full of guards.

A crowd collected. Everyone shouted and cursed, the driver of the gray roadster sprinted to another car that was parked with motor run-ning, parked in a second line of parking, and dashed down the street. The cop yelled and pulled his gun. There was some wild firing, screams, police whistles, pandemonium.

I worked through the tangled mass of traffic at the corner and started out after the armored truck, keeping pretty well back. The truck went easily and smoothly onward. At the corner, where the main out-of-town boulevard ran in, they stopped, and one of the men slipped to the sidewalk and scooped in the cloth signs, hung out two others, and they were on their way.

I sprinted ahead by a round-the-block detour and got a look at that new sign. I fancied I knew what it was, but I wanted to make sure.

"FEDERAL RESERVE—INTERURBAN SHIPMENT" read the new sign, and I chortled to myself at that. It was so slick it was greasy. They could take that armored truck any place they blamed pleased with that sign on it. By the time the police got the accident untangled, got in touch with the exhibit and found the car hadn't arrived, got the word spread out to the traffic cops . . . by that time the armored truck would have vanished from the face of the earth. There were a dozen similar trucks, engaged in banking transportation, keeping busy in the city—it would be one grand smear.

Then it happened. The truck hesitated, backfired, and coasted over to the curb. That was my cue. I swung around the block and stopped on a side street, with the engine running.

One of the men got out of the rear door and bent over the gas tank, then ran around again to the front. I figured he was switching on the auxiliary tank. There was the sound of the starting motor, but nothing happened beyond a slight cough.

I fancied there was much conversation going on in that truck just then. At length the carburetor filled again and the truck ran along for a few feet, then stopped. A man jumped from the driver's seat and sprinted to a car that was parked by the curb a block or so away. It was a little roadster, but apparently it was unlocked, for he got it going and dashed back to the truck. They were going to shift cargoes, to salvage what they could.

A machine came along, slowed down curiously, and was ordered to move along. Seconds were precious. In a few minutes that stalled truck would have a crowd of curious motorists rubbering at it. That would be fatal.

They swung open the heavy rear doors, backed the roadster . . . and then I got into action.

I opened the cut-out, raced the engine, and started the siren in a long, low, wailing scream. Then I waited. They didn't spot the car where it was hidden behind some drooping shade trees, but the sound did hit their ears, a sound associated with powerful police cars which tore around with wailing sirens and shotgun squads looking for trouble.

In consternation they looked at each other, and then the flight began. A second wail from my siren stirred things up a bit, and the roadster tore away from the stalled truck and out into the boulevard.

I had fancied I saw only two figures in that roadster, which would mean that one had been left behind, but I had no time to worry over details. It was now or never and I must act quickly. I swung my car around the corner and skidded to a stop beside the stalled truck. Quickly I jerked off the cap of the gasoline tank, pulled out the tight-fitting metal tube I had worked into the gasoline line, put back the cap, jumped into the truck, closed and locked the doors and looked about me.

The girl with the mole on her left hand was sitting on the driver's seat, her eyes wide, sparkling.

"You!" she exclaimed.

I had no time to analyze her tone, no opportunity to indulge in friendly conversation.

"You make a move or try to interfere and I'll throw you out on your ear," I told her, and meant it. She was a member of a gang that was out for my life, and there was to be no quarter given or asked. I had work to do, and to blunder at this stage of the game would be fatal. I had been warned specifically against this woman with the mole, and the man who gave me that warning had paid for his friendly interest with his life. He had been killed with the words still warm on his lips. Somewhere, somehow, there was a sinister influence exerted by this woman. Death and violence followed her every contact. For myself I was taking no chances.

Without a murmur, she slid off of the driver's seat and sat, her hands in plain sight, folded on her lap, looking at me curiously. Beyond that first exclamation there had been nothing to give me a clue as to her thoughts.

It was the work of an instant to start the motor and turn the heavy truck, and in that minute the two men who had fled in the roadster knew they had been duped. They were watching their backtrail for pursuit, wondering whether the police would stop to take possession of the abandoned truck or would give pursuit. They had seen me rush to the armored truck, do something to the gasoline tank, and then jump inside. In that brief instant they had recognized the deception that had been played on them, and had swung the roadster and started back.

I turned the truck and opened the throttle, roaring down the boulevard. The lighter roadster gained rapidly, and was soon alongside. Faces that were distorted with rage glared up at me. There came the crack of a pistol shot, and the bulletproof glass radiated a thousand fine lines of silvery cracks where the bullet struck, but the leaden missile did not penetrate. That finished my last worry. I made faces at the two helpless bandits without, twiddled my fingers at my nose, and finally, making a quick swerve of the heavy car, ran them clear into the opposite curb.

There was a crash as the heavy, railroad-iron bumper did its stuff and the light roadster crumpled like an eggshell, glanced from the curb to a telephone post, and the men pitched out to the cement sidewalk.

I did not look back. They may have escaped unhurt. They may have been seriously injured. They may have been killed. This was no picnic. This was war with no quarter given or asked.

Once more we entered the traffic of the business district. At my side the girl with the mole on her hand sat and watched me with a queer look upon her face. Her lips were slightly parted, her eyes almost starry, and they seldom left my face. Shut in there in that armored truck we were safe from attack of everything except a cannon or a bomb. Perchance, emissaries of the gang who had engineered the great robbery watched us as we thundered past. If so they were helpless.

I swung up to the curb of the place where the exhibit was to be held. There was a great crowd of excited people milling about. A squad of police held back the crowd. I saw old Redfern running about, frantic with excitement, his eyes bulging, hands waving . . . and then he caught sight of the truck backing up to the curb, and his eyes *did* bulge. Somewhere a police whistle shrilled, and there came the screech of a siren. Policemen began to cluster about the truck.

"Keep your face closed and start checking the stuff as it goes out," I told the girl with the mole, and flung open the doors.

"Get ready to handle this stuff," I yelled at the excited officer who thrust his head in at the door, and slammed a tray of choice platinum jewelry at him.

Mechanically, he took it, stood there, mouth open, eyes wide, seeking to interrogate me, and I slammed out another tray.

Watchmen and guards ran up, police officers milled about, and I had no words for any of them. I simply answered their questions by slamming out trays of choice jewelry, and the very apparent value of those goods was such that they mechanically turned and bore them into the place where the exhibit had been arranged.

I took the last tray in myself.

"Here's the list," said the girl with the mole, thrusting it into my hands; "and, oh, Ed! I had so *hoped* you would do just that!"

With that she was gone. A hell of a way for a member of a gang to congratulate the crook who had just outsmarted her of God knew how many thousand dollars.

I pattered on in with the tray, and an escort of cops clustered behind me. They didn't know exactly what it was all about, but this was once they figured they had Ed Jenkins dead to rights, and they didn't intend to let him live up to his reputation as a phantom crook by slipping through their fingers.

From somewhere behind me I caught the tail end of a hoarse whisper.

". . . too deep for me; but we'll make the pinch as soon as he starts for the door. With his record he's sunk. He can't alibi nothin'."

Up ahead there was a crowd of jewelry men and customers milling around, asking questions, gabbling away like a bunch of geese. I had the cops behind me and knew I'd be pinched when I started for the door. That meant I had to keep going straight ahead; and it meant I had to think fast. However, thinking fast is the thing that's kept me out of lots of jails.

I sat the tray down and climbed up on a chair.

"Silence, please!" I bellowed.

Everyone turned to rubber at me, and then I started my speech.

"Ladies and gentlemen," I said, "I am a crook!"

That got 'em. If I'd started to make an address of welcome or tell 'em a story they'd all have been buzzing with whispers of their own and I wouldn't have got their attention, but that single sentence made 'em stand stock still, and then I went on.

"But I am an honest crook, a man who has sought to make an honest living, to show that it is possible for a crook to go straight.

"I planned out this vast jewelry exhibition because I knew that it was a move in the right direction. The jewelry stores need an opportunity to exhibit to the select trade. The potential customers need to have a chance to study the latest styles in settings, to get up-to-the-minute information.

"Unfortunately, my assistant, the man upon whom I relied to sell space, to explain the idea to the merchants, turned out to be a crook. Knowing my record, he thought he could get away with the truckload of gems, and have the police blame it on to me. However, I managed to outwit this criminal and recover the entire truckload, and here it is, safe and sound, ready for the approval of the prospective purchasers."

I made a bow and stood there, watching the maps of the cops, wondering if I was going to make it stick.

"I think I shall purchase my season's supply of gems right now," said a woman whose voice carried to the farthest ends of the room. "I think this is a wonderful idea, but, really, we don't need the police here now, do we? Mr. Redfern, I wonder if you'd mind asking them to withdraw. It makes me feel sort of nervous and interferes with my purchasing."

It was Edith Jewett Kemper, and she was playing a trump card in the nick of time. I think I had the cops buffaloed at that, but when old Redfern charged down on them, waving his hands, sputtering, expostulating, it was a rout. The cops thinned out that door like mosquitoes before a smudge.

Redfern came back to me, his eyes shining, his hands outstretched.

"Wonderful! Wonderful!" he exclaimed. "Did you hear that Mrs. Kemper is going to purchase her *season's* supply of jewels? It's a great success. Everyone will follow suit. In fact, we will have to make her a little present, something to remember the occasion by."

I grabbed his arm.

"Yeah, in the meantime you'd better make out your check for the space. I'm goin' to get collected up right now so I won't have any books to keep."

Without a whimper he pulled out his checkbook.

"Payable to . . . ?" he asked.

"Just make it payable to Ed Jenkins," I told him. " 'The Down Town Merchants' Exhibit' was just a trade name."

He nodded and made out the check, dazed and happy.

A sergeant of police elbowed his way over, but he was smiling.

"Jenkins, you're all right!" he said. "I've had an anonymous tip these last two weeks to get you on suspicion of a big gem robbery, and here you were actually on the square. Bringing back that truckload was a wonderful thing. How did you do it?"

I shrugged my shoulders.

"Just by bein' honest, Sergeant, an' never lettin' that crook Schwartz get a chance. I was watchin' him like a hawk. Next time don't be so anxious to believe evil of me."

He shook his head as though he were in the middle of a dream and walked away, and, as he walked, I saw him pinch himself to find out whether he was really awake.

Helen Chadwick was over in a corner, away from the crowd, waiting.

"Ed, you won't be such a stranger, now that you've got this thing over with, will you?"

There was a wistful something in her voice, and I suddenly came down to earth, realized that in spite of any brilliant tricks I might play on the police or on other crooks, that I was, after all, a crook, myself. I realized also that no good could come to this girl from knowing me, and I cared so much for her that I wanted to protect her, even from myself.

"I'm going to get that other paper for you, Helen," I temporized, "and then we'll have a chance to sit down and talk other things over."

She shrugged her shoulders.

"You're the most obstinate brute I ever was engaged to," she said, and instantly became all vivacious chatter, all social small talk.

I grinned at her.

"Do I get any reward for that last paper, young lady?" I asked her.

She gave a quick glance around, then tilted her head, and pursed her lips.

"Come and get it," she challenged.

Fifteen minutes later, when I had started down the street to get those checks cashed, a dirty urchin thrust a paper in my hand.

"The man said there'd be an answer," he said, peering up at me with his young-old, wise eyes.

I unfolded the paper.

"You can't make it stick," read the note. "Other papers are outstanding and will be used in a way to ruin persons you would protect. Give this lad an answer, stating when and where you will turn over the commissions. I mean to have those space checks. That money is to come to me. Where do I get it and when?"

The note was unsigned. It didn't need a signature. I had jarred old Icy-Eyes out of his calm. I grinned, took a pencil from my pocket and started to scribble an answer, and then those words of Helen Chadwick's came to my mind. I chuckled and scribbled my message of defiance on the back of the note.

"COME AND GET IT," I wrote, and handed the paper back to the boy.

"The answer is on the back," I told him, and with that I started on my way, knowing that they would try to follow me, knowing also that I must thrust aside the ways of civilized society and vanish within the shadows, knowing that this conflict with the icy-eyed criminal would never cease until one of us had written "In Full of Account" against the life of the other. But in the meantime I had turned the tables, had got the police guessing, and had seen Helen Chadwick again—that joyous little flapper who was such a baffling combination of vivacious frivolity and courageous fortitude, that girl who was commencing to be so much in my thoughts.

Let Icy-Eyes come and get it. He would find a warm reception waiting him.

Cry Silence

Fredric Brown

FREDRIC BROWN (1906–1972) was born in Cincinnati, Ohio, and attended the University of Cincinnati and Hanover College before becoming an office worker from 1924 to 1936. He then took a job as a proofreader and reporter for the *Milwaukee Journal.* A chronic respiratory problem caused him to move to Taos, New Mexico, then Tucson, Arizona. While at the *Journal,* he sold his first short story and went on to publish more than three hundred stories in his lifetime, as well as nearly thirty novels, in both the science fiction and mystery genres.

Equally revered by fans of science and mystery fiction, Brown was one of the most original, creative pulp writers of his time, his stories often having astonishing twists and surprise endings, frequently leavened with humor. His first mystery novel, *The Fabulous Clipjoint* (1947), won an Edgar Allan Poe Award and introduced the detective team of Ed Hunter and his uncle Am, who appeared in six subsequent novels.

Brown wrote scripts for *Alfred Hitchcock Presents,* and several television dramas and films were made from his books, notably *Crack-Up* (1946, RKO, starring Pat O'Brien, Claire Trevor, and Herbert Marshall), based on his short story "Madman's Holiday," and *The Screaming Mimi* (1958, Columbia, starring Anita Ekberg, Phil Carey, and Gypsy Rose Lee), based on the novel of the same name.

"Cry Silence" was published in the November 1948 issue.

They scraped halfway through the thick door with a piece of loose concrete.

Cry Silence

Fredric Brown

Would you try to save your wife from a killer? Seems like a simple question, but to Mandy's husband, it was one to stump the experts.

IT WAS THAT OLD silly argument about sound. If a tree falls deep in the forest where there is no ear to hear, is its fall silent? Is there sound where there is no ear to hear it? I've heard it argued by college professors and by street sweepers.

This time it was being argued by the agent at the little railroad station and a beefy man in coveralls. It was a warm summer evening at dusk, and the station agent's window opening onto the back platform of the station was open; his elbows rested on the ledge of it. The beefy man leaned against the red brick of the building. The argument between them went in circles like a droning bumblebee.

I sat on a wooden bench on the platform about ten feet away. I was a stranger in town, waiting for a train that was late. There was one other man present; he sat on the bench beside me, between me and the window. He was a tall, heavy man with a face like granite, an uncompromising kind of face, and huge, rough hands. He looked like a farmer in his town clothes.

I wasn't interested in either the argument or the man beside me. I was wondering only how late that damned train would be.

I didn't have my watch; it was being repaired in the city. And from where I sat I couldn't see the clock inside the station. The tall man beside me was wearing a wristwatch and I asked him what time it was.

He didn't answer.

You've got the picture, haven't you? Four of us; three on the platform and the agent, leaning out of the window. The argument between the agent and the beefy man. On the bench, the silent man and I.

I got up off the bench and looked into the open door of the station. It was seven forty; the train was twelve minutes overdue. I sighed, and lighted a cigarette. I decided to stick my nose into the argument. It wasn't any of my business, but I knew the answer and they didn't.

"Pardon me for butting in," I said, "but you're not arguing about sound at all; you're arguing semantics."

I expected one of them to ask me what semantics was, but the station agent fooled me. He said: "That's the study of words, isn't it? In a way, you're right, I guess."

"All the way," I insisted. "If you look up 'sound' in the dictionary, you'll find two meanings listed. One of them is 'the vibration of a medium, usually air, within a certain range,' and the other is 'the effect of such vibrations on the ear.' That isn't the exact wording, but the general idea. Now by one of those definitions, the sound—the vibration—exists whether there's an ear around to hear it or not. By the other, the vibrations aren't sound unless there is an ear to hear them. So you're both right; it's just a matter of which meaning you use for the word 'sound.' "

The beefy man said: "Maybe you got something there." He looked back at the agent. "Let's call it a draw then, Joe. I got to get home. So long."

He stepped down off the platform and went around the station.

I asked the agent: "Any report on the train?"

"Nope," he said. He leaned a little farther out the window and looked to his right and I saw a clock in a steeple about a block away that I hadn't noticed before. "Ought to be along soon though."

He grinned at me. "Expert on sound, huh?"

"Well," I said, "I wouldn't say that. But I did happen to look it up in the dictionary. I know what it means."

"Uh-huh. Well, let's take that second definition and say sound is sound only if there's an ear to hear it. A tree crashes in the forest and there's only a deaf man there. Is there any sound?"

"I guess not," I said. "Not if you consider sound as subjective. Not if it's got to be heard."

I happened to glance to my right, at the tall man who hadn't answered my question about the time. He was still staring straight ahead. Lowering my voice a bit, I asked the station agent: "Is he deaf?"

"Him? Bill Meyers?" He chuckled; there was something odd in the sound of that chuckle. "Mister, nobody knows. That's what I was going to ask you next. If that tree falls down and there's a man near, but nobody knows if he's deaf or not, is there any sound?"

His voice had gone up in volume. I stared at him, puzzled, wondering if he was a little crazy, or if he was just trying to keep up the argument by thinking up screwy loopholes.

I said: "Then if nobody knows if he's deaf, nobody knows if there was any sound."

He said: "You're wrong, mister. That man would know whether he heard it or not. Maybe the tree would know, wouldn't it? And maybe other people would know, too."

"I don't get your point," I told him. "What are you trying to prove?"

"*Murder*, mister. You just got up from sitting next to a murderer."

I stared at him again, but he didn't look crazy. Far off, a train whistled, faintly. I said: "I don't understand you."

"The guy sitting on the bench," he said. "Bill Meyers. He murdered his wife. Her and his hired man."

· 29 ·

His voice was quite loud. I felt uncomfortable; I wished that far train was a lot nearer. I didn't know what went on here, but I knew I'd rather be on the train. Out of the corner of my eye I looked at the tall man with the granite face and the big hands. He was still staring out across the tracks. Not a muscle in his face had moved.

The station agent said: "I'll tell you about it, mister. I *like* to tell people about it. His wife was a cousin of mine, a fine woman. Mandy Eppert, her name was, before she married that skunk. He was mean to her, dirt mean. Know how mean a man can be to a woman who's helpless?

"She was seventeen when she was fool enough to marry him seven years ago. She was twenty-four when she died last spring. She'd done more work than most women do in a lifetime, out on that farm of his. He worked her like a horse and treated her like a slave. And her religion wouldn't let her divorce him or even leave him. See what I mean, mister?"

I cleared my throat, but there didn't seem to be anything to say. He didn't need prodding or comment. He went on.

"So how can you blame her, mister, for loving a decent guy, a clean, young fellow her own age, when he fell in love with her? Just *loving* him, that's all. I'd bet my life on that, because I knew Mandy. Oh, they talked, and they looked at each other—I wouldn't gamble too much there wasn't a stolen kiss now and then. But nothing to kill them for, mister."

I felt uneasy; I wished the train would come and get me out of this. I had to say something, though; the agent was waiting. I said: "Even if there had been, the unwritten law is out of date."

"Right, mister." I'd said the right thing. "But you know what that bastard sitting over there did? He went deaf."

"Huh?" I said.

"He went deaf. He came in town to see the doc and said he'd been having earaches and couldn't hear any more. Was afraid he was going deaf. Doc gave him some stuff to try, and you know where he went from the doc's office?"

I didn't try to guess.

"Sheriff's office," he said. "Told the sheriff he wanted to report his wife and his hired man were missing, see? Smart of him. Wasn't it? Swore out a complaint and said he'd prosecute if they were found. But he had an awful lot of trouble getting any of the questions the sheriff asked. Sheriff got tired of yelling and wrote 'em down on paper. Smart. See what I mean?"

"Not exactly," I said. "Hadn't his wife run away?"

"He'd murdered her. And him. Or rather, he was *murdering* them. Must have taken a couple of weeks, about. Found 'em a month later."

He glowered, his face black with anger.

"In the smokehouse," he said. "A new smokehouse made out of concrete and not used yet. With a padlock on the outside of the door. He'd walked through the farmyard one day about a month before—he said after their bodies were found—and noticed the padlock wasn't locked, just hanging in the hook and not even through the hasp.

"See? Just to keep the padlock from being lost or swiped, he slips it through the hasp and snaps it."

"My God," I said. "And they were in there? They starved to death?"

"Thirst kills you quicker, if you haven't either water or food. Oh, they'd tried hard to get out, all right. Scraped halfway through the door with a piece of concrete he'd worked loose. It was a thick door. I figure they yelled, after a while. I figure they hammered on that door plenty. Was there sound, mister, with only a *deaf* man living near that door, passing it twenty times a day?"

Again he chuckled humorlessly. He said: "Your train'll be along soon. That was it you heard whistle. It stops up by the water tower. It'll be here in ten minutes." And without changing his tone of voice, except that his tone got louder again, he said: "It was a bad way to die. Even if he was right in killing them, only a black-hearted son of a gun would have done it that way. Don't you think so?"

I said: "But are you sure he is—"

"Deaf? Sure, he's deaf. Can't you picture him standing there in front of that padlocked door, listening with his deaf ears to the hammering inside? And the yelling?

"Sure, he's deaf. That's why I can say all this to him, yell it in his ear. If I'm wrong, he can't hear me. But he can hear me. He comes here to hear me."

I had to ask it. "Why? Why would he—if you're right."

"I'm helping him, that's why. I'm helping him to make up his black mind to hang a rope from the grating in the top of that smokehouse, and dangle from it. He hasn't got the guts to, yet. So every time he's in town, he sits on the platform a while to rest. And I tell him what a murdering son of a gun he is."

He spat toward the tracks. He said: "There are a few of us know the score. Not the sheriff; he wouldn't believe us, said it would be too hard to prove."

The scrape of feet behind me made me turn.

The tall man with the huge hands and the granite face was standing up now. He didn't look toward us. He started for the steps.

The agent said: "He'll hang himself, pretty soon now. He wouldn't come here and sit like that for any other reason, would he, mister?"

"Unless," I said, "he *is* deaf."

"Sure. He could be. See what I meant? If a tree falls and the only man there to hear it is maybe deaf and maybe not, is it silent or isn't it? Well, I got to get the mail pouch ready."

I turned and looked at the tall figure walking away from the station. He walked slowly and his shoulders, big as they were, seemed a little stooped.

The clock in the steeple a block away began to strike for eight o'clock.

The tall man lifted his wrist to look at the watch on it.

I shuddered a little. It could have been coincidence, sure, and yet a little chill went down my spine.

The train pulled in, and I got aboard.

Arson Plus

Peter Collinson

PETER COLLINSON IS THE pseudonym of (Samuel) Dashiell Hammett (1894–1961), who was born in St. Mary's County, Maryland, and served in the Motor Ambulance Corps during World War I; he also served in the Signal Corps during World War II, mostly on the Aleutian Islands. He worked for the Pinkerton Detective Agency in several cities, including Baltimore, San Francisco (where he got a promotion for catching a man who had stolen a Ferris wheel), and Los Angeles, where he was involved in the rape case that ruined the then-famous comic actor Fatty Arbuckle; he was also once assigned to follow the notorious gangster Nick Arnstein. His years as a detective provided rich background for his crime stories, and he discovered early on that the pulp magazine market was a good one.

Although he is recognized as one of the giants in the history of the American hard-boiled school of fiction, Hammett produced only five novels and a modest number of short stories, especially when compared with the output of other successful pulp writers. After a few fairly trivial pieces for the *Smart Set* magazine, he wrote his first crime story and submitted it to *Black Mask* under the pseudonym Peter Collinson. In the underworld argot of the day, a "Peter Collins" was a nobody. Hammett added the "on" to make the name read, literally, "nobody's son."

"Arson Plus" is one of four stories sold to *Black Mask* under the Peter Collinson name, and the first Continental Op story. It was published in the October 1923 issue.

Arson Plus

Peter Collinson

This is a detective story you'll have a hard time solving before the end. Form your ideas of the outcome as you go along and then see how near you guessed it.

JIM TARR PICKED UP the cigar I rolled across his desk, looked at the band, bit off an end, and reached for a match.

"Fifteen cents straight," he said. "You must want me to break a *couple* of laws for you this time."

I had been doing business with this fat sheriff of Sacramento County for four or five years—ever since I came to the Continental Detective Agency's San Francisco office—and I had never known him to miss an opening for a sour crack; but it didn't mean anything.

"Wrong both times," I told him. "I get two of them for a quarter; and I'm here to do you a favor instead of asking for one. The company that insured Thornburgh's house thinks somebody touched it off."

"That's right enough, according to the fire department. They tell me the lower part of the house was soaked with gasoline, but God knows how they could tell—there wasn't a stick left standing. I've got McClump working on it, but he hasn't found anything to get excited about yet."

"What's the layout? All I know is that there was a fire."

Tarr leaned back in his chair, turned his red face to the ceiling and bellowed:

"Hey, Mac!"

The pearl push-buttons on his desk are ornaments as far as he is concerned. Deputy sheriffs McHale, McClump and Macklin came to the door together—MacNab apparently wasn't within hearing.

"What's the idea?" the sheriff demanded of McClump. "Are you carrying a bodyguard around with you?"

The two other deputies, thus informed as to who "Mac" referred to this time, went back to their cribbage game.

"We got a city slicker here to catch our firebug for us," Tarr told his deputy. "But we got to tell him what it's all about first."

McClump and I had worked together on an express robbery, several months before. He's a rangy, towheaded youngster of twenty-five or -six, with all the nerve in the world—and most of the laziness.

"Ain't the Lord good to us?"

He had himself draped across a chair by now—always his first objective when he comes into a room.

"Well, here's how she stands: This fellow Thornburgh's house was a couple miles out of town, on the old county road—an old frame house. About midnight, night before last, Jeff Pringle—the nearest neighbor, a half-mile or so to the east—saw a glare in the sky from over that way, and phoned in the alarm; but by the time the fire wagons got there, there wasn't enough of the house left to bother about. Pringle was the first of the neighbors to get to the house, and the roof had already fell in then.

"Nobody saw anything suspicious—no strangers hanging around or nothing. Thornburgh's help just managed to save themselves, and that was all. They don't know much about what happened—too scared, I reckon. But they did see Thornburgh at his window just before the fire got him. A fellow here in town—name of Handerson—saw that part of it too. He was driving home from Wayton, and got to the house just before the roof caved in.

"The fire department people say they found

signs of gasoline. The Coonses, Thornburgh's help, say they didn't have no gas on the place. So there you are."

"Thornburgh have any relatives?"

"Yeah. A niece in San Francisco—a Mrs. Evelyn Trowbridge. She was up yesterday, but there wasn't nothing she could do, and she couldn't tell us nothing much, so she went back home."

"Where are the servants now?"

"Here in town. Staying at a hotel on I Street. I told 'em to stick around for a few days."

"Thornburgh own the house?"

"Uh-huh. Bought it from Newning and Weed a couple months ago."

"You got anything to do this morning?"

"Nothing but this."

"Good! Let's get out and dig around."

We found the Coonses in their room at the hotel on I Street. Mr. Coons was a small-boned, plump man with the smooth, meaningless face and the suavity of the typical male houseservant.

His wife was a tall, stringy woman, perhaps five years older than her husband—say, forty—with a mouth and chin that seemed shaped for gossiping. But he did all the talking, while she nodded her agreement to every second or third word.

"We went to work for Mr. Thornburgh on the fifteenth of June, I think," he said, in reply to my first question. "We came to Sacramento, around the first of the month, and put in applications at the Allis Employment Bureau. A couple of weeks later they sent us out to see Mr. Thornburgh, and he took us on."

"Where were you before you came here?"

"In Seattle, sir, with a Mrs. Comerford; but the climate there didn't agree with my wife—she has bronchial trouble—so we decided to come to California. We most likely would have stayed in Seattle, though, if Mrs. Comerford hadn't given up her house."

"What do you know about Thornburgh?"

"Very little, sir. He wasn't a talkative gentleman. He hadn't any business that I know of. I think he was a retired seafaring man. He never said he was, but he had that manner and look. He never went out or had anybody in to see him, except his niece once, and he didn't write or get any mail. He had a room next to his bedroom fixed up as a sort of workshop. He spent most of his time in there. I always thought he was working on some kind of invention, but he kept the door locked, and wouldn't let us go near it."

"Haven't you any idea at all what it was?"

"No, sir. We never heard any hammering or noises from it, and never smelt anything either. And none of his clothes were ever the least bit soiled, even when they were ready to go out to the laundry. They would have been if he had been working on anything like machinery."

"Was he an old man?"

"He couldn't have been over fifty, sir. He was very erect, and his hair and beard were thick, with no grey hairs."

"Ever have any trouble with him?"

"Oh, no, sir! He was, if I may say it, a very peculiar gentleman in a way: and he didn't care about anything except having his meals fixed right, having his clothes taken care of—he was very particular about them—and not being disturbed. Except early in the morning and at night, we'd hardly see him all day."

"Now about the fire. Tell us the whole thing—everything you remember."

"Well, sir, I and my wife had gone to bed around ten o'clock, our regular time, and had gone to sleep. Our room was on the second floor, in the rear. Some time later—I never did exactly know what time it was—I woke up, coughing. The room was all full of smoke, and my wife was sort of strangling. I jumped up and dragged her down the back stairs and out the back door, not thinking of anything but getting her out of there.

"When I had her safe in the yard, I thought of Mr. Thornburgh, and tried to get back in the house; but the whole first floor was just flames. I ran around front then, to see if he got out, but didn't see anything of him. The whole yard was as light as day by then. Then I heard him scream—a horrible scream, sir—I can hear it

yet! And I looked up at his window—that was the front second-story room—and saw him there, trying to get out the window. But all the woodwork was burning, and he screamed again and fell back, and right after that the roof over his room fell in.

"There wasn't a ladder or anything that I could have put up to the window for him—there wasn't anything I could have done.

"In the meantime, a gentleman had left his automobile in the road, and come up to where I was standing; but there wasn't anything we could do—the house was burning everywhere and falling in here and there. So we went back to where I had left my wife, and carried her farther away from the fire, and brought her to—she had fainted. And that's all I know about it, sir."

"Hear any noises earlier that night? Or see anybody hanging around?"

"No, sir."

"Have any gasoline around the place?"

"No, sir. Mr. Thornburgh didn't have a car."

"No gasoline for cleaning?"

"No, sir, none at all, unless Mr. Thornburgh had it in his workshop. When his clothes needed cleaning, I took them to town, and all his laundry was taken by the grocer's man, when he brought our provisions."

"Don't know anything that might have some bearing on the fire?"

"No, sir. I was surprised when I heard that somebody had set the house afire. I could hardly believe it. I don't know why anybody should want to do that."

"What do you think of them?" I asked McClump, as we left the hotel.

"They might pad the bills, or even go south with some of the silver, but they don't figure as killers in my mind."

That was my opinion too; but they were the only persons known to have been there when the fire started except the man who had died. We went around to the Allis Employment Bureau and talked to the manager.

He told us that the Coonses had come into his office on June second, looking for work: and had given Mrs. Edward Comerford, 45 Wood-mansee Terrace, Seattle, Washington, as reference. In reply to a letter—he always checked up the references of servants—Mrs. Comerford had written that the Coonses had been in her employ for a number of years, and had been "extremely satisfactory in every respect." On June thirteenth, Thornburgh had telephoned the bureau, asking that a man and his wife be sent out to keep house for him; and Allis had sent two couples that he had listed. Neither had been employed by Thornburgh, though Allis considered them more desirable than the Coonses, who were finally hired by Thornburgh.

All that would certainly seem to indicate that the Coonses hadn't deliberately maneuvered themselves into the place, unless they were the luckiest people in the world—and a detective can't afford to believe in luck or coincidence, unless he has unquestionable proof of it.

At the office of the real estate agents, through whom Thornburgh had bought the house—Newning & Weed—we were told that Thornburgh had come in on the eleventh of June, and had said that he had been told that the house was for sale, had looked it over, and wanted to know the price. The deal had been closed the next morning, and he had paid for the house with a check for $4,500 on the Seamen's Bank of San Francisco. The house was already furnished.

After luncheon, McClump and I called on Howard Handerson—the man who had seen the fire while driving home from Wayton. He had an office in the Empire Building, with his name and the title "Northern California Agent, Instant-Sheen Cleanser Company" on the door. He was a big, careless-looking man of forty-five or so, with the professionally jovial smile that belongs to the salesman.

He had been in Wayton on business the day of the fire, he said, and had stayed there until rather late, going to dinner and afterward playing pool with a grocer named Hammersmith—one of his customers. He had left Wayton in his machine, at about ten thirty, and set out for Sacramento. At Tavender he had stopped at the garage for oil and gas and to have one of his tires blown up.

Just as he was about to leave the garage, the garage-man had called his attention to a red glare in the sky and had told him that it was probably from a fire somewhere along the old county road that paralleled the State road into Sacramento; so Handerson had taken the county road, and had arrived at the burning house just in time to see Thornburgh try to fight his way through the flames that enveloped him.

It was too late to make any attempt to put out the fire, and the man upstairs was beyond saving by then—undoubtedly dead even before the roof collapsed; so Handerson had helped Coons revive his wife, and stayed there watching the fire until it had burned itself out. He had seen no one on that county road while driving to the fire.

"What do you know about Handerson?" I asked McClump, when we were on the street.

"Came here, from somewhere in the East, I think, early in the summer to open that Cleanser agency. Lives at the Garden Hotel. Where do we go next?"

"We get a machine, and take a look at what's left of the Thornburgh house."

An enterprising incendiary couldn't have found a lovelier spot in which to turn himself loose, if he looked the whole county over. Tree-topped hills hid it from the rest of the world, on three sides; while away from the fourth, an uninhabited plain rolled down to the river. The county road that passed the front gate was shunned by automobiles, so McClump said, in favor of the State Highway to the north.

Where the house had been was now a mound of blackened ruins. We poked around in the ashes for a few minutes—not that we expected to find anything, but because it's the nature of man to poke around in ruins.

A garage in the rear, whose interior gave no evidence of recent occupation, had a badly scorched roof and front, but was otherwise undamaged. A shed behind it, sheltering an ax, a shovel and various odds and ends of gardening tools, had escaped the fire altogether. The lawn in front of the house, and the garden behind the shed—about an acre in all—had been pretty thoroughly cut and trampled by wagon wheels, and the feet of the firemen and the spectators.

Having ruined our shoe-shines, McClump and I got back in our machine and swung off in a circle around the place, calling at all the houses within a mile radius, and getting little besides jolts for our trouble.

The nearest house was that of Pringle, the man who had turned in the alarm: but he not only knew nothing about the dead man, but said he had never seen him. In fact, only one of his neighbors had ever seen him: a Mrs. Jabine, who lived about a mile to the south.

She had taken care of the key to the house while it was vacant; and a day or two before he bought it, Thornburgh had come over to her house, inquiring about the vacant one. She had gone over there with him and showed him through it, and he had told her that he intended on buying it, if the price, of which neither of them knew anything, wasn't too high.

He had been alone, except for the chauffeur of the hired car in which he had come from Sacramento, and, save that he had no family, he had told her nothing about himself.

Hearing that he had moved in, she went over to call on him several days later—"just a neighborly visit"—but had been told by Mrs. Coons that he was not at home. Most of the neighbors had talked to the Coonses, and had got the impression that Thornburgh didn't care for visitors, so they let him alone. The Coonses were described as "pleasant enough to talk to when you meet them," but reflecting their employer's desire not to make friends.

McClump summarized what the afternoon had taught us as we pointed our machine toward Tavender: "Any of these folks could have touched off the place, but we got nothing to show that any of 'em even knew Thornburgh, let alone had a bone to pick with him."

Tavender turned out to be a crossroads settlement of a general store and post office, a garage, a church, and six dwellings, about two miles from Thornburgh's place. McClump knew the storekeeper and postmaster, a scrawny little man named Philo, who stuttered moistly.

"I n-n-never s-saw Th-Thornburgh," he said, "and I n-n-never had any m-mail for him. C-Coons"—it sounded like one of these things butterflies come out of—"used to c-come in once a week t-to order groceries—they d-didn't have a phone. He used to walk in, and I'd s-send the stuff over in my c-c-car. Th-then I'd s-see him once in a while, waiting f-for the stage to S-S-Sacramento."

"Who drove the stuff out to Thornburgh's?"

"M-m-my b-boy. Want to t-talk to him?"

The boy was a juvenile edition of the old man, but without the stutter. He had never seen Thornburgh on any of his visits, but his business had taken him only as far as the kitchen. He hadn't noticed anything peculiar about the place.

"Who's the night man at the garage?" I asked him, after we had listened to the little he had to tell.

"Billy Luce. I think you can catch him there now. I saw him go in a few minutes ago."

We crossed the road and found Luce.

"Night before last—the night of the fire down the road—was there a man here talking to you when you first saw it?"

He turned his eyes upward in that vacant stare which people use to aid their memory.

"Yes, I remember now! He was going to town, and I told him that if he took the county road instead of the State Road he'd see the fire on his way in."

"What kind of looking man was he?"

"Middle-aged—a big man, but sort of slouchy. I think he had on a brown suit, baggy and wrinkled."

"Medium complexion?"

"Yes."

"Smile when he talked?"

"Yes, a pleasant sort of fellow."

"Curly brown hair?"

"Have a heart!" Luce laughed. "I didn't put him under a magnifying glass."

From Tavender, we drove over to Wayton. Luce's description had fit Handerson all right; but while we were at it, we thought we might as well check up to make sure that he had been coming from Wayton.

We spent exactly twenty-five minutes in Wayton; ten of them finding Hammersmith, the grocer with whom Handerson had said he dined and played pool; five minutes finding the proprietor of the poolroom; and ten verifying Handerson's story.

"What do you think of it now, Mac?" I asked, as we rolled back toward Sacramento.

Mac's too lazy to express an opinion, or even form one, unless he's driven to it; but that doesn't mean they aren't worth listening to, if you can get them.

"There ain't a hell of a lot to think," he said cheerfully. "Handerson is out of it, if he ever was in it. There's nothing to show that anybody but the Coonses and Thornburgh were there when the fire started—but there may have been a regiment there. Them Coonses ain't too honest-looking, maybe, but they ain't killers, or I miss my guess. But the fact remains that they're the only bet we got so far. Maybe we ought to try to get a line on them."

"All right," I agreed. "I'll get a wire off to our Seattle office asking them to interview Mrs. Comerford, and see what she can tell about them as soon as we get back in town. Then I'm going to catch a train for San Francisco, and see Thornburgh's niece in the morning."

Next morning, at the address McClump had given me—a rather elaborate apartment building on California Street—I had to wait three-quarters of an hour for Mrs. Evelyn Trowbridge to dress. If I had been younger, or a social caller, I suppose I'd have felt amply rewarded when she finally came in—a tall, slender woman of less than thirty; in some sort of clinging black affair; with a lot of black hair over a very white face, strikingly set off by a small red mouth and big hazel eyes that looked black until you got close to them.

But I was a busy, middle-aged detective, who was fuming over having his time wasted; and I was a lot more interested in finding the bird who struck the match than I was in feminine beauty. However, I smothered my grouch, apologized for disturbing her at such an early hour, and got down to business.

"I want you to tell me all you know about your uncle—his family, friends, enemies, business connections, everything."

I had scribbled on the back of the card I had sent into her what my business was.

"He hadn't any family," she said, "unless I might be it. He was my mother's brother, and I am the only one of that family now living."

"Where was he born?"

"Here in San Francisco. I don't know the date, but he was about fifty years old, I think—three years older than my mother."

"What was his business?"

"He went to sea when he was a boy, and, so far as I know, always followed it until a few months ago."

"Captain?"

"I don't know. Sometimes I wouldn't see or hear from him for several years, and he never talked about what he was doing; though he would mention some of the places he had visited—Rio de Janeiro, Madagascar, Tobago, Christiania. Then, about three months ago—sometime in May—he came here and told me that he was through with wandering; that he was going to take a house in some quiet place where he could work undisturbed on an invention in which he was interested.

"He lived at the Francisco Hotel while he was in San Francisco. After a couple of weeks, he suddenly disappeared. And then, about a month ago, I received a telegram from him, asking me to come to see him at his house near Sacramento. I went up the very next day, and I thought that he was acting very queerly—he seemed very excited over something. He gave me a will that he had just drawn up and some life insurance policies in which I was beneficiary.

"Immediately after that he insisted that I return home, and hinted rather plainly that he did not wish me to either visit him again or write until I heard from him. I thought all that rather peculiar, as he had always seemed fond of me. I never saw him again."

"What was this invention he was working on?"

"I really don't know. I asked him once, but he became so excited—even suspicious—that I changed the subject, and never mentioned it again."

"Are you sure that he really did follow the sea all those years?"

"No. I am not. I just took it for granted; but he may have been doing something altogether different."

"Was he ever married?"

"Not that I know of."

"Know any of his friends or enemies?"

"No, none."

"Remember anybody's name that he ever mentioned?"

"No."

"I don't want you to think this next question insulting, though I admit it is. But it has to be asked. Where were you the night of the fire?"

"At home; I had some friends here to dinner, and they stayed until about midnight. Mr. and Mrs. Walker Kellogg, Mrs. John Dupree, and a Mr. Killmer, who is a lawyer. I can give you their addresses, or you can get them from the phone book, if you want to question them."

From Mrs. Trowbridge's apartment I went to the Francisco Hotel. Thornburgh had been registered there from May tenth to June thirteenth, and hadn't attracted much attention. He had been a tall, broad-shouldered, erect man of about fifty, with rather long brown hair brushed straight back, a short, pointed brown beard, and healthy, ruddy complexion—grave, quiet, punctilious in dress and manner; his hours had been regular and he had had no visitors that any of the hotel employes remembered.

At the Seamen's Bank—upon which Thornburgh's check, in payment of the house, had been drawn—I was told that he had opened an account there on May fifteenth, having been introduced by W. W. Jeffers & Sons, local stock brokers. A balance of a little more than four hundred dollars remained to his credit. The canceled checks on hand were all to the order of various life insurance companies; and for amounts that, if they represented premiums, testified to rather large policies. I jotted down the names of the life insurance companies, and then went to the offices of W. W. Jeffers & Sons.

Thornburgh had come in, I was told, on the tenth of May with $4,000 worth of Liberty bonds that he wanted sold. During one of his conversations with Jeffers, he had asked the broker to recommend a bank, and Jeffers had given him a letter of introduction to the Seamen's Bank.

That was all Jeffers knew about him. He gave me the numbers of the bonds, but tracing Liberty bonds isn't the easiest thing in the world.

The reply to my Seattle telegram was waiting for me at the Agency when I arrived.

MRS. EDWARD COMERFORD RENTED APARTMENT AT ADDRESS YOU GIVE ON MAY TWENTY-FIVE GAVE IT UP JUNE SIX TRUNKS TO SAN FRANCISCO SAME DAY CHECK NUMBERS GN FOUR FIVE TWO FIVE EIGHT SEVEN AND EIGHT AND NINE

Tracing baggage is no trick at all, if you have the dates and check numbers to start with—as many a bird who is wearing somewhat similar numbers on his chest and back, because he overlooked that detail when making his getaway, can tell you—and twenty-five minutes in a baggage-room at the Ferry and half an hour in the office of a transfer company gave me my answer.

The trunks had been delivered to Mrs. Evelyn Trowbridge's apartment!

I got Jim Tarr on the phone and told him about it.

"Good shooting!" he said, forgetting for once to indulge his wit. "We'll grab the Coonses here and Mrs. Trowbridge there, and that's the end of another mystery."

"Wait a minute!" I cautioned him. "It's not all straightened out yet! There's still a few kinks in the plot."

"It's straight enough for me. I'm satisfied."

"You're the boss, but I think you're being a little hasty. I'm going up and talk with the niece again. Give me a little time before you phone the police here to make the pinch. I'll hold her until they get there."

Evelyn Trowbridge let me in this time, instead of the maid who had opened the door for me in the morning, and she led me to the same room in which we had had our first talk, I let her pick out a seat, and then I selected one that was closer to either door than hers was.

On the way up I had planned a lot of innocent-sounding questions that would get her all snarled up; but after taking a good look at this woman sitting in front of me, leaning comfortably back in her chair, coolly waiting for me to speak my piece, I discarded the trick stuff and came out cold-turkey.

"Ever use the name Mrs. Edward Comerford?"

"Oh, yes." As casual as a nod on the street.

"When?"

"Often. You see, I happen to have been married not so long ago to Mr. Edward Comerford. So it's not really strange that I should have used the name."

"Use it in Seattle recently?"

"I would suggest," she said sweetly, "that if you are leading up to the references I gave Coons and his wife, you might save time by coming right to it?"

"That's fair enough," I said. "Let's do that."

There wasn't a half-tone, a shading, in voice, manner, or expression to indicate that she was talking about anything half so serious or important to her as a possibility of being charged with murder. She might have been talking about the weather, or a book that hadn't interested her particularly.

"During the time that Mr. Comerford and I were married, we lived in Seattle, where he still lives. After the divorce, I left Seattle and resumed my maiden name. And the Coonses *were* in our employ, as you might learn if you care to look it up. You'll find my husband—or former husband—at the Chelsea apartments, I think.

"Last summer, or late spring, I decided to return to Seattle. The truth of it is—I suppose all my personal affairs will be aired anyhow—that I thought perhaps Edward and I might patch up our differences; so I went back and took an apartment on Woodmansee Terrace. As I was known in Seattle as Mrs. Edward Comerford, and as I thought my using his name might influence him a little, perhaps, I used it while I was there.

"Also I telephoned the Coonses to make tentative arrangements in case Edward and I should open our house again: but Coons told me that they were going to California, and so I gladly gave them an excellent recommendation when, some days later, I received a letter of inquiry from an employment bureau in Sacramento. After I had been in Seattle for about two weeks, I changed my mind about the reconciliation— Edward's interest, I learned, was all centered elsewhere; so I returned to San Francisco."

"Very nice! But—"

"If you will permit me to finish," she interrupted. "When I went to see my uncle in response to his telegram, I was surprised to find the Coonses in his house. Knowing my uncle's peculiarities, and finding them now increased, and remembering his extreme secretiveness about his mysterious invention, I cautioned the Coonses not to tell him that they had been in my employ.

"He certainly would have discharged them, and just as certainly would have quarreled with me—he would have thought that I was having him spied upon. Then, when Coons telephoned me after the fire, I knew that to admit that the Coonses had been formerly in my employ would, in view of the fact that I was my uncle's heir, cast suspicion on all three of us. So we foolishly agreed to say nothing about it and carry on the deception."

That didn't sound all wrong, but it didn't sound all right. I wished Tarr had taken it easier and let us get a better line on these people, before having them thrown in the coop.

"The coincidence of the Coonses stumbling into my uncle's house is, I fancy, too much for your detecting instincts," she went on, as I didn't say anything. "Am I to consider myself under arrest?"

I'm beginning to like this girl; she's a nice, cool piece of work.

"Not yet," I told her. "But I'm afraid it's going to happen pretty soon."

She smiled a little mocking smile at that, and another when the doorbell rang.

It was O'Hara from police headquarters. We turned the apartment upside down and inside out, but didn't find anything of importance except the will she had told me about, dated July eighth, and her uncle's life insurance policies. They were all dated between May fifteenth and June tenth, and added up to a little more than $200,000.

I spent an hour grilling the maid after O'Hara had taken Evelyn Trowbridge away, but she didn't know any more than I did. However, between her, the janitor, the manager of the apartments and the names Mrs. Trowbridge had given me, I learned that she had really been entertaining friends on the night of the fire—until after eleven o'clock, anyway—and that was late enough.

Half an hour later I was riding the Short Line back to Sacramento. I was getting to be one of the line's best customers, and my anatomy was on bouncing terms with every bump in the road; and the bumps, as "Rubberhead" Davis used to say about the flies and mosquitoes in Alberta in summer, "is freely plentiful."

Between bumps I tried to fit the pieces of this Thornburgh puzzle together. The niece and the Coonses fit in somewhere, but not just where we had them. We had been working on the job sort of lop-sided, but it was the best we could do with it. In the beginning we had turned to the

Coonses and Evelyn Trowbridge because there was no other direction to go; and now we had something on them—but a good lawyer could make hash of our case against them.

The Coonses were in the county jail when I got to Sacramento. After some questioning they had admitted their connection with the niece, and had come through with stories that matched hers in every detail.

Tarr, McClump and I sat around the sheriff's desk and argued.

"Those yarns are pipe-dreams," the sheriff said. "We got all three of 'em cold, and there's nothing else to it. They're as good as convicted of murder!"

McClump grinned derisively at his superior, and then turned to me.

"Go on! You tell him about the holes in his little case. He ain't your boss, and can't take it out on you later for being smarter than he is!"

Tarr glared from one of us to the other.

"Spill it, you wise guys!" he ordered.

"Our dope is," I told him, figuring that McClump's view of it was the same as mine, "that there's nothing to show that even Thornburgh knew he was going to buy that house before the tenth of June, and that the Coonses were in town looking for work on the second. And besides, it was only by luck that they got the jobs. The employment office sent two couples out there ahead of them."

"We'll take a chance on letting the jury figure that out."

"Yes? You'll also take a chance on them figuring out that Thornburgh, who seems to have been a nut all right, might have touched off the place himself! We've got something on these people, Jim, but not enough to go into court with them! How are you going to prove that when the Coonses were planted in Thornburgh's house— if you can even prove they were—they and the Trowbridge woman knew he was going to load up with insurance policies?"

The sheriff spat disgustedly.

"You guys are the limit! You run around in circles, digging up the dope on these people until you get enough to hang 'em, and then you run around hunting for outs! What the hell's the matter with you now?"

I answered him from half-way to the door—the pieces were beginning to fit together under my skull.

"Going to run some more circles! Come on, Mac!"

McClump and I held a conference on the fly, and then I got a machine from the nearest garage and headed for Tavender. We made time going out, and got there before the general store had closed for the night. The stuttering Philo separated himself from the two men with whom he had been talking Hiram Johnson, and followed me to the rear of the store.

"Do you keep an itemized list of the laundry you handle?"

"N-n-no; just the amounts."

"Let's look at Thornburgh's."

He produced a begrimed and rumpled account book and we picked out the weekly items I wanted: $2.60; $3.10, $2.25, and so on.

"Got the last batch of laundry here?"

"Y-yes," he said. "It j-just c-c-came out from the city t-today."

I tore open the bundle—some sheets, pillow-cases, table-cloths, towels, napkins; some feminine clothing; some shirts, collars, underwear, socks that were unmistakably Coons's. I thanked Philo while running back to my machine.

Back in Sacramento again, McClump was waiting for me at the garage where I had hired the car.

"Registered at the hotel on June fifteenth, rented the office on the sixteenth. I think he's in the hotel now," he greeted me.

We hurried around the block to the Garden Hotel.

"Mr. Handerson went out a minute or two ago," the night clerk told us. "He seemed to be in a hurry."

"Know where he keeps his car?"

"In the hotel garage around the corner."

We were within two pavements of the garage when Handerson's automobile shot out and turned up the street.

"Oh, Mr. Handerson!" I cried, trying to keep my voice level and smooth.

He stepped on the gas and streaked away from us.

"Want him?" McClump asked; and, at my nod, stopped a passing roadster by the simple expedient of stepping in front of it.

We climbed aboard, McClump flashed his star at the bewildered driver, and pointed out Handerson's dwindling tail-light. After he had persuaded himself that he wasn't being boarded by a couple of bandits, the commandeered driver did his best and we picked up Handerson's tail-light after two or three turnings, and closed in on him—though his machine was going at a good clip.

By the time we reached the outskirts of the city, we had crawled up to within safe shooting distance, and I sent a bullet over the fleeing man's head. Thus encouraged, he managed to get a little more speed out of his car; but we were definitely overhauling him now.

Just at the wrong minute Handerson decided to look over his shoulder at us—an unevenness in the road twisted his wheels—his machine swayed—skidded—went over on its side. Almost immediately, from the heart of the tangle, came a flash and a bullet moaned past my ear. Another. And then, while I was still hunting for something to shoot at in the pile of junk we were drawing down upon, McClump's ancient and battered revolver roared in my other ear.

Handerson was dead when we got to him—McClump's bullet had taken him over one eye.

McClump spoke to me over the body.

"I ain't an inquisitive sort of fellow, but I hope you don't mind telling me why I shot this lad."

"Because he was Thornburgh."

He didn't say anything for about five minutes. Then: "I reckon that's right. How'd you guess it?"

We were sitting beside the wreckage now, waiting for the police that we had sent our commandeered chauffeur to phone for.

"He had to be," I said, "when you think it all

over. Funny we didn't hit on it before! All that stuff we were told about Thornburgh had a fishy sound. Whiskers and an unknown profession, immaculate and working on a mysterious invention, very secretive and born in San Francisco—where the fire wiped out all the old records—just the sort of fake that could be cooked up easily.

"Then nobody but the Coonses, Evelyn Trowbridge, and Handerson ever saw him except between the tenth of May and the middle of June, when he bought the house. The Coonses and the Trowbridge woman were tied up together in this affair somehow, we knew—so that left only Handerson to consider. You had told me he came to Sacramento sometime early this summer—and the dates you got tonight show that he didn't come until after Thornburgh had bought his house. All right! Now compare Handerson with the descriptions we got of Thornburgh.

"Both are about the same size and age, and with the same color hair. The differences are all things that can be manufactured—clothes, a little sunburn, and a month's growth of beard, along with a little acting, would do the trick. Tonight I went out to Tavender and took a look at the last batch of laundry, and there wasn't any that didn't fit the Coonses—and none of the bills all the way back were large enough for Thornburgh to have been as careful about his clothes as we were told he was."

"It must be great to be a detective!" McClump grinned as the police ambulance came up and began disgorging policemen. "I reckon somebody must have tipped Handerson off that I was asking about him this evening." And then, regretfully: "So we ain't going to hang them folks for murder after all."

"No, but we oughtn't have any trouble convicting them of arson plus conspiracy to defraud, and anything else that the Prosecuting Attorney can think up."

Fall Guy

George Harmon Coxe

GEORGE HARMON COXE (1901–1984) was born in Olean, New York, and attended Purdue and Cornell before becoming a journalist and advertising man. His first stories were about his (undistinguished) college career, which appeared in *American Boy*, and then his mystery tales in *Detective Stories*. Although known today for his detective stories, he was also a prolific writer of sports, romance, adventure, and sea stories for a variety of pulp magazines. Later, he wrote for the top slicks, mainly war stories that he imbued with rich background material gleaned from his years as a special correspondent in the Pacific theater.

Coxe's first mystery novel, *Murder with Pictures* (1935), featured Kent Murdock, a newspaper photographer who was to be the protagonist in twenty-three of his more than sixty published novels in a career that spanned more than forty years. The novel served as the basis for a film of the same title, released by Paramount in 1936 and starring Lew Ayres and Gail Patrick.

Jack "Flashgun" Casey, Coxe's other famous detective character, was also a newspaper photographer, though tougher and less educated than Murdock. He made his debut in the March 1934 issue of *Black Mask*, and had successful careers in radio with *Flashgun Casey* (later *Casey, Crime Photographer*), running for more than a decade after its 1943 debut, and film, with *Women Are Trouble* (1936, MGM, starring Stuart Erwin) and *Here's Flash Casey* (1938, Grand National, with Eric Linden).

"Fall Guy" was published in the June 1936 issue.

Fall Guy

George Harmon Coxe

Somebody had to take it and Flashgun Casey was a natural.

T WAS THE FAG END of a dull day, and Casey was slouched behind his desk in the anteroom of the photographic department of the *Express* arguing with Tom Wade about the pennant chances of the Red Sox. When the telephone rang, he scowled at the interruption, hesitated, reached reluctantly for the offending instrument.

"Trouble, I'll bet," he growled.

He flipped the receiver into his hand and said: "Hello . . . yeah. Who? Norma?"

O'Hearn, who was leafing through an old movie magazine in search of the more undraped studies, winked at Wade and said:

"Umm. Norma."

"Sure," Casey was saying, grinning now. "I saw in the paper you were in town." He listened a few moments, added: "A favor? Sure. Anytime . . . Now? Okey, I'll be right over."

He planted the telephone on the desk with a flourish, gave a downward tug at his battered brown felt and swept his trench coat from a hat rack.

"Is she any good?" O'Hearn asked doubtfully. "This Norma."

"Quiet, Mugg," Casey said. Then, turning at the doorway: "If the Mayor wants me I'll be at the Carteret."

"Can you get in?" Wade asked, grinning.

"Listen," Casey said. "When I step in that hotel the manager nods."

"Yeah," cracked O'Hearn. "To the house detective."

Casey swung into the hall with a spring in his stride and a twinkle in his eye. He flipped a hand to the office boy who crossed his path, had good-natured answers for the elevator boy, the overalled pressmen in the car and the two circulation hustlers who got on at the second floor.

Without knowing it Casey sat, temporarily at least, upon that mythical and precarious spot known as the top of the world. There was no reason for this. It was just a mood. The mood was catching, and when the car stopped everybody was grinning.

Casey was like that. Big, thick through the chest and flat across the stomach, he was a burly figure with a rugged squarish face and craggy jaw. Gray peppered shaggy brown hair over the ears; his clothing was baggy but not cheap. His manner was often blunt, crabby; his dark eyes, without much illusion, were frequently sober. Sometimes he wore a grouch as a protective garment, but when he smiled he did a good job and seemed, somehow, to reflect a friendliness that was vital and genuine.

Whistling tunelessly, he bumped his cream-colored roadster out of its parking space at the curb, slid down Tremont Street through the gathering dusk of the June day. An afternoon rain had turned to a stubborn mist, leaving the pavement glossy and making shimmering red and green and orange lights of the traffic signal ahead of him.

He caught a green arrow at Boylston, and ten minutes later he was pounding briskly through the entrance of the Carteret. Answering the doorman's lofty, "Good evening, sir," he strode hard-heeled into the lobby as though he owned the place, bogged down slightly in ankle-deep carpet and bounced skilfully from a fat man's stomach when he winked at a marcelled blonde behind the magazine counter.

A silent elevator cushioned him to a stop on the ninth floor and he rapped a hard fist against a pastel-blue door marked Suite 9-B. He had a momentary wait; then the doorway was filled with a woman's silhouette and a vibrant contralto voice said:

"Flash."

"Norma." He got his hat off and took the firm, warm hand. "Gee, it's good to see you."

Silently she drew him into the entryway, took his arm, and they went into the room side by side. He saw from opened doorways beyond that there were at least three rooms to the suite. This first, the drawing room, was cream and green—hangings, upholstery, rug. Near the windows a man sat at a knee-hole desk which had apparently been moved in, because it did not go with the period furniture. There was a portable typewriter on the desk, a lot of scattered papers, a briefcase on the floor.

"Could you finish that some other time, Fred?" Norma asked.

"Surely." The man stood up, a slender, dark fellow with good clothes that he wore expertly. Definitely handsome in a rather brittle way, he gave Norma a reserved nod and a perfunctory smile as he withdrew.

"Martin—my husband—uses this as his office while he's in town," she explained, leading Casey to a Queen Anne love seat. "That's Fred Gilbert, his secretary."

Casey moved a damp polo coat from the chair, tossed it across the seat-back, sat down and studied briefly the woman opposite him. She was still just as attractive. Full-sized and meaty—the show-girl type—with auburn hair and liquid brown eyes. At least thirty, she remained beautifully put together; her jaw was clean and determined, with a rather pointed chin that was firm and smooth.

He had known her first as Norma Lamont, artist's model. Eight years ago that was. But even then she had been the sort that knew what she wanted and worked to that end. She had tried burlesque for a while, found she had a fair voice to go with her figure, and done a turn in vaudeville. Her first marriage, to her piano player, had not been much of a success from her viewpoint and she had gone West with a musical comedy after her divorce.

It was in Chicago that she met and married Martin Patten. Sure-shot Patten, they called him. Casey didn't know the man, but he knew of him. A well-known promoter and State Boxing Commissioner, Patten's name stood high in sporting circles, and his Eastern affiliations included a half interest in Norfolk Park, the local racing plant.

"I'm in trouble, Flash," Norma Patten said, and Casey, seeing her eyes upon him, knew that she spoke the truth.

A new and unaccustomed nervousness had put a jerkiness into her voice and tight lines around the mouth. She rose abruptly, went into an adjoining room and came back with a half dozen eight by ten photographs.

Standing in front of him she looked at them a moment, then fanned them out and showed them impulsively.

Casey's jaw went slack and his eyes widened. The photographs were of Norma Lamont in nude, or almost nude, poses. In two of these she grasped a bit of flowing chiffon about her; one showed her with a bath towel, apparently getting out of the tub. They were old, these pictures.

Casey saw that her face was younger, knew that they had probably been posed for various advertising clients.

Norma Patten whisked the pictures behind her. Casey stood up. In spite of himself he compared the rounded lines of this woman in her tailored dress with that glimpse of the nude pictures, and thought: Her figure is just as good now as it was then.

He was ashamed of the thought when he saw the trouble in her eyes, the way she tortured her red lower lip between her white even teeth.

"Blackmail?" he asked finally.

She nodded, then whirled and took the pictures into the adjoining room. When she returned she had a thick sheaf of fifty-dollar bills in her hand. She sat down and tapped them nervously against an open palm.

"A man brought the pictures yesterday," she began hurriedly. "He wants $25,000. Sorenson took them—years ago. I want you to take this ten thousand and see if you can buy the negatives back direct."

Casey's former jauntiness of manner and spirit fled and left his thick face somber, his dark eyes brooding.

"Wait a minute. How about your husband?"

"He knows. I had to tell him to get the money. He gave it to me—all of it."

"Then why doesn't he—"

"You don't know him, Flash." Norma Patten put a hand on his arm. "He doesn't know where the pictures came from, and I didn't dare tell him the name of the man who brought these copies. I told him I didn't know. We've been battling about it all day. If Martin knew where to go, well—I'm afraid of what he might do.

"I think he's planning some way to trap this man when he comes back, and he can't take the chance. If these pictures were printed, the publicity, the ridicule, would ruin him at home—everywhere. He—"

"Nobody'd dare print those," Casey argued. "You could sue."

Norma Patten shook her head wearily, spoke gently.

"No, Flash. Those were advertising studies, mostly. I was young, I needed the money. I had no great background; about all I had was a good figure and a determination to get to the top of the heap in any way I could. To collect on those pictures, I had to sign a release. Every model doing that sort of thing has to sign one—as a protection to the client.

"Well, Sorenson must have kept those negatives and the release. I've got to have both—particularly the release. I finally talked Martin into paying. I have the money. But if you go direct, Sorenson might take ten thousand. It would help to save that fifteen, and then I know Martin can't get mixed up in any trouble."

"I don't like it," Casey said. His brows drew down in a scowl and he rubbed the hinge of his jaw. He had never been intimate with Norma in the old days; she had always aimed a little higher than his prospects seemed to warrant. But he knew her, and had been at parties with her, accepted her as she was.

"Please. For old time's sake, Flash." The brown eyes were pleading, the lips parted, waiting breathlessly.

"I'm a chump to try it," Casey growled, "and a mug if I don't." He screwed morose eyes upon her. "Damn it, Norma! Why did you have to think of me?"

"I don't know anyone I could trust as I do you," the woman said simply. "And you couldn't be fooled about the negatives. You will try, won't you? Just try. It may not work. Sorenson may not have the negatives now. I don't know. But I've got to do something.

"The man, his name is Ambrose, who brought those prints, will call tomorrow and tell me what to do. He says if my husband is in on it, the deal is off. But Martin will *try* to be in on it and—"

"Okey," Casey grumbled, and snatched the sheaf of fifty-dollar bills. "But don't expect a miracle. Sorenson's a heel and if he's got the stuff maybe I can persuade him."

II

The mist had cleared and stars were a hazy counterpane against the dark blue sky. Along the quiet emptiness of Barlow Street two rows of ancient brown stone fronts marched in sedate columns that, under the cover of darkness, gave no inkling that most of them had gone commercial and been converted into small apartments and studios.

Casey parked his roadster in front of number 22 and stared morosely at the dimly lighted vestibule. Still grumbling over the job at hand, yet knowing there was no decent way he could have refused Norma Patten, he stepped to the sidewalk and started up the worn stone steps.

Scanning the vestibule mail boxes, he was about to reach for the inner door when it pulled away from his hand and a man popped through the opening. Without so much as a glance, he rushed past Casey and ran down the steps with coat tails flying. Casey grunted, stepped inside a musty-smelling hall and began to climb the ancient staircase.

Sorenson apparently rented the entire right side of the floor. A small sign directed Casey to enter at the door at the front of the hall, and he knocked here, noticed that light slid from a crack at the bottom and turned the knob.

He went in confidently, hesitated a moment as he noticed the disordered appearance of the office-like interior. Closing the door, he stepped towards the flat-topped desk flanked by barricades of steel filing cabinets, and had nearly reached the desk when he saw Sorenson.

The man was on his back on the floor with his neck cocked forward by his head, which was propped against one of the cabinets. Casey stiffened with his hands flat on the desk top, stared without breathing, then said:

"Sorenson."

The spoken word was not as silly as it sounded, because at that moment Casey was not sure. He swung around the end of the desk, knelt quickly beside the small, swart man with longish hair and a black tie that suggested a certain artiness, real or affected.

The black suit was mussed, disarranged; the collar was torn and there was a lump on one corner of the jaw, a bruise over the eye. It was not until Casey reached for an outstretched wrist that he saw the blood on the fabric of the coat. Opening this, he saw the wide reddish spot on the vest completely surrounding two tiny holes about four inches apart. There was no pulse.

Conscious, at last, that he was holding his breath, Casey exhaled noisily and stood up. For a moment a jumble of disordered thoughts vortexed crazily and he glanced about as he sought an answer.

Beyond the filing cabinet, the room had been arranged as a sort of waiting-room. There was a green rug, a leather divan, a few chairs, a table and two floor lamps. One of the chairs was overturned; so was one of the lamps. The drawer of one filing cabinet had been pulled clear out so that its load of manila folders had spilled on the floor; other drawers were open but still in the cabinets.

Ordinarily Casey's first move would have been to telephone the police. He had never kidded himself that he could outsmart the detective bureau, and he found it paid dividends to co-operate with fellows like Logan, Manahan, and Judson. But this time he was held back by his thought of Norma Patten.

Murder was something he wanted no part of. He cursed himself for coming here, cursed Norma for calling him up in the first place. Yet, now that he was here, he decided to look for the films. If he called the police first he might not get the chance to look, and he'd have too much explaining to do.

He went through the two connecting rooms of the studio, found them empty and came back to the waiting-room. As he passed the magazine table, he noticed an ashtray, and when he stopped to inspect the cigarette butts, he saw that one was of an ivory color. Scowling, he picked it up, sniffed it. It was a medicated brand.

He stared at it, twisted it in his fingers, finally put it back. Still scowling he stepped to the filing cabinets and began his search.

He had gone through one drawer and was starting on the second when he heard the quick rap of footsteps in the outer hall. Before he could do more than shut the drawer and jump to his feet, the door swung back and four men barged into the room and slid to a stop on the threshold.

The first man was the fellow who had run through the downstairs vestibule five minutes previous. Behind him stood Sergeant Haley and two plain-clothesmen.

"Well, well," Haley said and seemed to take a sneering enjoyment in the moment.

Trouble and dismay settled over Casey and he stood there, a burly, somber-eyed figure, as Haley approached.

Haley inspected the body briefly, glanced about, and said: "Looks like a .25. Got the gun?"

Casey said: "That's very funny," sourly.

Haley stood in front of Casey and bobbed his head. He was a tall, skinny man with shrewd green eyes and a perpetual sneer that fed on an ingrown grudge. His apparent dislike of the world in general became acute where Casey was concerned, and the animosity was mutual and of long standing; both men had long since accepted it.

"Well," Haley said again, "what're you waiting for? Let's have it."

"Have what?" Casey grunted.

"First—how you happen to be here?"

Casey did not hesitate long on his question. Possibly, had Lieutenant Logan been the questioner, Casey might have told the truth. But under Haley's sneering methods a sullen stubbornness welled up and he said:

"I got a tip—a phone call—and I came down to have a look."

Haley glanced about. "Where's the camera then?"

"I wasn't sure what it was so I didn't bring it."

"Baloney," lipped Haley. "What were you searching for?"

"Who was searching?" Casey bluffed.

"You were. Look at these drawers."

"You look," Casey said. "They were that way when I came." He glared at the wiry little man who stood looking on with eyes popping and jaw slack.

"You saw me downstairs," he rapped.

"Yes," the fellow gulped. "I—I'm a photographer. I do work for Mr. Sorenson now and then, and I had an appointment at nine o'clock. I came up here and—"

"There you are," Casey told Haley.

"He saw you downstairs," Haley leered, "but that ain't no alibi."

"Find out when he was killed," Casey said, "and I'll have an alibi." He tugged at his hat brim, buttoned his trench coat and started for the door.

"Hey," Haley called, "I'm not through with you. You've been here alone about five minutes. If you were on the level you'd've called Headquarters. I want to know things and you're gonna stick around until—"

"I am, huh?" Casey said. "Is it a pinch?"

"Never mind. Just do as I say."

Casey smiled, a mirthless gesture that, with the look in his hard, narrowed eyes, was ominous. The effect was part of his act. He wanted to get out, to have time to look around before Haley checked up on him, and he kept on with his bluff.

"Any time you want me at Headquarters to answer your questions you know where to find me," he said defiantly. "But I don't stay here and watch you fiddle around. I've got work to do."

Casey seldom bluffed. When he did he had the build and the manner to do it convincingly. And right now Haley wasn't quite sure of his ground. He advanced slowly, his thin face red and frustration in his eyes.

"You want to get tough about it?" he challenged.

"I don't have to," Casey said flatly. "I know my rights. If you want to keep me here, pinch me." He cocked a disdainful brow. "Otherwise—"

No more sure of his rights or his ground than Haley, Casey saw the sergeant hesitate. Then he opened the door and went out quickly with Haley's baffled threat ringing in his ears.

III

 he Hut is on the wrong side of Beacon Hill. The street it fronts is narrow, one-way, and hardly worthy of the term—street. The immediate neighborhood is sordid and decadent, with cubbyhole store fronts here and there, and two or three floors of tenements above. In the daytime, the cobblestones form a playground for smutty-nosed urchins; at night, to a casual passerby, it is just an alley.

Yet to the initiate, the Hut is a restaurant. There is a long, low room, dimly lighted and generally smoke-filled. The floor is rough planking and the tables are a hundred years old and look older. The food is good, and more expensive than the surroundings would lead you to believe. The only entertainment is a piano, presided over by the Professor, and, more recently, a girl who sings.

At a quarter of ten, there were but four tables occupied. Casey slid into one of the oaken booths and ordered rye and soda.

The girl was singing. In the half-light she seemed young and nice-looking rather than pretty. Her voice, although not strong or cultivated, was sweet. The accompaniment was soft, swinging, sort of dreamy and full of chords. Both local and visiting orchestra leaders came here for dinner frequently because the Professor could play; he had a left hand that piano players liked to match.

When the number ended, Casey summoned the waiter and told him he wanted to speak to the Professor. Shortly a stringy, sandy-haired fellow shuffled up to the booth. Seeing Casey, he smiled and said:

"Hello, Flash. How's it?"

"Sit down, Les. What'll you have."

The Professor—Les Boyden—slid down on the opposite bench and put up a palm. "Nothing, thanks," he said.

Casey lit a cigarette, studied Boyden over the match flame. The face was pleasant, but tired, with a look of a man who is not very well. A half smile was quite constant, but the blue eyes were pale and dull, and there was a weakness, somehow, to the mouth and jaw.

Norma Patten had once been Mrs. Les Boyden. Back when they had been a vaudeville team. Casey remembered this, and, seeking some lead on the Sorenson murder that might connect with Norma Patten, he had come here to see Boyden. He wanted time to think about this man, and he kept his voice casual and did not come to the point directly.

"How long you had the girl?" he asked.

"About three months."

"Where'd you get her?"

"She just came in." Boyden flipped a thin-fingered hand in an aimless gesture: "She came in and wanted to sing for her dinner. Honest."

He smiled at Casey, then looked away when the photographer eyed him questioningly without speaking.

"She was down to her last dime. Desperate. I guess this was her last stop on the way to the river. Anyway, she came in and was standing by the piano when I saw her."

There was a far-off look in Boyden's eyes and he continued in the absent tones of a man talking to himself.

"Well, I couldn't throw her out. She stuck around until I started another piece and then, damned if she didn't start to sing anyway." His eyes came back to Casey's. "She's been here ever since. She can sing, can't she?"

Casey nodded, and Boyden's manner brightened.

"And she's getting noticed. I'm dickering now for a spot on the radio. I think we might go places some day. She's got something. I don't know what it is. Something sort of genuine and sweet in her voice, like Kate Smith. I want you to meet her."

"Wait," Casey said.

But Boyden had already stood up, and in a minute or so he came back with the girl.

Boyden introduced Flash to her—Mary Nason.

She stood at the end of the booth as Casey rose. Her smile helped his first impression. Nice-looking, genuine. Her hair was dark and wavy and simply done. She had a trim little figure and nice hands and a rounded chin that looked firm and smooth. After a moment of conversation, Boyden said:

"About ten minutes, Mary, and we'll do a number for Flash." He watched her walk across the floor, then turned. "How do you like her?"

"She's nice," Casey said. "You like her too, huh?"

"Yeah," Boyden said, flushing slightly. "But I thought you might give her a plug sometime."

"You know Norma's in town?" Casey asked after a pause.

"Yes, I saw in the paper she was."

"Seen her?"

Boyden shook his head. Casey said casually: "Got a cigarette?"

"Only these." Boyden took out a brown paper package, shook out a cigarette wrapped in ivory-colored paper. "You wouldn't like them."

Casey took one, rolled it absently and said: "I always had a feeling she gave you a dirty deal."

"Perhaps—perhaps not. I guess it was my fault. I was in love with her and I married her. She was ambitious and had the determination to get what she wanted. When she made her mind up to do anything she went right ahead. She had what it takes and I didn't, that's all.

"I had ambitions too, but I wouldn't sacrifice everything else for them. I guess I never had enough guts or backbone to step with Norma." He shrugged, smiled weakly. "But that's all over. And no hard feelings. She saw a chance to get ahead alone and took it."

"You don't hold a grudge, do you?"

"No. Why? What're you trying to prove?"

"Somebody's been blackmailing her," Casey said, and his eyes narrowed in his study of Boyden's loose face. "With some old nude pictures Sorenson took. He was murdered tonight."

Boyden was smiling when Casey spoke, and the smile remained, a ghastly thing. It took him seconds to freeze out that smile and say:

"I asked you what you were tryin' to prove."

"I don't know," Casey said, and went on to tell how he had gone to try and buy the negatives and release from Sorenson. "And," he finished, "I think you were at Sorenson's place."

"Don't rib me, Flash," Boyden said, his face chalky. "Not about a thing like that."

"I wouldn't rib you," Casey said. "But I found a cigarette butt at his place." He lifted the cigarette in his hand. "Like this one."

Boyden swallowed with an effort. "Plenty of guys smoke them besides me."

"Some, but not plenty."

"It doesn't prove anything."

"Not a thing," Casey said. "That's why I came to ask." He sighed, pocketed the cigarette. "I may be wrong, but I always thought you had a yen for Norma in spite of the fact that she used you to climb. I thought maybe you might be helping out or something—like I was—and spill what you knew.

"But then again," he added dryly, "maybe you were just waiting for a chance to pay her back. You knew Sorenson. A few large coarse banknotes—say a cut of twenty-five grand—"

"Twenty-five?" Boyden husked.

"Yeah?" Casey said curiously, unable to analyze this new reaction. "A piece of that would help to put you and your singer over in a big way, wouldn't it?"

Boyden straightened up. His lips drew down; his eyes grew frosty.

"You're wasting your time," he said, "on a newspaper. You oughta go after Edgar Hoover's job."

"Okey," Casey said. He beckoned the waiter and paid his check. "But I was at Sorenson's looking for the negatives when the police crashed in. They didn't like my story—it wasn't very good. Sometime pretty soon I've got to give 'em the details."

"So"—he stood up—"*I* was just checking to see if I could find something to help my story."

There was a telephone in the dimly lighted foyer, and Casey stepped inside and called Norma Patten. When he had told her what had happened at Sorenson's he said:

"It's gonna be a mess, Norma, but there's one place I might try before I call it off. Who is this guy Ambrose that made the touch yesterday?"

"I think his name was Sol Ambrose," Norma Patten said.

"Oh, that one," Casey growled. "The shyster, huh? Okey, I'll see if I can find him on the way back to the Carteret."

"Please, Flash," Norma pleaded, "don't make it worse."

"I won't," Casey said. "I'll just give him a scare and see what happens."

IV

he so-called office building that served as Sol Ambrose's business address was a gloomy brick walk-up not far from Atlantic Avenue. Light from a frosted glass door spread an elongated rectangle across the dusty third-floor hall and up the cracked wall opposite. Casey opened the door without knocking and stalked in aggressively.

A plump, red-faced man with two chins and a shiny bald pate was hunched behind a book-filled desk. Small black eyes, nearly lost in the shadows, blinked angrily while Sol Ambrose half rose, poised, dropped back in his seat.

"Why don't you knock?" he asked resentfully.

Casey moved up to the desk, pushed some books out of the way and slid a thick thigh across one corner.

"Hello, Sol," he said levelly.

"I don't know you," Ambrose said.

"Don't let it bother you," Casey said. "I just stopped in to get those pictures you're holding for Norma Patten."

Ambrose blinked and his head seemed to shrink between hunched shoulders. He wet his lips and his eyes mirrored alarm as they swiveled helplessly about the room.

"Huh? What pictures?" he blustered.

"The ones you thought you'd get twenty-five grand for. I want the negatives and the release. And snap it up, I'm in a hurry."

Ambrose tried to outstare the burly figure perched on his desk, dropped his glance when he saw the bad look in Casey's eyes. Finally he cleared his throat, and with forced authority said:

"Beat it or I'll call the cops!"

"I said, snap it up!" Casey growled.

Ambrose reached for a telephone in nervous alarm. Casey slid off the desk, slapped the lawyer's hand aside. One long step put him behind the desk and, reaching down, he grabbed Ambrose's vest and jerked him erect with one hand.

"You've got two chances," Casey said, shaking the lawyer a bit for emphasis. "If you want to pass that stuff over I might pay you ten grand for it. If not, I'm gonna beat hell out of you, search this joint and drag you down to Headquarters."

Ambrose swallowed and his eyes bulged. Casey was still bluffing and he was still convincing—and here the odds were all his. Ambrose was not in a very good spot to argue. Thrice on the brink of disbarment he had a shady reputation and barely enough legitimate business to pay his rent. He opened his mouth, shut it; then Casey shook him again and rapped:

"Make up your mind!"

"I don't know nothing about it," Ambrose whined.

"You put the touch on her, didn't you?" Casey countered. He held the lawyer at arm's length and drew back his fist.

"But I haven't got those negatives."

"You know where they are."

"Suppose I do. What—"

That word was chewed off short. It was the last word Sol Ambrose ever spoke.

Casey was staring right at the lawyer's face.

He saw that face jerk sidewise, the red spot jump out on one corner of the forehead, the spatter of blood on the hand that gripped the vest; yet it was a full second before he realized what had happened.

There had been no warning, no sound of the door opening; even the roar of the gun seemed late. Somehow he was still waiting for Ambrose's next word: waiting, and staring into suddenly vacant eyes, and supporting a sagging weight with his left arm.

Casey broke the grip of surprise with latent action that tried to recover the lost second. He dropped Ambrose, forgot him and spun towards the door.

It was ajar. He thought he saw a wisp of powder smoke in the opening as he raced towards it. With no preconceived plan except to get a glimpse of the killer, he yanked the door open and dashed into the hall.

Too late he saw the out-thrust foot and realized the man had waited with his back against the wall for just such a headlong rush. Casey stumbled, crashed into the opposite wall and dropped to the floor. Before he could lift his head a gun muzzle jabbed into the nape of his neck.

"Up!" a whispered voice commanded. "Up. Easy, and with your face in the wall."

Casey stood up.

"Pull your hat down," the voice directed. "Over your ears."

Casey, prompted by the pressure of the gun and the knowledge he could not hope to reach the hand that held it, pulled his battered felt down over his ears with both hands. Another hand reached in front and tugged at the brim to make sure it was over his eyes.

"Now into the office—and keep your chin down or I'll knock it down."

Casey felt his way into the room. The gun was withdrawn. After the door closed he heard the man behind him, and a hand began to pat his trench coat pockets. Again the gun pressed against his spine while the hand tapped his hip pockets.

"No cannon?" the voice whispered.

Casey stiffened as something inside him froze. For the first time he was conscious of the bulging bulk in his inside coat pocket; that ten thousand dollars seemed to press against his chest and make it hard to breathe.

The hand moved up. Slapping the armpits and chest it tapped the pocket two or three times experimentally. And Casey stood there with the sweat coming out on his face, afraid to move lest he betray himself.

"What's this?" the voice said coolly, and a hand slid inside the coat.

The bulge vanished. Casey shot his eyes down past the rim of his hat at the bridge of his nose. All he could see was a gray coat sleeve, a lean, thin-fingered hand—and that sheaf of fifty-dollar bills.

Outraged anger rather than the fear of what might happen when he confessed his loss to Norma Patten motivated Casey's next move. It was a foolish play, risky, without much hope of success; but then when Casey was mad he was not always reasonable.

Whirling with a savage grunt, he ducked and dived behind him, arms outstretched. Apparently the man moved with the skill of an adagio dancer. Casey smacked the floor on his knees, brushed a slender leg but failed to grasp it; then the gun rapped down on his head and he went flat on the floor.

"Get up, chump!" the voice ordered grimly.

Casey heard a door open as he obeyed. Presently he felt the gun in his back again and he was being pushed through a doorway into what he felt was a closet.

He sensed the movement behind him. It was like a swish of air, intuitive rather than actual. He tried to duck; then pain exploded in his brain from a smash back of his ear. His knees crumpled and he went down. Behind him he thought he heard the door close and the bolt snap home.

At no time was Casey entirely unconscious. Half-stunned at first, he fought the dizziness in his head, wrenched off his hat and got to his knees. He remained that way a minute or so, and when the roaring in his ears abated, he could hear the killer searching the office. He stood up and oriented himself in the darkness, but he made no attempt to break out until he heard the man slam the outer door; then he put his shoulder against the closet door and tried to smash the panel or the lock.

He kept to these tactics for several minutes. The closet was so small he could not draw back for a real charge, could get no momentum.

Finally he rested, and while he devised another method he heard the office door open again. He listened. Someone was moving about. He could hear desk drawers open and close; a filing cabinet rasped on its metal slides.

Casey rapped on the door. The only result was a slap of heels on the floor and the clicking of the outer door. He cursed, arched his back against the rear wall of the closet, put one foot at a time beside the lock and, bent almost double, strained to straighten out.

The door creaked under the thrust of his powerful muscles. He rested, still wedged clear of the floor, took a breath and tried again. This time the lock ripped from the panel. The door flew open and he dropped heavily on his back.

Picking himself up, he went straight to the telephone and swept it into his hands. He barked a number, stood there, a burly, impatient figure with a trickle of blood on one ear and his eyes sultry and brooding.

When he got his connection he said: "Police Headquarters? Lemme speak to Lieutenant Logan."

V

uite 9-B at the Carteret had acquired a different aspect. Cigar smoke hung in a blue haze from the ceiling and the air had a stale, stuffy smell. Two plain-clothesmen, who looked bored and indifferent, leaned against the wall adjacent to the doorway. In the center of the room Sergeant Haley and Captain Judson were looking down at a slender hard-muscled man of forty-five or so; nearby, on the love seat, sat Norma Patten.

Casey, entering with Lieutenant Logan, stopped short and his surprise was apparent on his thick face. Because he trusted Logan, he had given him the whole story in Sol Ambrose's office; but he was unprepared for this sort of scene. Haley gave him the clue as to why the police were here in his first greeting.

"So—" He leered. "A tip was what took you to Sorenson's place, huh? I knew you were lying and I checked you. They told us at your office you'd come to the Carteret for a date with Norma." His green eyes narrowed scornfully and he turned to Logan. "Glad you picked him up."

Casey took a deep breath and anger boiled up inside him.

"He didn't pick me up," he grunted. "I called him."

"Sol Ambrose, the shyster, was knocked off about a half hour ago," Logan said quietly.

Haley gaped. Judson, a tall, long-jawed veteran, muffled a curse and sucked in his lips. The man in the chair gave no outward reaction at all, but Norma Patten gasped audibly and color drained from her cheeks, leaving them chalky except for the rouge spots.

"Tell them, Flash," Logan said crisply.

Casey told his story, told it with a smoldering stubbornness when he related how the ten thousand had been taken from his pocket. Norma Patten's eyes were sharp and accusing when he began to talk, and he avoided them until he finished; then he walked over to her and said thickly:

"I'm sorry, Norma. I guess I should have come back here from Sorenson's. But I thought I had a chance with Ambrose."

His voice got thready as memory recalled that moment when he felt the money leave his pocket.

"I *did* have a chance," he added sullenly. "Ambrose would've talked. That's why the killer plugged him when he did. He would've spilled something and—"

"It doesn't matter, Flash," Norma Patten said wearily. "Not now." She tried to smile, failed and dropped her eyes to the folded hands in her lap.

Judson rubbed his chin thoughtfully, pulling his lower jaw to one side. Haley bobbed his head and his eyes were gloating.

"What time did Ambrose get it?" he asked.

"About ten-thirty, I guess," Casey said glumly.

"And *he* took the ten grand, huh? Sure you didn't misplace it?"

Casey's eyes smoldered deep and hot beneath narrowed brows, but he said nothing. Haley turned to the man on the chair.

"Where were you at ten-thirty, Patten?"

"I don't remember exactly," Patten said levelly.

"There's ways of makin' guys like you remember," Haley threatened.

"And there's ways of putting smart cops in their places."

"Say, listen, you—" Haley began angrily.

"Pipe down!" Judson snapped. He glanced irritably at Haley and turned back to Patten. There was a worried look on his competent face and he seemed to be choosing his approach.

Casey thought he understood this uncertainty. Patten carried a lot of weight; even here in the East. Sitting there in the chair, apparently unconcerned about his position, he was a slender, gray man with a hard, tight mouth above an angular jaw. His suit was gray, so were his eyes; gray and icy hard. His straight hair and clipped mustache were gray-black.

To Casey it seemed that this man had something in common with his wife; they gave the impression that they got what they wanted out of life. And about Patten there was a quiet confidence, a surface covering for an inner hardness, and an air of one who was accustomed to success and could not be bluffed or pushed around.

Then Casey remembered something else. The hand that had taken the ten thousand dollars—slender, long fingered with a gray sleeve. Suspicion darkened his eyes. Patten had that kind of a hand and sleeve and—so had Les Boyden. The long, supple fingers of a piano player. The color of his suit Casey could not remember.

"Never mind this Ambrose thing now," Judson said finally. "What I'm interested in is Sorenson. You've got no alibi, Patten. Or if you have, you won't tell it. And that hand"—Judson reached down quickly and lifted Patten's right hand. From where he stood Casey could see that the knuckles were skinned. Patten smiled and his brows climbed. "What about it?" he asked easily.

"You knew about those pictures," Judson said. "And you went down to Sorenson's place to get them. You had a fight with him. Before you got through you plugged him."

"No!" Norma Patten cried. "He couldn't have—he didn't know where to go. I didn't tell him and—"

"He saw the pictures, didn't he?" Judson cut in. "He gave you the ten thousand?"

"Yes, but he couldn't know—"

"Why couldn't he?" Judson picked one of the photographs from a table, held it up to the light, tossed it back with a shrug. "Sorenson had a small stamp that perforated his pictures. He probably made these some time ago, and stamped them for identification. There's an S in each picture. If anybody was interested it wouldn't be hard to find out who S is in the photo studio line."

Norma Patten's eyes were wide and she gave her husband a quick enigmatic glance before she looked away.

"You've got your wires crossed, Captain," Patten said. "Mrs. Patten and myself both made mistakes on this thing. For obvious reasons I wanted those negatives and release." He gave his wife a cold, hard stare and Casey, seeing it, wondered how much he meant by it. "And I gave her the money, foolishly, because I thought I could get to the contact man when he came back. What I should have done was have her tell this guy that he'd have to do business with me."

He gave Judson a direct look from under his brows. "I can assure you if I had known about the details I wouldn't have bothered with the

photographer; I'd have gone right to this Ambrose lad and—"

"Maybe you did," Haley cut in.

Judson turned with a grunt of irritation. Haley shrugged and looked away. Patten continued evenly.

"Her mistake was to call this photographer in." He eyed Casey skeptically and sucked on his lips.

"Because it was my fault in the first place," Norma Patten said sharply, "and I thought maybe I could save you fifteen thousand."

"The point is," Patten added, "that we're out ten thousand—apparently—and haven't anything to show for it." He stood up, tall and straight and impressive in his unruffled manner. "Now if that fact, or anything else you have, leads you to believe that I killed Sorenson, or Ambrose for that matter, go ahead and arrest me. If not—"

He shrugged, waited a moment, his manner indicating that he considered the interview at an end.

"We're not ready for an arrest—yet," Judson said irritably. "But maybe we will be when we get through checking up on you."

"Any time you say, Captain. Just let me know and I'll be glad to come down to Headquarters—with a lawyer."

VI

An assignment that took Casey out of town to cover a kidnapping trial kept him busy most of the following day, and it was late afternoon before he returned to the city. A half hour later he trudged down the third-floor corridor at Police Headquarters to Logan's office and went in without knocking.

Logan was standing with his back to the door, staring out the lone window at the court below. He turned slowly, scowled, then returned to his window gazing without a word.

Casey put down his camera and plate-case and dropped wearily into a straight-backed chair beside the desk. His mood was grouchy and irritable. The work of the day had yielded but one routine picture, and at no time had he been able to shake off the blanket of resentment that had wrapped around him since last night.

His worry was no longer about Norma Patten or her husband, or who had killed Sorenson and Ambrose. Now that the matter was no secret it was, as far as he was concerned, a strictly police case—except for the ten thousand. That, no matter how he looked at it, seemed to be his fault, and he could not forget it.

The story of the killings had been fairly well hushed up. No newspaperman but himself knew of Patten's connection—or about the photographs. And since neither Sorenson nor Ambrose were of any great importance in the life of the city, the newspapers' accounts were not unduly lengthy, and there was little more than a hint that there might be a connection between the two deaths.

"Well, what the hell do *you* want?" Logan asked finally, coming over to the desk.

"Nothing," Casey said, "except the guy that lifted that ten grand from me."

"Then there really was a guy, huh?"

Casey shoved out his legs and eyed Logan morosely. "What're *you* sore at. I suppose when Norma Patten told me her story last night I shoulda grabbed a phone and let you in on it."

"You'd been better off."

"Damned if I wouldn't," Casey admitted disgustedly.

"You oughta know better than to try this amateur detective stuff."

"Detective stuff, hell!" Casey growled. "I was just a contact man—and I got a hunch Ambrose would've got knocked off whether I'd stopped there or not."

"Yeah," Logan said. "I wouldn't be surprised."

He sat down opposite Casey, sighed and lit a cigarette, a tall, good-looking man with black eyes and black hair. His oxford gray suit was immaculate, his linen was fresh and his shoes were neatly polished. Competent, hard without making a fuss about it, he knew his job—and he knew Casey.

There was, between these two, a mutual respect and admiration founded upon experience and a long association; and for once their glum and somber moods seemed to synchronize. Presently Logan got comfortable in his chair and began to talk.

"Why didn't you tell us you went down to the Hut to see the Professor last night?"

Casey looked up, momentarily startled.

"I don't know," he said, and sounded as if he meant it. "I wasn't sure where he fitted and—"

"We aren't sure now," Logan muttered. "But someplace, son; someplace. We found he'd been at Sorenson's studio earlier in the evening."

"And what's he say?" Casey asked, interested now.

Logan's brows knotted at the bridge of his nose and he waved the cigarette in a gesture of resentment and defeat. "We don't know. We can't find him. All we know is that he was packing a gun last night—a waiter saw it when he sat down at the piano once. But he is in this someplace or he'd be around."

Casey told about his talk with Boyden the previous night, and then asked: "How does Patten stand?"

"Number one," Logan said. "We've got a lot of things on that baby." He ground out his cigarette and sat up, eyes thoughtful. "We had him down here all morning. We're pretty sure he was at Sorenson's and we found a taxi-driver that took him to Ambrose's office building somewhere around ten-thirty. The driver can't be sure about the time."

"Pinch him?"

"Not yet." Logan spread his hands. "We've got to be careful. That guy is no lightweight. He knows a lot of right people around here, including the D.A. And the D.A. says watch him and see what happens.

"We've got a hundred plain-clothesmen out snooping around checking up; and every man in the department is looking for Les Boyden. When we find him we might be ready to go to town. Somebody besides Sorenson and Ambrose is in on this job and—"

"Figure it for me," Casey said.

Logan cocked a brow and his dark eyes were searching. "You haven't got any ideas, have you?"

"I don't want any," Casey said. "I'm just an amateur."

Logan grinned at the big photographer's grumbling manner and went on with his story.

"I figure it this way: Sorenson, Ambrose and the Professor cooked up this touch. The Professor got a dirty deal from Norma Patten. She used him as a stepping-stone, and she's the sort of woman that would get what she wants. And if he got the chance my guess is the Professor would grab an angle to pay off.

"He probably knew of those old modeling days, maybe about those same pictures. It was in the paper she was in town. So maybe he got in touch with Sorenson, or the other way around, and the two of them got Ambrose to make the touch.

"And"—Logan's voice got crisp and precise—"the only thing wrong with the picture was Sure-shot Patten. Nobody'd push that guy around much. I think he went gunning when he got the tip-off from the S-mark on those photographs.

"He probably didn't go to Sorenson's to kill him, but things happen like that sometimes. And after he got Sorenson he had to see Ambrose. When he found you there—bingo. He didn't know what Ambrose had to say and he was afraid to let him talk—to you." Logan hesitated thoughtfully. "I don't say that's right, understand. But it could be."

"So now," Casey said thoughtfully, "you're wondering if Patten got to Boyden, or whether Boyden is hiding out."

"Something like that."

Casey stood up and retrieved his plate-case and camera. "Well," he said, "I don't want any part of it. I got banged around, lost ten grand and

didn't even get a picture out of it. All I want is to know where that dough is."

VII

asey went back to the office to leave his camera and plate-case. He had dinner on his way home, arriving there about eight o'clock, and when he opened his apartment door he found Mary Nason, the singing girl he'd met at the Hut, sitting bolt upright in his wing chair, her hands gripping the arms.

She rose quickly when he shut the door and met him in the center of the room, a small, white-faced girl with a tightness around her lips and alarm in the depths of her brown eyes.

"Now what?" Casey said, and was rather gruff about it because he'd had enough trouble.

"It's Les. You've got to find him."

"Not me," Casey said. He detoured around the girl, went into the adjoining bedroom and got his pipe.

"But you've got to," the girl said, following at his heels. "He's in trouble and—"

"How do you know?"

"Because—well—he is."

"Then go to the cops. That's their business."

He went back to the living-room and sat down. The girl dropped into the wing chair, fumbled with the handbag in her lap for a moment. When she spoke again her voice was low and pleading.

"Please. You can help us."

"I gave him a chance last night," Casey said bluntly. "He wouldn't talk. You know what he was tryin' to do, don't you?" The girl shook her head, mute, and Casey told about Logan's theory of the twenty-five-thousand-dollar blackmail effort.

"I—I don't believe it," she gasped when he finished.

"Then why is he in trouble?" Casey's brows pulled down suspiciously. "You know where he is?" he added.

"Yes."

"Then why don't you go to him?"

"I don't know which apartment he's in. And—I'm afraid. I thought you would help me—I thought you were a friend of his." She leaned across the chair arm and went on hurriedly. "I don't know why he's gone. But it's something wrong. I know."

"It's a police job then," Casey said. Ordinarily he would have been more receptive to this plea, but at the moment the remains of his grouch still festered and the girl had not yet penetrated his protective shell. "In fact," he added, "I'll call 'em right now and then you won't need to worry any more."

He stepped to the telephone. Behind him as he lifted the receiver he heard the girl's gasp; then her voice, thin and cold, saying:

"Put that down or I'll shoot!"

Casey turned slowly, amazement in his eyes.

Mary Nason stood rigidly in the center of the floor, her young face taut and her mouth tight. A little .25 automatic trembled in her hand.

Casey frowned, made his voice casual. "Okey. If that's the way it is." He put down the telephone and came towards her slowly, the frown changing to a tolerant grin.

"You can't go to the police until I know why he has gone," Mary Nason breathed.

"Suit yourself," Casey said. He stopped in front of her, glanced down at the gun. "Can't you hold it steady?" he asked. And as her eyes dropped to watch her hand, he reached down quickly and twisted the automatic gently from her grasp.

The change in the girl was startling. She looked up at him and a whiteness came around her quivering lips. Then she was trembling, as though long, racking shudders passed through her. The sight of this raw emotion, the realization that her motive was so important that, knowing nothing of the game, she had forced herself to pull a gun, cracked Casey's callous crust.

He was at once ashamed of himself; yet troubled now on her behalf. Because he knew now

that he liked her, her simple genuineness, and he was afraid Les Boyden was involved more deeply than she dreamed. Drawing her back to the chair, he pushed her gently into it and said:

"Tell me the rest of it."

She began to sob softly, and Casey let her alone until she had recovered some of her composure. When at last she looked up, she began to speak hurriedly.

"Last night a man came to the Hut. I didn't see him at first because he talked with Les out in the foyer. When I went to look for Les and didn't see him, I went to the door. He was just getting into a taxi."

"Did you get a look at the man who was with him?" Casey asked her sharply.

"Not a good look. I just saw his back. He was about as tall as Les and slender. It seemed funny, his going out like that, but I didn't think he'd want me to run out on the street after him. I thought it might be business."

A dry sob interrupted her for a moment. "But he didn't come back. He wasn't at his rooms all night. And then I read about the Sorenson murder, and I'd heard Les say he was going to see Sorenson yesterday. So I didn't dare go to the police until—"

"How do you know where Les is?"

"I recognized the taxi-driver. He gave me the address." She gave a Randall Street number, adding: "And I thought you—"

Casey said: "All right," and stood up, pocketing the little automatic and remembering that Sorenson had been shot by just such a gun.

"Promise you won't tell the police," Mary Nason begged.

Casey shook his head. The thing was too mixed-up for him to try and figure out now, but if he could find Les Boyden it might be worth a look. It would be a sort of backhand favor for the girl maybe; and there was a chance of finding where that ten thousand dollars went. But he'd have to tip off Logan. He knew that, knew he was in no spot to handle a case like this alone.

"I can't promise that," he said. "But I'll look up this place, and then call up a personal friend of mine on the force. I'll promise you this: I'll get the best break I can for Les."

"All right," Mary Nason said weakly.

"If he's in a jam he's got to face it some time."

"Yes."

"You'd better run on home until—"

"I'd rather stay here," Mary Nason said. "Can I?"

"Sure," Casey said, making his voice confident. "And keep your chin up."

VIII

The number Mary Nason had given Casey proved to be a three-story apartment house built in the shape of an inverted U with little patches of lawn crisscrossed by the walks that led to the three doors on each wing and the two doors at the end section.

Without difficulty he located the janitor, a squat, beetle-browed man with a thick Irish brogue, and learned that the renting agent had brought a tall, slender man to look at apartment 3-B the day before. With this information he went to the nearest drug-store and called police headquarters.

When he had talked with Logan, he came back to the apartment court and opened the second door on the right. The stairs mounted in short, square turns, and there were two facing doors on each small landing. At the third, Casey stared at the brass 3-B tacked to the panel and listened.

Here, right under the roof, it was hot and stuffy. Moisture glistened on his broad face as he took the little automatic out and palmed it. Below him, the stairwell was a welter of sound while three radios—a dance band, a political speech and a light opera—fought it out in a discordance that made it impossible for him to concentrate. After a moment he knocked.

He knocked again before he got an answer, and then a voice said: "Who is it?"

"'Tis the janitorr," Casey said, trying to imitate the janitor's brogue.

A lock clicked. The door swung back and Casey stepped quickly into the opening. The automatic flipped up in his hand and he turned sidewise, jabbing the gun into the man's stomach as he slid up even with him.

For an instant as they stood there close together and immobile, Casey did not recognize this man. Then the handsome, dark face, the slender, immaculate figure clicked into place and he remembered. Norma Patten had introduced this fellow as her husband's secretary.

He said: "Hello, Gilbert. Back up!"

Gilbert backed and Casey heeled the door shut. Gilbert wet his lips, made a grotesque effort to smile which was little more than a baring of the white, even teeth.

"What's the idea?" he blustered finally.

"I don't know," Casey said flatly. "This is a big surprise to me; I was just looking for Les Boyden. Seen him?"

"Boyden?" Gilbert arched neat black brows, but his eyes weren't in the effort. "I don't think I know him."

"I do," Casey said. "Let's look. Just keep your hands in sight and play nice. I don't like trouble any more."

Les Boyden was in the adjoining bedroom. He was lying on the bed with his hands and feet tied, and when Casey shook him he saw that the fellow had been drugged and was in a comatose condition.

Casey's voice was hard and sultry when he pushed Gilbert back into the living-room.

"Well, that gives me one answer," he said. "You're the guy that called at the Hut for him last night. Why?"

Gilbert opened his mouth and shut it without speaking. His handsome face was very set and growing paler. His eyes were wary and uncertain and his hands moved nervously at his sides. Casey saw the bulge of a gun in one pocket, but he was content to keep this fellow covered until Logan arrived.

"You'll talk pretty soon," he added. "And then maybe we'll see if you're the louse that gunned out Ambrose and lifted that ten grand." Casey sucked in his lips and his eyes took on a dangerous glint that was partly anticipation. He knew he ought to wait for Logan, but he hated to do it.

"Because if you are," he added, "I'm gonna take a sock at you and even up for the grief and the raps you gave me. Suppose we go to Headquarters and talk it over."

"Suppose you drop the gun!"

Casey's nerves snapped taut at the curt authority in the new voice, and he stiffened rigidly, every muscle tense. Actually he was too startled to drop the gun. He didn't drop it; he turned his head. In the half-opened door was the grim-faced figure of Sure-shot Patten; in his right hand was a .38 automatic.

Even then Casey did not drop his gun. He knew better than to argue, and he dropped his arm, but he continued to stare while Patten sidled into the room and shut the door.

"I said, *drop it!*"

This time Casey let go of the gun and blew out his breath.

Patten came forward very slowly, very cautiously, as though he expected some hidden menace. When he got close, Casey saw the cold fury in the man's gray eyes. They seemed very small and bright and absolutely merciless; the lips and mustache had a flat, stretched look.

"So that's it, huh?" Casey said bitterly. He didn't know exactly what he meant, but he wanted to talk; and he felt the luxury of relief that he had called Logan. All he had to do was play along; so he thought of other things to say, and said them as they occurred to him.

"It was you and this louse, Gilbert, from the start, huh? Sorenson, Ambrose and Boyden ganged up for the touch and you slipped a cog and skidded into murder. Well"—his lids came down—"it'll take more than a flock of friends to get you out of this."

Patten's reaction to all this was peculiar. If he heard, he gave no sign. Not once did his expression change, and all the time those cold gray eyes kept moving, searching every corner of the room.

"Where's Norma?" he rapped suddenly.

"Norma?" echoed Casey hollowly; then glanced at the stone-faced Gilbert to see that the man's eyes were bright with new alarm.

"She called me," Patten pressed, "and I—"

A muffled pounding checked the sentence. Casey's jaw went slack and his eyes slid to a closed door in an inner hall, apparently a closet.

"Open it!" Patten ordered.

Casey stepped up and tried the knob. When he opened the door Norma Patten half fell into his arms. Her eyes were wide and startled, her auburn hair disheveled. A blue-checked scarf made a makeshift gag and she had apparently nearly freed her hands of the belt of her camel's-hair sport coat, which was wound around her wrists.

"Martin!" she gasped as soon as she could talk.

"Well," Patten said stonily.

"I was afraid you'd come and—I had to call you." Norma Patten stood with breast heaving and color high. She thrust her hands into her coat pockets and turned to face Fred Gilbert, the lines of her jaw hard and her eyes flashing. Then she turned back to her husband and began to talk.

"There," she said, pointing an accusing finger at Gilbert, "is your blackmailer. I didn't know it until he called me here. He made me telephone you. And if it hadn't been for Flash Casey he would have killed you and Les Boyden to make it look—"

Gilbert's voice cut like a whip.

"So I'm the sucker, huh?" He backed close to a chair, his chin outthrust and his handsome face livid as he faced Patten. "Well, I don't take this rap alone. I played the sap long enough; played the part and she made me like it. She's right about framing you and Boyden, but *she did the calling because*—"

Gilbert stopped with his mouth open, the next word ready but unuttered. In that instant the gun barked.

There had been no warning. Casey heard the shot and saw Gilbert's coat lift under the impact of the slug, but he didn't know who held the gun until it crashed again. Then he saw it in Norma Patten's hand. It was a little gun, a .25, like the one Mary Nason had; a woman's gun.

Between those two shots was not more than a fifth of a second, but it was long enough for Casey to do a lot of thinking.

Norma Patten, the woman who always got what she wanted. The thing had been a frame from the start, and he was the fall guy when it backfired. He remembered the damp polo coat on the Queen Anne love seat when he went to the Carteret. Norma had already been out—and she had killed Sorenson. Why—

He didn't know why. He was listening to the little automatic. It was still going off in snapping, spiteful barks. He heard the door open, sensed that it was Logan without turning. He dropped to one knee, groped for the gun he had dropped, found it, then didn't know just what to do with it.

There was blood on Gilbert's neck and shirtfront. He went back into the chair with a curious smile, a sagging jaw and a burning vacantness in his eyes. Then, suddenly, the rest of the drama happened all at once.

Gilbert straightened in the chair with a gun in his hand. Patten, who had wasted the first two seconds in openmouthed amazement, pulled his own gun towards his wife. Norma Patten screamed. Gilbert's gun roared, jumped in his hand and he dropped it as he collapsed.

Simultaneously another gun crashed and Casey thought it was Patten's until he saw the man's shoulder jerk and the automatic fly from his hand.

Gilbert slumped back in the chair. Norma Patten staggered and a red spot stained the left side of her fawn-colored dress. She was dead before she fell, but even then she went down gracefully, silently and was lost to Casey's sight behind the table.

For a long time no one spoke. The only sound was the noisy, tortured breathing of the unconscious Gilbert. Then windows began to bang up in the courtyard and excited voices bounced back and forth, raucous and shrill.

Logan stepped forward, gun in hand. Patten, holding tightly to his right arm, turned slowly

and looked at the lieutenant while the fury died in his eyes. Blood began to show through his clenched fingers and he finally said:

"Thanks, Lieutenant, for that shot of yours. If you hadn't got me I guess I'd've plugged her!"

"That's what I thought," Logan said thickly. "I couldn't see Gilbert's gun. I took you when I saw you meant business."

Except in the flicker of his eyes Patten showed no emotion. His appearance was unruffled. He still looked like a man accustomed to success, a man who could not be shoved around. His voice betrayed no inner misgivings.

"She had it coming," he said grimly. "She and that heel"—he nodded to the crumpled Gilbert—"have been chiseling for months. I had a private dick on their trail in Chicago and I was about ready to get clear.

"When she pulled this blackmail story I smelled a rat, and I gave her the money because I figured I could trap her and force the showdown. I thought I could persuade Sorenson to see it my way, but something went wrong and—"

He shrugged distastefully. "I'll give you what I know when we get this mess cleaned up."

Casey looked down at the little automatic in his hand. He put it away, wiped his sweaty face and blew out his breath with so much noise that Logan heard him and said dryly:

"And what's *your* story?"

"Me?" Casey sighed wearily and spoke disgustedly. "Where would I get a story? This is a job for you cops to dig out; it's too tough for an amateur like me.

"I get tangled up in all the grief and—hell, I don't even get a picture out of it. I'm just the fall guy."

IX

ater, in Logan's office, Casey stared moodily at his fingernails and said grouchily: "So I can't even tell the story to a rewrite man to make up for the pictures I didn't get?"

"Nope," Logan said cheerfully. "For once you're out of luck."

"For once, huh?"

"The D.A.'s clamping down," Logan said. "The story we're giving out is that Gilbert was the blackmailer. He shot Norma Patten and the police shot him."

"What police? You?"

"Lots of different police," Logan said, grinning. "Just the police."

"Well," Casey grumbled, "that gag has been worked before, I guess it'll work again."

"The truth," Logan went on, "would just make a big stink, and it wouldn't do any good. Patten was pretty clean from the start. Gilbert lived just long enough to clear him.

"Sorenson actually did blackmail Norma Patten. He came around with the story of the films and release and touched her for a thousand. Right then she and Gilbert got the idea. They had a hunch Patten was getting wise to them, and they saw a chance to get some getaway money.

"Norma figured Les Boyden was still sort of soft on her and she gave him the thousand and had him go to Sorenson and collect the negatives and release. We found 'em locked in her trunk. They thought that would be the end of Sorenson and Boyden. They intended to have Ambrose be a phony contact man and they planned to protect his identity from Patten.

"Well, Patten gave her the cash. When he saw the S-mark on the pictures he called on Sorenson, and beat hell out of him. The break was that for some reason Norma had gone to see Sorenson and was in the hall outside the door when the trouble was going on. When she went in Sorenson was picking himself up; Patten had told him he'd been touched for twenty-five grand and Sorenson, knowing the truth, got nasty and wanted half from Norma. Well, she plugged him when he got too tough."

Logan lit a cigarette and cocked one eye at Casey.

"That's where you came in. She played innocent to you because she knew she could trust you and because she wanted to have some help if she got in trouble. Your act was just to cover up. If anybody accused her she'd have your testimony that you went down with ten G's to buy the pictures, and that she didn't know he was dead.

"That was smart—until you ran into Haley and he traced you to her suite. Then the cat was out. Gilbert ran into you when he went to see Sol Ambrose and Patten got there too late, when you were in the closet. Gilbert had to silence Ambrose and he knew you carried the ten grand so he lifted it to get you in deeper and keep you in debt to Norma."

"I can guess the rest of it," Casey growled. "Norma knew that Patten was on the warpath. She and Gilbert were out the twenty-five grand they expected to collect. So they figured the best thing to do was to get Boyden, get Patten and make a plant that they'd shot it out.

"You'd've believed it too," he added. "You thought Patten was the guy you wanted, and you were looking for Boyden. If you had found them dead in that apartment with guns in their hands—"

"I guess you're right," Logan admitted. "It was a good plan at the beginning. Patten tracing Sorenson busted it wide open for them; and—I hate to admit it—you messed up the second idea. If you hadn't busted in on Gilbert while they were waiting for Patten, it would have been too bad for old Sure-shot. She was a tough baby, that Norma, but"—Logan grinned—"she sure had your number."

"Yeah," Casey groused. "Me, I'm just a softie. A fall guy. She rubs out Sorenson and then sends me down to make her look innocent. For old time's sake, she said, and I bit. That's what burns me."

"And let it be a lesson to you," Logan cracked. "After this, keep away from women—or get a chaperone."

"Yeah," groused Casey. "And you, you louse! I do all the work and dump the job in your lap and what does it get me? Grief—and funny answers."

Logan's black eyes mirrored a smile that was part admiration.

"But think of the fun you have."

"Yeah—and the dough I make."

The telephone shrilled, checking Casey's tirade, and when Logan answered it he said: "For you."

Casey groaned; "Oh, me." Then, accepting the telephone: "Two to one it's Blaine."

"I don't like the odds," Logan said, thereby proving his sagacity, because the city editor's voice cracked in Casey's ears the instant he answered.

"What the hell're you hiding out down there for?" Blaine demanded. "I've been looking all over for you."

"Why?" Casey said.

"Because I've got a job for you, you lug. There's a three-alarm fire at Sherry and Walton. Eddie's on his way down there with your stuff. Get going—and show something. You've been chasing around doing nothing for two days now, and I pay off on pictures."

Casey hung up, cursing softly. Logan said: "Anything wrong?"

"Naw," Casey said, buttoning up his coat in weary resignation. "Just the same old grief. That was the boyfriend reminding me that it's about time I took some pictures."

Doors in the Dark

Frederick Nebel

(LOUIS) FREDERICK NEBEL (1903–1967) was born on Staten Island, New York. He began his adult life as a blue-collar worker, working on the New York docks and on a tramp steamer. He lived in Canada for a while, selling his first pulp fiction to *Northwest Stories* before becoming a regular and prolific contributor to *Dime Detective*, for which he wrote the long-running Cardigan series, and, most of all, *Black Mask*, for which he created the Donny Donahue series and his most important works, those featuring tough captain Steve MacBride and the wisecracking and drunken crime reporter Kennedy.

Nebel sold the MacBride series to Warner Bros., which made nine films. However, Kennedy became a female journalist, Torchy Blane, and MacBride the object of her affections. The first film in the series, *Smart Blonde* (1937), was based on the *Black Mask* story "No Hard Feelings," though the remaining films simply used the characters without basing them on Nebel's stories. Other films were also based on his work, notably *Sleepers West* (1941), which became a Mike Shayne film, based on Nebel's novel *Sleepers East* (1934); *Fifty Roads to Town* (1937), based on his crime novel of the same name; and he wrote the story for *The Bribe* (1949), which starred Robert Taylor, Ava Gardner, Charles Laughton, and Vincent Price. The radio series *Meet MacBride*, based on the stories, made its debut on CBS on June 13, 1936.

"Doors in the Dark" first appeared in the February 1933 issue.

Doors in the Dark

Frederick Nebel

A STORY OF CAPT. STEVE MACBRIDE

Everyone said it was suicide, but Capt. MacBride smelled murder, and went on the trail alone.

THE SOUNDS OF MOTOR traffic on Marshall Drive rose in a muted, not unpleasant medley to the topmost floor of Tudor Towers. Eastward, the glow of midtown hung like a will-o'-the-wisp in the crisp winter sky. A breeze plucked fitfully at the northeast turret apartment.

MacBride, admitted by the oldish maid, brought with him into the warm apartment a breath of the cold outdoors and a vital sense of his own personality. He shook his head when the maid reached for his hat. His windy blue glance flicked her frightened gargoyle's face, darted away and leaped nimbly about the foyer as he trailed her short, rapid footsteps towards the living-room entry.

He saw Halo Rand standing at the far side of the room. The room was dimly, discreetly lighted. A parchment-shaded floor lamp stood back of the woman and built an amber halo about her amber hair.

"I'm so glad you came, Captain."

The Aubusson muffled the blunt fall of his heels as he went towards her extended hand. His spare-boned head dipped; in his eyes was a candid, straightforward look.

"Got here as quick as I could, Mrs. Rand."

The maid vanished with a breathless look flung over her shoulder.

Though Halo Rand's tall, slender body was relaxed, one knee slightly bent, there was an air of repressed excitement in her face. MacBride, holding her hand for a brief instant, felt tension transmitted to his own. He was aware of a vague, well-bred perfume.

"What's the matter, Mrs. Rand?"

She said: "Come." She led the way across the dropped living-room, up three steps to a mezzanine; opened a door and motioned the skipper into a large room furnished with leathers and hardwoods—a man's room.

"Dan's room," she said. "His den. Sit down, Captain."

He was strangely moved, puzzled; but he sat down. Halo Rand chose to stand, resting the fingertips of one hand on a mahogany desk. The other hand toyed with a string of pearls suspended from her neck.

"I may be foolish," she said, "but I'm afraid. I can't help it. I'm afraid for Dan. It's ten o'clock and he hasn't come home yet."

MacBride said: "Why are you afraid?"

Her violet eyes were luminous in the dim light. "He came home at noon today. I—I hardly recognized him. He looked—well, crushed. Dreamlike. And that isn't like Dan. You know that. Well, he walked in quietly, kissed me, though I think he barely saw me, and then went to this room. I was disturbed. I came and knocked on the door and asked what was wrong, and he said nothing was wrong and asked to be left alone. So I didn't bother him."

"What do you think was wrong?"

She breathed deeply, said in a hushed voice: "I don't know. But he was worried. That much

I do know. For the past two months, every now and then, he would sit and stare absently—and suddenly ask me what I had said. When I appeared curious, he'd rouse up and be his own self." She shook her head. "He never was the one to bring his business into the home."

"Think it's business?"

She shook her head wearily. "I don't know. I feel so helpless. That's why I asked you to come over. I knew you two were old friends. He's been hit hard in the market, you know. And I guess you know he's had trouble with the Colosseum. He is in debt heavily—but he hoped to pull out of it."

"Did he say where he was going?"

"No, he didn't. He came out of his room after an hour. I don't think he'd even taken his overcoat off. He came out and stood for a moment at the window. Then he said he was going out. He kissed me good-bye and held my hand for a minute, and then he went out. He said he'd be back at six. Well, he hasn't come."

MacBride slapped his knee. "Well, Mrs. Rand, I wouldn't get all worked up, if I were you. Maybe—"

"Wait," she said, and opened a desk drawer. "An hour ago I came in here. I don't know why. I don't think I expected to find anything. It was just chance. I—I opened this drawer. You remember the gun you gave him two years ago?"

"Yes."

"It's gone," she said. "It's not in his drawer."

MacBride stood up, muttered: "H'm."

"Emma, our maid, straightened this room yesterday. She said she saw the gun in this drawer yesterday. Now it's gone." Her eyes stared fixedly across the room. "That's why I'm afraid," she said. "That's why I asked you to come over."

She slumped a bit where she stood, brushed a hand across her forehead. MacBride's eyes were thought-fixed on the amber casque of her hair. He remembered the day she had ceased to be the *première danseuse* of Dubinoff's Ballet and had become Dan Rand's wife.

He said: "Just be calm, Mrs. Rand. You're imagining things. No use taking this thing so hard. I'll find him. He'll be okey. I'll phone you when I find him." There was a rough note of reassurance in his tone. A smile cracked his lean, spare-boned face. "Just take it easy."

They went into the living-room and she laughed brokenly. "I suppose I am a little fool. But I kept thinking about his finances. So many men nowadays, when they can't see their way ahead . . ." She made a limp, hopeless gesture.

"Not Dan," MacBride said. "He can take it. He always could take it and come up smiling."

She nodded. "I know. But lately—he hasn't been smiling."

They passed into the foyer and the oldish maid with the gargoyle's face appeared mysteriously and stood by the door.

The phone rang. The maid left the door and answered it and then said: "It's for you, Captain."

He went towards it, saying: "I left word at the office I'd be here." He picked up the instrument. "Hello . . . Yeah, Otto." He listened, and presently his brows bent, a shine appeared in his eyes. His low voice said: "Okey, Otto." He hung up, put the instrument down, staring hard at it.

Then he raised his bony head and looked at Halo Rand. A corner of his wide mouth twitched.

Kennedy, the eyes and ears of the Richmond City *Free Press*, slammed into the dusty little office at the base of the pier, ricocheted from door to wall to chair to desk, where he finally sprawled with a relieved sigh and calmly placed the telephone receiver to his ear, using the same hand to prop his head.

"Central 1000."

An astonished watchman stood spellbound against the wall. "Hey," he said. "Hey!"

"Now, now," Kennedy said with wrinkle-browed remonstrance. "Shush, shush. Don't you see I'm on the telephone?" He rolled over languidly on his back, propped his heels on the edge of the desk, his knees in the air, and held the telephone transmitter above his mouth.

The watchman dried his hands on a soiled towel. "This here is a private office and I'd like to know who the hell give you permission to use that phone!"

Kennedy said into the mouthpiece: "City desk, flower." He looked sidewise at the watchman. "Pardon me. I'm Kennedy of the *Free Press*. May I use your phone?"

"Sure—go ahead."

"Thanks . . . Hello, Abe," he said into the transmitter. "Kennedy. Dust out your ears and get a load of this. Daniel Cosgrove Rand, sportsman, fight promoter, owner of the Colosseum; dead, by his own hand, at 9:50 tonight, on River Road, near the foot of Pokomoke Street, in an abandoned warehouse. Shot heard, body found, by Patrolman Henry Pflueger. No witnesses. Got that? . . . Okey. More later."

He hung up, turned over on his stomach, put the phone down and pushed himself back off the desk to his feet. He was calm again, a little sallow-faced beneath his battered fedora. His roving, world-weary eyes alighted on a pint flask standing on a shelf above the desk.

"Is that," he said to the watchman, "something to drink?"

"Nah. Nah. That's rubbing alcohol." Kennedy reached up, took down the bottle, uncorked it and smelled it. He took two long swallows, corked the bottle, sighed and replaced the bottle on the shelf.

"Somebody's been kidding you, my good friend. That's gin." He buttoned his flimsy top-coat, said cheerfully: "Thanks for the use of your phone," and went out.

Winter wind, freighted with river damp, smote him and he shivered beneath his inade-quate topcoat. He strode, a scarecrow figure, along the edge of the river wall; saw red and green lights of tugboats moving, heard deep-toned whistles. Up ahead, in front of the aban-doned warehouse, the red-tinted lights of an ambulance glowed like swollen eyes. Figures moved in the glare of a spotlight, paced by their elongated shadows. Breath spumed whitely and hard heels struck and scraped on cold cobble-stones.

Kennedy said: "I thought I recognized your Harvard accent, skipper."

"Oh, you, huh?" MacBride said. He had just stepped from a police squad car. He blew his nose loudly into white, crisp linen. His cheeks were reddened by the cold; his eyes flashed like dark coals in the beam of the spotlight. "You always go where I go, huh?"

"Only this time I was here first. You're slip-ping, Cap."

A rotund man appeared in the entrance of the old warehouse. He blinked in the glare of the spotlight, then came forward with a bobbing, cheerful walk, a small black bag swinging in his hand.

"Hello, Doc," MacBride said.

"Dead, Steve—very dead," the ambulance doc-tor said. "In fact, he must have died instantly. Shot in the heart . . . Well, I must get going."

MacBride nodded. He set his jaw and sud-denly started off in a hard-heeled stride. The sound of his footfalls echoed in the large, bare warehouse. Far beyond, near the head of the wharf, he saw a lantern and several hand torches glowing; they made a wan, lonesome aureole of light around the shapes of several men. He walked through chill, damp air that seeped to his

marrow; heard, beneath the floor, the lapping of water among pilings.

He saw, as he drew nearer, the narrow chalky face of Eggleson, the Deputy Medical Examiner. Eggleson was standing spread-legged, torchlight spraying upward over his gaunt body to his nar-row face; and he was writing absentmindedly in a book. Patrolman Pflueger was in silhouette, arms akimbo, his back to MacBride. Moriarity and Cohen were kneeling, getting two lights from a match.

No one said anything as MacBride came up. He stopped, stood with hands thrust in overcoat pockets, slouching a bit, the torch- and lantern-light picking out sharply the bony irregularity of his face, the slitted eyes.

Then Kennedy's quiet voice from behind: "You knew him well, huh, skipper?"

"Yeah."

Patrolman Pflueger pointed: "There's the gun, Captain—layin' there."

"Yeah." MacBride's voice had a dull flat sound. "Yeah. I can recognize it from here. I gave it to him. You can see on the barrel: 'From Steve MacBride to Dan Rand.'"

Eggleson, the D.M.E., looked up from his notebook. "Suicide, Steve. Tough." He shook his head profoundly. "Tough, tough. He got pie-eyed drunk and then did the Dutch."

"Drunk, huh?"

"Pie-eyed. Can't you smell it?"

"Yeah."

Kennedy touched his arm. "Snap out of it, Steve."

"I liked him, Kennedy. I grew up with him. It's kind of swell to see a guy you grew up with make a name for himself. It ain't exactly the nuts when you find him dead." He wagged his bony head. "I never figured Dan would do the Dutch. He wasn't that kind. Not him. But . . ." He sighed, moved his broad shoulders. Then he flexed his hands, his voice picked up: "Moriar-ity, get the lead out of your pants. Get the Morgue bus down. . . . Hey, Pflueger, did you touch that gun?"

"Just by the barrel."

"I trained you, didn't I?"

"Yes, sir."

MacBride looked at Kennedy. "Hear that?" He bent down, caught hold of the gun by the barrel and lifted it. He wrapped the gun in a fresh handkerchief and slipped it carefully into his pocket.

"Who trained you, skipper?" Kennedy said.

"Experience . . . Hey, Moriarity, I thought I told you—"

"Okey, okey!" Moriarity started off at a fast walk.

Eggleson scoffed: "Suicide! It's as plain as the nose—"

"On my face." MacBride nodded. "I know. But I also knew"—he leveled an arm at the dead man—"Dan Rand. I guess if I want to take prints off this gun I have a right to!"

"What a man!" Eggleson sighed; then said: "Okey, Steve. Well, I'll be seeing you."

Police photographers came and took flashlight pictures of the body on the floor.

MacBride roamed through the warehouse, picking his way with the help of a torch borrowed from Pflueger. He pushed through a small door and stood on the pierhead, in the wind, watching the lights of river traffic. Kennedy came out and huddled in his topcoat, using MacBride's bulk to break the wind.

"Don't be a sap, Cap," he argued. "It was suicide plain and simple. You know Dan was in a bad way financially. Ever since he refused to let the Ricks-Gowanus boxfight take place in his Colosseum Cardiac boycotted him. It's cost Dan a lot of dough. He couldn't afford to lose it. Well, he lost it. And what happened?" He shrugged. "A Dutch out. He got drunk as hell and getting drunk either weakened or strengthened him to rub himself out. Depends on how you look at it."

MacBride remained silent, staring at the river lights.

Kennedy raised a cigarette to his mouth. The wind whipped sparks from its red end. His tone was lazy, ruminative: "He had an expensive wife . . . his apartment at Tudor Towers set him back $500 a month . . . a front to keep up." He

shrugged. "A guy like Rand would have hated to take one backward step in the scale of living."

"Yeah," said MacBride. "He hated defeat. And he could take it. I've seen him take it before."

"Sure. But a man can take it just so long, skipper, and then the lights go out. A short circuit in the nervous system."

MacBride turned. "I know, I know, Kennedy. You're using your head, you're reasoning things out. Swell! But I can't reason the same way because I knew Dan, I know he had guts. It's not like him to pull a stunt like this. It's all goofy! It's a cap that don't fit his head!"

Kennedy leaned back on his heels. "Listen, am I talking to a hard-headed cop or am I talking to a fat-head?"

MacBride growled, swung on his heel, yanked open the door and heaved into the warehouse. The lantern was swinging now in someone's hand. The Morgue bus had come and they were carrying out the body of Dan Rand.

Kennedy caught up with MacBride and said: "So don't make a horse's neck out of yourself just because you happened to play at cowboys and Indians with this guy when you were kids."

"I'm in the dark right now," MacBride ground out. "In the dark, get me?" His eyes shimmered between narrowed lids. "In a dark house. But I've got a feeling that there's a lot of doors around me in the darkness—and if I look hard enough, and take your wisecracks as just so much bushwha, I might find a streak of light— you know, at the bottom of a door."

"Listen to the man!"

"Razz me, sweetheart. I could take the razzberry when you were just a hope in your father's chest."

ohen was sitting on the desk, swinging a leg, flipping a coin in the air, when MacBride strode into the office next morning. The skipper removed his conservative blue overcoat, his conservative gray fedora, and hung them on a costumer in the corner. Crossing to the desk, rubbing his chilled hands smartly together, he stared down at the morning edition of the *Free Press. Dan Rand Commits Suicide*, the headlines said. MacBride looked at Cohen. Cohen continued flipping the coin.

"What's that, Ike, a new kind of endurance contest? . . . Come on, come on—with six chairs in this office, do you have to park yourself on my desk?"

Cohen stood up. "So I dusted the town last night, Cap. Rand hit *The Panama* at 2:30 yesterday afternoon, stayed an hour drinking alone. At 3:40 he walked into Joe Paloma's place, in Senate Street. Joe says he knocked off three highballs and left there about four o'clock. Plenty looking-glass drinking. At 4:30 he landed in Nick Raitt's place, on Division Hill. Rye highballs again; three. Nick said he didn't talk, didn't say a thing. Just looked at himself in the mirror and took on the liquor. Nick says he bailed out at about 5:30.

"At about a quarter of six he walked into the Old English Grill and got himself a meal and Al says he drank rye there. He was pretty crocked when he came in, but the food kind of straightened him out. He left the Old English at a little past seven and went down to Elmo Street, to Mike Cahill's place. He threw dice with Mike, but Mike says he kept his trap shut except to open it to pour in rye. He left Mike's place at 8:30.

"Tony Gatto, down in Jockey Street, says Rand sloped into his joint between eight and nine. He was pretty drunk. He took two highballs fast and left at about 9:15. Tony says Rand said: 'Well, Tony, I think I'll go home to my wife. Listen, Tony; never give up ship. Stick to it.' Tony didn't know what he meant. 'Some of us slide out, Tony,' Rand said. 'Some of us stick, hang on. I guess I'm that kind, damn my guts.' And he went out." Cohen shrugged. "So I guess Tony Gatto was the last guy to see him alive."

MacBride said: "Good work, Ike. Did you mark those places and times down?"

Cohen scaled a slip of paper onto the desk. MacBride studied the memoranda, mused

aloud: "What did Dan mean by that speech, Ike?"

"Hell, do drunks mean anything by the speeches they make? I read a book once—"

"Okey, okey. Suppose we don't go into that. Here"—he pointed to the telephone—"call McGovern and ask him if he got the prints off that gun yet."

Cohen telephoned the Bureau in the basement. Hanging up, he said: "In about half an hour."

MacBride took a turn up and down the room; stopped, eyed Cohen darkly. "You've got an idea I'm nuts, haven't you?"

"Well"—Cohen leaned on the desk—"it looks like suicide to me, Cap. Of course, if you want to make a case out of it, okey. I know about seventeen guys I could pick up, frame, box and deliver—"

"Do drunks mean anything by the speeches they make? . . . You asked me that, Ike. And I'll tell you. They do! Dan would, anyhow. He was going home to his wife. He might have thought about doing the Dutch. But in the end, tight as he was, he changed his mind." He leveled an arm. "When Danny Rand walked out of Tony Gatto's he was going home to his wife. He might have been flat broke, up to his ears in debt—but he was going to stick, kid—he was going to stick." He struck the desk with his fist. "Danny Rand didn't commit suicide!"

Cohen was unimpressed. He shrugged. "Okey, skipper, okey. He didn't commit suicide. Okey. Now tell me who bumped him off and I'll go out and pinch the guy—"

"Cut it, Ike!" MacBride chopped in savagely. In a quieter voice he said: "Scram. I'll call you if I want you."

He crammed a pipe, lighted up. He had fought the Medical Examiner's office tooth and nail for an autopsy. Halo Rand had sobbed. "An autopsy's cruel on his poor dead body," she had said. The Medical Examiner had chided, wheedled, opened a bottle of Napoleon brandy. But MacBride had stood his ground—grim-faced, obstinate, on a single track of thought and purpose.

He smoked out his pipe, knocked the ash into a tray. He sailed out of his office, went down to the central room, on down to the Bureau of Criminal Identification. McGovern, the fingerprint man, chewed a cigar beneath a brilliant light. The smoke foamed and rolled beneath the green eyeshade he wore, and he spoke laconically:

"No prints but Rand's on this gat, Steve. Nice gun. I always did like a .32."

MacBride muttered: "You're sure of that, Mac?"

"That's my business—being sure. But wait." He picked up the gun. "Smell it."

MacBride leaned down, sniffed. "What?" he said.

McGovern shrugged. "Smells—that's all. Can't you smell it?"

"I think I can. What's that mean?"

"Oh"—McGovern shrugged—"nothing, I suppose." He slapped palms softly together. "Suicide, Steve. You can't get away from it."

MacBride pointed: "Turn the gat over to Lewis. We ought to have that slug from the Morgue this morning." He turned on his heel, strode away; stopped, returned to the desk and picked up the gun again. He sniffed along the barrel, along the butt; sighed, shrugged and walked away again, a puzzled frown shadowing his forehead.

In the central room, Otto Bettdecken lowered a half-eaten liverwurst sandwich behind the desk and called: "Cap, a guy just called up from 313 Diamond Street. His name's Rossman. He said if you could come down there maybe he can tell you something."

"About what?"

"Well, he said he'd read the paper this morning—"

"Okey. Thanks, Otto."

The skipper hiked up the steps two at a time, barged into his office and saw Kennedy sitting at the desk. Kennedy was holding a glass in one hand, a bottle in the other; and he was grimacing painfully.

He said: "Honest, Cap, this last batch of liquor of yours is crummy—absolutely crummy." He was indignant.

MacBride grinned tightly, nodded. "I know, sweetheart. You got it out of that lower left drawer, didn't you? Swell! The good stuff is in the lower right—under lock and key. And I"—he thumbed his chest—"have the key!"

"Ah, my pal, my pal! Is it true that Rand was shot down by four Chinamen disguised as Princeton professors? I understand that there is a certain captain in Headquarters who insists that they were not four Chinamen; he says they were four dwarfs disguised as two dark, swart men wearing false hair eyebrows. This captain is principally known as an oboe player."

MacBride slapped on his hat, shrugged into his overcoat, said scornfully: "I hope you choke, Kennedy. And I hope if you ever get married your kids'll turn out to be saxophone players. In three words"—he reached the door, yanked it open—"nerts to you!"

In the central room he ran into Eggleson, the Deputy Medical Examiner. Eggleson's chalky face wore a dry, broad grin. "I hear, Steve, that only Rand's prints were on the gun. Tsk, tsk!"

MacBride said grimly: "You're just breaking down with regret, ain't you." And he went on, red-faced, warm with chagrin.

Cohegan was waiting at the wheel of the shabby squad car.

MacBride said: "Down to 313 Diamond Street, Bert."

"Okey."

MacBride climbed in, slammed the door. "The razzberry market is cheap these days," he rasped out.

"Me," said Cohegan soberly, "I like blueberries. My wife, now, she likes strawberries; but take a good bowl of blueberries—"

"You take 'em." MacBride sighed. He nipped savagely at the end of a cigar, cupped hands in the wind and lighted up.

The car purred across town, hit Broadway Avenue and weaved through traffic. It pushed westward past midtown hotels, shops, theaters. Its canvas top clapped and pattered in the wind, and the wind kept MacBride's cigar at a bright glow, tore smoke from his nostrils and whipped it away, reddened the right side of his face. Winter sunlight glittered on plate-glass windows, automobile radiators, the shields and buttons of white-gloved traffic officers. Pedestrians hurried. Discarded newspapers skipped and planed and looped above the sidewalks.

Cohegan made a left turn into Diamond Street, a narrow thoroughfare that sloped downhill, walled on either side with food shops, noisy radio stores, cut-rate drug-stores, pawnshops, novelty stores, cheap haberdashers. Number 313 was a pawnshop.

"Park here, Bert," MacBride said.

He climbed out, made a half-turn against the driving wind and strode into the pawnshop. Inside it was dim. Lights glowed dimly. Counters and showcases were cluttered with cheap odds and ends; and behind a brass wicket a small, pink-cheeked man was studying the inside of a watch.

"Your name Rossman?"

The little man was cheerful, bright-eyed. "Yes—yes, I'm Rossman."

"I'm Captain MacBride—"

"Oh, yes!" The little man laid down the watch, turned and shouted: "Charley! Charley, come here and take care a minute." And to MacBride: "Right in the back, Captain, if you don't mind."

MacBride strode to the rear of the store. Rossman met him at the end of the counter and bowed him into a small office where a coal stove glowed warmly. He closed the door quietly, changed spectacles and picked up a copy of the *Free Press*. A smile twinkled in his eyes, tugged at his lips.

"This," he said, pointing to the Rand story. "I read about it this morning, and I thought it over. I saw your name connected with it. I remembered that once you were kind to my son-in-law, Benny Lisk, and I thought maybe this would interest you." He paused, darted a shrewd, smiling look at MacBride. "I read here about the gun—the gun it says you gave him. I

looked a long time at Mr. Rand's picture here. Sit down, Captain."

MacBride sat down.

"This man," went on Rossman, striking the picture of Dan Rand, "came into my store at about two o'clock yesterday afternoon. I'm sure. I remember the face. And, Captain"—he dropped his voice significantly—"he wanted to buy a gun."

MacBride's face remained expressionless, but his eyes steadied on Rossman's cherubic face.

Rossman nodded. "So I sold him one. A .32 Colt automatic. And a box of 73-grain, metal case cartridges." He paused. "You see, Captain, I want no trouble with the police. Usually I don't sell guns to anybody, but this man had a permit to carry one. He loaded the gun here, and then, after he left, I found he didn't take the rest of the cartridges."

MacBride's eyes glowed. "Thanks, Mr. Rossman. I appreciate this a hell of a lot." He stood up, shook Rossman's hand vigorously. "This will help. This will help, Mr. Rossman. Any time you feel you're in a jam, let me know. I don't forget."

Leaving the room, he strode briskly through the shop, a hard windy glitter in his eyes and a firm jut to his jaw. Outside, he found the shabby squad car empty. He sent a sharp glance about the street, took a few steps, swore irritably; and then he saw Cohegan stroll casually out of a fruiterer's, eating a banana.

"Bert!"

Cohegan reached the car with his mouth full of banana.

MacBride jerked his chin, growled: "In, bozo!" And as they drove off: "Always on the muscle! Always on the make! If it's not fruit you're mooching, it's cigars, or socks, or candy for some jane you know, or liquor!"

Cohegan said soberly: "Where was we headed for now?"

There was a note of vengeance in MacBride's short laugh. "Back to H.Q., you racketeer!"

oriarity and Cohen were rolling dice on MacBride's desk when the skipper breezed into his office. His two aides did not look up. The dice clicked, tumbled; coins rang on the desk.

"Hot-cha!" Cohen exclaimed. "After it's over, Mory, you can borrow from me—at seven percent."

"What I found," MacBride said, rocking on his heels, "was that Dan Rand bought a gun. Bought a .32 Colt auto from a guy named Rossman in Diamond Street. Yesterday afternoon. And loaded it and walked out!"

The dice clicked and Cohen said: "You should never roll the bones, Mory; you were born unlucky."

"Now why did he buy that gun?" MacBride said impressively. "Why did he buy a gun when he had a perfectly good gun of his own? And how come the gun we found on him was the gun I gave him and not—not, you understand—the gun he bought? What happened to the gun he bought? Boy, oh, boy, if I— Lisyou apes!" he suddenly exploded. He caught up the dice and flung them against the wall.

Cohen whistled, picked up the money and dropped it into his pocket. Moriarity lighted a cigarette and said reasonably:

"It must have disappeared."

"It means this," MacBride hammered out, shaking a fist. "It means that I'm no fat-head! It means that maybe all the razzberry you and a lot of other guys shoveled at me is going to be dumped right back at you! It means," he said, thinning his voice, "that when Dan Rand walked out of his house at noon yesterday he didn't carry a gun. He went and bought one—"

"And with it," nodded Cohen, "committed suicide."

MacBride barked: "No!" He walked around the room and came back and barked again: "No!" He folded his arms. "This is murder. I know what to do about murder, wherever I find it. We'll see what kind of bullet they've taken out of Dan Rand and—"

The phone rang and MacBride scooped it up. "Okey," he said. He hung up. "Come on down. That was Lewis."

They went down to the basement. Lewis, the ballistics expert, was wiping off a gun.

He said: "There's the slug they took out of Rand. I matched it with this gun you gave him. It matches. There it is—a lead slug. Came out of a ninety-eight-grain Smith and Wesson cartridge." He laid the revolver down. "Suicide, I guess."

MacBride picked up the slug, studied it closely, then rolled it round and round between thumb and forefinger. His eyes flashed, his lips warped. He tossed the slug back to the desk.

"Murder," he clipped.

"Suicide suits me," Lewis said.

But MacBride was striding away. Moriarity and Cohen went along, exchanging hopeless glances. MacBride stopped short, swung about, returned to Lewis' desk and picked up the gun, thrust it into his pocket. He bore down on Moriarity and Cohen with a hard, preoccupied stare.

"Look at it this way, Cap," Moriarity said. "Maybe this guy Rossman made a mistake. Maybe it wasn't Rand after all."

"I'll bet that's just what happened!" Cohen said decisively.

MacBride went past them with his hard, fixed stare. He picked up Cohegan in the central room and they went outside and climbed into the car. MacBride sat motionless, staring ahead, while Cohegan started the motor and waited. After a while MacBride relaxed, looked about them as though surprised, then said:

"Okey, Bert. Drive to the Metals Building in Simpson Street." He leaned back, sighed as the car started. "I'm a sap," he muttered. "I get all steamed up over nothing."

The Metals Building was a seven-story brick affair, not new. The elevator was large, old, tarnished, and wheezed on the way up to the fifth floor. MacBride got out, slapped his heels down a linoleum covered corridor floor and stopped before a ground-glass door bearing the inscription: *Acme Sporting Enterprises, Inc.*

"Yes, sir?" chirped a blonde over a noisy typewriter.

"Mr. Cardiac." He champed the tip off a cigar. "MacBride's the name."

The girl flounced into one of two inner offices; reappeared in a moment and said: "Okey."

MacBride swung into the inner office, scaled his hat on the desk and flopped down into a leather-upholstered armchair; scowled down at his cigar and then licked a piece of the wrapper back into place.

"What do you think about Rand's suicide, Cardiac?"

Cardiac said: "Shocked. I was shocked. Sorry as hell to hear of it."

"Yes, you were!" MacBride chuckled sardonically.

Cardiac was a tall, handsome man, blond and rounded about the head. He had broad, neatly tailored shoulders, a jaw shaped like a spade, big white hands.

"Okey, then. I'm not sorry." He chuckled.

"That sounds better. With Dan Rand out of the way I suppose things will be easier for you, huh?"

"In what way?"

"Oh . . . I suppose it'll be easy for you to get control of the Colosseum. Listen, Cardiac." MacBride leaned forward. "Dan Rand hated you and you hated him. I'll tell you why he hated you. He didn't like your business methods. He kept you and your stable of fighters out of the Colosseum because he didn't believe in robbing the fight public. He had no use for set-ups. He believed the Ricks-Gowanus thing was a set-up.

"Before that, he crossed you on a number of other deals. He lost money doing it but he was willing to lose money to keep the fight game clean. You tried to stage fights in the old Hessler Arena. He stopped that by proving the place was a fire-trap. The only place big enough to make money in was the Colosseum, and he shut you out of there. You got back at him by talking other sport promoters into taking their jobs elsewhere—the smaller jobs, hockey, bicycle racing, wrestling. The Colosseum became an empty barn. He lost money and kept on losing it but no matter what you did you couldn't make him change his mind. Dan could always take it."

"Sure." Cardiac nodded. "Until finally he was flat broke and did the Dutch."

MacBride's eyes narrowed dangerously. "It always surprised me, Cardiac, the way all these small frys suddenly slid away from the Colosseum and pulled their stuff elsewhere. All of them!" He held aloft a rigid forefinger for a taut split-minute, then swung it levelly towards Cardiac. "I hope you've kept your nose clean, boy."

Cardiac delivered a bland smile. "You're steamed up about something." An eyebrow went up. "Will a drink help?"

"No . . . I'm dumb," he confessed. "When I look back, I see how dumb I am. The more I think of it, the funnier it seems. . . . I mean the way all these enterprises—wrestling, bike races, hockey, smokers—the way they all slipped away from the Colosseum to outlying dumps. You're the only man big enough in this town to've worked a racket like that, Cardiac!"

Cardiac looked bored. "Rave on, Skipper," he said offhand, waving a cigarette languidly.

There was a thump—and the gun lay on the table. And there was MacBride's blunt voice: "Ever see that?"

Cardiac folded his hands on his flat stomach, shook his head, said quietly: "No."

"It's the gat that killed Dan Rand."

"So-so! H'm . . . nice-looking gun. Suicide's queer—"

"Damn queer. So queer, Cardiac, that this time it's not suicide."

"Well, that is news!"

"Would you mind," said MacBride, "letting me see that nice silk pocket handkerchief?"

Cardiac tensed, his eyes flickered. He flexed his lips, then shrugged, chuckled jerkily. "Sure! Here." He tossed the handkerchief across the desk.

MacBride smelled it, making noises. Then he threw it back to Cardiac, rubbed his bony hand around the nape of his neck and sent a couple disgruntled smoke-puffs from one corner of his mouth. The skipper and Cardiac regarded each other for a long minute.

"Plan to get the Colosseum, don't you?" MacBride asked.

"I plan to organize a holding company and try to do business with the executors of Rand's estate."

"You wouldn't," MacBride said, "by any chance have already formed this holding company?"

"I was just thinking about it."

MacBride picked up a clipped sheaf of papers from a wire desk basket. "I've got good eyesight, Cardiac. It says here, 'Prospectus of the Colosseum Holding Company.'"

Cardiac nodded. "Yes, I know. I was just playing around with the idea this morning. Got down to the office early and ran off my ideas on the typewriter before my secretary arrived."

MacBride nodded, turned and went to the connecting door and opening it said to the blonde in the outer office, "Typewrite on a piece of paper, miss, one line—anything—and bring it in."

Cardiac was annoyed. "Why all the horseplay, Captain?"

MacBride, reading the prospectus, made no reply. In a moment the blonde entered with a sheet of paper. MacBride took it, slowly read the single line.

"Miss," he said, "how many letters have you typed since you arrived this morning?"

"Oh, about three."

"Thanks. You can go."

She went out, puzzled, a little frightened.

MacBride tossed the prospectus and the newly written sheet of paper on the desk.

"Take a look at them, Cardiac. You said you wrote that prospectus on the typewriter this morning. The girl said she's written only three letters this morning. Yet—look close, Cardiac—the typewriting on your prospectus is in fresh, heavy black type made by a brand-new ribbon. The line the girl just wrote is very faded—the ribbon hasn't been changed in weeks."

"Oh, nonsense!" Cardiac scoffed.

"Nonsense your grandmother! That prospectus wasn't written this morning, Cardiac. It was written weeks ago—maybe months ago. It was written because you had a good idea that pretty soon the Colosseum would be in the bag!"

Cardiac rose slowly, his mouth twisting, his pale eyes hard as chips of ice. "I'm getting tired of listening to a lot of hot air, MacBride!"

"You'll listen, baby—and like it. You're the only man big enough in this town to've wanted Rand's scalp."

Cardiac came around the desk, swaggering, a hard set to his spade jaw. "Watch those cracks, copper! I'm not taking dirty cracks from any cheap shamus." He held his hands out, palms up. "These hands are clean, skipper. Suppose you tuck your tail between your legs and scram."

The phone rang and Cardiac lifted it, growled "Hello" into the mouthpiece. Then his eyes blinked, he shook his head; clipped: "Call back. No, I'll call you back when— . . . No—no, not now!" His face colored, he seemed uneasy; he shouted: "I said I'll call you back!" He hung up violently. There were a few beads of sweat on his forehead.

MacBride said: "I'll be seeing you oftener." And went out.

acBride dropped into Tony Gatto's Jockey Street Club and found Kennedy drinking gin and Perrier at the bar. It was not quite noon, and Kennedy was the only customer. Tony Gatto stood behind the bar grinning, polishing a glass.

"No see you in a long time, Cap. How's t'ings?" Tony said.

"Hello, Tony. Bottle of ale . . . You ever drink water, Kennedy?"

"Sure. But I always put liquor in it to kill the germs. It turns out they weren't two dwarfs, Steve; just the Four Marx Brothers up to their old tricks—"

"Enough o' that, honeybunch." MacBride took a drink of ale; about-faced and hooked his elbows on the bar, his heel on the brass rail. "So all you mugs still think it's suicide." He clucked. "I'm continually grateful for the swell support I get from my friends. It just breaks my heart with gratitude. Some fine day I'm going to start out and systematically change the shapes of a lot of schnozzles in this man's town."

Kennedy also turned about, hooking elbows on the bar, a heel on the rail, and stood shoulder to shoulder with MacBride. Both stared at the blank wall opposite.

Kennedy said: "Ah," and took another drink. "How about the woman?" he asked.

"What woman?"

"Halo Rand."

MacBride said nothing. He took a long swallow of ale and cleared his throat; but still he said nothing.

"This gun business," Kennedy said. "If it's true that Rand bought a gun, that means his own gun wasn't in his desk at home."

"My, but you're a thinker, Kennedy!"

"And yet the gun found on him was the gun that wasn't in his desk and the gun he was supposed to have bought was—where?"

"So you still think it's suicide?"

"Come over to one of the booths."

They went to the rear of the bar, entered a small booth and drew the curtains. Kennedy flopped onto a chair, plunked down his glass.

"There's no reason," he said, "why a man would buy two guns to commit suicide. So we must believe that his own gun wasn't in his desk."

"It wasn't there when I went over."

"Right. We must believe that it wasn't there when Rand came home. If we believe that, then it stands to reason that somebody removed it."

"It was in the drawer on the day before."

"That narrows down the time element. It was removed between then and the time Rand came home."

"Why wouldn't Rand have mentioned it to his wife?"

"Maybe he thought she'd removed it for fear he might use it. Guys about to commit suicide are very clever. So he said nothing about it. He just went out and bought another." He dropped his voice. "What do you know about his wife?"

"Not much. I never saw Dan much in the home. I guess I met his wife only about three times. They seemed happy."

"A lot of people seem happy."

MacBride frowned. "Hell, I don't think she'd—"

"Okey, okey. It was just a thought I had. Only the way you talked, it seems to me she tried hard to stick it into your mind that he was hard up financially."

"He was!"

Kennedy smiled drolly. "I've been poking around this morning. I went down to Rand's office. I talked with his stenog. I got the names of the men who called on Rand yesterday morning. One of them was a man named Osgood—the only name I didn't recognize. So I looked up the business directory and found out a man named Charles Osgood was connected with the Packillac Motor Car Company. I sloped around and looked him up. Yes, he'd called on Rand. They'd had a long talk. When Osgood left it was practically settled that Rand was to sell his Colosseum to the Packillac people for $300,000."

MacBride barked: "Sell the Colosseum— What for?"

"The Packillac people intended to convert it into an assembling and distributing plant."

MacBride smacked the table. "Then it wasn't money! It wasn't money that worried him! It wasn't, then, suicide!"

"Hold on. We've got to believe that he intended to commit suicide. The sale could have been consummated through his estate. When he bought that gun, we must believe it was with the intention of committing suicide. Then, maybe, he changed his mind."

"So why, in the first place, if he had a chance to sell the Colosseum for $300,000—why did he even think about suicide?"

Kennedy was dry: "There might have been

another reason. Men do do the Dutch, you know, because of women. Not often. But now and then."

MacBride's voice was low, hoarse: "Then you've changed your mind about the suicide theory?"

"Blushingly," bowed Kennedy.

"Kennedy," MacBride said. "I always liked you. I never said I didn't like you, did I?"

Kennedy chuckled. "Old tomato! . . . How's the chances of buying me a drink?"

MacBride stood up. "Nah. Not this bellywash Tony sells. Here's the key to my private stock. Go back to my office. Lower right drawer."

"Where's your white whiskers, Santa Claus?"

The shabby phaeton rolled into the flagstone courtyard of Tudor Towers. A liveried chauffeur opened the door and MacBride stepped out, passed into the large, deftly lighted lobby. No hurry here; no noise: Tudor Towers was strictly residential, quietly austere. The elevator that carried the skipper to the top floor was a vehicle of black and chromium, noiseless in its ascent.

MacBride's hard heels were ably muffled by the thick cushioned runner in the corridor. The oldish maid with the gargoyle's face let him in. When he entered the living-room he saw Halo Rand sitting in a vis-à-vis couch beside a man wearing a correct morning suit, with a winged collar, dark-rimmed pince-nez. He was about fifty, black-haired, black-eyebrowed. He rose.

Halo Rand, wearing a black crêpe negligee, did not rise; but she said: "Captain MacBride, this is Dr. Landau." She had been crying. Her eyes were red-rimmed, her face sapped of color; and she was listless, tired.

Landau gripped MacBride's hand, eyed him with a dark, keen, direct look. "I am delighted to know you, Captain. I have heard a lot about you. I was just trying to console Mrs. Rand." He threw a profound look at her. "It is not easy, Captain."

"Family doctor?"

"Well, I've attended Dan Rand for quite a few years." He stopped, inhaled deeply, said in a low, level voice: "I am glad you came, Captain, when you did." He stared fixedly, remorsefully, into space. "You know, Dan Rand came to my office yesterday morning. We had a long talk together. He wasn't well, you know. It was marvelous, the way he kept it from everyone. But he was that way . . . proud; he hated pity. He'd been coming to me regularly and I'd been treating him, but finally, yesterday, he wanted to know the truth. I tried to evade telling the truth. But when a man like Rand becomes angry— And, well, he wanted to know. So I told him. Lungs." He nodded reflectively, bitterly. "I told him the truth. I told him to give up business. I said it was necessary for him to go west—New Mexico—if he hoped to prolong his life. He thanked me. He walked out of my office. So you see, Captain"—he shrugged—"what happens when a man demands the truth of a doctor."

Mrs. Rand said: "Do you want something, Emma?"

The maid was still hovering in the doorway. "N-no, madam."

"Then please go." For a brief instant Halo Rand seemed angry. Then it passed, and she relaxed, was limp again.

"That's news, Doctor," MacBride said.

"I daresay it is. Regrettable news. I hope you will understand my position. I hope you will understand that I tried to keep the truth from Rand a long time."

"Would this change of climate have helped him?"

"It would only have prolonged his life a little while. I daresay the poor chap took the bravest way out. I only regret that in a way I was responsible—"

MacBride scoffed. "Wasn't your fault."

They were silent for a moment and then Landau said: "Well, I shall have to get on."

When he had gone, MacBride sat down on a straight-backed chair and regarded Mrs. Rand.

He said: "Well, that seems to straighten out the motive for Dan's suicide."

"P-poor Dan," she said in a tiny voice, half sobbing.

"Only I came here," MacBride went on, "pretty firmly convinced that it wasn't suicide."

She looked up, startled. "Wasn't suicide!"

"Yeah."

"But—but if it wasn't—"

He said: "Mrs. Rand, your husband, when he left here at noon yesterday, went and bought a gun off a pawnbroker on Diamond Street. I have a complete description of the gun. It wasn't the gun we found in Dan's hand; that was the gun I gave him; it wasn't the gun that killed him."

"Oh!" She felt her throat. "You can't mean—"

He dragged out sardonically, half to himself: "It kind of bears the dirty earmarks of murder."

She sat bolt upright. "Murder!"

"Mrs. Rand, it appears that the gun I gave him was not in his desk drawer when he came home yesterday at noon. It appears that though he left this house and bought a gun with the intention of committing suicide, he changed his mind later in the day."

"But his gun must have been there!"

He thought this over. "No," he said, "it mustn't have been. He went out and bought another."

She was taut, white-faced, shaking. "This—this is all incredible, Captain!"

He was point-blank: "Is there another man in your life?"

She jumped to her feet, her eyes flashing. "How dare you say a thing like that?" she cried.

"My job," he said, rising, eying her levelly, "is not always the pleasantest under the sun. I asked you a question."

"It is so absurd that I don't feel called upon to answer it!"

He said: "Of course, you don't have to answer me—not now, anyhow. Later, you might."

Her eyes shimmered. For a long moment she stood tall, quivering, shiny-eyed. Then she burst into tears and covered her face and her handkerchief fell to the floor.

"How cruel you are! How utterly cruel!"

He bent, picked up the handkerchief, passed it in front of his face, sniffed, caught the faint odor of perfume. She took her hands from her face and stared at him with tears streaming from her eyes. He gave her back the handkerchief. She broke out into an incoherent hodgepodge of words, wringing her hands, shaking her head.

He raised palms towards her and said: "Please, Mrs. Rand."

She fell suddenly to the divan and fainted. The oldish maid came swiftly, silently, into the room; flicked a cold, contemptuous look at MacBride.

He offered: "I'll help you—"

"You needn't!" the maid snapped.

He colored, stepped back. "Very well. Tell Mrs. Rand I'll see her again—soon."

She snapped: "I will tell Mrs. Rand nothing of the sort!"

"Suit yourself," he said.

He pivoted and walked across the living-room, into the foyer; opened the door and went down the corridor to the elevator, his hands in overcoat pockets, his shoulders hunched and a dogged, obstinate look in his windy blue eyes.

Cohegan was asleep at the wheel.

MacBride punched him. "Well, sleeping beauty! . . ."

The shabby phaeton left a cloud of acrid exhaust smoke in the flagstone courtyard, hummed eastward on Marshall Drive.

fter all, Steve," the Police Commissioner said, "if there was another man in her life, and Dan committed suicide because of this, you can't—you really can't convict anyone of murder."

Pacing the floor grimly, MacBride threw up his hands in a violent gesture. "But it's murder! I say it's murder!"

Commissioner Sterns smiled drily. "I know. I know you've been going around saying that, but you haven't shown one shred of evidence that would hold in court. Very likely this pawnbroker made a mistake. Very likely it wasn't Dan Rand who bought that gun off him. I'm not trying to pigeon-hole anything, Steve. I—well, I just don't like to see you make a fool of yourself."

"Oh!" MacBride stopped, glared. "I just should be a strong, silent guy, huh? Well, listen to me, Harry. I've noticed that a strong, silent guy is usually that way because he don't know anything. I'm willing to beef around, talk my head off, *make* a fool of myself—if it'll get me anywhere."

"Trouble with you, Steve," Sterns said good-naturedly, "is that when a case concerns someone you knew and liked, why, you get all steamed up; you cause yourself a lot of heartache and headache. . . . Just because the gun happens to have an odd smell, you think that—"

"That's only one of the things, Harry."

He hammered his heels back to his office, crammed his pipe, lighted it and sat in his swivel-chair and filled the office with smoke. Somehow he couldn't bring himself to believe that Halo Rand had had a hand in it; and when Moriarity and Cohen drifted in, he said:

"Now if Dan Rand wanted to kill himself because his wife was in love with someone else, why would he have sold, or planned to sell, the Colosseum? He left everything to his wife. I asked his lawyers an hour ago. It seems to me that if he felt he was losing his wife to another man, he'd have left his estate to someone else. But he didn't. He meant, you apes—he meant to leave his wife well-fixed!"

Moriarity and Cohen exchanged subtle winks.

"You, Mory," MacBride clipped. "You go to the telephone company and find out about a telephone call Jim Cardiac received at 11:30 this morning. Find where it came from."

Moriarity went out and Cohen said: "Ah, so we're going to make Jim Cardiac the fall-guy."

"Razz on, Ike; razz on. Even the Commissioner's doing it. I'm getting used to it."

Moriarity returned in half an hour and said: "The call came from Southern 509—the Apex Laboratories, in the Marks Building, 199 South Endicott Street."

MacBride grabbed his hat, put on his overcoat and left his office. He ran into Kennedy in the central room, barged past him, went down to the basement and on into the garage. Cohegan was working on the phaeton's bright work.

"Knock off, Bert."

The skipper climbed in back, sat down and was joined in a moment by Kennedy.

"I don't remember asking you to join me, Kennedy."

"Oh, I'm sure you did."

"Where to, Cap?" Cohegan said.

"South Endicott Street—199."

The phaeton rolled out of the garage.

"How about the woman?" Kennedy said from beneath his hat brim.

"I think she's okey."

"She say she was?"

MacBride snorted, made no reply.

Kennedy said: "Where are we going now?"

"Call on Mr. Apex Laboratories . . . Hey, Cohegan, you color blind? That was a red light you passed through!"

"Oh, was it?"

The phaeton crawled through a midtown traffic jam, turned south past the Empress Theatre, entered South Endicott Street and pulled up before a narrow stone building.

"I'll be right down," MacBride said.

Reaching the elevator, he found Kennedy beside him.

"Me and my shadow!" he muttered.

"Think of all the guys who haven't got shadows. Up!"

They got out at the fourth floor and turned left. The legend *Apex Laboratories* was in black on the ground-glass panel of a door at the end of the corridor. The door was locked. There was a white card tacked to the wood: *Gone for the day. Phone Midland 214 or call at 26 Cypress if urgent.*

"Let's go, skipper."

MacBride complained: "Listen, Kennedy. Haven't you got a room of your own, or just some nice quiet place where you can go and sit for a while?"

"Sitting is a vice, skipper. Continuance of the practice leads to a multitude of evils."

They went down to the lobby, strode out to the phaeton. Cohegan was not in sight, but in a moment he was seen coming across the street with a package in his hands.

"Peanuts?" he offered soberly.

"Idea!" said Kennedy. "It stimulates the liquid appetite."

They climbed in and MacBride said: "I bet some fine day I manacle Cohegan to that wheel! . . . Drive to 26 Cypress."

Kennedy munched hot peanuts. "Translated into English, Steve, what would Mr. Apex Laboratories' name be?"

"I'll let him translate it."

Number 26 Cypress was a large fieldstone house in the West End; there was a broad lawn in front planted with shade trees. A driveway ran past the right side of the house, and on this side was a white porte-cochère. The phaeton was parked in the street. MacBride and Kennedy walked up the driveway and MacBride hammered a knocker on a broad, heavy door.

A vellum-skinned butler opened the door.

MacBride said: "I want to see the head of the Apex Laboratories. My name is MacBride."

"Have you an appointment?"

"No."

"Is the call professional?"

"Absolutely."

"Please step in."

They entered a high, dim foyer paneled in dark wood.

"Please take a seat," the butler said. "It won't be long."

He padded off down the hall, vanished.

MacBride and Kennedy did not sit down. They heard the low sound of voices somewhere near, behind a closed door. Kennedy roamed around, came back and pointed.

"In there, skipper. That's the talk-talk room. Mr. Apex Laboratories is probably busy."

"So am I."

MacBride went down the large foyer towards the door Kennedy had indicated. It was broad, heavy, and he stood eying it speculatively. Then he knocked. The low sound of voices ceased. After a moment the latch clicked, the door opened noiselessly.

MacBride stared; then his eyes narrowed, his low blunt voice said: "Hello, Dr. Landau."

"Why—Captain Mac—"

Kennedy chuckled: "You old translator, you!"

"Come on, Kennedy. . . . This is Kennedy, Doctor—of the *Free Press*—"

"Just a moment, Captain. Please! I am very busy and—"

"I won't take long."

Hard-eyed, MacBride elbowed Landau aside and entered a large, sumptuous room. Kennedy trailed amiably behind him. Landau closed the door quietly.

Cardiac was standing on the other side of a tremendous library table. In a large, straight-backed chair sat a youth dressed in tweeds.

"Cardiac," muttered MacBride.

"Hello, Skipper."

Landau removed his pince-nez, dabbed at his face with a handkerchief, came briskly from the door.

"Really, Captain, this is a most pleasant surprise—"

"Pleasant?" MacBride said dully.

"Naturally I didn't expect—"

"Just a minute." MacBride raised a palm. "I'll talk first." He flexed his lips, shot a dark glance at Cardiac, at the youth in tweeds, at Dr. Landau.

"You phoned Cardiac at 11:30 this morning, Doctor, didn't you?"

"Really, I can't remember—"

"You don't have to. You phoned him. That's settled. I was in his office then. Your phone call upset him. It upset him because I happened to be in the office and he couldn't talk to you then. Why couldn't he?"

The youth's eyes traveled slyly from one to another.

Cardiac cut in: "You're certainly making a nuisance of yourself, skipper. Why don't you get wise to yourself?"

"Why couldn't you talk to him, Cardiac? I know. Because I was there. Because the things you had to talk about were not for my ears. . . . Who's the pink-cheeked boy?"

"Mr. Avarill," Landau said.

MacBride said: "So you were Dan Rand's doctor, Landau? You were the man who told him he'd have to leave Richmond City? Was that the first time you told him?"

"Of course!"

"Hell! I don't believe it! His wife told me he'd been acting queer for the past few months. You told him before yesterday. And what happened? He wouldn't leave. He wouldn't leave his business interests. Do you use perfume, Doctor?"

"No."

MacBride looked around. "Someone in this room does. How about you, Mr. Avarill?"

The pink-cheeked boy grinned. "Why, Captain!"

MacBride crossed to him, bent down. "No, it's not you."

"My—! This is rich!" Cardiac exploded.

Kennedy was sitting on the edge of the large library table. He fished in his pockets for a cigarette, found none. He knocked open a large box on the table. It was empty. He knocked open another and found cigarettes; put one between his lips, started to strike a match, paused. He frowned, picked up the empty box, opened it and sniffed.

Landau complained: "You certainly make yourself at home, Mr. Kennedy."

"Don't I, though! . . . Nice sandalwood box, Doctor."

MacBride was standing at his shoulder. "That's what I smell," he said. He snatched the box from Kennedy's hand, inhaled. He tossed the box back on the desk and said: "That's the smell. That's the perfume I've been looking for."

Landau said warmly: "This is becoming ridiculous, Captain!"

"Is it?" MacBride snarled, turning on him. "It's the smell of sandalwood in the gun that killed Dan Rand. The gun was kept in that box for a while. The odor of sandalwood—if that's what Kennedy called it—was absorbed by the oil in the gun. It stayed with the gun, not as strong as the smell in the box—but it was there; it was faint but it was there!"

The pink-cheeked youth smiled brightly but said nothing. Cardiac lifted his chin, pursed his lips hard. Dr. Landau looked about the room in nervous fits and starts, shrugging, saying: "Of course . . . this is peculiar . . . I hardly know what to say . . . to think . . . but of course—"

"You had access to Rand's home," MacBride cut in. "When were you there last—before his death? And don't lie, because it'll be easy to check up."

Landau cleared his throat, touched his necktie. "I think—yes, I dropped in there for a few moments the evening before his—ah—death."

"How long do you consider a few moments?"

"Well"—he cleared his throat—"I daresay I was there for about—well—half an hour."

"In Dan's den?"

"I—ah—yes, of course: Dan's den. To be sure!"

MacBride said: "The gun was in his drawer during the day. The maid saw it when she was cleaning up. It will be easy for me to check up and find out if anyone was in that room between the time she cleaned up and the time you were there."

Cardiac picked up his coat, flung it over his arm. "I wouldn't take cracks like that from any cop, Doc. Remember, you don't have to answer him. . . . Well, I've got to run along."

MacBride turned. "Get back, Cardiac!"

"Now look here, you flatfoot—"

"Get back, Cardiac. I've stepped into something that's just burning my toes. Dan Rand was double-crossed by somebody—"

"I'd watch," drawled Kennedy, "the young Joe College over there. I don't like his smile."

Landau wrung his hands. "This is positively the most absurd situation I have ever—"

"Of course," said MacBride sarcastically, "sandalwood boxes are as common as egg crates in this burg! . . . You get the hell back there, Cardiac. I told you you're not leaving this room!"

"I'll be damned if I won't!" whipped back Cardiac. "If you want to hold me, shamus, go out and get a summons! I'm a busy man! I've got no time to play tag with a second-rate police captain!" He jerked his thumb. "Come on, Ralph. We're leaving."

The pink-cheeked youth rose cheerfully. "Right with you, Jim, old boy!"

MacBride pivoted, caught hold of the youth's vest and flung him back into the chair. The youth's teeth clicked. He jumped right up again. MacBride flung him into the chair a second time, and this time the chair went over, the youth sprawled on the floor. He lay there, propped on his elbows; he smiled wistfully, sadly, reflectively, a lock of golden hair curving down over one golden eyebrow.

MacBride roared: "When I tell you to sit down, mister, I don't mean stand up!"

"Captain, Captain!" Landau panted. "Don't—don't aggravate him that way. Don't—"

"And will you," ripped out MacBride, swiveling, "stop sticking your nose in my business! . . . Cardiac, come back here!"

Kennedy yelled: "Look out!"

MacBride swung around, his gun half drawn.

Landau cried out and dived for the youth. The youth was chuckling liquidly, resting on one elbow. The gun exploded in his other hand and stopped Landau in mid-career. MacBride fired and his slug nailed the youth to the floor. Landau started stumbling forward, choking. He gathered unbalanced speed, went careening across the room, knocked over a floor lamp, crashed head-on against the wall and slumped to the floor. The youth writhed on his back, chuckling wildly, beating his palms upon the floor.

A door banged.

"Cardiac," said Kennedy.

"You stay here!" MacBride said.

He broke into a run, yanked open the door, collided with the butler and fell down as the front door slammed shut. The butler cried out. MacBride untangled himself, rose, lunged for the front door and yelled:

"Cohegan!"

But Cohegan was not in the phaeton. Through the trees, MacBride saw Cardiac at the wheel; heard the blast of the motor and saw the car lurch forward, gather speed. He galloped down the graveled driveway, reached the sidewalk, turned left and stretched his legs in a hard-heeled run. Raising his gun, he did not fire. There were other automobiles moving in the street. But he fired in the air. Beyond was a main highway and he thought a cop might be in the neighborhood. Running, he fired again.

And then he heard, ahead, three blasts from another gun. He saw the phaeton whip from side to side; heard the scream of its brakes and the scream of other brakes as other cars sought to avoid it. Heeling over, the phaeton slammed across the curbstone; its radiator and hood doubled up like a folded accordion and the sound of the crash was drowned instantly in the roar of the explosion that followed. Flame daggered its way through smoke; bricks flew from the building into which the car crashed.

ennedy picked up the telephone, sat on the library table and swung his legs. "Central 1000," he said into the mouthpiece. His world-weary eyes traveled from the dead youth to the dead doctor, and he sighed. "City desk, flower." He lay down on the table, held the mouthpiece above him.

"Abe," he said, "this is that famous journalist and bon vivant, Kennedy. . . . So now dust your ears. Old Stephen J. MacBride did it again. . . . I'm telling you! Listen. A young punk named Ralph Avarill accidentally shot and killed Dr.

Amos Landau in the latter's home, 26 Cypress Street. . . . Yeah, the punk meant to kill the skipper, but things got balled up. Then MacBride knocked off the punk. At that moment Jim Cardiac took it into his head to lam, and MacBride high-tailed after him in the well-known MacBride manner. They're not back yet.

"Meantime, get a load of this nice little bedtime story. Landau told it to me and then died. The punk—Ralph Avarill—killed Dan Rand. He was a hop-head. . . . No, sweetness, not Rand; the punk. The punk was a friend of Cardiac's, and Landau was a silent backer of Cardiac's interests. Ostensibly a fine medico, he was also a dealer in dope and an addict himself. He met Dan Rand seven years ago at a boxfight where he attended a boxer who later died from the effect of a blow to the heart. He became Rand's personal physician.

"When this trouble between Rand and Cardiac began, grew hotter, Cardiac went to his silent partner Landau and wanted him to put Rand out of the way. Landau thought of a better method. He began working on Rand mentally, telling him he was a lunger and advising him to sell out all his business interests here and go West and live the simple life. Well, it didn't

quite work out. It wore Rand down, but he was a sticker. Finally Landau told him he would die if he didn't leave. But before he told him that—in fact, the evening before—he dropped in at Rand's apartment and while Rand was out of the room Landau swiped his gun, went home and put it in a sandalwood box until the punk called for it. Next day he told Rand his chances of living were mighty small. He thought Rand would go home and tell his wife and that his telling her would make an open and shut suicide case when the cops found the body. . . .

"What? . . . Sure, the punk was to tail Rand. And he did. Tailed him all afternoon and finally, at between 9:30 and ten o'clock, walked him to that abandoned warehouse and let him have it with the gun Landau had stolen from Rand's desk. And when Rand fell, his hand came out of his pocket and he dropped the gun he'd bought. The punk picked it up, left the other—Just a minute."

MacBride had come darkly into the room. "Tell him Cardiac's dead, Kennedy. Cohegan objected to the squad car being stolen."

"Where was Cohegan?"

"Down in a fancy grocery store on the corner, mooching apples."

Luck

Lester Dent

LESTER DENT (1904–1959) was born in La Plata, Missouri, but grew up on a ranch in Wyoming. While working as a Western Union telegraph operator, he learned that a coworker had sold a story to a pulp magazine for the princely sum of $450. As a reader of the pulps, he decided to try it himself and sold an action story, "Pirate Cay," to *Top Notch* for the September 1929 issue. Soon after, he moved to New York for a full-time writing job with Dell Publishing, then had the chance to launch a new series for Street & Smith. After staggering success with *The Shadow*, S&S hoped to duplicate it with a detective who used various gadgets to fight crime, and Dent created Doc Savage under the house name Kenneth Robeson; the first issue hit the stands in March 1933. The series lasted until 1949, with 181 issues, of which 159 were written by Dent.

After Doc Savage, the character for which Dent received the most acclaim was Oscar Sail, the loner boatman who appeared in only two *Black Mask* stories, "Sail" and "Angelfish," which have been relentlessly anthologized as outstanding examples of the hard-boiled pulp detective. He began a third story, "Cay," but when his editor, Joseph Shaw, left the magazine, he abandoned it. Dent wrote the earliest draft of "Sail" in the spring of 1936 on his schooner, *Albatross,* while anchored at Miami's City Yacht Basin—where "Sail" is set. He once told Frank Gruber, a prolific pulp writer himself, as well as a historian of the genre, that he had been forced to rewrite both stories so many times that he did not like the final product.

The story in this collection, "Luck," is an early draft of that first adventure about Oscar Sail. As there were numerous drafts, it cannot be said with authority that this is the first version, but it is safe to say that it is a very early one, and certainly one that Dent preferred to the published story. Thanks to the novelist and noted pulp scholar Will Murray, the agent for the Lester Dent estate, for the history of this important publication.

"Sail" was published in the October 1936 issue of *Black Mask*. "Luck" has never before appeared in print.

Luck

Lester Dent

THE FISH TREMBLED ITS TAIL AS the knife cut off its head, then red ran out of it and made a mess on the planks and spread enough to cover the wet red marks where two human hands had tried to hold to the dock edge.

Sail put the palm of his own hand in the mess.

The small policeman came from shore. He had shoved through the small green gate with the discreet sign, *Private Yachts—No Admittance,* at the shore end of the swanky pier, and was under the neat green canopy, tramping in the rear edge of the glare from his flashlight. His leather and brass glistened in the light. He was cautious enough to walk in the middle of the narrow long pier, but did enough stamping with his feet to show he was the law.

When he reached Sail, he stopped. His cap had a cock. His lower lip was loose on the left side, as if depressed by a pipe stem that wasn't there. He was young, bony and brown.

He asked, "That you give that yell?"

Sail picked up the hook and wet line. He held the hook close to his left palm. He grimaced at the small oozing rip in the brown callus of the palm. It was about the kind of a hole the fishhook would have made.

"Yeah?" the cop said vaguely. "You snagged the hand on a hook, eh? Made you yell?" The policeman toed the fish head's open mouthful of snake-fang teeth.

"Barracuda," he said, but not as if that was on his mind.

Red drops came out of the ripped palm, fat-tened on the lower edge, came loose and fell on the dock. Sail picked the fish up with his other hand. When he stood his straightest, he was still shorter than the small cocky policeman.

The officer splashed light on Sail. He saw the round jolly brown features of a thirtyish man who probably liked his food, who would put weight on until he was forty, and spend the rest of his life secretly trying to take it off. Sail's hair might have been unraveled rope, and looked as if it had been finger-combed. Some of the black had been scrubbed out of his black polo shirt. Washings had bleached his black dungarees; they fitted his small hips tightly and stopped halfway below the knees. Bare feet had squarish toes. Weather had gotten to all of the man a lot.

The officer hocked to clear his throat. "They don't eat barracuda in Miami. Not when you catch the damn things in the harbor, anyhow."

He didn't sound as if that was the thing bothering him, either.

Sail asked, "You the health department?"

The little policeman filled Sail's eyes with light. He said, "If that was a crack—" and changed to, "Was it you yelled?"

"Any law against a yell when you get a hook in your hand?"

The policeman popped his light into Sail's face again. Derision was around Sail's blue eyes and in the warp of his lips.

Loud music was coming from the moonlight excursion boat at the south end of the City Yacht Basin, but a barker spoiled the effect of the music, if any. Two slot machines alongside the lunch stand at Pier Six ate sailor nickels and chugged away.

A hundred million dollars' worth of yachts within a half-mile radius, the Miami publicity bureau said. Little Egyptian-silk-sail racing cutters that had cost a thousand a foot. A big three-hundred-foot Britisher, owned by Lady Something-or-other who only had officers with beards. And in-between sizes. Teak, mahogany, chromium, brass. Efficiency. Jap stewards as quiet as spooks. Blond Swede sailors. Skippers with leather faces, big hands and great calm.

The policeman pointed his flashlight beam at the boat tied to the end of the dock. The light showed the sloping masts, the black canvas covers over the sails, the black, neat, new-looking hull. Life preservers tied to the mainstays had *Sail* on them in gold leaf.

"What you call that kind of a boat?" the cop asked.

"Chesapeake five-log bugeye," Sail said. "Her bottom is made out of five logs drifted together with Swedish iron rods. The masts on bugeyes always rake back like that. She's thirty-four feet long in the water. You'll have trouble beating a bugeye for knocking around shallow water, and they're pretty fair sea—"

"Could it cross the ocean?"

"She has."

"Yeah? My old man's got the crazy idea he wants to go to the South Seas. He's nuts about boats."

"It gets you."

"This one yours?"

"Yes," Sail said.

"How old is it?"

"Sixty-eight years old."

"T'hell it is! That's older'n my old man. I don't think he'd want it."

"She'll take you anywhere," Sail defended.

"What's she worth?"

"Seventy-five thousand dollars," Sail said.

The policeman whistled. Then he laughed. He did not say anything.

Sail said, "There are some panels in the cabin, genuine hand carvings by Samuel McIntire of Salem. Probably they were once on a clipper ship. That's what makes her price stiff."

The cop did not answer. He switched off his light.

"All I can say is you let out a hell of a funny yell when you catch a fish," he said.

He took pains to stamp his feet while he walked away. By the time Sail got the effects of the flashlight out of his eyes, the officer was out of sight.

Sail held his hands close to his chest, fingers spread, palms in. There was barely enough breeze to make coolness against one side of his face. The music on the moonlit sailboat stopped. The barker was silent. Over in the Bayfront Park outdoor auditorium a political speaker was viewing something with alarm. After he had felt his hands tremble for a while, Sail went to his boat.

The boat, *Sail,* rode spring lines at the dock end. She had a thirty-four-foot waterline. Twelve-foot beam, two-foot draft with centerboard up, seven with it down. She was rigged to be sailed by one man, all lines coming aft.

The interior was teak, with inset panels of red sanders, fustic and green ebony, all hand-carved by a man who had died in 1811. How Samuel McIntire panels came to be in the bugeye, Sail did not know, but he had been offered a thousand dollars for each year of age for the boat and was hungry broke when he turned it down. It was not a money matter. Some men love dogs.

Sail slapped the fish into a kettle in the galley and, hurrying, put most of his right arm through a porthole, grasped a line, took half hitches off a cleat, and let the line go. The line snaked quietly down into the water, following a sinking live-box and its contents of live fish and crawfish.

Sail looked out of the hatch.

The young policeman had come quietly back to where the fish had bled and was using his flashlight. He squatted. After a while, he approached the dock end, moseying. Too carefully. When his flashlight brightened the bugeye's black masts and black sail covers, Sail was in the galley, making enough noise cutting up the fish to let the cop know where he was and what he was doing.

Sail waited four or five minutes before putting his head out of the hatch. The cop had gone somewhere silently.

Sail was still looking and listening for the policeman when he heard the man's curse and the woman's cry, short, sharp. The man's curse was something of a bray of surprise. The sounds came out of Bayfront Park, between the water-front yacht basin and Biscayne Boulevard. Sail, not stirring, but watching the park, saw a man running among the palms. Then the young policeman and his flashlight were also moving among the palms.

During the next five minutes, the policeman and his flash were not still long enough for him to have found anything.

Sail stripped naked, working fast once more. His body was rounding, the hair on it golden and long, but not thick. He looked at his belly as if he didn't like it, slapped it and sucked it in. The act was more a habit than a thought. He put on black jersey swim trunks.

Standing in the companion looking around, Sail scratched his chest and tugged the hair on it. His fingers twisted a little rattail of the chest hair. No one was in sight. He got over the side without being too conspicuous about it.

The water had odor and the usual things floated in it. He swam under the dock, searching. The tide was high slack, almost, but still coming in just a little, so things in the water were not moving away.

The pier had been built stout because of the hurricanes. There was a net of cross timbers underneath, and anything falling off the south side of the dock would drift against them. Sail found what he was seeking on the third dive.

He kept in the dark places as he swam away with it.

The little island—artificial, put there when they dredged the harbor—was darkly silent when Sail swam laboriously toward it. Pine trees on the island had been bent by the hurricanes, and some torn up. The weeds did not seem to have been affected.

Sail tried not to splash as he shoved through the shallows to the sand beach. He towed the Greek underwater. Half a dozen crabs and some seaweed clung to the Greek when Sail carried him into the pines and weeds. The knife sticking in the Greek, and what it had done, did not help. The pines scratched and the weeds crunched under the Greek when Sail laid him down. It was very dark.

Pulpy skins in a billfold were probably green-backs, and stiffer, smaller rectangles, business cards. Silver coins, a pocketknife, two clips for an automatic. The automatic holster empty under the Greek's left armpit. From inside the Greek's coat lining, another rectangle, four inches wide, five times as long, a quarter of an inch thick. It felt like hardwood. The Greek's wristwatch still ticked.

Sail put the business cards and the object from the coat lining inside his swim trunks, and was down on his knees cleaning his hands in the sand when the situation got the best of him. By the time he finished being sick, he had sweated profusely.

The water felt cold as he swam back the way he had come—under the docks and close to the seawall—with the Greek.

Sail clung to *Sail*'s chain bobstay until all the water had run off him that wanted to run off, then swung aboard and moved along the deck, keeping below the wharf level, and dropped down the hatch. He started to take the bathing suit off, and the girl said, "Puh-lease."

She swung her legs off the forward bunk. Light from the kerosene gimbal lamp did not reach all of her. The feet were small in dark blue sandals which showed red-enameled toenails. Her legs had not been shaved recently, but were nice.

Pink starting on Sail's chest and spreading made his tan look dark and uncomfortable, and he chewed an imaginary something between his large white front teeth as he squinted at the girl. He seemed about to say something two or three different times, but didn't, and went into the stateroom and got out of the swim trunks. The shadow-wrapped rest of her did not look bad as he passed. He tied a fish sinker to the trunks and dropped them through a porthole into the bay, which was dredged three fathoms deep here. He put on his scrubbed black clothes.

The girl had moved into the light. The rest of her was interesting.

"You probably think I'm a tart," she said. "I'm not, and I wish you'd let me stay here awhile longer. I have a good reason."

Sail scratched behind his right ear, raised and lowered his eyebrows at her, stalked self-consciously into the galley, pumped freshwater in a glass and threw it on the galley floor, then stepped in it. His feet now left wet tracks such as they had made when he came aboard. He seemed acutely conscious that his efforts to make this seem a perfectly sensible procedure were exaggerated. His hands upset a round bottle, but he caught it. He set it down, picked it up again, asked:

"Drink?"

She had crossed her legs. Her skirt was split. "That would be nice," she said.

Sail, his back to her, made more noise than necessary in rattling bottles and glasses and pinking an opener into a can of condensed milk. He mixed two parts of gin, one of crème de cacao, one of condensed milk. He put four drops from a small green bottle in one drink and gave that one to the girl, holding it out a full arm length, as if he didn't feel well acquainted enough to get closer, or didn't want to frighten her away.

They sipped.

She said, "It's not bad without ice, really."

"I did have an electric ice box," he told her, as if excusing the lack of ice. "But it and this salt air didn't mix so well."

Her skirt matched her blue pumps, and her yellow jersey was a contrast. Her long hair was mahogany, and done in a bun over each ear, so that her long oval face had a pure, sweet look. She drank again. Her blue leather handbag started to slip out of the hollow of her crossed legs and she caught it quickly.

Sail put his glass down and went around straightening things which really didn't need it. He picked up the *News* off the engine box. It was in two parts. He handed one part to the girl. That seemed to press the button. She threw the paper down and grabbed her blue purse with both hands.

"You don't need to be so goddamn smart about it!" she said through her teeth.

She started to get up, but her knee joints did not have strength, and she slid off the bench and sat hard on the black battleship linoleum. Sail moved fast and got his plump hands on the blue purse as she clawed it open. A small bright revolver fell out of the purse as they had a tug-of-war over it.

"Blick!" the girl squealed.

Blick and a revolver came out of the oilskin locker. The gun was a small bright twin to the girl's. Blick's Panama fell off slick mahogany hair, and disarranged oilskins fell down in the locker behind him. Blick had his lips rolled in until he seemed to have no lips. He looked about old enough to have fought in the last war.

"Want it shot off?" he gritted.

Sail jerked his hand away from the girl's purse as if a bullet was already headed for it. He put his hands up as high as the cabin carlins and ceiling would allow. His mouth and eyes were round and uneasy, and the upper part of his stomach jumped a little with each beat of his heart, moving the polo shirt fabric.

Blick gave Sail a quick search. He was rough. His lips were still rolled in, and a sleeve was still jammed up on one arm, above a drop of blood that was not yet dry.

The girl started to get up, couldn't. She said, "Blick!" weakly.

Blick, watching Sail, threw at her, "You hadda be a sucker and drink with him!"

The girl's lips worked over some words

before sounds started coming. "...was... I...know he...it doped."

Blick gritted at Sail, "Bud, she's my sis, and if she don't come out of that, I wouldn't wanta be you. Help me get her goin'!"

Blick dropped his sister's purse and gun in his coat pocket, got his Panama, then took the girl's right arm, letting Sail look into the little gun's muzzle all the while. "Help me, bud!"

Sail took his hands down. Sweat wetness was coming through his washed black polo shirt. He watched Blick's eyes and face instead of watching the gun. They walked the girl up the companion and onto the dock. Blick put his hand and small revolver into a trouser pocket.

"We're tight. Stagger!"

They staggered.

The orchestra on the moonlit excursion boat was still trying to entice customers for the moonlight sail. Yacht sailors, some of them with a load, stood in a knot at the end of the lunch stand, and out of the knot came the chug of the slot machines. Blick was tall enough to glare over his sister's head at Sail. His glare was not bright.

"What'd you give her?"

Sail wet his lips. The sweat had come out on his forehead enough to start running.

"Truth serum."

"You louse!"

Two sailors, one without his shirt, went past, headed for the slot machines.

Blick said, "Bud, I think I got you figured. You're a guy Andopolis rung in. He'd still try to get a boat and another guy."

Sail squinted out of one eye. Perspiration was stinging the other.

"Andopolis was the one who didn't digest the knife?"

"You ain't that dumb!"

"Was he?"

"You know that was Abel!"

Sail said, "Believe it or not, I'm guessing right across the board. Abel was to do the dirty work while you and the girl hung around on shore. Abel tried to take something from Andopolis on the dock. Abel had something that

had something to do with whatever he wanted. He tapped it inside his coat as he talked. Abel got knifed, let out a bellow, and went off the dock into the drink. Andopolis ran after he knifed Abel. You headed him off in the park. He got away and ran some more. You did a sneak to my hooker while the cop looked around."

"Did you guess all that?" Blick sneered.

They were nearing Biscayne Boulevard and traffic. On the *News* building tower, the neon sign alternately spelled *WIOD* and *NEWS*. Sail took a deep breath and tried to watch Blick's face.

"I'd like to know what Abel wanted."

Blick said nothing. They scuffed over the sidewalk, and Blick, walking as if he did not feel as if he weighed much, seemed to think to a conclusion which pleased him.

"Hell, Nola. Maybe Andopolis didn't spill to our bud, here."

Nola did not answer. She seemed about asleep. Blick pinched her, slapped her, and that awakened her somewhat.

A police radio car was parked at the corner of Biscayne and Blick did not see it in time. He said, as if he didn't give a damn, "Stagger, bud! This should be good."

Sail shoved a little to steer the girl to the side of the walk farthest from the prowl car. Blick shoved back to straighten them up. The result was that they passed close enough to the police machine to reach it with one good jump. Sail shoved Blick and Nola as hard as he could, using the force of the shove to propel himself toward the car. He grabbed the spare tire at the back and used it to help himself around the machine to shelter.

Blick's revolver went off three times about as rapidly as a revolver could fire. Both cops in the car brayed, and fell out of the car onto Sail.

Blick carried Nola to a taxicab forty feet down the street, and dumped her in. He stood beside the hack, aimed, and air began leaving the left front tire of the police car. The cops started shooting in a rattled way. Blick leaped into the taxi. An instant later, the hack driver fell out of his own machine, holding his head. The taxi took off. The two cops sprang up, and piled into their machine, one yelling:

"What about this one in the street?"

"Hell, he's dead."

The cops drove after the taxi, one shooting, his partner having trouble steering with the flat tire.

Sail, for a fat man, ran away from there very fast.

Sail planted his heaving chest against the lunch stand counter, held on to the edge with both hands, and stood there a while, twice looking down at his knees and moving them experimentally, as if suspecting something was wrong with them. The young man, who looked as youths in lunch stands somehow always manage to look, came over and swiped the counter with his towel.

"What've you got in cans?" Sail asked him, then stopped the answering recital on the third name. Beer suds overflowed the can before it hit the counter. Sail drank the first can and most of the next in big gulps, but slowed down on the third and seemed tied up in thought. He scraped at the tartar on a tooth with a fingernail, then started chewing the nail and got it down to the quick, then looked at it as if surprised. He absently put three dimes on the counter.

"Forty-five," the youth corrected.

Sail added a half and said, "Some nickels out of that."

He carried the nickels over to the mob around the slot machines. He stood around with his hands in his pockets. He tried whistling, and on the second attempt got a good result, after which he looked more satisfied with himself. His mouth warped wryly as he watched the play at the two machines. He took his nickels out, looked at them, firmly put them back, but took them out a bit later. When there was a lull, he shoved up to the slot machines.

The one-armed bandit gave him a lemon and two bars, with another bar just showing.

"You almost made it," someone said. "A little more and you'd have made the jackpot."

"Brother," Sail said, "you must be a mind reader."

He backed up, waited, still giving some attention to his private thoughts, until he got a chance at the other machine. It showed a bar, a lemon, a bar. Sail rubbed his forearms, looked thoughtful and walked off.

A telephone booth was housed at the end of Pier Four. Sail, when a nickel got a dial tone, dialed the 0, said, "Operator, I believe in giving all telephone operators possible employment, so I never dial a number. Give me police headquarters, please." He waited for a while after the operator laughed, said, "I want to report an attempted robbery," then told someone else, "This is Captain Sail of the yacht *Sail*. A few minutes ago, a man and a woman boarded my boat and marched me away at the point of a gun. I do not know why, except that the man was a drug user. I feel he intended to kill me. There was a police car parked at the corner of Biscayne, and when I broke away and got behind it, the man tried to shoot me, then drove off with the woman in a taxi, and two officers chased them. I want to know what to do now."

"It would help if you described the pair."

The man and woman Sail described would hardly be recognized as Blick and Nola.

"Could you come up to headquarters and look over our gallery?" asked the voice.

"Where is it?"

"Turn left off Flagler just as you reach the railroad."

When Sail left the telephone booth, the youth with the hot-dog-stand look was jerking the handle of one slot machine, then the other, and swearing.

"Funny both damn things blew up!" he complained.

Sail walked off wearing a small secret grin.

Two hours later, Sail pushed back a stack of gallery photographs in police headquarters and said in a tired, wondering voice, "There sure seem to be a lot of crooks in this world. But I don't see my two."

The captain at his elbow said heartily, "You don't, eh? That's tough. One of the boys in the radio car got it in the leg. We found the taxi. And we'll find them two. You can bet on that." He was a big brown captain with the kind of jaw and eyes that went with his job. He had said his name was Rader.

Sail rode back to the City Yacht Basin in a taxi, and looked around before he got out. He walked to *Sail*. While adjusting a spring line, he saw a head shape through the skylight. By craning, he saw the head shape was finished out by a police cap. Sail walked back and forth, changing the spring lines, which did not need changing, and otherwise putting off what might come. Finally, he pulled down his coat sleeves, put on an innocent look and went down.

One policeman waiting in the cabin was using his tongue to lather a new cigar with saliva. The tongue was coated. He was shaking, not very much, but shaking. His face had some loose red skin on it, and his neck was wattled.

The second policeman was the young bony cop with the warp in the end of his mouth. He still had his flashlight.

The third man was putting bottles and test tubes in a scuffed brown leather bag which held more of the same stuff and a microscope off which some of the enamel was worn. He wore a fuzzy gray flannel suit, had rimless, hookless glasses pinched tight on his nose, and had chewed up about half of the cigar in his mouth without lighting it. The cigar was the same kind the other policeman was licking.

Sail said, "I just talked to Captain Rader."

The warp got deeper in the end of the young cop's mouth. He switched his flashlight on and off in Sail's eyes, then hung it from the hook on his belt.

"What about?"

Sail told them what he had talked to Captain Rader about—the kidnapping, which he said he could not understand. In describing Nola and Blick, whom he did not name—he made no mention of having heard their names—he repeated the words he had used over the telephone.

When it was over, the young cop stepped forward, jaw first.

"All right, by God! *Now you can tell us the truth!*"

The shaking policeman got up slowly, holding his shiny damp cigar and looking miserable. "Now, Joey, that way won't do it."

Joey grabbed Sail's right wrist and squeezed it. "The hell it won't! Lewis says there was human blood on the dock along with the fish blood!"

The shaking policeman said, "Now, Joey."

Joey shouted, "A lot of people heard somebody let out a yip. Even over in the park where I was doing the vice squad's work, I heard it."

Sail held out his left hand to show the tear in the brown callus of the palm.

"A fishhook made that," he said. "You saw it bleed. There's your human blood on the dock."

Joey yelled, "Mister sailor, we've been checking on you by radio. You cleared from Bimini, the customs tells us. We radioed Bimini. You know what? You were asked to get out of Bimini. A gambling joint went broke in Bimini because one of their wheels had been wired and a lot of lads in the know made a cleaning. It ended up in a brawl and the gambling joint owner went to the hospital."

Joey shook his finger at Sail's throat. "The British police asked around and it began to look as if you had tipped the winners how to play. The joint owner claimed he didn't know his wheel was wired. It ended up with you being asked to clear out. The only reason you're not in the Bimini jug is because they couldn't figure any motive. You didn't get a cut. You hadn't lost any jack on the wheel. You didn't have a grudge against the owner. It was a screwy business, the British said, from beginning to end. But that's what they think. I think different. You know what I think?"

"I doubt if it would be interesting," Sail said dryly.

"I think you outfoxed 'em. You're a smooth article. That's what you think. But you can't pull this stuff here."

The shaking policeman said, "You haven't got a leg, Joey," between teeth clicks.

"I'll sweat the so-and-so until I got a thousand legs!"

The freezing policeman groaned, "You should have your behind kicked, Joey."

Joey released Sail's right wrist to frown at the other officer. "Listen, Mister Homicide—"

The shaking policeman got between Joey and Sail and stood there, saying nothing. Joey frowned at him, then sucked at his lower lip, pulling it out of shape.

"Hell, if you gotta run this, run it!" he said.

He turned and stamped up the companion, across the deck and, judging from the sounds, had some kind of an accident and nearly fell overboard getting from the boat to the dock, but finally made it safely.

The other policeman, grinning without much meaning in it, extended a hand which, when Sail took it, was hot and unnatural. After he held the hand a moment, Sail could feel it trembling.

"I'm Captain Chris of homicide," the officer said. "I want to thank you for reporting your trouble to Captain Rader, and I want to congratulate you on your narrow escape from those two. But next time, don't take such chances. Never fool with hop and guns. We'll let you know as soon as we hear anything of your attacker and his girlfriend or sister, whichever she was. I hope you have a good time in Miami in the meantime. We have a wonderful city. Florida has a wonderful climate." He shook with his chill.

The rabbity man, Lewis, who had not said anything, finished putting things in his bag, picked up a camera with a photoflash attachment which had been unnoticed on a bunk, and went up the companion, stepping carefully, as one who was not used to boats. He got onto the dock carefully with bag and camera. Captain Chris followed.

Sail said, "Quinine and whiskey is supposed to be good for malaria. But only certain quinines."

"Thanks," said Captain Chris. "But I think whiskey gave it to me."

They walked away, and young Joey was the only one who looked back.

The tide stood at flood slack, the water still, so that things did not float away. Something bright was bobbing on the water, and Sail got a light. He found five of the bright things when he hunted. Used photographic flashlight bulbs, with brass bases not corroded enough by the salt water for them to have been in long. Sail went below and looked around. Enough things were out of place to show the hooker had been searched. Fingerprint powder had not been wiped off quite well enough.

Sail catnapped all night, sleeping no more than a half hour soundly at any one time. He spent long periods with a mirror which he rigged to look out of the companion without showing himself.

On a big Matthews cruiser tied across the slip, somebody was ostensibly standing anchor watch. Boats lying at a slip do not usually stand on anchor. The watcher did not smoke and did not otherwise allow any light to get to his features. It was dark enough that he might have been tall or short, wide or narrow. The small things he did were what any man would do during a long, tiresome job, with one exception.

He frequently put a finger deep in his mouth and felt around.

Party fish boats making noise on their way out of Pier Five furnished Sail with an excuse to go on deck at about six bells. He stood there yawning, rubbing his head with his palms and making faces. He rubbed a finger across his chest and rolled up little twists and balls of dirt or old skin, after which he took a shower with the dock hose.

The watcher was not around the Matthews in the morning sun. Sail went below to don a pair of black shorts which washing had faded.

Sail's dinky rode in stern davits, bugeye fashion, at enough of a tilt not to hold seas or spray, and Sail lowered it. He got a brush and the dock hose and washed down the topsides, taking off dried salt that seawater had deposited on the hull. He dropped his brush in the water three different times; it sank, and he had to reach under for it.

The third time he reached under for the brush, he retrieved the stuff which the Greek's clothing had yielded the night before. The articles had not worked out of the nook between the dock cross braces underwater where Sail had jammed them after swimming back from the island where he had taken the dead Greek.

Sail finished washing down, hauled the dink up on the davits, and during the business of coiling the dock hose around the faucet in the middle of the dock, he worked his eyes. Any one of a dozen staring persons within view might have been the watcher from the Matthews. The other eleven would be tourists down for a gawk at the yachts.

Sail took the Greek's stuff out of the dink when he got the scrub brush. He went below. Picking the business cards apart was a job because they were soaked to pulp. He examined both sides of each card as he got it separated. One card said Captain Santorin Gura Andopolis of the yacht *Athens Girl* chartered for Gulf Stream fishing and that nobody caught more fish. The address was Pier Five. *I live aboard,* was written in pencil on the back.

The other twenty-six cards said the Lignum Vitae Towing Company had a president named Captain Abel Dokomos. The address was on the Miami River, and there was a telephone number for after six.

The piece of board was four by twenty by a quarter inches, mahogany, with screw holes in the four corners. Most of the varnish was gone, peeled rather than worn off, and so was some of the gold leaf. There were a letter and four figures in gold leaf: *K9420.*

Sail burned all of the stuff in the galley Shipmate.

A man was taking two slot machines away from the lunch stand as Sail passed on his way uptown. Later, he passed four places which had slot machines, and there was a play around all of them. Sail loafed around each crowd, but not as if he wanted to. He walked off from one crowd, then came back. In all, he managed to play three machines. The third paid four nickels and he played two back without getting anything. The slot in a dial telephone got one of the surviving nickels.

He told the operator he didn't dial as a matter of principle and asked for Pier Five, and when he got Pier Five, asked for Captain Santorin Gura Andopolis of the *Athens Girl.* It took them five minutes to decide they couldn't find Captain Andopolis.

After the telephone clanked its metal throat around the fourth nickel, Sail repeated the refusal to dial and asked for the number of Captain Abel Dokomos' Lignum Vitae Towing Company.

When he heard the answer, he made his voice as different as he could. "Cap'n Abel handy?"

"He hasn't come down this morning. Anything we can do?"

"Call later," Sail said.

The woman on the other end of the wire had been Blick's sister Nola, visitor aboard *Sail* the night before.

Sail selected a cafeteria which was a little overdone in chromium. The darkie who carried his tray got a dime. There was a small dab of oatmeal on the first chair Sail started to sit on. He broke his egg yolks and watched them run with an intent air. The fifth lump made his coffee cup overflow. He put almost a whole egg down with the first gulp from the force of habit of a man who eats his own cooking and eats it in solitude.

A boy wandered among the tables, selling newspapers and racing tip sheets. He carried and sold more tip sheets than newspapers. Sail took the coffee slowly with the spoon, getting a little undissolved sugar out of the bottom of the cup with each spoonful, seeming to enjoy it. The sugar lumps were wrapped in paper carrying the cafeteria's advertisement, and he unwrapped one and ate it after he finished everything before him. He put the papers in the coffee cup.

The man in a stiff straw hat eating near the door did not put syrup or anything sweet on his pancakes or in his coffee. And when he finished eating, he poked the back of his cheek absently with a finger, then put the finger in the back of his mouth to feel.

Sail got up and took a slow walk until he came to a U-Drive-It. There was a slot machine in the U-Drive-It. He tried it, and it paid off only in noise. He made a deposit and got a light six sedan. For three blocks, he drove slowly, looking out and appraising buildings for height. He picked one much taller than the others and parked in front of it. After starting into the building, he came back to look over an upright dingus, one of a row of the things along the curb. Small print said motorists could park there half an hour if they put a nickel in the dingus and turned the handle.

"The whole town's got it," he complained, and shook the device to see if it would start working without a nickel. It wouldn't and he put one in.

He said loudly, just before entering one of the tall building elevators, "Five!"

The fifth-floor corridor was not much different from other office building corridors. There were three real estate and one law office and some more.

The man who had felt his bad tooth in the cafeteria came sneaking up the stairs from the fourth floor and put his head around the corner. Sail was set. The man's straw hat sounded surprisingly like glass when it collapsed, and the man got down on all fours to mew in pain. Sail hit again, then unwrapped his belt from his fist. He blew on the fist, working the fingers.

"I've got to rush my friend to a place for treatment," he told the operator when the elevator cage came.

He thanked the operator and half a dozen other volunteer assistants while he started the rented car. He drove past the U-Drive-It. The proprietor was fussing with his machine.

Sail drove five or six miles by guess before he found a lonesome spot and got out. He hauled the man out. Sail's breathing was regular and deeper than usual; his eyes were wide with excitement, and he perspired. He wiped his palms on his clerical black shorts and bent over his victim.

The man with the bad tooth began big at the top and tapered. His small hands were callused, dirt was ground into the calluses, and the nails were broken. He had dark hair and a dark face, but got lighter as he went down, finishing off with feet in a pair of white shoes. He smelled a little as men smell who live on small boats with no baths.

His pockets held three hundred in nothing smaller than tens, all new bills, in a plain envelope. There was a dollar sixty-one in silver mixed up with the cashier's slip for his cafeteria breakfast. In ten or so minutes, he was scowling at Sail.

He said something in Greek. It sounded like his personal opinion of Sail or the situation.

Sail said, "Andopolis?"

"You know my name, so whatcha askin' for?" the man growled without much accent.

"You're here because I been getting too much attention," Sail said. "That oughta be clear, hadn't it?"

Andopolis felt his head, that part of his cheek over his bad tooth, then got to his feet. Sail took his belt out of his pocket and started threading it through the loops. Andopolis clutched his head, groaned, started to sit down, but jumped at Sail instead. Sail moved to one side, but not enough, and Andopolis hit his shoulder and the impact turned him around and around. Andopolis hit him somewhere else, and the whole front of his body went numb and something against his back was the ground.

"I'll stomp ya!" Andopolis yelled.

He jumped on Sail with both feet, and Sail was still numb enough to feel only the dull shock. His rounded body rolled under the impact, and Andopolis waved his arms to keep erect. Sail had his belt unthreaded. He laid it like a whip across Andopolis' face. Andopolis grabbed his face, and was wide open when he sat down heavily beside Sail.

When Andopolis came to, his wrists were fastened with the belt. Sail had his shirt unbuttoned and was examining the damage the other's feet had done. There was one purple print of the entire bottom of Andopolis' right foot, and a skinned patch where the other had slid off, with loosened skin tangled in the long golden hairs, but not much blood. He put back his head and shoulders and started to take a full breath, but broke it off in coughing. He sat down coughing, holding his chest, and sweated.

"Yah!" Andopolis gloated. "I stomp your guts good if you don't lay off me! What you been follerin' me for?"

Sail looked up sickly. "Followin' you?"

"Yah."

Sail, still sitting, said, "My Christian friend, you stood anchor watch on me last night. You haunted me this morning. But still I was following you, was I?"

"Before that, I'm talk about," Andopolis growled. "You follow me to Bimini in that black bugeye. I make the run from Bimini here yesterday. You make it too. What kinda blind fool you take me for? You followin' me, and don't you think I don't know him."

"It must have been coincidence."

"Don't feed me, mister."

"It just might be that nobody will have to feed you for long."

"Whatcha mean?"

"You were walking down the dock toward my boat last night when Abel jumped you. You sort of ruined Abel, and I covered up for you, but that's not the point. The point is, why were you coming to see me?"

"Aw, hell, I was gonna tell you about followin' me."

Sail coughed some, deep and low, trying to keep it from moving his ribs, then got up on his feet carefully.

"All right, now we're being honest with each other, and I'll tell you a true story about a yacht named *Lady Luck*."

Andopolis crowded his lips into a bunch and pushed the bunch out as far as he could, but didn't say anything.

Sail said, "The *Lady Luck*, Department of Commerce registration number K9420. She belonged to Bill Lord of Tulsa. Oil. Out in Tulsa, they call Bill the Osage Magician on account of what he's got that it seems to take to find oil. Missus Bill likes jewelry, and Bill likes her, so he buys her plenty. Because Missus Bill really likes her rocks, she carries them around with her. You following me?"

Andopolis was. He still had his lips pooched.

"Bill Lord had his *Lady Luck* anchored off the vet camp on Lower Matecumbe last November," Sail continued. "Bill and the missus were ashore, looking over the camp. Bill was in the trenches himself, and is some kind of a shot with the American Legion and the Democrats, so he was interested. The missus left her pretties on the yacht. Remember that. Everybody has read about the hurricane that hit that afternoon, and maybe some noticed that Bill and his missus were among those who hung on behind that tank car. But the *Lady Luck* wasn't so lucky, and she dragged her pick off somewhere and sank. For a while, nobody knew where."

Sail stopped to cough. He had to lie down on his back before he could stop, and he was very careful getting erect. Perspiration had most of him wet.

"A couple of weeks ago, a guy asked the Department of Commerce lads to check and give him the name of the boat, and the owner, that carried number K9420," Sail said, keeping his voice down now. "The word got to me. Never mind how. And it was easy to find you had had a fishing party down around the Matecumbes and Long Key a few days before you got curious about K9420. It was a little harder to locate your party. Two guys. They said you anchored off Lower Matecumbe to bottom-fish, and your anchor fouled something, and you had a time, and finally, when you got the anchor up, you brought aboard some bow planking off a sunken boat. From the strain, it was pretty evident the anchor had pulled this planking off the rest of the boat, which was still down there. You checked up as a matter of course to learn what boat you had found."

Andopolis looked as if more than his tooth hurt him.

Sail kept his voice even lower to keep his ribs from moving.

"Tough you didn't get in touch with the insurance people instead of contacting Captain Abel Dokomos, a countryman who had a towing and salvage outfit and no rep to speak of. You needed help to get the *Lady Luck*. Cap Abel tried to make you cough up the exact location. You got scared and lit out for Bimini. You discovered I was following you, and that scared you back to Miami. You wanted a showdown, and when Cap Abel collared you on the dock as you were coming to see me, you took care of that part of your troubles with a knife. But that left Abel's lady friend, or whatever she is, and her brother, Blick. They were in the know, too. They tried to grab you last night in the park after you fixed Abel up, and you outran them. Now, that's a very complete story, or do you think?"

Andopolis was a man who did his thinking with the help of his face, and there was more disgust than anything else on his features.

"You tryin' to cut in?" he snarled.

"Not trying."

"Then what—"

"Have."

The sun was comfortable, but mosquitoes were coming out of the swamp around the road to investigate.

"Yeah," Andopolis said. "I guess you have, maybe."

Sail put his shirt on, favoring his chest. "We've got to watch the insurance outfit. They paid off on Missus Bill's stuff. Over a hundred thousand. They'll have wires out."

Andopolis got up and held out his hands for the belt to be taken off, and Sail took it off. Andopolis said, "I thought of the insurance when I got Cap Abel. We used to run rum. The Macedonian tramp!"

"There's shoal-water diving stuff aboard my bugeye," Sail said.

"You don't get me in no water! Shark, barracuda, moray, sting rays. Hell of a place. If I hadn't been afraid, I'd have done the diving myself. I thought of that, believe me."

"That's my worry. It's not too bad, once you get a system." Sail felt his chest. "I guess maybe these ribs will knit in a while."

Andopolis looked much better, almost as if he had forgotten his tooth. "It's your neck. Okay if you say so."

"Then let's get going."

Andopolis was feeling his tooth when he got into the car. Sail had driven no more than half a mile when both front tires let go their air. The car was in the canal beside the road before anything could be done about it.

The car broke its windows going down the canal bank. The canal must have been six feet deep, and its tea-colored water filled the machine at once. Sail had both arms over his middle where the steering wheel had hit. So much air had been knocked out of him, and his middle hurt so, that he had to take something into his lungs, and there was only water. He began to drown.

The water seemed to be rushing around inside the car, although there was room for no more to come in. Sail couldn't find the door handles. The broken windows he did find were too small to crawl out of, but after exploring three, he got desperate and tried a small one. There was not enough hole. He pushed and worked around with the jagged glass, his head out of the car, the rest of him inside, until strange feelings of something running out of his neck made him know he was cutting his throat.

He pulled his head in, and pummeled the car roof with blows that did not have strength enough to knock him away from what he was hitting. It came to his mind to try the jagged glass again as being better than drowning, but he couldn't find it, and clawed and felt with growing madness until he began to get fistfuls of air. He sank twice before he clutched a weed on shore, after which the spasms he was having kept him at first from hearing the shots.

Yells were mixed in with the shot sounds.

Andopolis was on the canal bank, running madly. Blick and his sister were on the same bank, running after Andopolis, shooting at him, and having, for such short range, bad luck. They were shooting at Andopolis' legs. All three ran out of sight. Sound alone told Sail when they winged Andopolis and grabbed him.

Sail had some of the water out of his lungs. He swam to a clump of brush which hung down into the water, got under it, and managed to get his coughing stopped by the time Blick and Nola came up hauling Andopolis. Andopolis sobbed at the top of his voice.

"Shoot his other leg off if he acts up, Nola," Blick yelled. "I'll get our little fat bud."

Sail wanted to cough until it was almost worth getting shot just to do so. Red from his neck was spreading through the water under the brush.

"He must be a submarine," Blick said. He got a stick and poked around. "Hell, Nola, this water is eight feet deep anyhow."

Andopolis babbled something in Greek.

Blick screamed, "Shut up, or we'll put bullets into you like we put 'em into your car tires!"

Andopolis went on babbling.

"His leg is pretty bad, Blick," Nola said.

"Hell, let 'im bleed."

Air kept coming up from the submerged car. Sail tried to keep his mind off wanting to cough. It seemed that Blick was going to stand for hours on the bank with his bright little pistol.

"He musta drowned," Blick said. "Get that other leg to workin', Andopolis. You didn't know we been on your trail all night and all mornin', did ya? We didn't lose it when this Sail got you, either."

Andopolis whimpered as they hazed him away. Car sound departed.

Captain Chris, wide-eyed and hearty and with no sign of a chill, exclaimed, "Well, well, we began to think something had happened to you."

Sail looked at him with eyes that appeared drained, then stumbled the other two steps down the companion into the main cabin of *Sail* and let himself down on the starboard seat. Pads of cotton under gauze made Sail's neck and wrists three times normal thickness. Tape stuck to his face in four places, and iodine had run out from under one of the pieces and dried.

Young bony Joey looked Sail over and his big grin took the warp out of the corner of his mouth.

"Tsk, tsk," he said cheerfully. "Somebody beat me to it."

Sail gave them a look of bile. "This is a private boat, in case you forgot."

"He's mussed up and now he's tough!" Joey said. "Swell!"

"Now, now, let's keep things on an amiable footing," Captain Chris murmured.

Sail said, "Drag it!"

Joey popped his palms together, aimed a finger at Sail. "You got told about Lewis finding human blood in that fish mess on the dock last night. But try to alibi the rest. There was wet tracks in this boat. That was all right, maybe, only some of the tracks were salt water and the water spilled on the galley floor was fresh. We got the harbor squad diver down this morning. He found a box on the bottom below this boat with live fish in it. He found a bathing suit with a sinker tied to it. And this morning, a yachtsman beached his dink on the little island by Pier One and found a dead Greek. We sat down with all that and done our arithmetic, and here we are."

Sail's face began changing from red and tan to cream and tan, although the bandages took away some of the effect.

Captain Chris said, "Joey, you'd make a lousy gambler, on account of you show your cards."

Sail said in a low voice, "You're gonna get your snouts busted if you keep this up!"

Captain Chris looked unconvincingly injured. "I didn't think we'd have any trouble with you, Mister Sail. I hoped we wouldn't. You acted like a gentleman last night."

Sail had been seated. He got up, bending over first to get the center of gravity right. He pointed a thumb at the companion. "Don't fall overboard on your way out."

"I bet he thinks we're leaving!" Joey jeered.

A string of red crawled out from under one of the bandages on Sail's neck. His face was more cream than any other color. He reached behind himself into the tackle locker and got a gaff hook, a four-foot haft of varnished oak with a bright tempered-steel hook with a needle point. He showed Joey the hook and his front teeth.

He said violently, "I've got a six-aspirin headache and things to go with it! I feel too lousy to shy at cops. You two public servants get the hell out before I go fishing for kidneys."

Joey yelled happily, "Damn me, he's resisting arrest and threatening an officer!"

Sail said, "Arrest?"

"I forgot to tell you." Joey grinned. "We're going to—"

Sail asked Captain Chris, "Is this on the level?"

"I regret that it is," Captain Chris said. "After all, evidence is evidence, and while Miami is noted for her hospitality, we do draw lines, and when our visitors go so far as to use knives on—"

"I'm gonna hate to break your heart, you windbag!" Sail said angrily.

He took short steps, and not very fast ones, into the galley, and took the rearmost can of beer out of the icebox. He cut off the top instead of using the patent opener. When the beer had filled the sink with suds, he got a glass tube which had been waxed inside the can. He held out the two sheets of paper which the tube contained.

Joey raked his eyes over the print and penned signatures, then spelled them out, lips moving.

"This don't make a damn bit of difference!"

Captain Chris complained, "My glasses fell off yesterday during one of them infernal chills. What does it say, Joey?"

"He's a private dick assigned to locate some stuff that sank on a yacht. The insurance people hired him."

Captain Chris buttoned his coat, pulled it down over his hips, set his cap by patting the top of it.

"I'm afraid this makes it different, Joey."

Joey snorted. "I say it don't."

Captain Chris walked to the companion. "Beauty before age, Joey."

"Listen, if you think—"

"Out, Joey."

"Mister Homicide, any day—"

"Out!" Captain Chris roared. "You're as big a goddamn fool as your mother."

Joey licked his lips while he kept a malevolent eye on Sail, then took a step forward, but changed his mind and climbed the companion steps. When he was outside, he complained, "Paw, you and your ideas give me an ache."

Captain Chris sighed wearily while he looked at Sail. "He's my son, the spoiled whelp." He hesitated. "You wouldn't want to cooperate?"

"I wouldn't."

"If you get yourself in a sling, it'd be better if you had a reason for refusing to help the police."

Sail said, "All I get out of this is a commission for recovering the stuff. Right now, I need that money like hell."

"You'd still get it if we helped each other."

"Maybe. But I've cooperated before."

Captain Chris shrugged, climbed three of the companion's five steps, and stopped. "This malaria is sure something. I could sing like a lark today, only I keep thinking about the chills due tomorrow. Did you say a special quinine went in that whiskey?"

"Bullards. It's English."

"Thanks." Captain Chris climbed the rest of the way out.

When the two policemen reached the dock, Sail came slowly on deck and handed Captain Chris a bottle. "You can't buy Bullards here."

"Say, I appreciate this!"

"If my day's run of luck keeps on the way it has, you'll probably find your knife man in a canal somewhere," Sail said slowly.

"I'll look," Captain Chris promised.

The two cops went away with Joey kicking his feet down hard on the dock boards.

There was a rip in the nervous old man's canvas apron, and he mixed his words with waves of a pipe off which most of the stem had been bitten. He waved the pipe and said, "My, mister, you must've had a car accident."

Sail, holding to the counter, said, "What about the charts?"

"Yeah, there's one other place sells the government charts besides us. Hopkins Carter. But if you're going down in the keys, we got everything you need here. If you go on the inside, you'll want thirty-two-sixty and sixty-one. They're the strip charts. But if you take Hawk Channel, you'll need harbor chart five-eighty-three, and charts twelve-forty-nine, fifty and fifty-one. Here, I'll show—"

Sail squinted his eyes, swallowed and said, "I don't want to buy a chart. I want you to slip out and telephone me if either of certain two persons comes in here and asks for chart twelve-fifty, the one which has lower Matecumbe."

"Huh?"

Sail said patiently, "It's simple. You just tell the party you got to get the chart, and go telephone me, then stall around three or four minutes before you deliver the chart, giving me time to get over here and pick up their trail."

The nervous old man put his pipe in his mouth and immediately took it out.

"What kind of shenanigans is this?"

Sail showed him a license to operate in Florida.

"One of them private detectives, huh?" the old man said, impressed.

Sail put a ten-dollar bill on the counter.

"That one's got twins. How about it?"

"Mister, if you'll just describe your parties. That's all!"

Sail made a word picture of Blick and Nola, putting the salient points down on a piece of paper. He added a telephone number.

"The phone's a booth in a cigar store on the corner. I'll be there. How far is this Hopkins Carter?"

"Two blocks."

"I'll probably be there for the next ten minutes."

Sail, walking off, was not as pale as he had been on the boat. He had put on a serge suit more black than blue and a new black polo. When he was standing in front of the elevator, taking a pull at a flat amber bottle which had a crown and a figure 5 on the label, the old man yelled.

"Hey, mister!"

Sail lowered the bottle, started coughing, and called between coughs, "Now"—cough—"what?"

"Lemme look at this again and see if you said anything about the way he talked."

Sail moved back to where he could see the old man peering at the paper which held the descriptions. The old man took his pipe out of his teeth.

"Mister, what does that feller talk like?"

"Well, about like the rest of these crackers. No, wait. He'll call you bud two or three times."

The old man pointed his pipe at the floor. "I already sold that man a twelve-fifty. 'Bout half hour ago."

Sail pumped air out of his lungs in a short laugh which had no sound except the sound made by the air passing his teeth and nostrils. He said, "That's swell. They would probably want a late chart for their X-marks-the-spot. And so they've got it, and they're off to the wars, and me, I'm out ten percent on better than a hundred thousand."

He had taken two slow steps toward the elevator when the old man said, "The chart was delivered."

Sail came around. "Eh?"

"He ordered it over the telephone. We delivered. I got the address somewhere." He thumbed an order book. "*Whileaway*. A houseboat on the river below the Twelfth Street causeway."

Sail put a ten on the counter. "The brother."

He was a fat man trying to hide a big face behind two hands, a match and a cigar. He said, "Oof!" and his dropping hands dragged cigar ashes down his vest when Sail prodded him in the upper belly with a fingertip.

Sail said, "I just didn't want you to think you were getting away with it."

The fat man turned his cigar down at an injured angle. "With what?"

"Whatever you call what you've been doing."

"There must be some mistake, brother."

"There's been several. It'll be another if you keep on trying to tail me."

"Me, tailing you! Why should I do that?"

"Because you're a cop. You've got it all over you. And probably because Captain Chris ordered me trailed."

The plainclothesman sent his cigar between two pedestrians, across the sidewalk and into the gutter. "Mind telling me what you can do about it?"

Sail had started away. He came back, pounding his heels. "What was that?"

"I've heard all about you, small-fat-and-tough. You're due to learn that with the Miami Police Department, you can't horse—"

Sail put his hand on the fat man's face. The fingers were spread, and against the hand's two longest fingers, the fat man's eyeballs felt wet. Sail shoved out and up a little. The cop did not yell or curse. He swung a vicious uppercut. He kicked with his right foot, then his left. The kicks would have lifted a hound dog over a roof. He held his eyes. The third kick upset a stack of gallon cans of paint.

Sail got out of there. He changed cabs four times as rapidly as one cab could find another.

Whileaway was built for rivers, and not very wide rivers. She was a hooker that couldn't take a sea. A houseboat about sixty feet waterline, she had three decks that put her up like a skyscraper. She should never have been built. She was white, or had been.

Scattered onshore near the houseboat was a gravel pile, two trucks with nobody near them, a shed, junk left by the hurricane, a trailer with both tires flat, windows broken, and two rowboats in as bad shape as the trailer. Sail was behind most of them at one time or another on his way to the riverbank. There was a concrete seawall. Between Sail and the houseboat, two gigs, a yawl, a cruiser and another houseboat were tied to dolphins along the concrete river bulkhead. Nobody seemed to be on any of the boats.

Sail wore dark blue silk underwear shorts. He hid everything else under the hurricane junk. The water had a little more smell and floating things than in the harbor. He kept behind the moored boats after he got over the seawall, and let the tide carry him. He was just coming under the *Whileaway* bow when one of the square window ports opened almost overhead.

Sail sank. He thought somebody was going to shoot or use a harpoon.

Something large and heavy fell into the water and sank, colliding with him, pushing him out of the way and going on sinking. He had enough contact with it to tell the first part of it was a navy-type anchor. He swam down after it. The river had two fathoms here, and he found the anchor and what was tied to it. The tide stretched his legs out behind as he clung to what he had found.

Whoever had tied the knots was a sailor, and sailor knots, while they hold, are made to be easily untied. Sail got them loose.

It would have been better to swim under the houseboat and come up on the other side, away from the port from which the anchor and Nola had been thrown, but Sail didn't feel equal to anything but straight up. His air capacity was low because of his near drowning earlier in the day.

He put his head out of the water with his eyes open and fixed in the direction of the square port. No head was sticking out of the port. No weapon appeared. The tide had taken Sail near the stern of the *Whileaway* and still carried him.

He got Nola's head out. Water leaked from her nose and mouth. Sail got an arm up as high as he could, clutching. He missed the first sagging spring line, got the second. The rope with which the anchor had been attached to Nola still clung to her ankles. He tied one of her arms to the spring line so that her head was out.

Sail went up the spring line with his hands until one foot would reach the window sills. From there to the first deck was simpler.

Nola began to gag and cough. It made a racket.

Sail opened his mouth to yell at her to be quiet. She couldn't hear him yet, or understand. He wheeled and sloped into the houseboat cabin.

The furnishings might have been something once, but that had been fifteen years ago. Varnish everywhere had alligatored.

Sail angled into the galley when he saw it. He came out with a quart brass fire extinguisher which needed polishing, and a rusted ice pick. There had been nothing else in sight.

Nola got enough water out to start screeching.

Beyond the galley was a dining room. Sail had half crossed it when Captain Santorin Gura Andopolis came in the opposite door with a rusty butcher knife.

Andopolis was using a chair for a crutch, riding its bottom with the knee of the leg which Blick and Nola had put a bullet through. Around his eyes—on the lids more than elsewhere—were puffy gray blisters about a size which burning cigarettes would make. Three fingernails were off each hand. Red ran from the three mutilated tips on the right hand down over the rusty butcher knife.

Sail had time to throw the fire extinguisher and made use of the time, but the best he did was bounce the extinguisher off the bulkhead behind Andopolis.

Andopolis said thickly, "I feex you up, mine fran!" and deliberately reversed the butcher knife for throwing.

Sail threw his ice pick. It stuck into Andopolis' chest over his heart. It did not go in deep enough to bother Andopolis. He did not even bother to jerk it out.

Sail jumped for the door, wanting to go back the way he had come. His wet feet slipped, let him down flat on his face.

Feet came pounding through the door and went overhead. Sail looked up. The feet belonged to the plainclothes detective who had been in the hardware store which sold marine charts.

Andopolis threw his knife. He was good at it, or lucky. The detective put his hands over his middle and looked foolish. He changed his course and ran to the wall. His last steps were spraddling. He leaned against the bulkhead. His hands did not quite cover the handle of the butcher knife.

Andopolis hobbled to Sail on his chair. He stood on one leg and clubbed the chair. Sail rolled. The chair became two pieces and some splinters on the floor. Sail, still lying on the floor, kicked Andopolis' good leg. Andopolis fell down.

As if that had given him an idea, the detective fell. He kept both hands over the knife handle.

Andopolis used the two largest parts of the chair and flailed at Sail. On all fours, Sail got away. His throat wound was running again. He got up, but there was no weapon except the bent fire extinguisher. He got that. Andopolis hit him with the chair leg and his left side went numb from the belt down. He retreated, as lopsided on his feet as Andopolis, and passed into the main cabin.

Nola was still screaming. A man was swearing at her with young cocky Joey's voice. Men were jumping around on the decks and in the houseboat rooms.

Blick sat on the main cabin floor, getting his head untangled from the remains of a chair. His face was a mess. It was also smeared with blue ink. The ink bottle was upside down under a table on which a new chart was spread open. A common pen lay on the chart.

Andopolis came in following Sail. Andopolis crawled on one knee and two hands.

Blick squawked, "What's Nola yellin' for?"

Andopolis crawled as if he did not see Sail or Blick, had not heard Blick. A tattered divan stood against the starboard bulkhead. Andopolis lay down and put an arm under that. He brought out a little bright pistol, either Blick's or his sister's.

Captain Chris jumped in through the door.

Andopolis' small pistol made the noise of a big one. Blick, sitting on the floor, jumped a foot when there seemed no possible way of his jumping, no muscles to propel him upward. He came down with his head forward between his knees, and remained that way, even after drops began coming out of the center of his forehead.

Captain Chris had trouble with his coattails and his gun. Andopolis' little gun made its noise again. Captain Chris turned around faster than he could have without some help from lead, and ran out, still having trouble with his gun.

Sail worked the handle of the fire extinguisher. The plunger made *ink-sick!* noises going up and down. No tetrachloride came out. There was nothing to show it ever would. Then the first squirt ran out about a foot. The second was longer, and the third wet Andopolis' chest. Sail raised the stream and pumped. He got Andopolis's eyes full and rolled.

Andopolis fired once at where Sail had been. Then he got up on one foot and hopped for the door. His directions were a little confused. He hopped against a bulkhead.

Andopolis went down on the floor and began having a fit. It was a brief fit, ending by Andopolis turning over on his back and relaxing.

The wall had driven the ice pick the rest of the way into his chest.

Outside, Nola still screamed, but now she made words, scatteredly.

"Andopolis . . . killing Blick . . . tried . . . me . . . Andopolis . . . last night . . . Abel . . . knife . . . we . . . him . . . tell . . . broke loose . . . me . . . anchor . . . Blick . . ."

Sail ran to the table. The chart on the table had two ink lines forming a V with arms that ran to landmarks on Lower Matecumbe, and compass bearings were inked beside each arm, with the point where the lines came together ringed.

Sail left with the chart by the door opposite the one which he had come in by, taking the chart. He found a cabin. He tore the V out of the chart, folded it flat and tucked it under his neck bandages, using the stateroom mirror to adjust the bandages to hide the paper. He threw the rest of the chart out of a port on the river side.

Captain Chris was standing near dead Andopolis. Torn coat lining was hanging from under the right tail of his coat, but he had his gun in his hand.

"Where'd you go to?" he wanted to know.

"Was I supposed to stick around while you drew that gun?"

"The fireworks over?"

"I hope so."

Captain Chris put his gun in his pants pocket. "You're pinched. Don't say I didn't warn you."

Young Joey came in, not as cocky and not stamping his feet. Two plainclothesmen followed him, then two uniformed officers walking ahead of and behind the old man who sold the charts in the hardware store.

The old man pointed at Sail and said, "He's the one who asked about the feller who ordered the chart. Like I told you, I gave him—"

"Save it." Joey glared at Captain Chris. "We still ain't got nothing on this fat sailor, Paw. The girl says Andopolis is a party fisherman whose anchor pulled up part of a boat."

The girl had told about everything. Joey kept telling the story until he got to, "So Sail yanked the dame out, and now what've we got to hold him on?"

Captain Chris, looking mysterious and satisfied, told Sail, "Get your clothes on or we'll book you for indecent exposure along with the rest."

"What rest?"

"Get your clothes on."

Sail dressed sitting on the hurricane wreckage, brushed off the bottoms of his feet and put on socks and shoes. He looked up at Captain Chris as he tied the shoestrings.

"Kidding, aren't you?"

"Sure, sure!"

Sail bristled. "You've got to have a charge. Just try running me in on an INV and see what it gets you."

"I've got a charge."

"In a gnat's eye."

Captain Chris said with relish, "You've been playing the slot machines which are so popular in our fair city. You used a slug made of two hollow halves that fit together and hold muriatic or something that eats the works of the machines and puts them on the fritz. We found a box of the slugs on your boat. We have witnesses who saw you play machines before they went bad."

Sail wore a dark look toward the squad car. "This is a piker trick."

Captain Chris tooled the car over a bad street. "You put that gambling joint in Bimini on the bum, too. What's the idea?"

"Nuts."

"Now, don't get that way. I'm jugging you, yes. But it's the principle. It's to show you that it ain't a nice idea to football the cops around. Not in Miami, anyway. You'll get ten days or ten bucks is all. It's the principle. That, and a bet I made with Joey that if he'd let me handle this and keep his mouth shut, and you beat me to the kill, I'd jug you on this slot machine thing. Joey

wanted you jugged. Now, what's this between you and slot machines and wheels?"

Sail considered for a while, then took in breath.

"I even went to an institution where they cure things, once," he said. "Kind of a bughouse."

"Huh?"

"One psychologist called it a fixation. I've always had it. Can't help it. Some people can't stand being alone, and some can't stand being shut up in a room, and some can't take mice. With me, it's gambling. Can't stand it. I can't stand the thought of taking chances to make money."

"Just a lad who gets his dough the safe and sane method."

"That's the idea," Sail agreed, "in a general way."

The Maltese Falcon
Dashiell Hammett

DASHIELL HAMMETT (1894–1961) is arguably the most significant author of the hard-boiled private-eye novel in the history of American letters. Carroll John Daly is credited with inventing the genre, but it is Hammett who popularized it while elevating it to the level of serious literature.

By far his best-known work, and the most famous mystery novel ever written by an American, is *The Maltese Falcon*. After Hammett had written numerous short stories, novellas and two novels about the Continental Op, the series character that had made him both famous and successful, *The Maltese Falcon* was a major departure, the protagonist being the newly created but now iconic Sam Spade. Whereas the Op worked for a large firm and had a boss to whom he was answerable, Spade worked only with a partner who was murdered early in the novel, after which he was responsible to no one but himself and his sense of ethics.

Like most of Hammett's important work, *The Maltese Falcon* was originally published in *Black Mask*. It was a five-part serial running from September 1929 to January 1930; Alfred A. Knopf published it in book form on February 14, 1930.

The book was dramatically revised after serialization, with more than two thousand textual differences between the two versions. Some of the changes were made by copy editors at Knopf but the majority appear to have been made by Hammett himself. This is the first time that the original magazine version has been published since its initial appearance eighty years ago.

The Maltese Falcon

Dashiell Hammett

SPADE AND ARCHER

AMUEL SPADE'S JAW was long and bony, his chin a jutting V under the more flexible V of his mouth. His nostrils curved back to make another, smaller V. His yellow-gray eyes were horizontal. The V *motif* was picked up again by thickish brows rising outward from twin creases above a hooked nose, and his pale brown hair grew down, from high, flat temples, in a point on his forehead. He looked rather pleasantly like a blond Satan.

He said to Effie Perine: "Yes, sweetheart?"

She was a lanky, sunburned girl whose tan dress of thin woolen stuff clung to her with an effect of dampness. Her eyes were brown and playful in a shiny, boyish face.

She finished shutting the door behind her, leaned against it, and said:

"There's a girl wants to see you. Her name's Wonderly."

"A customer?"

"I guess so. You'll want to see her anyway; she's a knockout."

"Shoo her in, darling," said Spade. "Shoo her in."

Effie Perine opened the door again, following it back into the outer office, standing with a hand on the knob while saying:

"Will you come in, Miss Wonderly?"

A voice said, "Thank you," so softly that only the purest articulation made the words audible, and a young woman came through the doorway. She advanced slowly, with tentative steps, looking at Spade with cobalt-blue eyes that were both shy and probing.

She was tall. She was pliantly slender. Her erect, high-breasted body, her long legs, her narrow hands and feet, had nowhere any angularity. She wore two shades of blue that had been selected because of her eyes. The hair curling from under her blue hat was darkly red, her full lips more brightly red. White teeth glistened in the crescent her timid smile made.

Spade rose, bowing and indicating with a thick-fingered hand the oaken armchair beside his desk. He was quite six feet tall. The steep, rounded slope of his shoulders made his body seem almost conical, no broader than it was thick, and kept his freshly pressed gray coat from fitting very well.

Miss Wonderly murmured, "Thank you," softly as before, and sat down on the edge of the chair's wooden seat.

Spade sank into his swivel-chair, made a quarter turn to face her, and smiled politely. He smiled without separating his lips. All the V's in his face grew longer.

The tappity-tap-tap and the thin bell and muffled whir of Effie Perine's typewriting came through the closed door. Somewhere in a neighboring office a power-driven machine vibrated dully. On Spade's desk a limp cigarette smoldered in a brass tray filled with the remains of limp cigarettes. Ragged gray flakes of cigarette ash dotted the yellow top of the desk and the green blotter and the papers that were there. A buff-curtained window, eight or ten inches open, let in from the court a current of air faintly scented with ammonia. The ashes on the desk twitched and crawled in the current.

Miss Wonderly watched the twitching and crawling gray flakes uneasily. She sat stiffly on the very edge of her chair, her feet flat on the floor, as if she were about to rise. Her hands in dark gloves clasped a flat, dark handbag in her lap.

Spade rocked back in his chair and asked:

"Now what can I do for you, Miss Wonderly?"

She caught her breath and looked at him. She swallowed and said hurriedly: "Could you—? I thought—I—that is—" Then she tortured her lower lip with glistening teeth and said nothing. Only her dark eyes spoke now, pleading.

Spade nodded and smiled as if he understood her, but pleasantly, as if nothing really serious were involved. The same assurance was in his voice when he spoke.

"Suppose you tell me all about it, and then we'll know what needs doing. Better begin as far back as you can, as near the beginning."

"That was in New York," she said.

"Yes," he said.

"I don't know where she met him. I mean I don't know where in New York. She's five years younger than I, only seventeen, and we didn't have the same friends. I don't suppose we were ever as close as sisters should be. Mama and Papa are in Europe. It would kill them. I've got to get her back before they come home."

"Yes."

"They're returning the first of the month."

Spade's eyes brightened. "Then we've two whole weeks," he said.

"I didn't know what she had done until her letter came. I was frantic." Her lips trembled. Her hands mashed the dark handbag in her lap. "The fear that she had done something like this kept me from going to the police, and the fear that something had happened to her kept urging me to go. There wasn't anyone I could go to for advice. I didn't know what to do. What could I do?"

"Nothing, of course," Spade said amiably, "but then her letter came?"

"Yes, and I sent her a telegram asking her to come home. I sent it to General Delivery here. That was the only address she had given me. I waited a week, but no answer came, not a word from her. And Mama and Papa's return was drawing nearer and nearer. So I came to San Francisco to get her. I wrote her I was coming. I shouldn't have done that, should I?"

"Maybe not. It's not always easy to know what to do. Then you haven't found her?"

"I haven't found her. I wrote her that I would go to the St. Mark, and I begged her to come and let me talk to her even if she didn't intend going home with me. But she didn't come. I waited there three days, and Corinne didn't come, didn't even send me a message."

Spade nodded his blond Satan's head slowly, frowning sympathetically, his lips tightened together.

"It was horrible," she said, trying to smile. "I couldn't sit there like that and wait and wait, not knowing what had happened to her, what might be happening to her." She stopped trying to smile, and shuddered. "The only address I had was General Delivery. I wrote her another letter, and yesterday afternoon I went to the Post Office. I stayed there until dark, but I didn't see her. I went there again this morning, and still didn't see Corinne, but I saw Floyd Thursby."

Spade nodded again, but his frown had vanished. In its place was a look of sharp attentiveness.

"He wouldn't tell me where Corinne is," she went on, hopelessly. "He wouldn't tell me anything, except that she is well and happy. But how can I believe him? That is what he would tell me anyhow, isn't it?"

"Exactly," Spade agreed, "but it might be true."

"I hope it is. I do hope it is," she exclaimed. "But I can't go back home like this, without having seen her, without even having talked to her on the phone. He wouldn't take me to her. He said she didn't want to see me. I can't believe that. He promised to tell her he had seen me, and to bring her to see me if she would come—this evening at the hotel. He said he knew she wouldn't. He promised to come himself if she wouldn't. He—"

She broke off with a startled hand to her mouth as the office door opened.

The man who had opened the door came in a step, said, "Oh, excuse me," hastily took his brown hat from his head, and backed out.

"It's all right, Miles," Spade told him. "Come in. Miss Wonderly, this is Mr. Archer, my partner."

Miles Archer came into the office again, shutting the door behind him, ducking his head and smiling at Miss Wonderly, making a vaguely polite gesture with the hat in his hand.

He was of medium height, solidly built, wide in the shoulders, thick in the neck, with a jovial, heavy-jawed red face and some gray in his close-trimmed hair. He was apparently as many years past forty as Spade was past thirty.

Spade said:

"Miss Wonderly's sister ran away from New York with a fellow named Floyd Thursby. They're here. Miss Wonderly has seen Thursby, and has a date with him tonight. Maybe he'll bring her sister with him. The chances are he won't. Miss Wonderly wants us to help her find her sister and get her away from him and back home." He looked at Miss Wonderly. "Right?"

"Yes," she replied indistinctly.

The embarrassment that had gradually been driven away by Spade's ingratiating smiles and nods and assurances was pinkening her face again. She looked at the bag in her lap and picked nervously at it with a gloved finger.

Spade winked solemnly at his partner.

Miles Archer came forward to stand at a corner of the desk. While the girl looked at her bag he looked at her. His little brown eyes ran their bold, appraising gaze from her lowered face to her feet and up to her face again. Then he looked at Spade and made a silent whistling mouth of appreciation.

Spade raised two fingers from the arm of his chair in a brief warning gesture and said:

"Well, that should be easily enough managed. It's simply a matter of having a man at the hotel this evening to shadow him away when he leaves, and to keep on shadowing him till he leads us to your sister. If she comes with him, so much the better."

Archer said: "Yeh." His voice was heavy, coarse.

Miss Wonderly looked up quickly at Spade, puckering her forehead between her eyebrows.

"Oh, but you must be careful." Anxiety quivered in her voice. Her lips shaped the words with little nervous jerks. "I'm deathly afraid of him, and of what he might do. She's so young, his bringing her here from New York is such a serious— Mightn't he—mightn't he do—something to her?"

Spade smiled and patted the arms of his chair.

"Just leave that to us," he said. "We'll know how to handle him."

"But mightn't he?" she insisted.

"There's always a chance." Spade nodded judicially. "But you can trust us to take care of that."

"I do trust you," she said earnestly, "but I want you to know he's a dangerous man. I honestly don't believe he'd stop at anything. I don't believe he'd hesitate to—to kill Corinne if he thought it necessary to save himself. Mightn't he do that?"

"You didn't threaten him with arrest, did you?"

"I told him all I wanted was to get Corinne home before Mama and Papa came, so they'd never know what she had done. I swore to him that I'd never say a word to them about it if he'd help me do that, but that if he didn't Papa would certainly have him punished. I—I don't suppose he believed me, altogether."

"Can he cover up by marrying her?" Archer asked.

The girl blushed and said in confusion:

"He has a wife and three children in England. Corinne wrote me that, to explain why she'd gone off with him."

"They usually do," Spade said, "though not always in England." He leaned forward to reach for a pencil and pad of paper lying on the desk. "What does he look like?"

"He's thirty-five, perhaps, and as tall as you, and either naturally dark or quite sunburned. His hair is dark, too, and he has thick eyebrows. He talks in a rather loud, blustery way, and has a nervous, irritable manner. He gives an impression of being—of violence."

Spade, scribbling on the pad, asked without looking up: "What color eyes?"

"They're bluish gray, and watery, though not in a weak way. And—oh, yes—he has a marked cleft in his chin."

"Thin, medium, or heavy built?"

"Quite athletic. He's broad-shouldered and carries himself erect, what you would call a decidedly military carriage. He had on a light gray suit and a gray hat when I saw him this morning."

"What does he do for a living?" Spade asked as he pushed the pad back and laid down the pencil.

"I don't know," she said. "I've never had the slightest idea."

"When's he coming to see you?"

"At eight this evening."

"All right, Miss Wonderly. We'll have a man there. It'll help if—"

"Mr. Spade, could either you or Mr. Archer?" She made an appealing gesture with both hands. "Could either of you look after it personally? I don't mean that the man you send wouldn't be capable, but, oh! I am so afraid of what might happen to Corinne. I'm afraid of him. Could you? I'd expect to be charged more, of course." She opened her handbag with nervous fingers and put two hundred-dollar bills on Spade's desk. "Will that be enough now?"

"Yeh," Archer said, "and I'll handle it myself."

Miss Wonderly stood up, impulsively holding a hand out to him.

"Thank you. Thank you," she exclaimed, and then gave Spade the hand, repeating, "Thank you."

"Not at all," Spade said over it. "Glad to. It'll help some if you either wait for Thursby downstairs or come down with him when he leaves."

"I will," she promised, and thanked the partners again.

"And don't look for me," Archer cautioned her. "I'll see you all right."

Spade went to the outer door with Miss Wonderly. When he came back to his desk Archer nodded at the hundred-dollar bills there, growled complacently, "They're right enough," picked one up, folded it, and tucked it in a vest pocket. "And they had brothers in her bag."

Spade pocketed the other bill before he sat down. Then he said:

"Well, don't dynamite her too much. What do you think of her?"

"She's a sweet job. And you telling me not to dynamite her." Archer guffawed suddenly, without merriment. "Maybe you saw her first, Sam, but I spoke first." He put his hands in his pants pockets and teetered back on his heels.

"You'll play hell with her, you will." Spade grinned wolfishly, showing the edge of teeth far back in his jaw. "You've got brains, yes, you have." He began making a cigarette.

CHAPTER II
DEATH IN THE FOG

 telephone bell rang in darkness. The third time it rang bedsprings creaked, fingers fumbled on wood, something small and hard thudded on a carpeted floor, the springs creaked again, and a man's voice said:

"Hello . . . Yes, speaking . . . Dead? . . . Yes . . . Fifteen minutes. Thanks."

A switch clicked and a white bowl, hung on three gilded chains from the ceiling's center, filled the room with light.

Spade, barefooted in green and white checked pajamas, sat on the side of his bed. He scowled thoughtfully at the telephone on the table while his hands took from beside it a packet of brown papers and a sack of Bull Durham tobacco.

Cold, steamy air blew in through two open windows, bringing with it half a dozen times a minute the Alcatraz foghorn's dull moaning. A tinny alarm clock, insecurely mounted on a corner of Duke's *Celebrated Criminal Cases of America*, which lay facedown on the table, held its hands at five minutes past two.

Spade's thick fingers made a cigarette with deliberate care, sifting a measured quantity of the tan flakes down into curving paper, spreading the flakes so that they lay equal at the ends with a slight depression in the middle, thumbs rolling the paper's inner edge down and up under the outer edge as forefingers pressed it over, thumbs and fingers sliding to the paper cylinder's ends, holding it even while tongue licked the flap, left forefinger and thumb pinching their end while right forefinger and thumb smoothed the damp seam, right forefinger and thumb twisting their end and lifting the other to Spade's mouth.

He picked up the pigskin and nickel lighter that had been knocked off the table, worked it, and with the cigarette burning in a corner of his mouth stood up.

He took off his pajamas. The smooth thickness of his arms, legs and body, the sag of his big, rounded shoulders, made his body look like a bear's. It looked like a shaved bear's; his chest was hairless. His skin was childishly smooth and pink.

He scratched the back of his neck and began to dress. He put on a thin white union suit, gray socks, black garters, and dark brown shoes. When he had laced his shoes he picked up the telephone, called Graystone 4500, and ordered a taxicab. He put on a green-striped white shirt, a soft white collar, a green necktie, the gray suit he had worn that day, a loose tweed overcoat, and a dark gray hat.

The street door bell rang as he switched off the light.

Where Bush Street roofed Stockton before slipping downhill to Chinatown, Spade paid his fare and left the taxicab. San Francisco's night fog, thin, clammy and penetrant, blurred the street. A few yards from where Spade had dismissed the taxicab a small group of men stood looking up an alley. Two women stood with a man on the other side of Bush Street, looking at the alley. There were faces at windows.

Spade crossed the sidewalk between iron-railed hatchways that opened above bare, ugly stairs, went to the parapet and, resting his hands on the damp coping, looked down into Stockton Street.

An automobile popped out of the tunnel beneath him with a roaring swish, as if it had been blown out, and ran away. Not far from the tunnel's mouth a man was hunkered on his heels before a billboard that held advertisements of a moving picture and gasoline across the front of a gap between two store buildings. The hunkered man's head was bent almost to the sidewalk so he could look under the billboard. A hand flat on the sidewalk, a hand clenched on the billboard's green wooden frame, held him in this grotesque position.

Two other men stood awkwardly close together at one end of the billboard, peeping through the few inches of space between it and the building at that end. The building at the other end had a blank gray sidewall that looked down on the lot behind the billboard. Lights flickered on the sidewall, and the shadows of men moving among lights.

Spade turned from the parapet and walked up Bush Street to the alley where men were grouped. A uniformed policeman, chewing gum under an enamel sign that said *Burritt St.* in white against dark blue, put out an arm and asked:

"What do you want here?"

"I'm Sam Spade. Tom Polhaus phoned me."

"Sure you are." The policeman's arm went down. "I didn't know you at first. Well, they're back there." He jerked a thumb over his shoulder. "Bad business."

"Bad enough," Spade agreed, and went up the alley.

Halfway up it, not far from the entrance, a dark ambulance stood. Behind the ambulance, on the left, the alley was bounded by a waist-high fence, three strips of rough boarding. From the fence dark ground fell away steeply to the billboard on Stockton Street below.

A ten-foot length of the fence's top rail had been torn from a post at one end, and hung dangling from the other. Fifteen feet down the slope a flat boulder stuck out. In the notch between boulder and slope Miles Archer lay on his back. Two men stood over him. One of them held an electric torch's beam on the dead man. Other men with lights moved up and down the slope.

One of them hailed Spade, "Hello, Sam," and clambered up to the alley, his shadow running up before him. He was a barrel-bellied tall man with shrewd, small eyes, a thick mouth, and carelessly shaven dark jowls. His shoes, knees, hands and chin were daubed with brown loam.

"I figured you'd want to see it before we took him away," he said as he stepped over the broken fence.

"Yes. Thanks, Tom," Spade said. "What happened?"

He put an elbow on a fence post and looked down at the men below, nodding to those who nodded to him.

Tom Polhaus poked his own left breast with a dirty finger.

"Got him right through the pump, with this." He took a fat revolver from his coat pocket and held it out to Spade. Mud inlaid the depressions in the revolver's surface. "A Webley. English, ain't it?"

Spade took his elbow from the fence post and leaned down to look at the weapon, but he did not touch it.

"Yes," he said. "Webley-Fosbery semi-automatic revolver. That's it. Thirty-eight, eight shot. They don't make them any more. How many gone out of it?"

"One shot." Tom poked his breast again. "He must've been dead when he cracked the fence." He raised the muddy revolver. "You've seen this before?"

Spade nodded.

"I've seen Webley-Fosberys," he said indifferently, and then spoke rapidly: "He was shot up here, huh? Standing where you are, with his back to the fence. The man that shot him stands here." He went around in front of Tom and raised a hand breast-high with leveled forefinger. "Lets him have it and Miles goes back, taking the top off the fence and going on through and down till the rock catches him. That it?"

"That's it," Tom replied slowly, working his brows together. "The shot burnt his coat."

"Who found him?"

"The man on the beat, Shilling. He was coming down Bush, and just as he got here a machine turning around threw headlights up here and he saw the top rail off. So he came up and found him."

"What about the machine that was turning around?"

"Not a damned thing about it, Sam. Shilling didn't pay much attention to it, not knowing anything was wrong. He says nobody didn't come out of here during the time it took him to come down from Powell, or he'd've seen them. The only other way out would be under the billboard on Stockton. Nobody went that way. The fog's got the ground soggy, and the only marks are where Miles slid down and where this here gun rolled."

"Didn't anybody hear the shot?"

"For the love of God, Sam, we only just got here. Somebody must've heard it, when we find them." He turned and put a leg over the fence. "Coming down for a look at him before he's moved?"

Spade said: "No."

Tom halted astride the fence to look back at Spade with surprised, small eyes.

Spade said: "You've seen him. You'd see everything I could."

Tom, still looking at Spade, nodded doubtfully and withdrew his leg over the fence.

"His gun was tucked away on his hip," he said. "It hadn't been fired. There was a hundred and sixty-some bucks in his clothes. Was he working, Sam?"

Spade, after a moment's hesitation, nodded.

Tom asked: "Well?"

"He was supposed to be tailing a fellow named Floyd Thursby," Spade said, and described Thursby as Miss Wonderly had described him.

"What for?"

Spade put his hands into his overcoat pockets and blinked sleepy eyes at Tom.

Tom repeated impatiently: "What for?"

"He was an Englishman, maybe. I don't know what his game was, exactly. We were trying to find out where he lived." Spade grinned softly and took a hand from his pocket to pat Tom's shoulder. "Don't crowd me." He put the hand in his pocket again. "I'm going out to break the news to Miles's wife." He turned away.

Tom, scowling, opened his mouth, closed it without having said anything, cleared his throat, put the scowl off his face and spoke with a husky sort of gentleness:

"It's tough, him getting it like that. Miles had his faults same as the rest of us, but I guess he must've had his good points, too."

"I guess so," Spade agreed in a tone that was utterly meaningless, and went out of the alley.

In an all-night drugstore on the corner of Bush and Taylor streets Spade used a telephone.

"Precious," he said into it sometime after he had given central a number, "Miles has been shot. . . . Yes, he's dead. . . . Now don't get excited. . . . Yes . . . You'll have to break it to Iva. . . . No, I'm damned if I will. You've got to do it. . . . That's a good girl. . . . And keep her away from the office. Tell her I'll see her—uh—some time. . . . Yes, but don't tie me up to anything. . . . That's the stuff. You're an angel. Bye."

Spade's tinny alarm clock said three-forty when he turned on the light in the suspended bowl again. He dropped his hat and overcoat on the bed and went into his kitchen, returning to the bedroom with a wineglass and a tall, dark bottle of Bacardi. He poured a drink and drank it standing. Then he put bottle and glass on the table, sat down on the side of the bed facing them and rolled a cigarette.

He had drunk his third glass of Bacardi and was lighting his fifth cigarette when the street doorbell rang. The hands of the alarm clock stood at four thirty.

He sighed, rose from the bed, and went to the telephone box beside his bathroom door. He pressed the button that released the street door lock. He muttered, "Damn her," and stood scowling at the black telephone box, breathing irregularly while a dull flush grew in his cheeks.

The grating and rattling of the elevator door being opened and closed came from the corridor. Spade sighed again and moved toward the corridor door. Soft, heavy footsteps sounded on the carpeted floor outside, the footsteps of two men. Spade's face brightened. His eyes were no longer harassed. He opened the door quickly.

"Hello, Tom," he said to the barrel-bellied tall detective with whom he had talked in Burritt Street, and, "Hello, Lieutenant," to the man beside him. "Come in."

They nodded together, neither saying anything, and came in. Spade shut the door and ushered them back into his bedroom. Tom sat on an end of the sofa by the window. The lieutenant sat on a chair beside the table.

The lieutenant was a compactly built man with a round head under short-cut grizzled hair and a square face behind a short-cut grizzled mustache. A five-dollar gold piece was pinned to his necktie, and there was a small, elaborate diamond-set secret-society emblem on his lapel.

Spade brought two wineglasses in from the kitchen, filled them and his own with Bacardi, gave one to each of his guests, and sat down with his on the side of the bed. Spade's face was placid and incurious. He raised his glass, said, "Success to crime," and drank it down.

Tom emptied his glass, set it on the floor beside him, and wiped his mouth with the back of a muddy finger. He stared at the foot of the bed as if he were trying to remember something of which it vaguely reminded him.

The lieutenant looked at his glass for a dozen seconds, took a very small sip of the rum, and put the glass on the table at his elbow. He examined the room with hard, deliberate eyes, and then looked at Tom.

Tom moved uncomfortably on the sofa and without looking up asked:

"Did you break the news to Miles's wife, Sam?"

Spade said: "Uh-huh."

"How'd she take it?"

Spade shook his head. "I don't know anything about women."

Tom said softly: "The hell you don't!"

The lieutenant put his hands on his knees and leaned forward. His greenish eyes looked at Spade with a peculiarly rigid stare, as if their focus was a matter of mechanics, to be changed only by pulling a lever or pressing a button.

"What kind of a gun do you carry?" he asked.

"None. I don't like them much. There are some in the office, of course."

"I'd like to see one of them," the lieutenant said. "You don't happen to have one here?"

"No."

"You sure of that?"

"Look around." Spade smiled and waved his empty glass a little. "Turn the dump upside-down if you want. I won't squawk, if you've got a search warrant."

Tom protested: "Oh, hell, Sam!"

Spade put his glass on the table and stood up facing the lieutenant.

"What do you want, Dundy?" he asked in a voice hard and cold as his eyes.

Lieutenant Dundy's eyes had moved to maintain their focus on Spade's. Only his eyes had moved.

Tom shifted his bulk on the sofa again, blew a deep breath out through his nose, and growled plaintively:

"We're not wanting to make any trouble, Sam."

Spade, ignoring Tom, said to Dundy:

"Well, what do you want? Talk turkey. Who in hell do you think you are, coming in here trying to rope me?"

"All right," Dundy said in his chest. "Now sit down and listen."

"I'll sit or stand as I damned please," said Spade, not moving.

"For God's sake be reasonable," Tom begged. "What's the use of us having a row? If you want to know why we didn't talk turkey, it's because when I asked you who this Thursby was you as good as told me it was none of my business. You can't treat us that way, Sam. It ain't right, and it won't get you anywheres. We got our work to do."

Lieutenant Dundy jumped up, stood close to Spade, and thrust his square, pink face up at the taller man's.

"I've told you before your foot was going to slip one of these days."

Spade made a deprecative mouth, raising his eyebrows.

"Everybody's foot slips sometime," he said with derisive mildness.

"And maybe this is your time?"

Spade smiled and shook his head.

"No. I'll do nicely, thank you." He stopped smiling. His upper lip, on the left side, twitched over his eyetooth. His eyes became narrow and sultry. His voice came out deep as the lieutenant's. "I don't like this. What are you sucking around for? Tell me, or get out and let me go to bed."

"Who's Thursby?" Dundy snapped.

"I told Tom what I knew about him."

"You told Tom damned little."

"I knew damned little."

"Why were you tailing him?"

"I wasn't. Miles was, for the swell reason that we had a client who was paying good United States money to have him tailed."

"Who's the client?"

Placidity came back to Spade's face and voice.

"Now, now," he said reprovingly. "You know I can't tell you that until I've talked it over with the client."

"You'll tell it to me or you'll tell it in court," Dundy said hotly. "This is murder, and don't forget it."

"Maybe. And here's something for you to not forget, sweetheart. I'll tell it or not as I damned please. It's a long while since I burst out crying because policemen didn't like me."

Tom came over and sat on the foot of the bed. His carelessly shaven mud-smeared face was tired and lined.

"Be reasonable, Sam," he pleaded. "Give us a chance. How can we turn up anything on Miles's killing if you won't give us what you've got?"

"You needn't get a headache over that," Spade told him. "I'll bury my dead."

Lieutenant Dundy sat down and put his hands on his knees again. His eyes were warm green discs.

"I thought you would," he said. He smiled with grim content. "That's just exactly why we came to see you. Isn't it, Tom?"

Tom groaned, but said nothing articulate.

Spade watched Dundy warily.

"That's just what I said to Tom," the lieutenant went on. "I said, 'Tom, I've got a hunch that Sam Spade's a man to keep the family troubles in the family.' That's just what I said to him."

Spade put the wariness out of his eyes. He made them look bored. He turned his face to Tom and asked with great carelessness:

"What's itching your boy friend now?"

Dundy jumped up and tapped Spade's chest with the ends of two bent fingers.

"Just this," he said, taking pains to make each word very distinct, emphasizing them with repeated taps: "Thursby was shot down in front of his hotel just thirty-five minutes after you left Burritt Street."

Spade spoke, taking equal pains with his words:

"Keep your—damned dirty paws off me."

Dundy withdrew the tapping fingers, but there was no change in his voice.

"Tom says you were in too much of a hurry to even stop for a look at your partner."

Tom growled apologetically: "Well, damn it, Sam, you did run off like that."

"You didn't go to Archer's house to tell his wife," the lieutenant's accusing voice went on. "We called up and that girl in your office was there, and said you sent her."

Spade nodded. His face was stupid in its blankness.

Lieutenant Dundy raised the two bent fingers toward the private detective's chest, quickly lowered them, and said:

"I give you ten minutes to get to a phone and do your talking to the girl. I give you ten to fifteen minutes to get to Thursby's joint—Geary near Leavenworth—you could do it easy in that time. And that gives you ten or fifteen minutes of waiting before he showed up."

"I knew where he lived?" Spade asked. "And I knew he hadn't gone straight home after killing Miles?"

"You knew what you knew," Dundy replied stubbornly. "What time did you get home?"

"Twenty minutes to four. I walked around thinking things over."

The lieutenant wagged his round head up and down.

"We knew you weren't home at three-thirty," he said. "We tried to get you on the phone. Where'd you do your walking?"

"Out Bush Street a way and back."

"Did you see anybody that—?"

"No. No witnesses," Spade said and laughed, but pleasantly now. "Sit down, Dundy. You haven't finished your drink. Get your glass, Tom."

Tom said: "No, thanks."

Dundy sat down, but paid no attention to his glass of rum.

Spade filled his own glass, drank, put the empty glass on the table, and resumed his seat on the side of the bed.

"I know where I stand now," he said, looking with friendly eyes from one police detective to the other. "I'm sorry I got up on my hind legs. But you birds made me nervous, coming in and trying to put the work on me. Having Miles knocked off bothered me, and then you birds cracking foxy. That's all right now, though, now that I know what you're up to."

Tom said: "Forget it."

The lieutenant said nothing.

Spade asked: "Thursby dead?"

While the lieutenant hesitated Tom said: "Yes."

Then the lieutenant said angrily: "And you might just as well know it—if you don't—that he died before he could tell anybody anything."

Spade was rolling a cigarette. He asked, without looking up:

"What do you mean by that? You think I did know it?"

"I meant what I said," Dundy replied bluntly.

Spade looked up at him and smiled, holding the finished cigarette in one hand, his lighter in the other.

"You're not ready to pinch me yet, are you, Dundy?" he asked.

Dundy shook his head no.

"Then," said Spade, "there's no particular reason why I should give a damn what you think, is there?"

Dundy looked at Spade with hard green eyes and said nothing.

Tom said: "Aw, be reasonable, Sam."

Spade put the cigarette in his mouth, set fire to it, and laughed smoke out.

"I'll be reasonable, Tom," he promised. "How'd I kill this Thursby? I've forgotten."

Tom grunted disgust. Lieutenant Dundy said:

"He was shot four times in the back, with a .44 or .45, from across the street, when he started to go into his hotel. That's the way it figures, though nobody saw it."

"And he was wearing a Lüger in a shoulder holster," Tom added. "And it hadn't been fired."

"What do the hotel people know about him?" Spade asked.

"Nothing except that he'd been there a week."

"Alone?"

"Alone."

"What did you find on him? Or in his room?"

Dundy drew his lips in and asked:

"What'd you think we'd find?"

Spade made a careless motion with his limp cigarette.

"Something to tell you who he was, what his store was. Did you?"

"We thought you could tell us that."

Spade looked at the lieutenant with yellow-gray eyes that held an almost exaggerated amount of candor.

"I've never seen Thursby," he said, "dead or alive."

Lieutenant Dundy stood up looking dissatisfied. Tom rose yawning and stretching.

"We've asked what we came to ask," Dundy said, frowning over eyes hard as green pebbles. He held his mustached upper lip tight against his teeth, letting his lower lip push the words out. "We've told you more than you've told us. That's fair enough. You know me, Spade. If you did or you didn't you'll get a square deal out of me, and most of the breaks. I don't know that I'd blame you a hell of a lot for dropping him, but that won't keep me from nailing you."

"Fair enough," Spade agreed evenly. "But I'd feel better about it if you'd drink your drink."

Lieutenant Dundy turned to the table, picked up his glass, and slowly drained it. Then he said, "Good night," and held out his hand. They shook hands with marked formality. Tom and Spade shook hands with marked formality. Spade let them out. Then he undressed, turned off the lights, and went to bed.

CHAPTER III
THREE WOMEN

hen Spade reached his office at ten the following morning Effie Perine was at her desk opening the morning mail. Her boy's face was pale under its sunburn. She put down the handful of envelopes and the paperknife she held, and said: "She's in there." Her voice was low and warning.

"I asked you to keep her away," Spade complained irritably, though he too kept his voice low.

Effie Perine's brown eyes opened wide and her voice was sharp as his:

"Yes, but you didn't tell me how." Her eyelids went together a little, and her shoulders drooped. "Don't be cranky, Sam," she said wearily. "I had her all night."

Spade came over and stood beside the girl, putting a hand on her hair, smoothing it away from the part.

"Sorry, angel, I haven't—"

He broke off as the inner door opened.

"Hello, Iva," he said to the woman who had opened it.

"Oh, Sam!" she said.

She was a blonde woman of a few years more than thirty. Her facial prettiness was perhaps five years past its best moment. Her body, for all its sturdiness, was finely modeled and exquisite. She wore black clothes from hat to shoes. They had as mourning an impromptu air.

Having spoken, she stepped back from the door and stood waiting for Spade. He took his hand from Effie Perine's head and entered the inner office, shutting the door.

Iva came quickly to him, raising her face for his kiss. Her arms were around him before his held her. When they had kissed he made a little motion as if to release her, but she pressed her face to his chest and began to sob.

He stroked her round back, saying: "Poor darling."

His voice was tender. His eyes, squinting at the desk that had been his partner's, across the room from his own, were angry. He drew his lips back over his teeth in an impatient grimace and turned his chin aside to avoid contact with the crown of her hat.

"Did you send for Miles's brother?" he asked.

"Yes. He came over this morning." The words were blurred by her sobbing and his coat against her mouth.

He grimaced again and bent his head for a surreptitious look at the watch on his wrist. His left arm was around her, the hand on her left shoulder. His cuff was pulled back far enough to leave the watch exposed. It showed ten-thirteen.

The woman stirred in his arms and raised her

face again. Her blue eyes were wet, round, and white-ringed. Her mouth was moist.

"Oh, Sam," she moaned, "did you kill him?"

Spade stared at her with bulging eyes. His bony jaw sagged. He took his arms from around her and stepped back out of her arms. He scowled at her and cleared his throat.

She held her arms up as he had left them. Anguish clouded her eyes, partly closed them under eyebrows pulled up at the inner ends. Her soft damp red lips trembled.

Spade laughed a harsh syllable. "Ha," and went to the buff-curtained window. He stood there with his back to her, looking through the curtain into the court, until she started toward him. Then he turned quickly and went to his desk. He sat down, put his elbows on the desk, his chin between his fists, and looked at her. His yellowish eyes glittered between narrowed lids.

"Who," he asked coldly, "put that bright idea into your head?"

"I thought—" She put a hand to her mouth and fresh tears filled her eyes. She came to stand beside the desk, moving with easy sure-footed grace in black slippers whose smallness and heel-height were extreme. "Be kind to me, Sam," she said humbly.

He laughed at her, his eyes still glittering. "You killed my husband, Sam, be kind to me." He clapped his palms together and said: "Great God!"

She began to cry audibly, holding a white handkerchief to her face.

He got up and stood close behind her. He put his arms around her. He kissed her neck between ear and coat collar. He said: "Now, Iva, don't." His face was expressionless.

When she had stopped crying he put his mouth to her ear and murmured: "You shouldn't have come here today, precious. It wasn't wise. You can't stay. You ought to be home."

She turned around in his arms to face him, asking:

"You'll come tonight?"

He shook his head gently.

"Not tonight."

"Soon?"

"Soon."

"How soon?"

"As soon as I can."

He kissed her mouth, led her to the door, opened it, said "Good-bye, Iva," bowed, shut the door, and returned to his desk.

He took tobacco and cigarette papers from his vest pockets, but did not roll a cigarette. He sat holding the papers in one hand, the tobacco in the other, and looked with brooding eyes at his dead partner's desk.

Effie Perine opened the door and came in. Her brown eyes were uneasy. Her voice was careless. She asked: "Well?"

Spade said nothing. His brooding gaze did not move from his partner's desk.

The girl frowned and came around to his side.

"Well," she asked in a louder voice, "how did you and the widow make out?"

"She thinks I shot Miles," he said, only his lips moving.

"So you could marry her?"

Spade made no reply to that.

The girl took his hat from his head and put it on the desk, then leaned over and took the tobacco sack and the papers from his inert fingers.

"The police think I shot Thursby," he said.

"Who is he?" she asked, separating a paper from the packet, sifting tobacco into it.

"Who do you think I shot?" he asked.

When she ignored the question he said: "Thursby's the guy Miles was supposed to be shadowing for the Wonderly girl."

Her thin fingers finished shaping the cigarette. She licked it, smoothed it, twisted the ends, and placed it between Spade's lips.

He said, "Thanks, honey," put an arm around her slim waist and rested his cheek wearily against her hip, shutting his eyes.

"Are you going to marry Iva?" she asked, looking down at his pale brown hair.

"Don't be silly," he muttered. The unlighted cigarette bobbed up and down with the movement of his lips.

"She doesn't think it's silly. Why should she, the way you've played around with her?"

He sighed and said: "I wish to God I'd never seen her."

"Maybe you do now." A trace of spitefulness came into the girl's voice. "But there was a time."

"I never know what to do or say to women, except that way," he grumbled. "And then I didn't like Miles."

"That's a lie, Sam," the girl said. "You know I think she's a louse, but I'd be a louse too if I could have a body like that."

Spade rubbed his face impatiently against her hip, but said nothing.

Effie Perine bit her lower lip, wrinkled her forehead, and, bending down for a better view of his face, asked:

"Do you suppose she could have killed him?"

Spade sat up straight and took his arm from her waist. He smiled at her. His smile held nothing but amusement. He took out his lighter, snapped it on, and lit his cigarette.

"You're an angel," he said tenderly through smoke, "a nice rattle-brained angel."

She smiled a little wryly.

"Oh, am I? Suppose I told you that your Iva hadn't been home very many minutes when I arrived to break the news at three o'clock this morning?"

"Are you telling me?" he asked. His eyes had become alert, though his mouth continued to smile.

"She kept me waiting at the door while she undressed or finished undressing. I saw her clothes where she had dumped them on a chair. Her coat and hat were underneath. Her singlette, on top, was still warm. She said she had been asleep, but she hadn't. She had wrinkled up the bed, but the wrinkles weren't mashed down."

Spade took the girl's hand and patted it.

"You're a detective, darling, but"—he shook his head—"she didn't kill him."

Effie Perine snatched her hand away from him.

"That louse wants to marry you, Sam," she said bitterly.

He made a careless gesture of dismissal with one hand.

She frowned at him and demanded:

"Did you see her last night?"

"No."

"Honestly?"

"Honestly. Don't act like Dundy, sweetheart. It ill becomes you."

"Has Dundy been after you?"

"Uh-huh. He and Tom Polhaus stopped in for a drink at four o'clock."

"Do they really think you killed this what's-his-name?"

"Thursby."

He dropped what was left of his cigarette into the brass tray and began to roll another.

"Do they?" she insisted.

"God knows." His eyes were on the cigarette he was making. "They did have some such notion. I don't know how far I talked them out of it."

"Look at me, Sam."

He looked at her and laughed so that for the moment merriment mingled with the anxiety in her face.

"You worry me," she said, seriousness returning to her face as she talked. "You always think you know what you're doing, but you're too slick for your own good, and some day you're going to find it out."

He sighed mockingly and rubbed his cheek against her arm.

"That's what Dundy says, but you keep Iva away from me, sweet, and I'll manage to survive the rest of my troubles." He stood up and put on his hat. "Have the *Spade & Archer* taken off the door and *Samuel Spade* put in its place. I'll be back in an hour, or phone you."

Spade went through the St. Mark's long purplish lobby to the desk and asked a blond dandy if Miss Wonderly was in. The dandy turned away from Spade, and then back to him shaking his head.

"She checked out this morning, Mr. Spade."

"Thanks."

Spade walked past the desk to the alcove off the lobby, where a plump young-middle-aged man in dark clothes sat at a flat-topped mahogany desk. On the edge of the desk facing the lobby was a triangular prism of mahogany and brass inscribed *Mr. Freed*.

The plump man got up from his chair and came around the desk holding out his hand.

"I was awfully sorry to hear about Archer, Spade," he said in the tone of one trained to sympathize readily without intrusiveness. "I've just seen it in the *Call*. He was in here last night, you know."

"Thanks, Freed. Were you talking to him?"

"No. He was sitting in the lobby when I came in early in the evening. I didn't stop. I thought he was working and I know you fellows like to be let alone when you're busy. Did that have anything to do with his—?"

"I don't think so, but we don't know yet. Anyway, we won't mix the house up in it if we can help it."

"Thanks."

"That's all right. Can you give me some information about an ex-guest, and then forget I asked for it?"

"Surely."

"A Miss Wonderly checked out this morning. I'd like to know the details."

"Come along," Freed said, "and we'll see what we can learn."

Spade stood still shaking his head.

"I don't want to show in it," he said.

Freed nodded his sleek head and went out of the alcove. In the lobby he halted suddenly and returned to Spade.

"Barriman was the house detective on duty last night," he said. "He's sure to have seen Archer. Shall I caution him not to mention it?"

Spade looked at Freed from the corners of his eyes.

"Better not, Freed. That won't make any difference as long as there's no connection shown with this Wonderly. Barriman's all right, but he likes to talk, and I'd rather he didn't think there was anything to be kept quiet."

Freed nodded again and went away.

Fifteen minutes later he returned.

"She came here last Tuesday, registering from New York. She hadn't a trunk, only some bags. There were no phone calls charged to her room, and she doesn't seem to have gotten much mail, if any. The only visitor I could learn about was a tall dark man of thirty-six or so. They seem to have been together a lot. She went out at half past nine this morning, came back an hour later, paid her bill, and had her bags carried out to a car. The boy who carried them says it was a Nash touring car, probably a hired car. She left a forwarding address: the Ambassador, Los Angeles."

Spade said: "Thanks a lot, Freed," and left the St. Mark.

When Spade returned to his office Effie Perine stopped typing a letter to tell him: "Your friend Dundy was in. He wanted to look at your guns."

"And?"

"I told him to come back when you were here."

"Good girl. If he comes back let him see them."

"And Miss Wonderly called up."

"It's about time. What did she say?"

"She wants you to come to see her." The girl picked a slip of paper up from her desk and read the memorandum penciled on it: "She's at the Coronet, on California Street, apartment 1001. You're to ask for Miss Leblanc."

Spade said, "Give me," and held out his hand. When she had given him the memorandum he took out his lighter, snapped on the flame, applied it to the slip of paper, held the paper till all but one corner was curling black ash, dropped it on the linoleum floor, and mashed it under his shoe sole.

The girl watched him suspiciously.

He grinned at her, said, "That's just the way it is, dear," and went out again.

CHAPTER IV
THE BLACK BIRD

iss Wonderly, in a belted green crepe silk dress, opened the door of apartment 1001 at the Coronet. Her face was flushed. Her dark red hair, parted on the left side, swept back in loose waves over her right temple, was somewhat tousled.

Spade took off his hat and said: "Good morning."

His smile brought a fainter smile to her face. Her eyes, of blue that was almost violet, did not lose their troubled look.

She lowered her head, and said in a hushed, timid voice: "Come in, Mr. Spade."

She led him past open kitchen, bathroom and bedroom doors into a cream and red living room, apologizing for its confusion: "Everything is upside down. I haven't even finished unpacking."

She laid his hat on a table and sat down on a walnut settee. He sat on a brocaded oval-back chair facing her.

She looked at her fingers, working them together, and said:

"Mr. Spade, I've a terrible, terrible confession to make."

Spade smiled a polite smile, which she did not raise her eyes to see, and said nothing.

"That—that story I told you yesterday was all—a story," she stammered, and looked up at him now with miserable frightened eyes.

"Oh, that," Spade said lightly. "We didn't exactly believe your story."

"Then—?" Perplexity was added to the misery and fright in her eyes.

"We believed your two hundred dollars."

"You mean—?" She seemed to have no idea of what he meant.

"I mean that you paid us more than if you'd been telling the truth," he explained blandly, "and enough more to make it all right."

Her eyes lighted up suddenly. She lifted herself a few inches from the settee, settled down again, smoothed her skirt, leaned forward, and spoke eagerly:

"And even now you'd be willing to—?"

Spade stopped her with a palm-up motion of one hand. The upper part of his face frowned. The lower part smiled.

"That depends," he said. "The hell of it is, Miss— Is your name Wonderly or Leblanc?"

She blushed and murmured: "It's O'Shaughnessy, Brigid O'Shaughnessy."

"The hell of it is, Miss O'Shaughnessy, that a couple of murders"—she winced—"coming together like this get everybody stirred up, make the police think they can go the limit, make everything and everybody hard to handle, and expensive. It's not—"

He stopped talking because she had stopped listening and was impatiently waiting for him to finish.

"Mr. Spade, tell me the truth." Her voice quivered on the verge of hysteria. Her face had become haggard around desperate eyes. "Am I to blame for—for last night?"

Spade shook his head.

"Not unless there are things I don't know about," he said. "You warned us that Thursby was dangerous. Of course, you did lie to us about your sister and all, but that doesn't count: we didn't believe you." He shrugged his sloping shoulders. "I wouldn't say it looked like your fault."

She said, "Thank you," very softly, and then moved her head from side to side. "But I'll always blame myself." She put a hand to her throat. "Mr. Archer was so—so alive yesterday afternoon, so solid and hearty and—"

"Stop it," Slade commanded. "He knew what he was doing. They're the chances we take."

"Was—was he married?"

"Yes, with ten thousand insurance, no children, and a wife who didn't like him."

"Oh, please don't!" she whispered.

Spade shrugged again. "That's the way it was." He glanced at the watch on his wrist, and moved from his chair to the settee beside her. "There's no time for worrying about that now." His voice was amiable but firm. "Out there a flock of policemen and reporters and assistant district attorneys are running around with their noses to the ground. What do you want to do?"

"I want you to save me from—from all of it," she said in a thin, tremulous voice. She put a hand timidly on his forearm. "Mr. Spade, do they know about me?"

"Not yet. I wanted to see you first."

"What—what would they think if they knew about the way I came to you, with those lies?"

"That wouldn't mean anything to the police except guilt. That's why I've been stalling them till I could see you. I thought maybe we wouldn't have to let them know it all. We ought to be able to fake a story that will rock them to sleep, if necessary."

"Mr. Spade, you don't think I had anything to do with—the murders—do you?"

He grinned at her and said: "I forgot to ask you that. Did you?"

"No."

"That's good. Now what are we going to tell the police?"

She squirmed on her end of the settee and her eyes wavered between heavy lashes, as if trying and failing to free their gaze from his. She seemed smaller, and very young and oppressed.

"Must they know about me at all?" she asked. "I think I'd rather die than that, Mr. Spade. I can't explain now, but can't you somehow manage so that you can shield me from them altogether, so I won't have to answer their questions? I couldn't stand being questioned, Mr. Spade. I would rather die. Can't you?"

"Maybe," he said, "but *I'll* have to know what it's all about."

She went down on her knees at his knees. She held her face up to him. Her face was wan, taut, and fearful over tight-clasped hands.

"I haven't lived a good life," she cried. "I'm bad—worse than you could know—but I'm not all bad. Look at me, Mr. Spade. You know I'm not all bad, don't you? You can see that, can't you? Then can't you trust me a little? I'm so alone and afraid, and I've got nobody to help me if you won't help me. I know I've no right to ask you to trust me if I won't trust you. I do trust you, but I can't tell you. I can't tell you now. Later I will, when I can. I'm afraid, Mr. Spade. I'm afraid of trusting you. I don't mean that. I do trust you, but—but I trusted Floyd, and—I've nobody else, nobody else, Mr. Spade. You can save me. You've said you can save me. If I hadn't believed you could save me I would have run away today instead of sending for you. If I thought anybody else could save me would I be down on my knees to you? I know this isn't fair of me. But be generous, Mr. Spade. Don't ask me to be fair. You're strong, you're resourceful, you're brave. You can spare me some of that strength and resourcefulness and courage, surely. Help me, Mr. Spade. Help me because I need help so badly, and because if you don't where will I find anyone who can, however willing? Help me. I've no right to ask you to help me blindly, but I do ask you. Be generous, Mr. Spade. You can save me. You can. Won't you?"

Spade, who had held his breath throughout much of this speech, now emptied his lungs with a long sighing exhalation between pursed lips and said:

"You won't need much of anybody's help. You're good. You're very good. It's chiefly your eyes, I think, and that throaty sob you get into your voice when you say things like, 'Be generous, Mr. Spade.'"

She jumped up on her feet. Her face crimsoned painfully, but she held her head erect and she looked Spade straight in the eyes.

"I deserve that," she said. "I deserve it, but—oh!—I did want your help so much, and I do want it so much, and the lie was in the way I said it, Mr. Spade, and hardly at all in what I said."

She turned away from him, no longer holding herself erect. "It's my own fault that you can't believe me now."

Spade's face reddened and he looked down at the floor, muttering:

"Now you are dangerous."

Brigid O'Shaughnessy went to the table and got his hat. She came back and stood in front of him holding the hat, not offering it to him, but holding it for him to take if he wished. Her face was white and thin.

Spade looked at his hat and asked:

"What happened last night?"

"Floyd came to the hotel at nine o'clock, and we went out for a walk. I suggested that, so Mr. Archer could see him. We stopped at a restaurant in Geary Street, I think it was, for supper and to dance, and got back to the hotel at about half past twelve. Floyd left me at the door, and I stood inside and watched Mr. Archer follow him down the street, on the other side."

"Down? You mean toward Market Street?"

"Yes."

"Do you know what they'd be doing in the neighborhood of Bush and Stockton, where Archer was shot?"

"Isn't that near where Floyd lived?"

"No. It would be a dozen blocks out of his way if he was going from your hotel to his. Well, what did you do after they left?"

"I went to bed. And this morning when I went out for breakfast I saw the headlines in the paper and read about both of them being killed. Then I went up to Union Square, where I had seen automobiles for hire, and got one and went to my hotel for my luggage. After I found my room had been searched yesterday I knew I would have to move, and I had found this place yesterday afternoon. So I came up here and then phoned your office."

"Your room at the St. Mark was searched?" he asked.

"Yes, while I was in your office." She bit her lip. "I didn't mean to tell you that."

"You mean by that that I'm not to question you about it?"

She nodded timidly.

He frowned.

She moved his hat a little in her hands.

He laughed impatiently and said:

"Stop waving my hat in my face. Haven't I promised to do what I can?"

She smiled contritely, returned the hat to the table, and sat beside him on the settee again.

He said: "As for trusting you blindly, I've got nothing against that except that I won't be able to do much if I haven't some idea of what's going on. For instance, I've got to know something about your Floyd Thursby."

"I met him in the Orient." She spoke slowly, looking down at a pointed finger that traced 8's on the seat of the settee between them. "We came here together from Hongkong, last week. He was—he had promised to help me. He took advantage of my helplessness and dependence on him to—to betray me."

"Betray you how?"

She shook her head and said nothing.

Spade frowned impatiently and asked:

"Why did you want him shadowed?"

"I wanted to know how far he had gone. He wouldn't even tell me where he was staying. I wanted to find out what he was doing, who he was meeting, things like that."

"Did he kill Archer?"

She looked up at him, surprised.

"Yes, certainly," she said.

"He had a Lüger in a shoulder-holster. Archer wasn't shot with a Lüger."

"He had a revolver in his overcoat pocket," she said.

"You saw it?"

"Oh, I've seen it often. I know he always carried it there. I didn't see it last night, but I know he never wore an overcoat without it."

"Why all the guns?"

"He lived by them. There was a story in Hongkong that he had come out there, to the Orient, as bodyguard to a gambler who had had to leave the States, and that the gambler had since disappeared. They said Floyd knew about his disappearance. I don't know. I do know that he always went heavily armed, and that he never went to sleep without covering the floor around his bed with crumpled newspapers, so nobody could come silently into his room."

"You picked a nice sort of playmate."

"Only that sort could have helped me," she said simply, "if he had been loyal."

"Yes, if." Spade pinched his lower lip between finger and thumb and looked gloomily at her. The vertical creases over his nose deepened, drawing his brows together. "How bad a hole are you actually in?"

"As bad," she said, "as could be."

"Physical danger?"

"I'm not heroic. I don't think there's anything worse than death."

"Then it's that?"

"It's that as surely as we're sitting here"—she shivered—"unless you help me."

He took his fingers away from his mouth and ran them through his hair.

"I'm not Christ," he said irritably. "I can't work miracles out of thin air." He looked at his watch. "The day's going and you've given me nothing to work with. Who killed Thursby?"

She put a crumpled handkerchief to her mouth and said, "I don't know," through it.

"Your enemies or his?"

"I don't know. His, I hope, but I'm afraid—I don't know."

"How was he supposed to be helping you? Why did you bring him here from Hongkong?"

She looked at him with frightened eyes and shook her head in silence. Her face was haggard and pitifully stubborn.

Spade stood up, thrust his hands into his jacket pockets, and scowled down at her.

"This is hopeless," he said savagely. "I can't do anything for you. I don't know what you want done. I don't even know if you know what you want."

She hung her head and wept.

He made a growling animal noise in his throat and went to the table for his hat.

"You won't," she begged in a small choked voice, not looking up, "go to the police?"

"Go to them!" he exclaimed, his voice loud with rage. "They've been running me ragged since four o'clock this morning. I've made myself God knows how much trouble standing them off. For what? For some crazy notion that I could help you. I can't. I won't try." He put his hat on his head and pulled it down tight. "Go to them? All I've got to do is stand still and they'll be swarming all over me. Well, now I'll tell them what I know, and you'll have to take your chances."

She rose from the settee and held herself straight in front of him though her knees were trembling, and she held her white panic-stricken face up though she couldn't hold the twitching muscles of mouth and chin still. She said:

"You've been patient. You've tried to help me. It is hopeless and useless, I suppose." She stretched out her right hand. "I thank you for what you've tried to do. I—I'll have to take my chances."

Spade made the growling animal noise in his throat again and sat down on the settee.

"How much money have you got?" he asked.

The question startled her. Then she bit her lip and answered reluctantly:

"I've about five hundred dollars left."

"Give it to me."

She hesitated, looking timidly at him. He made angry gestures with eyebrows, mouth, hands and shoulders. She went into her bedroom, returning almost immediately with a thin sheaf of paper money in her hand.

He took the money from her, counted it, and said:

"There's only four hundred here."

"I had to keep some to live on," she explained meekly, putting a hand to her breast.

"Can't you get any more?"

"No."

"You must have something you can raise money on," he insisted.

"I've some rings, a little jewelry."

"You'll have to hock them," he said, and held out his hand. "The Remedial's the best place, Mission and Fifth."

She bit her lip, looking pleadingly at him. His yellow-gray eyes were hard and implacable. Slowly she put her hand inside the neck of her green dress, brought out a slender roll of bills, and put them in his waiting hand.

He smoothed the bills out and counted them, four twenties, four tens, and a five. He returned two of the tens and the five to her. The others he put in his pocket. Then he stood up and said:

"I'm going out and see what I can do for you. I'll be back as soon as I can, with the best news I can manage. I'll ring four times—long, short, long, short—so you'll know it's me. You needn't go to the door with me. I can let myself out."

He left her standing in the middle of the room looking after him with dazed blue eyes.

Spade went into a reception room whose door bore the legend *Wise, Merican & Wise*. The red-haired girl at the switchboard said: "Oh, hello, Mr. Spade!"

"Hello, darling," he replied. "Is Sid in?"

He stood beside her with a hand on her plump shoulder while she manipulated a plug and spoke into the mouthpiece: "Mr. Spade to see you, Mr. Wise." She looked up at Spade. "Go right in."

He squeezed her shoulder by way of acknowledgment, crossed the reception room to a dully lighted inner corridor, and passed down the corridor to a frosted door at its far end. He opened the door and went into an office where a small olive-skinned man with a tired oval face under thin dark hair dotted with dandruff sat behind an immense desk on which bales of paper were heaped.

The small man waved a cold cigar stub at Spade and said:

"Push a chair around. So Miles got his last night?" Neither his tired face nor his rather shrill voice held any emotion.

"Uh-huh. That's what I came in about." Spade frowned and cleared his throat. "I think I'm going to have to tell a coroner to go to hell, Sid. Can I hide behind the sanctity of my client's identity and secrets and whatnot, like a priest or a lawyer?"

Sid Wise lifted his shoulders and lowered the ends of his mouth.

"Why not?" he said. "An inquest is not a court trial. You can try, anyway. You've gotten away with more than that before now."

"I know, but Dundy's getting snotty, and it's a little bit thick this time. Get your hat, Sid, and we'll go see the right people. I want to be safe."

Sid Wise looked at the mass of papers on his desk and groaned, but he got up from his chair and went to the closet by the window.

"You're a son of a gun, Sammy," he said as he took his hat from its hook.

Spade returned to his office at ten minutes past five that evening. Effie Perine was sitting at his desk reading *Time*. Spade sat on the desk and asked:

"Anything stirring?"

"Not here. You look like you'd swallowed the canary."

Spade grinned contentedly.

"I think we've got a future. I always had an idea that if Miles would go off and die somewhere we'd stand a better chance of thriving. Will you take care of sending flowers for me?"

"I did."

"You're an invaluable angel. How's your woman's intuition today?"

"Why?"

"What do you think of Wonderly?"

"I'm for her," the girl said without hesitation.

"She's got too many names—Wonderly, Leblanc, and she says the right one's O'Shaughnessy."

"I don't care if she's got all the names in the phone book. That girl is all right, and you know it."

"I wonder." Spade blinked sleepily at Effie Perine. Then he chuckled. "Anyway, she's given up seven hundred bucks in two days, and that's all right."

Effie Perine sat up straight and said:

"Sam, if that girl's in trouble, and you let her down, or take advantage of it to bleed her, I'll never forgive you, never have any respect for you, as long as I live."

Spade smiled unnaturally. Then he frowned. The frown also was unnatural. He opened his mouth to speak, but the sound of someone coming in at the corridor door stopped him.

Effie Perine rose and went into the outer office. Spade took off his hat and sat in his chair. The girl returned with a card: *Mr. Joel Cairo.*

"This guy is queer," she said.

"In with him, then, darling," said Spade.

Mr. Joel Cairo was a small-boned dark man of medium height. His hair was black and smooth and very glossy. His features were Levantine. A square-cut ruby, its sides paralleled by four baguette diamonds, gleamed against the deep green of his cravat. His black coat, cut tight to narrow shoulders, flared a little over slightly plump hips. His trousers fit his round legs more snugly than was the current fashion. The uppers of his patent-leather shoes were hidden by fawn spats. He held a black derby hat in a chamois-gloved hand and came toward Spade with short mincing, bobbing steps. The fragrance of *chypre* came with him.

Spade inclined his head at his visitor and then at a chair, saying: "Sit down, Mr. Cairo."

Cairo bowed elaborately over his hat, said, "I thank you," in a high-pitched thin voice, and sat down. He sat down primly, crossing his ankles, placing his hat on his knees, and began to draw off his yellow gloves.

Spade rocked back in his chair and asked: "Now what can I do for you, Mr. Cairo?" The amiable negligence of his tone, his motion in the chair, were precisely as they had been when he had addressed the same question to Brigid O'Shaughnessy on the previous day.

Cairo turned his hat over, dropped his gloves into it, and placed it bottom up on the corner of the desk nearest him. Diamonds twinkled on the second and fourth fingers of his left hand, a ruby

that matched the one in his tie even to the surrounding diamonds on the third finger of his right hand. His hands were soft and well cared for. Though they were not large, their flaccid bluntness made them seem clumsy. He rubbed his palms together, and said over the whispering sound they made:

"May a stranger offer his condolences for your partner's unfortunate death?"

"Thanks."

Cairo bowed.

"May I ask, Mr. Spade, if there was, as the newspapers inferred, a certain—ah—relationship between that unfortunate happening and the death a little later of the man Thursby?"

Spade said nothing in a blank-faced definite way.

Cairo rose and bowed. "I beg your pardon." He sat down and placed his hands side by side, palms down, on the corner of the desk. "More than idle curiosity made me ask that, Mr. Spade. I am trying to recover an—ah—ornament that has been mislaid. I thought—I hoped—you could assist me."

Spade nodded with eyebrows lifted to indicate attentiveness.

"The ornament is a statuette," Cairo went on, selecting and mouthing his words carefully, "the black figure of a bird."

Spade nodded again, with courteous interest.

"I am prepared to pay, on behalf of the figure's rightful owner, the sum of five thousand dollars for its recovery." Cairo raised one hand from the desk and touched a spot in the air with the broad-nailed tip of an ugly white forefinger. "I am prepared to promise that—what is the phrase?—no questions will be asked." He put his hand on the desk beside the other and smiled blandly over them at the private detective.

"Five thousand is a lot of money," Spade commented, looking meditatively at Cairo. "It—"

Fingers drummed lightly on the door.

When Spade had called, "Come in," the door opened far enough to admit Effie Perine's head and shoulders. She had put on a small dark felt hat and a dark coat with a gray fur collar.

"Is there anything else, Mr. Spade?" she asked.

"No. Good night. Lock the door when you go, will you?"

"Good night," she said, and disappeared behind the closing door.

Spade turned his chair to face Cairo again, saying:

"It interests me some."

The sound of the corridor door closing behind Effie Perine came to them.

Cairo smiled and took a short, compact flat black pistol out of an inner pocket.

"You will please," he said, "clasp your hands together at the back of your neck."

The Maltese Falcon

Dashiell Hammett

CAIRO'S POCKETS

"OU WILL PLEASE clasp your hands together at the back of your neck."

Events had broken rapidly for Samuel Spade, of the firm of Spade & Archer, private detectives.

Twenty-four hours earlier a Miss Wonderly, young and beautiful, had come to Spade and Archer for help in finding her younger sister who had left their New York home with a man named Floyd Thursby. Thursby was coming to Miss Wonderly's hotel that night. Miles Archer went there to shadow him when he left, in hopes of thus being led to the sister.

At two o'clock the next morning Samuel Spade was awakened by the police. His partner had been shot and killed in an alley near Stockton and Bush streets. Spade went there, got what information he could from Detective-sergeant Polhaus, refused to give Polhaus any information beyond the name and description of the man Archer had been shadowing, and left without having gone within fifteen feet of his dead partner. At an all-night drugstore Spade telephoned his stenographer, Effie Perine, and sent her out to break the news to Archer's wife, Iva.

Two hours later Polhaus and Lieutenant Dundy came to Spade's apartment. Spade gave them short answers to their questions about his actions after leaving the alley and he refused to tell them for whom Miles Archer had been shadowing Thursby. He learned that Thursby had been killed in front of a Geary Street hotel shortly after he—Spade—had left the alley. Though Lieutenant Dundy suspected Spade of having killed Thursby to avenge his partner's murder they parted on friendly, if somewhat formal, terms.

Iva Archer came to Spade's office later that morning and asked him if he had killed her husband. Effie Perine told Spade she thought Iva had killed her husband so she could marry him, Spade.

Miss Wonderly phoned Spade from a California Street apartment to which she had moved, and he went to see her there. In a stormy interview she confessed that the story about her sister was untrue, that her real name was Brigid O'Shaughnessy and that Thursby had come to San Francisco with her from Hongkong. She begged Spade to help her, to shield her from the police and from another, graver danger. She would not tell him what this other danger was, except that if he did not help her she would certainly be killed. Spade finally agreed to help her and took what money she had left—five hundred dollars.

Late that afternoon into Spade's office came Joel Cairo, a swarthy small man, perfumed, bejeweled and overdressed, to offer Spade five thousand dollars for the recovery of a black statuette of a bird. While Spade was questioning Cairo about the bird Effie Perine left for the day, locking the outer door behind her. Then Cairo took a pistol from his pocket and pointed it at Spade. He said:

"You will please clasp your hands together at the back of your neck."

Spade did not look at the pistol. He raised his arms and, leaning back in his chair, intertwined the fingers of his two hands behind his head; but his eyes, holding no particular expression, remained focused on Cairo's dark face.

Cairo coughed a little apologetic cough and smiled nervously with lips that had lost some of their redness. His dark eyes were humid and bashful and very earnest.

"I intend to search your office, Mr. Spade," he said. "I warn you that if you attempt to prevent me I shall certainly shoot you."

"Go ahead." Spade's voice was as empty of expression as his face.

"You will please stand," the man with the pistol instructed him at whose thick chest the pistol was aimed. "I shall have to make sure that you are not armed."

Spade stood up, pushing the chair back with his calves as he straightened his legs.

Cairo went around behind him. He changed the pistol from his right hand to his left. He lifted Spade's coat tail and looked under it. Holding the pistol close to Spade's back, he put his right hand around Spade's side and patted his chest.

The Levantine face was then no more than six inches below and behind Spade's right elbow.

Spade's elbow dropped as Spade spun to the right. Cairo's face jerked back not far enough: Spade's right heel on the patent-leathered toes anchored the smaller man in the elbow's path. The elbow struck him beneath the cheekbone, staggering him so that he must have fallen had he not been held by Spade's foot on his foot.

Spade's elbow went on past the astonished face and straightened when Spade's hand struck down at the pistol. Cairo let go the pistol the instant that Spade's fingers touched it. The pistol was small in Spade's hand.

Spade took his foot off Cairo's to complete his about-face. With his left hand Spade gathered together the smaller man's coat lapels—the ruby-set green tie bunching out over his knuckles—while his right hand stowed the captured pistol away in a coat pocket. Spade's yellow-gray eyes were somber. His face was wooden except for a trace of sullenness around the mouth.

Cairo's face was twisted with pain and chagrin. There were tears in his dark eyes. His skin was the complexion of polished lead except where the elbow had reddened his cheek.

Spade by means of his grip on the Levantine's lapels turned him slowly and pushed him back until he was standing close in front of the chair he had lately occupied. A puzzled look replaced the look of pain in the lead-colored face.

Then Spade smiled. His smile was gentle, even dreamy.

His right shoulder lifted a few inches. His bent right arm was driven up by the shoulder's lift. Fist, wrist, forearm, crooked elbow, and upper arm seemed all one rigid piece, with only the limber shoulder giving them motion. The fist struck Cairo's face, covering for a moment one side of his chin, a corner of his mouth, and most of his cheek between cheek bone and jaw bone.

Cairo shut his eyes and was unconscious.

Spade lowered the limp body into the chair, where it lay with sprawled arms and legs, the head lolling back against the chair's back, the mouth open.

Spade emptied the unconscious man's pockets one by one, working methodically, moving the lax body when necessary, making a pile of the pocket's contents on the desk. When the last pocket had been turned out he returned to his own chair, rolled and lighted a cigarette, and began to examine his spoils. He examined them with grave and unhurried thoroughness.

There was a large wallet of dark soft leather. The wallet contained three hundred and sixty-five dollars in United States bills of several sizes; three five-pound notes; a much-viséd Greek passport bearing Cairo's name and portrait; five folded sheets of pinkish onion skin paper covered with what seemed to be Arabic writing; a raggedly clipped newspaper account of the finding of Archer's and Thursby's bodies; a postcard photograph of a dusky woman with bold cruel eyes and a tender drooping mouth; a large silk handkerchief, yellow with age and somewhat cracked along its folds; an American Express receipt for a package sent that day to Constantinople; and a thin sheaf of Mr. Joel Cairo's engraved cards.

Besides the wallet and its contents there were three gaily colored silk handkerchiefs, fragrant of *chypre*; a platinum Longines watch on a platinum and red gold chain, attached at the other end to a small pear-shaped pendant of some white metal, which rattled when shaken and was intricately carved and inlaid with black and green in overlapping geometrical patterns; a handful of United States, British, French, and Chinese coins; a ring holding half a dozen keys; a silver-and-onyx fountain pen; a metal comb in a leatherette case; a nail file in a leatherette case; a small street guide to San Francisco; a ticket for an orchestra seat at the Geary that evening; a Southern Pacific baggage check; a half-filled package of violet pastilles; a Shanghai insurance broker's business card; and four sheets of Hotel Belvedere writing paper, on one of which was written in small precise letters Samuel Spade's name and his business and residential addresses.

Having examined these articles carefully—he even opened the back of the watchcase to see that nothing was concealed inside—Spade leaned over and took the unconscious man's wrist between finger and thumb, feeling his pulse. Then he put the wrist down, leaned back in his chair, and rolled and lighted another cigarette.

His face while he smoked was, except for occasional slight and apparently aimless movements of his lower lip, so still and reflective that it seemed stupid. But when Cairo presently moaned and fluttered his eyelids Spade's face became bland, and he put the beginning of a friendly smile into his eyes and mouth.

Joel Cairo awakened slowly. His eyes opened first, but a full minute passed before they fixed their gaze on any definite part of the ceiling. Then he shut his mouth and swallowed, exhaling heavily through his nose afterward. He drew in one foot and turned a hand over on his thigh. Then he raised his head from the chair-back, looked around the office in confusion, saw Spade, and sat up. He opened his mouth to speak, started, clapped a hand to his face where Spade's fist had struck and where there was now a florid bruise.

He said through his teeth, painfully:

"I could have shot you, Mr. Spade."

"You could have tried," Spade conceded.

"I did not try."

"I know."

"Then why did you strike me after I was disarmed?"

"Sorry." Spade grinned wolfishly, showing his jaw teeth. "But imagine my embarrassment when I found your five-thousand-dollar offer was just hooey."

"You are mistaken, Mr. Spade. That was, and is, a genuine offer."

"What the hell?" Spade's surprise was genuine.

"I am prepared to pay five thousand dollars for the figure's return." Cairo took his hand away from his bruised face and sat up prim and business-like again. "You have it?"

"No."

"If it is not here"—Cairo was very politely skeptical—"why should you have risked serious injury to prevent my searching for it?"

Spade flicked a finger at Cairo's possessions on the desk. "You've got my apartment address. Been up there yet?"

"Yes, Mr. Spade. I am ready to pay five thousand dollars for the figure's return, but surely it is natural enough that I should first try to spare the owner that expense if possible."

"Who is he?"

Cairo shook his head. "I cannot reveal his name."

"The fellow you sent the package to Constantinople to?" Spade asked carelessly. "Inkinopolis or something?"

Cairo hesitated, then said: "That package will reach him, yes."

"What was in it?"

Cairo smiled. "You will have to forgive my not answering that."

"Will I?" Spade leaned forward, smiling with tight lips. "I've got you by the neck, Cairo. You've walked in and tied yourself up, plenty strong enough to suit the police, with last night's killings. Well, now you'll have to play with me or else."

Cairo's smile was demure, but not in any way alarmed.

"I made somewhat extensive inquiries about you before taking any action," he said, "and was assured that you were far too reasonable to allow other considerations to interfere with profitable business relations."

Spade shrugged.

"Where are they?" he asked.

"I have offered you five thousand dollars for the—"

Spade thumped Cairo's wallet with the backs of his fingers and said:

"There's nothing like five thousand dollars here. You're betting your eyes. You could come in and say, 'I'll pay you a million for a purple elephant.' But what the hell would that mean?"

"I see, I see," Cairo lisped thoughtfully, screwing up his eyes. "You wish some assurance of my sincerity." He stroked his red lower lip with a finger-tip. "A retainer, would that serve?"

"It might."

Cairo put his hand out toward his wallet, hesitated, withdrew the hand, and said:

"Will you take, say, a hundred dollars?"

Spade picked up the wallet and took out a hundred dollars. Then he frowned, said, "Better make it two hundred," and did.

Cairo said nothing.

"Your first guess was that I had the bird," Spade said in a crisp voice when he had put the two hundred dollars in his pocket and had returned the wallet to the desk-top. "There's nothing in that. What's your second?"

"That you know where it is, or, if not exactly that, that you know it is where you can get it."

Spade neither denied nor affirmed this: he seemed hardly to have heard it. He asked: "What proof can you give me that your man is the owner?"

"Unfortunately, very little. There is this, though: nobody else can give you any authentic evidence of ownership at all. And if you know as much about the affair as I suppose—or I should not be here—you know that the means by which it was taken from him show that his right to it was more valid than anyone else's—certainly more valid than Thursby's."

"What about his daughter?" Spade asked.

Excitement opened Cairo's eyes and mouth, turned his face pink, made his voice shrill.

"*He* is not the owner!"

Spade said, "Oh," mildly and ambiguously.

"Is he here, in San Francisco, now?" Cairo asked in a less shrill, but still excited voice.

Spade blinked his eyes sleepily and suggested:

"It might be better all around if we both put our cards on the table."

Cairo recovered composure with a tiny jerk.

"I do not think that would be better," he said. His voice was suave now. "If you know more than I, I shall profit by your knowledge, and so will you to the extent of five thousand dollars. If you do not, I have made a mistake in coming to you, and to do as you suggest would be simply to make that mistake worse."

Spade nodded indifferently and waved his hand at the articles on the desk, saying: "There's your stuff." And then, when Cairo was returning the articles to his pockets: "It's understood that you're to pay my expenses while I'm getting this bird back for you, and five thousand dollars when it's done."

"Yes, Mr. Spade. That is, five thousand less whatever moneys have been advanced to you, five thousand in all."

"Right. And it's a legitimate proposition." Spade's face was solemn except for wrinkles at the corners of his eyes. "You're not hiring me to do any murders or burglaries, but simply to get it back if possible in an honest and lawful way."

"If possible," Cairo agreed. His face also was solemn except for the eyes. "And in any event with discretion." He rose and picked up his hat. "I am at the Hotel Belvedere when you wish to communicate with me, room 635. I confidently expect the greatest mutual benefit from our association, Mr. Spade." He hesitated. "May I have my pistol?"

"Sure. I'd forgotten it."

Spade took the pistol out of his coat pocket and handed it to Cairo.

Cairo pointed the pistol at Spade's chest.

"You will please keep your hands on the top of the desk," he said earnestly. "I intend to search your offices."

Spade said: "I'll be damned." Then he laughed in his throat and said: "All right. Go ahead. I won't stop you."

CHAPTER VI
THE UNDERSIZED SHADOW

 or half an hour after Joel Cairo had gone Spade sat alone, still and frowning, in his office. Then he said aloud in the tone of one dismissing a problem, "Well, they're paying for it," and took a bottle of Manhattan cocktail and a paper drinking cup from a desk drawer. He filled the cup two-thirds full, drank, put the bottle back in the drawer, tossed the cup into the waste basket, put on his hat and overcoat, switched off the lights, and went down to the night-lit street.

An undersized youth of twenty or twenty-one in a neat gray cap and overcoat was standing idly on the corner below Spade's building.

Spade walked up Sutter Street to Kearney, where he went into a cigar store to buy two sacks of Bull Durham. When he came out the youth was one of the four people waiting for a street car on the opposite corner.

Spade went to Herbert's Grill in Powell Street for dinner. When he left the grill, at a quarter to eight, the youth was looking into a nearby haberdasher's window.

Spade went to the Hotel Belvedere, asking at the desk for Mr. Cairo. He was told that Mr. Cairo was not in. The youth sat in a chair in a far corner of the hotel lobby.

Spade went to the Geary Theater, failed to see Cairo in the lobby, and posted himself on the curb in front, facing the theater. The youth loitered with other loiterers before Marquard's restaurant below.

At ten minutes past eight Joel Cairo appeared, walking up Geary Street with his little mincing, bobbing steps. Apparently he did not see Spade until the private detective touched his shoulder. He seemed moderately surprised for a moment, and then said:

"Oh, yes, of course, you saw the ticket."

"Uh-huh. I've got something I want to show you." Spade drew Cairo back toward the curb a little away from the other waiting theater-goers. "The kid in the cap down by Marquard's."

Cairo murmured, "I'll see," and looked at his watch. He looked up Geary Street. He looked at a theater sign in front of him on which George Arliss was shown costumed as Shylock, and then his dark eyes crawled sideways in their sockets until they were looking at the kid in the cap, at his cool pale face with curling lashes hiding lowered eyes.

"Who is he?" Spade asked.

Cairo smiled up at Spade. "I do not know him."

"He's been tailing me around town."

Cairo wet his lower lip with his tongue and asked:

"Do you think it was wise, then, to let him see us together?"

"How do I know?" Spade replied. "Anyway, it's done."

Cairo took off his hat and smoothed his hair with a gloved hand. Then he replaced his hat carefully and said with every appearance of candor:

"I give you my word I do not know him, Mr. Spade. I give you my word I have nothing to do with him. I have asked nobody's assistance except yours, on my word of honor."

"Then he's one of the others?"

"That may be."

"I just wanted to know, because if he gets to be a nuisance I may have to hurt him."

"Do as you think best. He is not a friend of mine."

"That's good. There goes the curtain. Good night," Spade said, and crossed the street to board a westbound street car.

The youth in the cap boarded the same car.

Spade left the car at Hyde Street and went up to his apartment. His rooms were not greatly upset, but showed unmistakably that they had been searched. When Spade had washed and had put on a fresh shirt and collar he went out again, walked up to Sutter Street, and boarded a westbound car. The youth boarded it also.

Within half a dozen blocks of the Coronet Spade left the car and went into the vestibule of a tall brown apartment building. He pressed three fourth-floor buttons together. The street door lock buzzed. He entered, passed the elevator and stairs, went down a long yellow-walled corridor to the rear of the building, found a back door fastened with a Yale lock, and, leaving the lock unlatched, let himself out into a narrow court.

The court led to a dark back street, up which Spade walked for two blocks. Then he crossed over to California Street and went to the Coronet. It was not quite half past nine o'clock.

The eagerness with which Brigid O'Shaughnessy welcomed Spade suggested that she had not been entirely certain of his coming. She had put on a satin gown of the blue shade called Artoise that season, with chalcedony shoulder straps, and her stockings and slippers were Artoise.

The red and cream sitting-room had been brought to order and livened with flowers in squat pottery vases of black and silver. Three small rough-barked logs burned in the fireplace. Spade watched them burn while she put away his hat and coat.

"Do you bring me good news?" she asked when she came into the room again. Anxiety looked through her smile, and she held her breath.

"We won't have to make anything public that hasn't already been made public."

"The police won't have to know about me?"

"No."

She sighed happily and sat on the walnut settee. Her face relaxed and her body relaxed. She smiled up at him with admiring eyes.

"However did you manage it?" she asked, more in wonder than in curiosity.

"Most things in San Francisco can be bought, or taken."

"And you won't get into trouble? Do sit down." She made room for him on the settee.

"I don't mind a reasonable amount of trouble," he said with not too much complacence.

He stood beside the fireplace and looked at her with eyes that studied, weighed, judged her without pretense that they were not studying, weighing, judging her. She flushed slightly under the frankness of his scrutiny, but she seemed more sure of herself than before, though a becoming shyness had not left her eyes.

He stood there until it seemed plain that he meant to ignore her invitation to sit beside her, and then crossed to the settee.

"You aren't," he asked as he sat down, "exactly the sort of person you pretend to be, are you?"

"I'm not sure that I know what you mean," she said in her hushed voice, looking at him with puzzled eyes.

"Schoolgirl manner," he explained, "stammering, blushing, and all that."

She blushed and replied hurriedly, not looking at him now:

"I told you this afternoon that I've been bad, worse than you could know."

"That's what I mean," he said. "You told me that this afternoon in the same words, same tone. It's a speech you've practiced."

After a moment in which she seemed confused almost to the point of tears she laughed and said:

"Very well, then, Mr. Spade. I'm not at all the sort of person I pretend to be. I'm eighty years old, incredibly wicked, and an iron-molder by trade. But if it's a pose it's one I've grown into, so you won't expect me to drop it entirely, will you?"

"Oh, it's all right," he assured her. "Only it wouldn't be all right if you were actually that innocent. We'd never get anywhere."

"I won't be innocent," she promised with a hand on her heart.

"I saw Joel Cairo tonight," he said in the manner of one making polite conversation.

Gaiety went out of her face. Her eyes, focused on his profile, became frightened, then cautious. He had stretched out his legs and was looking at his crossed feet. His face did not indicate that he was thinking about anything.

There was a long pause before she asked uneasily:

"You—you know him?"

"I saw him tonight." Spade maintained his light conversational manner and did not look up from his feet. "He was going into the Geary to see George Arliss."

"You mean you saw him to talk to?"

"Only for a few minutes, till the performance started."

She got up from the settee and went to the fireplace to poke at the fire. Then she changed slightly the position of an ornament on the mantelpiece, crossed the room to get a box of cigarettes from a table in a corner, straightened a curtain, and returned to her seat. Her face was now smooth and unworried.

Spade grinned sidewise at her and said:

"You're good. You're very good."

Her face didn't change. She asked quietly:

"What did he say?"

"About what?"

She hesitated. "About me."

"Nothing." Spade turned to hold his lighter under the end of her cigarette. His eyes were shiny in a wooden Satan's face.

"Well, what did he say?" she asked with half-playful petulance.

"He offered me five thousand dollars for the black bird."

She jumped, her teeth tore the end of the cigarette, and her eyes, after a swift alarmed glance at Spade, turned away from him.

"You're not going to poke at the fire and go around straightening the room again, are you?" he asked lazily.

She laughed a clear girlish laugh, dropped the mangled cigarette into a tray, and looked at him with clear merry eyes.

"I won't," she promised. "And what did you say?"

"Five thousand is a lot of money."

She smiled as if she thought he was jesting, but when, instead of smiling, he looked gravely at her, her smile became confused, faint, and presently vanished. In its place came a hurt, bewildered look.

"Surely you're not really considering it," she said.

"Why not? Five thousand is a lot of money."

"But, Mr. Spade, you promised to help me." Her hands were on his arm. "I trusted you. You can't—" She broke off, took her hands from his sleeve and worked them together.

Spade smiled gently into her troubled eyes.

"Don't let's try to figure out how much you've trusted me," he said. "I promised to help you, but you didn't tell me anything about a black bird."

"But you must have known, or—or you wouldn't have told me about it. You do know now. You won't, you can't, treat me that way." Her eyes were cobalt blue prayers.

"Five thousand," he said for the third time, "is a lot of money."

She lifted her shoulders and hands and let them fall in a gesture that accepted defeat.

"It is," she agreed in a small dull voice. "It is far more than I could ever offer you, if I must bid for your loyalty."

Spade laughed. His laughter was brief and somewhat bitter.

"That is good," he said, "coming from you. What have you given me besides money? Have you given me any of your confidence? Any of the truth? Any help in helping you? Haven't you tried to buy my loyalty with money and nothing else? Well, if I'm peddling it, why shouldn't I let it go to the highest bidder?"

"I've given you all the money I have." Tears glistened in her white-ringed eyes. Her voice was hoarse, vibrant. "I've thrown myself on your mercy, told you that without your help I'm utterly lost. What else is there?" She suddenly moved close to him on the settee and cried angrily: "Can I buy you with my body?"

Their faces were a few inches apart.

Spade took her face between his hands and he kissed her mouth roughly and contemptuously.

Then he sat back and said: "I'll think it over." His face was hard and furious.

She sat still holding her numb face where his hands had left it.

He stood up and said: "——! There's no sense to this."

He took two steps toward the fireplace and stopped, glowering at the burning logs, grinding his teeth together.

She did not move.

He turned to face her. The two vertical lines over her nose were deep clefts between red welts.

"I don't give a damn about your honesty," he told her, trying to make himself speak calmly. "I don't care what kind of tricks you're up to, or what your secrets are. But I've got to have something to show that you know what you're doing."

"I do know. Please believe that I do, and that it's all for the best, and—"

"Show me," he ordered. "I'm willing to help you. I've done what I could so far. If necessary I'll go ahead blindfolded, but I can't do it without confidence in you. You've got to convince me that you know what it's all about, that you're not simply fiddling around by guess and by God, hoping it'll come out all right somehow in the end."

"Can't you trust me just a little longer?"

"How much is a little? And what are you waiting for?"

She bit her lip and looked down.

"I must talk to Joel Cairo," she said almost inaudibly.

"You can see him tonight," Spade said, looking at his watch. "His show will be out in a little while. We can get him on the phone at his hotel."

She raised her eyes, alarmed.

"But he can't come here. I can't let him know where I am. I'm afraid."

"My place," Spade suggested.

She hesitated, working her lips together, then asked:

"Do you think he'd come there?"

Spade nodded.

"All right," she exclaimed, jumping up, her eyes large and bright. "Shall we go now?"

She went into the next room. Spade went to the table in the corner and silently pulled the drawer out. The drawer held two packs of playing cards, a pad of bridge score-cards, a brass screw, a piece of red string, and a gold pencil. He had closed the drawer and was lighting a cigarette when she returned wearing a small dark hat and gray kidskin coat, carrying his hat and coat.

Their taxicab drew up behind a dark sedan that stood directly in front of Spade's street door. Iva Archer was alone in the sedan, sitting at the wheel. Spade lifted his hat to her and went indoors with Brigid O'Shaughnessy. In the lobby he halted beside one of the benches and asked:

"Do you mind waiting here a moment? I won't be long."

"That's perfectly all right," Brigid O'Shaughnessy said, sitting down. "You needn't hurry."

Spade went out to the sedan.

When he had opened the sedan door Iva spoke rapidly:

"I've got to talk to you, Sam. Can't I come in?" Her face was pale and nervous.

"Not now."

Iva clicked her teeth together and asked sharply: "Who is she?"

"I've only a minute, Iva," Spade said patiently. "What is it?"

"Who is she?" she repeated, nodding at the apartment building door.

He looked away from her, down the street. In front of a garage on the next corner an under-sized youth of twenty or twenty-one in neat gray cap and overcoat loafed with his back against a wall. Spade frowned and returned his gaze to Iva's insistent face.

"What is the matter?" he asked. "Has anything happened? You oughtn't to be here at this time of night."

"I'm beginning to believe that," she com-plained. "You told me I oughtn't to come to the office, and now I oughtn't come here. Do you mean I oughtn't chase after you? If that's what you mean why don't you say it right out?"

"Now, Iva, you've got no right to take that attitude."

"I know I haven't. I haven't any rights at all, it seems, where you're concerned. I thought I did. I thought your pretending to love me gave me some right, but—"

Spade said wearily:

"This is no time to be arguing about that, precious. What was it you wanted to see me about?"

"I can't talk to you here, Sam. Can't I come in?"

"Not now."

"Why can't I?"

Spade said nothing.

She made a thin line of her mouth, squirmed around straight behind the wheel, and started the engine, staring angrily ahead.

When the sedan began to move Spade said, "Good night, Iva," closed the door, and stood at the curb with his hat in his hand until it had been driven away. Then he went indoors again.

Brigid O'Shaughnessy rose smiling cheer-fully from the bench and they went up to his apartment.

CHAPTER VII
G IN THE AIR

 n his bedroom that was a living-room now the wall bed was up, Spade took Brigid O'Shaughnessy's hat and coat, made her comfortable in a padded rocking chair, and, after looking up the number in the telephone direc-tory, called the Hotel Belvedere. Cairo had not yet returned from the theater. Spade left his tele-phone number with the request that Cairo call him as soon as he came in.

Spade sat down in the armchair beside the table and without any preliminaries, without any introductory remarks, began to tell the girl about a thing that had happened three years before in the Northwest. He talked in a steady matter-of-fact tone, devoid of emphasis or pauses, though now and then he repeated a sentence slightly rearranged, as if it were important to relate each detail exactly as it had happened. His eyes while he talked looked at memories over her shoulder.

At the beginning she listened with only partial attentiveness, obviously more surprised by the story than interested in it, her curiosity more engaged with his purpose in telling the story than with the story he told; but presently, as the story went on, it caught her more and more fully, and held her, and she became still and receptive.

A man named Flitcraft had left his real estate office, in Tacoma, to go to luncheon one day and had never returned. He did not keep an engagement to play golf after four that afternoon, though he had taken the initiative in making the engagement a bare half hour before he went out to luncheon. His wife and children never saw him again. His wife and he were supposed to be on the best of terms. He had two children, boys, one five and one three. He owned his home in a Tacoma suburb, a new Packard car, already paid for, and the rest of the appurtenances of successful American living.

Flitcraft had inherited seventy thousand dollars from his father, and, with his success in real estate, was worth something in the neighborhood of two hundred thousand dollars at the time of his vanishing. His affairs were in order, though there were enough loose ends to indicate that he had not been setting his affairs in order preparatory to vanishing. A deal that would have brought him an attractive profit, for instance, was to have been completed the day after that on which he vanished. There was nothing to show that he had more than fifty or sixty dollars in his immediate possession at the time of his going. His time for months past could be at least roughly accounted for too thoroughly to justify any suspicion of secret vices, or

even of another woman, though of course either was possible.

"He went, like that," Spade said, "like a fist when you open your hand."

When he had reached this point in his story the telephone bell rang.

"Hello," he said into the instrument. "Mr. Cairo? This is Spade. Can you come up to my place, Post Street, now? Yes, I think it is." He looked at the girl, pursed his lips, and then said quickly: "Miss O'Shaughnessy is here and wants to see you."

She frowned a little and stirred in her chair, but said nothing.

Spade put down the telephone and told her:

"He'll be up in a few minutes. Well, that was in 1922. In 1927 I was with one of the national detective agencies in Seattle. Mrs. Flitcraft came in and told us somebody had seen a man who resembled her husband in Spokane. I went over there for her. It was Flitcraft, all right. He had been living in Spokane for a couple of years as Charles—that was his first name—Pierce. He had an automobile business that was netting him twenty or twenty-five thousand a year, a wife, a baby son, owned his home in a Spokane suburb, had all the trimmings that go with that kind of success, and usually got away to play golf after four in the afternoon during the season."

Spade hadn't been told very definitely what to do when he found Flitcraft. They talked in Spade's room at the Davenport. Flitcraft had no feeling of guilt. He had left his first family well provided for, and what he had done seemed to him perfectly reasonable. The only thing that bothered him was a doubt that he could make its reasonableness clear to Spade. He had never told anybody about it before, and thus had not had to attempt to make its reasonableness explicit. He tried now.

"I got it all right," Spade told Brigid O'Shaughnessy, "but Mrs. Flitcraft never did. She thought it was silly. Maybe it was. Anyway, it came out all right. She didn't want any scandal, and after the trick he had played on her, the way she looked at it, she didn't want him. So she divorced him on the quiet, and everything was swell all around.

"Here's what had happened to him. Going to lunch he had passed an office building—or the skeleton of one—that was being put up. A beam or something fell eight or ten stories to the sidewalk alongside him. It brushed close to him, but didn't touch him, though a piece of the sidewalk, a piece of brick or cement, was chipped off and flew up and struck him on the cheek. It only took a piece of skin off, but he still had the scar when I saw him. He rubbed it with his finger, thoughtfully, almost affectionately, while he told me about it.

"He was frightened, of course, he said, but he was more shocked than frightened. It was as if somebody had taken the lid off life and let him look at the works.

"He had been a good citizen, a good husband, and a good father, not by any outer compulsion, but simply because he was the sort of man who was most comfortable in step with his surroundings. He had been raised that way. The people he knew were like that. The life he knew was a clean, orderly, sane, responsible affair. Now a falling beam had shown him that life was fundamentally none of these things. He, the good citizen, could be wiped out between real estate office and restaurant by the accident of a falling beam. He knew then that men died at haphazard, like that, and lived only while blind chance spared them.

"It wasn't the injustice of it that disturbed him: he accepted that after the first shock. What disturbed him was the discovery that in sensibly ordering his affairs he had got out of step, and not into step, with life. He said he knew before he had gone twenty feet from the fallen beam that he would never again know peace until he had adjusted himself to this new glimpse of life. By the time he had finished his luncheon he had found his means of adjustment. Life could be ended for him at random by a falling beam; he would change his life at random simply by going off. He loved his family, he said, as much as he supposed was usual, but he knew he was leaving

them provided for, and his love for them wasn't of the sort that would make absence from them painful.

"He went to Seattle that afternoon," Spade said, "and from there by boat to San Francisco. For two or three years he roamed around the country and then returned to the Northwest, settling in Spokane. Presently he married. His second wife didn't look like his first, and you could find more points of difference than of likeness between them; but both were the sort of women who play fair golf and bridge, take pains with their guest rooms, and welcome new salad recipes. He felt that what he had done was reasonable. He regretted none of it. I don't think that he was conscious of having stepped back naturally into the groove he had left in Tacoma. But that's the part of it that I like best. He had adjusted himself to the falling beam, and then no more beams had fallen, and he had adjusted himself to their not falling."

"How perfectly fascinating," Brigid O'Shaughnessy said. She left her chair and stood in front of him, close. Her eyes were wide and deep. "I don't have to tell you how utterly at a disadvantage you'll have me, with him here, if you choose."

Spade smiled slightly without separating his lips.

"No, you don't have to tell me that," he agreed.

"And you know I'd never have placed myself in this position if I hadn't trusted you completely?" Her thumb and finger twisted a black button on his blue coat.

Spade said, "That again," with mock resignation.

"But you know it's so," she insisted.

"No, I don't know it." He patted the hand that was twisting the button. "My asking for reasons why I should trust you brought us here. Don't let's get ourselves confused. You don't have to trust me, anyway, as long as you can persuade me to trust you."

She studied his face. Her nostrils quivered.

Spade laughed. He patted her hand again and said:

"Don't worry about that now. He'll be here in

a moment. Get your business with him over, and then we'll see how we stand."

"And you'll let me go about it in my own way?"

"Of course."

She turned her hand under his so that her fingers pressed his. She said softly:

"You're a God-send."

Spade said: "Don't overdo it."

She looked reproachfully at him, though smiling, and returned to the padded rocker.

Joel Cairo was excited. His dark eyes seemed all irides, and his high-pitched thin-voiced words were tumbling out before Spade had got the door half open.

"That boy is out there watching the house, Mr. Spade, that boy you showed me, or to whom you showed me, in front of the theater. What am I to understand from that, Mr. Spade? I came here in good faith, with no thought of tricks or traps."

"You were asked in good faith." Spade frowned thoughtfully. "But I ought to've guessed that he might show up. He saw you come in?"

"Naturally. I could have gone on, but that seemed pointless, since you had already let him see us together."

Brigid O'Shaughnessy came into the passageway behind Spade and asked anxiously: "What boy? What is it?"

Cairo removed his black hat from his head, bowed stiffly, and said in a prim voice:

"If you do not know, ask Mr. Spade. I know nothing about it except through him."

"A kid who's been trying to tail me around town all evening." Spade spoke carelessly over his shoulder, not turning to face the girl. "Come on in, Cairo. There's no use standing here talking for all the neighbors."

Brigid O'Shaughnessy grasped Spade's arm above the elbow and demanded:

"Did he follow you to my apartment?"

"No. I shook him before that. Then I suppose he came back here to try to pick me up again."

Cairo, holding his black hat to his belly with both hands, had come into the passageway. Spade shut the corridor door behind him, and they went into the living-room. There Cairo bowed stiffly over his hat once more and said:

"I am delighted to see you again, Miss O'Shaughnessy."

"I was sure you would be, Joe," she replied, giving him her hand.

He made a formal bow over it and released it quickly.

She sat in the padded rocker she had occupied before. Cairo sat in the armchair by the table. Spade, when he had hung Cairo's hat and coat in the closet, sat on an end of the sofa in front of the windows and began to roll a cigarette.

Brigid O'Shaughnessy said to Cairo:

"Sam told me about your offer for the falcon. How soon can you have the money ready?"

Cairo's eyebrows twitched. He smiled. "It is ready." He continued to smile at the girl for a little while after he had spoken, and then looked at Spade.

Spade was lighting his cigarette. His face was placid.

"In cash?" she asked.

"Oh, yes," Cairo replied.

She frowned, put her tongue between her lips, withdrew it, and asked:

"You are ready to pay us five thousand dollars, now, if we give you the falcon?"

Cairo held up a wriggling white hand.

"Excuse me," he said. "I expressed myself badly. I did not mean to say I have the money in my pocket, but that I am prepared to get it on a very few minutes' notice at any time during banking hours."

"Oh." She looked significantly at Spade.

Spade blew cigarette smoke down the front of his vest and said:

"That's probably right. He had only a few hundred in his pockets when I frisked them this afternoon."

When her eyes opened round and wide he grinned.

Cairo bent forward in his chair. He barely failed to keep eagerness from showing in his eyes and voice.

"I can be quite prepared to give you the money at, say, half past ten in the morning. Eh?"

Brigid O'Shaughnessy smiled at him and said:

"But I haven't got the falcon."

Cairo's face was darkened by a flush of annoyance. He put an ugly white hand on either arm of the chair, holding his small-boned body erect and stiff between them. His dark eyes were angry. He did not say anything.

The girl made a mock-placatory face at him.

"I'll have it in a week at the most, though," she said.

"Where is it?" Cairo used politeness of mein to express skepticism.

"Where Floyd hid it."

"Floyd? Thursby?"

She nodded.

"And you know where that is?" he asked.

"I think I do."

"Then why must we wait a week?"

"Perhaps not a whole week. Whom are you buying it for, Joe?"

Cairo raised his eyebrows. "I told Mr. Spade. For its owner."

Surprise illuminated the girl's face. "So you went back to him?"

"Naturally."

She laughed softly in her throat and said: "I should have liked to have seen that."

Cairo shrugged. "That was the natural, the logical development." He rubbed the back of one hand with the palm of the other. His upper lids came down to shade his eyes. "Why, if I in turn may ask a question, are you willing to sell it to me, Brigid?"

"I'm afraid," she said simply, "after what happened to Floyd. That's why I haven't got it now. I'm afraid to touch it except to turn it over to someone else right away."

Spade, propped on an elbow on the sofa, looked at and listened to them impartially. In the comfortable slackness of his body, in the easy stillness of his features, there was no indication of either curiosity or impatience.

"Exactly what," Cairo asked in a low voice, "happened to Floyd?"

The tip of her right forefinger traced a swift G in the air.

Cairo said, "I see," but there was something of doubtfulness in his smile. "Is he here?"

"I don't know." She spoke impatiently. "What difference does that make?"

The doubt in Cairo's smile deepened. "It might make a difference," he said, and rearranged his hands in his lap so that, intentionally or not, a blunt forefinger pointed at Spade.

The girl glanced at the finger and made an impatient motion with her head.

"Or me," she said, "or you."

"Exactly. And shall we include, with more certainty, the boy outside?"

"Yes," she agreed and laughed. "Yes, unless he's the one you had in Constantinople."

Sudden blood mottled Cairo's face. In a shrill enraged voice he spoke a dozen words that were neither English, French, German nor Spanish.

Brigid O'Shaughnessy jumped up from her chair. Her lower lip was between her teeth. Her eyes were dark and wide in a tense white face. She took two quick steps toward Cairo. He started to rise. Her right hand went out and cracked sharply against his cheek, leaving the imprint of its fingers there.

Cairo grunted and slapped her cheek, staggering her sidewise, bringing from her a brief muffled scream.

Spade, wooden of face, was up from the sofa and close to them by then. He caught Cairo by the throat and shook him. Cairo gurgled and put a hand inside his coat. Spade grasped the smaller man's wrist, wrenched it away from the coat, forced it straight out to the side, and twisted it until the clumsy white fingers opened to let the black pistol fall down on the rug.

Brigid O'Shaughnessy quickly picked up the pistol.

Cairo, speaking with difficulty because of the fingers on his throat, said:

"This is the second time you've put your hands on me." His eyes, for all that the throttling pressure on his throat made them bulge, were cold and menacing.

"Yes," Spade growled. "And when you're slapped you'll take it and like it." He released Cairo's wrist and with a thick open hand struck the sides of his face three times, savagely.

Cairo tried to spit into Spade's face, but the dryness of his mouth made it only an angry gesture. Spade slapped the mouth, cutting Cairo's lower lip.

The door bell rang.

Cairo's eyes jerked into focus on the passageway that led to the corridor door. His eyes had become unangry and wary. The girl had gasped and turned to face the passageway. Her face was frightened.

Spade stared gloomily for a moment at the blood trickling from Cairo's lip, and then stepped back, taking his hand away from the Levantine's throat.

"Who is it?" the girl whispered, coming close to Spade; and Cairo's eyes asked the same question.

"I don't know," Spade replied in an irritable voice.

The bell rang again, more insistently.

"Well, keep quiet," Spade said, and went out of the room, shutting the door behind him.

Spade turned on the light in the passageway and opened the door to the corridor. Lieutenant Dundy and Tom Polhaus were there.

"Hello, Sam," Tom said. "We thought maybe you wouldn't've gone to bed yet."

Dundy nodded, but said nothing.

"Hello," Spade said good-naturedly. "You guys pick swell hours to go calling. What is it this time?"

Dundy spoke quietly: "We want to talk to you, Spade."

"Well?" Spade stood in the doorway, blocking it. "Go ahead and talk."

Tom Polhaus advanced, saying: "We don't have to do it standing here, do we?"

Spade stood still in the doorway and said: "You can't come in." His tone was very slightly apologetic.

Tom's thick-featured face, even in height with Spade's, took on an expression of friendly scornfulness, though there was a bright gleam in his small shrewd eyes.

"What the hell, Sam?" he protested, and put a big playful hand on Spade's chest.

Spade leaned against the pushing hand, grinned wolfishly, and asked:

"Going to strong-arm me, Tom?"

Tom grumbled, "Aw, for God's sake," and stopped pushing.

Dundy clicked his teeth together and said through them:

"Let us in."

Spade's lip twitched over an eyetooth. He said:

"You're not coming in. What do you want to do about it? Try to get in? Or do your talking here? Or go to hell?"

Tom groaned.

Dundy, still speaking through his teeth, said:

"It'd pay you to play along with us a little, Spade. You've got away with this and you've got away with that, but you can't keep it up forever."

"Stop me when you can," Spade replied arrogantly.

"That's what I'll do." Dundy put his hands behind him and thrust his hard face up toward the private detective's. "There's talk going around that you and Archer's wife were cheating on him."

Spade laughed. "That sounds like something you thought up yourself."

"Then there's not anything to it?"

"Not anything."

"The talk is," Dundy said, "that she tried to get a divorce out of him so she could put in with you, but he wouldn't give it to her. Anything to that?"

"Nothing."

"There's even talk," Dundy continued stolidly, "that that's why he was put on the spot."

Spade seemed mildly amused.

"Don't be a hog," he said. "You oughtn't try to pin more than one murder at a time on me. Your first notion that I knocked Thursby off because he'd killed Miles falls apart if you blame me for killing Miles too."

"You haven't heard me say you killed anybody," Dundy replied. "You're the one that's been bringing that up. But suppose I did. You could have blipped them both. There's a way of figuring it."

"Uh-huh. I could have butchered Miles to get his wife, and then Thursby so I could hang Miles's murder on him. That's a swell system, or will be when I get around to killing somebody else so I can accuse them of Thursby's murder. Am I supposed to keep that up? What are you going to do? Charge me with all the killings in San Francisco from now on?"

Tom said: "Aw, cut the comedy, Sam. You know damned well we don't like this any more than you do, but we got to do our work."

"I hope you've got something to do besides pop in here early every morning asking me a lot of damned fool questions."

"And getting damned lying answers," Dundy added deliberately.

"Easy now," Spade cautioned him.

Dundy looked him up and down and then looked him straight in the eyes.

"If you say there was nothing between you and Archer's wife," Dundy said, "you're a liar, and I'm telling you so."

A startled look came into Tom's small eyes.

Spade moistened his lips with the tip of his tongue and asked:

"Is that the hot tip that brought you here at this ungodly time of night?"

"That's one of them."

"And the others?"

Dundy drew down the corners of his mouth. "Let us in." He nodded significantly at the doorway in which Spade stood.

Spade frowned and shook his head.

Dundy's mouth-corners lifted a little in a smile of grim satisfaction.

"There must've been something in it," he told Tom.

Tom shifted his feet, and, not looking at either man, mumbled: "God knows."

"What's this?" Spade asked. "Charades?"

"All right, Spade, we're going." Dundy buttoned up his overcoat. "We'll be in to see you now and then. Maybe you're right in bucking us. Think it over."

"Uh-huh," Spade said, grinning. "Glad to see you any time, Lieutenant, and whenever I'm not busy I'll let you in."

A voice in Spade's living-room screamed: "Help! Help! Police! Help."

The voice, high and thin and shrill, was Joel Cairo's.

Lieutenant Dundy stopped turning away from the door, confronted Spade again, and said decisively:

"I guess we're going in."

The sounds of a brief struggle, of a blow, of a subdued cry, came to the men.

Spade's face twisted into a smile that held little of joy.

He said, "I guess you are," and stood out of the way.

When the police detectives had entered, he shut the corridor door and followed them back to the living-room.

CHAPTER VIII
HORSEFEATHERS

Brigid O'Shaughnessy was huddled in the armchair by the table. Her forearms were up over her cheeks, her knees drawn up until they hid the lower part of her face. Her eyes were white-circled and terrified.

Joel Cairo stood in front of her, bending over her, holding in one hand the pistol Spade had taken from him. His other hand was clapped to his forehead. Blood ran through its fingers and down under them to his eyes. A smaller trickle from his cut lip made three wavy red lines across his chin.

Cairo did not heed the detectives. He was glaring at the girl huddled before him. His lips were working spasmodically, but no coherent sound came from between them.

Dundy, the first of the three into the room, moved swiftly to Cairo's side, put a hand on his own hip under his overcoat, a hand on the Levantine's wrist, and growled:

"What are you up to here?"

Cairo took the red-smeared hand from his forehead and waved it close to the lieutenant's face. Uncovered by the hand, his forehead showed a three-inch ragged tear.

"This is what she did," he cried. "Look at it."

The girl put her feet down on the floor and looked warily from Dundy, holding Cairo's wrist, to Tom Polhaus, standing a little behind them, to Spade, leaning against the door frame. Spade's face was placid. When his gaze met hers, his yellow-gray eyes glinted for an instant with malicious humor, and then became expressionless again.

"Did you do that?" Dundy asked the girl, nodding at Cairo's cut head.

She looked at Spade again. He did not in any way respond to the appeal in her eyes. He leaned against the door frame and observed the occupants of the room with the polite air of an invited spectator.

The girl turned her eyes up to Dundy's. Her eyes were wide and dark and earnest.

"I had to," she said in a low, throaty, almost sobbing voice. "I was all alone in here with him when he attacked me. I couldn't—I tried to keep him off. I—I couldn't make myself shoot him."

"Oh, you liar!" Cairo cried, trying unsuccessfully to pull the arm that held the pistol out of Dundy's grip. "Oh, you dirty, filthy liar!" He squirmed around to face Dundy. "She's lying awfully. I came here in good faith, and was attacked by both of them, and when you came he went out to talk to you, leaving her here with this pistol, and then she said they were going to kill me after you left, and I called for help, so you wouldn't leave me here to be murdered, and then she struck me with the pistol."

"Here, give me this thing," Dundy said, and took the pistol from Cairo's hand. "Now let's get this straight. What'd you come here for?"

"He sent for me." Cairo twisted his head around to stare defiantly at Spade. "He called me up on the phone and asked me to come here."

Spade blinked sleepily at the Levantine and said nothing.

Dundy asked:

"What'd he want you for?"

Cairo withheld his reply until he had mopped his bloody forehead and chin with a lavender-barred silk handkerchief. By then some of the indignation in his manner had been replaced by caution.

"He said he wanted—they wanted—to see me. I didn't know what about."

Tom lowered his head, sniffed the odor of *chypre* that the mopping handkerchief had released into the air, and then turned his head to scowl interrogatively at Spade. Spade winked an eye at him and went on rolling a cigarette.

Dundy asked:

"Well, what happened then?"

"Then they attacked me. She struck me first, and then he choked me and took the pistol out of my pocket. I don't know what they would have done next if you hadn't arrived at that moment. I dare say they would have murdered me then and there. When he went out to answer the bell he left her here with the pistol to watch over me."

Brigid O'Shaughnessy jumped out of the armchair crying, "Why don't you tell the truth?" and slapped Cairo on the cheek.

Cairo yelled inarticulately.

Dundy pushed the girl back into the chair with the hand that was not holding the Levantine's arm, and growled: "None of that now."

Spade, lighting his cigarette, grinned softly through smoke and told Tom: "She's impulsive."

"Yeah," Tom agreed.

Dundy scowled down at the girl and asked:

"What do you want us to think the truth is?"

"Not what he said," she replied. "Not anything he said." She turned to Spade. "Is it?"

"How do I know?" Spade said. "I was out in the kitchen mixing an omelette when it all happened, wasn't I?"

She wrinkled her forehead, studying him with eyes that perplexity clouded.

Tom grunted in disgust.

Dundy, still scowling down at the girl, ignored Spade's speech and asked her:

"If he's not telling the truth, how come he did the squawking for help, and not you?"

"Oh, he was scared to death when I struck him," she replied, looking contemptuously at the Levantine.

Cairo's face flushed where it was not blood-smeared. He exclaimed:

"Pfoo! Another lie."

She kicked his leg, the high heel of her blue slipper striking him just below the knee. Dundy pulled him away from her while big Tom came to stand close to her, rumbling: "Behave, sister. That's no way to act."

"Then make him tell the truth," she said.

"We'll do that, all right," he promised. "Just don't get rough."

Dundy, looking at Spade with green eyes hard and bright with satisfaction, addressed his subordinate: "Well, Tom, I guess we'll take them in."

Tom nodded gloomily.

Spade left the door and advanced to the center of the room, dropping his cigarette into a tray on the table as he passed it. His smile and manner were amiable and easy.

"Don't be in a hurry," he said. "Everything can be explained."

"I bet you," Dundy agreed, sneering.

Spade bowed to the girl.

"Miss O'Shaughnessy," he said, "may I present Lieutenant Dundy and Detective-sergeant Polhaus?" He bowed to Dundy. "Miss O'Shaughnessy is an operative in my employ."

Joel Cairo said indignantly: "That isn't so. She—"

Spade interrupted him in a quite loud, but still genial voice:

"I hired her just recently, yesterday. This is Mr. Joel Cairo, a friend, anyhow an acquain-tance, of Thursby's. He came to me this afternoon and tried to hire me to find something Thursby was supposed to have on him when he was bumped off. It looked queer, the way he put it to me, so I wouldn't touch it. Then he pulled a gun—well, never mind that, unless it comes to a point of laying charges against each other. Anyway, after talking it over with Miss O'Shaughnessy I thought maybe I could get something out of him about Miles's and Thursby's killings, so I asked him to come up here. Maybe we put the questions to him a little rough, but he wasn't hurt any, not enough to have to cry for help. I'd already had to take his gun away from him again."

As Spade talked anxiety came into Cairo's reddened face. His eyes moved jerkily up and down, shifting their focus uneasily between the floor and Spade's bland face.

Dundy confronted Cairo and demanded brusquely:

"Well, what've you got to say to that?"

Cairo had nothing to say for nearly a minute while he stared at the lieutenant's chest. When he lifted his eyes they were shy and wary.

"I do not know what I should say," he murmured. His embarrassment seemed genuine.

"Try telling the facts," Dundy suggested.

"The facts?" Cairo's eyes fidgeted, though their gaze did not actually evade the lieutenant's. "What assurance have I that the facts will be believed?"

"Quit stalling. All you've got to do is swear to a complaint that they took a poke at you and the warrant clerk will believe you enough to issue a warrant that'll let us throw them in the can."

Spade spoke in an amused tone:

"Go ahead, Cairo. Make him happy. Tell him you'll do it, and then we'll swear to one against you, and he'll have the lot of us."

Cairo cleared his throat and looked nervously around the room, not into the eyes of anyone there.

Dundy blew breath through his nose in a puff that was not quite a snort and said:

"Get your hats."

Cairo's eyes, holding worry and a question,

met Spade's mocking gaze. Spade winked at him and sat on the arm of the padded rocker.

"Well, boys and girls," he said, grinning at the Levantine and at the girl with nothing but delight in his voice and in his grin, "we put it over nicely."

Dundy's hard square face darkened the least of shades. He repeated, peremptorily: "Get your hats."

Spade turned his grin on the lieutenant, squirmed into a more comfortable position on the chair arm, and asked lazily:

"Don't you know when you're being kidded?"

Tom Polhaus's face grew red and shiny. Dundy's face, still darkening, was immobile, except for his lips moving stiffly to say:

"No, but we'll let that wait till we get down to the Hall."

Spade rose and put his hands in his pockets. He stood erect so that he might look that much farther down at the lieutenant. His grin was a taunt, and self-certainty spoke in every line of his carriage.

"I dare you to take us in, Dundy," he said. "We'll laugh at you in every newspaper in San Francisco. You don't think any of us is going to swear to any complaints against the others, do you? Wake up. You've been kidded. When the bell rang I said to Miss O'Shaughnessy and Cairo, 'It's those damned bulls again. They're getting to be nuisances. Let's play a joke on them. When you hear them going, one of you scream, and then we'll see how far we can string them along before they tumble.' And—"

Brigid O'Shaughnessy bent forward in her chair and began to laugh hysterically.

Cairo started and smiled. There was no vitality in his smile, but he held it fixed on his face.

Tom, glowering, grumbled: "Cut it out, Sam."

Spade chuckled and said: "But that's the way it was. We—"

"And the cut on his head and mouth?" Dundy asked imperturbably. "Where'd they come from?"

"Ask him," Spade suggested. "Maybe he cut himself shaving."

Cairo spoke quickly, before he could be questioned, and the muscles of his face quivered under the strain of holding his smile in place while he spoke:

"I fell. We intended to be struggling for the pistol when you came in, but I fell. I tripped on the end of the rug, and fell while we were pretending to struggle."

Dundy said: "Horse feathers."

Spade said: "That's all right, Dundy, believe it or not. The point is that that's our story and we'll stick to it. The newspapers will print it whether they believe it or not, and it'll be just as funny one way as the other. What are you going to do about it? It's no crime to kid a copper, is it? You haven't got anything on anybody here. Everything we've told you was part of the joke. What are you going to do about it?"

Dundy put his back to Spade and gripped Cairo by the shoulders.

"You can't get away with that," he snarled, shaking the Levantine. "You squawked for help, and you've got to take it."

"No, sir," Cairo spluttered. "It was a joke. He said you were friends of his and would understand."

Spade laughed.

Dundy pulled Cairo roughly to him, holding him now by the nape of the neck and one wrist.

"I'll take you along for packing the gun, anyway," he said. "And I'll take the rest of you along to see who laughs at the joke."

Cairo's alarmed eyes jerked sidewise to focus on Spade's face.

Spade said: "Don't be a damned fool, Dundy. The gun was part of the plant. It's one of mine. I've got all the licenses you want."

Dundy released Cairo, spun on his heel, and his right fist clicked on Spade's chin.

Brigid O'Shaughnessy uttered a short cry.

Spade's smile flickered out at the instant of the impact, but returned immediately, with a dreamy quality added. He steadied himself with a short backward step, and his thick sloping shoulders writhed under his coat. Before his fist could come up, Tom Polhaus had pushed himself in between the two men, facing Spade, encumbering Spade's arms with the closeness of his barrel-bellied body and his own arms.

"No, no, for —— sake!" Tom begged.

After a long moment of motionlessness, Spade's muscles relaxed.

"Then get him out of here quick," he said. His smile had gone away, leaving his face sullen and somewhat pale.

Tom, remaining close to Spade, keeping his arms on Spade's arms, turned his head to look over his shoulder at Lieutenant Dundy. Tom's small eyes were reproachful.

Dundy's fist was still clenched in front of his body, and his feet were planted firm and a little apart on the floor, but the truculence in his face was modified by the thin rims of white showing between green irises and upper eyelids.

"Get their names and addresses," he ordered, "so we can get hold of them when we want them."

Tom looked at Cairo, who said quickly: "Joel Cairo, Hotel Belvedere."

Spade spoke before Tom could question the girl: "You can always get in touch with Miss O'Shaughnessy through me."

Tom looked at Dundy, who growled: "Get her address."

Spade said: "Her address is in care of my office."

Dundy moved forward, halting in front of the girl.

"Where do you live?" he asked.

Spade addressed Tom:

"Get him out of here. I've had enough of this."

Tom looked at Spade's eyes that were hard and glittering and mumbled:

"Take it easy, Sam." He buttoned up his coat and turned to Dundy, asking, in a voice that aped casualness, "Well, is that all?" and taking a step toward the door.

Dundy's scowl failed to conceal indecision.

Cairo suddenly moved toward the door, saying: "I'm going too, if Mr. Spade will give me my coat and hat."

Spade asked: "What's the hurry?"

Dundy said angrily:

"It was all in fun, but just the same you're afraid to be left here with them."

"Not at all," the Levantine replied, fidgeting, looking at neither of them, "but it's quite late and—and I'm going. I'll go out with you if you don't mind."

Dundy put his lips together firmly, but said nothing, though a light was glinting in his green eyes.

Spade went to the closet in the passageway and fetched Cairo's coat and hat. Spade's face was blank. His voice held the same blankness when he stepped back from helping the Levantine into his coat and said to Tom:

"Tell him to leave that gun of mine that he took from Cairo."

Dundy took Cairo's pistol from his pocket and put it on the table. He went out first, with Cairo at his heels.

Tom halted in front of Spade, muttered, "I hope to God you know what you're doing," got no response, sighed, and followed the others out.

Spade went after them as far as the bend in the passageway, where he stood until Tom had closed the corridor door.

CHAPTER IX
THE LIAR

pade returned to the living room and sat on an end of the sofa, elbows on knees, cheeks in hands, looking at the floor and not at Brigid O'Shaughnessy smiling weakly at him from the armchair. His eyes were sultry. The creases between brows above his nose were deep. His nostrils moved in and out with his breathing.

Brigid O'Shaughnessy, when it became apparent that he was not going to look up at her, stopped smiling and regarded him with some uneasiness.

Red rage came suddenly into his face, and he began to talk in a harsh, guttural voice. Holding his maddened face in his hands, glaring at the floor, he cursed Dundy for five minutes without break, cursed him obscenely, blasphemously, repetitiously, in a harsh, guttural voice.

Then he took his face out of his hands, looked at the girl, grinned sheepishly, and said: "Childish, huh? I know, but, by God, I do hate being hit without hitting back." He touched his chin with careful fingers. "Not that it was so much of a sock at that." He laughed and lounged back on the sofa, crossing his legs. "A cheap enough price to pay for winning." His brows drew together in a fleeting frown. "Though I won't forget it."

The girl, smiling again, left her chair and sat on the sofa beside him.

"You're absolutely the wildest person I've ever known," she said. "Do you always carry on so high-handed?"

"I let him hit me, didn't I?"

"Oh, yes, but a police official."

"It wasn't that," Spade explained. "It was that in losing his head and slugging me he overplayed his hand. If I'd mixed it with him he couldn't've backed down. He'd've had to go through with it, and we'd've had to tell that goofy story at headquarters." He stared thoughtfully at the girl, and then asked: "What did you do to Cairo?"

"Nothing." Her face flushed. "I tried to frighten him into keeping quiet until they had gone, and he either got too frightened or stubborn and yelled."

"And then you beaned him with the gun?"

"I had to. He attacked me."

"You don't know what you're doing." Spade's smile did not quite succeed in concealing annoyance. "It's just what I told you: you're fumbling along by guess and by God."

"I'm sorry," she said, face and voice soft with contrition, "Sam."

"Sure you are," he said, no longer showing annoyance. He took tobacco and papers from his pocket and began to make a cigarette. "Now you've had your talk with Cairo. Now you can talk to me."

She put a finger-tip to her mouth, staring across the room at nothing with widened eyes, and then, with narrower eyes, glanced quickly at Spade. He was engrossed in the making of his cigarette.

"Oh, yes," she began, "of course—" She took the finger away from her mouth and smoothed her blue dress over her knees. She frowned at her knees.

Spade licked his cigarette, sealed it, and asked, "Well?" while he felt for his lighter.

"But I didn't," she said, with short pauses between words as if she were selecting them with great care, "have time to finish talking to him." She stopped frowning at her knees and looked at Spade with clear candid eyes. "We were interrupted almost before we had begun."

Spade lighted his cigarette and laughed his mouth empty of smoke.

"Want me to call him up and ask him to come back?"

She shook her head without smiling. Her eyes moved back and forth between her lids as she shook her head, maintaining their focus on Spade's face. Her eyes were inquisitive.

Spade put an arm across her back, cupping his hand over the smooth bare white shoulder farthest from him. She leaned back a little into the bend of his arm.

He said: "Well, I'm listening."

She twisted her face around to smile up at him with friendly insolence, asking:

"Do you need your arm there for that?"

"No." He removed his hand from her shoulder, dropping it to the sofa behind her.

"You're altogether unpredictable," she murmured.

He nodded and said amiably: "I'm still listening."

"Look at the time," she exclaimed, wriggling a finger at the alarm clock perched atop *Celebrated Criminal Cases of America*, saying with its clumsily shaped hands, two-fifty a.m.

"Uh-huh. It's been a busy evening."

"I must go." She jumped up from the sofa. "This is terrible."

Spade did not get up. He shook his head and said: "Not until you've told me about it."

"But look at the time," she protested, "and it would take me hours to tell you."

"It'll have to take them then."

"Am I a prisoner?" she asked gaily.

"Besides, there's the kid outside. Maybe he hasn't gone home to sleep yet."

Her gaiety vanished.

"Do you think he's still there?"

"It's likely."

She shivered. "Could you find out?"

"I could go down and see."

"Oh, that's—will you?"

Spade studied her anxious face for a moment and then rose from the sofa saying: "Sure." He got a hat and overcoat from the passageway closet. "I'll be gone about ten minutes."

"Do be careful," she begged as she followed him to the corridor door.

He said, "I will," and went out.

Post Street was empty when Spade issued into it. He walked east a block, crossed the street, walked west two blocks on the other side, recrossed it, and returned to his building without having seen anyone except two mechanics working on a car in a garage.

When he opened his apartment door Brigid O'Shaughnessy was standing at the bend in the passageway, holding Cairo's pistol straight down at her side.

"He's still there," Spade replied to the question her face asked.

She bit the inside of her lip slowly, going back into the living-room. Spade followed her in, put his hat and overcoat on a chair, said, "So, we'll have time to talk," and went into the kitchen.

He had put the coffee pot on the stove when she came to the door, and was slicing a slender loaf of French bread. She stood in the doorway and watched him with preoccupied eyes. The fingers of her left hand idly caressed the body

and barrel of the pistol her right hand still held.

"The table cloth's in there," he said, pointing the bread knife at a cupboard that was one breakfast nook partition.

She set up the table while he spread liverwurst on, or put cold corned beef between, the small ovals of bread he had sliced. Then he poured the coffee, added to it Bacardi from a tall bottle, and they sat at the table. They sat side by side on one of the benches. She put the pistol on the end of the bench nearer her.

"You can start now, between bites," he said.

She made a face at him, complained, "You're the most insistent person," and bit a sandwich.

"Yes, and wild and unpredictable. What's this bird, this falcon, that everybody's steamed up about?"

She chewed the beef and bread in her mouth, swallowed it, looked attentively at the small crescent its removal had made in the sandwich's rim, and asked:

"Suppose I would not tell you. Suppose I wouldn't tell you anything at all about it. What would you do?"

"You mean about the bird?"

"I mean about the whole thing."

"I wouldn't be too surprised," he told her, grinning so that the edges of his jaw teeth were visible, "to know what to do next."

"And what would that be?" She transferred her attention from the sandwich to his face. "That's what I wanted to know: what would you do next?"

He shook his head.

Mockery rippled in a smile on her face. "Something wild and unpredictable?"

"Maybe, but I don't see what you've got to gain by covering up now. It's coming out bit by bit anyhow. There's a lot of it that I don't know, but there's some that I do, and some more that I can guess at, and give me another day like this and I'll be knowing things about it that you don't know."

"I suppose you do now," she said, looking at her sandwich again, her face serious. "But—oh, I'm so tired of it, and I do so hate having to talk

DASHIELL HAMMETT

about it. Wouldn't it—wouldn't it be just as well to wait and let you learn about it as you say you will?"

Spade laughed. "I don't know. You'll have to figure that out for yourself. My way of learning is to heave a wild and unpredictable monkey-wrench into the machinery. It's all right with me, if you're sure none of the flying pieces will hurt you."

She moved her bare shoulders uneasily, but said nothing. For several minutes they ate in silence, he phlegmatically, she thoughtfully. Then she said in a barely audible voice:

"I'm afraid of you, and that's the truth."

He said: "That's not the truth."

"It is," she insisted in the same low voice. "I know two men I'm afraid of, and I've seen them both tonight."

"I can understand your being afraid of Cairo," Spade said. "He's out of your reach."

"And you aren't?"

"Not that way," he said and grinned.

She blushed. She picked up a slice of bread thickly encrusted with gray liverwurst. She put it down on her plate. She wrinkled her white forehead, and she said:

"It's a black figure, as you know, smooth and shiny, of a bird, a hawk or falcon, about that high." She held her hands a foot apart.

"What makes it important?"

She sipped coffee and rum before she shook her head.

"I don't know," she said. "They'd never tell me. They promised me five hundred pounds if I helped them get it. Then Floyd said afterward, after we'd left Joe, that he'd give me seven hundred and fifty."

"So it must be worth more than seventy-five hundred dollars, anyway?"

"Oh, more than that," she said. "They didn't pretend that they were sharing it equally with me. They were simply hiring me to help them."

"To help them how?"

She lifted the cup to her lips again. Spade, not moving the domineering stare of his yellow-gray eyes from her face, began to make a cigarette.

Behind them the percolator bubbled on the stove.

"To help them get it from the man who had it," she said slowly when she had lowered her cup, "a Russian named Kemidov."

"How?"

"Oh, but that's not important," she objected, "and wouldn't help you." She smiled impudently. "And is certainly none of your business."

"This was in Constantinople?"

She hesitated, nodded, and said: "Marmora."

He waved his cigarette at her, saying: "Well, go ahead, what happened then?"

"But that's all. I've told you. They promised me five hundred pounds to help them, and I did, and then we found that Joe Cairo meant to desert us, taking the falcon with him and leaving us nothing. So we did exactly that to him first. But then I wasn't any better off than I had been before, because Floyd hadn't any intention at all of paying me the seven hundred and fifty pounds he had promised me. I learned that as soon as we got here. He said we would go to New York, where he would sell it and give me my share, but I could see then that he wasn't telling me the truth." Indignation had darkened her eyes to violet. "So that's why I came to you to get you to help me learn where the falcon was."

"And suppose you'd got it? What then?"

"Then I would have been in a position to talk terms with Mr. Floyd Thursby."

Spade squinted at her and suggested:

"But you wouldn't have known where to take it to get more money than he'd give you, the larger sum that you knew he expected to sell it for?"

"I did not," she said.

Spade scowled at the ashes he had dumped on his plate.

"What makes it worth all that money?" he demanded. "You must have some idea, at least be able to make a guess."

"I haven't the slightest idea."

He directed his scowl at her.

"What's it made of?"

"Porcelain or black stone. I don't know. I've never touched it. I've only seen it once, for a few

· 148 ·

minutes. Floyd showed it to me when we'd first got hold of it."

Spade mashed the remains of his cigarette in his plate and made one draught of the coffee and rum in his cup. His scowl had gone away. He wiped his lips with his napkin, dropped it crumpled on the table, and spoke casually:

"You *are* a liar."

She got up and stood at the end of the table, looking down at him with dark abashed eyes in a pinkening face.

"I am a liar," she said. "I've always been a liar."

"Don't brag about it: it's childish." His voice was good-humored. He came out from between table and bench. "Was there any truth at all in that yarn?"

She hung her head. Dampness glistened on her dark lashes.

"Some," she whispered.

"How much?"

"Not—not very much."

Spade put out a hand under her chin and raised her head. He laughed into her wet eyes and said:

"We've got all night before us. I'll put some more Bacardi into some more coffee, and we'll try again."

Her eyelids drooped.

"Oh, I'm so tired," she said tremulously, "so tired of it all, of myself, of lying and of thinking up lies, and of not knowing what is a lie and what is the truth. I wish I—"

She put her hands up to Spade's cheeks, put her open mouth hard against his mouth, her body flat against his body.

Spade's arms went around her, holding her to him, muscles bulging his blue sleeves, a hand cradling her head, its fingers half lost among red hair, a hand moving groping fingers over her slim back. His eyes burned yellowly.

The Maltese Falcon

Dashiell Hammett

H, I'M SO TIRED . . . SO tired of it all, of myself, of lying and thinking up lies, and of not knowing what is a lie and what is the truth. I wish—"

When Brigid O'Shaughnessy engaged Samuel Spade and Miles Archer, private detectives, to shadow Floyd Thursby she told them she was trying to find her sister, who had come to San Francisco from New York with Thursby. But when Archer, shadowing Thursby, and then, a little later, Thursby were shot to death in the streets that night, she confessed to Spade that she had lied, and that she and Thursby had come from Hongkong together. She refused to tell Spade why they had come, but threw herself on the private detective's mercy, telling him that unless he helped her she would certainly be killed too. She was obviously very frightened, and at length Spade took what money she had—five hundred dollars—and promised to do his best to shield her from both the danger she had mentioned and the police.

Lieutenant Dundy of the police suspected Spade of having shot Thursby to avenge his partner's murder. Iva Archer, Miles's widow, suspected Spade of having killed her husband. Effie Perine, Spade's stenographer, told him she thought Iva had killed her husband so she could marry Spade.

Late the following afternoon a swarthy Levantine who gave his name as Joel Cairo came to Spade's office and offered him five thousand dollars for the recovery of a small black figure of a bird that was supposed to have been in Brigid O'Shaughnessy and Floyd Thursby's possession. Cairo said he represented the bird's rightful owner, but would give Spade neither the owner's name nor any information about it. Spade agreed to find it and took a two-hundred-dollar retainer from Cairo.

When Spade left his office that evening he was shadowed by a boy of twenty or twenty-one. He met Cairo and pointed the boy out to him, but the Levantine denied any knowledge of the shadower. Spade eluded the boy and went to Brigid O'Shaughnessy's apartment. He told her of Cairo's offer and refused to help her any further unless she told him truthfully just what the whole affair was. She promised to do so after talking to Cairo, and Spade arranged a meeting between them at his apartment late that night.

At that meeting Brigid O'Shaughnessy told Cairo that the bird was where Thursby had hidden it and that she would turn it over to him for the five thousand dollars he had offered. She and Cairo both showed fear of someone they designated as "G"—who they believed had killed Thursby. Spade had learned this much, and that the girl and Cairo had been acquainted in Constantinople, when a quarrel broke out between them. Spade had to disarm Cairo and was choking him when Lieutenant Dundy and Detective-sergeant Polhaus arrived, to question Spade about information received that he and Iva Archer had been deceiving her husband. Spade denied this and, after coming to blows with Dundy, got rid of the police. Cairo, afraid to remain in the apartment, went away with the police.

Brigid O'Shaughnessy then told Spade that she, Thursby and Cairo had stolen the bird from a Russian named Kemidov in a Constantinople suburb and that she and Thursby had brought it to San Francisco when they found Cairo meant to double-cross them. In San Francisco, she said, she had learned that Thursby meant to double-cross her. She said she did not know what made the bird so valuable, insisting that she had only been employed by the men to help them. When Spade accused her of lying she admitted it. He demanded the truth from her.

Her eyelids drooped. "Oh, I'm so tired," she said tremulously, "so tired of it all, of myself, of lying and thinking up lies, and of not knowing what is a lie and what is the truth, I wish—" Then she came into Spade's arms.

Chapter X
THE BELVEDERE DIVAN

Beginning day had reduced night to a thin smokiness when Spade sat up. Brigid O'Shaughnessy's soft breathing had the regularity of utter sleep. Spade was quiet leaving bed and bedroom and shutting the bedroom door. He dressed in the bathroom. Then he examined the sleeping girl's clothes, took a flat brass key from the pocket of her coat, and went out.

He went to the Coronet, letting himself into the building and into her apartment with the key. To the eye there was nothing furtive about his going in; he entered boldly and directly. To the ear his going in was almost unnoticeable: he made as little sound as might be.

In the girl's apartment he switched on all the lights. He searched the place from wall to wall. His eyes and thick fingers moved without apparent haste and without ever lingering or fumbling or going back, from one inch of their fields to the next, probing, scrutinizing, testing with expert certainty. Every drawer, cupboard, cubbyhole, box, bag, trunk—locked or unlocked—was opened and its contents subjected to examination by eyes and fingers. Every piece of clothing was tested by hands that felt for telltale bulges and ears that listened for the crinkle of paper between pressing fingers. He stripped the bed of bedclothes. He looked under rugs and at the under side of each piece of furniture. He pulled down blinds to see that nothing had been rolled up in them for concealment. He leaned through windows to see that nothing hung below them on the outside. He poked with a fork into powder and cream jars on the dressing table. He held atomizers and bottles up against the light. He examined dishes and pans and food and food containers. He emptied the garbage can on spread sheets of newspaper. He opened the top of the flush box in the bathroom, drained the box, and peered down into it. He examined and tested the metal screens over bath-tub, wash-bowl, sink and laundry-tub drains.

Spade did not find a black bird. He found nothing that seemed to have any connection with a black bird: the only piece of writing he found was a week-old receipt for the month's apart-ment rent Brigid O'Shaughnessy had paid. The only thing he found that interested him enough to delay his search for a few minutes while he looked at it was a double handful of rather fine jewelry in a polychrome box in a locked dressing table drawer.

When he had finished he made and drank a cup of coffee. Then he unlocked the kitchen window, scarred the edge of its lock a little with his pocketknife, opened the window—over a fire escape—got his hat and overcoat from the living room settee, and left the apartment as he had come.

On his way home he stopped at a store that was being opened by a puffy-eyed, shivering, plump grocer and bought oranges, eggs, rolls, butter, and cream.

Spade went quietly into his apartment, but before he had shut the corridor door behind him Brigid O'Shaughnessy cried:

"Who is that?"

"Young Spade bearing breakfast."

"Oh, you frightened me!"

The bedroom door he had shut was open. The girl sat on the side of the bed, trembling, with her right hand out of sight under a pillow.

Spade put his packages on the kitchen table and went into the bedroom. He sat on the bed beside the girl, kissed her smooth shoulder, and said:

"I wanted to see if that kid was still on the job, and to get stuff for breakfast."

"Is he?"

"No."

She sighed and leaned against him.

"I awakened, and you weren't here, and then I heard somebody coming in. I was terrified."

Spade combed her red hair back from her face with his fingers and said:

"I'm sorry, angel. I thought you'd sleep through it. Did you have that gun under your pillow all night?"

"No. You know I didn't. I jumped up and got it when I was frightened." He cooked breakfast, and slipped the flat brass key into her coat pocket again, while she bathed and dressed.

She came out of the bathroom whistling "En Cuba."

"Shall I make the bed?" she asked.

"That'd be swell. The eggs need a couple of minutes more."

Their breakfast was on the table when she returned to the kitchen. They sat where they had sat the night before, and ate heartily.

"Now about that bird?" Spade suggested presently as they ate.

She put down her fork and looked at him. She drew her eyebrows together and made her mouth small and tight.

"You can't ask me to talk about that this morning of all mornings," she protested. "I don't want to, and I won't."

"It's a stubborn damned hussy," he said sadly, and put a piece of roll into his mouth.

The youth who had shadowed Spade was not in sight when Spade and Brigid O'Shaughnessy crossed the sidewalk to the waiting taxicab. The taxicab was not followed. Neither the youth nor another loiterer was visible in the vicinity of the Coronet when the taxicab arrived there.

Brigid O'Shaughnessy would not let Spade go indoors with her.

"It's bad enough to be coming home in evening dress at this hour without bringing company. I hope I don't meet anybody."

"Dinner tonight?"

"Yes."

They kissed. She went into the Coronet. He told the chauffeur: "Hotel Belvedere."

When he reached the hotel he saw the youth who had shadowed him sitting on a lobby divan from which the elevators could be seen. Apparently the youth was reading a newspaper.

At the desk Spade was told that Cairo was not in. He frowned and pinched his lower lip meditatively. Points of yellow light began to dance in his eyes. "Thanks," he said softly, and turned away.

Sauntering, he crossed the lobby to the divan from which the elevators could be seen, and sat down beside—not more than a foot from—the young man who apparently was reading a newspaper.

The young man did not look up from his paper. Seen at this scant distance, he seemed certainly less than twenty years old. His features were small, in keeping with his stature, and regular. His skin was very fair. The whiteness of his cheeks was as little blurred by any considerable growth of beard as by the glow of blood. His clothing was neither new nor of more than ordinary quality, but it, and his manner of wearing it, was marked by a hard masculine neatness.

Spade asked casually, "Where is he?" while shaking tobacco down into a paper curved to catch it.

The boy lowered his paper and looked around, moving with a purposeful sort of slowness, as of a more natural swiftness restrained. He looked with small hazel eyes under somewhat long curling lashes at Spade's chest. He said, in a voice as colorless and composed and cold as his young face:

"What?"

"Where is he?" Spade was busy with his cigarette.

"Who?"

"The fairy."

The hazel eyes' gaze went up Spade's chest to the knot of his maroon tie, and rested there.

"What do you think you're doing, Jack?" the boy demanded. "Kidding me?"

"I'll tell you when I am." Spade licked his cigarette and smiled amiably at the boy. "New York, aren't you?"

The boy stared at Spade's tie and did not speak. Spade nodded as if the boy had said yes, and asked:

"Baumes rush?"

The boy stared at Spade's tie for a moment longer, then the newspaper and returned his attention to it.

"Shove off," he said from the side of his mouth.

Spade lit his cigarette, leaned back comfortably on the divan, and spoke with good-humored carelessness:

"You'll have to talk to me before you're through, sonny. Some of you will, and you can tell G. I said so."

The boy put his paper down quickly and faced Spade, staring at his necktie with bleak hazel eyes. The boy's small hands were spread flat over his belly.

"Keep asking for it and you're going to get it," he said, "plenty." His voice was low and flat and threatening. "I told you to shove off. Shove off."

Spade waited until a bespectacled pudgy man and a thin-legged blond girl had passed out of hearing. Then he chuckled and said:

"That would go swell back on Seventh Avenue. But you're not in Romeville now. You're in my burg." He inhaled cigarette smoke and blew it out in a long pale cloud. "Well, where is he?"

The boy spoke two words, the first a short guttural verb, the second "you."

"People have lost teeth talking like that." Spade's voice was still amiable, though his face had become wooden. "If you want to hang around you'll be polite."

The boy repeated his two words.

Spade dropped his cigarette into a tall stone

jar beside the divan and with a lifted hand caught the attention of a man who had been for several minutes standing at an end of the cigar stand.

The man nodded and came toward them. He was a middle-aged man of medium height, round and sallow of face, compactly built, tidily dressed in dark clothes.

"Hello, Sam," he said as he came up.

"Hello, Luke."

They shook hands, and Luke said: "Say, that's too bad about Miles."

"Uh-huh, a bad break." Spade jerked his head to indicate the boy on the divan beside him. "What do you let these cheap gunmen hang out in your lobby for, with their tools bulging their clothes?"

"Yes?" Luke examined the boy with crafty brown eyes set in a suddenly hard face. "What do you want here?" he asked.

The boy stood up. Spade stood up. The boy looked at them, at their neckties, from one to the other. Luke's necktie was black. The boy looked like a schoolboy standing in front of them.

Luke said:

"Well, if you don't want anything, beat it, and don't come back."

The boy said, "I won't forget you guys," and went out.

They watched him go out. Spade took off his hat and wiped his damp forehead with a handkerchief. The hotel detective asked:

"What is it?"

"Damned if I know," Spade replied. "I just spotted him. Know anything about Joel Cairo, 635?"

"Oh, *her.*" The hotel detective leered. "I been watching him, but I ain't caught him doing anything he oughtn't to."

"How long's he been here?"

"Four days. This is the fifth."

"What about him?"

"Search me. I got nothing against him but his looks and that's enough."

"Find out if he was in last night?"

"Try to," the hotel detective promised, and went away.

Spade sat on the divan until Luke returned.

"No," Luke said, "he didn't sleep here. What is it, Sam?"

"Nothing."

"Come clean. You know I'll keep my clam shut, but if there's anything wrong we ought to know so we can collect our bill."

"Nothing like that," Spade assured him. "As a matter of fact, I'm doing some work for him. I'd tell you if he was wrong."

"You'd better. Want me to kind of keep an eye on him?"

"Thanks, Luke. It wouldn't hurt. You can't know too much about the birds you're working for."

It was twenty-one minutes past eleven by the clock over the elevator doors when Joel Cairo came in from the street. His forehead was bandaged. His clothes had the limp unfreshness of too many consecutive hours' wear. His face was pasty, with sagging mouth and eyelids.

Spade met him in front of the desk.

"Good morning," Spade said easily.

Cairo drew his tired body up straight, and the drooping lines of his face tightened.

"Good morning," he responded without enthusiasm.

There was a pause.

Spade said:

"Let's go some place where we can talk."

Cairo raised his chin.

"Please excuse me," he said. "Our conversations in private have not been such that I am anxious to continue them. Pardon my speaking bluntly, but it is the truth."

"You mean last night?" Spade made an impatient gesture with head and hands. "What the hell else could I do? I thought you'd see that. If you pick a fight with her, or let her pick one with you, I've got to throw in with her. I don't know where that damned bird is. You don't. She does. How in hell are we going to get it if I don't play along with her?"

Cairo hesitated, said dubiously:

"You've always, I must say, a smooth explanation ready."

Spade scowled. "What do you want me to do? Learn to stutter? Well, we can talk over here." He led the way to the divan. When they were seated he asked: "Dundy take you down to the hall?"

"Yes."

"How long did he work on you?"

"Till a very little while ago, and very much against my will." Pain and indignation were mixed in Cairo's face and voice. "I shall certainly take the matter up with the Consulate General of Greece and with an attorney."

"Go ahead, but it won't get you anything. What did they get out of you?"

There was prim satisfaction in Cairo's stiff smile.

"Not a single thing. I adhered to the course you had indicated earlier in your rooms." His smile went away. "Though I certainly wished you had devised a more reasonable story. I felt decidedly ridiculous repeating it."

Spade grinned mockingly.

"Sure," he said, "but its goofiness is what made it good. You're sure you didn't give them anything else?"

"You may rely upon it, Mr. Spade. I did not."

Spade drummed with his fingers on the leather seat between them.

"You'll be hearing from Dundy again. Stay dummied up on him and you'll be all right. Don't worry about the story's goofiness. A sensible one would have had us all in the cooler." He rose to his feet. "You'll want to sleep if you've been in the grease all night. See you later."

Effie Perine was saying, "No, not yet," into the telephone when Spade entered his outer office. She looked around at him and her lips shaped a silent word, "Iva." He shook his head. "Yes, I'll have him call you as soon as he comes in," she said aloud, and replaced the receiver on its prong.

"That's the third time she's called up this morning," she told Sam.

He made an impatient growling noise.

She moved her brown eyes to indicate the inner office door. "Your Miss O'Shaughnessy's in there. She has been waiting since a few minutes after nine."

Spade nodded as if he had expected that, and asked: "What else?"

"Sergeant Polhaus called up. He didn't leave any message."

"Get him for me."

"And G. called up."

Spade's eyes brightened. He asked: "Who?"

"G. That's what he said." Her air of personal indifference to the subject was flawless. "When I told him you weren't in he said, 'When he comes in, will you please tell him that G., who got his message, phoned and will phone again?'"

Spade worked his lips together as if tasting something he liked.

"Thanks, darling," he said. "See if you can get Tom Polhaus."

He opened the inner door and went into his private office, pulling the door to behind him.

Brigid O'Shaughnessy, dressed as on her first visit to the office, rose from a chair beside his desk and came quickly toward him.

"Somebody has been in my apartment," she exclaimed. "It is all upside down, every which way."

He seemed moderately surprised.

"Anything taken?"

"I don't think so. I don't know. I was afraid to stay. I changed as fast as I could and came down here. Oh, Sam, you must've let that boy follow you there."

Spade shook his head. "No, angel." He took an early copy of an afternoon newspaper from his pocket, opened it, and showed her a quarter-column headed:

SCREAM ROUTS BURGLARS

A young woman named Carolin Beale, who lived alone in a Sutter Street apartment, had been awakened at four that morning by the sound of somebody moving in her bedroom. She had screamed. The mover had run away. Two other women who lived alone in the same building had discovered, later in the morning, signs of the burglar's having visited their apartments. Nothing had been taken from any of the three.

"That's where I shook him," Spade explained. "I went into that building and ducked out the back door. That's why all three were women that lived alone.

"He tried the apartments that had women's names in the vestibule register, hunting for you under a phoney name."

"But he was watching your place when we were there," she objected.

Spade shrugged. "Maybe he's not alone. Maybe he went to Sutter Street after he began to think you were going to stay at my place all night. There are lots of maybes. But I didn't lead him to the Coronet."

She wasn't satisfied. "But he found it, or somebody did."

"Sure." He frowned at her feet. "I wonder if it could have been Cairo. He wasn't at his hotel all night, didn't get in till a few minutes ago. He told me he had been standing up under a quiz at headquarters all night. I wonder."

He turned, opened the door, and asked Effie Perine: "Got Tom yet?"

"He's not in. I'll try again in a few minutes."

"Thanks." Spade shut the door and faced Brigid O'Shaughnessy.

She looked at him with cloudy eyes. "You went to see Joe this morning?" she asked.

"Yes."

She hesitated. "Why?"

"Why?" He smiled down at her. "Because, my dear, I've got to keep in some sort of touch with the loose ends of this dizzy affair, if I'm ever going to make heads or tails of it." He put an arm around her shoulders and led her over to his swivel chair. He kissed the tip of her nose lightly and set her down in the chair. He sat on the desk in front of her. He said: "Now we've got to find a new home for you, haven't we?"

She nodded with emphasis. "I won't go back there."

He patted the desk beside his thighs and made a thoughtful face.

"I think I've got it," he said presently. "Wait a minute." He went into the outer office, shutting the door behind him.

Effie Perine reached for the telephone, saying: "I'll try again."

"Afterwards. Does your woman's intuition still tell you she's a Madonna or something?"

She looked sharply up at him.

"I still believe that no matter what kind of trouble she's gotten into she's all right, if that's what you mean."

"That's what I mean," he said. "Are you strong enough for her to give her a lift?"

"How?"

"Could you put her up for a few days?"

"You mean at home?"

"Yes. Her joint's been broken into. That's the second burglary she's had this week. It'd be better if she wasn't by herself. It would help a lot if you could take her in."

Effie Perine leaned forward, asking earnestly: "Is she really in danger, Sam?"

"I think she is."

She scratched her lip with a fingernail. "That would scare Ma into a green hemorrhage. I'll have to tell her she's a surprise witness or something that you're keeping under cover till the last minute."

"You're a darling," Spade said. "Better take her out there now. I'll get her key from her and bring whatever she needs from her apartment later. Let's see. You oughtn't to be seen leaving here with her. You go home now. Take a taxi, but make sure you aren't tailed. You probably won't be, but make sure. I'll send her out in another in a little while, making sure she isn't tailed."

CHAPTER XI
GUTMAN

he telephone bell was ringing when Spade returned to his office after sending Brigid O'Shaughnessy off to Effie Perine's house. He went to the telephone.

"Hello . . . Yes, this is Spade. . . . Yes, I got it. I've been waiting to hear from you. . . . Who? . . . Mr. Gutman? Oh, yes, sure . . . Now. The sooner the better . . . 12C . . . Right. Say fifteen minutes. . . . Right."

Spade sat on the corner of the desk beside the telephone and rolled a cigarette. His mouth was a hard, complacent V. His eyes, watching his fingers make the cigarette, smoldered over lower lids drawn up straight.

The door opened and Iva Archer came in.

Spade said, "Hello, honey," in a voice as lightly amiable as his face had suddenly become.

"Oh, Sam, forgive me! Forgive me!" she cried in a choked voice. She stood just inside the door, wadding a black-bordered handkerchief in her small gloved hands, peering into his face with frightened red and swollen eyes.

He did not get up from his seat on the desk corner. He said:

"Sure. That's all right. Forget it."

She came to him and put her hands on his shoulders.

"But, Sam," she wailed, "I sent those policemen there. I was mad, crazy with jealousy, and I phoned them that if they'd go there they'd learn something about Miles's murder."

"What made you think that?"

"Oh, I didn't, Sam, but I was mad, and I wanted to hurt you."

"It made things damn awkward." He put his arm around her and drew her nearer. "But it's all right now, only, don't get any more crazy ideas like that."

"I won't," she promised, "I won't. But you weren't nice to me last night. You were cold and distant and wanted to get rid of me, when I had come down there and waited and waited to warn you, and you—"

"Warn me about what?"

"About Phil. He's found out about—about you being in love with me, and Miles had told him about my wanting a divorce, though of course *he* never knew what for, and now Phil thinks we—you killed his brother because he wouldn't give me the divorce so we could get married. He told me he believed that, and yesterday he went and told the police."

"That's nice," Spade said softly. "And you came to warn me, and because I was busy you got up on your ear and helped this damn Phil Archer mess things up."

"I'm sorry," she whimpered. "I know you won't forgive me. I—I'm sorry, sorry, sorry."

"You ought to be," he agreed, "on your own account as well as mine. Has Dundy been to see you since Phil did his talking? Or anybody from the Hall?"

"No." Alarm opened her eyes and mouth.

"They will," he said, "and it'd be just as well to not let them find you here. Did you tell them who you were when you phoned?"

"Oh, no. I just told them that if they'd go to your apartment then they'd learn something about the murder, and hung up."

"Where'd you phone from?"

"The drug store up above your place. Oh, Sam, dearest, I—"

He patted her shoulder and said pleasantly:

"It was a dumb trick, all right, but it's done now. You'd better run along home and think up some things to tell the police. You'll be hearing from them. Maybe it'd be best to say, 'No,' right across the board." He frowned at something in the distance. "Or maybe you'd better see Sid Wise first." He took his arm from around her, took a card from his pocket, scribbled three lines on its back, and gave it to her. "You can tell Sid everything." He frowned. "Or almost everything. Where were you the night Miles was shot?"

"At home," she replied without hesitation.

He shook his head, grinning at her.

"I was," she insisted.

"No," he said, "but if that's your story it's all right with me. Go see Sid. It's up at the next corner, the pinkish building, room 827."

Her blue eyes tried to probe his yellow-gray ones.

"What makes you think I wasn't home?" she asked slowly.

"Nothing, except I know you weren't."

"But I was, I was." She bit her lip. Anger darkened her eyes. "Effie told you that," she said indignantly. "I saw her looking at my clothes and snooping around. You know she doesn't like me, Sam. Why do you believe things she tells you when you know she'd do anything to make trouble for me?"

"——, you women," Spade said gently. He looked at the watch on his wrist. "You'll have to trot along, precious, I'm late for an appointment now. You do what you want, but if I were you I'd tell Sid the truth or nothing. I mean, leave out the parts you don't want to tell him, but don't make up anything to take its place."

"I'm not lying to you, Sam," she protested.

"Like hell you're not," he said, and stood up.

She strained on tiptoe to hold her face nearer his.

"You don't believe me?" she whispered.

"I don't believe you."

"And you won't forgive me for—for what I did?"

"Sure I do." He bent his head and kissed her mouth. "That's all right. Now run along."

She put her arms around him. "Won't you go with me to see Mr. Wise?"

"I can't, and I'd only be in the way."

He patted her arms, took them from around his body, and kissed her left wrist between glove and sleeve. He put his hands on her shoulders, turned her to face the door, and released her with a little push.

"Beat it," he ordered.

The mahogany door of suite 12-C at the Alexandria Hotel was opened by the boy Spade had talked to in the Belvedere lobby.

Spade said, "Hello," good-naturedly.

The boy did not say anything. He stood aside holding the door open.

Spade went in. A fat man came to meet him.

The fat man was flabbily fat with bulbous pink cheeks and lips and chins and neck, with a great soft egg of a body that was all his torso, and pendant cones for arms and legs. As he advanced to meet Spade all his bulbs rose and shook and fell separately with each step, in the manner of clustered soap bubbles not yet released from the pipe through which they had been blown. His eyes, made small by fat puffs around them, were dark and sleek. Dark ringlets thinly covered his broad scalp. He wore a black cutaway coat, black vest, black satin ascot tie holding a pinkish pearl, striped gray worsted trousers, and patent-leather shoes.

His voice was a throaty purr. "Ah, Mr. Spade," he said with enthusiasm, and he held out a hand like a fat pink star.

Spade shook the hand and smiled, but said nothing.

Spade sat in a soft green chair. The fat man began to fill two glasses from bottle and siphon. The boy had disappeared. Doors set in three of the room's walls were closed. The fourth wall, behind Spade, was pierced by two windows looking out over Geary Street.

"We begin well, sir," the fat man purred, turning with a proffered glass in his hand. "I distrust a man that says when. If he's got to be careful not to drink too much it's because he's not to be trusted when he does."

Spade took the glass and, still smiling, made the beginning of a bow over it.

The fat man raised his glass and held it against a window's light. He nodded approvingly at the bubbles running upward in it. He said:

"Well, sir, here's to plain speaking and clear understanding."

They drank, and lowered their glasses.

The fat man looked shrewdly at Spade and asked:

"You're a close-mouthed man?"

Spade shook his head. "I like to talk."

"Better and better!" the fat man exclaimed. "I distrust a close-mouthed man. He generally picks the wrong time to talk, and says the wrong things. Talking's something you can't do judiciously unless you keep in practice." He beamed over his glass. "We'll get along, sir, that we will." He set his glass down on the table and held a box of Coronas del Ritz out to Spade. "A cigar, sir."

Spade took, and trimmed the end of, and lighted, a cigar. Meanwhile the fat man pulled another green plush chair around to face Spade's within convenient distance and pushed a smoking stand within reach of both chairs. Then he took his glass from the table, took a cigar from the box, and lowered himself into his chair. His bulbs stopped jouncing and settled into flabby rest. He sighed comfortably and said:

"Now, sir, we'll talk if you like. And I'll tell you right out that I'm a man that likes talking with a man that likes to talk."

"Swell. Will we talk about the black bird?"

The fat man laughed, and his bulbs rode up and down on his laughter.

"Will we?" he asked, and, "We will," he replied. His pink face was shiny with delight. "You're the man for me, sir, a man cut along my own lines. No beating about the bush, but right to the point. 'Will we talk about the black bird?' We will. I like that, sir. I like that way of doing business, sir. Let us talk about the black bird by all means, but first answer me a question, please, though maybe it's an unnecessary one, so we'll understand one another from the beginning. You're here as Miss O'Shaughnessy's representative?"

Spade blew smoke above the fat man's head in a long slanting plume. He frowned thoughtfully at the ash-tipped end of his cigar. He replied deliberately:

"I can't say yes or no. There's nothing certain about it either way, yet." He looked up at the fat man and his frown faded. "It depends."

"It depends on—?"

Spade shook his head. "If I knew what it depends on I could say yes or no."

The fat man took a mouthful from his glass, swallowed it, and suggested:

"Maybe it depends on Joel Cairo?"

Spade's prompt, "Maybe," was noncommittal. He drank.

The fat man leaned forward until his belly stopped him. His smile was ingratiating, and so was his purring voice:

"You could say then that the question is which one of them you'll represent?"

"You could put it that way."

"It will be one or the other?"

"I didn't say that."

The fat man's eyes glistened. His voice sank to a hoarse whisper, asking:

"Who else is there?"

Spade pointed his cigar at his own chest. "There's me," he said.

The fat man leaned back in his chair and let his body go flaccid. He blew his breath out in a long contented gust.

"That's wonderful, sir," he purred. "That's wonderful. I do like a man that tells you right out he's looking out for himself. Don't we all? I don't trust a man that says he's not. And the man that's telling the truth when he says he's not I distrust most of all, because he's an ass, and an ass that's going contrary to the laws of nature."

Spade exhaled smoke. His face was politely attentive. He said:

"Uh-huh. Now let's talk about the black bird."

The fat man smiled benevolently at Spade.

"Let's," he said. He squinted so that fat puffs crowding together left nothing visible of his eyes except a dark gleam. "Mr. Spade, have you any conception of how much money can be made out of that black bird?"

"No."

The fat man leaned forward and put a bloated pink hand on the arm of Spade's chair.

"Well, sir, if I told you—if I told you half—you'd call me a liar."

Spade smiled. "No," he said, "not even if I thought it. But if you don't want to take the risk, just tell me what it is and I'll figure out the profit."

The fat man laughed.

"You couldn't. You couldn't do it, sir. Nobody could do it that hadn't had a world of experience with things of that sort, and"—he paused impressively—"there aren't any other things of that sort." His bulbs jostled one another as he laughed again. He stopped laughing, abruptly. His fleshy lips hung a little apart, as laughter had left them. He stared at Spade with an intentness that suggested myopia. He asked: "You mean you don't know what it is?" Amazement took the throatiness out of his voice.

Spade made a careless gesture with his cigar.

"Oh, hell," he said lightly, "I know what it's supposed to look like. I know the value in life and money you people put on it. I don't know what it is."

"She didn't tell you?"

"Miss O'Shaughnessy?"

"Yes. A lovely girl, sir."

"Uh-huh. No."

The fat man's eyes were dark gleams in ambush behind pink puffs of flesh. He said indistinctly, "She must know," and then, "And Cairo didn't either?"

"Cairo is cagey. He's willing to buy it, but he won't risk telling me anything I don't know already."

The fat man moistened his lips with his tongue.

"How much is he willing to buy it for?" he asked.

"Ten thousand dollars."

The fat man laughed scornfully. "Ten thousand. And dollars, mind you, not even pounds. That's the Greek for you. Humph! And what did you say to that?"

"I said if I turned it over to him I'd expect the ten thousand."

"Ah, yes, *if*. Nicely put, sir." The fat man's forehead squirmed in a flesh-blurred frown. "They must know," he said only partly aloud, then: "Do they? Do they know what the bird is, sir? What is your impression?"

"I can't help you there," Spade confessed. "There's not much to go by. Cairo didn't say he did, and he didn't say he didn't. She said she didn't, but I took it for granted that she was lying."

"That was not an injudicious thing to do," the fat man said, but his mind was obviously not on his words. He scratched his head. He frowned until his forehead was marked by raw red creases. He fidgeted in his chair as much as its size and his size permitted fidgeting. He shut his eyes, suddenly opened them wide, and said to Spade: "Maybe they don't." His bulbous pink face slowly lost its worried frown and then, more quickly, took on an expression of ineffable happiness. "If they don't," he cried, and again: "If they don't, I'm the only one in the whole wide sweet world who does!"

Spade drew his lips back in a tight smile.

"I'm glad I came to the right place," he said.

The fat man smiled too, but somewhat vaguely. Happiness had gone out of his face, though he continued to smile, and caution had come into his eyes. His face was a watchful-eyed smiling mask held up between his thoughts and Spade. His eyes, avoiding Spade's, shifted to the glass at Spade's elbow. His face brightened.

"By Gar, sir," he said, "your glass is empty."

He got up and went to the table, and clattered glasses and siphon and bottle mixing two drinks. Spade was immobile in his chair until the fat man, with a flourish and a bow and a jocular, "Ah, this kind of medicine will never hurt you," had handed him his refilled glass.

Then Spade rose and stood close to the fat man, looking down at him. Spade's eyes were hard and bright. He raised his glass. His voice was sharp, challenging:

"Here's to plain speaking and clear understanding."

The fat man chuckled, and they drank. The fat man sat down. He held his glass against his belly with both hands and smiled up at Spade. He said:

"Well, sir, it's surprising, but it well may be a fact that neither of them does know exactly what that bird is, and that nobody in all this whole wide sweet world knows what it is, saving and excepting only your humble servant, Casper Gutman, Esquire."

"Swell." Spade stood with legs apart, one hand in his trouser pocket, the other holding his glass. "When you've told me, there'll only be two of us who know."

"Mathematically correct, sir." The fat man's eyes twinkled. "But"—his smile spread—"I don't know for certain that I'm going to tell you."

"Don't be a damned fool," Spade said patiently. "You know what it is. I know where it is. That's why we're here."

"Well, sir, where is it?"

Spade ignored the question.

The fat man bunched his lips, raised his eyebrows, and cocked his head a little to the left.

"You see," he said blandly, "I must tell you what I know, but you will not tell me what you know. That is hardly equitable, sir. No, no, I don't think we can do business like that."

Spade's face became pale and hard. He spoke rapidly in a low, furious voice:

"Think again and think fast. I told that punk of yours that you'd have to talk to me before you got through. I'll tell you now that you'll do your talking today or you are through. What are you wasting my time for? You and your lousy secret— I know exactly what that stuff is that they keep in the subtreasury vaults, but what good does that do me? I can get along without you. —— damn you. Maybe you could have got along without me if you'd kept clear of me. You can't now. Not in San Francisco. You'll come in or you'll get out, and you'll do it today."

He turned and with angry heedlessness tossed his glass on the table. The glass struck the wood, burst apart, and splashed its contents and glittering fragments over table and floor. Spade, deaf and blind to the crash, wheeled to confront the fat man again.

The fat man paid no more attention to the glass's fate than Spade did: lips pursed, eyebrows raised, head cocked a little to the left, he had maintained his pink-faced blandness throughout Spade's angry speech and he maintained it now.

Spade said, still furious:

"And another thing, I don't want—"

The door to Spade's left opened. The boy who had admitted Spade came in. He shut the door, stood in front of it with his hands flat against his flanks, and looked at Spade. The boy's eyes were wide open, and dark with wide pupils. Their gaze ran over Spade's body from shoulders to knees, and up again to settle on the handkerchief whose maroon border peeped from the breast pocket of Spade's brown coat.

"Another thing," Spade repeated, glaring at the boy: "Keep that gunsel away from me while you're making up your mind. I'll kill him. I don't like him. He makes me nervous. I'll kill him the first time he gets in my way. I'm afraid of him. I won't give him an even break. I won't give him a chance. I'll kill him."

The boy's lips twitched in a shadowy smile. He neither raised his eyes nor spoke.

The fat man said tolerantly:

"Well, sir, I must say you have a most violent temper."

"Temper?" Spade laughed crazily. He crossed to the chair on which he had dropped his hat, picked up the hat, and set it on his head. He held out a long arm that ended in a thick forefinger pointing at the fat man's belly. His angry voice filled the room: "Think it over, and think like hell. You've got till five-thirty to do it in. Then you're either in or out, for keeps."

He let his arm drop, scowled at the bland fat man for a moment, scowled at the boy, and went to the door through which he had entered. When he had opened the door he turned and said harshly:

"Five-thirty, then the curtain."

The boy, staring at Spade's chest, repeated the two words he had twice spoken in the Belvedere lobby. His voice was not loud. It was bitter.

Spade went out and slammed the door.

CHAPTER XII
MERRY-GO-ROUND

pade rode down from Gutman's floor in an elevator. His lips were dry and rough in a face otherwise pale and damp. When he took out his handkerchief to wipe his face he saw his hand trembling. He grinned at it, and said, "Whew!" so loudly that the elevator operator turned his head and asked: "Sir?"

Spade walked down Geary Street to the Palace Hotel, where he had luncheon. His face had lost its pallor, his lips their dryness, and his hand its tremor. He ate hungrily without haste, and then went to Sid Wise's office.

When Spade entered, Wise was biting a fingernail and staring at the window. He took his hand from his mouth, screwed his chair around to face Spade, and said:

"'Lo. Push a chair up."

Spade moved a chair to the side of the big paper-laden desk and sat down.

"Mrs. Archer come in?" he asked.

"Yes." The faintest of lights flickered in Wise's eyes. "Going to marry the lady, Sammy?"

Spade sighed irritably through his nose.

"——! Now you start that," he grumbled.

A brief tired smile lifted the corners of the lawyer's mouth.

"If you don't," he said, "you're going to have a job on your hands."

Spade looked up from the cigarette he was making and spoke sourly:

"You mean you are? Well, that's what you're for. What did she tell you?"

"About you?"

"About anything I ought to know."

Wise ran his fingers through his hair, sprinkling dandruff down on his shoulders.

"She told me she had tried to get a divorce from Miles so she could——"

"I know all that," Spade interrupted. "You can skip it. Get to the part I don't know."

"How do I know how much she——?"

"Quit stalling, Sid." Spade held the flame of his lighter to the end of his cigarette. "What did she tell you that she wanted kept from me?"

Wise looked reprovingly at Spade.

"Now, Sammy," he began, "that's not——"

Spade looked heavenward at the ceiling and groaned:

"Dear God, he's my own lawyer that's got rich off me and I have to get down on my knees and beg him to tell me things." He glowered at Wise. "What the hell do you think I sent her to you for?"

Wise made a weary grimace.

"Just one more client like you," he complained, "and I'd be in a sanatarium, or San Quentin."

"You'd be with most of your clients. Did she tell you where she was the night he was killed?"

"Yes."

"Where?"

"Following her husband."

Spade sat up straight and blinked. He exclaimed incredulously: "—— these women!" Then he laughed, relaxed, and asked: "Well, what did she see?"

Wise shook his head.

"Nothing much. When he came home for dinner that evening he told her he had a date with a girl at the St. Mark, taunting her, telling her that was her chance to get the evidence for the divorce she wanted. She thought at first that he was just trying to get under her skin. He knew——"

"I know the family history," Spade said. "Skip it. Tell me what she did."

"I will if you'll give me a chance. After he had gone out she began to think that maybe he might have had that date. You know Miles. It would have been like him to——"

"You can skip Miles's character too."

"I oughtn't to tell you a damned thing," the lawyer said. "So she got their car from the garage and drove down to the St. Mark, sitting in the car across the street. She saw him come out of the hotel, and she saw that he was shadowing a man and a girl—she says she saw the same girl with you last night—who had come out just ahead of him. She knew then that he was working, had been kidding her. I suppose she was disappointed, and mad; she sounded that way when she told about it. She followed Miles long enough to be sure he was shadowing the pair, and then she went up to your rooms. You weren't home."

"What time was that?" Spade asked.

"When she got to your place? Between half past nine and ten, the first time."

"The first time?"

"Yes. She drove around for half an hour or more after that, and then tried again. That would make it, say, ten-thirty. You were still out, so she drove back downtown and went to a movie to kill time until after midnight, when she thought she'd be more likely to find you in."

Spade frowned. "She went to a movie at ten-thirty?"

"So she said. The one on Powell Street that stays open till one in the morning. She didn't want to go home, she said, because she didn't want to be there when Miles came home. That always made him mad, it seems, especially if it was around midnight. She stayed in the movie until it closed." Wise's words came out slower now and there was a sardonic glint in his tired eyes. "She says she had decided not to go back to your place then. She says she didn't know whether you'd like having her drop in that late. So she went to Tait's—the one on Ellis Street—had something to eat, and then went home, alone."

Wise rocked back in his chair and waited for Spade to speak. Spade's face was expressionless. He asked:

"You believe her?"

"Don't you?" Wise replied.

"How do I know? How do I know it isn't something you fixed up between you to tell me?"

Wise smiled. "You don't cash many checks for strangers, do you, Sammy?"

"Not basketfuls. Well, then what? Miles wasn't home. It was at least two o'clock by then."

"Miles wasn't home," Wise said. "That made her mad again, because he didn't get home first to be made mad by her not being home first. So she took the car out of the garage again and went back to your place."

"And I wasn't home. I was down looking at Miles's corpse. ——! What a swell lot of merry-go-round riding. What next?"

"She went home, and her husband was still not there, and while she was undressing your messenger came with the news of his death."

Spade didn't speak until he had with great care rolled and lighted another cigarette. Then he said:

"I think that's an all-right spread. It seems to click with the known facts. It ought to hold."

Wise's fingers, running through his hair again, combed more dandruff down on his shoulders. He studied Spade's face with curious eyes, and asked:

"But you don't believe it?"

Spade plucked the cigarette from between his lips.

"I don't believe it or disbelieve it, Sid. I don't know a damned thing about it."

A wry smile twisted the lawyer's mouth. He shrugged wearily and said:

"That's right, I'm selling you out. Why don't you get an honest lawyer, one you can trust?"

"Oh, that fellow's dead." Spade stood up. He sneered at Wise. "Getting touchy, huh? I haven't got enough to think about; now I've got to remember to be polite to you. What did I do? Forget to genuflect when I came in?"

Sid Wise smiled sheepishly.

"You're a son of a gun, Sammy," he said.

Effie Perine was standing in the center of Spade's outer office when he entered. She looked at him with worried brown eyes and asked:

"What happened?"

Spade's face grew stiff.

"What happened where?" he demanded.

"Why didn't she come?"

Spade took two long steps and caught Effie Perine by the shoulders.

"She didn't get there?" he bawled into her frightened face.

She shook her head violently from side to side.

"I waited and waited, and she didn't come, and I couldn't get you on the phone, so I came down."

Spade jerked his hands from her shoulders, thrust them far down in his trouser pockets, said, "Another merry-go-round ride," in a loud enraged voice, and strode into his private office. He came out again. "Phone your mother," he commanded her. "See if she's come yet."

He walked up and down the office while the girl used the telephone.

"No," she said when she had finished. "Did—did you send her out in a taxi?"

His grunt probably meant yes.

"Are you sure she— Somebody must have seen her and followed her!"

Spade stopped pacing the floor. He put his hands on his hips and glared at the girl. He addressed her in a loud savage voice:

"Nobody followed her. Do you think I'm a —— damned schoolboy? I made sure of it before I put her in the cab, I rode a dozen blocks with her to be more sure, and I checked her another half dozen blocks after I got out."

"Well, but—"

"But she didn't get there. You've told me that. I know it. Do you think I think she did get there?"

Effie Perine sniffed. "You certainly act like a —— damned schoolboy," she said.

Spade made a harsh noise in his throat and went to the corridor door.

"I'm going out and find her if I have to dig up sewers," he said. "Stay here till I'm back or you hear from me. For God's sake let's do something right."

He went out, walked half the distance to the elevators, and retraced his steps. Effie Perine was sitting at her desk when he opened the door. He said:

"You ought to know better than to pay any attention to me when I talk like that."

"If you think I pay any attention to you, you're crazy," she replied, "only"—she crossed her arms and felt her shoulders, and her mouth twitched uncertainly—"I won't be able to wear an evening gown for two weeks, you big brute."

He grinned apologetically, said, "I'm no damned good," made an exaggerated bow, and went out again.

Two yellow taxicabs were at the Post and Montgomery Street stand when Spade stopped there. Their chauffeurs were standing together talking. Spade asked:

"Where's the red-faced blond driver that was here at noon?"

"Got a load," one of the chauffeurs said.

"Will he be back here?"

"I guess so."

One of his companions ducked his head toward the east. "Here he comes now."

Spade walked down to the corner and stood by the curb until the red-faced blond chauffeur had parked his cab and got out. Then Spade went up to him and said:

"I got in your cab with a lady at noontime. We went out Stockton Street and up Sacramento to Jones, where I got out."

"Sure," the red-faced man said, "I remember that."

"I told you to take her on to a Seventh Avenue number. You didn't take her there. Where did you take her?"

The chauffeur looked doubtfully at Spade and rubbed his cheek with a grimy hand.

"I don't know about this."

"It's all right," Spade assured him, giving him one of his business cards. "If you want to play safe, though, we can ride up to your office and get your superintendent's O.K."

"I guess it's all right. I took her to the Ferry Building."

"By herself?"

"Yeah. Sure."

"Didn't take her anywhere else first?"

"No. It was like this: after we dropped you I went on out Sacramento, and when we got to Polk she rapped on the glass and she said she wanted to get a newspaper, so I stopped at the corner and whistled for a kid, and she got her paper."

"Which paper?"

"The *Call*. Then I went on out Sacramento, and just after we'd crossed Van Ness she knocked on the glass again and said take her to the Ferry Building."

"Was she excited or anything?"

"Not so's I noticed."

"And when you got to the Ferry Building?"

"She paid me off, that was all."

"Anybody waiting there for her?"

"I didn't see them if they was."

"Which way did she go?"

"At the Ferry? I don't know. Maybe upstairs, or toward the steps."

"Take the newspaper with her?"

"Yeah, she had it tucked under her arm when she paid me."

"With the pink sheet outside, or one of the white?"

"Hell, cap, I don't remember that."

Spade thanked the chauffeur, said, "Get yourself a smoke," and gave him a silver dollar.

Spade bought a copy of the *Call* and carried it into an office-building vestibule to examine it out of the wind.

His eyes ran swiftly over the front-page headlines, and over those on the second and third pages. Then paused for a moment under SUSPECT ARRESTED AS COUNTERFEITER on the fourth page, and again on page five under BAY YOUTH SEEKS DEATH WITH BULLETS. Pages six and seven held nothing to interest him. On eight, 3 BOYS ARRESTED AS S. F. BURGLARS AFTER SHOOTING held his attention for a moment, and after that nothing until he reached the thirty-fifth page, which held news of the weather, shipping, produce, finance, divorces, births, marriages, and deaths. He read the list of dead, passed over pages thirty-six and thirty-seven—financial news—found nothing to stop his eyes on the thirty-eighth and last page, sighed, folded the newspaper, put it in his coat pocket, and rolled a cigarette.

For five minutes he stood there in the office-building vestibule, smoking and staring sulkily at nothing. Then he walked up to Stockton Street, hailed a taxicab, and had himself driven to the Coronet.

He let himself into the building and into Brigid O'Shaughnessy's apartment with the key she had given him. The blue gown she had worn the previous night was hanging across the foot of her bed. Her blue stockings and slippers were on the bedroom floor. The polychrome box that had held jewelry, and had been in the dressing table drawer, now stood empty on the dressing table's top.

Spade frowned at it, ran his tongue across his lips, strolled through the rooms, looking around, but not touching anything, then left the Coronet and went downtown again.

In the doorway of the building where Spade had his offices he came face to face with the boy he had left at Gutman's. The boy put himself in Spade's path, blocking the entrance, and said:

"Come on. He wants to see you."

The boy's hands were in his overcoat pockets. His pockets bulged more than his hands need have made them bulge.

Spade grinned, and said mockingly:

"I didn't expect you till five-twenty-five. I hope I haven't kept you waiting long."

The boy raised his eyes to Spade's mouth and spoke in the strained voice of one in physical pain:

"You louse! Keep on riding me and you're going to be picking iron out of your navel."

Spade chuckled. "The cheaper the crook, the gaudier the patter," he said cheerfully. "Well, let's go."

They walked up Sutter Street side by side.

The boy kept his hands in his overcoat pockets. They walked a little more than a block in silence. Then Spade asked pleasantly:

"How long have you been off the ——lay?"

The boy did not show that he had heard the question.

"Did you ever——?" Spade began, and stopped. A soft light began to glow in his yellowish eyes. He did not address the boy again.

They went into the Alexandria, rode up to the twelfth floor, and walked down the corridor toward Gutman's suite. Nobody else was in the corridor.

Spade lagged a little, so that, when they were within fifteen feet of Gutman's door, he was perhaps a foot and a half behind the boy. He leaned sidewise suddenly and grasped the boy from behind by both arms, just beneath the boy's elbows. He forced the arms forward so that the boy's hands, in his overcoat pockets, lifted the overcoat up before him.

The boy struggled and writhed, but he was impotent in Spade's grip. The boy kicked back, but his feet went between Spade's widespread legs.

Spade lifted the boy straight up from the floor and then brought him down hard on his feet again. The impact made little noise on the thick carpet. At the moment of impact Spade's big hands slid down and got a fresh grip on the boy's wrists.

The boy, teeth set hard together, did not for a moment stop straining against the man's hands, but he could not tear himself loose, could not keep Spade's fingers from crawling down over his own hands.

The boy's teeth ground together audibly, the sound mingling with the noise of Spade's breathing, as Spade crushed his hands. They were tensely motionless for a long moment. Then the boy's arms became limp. Spade released the boy and stepped back. In each of Spade's hands, when they came out of the boy's overcoat pockets, there was a heavy automatic pistol.

The boy turned and faced Spade. The boy's face was a ghastly white blank. He kept his hands in his overcoat pockets. He looked at Spade's chest and said nothing.

Spade put the pistols in his own pockets and grinned derisively.

"Come on," he said. "This will put you in solid with your boss."

They went to Gutman's door and Spade knocked.

CHAPTER XIII
THE EMPEROR'S GIFT

 utman opened the door. A glad smile lighted his fat face. He held out a hand and said:

"Ah, come in, sir. Thanks for coming. Come in."

Spade shook the hand and entered. The boy went in behind him. The fat man shut the door. Spade took the pistols from his pockets and held them out to Gutman.

"Here. You shouldn't let the lad run around with these. He'll get himself hurt."

The fat man laughed merrily and took the pistols.

"Well, well," he said, "what's this?" He looked from Spade to the boy.

Spade said, "A crippled newsboy took them away from him, but I made him give them up."

The white-faced boy took the pistols out of Gutman's hands and pocketed them. The boy did not speak.

Gutman laughed again.

"By Gad, sir," he told Spade, "you're a chap worth knowing, an amazing character. Come in. Sit down. Give me your hat."

The boy left the room by the door to the right of the entrance.

The fat man installed Spade in a green plush chair by the table, pressed a cigar upon him, held a light to it, mixed whiskey and carbonated water, put one glass in Spade's hand, and holding the other in his own, sat down facing Spade.

"Now, sir," he said, "I hope you'll let me apologize for—"

"Never mind that," Spade said. "Let's talk about the black bird."

The fat man cocked his head a little to one side and regarded Spade with fond eyes.

"All right, sir," he agreed. "Let's." He took a sip from his glass. "This is going to be the most astounding thing you've ever heard of, sir, and I say that knowing that a man of your caliber in your profession must have run across a lot of things."

Spade nodded politely.

The fat man screwed up his eyes and asked:

"What do you know, sir, about the *Order of the Hospital of St. John of Jerusalem,* later called the *Knights of Rhodes* and other things?"

Spade waved his cigar. "Not much, only what I can remember from history in school— Crusaders or something."

"Very good. Now you don't remember that Suleiman the Magnificent chased them out of Rhodes in 1523?"

"No."

"Well, sir, he did, and they settled in Crete. And they stayed there for seven years, until 1530, when they persuaded the Emperor Charles V to give them"—Gutman held up three puffy fingers and counted them—"Malta, Gozo, and Tripoli."

"Yes?"

"Yes, sir, but with these conditions: they were to pay the Emperor each year the tribute of one"—he held up a finger—"falcon in acknowledgment that Malta was still under Spain, and if they ever left the island it was to revert to Spain. Understand? He was giving it to them, but not unless they occupied it, and they couldn't give it or sell it to anybody else."

"Yes."

The fat man looked over his shoulders at the three closed doors, hunched his chair a few inches closer to Spade's, and reduced his voice to a husky whisper:

"Have you any conception of the extreme, the immeasurable wealth of the Order at that time?"

"If I remember, they were pretty well fixed," Spade said.

Gutman smiled indulgently.

"Pretty well, sir, is putting it mildly." His whisper became lower and harsher. "They were rolling in wealth, sir. You've no idea. None of us has any idea. For years they had preyed on the Saracens, had taken God only knows what spoils in gems, precious metals, silks, ivories, the top-cream luxuries of the East. That is history, sir. We all know that the Holy Wars to them, as to the Templars, were largely a matter of loot.

"Well, now, the Emperor Charles had given them Malta, and all the rent he asks is one insignificant bird per annum, just as a matter of form. What could be more natural than for these immeasurably wealthy Knights to look around for some way of showing their gratitude? Well, sir, that's exactly what they did, and they hit on the happy thought of sending Charles, for the first year's tribute, not an insignificant live bird, but a glorious falcon encrusted from head to foot with the finest jewels in their coffers. And, remember, they had fine ones, the finest out of Asia."

Gutman stopped whispering. His sleek dark eyes examined Spade's face, which was placid. The fat man asked:

"Well, sir, what do you think of that?"

"I don't know."

The fat man smiled.

"These are facts, historical facts; not schoolbook history, not Mr. Well's history, but history nonetheless." He leaned forward. "The archives of the Order from the twelfth century on are still at Malta. They are not intact, but what is there holds no less than three"—he held up three fingers—"references that can't be to anything else but this jeweled falcon. In J. Delaville Le Roulx's *Les Archives de l'Ordre de Saint-Jean* there is a reference to it, oblique to be sure, but still a reference. And the unpublished, because unfinished at the time of his death, supplement to Paoli's *Dell' origine ed instituto del sacro militar ordine* has a clear and unmistakable statement of these facts I am telling you."

"All right," Spade said.

"All right. Grand Master Villiers de l'Isle d'Adam had this foot-high jeweled bird made by Turkish slaves in the castle of St. Angelo, and sent it to Charles, who was in Spain. He sent it in a galley commanded by a French Knight named Cormier or Corvere, a member of the Order." His voice dropped to a whisper again. "It never reached Spain." He smiled with compressed lips and asked: "You know of Barbarossa, Redbeard, Khair-ed Din?"

"No."

"A famous admiral of buccaneers sailing out of Algiers then. Well, sir, he took the Knight's galley, and he took the bird. The bird went to Algiers. That's a fact. It's a fact that the French historian Pierre Dan put in one of his letters from Algiers. He wrote that the bird had been there for more than a hundred years, and that it had been carried away by Sir Francis Verney, an English adventurer who was with the Algerian buccaneers for a while, when he left Algiers. Maybe it wasn't, but Pierre Dan believed it, and that's good enough for me.

"There's nothing said about the bird in Lady Frances Verney's *Memoirs of the Verney Family during the Seventeenth Century*. I looked. And it's pretty certain that Sir Francis didn't have the bird when he died in a Messina hospital in 1615. He was stone broke. But, sir, there's no denying that the falcon *did* go to Sicily. It was there and it came into the possession of Victor Amadeus II some time after he became king in 1713, and it was one of his gifts to his wife when he married in Chambery after abdicating. That is a fact, sir. Carutti, the author of *Storia del Regno di Vittorio Amadeo II*, vouched for it.

"Maybe they—he and his wife—took it along with them to Turin when he tried to revoke his abdication. Anyhow, it turned up next in the possession of a Spaniard who had been with the army that took Naples in 1734, the father of Don Jose Monino y Redondo, Count of Floridablanca, who was Charles III's chief minister. There's nothing to show that it didn't stay in the same family until the end of the Carlist War in 1840. Then it showed up in Paris at just about the time that Paris was full of Carlists who had had to get out of Spain. One of them must have brought it with him, but whoever he was, he didn't know anything about its value. It had been painted or enameled over, the chances are during the Carlist trouble in Spain, to look like nothing more than a fairly interesting black statuette. And in that disguise, sir, it was kicked around Paris for seventy years, by private owners and dealers too stupid to see what it was under its skin.

"For seventy years, sir, this marvelous item was, as you might say, a football in the gutters of Paris, until in 1911, a Greek dealer named Charilaos Konstantinides found it in a curio shop. It didn't take Charilaos long to discover what it was, and to acquire it. No thickness of enamel could conceal value from either his eyes or nose. Well, sir, Charilaos was the man who traced most of its history, who identified it as what it is. I got wind of it, and finally got most of the story out of him, though I have been able to add a few details since.

"Charilaos was in no hurry to convert it into money at once. He knew that, enormous as its intrinsic value was, a far higher, a terrific, price could be obtained for it once its authenticity was established beyond doubt. Possibly he planned to do business with one of the modern descendants of the old order. There are, or were at that time, several: the English *Order of St. John of Jerusalem*, the Prussian *Johanniterorden*, and the Italian and German *Iangues* of the *Sovereign Order of Malta*."

The fat man raised his glass, smiled at its emptiness, and rose to fill it and Spade's.

"You begin to believe me a little?" he asked as he worked the siphon.

"I haven't said I didn't."

"No." Gutman chuckled. "But how you looked." He sat down, drank generously, and patted his mouth with a white handkerchief. "Well, sir, to keep it safe while pursuing his researches into its history, Charilaos had re-enameled the bird, apparently just as it is now.

One year to the very day after he had acquired it—that was perhaps three months after he had admitted his find to me—I picked up the *Times* in London and read that his establishment had been burglarized and him murdered. I was in Paris the next day." He shook his head sorrowfully. "The bird was gone. By Gad, sir, I was wild. I didn't believe anybody else knew about it. I didn't believe he had told anybody but me. A great quantity of stuff had been taken, which made me think that the thief had simply taken the falcon along with the rest of his plunder, not knowing what it was. Because I assure you that a thief who knew its value would not burden himself with anything else. No, sir, at least not anything less than crown jewels."

He closed his eyes and smiled complacently at an inner thought. He opened his eyes and continued:

"That was seventeen years ago. Well, sir, it took me seventeen years to locate that bird, but I did it. I wanted it, and I'm not a man that's easily discouraged when he wants something." His smile grew broad. "I wanted it, and I found it. I wanted it, and I'm going to have it." He drained his glass, dried his lips again, and returned his handkerchief to his pocket. "I traced it to the home of a Russian general, Kemidov, in a Constantinople suburb. He didn't know a thing about it. It was nothing but a black-enameled bird to him, but his natural contrariness—the natural contrariness of a Russian general—kept him from letting me have it when I made him an offer. Maybe in my eagerness I was a little clumsy, though not very. I don't know about that. But I do know I wanted it, and I was afraid this stupid soldier might begin to investigate, might chip off some of the enamel. So I sent some—ah—agents to get it. Well, sir, they got it, and I haven't got it." He stood up and carried his empty glass to the table. "But I'm going to get it. Your glass, sir."

"Then the bird doesn't belong to any of you," Spade asked, "but to a Russian named Kemidov?"

"Belong?" the fat man said jovially. "Well, sir, you might say it belonged to the King of Spain, but I don't see how you can honestly grant anybody else clear title to it, except by right of possession." He clucked. "An article of that value that has passed from hand to hand by such means is clearly the property of whoever can get hold of it."

"Then it is Miss O'Shaughnessy's now?"

"No, sir, except as my agent."

Spade said, "Oh," ironically.

Gutman, looking thoughtfully at the cork of the whiskey bottle in his hand, asked:

"There's no doubt that she has got it now?"

"Not much."

"Where?"

"I don't know exactly."

The fat man set the bottle on the table with a bang.

"But you said you did," he protested.

Spade made a careless gesture with one hand.

"I meant to say I know where to get it when the time comes."

The pink bulbs in Gutman's face arranged themselves more happily.

"And you do?" he asked.

"Yes."

"Where?"

Spade grinned and said:

"Leave that to me. That's my end."

"When?"

"When I'm ready."

The fat man pursed his lips, and, smiling with only slight uneasiness, asked: "Mr. Spade, where is Miss O'Shaughnessy now?"

"In my hands, safely put away."

Gutman smiled approvingly.

"Trust you for that, sir," he said. "Well, now, sir, before we sit down to talk prices answer me this: How soon can you, or how soon are you willing to, produce the falcon?"

"A couple of days."

The fat man nodded. "That is satisfactory. We— But I forget our nourishment." He turned to the table, poured whiskey, squirted charged water into it, set a glass at Spade's elbow and held his own aloft. "Well, sir, here's to a fair bargain and a profit large enough for both of us."

They drank. The fat man sat down. Spade asked:

"What's your idea of a fair bargain?"

Gutman held his glass to the light, looked at it as if he liked it, took another long drink, and said:

"I have two proposals to make, sir, and either is fair. Take your choice. I will give you twenty-five thousand dollars when you deliver the falcon, and another twenty-five thousand as soon as I get to New York; or I will give you one quarter—twenty-five percent—of what I realize on the falcon. There you are, sir: an almost immediate fifty thousand dollars or a vastly greater sum within, say, a couple of months."

Spade drank and asked:

"How much greater?"

"Vastly," the fat man repeated. "Will you believe me if I name the amount that seems the probable minimum?"

"Why not?"

"What would you say, sir, to half a million?"

Spade narrowed his eyes. "Then you think the dingus is worth two million?"

Gutman smiled serenely. "In your own words, why not?" he asked.

Spade emptied his glass and set it on the table. He put his cigar in his mouth, took it out, looked at it, and put it back in. His yellow-gray eyes were faintly muddy. He said:

"That's a hell of a lot of dough."

The fat man agreed: "That's a hell of a lot of dough." He leaned forward and patted Spade's knee. "That is the absolute, rock-bottom minimum, or Charilaos Konstantinides was a blithering idiot, and he wasn't."

Spade removed the cigar from his mouth again, frowned at it with distaste, and put it on the smoking stand. He shut his eyes hard, opened them again. Their muddiness had thickened.

"The—the minimum, huh? And the maximum?" he asked. An unmistakable *sh* followed the *X* in *maximum* as he pronounced it.

"The maximum?" Gutman held his empty hand out, palm up. "I refuse to guess. You'd think me crazy. I don't know. There's no telling how high it could go, sir, and that's the one and only truth about it."

Spade pulled his sagging lower lip tight against the upper. He shook his head impatiently. A sharp frightened gleam awoke in his eyes, and was smothered by the deepening muddiness.

He stood up, helping himself with his hands on the arms of the chair. He shook his head again, took an uncertain step forward, laughed thickly, and muttered: "—— damn you! The drops."

Gutman jumped up and pushed his chair back. His fat jiggled. His eyes were dark holes in a bulbous pink face.

Spade swung his head slowly from side to side until his dull eyes were, if not focused on, at least pointed at the corridor door. He took another unsteady step.

The fat man called sharply: "Wilmer!"

A door opened and the boy came in.

Spade took a third step. His face was grayish now, with jaw muscles standing out like tumors under his ears. His legs did not straighten again after his fourth step, and his muddy eyes were almost covered by their lids.

He took the fifth step.

The boy walked over and stood close to Spade, a little in front of him, but not directly between man and door. The boy's right hand was inside his coat over his heart. The corners of his mouth twitched.

Spade essayed his sixth step.

The boy's leg darted out across Spade's leg, in front. Spade tripped over the interfering leg and crashed face down on the floor.

The boy, keeping his right hand under his coat, looked down at Spade.

Spade tried to get up.

The boy drew his right foot far back, and kicked Spade's temple.

The kick rolled Spade over on his side. Once more he tried to get up, could not, and went to sleep.

The Maltese Falcon

Dashiell Hammett

PADE TRIED TO GET up, could not, and went to sleep.

When Brigid O'Shaughnessy engaged Samuel Spade and Miles Archer, private detectives, to shadow Floyd Thursby, she told them she was trying to find her sister, who had come to San Francisco from New York with Thursby. But when Archer, shadowing Thursby, was shot to death that night, and then Thursby was killed shortly afterward, she confessed to Spade that she had lied, that Thursby and she had come from Constantinople,

where, with a Levantine named Joel Cairo, they had stolen a black figure of a bird from a Russian named Kemidov. She was obviously in utter terror of someone she referred to as "G," whom she accused of Thursby's murder, and, though Spade could get little truthful information out of her, he took what money she had—five hundred dollars—and promised to shield her from both "G" and the police.

Lieutenant Dundy of the police suspected Spade of having killed Thursby to avenge his partner's death. Later, Dundy suspected him of having killed Archer, with whose wife, Iva, Spade had been on rather too-intimate terms. Iva and Archer's brother both suspected Spade of having killed Archer. Effie Perine, Spade's stenographer, thought Iva had killed her husband so she could marry Spade.

Joel Cairo came to Spade and offered him five thousand dollars for the bird. Spade arranged a meeting with Cairo and Brigid O'Shaughnessy in his apartment that night. The meeting broke up with quarrels between Cairo and Brigid and between Lieutenant Dundy and Spade. Brigid remained in Spade's apartment all night. While she slept he went to her apartment and searched it for the bird, but did not find it.

At Cairo's hotel the next morning, Spade met a boy who had tried to shadow him, and told the boy to tell "G" to get in touch with him. Later that morning Brigid came to Spade's office to tell him her apartment had been searched by someone. Spade sent her out to Effie Perine's house to stay until the trouble was over.

In response to a telephone message Spade went to see Casper Gutman, the "G" Brigid was afraid of. When Gutman learned that apparently Spade, Brigid and Cairo were all ignorant of the bird's real nature he refused to deal with him. Spade left in a rage, returning to his office to learn that Brigid had never reached Effie Perine's house. Spade learned that she had gone to the Ferry Building instead.

The boy who had shadowed Spade came to him with another invitation from Gutman. Spade went to Gutman's suite and was told that the bird was a jewel-studded gold figure made for Charles V by the *Order of the Hospital of St. John of Jerusalem* in the sixteenth century, now enameled over to conceal its value. Gutman offered Spade fifty thousand dollars in cash for the bird, but, when he learned that Spade could not deliver it to him for two or three days, he gave the private detective a drugged drink. Spade tried to get out of the suite before the drug overcame him, but was tripped by the boy. He fell, tried to get up. The boy kicked his temple.

Once more he tried to get up, could not, and went to sleep.

CHAPTER XIV
LA PALOMA

Spade, coming around the corner from the elevator at a few minutes past six o'clock in the morning, saw yellow light glowing through the frosted glass of his office door. He halted abruptly, set his lips together, looked up and down the corridor, and advanced to the door with swift, silent strides.

He put his hand on the knob and turned it with care that permitted neither rattle nor click. He turned the knob until it would turn no farther; the door was locked. Holding the knob as it was, he changed hands, taking it now in his left hand. With his right hand he took his keys from his pocket, carefully, so they would not jingle against one another. He separated the office key from the others and, smothering the others together in his palm, inserted the office key in the lock. The insertion was done without a sound. He balanced himself on the balls of his feet, filled his lungs, then clicked the door open and went in.

Effie Perine sat sleeping with her head on her forearms, her forearms on her desk. She wore her coat and had one of Spade's overcoats wrapped cape-fashion around her.

Spade blew out his breath in a muffled laugh, shut the door behind him, and crossed to the inner office door. The inner office was empty. He went over to the girl and put a hand on her shoulder.

She stirred, raised her head drowsily, and her eyelids fluttered. Suddenly she sat up straight, opening her eyes wide. She saw Spade, smiled, leaned back in her chair, and rubbed her eyes with the pointed tips of her fingers.

"So you finally got back?" she said. "What time is it?"

"Six o'clock. What are you doing here?"

She shivered, drew Spade's coat closer around her, and yawned. "You told me to stay till you came back or phoned."

"Oh, you're the sister of the boy who stood on the burning deck?"

"I wasn't going to—" She broke off and stood up, letting his coat slide down on the chair behind her. She looked with dark, excited eyes under his hat brim at his temple, and exclaimed: "Oh, your head! What happened, Sam?"

His right temple was dark and swollen.

"I don't know whether I fell or was slugged. I don't think it amounts to much, but it hurts like hell." He barely touched it with his fingers, flinched, turned his grimace into a bitter smile, and explained: "I went visiting, was fed knock-out drops, and came to twelve hours later all spread out on a man's floor."

She reached up and removed his hat from his head.

"It's terrible," she said. "You'll have to get a doctor. You can't walk around with a head like that."

"It's not so bad as it looks, except for the headache, and that might be mostly from the drops." He went to the cabinet in the corner of the office and ran cold water on a handkerchief. "Anything turn up after I left?"

"The District Attorney's office phoned. He wants to see you."

"Himself?"

"Yes, that's the way I understood it. And a boy came in with a message that Mr. Gutman would be delighted to talk to you before five-thirty, just like that."

Spade turned off the water, squeezed the handkerchief, and came away from the cabinet holding the handkerchief to his temple.

"I got that," he said. "I met the boy down-stairs, and talking to Mr. Gutman got me this."

"Is that the G. who phoned, Sam?"

"Yes."

"Well, what—?"

Spade stared through the girl and spoke as if using speech to arrange his thoughts:

"He wants something he thinks I can get. I persuaded him I could keep him from getting it if he didn't make the deal with me before five-thirty. Then—uh-huh, sure—it was after I told him he'd have to wait a couple of days that he fed me the junk. It's not likely he thought I was dead. He'd know I'd be up and around in ten or twelve hours. So maybe the answer's that he figured he could get it without my help in that time if I was fixed up so I couldn't interfere." He scowled. "I hope to —— he was wrong." His stare became less distant. "Any word from O'Shaughnessy?"

The girl shook her head no, and asked:

"Has this got anything to do with her?"

"Something."

"This thing he wants belongs to her?"

"Or to the King of Spain. Sweetheart, you've got an uncle that teaches history or something over at the university?"

"A cousin. Why?"

"If we brighten his life with an alleged histor-ical secret four centuries old, can he be trusted to keep it dark awhile?"

"Oh, yes; he's good people."

"Fine. Get your pencil and book."

She got them and sat in her chair. Spade ran more cold water on his handkerchief and, hold-ing it to his temple, stood in front of her and dic-tated the story of the falcon as he had heard it from Gutman, from Charles V's grant to the Hospitallers up to, but no further than, the enameled bird's arrival in Paris at the time of the Carlist influx. He stumbled over the names of authors and their works that Gutman had men-tioned, but managed to achieve some sort of pho-netic likeness. The rest of the history he repeated with the accuracy of a trained interviewer.

When he had finished, the girl shut her note-book and raised a flushed, smiling face to him.

"Oh, isn't this thrilling?" she said. "It's—"

"Yes, or ridiculous. Now will you take it over and read it to your cousin, and ask him what he thinks of it? Has he ever run across anything that might have some connection with it? Is it proba-ble? Is it possible, even barely possible? Or is it the bunk? If he wants more time to look it up, O.K., but get some sort of an opinion out of him now. And for God's sake make him keep it under his hat."

"I'll go right now," she said, "and you go see a doctor about that head."

"We'll have breakfast first."

"No, I'll eat over in Berkeley. I can't wait to hear what Ted thinks of this."

"Well," Spade said, "don't start boohooing if he laughs at you."

After a leisurely breakfast at the Palace, during which he read both morning papers, Spade went home, shaved, bathed, rubbed ice on his bruised temple, and put on fresh clothes.

He went to Brigid O'Shaughnessy's apartment at the Coronet. Nobody was in her apartment. Nothing had been changed in it since his last visit.

He went to the Alexandria Hotel. Gutman was not in. None of the other occupants of Gutman's suite was in. Spade learned that these other occupants were the fat man's secretary, Wilmer Cook, and his daughter Rhea, a brown-eyed fair-haired, smallish girl of seventeen, called beautiful by the hotel staff. Spade was told that the Gutman party had arrived at the hotel, from New York, ten days ago, and had not checked out.

Spade went to the Belvedere and found the hotel detective eating in the hotel café.

"Morning, Sam, sit down and bite an egg." The hotel detective stared at Spade's temple. "My God, somebody maced you plenty!"

"Thanks, I've had mine," Spade said as he sat down, and then, referring to his temple: "It looks worse than it is. How's my Cairo's conduct?"

"He went out not more than half an hour behind you yesterday, and I ain't seen him since. He didn't sleep here again last night."

"He's getting bad habits."

"Well, a fellow like that alone in a big city. Who put the slug to you, Sam?"

"It wasn't Cairo." Spade looked attentively at the small silver dome covering Luke's toast. "How's chances of giving his room a casing while he's out?"

"Can do. You know I'm willing to go all the way with you all the time." Luke pushed his coffee back, put his elbows on the table, and screwed up his eyes at Spade. "But I got a hunch you ain't going all the way with me. What's the honest-to-God on this guy, Sam? You don't have to kick back on me. You know I'm regular."

Spade lifted his eyes from the silver dome. They were clear and candid.

"Sure, you are," he said. "I'm not holding out. I gave you it straight. I'm doing a job for him, but he's got some friends that look wrong to me and I'm a little leery of him."

"The kid we chased out yesterday was one of his friends?"

"Yes, Luke, he was."

"And it was one of them that shoved Miles across?"

Spade shook his head. "Thursby killed Miles."

"And who killed him?"

Spade smiled.

"That's supposed to be a secret, but, confidentially, I did," he said, "according to the police."

Luke grunted and stood up, saying:

"You're a tough one to figure out, Sam. Come on, we'll have that look-see."

They stopped at the desk long enough for Luke to "fix it so we'll get a ring if he comes in," and then went up to Cairo's room.

Cairo's bed was smooth and trim, but paper in the wastebasket, unevenly drawn blinds, and a couple of rumpled towels in the bathroom showed that the chambermaid had not yet been in it that morning.

Cairo's luggage consisted of a square trunk, a valise, and a Gladstone bag. His bathroom cabinet was well stocked with cosmetics—boxes, cans, jars, and bottles of powders, creams, unguents, perfumes, lotions, and tonics. Two suits and an overcoat hung in the closet over three pairs of carefully treed shoes.

The valise and Gladstone bag were unlocked. Luke had the trunk unlocked by the time Spade had finished searching elsewhere.

"Blank so far," Spade said as they dug down into the trunk.

They found nothing there to interest them.

"Any particular thing we're looking for?" Luke asked as he locked the trunk again.

"No. He's supposed to have come here from Constantinople. I'd like to know if he did. I haven't seen anything that says he didn't."

"What's his racket?"

Spade shook his head. "That's something else I'd like to know." He crossed the room and bent down over the wastebasket. "Well, this is our last shot."

He took a newspaper from the basket. His eyes brightened when he saw it was the previous day's *Call*. It was folded with the classified advertising page outside. He opened it and examined that page. Nothing there stopped his eyes.

He turned the paper over and looked at the page that had been folded inside, the page that held financial and shipping news, the weather, births, marriages, and deaths. From the lower left-hand corner, a little more than two inches of the bottom of the second column had been torn out.

Immediately above the tear was a small caption, *Arrived Today*, followed by:

12:20 a.m.—Capac from Astoria.
5:05 a.m.—Helen P. Drew from
   Greenwood.
5:06 a.m.—Albarado from Bandon.

The tear passed through the next line, leaving only enough of its letters to make *from Sydney* inferable.

Spade put the *Call* down on the desk and looked into the wastebasket again. He found a small piece of wrapping paper, a piece of string, two hosiery tags, a haberdasher's sales ticket for a half dozen pair of socks, and, in the bottom of the basket, a piece of newspaper rolled into a tiny ball.

He opened the ball carefully, smoothed it out on the desk, and fitted it into the torn part of the *Call*. The fit at the sides was exact, but between the top of the crumpled fragment and the inferable *from Sydney*, half an inch was missing, suf-

ficient space to have held announcement of six or seven boats' arrival. He turned the sheet over and saw that the other side of the missing portion could have held only the meaningless corner of a stockbroker's advertisement.

Luke, leaning over Spade's shoulder, asked: "What's this all about?"

"Looks like the gent's interested in a boat."

"Well, there's no law against that, or is there?" Luke said while Spade was folding the torn page and the crumpled fragment together and putting them into his coat pocket. "You all through here now?"

"Yes. Thanks a lot, Luke. Will you give me a ring at the office as soon as he comes in?"

"Sure."

Spade went to the Business Office of the *Call*, bought a copy of the previous day's issue, opened it to the shipping news page, and compared it with the page taken from Cairo's wastebasket. The missing portion had read:

5:17 a.m.—Tahiti from Sydney and
   Papeete.
6:05 a.m.—Admiral Peoples from Astoria.
8:07 a.m.—Caddopeak from San Pedro.
8:17 a.m.—Silverado from San Pedro.
8:05 a.m.—La Paloma from Hongkong.
9:03 a.m.—Daisy Gray from Seattle.

He read the list slowly, and when he had finished he underscored Hongkong with a forefinger nail, cut the list of arrivals from the paper with his pocketknife, put the rest of the paper and Cairo's sheet into the wastebasket, and returned to his office.

He sat down at his desk, looked up a number in the telephone directory, and used the telephone:

"Kearney 1401, please . . . Where is the *Paloma*, in from Hongkong this morning, docked? . . ." He repeated the question. "Thanks."

He held the receiver hook down with his thumb for a moment, released it, and said:

"Davenport 2020, please . . . Detective bureau, please . . . Is Sergeant Polhaus there? . . . Thanks . . . Hello, Tom, this is Sam Spade. . . . Yes, I tried to get you yesterday afternoon. . . . Sure . . . Suppose you go to lunch with me. . . . Right."

He kept the receiver to his ear while his thumb worked the hook again.

"Davenport 0170, please . . . Hello, this is Samuel Spade. My secretary got a phone message yesterday that Mr. Bryan wants to see me. Will you ask him what time's most convenient for him? . . . Yes, Spade, S-p-a-d-e." A long pause. "Yes . . . Two-thirty, all right, thanks."

He called a fifth number and said:

"Hello, darling. Let me talk to Sid? . . . Hello, Sid, Sam. I've got a date with the District Attorney at half past two this afternoon. Will you give me a ring around four—there or here or both—just to see that I'm not in trouble? . . . The hell with your Saturday-afternoon golf: your job's to keep me out of jail. . . . Right, Sid. Bye."

He pushed the telephone away, yawned, stretched, felt his bruised temple, looked at his watch, and rolled and lighted a cigarette.

He smoked sleepily until Effie Perine came in.

She came in smiling, bright-eyed and rosy-faced.

"Ted says it could be," she reported, "and he hopes it is. He's going to look it up some more. He says he's not a specialist in that field, but the names and dates are all right, and at least none of your authorities or their works are out-and-out fictions. He's all excited over it."

"That's swell, as long as he doesn't get too enthusiastic to see through it if it's a lot of hooey."

"Oh, he wouldn't, not Ted! He's too good at his stuff for that."

"Uh-huh, the whole damned Perine family's wonderful," Spade said, "including you and the smudge of soot on your nose."

"He's not a Perine; he's a Christy." She bent her head to look at her nose in her vanity case mirror. "I must've got that from the fire." She scrubbed the smudge with the corner of a handkerchief.

"The Perine-Christy enthusiasm ignite Berkeley?" he asked.

She made a face at him while patting her nose with a powdered pink disc.

"There was a boat on fire when I came back. They were towing it out from the pier, and the smoke blew all over our ferryboat."

Spade put his hands on the arms of his chair.

"Were you near enough to see the name of the boat?" he asked.

"Yes. *La Paloma.* Why?"

Spade smiled ruefully.

"I'm damned if I know why, sister," he said.

CHAPTER XV
OFFICIALS

pade and Detective-sergeant Polhaus ate pickled pig's-feet at one of John's tables at the States Hof Brau.

Polhaus, balancing pale bright jelly on a fork halfway between plate and mouth, said:

"Hey, listen, Sam: forget about the other night. He was dead wrong, but you know anybody's liable to lose their head if you ride them like that."

Spade looked thoughtfully at the police detective.

"Was that what you wanted to see me about?" he asked.

Polhaus nodded, put the forkful of jelly into his mouth, swallowed it, and qualified his nod: "Mostly."

"Dundy send you?"

Polhaus made a disgusted mouth.

"You know he didn't. He's as bullheaded as you are."

Spade smiled and shook his head.

"No, he's not, Tom," he said. "He just thinks he is."

Tom scowled and chopped at his pig's foot with his knife.

"Ain't you ever going to grow up?" he grumbled. "What've you got to beef about? He didn't hurt you. You came out on top. What's the sense of making a grudge of it? You're just making a lot of grief for yourself."

Spade placed his knife and fork carefully together on his plate, and put his hands on the table beside his plate. His smile was faint and devoid of warmth.

"With every bull in town working overtime trying to pile up grief for me a little more won't hurt. I won't even know it's there."

Polhaus's ruddiness deepened. He said:

"That's a swell thing to say to me."

Spade picked up his knife and fork and began to eat. Polhaus ate.

Presently Spade asked:

"See the boat on fire in the bay?"

"I saw the smoke. Be reasonable, Sam. Dundy was wrong and he knows it. Why don't you let it go at that?"

"Think I ought to go around and tell him I hope my chin didn't hurt his fist?"

Polhaus cut savagely at his pig's foot. Spade said:

"Phil Archer been in with any more hot tips?"

"Aw, hell, Dundy didn't think you shot Miles, but what else could he do except run the lead down? You'd've done the same thing in his place, and you know it."

"Yes?" Malice glittered in Spade's eyes. "What made him think I didn't do it? What makes you think I didn't? Or don't you?"

Polhaus's ruddy face flushed again. He said:

"Thursby shot Miles."

"You think he did."

"He did. That Webley was his, all right, and the slug in Miles came out of it."

"Sure?" Spade demanded.

"Dead sure," the police detective replied in the tone of one without the least doubt. "We got

hold of a kid, a bellhop at his hotel, that had seen it in his room just that morning. He noticed it particular because he never saw one like it before. I never saw one. You say they don't make them any more. It ain't likely there'd be another around, and, anyway, if it wasn't Thursby's, what happened to his?" He started to put a piece of bread into his mouth, withdrew it, and asked: "You say you've seen them before. Where was that at?" He put the bread into his mouth.

"In England before the war."

"Sure, there you are."

Spade nodded and said:

"Then that leaves Thursby the only one I killed?"

Polhaus squirmed a little in his chair, and his face was red and shiny.

"—— sake, ain't you ever going to forget that?" he complained earnestly. "That's out. You know it as well as I do. You'd think you wasn't a dick yourself, the way you bellyache over things. I suppose you don't never pull the same stuff on anybody that we pulled on you?"

"You mean that you tried to pull on me, Tom—just tried."

Polhaus swore under his breath and attacked the remainder of his pig's foot.

Spade said:

"All right. You know it's out, and I know it's out. What does Dundy know?"

"He knows it's out."

"What woke him up?"

"Aw, Sam, he never really thought you'd—" The irony in Spade's smile checked Polhaus. He left the sentence incomplete and said: "We dug up Thursby's record."

"Yes? Who was he?"

Polhaus's shrewd small brown eyes studied Spade's face. Spade exclaimed irritably:

"I wish to God I knew half as much about this business as you smart guys think I do."

"I wish we all did," Polhaus grumbled. "Well, he was a St. Louis gunman the first we hear of him. He was picked up a lot back there for this and that, but he belonged to the Egan mob, so nothing much was ever done about any of it. I don't know how come he left that shelter, but they got him once in New York for knocking over a row of stuss games—his twist turned him up—and was in a year before Fallon sprung him. A couple of years later he did a short hitch in Joliet for pistol-whipping another twist that had given him the needle, but after that he took up with Dixie Monahan, and didn't have much trouble getting out whenever he happened to get in. That's when Dixie was almost as big a shot as Nick the Greek in Chicago gambling. This Thursby was Dixie's bodyguard, and he took the run-out with him when Dixie got in wrong with the rest of the boys over some debts he couldn't or wouldn't pay off. That was a couple of years back, about the time the Newport Beach Boating Club was shut up. I don't know if Dixie had anything to do with that. Anyway, this is the first time him or Thursby's been seen since."

"Dixie's been seen?" Spade asked.

Polhaus shook his head. "No." His small eyes became sharp, prying. "Not unless you've seen him, or know somebody's seen him."

Spade lounged back in his chair and began to make a cigarette.

"I haven't," he said mildly. "This is all new stuff to me."

"I bet you." Polhaus snorted.

Spade grinned and asked:

"Where'd you pick up all the news about Thursby?"

"Some of it's on the records. The rest—well, we got it here and there."

"From Cairo, for instance?" Now Spade's eyes held the sharp, prying gleam.

Polhaus put down his coffee cup and shook his head.

"Not a word of it. You poisoned that guy for us."

Spade laughed.

"You mean a couple of high-class sleuths like you and Dundy worked on that lily-of-the-valley all night and couldn't crack him?"

"What do you mean, all night?" Polhaus protested. "We worked on him for less than a

couple of hours, saw we wasn't getting anywheres, and let him go."

Spade laughed again and looked at his watch. He caught John's eye and asked for their check.

"I've got a date with the D.A. this afternoon," he told Polhaus while they waited for his change.

"He send for you?"

"Yes."

Polhaus pushed his chair back and stood up, a barrel-bellied tall man, solid and phlegmatic.

"You won't be doing me any favor," he said, "by telling him I've talked to you."

A lathy youth with salient ears ushered Spade into the District Attorney's office. Spade went in smiling easily, saying easily:

"Hello, Bryan."

District Attorney Bryan stood up and held his hand out across his desk. He was a blond man of medium stature, perhaps forty-five years old, with aggressive blue eyes behind black-ribboned nose glasses, the over large mouth of an orator, and a wide dimpled chin. When he said, "How do you do, Spade?" his voice was resonant with latent power.

They shook hands and sat down.

The District Attorney put his finger on one of the pearl buttons in a battery of four on his desk, said to the lathy youth who opened the door again, "Ask Mr. Thomas and Healy to come in," and then, rocking back in his chair, addressed Spade pleasantly: "You and the police haven't been hitting it off so well, have you?"

Spade made a negligent gesture with the fingers of his right hand.

"Nothing serious," he said lightly. "Dundy gets too enthusiastic."

The door opened once more to admit two men. The one to whom Spade said, "Hello, Thomas," was a sunburned stocky man of thirty with clothing and hair of a kindred unruliness. He clapped Spade on the shoulder with a freckled hand, asked, "How's tricks?" and sat down beside him. The second man was younger and colorless. He took a seat a little apart from the three and balanced a stenographer's notebook on his knee, holding a green pencil over it.

Spade glanced his way, chuckled, and asked Bryan:

"Anything I say will be used against me?"

The District Attorney smiled.

"That always holds good." He took his glasses off, looked at them, and set them on his nose again. He looked through them at Spade and asked: "Who killed Thursby?"

Spade said:

"I don't know."

Bryan rubbed his black eyeglass ribbon between thumb and fingers, and said knowingly:

"Perhaps you don't, but you certainly could make an excellent guess."

"Maybe, but I wouldn't."

The District Attorney raised his eyebrows.

"I wouldn't," Spade repeated. He was tranquil. "My guess might be excellent, or it might be crummy, but Mrs. Spade didn't raise any children dippy enough to make guesses in front of a district attorney, an assistant district attorney, and a stenographer."

"Why shouldn't you, if you've nothing to conceal?"

"Everybody," Spade blandly responded, "has something to conceal."

"And you have—?"

"My guesses, for one thing."

The District Attorney looked down at his desk, then up at Spade, settled his glasses more firmly on his nose, and said:

"If you'd prefer not having the stenographer here we can dismiss him. It was simply as a matter of convenience that I brought him in."

"I don't mind him a damned bit," Spade replied. "I'm willing to have anything I say put down, and I'm willing to sign it."

"We've no intention of asking you to sign anything," Bryan assured him. "I wish you wouldn't regard this as a formal inquiry at all. And please don't think that I've any confidence or even belief in those theories the police seem to have formed."

"No?"

"Not a particle."

Spade sighed and crossed his legs.

"I'm glad of that." He felt in his pockets for tobacco and cigarette papers. "What's your theory?"

Bryan leaned forward in his chair and his eyes were hard and shiny as the lenses over them.

"Tell me who Archer was shadowing Thursby for and I'll tell you who killed Thursby."

Spade's laugh was brief and scornful.

"You're as wrong as Dundy," he said.

"Don't misunderstand me, Spade." Bryan knocked on the desk with his knuckles. "I don't say your client killed Thursby, or had him killed, but I do say that, knowing who your client is, or was, I'll mighty soon know who killed Thursby."

Spade lighted his cigarette, removed it from his lips, blew his lungs empty of smoke, and spoke as if puzzled:

"I don't exactly get that."

"You don't? Then suppose I put it this way: where is Dixie Monahan?"

Spade's face retained its puzzled look.

"Putting it that way doesn't help much," he said. "I still don't get it."

The District Attorney took his glasses off and shook them a little for emphasis. He said:

"We know Thursby was Monahan's bodyguard, and went with him when Monahan found it wise to vanish from Chicago. We know Monahan welshed on something like two hundred thousand dollars' worth of bets when he vanished. We don't know—not yet—who his creditors were." He put his glasses on again and smiled grimly. "But we all know what's likely to happen to a gambler who welshes, and to his bodyguard, when his creditors find him. It's happened before."

Spade ran his tongue over his lips and pulled his lips back over his teeth in an ugly grin. His eyes glittered under pulled-down brows. His reddening neck bulged over the rim of his collar. His voice was low and hoarse and passionate:

"Well, what do you think? Did I kill him for his creditors? Or just find him and let them do their own killing?"

"No, no," the District Attorney protested. "You misunderstand me."

"I hope to —— I do," Spade said.

"He didn't mean that," Thomas said.

"Then what did he mean?" Spade asked.

Bryan waved a hand. "I only meant that you might have been involved in it without knowing what it was. That could—"

"I see." Spade sneered. "You don't think I'm naughty, you just think I'm dumb."

"Nonsense," Bryan insisted. "Suppose someone came to you and engaged you to find Monahan, telling you they had reason to think he was in the city. The someone might give you a completely false story—any one of a dozen or more would do—or might say he was a debtor who had run away, without giving you the details. How could you tell what was behind it? How would you know it wasn't an ordinary piece of detective work? And under those circumstances you certainly couldn't be held responsible for your part in it, unless"—his voice sank to a more impressive note, and his words came out spaced and distinct—"you made yourself an accomplice by concealing your knowledge of the murderer's identity or any information that would lead to his capture."

Anger was leaving Spade's face. No anger remained in his voice when he asked:

"That's what you meant?"

"Exactly."

"All right. Then there's no hard feelings. But you're wrong."

"Show me."

Spade shook his head. "I can't show you, now. I can tell you."

"Tell me."

"Nobody ever hired me to do anything about Dixie Monahan."

Bryan and Thomas exchanged glances. Bryan's eyes came back to Spade, and he said:

"But, by your own admission to the police, somebody did hire you to do something about Thursby, his bodyguard."

"Yes, about Thursby, his ex-bodyguard."

"Ex?"

"Yes, ex."

"You know that Thursby was no longer associated with Monahan? You know that positively?"

Spade stretched out his hand and dropped the stub of his cigarette into a tray on the desk. He spoke carelessly:

"I don't know anything positively except that my client wasn't interested in Monahan, had never been interested in Monahan. But I heard that Thursby took Monahan out to the Orient and lost him."

Again the District Attorney and his assistant exchanged glances.

Thomas, in a tone whose striving for matter-of-factness did not quite hide excitement, said:

"That opens another angle. Monahan's friends could have knocked Thursby off for ditching Monahan."

"Dead gamblers don't have any friends," Spade said.

"It opens up two new lines," Bryan said. He leaned back and stared at the ceiling for several seconds, then sat upright quickly. His orator's face was alight. "It narrows down to three things now. Number one: Thursby was killed by the gamblers Monahan had welshed on in Chicago. Not knowing Thursby had ditched Monahan—or not believing it—they killed him because he had been Monahan's associate, or to get him out of the way so they could get at Monahan, or because he had refused to lead them to Monahan. Number two: he was killed by friends of Monahan. Or number three: he sold Monahan out to his enemies and then fell out with them and they killed him."

"Or number four," Spade suggested with a cheerful smile: "he died of old age. You folks aren't serious, are you?"

The two men stared at Spade, but neither of them spoke. Spade turned his smile from one of them to the other, and shook his head in mock pity.

"You've got Arnold Rothstein on the brain," he said.

Bryan smacked the back of his right hand down into the palm of his left.

"In one of those three categories lies the solution." The power in his voice was no longer latent. His right hand, a fist except for the protruding forefinger, went up and then down to stop with a jerk when the finger was leveled at Spade's chest. "And you can give us the information that will enable us to determine the category."

Spade said, "Yes?" very slowly. His face was somber. He touched his lower lip with a finger, looked at the finger, and then scratched the back of his neck with it. Little irritable lines had appeared in his forehead. He blew his breath heavily out through his nose, and his voice was an ill-humored growl:

"You wouldn't want the kind of information I could give you, Bryan. You couldn't use it. It'd poop this gambler's-revenge scenario for you."

Bryan sat up straight and squared his shoulders. His voice was stern without bluster:

"You are not the judge of that. Right or wrong, I'm nevertheless the District Attorney."

Spade's lifted lip showed his eyetooth. "I thought this was an informal talk."

"I am a sworn officer of the law twenty-four hours a day," Bryan said, "and neither formality nor informality justifies your withholding evidence of crime from me, except of course"—he nodded meaningly—"on certain constitutional grounds."

"You mean if the information might incriminate me?" Spade asked. His voice was placid, almost amused, but his face was not. "Well, I've got grounds that suit me better than those. My clients are entitled to have their affairs kept confidential. Maybe I can be made to talk to a Grand Jury or even a Coroner's Jury, but I haven't been called before either yet, and it's a cinch I'm not going to publish any of my clients' secrets until I have to. Then again, you and the police have both accused me of being mixed up in the other night's murders. I've had trouble with both of you before. So far as I can see, my best chance of clearing myself is by bringing in the murderers, all tied up. And my only chance of ever catching them, and tying them up, and bringing them in, is in keeping away from you and the police, because neither of you show any signs of knowing what the hell it's all about."

He got up and turned his head over his shoulder to address the stenographer:

"Getting this all right, son? Or am I going too fast for you?"

The stenographer looked up at him with startled eyes and replied:

"No, sir, I'm getting it all right."

"Good work," Spade said, and turned to Bryan again. "Now if you want to go to the Board and tell them I'm obstructing justice and ask them to revoke my license, hop to it. You've tried it before and it didn't get you anything but a laugh." He picked up his hat.

Bryan began:

"Look here, you—"

Spade said:

"And I don't want any more of these informal talks. I've got nothing to tell you, and I'm —— damned tired of being called things by every crackpot on the city payroll. If you want to see me, pinch me, or subpoena me, or something, and I'll come down with my lawyer." He put his hat on his head, said, "See you at the inquest, maybe," and stalked out.

CHAPTER XVI
THE THIRD MURDER

pade went into the Hotel Sutter and telephoned the Alexandria. Gutman was not in. No member of Gutman's party was in. Spade telephoned the Belvedere. Cairo was not in, had not been in that day.

Spade went to his office.

A swart greasy man in notable clothes was waiting in the outer room. Effie Perine, indicating the swart man, said:

"This gentleman wishes to see you, Mr. Spade."

Spade smiled and bowed and opened the inner door. "Come in." Before following the man in Spade asked Effie Perine: "Any news on that other matter?"

"No, sir."

The swart man was the proprietor of a Market Street moving picture theater. He suspected one of his cashiers and a doorman of colluding to defraud him. Spade hurried him through the story, promised to "take care of it," asked for and received fifty dollars, and got rid of him in less than half an hour.

When the corridor door had closed behind the showman, Effie Perine came into the inner office. Her sunburned face was worried and questioning.

"You haven't found her?" she asked.

He shook his head and went on stroking his bruised temple lightly, in circles, with his fingertips.

"How is it?" she asked.

"All right, but I've got plenty of headache."

She went around and stood behind him, putting his hand down, stroking his temple with her thin fingers. He leaned back until the back of his head, over the chair-top, rested against her breast, and said: "You're an angel."

She bent her head forward, over his, and looked down at his face.

"You've got to find her, Sam. It's more than a day, and she—"

He stirred impatiently and interrupted her:

"I haven't got to do anything, but if you'll let me rest this damned head a minute or two I'll go out and find her."

She murmured, "Poor head," and stroked it in silence for a little while. Then she asked:

"You know where she is?"

The telephone bell rang. Spade picked up the telephone and said:

"Hello . . . Yes, Sid, it came out all right. . . . No . . . Sure. He got snotty, but so did I. . . . He's nursing a gamblers' war pipe dream. . . . Well, we didn't kiss when we parted. I declared my weight and walked out on him. . . . That's something for you to worry about. . . . Right. Bye."

He put the telephone down and leaned back in his chair again. Effie Perine came from behind him and stood at his side. She demanded:

"Do you think you know where she is, Sam?"

"I know where she went," he replied in a grudging tone.

"Where?" She was excited.

"Down to the boat you saw burning."

Her eyes opened until their brown was surrounded by white.

"You went down there." It was not a question.

"I did not," Spade said.

Effie Perine stamped her foot.

"Sam!" she cried angrily. "She may be—"

"She went down there," he said in a surly voice. "She wasn't taken. She went down there instead of to your house when she learned the boat had come in. Well, what the hell? Am I supposed to run around after my clients, begging them to let me help them?"

"But, Sam, when I told you the boat was on fire!"

"That was at noon, and I had a date with Polhaus and another with Bryan to keep."

She glared at him between tightened lids.

"Sam Spade," she said, "you're the most contemptible man God ever made when you want to be. Because she did something without confiding in you, you'd sit here and do nothing when you know she's in danger, when you know she might be—"

Spade's face flushed. He said stubbornly:

"She's pretty capable of taking care of herself. And she knows where to come when she thinks she needs help, and when it suits her."

"That's spite," the girl cried, "and that's all it is! You're sore because she did something on her own hook, without telling you. Why shouldn't she? You're not so damned honest, and you haven't been so much on the level with her that she could trust you implicitly."

Spade said:

"That's enough of that."

His tone brought a brief uneasy glint into her hot eyes, but she tossed her head and the glint vanished. Her boyish mouth was drawn taut and small. She said:

"If you don't go down there this very minute, I will, and I'll take the police down there." Her voice trembled on the last words, broke, and was thin and wailing: "Oh, Sam, go!"

He stood up cursing her. Then he said:

"——! It'll be easier on my head than sitting here listening to you squawk." He looked at his watch. "You might as well lock up and go home."

She said:

"I won't. I'm going to wait until you come back."

He said, "Do as you damned please," put his hat on, flinched, took it off, and went out carrying it in his hand.

An hour and a half later, at twenty minutes past five, Spade returned. He was cheerful. He came in asking:

"What makes you so hard to get along with, sweetheart?"

"Me?"

"Yes, you." He put a finger on the tip of Effie Perine's nose and flattened it. He put his hands under her elbows, lifted her straight up, and kissed her chin. He set her down on the floor again and asked: "Anything happen while I was gone?"

"Luke—what's his name?—at the Belvedere called up to tell you Cairo has returned. That was about half an hour ago."

Spade snapped his mouth shut, turned with a long step, and started for the door.

"Did you find her?" the girl called.

"Tell you about it when I'm back," he replied without pausing, and hurried out.

A taxicab deposited Spade at the Belvedere within ten minutes of his departure from his office. He found Luke in the lobby. The hotel detective came grinning and shaking his head to meet him.

"Fifteen minutes late," he said. "Your bird has fluttered."

Spade cursed.

"Checked out—gone, bag and baggage," Luke said. He took a battered memorandum book from a vest pocket, licked his thumb, thumbed pages, and held the book out open to Spade. "There's the number of the taxi that hauled him. I got that much for you."

"Thanks." Spade copied the number on the back of an envelope. "Any forwarding address?"

"No. He just come in carrying a big suitcase, and went upstairs and packed, and come down with his stuff, and paid his bill, and got a taxi and went without anybody hearing what he told the driver."

"How about his trunk?"

Luke's lower lip sagged.

"By God," he said, "I forgot that. Come on."

They went up to Cairo's room.

The trunk was there. It was closed, but not locked. They raised the lid. The trunk was empty.

Luke said: "What do you know about that!"

Spade did not say anything.

Spade went back to his office. Effie Perine's eyes questioned him.

"Missed him," he grumbled, and passed into his private room.

She followed him in. He sat in his chair and began to roll a cigarette. She sat on the desk in front of him and put her toes on a corner of his chair-seat.

"What about Miss O'Shaughnessy?" she demanded.

"I missed her, too," he replied, "but she had been there."

"On the *La Paloma*?"

"The *La* is a lousy combination," he said.

"Stop it. Be nice, Sam. Tell me."

He set fire to his cigarette, pocketed the lighter, patted her shins, and said:

"Yes, *La Paloma*. She got down there at a little after noon yesterday." He drew his brows down. "That means she went straight there after leaving the cab at the Ferry Building. It's only a few piers away. The Captain wasn't there. His name's Jacobi, and she asked for him by name. He was uptown on business. That would mean he didn't expect her, or not at that time, anyhow. She waited there till he came back at four o'clock. They spent the time from then till meal time in his cabin, and she ate with him."

He inhaled and exhaled smoke, turned his head aside to spit a yellow tobacco flake off his lip, and went on:

"After the meal Captain Jacobi had three more visitors. One of them was Cairo, and one was Gutman, and one was the kid who delivered Gutman's message to you yesterday. Those three came together, while Brigid was there, and the five of them did a lot of talking in the Captain's cabin. It's hard to get anything out of the crew, but they had a row, and somewhere around eleven that night a gun went off there, in the Captain's cabin. The watchman beat it down there, but the Captain met him outside and told him there was nothing the matter. There's a fresh bullet hole in one corner of the cabin, up high enough to make it likely that the bullet didn't go through anybody to get there. As far as I could learn, there was only that one shot fired. But as far as I could learn wasn't very far."

He scowled and inhaled smoke again.

"Well, they left at around midnight, the Captain and his four visitors, all together, and all of them seem to have been walking all right. I got that from the watchman. I haven't been able to get hold of the Custom House men who were on duty there then. That's all of it. The Captain hasn't been back since. He didn't keep a date this noon with some shipping agents, and they haven't found him to tell him about the fire."

"And the fire?"

Spade shrugged. "I don't know. It was discovered in the hold, aft—in the rear basement—late this morning. The chances are it got started sometime yesterday. They got it out all right, though it did damage enough. Nobody would talk about it much while the captain's away. It's the—"

The corridor door opened. Spade shut his mouth. Effie Perine jumped down from the desk, but a man opened the connecting door before she could reach it.

"Where's Spade?" he asked.

His voice brought Spade up erect and alert in his chair. It was a voice harsh and rasping with agony and with the strain of keeping two words from being smothered by the liquid bubbling that ran under and behind them.

Effie Perine, frightened, stepped out of the man's way.

He stood in the doorway with his soft dark hat crushed between his head and the top of the door-frame: he was nearly seven feet tall. A black overcoat cut long and straight like a sheath, buttoned from throat to knees, exaggerated his leanness. His shoulders stuck out, high, thin and angular. His bony face—weather-coarsened, age-lined—was the color of damp sand and was damp with sweat on cheeks and chin. His eyes were dark and bloodshot and mad above lower lids that hung down to show pink inner membrane.

Held tight against the left side of his chest by a black-sleeved forearm that ended in a yellowish claw was a brown-paper-wrapped parcel, bound with thin rope—an ellipsoid somewhat larger than an American football.

The tall man stood in the doorway and there was nothing to show that he saw Spade.

He said, "You have," and then the liquid bubbling came up in his throat and submerged whatever else he said.

He put his other hand over the hand that held the ellipsoid. Holding himself straight, rigid, and not putting his hands out to break his fall, he fell forward as a tree falls.

Spade, wooden-faced and nimble, sprang from his chair and caught the falling man. When Spade caught him the man's mouth opened and a little blood spurted out and the brown-wrapped parcel dropped from the man's hands and rolled across the floor until a foot of the desk stopped it. Then the man's knees bent, and he bent at the waist and his thin body became limber inside the sheathlike overcoat, sagging in Spade's arms so that Spade could not hold it up from the floor.

Spade lowered the man gently until he lay on the floor on his left side. The man's eyes, dark and bloodshot but not now mad, were wide open and still. His mouth was open as when blood had spurted from it, but no more blood came from it, and all his long body was as still as the floor on which it lay.

Spade said:

"Lock the door."

While Effie Perine, her teeth chattering, fumbled with the corridor door's lock, Spade knelt beside the thin man, turned him over on his back and ran a hand down inside his overcoat. When he withdrew his hand presently it came out smeared with blood. The sight of his bloody hand brought not the least nor briefest of changes in Spade's face.

Holding that hand up where it would touch nothing, he took his lighter out of his pocket with his other hand. He snapped on the flame and held the flame close to first one and then the other of the thin man's eyes. The eyes—lids, balls, irises and pupils—remained frozen, immobile.

Spade extinguished the flame and returned the lighter to his pocket. He moved on his knees around to the man's side, and using his one clean hand, unbuttoned the tubular overcoat and opened it. The inside of the overcoat was wet with blood and the double-breasted blue jacket beneath it was sodden. The jacket's lapels where they crossed over the man's chest and both sides of his coat immediately below that point were mangled as if chewed.

Spade rose and went to the washbowl in the outer office.

Effie Perine, wan and trembling and holding herself upright by means of a hand and her back against the door, whispered:

"Is—is he—?"

"Yes. He's been shot through the chest, maybe half a dozen times."

Spade began to wash his hands.

"Oughtn't we—?" she began, but he cut her short.

"It's too late for a doctor now, and I've got to think before we do anything." He finished washing his hands and began to rinse the bowl. "He couldn't have gone far with those in him. If he— Why in hell couldn't he have stood up long enough to tell us something?" He frowned at the girl, rinsed his hands again and picked up a towel. "Pull yourself together. For God's sake, don't get sick on me now." He threw the towel down and ran fingers through his hair. "We'll have a look at that bundle."

He went into the inner office again, stepped over the dead man's legs, and picked up the brown-paper-wrapped parcel. When he felt its weight his eyes glowed. He put it on his desk, turning it over so that the knotted part of the rope was uppermost. The knot was hard and tight. He took out his pocket knife and cut the rope.

The girl had left the door and, edging around the dead man with her face turned away, had come to Spade's side. As she stood there, with her hands on a corner of the desk, watching him pull the rope loose and push aside the brown paper, excitement began to supplant nausea in her face.

"Do you think it is?" she whispered.

"We'll soon know," Spade said, his big fingers busy with the inner husk of coarse gray paper, three sheets thick, that the brown paper's removal had revealed. Though his face was hard and dull his eyes were shining.

When he had put the gray paper out of his way he had an egg-shaped mass of pale excelsior wadded tight. His fingers tore the wad apart and then he had the foot-high figure of a bird, black as coal and shiny where its polish was not dulled by wood-dust and fragments of excelsior.

Spade laughed. He put a hand down on the bird, a hand whose wide-spread fingers had ownership in their curving. He put his other arm around Effie Perine and crushed her body to his.

"We've got the damned thing, angel," he said.

"Ouch! You're hurting me!"

He took his arm away from her, picked the black bird up in both hands, and shook it to dislodge clinging excelsior. Then he stepped back, holding it up in front of him, blowing dust off it, regarding it triumphantly.

Effie Perine made a horrified face and screamed, pointing at his feet.

He looked down at his feet. His last backward step had brought his left heel into contact with the dead man's hand, pinching a quarter inch of flesh at a side of the palm between heel and floor.

Spade jerked his foot away from the hand.

The telephone bell rang.

He nodded at the girl. She turned to the desk, and put the receiver to her ear. She said:

"Hello . . . Yes . . . Who? . . . Oh, yes!" Her eyes became large. "Yes . . . Yes . . . Hold the line. . . ." Her mouth suddenly stretched wide and fearful. She cried, "Hello! Hello! Hello!" into the telephone. She rattled the hook and cried, "Hello!" twice. Then she sobbed and jumped around to face Spade, who was close beside her now.

"It was Miss O'Shaughnessy!" she said wildly. "She wants you. She's in danger. She's at the Alexandria. Her voice was—oh, it was awful, Sam!—and something happened to her before she could finish. Go help her, Sam!"

Spade put the falcon on the desk and scowled gloomily.

"I've got to take care of this fellow first," he said, pointing his thumb at the thin corpse on the floor.

She beat his chest with her fists, crying:

"No, you've got to go to her. Don't you see, Sam? He had the thing that was hers, and he came to you with it. Don't you see? He was helping her, and they killed him, and now she's— Oh, you've got to go, Sam."

"All right." Spade pushed her away and bent over his desk, putting the black bird back into its nest of excelsior, bending the paper around it, working swiftly, making a larger and clumsy package. "As soon as I've gone, phone the police. Tell them how it happened, but don't drag any names in. You don't know. I got the phone call, and I told you I had to go out, but I didn't say where." He cursed the rope for being tangled, yanked it into straightness, and began to bind up the package.

"Forget this thing. Tell it as it happened, but forget he had a bundle." He chewed his lower lip. "Unless they pin you down. If they seem to know about it, you'll have to admit it. But that's not likely. If they do, then I took the bundle away with me, unopened." He finished tying the knot, and straightened up with the parcel under his left arm. "Get it straight, now. Everything happened the way it happened, but without this dingus unless they already know about it. Don't deny it—just don't mention it. And I got the phone call—not you. And you don't know anything about anybody else having any connection with this fellow. You don't know anything about him, and you can't talk about my business until you see me. Got it?"

"Yes, Sam. Who—do you know who he is?"

He grinned wolfishly.

"Uh-uh," he said, "but I'd guess he was Captain Jacobi, late master of *La Paloma*." He picked up his hat and put it on. He looked thoughtfully at the dead man and then around the room.

"Hurry, Sam," the girl begged.

"Sure," he promised absent-mindedly, "I'll hurry. Might not hurt to get those few scraps of excelsior off the floor before the police come. And maybe you ought to try to get hold of Sid. No." He rubbed his chin. "We'll leave him out of it for a while. It'll look better. I'd keep the door locked till they come." He took his hand away from his chin and rubbed her cheek.

"You're a damned good man, sister," he said, and went out.

Chapter XVII
SATURDAY NIGHT

Carrying the parcel lightly under his arm, walking briskly, with only the ceaseless shifting of his eyes denoting wariness, Spade went, partly by way of an alley and a narrow court, from his office-building to Kearney and Post streets, where he hailed a passing taxicab. The taxicab carried him to the Pickwick Stage terminal in Fifth Street.

He checked his parcel at the Parcel Room there, put the check into a stamped envelope, wrote *M. F. Holland* and a San Francisco Post Office box number on the envelope, sealed it, and dropped it into a mail box. Then he entered another taxicab and was driven to the Alexandria Hotel.

Spade went up to suite 12-C and knocked on the door.

The door was opened, when he had knocked a second time, by a small fair-haired girl in a shimmering yellow dressing gown, a small girl whose face was white and dim, and who clung desperately to the inner knob with both hands and gasped:

"You're Mr. Spade?"

Spade said, "Yes," and caught her as she swayed.

Her body arched back over his arm, and her head dropped straight back, so that her short fair hair hung down from her scalp and her slender throat was a firm curve from chin to chest.

Spade slid his supporting arm higher up her back and bent to get his other arm under her knees, but she stirred, resisting, and between parted lips that barely moved blurred words came:

"No! Ma'e me wal'!"

Spade made her walk. He kicked the door shut and he walked her up and down the green-carpeted room, from wall to wall. One of his arms around her small body—that hand under her armpit—his other hand gripping her other arm, held her erect when she stumbled, checked her swaying, kept urging her forward, but made her tottering legs bear all of her weight they could bear.

They walked across and across the floor, the girl faltering, with incoordinate steps; Spade surely, on the balls of his feet, with balance unaffected by her staggering. Her face was chalk-white and eyeless; his sullen, with eyes hardened to watch everywhere at once.

He talked to her, monotonously:

"That's the stuff. Left, right, left, right. That's the stuff. One, two, three, four, now we turn." He shook her as they turned from the wall. "Now back again. One, two, three, four. Hold your head up. That's the stuff. Good girl. Left, right, left, right. Now we turn again." He shook her again. "Walk, walk, walk, walk. One, two, three, four. That's the girl. Now we go around." He shook her, more roughly, and increased their pace. "That's the trick. Left, right, left, right. Speed it up. We're in a hurry. One, two, three . . ."

She shuddered, and swallowed audibly. Spade began to chafe her arm and side, and he bent his mouth nearer her ear.

"That's fine. You're doing fine. One, two, three, four. Faster, faster, faster, faster. That's it. Step, step, step, step. Pick them up and lay them down. That's the stuff. What'd they do, dope you? The same stuff they gave me?"

Her eyelids twitched up then for an instant over dulled golden-brown eyes, and she managed to say all of, "Yes," except the final consonant.

They walked the floor, the girl almost trotting now to keep up with Spade, Spade slapping and kneading her flesh through yellow silk with both hands, talking and talking while his eyes remained hard and aloof and watchful.

"Left, right, left, right, left, right, turn. That's the girl. One, two, three, four. Keep the chin up. That's the stuff. . . ."

Her lids lifted again, a bare fraction of an inch, and under them her eyes moved dully from side to side.

"That's fine," he said, crisply, dropping his monotone. "Keep them open! Open them wide, wide!" He shook her.

She moaned in protest, but her lids went further up, though her eyes still were without inner light.

He raised his hand and slapped her cheek half a dozen times in quick succession.

She moaned again and tried to break away from him. His arm held her, swept her along beside him from wall to wall.

"Keep walking," he ordered in a harsh voice, and then: "Who are you?"

Her, "Rhea Gutman," was thick, but intelligible.

"The daughter?"

"Yes." Now she was no farther from the final consonant than *sh*.

"Where's Brigid?"

She twisted convulsively around in his arms and caught at one of his hands with both of hers.

He pulled his hand away quickly and looked at it. Across its back was a thin red scratch, an inch and a half or more in length.

"What the hell?" he growled, and examined her hands. Her left hand was empty. In her right hand, when he opened it, lay a three-inch jade-headed steel bouquet pin. "What the hell?" he growled again, and held the pin up in front of her eyes.

When she saw the pin she whimpered and opened her dressing gown. She pushed aside the cream-colored pajama coat under it, and showed him her body below her left breast—white flesh crisscrossed with thin red lines, dotted with tiny red dots, where the pin had scratched and punctured it.

"To keep me awake . . . to walk . . . till you came . . . She said you'd come . . . were so long coming!" She swayed.

Spade tightened his arm around her and said: "Walk!"

She fought against the arm, squirming around to face him again.

"No . . . tell you . . . sleep . . . you go to her. . . ."

"Brigid?" he demanded.

"Yes . . . took her . . . Burlingame . . . 26 Ancho . . . hurry . . . too late."

Her head fell over on her shoulder.

Spade pushed her head up, roughly.

"Who took her? Your father?"

"Yes . . . Wilmer . . . Cairo . . ." She writhed, and her eyelids twitched but did not open. ". . . kill her . . ."

Her head fell over again, and again he pushed it up.

"Who shot Jacobi?"

She did not seem to hear the question. She tried pitifully to hold her head up, to open her eyes. She mumbled: "Go . . . she . . ."

He shook her brutally.

"Stay awake till the doctor comes."

Fear opened her eyes and pushed for a moment the cloudiness from her face.

"No, no," she cried thickly, "Father . . . kill me . . . swear you won't . . . he'd know . . . I did . . . for her . . . promise you won't . . . sleep . . . all right . . . morning."

He shook her again.

"You're sure you can sleep it off all right?"

"Ye'." Her head fell down.

"Where's your bed?"

She tried to raise a hand, but the effort had become too much for her before the hand pointed at anything except the floor. With a sigh of a tired child she let her whole body relax and crumple.

Spade caught her up in his arms, scooped her up as she sank, and, holding her easily against his chest, went to the nearest of the three doors.

He turned the knob far enough to release the catch, pushed the door open with his foot, and went into a passageway that ran past an open bathroom door to a bedroom. He looked into the bathroom, saw it was empty, and carried the girl into the bedroom. Nobody was there, but the clothing that was visible, and things on the chiffonier, said it was a man's room.

Spade carried the girl back to the green-carpeted room and tried the opposite door. Through it he passed into another passageway, past another empty bathroom, and into a bedroom that was feminine in its accessories.

He turned back the bedclothes and laid the girl on the bed, removed her slippers, raised her a little to slide the yellow dressing gown off, fixed a pillow under her head, and put the covers up over her.

Then he opened the room's two windows and stood with his back to them, staring at the sleeping girl. Her breathing was heavy but not troubled. He frowned and looked around, working his lips together. Twilight was dimming the room. He stood there in the weakening light for perhaps five minutes. Finally he shook his thick sloping shoulders impatiently and went out, leaving the outer door unlocked.

Spade went to the Pacific Telephone and Telegraph Company's Powell Street station and called Davenport 2020:

"Emergency Hospital, please . . . Hello, there's a girl in suite 12-C at the Alexandria Hotel who has been drugged. . . . Yes, you'd better send somebody to take a look at her. . . . Yes, this is Mr. Hooper of the Alexandria."

He put the receiver on its prong and laughed. He called another number and said:

"Hello, Frank. This is Sam Spade. . . . Can you let me have a car to go down the peninsula right away? . . . Just a couple of hours. And give me a driver that will keep his mouth shut, will you? . . . Right. Have him pick me up at John's, Ellis Street, as soon as he can make it."

He called another number, his own office's, held the receiver to his ear for a little while without saying anything, and replaced it on its hook.

He went to John's Grill, asked the waiter to hurry his order of chops, baked potato, and sliced tomatoes, ate hurriedly, and was smoking a cigarette with his coffee when a thick-set youngish man with a plaid cap set askew above pale eyes and a tough cheery face came into the Grill and to his table.

"All set, Mr. Spade. She's full of gas and raring to go."

"Swell." Spade emptied his cup and went out with the thick-set man. "Know where Ancho Avenue, or Road, or Boulevard, is in Burlingame?"

"Nope, but if she's there we can find her."

"Let's do that," Spade said as he sat beside the chauffeur in a dark Cadillac sedan. "Twenty-six is the number we want, and the sooner the better, but we don't want to pull up at the front door."

"Correct."

They rode a half dozen blocks. The chauffeur said:

"Your partner got knocked off, didn't he?"

"Uh-huh."

The chauffeur clucked. "She's a tough racket."

"Well, hack-drivers don't live forever."

"Maybe that's right," the thick-set man conceded, "but, just the same, it'll always be a surprise to me if I don't."

Spade stared ahead at nothing and thereafter, until the chauffeur became tired of making conversation, replied with uninterested yeses and noes.

At a drugstore in Burlingame the chauffeur learned how to reach Ancho Avenue.

Ten minutes later he stopped the car near a dark corner, turned off the lights, and waved his hand at the block ahead.

"There she is," he said. "She ought to be on the other side, maybe the third or fourth house."

Spade said, "Right," and got out of the car. "Keep the engine going. We might have to leave in a hurry."

He crossed the street and went up the other side.

Night had settled. Far ahead a lone streetlight burned. Warmer lights dotted the night on either side, where houses were spaced half a dozen to a block. A high thin moon was cold and feeble as the distant streetlight. A radio droned through the open window of a house on the other side of the street.

In front of the second house from the corner

Spade halted. On one of the gateposts that were massive out of all proportion to the fence flanking them, a 2 and a 6 of pale metal caught what light there was. A square white card was nailed above them. Putting his face close to the card, Spade could see it was a FOR SALE OR RENT sign.

There was no gate between the posts. Spade went up the cement walk to the house. He stood still on the walk at the foot of the porch steps for a long moment. No sound came from the house. The house was dark except for another pale square card on its door.

Spade went up to the door and listened. He could hear nothing. He tried to look through the glass of the door. There was no curtain to keep his gaze out, but inner darkness. He tip-toed to a window, and then to another. They, like the door, were uncurtained except by inner darkness. He tried both windows. They were locked. He tried the door. It was locked.

He left the porch and, stepping carefully over unfamiliar ground, walked through weeds around the house. The side windows were too high to be reached. The back door and the one back window he could reach were locked.

Spade went back to the gatepost, and, cupping the flame between his hands, held his lighter up to the FOR SALE OR RENT sign. It bore the printed name and address of a San Mateo real estate dealer, and a line penciled in blue: *Key at 31.*

Spade went back to the sedan and asked the chauffeur:

"Got a flashlight?"

"Sure." He gave it to Spade. "Can I give you a hand at anything?"

"Maybe." Spade got into the sedan. "We'll ride up to number thirty-one. You can use your lights."

Number 31 was a square gray house across the street from, but a little farther up than, 26. Lights glowed in its downstairs windows.

Spade went up on the porch and rang the bell. A dark-haired girl of fourteen or fifteen opened the door. Spade, bowing and smiling, said:

"I'd like to get the key to number twenty-six."

"I'll call Papa," she said, and went back into the house calling: "Papa."

A plump red-faced man, baldheaded and heavily mustached, appeared, carrying a newspaper.

Spade said: "I'd like to get the key to twenty-six."

The plump man looked doubtful. He said:

"The lights are not on. You couldn't see anything."

Spade patted his pocket. "I've a flashlight."

The plump man looked more doubtful. He cleared his throat uneasily and crumpled the newspaper in his hand.

Spade showed the man one of his business cards, put it back in his pocket, and said in a low voice:

"We got a tip that there might be something hidden over there."

The plump man's face and voice were eager.

"Wait a minute," he said. "I'll go over with you."

When he came back a moment later he carried a brass key attached to a yellow and red tag. Spade beckoned to the chauffeur as they passed the sedan, and the chauffeur joined them.

"Anybody been looking at the house lately?" Spade asked.

"Not that I know of," the plump man replied. "Nobody's been to me for the key in a couple of months."

The plump man marched ahead with the key until they had gone up on the porch. Then he thrust it into Spade's hand, mumbled, "Here you are," and stepped aside.

Spade unlocked the door and pushed it open. There was silence and darkness.

Holding the flashlight, dark, in his left hand, Spade went in. The chauffeur came close behind him, and then, at a little distance, the plump man followed them.

They searched the house from bottom to top, cautiously at first, then, finding nothing, boldly. The house was empty, unmistakably, and there was nothing to show that it had been visited in weeks.

Spade, saying, "That's all, thanks," and, "Good night," left the sedan in front of the Alexandria. He went into the hotel, to the desk, where a tall young man with a dark grave face said: "Good evening, Mr. Spade."

"Good evening." Spade drew the young man to one end of the desk. "These Gutmans up in 12-C—are they in?"

The young man replied, "No," darting a quick sharp glance at Spade. Then he looked away, hesitated, looked at Spade again, and murmured: "A funny thing happened a couple of hours ago. Somebody called the Emergency Hospital and told them there was a sick girl up there."

"And there wasn't?"

"Oh, no—there was nobody up there. They went out earlier in the evening."

Spade said: "Well, these practical jokers have to have their fun. Thanks."

He went to a telephone booth, called a number, and said:

"Hello . . . Mrs. Perine? . . . Is Effie there? . . . Yes, please . . . Thanks.

"Hello, angel! What's the good word? . . . Fine, fine! Hold it. I'll be out in twenty minutes. . . . Right."

Half an hour later Spade rang the doorbell of a two-story brick house in Seventh Avenue. Effie Perine opened the door. Her boyish face was tired and smiling.

"Hello, boss," she said. "Enter." Then she said in a low voice: "If Ma says anything to you, Sam, be nice to her. She's all up in the air."

Spade grinned reassuringly and patted her shoulder.

She put her hands on his arm. "Miss O'Shaughnessy?"

"No," he growled. "I ran into a plant. Are you sure it was her voice?"

"Yes."

He made an unpleasant face. "Well, it was hooey."

She took him into a bright living-room, sighed, and slumped down on one end of a Chesterfield, smiling cheerfully up at him through her weariness.

He sat beside her and asked:

"Everything went O.K.? Nothing said about the bundle?"

"Nothing. I told them what you told me to tell them, and they seemed to take it for granted that the telephone call had had something to do with him, and that you were off trying to clear it up."

"Dundy there?"

"No. Hoff and O'Gar, and some others I didn't know. I talked to the Captain, too."

"They took you down to the Hall?"

"Oh, yes, and they asked me loads of questions, but it was all—you know—routine."

Spade rubbed his palms together.

"Swell," he said, and then frowned, "though I guess they'll think up plenty outside of routine to put to me when we meet. That damned Dundy will anyway, and Bryan." He shrugged. "Anybody you know, outside of the coppers, come around?"

"Yes." She sat up straight. "That boy—the one who brought the message from Gutman—was there. He didn't come in, but the police left the corridor door open when they came in and I saw him standing there."

"You didn't say anything?"

"Oh, no. You had said not to. So I didn't pay any attention to him, and the next time I looked he was gone."

Spade grinned at her. "Damned lucky for you, sister, that the coppers got there first."

"Why?"

"He's a bad egg, that lad—poison. Was the dead man Jacobi?"

"Yes."

He pressed her hands and stood up.

"I'm going to run along. You'd better hit the hay. You're all in."

She rose.

"Sam, what is—?"

He stopped her words with a hand over her mouth.

"Keep your questions till Monday," he said. "I want to sneak out before your mother catches me and gives me hell for dragging her lamb through gutters."

Midnight was a few minutes away when Spade reached his home. He put his key into the street door's lock. Heels clicked rapidly on the sidewalk behind him. He let go the key and wheeled. Brigid O'Shaughnessy ran up the steps to him.

She put her arms around him and hung on him, panting: "Oh, I thought you'd never come!" Her face was wan, distraught, shaken by the tremors that shook her from head to foot.

With the hand not supporting her he felt for the key again, opened the door, and half lifted her inside.

"You've been waiting?" he asked.

"Yes." Panting spaced her words. "In a—doorway—up the—street."

"Make it all right?" he asked. "Or shall I carry you up?"

She shook her head against his shoulder.

"I'll be—all right—when I—get where—I can—sit down."

They rode up to Spade's floor in the elevator, and went around to his apartment. She left his arm, and stood beside him, panting, both hands to her breast, while he unlocked his door. He switched on the passageway light. They went in.

He shut the door, and with his arm around her again half-carried her toward the living-room. When they were within a step of the living-room door, the living-room light went on.

The girl cried out and clung to Spade.

Just inside the living-room door, fat Gutman stood smiling benevolently at them.

The undersized youth Gutman had called Wilmer came out of the kitchen behind them. Black pistols were gigantic in his small hands.

Cairo came out of the bathroom. He too had a pistol.

Gutman said:

"Well, sir, we're all here, as you can see. Now let's come in and sit down and be comfortable and talk."

To our readers:

I read this story just as you have read it—installment by installment. When I got this far I was as uncertain as you are how the story comes out, or who killed Archer and Thursby. I had ideas, of course, just as you probably have. It wasn't until, practically speaking, the very last word of the last installment (the installment you will read next—in the January issue) that I knew the answer; and it took me completely by surprise.

As a matter of fact, when I finished reading the last installment I was breathless and almost overwhelmed. In all of my experience I have never read a story as intense, as gripping or as powerful as this last installment. It is a magnificent piece of writing: with all the earnestness of which I am capable I tell you not to miss it.

THE EDITOR

The Maltese Falcon

Dashiell Hammett

WELL, SIR, WE'RE all here, as you can see for yourself. Now let's come in and sit down and be comfortable and talk."

When Brigid O'Shaughnessy engaged Samuel Spade and Miles Archer, private detectives, to shadow Floyd Thursby for her she told them she was trying to find her sister, who had come to San Francisco from New York with Thursby. But when Archer and Thursby were shot to death on the streets that night she confessed to Spade that she had lied, that she and Thursby had come from Constantinople, where,

with a Levantine named Joel Cairo, they had stolen a black figure of a bird from one Kemidov, a Russian general. She was obviously in utter terror of someone she called "G," whom she accused of Thursby's murder, and, though Spade could get little truthful information out of her, he took what money she had—five hundred dollars—and promised to shield her from "G" and the police.

Lieutenant Dundy of the police suspected Spade of having killed Thursby to avenge his partner's death. Later, Dundy accused him of having killed Archer, with whose wife, Iva, Spade had been on too-intimate terms. Iva and Archer's brother both apparently suspected Spade of having killed his partner. Effie Perine,

Spade's stenographer, told him she thought Iva had killed her husband so she could marry Spade.

Joel Cairo came to Spade and offered him five thousand dollars for the recovery of the black bird. Casper Gutman, the "G" of whom Brigid was afraid, and the man for whom Cairo and Brigid had been supposed to get the bird in the first place, offered Spade a much greater sum for it, and told him it was a jewel-studded gold figure made by the *Order of the Hospital of St. John of Jerusalem* for Charles V in the sixteenth century, and later enameled to conceal its value.

Brigid disappeared on her way to Effie Perine's house. Spade traced her to the waterfront and later learned that Cairo had been interested in the arrival of *La Paloma*, a boat from Hongkong. Later he learns that she, Cairo, Gutman, and the boy Wilmer met on the *Paloma* spent most of an evening there, and left at midnight with the captain. That afternoon the captain of *La Paloma* staggers into Spade's office carrying the black bird under his arm and half a dozen bullets in his chest. He dies before he can tell Spade anything.

Immediately thereafter the telephone rings and Brigid O'Shaughnessy cries over it for help, saying she is in Gutman's suite at the Alexandria Hotel. Spade checks the black bird at a parcel room, mails the check to himself, and goes to the Alexandria. Gutman's daughter is the only occupant of his suite. She tells him she has been drugged, tells him Brigid has been taken to a house in Burlingame, and collapses. Spade goes to Burlingame and finds he has been sent on a wild-goose chase.

When Spade returns to his apartment he finds Brigid waiting outside for him. He takes her in. Gutman, Cairo, and the boy Wilmer are concealed in his apartment. They cover him with their guns and Gutman says:

"Well, sir, we're all here, as you can see for yourself. Now let's come in and sit down and be comfortable and talk."

CHAPTER XVIII
THE FALL-GUY

Spade, with his arms around Brigid O'Shaughnessy, smiled meagerly over her head and said:

"Sure, we'll talk."

Gutman's bulbs jounced as he took three waddling, backward steps away from the door.

Spade and the girl went in together. The boy and Cairo followed them in. Cairo stopped in the doorway. The boy put away one of his pistols and came up close behind Spade.

Spade turned his head far around to look down over his shoulder at the boy, and said:

"Get away. You're not going to frisk me."

The boy said:

"Shut up. Stand still."

Spade's nostrils went in and out with his breathing. His voice was level:

"Get away. Put your paw on me and I'm going to make you use the gun. Ask your boss if he wants me shot up before we talk."

"Never mind, Wilmer," the fat man said. He frowned indulgently at Spade. "You are certainly a most headstrong individual. Well, let's be seated."

Spade said, "I told you I didn't like that punk," and took Brigid O'Shaughnessy to the sofa by the windows. They sat close together, her head against his left shoulder, his left arm around her shoulders.

She had stopped trembling, had stopped panting. The appearance of Gutman and his companions seemed to have robbed her of that freedom of personal movement and emotion which is animal, leaving her alive, conscious, but quiescent as a plant.

Gutman lowered himself into the padded rocking chair. Cairo chose the armchair by the table. The boy Wilmer did not sit down. He stood in the doorway where Cairo had stood, letting his one visible pistol hang down at his side, looking under curling lashes at Spade's body. Cairo put his pistol on the table beside him.

Spade took off his hat and tossed it to the

other end of the sofa. He grinned at Gutman. The looseness of his lower lip and the droop of his upper eyelids combined with the V's in his face to make his grin lewd as a satyr's.

"That daughter of yours has a nice belly," he said, "too nice to be scratched up with pins."

Gutman's smile was affable, if a bit oily.

The boy in the doorway took a short step forward, raising his pistol as far as his hip.

Everyone in the room looked at him. In the dissimilar eyes with which Brigid O'Shaughnessy and Joel Cairo looked at him there was, oddly, something identically reproving.

The boy blushed, drew back his advanced foot, straightened his legs, lowered the pistol, and stood as he had stood before, looking under lashes that hid his eyes at Spade's chest. The blush was pale enough, and lasted only an instant, but it was startling on his face that habitually was so cold and composed.

Gutman turned his sleek-eyed fat smile on Spade again. His voice was a suave purring:

"Yes, sir, that was a shame, but you must admit that it served its purpose pretty well."

Spade's brows twitched together.

"Anything would've," he said impatiently. "Naturally I wanted to see you as soon as I had the falcon. Cash customers—why not? I went to Burlingame expecting to run into this sort of meeting. I didn't know you were blundering around, half an hour late, trying to get me out the way so you could find Jacobi again before he found me."

Gutman chuckled. His chuckle seemed to hold nothing but satisfaction.

"Well, sir," he said, "in any case, here we are, having our little meeting, if that's what you wanted."

"That's what I wanted. How soon are you ready to make your first payment and take the bird off my hands?"

Brigid O'Shaughnessy sat up straight and looked at Spade with surprised blue eyes. He patted her shoulder inattentively. His eyes were steady on Gutman's. Gutman's twinkled merrily between sheltering fat-puffs.

He said, "Well, sir, as to that," and put a hand inside the breast of his coat.

Cairo, hands on thighs, leaned forward in his chair, breathing between parted soft lips. His dark eyes had the surface shine of lacquer. They shifted their focus warily from Spade's face to Gutman's, from Gutman's to Spade's.

Gutman repeated, "Well, sir, as to that," and took a white envelope from his pocket.

Ten eyes—the boy's now only half hidden by his lashes—looked at the envelope.

Turning the envelope over in his swollen hands, Gutman studied for a thoughtful moment its blank white front and then its back, unsealed, with the flap tucked in. He raised his head, smiled amiably, and scaled the envelope at Spade's lap.

The envelope, though not bulky, had sufficient weight to fly true. It struck the lower part of Spade's chest and dropped down on his thighs. He picked it up deliberately and opened it deliberately, using both hands, having taken his left arm from around the girl. The contents of the envelope were thousand-dollar bills, smooth and stiff and new. Spade took them out and counted them. There were ten of them. Spade looked up smiling. He said mildly:

"We were talking about more money than this."

"Yes, sir, we were," Gutman agreed, "but we were talking then. This is actual money, genuine coin of the realm, sir. With a dollar of this you can buy more than ten dollars' worth of talk." He shook his bulbs with silent laughter. Then the commotion stopped and he said, more seriously, yet not altogether seriously: "There are more of us to be taken care of now." He moved his twinkling eyes and his fat head sidewise with a little jerk to indicate Cairo. "And—well, sir, in short—the situation has changed considerably."

While Gutman talked Spade had tapped the edges of the ten bills into alignment and had returned them to their envelope, tucking the flap in over them. Now, with forearms on knees, he sat hunched forward, dangling the envelope, from a corner held tightly by finger and thumb, down between his legs. His reply to the fat man's words was careless:

"Sure. You're together now, but I've got the falcon."

Joel Cairo spoke. Ugly white hands grasping the arms of his chair, he leaned forward and said primly, in his high-pitched thin voice:

"I shouldn't think it would be necessary to remind you, Mr. Spade, that, though you may have the falcon, yet we certainly have you."

Spade grinned.

"I'm trying to not let that worry me," he said. He sat up straight, put the envelope aside—on the end of the sofa—and addressed Gutman: "We'll come back to the money later. There's another thing that's got to be taken care of. We've got to have a fall-guy."

The fat man frowned without comprehension, but before he could speak Spade was explaining:

"The police have got to have a victim, somebody they can stick for those three murders. We—"

Cairo, speaking in a brittle, excited voice, interrupted him:

"Two—only two—murders, Mr. Spade. Thursby undoubtedly killed your partner."

"All right, two," Spade growled. "What difference does that make? The point is, we've got to feed the police some—"

Now Gutman broke in, smiling complacently, talking with good-humored assurance:

"Well, sir, from what I've seen and heard of you, I don't think we'll have to bother ourselves about that. We can leave the handling of the police to you, all right. You won't need any of our help."

"If that's what you think," Spade said, "you haven't seen or heard enough."

Gutman's good humor was undisturbed. He remonstrated:

"Now, come, Mr. Spade, you can't expect us to believe at this late date that you are the least bit afraid of the police, or that you are not quite able to handle—"

Spade snorted with his throat and nose. He bent forward, resting forearms on knees again, and interrupted Gutman irritably:

"I'm not a damned bit afraid of them, and I know how to handle them. That's what I'm trying to tell you. The way to handle them is to toss them a victim, somebody they can hang the works on."

"Well, sir, I grant you that that's one way of doing it, but—"

" 'But' hell!" Spade said. "It's the only way." His eyes were hot and earnest under a reddening forehead. The bruise on his temple was liver-colored. "I know what I'm talking about. I've been through it all before, and I expect to go through it again. At one time or another I've had to tell everybody from the Supreme Court down to go to hell, and I've got away with it. I got away with it because I never let myself forget that a day of reckoning was coming. I never forget that when the day of reckoning comes I want to be all set to march into headquarters, pushing a victim in front of me, saying: 'Here, you chumps, here's your criminal.' As long as I can do that I can put my thumb to my nose and wiggle my fingers at all the laws in the book. The first time I can't do it my name's Mud. There hasn't been a first time yet. This isn't going to be it. That's flat."

Gutman's eyes flickered, and their sleekness became dubious, but he held his other features in their bulbous pink smiling complacent cast, and there was nothing of uneasiness in his voice. He said:

"That's a system that's got a lot to recommend it, sir, by Gad it has. And if it was anyway at all possible this time I'd be the first to say: 'Stick to it by all means, sir.' But this just happens to be a case where it's not practical. That's the way it is with the best of systems. There comes a time when you've got to make exceptions, and a wise man just goes ahead and makes them. Well, sir, that's just the way it is in this case, and I don't mind telling you that I think you're being very well paid for making an exception. Now maybe it will be a little more trouble to you than if you had your victim to hand over to the police, but"—he laughed and spread his hands—"you're not a man that's afraid of a little bit of trouble. You know how to manage things, and you know you'll manage to land on your feet in the end, no matter what happens." He pursed his lips, partly closing one eye. "And maybe it might be that we could add a little something more to what's in that envelope."

Spade's eyes had lost their warmth. His face was dull and lumpy.

"We'll talk about the money later," he said in a low consciously patient tone. "We're talking about the police now, or I am, and I know what I'm talking about. This is my city and my game. I could manage to land on my feet—sure, this time, but the next time I tried to put over a fast one they'd stop me so quick I'd swallow my teeth. Hell with that. You birds'll be in New York, or Constantinople, or someplace else. I'm in business here."

"But surely," Gutman began, "you can—"

"I can't," Spade said earnestly. "I won't. I mean it." He sat up straight. A pleasant smile illuminated his face, erasing its dull lumpishness. He spoke rapidly, in an agreeable, persuasive tone: "Listen to me, Gutman. I'm telling you what's best for both of us. If we don't give the police a fall-guy it's ten to one they'll get news of the falcon sooner or later. Then you'll have to duck for cover with it, no matter where you are, and that's not going to help you make your fortune off it. Give them a fall-guy, and they'll stop right there."

"Well, sir, that's just the point," Gutman replied, and still only in his eyes was uneasiness faintly apparent. "Will they stop right there? Or won't your fall-guy be a fresh clue that as likely as not will lead them straight to the falcon? And, on the other hand, wouldn't you say that they were stopped right now, and that the best thing for us to do is to leave well enough alone?"

A forked vein began to swell in Spade's forehead.

"——! You don't know what it's all about either," he said in a restrained tone. "They're not asleep, Gutman. They're lying low, waiting. Try to get that. I'm in it up to my neck, and they

know it. That's all right as long as I do something when the time comes. But it won't be all right if I don't." His voice became persuasive again. "Listen, Gutman, we've absolutely got to give them a victim. There's no way out of it. Let's give them the punk." He nodded pleasantly at the boy in the doorway. "He actually did shoot both of them—Thursby and Jacobi—didn't he? Anyway, he's made to order for the part. Let's pin the necessary evidence on him and turn him over to them."

The boy in the doorway tightened the corners of his mouth in what may have been a minute smile. Spade's proposal seemed to have no other effect on him.

Joel Cairo's dark face was openmouthed, open-eyed, yellowish, and amazed. He breathed through his mouth, his round effeminate chest rising and falling, while he gaped at Spade.

Brigid O'Shaughnessy had moved away from Spade a little and had twisted herself around on the sofa to stare at him. There was a suggestion of hysterical laughter behind the startled confusion in her face.

Gutman remained still and expressionless for a long moment. Then he decided to laugh. He laughed heartily and lengthily, not stopping until his sleek eyes had borrowed merriment from his laughter. When he stopped laughing he said:

"By Gad, sir, you're a character, that you are." He took a white handkerchief from his pocket and wiped his eyes. "Yes, sir, there's never any telling what you'll do or say next, except that it's bound to be something astonishing."

"There's nothing funny about it." Spade did not seem offended by the fat man's laughter, nor in any way impressed. He spoke in the manner of one reasoning with a recalcitrant, but not altogether unreasonable, friend. "It's our best bet. With him in their hands, the police will—"

"But, my dear man," Gutman objected, "can't you see? If I even for a moment thought of doing it— But that's ridiculous too. I feel toward Wilmer just exactly as if he were my own son. I really do. But if I even for a moment thought of doing what you propose, what in the world do you think would keep Wilmer from telling the police every last detail about the falcon and about you and me and all of us?"

Spade grinned with stiff lips.

"If we had to," he said softly, "we could have him killed resisting arrest. But we wouldn't have to go that far. Let him talk his head off. I promise you nobody'll do anything about it. That's easy enough to fix."

The pink flesh on Gutman's forehead crawled in a frown. He lowered his head, mashing his chins together over his collar, and asked: "How?" Then, with an abruptness that set all his fat bulbs to quivering and tumbling against one another, he raised his head, squirmed around to look at the boy, and laughed merrily. "What do you think of all this, Wilmer? It's funny, eh?"

The boy's eyes were cold hazel gleams under his lashes. He said in a low distinct voice: "Yes, it's funny, the —— —— —— ——."

Spade was talking to Brigid O'Shaughnessy: "How do you feel now, angel? Any better?"

"Yes, much better, only"—she reduced her voice until the last words were inaudible two feet away—"I'm frightened."

"Don't be," he said carelessly and put a hand on her round gray-stockinged knee. "Nothing very bad's going to happen. Want a drink?"

"Not now, thanks." Her voice became barely audible again. "Be careful, Sam."

Spade grinned and looked at Gutman, who was looking at him. The fat man smiled genially, saying nothing for a moment, and then asked: "How?"

Spade was stupid. "How what?"

The fat man considered more laughter necessary then, and an explanation:

"Well, sir, if you're really serious about this—this—suggestion of yours, the least we can do, in common politeness, is to hear you out. Now how are you going about fixing it so that Wilmer"—he paused here to laugh again—"won't be able to do us any harm?"

Spade shook his head.

"No," he said, "I wouldn't want to take advantage of anybody's politeness, no matter how common, like that. Forget it."

The fat man puckered up his facial bulbs.

"Now, come, come," he protested, "you make me feel decidedly uncomfortable, sir. I shouldn't have laughed, and I apologize most humbly and sincerely. I wouldn't want to seem to ridicule anything you'd suggest, Mr. Spade, regardless of how much I disagreed with you, for you must know that I have the greatest amount of respect and admiration for your astuteness. Now, mind you, I don't see how this suggestion of yours can be in any way practical—even leaving out the fact that I couldn't feel any different toward Wilmer if he was my own flesh and blood—but I'll consider it a personal favor, sir, as well as a sign that you've accepted my apology, if you'll go ahead and tell me the rest of it."

"Fair enough," Spade said. "Bryan is like most district attorneys. He's more interested in how his record will look on paper than in anything else. He'd rather drop a doubtful case than try it and have it go against him. I don't know that he ever deliberately framed anyone he believed innocent, but I can't imagine his letting himself believe them innocent if he could scrape up, or twist into shape, proof of their guilt. To be sure of convicting one man he'll let half a dozen equally guilty accomplices go free, if trying to nail them all might confuse his case.

"That's the choice we'll give him, and he'll gobble it up. He wouldn't want to know about the falcon. He'll be tickled to death to persuade himself that anything the punk tells him about it is a lot of hooey, an attempt to muddle things up. Leave that end to me. I can show him that if he starts fooling around trying to gather up everybody, he's going to have a tangled case that no jury will be able to make heads or tails of; while if he sticks to the punk he can get a conviction standing on his head."

Gutman wagged his head sidewise in a slow smiling gesture of benign disapproval.

"No, sir," he said, "I'm afraid that won't do, won't do at all. I don't see how even this district attorney of yours could link Thursby and Jacobi and Wilmer together without having to—"

"You don't know district attorneys," Spade told him. "The Thursby angle is easy. He was a gunman and so's your punk. Bryan's already got a theory about that. There'll be no catch there. Well, ——! They can only hang the punk once. Why try him for Jacobi's murder after he's been convicted of Thursby's? They just close the record by writing it up against him, and let it go at that. If, as is likely enough, he used the same gun on both of them, the bullets will match up. Everybody will be satisfied."

"Yes, but," Gutman began, and stopped to look at the boy.

The boy advanced from the doorway, walking stiff-legged, with his legs apart, until he was between Gutman and Cairo, almost in the center of the floor. He halted there, leaning forward slightly from the waist, his shoulders raised toward the front. The pistol in his hand still hung at his side, but his knuckles were white over its grip. His other hand was a small, hard fist down at his other side. The indelible youngness of his face gave an indescribably vicious, an inhuman, turn to the white-hot hatred and the cold white malevolence in his face. He said to Spade in a voice cramped by passion:

"You ——, get up on your feet and go for your heater."

Spade smiled at the boy. His smile was not broad, but the amusement in it seemed genuine and unalloyed.

The boy said: "You ——, get up and shoot it out if you've got the guts. I've taken all the riding from you I'm going to take."

The amusement in Spade's smile deepened. He looked at Gutman.

"Young Wild West," he said in a voice that matched his smile. "Maybe you'd better remind him that shooting me before you get your hands on the falcon would be bad for business."

Gutman's attempt to smile was not successful, but he kept the resultant grimace on his mottled face. He licked his dry lips with a dry tongue. His voice was too hoarse and gritty for

the paternally admonishing tone it tried to achieve.

"Now, come, Wilmer," he said, "we can't have any of that. You shouldn't let yourself attach so much importance to these things. You—"

The boy, not taking his eyes from Spade, spoke in a choked voice out the side of his mouth: "Make him lay off me, then. I'm going to plug him if he keeps it up, and there won't be anything that will stop me from doing it."

"Now, Wilmer," Gutman said, and turned to Spade. His face and voice were under control. "Your plan is, sir, as I said in the first place, not at all practical. Let's not say anything more about it."

Spade looked from one of them to the other. He had stopped smiling. His face held no expression at all.

"I say what I please," he told them.

"You certainly do," Gutman said quickly, "and that's one of the things I've always admired in you. But this matter is, as I say, not at all practical, so there's not the least bit of use of our discussing it any further, as you can see for yourself."

"I can't see it for myself," Spade argued, "and you haven't made me see it." He frowned at Gutman. "Let's get this straight. Am I wasting time talking to you? I thought this was your show. Should I do my talking to the punk? I know how to do that."

"No, sir," Gutman replied, "you're quite right in dealing with me."

Spade said: "All right. Now I've got another suggestion. It's not as good as the first one, but it's better than nothing. Want to hear it?"

"Most assuredly."

"Give them Cairo."

Cairo hastily picked his pistol up from the table beside him. He held it tight in his lap with both hands. Its muzzle pointed at the floor a little to one side of the sofa. His face had become yellowish again. His black eyes darted their gaze from face to face. The opaqueness of his eyes made them seem flat, two-dimensional.

Gutman looked as if he did not believe he could have heard what he had heard. He asked: "Do what?"

"Give the police Cairo."

Gutman seemed about to laugh, but he did not laugh. Finally he exclaimed: "Well, by God, sir!" in an uncertain voice.

"It's not as good as giving them the punk," Spade said. "Cairo's not a gunman, and he carries a .38, while Jacobi and Thursby were cut down by larger bullets. That means we'll have to go to some trouble framing him, but that's better than giving the police nobody."

Cairo cried in a voice shrill with indignation: "Suppose we give them you, Mr. Spade, or Miss O'Shaughnessy? How about that if you're so set on giving them somebody?"

Spade smiled at the Levantine and answered him calmly:

"You people want the falcon. I've got it. I'm asking for a fall-guy as part of my price. As for Miss O'Shaughnessy"—his dispassionate glance moved to her white perplexed face for a moment and then back to Cairo, and his shoulders rose and fell a fraction of an inch—"if you think she can be rigged for the part I'm perfectly willing to talk it over with you."

The girl put her hands to her throat, uttered a short, strangled cry, and edged away from him.

Cairo, his face and body twitching with excitement, exclaimed:

"You seem to forget that you are not in a position to insist on any price."

Spade laughed, a harsh, derisive snort.

Gutman said, in a voice that tried to make firmness ingratiating: "Come, now, gentlemen, let's keep our discussion on a friendly basis; but there certainly is"—he was addressing Spade—"something in what Mr. Cairo says. You must take into consideration the—"

"Like hell I must." Spade flung his words out with a brutal sort of carelessness that gave them more weight than they could have got from dramatic emphasis or from loudness. "If you kill me, how are you going to get the bird? If I know you can't afford to kill me till you have

it, how are you going to scare me into giving it to you?"

Gutman cocked his head to the left and considered these questions. His eyes twinkled between puckered lids. Presently he gave his genial answer: "Well, sir, there are other means of persuasion besides killing or threatening to kill."

"Sure," Spade agreed, "but they're not much good unless the threat of death is behind them to hold the victim down. See what I mean? If you try anything I don't like, I won't stand for it. I'll make it a matter of your having to call it off or kill me, knowing you can't afford to kill me."

"I see what you mean." Gutman chuckled. "That is an attitude, sir, that calls for the most delicate judgment on both sides, because, as you know, sir, men are likely to forget in the heat of action just what they can and can't afford and let their emotions carry them away."

Spade was all smiling blandness.

"That's the trick, from my side," he said, "to make my play strong enough that it ties you up, but not strong enough to make you mad enough to bump me off against your better judgment."

Gutman said fondly: "By Gad, sir, you're a character."

Joel Cairo jumped up from his chair and went around behind the boy and behind Gutman's chair. He bent over the back of Gutman's chair and, screening his mouth and the fat man's ear with his empty hand, whispered.

Gutman listened attentively, shutting his eyes.

Spade grinned at Brigid O'Shaughnessy. Her lips smiled feebly in response. There was no change in her eyes: they did not lose their numb, fearful stare.

Spade turned to the boy. "Two to one they're selling you out, son."

The boy did not say anything. A trembling in his knees began to shake the knees of his trousers.

Spade addressed Gutman: "I hope you're not letting yourself be influenced by the guns these pocket-edition desperadoes are waving."

Gutman opened his eyes. Cairo stopped whispering and stood erect behind the fat man's chair.

Spade continued: "I've practiced taking them away from both of them, so there'll be no trouble there. The punk is—"

In a voice choked horribly with emotion, the boy cried, "All right!" and jerked his pistol up in front of his chest.

Gutman flung a fat hand out at the boy's wrist, caught the wrist, and bore it and the gun down while Gutman's fat body was rising in haste from the rocking chair. Joel Cairo scurried around to the boy's other side and grasped his other arm. They wrestled with the boy, forcing his arms down, holding them down, while his small wiry body writhed futilely against them.

Words came out of the squirming group: fragments of the boy's incoherent speech— "right . . . go . . . —— . . . smoke"—Gutman's, "Now, now, Wilmer!" repeated many times; Cairo's, "No, please, don't," and "Don't do that, Wilmer."

Wooden-faced and dreamy-eyed, Spade got up from the sofa and went over to the group. The boy, unable to cope with the weight against him, had stopped struggling. Cairo stood partly in front of him, talking to him soothingly, still holding one of his arms.

Spade pushed Cairo aside, gently, and drove his left fist against the boy's chin. The boy's head snapped back as far as it could while his arms were held, and then sank forward. Gutman began a desperate, "Hey! Y—" Spade drove his right fist against the boy's chin.

The boy collapsed against Gutman's great round belly as Cairo dropped his other arm. Cairo sprang at Spade, clawing at his face with the curved stiff fingers of both hands.

Spade blew his breath out sharply and pushed the Levantine away. Cairo sprang at him again. Tears were in Cairo's eyes and his red lips worked angrily, forming words, but no sound came from between them. Spade laughed grimly at him, grunted, "——! You're a darb," and

cuffed the side of his face with a big open hand, knocking Cairo over against the table.

Cairo regained his balance and sprang at Spade the third time. Spade stopped him with both palms held out on long stiff arms against his face. Cairo, failing to reach Spade's face with his shorter arms, thumped Spade's arms.

"Stop it," Spade growled. "I'll hurt you."

Cairo cried, "Oh, you big coward!" and backed away from him.

Spade stooped to pick up Cairo's pistol from the floor, and then the boy's. He straightened up, holding them in his left hand, dangling them upside down by their trigger-guards from his forefinger.

Gutman had put the unconscious boy in the rocking chair, and stood looking down at him with troubled eyes in an uncertainly puckered face. Cairo was on his knees beside the chair, chafing one of the boy's limp hands.

Spade leaned over and felt the boy's chin with his fingers. "Nothing broken," he said. "We'll spread him on the sofa." He put his right arm under the boy's arm and around his back, put his left forearm under the boy's knees, lifted him without apparent effort, and carried him to the sofa.

Brigid O'Shaughnessy got up quickly and Spade laid the boy there. With his right hand Spade patted the boy's clothes, found the boy's second pistol, added it to the others in his left hand, and turned his back on the sofa. Cairo was already sitting beside the boy's head.

Spade clinked the pistols together in his hand and smiled cheerfully at Gutman.

"Well," he said, "there's our fall-guy."

Gutman's face was grayish and his eyes were troubled. He did not look at Spade. He looked at the floor and he did not say anything.

Spade said: "Don't be a damned fool again. You let Cairo whisper to you, and you held the kid while I pasted him. You can't laugh that off, and you're likely to get yourself shot trying to."

Gutman moved his feet uneasily on the rug and said nothing.

Spade said: "And the other angle to it is that you'll either say yes right now or I'll turn the falcon and the whole —— damned lot of you in."

Gutman raised his head and muttered through his teeth: "I don't like that, sir."

"You won't like it," Spade said. "Well?"

The fat man sighed and made a wry face and replied wearily: "You can have him."

Spade said: "That's swell."

CHAPTER XIX
THE RUSSIAN'S HAND

he boy lay on his back on the sofa, a small figure that was, except for its breathing, altogether corpse-like to the eye.

Joel Cairo sat beside the boy, bending over him, rubbing his cheeks and wrists, smoothing his hair back from his forehead, whispering to him, and peering anxiously down at his white, still face.

Brigid O'Shaughnessy stood in an angle made by table and wall. One of her hands was flat on the table, the other to her breast. She pinched her lower lip between her teeth and glanced furtively at Spade whenever he was not looking at her. When he looked at her she looked at Cairo and the boy.

Gutman's face had lost its troubled cast and was becoming rosy again. He had put his hands in his trouser pockets. He stood facing Spade, watching him without curiosity.

Spade, idly jingling his handful of pistols, nodded at Cairo's rounded back and asked Gutman: "It'll be all right with him?"

"I don't know," the fat man replied. "That part of it will have to be strictly up to you, sir."

Spade's smile made his V-shaped chin more salient. He said: "Cairo."

The Levantine screwed his dark, anxious face around over his shoulder.

Spade said: "Let him rest awhile. We're going to give him to the police. We ought to get the details fixed before he comes to."

Cairo asked bitterly: "Don't you think you have done enough to him without that?"

Spade said: "No."

Cairo left the sofa and went close to the fat man.

"Please don't do this thing, Mr. Gutman," he begged. "You must realize that—"

Spade interrupted him: "That's settled. The question is, what are you going to do about it? Coming in, or getting out?"

Though Gutman's smile was a little sad, even wistful in its way, he nodded his head. "I don't like it either," he told the Levantine, "but we can't help ourselves now. We really can't."

Spade asked: "What are you doing, Cairo? In or out?"

Cairo wet his lips and turned slowly to face Spade. "Suppose," he said, and swallowed. "Have I— Can I choose?"

"You can," Spade assured him seriously, "but you ought to know that if your answer is *out* we'll give you to the police with your boy-friend."

"Oh, I say, Mr. Spade," Gutman protested, "that isn't—"

"Like hell we'll let him walk out on us," Spade said. "He'll either come in or he'll go in. We can't have any loose ends hanging around." He scowled at Gutman and exclaimed irritably: "—— ——! Is this the first thing you guys ever stole? You're a fine lot of lollipops. What are you going to do next—get down and pray?" He directed his scowl at Cairo. "Well, what's the answer?"

"You give me no choice." Cairo's narrow shoulders moved in a hopeless shrug. "I come in."

"Good." Spade looked at Gutman and at Brigid O'Shaughnessy. "Sit down."

The girl sat down gingerly on the end of the sofa by the unconscious boy's feet. Gutman returned to the padded rocking-chair and Cairo to the armchair. Spade put his handful of pistols on the table and sat on the table-corner beside them. He looked at the watch on his wrist and said:

"Two o'clock. I can't get the falcon till daylight. We've got plenty of time to arrange things."

Gutman cleared his throat.

"Where is it?" he asked, and then hastily explained: "I don't really care, sir. What I had in mind was that it would be best for all concerned if we did not get out of each other's sight now until our business has been transacted." He looked at the sofa, and at Spade again, sharply. "You have the envelope?"

Spade shook his head, looking at the sofa, and then at the girl. He smiled with his eyes and said: "Miss O'Shaughnessy has it."

"Yes, I have it," she murmured, putting a hand inside her coat. "I picked it up. . . ."

"That's all right," Spade told her. "Hang on to it." He addressed Gutman: "We won't have to lose sight of each other. I can have the falcon brought here."

"An excellent idea," Gutman purred. "Then, sir, in exchange for the ten thousand dollars and Wilmer, you will give us the falcon and an hour or two of grace, so we won't be in the city when you turn him over to the authorities."

"You don't have to duck," Spade said. "It'll be airtight."

"That may be, sir, but nevertheless we'll feel a lot safer well out of the city when Wilmer is being questioned by your district attorney."

"Suit yourself," Spade replied. "I can hold him here all day if you want." He began to roll a cigarette. "Let's get the details fixed. Why did he shoot Thursby? And why and how and where did he shoot Jacobi?"

Gutman smiled indulgently, shaking his head and purring: "Now, come, sir, you can't expect that. We've given you the money and Wilmer. That is our part of the agreement."

"I do expect it," Spade said. He held his lighter to his cigarette. "A fall-guy was what I asked for, and he's not a fall-guy unless he's a cinch to take the fall. Well, to cinch that I've got to know what's what." He pulled his brows

together. "What are you squawking about? You're not going to be sitting so damned pretty if you leave him with an out."

Gutman leaned forward and wagged a fat finger at the pistols on the table beside Spade's legs.

"There's ample evidence of his guilt, sir. Both men were shot with those guns. It's a very simple matter for the police department experts to determine that the bullets that killed the men were fired from those guns. You know that—you've mentioned it yourself. And that, it seems to me, is ample proof of his guilt."

"Maybe," Spade agreed, "but the thing's more complicated than that, and I've got to know what happened so I can be sure that the parts that won't fit in are covered up."

Cairo's eyes were round and hot.

"Apparently you've forgotten that you assured us it would be a very simple affair, Mr. Spade," he said. He turned his excited dark face to Gutman. "You see! I advised you not to do this. I don't think—"

"It doesn't make a damned bit of difference what either of you think," Spade said bluntly. "It's too late for that now, and you're in too deep. Why did he kill Thursby?"

Gutman interlaced his fingers over his belly and rocked his chair. His voice, like his smile, was frankly rueful.

"You are an uncommonly difficult person to get the best of," he said. "I begin to think that we made a mistake, sir, in not letting you alone from the very first. By Gad, I do!"

Spade moved his cigarette carelessly. "You haven't done so bad. You're staying out of jail and you're getting the falcon. What do you mean?" He put his cigarette into a corner of his mouth and said around it, "Anyhow, you know where you stand now. Why did he kill Thursby?"

Gutman stopped rocking his chair. "Thursby was a notorious gunman, and Miss O'Shaughnessy's ally. We knew that removing him in just that manner would make her stop and think that perhaps she would do better to patch up her differences with us, besides leaving her without so violent a protector. You see, sir, I am being candid with you."

"Yes. Keep it up. You didn't think he might have the falcon?"

Gutman shook his head so that his round cheeks wabbled.

"We didn't think that for a minute," he replied. He smiled benevolently. "We had the advantage of knowing Miss O'Shaughnessy far too well for that and, while we didn't then know that she had left the falcon with Captain Jacobi in Hongkong, to be brought over on the *Paloma* while they took a faster boat, still we didn't think for a minute that, if only one of them knew where it was, Thursby was the one."

Spade nodded thoughtfully and asked:

"You didn't try to make a deal with him before you gave him the works?"

"Yes, sir, certainly we did. I talked to him myself that night. Wilmer had located him two days before, and had been trying to follow him to wherever he was meeting Miss O'Shaughnessy, but Thursby was too crafty for that, even if he didn't know he was being followed. So that night Wilmer went to his hotel, learned he wasn't in, and waited outside for him. I suppose Thursby returned immediately after killing your partner. Be that as it may, Wilmer brought him to see me. We could do nothing with him: he was quite determinedly loyal to Miss O'Shaughnessy. Well, sir, Wilmer followed him back to his hotel and did what he did."

Spade thought for a moment. "That sounds all right. Now Jacobi."

Gutman looked with grave eyes at Spade and said: "Captain Jacobi's death was entirely Miss O'Shaughnessy's fault."

The girl gasped, "Oh!" and put a hand to her mouth.

Spade's voice was heavy and even. "Never mind that now. How did it happen?"

After a shrewd look at Spade, Gutman smiled.

"Just as you say, sir," he said. "Well, Cairo, as you now know, got in touch with me—or rather I sent for him—after he left police headquarters the night—the morning—he was up here. We

recognized the mutual advantage of pooling forces at that time." He directed his smile at the Levantine. "Mr. Cairo is a man of nice judgment. The *Paloma* was his thought. He saw the notice of its arrival in the papers, and remembered that in Hongkong he had heard that Miss O'Shaughnessy and Jacobi had been seen together. That was when he was trying to find her there, and he thought at first that she had left on the *Paloma*, though later he learned that she hadn't. Well, sir, when he saw that in the paper, he guessed just what had happened: she had given the bird to Jacobi to bring here for her. Jacobi did not know what it was, of course. Miss O'Shaughnessy is too discreet for that."

He beamed at the girl, rocked his chair twice, and went on: "Mr. Cairo and Wilmer and I went to call on Captain Jacobi, and were fortunate enough to arrive before Miss O'Shaughnessy had left. In many ways it was a difficult interview, but finally by midnight, we had persuaded Miss O'Shaughnessy to come to terms, or so we thought. We then left the boat and set out for my hotel, where we were to pay Miss O'Shaughnessy and receive the bird. Well, sir, we, mere men, should have known better than to suppose we were capable of coping with her. *En route*, she and Captain Jacobi and the falcon slipped completely through our fingers." He laughed merrily. "By Gad, sir, it was neatly done."

Spade looked at the girl. Her eyes, large and dark with pleading, met his. He asked Gutman:

"You touched off the boat before you left?"

"Not intentionally, no, sir," the fat man replied, "though I dare say we—or Wilmer at least—were responsible for the fire. He was out trying to find the falcon while the rest of us were talking in the cabin, and he may have been careless with matches."

"That's fine," Spade said. "If any slip-up makes it necessary for us to try him for Jacobi's murder we can also hang an arson charge on him. All right. Now about the shooting?"

"Well, sir, we dashed around town all day trying to find them, and we found them late this afternoon. We weren't sure at first that we had found them. All we were sure of was that we had found Miss O'Shaughnessy's apartment, on California Street. But when we listened at the door we heard them moving inside, so we were pretty confident we had them, and rang the bell. When she asked us who we were and we told her, we heard a window going up.

"We knew what that meant, of course, so Wilmer hurried downstairs as fast as he could and around to the back of the building to cover the fire escape. And when he turned into the alley he ran right plumb smack into Jacobi running away with the falcon under his arm. That was a difficult situation to handle, but Wilmer did every bit as well as he could. He shot Jacobi, more than once, but Jacobi was too tough to either fall down or drop the falcon, and he was too close for Wilmer to keep out of his way. He knocked Wilmer down and ran. And this was in broad daylight, you understand, in the afternoon. And when Wilmer got up he could see a policeman coming up from the block below. So he had to give it up. He dodged into the open back door of the building next to the Coronet, into the street, and then in to join us, and very fortunate he was to make it safely.

"Well, sir, there we were, stumped again. Miss O'Shaughnessy had opened the door for Cairo and me after she had seen Jacobi safely out the window, and she—" He smiled at a memory. "We persuaded—that is the word, sir—her to tell us that she had told Jacobi to take the falcon to you. It looked very unlikely that he'd live to get there, even if he wasn't picked up by the police on his way, but that was the only chance we had, sir. And so, once more, we persuaded Miss O'Shaughnessy to give us a little assistance. We had her phone you in an attempt to draw you away from your office before Jacobi got there, and we sent Wilmer after him. Unfortunately, it had taken us too long to decide, and too long to persuade Miss O'Shaughnessy to—"

The boy on the sofa groaned and rolled over on his side. His eyes opened and closed several times. The girl stood up and moved into the angle of table and wall again.

"—to co-operate with us," Gutman concluded hurriedly, "and so you had the falcon before we could reach you."

The boy put one foot down on the floor, raised himself on an elbow, opened his eyes wide, put the other foot down, sat up, and looked around. When his eyes focused on Spade, bewilderment went out of them.

Cairo left the armchair and went over to the boy; he put his arm on the boy's shoulder and started to say something.

The boy rose to his feet quickly, shaking the arm off his shoulder. He glanced around the room once and then fixed his eyes on Spade again. His face was set hard, and he held his body so tense that it seemed drawn in and shrunken.

Spade, sitting on a corner of the table, swinging his legs carelessly, said:

"Now listen, kid: if you come over here and start cutting up I'm going to kick you in the face. Sit down and shut up and behave, and you'll last longer."

The boy looked at Gutman.

Gutman smiled benignly at him and said: "Well, Wilmer, I'm sorry to lose you indeed, and I want you to know that I couldn't be any fonder of you if you were my own son; but, well, by Gad, if you lose a son it's possible to get another—and there's only one Maltese falcon."

Spade laughed.

Cairo leaned over and muttered in the boy's ear. The boy, keeping his cold hazel eyes on Gutman's face, sat down on the sofa again. The Levantine sat beside him.

Gutman's sigh did not affect the benignity of his smile. He said to Spade: "When you're young you simply don't understand things."

Cairo had an arm around the boy's shoulder again, and was whispering to him.

Spade grinned at Gutman and addressed Brigid O'Shaughnessy: "I think it'd be swell if you'd see what you can find us to eat in the kitchen, with plenty of coffee. Will you? I don't like to leave my guests."

"Surely," she said, and started toward the door.

Gutman stopped rocking. "Just a moment, my dear." He held up a thick hand. "Hadn't you better leave the envelope in here? You don't want to get grease spots on it."

The girl's eyes questioned Spade, who said in an indifferent tone: "It's still his."

She put a hand inside her coat, took out the envelope and gave it to Spade. Spade tossed it into Gutman's lap, saying: "Sit on it if you're afraid of losing it."

"You misunderstand me," Gutman replied suavely. "It's not that at all, but business should be transacted in a businesslike manner." He opened the flap of the envelope, took out the thousand-dollar bills, counted them, and chuckled so that his belly bounced. "For instance, there are only nine bills here now." He spread them out on his fat knees and thighs. "There were ten when I handed it to you, as you well know." His smile was broad and jovial and triumphant.

Spade, looking at Brigid O'Shaughnessy, asked: "Well?"

She shook her head sidewise with emphasis. She did not say anything, though her lips moved slightly, as if she had tried to. Her face was frightened.

Spade held his hand out to Gutman, and the fat man put the money into it. Spade counted the money, nine thousand-dollar bills, and returned it to Gutman. Then Spade stood up, and his face was dull and placid. He picked up the three pistols on the table. He spoke in a matter-of-fact voice.

"I want to know about this. We"—he nodded slightly to indicate the girl—"are going in the bathroom. The door will be open, and I'll be facing it. Unless you want a three-story drop from the windows there's no way out of the room except past the bathroom door. Don't try to make it."

"Really, sir," Gutman protested, "it's not necessary, and certainly not very polite of you to threaten us in this manner. You must know that we've not the least desire to leave."

"I'll know when I'm through." Spade was patient but resolute. "This trick upsets things.

I've got to find the answer. It won't take long." He touched the girl's elbow. "Come on."

In the bathroom Brigid O'Shaughnessy found words. She put her hands up flat on Spade's chest and her face up close to his and whispered:

"I did not take that bill, Sam."

"I don't think you did," Spade said, "but I've got to know. Take your clothes off."

"You won't take my word for it?"

"No. Take your clothes off."

"I won't."

"All right. We'll go back to the other room and I'll have them taken off."

She stepped back with her hands to her mouth. Her eyes were round with horror. "You would?" she asked through her fingers.

"I will," he said. "I've got to know what happened to that bill, and I'm not going to be held up by anybody's maidenly modesty."

"Oh, it isn't that." She came close to him and put her hands on his chest again. "Can't you see that if you make me you'll—you'll be killing something?"

He did not raise his voice. "I don't know anything about that. I've got to know what happened to the bill. Take them off."

She looked at his unblinking yellow-gray eyes and her face became pink and then white again.

"Very well," she said.

He sat on the side of the bath-tub watching the opened door. No sound came from the living-room. She removed her clothes swiftly. In her mien was pride without defiance or embarrassment.

He picked up each piece and examined it with fingers as well as with eyes. He did not find the thousand-dollar bill. When he had finished, he stood up, holding her clothes out in his hands to her.

"Thanks," he said. "Now I know."

She took the clothing from him. She did not say anything. He picked up his pistols. He shut the bathroom door behind him and went into the living-room.

Gutman smiled amiably from the rocking chair. "Find it?" he asked.

Cairo, sitting beside the boy on the sofa, looked at Spade with questioning opaque eyes. The boy did not look up. He was leaning forward, head between hands, elbows on knees, staring at the floor between his feet.

Spade told Gutman: "No, I didn't find it. You palmed it."

The fat man chuckled. "I palmed it?"

"Yes," Spade said, jingling the pistols in his hand. "Do you want to say so, or do you want to stand for a frisk?"

"Stand for—?"

"You're going to admit it," Spade said, "or I'm going to search you. There's no third way."

Gutman looked up at Spade's hard face and laughed outright.

"By Gad, sir, I believe you would. I really do. You're a character, sir, if you don't mind my saying so."

"You palmed it," Spade said.

"Yes, sir, that I did." The fat man took a crumpled bill from his vest pocket, smoothed it on a wide thigh, took the envelope holding the nine bills from his coat pocket and put the smoothed bill in with the others. "I must have my little joke every now and then, and I was curious to know what you'd do in a situation of that sort. I must say you passed the test with flying colors, sir. It never occurred to me that you'd hit on such a simple and direct way of getting at the truth."

Spade sneered at him without bitterness. "That's the kind of thing I'd expect from somebody the punk's age."

Gutman chuckled.

Brigid O'Shaughnessy, dressed again except for coat and hat, came out of the bathroom, took a step toward the living-room, turned around, went back to the kitchen, and turned on the light.

Cairo edged closer to the boy on the sofa and began whispering in his ear again. The boy shrugged irritably.

Spade, looking at the pistols in his hand and then at Gutman, went out into the passageway to the closet there. He opened the door, put the pistols inside on the top of a trunk, shut the door, locked it, put the key in his pants pocket and went to the kitchen door.

Brigid O'Shaughnessy was filling an aluminum percolator.

"Find everything?" Spade asked.

"Yes," she replied in a cool voice, not raising her head. Then she set the percolator aside and came to the door. She blushed, and her eyes were large and moist and chiding. "You shouldn't have done that, Sam," she said softly.

"I had to find out, angel." He bent down, kissed her mouth lightly and returned to the living-room.

Gutman smiled at Spade and offered him the white envelope, saying: "This will soon be yours; you might as well take it now."

Spade did not take it. He sat in the armchair and said: "There's plenty of time for that. Besides, we haven't done enough talking about the money end yet. I ought to have more than ten thousand."

Gutman said: "Ten thousand dollars is a lot of money."

Spade said: "You're quoting me, but it's not all the money in the world."

"No, sir, it's not. I grant you that. But it's a lot of money to be picked up in as few days, and as easily, as you're getting it."

"You think it's been so damned easy?" Spade asked and shrugged. "Well, maybe, but that's my business."

"It certainly is," the fat man agreed. He screwed up his eyes, moved his head to indicate the kitchen, and lowered his voice. "Are you sharing with her?"

Spade said: "That's my business, too."

"It certainly is," the fat man agreed once more, "but"—he hesitated—"I'd like to give you a word of advice."

"Go ahead."

"If you don't—I dare say you'll give her some

money, in any event; but if you don't give her as much as she thinks she ought to have, my word of advice is—be careful."

Spade's eyes held a mocking light. He asked: "Bad?"

"Bad," the fat man replied.

Spade grinned and began to roll a cigarette.

Cairo, still muttering in the boy's ear, had put his arm around his shoulders again. Suddenly the boy pushed his arm away and twisted around on the sofa to face Cairo. The boy's face held anger and disgust. He made a fist of a small hand and struck the Levantine's mouth with it. Cairo cried out as a woman might have cried and drew back to the very end of the sofa. He took a silk handkerchief from his pocket and put it to his mouth. It came away daubed with blood. He put it to his mouth again and looked reproachfully at the boy. The boy snarled, "Keep away from me," and put his face between his hands again. Cairo's handkerchief released the fragrance of *chypre* in the room.

Cairo's cry had drawn Brigid O'Shaughnessy to the door.

Spade, grinning, jerked a thumb at the sofa and told her: "The course of true love. How's the food coming along?"

"It's coming," she said, and returned to the kitchen.

Spade lighted his cigarette and addressed Gutman: "Let's talk about the money."

"Willingly, sir, with all my heart," the fat man replied, "but I might as well tell you frankly right now that ten thousand is every cent I can raise."

Spade exhaled smoke. "I ought to have twenty."

"I wish you could. I'd give it to you gladly, if I had it, but ten thousand is every cent I can manage, on my word of honor."

"All right, then, call it fifteen thousand."

Gutman smiled and frowned and shook his head. "Mr. Spade, I've told you frankly and candidly and on my word of honor as a gentleman that ten thousand dollars is all the money I've got, all I can raise."

"Sure you told me that. But you didn't say positively."

Gutman laughed and said: "Positively."

Spade said gloomily: "That's not any too good, but if it's the best you can do, give it to me."

Gutman handed him the envelope. Spade counted the bills and was putting them in his pocket when Brigid O'Shaughnessy came in carrying a tray.

The boy would not eat. Cairo took a cup of coffee. The girl, Gutman, and Spade ate the scrambled eggs and bacon and toast and marmalade she had prepared, and drank two cups of coffee apiece. Then they settled down to wait the rest of the night through.

Gutman smoked a cigar and read *Celebrated Criminal Cases of America,* now and then chuckling over or commenting on the parts of its contents that he found interesting. Cairo nursed his bruised mouth and sulked on his end of the sofa. The boy sat with his head in his hands until a little after four o'clock. Then he lay down with his feet toward Cairo, turned his face to the window, and went to sleep. Brigid O'Shaughnessy, in the armchair, dozed, listened to the fat man's comments, and carried on a wide-spaced, desultory conversation with Spade.

Spade lolled and smoked cigarettes and moved, without fidgeting or nervousness, around the room. He sat sometimes on an arm of the girl's chair, on the table corner, on the floor at her feet, on a straight-backed chair. He was wide awake, cheerful and full of vigor.

At half past five he went into the kitchen and made more coffee. Half an hour later the boy stirred, awakened, and sat up yawning. Gutman looked at his watch and questioned Spade:

"Can you get it now?"

"Give me another hour."

Gutman nodded and returned his attention to his book.

At seven o'clock Spade went to the telephone and called Effie Perine's number.

"Hello, Mrs. Perine? . . . This is Mr. Spade. Will you let me talk to Effie, please? . . . Yes, it is. . . . Thanks." He whistled two lines of "En Cuba," softly. "Hello, angel. Sorry to get you up . . . Yes, very. Here's the plot: in our Holland box at the post office you'll find an envelope addressed in my scribble. There's a Pickwick Stage parcel-room check in it—for the bundle we got yesterday. Will you get the bundle and bring it to me, P.D.Q.? . . . Yes, I'm home. . . . That's the girl—hustle. . . . Bye."

The street doorbell rang at ten minutes of eight. Spade went to the telephone box and pressed the button that released the door. Gutman put down his book and rose smiling.

"You don't mind if I go to the door with you?" he asked.

"O.K.," Spade told him.

Gutman followed him to the corridor door. Spade opened it. Presently Effie Perine, carrying the brown-wrapped parcel, came from the elevator. Her boyish face was gay and excited, and she came forward quickly, almost trotting. After one quick glance she did not look at Gutman. She smiled at Spade and gave him the parcel.

He took it, saying: "Thanks a lot, lady. I'm sorry to spoil your day of rest, but this—"

"It's not the first one you've spoiled," she replied, laughing, and then, when it was apparent that he was not going to invite her in, asked: "Anything else?"

He shook his head. "No, thanks."

She said, "Bye-bye," and went back to the elevator.

Spade shut the door and carried the parcel into the living-room. Gutman's face was red and his cheeks quivered.

Cairo and Brigid O'Shaughnessy came to the table as Spade put the parcel there. They were excited. The boy rose, pale and tense, but he remained by the sofa, staring under curling lashes at the others.

Spade stepped back from the table, saying, "There you are."

Gutman's fat fingers made short work of cord and paper and excelsior, and he had the black bird in his hands.

"Ah," he said huskily, "now, after seventeen years!" His eyes were moist.

Cairo licked his red lips and worked his hands together. The girl's lower lip was between her teeth. She and Cairo, like Gutman, and like Spade and the boy, were breathing heavily. The air in the room was chilly and stale and heavy with tobacco smoke.

Gutman set the bird down on the table again and fumbled at a pocket.

"It's it," he said, "but we'll make sure."

Sweat glistened on his round cheeks. His fingers jerked as he took out a gold pocket-knife and opened it. Cairo and the girl stood close beside him, on either side. Spade stood back a little, where he could watch the boy as well as the group at the table.

Gutman turned the bird upside down and scraped an edge of its base with his knife. Black enamel came off in tiny curls, exposing blackened metal beneath. Gutman's knife blade bit into the metal, turning back a thin curved shaving. The inside of the shaving, and the narrow plane its removal had left, had the soft gray sheen of lead.

Gutman's breath hissed between his teeth. His face became turgid with hot blood. He twisted the bird around and hacked at its head. There, too, the edge of his knife bared lead. He let knife and bird bang down on the table while he wheeled to confront Spade.

"It's a fake," he said hoarsely.

Spade's face had become somber. His nod was slow, but there was no slowness in his hand's going out to catch Brigid O'Shaughnessy's wrist. He pulled her to him and grasped her chin with his other hand, raising her face roughly.

"All right," he growled down into her frightened face. "You've had *your* little joke. Now tell us about it."

She cried: "No, Sam, no! That is the one I got from Kemidov. I swear—"

Joel Cairo thrust himself between Spade and

Gutman and began to emit words in a shrill, spluttering stream:

"That's it, that's it! It was the Russian! I should have known! What a fool we thought him, and what fools he made of us!" Tears ran down the Levantine's cheeks and he danced up and down. "You bungled it!" he screamed at Gutman. "You and your stupid attempt to buy it from him! You fat fool! You let him know it was valuable, and he found out how valuable, and made a duplicate for us. No wonder we had so little trouble stealing it! No wonder he was so willing to send me off around the world looking for it! You imbecile, you bloated idiot!" He put his hands to his face and blubbered.

Gutman's jaw sagged. He blinked vacant eyes. Then he shook himself and was—by the time his bulbs had stopped jouncing—again a jovially smiling fat man.

"Come, sir," he said good-naturedly, "there's no need of going on like that. Everybody errs at times, and you may be sure that this is every bit as severe a blow to me as to anyone else. Yes, that is the Russian's hand—there's no doubt of it. Well, sir, what do you suggest? Shall we stand here and call each other names? Or shall we"— he paused, and his smile was a cherub's—"go to Constantinople?"

Now Cairo's jaw sagged while Cairo's eyes bulged. In a little while he stammered: "You are—?" Amazement that came with full comprehension seemed to rob him of further words.

Gutman patted a fat cheek gently with a fat hand. His eyes twinkled. His voice was a complacent throaty purring:

"For seventeen years I have wanted that little item, and have been trying to get it. If I must spend another year on the quest, well, sir, that will be an additional expenditure in time of only"—his lips moved silently as he calculated—"five and fifteen-seventeenths percent."

The Levantine giggled and cried: "I go with you!"

Spade suddenly released the girl's wrist and looked around the room. The boy was not there. Spade went into the passageway. The corridor door was open. Spade made a dissatisfied mouth, shut the door, and returned to the living-room.

He leaned against the door-frame and looked at Gutman. He looked at him for a long time, sourly. Then he spoke, mimicking the fat man's throaty purr:

"Well, sir, I must say you're a swell lot of thieves."

Gutman chuckled.

"We've nothing to boast of, and that's a fact, sir," he said. "But, well, we're none of us dead yet, and there's not a bit of use of thinking the world's come to an end just because we've run into a little setback." He brought his left hand from behind him and held it out at Spade, pink smooth hilly palm up. "I'll have to ask you for that envelope, sir."

Spade did not move. His face was wooden. He said:

"I held up my end. You got your dingus. It's your hard luck, not mine, that it wasn't what you wanted."

"Now, come, sir," Gutman said persuasively, "we've all failed, and there's no reason for expecting any one of us to bear the brunt of it. It's simply one of those unfortunate happenings, and—" He brought his right hand from behind him. In the hand was a small pistol, an ornately engraved and inlaid affair of silver and gold and mother-of-pearl. "In short, sir, I must ask you to return my ten thousand dollars."

Spade's face did not change. He shrugged phlegmatically and took the envelope from his pocket. He started to hold it out to Gutman, hesitated, opened the envelope and took out one thousand-dollar bill. He put that bill into his pants pocket. He tucked the envelope's flap in over the other bills and held them out to Gutman.

"That'll take care of my time and expenses," he said.

Gutman, after a little pause, imitated Spade's shrug and accepted the envelope. He said:

"Now, sir, we will say goodbye to you, unless"—the fat puffs around his eyes crinkled— "you care to undertake the Constantinople expedition with us. You don't? Well, sir, frankly, I'd like to have you along. You're a man to my liking, a man of many resources and of nice judgment. Because we know you're a man of nice judgment we know we can say goodbye with every assurance that you'll hold the details of our little enterprise in confidence. We know we can count on you appreciating the fact that, as the situation now stands, any legal difficulties that came to us in connection with these last few days would likewise and equally come to you and the charming Miss O'Shaughnessy. You're too shrewd not to realize that, sir, I'm sure."

"I understand that," Spade replied.

"I was sure you would. I'm also sure that, now there's no alternative, you'll somehow manage the police without giving them a fall-guy."

"I'll make out all right," Spade replied.

"I was sure you would. Well, sir, the shortest farewells are the best. Adieu." He made a portly bow. "And to you, Miss O'Shaughnessy, adieu. I leave you the *rara avis* on the table as a little memento."

CHAPTER XX
IF THEY HANG YOU

or all of five minutes after the outer door had closed behind Joel Cairo and Casper Gutman, Spade, motionless, stood staring at the knob of the open living-room door. His eyes were gloomy under a forehead drawn down. The clefts at the root of his nose were deep and red. His lips protruded loosely, pouting. He drew them in to make a hard V and went to the telephone. He had not looked at Brigid O'Shaughnessy, who stood by the table looking with uneasy eyes at him.

He picked up the telephone, set it on its shelf again, and bent to look into the telephone directory hanging from a corner of the shelf. He turned the pages rapidly, found the one he wanted, ran his finger down a column, straightened up, and lifted the telephone from the shelf again.

He called a number and said:

"Hello, is Sergeant Polhaus there? . . . Will you call him, please? This is Samuel Spade." He stared into space, waiting. "Hello, Tom, I've got something for you. . . . Yes, plenty. Here it is: Thursby and Jacobi were shot by a kid named Wilmer Cook, from New York, I think." He described the boy minutely. "He's tied up with—working for—a man named Casper Gutman." He described Gutman. "That fellow Cairo you met here is in with them now also. . . . Yes, that's it. . . . Gutman and the kid have been staying at the Alexandria, suite 12-C. They've just left here, and they're blowing town, so you'll have to move quick; but I don't think they're expecting a pinch. . . . There's a girl in it, too— Gutman's daughter." He described Rhea Gutman. "Watch yourself when you go up against the kid. He's supposed to be pretty good with the gun. . . . That's right, Tom; and I've got some stuff here for you. I think I've got the guns he used. . . . Right. Step on it—and luck to you."

Spade slowly replaced receiver on prong, telephone on shelf. He licked his lips and looked down at his hands. Their palms were wet. He filled his deep chest with air. His eyes began to glitter between straightened lids. He turned and took three long, swift steps into the living-room.

Brigid O'Shaughnessy, startled by the suddenness of his approach, let her breath out in a little laughing gasp.

Spade, face to face with her, very close to her, tall, big-boned and thick-muscled, coldly smiling, hard of jaw and eye, said:

"They'll talk when they're pinched—about us. We're sitting on dynamite, and we've got only minutes to get set for the police. I can swing it if I'm sure I know what's what. Give me all of it—fast. Gutman sent you and Cairo to Constantinople?"

She started to speak, hesitated, and bit her lip.

He put a hand on her shoulder.

"—— damn you, talk!" he said. "I'm in this with you, and you're not going to gum it. Talk. He sent you to Constantinople?"

"Y-yes. He sent me. I met Joe there, and—and asked him to help me. Then we—"

"Wait. You asked Cairo to help you get it from Kemidov?"

"Yes."

"For Gutman?"

She hesitated again, squirmed under the hard, angry glare of his eyes, swallowed, and said:

"No, not then. We thought we would get it for ourselves."

"All right. Then?"

"Oh, then I began to be afraid that Joe wouldn't play fair with me, so—so I asked Floyd Thursby to help me."

"And he did. Well?"

"Well, we got it and went to Hongkong."

"With Cairo, or had he been ditched before that?"

"Yes. We left him in Constantinople, in jail—something about a check."

"Something you fixed up to hold him there?"

She looked shamefacedly at Spade and whispered: "Yes."

"Right. Now you and Thursby are in Hongkong with the bird."

"Yes, and then—I didn't know him very well—I didn't know whether I could trust him. I thought it would be safest—anyway, I met Captain Jacobi and I knew his boat was coming here, so I asked him to bring a package for me—and that was the falcon. I wasn't sure I could trust Floyd, and that was safer than running the risk of having it where he could get it."

"All right. Then you and Thursby caught one of the fast boats over. Then what?"

"Then—then I was afraid of Gutman. I knew he had people—connections—everywhere, and he'd soon know what we had done; and I was afraid he'd have learned that we had left Hongkong for San Francisco. He was in New York, and I knew if he heard that by cable, even some time after we'd left, he could get here by the time we did. And he did. I didn't know that then, but I was afraid of it, and I had to wait here until Captain Jacobi arrived. And I was afraid Gutman would find me, or find Floyd, and buy him over. That's why I came to you and Mr. Archer and asked you to watch him for—"

"That's a lie," Spade said. "You had Thursby hooked, and you knew it. He was a sucker for women. His record shows that: the only falls he ever took were over women. And, once a chump, always a chump. Maybe you didn't know his record, but you'd know you had him safe."

She blushed and looked timidly at him.

He said: "You wanted to get him out of the way before Jacobi arrived with the loot. What was your scheme?"

"I—I knew he'd left the States with a gambler, after some trouble. I didn't know what it was, but I thought that if it was anything serious and he saw a detective watching him, he'd think it was on account of the old trouble, and would be frightened into going away. I didn't think—"

"You told him he was being shadowed," Spade said confidently. "Miles hadn't many brains, but he wasn't clumsy enough to be spotted the first night."

"I told him, yes. When we went for a walk that night I pretended to discover Mr. Archer following us, and pointed him out to Floyd." She sobbed.

"But please believe, Sam, that I wouldn't have done it if I'd thought Floyd would kill him. I thought he'd be frightened into leaving the city. I didn't for a minute think he'd shoot him like that."

Spade smiled wolfishly with his lips, but not at all with his eyes. He said:

"If you thought he wouldn't you were right."

The girl's upraised face held utter astonishment.

Spade said: "Thursby didn't shoot him."

Incredulity joined the astonishment in the girl's face.

Spade said: "Miles hadn't many brains, but ——! He had had too many years' experience as a detective to be caught like that by a man he was shadowing. Up a blind alley, with his gun tucked away on his hip? Not a chance. He was as dumb as any man ought to be, but he wasn't that dumb. The only two ways out of the alley could have been watched from the edge of Bush Street over the tunnel. You'd told us Thursby was a bad actor. He couldn't have tricked Miles into the alley like that, and he couldn't have driven him in. He was dumb, but not dumb enough for that."

He ran his tongue across the inside of his lips and smiled affectionately at the girl. He said:

"But he'd have gone up there with you, angel, if he was sure nobody else was up there. You were his client, so he would have had no reason for not dropping the shadow on your say-so, and if you had caught up with him and asked him to go up there, he'd've gone. He was just dumb enough for that. He'd've licked his lips and looked you up and down and gone—and then you could have stood as close to him as you liked in the dark and put a hole through him with the gun you had got from Thursby that evening."

Brigid O'Shaughnessy shrank back from him until the edge of the table stopped her. She looked at him with horrified wide eyes and cried:

"Don't—don't talk to me like that, Sam! You know I didn't! You know—"

"Stop it." He looked at the watch on his wrist. "The police will be blowing in any minute now, and we're sitting on dynamite. Talk."

She put the back of a hand to her forehead. "Oh, why do you accuse me of such a terrible—?"

"Will you stop it?" he demanded in a low, impatient voice. "This isn't the spot for the schoolgirl manners. Listen to me. The pair of us are sitting under the gallows." He took hold of her wrists and made her stand up straight in front of him. "Talk!"

"I—I— How did you know he—he licked his lips and looked—?"

Spade laughed harshly.

"I knew Miles, but never mind that. Why did you shoot him?"

She twisted her wrists out of Spade's fingers and put her hands up around the back of his neck, pulling his head down until his mouth all but touched hers. Her body was flat against his from knees to chest. He put his arms around her, holding her tight to him. Her dark-lashed lids were half down over velvety blue eyes. Her voice was hushed, throaty:

"I didn't mean to, at first. I didn't, really. I meant what I told you, but when I saw Floyd couldn't be frightened, I—"

Spade shook her roughly. He said: "That's a lie. You asked Miles and me to handle it ourselves. You wanted to be sure the shadower was somebody you knew and who knew you, so they'd go with you. You got the gun from Thursby that day—that night. You had already rented the apartment at the Coronet. You had trunks there, and none at the hotel, and when I looked the apartment over I found a rent receipt dated five or six days before the time you told me you had moved in."

She swallowed with difficulty, and her voice was humble:

"Yes, that's a lie, Sam. I did mean to, if Floyd— I—I can't look at you and tell you this, Sam." She pulled his head farther down until her cheek was against his cheek, her mouth by his ear, and whispered: "I knew Floyd wouldn't be easily frightened, but I thought that if he knew somebody was shadowing him, either he'd— Oh, I can't say it, Sam!" She clung to him, sobbing.

Spade said: "You thought Floyd would tackle him, and one or the other would be killed. If Thursby was the one, then you were rid of him. If Miles was, then you could see that Thursby was caught, if he didn't go away then, and you'd be through with him. That it?"

"Something like that."

"And when you found that Thursby didn't mean to tackle him, you borrowed the gun from him and did it yourself. Right?"

"Y-yes."

"And then you thought Thursby would be nailed for the killing."

"Yes, and—and they'd hold him at least till after Jacobi had come and I'd had a chance to get the falcon."

"And you didn't know then—you didn't even suspect—that Gutman was here hunting for you; or you wouldn't have wanted to shake your gunman. You knew Gutman was here when you learned Thursby had been shot. Then you knew you needed another protector, so you came back to me. Right?"

"Yes, but, oh! Sweetheart, it wasn't only that. I would have come back to you sooner or later. From the first instant I saw you I knew—"

Spade said tenderly:

"You're an angel. Well, if you get a good break, you'll be out of San Quentin in twenty years, and you can come back to me then."

She took her cheek away from his, drawing her head far back to stare up at him without comprehension.

He was pale. He said tenderly: "I hope to —— they don't hang you, precious, by that sweet neck." He slid his hands up to caress her throat.

In an instant she was out of his arms, back against the table, crouching, both hands spread over her throat. Her face was wild-eyed, haggard. Her dry mouth opened and closed. She said in a small parched voice: "You're not—" She could not get more words out.

Spade's face was yellow-white now. His mouth smiled and there were smile wrinkles around his glittering eyes. His voice was soft, gentle. He said:

"I'm going to send you over. The chances are you'll get off with life. That means you'll be out again in twenty years. You're an angel. I'll be waiting for you." He cleared his throat. "If they hang you I'll always remember you."

She dropped her hands and stood erect. Her face became smooth and untroubled except for the faintest of dubious glints in her eyes. She smiled back at him, gently.

"Don't, Sam, don't say that even in fun. Oh, you frightened me for a moment! I really thought you— You know you do such wild and unpredictable things that—" She broke off, thrust her face forward, and stared deep into his eyes. Her cheeks and the flesh around her mouth shivered, and fear came back in her eyes. "What—? Sam!" She put her hands to her throat again and lost her erectness.

Spade laughed. His yellow-white face was damp with sweat and, though he held his smile, he could not keep softness in his voice. He croaked:

"Don't be silly. You're taking the fall. One of us has got to take it—after the talking Gutman and Cairo will do. They'd hang me sure. You're likely to get a better break. Well?"

"But—but, Sam! You can't! After what we've been to each other you can't—"

"Like hell I can't."

She took a long, trembling breath. "You've been playing with me? Only pretending you cared? You didn't, at all? You didn't—you don't—l-love me?"

"I think I do," Spade said. "What of it?" The muscles holding his smile in place stood out like wales. "I'm not Thursby. I'm not Jacobi. I won't play the sap for you."

"That is not just," she cried. Tears glistened in her eyes. "It's unfair. It's contemptible of you. You know it was not that. You can't say that."

"Like hell I can't," Spade said. "You came into my bed to stop me from asking questions. You led me out for Gutman and Cairo yesterday with that phoney call for help. Last night you came here with them, and waited for me outside, and came in with me. You were in my arms when the trap was sprung, so that I couldn't have gone for a gun if I'd had one on me, and couldn't have made a fight of it until too late if I had wanted to. And, if they didn't take you away with them, it was only because Gutman's got too much sense to trust you except for short periods when he has to, and because he thought I'd play the sap for you and, not wanting to do anything to hurt you, I couldn't do anything to hurt him."

Brigid O'Shaughnessy blinked her tears away. She took a step toward him and stood there looking him in the eyes, straight and proud.

"You've called me a liar," she said. "Now

you're lying. You're lying if you say that, in spite of anything I've done. Down in your heart you don't know I love you."

Spade made a short, abrupt bow. His eyes were becoming bloodshot, but there was no other change in his damp and yellowish, fixedly smiling face.

"Maybe I do," he said. "What of it? I should trust you? You who arranged that nice little trick for—for my predecessor, Thursby? You who knocked off Miles, a man you had nothing against, in cold blood, just like swatting a fly, for the sake of ruining Thursby? You who've never played square with me for half an hour at a stretch since I've known you? I should trust you? No, no, darling. I wouldn't do it, even if I could. Why should I?"

Her eyes were steady under his, and her hushed voice was steady when she replied:

"Why should you? If you have been playing with me, if you do not love me, there is no answer to that. If you did, no answer would be needed."

Blood streaked Spade's eyeballs now, and his long-held smile had become a frightful grimace. He cleared his throat huskily and said:

"Making speeches is no damned good now." He put a hand on her shoulder. The hand trembled. "I don't care who loves who. I'm not going to play the sap for you. I won't walk in Thursby's and Jacobi's and God knows who else's footsteps. You killed Miles and you're going over for it. I could have helped you by letting the others go and standing off the police the best way I could. It's too late now. I can't help you, and—I wouldn't if I could."

She put a hand on his hand on her shoulder.

"Don't help me, then," she whispered. "But don't hurt me. Let me go away now."

"No," he said. "I'm sunk if I haven't got you to hand to the police when they come. That's the only thing that can keep me from being sunk with the others."

"You won't do that for me?"

"I won't play the sap for you."

"Don't say that, please." She took his hand from her shoulder and held it to her face. "Why must you do this, Sam? Surely Mr. Archer wasn't as much to you as—"

"Miles," Spade said hoarsely, "was a —— —— —— ——. I found that out the first week we were in business together, and I intended to kick him out as soon as the year was up. You didn't do me a damned bit of harm by murdering him."

"Then what?"

Spade pulled his hand out of hers. He no longer either smiled or grimaced. His wet yellow face was set hard and deeply lined. His eyes burned madly. He said:

"Listen. This isn't a damned bit of good. You'll never understand me, but I'll try once more, and then we'll give it up. In my part of the world when your partner's killed you're supposed to do something about it. It doesn't make any difference what you thought of him. He was your partner and you're supposed to do something about it. Then it happens that we were in the detective business. Well, when one of your employees, or a partner, or anybody connected with your detective business is killed, it's bad business to let the killer get away with it. It's bad all around, bad for that one agency, and bad for every detective—bad all around. Third, I'm a detective, and expecting me to run any criminal down and then let him go free is like asking a dog to catch a rabbit and then let it go. It can be done, all right, and sometimes it is done, but it's not the natural thing."

"But—"

"Wait till I'm through and then you can talk. Fourth, no matter what I wanted to do now, it would be absolutely impossible for me to let you go now without having myself dragged in with Gutman, Cairo and the kid. Next, I've no reason in God's world to think I can trust you, and if I did this, and got away with it, you'd have something on me that you could use if you ever happened to want to. That's five of them. The sixth would be that, since I'd also have something on you, I couldn't be sure you wouldn't decide to shoot holes in *me* some day. Seventh, I don't like the idea of even thinking that there might be one chance in a hundred that you'd played me for a sucker. And eighth—but that's enough. All those on one side. Maybe some of them seem unimportant, but look at the number of them. Now on the other side we've got what? All we've got is the fact that maybe you love me and maybe I love you?"

"You know," she whispered, "whether you do or not."

"I don't. It's easy enough for me to be nuts about you." He looked hungrily from her hair to her feet and up to her eyes again. "But I don't know what that amounts to. Does anybody ever? But suppose I do: what of it? Maybe next month I won't. I've been through it before—when it lasted that long. Then what? Then I'll remember you and I'll think I played the sap. And if I did it and got sent over, as I probably would, then I'd be sure I'd been the sap. Well, if I send you over I'll be sorry as hell—I'll have some rotten nights—but that'll pass."

She raised her hands to his cheeks and drew his face down.

"Look at me," she said, "and tell me the truth. Would you have done this if the falcon had been real, and you had been paid your money?"

"What difference does that make now? Don't be too sure that I'm as crooked as I'm supposed to be. That kind of a reputation might be good business, bringing in high-priced jobs and making dealings with the enemy easier."

She looked at him, saying nothing.

He moved his shoulders slightly and said: "Well, a lot of money would have been at least one more item on the other side of the scales."

She put her face up to his face. Her mouth was partly open, with lips thrust a little out. She whispered: "If you loved me you'd need nothing more on that side."

Spade set the edges of his teeth together and said through them: "I won't play the sap for you."

She put her mouth against his, slowly, her arms around him, and came into his arms.

She was in his arms when the doorbell rang.

Spade, left arm around Brigid O'Shaughnessy, opened the corridor door. Lieutenant Dundy, Detective Sergeant Polhaus and two other detectives were there.

Spade said: "Hello, Tom. Get them?"

Polhaus said: "Got them."

"Swell. Come in. Here's another one for you." Spade pressed the girl forward. "She killed Miles. And I've got some more exhibits—the boy's guns, one of Cairo's, a black statuette that all the hell was about, and a thousand-buck bill that I was supposed to be bribed with." He looked at Dundy, drew his brows together, leaned forward to peer insolently into the Lieutenant's face, and then burst out laughing. "What the hell's the matter with your little playmate, Tom? He looks heartbroken." He laughed again. "I bet, by God, when he heard Gutman's story he thought he had me at last!"

"Cut it out, Sam," Tom grumbled. "We didn't think—"

"Like hell he didn't," Spade said merrily. "He came up here with his mouth watering, though you'd have sense enough to know I'd been stringing Gutman."

"Cut it out," Tom grumbled again, looking uneasily sidewise at his superior. "Anyways, we got it from Cairo. Gutman's dead. The kid shot him up just before we got there."

Spade nodded.

"He ought to have expected that," he said.

Effie Perine put down her newspaper and jumped up from Spade's chair when he came into the office at a little after nine o'clock Monday morning.

He said: "Morning, angel."

"Is that—what the papers have—right?" she asked.

"Yes, ma'am." He dropped his hat on the desk and sat down. His face was pasty in color, but its lines were strong and cheerful, and his eyes, though shot with blood, were clear.

The girl's brown eyes were peculiarly enlarged and there was a queer twist to her mouth. She stood beside him, staring down at him.

He raised his head, grinned, and said mockingly: "So much for your woman's intuition."

Her voice was queer as the expression on her face. "You did that, Sam, to her?"

He nodded. "Your Sam's a detective." He looked sharply at her. He put his arm around her waist, his hand on her hip. "She did kill Miles, angel," he said gently, "offhand, like that." He snapped fingers of his other hand.

She moved away from his encircling arm as if it had hurt her.

"Don't, please, don't touch me," she said brokenly. "I know—I know you're right. You're right. But don't touch me now—not now."

Spade's face became pale as his collar.

The corridor door's knob rattled. Effie Perine turned quickly and went into the outer office, shutting the door behind her. When she came in again she shut it behind her.

She said in a small, flat voice: "Iva is here."

Spade, looking down at his desk, nodded almost imperceptibly.

"Yes," he said and shivered. "Iva. Well, send her in."

Ten Carats of Lead
Stewart Sterling

STEWART STERLING, THE PSEUDONYM of Prentice Winchell (1895–1976), was born in Illinois but lived for many years in Florida. He began his career as a journalist and editor of trade publications before becoming the writer and producer of more than five hundred programs for radio, mostly mystery series, as well as writing for film and television. Among his many radio shows were *Bill Lance* (which ran on West Coast stations in 1944 and 1945) and the early series *The Eno Crime Club*, which first aired on CBS on February 9, 1931, as a five-times-a-week show; it underwent several format and title changes during its five-year run. Written by Sterling, it featured pure detective stories about Spencer Dean, known as "the Manhunter"; beginning in 1954, Sterling wrote a series of nine mysteries under the Spencer Dean pseudonym. His best-known screenplay was *Having Wonderful Crime* (1945), very loosely based on the 1943 John J. Malone novel by Craig Rice, starring Pat O'Brien, George Murphy, and Carole Landis.

Of his more than four hundred mystery stories, forty are about Chief Fire Marshall Ben Pedley, the tough investigator who hunts down arsonists with single-minded intensity; he also starred in nine novels, beginning with *Five Alarm Funeral* (1942). His other major series detectives are Gil Vine, a hotel dick at the Plaza Royale, in eight books, and department store detective Don Cadee in the Spencer Dean novels. Other Winchell pseudonyms are Jay de Bekker and Dexter St. Clair.

"Ten Carats of Lead" was published in the August 1940 issue.

Ten Carats of Lead

Stewart Sterling

It was a case for the Homicide men according to all the rules, but Mike Hansard of the headquarters hockshop squad knew it had germinated under the three gold balls of his own special province, and that it could only end when he pulled the correct "blue card" from his "suspected" file.

CHAPTER ONE

DEATH ON THE DIAMOND EXCHANGE

MIKE HANSARD STOOD just outside the door as two white-clad interns wheeled the operating carriage into the wardroom. They left the room silently without bothering to transfer the man in the short-sleeved hospital shirt to the cot.

A grave-eyed nurse touched Hansard on the sleeve. "He won't be out of it for half an hour. You might have a little while with him, then."

The plainclothesman eyed the strained, weather-beaten face on the pillow. "No chance to pull through?"

She shook her head. "An ordinary man would've died on the table. He . . ."

"Yeah." Mike's jaw was rocky. "Guy gets toughened up after twenty years on a beat. Makes it that much harder to check out."

The nurse moved quietly down the long corridor. Mike sat down on the cot.

The dying man groaned, stirred a bandaged arm uneasily. Mike had a similar bandage on his own arm, where they'd made the transfusion. But he didn't have three bullet holes in his guts, the way Tom MacReady did. Mike

The staccato bark of an automatic rifle echoed hollowly in the empty street

would have given a lot more than a pint of blood to help Tom, if he'd had the chance.

MacReady had gone to bat for him plenty of times. There was that night when Mike was new to harness, and the Cassati crowd had cornered him in a blind alley and put the lead to him. Tom hadn't even been on duty, but he'd heard the gunfire and come in blasting, just as Joe Cassati was about to dot Mike's eye. There would be a three-inch scar, somewhere on MacReady's chest, under those bandages, that the older man had carried ever since as a memento of Cassati.

Mike had been close to Tom in those rookie days. They both reported to the reserve-room in the same precinct house. Both had similar ambi-

tions. But Mike had passed his qualifying examinations and gone on up. Tom just couldn't seem to make the grade, but that was just because some of the gold-braid boys couldn't get it through their thick skulls that MacReady had what it takes to be a first-class detective and then some.

They knew now—too late. And they'd be out in force at the funeral, to give honor to a cop who'd faced a murderous pistol fire in performance of his duty. Hansard ground out his cigarette and cursed helplessly. A hell of a lot of good official honors would do Tom's widow and ten-year-old kid!

he man on the pillow muttered incoherently and rolled his head from side to side. He opened his eyes, stared vacantly up at the detective. It was another five minutes before there was a light of recognition in his gaze; then he reached out feebly for Hansard's hand.

"Hello, Mike," he whispered hoarsely.

"How you feel, Tom?"

MacReady grimaced. "Not so bad. I guess they . . . fixed me up O.K."

"Sure." Mike grinned cheerfully. What they had fixed Tom up with had been a load of morphine. That was all they could do. "Feel like telling me what happened?"

The wounded man closed his eyes. "Ain't much I can tell, Mike. I'm coming along Hester Street. To see if old lady Kruger got her coal from the relief. When I get to the corner opposite Dumont's jewelry store—" He groaned, tried to put a hand to his belly, fumbled at the bandages for a little, then stiffened and lay still.

Hansard lit a cigarette, held it to MacReady's lips. "Take a drag, Tom."

The patrolman inhaled greedily, let the smoke dribble slowly from his nostrils. "I see these two punks and a dame huddled in front of Dumont's window. When they spot me, they move on kind of sudden. So I go over to give a peek." His voice was weaker, his lips looked like blue steel. "When I get up close, I see this Red Cross poster stuck on the outside of the window. . . . Ah! It does hurt!"

"Take it easy, old-timer."

"The old gray mare, Mike, ain't what she used to be." Sweat glistened on MacReady's face. He went on, slowly. "Knew that poster was screwy. Stuck over hole in the glass. They'd used a glass cutter and a suction cup. Half the junk was gone out of the window. So I . . . went after 'em."

"You get a look at them, Tom?"

MacReady licked his lips. "Couldn't see 'em clear. Light was bad. They went . . . up the Bowery. Turned in that alley. Middle of the block." A trickle of pink saliva ran out of the corner of his mouth. "When I hit the corner . . . they jumped me. Didn't get a chance . . ." His voice trailed off into nothing, but his lips continued to work.

Hansard put his ear close to MacReady's mouth.

"Be a while," the patrolman was gasping, "before I . . . get back . . . to roll call."

"A little while, Tom. Yeah."

"You'll have to . . . look after it, Mike." MacReady's eyes opened suddenly, very wide. He hoisted himself up convulsively, on one elbow. "They assigned you . . . to the case . . . didn't they, Mike? It's a hockshop case . . . ain't it?"

"Sure it is. Inspector put me on it personal."

"That's O.K. . . . then." The patrolman fell back limply. "Long as . . . you're on it, Mike." His eyes glazed. He fought to focus them on the man bending over him. "When'll . . . Mary and Steve . . . be over . . . to see me?"

"Ought to be here any minute, Tom. Any minute, now."

There wasn't any answer. The faded blue eyes stared fixedly up at the ceiling.

Hansard took out his watch, rubbed the back to mirror brightness on his vest, held it to MacReady's lips. After a minute he put the watch back in his pocket.

"You sure got lousy breaks, pal. You sure did. I don't know if anything can be done to balance the books for you, but I'll give it a try, Tom."

He rang the bell on the wall.

n the shadow of the El, the street was dark and gloomy, but the opposite side of the Bowery was a blaze of naked electric bulbs over dazzling displays of silverplate and glittering rows of gaudy

gems. One jewelry store crowded against another, elbowing for space in this brilliant white light of Little Maiden Lane.

As Mike stalked toward the sign—DUMONT'S——DIAMONDS—he saw a bulky-shouldered man lounging in the doorway. When Hansard angled toward the Red Cross poster on Dumont's window, the man stepped out into the light. His eyes were narrow slits in a brick-red face. He had his right hand in his coat pocket and his voice was brusque.

"Keep movin', mister . . . right along, now. Right along."

Hansard didn't even bother to show his badge. "Crysake, don't you Ames dummies know a cop when you see one?"

The representative of the Ames Patrol took his hand out of his coat pocket. "I ain't takin' no chances. Buddy of mine had the switch snapped on him a little while ago, right up there on the corner."

"Yeah. An' he might be alive now if you stuck to your post, way you're supposed to, shamus," Mike said curtly. "What's your name?"

"Brundage." The Ames man was surly. "Don't be telling me my business. I know what I'm supposed to do and what I ain't. I been assigned to this corner for two years. Me an' Tom MacReady always got along jake. He never made no complaint. An' none of our subscribers got any squawk—"

"MacReady ain't exactly in a position to complain. Far as your customers are concerned, why should they holler? They're covered by insurance, aren't they?" Hansard went over to the window, ripped off the poster, looked at the six-inch hole the glass-cutter had made. "But that isn't saying there aren't going to be plenty of beefs about this. There've been too many of these glass-cutter jobs in the last two-three weeks. It'll be the same mob back of all of 'em. Now they've gone up against a chair job, everybody'll get put on the pan about it. Where was you when the fireworks went off?"

Brundage jerked his thumb over his shoulder. "Down on Hester. Kid came up and told me somebody'd heaved a brick at Thomasini's window. That We Buy Old Gold joint. So I beat it down there. It was a false alarm. So then I hear the shooting and hike back." He shifted uneasily under Hansard's cold stare. "I called an ambulance for MacReady."

"Yeah?" Hansard morosely studied the vacant spaces in Dumont's display. The robbers had been smart. They hadn't taken any watches or any of the cheap "slum" that's used to catch the eye of the passerby. The stuff that was missing was mostly rings, he decided.

"Got a key, Brundage?"

The Ames man produced a ring attached to his belt with a steel chain. "I ain't s'posed—"

"Suppose my eye!" growled the plainclothesman. "Open up!"

Brundage used a key. Hansard went in first, inspected the alarm box on the wall, saw it hadn't been tampered with. Then he found a phone, got through to headquarters.

"Extension four-oh-two . . . Ed Schmidt . . . Ed? I'm down at Dumont's. Put through a thirty-one, will you? All cars. Rush. Have 'em contact every hockshop in the city. Notify us of anyone trying to pawn any solitaires worth over—say, fifty bucks. Or any unset stones more than a quarter carat. They'll probably pry the stones out of the settings. . . . I know, I know. It's a hundred-to-one shot. Still and all, it's one of those things we gotta cover, Ed." He hung up.

Brundage shook his head dubiously. "You ain't gonna lay the finger on the lads who did this job just by puttin' the peep on the hockshops. This mob was from out of town."

"Why do you think so?"

"I seen their car."

"Where?"

"Couple of blocks down. Green sedan with Jersey pads."

Hansard swore and reached for the phone again. "Why the hell didn't you say so when I was talking to headquarters! How did you know it was their car?"

"Well, I don't—for sure. But it was there when I beat it down on Hester, and it wasn't there when I got back. Then that old hag selling pretzels down on the corner claims there was two guys and a frill came running over to the sedan and drove away like a bat outa—"

"Hello, Ed? Something to add to that alarm. All cars to notify all men on post. Pick up a green sedan. . . . What make, Brundage?"

"Buick, near as I noticed."

". . . a Buick, maybe, Ed. Or any other green sedan with Jersey plates. Two men and a girl in it . . . Nah, this Ames dope I'm talking to never heard about getting a license number. So long."

The headquarters man reached out, caught the private guard's necktie, yanked him close. "How many times you been told to take the plate numbers of any car parks near the Diamond Exchange after closing hours?"

"Leggo," snarled Brundage, "you're chokin' me! I don't know when that sedan parked there. They's a lot of Jersey hockers come over to do business before closing hours an' leave their cars around here while they grab a bite. Anyhow, I told you I was in a hurry to check up on that rock throwin'. If it hadn't been for that—"

"Yah!" Hansard sent him reeling back against one of the glass cases. "You don't stay on your post. You don't check on parked cars. You'd ought to have your watchman's license revoked. You had sense enough to notify the proprietor, here?"

"I tried to get Dumont on the phone. He wasn't home."

"Where's he live?"

"Over in Brooklyn."

"Well, try him again. Send him a wire—collect. Ask the phone company to give him a bell every five minutes until they get him. But get him over here."

"I'll do the best I can."

"And soon as you see him, get me a complete checklist of all the ice that was glommed. I want the number of stones in each ring, the carat weights, settings—"

"Sure, I know."

"You don't know your rump from a hole in the ground. If you get hold of anything phone it in to headquarters, extension four-oh-two. And don't be leaving Dumont's here to run around and see if you can locate somebody who can give you a description of those three. We'll take care of that without any amateur kibitzing."

Hansard got out of the store, up to the corner of the alley. He half expected some of the Homicide boys to be down there, but maybe the word hadn't gotten through that MacReady had died. Or perhaps they'd come and snapped their photographs and were now combing the district for eyewitnesses. . . .

The sharp contrast between the blinding brilliance of the row of windows at the Diamond Exchange and the utter pitch-blackness of the alley made it difficult for him to adjust his eyes quickly. He slipped on something greasy underfoot.

He put his flash on it and his nostrils flared in repugnance. This was where Tom had taken it. He swung the circle of light up and down the cobblestones. Besides MacReady's blood, there was nothing to see except a couple of those small, white, slotted cards in which rings are displayed. Each card bore the caption—*Absolutely Perfect Blue-White——22-Carat Setting—Latest Style.*

A couple of chunks of limestone had been chipped from the building wall by flying lead but there was nothing else.

CHAPTER TWO
THE GIRL IN THE HOCKSHOP

Mike strode grimly through the alley, over to Centre Street, up to the block-long white stone building at Number 240.

He went down a freshly scrubbed corridor smelling of antiseptic, turned in at a door marked—*DETECTIVE BUREAU——LOST PROPERTY DIVISION.*

There was a long counter running across the

front of the room, behind it half a dozen small oak desks. There was only one man in the office, a thin, sharp-featured individual with glossy black hair, shaggy eyebrows and an expression of perpetual surprise on his face. He sat in a swivel chair, with his feet up on the lower drawer of his desk. This was Ed Schmidt, Hansard's working partner. He was drawling into a telephone.

"Yeah, that's what I said. Report by phone and pronto. That don't mean you shouldn't send in the regular descriptive cards on everything that's been hocked in your shop today. If I don't get a brown envelope with a bunch of those cards from you in the morning I'll know you've either gone out of business or you're trying to give us the runaround, Abe. But about those solitaires— it's important. They're hot as the electric chair."

Hansard sat at his desk and gloomily fingered the day's list of property, lost and stolen. There were wallets reported from the midtown section. Their only chance of recovery lay across the hall in the offices of the pickpocket squad. Another epidemic of lost dogs in the Washington Heights area probably meant that the old "dog racket" was being worked again. And there was the usual assortment of missing handbags, wrist-watches and briefcases—mostly testimonials to their owner's forgetfulness.

None of these held any interest for Mike. He would let the other boys on the squad look after them. By that tacit understanding which goes without expression in the police department, it was accepted that Hansard was after the mob that had shot down his friend, and that he would let nothing interfere with that job until it was done.

He knew that the likelihood of his finding the killers was remote, unless he had a streak of luck. For there would be little doubt that this was the work of the same crowd that had bedeviled the pawnshop squad for nearly three weeks, with window-hole robberies from one end of Manhattan to the other.

"Mike," called the other man, hanging up the phone, "I got that file of lugs who've been involved in window robberies, from the Bureau of Identification. Covers twelve years. About sixty guys. But more than half of 'em are doing their homework up at Stone College."

"Let me have a look-see, Eddie." Mike shuffled over the identification cards, with full-face and profile photos. "None of these answer the descriptions given by any of the bystanders at the other robberies, huh, Ed?"

"Not as near as I can make out. But we might as well go through the routine."

"Let Homicide do it, Eddie. They can put more men on it than we can. And anyhow, I got an idea it's a waste of time. I think this is a new mob, just organized."

"The way they're going at it, Mike"— Schmidt came over and put a police flyer from San Francisco headquarters on Hansard's desk—"it looks to me as if they're old hands. Seven jobs, they've pulled. Nobody's caught 'em. Nobody's even got a cast-iron description. That takes some experience."

"Yeah. I guess so, Eddie." Mike studied the flyer.

It was an old one. It stated that all police departments should be on the lookout for William Sexton, recently a resident of San Francisco. Sexton was an expert at window work, had cleaned out five jewelry stores in one night and departed for places unknown. His method had been to use a couple of stooges to stand on either side of him, apparently inspecting the contents of a show-window, while he used a window-glass cutter, calmly inserted a cane with a wad of chewing gum on it and picked up such items as his fancy dictated. After the desired merchandise had been abstracted, the busy Mr. Sexton would calmly paste a poster of some sort over the small hole and depart.

"This looks good," Mike grunted. "Only there's no photo."

"Good reason why," Schmidt pointed out. "They never caught him. They picked up that dope from stoolies. Wouldn't you say this Sexton might be our man?"

"It's a thought. All we got to go on is—five-feet-six or -seven, hundred and sixty pounds or thereabouts, brown hair, brown eyes. I can't walk from here to Broome Street without bumping into half a dozen guys would answer that description. Tell you what, Ed. Wire Frisco. Ask 'em if they've got any later dope on this punk."

"O.K."

"And send out a teletype to all states we got working agreements with, giving his description. Include the green sedan in the Jersey notice. And warn all of 'em to be on the lookout for anybody trying to hock or sell unset ice."

"Anything else, Mike?"

"Yeah. Check over the lists of arrests MacReady made, the last four-five years. See if any of those bums had any jewelry-store robberies in their records. I have a hunch maybe this slob who shot him did it because Mike knew him and put the pinch on him at some previous time."

The phone rang. Schmidt answered. "Yeah? Hold the line a second, Elias." He put his hand over the receiver. "Litzman calling. Up on Sixth Avenue. Says there's a floozie trying to put the bite on him for two hundred bucks on a rock worth six or seven C's anyway. Wants to know what to do with her."

"Tell him to stall her. Kid her along. Haggle with her. Tell him if he lets her go before I get up there, I'll dig that old receiver charge up and slap him in the jug for sure." Mike grabbed his overcoat, got to the door. "And, Ed—"

"Yuh?"

"Tell him to work it so he gets her prints. On his showcase. Or maybe a fountain pen."

He got into the corridor before Schmidt yelled: "Want me to notify the radio Rollos?"

"No," Mike called back. "I'll do that. If I need 'em."

ansard's coupe hit nothing but the high spots on the way uptown. This might be a wrong lead, of course. No telling whether the skirt at Litzman's was the same one Tom MacReady had spotted down on Little Maiden Lane. But if she wasn't,

it was a damn queer coincidence. Women didn't do much legitimate pawning late at night. That was a male trick, for booze money. Women usually did their hocking in the daytime, when they could buy something they needed with the money they got. But if this was the same dame, seconds might count. Litzman might not be able to stall her off for long. She'd be sure to get suspicious.

Still, there was something screwy about the set-up. That window-job had certainly been done by a professional mob of heisters. Yet no gem thief would be dumb enough to suppose he could get away with pawning a piece of glitter within a couple of hours after the stuff had been lifted.

It was ten minutes past nine when Mike got out, a block below Litzman's. He forced himself to stroll leisurely toward the hockshop—past a couple of employment agencies.

It wouldn't do to come tearing into the shop. There might be a lookout waiting outside, or across the street. That was why he hadn't wanted the radio cars notified. A lookout would have spotted police cars before they could have closed in and given the alarm.

He turned in, hesitantly, under a dingy sign from which hung three tarnished gilt balls. The window was plastered, inside, with a miscellaneous network of watches, binoculars, shotguns, revolvers, banjoes, carpenter's levels, flutes, fishing rods. Phony "flash wares" bought at auction, Hansard knew, for sale to overwise suckers.

The girl was still there. She was talking earnestly to Elias down at the far end of the counter. A bleached-out aluminum blonde with plenty of curves where they counted, and a pinched, sharp little face with too much rouge and lipstick on it. She wore a short seal jacket over a thin blue silk dress, and if Mike Hansard was any judge, she was scared silly about something.

"Won't you please hurry," she was saying, shrilly, to the two men behind the counter. "I tell you I've got to catch a train."

Old Elias Litzman looked at her mildly over his steel-rimmed spectacles and fingered his scraggly beard thoughtfully. "In a transaction of this size, it is necessary to make out the papers correctly. I have my pawnshop license to protect—"

"I understand. But I've given you all the information you've asked for."

"How do you spell your first name, Miss Sampson? Or here"—the pawnbroker deferentially handed her his pen—"if you will just fill this in yourself. Full name and address. Phone number, if you have one . . ."

The girl wrote eagerly.

Hansard rested his elbows wearily on the counter, took his watch out of his pocket as if he were greatly embarrassed.

The younger Litzman came up to him, briskly. "You wish to make a loan, gentleman?" He slid a slip of white paper under Mike's hand.

"Like to get about five-six bucks on the turnip. It's worth twenty-five, at least."

On the slip he read—

Stones: One diamond
Weight: One and one-half carats
Setting: 22k. yellow gold
Inscriptions: None
Maker's name: None

Mike tucked the pawnbroker's record unobtrusively away in his pocket. "I got to have five dollars, anyway." Under his breath he added: "*Nobody with her, Sol?*"

Sol Litzman examined the watch's movement with professional disdain. "Five I couldn't let you have. Watches like them are positively a drag on the market, these days. Maybe three." He whispered: "*All alone, Mr. Hansard.*"

"You can sell it for fifteen. A fella offered me fifteen."

Sol shrugged, scornfully. "You should have taken it."

"Gimme five seeds on it." Mike murmured: "*Ever seen her before?*"

"Where'd you get this watch, mister? You're so anxious to get rid of it, maybe it ain't yours. *Never laid eyes on her, so help me.*"

"It's mine," Hansard grumbled. "Those are my initials, inside the case, there. *What's her say-so?*"

"*Claims she's a showgirl. Used to be in burly. Out of a job. Claims she's had the ring couple of years, guy gave it to her.*" Sol laid the watch on the counter, with an air of finality. "Three-fifty is absolutely our outside limit, my friend. Take it or leave it."

"I'll split the difference. Make it four, huh? *You think she's leveling, Sol?*"

"Well, so I'll do it. If you don't come back and redeem it, I lose money, I'm telling you. *We put the ring under the glass, Mr. Hansard. She's lying, positively. Ring ain't ever been worn by nobody. Anyway, showgirl's rings always got a little greasepaint on 'em that hold the dust under the setting points. There ain't no dust of any sort under the points on this ring.* Write out your full name and address, please."

Mike spoke without moving his lips. "*How much will she take?*"

"Here's four dollars, mister. *She come down to a hundred-fifty.*"

"Much obliged. I'll be back for the watch. *Give it to her. I'll be responsible for it.*"

Sol turned toward the green steel cabinet back of the counter. As he did so, he nodded almost imperceptibly to his father. And as the plainclothesman slouched toward the door, he could hear old Elias saying: "I take a chance, young lady. Actual I ain't got a right to let you have the money. But you say you got to get to San Francisco. You give me your word. Absolutely you redeem the ring, so I make an exception. . . ."

ansard glanced back through the intervening lacework of opera glasses, ukeleles, cocktail sets, drawing instruments. The girl's head was thrown back. She was drawing a deep breath as if a terrible load had been lifted from her shoulders. This could be the frill MacReady had seen. It was the

type of ring that had been stolen from Dumont's place. He had been able to tell from the vacant spots in the jeweler's window that most of the rings had been "engagement specials."

He surveyed the street. Between Forty-sixth and -seventh there was only an elderly couple strolling leisurely. No cars at the curb, just a battered baker's truck parked in front of a Coffee Pot, down at the next corner.

Mike slid into the doorway next to Litzman's. He'd tail her, see who she met, where she went. Maybe the mob had been desperate for dough, had to make a fast touch to get out of town. In that case . . .

She was coming. She was almost running as she pushed open the door, but she glanced warily up and down the block before she walked quickly downtown.

She got about ten paces when the baker's truck moved jerkily out from the curb.

The man behind the wheel was a horse-faced individual with an ugly scar slashing down from one corner of his mouth. Hansard saw the glint of metal in the driver's hand.

That was enough warning for Mike.

"Hey, kid," he yelled. "Watch that truck!"

She saw it at the same instant, screamed, turned and fled back for the shelter of the pawnshop doorway.

The truck speeded up. Little jets of orange flame began to spit from a hole in the side panel of the truck. Glass shattered above Hansard's head as he put out a foot, tripped the girl so she sprawled flat on the sidewalk.

The staccato bark of an automatic rifle echoed hollowly in the empty street. The heavy flat report from Mike's Police Positive crashed thunderously through the more brittle sound of the rifle fire.

Something licked out with a hot tongue at his cheek. He dropped to one knee and aimed carefully as the gray truck roared past.

The door and window of the pawnshop disintegrated in a jangling shatter of broken glass.

At his feet the girl squealed, once—and lay still.

Mike fired at the driver, saw the windshield smash, put another bullet halfway down in the front door by the driver's seat. Then the truck was past. Lead smacked into the door jamb beside him as he thumbed fresh cartridges into his pistol, sent a burst of slugs at a rear tire. He heard the tire go, saw the truck swerve crazily around a corner.

A police whistle shrieked. Behind him, heavy feet pounded on pavement. Hansard stood up, flipped his left hand in the horizontal palm-up, fingers-back gesture that says, "I'm a cop," everywhere.

A harsh voice behind him grated: "Which way they'd go?"

"'Round the corner," snapped Mike. "Gray truck. Tire gone. Watch it. They got a chatter gun—"

The patrolman raced for the corner.

ansard knelt beside the girl. His attempt to protect her had failed. One of those half-inch slugs from that automatic rifle had ricocheted from the metal casing of the pawnbroker's window, caught her in the throat. She was still alive but when she tried to speak, a red froth bubbled from her lips and her eyes glazed.

Behind Hansard, old Litzman was screeching like a maniac. "Look, *nu!* Look what you done. A tip-off I give you and right away is shooting, is killing. . . ."

"Shut up, Papa," yelled his son. "You ain't hurt. That poor girl, she's dead."

A radio car came down the avenue with a banshee wail, slid to a screaming stop. Two uniformed men came over cautiously, guns drawn.

Mike said: "Hansard. Headquarters hockshop squad. Shield one-seven-two-one."

One of the officers had a sergeant's chevrons on his sleeve. He glanced down at the girl, looked up at the left side of Mike's face. "They get you bad?"

Mike put his fingers up, touched his cheek. It was warm and wet. There was a jagged cut a couple of inches long where a splinter of glass had ripped him.

"Cut myself shaving," he gritted. "Tell the broadcasting boys to put out a thirty-one for an old Ford truck. Gray panel job. Two men, both armed. One's a guy with a long, narrow face. He's got an inch scar at the right side of his mouth. I didn't see the other guy. He's the one hit this kid with the stutter gun."

The sergeant motioned to his partner. "Phone inside. Headquarters, first. Then a meat-wagon." The patrolman pushed open the shattered door, got in to the telephone.

The muscles in Mike's jaws twitched. "Same two who put the clutch on a flock of stones in a Bowery jewelry store and knocked off Tom MacReady, coupla hours ago, Sarge. The blonde here was in on the heist. She pulled a fast one on her pals, must've wanted to take a powder. She tried to hock a piece of ice here with Litzman. They followed her. When she came out of the shop, they drove up and let her have it. I winged the lug who had the wheel." He bent down and picked up the girl's gilt-mesh bag.

The sergeant sheathed his gun. "Where'd this truck come from?"

Hansard jerked his head toward the Coffee Pot. "Parked in front of the scoff-shop down there. Might be some of the boys inside got an idea where it came from, but I doubt it. This was the same outfit who were supposed to be riding around in a green Buick sedan. The truck was probably stolen, half an hour ago."

"I'll drop in the lunch counter." The sergeant bent over to get a good look at the girl's face. "This dame didn't work this part of town. I'll guarantee that."

"Might not be from New York at all." Mike's face was stern. "But the fingerprint boys'll find out. This mob that knocked her off has gone kill-crazy. If we don't put the clamps on 'em—"

"Yeah." The sergeant pulled out his report book. "They might've holed in, right close by here. We'll give this precinct a going over. Don't

worry about that. I knew Tom MacReady. He was a right cop."

"One of the best," Mike agreed.

The other officer ran out of the hockshop. "Tunnels and ferries and bridges all blocked. There'll be an ambulance here in a couple of minutes."

"Thanks." Mike stepped over the girl's body. "Get something to cover that up, will you? I'm going inside a minute. I'll stick around till Homicide gets here, anyway."

CHAPTER THREE
LILY DOESN'T WORK HERE ANY MORE

 nside old Elias was blubbering incoherently, in a frenzy of fear. Sol was still trying to calm him. Mike spilled the contents of the girl's bag out on the counter-top. Lipstick, cigarettes, gum, an address book full of phone numbers, a couple of old letters without the envelopes, a purse, some hairpins and a few keys.

Mike opened the purse. There was a roll of bills, a couple of dollars in silver. He tossed the currency across the counter.

"Tear up that ticket, Sol. Here's the dough. Lemme have the ring."

The younger Litzman took the money as if it was a scorpion, went to the safe. Mike pawed over the miscellany on the counter, put the stuff back in the bag. The letters were addressed to *Dearest Daughter* and were signed *Mama*. There wasn't anything in them to tell who the daughter was, or where she lived or anything about her except that her mother was glad she was so well and happy with her work.

The names in the address book were Phils and Johns and Pauls and Bobs—no women. Most of the phone exchanges were in the mid-town office section.

Tucked away in the back of the book, where

he hadn't noticed it before, was a little piece of blue paper about three inches long and an inch wide. It was a remitter's receipt from the American Express Company for a money order. It was for twenty bucks, was made out to *F. O. Marshal,* signed by *L. Marsh.*

He went over to the telephone, worked the dial. After a second Schmidt came on.

"Ed? Saw some wood for me, will you? . . . Yeah . . . I want to know who L. Marsh was. The skirt who was with the two who put the burn on MacReady. They just fixed her up with a slug, too. L. Marsh is the name. I don't know anything about her except she's a five-buck floozie. But she sent an express money order to someone named F. O. Marshal on April twenty-second. Number is 1317522. Get me an address, Ed. . . . Yeah, I'm still at Litzman's."

Outside the ambulance slid to the curb with bell clanging and bloodshot headlights. The emergency intern came in and swabbed off Mike's cheek with something that stung like fire.

"Y'oughta come back to the hospital. Have this treated right, officer."

"Later, maybe. Just do your stitch-in-time stuff, Doc. I got a rush job on hand."

The intern got out the needle.

Sol brought the ring to the plainclothesman while the suture was being threaded into the flesh of Mike's cheek.

"It ain't the plate glass, Mr. Hansard, or the damage inside the shop here. But nobody'll come near us now. A thing like this'll ruin us, honest. Especially if it gets out that the poor girl was borrowing a little money from us and got murdered like that, right after. Couldn't you tell those newspaper men that it was accidental, that she just happened to be in front of our place of business. . . ."

Mike couldn't talk back. He mumbled, "No," as well as he could.

"There you are, Officer." The intern slapped gauze and collodion over the wound. "Come around in a couple days and have it dressed."

"Sure." Hansard grinned lopsidedly. "That'll be fun."

The intern went out to help put the girl's body on a stretcher.

Sol held out his hands, despairingly, to Mike. "Suppose those killers come back. Maybe they'll think Papa and I could identify them."

"They know damn well *I* can. So they'll come after me first. Long as I'm alive you don't have to work up a sweat about it. There's your phone. Maybe that's Ed Schmidt."

It was. "Jeeze Mike, I just got the news over the short-wave. They get you bad?"

"Only a scratch, Ed. You get that address?"

"Yeah. I don't know if it's the right one. But the Express people say Lily Marsh lives at Four-seventy-eight West Seventy-second Street. Know what that is?"

"Riding academy, Ed?"

"That's what they tell me. I wouldn't know. I'm a married man, myself. But you're white, single and over twenty-one, so—"

"Go to hell, Eddie. Any other stuff come in?"

"Not from hockshops. Word about the truck."

"What?"

"Picked up what was left of it on West Forty-eighth. They'd folded it over a hydrant. Bloodstains on the upholstery of the driver's seat. You must've nicked one of 'em."

"I hope. That wouldn't even up the score, either. Any report from that stupe in the Ames Patrol?"

"Yeah. He's got Dumont down at the store. Want me to cover it?"

"No. Stick to that phone for the time being. I'll have a look at the Marsh hangout and then run down to Dumont's."

The Homicide boys rolled up in two black cars, brought out their print kits and cameras, questioned Mike for a few minutes. Then he left them there, with the assistant medical examiner making chalk marks around the body. He got to his car, tramped on the button up through Central Park, turned west at Seventy-second.

he ground floor of Number 478 was occupied by a glorified lunch counter, with shiny red-leather stools and lots of chromium and glass brick. There was a big neon sign flashing over the door. Every couple of seconds the crimson-and-green tubing proclaimed—*THE MEATING PLACE . . . Where Gourmets Gather . . .*

There was a little hallway off at one side, a row of letter boxes with name cards in them. None of the cards bore the name of Marsh or Marshal.

Mike went up a carpeted flight. At the head of the stairs, behind an oval marble-top table, sat an enormously fat woman in a black lace dress. Her eyes peered out slyly from puckers of pink flesh. There was no way of telling where her chin ended and her bosom began. She patted a crown of permanent curls with pudgy fingers covered with diamonds, and leered ingratiatingly.

"Evening, sweetheart. Which one of the girls did you wanna see?"

Mike grinned amiably. "Lily Marsh. She in?"

The madame's lips made an O! "She ain't, honey. But maybe you'd like t' make the acquaintance of a cute little redhead. She's—" The fat woman stopped and squinted at the gold badge Mike was holding in the palm of his hand. Then she giggled. Her jowls shivered with merriment. "You're a man who can take a joke, aren't you, Officer? I like a man who can stand for a little kidding once in a while." She reached down, pulled up her skirts, brought out a wad of bills from its stocking hideout.

Hansard waved a hand. "Once in a while. But not tonight. Which is Lily's room?"

She put both hands flat on the marble, levered herself erect. "You ain't gonna get rough, or anything like that, are you?"

"Not unless I have to." Mike's smile was still agreeable but his eyes were frosty. "Which room?"

"Front, right." The stout woman pointed. "Want a key?"

"I don't want to kick the door down." He held out his hand. From somewhere in the folds of her dress she produced a flat key. "Just sit right down there again. Act natural. Don't bother to tip off anybody. Just go right on as if I wasn't around. Probably in a few minutes I won't be."

"I always play ball, Officer. It's the safest way."

He went toward the front of the house, used the key. He kicked the door open, stood to one side. The room was pitch-dark, the shades were drawn in the windows looking down onto the street, although through them Mike could see the dull claret glare of the *MEATING PLACE* sign at regular intervals. There was an odor of musky perfume.

He held his gun in his right hand, felt around for the light switch with his left. An unseen hand gripped his left wrist, jerked him off balance!

Mike wrenched himself free, but not before a two-foot length of lead pipe had smashed down across the back of his neck, half stunning him. He crashed forward, to his knees. A foot stamped savagely on his gun-hand, crunching the knuckles. The shoe, which had come within the detective's blurred vision, booted the revolver out of his grasp.

The door slammed behind him; light flooded the room from rose-shaded bulbs in the ceiling. Hansard gazed up, groggily. Two men stood over him. One was short and squat. His arms were so long his hands hung almost to his knees. His face was long and narrow. There was a scar twisting down the right corner of his mouth. The left sleeve of his coat had a jagged tear in it. The fabric was soaked with something that looked like port wine.

The other man was tall and slender, with a boy's pink cheeks and flax-colored hair that waved as if it had been marcelled. He wore a suit of pearl-gray gabardine, a wine-red shirt and an apple-green tie. Neither of the two faces above him had been among the photographs Ed

Schmidt had taken from the Bureau of Identification, Hansard decided.

The tall youth spoke languidly. "Don't waste time giving him the toe, Gorilla. Use the pipe."

The squat man grunted, swung clumsily with the chunk of lead. Mike did his best to roll away from the blow, but took it on the shoulder. His left arm felt as if it were paralyzed.

"He's one of them he-guys, Babe," spat the Gorilla. "Got guts."

"Never mind his guts, George. I want his brains smeared on the carpet. And make it snappy. He might have a partner hanging around somewhere."

Mike wished to God he'd *had* sense enough to lug Ed Schmidt along. Maybe he could summon help, if that fat dame in the hall wasn't in on the play. He tried to cry out, but the smash on the back of his neck had done something to his vocal cords. He could only whisper.

The Gorilla could still talk all right, though. "Can't I have a little fun with him, Babe? It ain't every day—"

"Kill him! Kill him now," insisted Babe in an ugly high-pitched squeak. "Cave his skull in. Knock his teeth out afterwards, for souvenirs, if you want to. I don't give a damn. But finish him off, first."

Gorilla George measured his distance, swung down his arm.

Mike twisted, rolled, stumbled to his feet.

Babe was leveling a gun at him, five feet away. The detective could see the bright blue eyes sighting along the barrel.

There was no time to make a decision. Babe would put a shot through his heart in another split second. And if the slug missed, the Gorilla would be on him and next time that lethal pipe would smash home.

Mike acted almost without thinking. As Babe's finger tightened on the trigger and the Gorilla's grunt of rage came close behind him, Hansard leaped.

Through the window . . .

He took shade, curtain and sash with him. The glass crash was loud enough to smother the crack of Babe's gun. Mike didn't feel the impact of a bullet. But at that particular instant he didn't think it mattered much. One way or another, he was probably checking out. Unless his estimate of distance had been exactly right!

He could hear the warning yells of pedestrians below as he burst out over the sill. It wouldn't do any good to brace himself, but he couldn't help it. Something came up, slammed into him with terrific force. He grunted with the shock, but it wasn't the sidewalk, and it hadn't knocked him goofy.

He'd guessed right, then. The narrow, flat surface beneath him, that had stopped his fall, was the top of the *MEATING PLACE* sign. It was directly under Lily's window.

Women screamed from below. Mike twisted around to look down. There was a vicious stab of agony at his right side. That must be a cracked rib. The pain made him dizzy. He put out a hand to steady himself, knocked aside a length of hot tubing, saw the sign beneath him flicker and dim.

He gritted his teeth, got his knees under him, crawled backward till his heels touched the building.

A traffic cop sprinted across Seventy-second Street, shouting: "Don't move! Stay right where you are. . . . Keep your head now. I'll get you!"

Hansard stood up, teetered precariously on the foot-wide top of the sign. He knew the traffic man, hollered: "Never mind me, Allison. Watch below there. Don't let anybody in or out."

"Got you, Mike." The policeman bellowed gruff commands at the gathering crowd.

Mike rested his elbows on the sill above him, muscled himself up. He hadn't taken all of the windowpane with him. He had to kick some of it out before he could climb back into Lily's room.

The light was still on, his gun still on the floor, over in the corner where Gorilla George had kicked it. He picked it up.

The fat woman stood in the doorway, dry

washing her hands and whining: "I thought you said there wasn't gonna be any roughhouse?"

Mike ignored it. "Where'd those two punks go?"

"Those men who ran out into the hall just now?"

Mike's lips tightened. "Don't stall. Where are they?"

She pointed to the stairs. "They went down. I didn't know you were after them. I couldn't have stopped them, anyway."

"I'll say you couldn't. You know 'em!"

"Never saw either of them before tonight, in my life. Honest to God."

"All right," he growled. "If you see either of them again, and don't report it to the precinct, you'll take a good long vacation at the city's expense." He went up to third and top floor, made sure there was no trap to the roof.

Allison yelled up to him: "Mike! Janitor down here says a couple of mugs beat it out back into Seventy-first, through the basement, a minute ago. One was a kind of ape-man with a scar on his face. The other one just a real sweet thing. They the ones?"

"That's the pair." Mike came down, described Gorilla George and the Babe in lurid detail. "Phone that dope in to the dispatcher. Tell every man on duty to pick up either one of those lugs on sight."

"They got guns, Mike?"

"They sure have. And they like to use 'em on a man's back. They'd have used one on me, right away, except they didn't want to attract too much attention here in a crowded district. The Babe shot at me, as it was."

"You look like you been in another fracas, somewhere, Mike. Get chewed up a little?"

Mike put his hand up to his cheek. The cotton and collodion bandage was still there. "Rather be chewed up than boarded up, Allison. I still got my luck. Never mind filing an accident report. But after you finish with that alarm, you might phone Homicide and tell 'em what happened up here. Those punks must have a hangout in town somewhere. They know their way

around too well to be strangers. So maybe some stoolie can help us out."

He went back to Lily's room, closed the door. There was no doubt this was the blonde's "place of residence," even if she didn't always sleep here. There was another one of those letters in the bureau drawer, in the same handwriting, signed, *Mama*, but very little else. On the dresser was a pyroxylin toilet set in flamboyant lavender and gilt.

Mike thoughtfully stuck the hairbrush in his pocket, went out and locked the door. He'd never seen a set just like that one. The fact might be worth a little nosing around.

He tossed the room key on the marble table. The fat woman eyed him fearfully.

"Lily won't be back," Mike said, curtly. "She's got a date with an undertaker. Keep everybody out of this room until an officer tells you different."

CHAPTER FOUR
KREDIT KORNER CLUE

When he went down and climbed in his car, it hurt him to sit straight behind the wheel. He found he could get by if he twisted sideways a little. That rib would give the sawbones a little something extra to play with when he went to have his cheek dressed.

The part the girl had played in the robbery and killing had been cleared up a little. She had undoubtedly been a pickup, hooked into the crime without knowing what it was all about. Probably they'd given her the one ring as her part of the payoff. But when MacReady had spotted them, been murdered for his alertness, the girl got cold feet and tried to run out.

That still didn't clear up the main problem. Who was behind this business? Neither the Babe or Gorilla George were more than cheap choppers. They wouldn't be likely to have planned this whole series of window jobs on their own.

Mike stopped in at a bar opposite the *News* building and ordered rum—a double Demerara, straight. He felt better directly he'd downed it.

When he got down to Little Maiden Lane, Brundage, the Ames Patrol Service guard, was inside the jewelry store with a small, dapper, apple-cheeked man in pince-nez who wore a Vandyke that looked as if it were made of old manila rope.

He bobbed his head to Hansard, held out a neatly manicured hand and said: "I am Ramon Dumont. You are from headquarters, Lieutenant . . . ?"

"Yeah. Just Detective Hansard. Hello, Amesy."

"Hello." Brundage stared. "Judas Priest! They marked you up, didn't they? I heard about it from the harness bull who took MacReady's beat."

"I'm still a hell of a lot better off than Tom. You make out that missing property list, Mr. Dumont?"

"I have it here. The total amount is near seven thousand. But of course the thieves cannot realize any sum such as that."

"Don't bet on it," said Mike. "They might have ways and means." He put the list in his pocket, took out the hairbrush. "You sell this?"

Dumont examined it. "No. It is not an item we carry."

The Ames man goggled. "Nobody'd be fathead enough to risk ten years in the pen for a hunk of junk like that, Hansard."

"I didn't think it was stolen, shamus." The detective tossed the brush on the showcase. "But it belonged to the skirt who was in on the robbery here. Figured maybe she'd bought it down here, used it as an excuse to case the store."

The little jeweler laid a finger alongside his nose, cocked his head quizzically. "As I say, it is not out of our stock. But it is possible"—he dived under the counter, disappeared from sight—"I might, perhaps, be able to tell you who is the manufacturer."

"That might help," Hansard agreed.

Dumont began to paw over illustrated pages in a catalogue.

Brundage said in an undertone: "I phoned a copy of the loot list to our Jersey office."

"Can't do any harm," Mike said wearily. "Won't do any good, either."

"That's what you Centre Street wiseys think." Brundage was nettled. "The Newark cops just give out with a stolen-car bulletin. Guess what car?"

"Don't tell me," Hansard said sarcastically, "it's that green sedan you saw?"

"Exactly," retorted Brundage. "And from the way you described that lug with the scar on his puss, I'd say he's one of the old Newark mob. A rat called Chuck Scanlon."

"You must be out of practice, Amesy. You're not calling your shots so good. The crut who put the bump on that blonde is named Gorilla George. I don't know if he comes from Newark or not, but I've good reason to believe he's still in New York."

"Well, for Crysake." Brundage glowered angrily. "How you expect us to be any use on a job like this, if you keep all the info to yourselves?"

"I don't, fella. I don't. This is a cop case. A blue's been knocked off. It's a personal matter with those of us who knew MacReady, to get the guys who dropped him, Brundage. That lets you out."

"In a pig's whinny, it does. I been assigned by my office to follow through on this job. The insurance outfits are beginning to raise hell with Ames. So it's a personal matter with us, too."

The jeweler said excitedly: "Here it is. I've found it. It is a new design. The manufacturer is the Nik-Nak Novelty Company. They're up in Attleboro, Massachusetts."

Mike said briskly: "I hope they don't go to bed before ten o'clock up in Attleboro."

He reached for the phone and dialed headquarters. "Eddie," he said, when he got his partner's extension, "we might have a lead. Up in the Marsh mouse's furnished room, I find a very gaudy piece of jewelry. A toilet set. It was made by Nik-Nak Novelty, up in Attleboro. According to their new catalogue, it's listed as number 27VO and is called *Passionelle*. Hot stuff, eh? Well, I figure maybe one of the killers might have given it to her. If so, it might help a lot to know where he bought it. Or stole it. Get on to Attleboro. I know it's late, but get the cops up there to locate somebody who can tell you who bought sets like that, around New York. And hustle, Eddie. Hustle."

Then he went to work on the loot list.

"Twenty-two solitaires, up to one and a half carats," he read. "Five bar-pins, mostly mellees. One platinum brooch with two rubies and six mellees. One yellow-gold brooch with a small cabochon emerald and five genuine pearls. One pair of diamond cuff-links, yellow-white stones, gold lovers'-knot setting." He glanced up curiously at Dumont, who was stroking his beard daintily. "Didn't look to me like there were that many empty spots in the display."

The jeweler shrugged. "I do not dress the window myself, naturally. But here is the clerk's notation for the close of business, last night." He took a typed sheet of paper from his pocket, unfolded it on the showcase. "I have crossed off the items which are still in the window. Those which I have not checked are obviously missing. If there has been any mistake it is obviously . . . ah . . . simply an oversight."

"You don't say." Hansard stuck the display record in his pocket, along with the list of stolen merchandise. "You want to be a little careful about oversights in a matter like this. Might get someone to wondering if maybe you don't know more about the robbery than you're telling."

Dumont was horrified. "But not at all. The list I gave you is accurate, to the best of my knowledge, I assure you. I cannot permit you to make insinuations. . . ."

Brundage tapped on the showcase with a scowl of importance. "The insurance companies will have to prosecute if you're making a false claim, Mr. Dumont. I'm warning you."

"So!" The jeweler hissed, resentfully. "You intend to intimidate me, to induce me to present a less complete list of my losses. Well"—his manila-rope beard stuck out at right angles to his neck—"you will not frighten Ramon Dumont. No. Not one little bit—"

The phone rang sharply. Mike got it.

"I caught the sales manager in his office, working late, Mike. He checked his order book, and the Nik-Nak people sold that particular number to twenty-four jewelers in the metropolitan area."

"We haven't got time to fine-tooth twenty-four stores, Ed. Look up their cards."

"I already done it," Schmidt announced. "There's only two of the twenty-four on our blue list."

"Which two?"

"Salvatore Monterro, down on Nassau Street, and that big outfit up in Harlem. Nathan Kutwik."

"Ah! Maybe you got something there, Eddie. Grab your hat. I'll pick you up down front, in five minutes."

He left Brundage cross-questioning the jeweler, ran his coupe up to headquarters. Schmidt was waiting. "Pile in, pal."

"Holy cats, Mike. What smacked you?"

"Glass out of Litzman's window. I want to do a little smacking back."

"Can't blame you for that."

"They laid for me up at the blonde's hangout, too, Ed. Wanted to put me out of the picture because they weren't sure how much the blonde had told me before she died."

"How much did she tell you?"

"Not one damn thing. But I dug the Nik-Nak lead up in her room."

"It smells like trouble, Mike. Wouldn't it be an idea to let the Homicide babies do the dirty work up in Harlem?"

"A lousy idea. They'll be on the Litzman end, anyhow. But this business is right down our alley. We know this Kutwik is a chiseling fence, or he wouldn't be on the suspected file. Maybe he's been engineering all of these window-hole jobs."

"His place'll probably be closed, this hour."

"Might. Might be open, too. They do more business in Harlem around midnight than they do in the daytime."

When they rolled up in front of a dazzling corner in the heart of Harlem Mike got out of the coupe. The luminous sign said— *YOUR Kredit Is Good at Kutwik's Korner.*

"You can watch through the window, from here, Eddie. Don't let anybody climb on my back." Mike went inside.

There was only one man in the store, a tall, powerfully built individual with expressionless gray eyes and skin the color of tallow. "Something I can do for you, sir?"

"Maybe. I'm a police officer. You're Nathan Kutwik?"

The big man's eyes narrowed. "I am."

"Then you'll know about a girl who bought a dresser-set here a little while ago."

Kutwik pulled down the corners of his mouth and rotated his head slowly, from left to right. "I can't be expected to remember every person—"

"You remember this blonde. Friend of the Babe's and Gorilla George."

A pendulum clock on the wall ticked off several seconds before Kutwik answered. "These persons you mention. I can't seem to recall—"

Hansard shrugged. "Maybe they're the ones who're lying, then. They claim to know you, all right."

"That's quite possible." The expressionless eyes stared insolently at Hansard. "I have been here on this corner for several years now."

"Yeah. We been watching you for several years, too. You shouldn't have any trouble remembering these lads. They say they been doing business with you for quite some time."

Kutwik picked up a cocktail shaker made of ruby glass in the shape of a barrel, ringed with silver hoops. "What sort of business?"

"Stones. Their statement says they just left a bunch of stuff with you." Mike was casual about it. As yet there was no indication his bluff was working. "I'm just waiting for the search warrant to come over from the station."

The proprietor of the Kredit Korner waved a bloodless hand. "Help yourself. You don't need a warrant in my store. Go right ahead."

The plainclothesman played his last card. "If it was only some hot ice we were after, I'd take you up on that. But this is a homicide case, Kutwik."

"Oh!" The jeweler set down the shaker, softly. "Someone has been killed?"

"The girl I just told you about. And a cop. You know how it is with the commissioner. When a policeman's been murdered we put on plenty of pressure, but we have to do everything strictly legal, to be sure no pratt of a lawyer can beat a conviction."

Kutwik took out a silk handkerchief, wiped his mouth. "This killing, now. It was in connection with those diamonds?"

"That's right. And the party who's fencing them is going to be charged as an accessory. It's a chair-job for someone. But of course, if you're in the clear, it won't worry *you.*"

"Suppose"—the big man put both palms on the top of the showcase, bent over until his face was only a foot from Hansard's—"an honest business man had been deceived about the ownership of certain gems, and was quite unaware of the manner in which they came into the possession of certain parties attempting to sell them—"

"Go ahead. I'm supposing. . . ."

"Do you think the police would take this fact into consideration, my friend?"

Hansard smiled tightly. "They might. If the business man could help us to get a conviction."

Kutwik sighed. "I give you my word of honor

I knew nothing of this killing. Naturally, under such circumstances, I would immediately have turned the stones over to the authorities."

"I bet you would," said Hansard, curtly. "Let's see 'em."

The jeweler emerged from behind the counter, walked with a curious shambling gait to the door of the Kredit Korner, locked it. Mike grinned to himself. That would give Schmidt something to fret about.

The big man came back, beckoned to Hansard, led the way to a partition at the rear of the store. On the way, the detective gave the once-over to the big steel safe which stood under an electric light out where any passing policeman could make sure it hadn't been tampered with. Evidently the jeweler didn't trust his privately purchased goods to its security!

There was a tiny cubbyhole of an office, a big glass-topped desk and a modernistic lamp of varnished wood and copper. Kutwik snapped on the light, sat down in a padded chair.

"Let's be open and above-board, my friend."

"Let's," Mike agreed.

"Perhaps there is . . . um . . . a reward for the arrest of these men you tell me about."

Mike stared. "Sure. Jewelers Association reward. Twenty-five hundred bucks or so, last time I heard. For evidence leading to conviction. Why?"

"As I understand it, you policemen are not qualified for such a reward, if you capture the criminals?"

"So which?"

Kutwik spread his palms, blandly. "Possibly we could work out some arrangement. You and I, eh? I give you the information; you see to it that I receive the reward. Then we split—"

Hansard shook his head in admiration. "You got your nerve. Putting a program like that up to me. Why, you putty-puss, you'll be getting all

the reward that's coming to you if you miss getting indicted for complicity in murder. Now cut out the horse and show me the glitter."

Kutwick sighed, pulled the lamp over in front of him. "You cops are so stupid about money matters. Who will it hurt if you and I split that twenty-five hundred?" There was no answer from the hockshop cop, so the jeweler grasped the base of the lamp in his left hand, twisted the top with his right.

The lamp unscrewed, the top lifted off, and there was a niche in the wooden base about the size of a bird's nest. There were a lot of shiny eggs in it, round little gold eggs with diamonds in them.

Hansard laid them out on the desk. "All here but one," he announced. "I got that one in my pocket already."

"They wanted three thousand dollars for the lot," Kutwik murmured, resentfully. "Claimed they'd brought it over from Naples and smuggled it in."

"Don't give me any of that guff." Hansard scooped up the jewelry, dumped it in his coat pocket. "You knew where it came from. Probably you bought it, at that."

"Oh, I deny it, absolutely. I asked for time to make an appraisal."

"Did, eh? Tell me why a crook should trust you with five or six thousand dollars' worth of rocks. Unless, of course, they'd done business with you before on the same basis."

The fence arched his eyebrows, superciliously. "I am a reputable dealer. I wouldn't be likely to run away."

"Not unless you could make a dollar by doing it. All right. When were these rats coming back for their cheese?"

"Tomorrow morning, Officer."

"Didn't they leave any address, anyplace you could get hold of them?"

Kutwik looked startled. "Why do you ask me? You have them under arrest, haven't you?"

"I didn't say so, mug. But I'll have you in a cell in no time at all, unless you answer my questions."

The jeweler groaned. "They mentioned a Nevins Street number. Over in Brooklyn 24781, if I remember correctly. But they were most particular that I shouldn't attempt to contact them."

Hansard wrote it down. "O.K., mister. I'll get over there and give a gander. You better close up shop now."

"I'd intended to."

"One more thing." Mike reached for the phone, dialed Spring 7-1000. When he got the switchboard man, he rattled off: "Hansard talking, hockshop squad . . . I'm up at 9744 Lenox Avenue. Jewelry store. Nathan Kutwik. Got that? The phone is Edgecombe 7-0741. Put a tap on the wire, right away, will you? Want a record kept of all conversations, numbers called, the works."

He hung up with the operator's comment still ringing in his ears. "What's the matter with you, Hansard? You know we got to get a court order before we do any wire-tapping."

Mike started for the front door.

"Where you live, Kutwik?"

"At the Concourse Savoy. On the Grand Concourse."

"You better beat it right up there. Stay there till I give you a ring."

The jeweler unlocked the door. "You won't double-cross me, Mr. Hansard. After my helping you, this way?"

The detective clucked derisively. "*Tchk, tchk.* You're a guy should talk about double-crossing! I'll promise you nothing except an even break. And you won't get that if you don't keep your nose clean from here on in."

CHAPTER FIVE
TEN CARATS OF LEAD

He went out, swung briskly past Schmidt, without speaking. After he'd gone halfway down the block, he flailed one arm in a come-on motion without turning around. His partner got it, slid the car up alongside.

"No dice, huh, Mike?"

"Plenty dice. I got the junk in my pocket."

"Ain't you going to arrest Kutwik?"

"Not yet, Ed. I'm not sure he's really working with these choppers. But we'll find out. You stick here, at this end of the block. I'll drive around to the other end. We tail him. If he comes your way, I'll see him and pick you up. If he heads my way, you're on your own. You better check in with H.Q."

Hansard dropped his partner, drove on around the block. The lights at the Kredit Korner were just going out as he hit the end of the street. A minute later the jeweler stepped out of the door. He glanced cautiously up and down the block, hurried toward Schmidt's corner. Mike followed with the car, keeping well behind him.

Kutwik turned down Seventh Avenue. By the time Mike saw Ed Schmidt, the fence was nowhere in sight.

"That yellow," Schmidt snapped. "Headin' downtown. That's him!"

Mike grunted. "He's taking one hell of a roundabout route to get to the Concourse, isn't he?"

Through the northwest corner of Central Park, they trailed the taxi to a short crosstown block between Columbus and Broadway. Mike stopped the coupe before the taxi ceased moving. When Kutwik got out of his cab and scanned the street, there was no indication anyone had been trailing him.

The jeweler paid off, hurried into a three-story brownstone house.

Schmidt said: "That's one of those remodeled joints with a couple of apartments on each floor. How do we know which one he's in?"

"We don't, Eddie. You stay here. Collar him if he comes out. If you get rough about it, nobody could blame you. Cuff him to the wheel and then hit the hall. Wait there until you hear a racket, somewhere. That'll be me. If you don't hear a rumpus in a couple of minutes, make one yourself and get some help."

"How'll you know where to head in, Mike?"

"I'll have to pull a Peeping Tom act. Up the

fire-escape, at the rear. If he's not in one of the rear flats I'll go to the roof and come down inside."

"Don't climb into some dame's room by mistake, pal."

Mike told him to go to hell, got around back past a row of ash cans, using his flash, found the iron ladder leading up past the rear windows.

There were lights on all three floors. The voices on the first floor were female, those on the second an old man and a child.

But when Hansard put his ear to the window on the top floor he heard Kutwik say: "I don't want any part of it, Babe. I don't mind running a few legitimate risks. But this hot-squat stuff is too much for me."

The high-pitched voice of the Babe cut in. "You soft-bellied ——! What do you think you can do about it now?"

"All I want is my money back. I'll give you the stuff. You can get rid of it outside the state."

The Babe cursed him obscenely. "You got as much chance of getting back that grand as you have of staying in the clear if George or I get picked up, Nate. The junk was worth three thousand, any way you wanted to figure it. You chiseled us down to one and now you want to welsh on that."

"All right." Kutwik sounded tired. "Forget the cash. Come up tomorrow and take the junk back. I don't want it. It's too hot for me. I'd rather take the loss and throw the stuff down the sewer."

"Why didn't you bring it with you tonight, if you're so damn anxious to get rid of it?"

The jeweler said: "I don't want to touch it again. Much less carry it around where they could frisk it off me. You come up in the morning and get it. If you don't, I'll heave it in the river. I'm telling you."

Mike squatted on the fire-escape and grinned sourly as he patted the bulge in his pocket where the rings were. The old buzzard was still after

that reward, figured that by getting Babe and the Gorilla to return to the Kredit Korner in the morning, he'd square himself with the authorities and be able to claim at least a part of the twenty-five hundred. He wouldn't miss the thousand bucks he'd paid over to the Babe so much, then.

There was no more talking from within. Somewhere in the apartment a door slammed. Mike got out his jack-knife, went to work on the catch of the window. It was a gamble, busting into a crook's flat this way. But it would be even more of a gamble if he and Eddie tried to crash the front door. And maybe this rear window wasn't being watched.

It wasn't. He slipped the catch with the blade, put his fingers on the pane, pushed up gently. The window came up with no noise. He got out his gun, shoved the shade aside, stepped quietly over the sill. Then he closed the window softly. The Babe might notice a draft from an unaccustomed source.

The room he was in looked like a boudoir. Rose-pink spread on the bed, fluffy drapes at the windows, a dressing-table with a vanity mirror. But no women's clothes . . .

He stepped to the door leading into the hall. There was a rattling of ice in a glass, the sound of a syphon. Mike moved out into the hall.

The Babe, in a pair of vivid blue lounging pajamas, was mixing a drink. He was lifting it to his lips when Mike said: "Hang onto it, sweetheart. With both hands. *Get both hands on that glass, fast!*"

The Babe did as he was told, watching Hansard with sullen eyes.

Mike stepped close to him, jabbed him gently with the muzzle of his pistol. "Turn around, Babe. Up against the wall there." He got the bracelets out of his hip pocket, clipped one-half of the nickeled cuffs to the killer's left wrist.

There was a buzz out in the front of the apartment, another and another.

"That will be Georgie the ape-man, huh?"

Mike snapped the other half of the handcuffs around a steam riser in the corner of the kitchen. "You stay here, beautiful. I'll go let him in. And if you yell or anything like that, I'll put a dent in that classic nose of yours."

Hansard went through the hall, past a daintily furnished living-room, to the front door. There was the sound of a key in the lock. Mike didn't wait. He jerked the door open.

Gorilla George fell into the room, his jaw gaping in astonishment. Hansard had his share of the same feeling. For behind the Gorilla, a look of grim determination on his red face and an automatic clutched in his fist, was Brundage, the Ames patrolman!

Things happened fast. The Gorilla let the momentum of his plunging entrance carry him into a dive for Mike's knees. Hansard chopped down with the barrel of his revolver, caught the ape-man beside the ear with force enough to crack the skull of an ordinary individual.

But the Gorilla didn't stop. He got those long arms around Hansard's knees, threw him heavily.

From the kitchen came a cry. "George. He's got me cuffed here!" The words spurred the scar-lipped man to a frenzy. Mike shot him once, through the shoulder, but George smashed a clubbed fist to the plainclothesman's jaw, wrenching his head to one side and sending a spasm of pain through him from the cracked rib.

Then Brundage took two quick steps, put the muzzle of his automatic in the Gorilla's right ear, pulled the trigger. The body collapsed on top of Hansard.

"Crysake, Brundage," Mike muttered. "You didn't have to do that."

The Ames man blew the smoke out of his pistol barrel. "He'd have killed you, wise guy. He was heading upstairs to do just that, when I ran into him."

Mike got painfully to his feet. "Didn't you run into my partner, too? I left him down there, on guard."

"Sure." Brundage turned the Gorilla over with his toe. "But he wanted to phone for some more of you John Laws, so I told him to go ahead. Then when I got in the building, I'm trying to find which apartment belongs to this Babe

Tyler, who used to buddy around with Dumont, an' who should come along but this rat? So I bring him up with me."

"George!" screamed the Babe, from the kitchen. "Where did he hit you, George? If that —— got you, I'll burn his eyes out!"

Mike nodded toward the kitchen. "Georgie's boy-friend, or something. The one who drilled Tom MacReady."

Brundage stuck out his jaw belligerently. "I'd like a crack at that punk. I'll run him over to the precinct house for you. You ain't in no shape to manhandle him, fella."

Hansard said: "I'll be O.K. Bent a rib last time I had an argument with these two. But you can help me with him, unless you've got ideas about collecting any part of that Jeweler's Association reward?"

The Ames man shook his head. "I ain't eligible. All I'm doin' is tryin' to protect my job. That's why I hammered Dumont until I dragged the Babe's address outa him. Gimme the cuff-keys. I got a couple of new grips I want to show that scut."

Hansard took a key from his vest pocket, tossed it to him. "Don't bang him around too much. Prosecutor'll give us trouble, if you do."

Brundage went into the kitchen.

Mike waited until the private patrolman was out of sight, then followed on tiptoe. He peeked around the corner.

Brundage was having trouble with the lock on the handcuffs.

"Hurry up," whispered the Babe. "And give me a gun."

"Left-hand pocket," muttered the Ames representative. "This key don't fit."

"Damn right it don't," Mike snapped. "You don't think I was sap enough to fall for that line of horse, do you?"

Brundage snarled, fired. But his aim was spoiled by the Babe, who was desperately trying to tug the extra pistol from Brundage's pocket.

ike took his time, steadied himself against the door jamb, shot Brundage in the navel. He had to put another slug in the same place before the private cop sank to the floor and dropped his gun.

The Babe had managed to get the automatic from Brundage's coat before the Ames man fell. He lifted it, sighted.

Hansard came in fast, knocked the muzzle aside, clipped the Babe once across the teeth with the barrel of his own .38.

The killer moaned and sagged limply against the chain of the handcuffs.

Brundage rolled over on his side. "They'll get you for this, copper. My people'll get you."

"Sure they will, Amesy." Mike ran water in the sink, put his head under it, said sputteringly: "They'll get me to accept a medal for turning up a traitor. As well as a guy who's wanted by the Frisco police."

"You're crazy. Ain't . . . first time . . . cop's gone . . . gun-crazy." Brundage put a hand to his belly. Somehow the gesture reminded Mike of Tom MacReady on the operating carriage.

"No." Mike wiped his face on a dish towel. "I might have been a little dumb. But not wacky. I had sense enough to figure out that the louse behind all these window-hole robberies must be somebody who knew a lot about the kind of stuff in jewelry-store windows and when the Ames men wouldn't be around and what time the harness bulls would be on a different part of their beats. A guy like Dumont wouldn't know all those angles. He wouldn't be able to find out, either. And naturally, a couple of torpedoes like the Gorilla and the Babe here wouldn't have that information. But you would. And working with Kutwik, you'd gotten away with it for a long

time. Using a different mob of killers every so often and knocking them off yourself, when you were through with them, I suppose."

The Babe whimpered: "George. You shot George?"

"Not me," Mike said. "I would have, only your boss beat me to the punch."

The youth in the pajamas reached over, clawed savagely at Brundage's face. Mike bent down, clipped him.

"Mike! Where are you, Mike?" It was Schmidt's worried voice, calling from the front door.

"In the kitchen," Hansard shouted.

Schmidt came running in. "Holy cow!" he breathed as he saw the two men on the floor in the corner. "Good thing I sent for an ambulance, huh?"

"What'd you do that for, Ed?"

"That jeweler, Kutwik. I went away from the car and left that Ames gent to watch him. When I come back, the Ames lad is gone and Kutwik has a hole as big as your thumb, in his chest."

"I hope he'll live," Mike growled, "to testify against this crooked private cop. His name isn't Brundage, of course. It's Sexton. But it won't make much difference. The Babe will go to town on the stand. Brundage, or Sexton, bumped the Babe's boy-friend."

"Jeeze, Mike! What a shambles! Which one shot the blonde?"

"The Babe, there. On Brundage's orders, no doubt. The girl got panicky when Tom was shot and tried to skip. They had to blot her out or the game was up." He went over to the half-conscious youth, ran his fingers through the marcelled hair. "Know what I was wondering, Eddie?"

"What, Mike?"

"How this baby will look with his head shaved."

Murder *Is* Bad Luck
Wyatt Blassingame

WYATT (RAINEY) BLASSINGAME (1909–1985) was born in Demopolis, Alabama, and graduated from the University of Alabama. Eager to travel, he hit the road and was given the nickname "Hobo." He got a job with a newspaper but lost it within a year because of the Depression. He eventually found his way to New York City in 1933, where his brother Lurton, a literary agent, showed the young writer a stack of pulp magazines and told him to take them home and study them, as they were buying stories. Six weeks later, Wyatt, who had never even heard of the pulps, sold his first story. Although he was a slower writer than many of his contemporaries, he still sold four hundred stories to the pulps before serving as an officer in the U.S. Navy during World War II, and about six hundred throughout his career. The service gave him background for several books, and he graduated to the better-paying slick magazines like *The Saturday Evening Post*, *Colliers*, *American*, and *Redbook*. When the fiction markets began to dry up, he turned to writing nonfiction articles, mainly on travel, and juveniles, mostly about animals and American history. His only book of mystery fiction was a short-story collection, *John Smith Hears Death Walking* (1944). Perhaps his best-known mystery character was Joe Gee (a short name he liked because he could type it quickly but which still counted as two words), who couldn't sleep while he was on a case. He also wrote many pulp stories under the pseudonym William B. Rainey.

"Murder *Is* Bad Luck" was published in the March 1940 issue.

Murder *Is* Bad Luck

Wyatt Blassingame

FOR ME THIS MAN McCracken was bad luck. Like a black cat or the number thirteen for some people. He didn't want to be bad luck any more than a cat does. He just *was*.

To start with, he lost me my chance at the daily double. It was New Year's Day, and the Fair Grounds was jammed with people. Christmas week had made a cut in my paycheck and I was trying to get well with ten bucks on the double, which my old agent, who is still around chiseling the boys out of their fees, had put down for me. I'm a track cop and not supposed to

bet. Extra Trouble had taken the first one all right, and now if Doomsday came through, the payoff would be $22.40 for each two-buck ticket.

I hadn't gone to the paddock, so I didn't see Doomsday until the horses were on the track. And when I saw him I leaned over to Dud Harris, who is a rat-faced private detective and a louse and happened to be standing beside me.

It started at a New Orleans racetrack, that chain of strange events of which the links were murder and mystery.

"He's got a needleful," I said.

"So it would seem indeed," Dud said.

Doomsday was wet with sweat, with foam white along his neck and around his mouth, and he was tiptoeing along, chiefly on his hind legs. He made a couple of breaks toward the infield and he took a nip at the number four horse's rump. The boy on him, an apprentice who'd been riding about three months, was so scared you could tell it by looking at him. As they paraded past—I was standing at the rail near the finish line—I yelled to Johnny on the lead pony and he turned around, meaning to get a hand on Doomsday's reins.

And then some damn fool threw a New Year's firecracker right over on the track!

The guy who threw it was standing a few yards from me, and I saw his hand go up in the air, the sparks sizzling off the fuse. A man close to him—later I learned it was this man McCracken, who at the time I had never seen—yelled, "Hey!" and grabbed the thrower's wrist, and the firecracker, instead of sailing up the track, went straight out between Doomsday's feet.

It and the horse exploded together. Doomsday made two corkscrew turns, and, on the second one, the jockey took off like a pebble out of a slingshot. Then the horse came straight at the rail, fear-crazy, and jumped it. The crowd was so thick that persons against the rail didn't have a chance. The fall broke Doomsday's right foreleg and his neck, or only God knows what would have happened; but he had already done damage enough. There was one man killed, another with a dislocated shoulder, a woman with a bloody nose, and my ten bucks gone to hell. The drunk who'd thrown the firecracker wasn't hurt.

The man with the dislocated shoulder was this McCracken. David McCracken, he

said his name was, and he said the dead man was a friend of his named Andrews. Doomsday had come right down on top of this Andrews, crushed his skull and broken his neck. I was told to go along to the hospital with the injured man and learn just how bad the lawsuit was going to be.

When I finally got to talk with McCracken he turned out to be a pretty nice fellow; an average-sized blond man with an average face. He said he realized the track wasn't to blame—and the drunk who'd thrown the firecracker didn't have money enough to be sued. All McCracken asked for was money for his doctor's bill and a pass to the track.

He couldn't tell me very much about the dead man, a fellow named Arthur Andrews, except that Andrews had been a small-time commercial artist and writer. "Told me he did articles on outdoor life and illustrated them himself," McCracken

said. "He's got a wife somewhere in New York City, I can probably find her address for you." It seemed this McCracken was a bachelor who lived on a comfortable but fairly moderate income and spent his time wandering around the world. He had met Andrews two weeks before at a little fishing camp near the mouth of the Mississippi; they'd got to be friends and had come to New Orleans together for New Year's.

The police checked this as a matter of routine and proved it was true. To everybody's surprise

Andrews' wife didn't sue the track for a dime. She just had her husband's body sent to New York and buried it. The only person who sued was the woman who'd got a bloody nose. She said her beauty had been ruined forever and she sued for a hundred thousand dollars. I said I was going to sue because my ten bucks had been on Doomsday, but the stewards reminded me they couldn't have been because a track cop isn't allowed to bet.

So that, we thought, was that. But it wasn't.

I saw McCracken a few times. Twice he asked me up to his hotel to poker games, and both times I lost. For me he was plain bad luck.

It was about two weeks later that the girl turned up at my apartment and asked if I could find David McCracken. "He's my uncle," she said, "and I've got to find him, and he seems to have disappeared all of a sudden."

I looked the girl over and decided maybe McCracken wasn't such bad luck after all. She wasn't more than five feet tall, with black hair cut in a long bob, and she was cute and sleek as a two-year-old. I like small women because I'm little myself. I'm too heavy to ride anymore, though I rated with the best for three years, and I brought home Morning Glory in the Derby; but I still don't reach over five feet six without jumping . . . and this girl was small, but oh my!

"The clerk at Uncle's hotel told me to come to you, Mr. Rice," she said. "He said you knew my uncle personally and that you were a detective and could find him, if anybody could."

"Maybe he's left town," I said.

"He was here three days ago when I arrived and telephoned him. He said he would come over to my hotel to see me—and he never got there. No one has seen him since, but his hotel says he has phoned several times to ask if he had any mail. And he's still registered there." She looked me squarely in the eyes. "If you could find him, it might be worth money to both of us. He'll be getting six months' income in a few days, and I want to make a touch. I'll pay you ten percent of what I wiggle out of him."

I'd had a sure thing in the fourth that after-noon and consequently was wondering what I would use for money the rest of the month, so pay on the side sounded good. And it wouldn't have mattered anyway—and you'd understand that if you'd seen the girl. I have my weaknesses.

"I was just going to dinner," I said. "Come along and you can explain in detail."

I went by and nicked my old agent for thirty, and the girl and I went to a place in the Quarter where they boil shrimp the way I like them. I said we should have a drink before eating and she said she'd drink a martini. I took a *pousse l'amour*. I ate there fairly often so the waiter didn't even blink, but the girl did when she saw the drink.

"What's in there?" she asked.

"Nothing but maraschino, the yolk of an egg, vanilla cordial, and brandy."

"Oh," she said. "That's all?"

"That's all. Now tell me about this missing uncle of yours."

"I'm his only niece; in fact, I'm the only relative he has." She smiled. Her lips were full, the lower one puckering down a little, the way I like them. They were bright red and her teeth were white. She was a honey. "My name's Mary Swanson and I'm a junior in medical school."

"What?" I said. "Huh?"

She laughed. "Everybody looks that way when I say I'm studying medicine, but I am. I won't be much longer, though, if I don't find Uncle David and put the bee on him. He wasn't very definite in his last letter, so I decided I'd come down—from St. Louis—and try to talk him out of a thousand dollars. After all, I'm his only living relative, and I happen to know that he gets half his income every year about the first of February. But I've got to be back at school in a couple of days, and I haven't been able to find him."

"He's hiding out on you."

She shook her head. "I don't think so. He's always been generous with me. I've never had to ask him for money before. But he did sound strange when I talked to him over the phone—kind of frightened. I'm afraid something has happened to him."

She took another martini and I had a brandy scaffa, which is made of raspberry syrup, maraschino, green chartreuse, and brandy, the liquors kept in separate layers. She said it was pretty, but that she didn't want to sample it. Which was probably my loss.

I asked why she hadn't gone to the police about her uncle.

She sipped at her drink and then looked up, half serious and half grinning. "I'm afraid my uncle's got himself mixed up in some kind of personal affair. Nothing bad, but—well, I have my reasons."

I said that I could understand, and that Sandy Rice was to be relied on to be discreet in matters of this kind. And she said, "I'm sure you are, Mr. Rice."

And I said, "Call me Sandy."

So we ate dinner, and afterwards she drank cognac and I took a brandy sangaree, which is a mild concoction of sugar and water and brandy and port wine with nutmeg sprinkled on top.

It was cold when we went outside. The wind whipped down Conti Street, and Mary—she was Mary by now and I didn't even remember her last name—put her hand in my elbow. "Let's go over to your uncle's hotel," I said. "If we don't learn anything, we can take in the first show at the Blue Room without getting out in the cold again."

Sam, the night clerk at the hotel, said, "McCracken phoned a couple of times to know if he had any mail, but I haven't seen him the last three nights. I told the girl you were the guy to help her." Mary was standing several yards behind me. Sam said, "Nice, huh?" and leered out of one corner of his eye like a cop who has caught you speeding but doesn't want to write a ticket. "One good turn deserves another, Sandy."

I said, "There is some rumor that Old Cactus will take the fourth tomorrow, but I wouldn't put more than two bucks on it."

"Thanks."

It was my inning now.

"How about giving me the key to McCracken's room and letting me go up and look around?"

"I like this job," Sam said. "I don't want to lose it."

"Is it still the same room?"

"Yes. Five twelve."

I said, "If the odds go below five to one, tomorrow might not be Old Cactus' day after all."

"You are a hell of a detective," Sam said. "You protect the people's interests, don't you?"

"I work for the track. I investigate what they tell me to. I can't help rumors."

I told Mary to wait for me in the lobby. I rode up to the fifth floor and went up to five twelve, the first door around the bend in the hall. There are quite a few keys on my key ring and they will open a lot of doors, but none of them opened this one. Wondering why, I tried the knob. The door was already unlocked. I stepped inside and closed the door again.

It was dark in the room, just a little gray haze coming through the windows. I moved to the left, feeling for the light switch, and my foot touched something big and heavy and rubbery. My hand touched the switch at the same time and I clicked it on. I looked down at the thing at my feet.

It was a man. He lay on his back with one arm flung back. The coat was messy with blood and the knife was still there under his left shoulder blade. Blood was bubbling slowly around it, but he was dead, plenty. And they tell me that when a corpse is still bleeding, then it hasn't been a corpse more than a few minutes.

I looked at the dead man's face, and I had never seen him before. Then I looked up and saw that the door to the adjoining room was open.

It was very still and very quiet; that kind of quiet stillness that comes just before a big race when there is actually some movement and sound all around you but you don't hear it or see it anymore. It was the kind of stiff quietness that you feel.

When McCracken and Arthur Andrews—the man who had been killed in the accident at the track—had come here they had taken adjoining rooms, and after Andrews' death, McCracken had kept both rooms. The one beyond the open door was dark except for the yellow rectangle of light on the floor.

I didn't know what to do. I didn't have a gun and I didn't have any business here—though Sam, the desk clerk, knew damn well I had come up—and I didn't know if there was anybody in that dark room beyond the door. But there wasn't much time to think and I did a fool thing . . . maybe Mary and I shouldn't have stopped in that bar on the way to the hotel where I put down an East India cocktail of raspberry syrup, caroni bitters, red curaçao, maraschino, and a double brandy. Anyway, I reached down and took the knife out of the dead man's back—it was really stuck in there. I had to pull hard to get it loose. Then I circled the bed and went through that open door into the room beyond.

I could see the outline of the room, but nothing else. I turned on the light to make sure. The room was empty.

I tried the door opening into the hall. It was unlocked.

When I looked down, I saw that several drops of blood had dripped from the knife blade onto the floor. The palm of my hand was sticky, and all at once I felt a little sick at the pit of my stomach. I realized I had been so scared the backs of my knees were aching.

I returned to the room where the dead man lay. Somebody knocked on the door, two sharp raps, and then the door opened and a man came in. He said, "Ah, David, if you won't answer my letters, I—" Then he stumbled over the dead man.

He was a tall, thin, hawk-nosed man and he looked as if he was accustomed to having his own way. He certainly had control of himself. He took a half step back from the corpse and his mouth, which wasn't much more than a white slit in his face to start with, got tighter and whiter. He reached in the inside pocket of his expensive gray topcoat and took out a .25 automatic. The gun was about as big as a pack of cigarettes, but it was big enough. With his left hand he reached back of him and closed the door into the hall.

"Drop that knife," he said. And when I did, "Where's David McCracken?"

I just stood there. There wasn't much else I could do. "I don't know," I said.

The newcomer stared hard at me.

"This is his room, isn't it? Where is he?"

"It's his room all right, but he's not here. I don't know where he is."

"Was he here when you killed this man?" His eyes flickered down to the body and back at me again, hard and black. "That's impossible. This man hasn't been dead more than ten minutes." He had a deep voice but it was sharp and hard and very distinct. Except for one of these Boston accents, he would have made a swell race announcer. He said, "What are you doing in McCracken's room?"

"I was looking for him."

"And this man?" He gestured at the corpse without taking his eyes off me. That fishy stare was getting me.

"I found him here."

"Who is he? What is his connection with Mr. McCracken? And who are you?"

I was getting over the shock of looking into the gun muzzle and felt sure the man wasn't going to shoot. I said, "I'm a detective, of sorts. The guy on the floor I don't know. Do you?"

We faced one another for about four seconds, the tall man trying to make up his mind about something. I had already made up my mind; I wished to God I had never heard of David McCracken.

The man said, his mind made up, "Back over to that phone in the corner and tell whoever answers that you have killed a man in room five-twelve and to send the police."

"Wait a minute!" I said. "You're jumping the bell. I didn't kill him. I never saw the guy before."

He said, "Phone," and meant it.

The switchboard girl answered and I said, "Put Sam on the line."

The tall man snapped, "You can talk to whoever answers!"

"To hell with you." I was certain now he wasn't going to shoot. I said, "Sam, I'm up in McCracken's room. The door was unlocked; that's how I got in. And there was somebody ahead of me. A guy with a knife stuck in his back."

Sam made muffled moaning sounds like a man who has bet next week's pay on the favorite and watched him run last.

"And now there's somebody else up here, some nut with a gun who thinks I did the killing. . . . No, I never saw either of 'em before. You better phone Lieutenant Murphy."

I hung up and the tall man and I stood there looking at one another. With his left hand he reached in his pocket and got out an ivory-tipped cigarette and a gold lighter and lit up. He never took his eyes off me and he never moved the gun.

Someone knocked on the door. I thought it was the house dick. The tall man said, "Come in," but the door was already opening, a woman coming through, saying, "Art, darling, I've—" and then she stumbled over the body.

She screamed. It wasn't a loud cry. It was choked, like a man trying to yell after a horse has kicked him in the belly. Her eyes got too big for their sockets and I thought they were going to spill over. Her face got so white the make-up looked like smeared blood. She staggered back against the wall.

The tall man snapped at her, "Whom were you looking for?" You could be certain he said "whom" because that's the way he pronounced words.

The woman didn't say anything. She just stared at the corpse as though she was going to be sick.

"You were looking for Mr. McCracken?"

She looked up at him, and then at me. She was breathing hard. She was still frightened, but her face wasn't so twisted with fear anymore and I began to notice that she was good-looking, very good-looking indeed, if you like redheads, and I do. Blondes, brunettes, and redheads. She was a little tall for me, slender, but full where she should be. She had a kind of bright, show-off beauty, and my guess was she'd been a chorus girl.

"Yes," she said after a while. "David McCracken."

"You're lying!" the tall man snapped. He sounded damn sure of himself.

And about that time the house dick came in, and a few minutes later Lieutenant Murphy and a whole flock of boys from Headquarters.

Now the fun would begin. Fun for everyone but me.

The tall man pointed at me and told them, "I knocked on the door and entered and found this man with the bloody knife in his hand."

Murphy is a big man with pink cheeks and pale, heavy-lidded eyes, and a brother-in-law who is a politician, or else he never would have got on the force, no less be a lieutenant. When he looked at me I knew he was still remembering a sure thing I had given him a couple of weeks back. The sure thing had run fourth. (That's the hell of being connected with the track; persons keep after you to put them onto something, and if you don't they hate you for a cheapskate, and if you do—and it comes in—they forget you; and if it doesn't come home, they say you touted them wrong intentionally. Hell, if I could find one really sure thing a season, I wouldn't be working for a living.)

I said, "Now look, Pete. I never saw this guy on the floor before in my life. I didn't kill him. Why don't you ask this tall bird what he's doing here and what he's carrying a gun for?"

The tall man said his name was Linden Blumberry and he was from Boston. "I am Mr. David McCracken's lawyer and the administrator of his estate. For several weeks I have been trying to persuade Mr. McCracken to come to Boston to complete the sale of some bonds of his for which I have obtained an offer. For some strange reason he has refused to come there. So I came to him."

"Carrying a gun?" I said.

He looked down a thin nose at me before he decided to answer. "And a certified check for five thousand dollars to complete the sale. Of course I carried a gun."

I told Murphy about McCracken's niece, and how I had come up to his room and knocked on the door, which was ajar, I said, and which swung open when I knocked; and from there I went on with the exact truth.

Murphy snorted and the fingerprint man said, from the next room, "Only one set of prints on this knife, I think, Lieutenant. I can make sure after I get it down to Headquarters." And that set would be mine!

The M.E. said the dead man had been killed sometime within the last forty minutes, and Murphy looked at me and nodded his head.

The red-headed girl said her name was Nell Parker, and she had known McCracken in New York, had written to him occasionally. She had come south for the winter, arriving in New Orleans that very day, and had called on McCracken.

Both she and Mr. Linden Blumberry said they had never seen the dead man before.

Murphy had the hotel manager and Sam, the night clerk, in the room by now. Sam looked worried. "I didn't give anybody the key to Mr. McCracken's room," he kept saying. "I don't know how the door could have been opened."

"You didn't have any idea that Sandy Rice was coming up here?" Murphy asked.

"No, sir. There've been lots of persons phoning and asking about Mr. McCracken lately, but I just told them he wasn't in. I would have told this gentleman," he nodded toward Linden Blumberry, "when he asked for Mr. McCracken's room number, but he walked off before I could explain."

"What did you think Sandy Rice wanted with McCracken?"

"Well, Sandy used to play poker up here sometimes, I think. I—" Sam began to stammer; and Murphy started looking at me with his mouth grinning and his pale eyes cold.

"Gambling," he said. He had it all worked out now. Somehow the gambling would furnish a motive; and I'd practically been caught in the act of murder. They'd make a cinch case out of it. I'd have a chance like a three-legged mule in a match race with Johnstown.

"Damn it!" I said. "Let's get Mary up here and she'll tell you—"

"Mary?" Murphy asked.

"McCracken's niece, you idiot. She's downstairs in the lobby. She'll tell you what I was doing."

He told the other cops to keep their eyes on Blumberry and the red-headed girl and the corpse, and we would be right back. We rode down on the elevator. Pete said, "I lost twenty bucks on that pig you touted me on. I hope to Gawd you try something cute."

There wasn't any need to argue with him. He wasn't much better than a half-wit anyway.

We started across the lobby. I couldn't see Mary anywhere. "Where is she?" Pete said.

A man and woman in evening clothes passed us. The woman wore one of these dresses without any shoulder straps at all—the kind that looks like it has already started to fall off and is halfway gone. Pete said, "My Gawd! Look at that!" and turned to watch.

It was then I saw another couple going out the street door at the far end of the lobby. Mary and David McCracken! I started to run after them.

Halfway across the lobby, I heard Pete bellow, just a roar of sound at first, changing into, "Hey! Hey, you!" and of all things, "Halt!"

Mary and Dave McCracken were already out of sight, but I wasn't going to lose them. I kept going.

I was running, five yards from the door, the Negro doorman staring at me and at Pete, who was following across the lobby. All at once the Negro's face went a sort of ash gray and he went straight up and came down running. At the same time a hole popped in the door—and then I heard the shot. I hadn't thought that idiot Pete would shoot, but now I was going too fast to stop. The second bullet whined at my ear as I plunged down the steps.

A quarter block down the lighted street I saw McCracken helping Mary into an automobile. She had stopped, half in and half out, and was staring back toward the sound of the shots. I yelled, "Hey! Wait!"

McCracken shoved her. He shoved her so hard she must have bounced against the other side of the car. He dived after her.

I saw I couldn't catch him on foot, so I angled for one of the cabs lined up in front of the hotel. Behind me there was a crash as Pete Murphy came through the hotel door, waving his gun. The driver of the cab I was going for took one look and went out the other side and I jumped under the wheel. I got the taxi going just as that half-witted cop let go with another bullet. I heard it smack into the rear of the car.

There was only one car between McCracken and me. I figured I'd catch him easy enough. By this time I was mad as hell, getting shoved around and accused of murder and shot at. I put my foot down hard on the gas.

The streetlight was green, and McCracken went straight across Canal into Dauphine Street. I knew I had him. He was going the wrong way on a one-way street. The first block was almost empty of traffic, but if he turned, he'd have to slow down; and if he went straight, he'd jam up in traffic.

And then my motor gave a couple of *sputs* and died. Pete Murphy had shot a hole in the gas tank. My luck with McCracken was holding steady. Less than a block behind me cops were blowing whistles and running and waving guns and people were yelling.

I left the taxi where it stopped. In fact, I left it before it stopped.

he joint I picked was called The Purple Door. I had never been there but once, and nobody knew me, and they had closed booths along the rear wall. I went past the bar, across what they called a dance floor where a three-piece Negro orchestra was blowing its lungs out, and into a booth. I sat down and one of the house girls sat down opposite me.

"Run along," I said. "I got trouble."

"You waiting for one of the other girls?"

"I'm waiting for a drink."

"Well, you want to buy me one, don't you?"

"No," I said, "I don't. I just want to sit here and do some deep thinking."

A waiter stuck his head in the booth and the girl said, "Hey, Doug, this guy don't want to buy me a drink."

"What's he want?" Doug demanded. "Hold his own hand? You can do that outside, squirt."

I was deciding that with the cops looking for me I would be less conspicuous in the French Quarter with a girl than without one, so I said, "All right, I'll buy her a drink. What you want, baby?"

"I know what she wants," Doug said. "What about you?"

"A Roman punch."

"A what?"

"If the bartender don't know how to make it, tell him to look it up. He can read, can't he?"

Doug spat out of one corner of his mouth. "What difference's it to you? You ain't big enough to complain."

He went off and the girl said, "It's a cold night, ain't it?" and I didn't say anything. I had a lot of hard thinking to do. I had a murder charge hanging over me and I was guilty of stealing a taxi. I had run away from the scene of the crime and Pete Murphy would be sure I was guilty; once he got me in jail, that would be the end of it. From there to the hot seat would be shorter than the road from the betting ring to the poor-house. Once they got me in jail it would all be over—so I had to keep out of jail and learn who had murdered the man in the hotel room—and I didn't even know who the murdered man was!

The waiter brought our drinks. He looked at my Roman punch and at me and shook his head and went away again. The girl said, "My Lord! What's in there beside a fruit salad?"

"A mixture. Raspberry syrup, lemon juice, orange juice, curaçao, rum, and brandy. I like the brandy."

"I been working in this joint for six months," she said, "and this is the first time I ever thought I got the best of it by drinking this colored water they serve us girls."

I said, "Uh," and went back to figuring what I had ahead of me. I couldn't go home, because the cops would be watching the place, and I couldn't go to the track tomorrow because they'd be there too. I tried to think of Mary's last name and I couldn't remember it—and she hadn't told me which hotel she was staying in. But obviously the thing to do was find her and McCracken, because I felt sure McCracken would at least know the corpse in his hotel room. But how to find McCracken?

The waiter stuck his head in the door. "You ready for a drink, buddy? That ain't a park bench you're setting on."

The girl said, "I'll take another one."

"A brandy flip," I said.

The waiter brought it and when I took a sip the girl said, "You're drunker than I thought you were; you wouldn't drink that thing sober."

"I like it. There's nothing in it but hot ale and egg and sugar and nutmeg and brandy."

"Oh," she said. "You're one of these straight whiskey drinkers, huh?"

I said, "I love to buy you whiskey, or that colored water they serve you girls for whiskey. But I'd love it better if you kept quiet. I got some thinking to do."

"It's oke with me. I get paid by the drink."

"It's a wonder that pink water don't rot your stomach out," I said, and then went back to my thinking. I tried to remember everything that had ever happened to me which had any

connection with David McCracken. It was a dismal list, all bad. I tried to remember everything that had happened tonight from the time Mary rang my doorbell and asked if I could find her uncle. I thought about this a while and said to the girl:

"Excuse me, baby, but I got to make a phone call. Just wait for me."

The Negro orchestra was blowing so loud it shook the phone booth, but I finally got Sam, the hotel clerk. He was an inquisitive cuss, and I figured that by this time he would know everything the police did. I asked him if the cops had identified the corpse.

"Sure," he said. "Where are you?"

"You just answer questions and one of these days I'll give you a winner."

He said the stiff was identified as a Roscoe Jancey, a member of a New York brokerage firm.

"How much money did he have on him?" I asked.

"Fourteen bucks and twenty cents. But at the St. Charles—that's where he was staying—he'd put five hundred in the safe."

"Did he have any big certified checks on him, or in the safe?"

"There's none listed," Sam said. "What's your idea?"

"That lanky Boston lawyer, Linden Blumberry, brought down a big check for McCracken. And you said the dead man was a broker. I thought maybe he'd brought one too."

Sam was quiet a moment before he said, "He didn't bring the one Mr. Blumberry had. That was on a Boston firm and had to be countersigned by Blumberry himself."

"Not that one," I said. "But there may be some damn fool who wanted to steal the one he did bring." And I hung up and went back to the booth and finished my brandy flip.

The waiter stuck his head in and looked at the empty glass, and then at me with some new respect. He said, "Little man, what now?"

"A metropolitan cocktail."

The girl said, "When you make mine this time, use the big eyedropper to put the liquor in my water. I got to have something to help me stand up under this guy's conversation. I swear to Gawd he's about to talk my ear off."

Doug brought the drinks back and put mine gently on the table. "I'll bring the lilies with the next one," he said. The guy underestimated me.

"You don't have to worry as long as I stick to straight brandy," I said. "I always stick to brandy when I'm drinking fairly steady."

"Oh," the girl said. "So that's straight brandy?"

"With gum syrup, caroni bitters, and French vermouth thrown in," the waiter said. "The bartender's sprained his back looking under the shelf for bottles that ain't had the dust off 'em since he bought this place." He closed the booth door and went away.

The girl said, "How'd you ever learn the names of all them drinks? You read 'em in a book somewhere? Or'd you used to be a bartender?"

"I used to be a jockey," I said. "I was raised around horses; I never had more than two bits at a time until I was sixteen and started riding; and all at once I was in the big money. Of course, after three years I was too heavy and out of the money again, but when I had it, I had plenty. I had to train most of the time, but on Saturday nights I'd go out with the other jockeys and, because we didn't know any better, we'd order whatever looked the fanciest and cost the most. I got to where I liked the things."

She said, "I been drinking this pink water a long time, but I ain't got to like it yet."

"Won't they let you drink anything else?"

"Yeah, if the customer'll buy it. But this is almost all profit and I get a bigger cut off one of these than off something costs more. Besides, you can drink these all night."

That reminded me that I couldn't sit here gossiping all night, so I started figuring on my problem again. But I didn't get anywhere. I wanted to find McCracken and I didn't know how to go about it . . . until about fifteen minutes later, when I got my first break. The door of the booth opened and there was the rat-faced private detective named Dud Harris, the same

guy who'd been beside me at the track the first time I ever saw McCracken.

He grinned and showed his rat teeth and said, "I am a very smart detective, Sandy. I am indeed the smartest detective in Lousiana. I find you in ten minutes when all the cops in New Orleans are sitting around waiting for you in other places. I am very smart indeed." He was very pleased with himself.

"If you're so damn smart," I said, "why can't you see I've got company?" There wasn't any sense in spreading the news that the cops were looking for me.

"Do not worry about her. My car is outside, so let us depart. I have news for you." I'm not lying; that's the way he talked. In Omaha once I saw an amateur play where the characters talked the way Dud Harris did, but, in addition, Dud always had his pointed teeth sticking down below his narrow, mustached lip. He was one of these people you want to sock without knowing why. But he was smart, and if he said he had news, it was probably worthwhile. Anything right then was worth trying.

e drove down St. Louis to Canal and out toward Lake Pontchartrain. I asked how he'd found me.

"I have been talking with our mutual friend, the night clerk, Sam. He told me you had phoned."

"I didn't tell him where I was."

"No. But Sam is a very observing young man, though not smart. He said you were calling from an establishment which had a very loud and raucous band. I concluded it would not be any of the places you frequent, because you feared the police would be looking for you there. And yet I thought you would be in the Quarter. I found you in the third dive I investigated."

"Why were you looking for me?"

"I thought perhaps you were interested in locating Mr. David McCracken."

I turned around on the seat and looked at him. He was whistling softly through his teeth, staring straight ahead at the street and seeming very pleased with himself.

"Do you know where McCracken is?"

"I do," he said. "Indeed I do."

"Where?"

"That is a long story, Sandy. I was hired two days ago, by a Mr. Roscoe Jancey, of New York City, to locate Mr. David McCracken. Tonight, having accomplished the job with my usual ease, I was embittered to learn that Mr. Roscoe Jancey is now a corpse who will never pay my fee. But it occurred to me, after hearing the story, that you might be willing to take Mr. Jancey's place. It occurred to me that locating Mr. McCracken might help you to prove you had not murdered Mr. Jancey."

"How do you know I didn't?"

"I am a student of human nature," Dud said. "You are not capable of cold-blooded murder."

I promised that I would borrow a hundred bucks in the morning and pay him—that was the price he insisted on, and I wasn't in any spot to argue. He gave me an address which was only a couple of blocks from the point we were passing, and at the next corner he stopped and let me out.

I watched the red tail-light of his car as he drove away. The idea that Dud Harris was mixed up in this was something new. Maybe he was right that I couldn't commit a cold-blooded murder, but I'd bet that Dud could stab a man in the back any time he needed to.

The house McCracken was supposed to be in was between City Park and Canal, a small place with shrubs growing in the yard. The blinds were pulled, so that at first I thought there were no lights inside; then I saw a narrow yellow thread under the front door. It was cold and the wind flapped my top coat against my knees as I started up the walk.

I wished suddenly I had a gun. I had a creepy feeling that I was going to need one. But I didn't have one with me, and I couldn't go home to get one because the cops would be watching my apartment house.

I went up the steps quietly and tried the knob without knocking. The door swung open.

I stood in the doorway looking in.

David McCracken was walking across the floor with a half-filled glass of whiskey and soda in his hand, walking like a man who has been at it a long time, back and forth. He looked worried and frightened. He spun around as I entered, turning so fast some of the liquor spilled from his glass. "What—What . . ." His mouth hung open.

I let him have it. I said, "I want to know why you killed that man in your hotel room."

He'd been frightened before, but now he looked as though he was going to faint. His face got green and he just stammered without making any sense. He didn't seem able to say anything but, "What? What? What?"

"The dead man in your hotel room," I said. "A Roscoe Jancey. Why did you kill him?"

The whiskey glass slid out of his hand and broke on the floor. He didn't notice it. His mouth was working with froth coming out of it like he was a horse who'd run the mile and a quarter in mud. Finally he said, "I didn't kill anybody. I haven't been in that room in three days." He swallowed hard. "Who'd you say was killed?"

"Roscoe Jancey, of New York."

"I never heard of him."

I was watching him when he said it, and I would have sworn he was telling the truth. It gave me an empty feeling in the stomach, because I'd counted on something here that would help. This made the whole mess crazier than ever.

And then the door on the far side of the room opened and Mary came in, looking as pretty and cute as a puppy. She was smiling with her mouth, but her eyes were a little worried. Her black hair waved smooth down to her shoulders and she must have just finished putting on fresh make-up. "I thought I heard your voice," she said. "What was all the excitement in front of the hotel just as Mr. Smith and I were leaving?"

"You didn't want to see."

"I wanted to. But Mr. Smith said that if I wanted to find Uncle Dave I'd have to hurry."

I stared at her, trying to make sense out of her words. "*Who* said *what?*"

"Mr. Smith said he'd take me to Uncle Dave, but there wasn't any time to waste. I knew you'd understand."

"I don't. Isn't Dave McCracken your uncle?"

It was her turn to stare.

"Why, of course."

I was really confused now.

"Then you mean this man here isn't McCracken?"

"Certainly not. But he said he knew where Uncle Dave—"

McCracken jumped. I never saw anybody move so fast. I was spinning sideways but he got his left hand on my coat, and held on. He was bigger than I was and the top coat handicapped me. I hit him twice in the face with all I had, but he still held on. And then he had the gun out of his hip pocket and slammed me over the head with it.

The room began to spin around in easy circles, but I could tell I was on hands and knees, and I could feel the blood running down my forehead from the cut the gun had made. I heard somebody screaming, away off, it seemed; and then I knew it was right there in the room with me. It was Mary. She was backed into a corner and McCracken was going for her.

I tried to get up and I stumbled and fell. My head hit the arm of a chair. I went down flat— and cold.

I came to on the floor where I had fallen. My wrists and ankles were tied and I was gagged and my head hurt like hell. There was dried blood in my eyes and I couldn't see very clearly.

I blinked a few times and twisted around and there was Mary on the floor across the room from me. She was tied up the same way I was and her hair wasn't in smooth waves anymore; but she was conscious and she didn't seem to be hurt. She tried to grin at me, which is quite a job when you have a lemon in your mouth with a handkerchief tied outside to keep it there.

My head hurt worse than a homebrew hangover, but I started wiggling around, trying to get loose. McCracken had been hurried and frightened and he'd done a lousy job of tying me up with some neckties. In five minutes I knew I was going to make it. It took about fifteen minutes altogether. Then I untied Mary.

"Well, well," she said, "fancy meeting you here." She began to laugh. She was scared almost sick, but she was fighting against it. That girl had what it takes.

"Where'd McCracken go?" I asked.

"Who?"

"McCracken. At least, he's the fellow I knew as David McCracken. You called him Smith."

"That's what he told me his name was. The one thing I'm certain of; he's not my uncle."

"Where'd he go?"

"I don't know. But don't you think we better leave here before he comes back? He might," she swallowed, "might do worse next time."

"Wait a minute. Maybe I can find a gun." I searched the house and the only thing of interest was a small batch of drawings done in pencil. They were pretty good. One of them showed a horse and jockey and under the picture was written: *Sandy Rice on Morning Glory.*

I said, "Well, I'll be damned!" But I didn't find a gun.

Mary and I walked two blocks before we located an all-night drug store and I phoned for a cab. My watch showed ten minutes after four. It was cold, that wet kind of New Orleans cold that soaks through you so you feel as cold in the middle of your stomach as outside.

Mary was explaining, "I was waiting for you in the lobby. You must have been gone nearly a half hour. And the clerk who'd been at the desk—"

"Sam?"

"I think that's the one. He'd left the desk a

few minutes before. Then this Mr. Smith, or whatever his real name is, came up and asked for my uncle's mail. I heard him and so I asked him if he knew where Uncle Dave was. He looked frightened, and then he said yes, he knew where Uncle Dave was, and he'd take me to him. As we were getting in his car we heard the shooting and I saw you run out; but Mr. Smith shoved me into the car. He said Uncle Dave was already in trouble and couldn't afford any more. He brought me to that house, and he said for me to wait until Uncle Dave came. After two or three hours you came in."

We were waiting for the cab, drinking black scalding coffee at the soda fountain. I asked, "After he bopped me, what?"

"He tied me up; he didn't hurt me once I quit fighting. Then he tied you and walked up and down the room like he didn't know what to do next, until finally he turned around and said he would be back later, and went dashing out the door."

It looked to me as though I had part of this crazy matter worked out; but I still couldn't be sure. I told Mary about the murder and she said she had never heard of a Roscoe Jancey; as far as I could tell the world wasn't going to miss Roscoe Jancey very much. Nobody seemed to have heard of him. He was a hell of a man to get sent to the electric chair about.

"What about a Mr. Linden Blumberry?" I asked.

"I know him. He had charge of Uncle David's estate. And by the way, when I was waiting for you in the lobby I thought I saw him coming down the stairs, but then somebody got in the way and, when I looked again, I decided I was wrong."

"He was there." The cab was blowing outside and we went out to it. It was cold in the taxi and we sat close together. "Downtown," I told the driver. And then I asked Mary, "What about this Blumberry?"

"I always had an idea he'd be crooked if he needed to."

"Well, he's a lawyer, isn't he?"

She laughed and said I must not like lawyers and I started to tell her about the time I got sued for breach of promise by a girl I had never seen but once in my life—that was when I was riding and in the money—but I skipped it. I asked her if she had ever heard of a Nell Parker, a good-looking redhead.

Mary looked up at me, frowning a little. "No . . . Why?"

"The redhead who came rushing into your uncle's hotel room tonight said that was her name."

Mary was quiet a moment. "When you asked me why I didn't go to the police about my uncle," she said, "I didn't tell you the exact truth—at least not all of it. Maybe I should."

"It's about time."

"When I telephoned Uncle David the day I got to New Orleans, the first thing he said when he heard my voice was: 'Nell, darling!' He said it in a way Uncle David has assured me he never spoke to women. He was pretty much of a Puritan. When he didn't turn up, I thought perhaps this Nell was mixed up in it somewhere, and if I went to the police and they found him—and her—he might not be in the humor for lending me money. I thought it was better to find him privately."

"I think it's time we found her," I said.

"Do you believe Uncle David's with her?"

I looked at her squarely. "I believe your Uncle David is dead. I believe he has been dead for a month."

The morning papers were on the street by now. I read that I was wanted on suspicion of murder. From what Lieutenant Pete Murphy had told the reporters, there didn't seem to be much suspicion; Pete was sure. Cops were ordered to shoot if necessary. It gave me a sort of weak feeling in the stomach.

The paper also listed the names and addresses of everybody mixed in the affair. Nell Parker was staying in a small apartment hotel in the French Quarter. We went there.

It was one of these old places with a courtyard. Fog was coming in from the river and you could smell the river and once or twice hear a ship's horn moaning. There was a kind of gray light mixed in with the fog, but you still had to feel your way along. Inside the house it was almost as bad; a hall down each floor that was almost as wide as the rooms on either side and just a small globe at the end. The whole building had a damp cold smell.

"How'll you know which room is hers?" Mary was whispering, though I had told her not to.

"I'm guessing there'll be somebody awake in her room, and talking." So I went from door to door, listening. It was on the second floor at the back I heard the voices.

A man was saying, "—never meant to let myself in for murder! They'll pin it on me sure! We've got to get away from here!"

A woman said something I couldn't understand.

Then the man said, "We've got enough. We've got insurance."

I didn't know what to do. If I went for the cops and this man and woman got away, I was a sure thing for the electric chair. And once the cops got their hands on me, they weren't likely to look farther; it would take a long time to convince them, probably too long. But I didn't have a gun.

I decided to take the chance this fellow wouldn't shoot. I motioned to Mary to stand back, raised my hand, and knocked on the door.

The voices in the room stopped as though I had hit them with a hammer. There wasn't a sound at all. Way down the river somewhere a foghorn tooted.

I knocked on the door again.

There was about ten seconds of quiet and I thought, "Maybe they are taking it on the lam out the window," then I heard the clacking sound a woman's mules make and the door was unlocked and opened. The redhead from the hotel stood there, wearing a negligée. I moved with the door as it opened and got inside before she could stop me.

Except for the redhead, the room seemed empty. But on the far side there was a closed French window onto a balcony. I thought I saw something move there, a little gleam of light on metal. I kept wondering if the man was going to shoot, and I had the weak sensation you get as you start down the highest drop on a roller coaster.

The redhead said, "What the devil do you want?"

"I'm looking for your husband."

She took a long breath. It made her breasts stand tight against the silk negligée. "For who?"

Arthur Andrews supposedly had been killed at the race track the time I first saw McCracken. But I felt sure now he was alive. I looked at the window.

"For Mr. Arthur Andrews," I said. The light glint outside moved and I said quick, loud: "I know he didn't kill that man at the hotel. I just want him to help me prove it."

Her face got very pale, but set. She had green eyes like those of a cat. "Didn't you kill him?"

"No," I said.

"Then who did?"

I'll admit it was part guess work, but I had to give her and Andrews something because I needed them. The whole thing had to come clean before the cops would believe me. And I didn't know who was on the balcony. I knew part of it but not all. I didn't know I was practically trying to commit suicide.

I said, "The real McCracken's lawyer killed him. That Mr. Linden Blumberry."

On the balcony the light beam moved fast. A man yelled and I dived sideways. There was a hole in the glass window with lines spider-webbing out from it and the sound of the gun came smashing through.

I was rolling sideways, trying to get out of range, when the second shot blasted. The bullet ripped into the floor by my face. Then I got both hands on a straight chair and flung it. It was a big chair, but when you're scared as I was, you're stronger than you think.

The window went out with a crash. And there was another sound that wasn't part of the window breaking; that kind of screeching noise a nail makes when it's pulled out of wood, and the crackle of iron.

A man screamed. He really screamed. Then there was a kind of soggy bump and the scream stopped with it.

I stood up and was surprised my knees would hold me, and even more surprised that my stomach didn't give way and let my shoulders settle down on my knees. But somehow I got over to the balcony. There was a man standing there looking down where the rail was gone. As I came up the man turned around. It was David McCracken. At least, he was the fellow I had thought was McCracken; the fellow who told Mary his name was Smith. His name actually was Arthur Andrews.

I looked down to where there was something dark in the courtyard. "Who's that?"

"I don't know. When you knocked, I ducked out here and he was here. I'd never seen him before. When he tried to shoot you I grabbed him. We were wrestling and—and . . ." He swallowed.

We went down and looked at him. It was Linden Blumberry, the lawyer. He wasn't dead, but he wasn't going to get up soon. His back was broken.

ary was ready to go back to medical school and I had said I would take her to the train. We started a couple of hours early so as to have time for a drink or two. Mary was sipping a martini and I was drinking gin with her, a Kinney fifty-fifty, which is a smooth mixture of rum, grapefruit juice, the white of an egg, and gin.

Mary said, "Now tell me how you knew that Mr. Blumberry, Uncle Dave's lawyer, had killed that man."

I said I hated to admit it, but it was part guess work. "But I did have some things to go on. When he found me in the room with the corpse,

he said the man hadn't been dead more than ten minutes. But he hadn't even touched the body, except to stumble against it. He'd hardly glanced at it—and it had stopped bleeding. In that light he couldn't even tell if the blood was dry or not. I wondered from the first how he could be so sure."

"And you guessed from that?"

"With what you told me. You said you saw Blumberry coming down the hotel stairway. In other words, he had already been upstairs, and was walking down again. Yet he claimed to have come up only once, in the elevator. All I needed was a motive. The cops have got that straight now."

"Explain it," she said.

"It was some kind of South American government bond which had been defaulted years ago and was considered worthless. I don't understand much about these things, but it seems this government was trying to get some fresh American cash and, to make a good impression, they were going to redeem those old bonds. Your uncle had nearly a hundred thousand dollars in them. The redemption had been kept under cover and Blumberry was trying to buy them from your uncle for five thousand, buying them under another name and selling your uncle on the idea he'd found a sucker. The trouble was, your uncle was supposed to go to Boston to close the deal. And he couldn't go because he was dead. And Andrews couldn't go because he'd be recognized as a fake."

"You mean that when the accident happened at the track, Mr. Smith, or Andrews, or whatever his name was, told the police that Uncle Dave, the dead man, was named Andrews, while he pretended to be Uncle Dave?"

"That's it. Andrews and your uncle had actually met in that fishing camp, just as Andrews told me. They got to be friends and came to New Orleans together. Your uncle had told Andrews enough about his affairs for Andrews to know your uncle lived on an income, and that a good part of it was soon due. Andrews himself was in a tough hole financially. When the accident happened he saw his chance. He and your uncle were about the same size, both blond. They didn't look particularly alike, but they looked enough alike for a vague description to fit either one of them. And nobody knew them.

"Everybody took Andrews' word for it that he was McCracken. He wrote his wife in New York, and when your uncle's body arrived, Mrs. Andrews buried it just as if it were her husband, and collected his insurance. The insurance company didn't investigate. They had the word of the New Orleans authorities that Andrews had been killed in an accident. Andrews was waiting for your uncle's checks to arrive. He had some old signatures of your uncle's which he could trace as endorsement—and that would be that. Then he could leave, change his name again, and your uncle would vanish. Or with good luck he could just keep on living on your uncle's income."

"And then?"

"Then this matter of the bonds turned up. Andrews wouldn't go to Boston, so Blumberry came here. I think he came intending to kill your uncle, but he swears no. With your stubborn uncle out of the way it would have been easy to persuade you, the heir, to sign over the bonds. Unless he meant to kill your uncle, there wasn't any need for having those skeleton keys that would open his hotel room, for walking up the stairs so he wouldn't be seen, for having the knife ready.

"What Blumberry didn't know was that you had come to New Orleans two days before and phoned and frightened Andrews so bad he was hiding, but still trying to collect the mail with the checks in it. So Blumberry went up and waited in your uncle's room for him to come. It was this Roscoe Jancey who came instead."

"What was he doing?"

"He was a member of a New York firm that was interested in the bonds. For two days he'd been trying to locate McCracken, or the man he thought was McCracken. He'd hired a private detective. Finally he got the idea the desk clerk was lying and that McCracken was in his room all the time. So he went up and turned the doorknob and went in.

"Blumberry says they argued and learned they were there on the same business and finally fought. Personally I think Blumberry was standing by the door and let him have it as he came in, thinking Jancey was your uncle, and not seeing his mistake until too late. Anyway, he killed him.

"He must have just been slipping down the stairs as I came and he saw me. He was sure you saw him as he started across the lobby, and realizing that would break his story of not having been there, he marched up to the desk, asked for McCracken's room number, and headed for the elevator. He knew I would probably still be in the room, and he might be able to make me a fall guy for the killing."

"But what was he doing on Andrews' balcony later?"

"He had begun to guess the truth after the redhead came in asking for Art. I'd forgotten about her saying, 'Art, darling,' until I found the drawings in that house near City Park. Then I remembered that Arthur Andrews had been a small-time artist.

"Anyway, Blumberry figured if he was right, and if somebody was pretending to be McCracken but wasn't, and if he could turn that fellow over to the police, all would be swell. He would have the real McCracken dead and he would have somebody convicted of Roscoe Jancey's death—because it would look as if Jancey had recognized Andrews as a fake and Andrews had killed him.

"Blumberry traced Andrews the same way I did, by his wife's address in the paper. She'd given the cops her maiden name, but she'd had to give them her right address. Blumberry crawled up to the balcony to get a look; about that time I scared Andrews into hiding on the balcony, and there they were together, both listening to what I told the redhead."

Mary asked what they were going to do to Andrews.

"I don't know. A mild jail term. I'll do what I can to help, because he came through for me on the balcony. He wasn't a killer, not even when he had you and didn't know what to do with you. He was afraid you'd find out he was pretending to be McCracken. Even after I arrived and we both knew he was a fake, he didn't kill us."

Mary and I both got to thinking about how we felt when we thought he was going to kill us, and we polished off our drinks in a hurry.

I felt better, then, and warmed up.

"I think we'll have another," I said. "To McCracken."

"You mean Smith."

"Another one for Smith," I said. "And then one for Andrews, so we'll have him right under whatever name he prefers."

Her Dagger Before Me
Talmadge Powell

TALMADGE POWELL (1920–2000) was born in Hendersonville, North Carolina, and attended schools in North Carolina, Tennessee, New York, and California, studying creative writing at the University of North Carolina. He settled into a career as a professional writer fairly early, selling his first mystery story to *10-Story Detective,* which ran in January 1944. Although he produced stories in various genres, more than two hundred of his pulp and digest-size magazine stories were in the mystery, crime, and detective field, both under his own name and using various pseudonyms, including Jack McCready, Anne Talmadge—for the novel *Dark Over Acadia* (1971)—Robert Hart Davis, Robert Henry, Milton T. Lamb, and Milton Land. For four novels about Tim Corrigan, he employed the familiar Ellery Queen byline used by several other writers. His short-story-writing career spanned four decades, and many of his original, character-driven tales were adapted for *Alfred Hitchcock Presents*; they were collected in *Written for Hitchcock* (1989).

Of the nine mystery novels under his own name, five were about Ed Rivers, a tough but goodhearted Tampa-based private eye, including his first book, *The Killer Is Mine* (1959), followed by the much-praised *The Girl's Number Doesn't Answer* (1960), as well as *With a Madman Behind Me* (1962), *Start Screaming Murder* (1962), and *Corpus Delectable* (1964).

He was the guest of honor at Pulpcon in 1996.

"Her Dagger Before Me" was published in the July 1949 issue.

Her Dagger Before Me

Talmadge Powell

CHAPTER ONE
COLD MEAT

I HAD BEEN ON a divorce case, shadowing a man most of the night before; so I didn't do anything about the screaming telephone for the first few seconds except try to swim back down in the sticky molasses of sleep and wish whoever was calling would go away.

The phone kept snarling. After a minute I was wide awake and in that state going back to sleep in the muggy, noonday Florida heat was

out of the question. I heaved myself on the edge of the bed and shouted at the phone, "All right, I'm coming!"

The apartment was sodden with heat; I've been in Tampa a long time but I never got used to the heat.

While I'm padding toward the phone, I might as well tell you who I am.

EXCITING MYSTERY NOVELETTE

Pleasure-hungry Allene's gay step-mother had nothing but time, a gigolo,
and money on her hands—Allene's money!

*I found Osgood
by the water.*

The name is Lloyd Carter, age forty-four. I'm beginning to add an inner tube around my middle, and I don't like to be kidded about the way I'm starting to bald on the crown of my head. I live in a run-down apartment on the edge of Tampa's Ybor City. The bed is lumpy, the furniture old. It's just a place to sleep. I got in the private detective business twenty-one years ago. I never intended to make it a lifetime career, but I guess now I will.

I've never married, which is maybe what put the pickles in my disposition. I had a girl when I was young, in New York, that I might have married, but she ran off with a punk I was trying to nail. He was cornered in Indiana by state police, made a run for it, but a fast freight got in the way of his automobile. She was in the car.

New York wasn't the same after that, and I came south. I've been with Southeastern Detective Service over sixteen years. . . .

I picked up the telephone.

"Lloyd?"

It was the old man's voice. Henry Fayette, who ram-rodded Southeastern, should have retired a long time ago. He's seen too much of the seamy side of life streaming through his agency. It's in his voice. But he never could retire because he's a spender and is always scratching hard to keep the wolf at arm's length.

"Lloyd," his tired voice said, "I want you to come to the office right away."

I didn't argue. He'd known how late I'd worked last night. If he hadn't had to call me, he wouldn't have.

I went in the bedroom and dressed. Baggy slacks, sweaty sport shirt. And the knife under my left armpit. I'm naked without the knife. My work puts me across the tables now and then from Ybor City characters. The only weapon some of those lads understand is a knife.

I was going to have to get my laundry out today. I wrote a note for the girl, left it on the kitchen table. I opened the icebox, drank a pint of beer, and headed for the office. The heat was terrible. Already beads of sweat were like a film of hot oil all over me.

The agency's offices are in a sagging brick building that was young when Tampa was young, on the lower end of Franklin Street. I opened the door to Henry Fayette's office. He was behind his desk, a tall, gaunt, rawboned gray man in a gray tropical suit. He stood up. The girl sitting at the end of his desk watched me cross the office. Without looking directly at her, I sized her up.

She wasn't exactly plain, but she wasn't beautiful, either. She was tall and slim, with a nice enough figure and face and rather drab brown hair. Just a girl who could lose herself in a crowd, with a sort of hungry look on her face that might mean she was hungry for food—or love. Her clothes, white linen frock and bag, indicated she had enough money to eat regularly.

The chief introduced us. Her name was Allene Buford.

"Lloyd," Henry Fayette said with a small, tired gesture of his hand, "Miss Buford wants us to do something about her step-mother and a chap named Buddy Tomlinson. You might repeat the details, Miss Buford, to Lloyd as you told them to me."

She sat on the edge of her chair, hands in her lap, and gave me the details. Her voice was calm, even, but it was belied by the cold fire deep in her eyes.

It was about the average sordid mess. This Allene Buford's father had been a fairly wealthy man. Allene's mother had died ten years ago, and her father had remarried six years later, all of which was normal enough. But the sordid part began when the old man died. In his will, he left provisions for Allene to have an income, not too large. The bulk of his fortune, Emagine Buford, Allene's step-mother, was to hold until the girl was thirty—seven years from now.

"My father seemed to have some foggy idea that I wouldn't be capable of handling almost a million dollars until I was at least thirty."

"And what happens then?" I asked her.

"Emagine is to come into two hundred thousand. I am to have the rest of the money." Her face tightened, and I leaned back with a sigh, knowing that now we were getting around to the sordid part.

Emagine Buford and her step-daughter had come south for the winter, to St. Petersburg, the resort city across the bay from Tampa. She had joined the throngs, a woman who had outlived her responsibilities. Who had nothing but time, money, and restlessness on her hands. She'd met Buddy Tomlinson. From Allene's description, he was one of those boys who had perpetual youth, a husky physique that, at forty-five, was still trim, a disarming smile, coal black hair, and one of those little-boy faces.

The fact that she was almost fifteen years Buddy's senior hadn't worried Emagine any. "She's like a school girl," Allene said, "with her first beau. She's buying bathing suits and evening gowns and seeing Buddy Tomlinson constantly."

"And where do I enter? What do you want me to do?" I looked at her over the flame of my lighter as I touched it to a fag.

Allene looked steadily at me. "I want you to mark up Buddy Tomlinson so he'll never be handsome to any woman again!"

A second or two ticked away. She saw the old man about to speak. "Of course," she said, "I know you can't be hired to do that. But I know Buddy's trying to marry Emagine. He has plenty of chance of success. My money is melting away fast enough in her keeping, and if Buddy marries her, there won't be anything for me when I'm thirty!"

"Could Tomlinson and Emagine manage that?" I asked the old man.

"You know anything can be managed with enough money and the right lawyers," he stated flatly.

"But it's my money!" For the first time a bit of panic showed in Allene's face. "He was my father; he made the money. Now it's my money! You can't let them do that to me!"

"Will you wait outside for a minute, Miss Buford?" Fayette asked. The girl looked at him, then got up and went out of the office.

"Lloyd," Fayette said when she had closed the door behind her, "I want you to drive over to St. Pete with her. This is a sort of personal thing with me. I've known Emagine Buford for a long time. She used to live in Tampa. Then she went north to work, met and married Ollie Buford. Since she's been back in Florida I've visited her a time or two at her place in St. Pete. That's why the girl came here to us, I guess.

"Emagine's going through a phase in her second childhood, to my way of thinking, but I don't want anything to happen to her. I want her to have a chance to wake up. See what kind of man Tomlinson is. See if he'll scare. Then scare him."

"I'm flat," I said.

He grimaced, pulled out his wallet, hesitated, and handed me the lone twenty from the worn leather sheath. "Use my car. It's parked in back of the building. See Buddy Tomlinson, phone me back, and take the rest of the day off."

I said thanks. When I left his office, he was punching tiny holes in his desk blotter with the tip of his letter opener. . . .

The girl rode with her head slightly back, catching the breeze that blew in the gray sedan. Her hair rippled. Her lips were parted a little as she looked out over the bay. "Tomlinson has a beach place," she said. "On Coquina Key. We'll probably find him there."

That was about all the talking we did. But I kept looking at her. She wasn't beautiful. Yet there was—something.

Coquina Key isn't the real name for the island, but we'd better call it that. It's one of that long chain of islands west of St. Petersburg, all connected by bridges and causeways, that separate Boca Ciega bay from the Gulf of Mexico.

We drove through the snarled, slow traffic of St. Petersburg, took the Central Avenue causeway, stopping once at the toll gate and then driving on across the white, four-lane parkway that had been pumped up out of Boca Ciega bay. Then we were on the keys.

The islands are a lot alike, long fingers of land stretching north and south for miles, but just wide enough crosswise to separate Boca Ciega from the Gulf. Where they're settled, the keys are built up heavily, with cabanas, frame boat houses, frame cottages, and a development here and there of bungalows. But in the unsettled stretches, the islands are desolate, white sand and shell and, closer to the boulevard, grown over with weeds, scrub pines, cabbage palms, and palmetto. Over the whole put a vast blue sky, torrid sun, surround with sparkling blue water and whispering surf on the white beaches, populate with easy-living people, put a fleet of fishing boats in the inlets, with a fine cabin cruiser at a private pier on a private beach here and there—and you've got the picture.

Toward the lower end of Coquina Beach we turned off the boulevard on Sunshine Way. The street was wide, white concrete, curving gently toward the cluster of squat bungalows half a mile down the island. It looked like a brand-new development, the white land so clean it was barren. Here and there small Australian pines and royal palms had been set out.

Buddy Tomlinson lived in the CBS—stucco over cement block—near the end of the street. The whole row of houses was painted a light pink. I opened the car door. Allene opened hers.

"Hadn't you better wait out here?"

"No," she said, "I'm coming in."

I shrugged and we went up the walk together. I rang the chimes on the oak-stained door. Nothing happened. In the bungalow next door I could hear warm laughter, and in the background a radio playing softly.

I rang four times in all. Then I walked around the side of the bungalow and looked in a window. I looked away quick, closed my eyes for a second. The first thing I saw when I opened them was Allene's profile. She was standing close to me, looking through the window, as I had done.

"He's dead," she said calmly.

I didn't ask if it was Buddy Tomlinson crumpled in there in the living room. The description fitted like a glove. Allene had her wish. He'd never be beautiful to any woman again.

"Well," Allene said, "we won't have to worry about him any longer." Then her eyes rolled up in her head. Her face was very white. And before I had time to think, she was keeling over.

I caught her, carried her out to the car. There was a half-empty pint in the glove compartment. I figured that ought to bring her to. "You," I told her limp form, "are one hell of a funny sort of dame!"

I was tilting the pint bottle to Allene's lips when a nearby male voice said, "Anything wrong?"

I looked at the bungalow that was next door to the one in which Buddy Tomlinson lay dead. I remembered the music and casual laughter I'd heard.

Now the music was silenced. A man and woman stood together just outside the screen door of the bungalow, on the small, hot flagstone terrace. I noticed the screen door behind them was one of those fancy jobs with a huge, white silhouette of a flamingo on it.

The man and woman were watching me warily, thinking, no doubt, that Allene and I were a pair of drunks out celebrating.

There was just one word for the girl standing on the terrace: sleek. She was wearing a white play suit that was startling against her dark tan. She had a sultry-looking face, with wide, red lips. Her hair was midnight black, cut with bangs. She was holding her hands at her sides in a sort of theatrical way, the way models do, pointing very slightly outward.

The man beside her was tall and athletic, dressed in an expensive T-shirt that was a riot of colors, cream-colored slacks, and tan sandals. His arms and face were freckled, his hair a crinkly, close-cropped, light blond mass on his head.

He and the girl watched as I took the bottle from Allene's lips. Allene sat up, mumbling a groan. Her lids fluttered. "I'm all right," she said weakly, shaking her head.

I got out of the car. The strapping young blond experienced a tightening in his face. To put him at ease, I said, "The lady simply fainted."

"That's too bad," the girl in the white play suit said. "Is there anything we can do to help?"

"Phyllis!" the man said, obviously annoyed.

"Oh, they're all right, Baxter!" she said crossly.

Then to me: "We saw you carrying the girl to the car. We thought you might be drunk!" She giggled and made dainty, studied gestures with her hands. They were graceful long hands. She probably realized it. She probably made use of them with every word she said.

"Do you know the man next door?" I asked.

"Buddy? Sure," Baxter said. "But Phyllis and I haven't seen him around since we came in from our sail, if you're looking for him—"

"I'm not looking for him," I cut in. "Have you got a phone?"

Baxter frowned. "Yes, here in the living room."

"I'd like to use it."

Baxter looked annoyed. Phyllis told me to go ahead. They followed as far as the doorway, stood there while I phoned. Maybe Baxter was afraid I'd carry off the ivory bookends on the table near the phone.

The Gulf beaches are not incorporated in the City of St. Petersburg, which allows the beaches to sell alcoholic beverages on Sunday and a later curfew for their nightspots. So I put in a call to Sheriff Ben Aiken. What I told him jarred a few morose curses out of him, and he said he'd be right out.

When I turned from the phone, Phyllis' hands were fluttering about her throat. Baxter's face looked tight—and somehow mean.

"Buddy Tomlinson is dead?" Phyllis said, as if it was simply too, too horrible for her to realize.

I was in no mood for details, and simply nodded. I went back out to the car and sat down on the running board on the shady side and lighted a cigarette. "Can I have one?" Allene said. I gave it to her.

"What will they do with him, Lloyd?"

"Take him to an undertaking parlor. I think Doc Robison has got the corner on that trade for the county."

"I wonder who killed him?"

"I wouldn't know." I didn't particularly care. I sat and smoked chain fashion, and at last Ben Aiken arrived.

There were two other men with Ben, but they were just faces. He was the whole show. He was a big, fat man, with a lot of gut hanging over his belt. His pants were even baggier than mine and his shirt was pasted to his big, sloping shoulders with sweat. He had a large, florid face with a tiny button nose in the middle of it, and a sweating bald head.

I sat there in the open door of the car, watching the house. I couldn't see much, but I could hear Ben and the other two men working inside. Shortly the county coroner drove up. He was swallowed by Buddy Tomlinson's bungalow.

After a while, Ben Aiken came out. He came over to the car, questioned Allene and me. I told him the short, simple story of my finding Buddy Tomlinson. To keep myself clean, I told him why Allene had hired me. She was sitting on the car seat behind me, at a higher level, of course. When I brought her step-mother's name into it, the toe of her shoe bit in my spine.

Aiken got nothing more out of her. He questioned the couple from next door. Phyllis' last name was Darnell. She had been married, she said, but was a divorcée. Baxter's full name was Baxter B. Osgood. Yes, he and Phyllis both had known Tomlinson. No, they hadn't seen him since yesterday afternoon when they'd all been drinking at the Pelican Bar and Grill, half a mile down the beach. He and Phyllis had had a morning date to go sailing. They'd sailed and swum and come back here just before Allene and I rolled up.

When he'd finished with them, Ben motioned me off to one side. "You got any ideas on this thing, Lloyd?"

"No, I'm off it. I was supposed to warn Buddy Tomlinson off Emagine Buford. Now Buddy doesn't need it."

"You think the gal is holding anything back?" He cut a side glance at the car where Allene was still sitting stiffly.

"If she's holding out on you, she's holding out on me, too."

Ben sighed and mopped his face. "May be one of them long drawn cases. I got to trace this

Buddy Tomlinson backward, find out who he was, where he's been keeping himself, in whose company, and so on. I might find a motive somewhere along the line.

"Funny kind of kill. You didn't get a good look in there, did you, Lloyd?"

I hadn't. But I didn't say anything. I just stood passive and let Ben get it off his chest. I knew that in talking it in his confidential whisper, he was setting the details in his mind.

"Nothing in the whole bungalow had been hurt—except Tomlinson. You saw the wound in his face, Lloyd. He was shot in close. The side of his right palm was mutilated. Looked like somebody was threatening him with a gun. He made a grab for it and the shooting started."

"What does that give you?"

"Nothing much. It must mean he was shot with a revolver. Don't need to tell a man like you that an automatic won't fire with pressure on the killing end of it. Ejector won't work, gun won't cock, gun jams up. We're hunting the slug. From Tomlinson's cheek looks like a thirty-eight. So maybe when I find out where he's been keeping himself, who he's been seeing, I might find out somebody who owns a revolver like that."

"You need me for anything else, Ben?"

"I guess not."

"Then I'm going back to Tampa. I'll drop the girl in St. Pete. She'll probably want to talk with her step-mother."

"She won't have much privacy." Ben grinned. "There's a phone in Tomlinson's bungalow and I'm gonna have city Homicide look in on Mrs. Emagine Buford." He mopped his face some more. "Hell to work in this heat. I'll see you around, Lloyd."

I got in the car and drove off. The last I saw of the scene, Baxter Osgood and Phyllis Darnell were still standing on Osgood's flagstone terrace, watching Ben Aiken waddle his way into the Tomlinson bungalow. Somehow, they looked scared.

I drove Allene to the Morro Hotel, in the northeast section of St. Pete. The drive along Tampa Bay was wide, beautiful, lined with fine houses and hotels. A few boats were out sailing on the bay, the small, white triangles of their sails tilted over in the light breeze.

The Morro was built like an old Spanish castle. When I braked before it, I saw a black car at the curb. Allene saw it, caught her lip between her teeth. She turned her face to me as she got out of the car. "I'd like to see you again sometime," she said.

I looked at her for a minute. "I'll phone you this weekend."

She closed the car door, went running up the wide, palm-lined walk. She was staying here at the Morro with her step-mother, but I didn't know the phone number and I decided I didn't like to thumb through the phone books. It was just as well. I was twenty years her senior.

I drove back to Tampa and went to the office. The old man wasn't there and I mumbled talk with the girl behind the reception desk until he came in. He went into his private office and I told Fayette everything that had happened. His chiseled, rawboned face looked gaunt. He sank behind his desk. "What'd you find out about Tomlinson?"

"Nothing, except that now he's just a dead pretty boy. It ain't our case. I'll see you tomorrow."

I caught a bus and rode up through the squalor of lower Nebraska to my apartment. I bought a twenty-five-pound block of ice at the ice house on the corner, carried it up to my apartment. I put the ice in a dishpan, set the dishpan on a center table in the bedroom. I plugged in the electric fan and set it behind the pan, so that the air was blowing over the ice, over the bed.

I sat down on the edge of the bed. The air was cool and good for a second or two, until I got used to it. I reached under my left armpit and pulled out the knife. It was long, keen, and gleaming with a six-and-a-quarter-inch blade. I knew what was bothering me, now.

A living, breathing, feeling man had been killed.

I slung the knife. It flashed, struck the door-jamb, stood out from the wood, quivering.

I flopped over on the bed and went to sleep.

It was a hell of a hot day.

CHAPTER TWO
KNIFE FOR HIRE

I didn't sleep long. I woke with a mouthful of cotton, sweat drenching me, a heat-thickened pulse pounding in my head. I ran my tongue around my gums, realized that somebody was knocking on the door. As I went to answer, I plucked the knife from the door jamb, put it back in its sheath under my armpit. I looked at my watch. It was 4:40 in the afternoon.

When I opened the door, Phyllis Darnell had her hand raised to knock again. She'd changed from the white play suit, wearing now a yellow silk dress that really set off her complexion, lazy black eyes, and midnight hair.

"Oh!" she said, as if the opening of the door had startled her. She made vague gestures in the air with her hands. If it hadn't been for that way she had of using her hands, she'd have been a very beautiful woman.

"You wanted to see me?"

"Yes, Mr. Carter. Are you busy?"

"It depends. I guess you want to hire a detective?"

"Why do you say that?"

"Well, my looks didn't bring you here, did they?"

Ice flaked in her eyes. "No, your looks didn't bring me here. Are you going to ask me in or not?"

"Why not?" I held the door wide. When she came in and I'd closed the door, I said, "You care for beer?"

"No."

"Well, excuse me a moment. Make yourself at home."

She followed me out to the kitchen. I opened the icebox, counted the bottles of beer. The girl who'd come in to clean while I'd been out had been thirsty again. I opened a bottle of beer, killed half of it, said, "I'm listening."

"I really don't know how to begin, Mr. Carter. I really don't!" She wrung her hands, real fright coming to life in her eyes. "It's very awkward."

"I've heard awkward things before. Sit down. Iced tea?"

She shook her head, then nodded. "Yes, I'll have a glass of tea."

I put water on to boil.

"How'd you find me, Mrs. Darnell?"

"I asked that sheriff. From the way he talked to you when he arrived at Buddy Tomlinson's bungalow, I knew you were a detective. He told me where you worked, where you lived. You weren't in your office, neither was your boss, and the girl at the reception desk."

"Okay, okay. I guess you wanted to talk to me about Tomlinson?"

"I yes—no. I mean, in a way I did." She glanced about the kitchen as if seeking a way out, a way to stall. "I see the water is simmering, Mr. Carter."

So it was. I took the battered aluminum pot off the flame, dropped in a tea bag, chipped ice and put it in a glass, and poured the tea over it. I set out cream, sugar, and scratched in the back corner of the icebox for the lone, wilted lemon there. Slicing the lemon, I said, "Why don't you just tell me straight off? Why beat around the bush? Buddy Tomlinson has been murdered and it's put you on the spot somehow. You want me to remove you from said spot. All right, what is it?"

The way she whitened beneath her deep tan gave her the appearance of wearing a heavy coat of dark powder. Her hands were trembling. "I— I really don't know what to say. I really don't."

I set the tea before her, sat down across the table, and finished my beer. Then I just sat there, not speaking, not moving.

When the silence began to eat away her nerves, she said shrilly, "I lied this morning! I'm married—but I'm not a divorcée. And I had every reason in the world for wanting to kill Buddy Tomlinson!"

She began to cry softly. She took out a wispy handkerchief, made dabs at her eyes.

"I really hate to say this. I really do. You see, Mr. Carter, I have a husband in Augusta, Maine. But we're not divorced, and never intend to be. I really don't know how I'm going to explain this to you. Oh, I've been a fool! I can hardly explain it to myself.

"I love my husband deeply and I am sure I mean more to him than life itself. I won't try to excuse myself. But every year I take a vacation, to Florida, the West Coast, South America, or Cuba. My poor, trusting husband! His business keeps him tied to his desk, but he insists that I might as well escape a few weeks of northern winter every year. It's on these trips that I present myself as an unmarried woman or a divorcée. That way one interests a better class of men than if one admitted being a married woman. Somehow that way it always seemed in my mind to cheapen my husband less."

She was looking down at her hands, momentarily quiet in her lap, waiting for me to speak. To condemn her, maybe. I opened another cold beer and didn't say anything.

"Drink your tea," I said.

It wasn't very good tea, but she drank it gratefully. I finished my beer and said, "Buddy Tomlinson was one of those men?"

She nodded mutely.

"You certainly made a mistake about classifying men in his case!"

She shuddered under the sentence as if it was a blow of my hand, but she continued to look silently down.

"How'd you meet Tomlinson?"

"Through Baxter Osgood. They seemed to be close friends. Baxter Osgood owns a small beer garden on Coquina Beach. I was there one night—he introduced me to Buddy."

"And you were promptly swept off your feet."

"You aren't a woman. You didn't know Buddy Tomlinson," she said in a stricken voice. "Now he's dead, and the letters have disappeared."

"You made the mistake of writing him some mush notes?"

Her face flooded red. "He was in Bradenton for a week. He begged me to write him every day. He was so sweet, so boyish." Her voice thickened with a violent anger; her hands played on the table top. "Something I said must have caused him to suspect that I wasn't really divorced."

"Can you recall what you might have said?"

"I— No. One night—just before he went down to Bradenton—we drank quite a bit. I was drunk when he took me to my hotel. I must have talked of my life in Augusta."

"Afterwards he wanted money for the letters?"

She nodded again, swallowing in such a way her throat constricted with the action. "I gave him almost five hundred dollars—but he didn't give me the letters back. I knew then that I was in a deadly game, that my life in Augusta depended on what I did. I hoped to wheedle the letters out of him. Now he's dead. Can't you see what might be the results if those letters come to light? My husband's life ruined, a possible murder charge against me. Mr. Carter, you must help me. I can't afford to be drawn openly into this kind of mess."

I opened a third beer. She was in a jam, all right. If those letters had been worth five hundred before Buddy Tomlinson's death, now they were worth every nickel she could lay her hands on, and somebody evidently knew that. If the police had discovered the letters, they'd have taken her in for questioning by this time. I said, "Any idea who Tomlinson might have boasted to? Who might have known about those letters?"

"No—unless it's Baxter Osgood. I don't think he makes all his money out of that beer garden he owns. I think there was something more between him and Buddy than mere friendship."

"Business deals?"

"Perhaps."

"All right," I said, "I'll do what I can to help you. But get one thing straight. This is murder. Contrary to what the public thinks, private dicks don't like to get mixed in murder. If we have to wade through murder the cost is high."

"I know," Phyllis Darnell said. "I'll pay."

"I'm not worrying. After all, I'll have the letters, won't I?"

I ushered her out, showered, and went over to Mac's garage, where my coupe had been laid up with a ring job. Greasy, limp from the heat, Mac had just finished the job. He wiped his hands on a piece of waste and told me the old crate was ready to roll. I made arrangements to see him on the fifteenth and drove down to the office.

The old man was locking his private office, getting ready to leave for the day. I told him to unlock again, explained the case.

He unlocked the door, walked across his office saying, "A murder case? I don't like it, Lloyd. I never liked a murder case."

"I know."

"The official boys have everything to work on a murder case, labs, organization, everything. A private agency small as ours ain't equipped for it."

"I know."

I opened his desk drawer, took out the .38 police special that always nestled there. I pulled out a corner of my shirttail, tucked the gun in my waistband, and tucked the shirt back in over the gun. You'd never know it was there. A box of loads was in the corner of the drawer. I dropped a handful of them in my pocket.

The old man was already on the phone, talking long-distance.

I sat down and smoked until he finished.

He pushed back the phone, shadows over his rawboned, gaunt face.

"Ben Aiken's glad we're going to cooperate," Fayette said.

"That's good. He give you much?"

Henry Fayette nodded, his frown deep and sour. He jabbed at his desk blotter with his letter opener. "This Buddy Tomlinson was quite a guy. Convicted once in Miami on a larceny charge. Charged once with blackmail in Baltimore, Maryland, but got off for lack of evidence. Nabbed once in Brownsville, Texas, for being mixed in the marijuana racket, but beat that rap too. Miami had his whole previous record.

"Tomlinson came to St. Petersburg almost a year ago in company with an unknown woman who can't be located. There's nothing on the St. Pete blotter against him except a charge of driving intoxicated, for which he was fined.

"He was killed between twelve midnight and one o'clock last night, which means that he lay in his bungalow during that time without being found. The murder gun has not been located, but Aiken has got him an important witness. Guy by the name of Baxter B. Osgood. He the one you met over there?"

I nodded. "Osgood owns a beer garden on the beach. He lives in the bungalow next to Tomlinson's. An athletic, freckled, blond guy. He could be plenty mean, I guess."

The old man traced a pattern on the desk blotter with the opener. "Osgood says he was awakened last night about twelve thirty. Says he dreamed a backfire woke him, now realizes it must have been the shot in Buddy Tomlinson's bungalow. Osgood says his bedroom window faces the Tomlinson house, and that from that window he saw a woman leaving Tomlinson's bungalow. There was a bright moon. You know that moon at the beach, turning night into day. Osgood recognized the woman by the red swagger coat she was wearing, and her hat. The hat had a couple of tall feathers sticking up out of it."

Fayette flung the opener on the desk; his face was gray. "Dammit, I told you she was an old friend of mine." Accusation flamed on the old man's face, then he shook his head as if clearing it. "I'm upset. I can't blame you. I got no reason to blame you, Lloyd."

"You mean the woman Baxter Osgood recognized leaving the Tomlinson bungalow is Emagine Buford?"

Fayette nodded. In his quiet, flat voice he said, "Ben Aiken's jailed her—charged her with first-degree murder."

I whistled softly. It didn't help the old man's feelings any.

It was pretty late in the day to do anything much, but Fayette insisted on driving over to St. Pete, to talk to Emagine Buford. We took my coupe. The thing I wanted out of this case was those letters of Phyllis Darnell's. That's what we'd get paid for. But the letters were somewhere in the pattern of Buddy Tomlinson's death, and I knew we were going to have to sift through that pattern to find them. I didn't like a damn thing about the case.

It's only half an hour's drive from Tampa to St. Pete by way of Gandy Bridge, and it was still daylight when we got in the Sunshine City, though the sun had dropped in the Gulf, leaving behind it vast streamers of crimson and gold in the western sky.

We wasted fifteen minutes talking over the case with the St. Pete men. Then we went back to Emagine Buford's cell.

She had been crying, and her face was swollen, but even so you could see that she had been a raving beauty in her day. As Allene had said of her step-mother, Emagine was well preserved, slim, with a small, unlined face, and hair dyed to a nice shade just darker than auburn. She didn't look a day over a young forty.

She managed a smile when the old man entered her cell. "It's unfortunate that you have to visit me here, Henry."

Fayette said, "We want to help you. This is Lloyd Carter. Mrs. Buford, Lloyd."

We each said it was a pleasure, and Emagine sank on the edge of her cot. She looked at the old man with hope and trust. They talked for two minutes. She wasn't able to tell us a thing more than the county men had. She had been home asleep, she claimed, when Buddy Tomlinson had been murdered. She hadn't seen him since the night before his death. She spoke of him with a mixed tenderness and hot, new-born hatred.

The old man told her that we'd do our best, and we left her.

That was that, for my money. Outside headquarters, Fayette mopped his face with a big red bandanna and said we might as well eat.

We went to eat.

It was just after 8:30 when I got back to my apartment house in Tampa. The place had no garages; so if you owned a car, you left it at the curb. I locked the coupe, and walked in the apartment house. I was halfway up the flight of stairs when the door opened in the lower hall and my landlady's nasal drawl came to me. "Is that you, Mr. Carter?"

I bent over the stair railing, looking down the hall. She was standing in her doorway. "There's a woman in your apartment," she said. "Said she had to see you. I let her in to wait."

She slammed her door.

I went on up the stairs, down the hall, and opened my apartment door. Allene Buford stood up when I entered.

She'd turned on the small lamp over near the corner, and the soft light silhouetted her. I remembered her as I'd first seen her in the old man's office earlier in the day: not plain, but not beautiful either. Now, with the light behind her like that, a light not bright enough to glare at her or to show up the room in which she was standing, she almost made the grade. She was almost beautiful.

"Are you mad at me, Lloyd?"

"For coming here? I don't think so."

"I'm glad," she said in her calm, colorless voice. She took a turn up and down the room. I closed the door and stood watching her. "I couldn't stand it in the empty hotel room any longer," she said. "I thought I hated her, Lloyd, but she was so pitiful when the police came and took her."

She came over closer to me. "Emagine and I never got along, but when she was gone I sat in the room there in the Morro for a while, remembering the fights we'd had. The things I'd said to her. I couldn't stand the room any longer. I called one of the St. Petersburg detectives. He didn't know you, but had a buddy who did. So I got your address and drove over."

A moment of silence passed.

"Lloyd, will you take me some place?"

"Where would you like to go?"

"Any place there's some music, a glass of wine, something to eat."

She caught my arm. "Lloyd, they won't send her to the electric chair, will they?"

"I don't know."

"But what if she didn't do it?"

"It looks pretty much like she did. Murder is a funny thing. Sometimes cops flounder around a lot on a murder case, because they haven't got direction. But once they get direction, once they know what they're looking for and who it's to be used against, they usually dig up evidence."

I sensed a shudder rippling over her.

"Let's go have that glass of wine."

We went down, got in the coupe, and drove over to Club Habana, a small, quiet place with Cuban music, fair wines, and fairly good food.

I sipped a beer, danced with her, watched her eat her dinner. She ate the spicy Cuban food as if she'd been too nervous and distraught to eat before. Now that she'd let down, she'd discovered she was famished. But that other hunger, that longing in her eyes—it was still there when she'd reached her coffee. It had been there always, I guessed, lonely, without an anchor.

We danced a few more times. We talked for a while. She told me about her home town, her girlhood. "I was walled off," she laughed, "by high walls of greenbacks." She reached over and clutched my hand. "I feel much better now, Lloyd. I think I'd better go back to St. Pete. But tomorrow—couldn't we do something then?"

"I dunno, I—"

"Show me Florida, Lloyd! Not the Florida the tourist sees, but the backways, the way the swamp people live, the farms, and villages."

"Sometime," I said.

She didn't take her hand off mine. She leaned toward me, her mouth parted a little, the soft, blue light of the Cabana glinting faintly on the tips of her teeth. I could see a pulse beating in her throat and the almost invisible sheen of per-spiration on her forehead. Very softly the band was playing a tender Cuban love song.

I kissed her softly on the lips. She leaned back, said quietly, "Thank you, Lloyd." Then she gathered her handbag, stood up, and we left the place.

She said she'd take a taxi to St. Pete, and I deposited her in one, and drove on back to my apartment.

The heat was still like a blanket, even though the night was a bit older. I had a cold beer in the kitchen. Cold beer was the only thing I'd ever found to help against the heat, but even that was a losing contest. The beer didn't keep you cool long enough.

I wondered if I'd ever get used to Tampa heat.

I went in the bedroom. The ice I'd put in the pan on the center table that afternoon had long since melted, but the fan was still running, sending a stream of sluggish hot air over my face. I didn't lie down. I simply sat on the edge of the bed, trying to get my thoughts straight. I couldn't go to sleep; so I got up and went back down to the coupe.

I started the motor, let it idle for a minute. Then I pointed the nose toward St. Pete and Coquina Key.

It was a little after 11:00 when I rolled down the boulevard on the island. A huge moon bathed Coquina Key in silver light. White surf broke against the beach, and out in the water, moon rays lay in a great elongated splash, a pool all their own. Stars were out by the millions in a sky that was pure black velvet.

I braked in the business section of the Key. It was pretty grubby, most of the buildings of frame wooden construction, a cluster of boat houses down at the inlet, along with some bait houses. Cabanas and cottages were stacked over the area, close together. Everything there was dark, except for a bar, a chicken-in-the-basket place, and Baxter Osgood's beer garden.

CHAPTER THREE
KILL ONE, SKIP ONE

The beer garden was crowded with people in rumpled sport shirts and slacks and cool cotton dresses. It was hot, smoky, wet and rank with the odor of beer, turgidly alive with sluggish conversation and the rasping of a juke box. I bought a beer at the bar and asked if Baxter Osgood was around.

"I'm right here," Osgood said, practically at my elbow.

I turned around to look at him. He moved up to the bar beside me, sat down on a stool.

"I saw you come in, Carter."

"The beer isn't cold," I said.

"No? Why don't you buy someplace else?"

"I couldn't—not the product I'm in the market for."

"No?" he said again. "What is it you're wanting to buy?"

"Letters," I told him.

He watched the dancing for a few seconds. "I don't know what you're talking about."

"I know you don't, Mr. Osgood."

"How much are you paying for this product?"

"Enough—but not too much."

He yawned against the back of his hand. "I've got to run over to the house for a minute. Like to come along—just for the ride?"

"Sure," I said. "I'll come along, just for the ride."

We went outside. His car was angle parked at the curb, a blue convertible. We got in, and he drove down the boulevard, turned off on Sunshine Way, braked before his bungalow.

"Every time I look at the house next door," he said as we got out of the car, "I think of Mr. Tomlinson."

"Too bad about Mr. Tomlinson, but I understand they've got the woman who killed him."

"I thought you might be interested in it—say in an academic way."

"Not even in an academic way."

"Just in letters, huh?"

"You said it."

He keyed open the front door. The house was like an oven; he turned on lights, opened windows, threw the switch on an attic fan. Cooler night air began to rush through the place.

Osgood walked over to the knee hole desk, stuck a cigarette in his mouth, and picked up a box of matches that was on the desk. He turned halfway back toward the desk, dropped the matches on it, and opened the drawer and pulled the gun, all in one liquid motion.

He laughed faintly. The gun was leveled at my middle.

"Well," I said, "every man is entitled to one mistake."

"Yes—one."

He came halfway across the room toward me. "Turn around, Carter."

I stood still, and he jerked the gun up. His words didn't bother me—the sudden message in his eyes did. I turned around.

He came up behind me as if to frisk me. He hit me on the crown, where I'm starting to bald. I don't remember much after that.

I think I tried to get out of the house. Common sense tells me I tried to pull Henry Fayette's .38 out of the waistband of my pants. Putting it together later as it must have been, I think I crawled as far as the kitchen. There I passed out for a moment, and he must have unlocked the kitchen door and dragged me outside. I tried to stir on the powdery sand of the back yard. He hit me again, on the back of the head.

The next thing I sensed was a slow melting of black nothingness into a quivering curtain of heavy gray fire, if there ever was any such thing, against the walls of my eyeballs. As the black faded, feeling came in to take its place. My head was a pincushion of pain; my heart was laboring; and I was sucking in mouthfuls of cool, clean air. It was very early morning.

Ten or fifteen minutes later I sat up slowly. I was still in Baxter Osgood's backyard. I stumbled to my feet, staggered to the kitchen door, opened it. The old man's gun had still been in my waistband. Now it was in my hand. I intended to fix Osgood so he'd never beat another man again. In my state, I was no match for a fever-ridden midget, but that didn't occur to me. I had a gun, I was on my feet, and Osgood deserved every damn thing I could dish out.

But he wasn't in the house. The place was pretty well messed up, with drawers pulled out and stuff strewn over the floors. I decided he'd grabbed a few valuables and skipped. Then I looked out the window, saw his convertible still parked on the edge of the street. I tried to make sense out of it, but didn't feel up to it.

As the anger burned out of me, I didn't feel up to anything. I went in his kitchen, started some coffee making. I looked in his refrigerator. Two bottles of beer were in it. I drank both of them.

I followed the beer a few minutes later with two cups of scalding black coffee. I ate a piece of bread and butter, a slice of cheese, and followed that with another cup of coffee.

I went to the living room, opened the front door. My head was still aching and spinning like crazy. I wondered if I had a concussion. The sun was just over the lip of the earth in the east, rising in that burst of orange and crimson you see nowhere but in Florida.

Low in the air, over the edge of the beach, a cluster of gulls were wheeling and screaming.

I did a double take at that group of gulls, stared at them a few seconds, then went stumbling toward the strip of beach as fast as I could go.

Baxter Osgood was lying on his face, the water almost lapping the tips of his upflung hands. He'd been shot in the right temple, and near his hand lay a .38-caliber revolver.

I squatted on my heels beside Osgood's body and tried to figure the way it had happened. He'd left me in the back yard, entered the house to get something. Somebody had arrived.

He and the somebody had walked down here, and the somebody utterly without warning had

shot him, then with panic gnawing, the somebody had wiped the gun, pressed Osgood's prints on it, and left it where it might have fallen from his hand. I was pretty sure the gun was the same that had killed Buddy Tomlinson.

It was just a hunch, but granting the hunch, and granting that Ben Aiken fell for the suicide picture, Aiken would conclude that Osgood had killed Tomlinson because one of their shady deals went sour, then in panic had killed himself.

There was one other point. The murderer evidently hadn't known I was in the back yard. My coupe wasn't at Osgood's house, but up at his beer joint. There was no other evidence that I was lying in the back yard unconscious when the murderer had called on Osgood.

I turned Osgood over, remembering the way his bungalow had been searched. I patted his torso, his waist.

The money belt was one of those jobs that blends right in with the body lines. If you weren't careful, you could search him and miss it. I tore his shirt open, took the belt off him.

Osgood's belt contained five thousand dollars in money and a few sheets of paper that upon reading I knew were the letters that Phyllis Darnell had written to Buddy Tomlinson.

I went back in the house and phoned Ben Aiken.

An hour after that, a small crowd of people was gathered in a room in St. Pete's old, sun-baked city hall.

They all looked at me when I entered. I had my head bandaged, three aspirins under my belt, pile drivers still in my skull, and a feeling like a wad of cotton in my throat.

I looked over the silent room. Ben and a city dick were there, along with a stenographer, who was a big, brawny man. Henry Fayette was standing beside the chair that held Emagine Buford, who'd been taken from her cell. Allene Buford stood near the windows, and Phyllis Darnell stood with her back to the wall near Emagine's chair.

I tossed Phyllis Darnell's letters on the scarred table. Her gaze rabbited around the room, her hands fluttering to her throat. "Go ahead," I said, "and pick them up. My boss will render you a bill later. For my money, you're a dirty little tramp, Mrs. Darnell, but Ben has agreed to keep the letters confidential. Not because of you—because of that poor devil up in Augusta, Maine."

"Then you know that I didn't kill Buddy Tomlinson? You really do know!" Phyllis held her hands pressed tight against her throat.

I looked at Allene. She took a step or two toward me. That wad of cotton fluffed out in my throat. "We know who killed Tomlinson and Osgood both, don't we, Allene?"

She stopped, then began moving again, circling around the room. "Are you joking with me, Lloyd?"

"I wish I was. I wish it more than you know, though maybe not for the reason you think. You knew Tomlinson had a good chance of getting his hands on the Buford money through Emagine, unless something was done about him. You went to his bungalow, maybe planning to kill him, maybe not. But you did kill him. Osgood saw you leaving. You were wearing Emagine's hat and coat, and he thought it was Emagine at first. But when he heard her story, he was inclined to believe it and guessed it had been you.

"You had killed Tomlinson to hold on to your money, Osgood reasoned. If Emagine went to the chair, it would not only leave you clear, Allene, but would remove her as the last obstacle between you and the Buford fortune. It looked sweet from where Osgood sat. He dug you for five grand, but when you'd had time to think, you knew it was no good. It would never be any good as long as Osgood was alive. So you killed him too.

"When I found Osgood dead on the beach, I started trying to think of the whole thing as he would have thought. You were the only answer, Allene. You were the one who could have easily gotten Emagine's hat and coat. You had motive. And I'm afraid they'll pin it on you. There must be some of your fingerprints on the five grand I took off of Osgood. There'll be so many more

things when they start looking and digging, Allene."

She looked from face to face, her hands knotted at her sides. Then she wheeled and lunged for the door. But the knife was quicker. The knife flashed in my hand, thudded in the door, close to her face. It paralyzed her. It paralyzed everyone in the room. She came to life first. She grasped the knife and pulled it from the wood. "You'd do this to me, Lloyd?"

That wad of cotton in my throat choked me.

"What else could I do?" she whispered. "I'd never had but one thing in a lousy life—that money. That damned filthy Buford money—and now I was going to get cheated out of that. I didn't mean to kill Buddy Tomlinson. I only wanted to scare him. But he grabbed at the gun—and it went off. I thought that if I hired a detective to warn Buddy away from Emagine, Buddy's body would be found and no one would ever think I had known he was dead. I thought that would take suspicion from me, and once Buddy's body was found, the detective would have no more to do with the case.

"After that, it seemed easier. It was much easier to kill Osgood. Yes, killing gets easier all the time—"

She sliced the word off with the knife. A spasm crossed her face, telegraphing a wave of horror over the room. A little cough bubbled in her throat.

I had never thought she'd use the knife for that. I'd only wanted to scare her, to bring her up at the door before Ben and his men began pulling guns. I'd wanted her to stop, to think. To talk. To cop a plea. To live.

She had saved my life. It was the only possible way I could have saved hers.

But she'd used the knife on herself.

I caught her in my arms as she crumpled, laid her gently on the floor. The scene in the room was breaking apart, people moving, converging on her. Her eyes flicked open. "Why couldn't it have been different, Lloyd? Why couldn't you have showed me Florida—the—part—the tourist never sees?"

Tears welled in her eyes. A spasm shuddered over her.

I stood up, fighting the moisture in my eyes. Distantly, I heard Emagine Buford say, "In a way, I'm not surprised. She was always sort of—"

"Shut up!" I screamed.

Somehow I got out of the room. I walked down the corridor outside, not seeing its walls, not feeling its floor under my feet.

Only remembering. That longing that was almost pain. That terrible, pitiful hunger. Even death hadn't erased it from her face, and I knew at last why Allene Buford had never been quite beautiful. . . .

One Shot

Charles G. Booth

CHARLES G(ORDON) BOOTH (1896–1949) was born in Manchester, England, then emigrated to Canada before settling in Los Angeles in 1922 to become a screenwriter for 20th Century Fox. While he was a popular and successful pulp writer and novelist in his time, even his best works, such as *Gold Bullets* (1929), *Murder at High Tide* (1930), *The General Died at Dawn* (1941), and *Mr. Angel Comes Aboard* (1944), are seldom read today.

The motion pictures that he wrote, however, as well as those based on his novels, are a different matter, still commonly found on late-night movie channels. *The House on 92nd Street* (1945) was released shortly after World War II as a thinly disguised film version of the FBI's success in bringing down the largest Nazi espionage organization in the history of the United States, the Duquesne Spy Ring, in 1941. A black-and-white noir semidocumentary, it featured an introduction by J. Edgar Hoover and real-life FBI agents in several scenes. Booth won an Academy Award for Best Original Motion Picture Story and was nominated for an Edgar Allan Poe Award for Best Motion Picture Screenplay (with cowriters Barré Lyndon and John Monks Jr.). It starred Lloyd Nolan and William Eythe. Films based on Booth's novels are *Johnny Angel* (1945, with a screenplay by Steve Fisher and Frank Gruber, based on *Mr. Angel Comes Aboard*) and *The General Died at Dawn* (1936, with a screenplay by Clifford Odets).

"One Shot" was published in the June 1925 issue.

One Shot

Charles G. Booth

PETER STODDARD FOUND NAT Hammond's letter waiting for him on his return to Los Angeles. Stoddard had never liked Hammond over much—few people did, for that matter; nevertheless, he opened the letter with a good deal of anticipation. He knew of only one reason why the celebrated engineer should write him.

Stoddard was something of an authority on antiques. Twelve months before, he had offered to purchase the famous Parsee Sunrise from Walter Hammond, Nat's brother, on behalf of Philip Andrea, the South American collector. Andrea was a friend of his. But notwithstanding the tragic accident that had wrecked Walter

Hammond's brilliant brain and left him broken in body and spirit two years prior to that, he had continued to adore the antique and the beautiful, and Stoddard could not induce him to part with the ancient symbol of the Parsee faith at any price. Walter Hammond had died six months ago.

Stoddard, also, was an engineer. He had won his spurs early in life, for he was still under thirty-five. But his was not the spectacular renown of the Hammond Brothers, builders of the Tse Chen railroad; rather, it was that solid, unobtrusive eminence such as men achieve by dint of their dogged refusal to admit themselves inferior to any contingency life may have in store for them. He was a tall, strongly built man with a rugged, kindly face tanned to a leathery hue by wind and sun. One sensed in him qualities of permanency and dependability leavened by a queer boyishness that endeared him to those who knew him intimately.

Stoddard was keenly observant in his undemonstrative way; and as he opened the letter, it occurred to him, as it had often done in the past, that he had never met brothers so opposite in their natures and in their outlook upon life as the two Hammonds.

Walter had been the artist, the thinker, the brains of that extraordinary partnership. Stoddard recalled him as he had seen him before the accident: clear-eyed and clear-skinned, well-shaped head, figure tall and lithe and slender like an athlete's; generous to a fault and contemptuous of the commercial aspect of his profession. And then, after the Tse Chen accident: broken and bent and vacant-eyed, handsome face all twisted and awry, inarticulate in his speech and cherishing the beautiful things he had always loved, with the pathetic passion of a slum child for a broken toy.

Nat, on the other hand, was a great chunk of a man, domineering and brutal, calculating and cynical, as hard as nails and as tough as leather. How Walter had endured him Stoddard never really understood. Flesh and blood, he supposed.

The letter, Stoddard saw, had been written at Hammond's place in the foothills, an old Spanish house near San Paulo, a small interior town some fifty miles east of Los Angeles. As he had surmised, it was in reference to the Parsee Sunrise. The letter ran:

Dear Stoddard:

Probably you are aware that my brother, Walter, died here last spring. I am sole executor of his estate, and there are one or two things which I think it advisable to get rid of. Among them is that Parsee Sunrise over which Walter made such a fool of himself a

year ago. If you still want the thing, the price is twenty thousand dollars. I shall not be in Los Angeles for several weeks. Drop in to see me if you are out this way.

Yours, etc.,
Nat Hammond

Twenty thousand dollars! Pretty high, even for the Parsee Sunrise. Nevertheless, Stoddard knew that old Andrea would gladly pay it. The Sunrise was a jeweled symbol of the Parsee fire worshipers, ritualistic in purpose, extraordinarily beautiful in design. It was fashioned to represent the rising sun: some three inches across, its center was set with magnificent pigeon's blood rubies from which radiated sapphire tongues of flame. Walter Hammond had acquired it in India from a converted Parsee—one of that remnant of the descendants of the followers of the ancient Persian, Zoroaster.

Stoddard's satisfaction at the prospect of securing the Sunrise was lessened somewhat by the contempt of Walter's love of beauty expressed in Hammond's letter. Well, Walter Hammond could no longer adore his beloved Parsee symbol—far better that Andrea should have it than that it should remain in Nat Hammond's unappreciative hands.

And then, as Stoddard turned the typewritten letter over, these considerations were suddenly and dramatically swept from his mind. He found himself staring down at a pen-written postscript appended to the back of the note. The character of the handwriting—small, neatly printed script, totally unlike Hammond's sprawling signature—was scarcely less intriguing than the text. To his amazement he read:

Mr. Stoddard! Don't buy the Parsee Sunrise—please!

That was all.

Peter Stoddard was ever a man of brisk action, and nine o'clock that evening found him driving into San Paulo. It must be admitted that his quest for the Parsee Sunrise was overshadowed by the extraordinary postscript that had been added to Hammond's letter. The engineer had not penned it, of course. Who had, then? This diverting question, and his inability to answer it, had alternatively puzzled and delighted him ever since he had read the postscript. That queer boyish streak in his otherwise staid and responsible nature had dressed it in the iridescent garb of romance.

At one of the hotels Stoddard was informed that Hammond's place was some ten miles northeast of the town. He was instructed to proceed over the county highway, then turn east along the second dirt road. Two giant eucalyptus trees marked the entrance to the estate.

A strong wind had risen in the past half hour; before it drove scudding banks of cloud that spread a pitch-black pall across the sky. As Stoddard's roadster swept along the purple highway, so dense had the night become that impenetrable walls of blackness seemed to enclose him on three sides. The fan-shaped glare from the headlights of his car alone gave him any sense of dimension. The wind, rising steadily, clawed at his face, whipped the red into his cheeks; he was compelled to narrow his eyes to slits, thus increasing his visual difficulties.

After some twenty minutes of this difficult going, Stoddard perceived an opening in the continuity of wire fencing on his right. Swinging his car, he found himself bounding over a rutted, weed-grown road which apparently extended into the invisible mountain range bulking hugely before him. The grade rose steeply. The scent of deciduous orchards assailed his nostrils. He slowed down and began to peer ahead, seeking the two eucalyptus trees. Presently he saw them: vague and indistinct in the all-pervasive gloom, and creaking and groaning and whispering in the howling wind.

Stoddard swung into the drive and slowed down to a crawl. He found himself in an avenue of smaller eucalyptus trees that whipped his nostrils with their pungent scent. As the machine glided up the cindered drive, headlights cutting a white swath before it, the Hammond house emerged from the pall of darkness that enveloped the estate. It was a white, sprawling, flat-topped structure with cool porches and shadowy terraces, ivy-covered and embowered in a profusion of subtropical plants and shrubbery. A light burned dimly in a single window.

Stoddard stopped his roadster in front of the house, alighted, and hammered on the stout oak front door with a bronze knocker which he found fastened thereto. A dull booming noise like muffled thunder seemed to emerge from the interior of the house. He waited, but there came no response. He repeated the summons. . . . Still no response. For the third time he wielded the bronze knocker. Then he glanced at his watch. Nine forty-five! The wind swished and howled in the trees now, and ran shrieking around the corners of the building. . . . No response!

Stoddard stepped back and regarded the house contemplatively. It had a somber, menacing appearance in the brooding darkness; an atmosphere of evil seemed to enfold it and press down upon it. Once again he evoked muffled thunder from the bronze knocker, and waiting, listened attentively. A full minute elapsed. Still the house retained its tomb-like silence.

A cinder path skirted the front of the house. Stoddard ran softly along it toward the lighted window. A queer, apprehensive feeling was taking possession of him. Stopping in front of the window—it consisted of two long French doors—he saw that it was approached by a small porch. To this he quickly ascended. Curtains were drawn across the glass doors, but there remained an inch or so of space between them, affording a limited view of the room.

At what he saw, Stoddard caught and held his breath; his face whitened to the lips; his heart seemed to stop beating.

The room was evidently a library. Books lined two walls; there were several comfortable chairs; a fire crackled in a cobblestone grate. Against one of the walls stood an antique desk, richly carved. Stoddard could see only the front of the desk. Before it, in an arm chair, sat a man with his body slumped forward, head and shoulders sprawled over the left-hand front corner of the desk. The left side of his face lay on the edge of the desk. Stoddard glimpsed a smear of red against the light grey of his coat. His body was limp and strangely still.

Nat Hammond was dead. Of course, Stoddard knew this intuitively. But so devastating to his mental poise was the shock of thus finding the man he had come all these miles to see, that for a moment or two he could merely stare at him, incapable of thought or movement or speech. Then a gust of fury shook him. Hammond had been shot down like a dog—perhaps within the last few minutes. Casting caution to the winds, he shook the French doors vigorously. They were locked. He took off his cap, pulled it over his hand, and drove his fist through one of the center panes of the doors. In a moment he had drawn the bolt, pushed the door open, and stepped into the room.

Hammond had been shot through the heart. His body was still warm. Stoddard gently raised his head and shoulders, and leaned them back in the chair. The man's heavy, domineering face was set and rigid; it expressed a profound amazement, as if death had revealed its mystery to him while he was yet alive.

Stoddard glanced swiftly around the room. There were no indications of a struggle, nor did he see a weapon of any sort. The door was shut. He closed and bolted the French doors.

Stoddard stood in the middle of the room debating with himself what he should do. The police must be notified, of course. But it was within the bounds of possibility that Hammond's murderer was still in the house, in which event he must be apprehended at once. Stoddard's mind was quickly and coolly made up. First, he would search every room in the place; then he would telephone to the police. He was unarmed, but Stoddard was one of those rare men who seem to have been born absolutely fearless. The risk he would run simply did not occur to him.

Stoddard remained where he was, however.

His big body tensed suddenly and his rugged face grew as hard as flint. He leaned forward, listening intently, grey eyes fixed on the door. He had just discovered that he was not alone in the house. A small sound had come from the hall or room beyond the door: an inarticulate sound like the suppressed sob or a gasp of pain or terror. Stoddard measured the distance between himself and the door. Then his body flexed and he sprang forward, covering the intervening several yards at a single bound, caught the door handle, and jerked the door open.

A gasp of amazement broke from his lips; he fell back in consternation. A girl had tumbled headlong into the room. She recovered herself, and shrank back against the wall. Stoddard stared at her speechlessly, the color ebbing and flowing in his bronzed cheeks.

She was undeniably pretty; he realized this in spite of the consternation that transfixed him. Her eyes were large and dark and luminous, and her oval face, notwithstanding its deathly pallor, had an intriguing piquancy about it. Her dark bobbed hair fell around her well-shaped head in charming disarray. He saw that terror and horror dominated every fiber of her being; she seemed to shrink visibly as he stared down at her. Stoddard was the first to speak.

"Hammond is dead," he said, huskily. "Do you know when it happened?—who did it?"

She must have found some reassuring quality in his voice, for the terror in her eyes receded a little. A moment or two elapsed before she replied.

"Ten minutes ago." the girl whispered, jerkily. "I was in my room—I heard the shot—I found him—tumbled over his desk—" She stopped shuddering and covered her face with her hands. "I don't know who!—why!—anything!"

Stoddard nodded understandingly.

"Did you hear anyone trying to get away—afterward?"

"No! There was no one in the house but Uncle Nat and I. Whoever did it—must have got out through those doors!"

She indicated the French doors by which Stoddard had entered the library.

The engineer shook his head emphatically.

"Those doors were bolted! He didn't get out that way! He couldn't have! I had to break one of them to unfasten the bolt."

The girl stared at him incredulously.

"You are Hammond's niece?" Stoddard went on.

She nodded, still keeping her dark eyes fixed upon him.

"I am Julia Hammond. Walter Hammond was my father. You are Mr. Stoddard, I suppose. Uncle Nat said you were coming about—the Parsee Sunrise."

There seemed the merest edge of contempt in her tone as she mentioned the antique symbol. Stoddard let it pass without comment, however.

"About how much time elapsed between the firing of the shot and your entrance into this room?" he went on. "I must ask these questions, you know," he added gently, noticing signals of distress in her eyes. "We've simply *got* to find out who did it!"

Julia nodded.

"Yes—I know," she whispered. "I ran in at once—a few seconds, that's all."

Stoddard was incredulous now.

"But how could he have got away in so short a time without your seeing him?"

Tears suddenly welled up into the girl's dark eyes.

"I don't know! I don't know how he got away!" she sobbed, with such emphasis that Stoddard was startled. "Uncle Nat and I were alone in the house. Mrs. Bell, the housekeeper, is visiting in Los Angeles over the weekend. Tyson, the man around the place, has gone to San Paulo for the car—it is being overhauled. He'll be back soon. Someone must have got into the house, shot Uncle Nat, and got away. I don't know how he got in, or who it was!"

Her voice had risen hysterically; she broke into a paroxysm of sobbing.

Stoddard's protective instincts were thoroughly aroused now. He longed to utter some word of comfort, but he was essentially an outdoor man and he could think of nothing adequate to the situation; so he simply waited for the girl's outburst to subside. Stoddard was as ignorant of women as he was wise in the ways of men, but he had an unusually keen brain and he thought he detected in the girl's behavior a note of panic which her natural distress at her uncle's tragic end did not account for satisfactorily. Moreover, how Hammond's murderer could have got out of the house—provided, of course, he was not still in it—without Julia seeing him was utterly beyond Stoddard's understanding. The engineer puzzled over these points until he found Julia looking up at him.

"I'm sorry I broke down like that," she said quietly. "What shall we do?"

"I'm going to search the house," Stoddard declared. "If the man we want isn't hiding in it he must have got out through a door or window somewhere! You had better stay here."

Julia shook her dark head decidedly.

"No, I'm going with you! I simply *couldn't* stay here!"

She led the way into the hall, and snapped on a light. Stoddard preceded her to the front door. It was bolted on the inside. Julia said nothing. Stoddard felt a queer chill run over him. They began a tour of the house, commencing with the drawing-room. The windows of the latter were fastened—on the inside. They passed into the dining-room and then into the living-room. In these rooms also the windows were fastened.

"Uncle Nat had Tyson bolt them on account of the wind," Julia explained tonelessly.

Stoddard did not reply. There seemed nothing to say. A sense of emptiness possessed him; he felt as if the atmosphere of the place were choking him. He avoided Julia's eyes. They continued their rounds of the house in silence, coming into each of the five bedrooms and the two bathrooms in turn. All the windows were bolted. Finally they entered the kitchen. The single window was fastened and the back door which led into an outhouse was bolted on the inside. There was no basement. Every means of egress from the house was secured on the inside.

"I bolted the kitchen door after Tyson went to San Paulo," Julia said, in the same toneless voice. "Uncle Nat has one or two valuable antiques, our house stands alone, and he was always very particular about having the doors locked and bolted, especially at night."

Stoddard said nothing. Not until this moment had he permitted himself to contemplate the conclusion that had been hammering at his brain since they had found the front door bolted. Julia was looking at him unhappily, searching his face for some key to his thoughts. Stoddard contrived to avoid meeting her eyes. It was inconceivable that she had taken her uncle's life, yet he was compelled to consider the evidence of his senses. His respect for the principles of logic, inculcated in him during a lifetime of professional experience, was not to be lightly put aside. Julia had known they would find the windows and doors bolted before they had begun to examine them! This, of course, accounted for that panic-stricken note he had detected in her breakdown in the library.

Then a revulsion of feeling set in. Julia could not have done this monstrous thing! Such a theory was too fantastically horrible for sane and reasonable thought. There *must* be some logical explanation that did not offend every canon of decency. Stoddard forced himself to meet her wide, searching eyes. His suspicions were sacrilege; he swept them out of his mind. Julia caught him by the arm.

"Mr. Stoddard," she began, "I heard you knocking at the front door! I didn't dare to open it! I was terrified—I couldn't think! My uncle had been shot down, and I was the only one in the house with him—so far as I knew. I felt sure that every window and door was fastened on the inside—and I had seen no one—heard no one! I was nearly frantic. You know what it means! They'll say I—did it!" Her voice broke; then she went on more quietly. "I can't think how it has been done—men don't pass through adobe walls and locked doors!" She gripped Stoddard's arm in a sudden access of terror. "You don't think— you don't think I did it, Mr. Stoddard?"

"No!" Stoddard shouted. He caught the girl by the shoulders. Their eyes held and kindled; an indissolvable bond of understanding seemed to draw them together. "You didn't do it, Julia, and nothing will ever make me think you did!"

A sob of relief broke from the girl's lips. Stoddard was seized with a nearly irrepressible desire to draw her to him. He contented himself with merely pressing her hand reassuringly.

"You must phone the police," she whispered.

Stoddard had forgotten the police. Julia was right, of course. The sooner he got in touch with the authorities, the better. Just then he heard the purr of an engine in the drive outside, followed by the creak of a stopping car.

"Tyson," Julia stated.

There came a slow, dull knock on the kitchen door. Stoddard shot back the bolt.

Tyson was a little wisp of a man with disheveled grey hair, small eyes of a curious faded blue, rather shrewd in their expression, and a wizened skin that reminded Stoddard of a last year's apple. He was quite old—seventy, at least: his small, thin body was stooped with age, though a sinewy strength like that of an old gnarled stick still clung to it tenaciously. At sight of their grave faces, a look of apprehension leaped into his faded eyes.

"What's wrong?" he queried in a thin, cracked voice.

Stoddard looked at him gravely for a moment without speaking. The kitchen grew very still and quiet, and the old man seemed to grasp something of the gravity of the situation.

"Mr. Hammond—" he began in a trembling voice.

Stoddard nodded.

"Mr. Hammond is dead," he stated, slowly. "He has been shot."

Tyson's eyes almost started out of their sockets; his russet color faded and he caught at the table to support himself. Stoddard watched him narrowly.

"Dead!" Tyson muttered, as if he found the fact unbelievable. "Dead!" Then he shot a sharp, penetrating look at Stoddard. "Who did it?" he croaked.

"We are trying to find out," Stoddard

returned gravely. "Did you meet anyone in the drive or on the road?"

Tyson shook his head emphatically.

"I saw no one," he quavered shrilly.

The engineer silently led the way into the library. Julia was still deathly white, but into her face had come an impassive expression that suggested little of the terror and misery behind it. Tyson stared at the body of his master in silence, a look of unutterable horror in his faded eyes.

Stoddard picked up the telephone and got in touch with the office of the San Paulo Town Marshall. The latter, it appeared, was out. He would return within the next half hour and would come at once. Stoddard put the instrument down, thankful for the small respite.

Tyson was still staring at Hammond's body in frozen silence and Stoddard dismissed him impatiently. The old man went off to his kitchen mumbling indistinguishably to himself. Two chairs were drawn up before the fireplace, and Stoddard dropped into one of them. Julia seemed on the verge of taking the other when she cast a shuddering glance at the limp figure by the desk. She went to the switch and snapped out the light. Then she took the vacant chair.

"You don't mind—the dark!" she whispered, tremulously. "I can't bear the light—with him there."

Stoddard nodded understandingly. The dying firelight played redly on Julia's dark head. They regarded each other unhappily. Neither of them spoke. The silence seemed to knit them closer together. Outside, the wind still swished dismally in the tree tops. Suddenly, Stoddard took Hammond's letter from his pocket and showed the postscript to the girl.

"Why did you write that, Julia?" he asked, gently.

She looked at him searchingly for a moment.

"I was doing secretarial work for Uncle Nat."

"And you didn't want me to buy the Parsee Sunrise?"

Julia's eyes grew humid with expression.

"I wonder if I can make you understand, Mr. Stoddard," she went on, slowly. "Uncle Nat hated beauty—my father loved it—passionately. After

the accident—you remember?—he simply adored that Parsee symbol. It was pitiable to see him with it. Last year when Uncle Nat wanted him to sell it to you, he went into hysterics and made me promise to keep it—always. Just before he died he made me promise again. Uncle Nat has charge of my estate until I am twenty-five—next June—and he insisted on selling the Sunrise. I begged him not to. He called me a silly fool—said the market was just right for disposing of antiques—and he wrote that letter to you. He gave it to me to mail. I was desperate and I added that absurd postscript. I might have known that it would bring you quicker than anything else!

"Uncle Nat had no feeling, no love, no tenderness in him!" Julia continued bitterly. "Sometimes I positively hated him!" She leaned forward. "Do you know, Mr. Stoddard, I can't help thinking that that Parsee Sunrise has something to do with his death!"

This had already occurred to Stoddard, and he nodded silently. Julia's explanation had increased his fears on her behalf. If she repeated it to the police an ambitious prosecuting attorney would easily find in her dislike of Hammond and in her desperate determination to prevent him from selling the symbol a motive strong enough to account for the crime.

"Julia," he began, earnestly, "I had to break that window to get into the room! We've got to tell the San Paulo marshal that I found it broken and open! We must give the impression that someone got in, shot Nat Hammond, and got out that way! And we are not going to say anything about your trouble with Hammond!"

But Julia shook her head emphatically.

"No, Peter." She smiled, using his first name with a tenderness that thrilled him. "We are going to tell the truth—all the truth—nothing else! Don't you understand? If we lie, they'll find us out somehow and that will make it all the worse."

"But appearances are so strongly against you!"

"I know. That is why I'm going to tell the truth, Peter. Nothing but the truth. It is the best way. You'll stand by me, won't you?"

A lump rose in Stoddard's throat and he could not command his tongue. He caught her hand in his and pressed it tightly. The contact seemed to tell her more than a hundred expressions of loyalty could have done. . . .

Stoddard leaned back in his chair and ran a weary hand through his hair. His brain ached with the strain of its continuous application to this impossible problem he had set out to solve. Every facet of the riddle had an adamantine hardness that defied his mental powers as resolutely as Lucifer ever defied the hosts of heaven. He felt as if he were traveling along the convolutions of a maze—a maze with neither entrance nor exit. Well, there was an opening somewhere and he must find it. He must!

Stoddard shut his eyes to ease the throbbing in his head. The house was silent. Outside, the wind had dropped to a thin wail. The fire in the grate had sunk to a bed of red embers. He did not move. Neither did Julia. She was staring into the grate, chin cupped in her hands, waiting. . . . Some time passed. Then, suddenly, Stoddard heard a tiny whisper of sound like the quick patter of infinitesimally small feet on the floor near the antique desk.

Cautiously turning his head he strained his eyes at the place from where he thought the sound had come. But the shadows were too thick; he could see nothing. The noise continued. Stoddard's hard-muscled body grew rigid; his hands clamped down on the arms of his chair. Still he could not identify the sound! Apparently, Julia had not noticed it. She was still gazing into the red-embered grate.

The sound possessed Stoddard body and soul. Identify it he must! Setting his eyes on the whereabouts of the light switch he tensed his body and sprang at a single bound across the intervening floor space. His hand closed on the switch; light flooded the room.

There came a sharp yelp of pain. Three streaks of white whizzed across the floor and vanished behind the antique desk. Stoddard gaped at them in amazement. Mice! White mice! A wave of exasperation swept over him. He had

made a fool of himself over these! Then he saw Julia smiling wryly up at him and he grinned sheepishly.

"They are quite wild, now," she said. "Father got them—after the accident. He thought the world of them and he trained them to do the prettiest tricks! Tyson promised to look after them, but Uncle Nat, of course, ordered them destroyed. Tyson simply worshiped Father and he left their cage open—on purpose, I'm afraid—and they got away. That desk was Father's—he used to let them have the run of it. Uncle Nat had Tyson set traps—you'll find one behind the desk. Probably there's a mouse in it."

Stoddard fumbled behind the back of the desk and drew out an old-fashioned mousetrap of the box type. In it was a tiny white mouse, stiff with terror.

"I am sure Tyson lets them go after he catches them," Julia continued. "The place is overrun with them and they never seem to get any less. Tyson was with Uncle Nat and Father for thirty years—he went with them everywhere—and he considers himself a privileged person. I'm sure he couldn't be persuaded to kill the little things. He adored Father."

Scarcely conscious of what he was doing, Stoddard knelt down, opened the trap and shook the tiny rodent out onto the floor. It streaked across the room and vanished behind the antique desk. His mind pivoted upon that last remark of Julia's. She had said that Tyson had adored her father! Could it be possible that Tyson had shot Nat Hammond because of some fancied or magnified wrong done to Walter Hammond by his brother?

Stoddard's heart leaped at the thought. Then he dismissed the notion. It was absurd, of course. Tyson was driving back from San Paulo at the time the shot was fired. Moreover, every door and window in the house had been locked on the inside—Stoddard shook his head in a gesture of rage and despair. His brain was numb; he could not think coherently. Setting aside the trap he looked at Julia.

"Do you know where the Parsee Sunrise is?"
Julia shook her head.

"No, I don't. Uncle Nat hid it away. I never could find it."

"Did Hammond have a pistol of any sort?"
Julia nodded.

"Yes, a small automatic. I don't know where he kept it. I think he was afraid of Father getting it."

Stoddard glared malevolently at the antique desk. A curious feeling that it was in some way connected with Hammond's death came upon him. More than ever did it seem a sinister presence, brooding over the room.

To distract his unhappy thoughts he commenced a thorough search of the five drawers of the desk. Perhaps he might find the Parsee Sunrise. The drawers were crammed with a miscellaneous litter of papers, appertaining to Hammond's business affairs, personal and private. . . . When he had finished several minutes later he had found no sign of the ancient symbol.

His brain had cleared, however, and he eyed the desk thoughtfully. Then he began to run his fingers slowly and heavily over the top of the desk, studying with particular care the beautiful grain of the wood. Nothing resulted from this proceeding and he turned his attention to one of the massive legs that supported the desk.

At that moment a powerful car throbbed up the cinder drive and slurred to a stop in front of the house. Heavy feet approached and someone hammered authoritatively on the front door. Tyson shambled out of the kitchen. Stoddard looked up; the color receded from his cheeks.

"The San Paulo marshal!" he whispered.

Julia nodded. She had gone deathly pale. Stoddard caught her hands tightly between his.

"We've got to tell him that I found this window open!" he stated, emphatically.

"No!" The fierceness of her tone startled Stoddard.

"If you do, I'll tell him the truth of it, anyway! We won't accomplish anything by deceit. I

know!" Her voice softened. "Peter—don't worry. Things will come out right, you'll see."

A sudden impulse to press her hand to his lips overcame Stoddard. As he yielded to it the look in her dark eyes seemed to leap out at him. Her lips trembled; she withdrew her hand gently, as a heavily built man with a hard, shrewd face and frosty blue eyes strode into the room.

Tyson hovered near the door. The marshal went directly to Hammond's body and glanced at it coolly and appraisingly; then he addressed himself to Stoddard.

"Bartlett is my name," he stated, in a crisp voice. "I am the San Paulo city marshal." He said this as if he wished to leave no doubt of it in their minds. "What's happened here?"

Stoddard had intended to gloss over the evidence so damaging to Julia's case as much as possible—not that he expected to accomplish anything by so doing—but before he could utter a word Julia plunged into a vividly phrased recital of what they knew of the affair. She quickly explained Stoddard's presence in the house, how he had effected an entrance, and her relationship to Hammond. The possible connection of the Parsee Sunrise with the shooting she touched on briefly, also. Then, as if her case were not black enough already, she specifically mentioned that they had searched the house and found no one, and that every window and door had been fastened and bolted on the inside. Frankness, her only card, she played skillfully. She finished with a little hopeless gesture that wrung Stoddard's heart.

Throughout Julia's explanation, Bartlett had maintained a rigid silence. Little darts of suspicion had leaped into his frosty eyes and his lips had curled ironically once or twice. Stoddard had observed these signals of the marshal's disbelief and his rugged face grew haggard as he waited for the man to express himself.

But whatever opinions he had formed, Bartlett, for the moment, kept to himself. He fired a stream of pertinent questions at Julia. She answered them coolly and quietly, sitting in the chair in front of the fireplace. The occasional twitching of her hands and the deathly pallor of her face were the only outward manifestations of the stress she was under.

"Every window and door locked on the inside, hey?" Bartlett snapped.

"Yes."

"And you searched every room in the house?"

"Yes."

Bartlett grunted indistinguishably. Then he took a black bound notebook from his pocket and penciled rapidly on its pages. Stoddard hung on his movements fearfully and breathlessly. Finally, he could stand it no longer.

"Look here, Bartlett!" he burst forth, huskily. "You don't believe she did it, do you? It looks bad, I know! But, good Lord, man! She *couldn't* have done it! *Look* at her!"

In his desperate eagerness to impress the marshal Stoddard stepped forward and caught him fiercely by the arm.

But the other shook him off, chuckling grimly.

"If she didn't do it, I'd like to know who did! Every window and door locked and bolted and the girl and Hammond alone in the house! Two and two still make four, Stoddard! You can't get away from it!"

Julia uttered a cry and covered her face with her hands. Stoddard's arm dropped limply to his side. He had expected this, of course; nevertheless, Bartlett's reasonable deductions left him weak and trembling, all his rugged strength sapped out of him. Julia had intrigued him as no other woman had ever done, and if he could have shifted her burden to his own broad and capable shoulders he would gladly have done so. He had known her scarcely more than an hour; but into that time had been packed the emotional experiences of a lifetime.

Tyson, still in the doorway, took a shambling step forward. Then he stopped, a look of horror creeping into his faded eyes. His lips mumbled soundlessly and his old teeth clicked together like castanets. Bartlett returned to his notebook.

"That Parsee trinket—what's it worth?" the marshal demanded abruptly after a moment.

"Twenty thousand dollars," Julia whispered in dead tones.

The Parsee Sunrise. Stoddard caught his breath sharply. A little train of thought had flared up in his mind. If the ancient symbol had been stolen, and he could establish that fact, the existence of a third party might be argued— surely a point in Julia's favor. He stared at the antique desk thoughtfully. It seemed to leer back at him.

The desk had been manufactured in a day of political intrigue—probably for someone of importance—when combination lock safes were unknown and a secret compartment in a private desk was a highly desirable feature. Stoddard had examined the grain of the top of the desk in the hope of discovering a concealed chamber of some kind, feeling sure that if there was one the Parsee symbol would be inside it. Now he began to run his fingers painstakingly over the right-hand front leg, as he had been about to do when Bartlett arrived.

Several minutes elapsed. The marshal continued to make notes in his black bound book. Julia had not moved from her chair in front of the fireplace. Tyson was still standing within the door, mumbling soundlessly to himself. Stoddard began on the left front leg of the desk. Suddenly, Bartlett closed his book with a snap, pocketed it, and turned to Julia.

"Get your things together," he commanded, tersely. "I'm going to take a look around the house. Then we start for San Paulo. The sheriff and the D.A.—"

"No!"

The single word, uttered by Stoddard, had the effect of a pistol crack. A cry of exultation broke from his lips, and he pointed dramatically down at the top of the antique desk. Then Bartlett and Julia and Tyson rushed forward. Stoddard met them with an ecstatic look on his rugged face and his left hand closed fiercely, triumphantly, on Julia's arm.

A section of the top of the desk, some eight inches long and five inches wide, stood erect, revealing a compartment perhaps four inches deep. There was a hole in one corner of the compartment. Near it lay the Parsee Sunrise, glittering like a constellation of minute stars. A bundle of papers, their edges serrated as with the fretting of tiny teeth, lay on the bottom of the compartment partly supporting an automatic pistol that had been carelessly thrust into the compartment in such a way that its muzzle pointed directly at where Hammond's body must have been before he fell forward, and his death agony shut down the cunningly concealed section he had just released.

Entangled with the trigger guard and hair trigger of the pistol was a common mousetrap, baited with cheese. And caught by the leg in the trap Nat Hammond had set for it was one of Walter Hammond's white mice! In futile terror it had dragged the trap across the trigger as Hammond had opened the compartment. The roar of the shot that had killed Hammond had stilled its tiny heart.

The Dancing Rats

Richard Sale

RICHARD (BERNARD) SALE (1911–1993) was born in New York City and educated at Washington and Lee University (1930–1933), where he had already begun to write professionally, selling early stories to the pulps, including "The White Cobra" to *The Shadow* magazine in 1932. He went on to write more than 350 stories, mostly mystery fiction, for all the major pulp magazines, including *Black Mask, Thrilling Mystery, Argosy,* and *Detective Fiction Weekly,* for which he created his most successful series character, the newspaper reporter–cum–detective Joe "Daffy" Dill, whose adventures also featured Bill Hanley and Candid Jones. He also wrote stories for all the major slick magazines.

His first novel, *Not Too Narrow . . . Not Too Deep* (1936), is an adventure tale of ten convicts who escape from a French penal colony (a renamed Devil's Island) and a mysterious stranger who accompanies them. It was filmed by MGM in 1940 as *Strange Cargo,* starring Clark Gable, Joan Crawford, and Peter Lorre. His finest novels are *Lazarus #7* (1942) and *Passing Strange* (1942). He had an active career in the film industry as a writer, with such credits as *Mr. Belvedere Goes to College* (1949), *A Ticket to Tomahawk* (1950), *Suddenly* (1954), a suspense film with Frank Sinatra, and *Torpedo Run* (1958), which he also directed. With his wife, Mary Anita Loos, he wrote *Gentlemen Marry Brunettes* (1955) and other films.

"The Dancing Rats" was published in the June 1942 issue.

The Dancing Rats

Richard Sale

A NOVELETTE

Kita was pointing the gun almost into Nick's face when Captain Malta fired.

What was the mysterious and terrible disaster that threatened to wreak havoc in Oahu, reduce the Pacific fortress to impotency and throw the shadow of death across every mother's son on the island? Dr. Nicholas Adams, summoned from his work at the leper colony of Molokai, had just forty-eight hours to find out!

CHAPTER ONE
THE EPISODE OF MR. SZE

HE WIRELESS HAD been burning a hole in Nick Adams' pocket ever since it had been delivered to him at the Cardwell Institute's labs over on the island of Molokai.

Nick had been checking the progress of the Institute's fight against leprosy there when the war broke. And although the perfidy at Pearl Harbor had been a memory for some time now, he had remained on Molokai's north coast, checking experimentations with Brooke Carteret, a fine leprosy medico.

The wireless, however, took his interest away from Molokai abruptly, and returned it to Oahu. Even in the baby clipper plane of the Inter-Island Steam Navigation Company, he could not restrain himself from pulling the thing out once more and rereading it. He knew every word by heart then, as the soiled and frayed message indicated, but it was so damned provocative, he couldn't resist staring at it.

It said:

REQUIRE YOUR IMMEDIATE ASSISTANCE IN MATTER OF VITAL

IMPORTANCE STOP SECRECY ESSENTIAL STOP DISASTER IMMINENT IN OAHU IN FORTY EIGHT HOURS UNLESS YOU AND I STOP IT COME AT ONCE EXPLAIN WHEN SEE YOU WIRE INSTRUCTIONS SIGNED COLONEL JOHN VENNER US MEDCORPS SCHOFIELD BARRACKS

Nick blinked again and frowned. The plane was empty except for himself. The IISNC operated steamships among the islands, and due to the fact that Molokai held the leper colony, it was not included among the normal stops for tourists. But the company also operated several twin-motored clippers of the old Pan-American type, and one of these had flown him out, and a second—which he now rode—had been wirelessed for, to fly him back.

From northern Molokai to southern Oahu where Honolulu sat upon the sea was no great shakes of a trip, a matter of hours, and they were due to come in at any time. He folded the message and put it away and then watched out the plane window for the sight of Diamond Head rising precipitantly from the sea.

Dr. Nicholas Adams, chief of the field staffs of the Cardwell Institute through the western Pacific—if you wanted to get formal about it—was no *malihini* to the Hawaiian Island. No stranger. He knew that his identity was well known in Honolulu, as it was in various other places such as Singapore, Shanghai, Manila and Batavia, indeed in any portion of the western Pacific where there was disease. But he could not help wondering who the devil Colonel John Venner was, and how the devil Venner had known that he was on Molokai.

As for the message itself, it was intriguing, but at the same time, it was extremely dubious. The only disaster which could be imminent in Oahu was of the same ilk as had struck it once before—those Japanese planes winging death out of the sky in the dawn. And if Venner had come by such inside information, of what use was a non-military medico like Nick Adams going to be in averting it? It was more the Army and Navy's job.

So, obviously, it was not a Japanese attack which Venner meant. It was something else. Nick made no attempt to fathom what, because he could only conjecture, and rather wildly at that.

Probably Venner had got in touch with the Cardwell Institute labs on Bishop Street in Honolulu and learned from Paul Cameron—the local head of the organization in Oahu—that Nick

Adams was at Molokai. Then Venner had wirelessed.

In any case, he had got Nick's goat, and Nick had replied by wireless when and how and where he would be arriving. He assumed that Colonel Venner would meet him and break this strain of curious impatience which held him.

From the window of the plane, Nick finally made out Koko Head, and then beyond that, the majesty of Diamond Head. An Army patrol plane, looking sleek and deadly, had picked them up some time before, established their identity and sent them on. Thus forewarned, no other planes interrupted their flight, but Nick hoped that each of the ground crews who undoubtedly had an A.A. gun trained on them would also recognize the inter-island plane, a good Hawaiian fixture, and not be too precipitous.

They glided lower, and the Aloha Tower by the Matson pier flashed by. Honolulu sat in the sun peacefully, and the blue sea broke white along the shore from Waikiki to Fort Kamehameha. Then they were down, gliding to a perfect landing on the sea and taxiing up to the ramp of the Inter-Island airport.

When Nick reached the waiting-room, there was no sign of any Army man waiting for him. There was only one man there, an Oriental of one sort or another—it was difficult to tell Japanese from Chinese—and Nick ignored him and stepped out to see if Colonel Venner might be waiting in a car at the parking space.

"Dr. Adams, sah?"

Nick turned, blank-faced. From Hawaii west, you always blank-faced when you were surprised. It was a trick of the Asiatics, friend and foe alike. He said, "Yes?"

"This humble person begs your forgiveness," said the man who had spoken, the same Oriental, "but I have been sent to meet you. Colonel Venner is occupied. He asked me to pick you up. Will you honor me, sah?"

Nick found himself bordering on a reaction of wariness. The stranger was a Chinese, a long lean-cheeked Cassius sort of Chinese, with teeth that were almost as yellow as his skin. It was not only that the man's dark eyes were dishonest, they were sinister. They were like onyx jewels, touched with a cold glitter, nor were they shifty—they met his own directly, hard and uncompromising. But the fellow's hands intrigued Nick even more. They were fine hands for a strangler. From wrist to finger base, the measured distance must have been six full inches, and the tapering fingers, delicately manicured, were weirdly long and graceful, the left pinkie wearing an opal set in gold.

"I'm Nicholas Adams," Nick said. "Who are you?"

"This worthless one is known as H. H. Sze," replied the Chinese. He pronounced his surname *T'see*. "I am an officer with the Commission of Health in Honolulu, Doctor."

"And you came for me?" Nick said.

"Forgive me, yes." Mr. Sze did not have a semblance of expression on his face. "Colonel Venner asked me to get you. This is my car. I shall take you to him at once."

"What's it all about?" Nick said. "Go ahead. Get in."

"Forgive me—after you, sah," Mr. Sze replied. His striped seersucker suit looked as if it had been slept in. It needed a starching badly. He waited for Nick to sit in the car, then got in himself, on the edge of the seat, his face always blank, his hands on the wheel, lightly, as if he held them ready to move.

"This humble one must apologize for any celerity," Mr. Sze said. He drove off and took the Waiana Road. "Forgive me, we do not have much time. I will explain quickly."

"Do," Nick said. He lighted his pipe unhurriedly and watched Mr. Sze.

"It is an epidemic, and you are needed, sah," Mr. Sze said smoothly. "I believe you and the commissioner are old friends?"

"Yes," Nick said. "How is he?"

"Commissioner Hartly is in the most beautiful health, and had honored this humble one in conveying his personal profound wishes for your own health, and his gratification at your presence so close to us. He and Colonel Venner dispatched me this morning to take you from the plane. It is so very, very urgent, you see."

"Very interesting," Nick said. He was positive Mr. Sze was lying through his teeth. "What seems to be the trouble?"

"Beriberi," said Mr. Sze. "It is sweeping through the pineapple estates north of Wright Field like a pestilence. It is very bad. The honorable commissioner said that the most sagacious Dr. Adams would know what to do—"

"Contagious, eh?"

"The *Kanakas* are sick and dying," Mr. Sze said. "The *Kahunas* do nothing." His voice was very dramatic, although his face remained as blank as stone. "Forgive me—like a sweeping pestilence—"

"You certainly like to be forgiven, don't you?"

"Forgive me, a habit of speech—"

ick pointed the stem of his pipe at Mr. Sze. "You are a very extraordinary health officer, Mr. Sze."

"Thank you, sah," Mr. Sze said, bowing his head. "I am only a humble servant—"

"And I didn't mean it as a compliment," Nick said coldly. "You can go back and tell the commissioner that beriberi is not contagious. It is a painful disease which comes from the eating of polished rice and a lack of vitamin B. Or were you confused in the press of things?"

Mr. Sze said nothing at all. He did not look nonplussed. Resigned if anything. The trouble was you couldn't tell how he looked. He had learned the poker face trick so exceptionally well, it was the only face he wore.

The car was slowing down, and the outskirts of the low-lying town of Waiana began to show themselves ahead.

Nick said: "The truth of the matter is you

don't know Commissioner Hartly at all and he never sent you after me. . . . What's your game, Mr. Sze?"

Mr. Sze did not reply. He met Nick's eyes with his own cold stare and let it go at that.

"When we reach Waiana—and it's here now—I'm going to turn you over to the police, Mr. Sze, unless you tell me what your game is."

"This unwitting person—"

"Oh, for Lord's sake, skip the obsequious formalities, Sze. Let's not kid each other."

Mr. Sze did not object. He said: "Forgive me. Am I such a poor actor?"

"No, but your research was poor. What's the idea?"

"Too bad, really too bad," Mr. Sze said. "I'm so very sorry. I know so little of medicine and I was given such little time. It would have been more harmonious if we had reached an understanding through my little thespia. Now I regret, sah, that it will be more difficult."

"I don't like you," Nick Adams said bluntly. "And I don't like your methods. I'm turning you over to the police."

The car jolted to a halt, brakes squealing. Nick started to open the door. Mr. Sze, still blank-faced, said quietly: "Forgive me, please do not touch it, sah, or I will be compelled to shoot you."

Nick paused. He glanced around, saw that Mr. Sze had a pistol in his right hand. The polished steel barrel caught up the reflection of the sun with dazzling flashes of fire. There was nothing to be said under the circumstances.

"I am going to a little place in Waiana here," Mr. Sze remarked. "Forgive me, but you will honor me with your presence."

"You go to the devil," Nick said. "You can't frighten me."

"That is to be regretted if true," Mr. Sze said, his face serenely empty. "If so, I must shoot you and run. I was ordered to detain you peaceably, sah, and if that failed, I could use my own discretion, as long as the purpose was achieved. I have no choice in this instance but to shoot you if you do not cooperate. Forgive me, it makes no

difference to me one way or the other. I leave the choice to you."

Nick was flabbergasted. "Of all the damned silliness," he said. "If it's robbery—"

"We are not concerned with money," Mr. Sze said. "Please leave your bags, sah. Sit still; you are to be a prisoner. It is a happy occasion that you are being so very sensible." He started the car again. "I will put the pistol in my pocket with my hand around it. You will drive with me. Obey me. I sincerely trust you will behave like a gentleman, for if so, there will be no regrettable violence. Nothing will happen if your behavior is exemplary. Please, sah, now."

Nick was scarlet with anger and frustration. The man was bluffing probably, and yet Nick didn't want to take a chance, not with a pair of eyes like that. If he could only have seen some expression in the face he might have been able to make a few guesses, but the face was void. He dropped his bags, grimly, desperately, and sat back.

Mr. Sze drove. On the edge of Waiana, he turned off the main road and presently stopped the car in front of a small cottage, placing the right side of the car so close to the wall that Nick could not get out on that side. Mr. Sze opened the door on his side and got out and stood behind the door.

"That is very excellent," Mr. Sze said. "With haste, if you please, Dr. Adams, we have so little time. That way out."

"Oh, all right, damn you, I'm coming," Nick said grimly.

Mr. Sze waited. There was no sign of the pistol, no need for sight of it. When he neared the end of the seat, Nick saw that Sze's position behind the door was vulnerable. His own nerve was good. When he came abreast of it, he dropped both of his bags, braced both feet against the half-opened door and slammed the door wide open, grateful that it was steel. It struck Mr. Sze with a shuddery thud, knocked the Chinese down. Nick touched the starter, put the car in gear, drove off. He had a momentary glimpse of Sze rolling on the ground. He waited to be shot at. No shots however. In the mirror he saw Mr. Sze, his face void of anger. Nick was a little dismayed at Mr. Sze's lack of expression. It was very unreal. No fury, no despair, no frustration, nothing. He stood on the street, regaining his feet, like an innocent tourist, hands in his pockets, and watched the car go. It was a chilling sensation to see him. Then Mr. Sze disappeared, along with the confused and unimpressive patterns of Waiana, and the car was rolling southwest toward Honolulu. There was no point in calling the police now. Oahu was an island. Sze would not get away. There was the cottage too. Nick hoped fervently that he would never meet Mr. Sze again. It had been a very unpleasant experience.

CHAPTER TWO
THE DEVIL IS LOOSE!

s far as Koko Head, he had worried about Venner's telegram. Now he worried about H. H. Sze. Life could be incredible sometimes. It had happened before. You could get along for a year without the slightest deviation in a monotonous routine, and then, for no reason at all, you were whisked into a maelstrom.

Consideration of Venner's telegram was really *de trop* because he could only conjecture. The wire was a trifle spectacular and melodramatic and Nick conservatively doubted that disaster of any kind except typhoon, earthquake or hurricane could be imminent within forty-eight hours. How could you put a time limit on disaster? And why the devil was he so important to Venner? It did not read, *Request your assistance.* Oh, no, it was *Require your assistance.* A very urgent touch. He reminded himself not to be angry with Venner when the disaster turned out to be a phantom. The average person was secretly addicted to exaggeration, and it had

taken Nicholas Adams many years of painstaking research to speak the facts of a fact and not what might be startling about a fact.

He could not however dismiss Mr. Sze as easily. Mr. Sze had been in earnest. The pistol had been real.

He thought, What did the bandit want with me? Is the prestige of the Cardwell Institute so great that he had visions of kidnaping and a glowing ransom? He seemed too practical for such an idea. And he knew about Venner—and the wireless!

It was true, as he was well aware, that the Cardwell Institute did enjoy a prestige in Hawaii akin to that jealously guarded by the old guard mercantile firms whose ancestry dated back to the pre-treaty days of iron men and sailing ships, and all this because lives were saved by it.

Lord knows that was true enough. Nick himself had been saving fifty thousand lives a year now for many years, and he could get tired of saving lives. They didn't want to be saved. You showed a cause and a result. Like the hookworm in Malaya. It didn't make any difference usually. The boys were too damned lazy to use the latrines, and too damned anemic from hookworm to worry about death. So you broke out the thymol and gave them the works one more time and for a while you got it well under control again. . . . But give it a year.

Nick Adams had never been too philosophical. There had been nothing philosophical about his reply to the young Japanese medico who, during the aftermath of *the* Japanese earthquake, had asked him, "How can you Americans be so generous with this money and all these supplies and medicines? You will forgive my distrust but is there not some hidden reward for you, in this dispensation?"

"Sure," Nick had said baldly. "There is balm in Gilead for an old man's soul. The gentleman who founded this Institute, Alexander Cardwell the First, made some ninety millions of dollars stealing railroads from other gentlemen. And when he wizened and saw the yawning grave before him, he repented, and wished to gather a smattering of honor unto his perfidious name. So for all this, you are to remember Cardwell *San* as a gentleman and a scholar and a great humanitarian instead of a robber baron and bandit. Do I make myself clear?" Such logic however was beyond the understanding of a Japanese.

Well, the old man was eight years buried now, and the fact remained that what had started out as a vanity had become one of the most renowned and powerful healing organizations on earth, the Rockefeller Institute being the only comparable group.

Nick dropped his chin onto the palm of his hand and stared gloomily out of the car window.

"Damn that Sze!" he growled. "What the devil did he want with me anyhow?"

At Pearl City, he abandoned the car. He was glad to be out of it. He took his bags and walked down the *alanui* until he found a taxicab which he instantly hired. He told the Hawaiian driver: "The Royal Hawaiian and *wikiwiki*!"

But before he reached the hotel, he saw that the driver had taken Bishop Street and he was half prompted to stop off at the Cardwell Institute laboratories and see his friend Paul Cameron. On second thought, he decided to ring Cameron from the hotel.

He did this. After registering and being given his room facing southward on Waikiki Beach and the ocean, from which, nevertheless, he could still see the wreckage in the city where Jap bombs had dropped, he telephoned the labs. Dr. Cameron came to the hotel at once.

"In the name of heaven, Nick," Cameron exclaimed, shaking hands with him. "When did you get in?"

"When did I get in?" Nick said. "Didn't you get my message?"

"Message?"

"Paul, the very devil is loose on this island. Something is very much wrong. I wirelessed you from Molokai, asking you to meet me at the plane, along with Colonel Venner. I wanted your advice about a grave matter. You didn't—"

"But I never got your message, Nick," Cameron said. He was a tall thin man with a severe face. His nose and mouth were sharp, and he had fever-hollowed cheeks, picked up from his work of many years in Singapore on malarial control of the swamps of the island. His eyes were brown and soft and very remote. "Mind you, I'm glad to see you, Nick, but I didn't expect you. You told us you'd be out there with the lepers of Molokai from three to five months—"

"Yes, I know, but this strange thing came up—we'll talk about it. How are Dr. Wing and Andrews?"

"Both fine." Cameron sighed. "Of course, since the Japs bombed Pearl Harbor, the whole place has become an armed camp, no chance for amenities or social graces—"

"That's as it should be," Nick Adams said. "Tell me something. Did you ever hear of a man named John Venner? A colonel in the medical corps? He's stationed at Schofield Barracks."

"I know who he is," Cameron said. "But Wing is the man to tell you about Venner. Wing is a good friend of his. I think Venner is in charge of the new military hospital out near Wright Field. The Stafford in Wahiawa. Look here, Nick, why don't you quit this hotel and bunk in at my place during your stay—"

"No, thanks," Nick said. "Appreciate it, Paul, but I'm going to be on the move for a while, and I want to have a free hand. Suppose you have dinner here with me tonight? I want to tell you something very odd. But first I want to check on it."

"Very well," Cameron said. "See you tonight."

ick was worried. He wished he knew where Venner was. Naturally, in a telegram, Venner couldn't tell all, and yet it was confusing not to know where you stood. There had been no sign of the Army man.

Why hadn't Venner met him? The wireless must certainly have reached him. It had been sent very early that morning, and it was now late afternoon. He wondered if Venner perhaps had planned to drop in at the hotel. How the devil would the fellow know which hotel? The Royal Hawaiian, probably, and yet there were at least six other very fine hotels. Venner had certainly been told which plane it was. No chance to have got mixed up.

Nick chewed the side of his mouth nervously. It was very hot, and his shirt was shapeless, the collar wet from perspiration. *Disaster imminent in Oahu within forty-eight hours unless you and I stop it.* What the devil! Oahu just wasn't built for a disaster in forty-eight hours unless Venner were a prophet with a secret volcano or a rattling earthquake or a whistling typhoon up his sleeve. As far as the wars went, Oahu was damned near impregnable. As near impregnable as a fortress could be. Because no fortress manned by men could ever be impregnable. How could two men who had never even met each other avert a disaster that was due to pop within forty-eight hours? It wasn't forty-eight hours any more either. It was less than that. Considering there wouldn't be time to waste, why hadn't Venner shown up?

He wearily dismissed the thing from his mind for the moment and closed his eyes. Finally he picked up the telephone and asked to be connected with the new Stafford Hospital in Wahiawa. He got through immediately but still could not reach Colonel Venner. The colonel was not at Wahiawa. Nick thanked the woman for the information, hung up and started frowning again. Almost instantly, the telephone rang.

"Colonel John Venner to see you, sir."

"Send him up at once," Nick said. He spoke much too loud in his relief.

He got a towel from the bath and wrapped it around his throat to soak up the sweat and spare the collar of his linen suit. He felt much better now. When the knock came on the door, he said: "Come in, please."

The man who came in was tall and heavily built, red-faced, mustached. He was forty or so but Nick had the distinct impression that he was trying to look younger.

"Colonel Venner?" he said.

"Right," said the officer. He smiled broadly and shook hands. He had an iron grip. He was dressed in a smart uniform, and there were some decorations over the heart, and a medal. Over the shoulders were the oak leaves. And on the collar of the tunic was the Medical Corps standard. "Dr. Adams, I owe you the most profound of apologies."

"Have a seat," Nick said. "I expected you at the airport. But I thought you might find me here. I don't mind saying that your telegram has intrigued me insidiously ever since I got it. I came down from Molokai, at once. I'm at your service, Doctor."

"That's very decent of you," said the officer. "It makes it so much the harder for me to tell you that—well—it's done."

"What's done?"

"What I mean to say, Doctor, is that I no longer have any need for you. I had stumbled on a rather heinous and far-flung plot and I admit to the fact that I was terrified by it. I had heard that you were in Molokai, and knowing your reputation—there were lesser medicos I could have had to assist—I wired you at once. Then by an unbelievable stroke of luck, I came into some facts which exploded the whole plot. I had the malcontents arrested and the entire incident is closed."

"You mean I missed the whole thing?"

"Quite." The officer smiled. "You regret that?"

"Certainly," Nick said, disappointed. "I'd anticipated so much of it—you haven't told me what it was and why you wanted me?"

"And I am afraid I cannot tell you now," he replied.

"Hell, man, have a heart."

"I'm terribly sorry," said the colonel. "But secrecy is absolutely vital. And since the affair is closed, it would be better if no one but the superiors here knew. Not a good story to get around.

Might give people ideas, you know. Your expenses down here will be taken care of, Doctor, and you have our eternal gratitude for your prompt action."

"Oh well," Nick said, "I rather thought it would be a phantom anyhow."

"I hope we didn't pull you away from something as important. In any case—"

"Leprosy at Molokai."

"I was going to say, in any case, you are free to return. And I assure you—"

Nick was weary of his politeness. "Never mind, Doctor, that's all right. We'll say no more about it. But I don't think I'll be going back to Molokai. I'd like very much to visit your new hospital, if I may."

"Of course you may!" said the colonel. "Suppose I give you a buzz. You could come out to Wahiawa for tea, and I'd show you through. We have all the military cases. Most interesting. When could you come out?"

Nick said, "Any time."

"Well—" said the colonel, "I'm going to be rather busy until Thursday. Suppose I give you a ring on Thursday?"

"Suppose you do," Nick said. He was annoyed.

"Righto. Call you Thursday then. And again, many thanks for dashing down here so diligently. Like a fire wagon going to a fire!"

"I've had to put out many fires," Nick said. "Sometimes I have to work fast. Good-bye, Colonel."

He showed the fellow to the door, and when he opened the door the edge of it struck another man outside who had been on the point of knocking. The colonel brushed by quickly and went down the hall. He did not wait for the elevator, but descended by the stairs. Nick took the second man by the shoulders and said: "Eddie Wing! The only man in the world I am always glad to see. Come on in, Eddie."

Dr. E. V. Wing was little, young and irrepressible. He was so small that a strong breeze could have blown him away. He was a native Hawaiian, with the C.I. labs.

"It is very delightful to see you again, sweetheart," Dr. Wing said. "I missed you."

"I've missed you too," Nick said. "I guess I got pretty used to you, Eddie. You look fine."

"As ever," Dr. Wing said, cheerfully. "Cameron said you were back. I thought I'd better come right over and apologize. I'm the guy who got you into this thing, Nick. I mean—the reason you came back to Oahu. I told Venner where you were. He knew you were in the islands. He asked me where. . . . It *is* good to see you, palsy. I hope I did not interrupt you and the officer? I should have telephoned. Paul said you were in, and I took the liberty of coming over at once."

Nick said: "You didn't interrupt anything but a lot of beating about the bush. I'll tell you about it later. Colonel Venner of the Medical Corps just came to see me to beg off demanding my assistance."

Eddie Wing blinked, silent for a moment. "Are *you* kidding?" he said. "You mean that the officer who just left—"

"Yes! That was Venner! Brought me all the way down here on an emergency and then ditched me after I got here." Nick smiled wryly.

"Nicholas," Eddie Wing said, "I am afraid you have been duped."

Nick frowned. "I have a weakness for getting duped."

"I mean that the guy who just left here was *not* Colonel Venner. If he said so, he's a phony."

"Eddie, are you sure? He—"

"Your humble pardon, Nick-ole-ass, but these ferret eyes can see pretty well!"

"Then who the devil—" Yes, and what the devil and why the devil and a lot of other queries sprung into his mind. All went unanswered. Nick stared at the door blankly, trying to arrange his thoughts in some sort of pattern, but they would not fall into line. He picked up the telephone and said: "Get me Army Intelligence at Schofield, please."

The desk clerk wanted to ask if something

was wrong but he didn't. Presently the station answered. Nick said: "Lieutenant Kerry, please." Allan Kerry was an old friend.

"Kerry here," Kerry said. "Army Intelligence."

"Kerry, this is Nicholas Adams. I'm at the Royal Hawaiian."

"Yes, Doctor?"

"I've just had an unusual experience. A gentleman dressed in the uniform of the United States Army, rank of colonel, visited me and passed himself off falsely as one John Venner. I wondered if you people wanted to do something about it."

"Silly boy!" said Kerry. "I'll give you Captain Malta. He's in charge of that sort of thing. Hold on."

Captain Malta had a kettle drum voice which rattled from the depths of his diaphragm without effort. "Do you have this guy with you still?"

"No, I'm sorry, he's gone. I can give you a pretty good description."

"Do that," Captain Malta said. "We'll see if we can't pick him up. I'd like to see him."

Nick described the impostor accurately. "Understand, I just *could* be mistaken. Perhaps it really was Venner. But the chances are a hundred to one it was an impostor."

"There are no chances involved," Captain Malta said. "Thank you for your information, Doctor. I'll see you personally soon."

"Very well," Nick said and, curiously, "How do you know there are no chances involved?"

"Because Colonel John Venner happens to be dead," replied Captain Malta. "He was murdered in the dark sometime late last night and we only recovered his body at noon today."

"What?" Nick whispered, awed.

"So it *was* an impostor."

"Yes," Nick said in a low voice. "Good-bye, Captain." He hung up the telephone and sat down, his eyes troubled.

 or a few minutes, Nick Adams said nothing. Eddie Wing smoked a cigarette detachedly. Nick went to the window and looked out upon the ocean. It kept coming home to him that the baby had been left on his doorstep. In one way, he was being released from any obligation. What the devil, he knew nothing at all about the forty-eight-hour disaster; he had kept his word to Venner, come down to Honolulu at once. If Venner was dead, how could anyone expect him to keep on with the mystery? On the other hand, several things he had not appreciated began to make themselves clear.

First, H. H. Sze's attempt to divert him from the plane to Waiana finally took on an aspect of logic. By itself it was incredible. But when you put it with the word of the impostor officer who had assured him the case was closed, it made sound sense. Sze had been commissioned to get him off the plane and hidden because someone knew he was coming to Honolulu and didn't want him there. This failing, the bogus Venner had arrived instantly to assure him the "plot" had been nipped in the bud, and that he was free to return to Molokai. The red-faced officer had made a great point of telling Nick that he was free to go. Not free to remain and enjoy his visit in Honolulu. Free to go back.

They didn't want him in town. He didn't know a damned thing, and yet they were afraid of him.

That line of reasoning really made up his mind. He felt rather useless and helpless, but since they considered him such a potential menace to the catastrophic plans Venner had stumbled on, he would stay and try to do a job of it. He had no idea where to begin. But it was his baby and he adopted it on the spot.

The imminent disaster was, obviously, no longer forty-eight hours away. Colonel Venner had set that hour in his telegram at 8:33 the evening before. It was now nearly six p.m. Almost twenty-two hours had elapsed since the telegram had been dispatched. Twenty-two from forty-eight equaled twenty-six. A little more than a full day.

Nick felt panic-stricken.

"Eddie," he said, "you've got to help."

"I knew that," Eddie Wing said. "Say the word, sweetheart. *E hele kaua!*"

"Read this." Nick gave him the telegram. *Secrecy essential.* Well, by God, you had to trust someone. There was no one in the East or the West he could have trusted as much as Eddie Wing. Dr. Wing read the message without expression, paused to consider it with eyes closed, and then returned it to Nick.

"I am not surprised," he said. "Some fun, chum!"

"Some fun," Nick said. "But this may surprise you. I was just talking with Captain Malta of Army Intelligence. He told me that your friend Colonel Venner is dead."

"Dead?" Wing said, in a whisper.

"Yes. I'm sorry, Eddie. He's dead. *Make.* He was murdered last night. They found his body today at noon. I don't have any details."

Eddie Wing's face became hard. "Tough, Nick. He was a swell guy. Good medico. And the culprit?"

"Anonymous and at large."

Eddie Wing said slowly, after a long breath: "Guess I'd better talk. I had lunch with Colonel Venner yesterday. He was scared. He mentioned your name. He had never met you. But he was familiar with your work in Cairo, where he had been stationed before the war. Not only familiar, he was fervent concerning it. He said he wished you were here. I mentioned that you were, that I had the dope on your location in Molokai. He asked for it. And thus it began. Yowzuh."

Nick sat down. "There's an angle here," he said. "Maybe we can talk something out of it. Eddie, you've got to use the old bean. Remember everything. Did he say anything which might give us a clue to this message he sent? Please think about it."

"You are going to continue with the case, sweetheart?"

"What else can I do?" Nick said. His voice was hard. "The man was depending upon my help. No one else seems to have had any word of it. I can't just let it ride. If he meant what he said, something rotten is breeding. If he was a friend of yours, I can't take his message lightly. I've got to work on it."

"He was murdered for his pains," Wing said.

"Oh hell, that part of it doesn't bother me," Nick said. His chin began to point out a little. "I've never been afraid and God knows there have been more things to fear than men in the pest-holes of the earth."

"You've got something there," Wing said. "O.K., Nick, can do. *Hiki no.* Now get this. Dr. Venner was disturbed at luncheon. Greatly disturbed. I didn't ask him what was none of my affair, but presently he told me that he had unearthed a ghastly business. What were his words? 'If I don't break this thing cleanly, every mother's son in Oahu will walk in the valley of death within two days.' A very close translation."

"What did you suggest?"

"I suggested that perhaps his problem was meant for the Army Intelligence, and I pointed out the impossibility of a single man attempting to handle a threat of such proportions. But he disagreed with me. He was afraid that the Intelligence might muddle it, and that if it were ever muddled, the result would be catastrophic." Wing blinked. "Boy, can I sling the lingo!"

"He should have confided in either the Intelligence or the police," Nick said. "As a result we're left with our hands tied. You can be too secretive. Look at this blank wall we start from."

"He was afraid of panic."

"Panic?"

"Panic. Mob panic."

"How could he have— Eddie, look here. Did he say anything—*anything*—as to how he found it out—what it was—"

"No," Eddie Wing said. "He didn't trust me with such information. But whatever it was, it was real to him. He could barely eat."

Nick pounded his fist into his hand and stalked around the room. It didn't help much.

My God, he thought desperately, I want something to work with!

"I have been thinking," Eddie Wing said. "John was very close to his aide, Bertram Woolton, a sergeant. From Brooklyn. Not a medico. Maybe the sergeant—"

"Good. We'll get in touch with him at once. The Schofield Barracks?"

"Yowzuh. Sergeant Woolton was on Venner's staff at the Stafford Hospital. I think he drove the car and such."

"Will you drive out with me?"

Dr. Wing studied him very carefully. "No," he said finally. "No can do, Nick."

"Eddie, you're not afraid?" Nick scoffed.

"Who, me? No, palsy. Got another date."

Nick said, nodding: "I'll drive out alone. If this doesn't give us anything, we'll have to work backwards from Venner's body. That's outright detective work and doubtless the trail won't be any too fresh. But I'll do what I can."

"O.K.," Eddie Wing said. "But look, Nick. Be very careful and don't forget for an instant that Colonel Venner is dead as a red herring from following this same road you're starting on."

"I'll remember," Nick said.

CHAPTER THREE
THE DAY BEFORE DOOMSDAY

The Stafford Hospital was located out in Wahiawa, east of the barracks and Wright Field. Nick Adams was taken pleasantly by the sight of it, for it was a fresh and new building, impressive in architecture and set against an excellent job of landscaping, the lawns studded with giant palms. He went in and stopped at the information desk and asked if he could see Sergeant Bertram Woolton.

The reception nurse was a big-boned, pink-faced woman with straight hair and a strong jaw. The plaque on her desk said *Miss Farrar*. She smiled very faintly and remarked: "Then you would be Dr. Nicholas Adams of the Cardwell Institute?"

"That's correct," Nick said, surprised. "How the devil—"

"We expected you, Doctor. Captain Malta is at the hospital, and wishes to see you. I was to send you in to him when you arrived. I believe he's in the waiting room on the second floor. As for Sergeant Woolton, Doctor, he isn't in the hospital. He is not a medico, as you may be aware. He is simply on Colonel Venner's staff, an aide-de-camp," she explained.

"Any idea where I might locate him?"

"Probably at the barracks."

"Thanks very much," Nick said. "I'll give it a try."

"You won't forget Captain Malta?"

"I'll go right up and see him."

Nick passed her desk to the elevator without another word. He was impressed. Of course Captain Malta had been in touch with Eddie Wing in some way and had learned he was going out to the Stafford. But even so, they rather kept track of him. Considering they were the right people, he was not displeased at all.

On the next floor he found a gentleman writing on a small scratch pad in the waiting-room. It was obviously Captain Malta, in uniform. He was quite an elderly man, his eyebrows dead white, his hair white, his skin coppery. His face was characteristically long and mild where it should have been severe, but his gray eyes were shrewd and sharp and his mouth had a wry practical twist.

"Captain Malta?"

"Dr. Adams, I believe. A real pleasure for me, Doctor."

They shook hands. Nick said, with a smile: "You don't look like your voice, Captain. Glad to meet you."

"Sit down," Captain Malta said. "Why did you come out here, Adams?"

"Same reason as you," Nick said. "Only how did you know I was coming?"

"Oh, that. Dr. Wing called and asked for police protection for you. Naturally they called me out here to report it. Anything to do with the Venner case comes to me. Did you know you had a sergeant of police on your trail?"

"Not in the slightest!" Nick said, surprised. "Damn Eddie, so that was the engagement he had! I can take care of myself, Captain."

"I should have thought Colonel Venner could take care of himself too."

Nick shrugged off the inference.

"Now, Doctor," Captain Malta said, "are you after Woolton?"

"Yes."

"So am I. I wouldn't be surprised if he were after you. He's not at the barracks. So I imagine he's downtown and moving rather cautiously after what happened to Dr. Venner. You and I have some things to talk about. There are elements here beyond me. Here is the picture as I have been able to gather it together. First, I have not located the gentleman who posed as Venner and I haven't the faintest notion what his purpose would be."

Nick told him what the purpose might be and mentioned the episode with H. H. Sze at Waiana.

Captain Malta shook his head. "Venner made a great mistake in not working with the Army. We'd have co-operated one hundred percent. As it is, we're batting with a split stick."

Nick handed him the telegram. "The reminder has chastened me, Captain. Perhaps you'd better have a look at this."

Captain Malta glanced at it. "I've seen a copy at the R.C.A. offices on South King Street."

"Captain, you're amazing! How did you know—"

"Found your wireless in reply to the one he sent. Right on his desk at his quarters, unopened. He was murdered before he ever received it. Naturally I could tell from your wire something of what he had sent and got in touch with R.C.A. Rather startling, wasn't it? Forty-eight-hour disaster."

"Twenty-five hours now," Nick said. "And we sit wasting time."

"You are never wasting time when you are thinking," Captain Malta said. "A culprit can be captured in sixty seconds if you know where to take him and what for. So please let's discuss this. What sort of disaster did you think Venner insinuated?"

"I don't know," Nick said. "There was no way of telling. He mentioned the idea to Dr. Wing at lunch yesterday and said something about secrecy being essential to avoid panic among the people. So that would make it a universal disaster. I'd considered an artificial epidemic of cholera. You see, the impregnable fortress of Oahu is impregnable only so long as the men and women inside the fortress are able to man it. A sweeping epidemic of cholera would wreak havoc. I'm not much of a cholera man myself, never was much interested in the disease because its causes and its remedies were so simple."

"Well, now," Captain Malta said, frowning heavily, "you may have hit the nail on the head."

"It would be the easiest sort of thing to start rolling, and the easiest way of reaching the entire populace of Oahu Island. It's a horrible idea, but it's quite possible it wouldn't work."

"It's not contagious, is it?" the captain asked.

"Oh no. You have to drink cholera to catch it. It's in the water. That's what I mean about it not working. You have a high percent Chinese and Japanese population on the island. The Chinese learned about cholera hundreds of years ago when they became a nation of tea drinkers. In other words, I'm quite sure your Chinese population would not come down with it because they boil their water for tea. We Americans ourselves are coffee drinkers so that the disease would not be apt to decimate us, and the moment you had more than the average cases, you'd warn everyone to boil water and you would nip it in the bud. It's not contagious. There's the crux. So I'm almost certain you can discard the premise," Nick said. "And that leaves me absolutely without another theory, because that is the only epidemic I know of which could possibly be started artificially."

"Then we must look for a different disaster.

Now see if what I have to tell you suggests anything to you. Today is Tuesday. Monday morning, a soldier from Schofield Barracks named Robert MacFerson reported in here at the hospital, violently ill. The nurse on duty downstairs—Miss Farrar I think her name is—she said he was in poor shape, to express it mildly. Dr. Venner brought him up to Isolation and put him off in a room by himself with a nurse—Miss Agatha Wilson. Then Dr. Venner came down with his aide, Woolton, and said that no one was to see the patient without his permission. By Monday noon, the patient apparently failing, Dr. Venner went down to Honolulu. Where he went we have no idea. Why he left a dying man is also something I don't understand.

"You say that he lunched with Dr. Wing. This wasn't all, obviously. He never returned to the hospital. He was alive to send you the radiogram at 8:33 p.m. but he never returned to Stafford Hospital."

Nick said: "It's possible he deserted his patient and went downtown because of the urgency of the terrible secret he had unearthed. If the patient were in a hopeless condition—though why he isolated the patient so thoroughly interests me. Captain, I think it might do us no harm to visit the Isolation Ward and see the patient."

"Oh, he's probably dead," Captain Malta said.

"Do you know what was wrong with him?"

"Not an iota."

"Well, couldn't we have a word or two with Miss Agatha Wilson? The nurse would certainly have his nursing charts all handy."

"Of course," Captain Malta said suddenly and grimly. "We've been fools! Of course that's it! This all began when MacFerson reported in. Up to that time, obviously, there had been no intimation of any disaster. Venner was going about his business normally here. But *after* MacFerson reported in, things began to pop."

"I don't quite get it, Captain," Nick said.

"Don't you see, Adams? A dying man always relieves his sinful soul, and if MacFerson were part of this plot, or even were aware of it, he might have poured out his soul to Venner and revealed the very crux we're after. Consider it, Venner's isolating him, the secrecy involved, Venner rushing downtown, seeing Wing, speaking of disaster, trying to find you, finally wirelessing you in desperation. It all goes back to this MacFerson patient and stops. There is nothing beyond MacFerson."

"In that case, let's see the man or corpse as the case may be," Nick said, jumping to his feet. "And Miss Wilson should be able to unburden herself to a great extent. Where is Isolation, Captain?"

 solation was on the third floor. They took the elevator up, and reported to a Dr. Hugh Hollister, a grumpy little man with spectacles and a reddish mustache. He and Malta seemed to know each other.

"It's Venner's patient, Hugh," Captain Malta said. "The Robert MacFerson in Isolation. I beg your pardon, this is Nicholas Adams of the C.I. offices. Adams, this is Dr. Hollister, in charge here now."

"How do, Doctor," Hollister grumbled. "Glad to meet you. Heard a lot about you. If you want to see MacFerson you're out of luck."

Nick's heart fell. "Even if he's dead—"

"I wouldn't know about that," said Hollister. "But I'm damn sick of John's hocus-pocus on this thing. Why, he left strict orders that no one was to take a look at MacFerson unless he ordered it in writing. And since he's the commanding officer, that's the way it was. Of course, Wilson was his pet nurse, and he trusted her implicitly, along with Woolton."

"I'd like to talk with her," said Nick.

"You can't," said Hollister. "She's gone."

"Gone?" Captain Malta said sharply. "What the devil are you talking about, Hugh? Gone where?"

"Well, you don't have to be popping off at me! Tell it to John Venner! It's all his fault, this whole abracadabra. Agatha Wilson went out with MacFerson, about an hour ago."

"With *MacFerson*?" Nick exclaimed, appalled.

"Are you surprised?" Dr. Hollister grumbled. "My word, I'd have expected you, at least, to know all about it. MacFerson was switched down to the Cardwell Institute laboratories for further treatment. Don't ask me what kind of treatment, I don't even know what was wrong with him. All I know is an efficient sort of snob from the government offices, a colonel at that, came in here with a release for the patient signed by John Venner, along with credentials from the Cardwell Institute verifying MacFerson's removal and admittance to the C.I. labs."

"Who signed the Cardwell Institute papers?" Nick asked sharply, his hands trembling.

"Why, Paul Cameron, of course! He's the chief down there—"

Captain Malta took a chair, sighing quietly, his face looking most indulgent despite the reverses. "Then MacFerson is really gone, Hugh? And Miss Wilson with him?"

"All signed out. They left in a private ambulance which was waiting down in the emergency courtyard."

"Hand me the phone, please, Hugh. . . . You can have it when I'm finished, Adams."

Captain Malta telephoned Central Police station and asked to have the ambulance checked. He sent two men over to the Cardwell Institute labs. Dr. Hollister looked amazed. "Now," Malta said quietly, still holding the phone, "what did your snobbish colonel look like, Hugh?"

Hollister began an elaborate description, which proved to be unnecessary, for even from the briefest details, Nick recognized the fellow as the same pink-skinned gentleman who had visited him at the Royal Hawaiian, posing as John Venner. He considered the man's efficiency, for if the impostor had managed to sign out MacFerson only an hour before, he had still been able to pop in on Nick and explain that the case

was closed. The man had cold nerve. Malta said into the phone: "Yes, it's Zeller again. You've got to find him. I'd report it to Intelligence also, since we're more interested in him than they are. . . . Yes . . . Yes, in thirty minutes or so, I'll be there. Good-bye." He hung up.

Nick said: "You know the man?"

"Yes. Fritz Zeller, a German agent. Intelligence knows him a bit better and would like to nip him. It's a firing squad when they do. He's a damned clever lad. You wished to call Cameron, didn't you?"

"Yes," Nick said. He took the telephone, got through to Paul Cameron at his home. "Paul," he said, "did you sign credentials acknowledging that a patient from the Stafford named Robert MacFerson was to be treated and admitted to the C.I. labs?"

Dr. Cameron was silent a moment. "Say it again, Nick."

After he had repeated it, Cameron said, perplexed: "I'm afraid not, Nick. I didn't know what the devil you were talking about for a moment. You sound rather perturbed."

"There's been a forgery then," Nick said. "That's all. I'll explain it all later, Paul. Goodnight." He hung up. He sighed heavily. "You can assume the worst," he murmured.

"I already had," Captain Malta replied dryly. "And you needn't look so pop-eyed, Hugh."

"I think you're both quite mad," said Dr. Hollister, awed. "A touch of sun?"

"Johnny Venner is dead, murdered," Captain Malta said. "And don't ask me for explanations. You ponder it and it ought to explain our behavior here."

"Are you sure the charts are gone?" Nick asked desperately.

"Yes, she took them with her— Murdered? John murdered?"

"Let's get out of here," Captain Malta said. "This chap will hold us for hours asking details. Read the newspapers, Hugh, and thanks for all the help."

They went downstairs. Nick said, in admiration: "You've done a good job on this thing, Captain."

"Not at all," Captain Malta said. "This has all been routine. Don't be impressed. Actually it has accomplished little. As for my having covered so many details, remember I've been at it longer than you, ever since we found Venner's body at Maili by the tracks of the Oahu railroad. He was found shot through the head, stark naked, all identification removed. I recognized him of course. He was not meant to be found so soon, being in a stream. There were some chains still on one leg, but the heavier weights had dropped off. Where did you plan on going now?"

"To Schofield Barracks," Nick said. "To find Sergeant Woolton."

"I'll save you the trip," said Captain Malta. "He's not there."

"Not there? Where is he?"

"I wish I knew. If he is still alive, I think he may be hiding out. Possibly he wishes to reach you, since he must have known that Venner had wired you. I would like you to go back to town. I want you to be convenient for Woolton to find."

Nick had a cold thought. "The weights and chains might have hung onto him. He could be at the bottom of the ocean."

"Anything is possible," said Captain Malta, his white bushy brows jerking as he moved them. "We should try to be optimistic. It's the least we can do. Come along, Adams, I'll drive you back to town myself. I'd like you to meet the man I've put on you, for safety's sake. His name is Crowell. He's a nice fellow, seen service in New York's finest."

Sergeant Crowell was waiting in the lobby downstairs. He was a cheerful soul, moon-faced, and with a glistening gold tooth in the front of his mouth.

"Highly pleased to make your acquaintance, sir," he said, shaking hands.

"We're going back together," Malta said. "You follow. Nothing on the way out?"

"No one followed him, Captain."

"Very good. Keep a weather eye on the doctor. I have a feeling he's going to be worth his weight in gold before long."

Nick was gloomy. "It will have to be before long. It's nearly eight o'clock. That gives us a solitary day, according to Venner's own time limit. Not many hours, Captain."

"True," Malta said. His voice was low but his eyes were hard. "Still, empires have vanished in less time. We've a chance, we've a chance." But he did not sound enthusiastic.

CHAPTER FOUR
THE EMPTY CARTON

There had been no calls for him at the hotel. No Woolton, to his intense disappointment. While he was still at the desk, he saw Dr. Cameron come in. He glanced at his wristwatch, saw it was only a few minutes past eight. He joined Cameron.

"Paul," he said. "It may be a hit-and-run meal. I'm expecting a very important call and I can't risk missing it."

"That's all right, Nick," Cameron said, his voice cool. "Although I did want to tell you a personal decision I made today."

"We'll have time for that, surely," Nick said. "Go ahead. I'll tell them at the desk that I'm inside and if there are any calls they can page me there. I'll eat with you and then go up to my room and change my things."

He joined Paul Cameron at a table a few moments later.

Nick turned to Cameron, who did not look well, nor did he look ill. His cheeks were very hollow, and his color was not good, and from the twitching of his fingers, he seemed to be tense and nervous. "What was your news, Paul?" Nick said.

"I've tendered my resignation from the Institute," Cameron said. "Effective immediately."

"What?" Nick exclaimed sharply. "Your resignation? Have you gone crazy, Paul?"

"I put it in writing by mail, but I also cabled the New York office of my decision," said Cameron, his voice dead.

"But Paul, in the name of heaven—"

"I had an offer from the University of Southern California, a doctor of pathology there, my own department, much free time for any experimentation I desire. In other words, a free hand. So I've accepted. I'm tired of malaria. I've done all I can do with it. I want a go at the lepra bacilli. I'm going to try and find the way the blight is communicated."

"I'm terribly disappointed," Nick said gravely. "It's such a poor time to lose a man like you."

"Very kind of you, Nick."

"Oh, the hell with kindness—you've spoiled the night for me. They'll have a struggle getting another fellow like you."

"There are better than I," Cameron said. His eyes were abnormally bright, and he could not sit still.

"That's not true. I can't believe it still."

"Its causes are not easily explained, Nick. They're bound up in my own life. Tonight I am finishing here a task I dedicated myself to many, many years ago when I was very young. Tomorrow I will start on a new task, and a new dedication, and perhaps my life will not be, in the future, the inhibited turmoil it has been in the past."

Nick shrugged. "I don't know what you mean, but of course you know what you're doing."

"Out of the whole thing, I'm grateful for your friendship, Nick."

"You sound as if you were resigning from that too."

A waiter stopped by and bowed politely. "Telephone call for doctor, please."

"Which doctor?" Nick said, starting to rise.

"Dr. Cameron, *tuan*."

Cameron rose. He seemed relieved. "Be right back." He left.

Cameron returned in a few moments, his face somber. "I'm very sorry, but I'll have to run. I know you're busy, Nick, too, so suppose you come to the labs tomorrow?"

"Very well," Nick said. "See you tomorrow."

"Good-night, Nick."

"'Night, Paul."

Almost instantly, the waiter came over again. "Pardon. Dr. Adams? You are wanted at the front desk, sir."

Nick signed the check hurriedly and walked out briskly. At the front desk, the clerk said: "The telephone call you were expecting, Doctor."

"Good!" Nick said, elated. "I'll take it up in my room. Tell the gentleman to hold on."

"Very well, Doctor. And just a moment. Your friend, Dr. Cameron, dropped this package as he was leaving. Will you be able to return it to him?"

Nick took the small carton, about the size of a toothpaste tube box, nodded, said he would return it to Cameron, and then ran for his room.

Nick unlocked the door and went in. The moonlight through the window looked very beautiful. The telephone was ringing. He hurried to the phone without turning on the lights, and sat on the edge of the bed as he answered it.

"Hello?"

"Nicholas?"

"Hello, Eddie." Nick's voice dropped in disappointment.

Eddie Wing sounded serene, as was his way. "Sweetheart, I would appreciate the pleasure of your company this evening for the dropping of a few pearls of wisdom and the eating of some *poi*."

"Eddie—thanks, but you know—"

"*Huapala*—I insist." Eddie was firm. "I have a friend here who is most anxious to meet you. In fact, visiting me might coincide perfectly with your plans for the night."

Nick began to warm. "This friend wouldn't be a denizen of Brooklyn by any chance?"

Eddie Wing said whimsically: "I do believe he mentioned the fact. We may expect you then, Nicholas?"

"Yes," Nick said. "Bless your heart, Eddie."

"Bless my foot!" Eddie said. "Come on over."

"At once."

Nick hung up. Sergeant Woolton had been found! Dr. Venner's aide-de-camp was at Wing's house! It was marvelous good luck, and Nick began to feel the pulse of optimism in his veins. He started for the door hastily, not bothering to change, but hearing a faint click behind him, he paused at the door, his back against it. There was an amused chuckle in the dark. Nick's heart jumped. He reached for the light—hesitated.

A voice as liquid as oil said: "Please, sah, forgive me, but you may turn on the light."

Nick flipped the switch. When the room blazed, he found Mr. H. H. Sze lying on the bed. Mr. Sze was not reclining exactly. He was half erect, his shoulders against the headboard, a pillow under them, and his knees were high against his chest. He was dangling his pistol carelessly, his index finger crooked under the trigger guard. "Good evening, sah," he said, his face with less expression than a judge's. "Forgive this worthless one such informality." He rose mockingly to his feet and bowed.

"Well, Mr. Sze," Nick said. He halted, at a momentary loss for words. "We meet again. I had high hopes I'd avoid another visit from you."

"Forgive me," said Mr. Sze, "but your so clever escape at Waiana was so very much a challenge to me. You are armed, sah?"

"No."

"Forgive me, sah, if I make certain for myself." Gracefully he moved behind Nick. Nick stood stock-still while those long fingers probed his person for a gun, and found none. "You have something of great importance in your hand, sah?"

"Since I haven't seen it yet, I wouldn't know," Nick said.

"Forgive me, sah, I will see for myself."

Mr. Sze took Cameron's carton from Nick and opened it. He did not just rip it open. He inserted one of his long index fingers under the flap and very evenly raised the flap. There was nothing inside. The carton was empty.

Mr. Sze looked at the thing blankly. It could not have meant anything to him, but with his lack of facial expression, Nick wasn't able to make any guesses. Mr. Sze shrugged. "So very sorry, sah." He dropped the carton on the bed.

"Quite all right," Nick said. "I'm sorry I don't have a lot of personal papers you could peruse. It would probably do your heart good. Or can you read, Mr. Sze?"

Mr. Sze's eyes glittered. "Forgive me, Doctor, but this witless one has earned the accomplishment. This humble one is aware that he would normally be your inferior." He drew himself erect. "But a pistol, sah, is the great equalizer. One man, yellow or white, is as good as another."

"Ah," Nick said, stalling, "a philosopher."

"Forgive me, sah, but you are right. I am a philosopher. But this poor one is also a realist. You are my prisoner, if you please, and this time you must not escape, you must not offer resistance, Doctor, because this time—forgive me—I will take no chances."

"What are your plans for me?" Nick said heavily. He was not afraid, his voice was quite steady, and he felt very cool.

"Forgive me, sah, this unfortunate one does not make the plans. If it were left to me to make the plans, you would be fermenting in Waiana, sah, for when a man is considered dangerous to a cause, there is no wise recourse but to slay him. To do otherwise is to be careless, sentimental, or merciful, none of which are compatible with destiny. Forgive me, it is un-Christian, but this realist belives that the meek will inherit only the grave.

"I am not of those meek, sah, forgive me the personal mention. This person believes you should have perished in Malacca. This person believes that you should perish now. But others have seen fit to forbid imperiling your life. And elaborate precautions have thus been taken for your safety. Indeed, sah, the star which blessed your birth will take you from this city tonight, for which, Christianly, you should offer your gratification to the Deity. Those who are left in Oahu on the morrow will not offer prayers to the Deity this side of hell."

Nick felt the goose pimples studding his flesh. He managed to ask: "And these precautions, Mr. Sze?"

"Forgive me, sah, I have the drug herewith. You are to drink a glass of water in which is dissolved two tablets from this bottle. I have been given to understand that they will render you unconscious within a brief time. When you recover your senses, sah, you will be enroute south by small boat to Lanai, properly warned that should you show yourself in this locality again, immediate death would result. Forgive me, sah."

"For God's sake," Nick said huskily. "I forgive thee. Don't keep saying that. What guarantee have I that the drug isn't nitric acid or the like?"

"None, sah."

Nick walked to the bed and sat down and put his head in his hands. "And if I refuse, you shoot?"

"Forgive, sah," Mr. Sze said, eyes inflexible, "but that would be my pleasure."

Nick raised his head. He dropped his eyes to the carton on the bed, the empty carton which the clerk had given him. He could just see the legend on the face of the box. The drug had a Cardwell Institute label on it, a number, and the words *Haffkine Vaccine*.

Five silent seconds passed while his brain absorbed the words. They transfixed him. He went rigid, his mouth agape, his eyes dilated, his face paling. It struck home, the whole rotten terrifying business hit into the pit of the stomach with force which stiffened his muscles and knotted a nausea in his throat. The realization welled up in his mind in a roaring crescendo, and he saw the past flit by in rapid succession, from the second century through the twentieth, in the twinkling of an eye. Here was a plot he would not have believed possible, a plot where artificiality was almost fantastic, and yet the simple legend on the carton, like a thunderbolt, declaimed the fact. All at once, the pieces fitted together, the entire jigsaw puzzle coincided its multitudinous parts perfectly.

In the lightning swift procession of the past, he saw Imperial Rome decimated, the houses filled with dead, the streets with funerals, the air with lamentations. He saw the Italian boot gripped in the thing, Genoa, Siena, Pisa prostrated, nearly all the population struck down, the city of Florence taken in storm, perishing in the twinkling of an eye. He saw the Channel crossed, and London blighted and seventy thousand men and women dying swiftly and terribly. He saw the red crosses on the doors of Drury Lane and the words *Lord Have Mercy on Us* inscribed thereon, as Samuel Pepys had seen. He saw the dancing rats, red-eyed, sick and dying, coming down the centuries, to Hong Kong, Manila, Bombay. He saw the flea, *Pulex cheopis*, and the cry echoed in his mind like the beat of a kettle drum: Plague, PLAGUE, *PLAGUE*!

All this from the simple legend on the carton. The two words *Haffkine Vaccine* explained so much. Back in time, recent enough to be called contemporary, a professor named W. M. Haffkine of Bombay had developed a vaccine for bubonic plague which aroused the immunity forces of an individual against the Black Death, although the time of immunity was extremely brief. Nick had used it often, injecting himself before going into plague foci to stamp out the pestilence. A man like Cameron, working in Honolulu where plague was not endemic, could never have had a sane reason for such an injection unless he was working with plague.

It raced through Nick's mind, feverishly, as he sat on the bed, all in brief seconds, for Mr. Sze did not seem aware of any prolonged stalling. *Disaster imminent in forty-eight hours.* MacFerson must have been part of the plot, come down with the buboes, and in his dying terror, had blurted it all out to Colonel Venner.

It was madness, he would not have believed it could be handled artificially, and yet, of them all, it was the surest and most sweeping pestilence. It was the sort of thing which could decimate half of the entire garrison of the island, make the naval base almost uninhabitable, the crowded native sections a pyre of dead, wipe out the man-power in the military barracks. It was difficult to control when it erupted, naturally. Artificially begun, with varied and numerous foci, with thousands of rats and fleas—the image stunned him. The Black Death was omega; there was scarcely any survival if you were struck. You could bury a man in the morning and be buried yourself that evening.

Everything seemed clearer. Venner's mentioning qualifications for the job, and speaking of his Cairo work. What the devil, he'd been in Cairo many times and done much work, but he knew now that Venner had meant his work in Cairo when he had hunted incessantly for the focus, found it and destroyed it. The greatest rat catcher in Egypt, they had called him.

Nick had never liked working on plague. It was hazardous, its mortality breathtaking. He remembered when he had stood in a Cairo cellar and seen his covered legs swarming with fleas from the dancing, dying rats in that black hole.

Mr. Sze said suddenly: "Forgive me, sah, time passes, and you must reach a decision."

"Get me the glass of water and put in your chloral hydrate," Nick said. He rubbed his hands against each other hard, thinking, watching Mr. Sze with caution.

Mr. Sze did not have to leave the room. He poured a glass of water from the Bombay cooler on the side table and dropped the two pills into the water, where they dissolved. He was standing fairly close to the bed. Nick shifted his weight forward so that his feet, curling under the bed, would be able to raise him quickly. Then Mr. Sze, gun in his right hand, glass of water in his left, said: "Forgive me, sah, your potion is ready, if you please."

"Can it be," Nick remarked casually, "that you have canine blood, Mr. Sze? Are you related then to the Ming dogs?"

"Forgive me, sah," Mr. Sze replied, mouth hard, "is it a poor joke?"

"A poor joke," Nick said, and then he drove it home. "I just happened to notice the flea on your leg."

he glass of water dropped with a crash. For the first time in their acquaintance-ship, Nick saw expression on the face of H. H. Sze. A gnarled pattern of inter-mingled terror and repugnance broke down the passive structure of the Chinese's countenance, and he threw his head and eyes down, without any thought but of his own survival, to see the flea—in his mind the only flea—the plague flea.

Nick thought, coming up from the bed, that he took an eternity. He had been tensed, tuning his body for just that moment. He put all pressure on the balls of his feet and shot up from the bed, his right fist out like a ramrod. He had meant to catch Mr. Sze on the jaw, but he miscalculated and struck the Chinese square in the face with force which drove a sharp pain through his hand, and lifted the man over backwards to the floor.

Mr. Sze made no sound, but Nick could see the Chinese had not dropped the gun.

Nick kicked at the gun hand, caught the barrel of the pistol with his toe, sent the gun spinning across the room. It struck the wall a savage blow and detonated. The sound was sharp and frightening. He did not see where the bullet went. He ran across the room, imagining he heard Mr. Sze coming to, for possession of the pistol. Nick picked it up, breathless, and wheeled. But Mr. Sze lay on the floor, on his back, where he had first fallen, his nose bleeding profusely, his eyes closed.

I've killed him, Nick thought, appalled.

There was, however, a strong pulse. Holding the gun and watching the Chinese, Nick picked up the telephone. "I want a policeman," he said. It was a classic phrase in the forepart of every American telephone directory. He supplemented it. "Page a Sergeant Crowell; he may be in the lobby. Then call Army Intelligence, Captain Malta; I've caught a gunman in my room."

The desk clerk couldn't say a word.

Nick hung up, his hands shaking from excitement. He couldn't catch his breath. Good Lord, it was a mess. It was no time to be respectable, even though he gave his respectability a momentary thought worrying about it. Someone called him from the door. "Are you all right, sir? Open up in here!"

He opened the door. Sergeant Crowell strode in, his face screwed tight, a revolver in his hand. "Heard the shot," he said.

"You heard the shot? Then you couldn't have been downstairs."

"I was in the lobby," Sergeant Crowell said. "Sounded like a blasted cannon. Is that the one, the sloe-eyed —— sir?"

"His name is H. H. Sze," Nick replied. He gave Crowell the gun. "You can arrest him. I've no time to wait for details at this point. Please get in touch with Captain Malta and tell him to meet me at the home of Eddie Wing. Can you remember that? Wing's home. And whatever you do, don't let this man escape."

Sergeant Crowell cocked his head grimly. "That point you don't have to think about twice, sir. With me they don't escape alive."

Nick retrieved the vaccine carton, put it in his pocket, and fled. He took a cab and drove quickly to Dr. Wing's home, which was located out in Nuuanu Valley not far from the Country Club. From the outside, the stucco house was ordinary, but its interior was carpeted with luxuriantly deep rugs, the walls studded with Hawaiian objets d'art, the furniture polished teakwood, the place alive with books of many languages. There was a musty richness about Eddie Wing's home which did not match his youth. "Nicholas," he said. "Welcome to Stony Broke. Come in, please, quickly—"

"It's plague," Nick breathed, unable to contain himself. "It's plague, Eddie, bubonic plague. Look at this." He thrust the carton at Wing. "Paul Cameron inoculated himself with this stuff tonight. It means he's either working with plague or trying to break this thing himself, and the second possibility is an impossibility. I'm convinced. He's been in and out of the thing vaguely ever since I found it. His signature was forged to the credentials Zeller used to get MacFerson and his nurse out of the hospital. Now I don't think it was a forgery at all. His resigning his post here—leaving tomorrow himself—it all fits, don't you see? He's in it! My God, I can't believe such a thing, but he's in it!"

"*Huapala,* catch your breath," Eddie Wing said, his voice a whisper in comparison with Nick's hoarseness. "You're too excited. Come upstairs quickly. Sergeant Woolton is here, and he has news. I don't believe it's plague. You can't use plague in artificial fashion. Too dangerous."

"Yes?" Nick said. "It's plague, all right! If it hadn't been plague, I might not be here. It was plague to the damned gunman who— Where is Woolton, Eddie? I'm out of hand."

"Upstairs in the forward bedroom. Go ahead—scramble! Go right up and visit with him, but don't let him get excited. He's wounded."

Nick nodded and ran up the stairs. He knew the guest-room well, had spent many nights in it. There was a faint scent of sandalwood upstairs. He opened the guest-room door, went in, and found Sergeant Woolton reposing in bed, a young man, brawny and huge, with a big face, big hands and wild hair. He sat up instantly, his face showing some pain, and he said: "Hello, pal, who are you?"

"I'm Nicholas Adams," Nick said, "Woolton?"

"That's the name, Doc. My friends call me Boitie."

"You're wounded?"

"Yeah, Doc, the —— slipped me one. Square in the groin, but that won't stop me. It didn't stop me when I caught it. I wish to hell you could patch me up for the final because I'm a fighting man, Doc, and I'd like to be in this thing for the windup."

"You take it easy," Nick said. "Let's see it."

It was a serious wound. Eddie Wing had already attended to the extraction of the bullet. If there was going to be peritonitis, Bertie Woolton was in trouble. But he didn't seem to mind. His energy, under the circumstances, was amazing. "Will I make the grade, Doc?"

"Yes, if you give yourself a chance and stay strong."

"Good. I'll moider 'em when I get out."

Nick replied: "How did you get shot and who shot you?"

"Jap named Kita shot me because I got too nosy," said Woolton, his voice strong. "Oh, he was a sneaky little monkey. I never got a shot at him. I'm glad you came down, sir. I knew the colonel was going to wire you. That was the last I saw of him, when he went to R.C.A. on King. 'Boitie,' he says to me, 'you keep your glimmers on Kita until you hear from me. Kita knows where the focus is and Kita will lead you there.' "

Nick said: "Now talk slowly and take it easy. You'd better start at the beginning, Woolton."

"O.K.," Woolton said, nodding. He leaned back in bed and rested a moment. "Began yesterday morning. Punk named Robert Mac-Foison reported in at Stafford ill. Slinky little rat. Colonel Venner put him to bed. MacFoison was fulla lumps. Colonel got Miss Wilson, told me to get out. I ain't a butcher, y'see."

"Yes, I know."

"Next thing, the colonel comes dashing out like an M-3 heading for Libya. 'Boitie,' he says, 'hell to pay. We've gotta woik fast, lotsa woik, Boitie, before they toin this island into a pest-hole.' "

Nick said: "Did Venner tell you what MacFerson had related to him?"

"If you'll hold your hat, Doc, I'll tell you exactly like I was told. And this man-hole in my belly hoits." He stirred restlessly. Nick knew that Bertie Woolton couldn't be killed by one wound. The fellow's strength and *sang froid* were wonderful. "Now the colonel didn't talk much. 'What it is,' he says, 'I can't tell you, Boitie. But in brief, this MacFoison was part of a plot to spread a lot of death around this island where it would do the most good. The punk was gonna introduce the Schofield Barracks to this screwy blitz. That was his job. And he came down with the same sickness he had planned for his pals.' " Woolton frowned. "It *was* a sickness of some kind."

"I know what it is now," Nick said. "I don't like to be impatient under the circumstances, Woolton, but time is precious."

"Sure, pal." Woolton nodded. "I'll blitz it. So the colonel says: 'I'm going down for a snort with Doc Wing because there is only one mug for this job and that's his pal Nicholas Adams'—you. 'I've got to get Adams here at once,' he says, 'because MacFoison said inoculation has already begun, and they plan to loose the sickness on the island within forty-eight hours, when the rats are thoroughly infected.' I didn't know what the hell he was talking about, I'm a fighting man, I ain't a sawbones."

"You're making fine sense," Nick said. "Keep going, Woolton. Did he know where the focus was?"

"Focus, focus, he said focus too. What's a focus?"

"A focus is the center. It's where they would have these infected rats."

"No, my fran', that he didn't know. That yellow rat MacFoison got hold of himself, Doc. He'd been outa his head for fear and spouting all this dope, and all of a sudden, MacFoison got leery that the colonel wouldn't save him. So he shut up like a clam and said he would give out no more singing unless Colonel Venner saved him from the lumps. The colonel threatened him with every torture this side of Canarsie, but MacFoison wouldn't open up. Foist, he'd been afraid of what he had, then he was afraid of the colonel leaving him to die. Colonel Venner said there was nothing he could do anyhow."

"What was MacFerson's job in the thing?" Nick asked.

"He was going to infect Schofield Barracks."

"But how?"

"I don't know," Woolton said. "How the hell would a man infect a barracks? You should know, Doc."

"He'd have to transport infected rats by truck," Nick said.

"Truck?" said Woolton. "You're within a smell of it, Doc. Because MacFoison had raved about some people, see? He'd mentioned a man named Zeller and a man named the Chief, and a man named Kita. The colonel told me that I was to find Kita and that Kita was a trucker, and that I was to follow Kita until he led me to the focus."

"And you found Kita?"

"He had a trucking agency on Chulia Street. There was a spot over the road from the garage and I hung in there with a bottle until it was a dead marine. Then the Nipper came out of the garage. He drove his own car. I chased him in a taxi. He went down to Bishop Street and stopped in front of a place called Laboratories, Limited. That was when I caught my slug. Kita saw me leave the cab, and if I'd not been in uniform, it woulda been different. I ducked into an alley and thought I'd lost the Nip, but I hadn't. I was rounding the corner behind the stores when I caught one. I heard the shot and he just got me toining—see how it hit me—and I went down. Then I got up and I could still walk but I knew I couldn't get far. There was a parking space behind the alley, and six trucks lined up with Kita's name on the side of them. They had tarpaulin over the back so I crawled under there. The trucks was empty."

"When was this?"

"Round noon, Doc, because the heat was filthy the rest of the day. The trucks stayed there. I could hear them looking for me, but I hadn't bled outside my clothes and there was no trail. When it got dark, I managed to get out the alley, into a cab. I came right to Dr. Wing's place, because I figured he'd know where the colonel was. Then I heard they'd bumped off the colonel. That's all."

Nick shook his head. "Woolton," he said, his face alive, "you're terrific."

"I'm dead tired," Woolton said. He smiled. "Thanks, pal. It's your show now. Make it a lulu and slip the sloe a slug from his pal Boitie."

CHAPTER FIVE
THE MEN BEHIND THE RATS

There was no time to waste. Nick was aware that Eddie Wing had been in the room with them for most of it, but had disappeared. Nick went downstairs to find Captain Malta in the hall with Wing, a Colt H-5 at his hip. "In a minute," Nick said. "We can break it open if we're not too late." He picked up the telephone and called the Quarantine station in Honolulu. "This is Dr. Nicholas Adams of the Cardwell Institute," he began formally, so that they would place him. He knew Dr. Jeremiah Riggs down there very well. He asked for Dr. Riggs, and they switched the call to Dr. Riggs' home. It took some minutes, and Nick was in a nervous frenzy. "Hello, Riggs? This is Nick Adams! Yes, in Honolulu, but listen, Jerry, I haven't time for amenities. I want you—please understand this, it's most urgent— I want you to get together the fumigation equipment—yes, hydrocyanic gas and sulphur and anything you have, bring it all, I'm not sure what sort of situation there may be—to the Laboratories Limited on Bishop Street. . . . I mean every word, Riggs, there's a bubonic plague focus there. Thanks, Jerry, thanks very much." He hung up.

Captain Malta said: "Bishop Street, Doctor? The shopping center?"

"Yes."

"I'll be damned!" said Captain Malta, his face red, and his eyebrows bristling. "Plague! This is out of my line, Adams!"

"No time to talk," Nick said. "Let's go. Do you have men?"

"Not with me." Captain Malta telephoned headquarters. "Give me a company at once," he said. "Laboratories Limited on Bishop Street. The men are to deploy with arms covering the entrance."

"There's a trucking exit in the rear," Nick said. "That's most important. Make certain the men who cover that section are protected on hands and legs from any flea bites. Make certain of that, Malta, or it may mean death for them."

Malta relayed the information and received some in return. "He did? . . . I'll leave word here then for him to follow. Yes, at once." He hung up. "Sergeant Crowell brought in a prisoner at Central station and said that he had information for me. He's on the way over. Dr. Wing, will you inform the sergeant that I've left with Dr. Adams for—"

"I imagine," Dr. Wing said quietly, "your sergeant is just arriving. There is a car racing down the road."

He was right. Sergeant Crowell was in the car, and he brought it to a roaring halt in front of the house behind Captain Malta's car. Sergeant Crowell jumped out. Captain Malta said tersely: "Headquarters said you had important information for me."

"Yes, Captain, I have. On that gunman—Mr. Sze, Doctor—I found these inter-island boat tickets for Lanai. He was taking the morning boat, two tickets."

"He was to take me," Nick said. "At least he said so."

"Yes, sir, but it ain't what I mean. Look here, on the other side is the address where the tickets were sent to him. Care of the Laboratories, Limited, Bishop Street. I thought—"

"Good job," Malta snapped. "Fortunately, we're a bit ahead of you, we already have the address. Let's be going."

Nick and Eddie Wing got in Malta's car as the engine started. Nick shut out everything but the job. It came easily to him, he had done it often before when he had a patient. You could be thinking of a thousand important things, and suddenly you saw your patient, and in a twinkling, you had detached yourself from everything but the patient and your treatment of him. Oahu was the patient this night and, not unlike those distant days when he had interned at Lenox Hill in New York, he was answering an emergency call, and all that was lacking was the clanging bell of an ambulance.

"I can't impress upon you the value of secrecy," Nick Adams told Captain Malta, as they drove into town together. "I fully understand now why Venner was so mysterious. I don't mind your knowing that we have bubonic plague in Oahu, Captain, and I pray to God we stamp it out before the night is over. Naturally Dr. Riggs and his disinfecting crew are going to know, too, and I suppose Intelligence will be informed. But other than that, I would hush any publicity on the matter, for it ought to be fairly plain to you that such a plot suggests itself again, or suggests others, and that isn't so good. Also, the population might be too close to a panic line on any other incident, which may transpire, for war is war and other incidents will come along."

"I understand thoroughly," Captain Malta said. "I'm even inclined to think I would have acted as Colonel Venner did. It was just his own incredible bad luck in being murdered that prevented a successful conclusion to the thing, as he had planned it. Plague! I don't know much of these things—that's the one with rats?"

"Yes," Nick said. "That's the one with rats. That's the one that wiped off half the population of Europe some centuries ago. That's the one they worry about even in the United States at ports like Mobile or New Orleans or San Francisco."

"Could it—really work?" Captain Malta asked, his voice awed. "It's hard to think—"

"It may still work," Nick said. "If they've loaded those trucks with infected rats to establish various foci at the naval base, at various barracks, at the docks, and in the Chinese quarter, not I nor twenty like me will stop the fire once it begins to burn!"

"But exactly how do the rats do it? Why is it so difficult? It's easy enough to trap a rat."

"The rat doesn't do it. The rat is the carrier. There are two types of fleas that do it, they are infected, *cheopis* and *asta*. They climb onto a rat, live on him, infect him. When he dies, they hide in the dust and leap onto the next living thing that comes by. Since the long-tailed black *mus rattus* makes his home with man, he brings the flea into man's quarters, and you have plague. In septicemic plague, there is a ninety percent mortality, and no treatment of any avail. The ten percent are just lucky. In pneumonic plague, man can then directly contaminate man by merely coughing! The possibilities are gruesome to look upon. As for trapping the rat, Captain, I will pay you a fine reward if you will find me the resting place of the rat. Like the elephant, the rodent burying ground has never been found. Think of it, there is one rat for every two persons in the world, and yet his tomb has never been found. A famous scientist connected with the Rockefeller Institute once spent much time in Manila, trying to find the rat's grave, and never succeeded. It is most difficult to catch a dead rat, Captain, and in this case, it is the dead rat who is likely to have carried the sinister boarders who strike plague."

Captain Malta made no comment. His silence was one of dismay. They turned into Bishop Street and proceeded to the address. They found that the constabulary had already done an excellent piece of work. The street was roped off on either side, and the quarantine fumigating equipment stood by, waiting, the truck with the big pumps, hoses and cylinders of deadly hydrocyanic gas.

A tall dignified man with a fine mustache met Malta, and the captain introduced the newcomer as Major Henry Dinwoody, commanding the soldiers who had been rushed to the scene. "We must move quickly," Dinwoody said. "It's possible they aren't aware of us yet. This was done quickly and quietly."

"Is the rear covered?" Nick asked.

"Quite thoroughly."

"And they aren't aware?"

"No, Doctor," Dinwoody said. "They are loading small crates into the trucks."

Nick shuddered and said: "Let's go, Captain. Don't storm the place, Major. Just make certain that no one leaves the front entrance. And have the fumigating crew ready to pump. If there are any other people in these shops along the way, get them out, and force them to leave until we are finished. It will take time."

 aptain Malta joined Nick. They were directed to the alley, followed it in the dark until they reached the area way behind the stores. They approached the rear of Laboratories Limited, and were quietly halted by a tough sergeant, looking queer with white gloves and white leggings. He recognized Malta and apologized. They had reached the line.

"What arrangements have you made?" Captain Malta asked the sergeant.

"I blow my whistle and we go in with the bayonet," the sergeant said. He was very tall.

Nick watched. Bare-legged, bare-armed coolies, who didn't even realize what they were doing, earning their daily shilling, were bringing small wire-netted crates from the sliding rear door of the building and piling them one on top of the other in the rear of the various trucks.

Close by the door, his arms folded stoically, stood a little man. Nick assumed it was the same Mr. Kita whose name adorned the trucks.

Captain Malta passed a pistol and a flashlight

to Nick. Nick rejected the pistol. — "Never killed a man in my life"—but took the torch. Nick said: "No point waiting, Captain. Leave the trucks as they are; don't have your men touch them. Take every man in sight prisoner. The important thing is for me to get inside and seal that building. This is it, no doubt of it."

"Blow your whistle, Sergeant," Captain Malta said.

The sergeant took a breath and blew piercingly on his whistle. Soldiers evolved out of the darkness in more quantity than Nick had ever expected. He found himself running, right in the vanguard, striving for the open door before Kita leaped in and closed it. There would be the devil to pay if they couldn't get in.

Kita, surprised by the whistle and the sudden rush of men, threw his head one way and another and started shooting. Nick had not even seen him take a gun out, but the shots were vivid enough. His stomach was terrified, a rocklike knob, but his legs kept moving and his head was cool enough. He had a momentary vision as he approached the door of Kita pointing a gun almost directly into his face. *It couldn't happen to me,* Nick thought in a flash, *not me!*

Captain Malta, just behind him, fired at Kita and killed the Jap before Kita ever pulled his trigger. The proximity of Malta's pistol to Nick's ear was such that Nick thought he had burst an eardrum. His left ear rang and kept ringing but other than that internal ring, it was as deaf as a stone. He saw the coolies yelling and chattering in a frantic fear. They were quickly taken, no resistance offered. *Poor souls,* he thought, *they've lived with death tonight and don't even know it.* He wondered how many of them had been infected by the valveless epipharynx of the plague flea.

When he reached the door, he turned and went in. It was damned reassuring to have a man like Captain Malta at his side. The place was well lighted when they went in, but almost instantly, the fluorescent tubes died, and the building plunged into darkness. Nick had had a quick vision of the interior, and the room in which he

stood he knew to be a former loft, now containing shelves in quantity separated by little alleys, and the shelves which rose from the floor to a six-foot height were filled with meshed cages in which the oddly sinister scuffle of the rats could be heard. Some of the beasts were squealing. It was ugly.

"There's a staircase on the left," Nick panted. "Must go up to the laboratory itself. No one can get out?"

"No one," Captain Malta said grimly.

"I'll take the staircase, they must be up there!"

"Let me go first, Adams, you're not armed!"

"No, no, it's all right."

Nick found the staircase with his electric torch. The stairs were old and creaky and he heard each one of his own steps as he ascended. A voice ahead of him called, "Adams?"

"Yes," he said. "Yes."

A rough hard hand grasped him, swung him around and pulled him. The torch fell from his hand. Nick felt the cold barrel of a gun against his cheek—in the dark his assailant had meant for it to be against his head. There was a grunt. He heard Captain Malta trip on the stairs and curse. Then Malta called: "Adams, are you safe?"

Nick's assailant said: "Is that you, Malta?"

"Yes."

"I want safe conduct," the man said. He was strong. "This is Zeller speaking. I'm holding Adams here. If you don't give me safe conduct, I'll kill him. I'll take him with me and release him when I get clear."

"Has he got you, Doctor?"

It occurred to Nick that he had a golden opportunity. The gun was hard against his cheek. He jerked his head backwards and found the right side of Zeller's thumb cushion against his mouth. He bit it as savagely as any animal, and he felt his teeth go deep. Zeller roared at the pain and futilely pounded Nick's back with his fist. Then Captain Malta's torch spotlighted them both. At that moment, the pressure of Nick's teeth opening the muscles of Zeller's hand, Zeller dropped his gun. It clattered down the stairs. Captain Malta raised his gun as Nick released Zeller's hand.

"*Kamerad,*" Zeller said. He did not raise his hands. He shook the one which had been bitten. "*Kamerad,* Malta. I am taken." He said it very quickly, not frightened, but quickly nevertheless, for Malta was not being merciful in the press of things.

"This is a dangerous man," Captain Malta said, "and I don't want to lose him in this melee. Can you wait a few seconds, Adams, while I deliver him to a guard downstairs?"

"Go ahead, I'll wait."

A gun in his back, Fritz Zeller said, his voice ugly: "I trust you have not infected me, Adams."

"You never know," Nick said. "Better have a Pasteur treatment, although a chap like yourself should certainly have built up an immunization against rabies."

"We should have wiped you off early," Zeller said. He went down the stairs with Malta behind him, grumbling something about the damned stubborn Dutchman.

Alone, Nick Adams stood on the landing. His eyes had become more accustomed to the darkness, and that, coupled with the reflection of the electric torches on the floor of the loft below, showed him a door with an opaque glass upper half, marked *Private* and closed. He was wary. Then he called: "Paul! Paul Cameron!"

There was a voice beyond the door. "Nick?" Cameron's voice, but not cold and impersonal as it had always been. It was a tired voice, quivering with emotion.

"It's no use, Paul," Nick called. "It's finished, Paul."

The door opened. Cameron said: "Come in quickly."

Nick shivered and went in. He heard Cameron lock the door. They stood in the darkness. He heard Cameron moving. "Walk directly ahead," said Cameron wearily. "You'll find a chair. You're a fool. You realize I could kill you

as easily as I'd step on a spider? I've a Mauser here, Nick, in my hand."

"Why would you kill me?" Nick said. "I'm the only friend you have left in this world."

"Sit down," Cameron said. "Sit down."

Nick found the chair and sat. He wished, vainly, that he could see Cameron's face, for the voice was tortured. He was not afraid. He said: "In the name of God, Paul, why did you do it?"

He heard a sigh. "It was so perfect," Cameron whispered. "Damn you, Nick. Damn you, damn you. You've ruined a lifetime, you've destroyed a dream. . . . No, *I* have. I've done it myself, committed hara-kiri because I was still capable of one human frailty. From the beginning Sze and Zeller wanted to murder you, but I would not sanction it. I should have stayed in character and let them finish you, and tonight, Oahu would have begun its decline and fall. Oh my God, why were you my friend in the beginning?" His voice broke, then choked into silence.

There was a long and tense pause. Outside on the landing, Captain Malta called: "Adams! Where are you?" Then the door rattled.

Cameron fired at the door without warning, and the shot raised Nick's hair and took his breath away. He had not expected it. Cameron said: "You had better explain to your friend, Nick. I'll kill any man who comes through that door now. I'm not to be taken alive tonight."

"Malta!" Nick called feverishly. "Don't come in! I'm in here, I'm all right. Please don't come in."

"You may tell him that you will be out presently unharmed," Cameron said. "I want to talk with you, Nick."

"I'll be out in a few minutes unharmed," Nick said. "Please be patient, Captain."

"Are you saying that at gunpoint?" Malta called sharply.

"No, no," Nick said. "He could shoot me if he wished. Please stand by, Captain."

The logic was plain. "Very well, Adams."

"I am sitting here," Cameron said huskily in the dark, "and wondering what is being thought in that neat and honest mind of yours, Nick."

"Incredulity mostly."

"You hate me," Cameron said in a tight voice.

"I'm incapable of hate," Nick said. "But I can't forgive you this, for any reason, because you are a doctor. I could forgive no man who had sworn his fidelity by the Hippocratic oath such a black rotten plot. It was your job to save lives, not extinguish them. It was your job to put everything else in life aside—all your personal wishes—and save, not destroy."

"You'd never understand," Cameron said.

"Right. A chauvinist perhaps. But not a doctor."

ameron's teeth were gritted and his voice was fierce. "I've owed them this, the *verdamnt* Yankees, owed them it since April 1917. If they had stayed at home, tended their own business, we would not be at war today; we Germans would have won the first war, as it was intended we should! But you Yankees interfered; you did not defeat us, you tired us, and you postponed the war for twenty years. This time, I swore I would take care of you."

He coughed. Nick stunned, said: "*We Germans,* did you say?"

"Yes. We Germans. I am a German. First, last, always. I saw the pattern of things to come so far back when my kin and friends were killed by American soldiers. I saw what would happen. The Armistice confirmed this. I knew at once I must work from within. The opportunity would come. I even assumed United States citizenship. Then the opportunity came. I saw what would happen—the same story again—but this time *we* had Japan with us. Oahu, the impregnable Pacific fortress—there was an objective to reduce!"

Nick grimaced at the sound of jubilance in Cameron's hard voice.

"After the attack on Pearl Harbor, I knew more than ever that the base could not be taken from the outside unless first it was softened up on the inside. *That* was my task. Fortunately, I had been working on the premise long before the Japanese flew in from the west and decimated your fleet—"

"How in God's name—"

Cameron raised his hands. "It took time and patience. I began a year ago, almost, with fifty rats, male and female. As you know, their gestation period is twenty-one days, and in three months, the newborn can also breed, so that by the end of the year when I reached a figure of five thousand rats, all *mus rattus,* the time had come to inoculate them. These rats had all been maintained in the lofts below in their cages, well fed and uninfected, as far as we could help. I imported *cheopis* and *asta* fleas from Haifa and Jaffa, from India and from Manila. In other words, under the seal of the Cardwell Institute I imported the *bacillus pestis.* The time had come. I proceeded to infect every rat in the loft with fleas, allowed a suitable incubation period for the vermin to sicken. Tonight they are alive with plague. In hours—"

"That's over," Nick said harshly. "Do you hear? Finished."

Cameron said grimly: "It would have been ghastly, Nick. But it would have served its purpose. The Japanese did not have to take Oahu. They had only to reduce it to impotency, drive the U.S. fleet back to the coast, knowing it constituted no threat to their lines of communication. . . . I could have accomplished that, almost alone. But it is finished, as you say, and I am finished. I am very tired."

"What happened to MacFerson?" Nick said.

"Gone in the sea. That was Zeller's department. Venner was Zeller's department. There was another, an American sergeant. Kita shot him in the stomach. I don't know where he died. You were Zeller's department, he put Sze on you. But I forbade violence. . . . In one way"—he spoke very slowly now—"I am glad that no cause contributed to my failure but the cause of friendship. The Jekyll frustrated the Hyde. There is something reassuring in the thought."

His voice hardened. "Rid the earth of malcontents, Nick, when you look for disease, for they are disease and while they exist, the meek shall never inherit the earth. Please leave me now, and I give you fair warning, don't let me see you again."

"You're going to give yourself up, Paul. Don't be a fool. You're surrounded here, we're sealing the building, you're alone."

"Get out, Nick. Tell Malta to try and take me. I've six bullets left in the pistol, good for six men."

Nick rose and felt his way to the door. "Goodbye, Paul," he said. There was no point persuading. He knew from Cameron's voice.

Nick unlocked the door and stepped out. The door was slammed and locked behind him. He ran into Malta's arms. Captain Malta said, "Adams!"

"I'm all right."

"Where is he?"

"In there."

"I've got to bring him out."

"You haven't a chance. No windows, he's in a closed room. He'd shoot you the instant you opened the door. He won't give himself up."

"I want that man," Malta said.

"Come along," Nick said. "The man is finished but the rats are not. The plague is more important than the man who fashioned it. I promise you that you'll have Cameron, but first I want the life of every rat and flea in this pesthole. Tell your men to seal all windows, seal all doors, check the roof and sides for ventilators. The building is to be made as air-tight as possible. And remove all inhabitants from the buildings around in an area of five hundred yards."

"Very well, Adams."

Nick descended the stairs to the floor of the loft. There were electric torches flashing around. He saw the crated rats, red-eyed, scuffling, squealing, panicky. His skin crawled. He walked out of the place quickly. He borrowed a light to look at his trousers but they were devoid of fleas. The chances in that hole were terrific. He watched the men sealing up the building. When Captain Malta came out, Nick said: "These trucks will have to be driven some place and burned. They're thoroughly infected at this point and we can't openly spray them with the gas. It's too deadly."

Captain Malta ordered the soldiers to drive the trucks out toward Barber's Point and to set them all together out there and await instructions. "I'll call the Army post and ask them if they can't use a flame-thrower on the blasted things. That's quick fire to kill everything in a hurry."

They went around through the alley to Bishop Street and soon the report came that the place was sealed. The quarantine crew made a quick inspection of their own, then ran a hose into the building. The pumps started, and the hydrocyanic gas went in.

"But Cameron!" Malta said suddenly. "What about Cameron?"

Nick stared at the closed building. His face was dull and unexpressive. "You have no worries about Cameron," he said. "Hydrocyanic is quick and painless." He slumped. "There's nothing else for me to do here, Captain. I'd rather not stay around."

Captain Malta looked up to the boarded windows on the second floor. Then he nodded. "Yes," he said. "I see your point. I think we've no further need for you at this time, Doctor. Good-night."

There was a single shot, sharp and clear. It came from the building. . . .

"Good-night," Nick said.

"Well, sweetheart," said Dr. Eddie Wing, who drove him away from the scene, "spend the night with me?"

"No," Nick said. "Thanks, Eddie. I'm going back to the Royal Hawaiian. I want to see about passage."

"East?"

"Yes. I'm going home to the States."

Eddie Wing smiled grimly. "What are you going to do there, Nick?"

"Now is the time for all good men to come to the aid of the country," Nick said. He smiled too. "I guess we've got to take a moratorium on saving lives, Eddie. First you kill the bug; then saving a life becomes easy. I'm going to offer my services to the Medical Corps. Perhaps I can help in isolating and destroying the *pestis Japanicus*."

"And the *pestis Germanicus*," Eddie Wing said.

"And the *ladybug Italia*," Nick said.

Bracelets

Katherine Brocklebank

KATHERINE BROCKLEBANK was unique in the history of *Black Mask* magazine, and a rara avis in the detective pulp fiction world in general. In the first place, she was a woman and, unless cloaked behind initials or a male pseudonym, the only one identified in the thirty-two-year history of *Black Mask*, even when it was under the control of a female editor, Fanny Ellsworth, from 1936 to 1940. Second, she created a female series character, Tex of the Border Patrol, who appeared in four stories late in the 1920s. Readers of *Black Mask*, as was true of all the detective pulps, demonstrated in their letters to the editor that they didn't particularly care for either female protagonists or authors. While there were some exceptions in other popular magazines, fiction by or about women (except as sidekicks or girlfriends, or the occasional villain) represented a tiny fraction of the thousands of detective stories published annually in the golden age of the pulps (which was between the two World Wars).

"Bracelets," the first story about Tex of the Border Patrol, was published in the December 1928 issue. The other three *Black Mask* stories in which she starred were "White Talons" (January 1929), "The Canine Tooth" (June 1929), and "The Silver Horseshoe" (July 1929).

Bracelets

Katherine Brocklebank

A tale of Tia Juana after the closing hour of the Border and all the good folks have gone home.

TEX WATCHED FROM THE CORNERS of her eyes, watched, with a tight little pucker around her heart.

The girl seemed so young, so incongruous in that blatantly obvious setting. She was like a flower from an old-fashioned garden and yet there she was in the ribald atmosphere of the Blue Fox—where Pancho, the shifty-eyed Mexican proprietor, rubbed his palms together and smiled his oily smile to his patrons; where Eddie swung his bamboo cane to the syncopated time of his moaning Hopa-Holi orchestra—Eddie

who wore a chocolate brown suit to match his complexion, a screaming orange tie and a straw hat, who sang the latest popular ballads in a voice—untrained, crooning—as insidious as the ether-doped drinks that the silken-voiced bartenders slid across the bars of Old Town, that were now world-famous, polished to a dull red glow by the elbows of many nationalities.

Tex shifted her eyes to the long mirror back of the bar, noting her titian wig with an inward smile of satisfaction. Strangely enough her greenish gold eyes took on a copper glint. Her wide, good-humored mouth had turned to one of hard wisdom under the clever manipulation of a vivid lip-stick. The orange rouge, slapped carelessly on either cheekbone, gave the finishing touch to a Border percentage girl, calloused, eager—pathetic.

She eased away from the obese gentleman from Kansas City, who pawed her with maudlin intensity, and edged a little nearer to the girl. Her eyes traveled slowly over her, cognizant of the soft green silk dress; the skirt a bit longer than was smart, the floppy affair of black straw that shadowed her face. She seemed like a slender flower-stalk as she leaned against the bar, her arms draped across its stained surface, her fingers playing nervously with the string of bracelets she wore on her left wrist.

Tex noticed particularly the girl's hands. Narrow and white with long, thin fingers that were never still—fingers that hovered constantly over the bracelets—bracelets that caught and held Tex's attention. There were eight of them, Chinese, of intricate design, amber and gold, carved ivory, jade. They made a peculiar clanking sound whenever the girl moved her arm.

Tex let her gaze rove blearily along the string of heterogeneity that lined the bar: percentage girls, cheap, faded creatures with gold-filled teeth who wheedled unwilling male sightseers into buying them drinks; thrill-hunters; society matrons with a veneer of hauteur washed off by Border hooch; flappers; groggy daddies whose wives were abroad for the summer; doubtful ladies in shoddy evening clothes; crafty-eyed Mexicans; derelicts; law-dodgers.

Slowly Tex's eyes came back to the girl and the vain little fish-faced man who stood beside her. They had come in together and Tex knew from things she had heard—never mind how or where—that this must be "The Eel." A clever crook was The Eel, who had so far eluded the police, who was always under suspicion but had never been caught with the goods. He claimed to be Mexican, although his intimates knew that he was half Chinese. Under an assumption of intoxication Tex studied him closely. With his oily, mud-colored skin, slick black hair and opaque slanting eyes he resembled his pseudonym, and Tex imagined she'd want to wash her hands after touching him. He looked—slimy.

Tex lurched against the girl. "'Lo," she gurgled in her slightly husky voice.

The girl looked up at her, startled. "'Lo," she answered involuntarily, without smiling.

The Eel bent forward, giving Tex a sharp glance of mistrust, but when he saw her grinning at him vacantly he turned back to the girl and continued his low-toned conversation.

Tex edged a little nearer, endeavoring to hear his whispered words. He stopped short and Tex felt instinctively that he was regarding her with suspicion in the bar mirror. She hooked her arm in the girl's in a sudden burst of alcoholic familiarity and felt the girl grow rigid—with fear? Tex wondered. "Have thish one on me, dearie," said Tex.

The girl relaxed and smiled wanly. "Oh— thank you." She pushed her empty glass across the bar.

"M'boyfren'll buy fur the crowd—won' yuh, honey?" Tex swayed toward the inebriated obesity from Kansas City, but he was slumped over the bar, oblivious to the percentage girls' ever consuming thirst.

Tex shrugged. "Nev' mind, dearie, Ah's good sport. Ah'll buy—mahshelf." She opened her stringy bead bag a crack and peered blearily into its shabby depths.

"Aw, lay off, will yuh?" The Eel scowled darkly at her, flipped a coin to the bartender, grasped the girl by the arm, and pushed her through the crowd of black-bottom maniacs on the dance floor to the door.

Through the medium of the bar mirror Tex watched them vanish into the one main street, a street that was already growing dusk, a street that, after dark, was deserted, stealthy, dangerous—for those visitors who are foolish enough to loiter.

Tex loitered, loitered until the music stopped abruptly with harsh discordance; until the last stream of sightseers stampeded for the Border; until the gambling halls and open-fronted cantinas closed with mock modesty and a final sly wink of lights; until night shrouded the wicked little town with brooding silence and skulking shadows.

With a cold shiver of apprehension Tex lurched past Cæsar's Bar and Paul's. She felt as if eyes watched from yawning black doorways, darkened windows—eyes that were hostile, suspicious, sinister.

She hugged her beaded bag under her left arm, her right hand clasped over it, and felt the reassuring hardness of the small, snub-nosed pistol, with its Maxim silencer, as it snuggled securely within the torn lining.

She turned into the dimly lighted entrance of the San Francisco Cantina and stumbled up the cheaply carpeted stairs to her room. She closed the door with a bang and hiccoughed as she switched on the light. From under lowered lids she made a hasty survey of the small, bare room, then flung herself full-length on the bed, her purse held tightly across her breast.

One hour crawled by on furtive, dragging feet. Two. And still Tex lay on her springless wooden bed, feigning drunken slumber.

A slight breeze riffled in through the window stirring the sagging lace curtain to shake some of its dust in Tex's nose. She suppressed a sneeze and turned it into a snore with a choked sort of snort on the end of it.

A little longer she listened to the swishing of the curtain as it flapped wearily in and out of the window. Then she thought she heard another sound. A shuffling sound, soft, guarded, muffled.

Slowly she sat up, swinging her feet quietly over the edge of the bed and eased them to the carpetless floor. Silently she crept across the room to the door and paused, tensing, listening, her bead bag clutched in her right hand.

At first there was nothing—just silence— then a faint hissing sound. Tex leaned nearer to the crack and a few whispered words drifted in to her.

"But, Señor Jefe, she ees wan of my percentage girls. Mucho good wan, too. You make wan beeg mistake. She ees not what you t'ink." The voice was Pancho's—Pancho of the Blue Fox.

"Well, I ain't takin' no chances. She talks like that Texan female dick. . . . Anyway—we'll leave him for her."

In her startled surprise Tex lost the rest of the sentence. She gripped the bead bag more tightly. Damn that Texas drawl of hers! For a second she wished she had heeded her chief's warning and brought Bobbie with her. Then she laughed softly, a shaky little laugh. She'd been in tight corners before since she'd entered the secret service four years ago, and through her quick wit and clear reasoning she had always managed to extricate herself—with honors—and part of the trapped underworld. That was why the chief had chosen her to unravel the skein of mystery that tangled around the strange death of Melville Hewett, a wealthy San Francisco merchant, and the disappearance of his son, Arthur. The Eel had been seen coming out of Hewett's home the night before the murder.

Tex was suddenly aware of a curious absence of sound. She waited a moment, holding her breath, her left hand on the door-knob. Then with a swift, cat-like movement, she pulled the door toward her. It opened abruptly, as if someone were pushing against it. She flashed her hand inside her bag, her fingers closing around the pistol, but suddenly recoiled with a stifled cry as a man's body plunged inward and fell forward on his face.

There was something peculiar about his swollen, twisted limbs. Something that vaguely reminded Tex of another man. Who was it? Then in a flash she knew. Melville Hewett had looked that same way.

With a revulsion of feeling toward touching anything lifeless, that she had never been able to overcome, she turned the man on his back.

Staring up at her with glassy eyes, with the contorted features of one who has died in agony, was Bobbie; Bobbie, who was the youngest member of the department and whom the chief had evidently sent to protect her.

Tex straightened, her eyes clouded with unexpected tears, and her heart felt sick. Bobbie was such a youngster. So straight and clean. Damn them! Her hot Texan blood began to boil. She'd get them for this!

She leaned over him again, examining him more closely, pondering. There were no marks of violence. No blood. Then the glint of a green circlet on his left wrist caught her eye. The bracelet was of jade, carved, Chinese. Attached to it by a slender gold chain was a small folded paper. Tex stiffened, for instinctively she knew it was a message for her. She spread the paper out and read the illiterate, scribbled words—*Ull git yuse next if u dont lay off.* At the end, instead of the signature, was a green seal. Tex scrutinized it intently, her eyes narrowing as she turned the paper around. The seal evolved into a bracelet as she examined it. A bracelet with the head of a snake and the tail of a fish. She smiled, a grim twisting of her painted lips. The Eel was an egomaniac. He couldn't resist the temptation of becoming his own press agent.

A low, husky sound issued from the slim, round throat of Tex; a cry of comprehension, relentless rage, warning.

Through the crooked back streets of Old Town, Tex slid cautiously, like some stalking shadow, through streets that seemed to be winding, dirt-smeared menaces leading into oblivion.

She was following her hunch. A hunch that beckoned her to Pancho's crumbling adobe that crouched, like some hunted animal in the treacherous sands of the desert, one mile south of Tia Juana.

From time to time she glanced nervously over her shoulder. Silence trailed back of her—heavy, oppressive. And before her? Nameless peril. A little demon of fear clutched at her heart, squeezing it until she could hardly breathe. A peculiar tingling sensation ran along her arms and twitched the ends of her fingers. She knew the symptoms. She had had the same feeling when she was about to take off for the five-foot hurdles back in Texas. A breathless sort of feeling. A feeling that a hunter must have just before the kill.

Pancho's adobe loomed unexpectedly before her, a darker shadow in the surrounding gloom.

It was long, low and narrow. A wide chimney of rotting stones in the back; two thick, weather-scarred doors of solid wood in front; a narrow, deep-set window near the slanting mud roof at either end. No sound came from the adobe and no light penetrated the thick wooden openings.

Tex crept up to the door nearer her and gently pushed against it. It gave silently under her weight. Quickly, quietly she stepped into the long, low-ceilinged room into which it directly opened, her bead bag hugged under her left arm. She blinked at the sudden light although it was only a feeble flicker from three tallow candles that hung in a rusty iron chandelier suspended from a single wooden beam that ran the length of the room.

Swiftly she took in her surroundings. In a shrouded corner was a cot with something moaning under a pair of soiled blankets. Near it drooped the girl with the bracelets, sobbing softly in a suppressed sort of hopelessness.

Tex closed the door quietly and advanced toward the cot.

At the slight sound of her steps the girl looked up, her eyes widening in terror, her narrow white hands flying to her mouth to stifle the cry that sprang to her lips, the bracelets crowding together, clicking, clanking. Then the fear slowly faded from the girl's face. "Oh, it's— you," she said dully.

Tex nodded and grinned. "Sure." She slid a little nearer and stared down at the white face on the pillow. "Arthur Hewett," she whispered. "Doped and kept doped for days," she added to herself.

At that the girl seemed to waken as from heavy stupor. "How did you know? Who are you?" She sprang up facing Tex.

Tex thought rapidly. She must move cautiously—and—quickly. The girl was suspicious, yet Tex felt that through her she would gain the key to the mystery.

"He looks like his pitcher, don't he?" Tex answered the first question, ignoring the second. She lolled against the burnt brick wall, swinging her bag back and forth, searching furtively the other three corners of the room. "Gotter swig er hooch round this heah dump?" she finally asked, turning back to the girl.

The girl shook her head, slumping back into the chair, her long fingers playing nervously with her bracelets.

"Now, ain't that too bad?" murmured Tex, watching her from under lowered lids. "My, ain't them bracelets pretty?" She stretched an experimental hand toward the girl's left wrist.

The girl drew back sharply, alarm in her shadowed eyes, her fingers curling protectively around the eight circlets.

Tex assumed a sullen tone. "Ah—what'd'yuh take me fur? A cheap dip?" She glanced toward the two doors. "Hell! Ah'd give mah best gold inlay fur a shot er hooch."

A pale little smile hovered around the girl's lips. "I'm sorry—but there isn't any here—only—" She chopped her sentence off abruptly with a little gasp of fright.

"Only what?" prodded Tex quietly, successfully cloaking her eagerness. "If thar's anything that'll take the place—er hooch—hand it ovah, honey, 'cause Ah'm lower than a snake's hips."

"Snakes!" whispered the girl in deadly fear, and Tex leaned toward her suddenly.

"Gawd! Thar ain't no snakes—heah?" Under the pretense of dismay she studied the girl intently. Snakes? The deaths of Hewett and Bobbie strangely resembled the deadly bites of rattlers. The swollen limbs; the discolored flesh; the almost invisible twin red marks on the left wrists. And yet there had been no snakes.

The girl recovered herself and regarded Tex a little doubtfully. "No—no—of course not." She turned to soothe the moaning man with gently caressing hands, the bracelets huddling down toward her slender hand. She turned back to Tex. "How did you know of this place?" she demanded unexpectedly, a sharp note in her usually low tones.

Tex didn't answer at once. Instead she hitched a little nearer to the bed, keeping her back to the wall, facing the two doors. "Listen, honey," she murmured at last, "Ah come heah to help you." A crooning note slid into her throaty voice and she glanced significantly toward the wasted form of Arthur Hewett.

The girl's eyes followed hers and returned, poignant pain suffusing their shadowed depths. She gazed up at Tex, hesitating, seeming to consider.

And Tex waited, outwardly calm, in no hurry. Inwardly at a high-pitched, nervous tension, her ears cocked for any outside disturbance, her eyes darting to the doors, the windows, around the room, back to the girl and the moaning man. If, as she surmised, the girl was weak, guarding some secret, through love—or fear—she would break under Tex's soft persuasion.

"Oh, I'm afraid—afraid." The words were so low Tex had to stoop to catch them.

The girl clasped her hands tightly in her lap and swayed back and forth.

"Afraid of what—of—who?" prompted Tex. Lord, if the girl would only hurry! A cold feeling of playing for time shivered through her. She hugged her bag more closely under her left arm, the fingers of her right hand curling about the broken clasp. Seconds seemed to leap at her—crowding—crowding—

Presently the girl spoke, her words low, halting—as if being dragged through unwilling lips. "Oh, if you could take—Arthur away—away—where it's safe—safe." She stared up at Tex, repeating the last word in a sort of frenzied appeal.

Tex suddenly put out her hand and grasped the girl's left wrist. The bracelets slid away from her fingers, slipping along the girl's arm as if they were something animate—alive.

For an instant the very intensity of her gaze held the girl irresolute, tractable, willing. "Ah'll take Arthur where it's safe—but—first—you must tell me about—these." She gave the girl's arm a little shake before letting go and the bracelets rattled together.

"I—can't. I'm—afraid—" Her voice trailed off into a sobbing whisper.

"For Arthur!" There was a breathless

urgency to Tex's guarded tones as her eyes glanced from the doors to the girl and back again.

"For Arthur!" echoed the girl, a curious little trill creeping into her voice. Her teeth bit into her lower lip and her long, thin fingers twined about the bracelets. She looked down at her restless hands while her words jerked out, automatically, as if some irresistible force were driving her. "I came from a little country town—two years ago. I couldn't get work—and—Jefe found me—starving. He planted me in—Melville Hewett's home—as a maid. Then Mr. Hewett made me his ward. I guess he felt sorry for me—and—he was so good to me—I—I—didn't want to go on—but I was afraid—of—Jefe—"

"Go on with what?" interrupted Tex, every faculty strained for the slightest sound of movement from the stillness of the desert. The shadowy room, like herself, seemed to be holding its breath—waiting—waiting—

The girl sent her a lightning glance of doubt, then went on, a new note calming her voice. A note of fatality—resignation. "Go on with the plans to rob Mr. Hewett—then—I—met—Arthur—" She turned her attention to the man on the cot, seeming to forget everything else. "They have kept him under morphine—to try to make him sign—"

"Sign what?" Tex shifted her position a little, her eyes on the doors.

"The paper—that Jefe had drawn up in his own name—"

"Then Arthur inherited his father's fortune?" Tex asked the question out of the side of her mouth. Her vigilance was directed toward an almost inaudible sound just beyond the doors.

"Yes."

"And after he signs they intend to—"

"Yes—yes. Oh, God!" The girl's voice rose to a high key of hysteria.

"Sh—" Tex wheeled on her suddenly, a cautioning finger to her lips. "Quick! Tell me what you're hiding!" she whispered, her fingers pressing into the girl's arm.

For one pulsating instant the girl hesitated, her eyes as she gazed up at Tex veiled, defiant; then her shadowy lids drooped over them and she slid her bracelets up and down with agitated fingers. "It's—it's—a paper Mr. Hewett made Jefe give him—"

"Where's this paper now?"

"Arthur gave it to me—to hide—"

"Where did you hide it?"

The girl stretched her hands toward Tex in a gesture of desperate entreaty. "Oh, you *will* take Arthur where he'll get well—and be—safe?"

Tex lapsed back into her soft drawl, successfully cloaking her impatience. "Sure, honey, Ah promised, but you didn't tell me where you hid the paper."

"I hid it in—" The girl's eyes widened in terror as they shot past Tex to the doors.

Tex followed her gaze to the door nearest her. Slowly—quietly it was being pushed inward. Tex stiffened imperceptibly, her bead bag gripped tightly in both hands. Her mouth suddenly went dry and an icy finger seemed to trail along her spine.

Into the dim circle of light slid The Eel, his hands in his pockets, his crafty features set in an oily, unreadable mask.

Pancho followed him, an ugly grin pulling at his thick lips. A sharp-edged stiletto in his hand. "Better keel 'er now, eh, Jefe?" he flung at The Eel in a sort of gloating snarl.

"Naw, not that way, yuh'd get caught bang ter rights an' take a fall to the big house." The Eel stared at Tex, his deep, expressionless eyes glittering in the half-light like a snake's.

"'Lo," ventured Tex, her heart pounding against her side.

Pancho grunted, examining his knife.

The Eel glided toward Tex, a sinister smile stretching his narrow, fish-like mouth. "I got a more artistic way ter bump off them that gets in my way."

Tex's hand slid cautiously into her bag. She could shoot her way out if it was necessary but that would mean defeat. She wanted an explanation of the mystery; a confession if possible. And she felt that The Eel's tremendous ego would be his downfall. He was so cocksure of himself. So confident that he could always squirm from under any police trap set to ensnare him.

Tex forced a laugh through stiff lips. "Say, fellah, who you goin' to bump off—an' if so—why—an'—how?"

The Eel stopped a few feet from her and regarded her with a sly smirk. "Thought yuh'd like a bracelet." He brought his hand out of his pocket, gingerly holding a jade circlet toward her.

A little gasp came from the girl but the two men were too engrossed in watching Tex to heed it.

The Eel came closer, almost touching her arm with the green bangle. She made no move to take it, although an involuntary shudder ran through her body.

"For God's sake, Jefe, don't—don't!" The girl's voice shivered upward into a thin shriek.

He wheeled toward her, a grin that was baleful in its significance twitching his lips. "Aw, don't worry none, sister. I got one fer yuh, too."

The girl shrank further into the shadows, her slim fingers clutching at each other in a frenzy of fear.

Then Tex spoke softly, in a sort of deadly calm, her Texan drawl more noticeable than ever, her greenish gold eyes flashing in the wavering half-light as she held The Eel with her steady stare. "Ah—don't—want—your bracelet. Ah—never—did—like 'em. But—Ah'm kinda curious—What's in 'em?" This last was a random shot but it had the desired effect. She heard the girl's sharp intake of breath; noted the slight movement of startled surprise from Pancho. Her eyes, however, never left The Eel.

No change of expression came over his evil mask of a face. Only a trifle more expansion of his narrow chest. "I don't mind tellin' yuh because yuh ain't goin' ter live long enough ter spill it, see?" He paused dramatically to let this sink in.

Tex merely nodded and presently The Eel went on, wallowing in his own conceit. Tex smiled inwardly.

"*I* invented it, see? The hollow bracelets. First fer smugglin' in dope, then out of my own head popped another idea. Poison, from my friend the rattler. A Chink learned me how ter take it out of the snake." He stopped talking and grinned maliciously, fingering the jade bracelet.

Tex guessed that the "Chink" was himself. She stared at the bracelet, then at him, simulating awe, horror, admiration. "Lordy," she whispered, "It sure takes a heap of *brains* to figure that out!"

He seemed to expand more than ever.

Tex waited, her hand grasping the pistol inside her bag.

The Eel was so absorbed in his own achievement that he didn't notice, and Pancho's mind was diverted, watching The Eel in fascinated horror, his stiletto in his belt.

There was no movement from the girl and Tex wondered what she was doing. She didn't dare look, take her vigilant attention from Jefe. The green bangle made her feel creepy, as if a snake were actually crawling over her body. She moistened her dry lips with the tip of her tongue and forced herself a step nearer The Eel.

Instantly Pancho lunged toward her, his hand flashing to his dagger.

"Aw, lay off, will yuh," Jefe snapped irritably. "Put up yuh jack-knife." He again addressed himself to Tex. "Now I'll show yuh how I put Hewett an' yuh little dick friend out of the way." He turned the bracelet around carefully and pointed to two sharpened gold points on the inside. "Them," he explained, "represents the fangs, an' when pushed onter the arm it releases this little spring, stabbin' the flesh at the same time and the poison pours inter the holes, see?" A maniacal laugh fell from his twisting lips.

Tex shivered.

"An' yuh don't like bracelets?" He turned to the girl with a sinister grin. "But Mame here does. Don't yuh, Mame?"

The girl gave a cry of terror.

Pancho laughed and at a signal from The Eel sprang in front of Tex, grasping the girl around the waist, pinioning her wildly fighting arms to her sides and propelling her toward the advancing Jefe.

"I'll show yuh how it works," bragged The Eel, looking at Tex over his shoulder. "Then yuh'll know in advance just how yuh'll act, see?" He gripped the girl's wrist.

She wriggled and jerked in a panic of fear. "Don't! Don't!" She turned tragic, horror-stricken eyes to Tex. "For God's sake, stop him!"

Tex stood motionless, her heart thumping against her chest, her eyes riveted on the green bracelet.

The Eel paused and thrust his evil face close to the girl's. "Hand over that paper an' I'll let yuh off."

"What paper?" the girl parried faintly.

"Yuh know what paper! The one Hewett took off of me."

The girl hesitated, her apprehensive eyes darting about the room. When at last she spoke it seemed to Tex that the words were meant for her. "The—the—one where you admitted killing Hewett's partner—and threatened to kill Hewett—in the same way—if he refused to give you one hundred thousand dollars? Well—I—I—destroyed it."

"Yuh lyin'! Come clean or—" The Eel held the bracelet close to her face.

A little moan trembled from her lips and she tried to pull away; then suddenly she lifted her head and looked at The Eel squarely with a pathetic show of bravado. "Yes—I have—the—paper—but—I won't give it to you!—I promised—Arthur." The last word was a faint whisper, almost a prayer, and the thought flashed through Tex's seething mind that this girl, weak, misguided, had somehow gained a noble strength through her love for Arthur Hewett.

With his thin lips stretched over his teeth in a half snarl, The Eel sprang at the girl, grasping her wrist while Pancho laughed and held her waist with his great hairy hands.

"Yuh last chance, yuh fool," hissed Jefe. "Hand over that paper!"

The girl seemed to wilt, her head drooping forward as if too heavy to hold erect, although her words rang out clearly in the silently waiting room. "No! You—murderer!"

"Hold her arm out, Pancho," ordered Jefe, and the green bangle touched her slender clenched hand.

"Oh, God! Oh, God!" she murmured hopelessly, despairingly.

Tex eased a little to one side so that Pancho's broad back was between her and the girl.

"She's too good ter live," continued The Eel, and laughed. A sound that reminded Tex of a hyena she had once heard in the zoo—mirthless, blood-chilling.

Then with his laugh another sound mingled—slyly apologetic. A sort of muffled plop.

An expression of wonder spread over Pancho's crafty features as he loosened his hold on Mame and slumped grotesquely to the brick floor.

"What the hell?" muttered The Eel, staring at the inert body of Pancho; then he raised his eyes to a thin stream of smoke that was drifting from the mouth of a small pistol encased in Tex's steady fingers. His gaze traveled on upward until it encountered the unflinching gold-green eyes of Tex.

"Ah'd—rather take you—alive," she murmured with a faint smile.

For a moment he stared at her, expressionless, immovable; then without the slightest warning he sprang straight at her, knocking the pistol to the floor, curling his fingers about her wrist. Holding the jade bracelet lightly, gingerly, between the thumb and fingers of his right hand.

A little quiver of panic shivered through Tex, then her cold, sane reasoning came to her rescue. She held The Eel's eyes with her own while she eased her left hand toward the green menace and with a swift movement of her strong fingers snatched the bracelet from him. He lunged for it. She met the darting hand with a movement as swift as his own. His slender fingers entered the circlet; the needle-like prongs cut and tore. He gave a cry of rage and terror, clawing frantically at the poisonous manacle, but the more he pulled at it the deeper sank the sharp gold points into his punctured flesh.

His writhing agony was horrible to see. It made Tex a little sick. She stooped to recover her pistol and regarded the girl who sagged against the cot and stared at her with a dazed look in her shadowy eyes.

"In which bracelet did you hide the paper?" asked Tex unexpectedly.

The girl fingered the bangles with fluttering fingers. "This one," she answered automatically, caressing a beautifully carved circlet of mellowed ivory. "It's—Arthur's favorite."

Tex caught the girl by her shoulders and gently shook her. "Gather yourself," she admonished, not unkindly, "and go quickly to Tia Juana. Phone to my chief, J. C. Gilbert. Here's his number. Tell him Tex has sent for him. To come to Pancho's at once—and to bring a doctor." She gave the girl a little push toward the door. "Hurry!"

Slowly Mame pulled the heavy door toward her, paused and looked back at Tex with a slight pleading gesture of her slim white hands. "You'll take care of—Arthur?"

Tex nodded, still the girl lingered.

"When he wakes—you'll tell him—that—my—my—love for him—was greater—than—than—my—fear?"

A lump rose in Tex's throat and she had to swallow it before answering. "Ah'll—tell him," she said softly.

Mame left reluctantly, slipping quietly out into the darkness, closing Tex in the shrouded room.

The candles burned low, dripping over the edges of their rusty iron holders.

Tex allowed her eyes to wander around the dimly flickering room, to slide quickly over the lifeless body of Pancho, on to the twisted form of The Eel, that even in death seemed to coil, like a snake. She turned with a lightening spirit to Arthur Hewett. He was breathing evenly, calmly.

She dropped wearily into the chair near the cot and slipped her pistol back into the frayed depths of her bead bag. Her fingers touched the cool hardness of a pair of handcuffs. "Bracelets," she murmured, and a little exultant cry trickled from her throat.

Diamonds Mean Death

Thomas Walsh

THOMAS (FRANCIS MORGAN) WALSH (1908–1984) was born in New York City and received his BA from Columbia University in 1933, the same year in which he sold his first short story, "Double Check," to *Black Mask*. He sold several additional stories to *Black Mask*, one of which was honored by Joseph T. Shaw when he selected "Best Man" (October 1934) for his groundbreaking anthology *The Hard-Boiled Omnibus* (1946), which he regarded as the best work produced during his tenure as editor of *Black Mask*. Walsh went on to sell numerous stories to *Collier's*, *The Saturday Evening Post*, and *Ellery Queen's Mystery Magazine*, one of which, "Chance after Chance," won the Edgar Allan Poe Award in 1978. The first of his eleven New York police novels, *Nightmare in Manhattan* (1950), had previously won the Edgar for Best First Novel. It was filmed in the same year by Paramount as *Union Station*, starring William Holden, Nancy Olson, and Barry Fitzgerald. The exciting screenplay, for which Sydney Boehm was nominated for an Edgar, remained extremely faithful to the novel, although the locale was changed from New York's Grand Central Station to Chicago's titular crossroads, and the kidnapping victim was a blind teenage girl instead of a young boy. Walsh's *The Night Watch* (1952) also served as the partial basis, with Bill S. Ballinger's *Rafferty*, for the Columbia film noir *Pushover* (1954), which starred Fred MacMurray as a good cop gone bad, and Kim Novak in her first major role.

"Diamonds Mean Death," Walsh's last *Black Mask* story, was published in March 1936.

Diamonds Mean Death

Thomas Walsh

There is a trick even to the trade of murder.

IN THE YELLOW CONE of light thrown down by the lamp behind her, the girl's dark face looked lovely and eager, a pale, glowing cameo sharp cut against the shadows at her back.

The two men seated across the table watched her with varying emotions—Major Geoffrey Russell with very clear, slightly amused blue eyes, a smile faint on his lips, a cigarette graceful in his long fingers. Joe Keenan was not smiling; he sat at the end of the table, sharp face watch-ful, gray eyes shining coldly, with small glints of color, as if the diamonds heaped carelessly on the cloth before the girl were reflected there in pin-points of ice.

None of the three spoke. There was a slight clicking sound as the girl's fingers flashed through the stones, selecting one, holding it to the light for an instant, then passing on to the next.

In the corners of the room shadows held steady, cut in sharp patterns by the yellow glow of the lamp. Thick drapes concealed the win-dows at the far side, and occasionally Joe Keenan's restless gaze flicked to them. Heavily lifeless, they hung there without motion, and through them only a few night sounds, mournful with distance, pierced in from the woods outside.

Joe Keenan's eyes had kept steadily attentive on those drapes for the past twenty minutes, even when he had apparently been looking elsewhere. But there had been no movement from them, and no sound, and gradually his right hand had relaxed on his thigh, six inches from the automatic in his topcoat pocket.

Bending forward into the light as he lit another cigarette, Major Russell smiled at him, offered him his case. He was a bulky, muscular man of forty, rather tall, with skin tanned to a deep leathery tinge, and a short, square-cut beard of flaming auburn, through which his teeth showed very white when he smiled. Keenan took a cork-tipped cigarette from the extended case and nodded thanks; he was lighting it when a sharp breath of admiration from the girl drew his eyes.

In her hands, almost reverently, she cupped a tawny yellow diamond that seemed to Keenan as large as a hazelnut. "It's real," she said, turning to him with shining eyes. "They're all genuine, Joe. I can't really believe it."

"Genuine?" Major Russell laughed shortly; the blue eyes twinkled. "You may be sure I made quite certain of that, my dear. They're genuine, right enough."

He smiled again, reminiscently, spun the tawny diamond in the air, caught it with one hand and tossed it to the heap of others by the girl. "And if you care to buy them the lot will cost you just thirty-five thousand dollars. May I add that I think it is a very reasonable and fair price, Miss Bridges?"

"Fair?" Ellen Bridges' dark glance came up and studied him thoughtfully. "More than fair—much more, Major. It is that"—she smiled faintly in turn—"which makes one think. In open market your stones would bring close to eighty thousand dollars."

Joe Keenan's gray eyes narrowed on the Englishman. He said, "That's the queer part. You claim they're straight and yet you won't peddle

them yourself. So by selling them to Miss Bridges here you're taking a loss of forty-five thousand dollars. There are two answers to that—you're crazy or you're crooked. Me, I don't think you're crazy. Those stones are hot."

"Hot?" The bearded man frowned as if puzzled.

"Stolen," Ellen Bridges explained, with a faint smile. "You mustn't mind Joe Keenan; he has a bad habit of saying just what he thinks."

Major Russell smiled slightly. "Perfectly all right. Naturally I did not expect you to buy until I satisfied you as to the legal ownership. It is unfortunate that, strictly speaking, there is none—none that could be proved before a court of law."

His voice was clipped, British, decisive; but his eyes kept friendly enough. "The information I am about to give you is, of course, confidential. Having Mr. Keenan present is something I had not anticipated—I had preferred you came alone."

"Mr. Keenan's an old family friend," Ellen Bridges said. "And he's also an excellent private detective. My father employed him often when he was alive. I asked him to come with me tonight, Major, so if there is a fault it's mine."

"All right," the Englishman said heartily. "Perfectly all right, my dear. I must apologize for my nerves tonight. They're a bit jumpy. But to begin—" He knocked ash from his cigarette, drew on it thoughtfully, was silent a moment. "You see, I've knocked about the world a good bit in my time—never was one for standing still. A new place always called me on somehow. India, Brazil, the Sahara—I've seen them all. No regrets. A year ago this June it was Africa.

"I was knocking around the interior with no very definite object in view, just a small commission or two to keep me busy—trapping animals for zoos, that sort of thing. A living in it with luck but not much else. I was working my way over by easy stages to the coast, fed up with the existence, and anxious to see some white faces for a change.

"There were four black boys with me—four

filthy, thieving devils I could cheerfully have murdered. No other human soul within miles. It was depressing country, rocky, practically waterless, damnably hot and pretty well deserted. Then one afternoon, as we pushed through a narrow cut in the side of a hill, one of my black boys stumbled on the body of a man—a white man."

He paused to blow a long stream of smoke towards the ceiling. "He'd been there for years, I suppose, so there wasn't much left of the poor chap then. A few bones, one or two rags of clothing, and a leather pouch that the sun had caked as dry as a rock." Somberly he nodded towards the diamonds. "And they were in that pouch. I found nothing else around to give me the slightest clue to his identity.

"Anyone not entirely new to Africa could read part of the story easily. We were about a hundred miles distant from the diamond fields, in a district rather sparsely traversed, due mostly to its lack of water; and in view of the fact that it was so little traveled it seemed evident to me that our man had been trying to reach one of the northern ports secretly. The laws on I.D.B.s—illicit diamond buyers—are very strict in British Africa. This poor devil had somehow gained possession of the stones—how we do not know—and gambled his life on getting away with them." The Englishman nodded soberly. "He lost, and I'm afraid it wasn't a pleasant death."

Ellen Bridges shivered. "Dreadful."

Major Russell looked at her gravely. "All this, you understand, is pure conjecture on my part. After we reached the coast I made inquiries—judicious ones—but learned nothing at all about who the man might have been, or where he could have found the diamonds. Perhaps my moral code is twisted, but I couldn't see handing the stones over to the government as a gift. No one knew about them, I thought; certainly no one could prove ownership; and so, in the end, I held on to them myself.

"The night before I left Jo'burg my room was ransacked—trunks turned inside out, clothes tumbled around, pictures taken from the walls. One of my black boys must have had a glimpse of what the pouch contained and sold his information to some rascal in Jo'burg, perhaps with a thought of sharing the proceeds. Fortunately, however, I happened to be carrying the stones with me that night, and on the boat I had no trouble.

"Eventually I came to America to dispose of them. The morning after I landed a man came to my hotel. He'd got wind of what I was about, perhaps from the fellow who went through my room in Johannesburg. He told me coolly what I was carrying, and offered ten thousand for the lot. I refused; and on that he threatened to tell the British authorities the whole story. I threw him out and left the hotel immediately, taking this cottage as a quiet place where no one would find me. Well"—he crushed out his cigarette and looked up with a faint smile—"that's the story. If it isn't very convincing the fault is mine as narrator. The details, I assure you, are true."

Keenan's gray eyes studied him a moment. "And you never found out who this man was that came to your hotel in New York?"

"Later I did." The major pursed his lips. "Not an estimable character. A disposer of stolen goods—I believe the term is fence over here. His name was Peale. Perhaps you know him."

"Jerome Peale?" Keenan nodded. "A little. Not anyone to fool with. Bad."

"I gathered that," the major said, looking at his watch and then up at Ellen Bridges. "That is why I left the hotel. Even in Africa we have heard of your one-way rides." White teeth flashed inside the beard. "But he doesn't concern us now. Shall we consider the bargain settled?"

The girl nodded. "You'll want cash, of course. I can have it here by noon tomorrow. Will that do?"

"Excellently," the bearded man said, rising. "You see, I have neither the time nor the connections to dispose of the stones singly. It seemed best to get in touch with someone running a legitimate jewelry business—that is why I got in touch with you, Miss Bridges. Naturally you are very welcome to any profit you may make over the purchase price." He smiled, bowed. "Until tomorrow at twelve then?"

Joe Keenan rose after him, his hard gray eyes puzzled. The major's story seemed plausible enough—it might be a shade too plausible. Was that the catch, the warning, that jerked uneasily at his mind?

As he followed the girl towards the door he was frowning, unsatisfied—something in all this didn't ring true. A man would not throw forty thousand dollars to a stranger because he had no time. A man—

Somebody behind him said: "Hold it."

It was a quiet voice with a low snarling edge to it. Before Keenan the major stopped suddenly, with an instant's stiffness, so that one of his hands, halfway to the knob, froze in the air, the fingers spread, the thumb straight up. Keenan did not move; the girl gave a soft cry.

"You'll turn," the voice said. "All of you with your hands up. Over your head. And slow."

There was a closet set flush against the wall of the room they had just left. Its door was open now and a man stood there—a gaunt man with a long dark face and a mouth that twitched unpleasantly.

"Peale," Major Russell said, in an incredulous voice.

"Peale," the gaunt man repeated nastily. "Everything fine, huh? Or it was until I dug up the van that moved your trunks." His eyes widened, narrowed swiftly as Joe Keenan turned around. "Keenan—what are you doing here?" His glance swept over the girl without recognition, and the first touch of surprise in his features changed to an expression of bitter mirth. "Joe Keenan! Don't tell me the boy friend here got—"

Major Russell interrupted him in a cold voice. "You shouldn't have tried to do anything like this, Peale. I don't see what—"

"Maybe you don't," Jerome Peale snarled, dark flame spouting up in his eyes. "Maybe pretty soon you won't see anything at all. Dead men are funny that way."

Standing at the girl's right, Major Russell's blue eyes remained calm, steady, unafraid. "Killing me won't help, you know. There's—"

"Shut up!" Peale raised the automatic; his eyes blackened with hate. After a moment the Englishman shrugged, subsided. Turning slightly to Keenan, Peale went on in the same low snarl: "I had you pegged for a square guy, Joe. You have that name and everyone knows it. If the skirt's with you there's a chance for you to blow now. I'll figure you were like me; dumb enough to—"

At Keenan's left there was a flicker of motion, a blur of silver that crossed the corner of his eye too swiftly to be defined. Before him Peale swung around his automatic, with his mouth open above it twisted down and sidewise in the gaunt face. His eyes glittered, black and venomous with rage, but in the split second that it took him to bring the gun up terror spread swiftly in them, transfixing the irises, widening the lids.

There was a sharp, distinct crack, like wood snapping. It was gone in an instant, without echo. Peale stared ahead stupidly, with the terror fixed in his eyes and an irregular brown smear high up in his forehead, just under the hair. Then he swung forward stiffly, with all his body rigid, and crashed face down to the floor.

"A mad dog," Russell said, breathing softly. "He would have killed me." In his right hand there was a small pistol not as large as Keenan's palm, with a wisp of smoke drifting up from the barrel. It looked like a top, a child's cap pistol. But at five feet it could kill a man. It had, Joe Keenan thought grimly, as he gripped Peale's shoulder and turned him on his back.

The gaunt man must have died instantly. His eyes were still open, staring, his mouth open too, in surprise, in terror.

"He's dead?" Ellen Bridges whispered shakily.

Keenan rose, nodding. Through the glass upper half of the front door he could see a deserted stretch of road, with trees nodding in the night wind, quietly, on the far side. Probably the shot had not been audible outside; even if it had, there was no one there to hear it. A cottage on a lonely road on Staten Island, two miles from the nearest village, was a safe place for killing. Keenan twisted his lips sourly as the thought struck his mind that that idea had come to him earlier in the evening. A swell place for murder!

Major Russell put the small pistol in the pocket of his jacket. His voice, his actions, were calm and unexcited. "Self-defense," he said quietly. "The man was going to kill me—you both heard him say that. If you want to call the police there's a phone here."

Staring down at the dead man, Keenan shrugged his shoulders after a moment. "Peale asked for what he got. I'm not hopped up about hick cops nosing around and asking Miss Bridges a lot of questions. And they can't do him any good now."

"I had hoped you'd see it that way," Major Russell said. "I had no choice. After you leave I'll get him in my car and drop him off in some lonely stretch of woodland. Then there won't be any trouble, any questions. That way, I believe, will be wisest for ourselves and our business."

Ellen Bridges shuddered, keeping her glance away from the fixed black stare of the dead man. "Do anything," she said, gripping Keenan's arm. "But let's get out of here immediately, Joe."

The bearded man nodded, gravely calm. He held the outer door open for them, said good night quietly, and closed it without sound after they had passed through. That guy, Joe Keenan decided, had plenty of guts; through his obscure sense of dislike for the man he felt something like admiration.

In the front seat of the roadster Ellen trembled against him. She whispered: "Oh, it's horrible, death like that! One minute he was alive talking to us; and then the next—"

"Don't let it get you," Keenan told her.

"Jerome Peale wasn't a kid. He had it coming that way for a long while."

"I suppose so." She was silent a few seconds while the needle of the speedometer flickered up to fifty-five and steadied there. Then she said in a small voice: "I'm afraid I got you in this jam, Joe. I know you didn't want to come over here tonight; you only agreed to because you were afraid something might happen to me."

"Forget that," Keenan grunted. "Your father was a mighty good friend of mine."

"Is it just because of my father?" she asked softly, looking up at him. "Don't I count at all, Joe?"

Keenan shifted in his seat, looked down at her quizzically.

"You're a fresh kid that ought to be whaled. If you're asking for advice, I'll tell you not to touch those diamonds with a ten-foot pole. They smell bad even with the story we got."

"You're suspicious of everybody," the girl told him petulantly.

"After all, they don't really belong to anyone. So why shouldn't I buy them as well as someone else? If there were a legal owner, it would be different. But as it is—"

"As it is," Joe Keenan said irritably, "you won't take advice. This seems like adventure and fun, so you're going through with it. You're still young enough to think a British accent is wonderful."

"Major Russell's a gentleman," she flashed. "Of course I believe his story."

"I don't," Keenan said. "And you're still sure you know it all. I wish you luck."

"You're—you're detestable," the girl blazed. Sullenly she turned away and looked through the window, refusing to speak even on the thirty-minute ferry ride to Manhattan.

Letting her out in front of her apartment, Keenan said, "Good night." But he was not answered, and his lean face frowned after her. Women were queer people. And when the one you had to take care of was an obstinate, silly kid like that . . . He sighed. Well, it was a tough job. Joe Keenan wouldn't have touched it for money;

but his friendship for her dead father was something that could not be written off or canceled. And if she wasn't so willful, she might even be a nice kid. Then Joe Keenan caught his thoughts there with an irritated grunt, and slammed in his gear.

wenty minutes later he reached his own place. It was an old private house in the quiet upper seventies, remodeled into apartments, with a tall stoop in front and a light showing at the top behind glass vestibule doors. On the second landing he inserted a key in the lock on the left, turned it, and went in.

When he snapped on the button of the light-switch, lamps sprang instantly to life in three corners of the inner room. The light was soft, subdued, but quite clear, and the man sitting in the easy chair that faced the door, faced Joe Keenan, blinked at it once.

He was a short man, fat, wearing a derby hat steeply slanted over one ear and a blue overcoat below that. There was an automatic in his right hand that rested negligently on one arm of the chair. Keenan's steady gray eyes went over him without nervousness, without haste.

The fat man said: "Sit down. Just keep your hands away from your pockets and act sensible. We're friends, Joe—I even been sampling your Scotch. It's good."

"Next time take rye," Keenan grunted. "The Scotch is for friends. I don't lay out four bucks a fifth for punks."

The fat man said, "Okey," good-naturedly. But when he rose and backed to the window his eyes were small and watchful, and they did not shift while he felt behind him with his free hand, grabbed the shade cord and pulled it down to the bottom, then released it with a snap that sent it spinning to the top. Coming back, he held his gun close in to his side, where it could not be seen from outside.

"Look," he said. "Nobody's slippin' you the works unless you ask for it. Do what you're told and everything will be fine. There ain't anything to this unless you're dumb enough to make a break now."

In the street a car motor roared briefly and then throttled down. The front door below opened and closed, and light fast steps pattered on the stairs. In a moment the door behind Keenan opened; a young man, hard faced, dapperly dressed, came in and shut it after him.

"Frisking job," the fat man said. "From behind and careful. Don't miss anything."

In back of Keenan the second man opened his coat, ran swift fingers over him. He removed the automatic and then probed the empty shoulder-holster, patted trouser legs with a practiced deftness.

"Okey," he said, when he straightened. "Nothing on him, Feeney."

Feeney grunted. "Then get back to the car. When the street's clear honk twice and we'll go down."

Keenan took a cigarette from a box on the table, snapped a lighter against it. The fat man's pudgy face grew ugly at the action.

"Ask the next time," he growled.

"This isn't a ride?" Keenan asked.

"Uh-huh." Feeney nodded. He chuckled suddenly. "But not the kind you're thinkin'. We got nothin' against you. Keep on actin' nice and in a day or two you're turned out all rested up. Nothin' to get fretted about, Joe."

Keenan's black brows drew together. "Why?"

Feeney took a bottle of Scotch from a table drawer, put it in his overcoat pocket, and patted the flap down gently. "Company, Joe. Don't worry about why. If we wanted to jolt you it could be done here, easy and nice, with a rope around your neck and no squawk. Since we ain't doin' that you oughta see we don't want to crate you. Not unless you get tough and ask for it."

Outside a car horn honked twice. Feeney straightened the derby with his left hand and motioned with the automatic gently towards the door. They went down the steps in single file, and descended the outer stoop in the same order, meeting no one. There was a small sedan purring at the curb, with the back door open.

"In," Feeney grunted, the automatic close against Keenan's back, where the shine of it was hidden. Keenan bent and entered, with the fat man right after him; from the front seat the driver leaned back and pulled the door shut.

They drew away from the curb, swung south on Lexington Avenue, and began to slip smoothly by dark, empty streets. On Sixtieth they turned east, slipping under the black shadow of the elevated structure on Second Avenue to the ramp of the Queensboro Bridge.

Feeney was half facing him, with the gun against his side, low, hidden by both their bodies. The dark span of the bridge unrolled before them under the long line of lights; moving very fast, they flashed off the Long Island side and threaded out Queens Boulevard. It was after one, store fronts dark, pavements empty.

Joe Keenan's mind tried to consider it all calmly, without fuss. It was possible that Feeney and his friend might be Jerome Peale's men. If they were, how had they heard about his death so soon? And if he was to be killed in reprisal for Peale, why hadn't they murdered him back in his apartment, where, as Feeney had said, it could have been done quietly, safely? Thinking it over, Keenan decided they weren't Peale's men; at least it didn't seem likely. And if they weren't, what did they want him for; what were they going to do?

He couldn't hit on any answers. In the front seat, keeping the speedometer gyrating uneasily at fifty-five, the hard-faced man swung left from the Boulevard to one of the Parkways, and they raced away from monotonous rows of two-family houses to dark open stretches of woodland. An hour went by; the road lost its wide smoothness, narrowed to a single lane affair with trees crowded close on either side. Joe Keenan's sharp face tightened; his light-colored irises seemed to draw in and compact. In a day or two he'd be freed, Feeney had said. What was going

to happen during that time? What was so important that he must be kept out of the way?

His mind flashed to Ellen Bridges, to Major Russell. Were Feeney and his friend after the diamonds—and the thirty-five thousand in cash the girl was to bring to the Englishman tomorrow at twelve? For if Peale had known where the Englishman was hiding out mightn't others know too? And if they knew, if they planned— A small lump of muscle formed along his jawbone. Ellen Bridges, alone, helpless—murdered, probably, as soon as they took the money from her.

The thought roused him to a cold rush of anger, and in the wake of that, desperately and almost without hope, an insane determination. Under Feeney's careful eyes he got a cigarette from his pocket, then fumbled for a match.

Before them the road swung up the hill in a sharp S curve, indicated by a sign that flashed past his eyes. In the front seat the hard-faced man had not yet circled the wheel for the first turn; he was bent slightly forward, the base of his skull showing under close-cropped hair. Striking the match, Keenan saw it, and his plan clicked into place in his brain. Desperate, insane maybe—but a chance.

Feeney watched him, wary, alert, as the tiny match flame speared up through the darkness. Holding the match cupped, his left hand concealing the right, Keenan got his middle finger under the sliver of wood and rested it there. When the man in front slowed for the turn—

He slowed. Keenan lifted his face from his cupped hands, leaving the match still burning, and blew a thin funnel of smoke casually upward. The wariness in Feeney's eyes relaxed—and at that instant Joe Keenan's middle finger flipped the burning match straight between his eyes. With the same movement his left hand swung out and down with the weight of his body behind it to crash solidly against the base of the driver's skull.

Blinded by the match, the fat man fired twice. But Keenan's lean body had flung itself forward and down the instant before the shots, to its knees against the front seat. Feeling the breath of the shots on his neck he whirled and brought his right fist up slashing, from the floor to the point of the fat man's chin. It was a terrific blow that almost lifted Feeney completely out of his seat; his eyes lost focus, lost consciousness, as he slumped limply back.

It all happened in a moment, in a blur of motion, as the car yawed across the road. Keenan spun to the wheel, knocking the sprawled out form of the driver from it as the concrete guarding wall on the left side of the road shot into view. They crashed with a grating scream of sound from the front fender as it crumpled like paper against the solid barrier. Keenan was slammed forward, bruising his chest on the front seat; glass fell in a showery tinkle as one of the headlights smashed. Then he yanked back the brake, and they stopped.

A car topped the hill and raced down towards them as he clambered out to the running-board. Ten feet off it slowed, and a startled white face looked out at Keenan, at the automatic he picked from the floor, where the fat man had dropped it. Then the car was past, racing on again with an accelerated roar of sound.

The fat man, Feeney, was moaning, rolling his head loosely from side to side as Keenan pulled him out. The driver was still out cold, and Keenan laid them flat on the grass, by each other, and went back to the car. When he slipped behind the wheel the motor responded readily enough, and he put it in reverse, circled it in the road, and left it facing back the way they had come.

As he got out of the car again, Feeney was sitting dazedly up, propped by his arms. He cursed sullenly, indistinctly, as he rubbed his jaw. The coldness in Keenan's gray eyes hardened and became more evident; looking up, Feeney saw that coldness and stopped suddenly.

Keenan said in a quiet voice: "That's fine. Be nice, fellow. Who wanted me snatched? Who hired you and your friend for the job?"

"Go to hell," the fat man snarled, with an attempt at bravado. He tried to hold Keenan's stare and failed; after a moment his own flinched uneasily away. He began to lick his lips.

Holding the grip of the automatic, Keenan weighed the barrel in his free hand. He went on in his quiet tone: "Maybe you've never been pistol whipped. It isn't nice. Me, I'd talk. Who hired you?"

Feeney did not answer. Joe Keenan's eyes glittered and grew small. He asked again, curiously soft: "Who hired you?"

"Listen," the fat man wheezed, his eyes pathetically earnest. "I never had a thing against you, Keenan. I told you that. We weren't going to hurt you. Honest to—"

Down the road there was a faint motor sound that grew rapidly louder. As Keenan turned two motorcycles whined around the curve of the hill and squealed to a stop opposite the parked car. A big state trooper swung off one and crossed the road cautiously, his partner coming at the car from the side.

"Drop your gun," he told Keenan. "What's going on here?"

Keenan obeyed, gave his story briefly. The auto that had raced by five minutes before would have reported them in the next town, of course. And if he had had only five minutes longer with the fat man—Feeney would have talked; he'd have been glad to. And now nothing had been cleared up; the motive behind it all remained as vague, as apparently pointless as ever.

In the troopers' barracks Keenan gave his story again, presented credentials. But it was five o'clock before he was free to go, and the fat man and his friend had been led away to cells. They both kept obdurately silent; they knew nothing, could tell nothing.

In the chilly station, where he had to wait two hours for the earliest commuters' train, Keenan went over it again in his mind. And presently it began to hang cloudily together. It was robbery, of course; get him out of the way and in the morning they could have picked up Ellen Bridges easily enough, after she had drawn the money from the bank.

But who besides Russell knew of that? Of course, there was no surety that Peale had come to the house alone; perhaps some of his accomplices had been there, staying in hiding until he and the girl had gone. They could have murdered Russell last night and taken the stones; they could even be waiting there at the cottage for the girl to come.

On the train he dismissed it tiredly. The vital part, the thing that would have made it jell, was missing. And, without that, it was useless racking his brains. At his own apartment he showered quickly, shaved, and changed his clothes. Then he got out his roadster and met Ellen Bridges at her store on upper Fifth Avenue.

She greeted him coolly, and said she did not need his help. Without answering her, Joe Keenan grasped her arm and drew her out to his roadster. He drove to the bank and went inside with her, studied the street outside carefully before allowing her to emerge again, for that disturbing sense of uneasiness still clung to him. But nothing untoward happened; they wound their way downtown and caught the eleven-o'clock ferry. On the ride across Keenan told her the events of the previous night, and before he was half through her coolness vanished in a swift rush of solicitude.

"They might have killed you, Joe. You shouldn't have—"

"But they didn't," he pointed out. "And I've got a hunch that I've figured the lay all wrong. I'm going to drop you on the other side, Ellen. If they've killed Russell and are waiting there—"

She said, firmly, "I'm going with you. And it's not going to do you the slightest bit of good to argue about it."

It didn't. Three-quarters of an hour later, when he stopped the car before Major Russell's bungalow, she was still sitting determinedly by his side. In a moment the major himself appeared in the doorway, younger, more

somber, against the morning sunlight. He bowed to Ellen, gave Keenan a quick, hard grip. Leading a way to an inner room he took a chamois bag from a wall safe and upended it on the table. "The stones are there, my dear. If everything else is ready—"

The girl nodded. "I have the cash. We were afraid something had happened to you, Major. I was nervous all the way down."

"To me?" White teeth flashed in a smile. "Why should it? No doubt that unpleasantness last night worked on your mind. Now if you would like to examine the stones—" He pushed them across the table to her.

Keenan watched him, the uneasiness, the sense of mistrust, moving in his mind again. When the girl began: "That's hardly—" he cut in emotionlessly: "Examine them."

"By all means." The major's voice was hearty. "We must be businesslike, my dear." His hand flung out, tossed over the huge tawny diamond Keenan had seen the night before. "Begin on that beauty."

Looking at Keenan, the girl flushed angrily. "Of course I know, Major, that—"

"Examine them," Joe Keenan said.

She gave him a cold, annoyed glance. Major Russell bowed, his blue eyes amused. "Perfectly all right, my dear. Mr. Keenan is merely being a good business man. Please do as he suggests."

Her head bent for a long moment; when she raised it again and put away her glass her tone was apologetic. "Of course it's the one I saw last night." From the leather portmanteau at her side she drew neatly rectangular folds of bills. "And here is your money. Count it if you wish."

The major bowed gallantly. "I never doubt a lady, my dear. Perhaps"—his eyes dwelt with a thin trace of mockery on Keenan—"I am not what you call a smart guy over here." Carelessly he riffled fingers through the heap of diamonds, and Keenan, his gaze lowered, watched them, fascinated by their flickering swiftness. "You may get in touch with me this week at the Savoy. I'll do all I can to help in case of any difficulty."

Ellen Bridges flashed him a smile, but Joe

Keenan's sharp face was set in an ugly scowl. Smart guy! Last night Jerome Peale had said something like that. What was it? He had figured Joe Keenan was like him, dumb enough to—Russell had shot him there, before he could finish. Dumb enough to what?

he major was smiling at him, offering his hand. Joe Keenan ignored it. He asked out of straight lips: "You're a good shot, Major?"

Russell smiled faintly, his eyes puzzled. "Tolerable. I've won a match here and there. Nothing spectacular."

"Yeah." Keenan nodded slowly. "You're a good shot, maybe a swell shot. Last night you killed Peale, although a good shot wouldn't have had to do that. He could have shot Peale's arm, his side."

"Forgive me," Russell said coldly, "if I don't see the point."

"You'll see it," Keenan said grimly. "You killed Peale because he was going to talk. He was saying he figured I had been dumb enough to—then you shot him. If he'd finished I think he'd have said dumb enough to let you fool me the way you did him. And you killed Peale to shut his mouth, not to protect yourself. Winging him in the arm would have done that."

Gravely, without surprise, the Englishman faced him, a big man, tanned and quiet, calm, steady eyed. "So you see a catch," he said. "Are you sure there is one?"

Keenan growled: "It was there from the start. You're pretty fast with your hands. I've seen worse sleight of hand men on the stage. Maybe you were in that racket at one time but this paid you better. Every time you pulled it off it meant thirty or forty grand. I never figured out how you could get a gun out so fast while Peale was swinging his around; but say it was in your sleeve—it was plenty small enough to fit there—and a decent magician could flick it out faster than light.

"And a decent magician," he went on, "could let Miss Bridges look at the big diamond now, the genuine one, and then switch it with a fake that looked exactly like it when you took it away from her to replace it in the pile. Satisfy us that one was good and you knew we wouldn't bother to look at the rest."

There was a pause. Ellen Bridges' dark eyes flickered from Keenan to the bearded man, to the stones. She reached out to the tawny one and silence lasted for three breaths. Then she cried: "Oh, it isn't the same. It's paste!"

Keenan's smile was grim. "A swell racket, Russell. You had two ways to work it. The first was to get rid of me and slug the girl when she came here alone with the money. The other was to switch the stuff, and when your punks missed up on me last night you had to work it this way to get the money. You fooled Peale and lots of others. When he started to squawk last night, kidding me for being a smart guy before he gave the inside, probably, on how you had switched the stuff on him too, you fed him a steel slug to shut his mouth."

Russell said: "Yes," in a clipped, hard sound. His eyes had lost all depth, become pinpoints of blued metal. His right arm was before him, raised slightly, the sleeve hanging loose. "You are right. I'm fast with my hands, Keenan—fast enough to kill you before you can wink an eye. That's why you and the girl will get up very carefully and back into the closet. That's why you'll keep your hands over your head."

Russell was standing close against the other side of the table. Keenan sat directly across from him, carelessly slouched in his chair, long legs doubled.

"Get up," Russell said softly. "You and the girl. Don't move your hands."

"Please," Ellen Bridges whispered. "Do what he says, Joe. The money isn't—"

Joe Keenan remained still. One of his hands was on the table—the other, the right, was hooked by a thumb in the top pocket of his coat. His gray eyes, narrowed and hard, watched Russell's face. He did not answer him.

There was a silence with only the sound of

the girl's breathing in it. There was something impassive but alert and poised in the stiff erectness of Russell's body; he looked at Keenan for a long moment, expressionlessly. He said: "You're a fool," and his lips drew back slightly, tautly, into the lean brown cheeks.

Keenan saw the flicker in his eyes that preceded motion. Keenan made a little sidewise shrug as if about to get out of the chair. Watching Russell, his long legs, beneath the table, straightened, spread a little. Then, suddenly, he shot his body, feet first, beneath the table.

Keenan's toes hooked around Russell's ankles. He jerked inward, and the Englishman slammed over backward on to the floor.

Keenan scrambled upward, pushing with his left hand, the table before him as lead smacked lightly into the wood. Keenan flashed a glance around the table edge. Russell, on his back, the tiny pistol in his right hand, swung it for a second shot, and again the lead smacked without weight into the table. Keenan flipped his hand out and the big automatic spouted flame.

The blue eyes emptied suddenly of light, of life—for an instant they looked back at Keenan with a blank, dead glitter. Then he collapsed fast, limply, and did not move at all.

Keenan's lean dark face stared down at him. He put his automatic back and got up and crossed to the phone in one corner.

"Police headquarters," he said, into the mouthpiece, winking solemnly at Ellen Bridges' white face over it.

It was late afternoon when he got into the roadster with the girl, reversed it around the police car parked outside it, and swung out to

the road. Shaking a little, she pressed into his arm.

"You—you're a fool," she whispered, looking up at him. "He might have shot you—killed you. I'm still shivering inside. Why did you do it?"

"Why?" Keenan moved his shoulders slightly. "Maybe just because I didn't like the guy. There was a contraption inside his sleeve that held the small pistol—all he had to do was jerk his elbow and a spring snapped the gun down into his hand faster than you could watch it. An outfit like that is part of the equipment of a sleight of hand man, only usually guns aren't in them. Close enough a toy like that could kill any man the way it killed Peale."

"It could have killed you," Ellen Bridges said softly. "And the money wouldn't have meant that much to me, Joe."

Keenan said: "It wasn't the money. With an outfit like that, a man didn't have a chance. Major Russell was a rat. There's just one thing to do with a rat, Kitten. I figured that staring him down like that would knock him off balance, make him panicky. When Russell was on the short end of a hundred to one chance he was cool; and a heel like him had had it all in his favor so long that he'd forgotten what it was like to play it even up."

Shivering, Ellen Bridges came close into his shoulder, put her hand over his on the steering wheel.

"And it wasn't me?" she asked, after a while. "Not even a little bit?"

Keenan looked down at her, his gray eyes amused.

He said: "That's one you have to figure out, Kitten."

Murder in the Ring
Raoul Whitfield

RAOUL (FAUCCONIER) WHITFIELD (1896–1945) was born in New York City and traveled with his family extensively, spending much of his youth in the Philippines. During World War I, he served with the U.S. Army Air Corps in France as a pilot. When he returned to the United States, he went to learn the steel business (he was related to Andrew Carnegie), then worked as a newspaper reporter and began to write fiction for pulp magazines. He used his flying background to write aviation stories for the pulps in the early 1920s, then sold his first mystery to *Black Mask* for the March 1926 issue. He went on, in a serious burst of prolificity, to write nearly ninety stories, under his own name and as Ramon Decolta, for *Black Mask* between that first effort and his last one, only eight years later, for the February 1934 issue. During that time, he also wrote five mystery novels: three under his own name, *Green Ice* (1930), *Death in a Bowl* (1931), and *The Virgin Kills* (1932); and two under the pseudonym Temple Field, *Five* (1931) and *Killer's Carnival* (1932). As Whitfield, he wrote four juveniles, all with aviation backgrounds: *Wings of Gold* (1930), *Silver Wings* (1930), *Danger Zone* (1931), and *Danger Circus* (1933). His *Black Mask* story "Man Killer," which was published in the April 1932 issue, was filmed as *Private Detective 62* by Paramount in 1933; Michael Curtiz was the director, and the comic crime story starred William Powell and Margaret Lindsay.

"Murder in the Ring" was published in the December 1930 issue.

Murder in the Ring

Raoul Whitfield

A fighter with promise of the big money and a gang that wants the split.

GUS MONKLY WATCHED Pardo crowd the blond slugger into a neutral corner, work his huge arms like battering rams. The Garden crowd was on its feet—the arena was shrill with sound. Across the ring Gus saw Eddie Feese, his white face twisted as he shouted at his blond fighter. There was a sudden silence from the crowd—Gus got his eyes on Pardo again. The seven-foot giant was stepping back. He was grinning. Mike Connell sagged forward as Pardo backed away. He went to his knees.

The crowd roared again. Pardo lowered his guard and glanced towards Gus. The manager's face twisted with fear. Connell pitched upward and forward. The referee had his back turned to the blond fighter; he was waving Pardo to a neutral corner.

Connell ripped up a short right arm, and then the referee was between the two men. Pardo muttered something as the referee stepped away. The dark-haired fighter shoved a huge right glove in Connell's face, stepped around to the right. Connell was trying to weave, but he was groggy. He led with a left that was short, threw over a hard right. The right glanced off Pardo's left shoulder. The giant shot his own right, straight for the chin.

It landed with a sound that could be heard all over the Garden. Connell went down like a slaughtered steer. Resin dust rose from the canvas. The referee waved Pardo back. Once again the big, black-haired fighter glanced towards Gus Monkly. The manager swore at him, but his curses were lost in the roar of the crowd.

Pardo backed into the wrong corner, and the referee pointed to a neutral one. Pardo stared stupidly at the man in white. Then he went across the ring to the neutral corner. The referee stood beside Connell, picked up the pounded count from Snyder. At "ten" he straightened, raised his arms high, pointed towards Pardo. The crowd yelled wildly.

Gus Monkly stood up and frowned at Jerry Gold. Gold grinned and said in a husky voice:

"He's put you in line, Gus—the next shot will do the trick. Good for—a half million if he gets by Bolley."

Gus kept on frowning towards the winner of the final go. Pardo stood in the center of the ring, grinned sheepishly, and tapped his gloves together, above his head. The crowd cheered and jeered. Seconds dragged the unconscious figure of Mike Connell from the resin, towards his corner. The radio announcer stood at the edge of the ring and shouted at Pardo.

Gus muttered grimly: "What the hell—that palooka's too dumb to talk at a mike! Hey, Berry!"

Lou Berryman stood inside the ropes and grinned at Pardo's manager. Gus kept on frowning.

"Get him out of there!" he shouted at Berryman. "Get him downstairs, Berry. Stay along with him—get him out of there!"

Berryman nodded and went over near the towering Pardo. He grabbed him by a wrist and pointed towards the exit corner of the ring. The radio announcer started to rave at Berryman. Gus Monkly fought his way to a spot close to the mike. He leaned down, and the announcer grinned at him. He lifted the mike high.

Gus breathed heavily through his nose. "This is Giant Pardo—" he announced thickly. "I just—wanna say—he give me—a sweet scrap, he did! Mike's a good boy—but I guess I was—better! I'm gonna be—fightin' the champ yet—s'long folks!"

Gus stepped away from the microphone. The announcer glared at him.

"What the hell's the idea?" he muttered. "You can't get away with that stuff!"

Monkly narrowed his beady little eyes. "No?" he questioned. "Lay off, boy. Didn't you get what you wanted? They won't know the difference. Pardo—he can't talk. He's a scrapper."

He turned away, with the announcer muttering at him. A short, red-faced individual gripped him by the arm.

"What do you mean—that bum's a scrapper?" he asked. "Better take him out in the sticks for a while, Gus. It'll be healthier."

Gus grinned at the short one. "Want a piece of him?" he asked. "Like hell you don't. I'll cut you forty percent of him—for fifty grand."

Charlie Russel threw back his red face and laughed. Then suddenly he stopped laughing.

"If he gets by Bolley—come and see me, Gus."

The manager swore. "Do I look that way?" he snapped. "If he gets by Bolley come and *try* to see me. The line forms on the right."

He fought his way towards the aisle that led to the dressing rooms. The Garden crowd was using the exits. Mike Connell was being carried through the ropes. Eddie Feese caught Gus's eye and called over to him.

"It was—just a lucky one."

Gus Monkly chuckled hoarsely. "Sure," he yelled back. "Lucky Pardo didn't hit him real hard!"

He went along the aisle, grinned at the big Garden copper who kept the crowd moving in another direction. As he went past the officer, Riley said:

"You got a money fighter, Gus. All yours?"

Gus nodded. "All mine, Irish," he replied. "I'm going to clean up on him."

The copper grunted. "If he gets by Bolley," he corrected.

The manager chuckled again. "They can't stop that right, Irish," he stated hoarsely. "It's worse than that dynamite Cotti serves over the bar. They can't stop him, Irish."

The Garden copper shrugged. "I've seen a lot of 'em stopped in here, Gus," he said. "But I hope you're right. It's a sweet spot for a clean-up."

Gus Monkly went along the corridor that led to the dressing rooms. Humans spoke to him, patted him, grinned at him. Gus grinned back. He used words in reply. But he wasn't caring much. He was thinking about Pardo. A palooka with a punch. A big guy he'd grabbed at the right time. He tapped on the door of Pardo's dressing room—Berryman opened it. Gus went inside and Berryman slammed the door in the faces of the three or four guys.

Pardo sat on the edge of the training table and grinned at the manager.

"Not so rotten, eh?" he said in a voice that was husky and flat. "He ain't dead?"

Gus Monkly frowned at his fighter. "He damn' near finished you," he snapped. "You got to cut out looking at me every time you knock a guy off his feet, see?"

Pardo looked hurt. He held huge, taped hands close together and looked down stupidly at them. He weighed two hundred and sixty-four—and towered above the handlers crowded into the dressing room. He had thick lips and dumb, dark eyes.

Gus looked at Berryman and said: "Get him fixed up right—and let him feed the way he likes. There'll be a crowd hanging around the lobby to see him come out. Go out that way and stroll around a little. I'll see you tomorrow at ten, at the hotel."

He turned his back on the men in the room, moved towards the door. Before he reached it he faced Pardo and grinned at the fighter.

"That wasn't so rotten, Big Boy," he said. "But remember—Bolley won't let you get him on the ropes like Mike did."

Pardo made a hoarse sound with his lips. He swung the upper part of his huge body from side to side, showed broken teeth, grinned. He flicked his broken nose with the back of a huge hand.

"I'll make a bum outa Bolley," he muttered.

Gus said: "Yeah? Well, ain't that nice! We ain't got him yet, Big Boy."

Pardo grinned. "That's your job," he said. "You get him—I'll kill him."

Gus whistled softly. "Sure, sure," he agreed, and went from the dressing room.

When he got in the corridor again he moved slowly towards a Forty-ninth Street exit. He lighted a cigar and swore softly.

"I get him—and the Big Boy kills him!" he breathed to himself. "Now, *that* ain't just what I'd call dumb."

CHAPTER II

erryman ran stubby fingers over his bald head and watched the swinging doors of the speakeasy nervously. The doors separated a narrow hallway from the bar and the few tables along the side wall. Berryman took the fingers away from his head and tapped the surface of the table. Gus Monkly sipped his beer and shoved a cigar around between his narrow lips. The half-moon scar on his right cheek twitched a little more than usual, and his beady eyes were a little brighter than at most times.

Berryman said: "Bolley'll lick him, sure as hell. Jeez—but I hate to see that coin get away from us, Gus."

The manager grinned at Pardo's chief second. He said in his husky, flat voice:

"Yeah—away from *us*? How do *you* cut in, Berry?"

The second showed yellow teeth in a swift grin. He said very softly:

"Be wise, Gus—hand over a piece to me. It'll be easier."

Monkly sat up a little in his chair and moved his head forward. He stopped sipping the beer. His beady eyes got narrow.

"Let's get it over with, Berry," he said in a hard tone. "You've got somethin' on your mind. It's been there a week or so. Spill it loose."

The second kept tapping on the dirty table

surface and watching the swinging doors. Gus leaned forward a little more.

"Get it out, Berry!" he advised. "You're a pretty expensive second for me to carry."

A little red went out of Berryman's face. He got very quiet.

"I'm pretty cheap, Gus," he corrected. "I'm cheap as hell."

The swinging doors opened; a short, plump blonde came in. She spoke to the bartender, waved her left hand towards the table at which Gus and Berryman sat. Her right arm was held close to her side. She walked over, and Gus kicked out a chair. He didn't speak.

Berryman said: "Hello, Edna—where's Hurry?"

The blonde looked at Gus and didn't answer the second. She leaned towards the manager and said cheerfully:

"That was a nice scrap your wop put up last night. Maybe he's a champ, eh?"

She laughed without looking happy. There was too much color on her face skin and the wrong shade on her lips. She had dull gray eyes, and they were too black underneath.

Gus said: "Maybe, yeah."

The girl made the laughing sound again. She looked at Berryman and answered his question.

"Hurry'll be along pretty quick. He had to make a trip to Philly, after the scrap."

Gus Monkly sucked in his breath and reached for the beer. The girl said:

"Yeah, I'll have something. Damn' nice of you two chiselers to think of it!"

Berryman called the waiter. The girl ordered whiskey and White Rock. Gus said in a tone that was too soft:

"What do you mean—chiselers?"

The blonde smiled without parting her rouged lips.

"I figured maybe you might not sell Hurry the hunk he's counting on," she said slowly.

Gus Monkly frowned at her and stretched his arms. He stopped frowning, grinned.

"You talk too damn' much, Edna," he said. "I'm out of beer, anyway."

She nodded. "How much have you made on that wop, Gus?" she said softly.

Gus looked at his fingernails and said that he'd taken a bad trimming on the World Series games. Berryman watched the swinging doors and said nothing. The girl kept her eyes on Monkly and smiled. Her smile wasn't too pretty.

"Well, you get the idea," she said. "When Hurry parks himself close to you—don't stall. What he's looking for is the answer."

Gus said disagreeably: "I don't know what you're gabbing about, Edna. If Hurry's got the hunch that—"

He stopped. The swinging doors moved and a man came through. He came through slowly. He was a big man, with broad shoulders and a moon face. He looked a lot like Paul Whiteman. Berryman got up and pulled over a chair from another table. Gus straightened up and got a smile on his face. The blonde said:

"Gus has been worried about you, Hurry."

The big man moved towards the table. He didn't move his arms as he walked, and his pace was slow. He smiled gently.

"Well, ain't that nice," he stated in a homey tone. "I don't like having people worried about me."

He sat down, and when the waiter brought the blonde her whiskey and White Rock he ordered the same. He turned his small eyes on Gus and chuckled. He chuckled like a traveling salesman about to tell a story.

"Maybe that guy can fight, Gus," he said. "Maybe he can get past Bolley."

Gus widened his eyes and looked surprised. "Don't be that way, Hurry," he said softly. "Giant Pardo—fight? Quit kiddin'—Bolley'll kill him."

Hurry smiled almost gently and took his eyes away from the beady ones of Monkly. He looked down at the rigid right arm of the girl.

"How's the arm, Kid?" he asked.

Edna Harms shook her head. She sipped whiskey and said slowly:

"I hate gettin' that slug from a guy that was quittin' you, Hurry. Maybe I'll be able to swing it again sometime. The doc ain't sure."

Hurry stopped smiling and said to Gus:

"Remember the afternoon the Kid took that slug, Gus?"

Gus Monkly's narrow lips twitched. He remembered the afternoon well enough. There had been a lot of times he would have liked to forget it. He said to Hurry:

"Listen—I picked the wop up when I worked loose from Chi. He's dumb, Hurry. He's just a little too dumb. Mike almost came back and finished him tonight. The referee happened to be in the way."

Hurry Lassen tapped the leather of his right shoe on the wood beneath the table. He let his moon face grin but he talked hard.

"*I* happen to be in the way—right now, Gus."

The manager wet his lips with his tongue, looked at Lou Berryman. He said in a voice that was a little strained:

"I've only got forty percent of him, Hurry. Berry's got forty. A guy named Langdon's got the rest. He greased me so that I could get the Big Boy away from the little lake town where I found him. He runs a small club there."

Hurry sat back in his chair and looked at the drink the waiter had brought. He whistled a little. The girl looked at him.

"He's lyin', Hurry," she said in a tone that had a lot of hate in it.

Gus turned his head towards her and said in a nasty voice:

"Now you keep out of this, Edna. It ain't healthy to lie to Hurry, and I know it."

Lassen raised his eyebrows and looked at Lou Berryman. He said in a voice that was half amused:

"So you've got a forty percent cut in this Giant Pardo, eh?"

Berryman nodded. He tried to smile. Gus spoke softly.

"Berry's been pretty nice with me, Hurry. I gave him the cut cheap. But we didn't figure the Big Boy would even scrap in the Garden ropes."

The girl laughed bitterly. "They're both lyin', Hurry," she said. "They blundered into a money fighter—that big bozo will slam Bolley down. The next scrap will mean half a million.

It'll be with the champ—and the champ's making a come-back. An outdoor shot, Hurry."

Hurry's moon-like face stopped smiling. He nodded his head slowly.

"Want to sell your forty percent, Berryman?" he asked in a cold tone.

The second glanced towards Gus. Hurry followed the glance with contempt in his eyes. Gus yawned and reached for a cigarette. Berryman shook his head.

"It's a gamble," he said shakily. "He might take Bolley—then my cut would be worth plenty. Or he might get licked and go hitting the sticks again. It's a gamble."

"Once in a while," Hurry said slowly, "I like to gamble. Twenty-five grand for your forty."

Berryman looked at Gus again. The moon-faced one stopped tapping his foot on the wood of the floor, leaned across the table and got big fingers around the gray-striped tie that the second wore. He jerked Berryman's shoulder and head towards him.

"You dirty liar!" he snapped coldly. "You don't *hold* a cut on that slugger!"

Berryman's face got white. Gus Monkly got to his feet, shoving back his chair. The blond girl swung around and kept her left arm low.

"You be good!" she warned. "I'll give you the works quicker than hell—"

Hurry Lassen raised his right hand and closed the fingers. He struck without much effort, but the blow sounded as though Berryman's jaw was broken. The second slipped off the right side of his chair and hit the wood of the speakeasy heavily. Beyond the swinging doors someone swore loudly; there was the metallic sound of a bar dropping against steel.

Gus kept his beady eyes on the girl. He didn't speak. Hurry got up from his chair and wiped his right-hand knuckles with the fingers of his other hand. On the floor, Berryman groaned.

The girl said: "He had that comin', Hurry. How about Gus?"

A man with a mop of black hair swung open the doors and started to talk. Hurry turned around and the man stopped talking. He said, after a few seconds' silence:

"Hell—I didn't figure you were in, Hurry. I was in back when you—"

Lassen nodded his head and smiled. "Keep that bar on the door until I get through," he said.

The waiter stood back of the polished wood and kept his eyes on Hurry. Gus looked at the girl.

"Take that rod off me, Edna," he breathed. "I don't get this slamming down—"

Lou Berryman pulled himself to his feet, and kept his hands over his face. Hurry said sharply:

"Burke!"

A medium-sized man with gray hair and a brown-skinned face came in through the swinging doors. Hurry smiled at him, but kept his eyes on Berryman.

"Get Berry's rod," he ordered. "Take him in back and stay with him. Let him wash his face, but don't let him use brains. That is, if he has any."

Burke elbowed the second away from the table. Hurry Lassen said pleasantly to Gus Monkly:

"Sit down—put your hands out where I can see them. Keep that rod in your lap, Edna. I got a question you didn't hear the first time. You didn't hear it—and Berry didn't have the right answer."

Gus Monkly lifted an empty beer glass with fingers that didn't shake, and tried to moisten his thin lips. He set it down and smiled at Hurry.

"You can't get a cut in on Pardo—not by slugging," he said.

Hurry leaned his broad shoulders and big head across the table surface. He said coldly:

"The beer racket got too tough for you, Gus. And when you pulled out you left me holding the bag. We needed guts and guns—and you took a little of each with you. You cost me money. I figured on getting some of it back. I'll gamble for it. Twenty grand for a forty percent cut-in on Pardo."

Gus swore. "You just offered Berry twenty-five grand," he stated grimly.

The round-faced one grinned. "*He* didn't have it to sell," he replied. "And it was different—five minutes ago."

The manager shrugged. "If Pardo loses to Bolley, he won't be worth twenty grand to you. I don't get it all, Hurry. The big boy gets his share."

The girl laughed. Hurry kept on grinning.

"I'll bet you treat him square," he said mockingly. "You get sixty percent of what's left after you settle with him, Gus—I get forty. That guy you said got twenty—he don't. I've got a good shyster we can get tonight—he'll fix the papers."

Gus narrowed his little eyes on Lassen's. He shook his head.

"What I've got of that palooka—I'm keeping," he said slowly. "I don't owe you anything, Hurry. I played with you—and I quit clean. I dug up Pardo. He's dumb as hell. What he knows, I taught him."

The blonde chuckled. "And he's still dumb as hell!" she muttered.

Hurry nodded agreeably. "Just the same," he said quietly, "I've got a hunch he's going to take Bolley."

Gus shook his head. "We may pick up a few grand in the sticks, after Bolley takes *him*," he said. "But you'd be making a bad buy-in, Hurry."

Hurry lighted a cigarette, and started tapping the floor with a foot again. Gus was getting nervous. The girl said:

"Take him in back and give him the works, Hurry. He's lyin'—and he's yellow. He got me this slug in the arm—"

The moon-faced one shook his head. He smiled at the manager.

"You were slow shiftin', Kid," he said. "Gus used to be real fast at the wheel. We got out of places in a hurry—when Gus was workin' with us."

There was a little silence. The blonde shifted around and swore.

"Giant Pardo looks good," she said. "I've seen a flock of big boys. Get your cut, Hurry. Gus is a rat."

The manager swung on the blonde. "The next slug won't get you in the arm, Edna," he stated coldly. "You hate out loud. Not so good."

Lassen frowned. "Gus is all right, Kid," he told the girl. "It would be just too bad if his big boy didn't get inside the ropes with Bolley."

The manager sat back in his chair and kept his eyes on Hurry's. His hands were on the surface of the table, near the beer glass.

"If anything happens to Pardo—I'll know who made it happen," he said slowly.

Hurry tilted his chair away from the table and looked pleased with himself.

"Sure—but will you be able to *prove* it?" he mocked.

Gus sucked in his breath sharply, leaned forward and spoke in a hard, low voice.

"You keep off, Hurry. I'm square with you. I'm gamblin' on the Giant—and I'm playin' it alone. You stay outside, see?"

The big man leaned back and nodded. He spoke in a pleasant voice.

"You got a week to fix me up, Gus. I'm staying near here, and Callahan can tell you where. I'll see that he does. I'm paying twenty grand for a forty percent share of your take on Giant Pardo. I don't care how much your take is. It's plenty, I know that. I'll gamble that your boy gets the big shot with the champ. If you don't see it my way—"

He shrugged. Gus's voice got a little high.

"You lay off Pardo!" he said. "If you fix him so he can't—"

He stopped as Hurry shoved back his chair slowly and got to his feet. The blonde threw a neck piece over her left arm and hand, got up. She said softly:

"Better be good, Gus. You might be takin' the count yourself. It ain't so easy to get over the ropes—"

Gus Monkly spoke through lips that were pressed together.

"I ain't inside the ropes—"

Hurry Lassen said from a spot beside the swinging doors:

"No? Well, do some thinking, Gus."

He went outside. The girl followed him. The waiter came around and looked at Gus.

"How about the drinks?" he asked.

The manager paid for them, got up and went into the back room. Burke was gone; Berryman was holding a wet rag to his jaw. He said thickly:

"That dirty—killer—"

Gus swore softly. He said: "You stay here— I'll get you a drink. We've got to watch ourselves, Berry. It don't look so good."

Lou Berryman cursed thickly. Gus Monkly went back along the bar and ordered two drinks. The waiter frowned at him when he set them down, glanced towards the table at which the four of them had been seated.

"They come tough in Chi," he observed. "That Lassen—he don't feel good tonight."

Gus lifted the drinks and smiled with his beady eyes on the yellow-red liquid:

"He might be feelin' worse," he said slowly, "*some* night!"

CHAPTER III

Little Andy came into Bryant's gym and stood near the mats piled along the wall. He watched Giant Pardo swinging lazily at a punching bag, moved his eyes towards the figure of Gus Monkly. Pardo's manager stood alone, a short distance from a group of sports writers who were watching the big fighter.

Little Andy was small; he had red hair and blue, watery eyes. They went to the slightly crouched form of Pardo. He smiled.

"Big brute," he breathed. "But the slugs fix 'em all."

He leaned against a mat standing on end, half rolled. After a few minutes Gus Monkly called to his fighter.

"All right, Giant—that'll do. Get a shower and rub. I'll see you around here. Make it fast."

Pardo stopped his slow-motion punching and

turned towards his manager. He grinned. Gus looked towards the wall and the mats. He saw Little Andy; his body stiffened. The little fellow made a motion with his head. Gus stared at him. Little Andy leaned against the mat and waited. He smiled pleasantly.

Pardo went away from the punching bag, towards the dressing rooms. A few of the sports writers went with him. Gus moved over and stood looking at Little Andy. They were some distance from the nearest humans.

"You got guts—comin' up here," Gus said tightly.

Little Andy continued to smile. It was a lip smile; his eyes held a vacant expression.

"Boss sent me," he replied. "He told me not to get hurt. He gave me a message for you."

Gus said: "Yeah?"

The little fellow nodded. "That's right," he replied. "He said to tell you that if he didn't get a cut of that prize hunk of beef—there was a jingle you had better read."

The manager frowned. "Yes?" he said. "What jingle?"

Little Andy scratched his head and smiled with his eyes, this time.

"Something about 'the kid's last fight,'" he said very slowly.

Gus Monkly stood close to the little fellow and swayed a bit. He sunk his head down on his shoulders. The half-moon scar on his cheek twitched. He said softly and not too steadily:

"Listen, Andy—this is a money scrap. The big ones are getting aboard. If Hurry does anything that ain't just nice—"

The little fellow looked blank. "That was the message, Gus," he said. "That was my job. No use talkin' to me."

The manager straightened. He stared at the blue eyes of Little Andy. There had been a time when Andy had been sitting right alongside of Hurry Lassen. Gus had the idea he was still sitting there.

"All right—all right," he replied. "Tell the boss I listened to you, but I didn't get the idea."

The little fellow widened his blue eyes, swore softly.

"Jeez!" he breathed. "I figured you was just as green in the fight game as the paper boys have been sayin'. But I didn't figure you was green in other things, Gus."

The manager smiled. "Bolley'll take the big boy," he said. "What coin I make—that'll be made in the sticks, after Pardo is flattened. It won't be too much, and I ain't going to split it up any."

Little Andy whistled softly. "For a guy who figures his scrapper is going to lose, refusing a twenty-grand buy-in—that looks dumb, eh?"

Gus shook his head. "I don't want to get in a jam," he said. "I don't want to be worried about things. I'm saving the boss coin. And I ain't runnin' with the mob, anyway."

Little Andy shrugged. "*You're* pickin' the spots," he said carelessly. "Well—s'long."

He went out and down the stairs that led from Bryant's gym. Gus stared after him, swearing to himself. When he turned towards the dressing rooms Lou Berryman came up to him. He was scowling. In his right hand he held a yellow slip of paper.

"Hell, Gus," he said, "I got to get back to Chi. My sister got hit by a truck—she's dying."

The manager narrowed his eyes on those of the chief second. He said softly:

"Yeah? Say—that's tough."

Berryman nodded, keeping his eyes away from Monkly's. He raised the telegram a little.

"It sure is," he said slowly. "With the big scrap on tomorrow night."

Gus reached for the wire, read it. He handed it back.

"That's tough, Berry," he repeated. "Yeah—I'm sorry. But you might get back in time—there might be a mistake."

The second nodded, scowling down at the yellow sheet of paper.

"The big boy's right, anyway," he said. "And if I can get back—you know I will, Gus."

The manager looked beyond Berryman and nodded his head.

"Sure, I know you will," he said quietly, but his voice held a peculiar tone.

Berryman said: "I'd better get going right away."

Gus Monkly nodded. He reached into a pocket and drew out a roll of bills. He handed the chief second several of them. They were new and crisp.

"I'm sorry, Berry," he said. "That enough?"

The second nodded. "Connors can handle Giant—if I don't get back," he said. "He knows what the big boy needs. But I'll try to make it."

The manager nodded. Berryman met his gaze with half-closed eyes, turned away. He went from the gymnasium. Gus went into the dressing room and found Connors standing near a locker and humming to himself. Connors was a big man, with Irish features and a flat nose. He was an ex-pug.

"Berry's gone to Chicago," Gus said slowly, and smiled a little. He touched the half-moon scar with his fingertips, lightly. "His sister's dying."

Connors swore softly. "Sick—or was it something sudden?" he asked.

Gus smiled more broadly. "Sudden—she got hit by a truck," he said. "You'll be handling the big boy, unless he gets back in time."

Connors nodded. "I'll do what I can," he said. "You know, Gus—the palooka's got a chance, maybe. Bolley's a sucker for a straight right. Bell made a bad match, the way I see it. We got a chance to take that guy."

Gus nodded. "I'm puttin' coin on it," he said. "Got any relatives in Chi, Connors?"

The handler narrowed his eyes, shook his head. Gus reached into his pocket and slipped the man several bills. He said in a low tone:

"Keep it quiet—that you're going to be boss in Pardo's corner. Don't even tell him—not yet. I'll do that stuff. And don't talk much, Connors."

The handler nodded. "Maybe Berry'll get back," he said slowly.

"Yeah," the manager replied. "He might."

He went around to the table on which Giant Pardo was being rubbed down. The fighter grinned at him.

"I'm gonna take—this guy, Gus," he said hoarsely.

The manager nodded. "Sure you are, Big Boy," he replied. "Like Sherman took Rome. Sure you are. But you got to quit lookin' for me, after you knock him down, see?"

The big slugger nodded with his head flat on the table surface. The rubbers were working on his legs.

"Me—I go to a neutral corner," Pardo said thickly.

Gus Monkly nodded. "The right'll do it," he said. "And we'll both be sittin' pretty and waitin' for a crack at the champ. We won't wait too long, at that. He'll be coming. How do you feel?"

The slugger grinned. "I feel swell," he returned. "How are they bettin'?"

Gus grunted. "Three to one—with you on the short end. But that's because Bolley took the nigger. You'll get him, Big Boy."

Pardo nodded again. "I feel swell," he said.

Gus grinned. "You stick with Connors and Eddie—all the time until tomorrow night," he said slowly. "We don't want no accidents."

The Giant sat up and blinked at his manager. He asked hoarsely:

"What kind of accidents?"

Gus slapped him playfully across the back of his big head.

"You might meet up with a blonde," he kidded. "You stick with Connors and Eddie."

The big slugger chuckled. He rubbed his broken nose with big knuckles.

"Hell," he breathed, "with the blondes!"

Gus nodded and went away from the dressing room. In the gym he spotted Connors, went to his side.

"Stay close to the big boy," he ordered. "Keep him here, or at the hotel—or at a picture show."

Connors nodded. "I'll watch him," he said. "I'm layin' coin on him."

Gus went down the stairs and into the street. It had started to snow. He turned towards Ninth Avenue. What he wanted was a drink. And he didn't want it at Cotti's place. If he could keep clear of Hurry Lassen, until after tomorrow night—

He smiled a little. It would be easy, after that. He'd get Pardo out of sight, out of the city. They could lay low. He knew a few tricks that would throw Hurry off the track, if he tried to trace them. And then they'd sign the big contract, the money contract. Or maybe, if things got too tough, he'd sell Pardo. With the big shot in sight he might get two hundred grand. Two hundred grand! Gus wet his thin lips with the tip of his tongue. That was money—big money.

He reached Eighth Avenue, walked northward a square, turned westward again. Halfway between Ninth and Tenth he stopped and lighted a cigarette. When he got near the corner of Tenth he looked across the street and saw the cheap hotel run by the brother of Lou Berryman. He smiled grimly.

He crossed back of a cab that was going speedily towards the Hudson. There was a lot of noise in the street, which was in the lower fifties. The hotel had signs in front, but no names on them. It was an old building with a dingy entrance. Gus went inside and walked towards a small desk. There was no one behind it. He heard footfalls on the stairs that rose from the rear of the small lobby.

There was a wash-room near the stairs—he stepped into it. The footfalls grew louder; human weight on the steps made them creak. A voice said:

"You won't be back for the fight, Lou?"

Gus swore softly. He recognized the voice of Al Berryman, Lou's brother. It had a peculiar grating quality.

Lou replied thickly: "Hell, no! And if *you're* wise—"

The words died. Gus got his body flat against a wall of the wash-room and waited. The footfalls were growing fainter now; they died away completely. Gus stepped into the poorly lighted lobby and saw the back of his chief second. A small bag dangled from Berryman's right hand. He moved away and his brother came back into the hotel. Gus slipped into the wash-room again. He could hear Al moving around behind the desk.

He waited almost ten minutes, then went down the stairs which he had descended before, and moved over damp concrete towards the basement steps. They led up to the street level, not far from the entrance.

He was almost beside the grilled gate at the front basement entrance, when he heard the sound behind him. It was a faint sound, a swishing sound. There was the brief noise of breath sucked in quickly.

Gus Monkly bent his head forward, dropped to his knees. His body was pivoting; his right hand was reaching for his automatic, when the crashes sounded. There were two of them. They filled the basement with their roar.

The manager swore brokenly, got hands before his eyes, pitched to one side. He lay motionlessly, with his body huddled. A figure came close to him, breathing quickly. There was the faint odor of cheap perfume. Then the figure was gone.

He heard shouts from the top of the steps, near the wash-room. A car door slammed, in the street. There was the sound of an engine running at high speed through the gears. Al Berryman's grating voice sounded again:

"What's wrong—down there?"

Gus Monkly got slowly to his feet. He went outside, went up the stairs that led to the street level. A tan taxi was speeding towards Ninth Avenue. A small boy stared at him with wide eyes.

Across the street were two men; they had stopped and were looking at him. Gus narrowed his eyes on them for several seconds. He said to the boy:

"Who got in—that cab, Kid?"

The boy looked cold. The two men across the street walked on towards the Hudson. Gus handed the boy a quarter and brushed off his brown coat.

"See who got in—the cab?" he asked again.

The boy spoke in a high-pitched voice.

"A lady," he said. "She was nice."

Gus straightened up and swore softly. "Yeah?" he muttered. "A lady, eh?"

The boy narrowed dark eyes on Gus's small ones. He nodded his head.

"Guess you don't know that," he said with sarcasm. "Guess you didn't hurt her."

The manager stared at the boy. "Hurt her?" he repeated.

The boy scowled at him. "She had a hurt arm," he said, raising his voice a little. "She was holding it, an' she didn't move it any."

Gus Monkly looked towards Ninth Avenue and muttered something beneath his breath. The boy said:

"There was a lot of noise—"

The manager grinned at the boy. He spoke in a cheerful tone.

"She didn't want to be kissed, Kid—some gals are like that. She got away—and maybe she bumped her arm against the door."

He went towards the entrance of the hotel, and met Al Berryman on the way in. Al was taller than his brother, and thinner.

"What happened?" he asked in his grating voice. "You use that gun?"

Gus stared at him stupidly. "What's wrong with you—drinking again?" he asked. "What gun?"

Al looked up and down Gus's overcoat. He narrowed bloodshot eyes.

"You're all dirty," he said. "I heard two shots."

Gus brushed at his coat with both hands. "The damn taxis," he said. "They never clean 'em."

Al Berryman went past Gus and reached the street. He looked east and west, stood with a hand in his right pocket. Then he moved out of sight. Gus looked through the opened door at the snow, went a few feet and closed it. He moved to the desk and thought about the blonde, Edna. It had been dark down below. She had fired two shots. Had they been meant for Lou Berryman—or himself? Or had the slugs been intended for some other person?

Gus listened to Al coming up the stairs. When the hotel owner came up to him his face was white. He said shakily:

"Look at—this!"

There was a piece of lead in the palm of his right hand. It had flattened out against something that had left a rusty color on it. Gus said slowly:

"What is it, Al?"

Al Berryman swore fiercely at him. "You don't know!" he sneered.

Gus said in a calm voice: "Where's Lou—I want to see him. Right away."

Al Berryman walked back a few feet towards the counter, but he kept his face turned towards Gus. His right hand moved inside the pocket.

"You don't know where Lou is, eh?" he said mockingly.

Gus shook his head. "He said he might have to go to Chi in a hurry," he replied. "Said your sister got hit by a truck. I was tryin' to find out if he went."

Al Berryman smiled without moving his eyes away from Monkly's. Over on Tenth Avenue there was the sharp sound of a back-fire. Al jerked his body nervously. He stopped smiling.

"Think you'd find out—down in the basement, Gus?" he snapped.

The manager said: "What basement—what the hell are you talking about, Al? You've been hitting the stuff hard."

Al Berryman smiled again. His face was very white.

"I ain't drinking—not these days," he said slowly. "This yours?"

He took his left hand from the pocket of his soiled suit. In the fingers he held a leather case. There was still one long cigar in it.

Gus whistled softly. "Sure it is," he said. "Where'd you get that? I've been looking for it since that stud game up here the other night."

Al Berryman's voice pitched higher. "You're not coming through, Gus," he said. "This wallet wasn't down there an hour ago."

Gus Monkly reached out and took the wallet. He started to put it back in the upper pocket of his coat, checked himself. There was a dirty mark beneath the pocket. Al's bloodshot eyes were on his.

"You were down there!" he stated. "If you get me in bad, Gus—"

The manager shoved the wallet in his pocket. He put the cigar in his mouth, lighted it. It was crushed and didn't draw well. He said slowly:

"I'm not taking any orders from you, Al. I'm asking you about Lou. Did he leave for Chi?"

Berryman nodded. His eyes were frowning into those of Monkly.

"He just left," he said in a surly tone.

Gus sighed heavily. He turned a little. Al Berryman took his right hand out of the suit pocket. Gus moved like a cat. He got fingers over Al's right wrist, lifted his arm. His right hand went into Berryman's pocket, pulled loose the gun. Gus backed away, smiling.

"Where did Lou go— and *why* did he go?" he said slowly. "Don't hold back, Al."

Al Berryman's eyes were staring at him, wide with fear. Gus said:

"Better be careful, Al. I've got a big money shot just ahead of me. You know that. It means a lot. Lou's been living here with you—and you know things. You always knew things in Chi. You two may have a sister in that burg—but she wasn't hit by any truck. Come on—what's Lou's game?"

Al Berryman stood motionless near the desk and shook his head from side to side. From the floor above there came the faint sound of whistling. A door slammed. Gus moved his head forward a little and said in a very hard tone:

"Hurry Lassen hates my guts. He hates Lou's too. But he could slam Lou down, where he had to go easy with me. And maybe Lou would see things different like, see? That's what I want to know."

He moved the gun a little. Al Berryman swallowed hard. He shook his head again.

"Lou went—to Chi. A truck hit—"

"Shut up!" Gus snapped. "I'll put a slug in you, sure as hell—if you lie! Lou did one thing— or another. He got yellow—and ran like a rat. He's looking for a crawl spot. Or he went over— to Hurry!"

Al Berryman said in his grating voice:

"Ella—got hit by a truck—"

He checked his words as Gus walked up close to him and shoved the muzzle of the gun against his stomach. He spoke softly.

"You're going out. I think you're riding with Hurry, and you've got to go out. You should have had the dose before. Walk to the stairs in back—go down. If you've got anything to think about—"

Berryman's eyes stared into the beady ones of the fight manager. He said slowly, shakenly:

"For God's sake, Gus—don't do it—"

The whistling up above grew louder. Gus Monkly shoved the gun forward a little. Berryman's body stiffened. Gus said:

"Get moving—"

Al Berryman made a choking sound. He said weakly:

"It's—Pardo, Gus. They're going to—"

His face was ghastly. His voice was a little whisper.

"Lou—made a duck—Hurry was coming right after—"

Al Berryman's body jerked, relaxed. It

slumped towards the floor. Gus got an arm around the man, dragged him back of the desk to a battered chair. He touched Al's right wrist—there was no pulse beat.

The fight manager swore softly. He wiped the gun off with his handkerchief, wiped it carefully. He slipped it into a pocket of Al's faded suit. Then he went around to the front of the desk, looked towards the door that led to the street. It was still closed.

Upstairs he heard the wavering voice of the hotel porter, Conlon. The porter was calling Al's name. Gus smiled grimly and went towards the rear stairs again. As he went down he heard Conlon call in a louder, shriller voice:

"Hey, Al! How about them chips in number eight?"

Gus went along the concrete floor of the basement, reached the street. It was snowing hard. He walked towards the river, watching the cabs. A man on horseback, riding ahead of a huge locomotive, appeared faintly through the snow. Gus turned southward, hailed a cab at the next square.

"The Manger," he told the driver. "And take it easy—I've got a bad heart."

The driver grinned, nodded. Gus Monkly settled back in the seat and shook the snow from his soft hat. He said, half aloud:

"That's a hell of a lot better—than no heart—at all."

CHAPTER IV

 iant Pardo was playing pinochle with Eddie Leach, one of the handlers, when Gus got inside the room. He grinned at the manager.

"It's snowin' out, Gus," he said.

Gus grunted. "You've been peeking," he replied. "Feel all right?"

The big slugger nodded. "I feel swell," he replied. "I like it cold."

Gus swore. "Not too cold, big boy," he reminded. "That's the way we want Bolley to like it—cold."

The big slugger blinked stupidly. "Yeah," he said. "Sure, Gus."

The manager said: "Where's Connors?"

Eddie Leach gestured towards one of the connecting rooms.

"Readin' about how good Bolley is," he stated. "Or maybe he's washin' his neck. It's the right month."

The Giant threw back his big head and roared with laughter. Things rattled in the room. Gus frowned at his fighter, then grinned.

"Yeah," he agreed. "The right month, eh?"

Pardo rocked from side to side with laughter. Gus grinned at the fighter until he turned his head away. Then he frowned. He went across the room and met Connors at the doorway.

"What's goin' on?" the second muttered.

Gus forced a grin. "Eddie told a joke," he stated. He walked past Connors, said in a low voice: "Come on in and shut the door—I'll tell another one, not so funny."

Connors closed the door. Gus took off his coat, tossed it over the back of a chair. He threw his hat on top of it, went over and sat on the edge of the bed.

"Listen, Connors," he said in a low tone, "you stickin' with me?"

Connors narrowed his eyes. "Sure," he replied. "Why not?"

Gus lighted a cigarette and shrugged. He kept his small eyes on the blue ones of Connors, and didn't reply for several seconds. When he spoke his voice was toneless.

"Lou Berryman isn't heading for Chi because his sister got hit by a truck, Connors. Maybe he isn't heading that way at all. He ran out on me. He got yellow."

Connors whistled softly. "Say, Gus," he said slowly, "is this fight on the level?"

Gus Monkly looked hurt. "You're damn right it is," he stated. "This ain't the sticks—this is the Garden. The fight's on the square. But that don't mean—"

He checked himself. He narrowed his eyes to little slits.

"I got to have you—with me, Connors," he said. "You don't run with the mob. You stickin'?"

The handler swore. "Come on," he muttered. "Give it to me. What was Lou's game?"

Gus said slowly: "Hurry Lassen slammed him down, a few nights ago. He got worried. Lou was in Hurry's mob, working beer, in Chi. He and I—we quit. Things were getting tough, and Hurry was playing around. He's got a blonde now. She comes close to running things. And she figures Hurry should have a slice of the Giant. Forty percent cut-in."

Connors said: "Yeah?" very slowly.

Gus said: "Lou figured he should have a hunk of Pardo, too. But he wasn't coming after me too hard. We meet up with Hurry, and I hand him the line that the boy's all sliced up. Lou admits he's got a share—and Hurry knows he's lying. He slams him down. The blonde sits there and thinks a little for him. Hurry tries to throw a scare my way. He wants forty percent of my take on the Giant—and he sent Little Andy around to tell me that if he don't get it before the scrap with Bolley—it'll be Pardo's last fight."

Connors sat down in a chair and shook his head from side to side. He swore huskily. Gus said:

"Then Lou comes along with a fake wire—and makes a duck. He got yellow. He's been staying at his brother's hotel. I went over to see if he was really walking out—and the blonde tried to rub me out, down in the basement. I put a gun on Al Berryman—he was getting set to spill something, and his pumper went bad. He's dead."

Connors got up and walked around. Gus said slowly:

"I've got to have help, Connors—that's why I'm giving it to you straight. If Pardo gets the nod over Bolley—he'll get the works!"

Connors said grimly: "We got to hide him out. He's got a chance to win, Gus."

The manager grunted. "Chance, hell!" he breathed. "Bell made a rotten match. He needs the coin. Bolley's a sucker for a right—and Pardo's got the right. I've been stallin' around, Connors. The big boy's in right now. But the hell of it is—"

Gus got up and went over to the window. The handler said softly:

"You could sell him the cut, Gus."

The fight manager swung around, his beady eyes glittering.

"I'm not yellow," he said harshly. "I dug up this palooka. He was opening oysters in a lousy town. He was so dumb he'd been fired from one fish joint because he couldn't count up to six. He was giving the customers five shells. I taught him something. I ain't letting Hurry come in. If the boy gets over—he's worth big money. If Hurry gets in on big money—the other guy gets sick. Sometimes he don't get well again."

Connors nodded slowly. "Pardo'll take Bolley," he muttered. "We can fix up a way of gettin' him out of the Garden without being seen. We can hide him out—"

The fight manager smiled grimly. "Yeah?" he said. "Well, that's what I'm looking for. Hurry's a killer—and he hates my guts. That means he hates anything I touch—except maybe the dirt he'd like to shove me into. We got to be careful."

Connors said slowly: "Or it's no coin for you, eh? And the long count—for Pardo."

The manager said tonelessly: "See what you can dope out. If Hurry gets Pardo—I'll get him. Jeeze—I'll get him for it, Connors!"

The handler closed his eyes and said slowly:

"We're safe—while we've got the Giant in the Garden. If we can sneak him out—"

Gus Monkly spoke softly. "Pardo's going to kayo Bolley, Connors. He'll give him the count. And I know Hurry. He'll go through hell to square it with me for—"

Connors said quietly: "Why don't he gun *you* out, Gus?"

The manager's half-moon scar jerked a little. He laughed harshly.

"That's easy," he said. "He wants me to walk around and remember. To think about the coin I *almost* got my fingers on, see? He wants to let me know he can still boss jobs, see? He's a killer—and he's a cold killer."

Connors didn't say anything. Gus got to his feet, started towards the door. He turned suddenly.

"Don't get talking, Connors. You're sitting in now. Keep your face tight. I'll fix you so it'll be worthwhile."

Connors nodded. "We'll lick 'em, Gus," he said grimly. "But we've got to use brains."

The fight manager took the cigarette from between his thin lips and looked at the ash.

"Brains—and maybe some other things," he said softly, and went into the other room.

Eddie Leach grinned at him. "Is he usin' soap?" he asked.

Giant Pardo chuckled. He stood up and put his big arms out. He swung at the air. Gus said grimly:

"You look great, big boy. I'm feelin' sorry for Bolley."

Eddie lighted a cigarette. "He'll murder him," he said.

The scar on Gus's face twitched. He stiffened a little. Then he grinned.

"Sure," he said. "And say, Giant—Lou's sister got sick in Chi. He had a wire. If he don't get back for the fight, Connors will be in your corner."

Pardo grinned. "To hell with seconds," he announced. "I'll kill this guy."

"Yeah," Gus stated. "But you got to quit grinnin' at me, after you knock a guy down."

The big slugger chuckled. "I go to a—neutral corner," he said thickly in singsong fashion. "I won't look at you, Gus."

The manager nodded. Eddie Leach pulled on his cigarette and said softly:

"At three to one—it's nice, Gus—it's—a killing!"

CHAPTER V

he Garden was packed; they were standing three deep in the rear of the mezzanine and balcony. The ringside was filled; there was a buzz of voices as Joe Humphrey climbed through the ropes. The buzz became a roar as the big form of Chuck Bolley came along the aisle from the dressing rooms.

Bolley was almost as tall as Pardo; he had reddish hair and a pale face. He'd been fighting for five years and had spoiled the chances of more potential champs than any other scrapper in the heavyweight division. He raised his long arms above his head, tapped his gloves together. He towered above his handlers. Schenck, his brown-faced manager, was dwarfed as he stood beside him.

There was another roar as Giant Pardo came into the ring. Pardo was grinning; he leaned down suddenly and spoke to Connors at his side.

"It's a—good crowd, Connors."

The second grinned up at him. "You got a punch and they know it," he replied. "And Bolley'll know it, too!"

Pardo nodded. "Sure," he agreed.

Joe Humphrey was introducing fighters who had climbed inside the ropes. The crowd was impatient; they shouted above the announcer's clear voice. They drowned him out. Humphrey raised both hands as the gong clanged again and again. He pointed towards Giant Pardo seated on the stool in his corner.

". . . the big boy from the Great Lakes, Giant Pardo!"

Pardo stood up and tapped leather at the crowd, turning slowly. Bolley sat across the ring and glared at him. The crowd cheered wildly. Pardo sat down as Humphrey faced his opponent.

". . . that slugger from the Northwest, Red Bolley!"

The cheers were greater in volume as Bolley

got up and went towards the center of the ring. He moved more gracefully than Pardo, swung more rapidly as he tapped his gloves above his head. Johnny Parks, the referee, went to the center of the ring. The fighters moved out to his side. Schenk was with Bolley, but Gus Monkly was not inside the ropes. Connors and Eddie Leach stood beside the big boy.

The referee gave instructions that both sluggers knew by heart. And Gus Monkly sat in an aisle chair, just back of Pardo's stool, staring towards the ring—and thinking about Hurry Lassen.

The referee turned away. The fighters went to their corners. Gus Monkly stared across the ring, turned his eyes on the chairs. He didn't see the blonde girl or Hurry. He didn't see any of the mob. And that bothered him. His nerves were jumpy. The stools were being swung through the ropes; the handlers were climbing out of the ring. The gong clanged.

Bolley came out fast and swung a left that missed the Giant's chin by inches. Pardo was short with a choppy right to the body. Bolley tried another right that Pardo smothered with his glove. They went into a clinch. Pardo seemed stronger than Bolley, though he weighed only two pounds more. He shoved the red-haired fighter away from him and shot out a straight right. It caught Bolley over the left eye and knocked him off balance. The crowd roared.

Gus leaned forward in his chair and shouted hoarsely:

"Get in there! Watch yourself—"

Pardo moved forward and shot another right. Bolley twisted to one side. He was hurt and holding his guard high. Gus shouted:

"To his belly, Giant—to his belly!"

Pardo tried a short left to the head. He missed. Bolley got in close and hung on. There was red over his left eye. Gus glanced towards Connors and saw the Irishman signaling Pardo to shove the red-haired fighter away, and work on his stomach. But Giant didn't seem to see Connors. Gus muttered:

"He's too—dumb—"

The referee broke them. Bolley backed away and brushed his left eye with the back of his right glove. Pardo followed him up and shot two lefts to the head, neither of which landed.

Bolley stepped in and landed a hard left to the body. Pardo lowered his guard and Bolley feinted with his right, shot a hard left to the mouth. Pardo shook his head and started to back away. Bolley came in fast and brought up an uppercut that just missed Pardo's chin.

Gus leaned forward and shouted hoarsely. His words were drowned in the roar of the crowd.

"Get inside—get in close, Big Boy!"

Bolley landed two lefts to the body and missed a hard right to the head. Pardo crouched and shot out a straight right. It caught Bolley high on the forehead, knocked him back, off balance. The red-haired slugger's face was streaked with red from his cut eye. He covered up and backed away as Pardo went after him slowly. The gong clanged.

Gus muttered to himself: "The palooka's slow—but Red's gettin' tired already. If Pardo can get in a right—"

He watched Bolley drop to his stool. The Giant was standing in his corner and grinning at Gus. The manager swore at him as Connors jerked him down. A voice at Gus's side said:

"Got a winner, Gus?"

The manager stiffened, turned. The blonde was across the aisle now. She was going to her seat. Beside her was Burke. He didn't look at Gus. Edna looked pale, but there was a smile on her thin face.

On the opposite side of the ring a man was sliding past people to his seat. He was a small man. Little Andy.

Gus Monkly smiled with his thin lips. Three of the mob were present. But Hurry wasn't in sight. The semifinal had been a good scrap; most of the crowd had come in time to see it. But this mob was arriving late. Why?

The bell clanged for the second round. Pardo was out before Bolley had left his stool. There was a white line over the red-haired slugger's bad eye. Bolley came out in a crouch, and started weaving almost immediately. The crowd jeered. Pardo shot a swinging left, and Bolley got his head underneath it. He came in close and pawed at the Giant with both hands. Pardo shot a short right. His mouth was bleeding slightly; there was a half grin on his face. Bolley tried a right and left, fell into a clinch. Pardo broke away, and Bolley caught him on the head with a light left.

Pardo walked in and started throwing rights and lefts to the body. The crowd roared; Gus leaned forward in his chair. Bolley tried to get into a clinch but the Giant shoved him away. He drove a hard left to the body, and when Bolley sagged forward he stepped back and landed a heavy left to the face. Bolley was on the ropes now, crowded against them by Pardo. The crowd was howling fiercely, remembering the way the Giant had finished Mike Connell.

Bolley bent forward and tried to clinch. Suddenly he shoved Pardo away from him and snapped out a hard left. It caught Pardo with his arms out, knocked him back. Bolley leaped forward and brought one up from the floor. It missed Pardo's chin by an inch.

Gus Monkly saw the expression on his slugger's face—saw the grin fade, the eyes narrow. Pardo was facing the ropes almost directly in front of his manager. Gus caught one flashing glimpse of Pardo's eyes—sensing the kill punch. And then the Giant shot the right. It had everything behind it—straight from the shoulder.

The gloved fist caught Bolley flush on the jaw, off balance. There was a screaming roar from the crowd—then silence. Bolley slumped forward. He hit resin heavily—there was no movement to his body. Pardo backed away, looked towards Gus. He started to grin, then turned towards his corner. Connors waved him off—he went to a neutral corner. The referee started the count.

Gus stood up and shouted hoarsely. At ten Bolley had not moved a muscle. He was out cold. The Garden was filled with sound as Johnny Parks pointed towards Giant Pardo. Gus caught a glimpse of Connors waving his arms wildly.

Men were climbing into the ring—handlers of the fighters. Pardo came out from the neutral corner as Bolley's seconds lifted him from the resin. He raised his gloved hands—the crowd shouted wildly. Gus stared at the ring—there were a half dozen humans inside the ropes now. More were climbing in. He saw Humphrey swing a leg over the ropes. A photographer climbed inside. Connors turned and grinned broadly at Gus.

"What a right!" he shouted hoarsely. "What a—"

His voice was drowned by the shouts of the crowd. A hand gripped Gus's left shoulder. He swung around. Burke was standing back of him. There was a faint smile on his face.

"You win, Gus," he said. "But it's—like this—"

A flashlight boomed; the din of the crowd was dying. From the balcony there came a sudden hush. Gus kept his eyes on Burke.

"It's like this, Burke," he said, "you'd better be careful—"

Burke grinned and turned away. Gus looked across the aisle, failed to see the blonde Edna. He turned his face towards the ring. There was a crowd in the center of it, but the figure of Giant Pardo did not tower above the other humans. He saw the referee bending down. Connors swung towards the ropes, his face white and twisted.

"Gus!" he shouted. "Come—up here!"

Gus Monkly reached the corner that had been his fighter's. He swung through the ropes. A uniformed cop stared at him. He saw Doc Bailey bending down, shoved his way to the doctor's side.

Giant Pardo lay on his back. His eyes were wide open. His great arms were flung wide. There was a half smile on his face. His chest was soaked with water—his dark hair wet with it. Over his heart was a small reddish brown spot. A thin stream of blood had streaked down from it, towards his trunks.

Bailey looked at Gus. He shook his head slowly. There was a darker color around the skin of the heart. Bailey said quietly:

"He's dead, Monkly. Shot through the heart."

Gus Monkly stared at the wide eyes of Pardo. He straightened a little. He said slowly:

"Through the heart—but that would mean a sweet piece—"

Bailey said: "Powder burns on the skin. The murderer was in the ring, Monkly. He was inside—the ropes!"

Gus straightened; his eyes met the blue, staring ones of Connors. The second said fiercely:

"They got him—"

Gus reached out strong fingers and gripped Connors's right wrist. He said in a hard, low voice:

"Take it easy. Don't talk—"

There were several officers in the ring now. They were moving about, questioning seconds, officials, photographers. A handsome man in evening dress, with a black mustache he touched nervously, came close to Gus.

"You were—Pardo's manager?" he asked. "I'm Watterman, police commissioner. Your man—was he ever threatened?"

Gus shook his head. His eyes held little expression. He looked at the immaculate police commissioner, but did not see him. Watterman said:

"Keep everybody inside the ropes, you officers. Monkly—recognize anyone here that might have reason for murdering your fighter?"

Gus shook his head and said: "No. But how could he have been shot—"

Bailey spoke up. "There was a lot of confusion. Eight or ten persons—perhaps a dozen were in the ring. There was a flashlight explosion—"

Colter, in charge of the Garden, was standing beside Bailey. He said in a grim tone:

"We don't allow photographers in the ring, unless it's a championship fight. There was no permission given for a photographer—"

Watterman said grimly: "Where's that picture man?"

He turned away from Gus. The manager went over to the ropes and leaned against them.

He looked towards the spot where he had seen Little Andy. The man wasn't there now. He hadn't seen Hurry Lassen at all. Connors came to his side and swore bitterly.

"Poor damn kid!" he muttered. "He might have been—champ—"

Gus said in a hard voice: "He wouldn't have been. Rawlton would have kayoed him. But he was in a sweet spot—"

He checked himself, turned his back to the crowd milling around in the seats. Those in the mezzanine and balcony were not making for the exits. They were staring down at the ring. Humphrey's voice sounded above the buzz in the Garden.

"The winner—Pardo—one minute and ten seconds—in the second round—"

A voice boomed down from the balcony: "What's the matter—with Pardo?"

Bailey came to Gus's side. "The camera's still there—but there's no photographer," he said grimly. "It was a frame-up. They used the flash to kill the gun color, if there was any. And the sound to kill the sound. Maxim-silencer. Thirty-eight, probably. The murderer stepped close to him—let him have it. Got clear in the confusion. Probably two of them. You sure you don't know anything about—"

Gus Monkly narrowed his beady eyes and looked beyond Bailey, towards the figure of the dead fighter. He said in a dull, low voice:

"Me—I don't know—a thing. Not a damn thing, Bailey!"

CHAPTER VI

 hey sat in the room at the Manger. It was almost dawn; they had been released by the police an hour ago. There had been many questions— but the answers had been unimportant. Gus Monkly smoked a cigarette, and kept his eyes half closed. Connors lay on the bed and swore softly at inter-

vals. It was raining outside; the drops beat against the window.

Gus said slowly and in a voice that showed no emotion:

"He did what he said—he'd do. Only he did it quicker—than we figured. He got the big boy, but that don't count so much. I made that kid what he was. The champ would have dropped him—he'd have worked the sticks for a while—and then some doll would have grabbed what coin he had left. He'd have ended up opening oysters, where I found him. That don't count. But something else—does count—"

Connors said bitterly: "He was a good kid. Dumb but good. I hate the guys that finished him. If you're going after them—"

Gus nodded his head slowly. "I ain't yellow," he said. "I'm going after them—just once. It'll be that way. Just once."

"He was dumb—but he was tryin'," Connors said fiercely. "God—I hate 'em for that."

The manager nodded his head again. "Two hundred grand—" he breathed. "They took it away from me, Connors. They killed to do it. Because I wouldn't let 'em cut in. Two hundred grand!"

Connors sat up, swung his legs over the edge of the bed.

"That blonde—she tried to get you, in the basement of Berryman's hotel. That might have given them a chance—with you out of the way. But why didn't they try again—for you?"

Gus said slowly: "Maybe Hurry didn't know about that. He's got plenty of coin. He wants to hurt me, break me. I was square with him. But I walked out too soon. He needed me. He wanted to get even, get square. And he did."

The manager stood up and looked down at Connors. The Irish handler's blue eyes were narrowed on his. There was hatred in them. Gus said steadily:

"I guess you're right, Connors—Pardo was tryin'. He was a good kid. We got to square things up. He was a scrapper, but they didn't give him a chance. We've got to *take* one—to square things."

Connors said nothing. The manager went over to the window.

"Maybe the mob made a break for it—maybe they didn't. I've got a hunch they're sittin' tight—and waiting for me to come to them. *Figuring* I'll come to them. Or maybe they think I'm yellow—like Lou Berryman."

"He didn't have a chance!" Connors breathed bitterly. "The dirty rats—"

Gus shook his head slowly. "You've got to take it easy, Connors," he warned. "They're killers. And they're cold. You've got to be the same way."

Connors said in a calmer voice: "You could turn 'em up—tell the bulls what you know."

Gus Monkly laughed harshly. "Where's the proof?" he asked. "Hurry's got enough coin to beat a dozen charges like this one. Burke was talking to me when Pardo got the dose. The blonde had been sitting right across from me. Little Andy was on the other side of the ring. They'd all have alibis. And I didn't see Hurry. He'd have one—and it would be air-tight. Turn 'em up? Not a chance."

Connors swore. "And they might remember something on *you*," he said.

Gus nodded. "They *would*," he replied. "No, that ain't the way, Connors. The thing is to just walk in on 'em. Maybe we can walk out—maybe not. Maybe we can do the job right."

The phone bell rang. Gus looked towards the table on which it rested. He said grimly:

"The bulls—pretty sure."

He went over and lifted the receiver. He made his voice sound sleepy.

"Yeah," he said. "Monkly."

His body got straight—he sucked in his breath sharply. Then he relaxed. He listened for a few seconds. Once he said: "No," in a husky voice. After a half minute he said: "Yeah—I know the spot. In thirty minutes. But if you're lying, Edna—" He hung up abruptly.

When he faced Connors there was a twisted smile on his thin lips. He touched the half-moon scar gently.

"The blonde—Edna," he said. "She's waitin'

for me, downtown. She's alone—and she's got something big to say. She swears to God it's all right. Hurry's crossed her up. What she's got to say will mean a lot to me. If I don't come down—I'm on the spot. If I do come down, she's got a line that'll help me beat it. That's all."

Connors said in a half whisper: "It's a plant. They'll gun you out. They're getting yellow."

"Just the same—I'm going down." Gus's voice was steady. "I knew a moll once that lied all her life—and then told one truth. It helped. Edna's tricky as hell. Maybe she's got that way with Hurry. It's a gambling chance."

"You're on the short end," Connors muttered. "I'm riding down with you."

Gus smiled a little with his eyes. "You're twenty-one," he said. "It might help."

Connors read a morning paper as the cab moved eastward towards the Hudson. He said grimly:

"Its all over the paper—the kill story. The bulls are running around in circles. Watterman was at the ringside, and he's raising hell. They haven't picked up anyone who remembers what the man that climbed into the ring with the camera looked like. A handler named Lester, workin' with Bolley—he thinks he saw a flash. Another guy says he saw a short, thickset bird standing close to Pardo, just before the flash went off."

"The coppers won't get anywhere," Gus said softly. "There was too much excitement. Maybe even the big boy didn't see the killer. There wouldn't be much flash—and with that flashlight racket and the cheering—the sound of the gun—"

Connors tossed the paper on the floor of the cab. It had stopped raining, and was getting colder. Gus looked down at the large-sized picture of Pardo, posed in his fighting togs.

"Two hundred grand—maybe more!" he breathed fiercely.

Connors said slowly: "How do we—work this, Gus?"

The fight manager shrugged. "It's a small hotel," he said. "Edna's aunt runs it. She wouldn't let any of the mob hang out there, six

months ago. But she may have changed her mind. There's one entrance—one exit. I've used 'em both—the place was raided for booze once, when I was inside. There's a small bar in the back room. The aunt isn't inside much of the time. A fat bird named Lippe keeps things going. He's dumb, and handy with a blackjack."

Connors said slowly: "A rod can beat a blackjack, any time."

Gus shook his head. "That isn't our line," he stated. "Let me do the gabbing. I've got a hunch that Edna's on the level this time. Give her a chance—it may help."

Connors kept his left hand inside the pocket of his brown coat and swore softly.

"We're both going to get finished, maybe," he said in a peculiarly dull voice.

Gus said: "Yeah—maybe. We ain't there yet. You can drop out, Connors. You ain't mixed up in this too much. You can ease out."

The handler swore again. "Giant was a good kid," he repeated. "They never gave him a break. The bulls won't do anything. I want this chance."

The cab turned southward on Tenth Avenue. When it turned westward again, a few squares distant, Gus tapped on the glass that separated the driver from the rear of the cab.

"Pull in," he ordered. "This is right."

When the cab was a half block distant Gus led the way across the street. There was slush under-foot; Connors slipped once and swore grimly. Gus said with irony in his voice:

"Careful—don't get hurt!"

He turned in abruptly at the entrance, narrow and dark, of a three-story brown house. The brick was dirty and in need of repair. There was a bell at one side of the entrance—he pressed it.

There was the sound of a lock snapping. The door opened a little. Gus said quietly, steadily:

"It's Gus, Lips. Edna called me."

There was a muttered sound from beyond the door. It opened a little more. Gus sighed and squeezed through the opening. The fat one started to close the door, but Gus said slowly:

"Wait—I got one good guy with me."

The fat man muttered again. Connors slid inside. Gus took his Colt from a coat pocket and pressed it against the fat man's side. The hallway was almost dark.

"You go first, Lips," he said. "I hate to see you get quiet. Take us to Edna."

Lippe said huskily. "This is—a hell of a note. Pullin' a rod on me!"

Gus said: "I ain't using it, Lips. It's just—for fun."

The fat man led the way towards the back room. He went inside with Gus close behind him. Connors stayed near Monkly. The room was small, lighted by one hanging bulb. There was a small bar. At one end of it was a dirty tray, with two empty, tall glasses on it. There were two tables in the room—they had white surfaces that glistened in the light.

Edna sat beside one of the tables. Her back was to the door that led to the narrow passage going towards the rear. One arm rested on the table, the other rigidly at her side. She looked shorter, heavier than ever. Her face was strangely thin—there was a bluish bruise over her right eye. She wore a dark suit, and her face seemed very pale. She smiled a little.

"Hello, Gus," she said. "Come on over. Sit down."

Gus smiled with his thin lips. "Take a look back of the bar, Connors," he said. "Lips—you go over there and sit down. Keep your hands in sight."

He pointed towards the other table. The bartender swore and did as he was told. The girl narrowed her eyes on Connors. She said bitterly:

"Hell—there's no one here. Just Lips and myself. And Lips is wise to everything."

Gus said: "Sure, Edna."

He went close to her, pulled out a chair and placed it so that it faced the doorway through which they had come. He could see the rear exit without turning his head. He put the gun in his right coat pocket and said to Connors: "All right?"

Connors said: "All right, Gus. I'll stick here by the bar."

Gus nodded. He smiled at the girl. Lippe was making a heavy noise as he breathed. Gus said:

"Well—get started whining, Edna."

She shook her head. There was an empty glass in front of her.

"How about a drink?" she asked in a shaken voice, and moved her left arm a little.

Gus shook his head. "Not doing it—right now," he stated. "Pretty rotten with your left hand, eh?"

She widened her eyes a little. There wasn't as much rouge on her lips as usual. They looked gray. She said:

"I don't get you, Gus."

He smiled. "You *didn't* get me," he corrected. "But you made too much noise, in that basement. You *tried* damn' hard."

She looked puzzled. Her right arm moved a little, above the elbow.

"I don't get you, Gus," she said again.

The fight manager said nothing. His eyes were narrowed on hers. She shrugged, said slowly:

"Something went wrong, Gus. I got the dirty end. No man can kick me around."

She raised her left-hand fingers and touched the bruise on her forehead. She said bitterly:

"Damn Hurry—I'd see him burn for what—"

She stopped. Gus smiled and said: "You could almost play the Palace, Kid. You can almost act."

She stiffened in the chair. Her voice dropped; she looked beyond Gus, towards Connors.

"I told you to come—alone," she said.

Gus Monkly nodded. "And I didn't," he replied. "What about it?"

She shivered a little. His tone was hard, and his eyes were hard.

"It's all—right," she replied. "Something slipped up, Gus. Hurry didn't—get your man."

The fight manager smiled a little. "No?" he said. "You got me down here to tell me that."

She nodded. "That—and something else," she said. "God knows I'm not trying to make it easy for Hurry." She leaned towards him and said fiercely: "I hate him, Gus. I swear I do—I hate his insides!"

Gus nodded. He kept on smiling coldly. "Sure you do—and you got me down here to tell me that."

She relaxed a little. "I'm sick," she said slowly. "I'm terrible sick, Gus. I want to get away—to get out of here."

The fight manager stopped smiling. "Yeah?" he said. He got up from the chair suddenly, and moved back a little. Lippe straightened at the table, staring at the manager.

Gus said: "All right, Kid—I'll see that you go away. I've got your ticket—"

He took his gun from the pocket. The girl's eyes were filled with fear. She cried shrilly:

"No—no! For God's sake. Gus—I got you here to tell you—who finished—Pardo!"

The fight manager let his small eyes open a little. He held the Colt low.

"All right," he said. "Spill it!"

The girl's face was twisted, white. The bluish bruise stood out clearly in the white light from the unshaded bulb. Lippe was breathing heavily in the silence before she spoke. She said hoarsely:

"There he is—Connors!"

Gus Monkly turned his head slightly. Connors's eyes were on the girl, blue pinpoints in the white light. His lips moved very little.

"You dirty liar!" he said.

The girl rose suddenly from her chair. She faced Connors. Her body was tense. She extended her right arm, pointed a finger at him. Her left arm was close against the dark cloth of her suit.

"Don't crawl, Connors!" she said harshly. "You got Lou Berryman in the clear, when we were right on top of him. Hurry fixed it with you. And you got Giant Pardo. I saw you!"

Gus Monkly turned his body a little towards the second. He swayed a bit, from side to side. But he kept the muzzle of his gun on the girl's figure. Connors said again:

"You dirty, yellow liar!"

The girl dropped her right arm. "You were in the ring!" she said. "Gus had to have someone with him. You weren't in the mob in Chi. He

thought you were all right, I suppose. You can play pretty white, I guess. After the kayo—you went towards Giant with a towel in your hands. You gave Pardo the works!"

Gus drew in his breath slowly. Lippe swore hoarsely, across the room. Gus said slowly:

"How about it—Connors?"

The second laughed throatily. He gestured towards the blonde in a careless manner, using his right hand. The left was still out of sight.

"She's tryin' to frame me," he said grimly. "She's a rat, Gus. We'd better let her have—"

The girl broke in. "I'm givin' it to you straight, Gus. Connors is workin' for Hurry. Don't I know? Hurry was afraid you'd hide Pardo out. You had a winner. He was down the aisle, near the dressing room. He was waiting—in case Connors lost his nerve. But he didn't lose it. He did for Pardo, I'm tellin' you!"

Her voice had risen shrilly. Connors's eyes had ceased to be pinpoints now. They were wider. He chuckled huskily.

"What's her game, Gus?" he asked. "Why's she trying to put it on me?"

Gus said in a cold tone: "Take your hand away from the rod, Connors."

The handler stared at him. His left-hand pocket was away from the fight manager. He didn't move. Gus spoke very quietly:

"Show me your left, Connors."

Connors took his left hand from the pocket of his coat. He said bitterly:

"Hell, Gus—you ain't falling for her line? It's a frame—she's trying to get us spilling lead at each other. She's sitting in with Hurry—and this is a try for an easy out."

Gus said with a faint smile in his eyes:

"All right, Connors—but it won't work. We won't spill lead—not at *each other*."

The blonde stared at Monkly. "He did it, Gus!" she said. "I'm tellin' you—I saw him go for Pardo, with the towel. They used the flashlight to drown the sound—"

Gus said: "Sure, I know, Kid. Now you sit down. Connors—move over and sit down next to her. Face me—"

He watched Connors go over and sit down next to the blonde. There was a sound something like a door shutting, somewhere in the hotel. Gus looked at Lippe and said quietly:

"If anyone comes in here—you'll get it first, Lips. Remember that!"

The fat man wet his lips and started to speak. But he said nothing. Gus looked at the girl. There was terror in her eyes.

"You damn' near got me, at Berryman's place," he said. "What's the answer?"

She shook her head. "I was after Lou," she said thickly. "I thought he came downstairs. I squeezed lead twice—and got clear in a cab. Hurry wanted Lou out of the way. He knew he was yellow—and he was afraid he'd run out, or play with you. Lou was supposed to do the job on Pardo."

Gus said: "Yeah?"

The blonde nodded. "It was a hate kill, Gus. You quit the racket in Chi. They needed you. You ran into something nice, and wouldn't give Hurry a piece. He'd staked you. He didn't need the coin, but he got hating you—for not coming through. When Lou started to go yellow—he picked me to stop him."

Gus said: "Why?"

She shrugged. "He figured I could do it with my left—and no one on the inside would be wise. I can't move the right arm. He figured I'd be safe."

Gus said in a low tone: "And Connors did the job on Pardo, with a Maxim-silenced gun under a towel—inside the ropes?"

The girl looked at Connors and replied in a hard voice:

"He did it, Gus."

Connors ran the back of his left hand across his broken nose. He smiled nastily.

"She's a lyin' moll," he said calmly. "Get it right, Gus."

Gus Monkly nodded. "It'll be that way," he said. "Listen, Edna—if Connors was working for Hurry—why did they pull the job in the ring? Why didn't they wait? I'd have sent Pardo with Connors—"

He stopped, smiling grimly. Edna Harms swore softly.

"You know that answer—you ain't that dumb," she said. "You'd know who did the job—if they waited. They wanted to work it smooth—and when it would hurt most. And they didn't want you to know about Connors."

Gus said in a soft tone: "With Connors workin' for Hurry they could have fixed it so that Giant would lose the scrap."

The girl smiled bitterly. "Hurry was betting on Giant," she said. "At three to one he cleaned up plenty. And then he put the job over—"

"She's lying, Gus." Connors's voice held a shaken note. "You know she's lying."

Gus looked at the girl and said in a tone that was low and smooth:

"You're spilling the works, Edna—why?"

Her voice held a lot of hate. She looked beyond Gus, towards the dirty mirror back of the bar.

"There's a guy named—never mind that, Gus. I wanted to slide out of the mob, three months ago. I've been good to Hurry—he ain't been so damn' good to me. I wanted to quit, like you did. This guy that made me want to quit—he ain't so good. But he ain't rotten, like Hurry. I couldn't get clear—Hurry wouldn't let me go. I kept trying. Hurry said if I helped with this deal he'd let me out. I played along. Tonight he squealed on me."

Gus said slowly: "To this—guy—you wanted to quit for?"

The girl nodded. Lippe spoke in a husky voice.

"That's straight, Gus. That's straight."

Connors's eyes were little blue points of fire. He said sharply:

"It's a ——damn' lie! It's a frame."

The girl shook her head. "You didn't know how much I knew," she said. "You came along to help Gus—and you came along to get me out of things. You didn't think I'd have guts enough to tell him—the truth."

Gus moved his right hand a little. "Hurry threw you over," he said. "He got me fixed—and threw you over. He squealed about you—to the guy you wanted to quit the racket for."

Edna said: "Damn him—I just wanted—to quit. It's a rotten racket."

Gus said slowly: "I think you—told the one truth, Kid."

Connors stiffened his body; he stared up at the fight manager. He said fiercely:

"You ain't falling for the line, Gus. For God's sake—you don't think—"

Gus smiled just a little. "Yeah," he said in a soft tone. "You did the job, Connors. You talked about Giant being a good guy—but you did the job. Sure as hell—you did it."

The girl started to cry. Gus said sharply:

"Don't do that, Kid! Where's Hurry—and Little Andy—"

The blonde stopped crying and looked at Gus. Her voice was broken when she spoke.

"They split up—after the kill—got out of the burg. They had coin—they didn't leave me any—"

Connors turned his head towards the fight manager, shook it from side to side.

"Jeeze, Gus," he breathed, "I'm tellin' you it's a fix! If you don't—"

"All right," the manager cut in softly. "All right, Connors. It's a fix."

The girl said: "Burke went—with them. They cleaned up plenty—and they got your—"

She stopped, said softly: "And he squealed on me. He hit me, Gus. He went to—"

Connors's eyes were looking down towards the white surface of the table. The manager spoke in a steady tone.

"Don't get careless, Connors. Keep your hands where I can see them. We're just—talkin'."

Connors swore. "She's just—lying!" he said huskily. "She's killing time, maybe. If we stick here they'll walk in on—"

Gus Monkly smiled. "Edna and me—we've got plenty of time," he said. "You—maybe *you* ain't got so much."

Connors's eyes widened. His lips parted—he stared at Gus. He said:

"Now listen, Gus—I'm telling you—"

The fight manager said slowly: "Never mind, Connors. You slipped that gun to the guy working with you, in the ring. But you hung on to the towel. I got a look at it. The gas burned it a little. I couldn't be sure about that, so I played along. I treated you like you were a white guy, Connors."

His voice got suddenly hard. "But that's done now. You killed, Connors—and you won't get free. Maybe the others won't, either. You can't tell. I don't know about that. But I know about *you*!"

Connors relaxed in the chair and stared at the fight manager. He shook his head slowly. An amazed smile showed in his eyes.

"You're falling for her line!" he said hoarsely. "I'll be damned if you ain't falling for—"

His body moved forward—the table came up from the floor. The girl screamed as the white surface battered against her head. Gus Monkly stepped to one side and squeezed the gun trigger.

The bullet ricocheted from the iron leg nearest him. Connors's gun crashed. Gus felt a hot pain over his left thigh. He squeezed the trigger a second time. Connors cried out. But his gun crashed again.

Gus Monkly felt as though he had been lifted away for a little while—hot waves ran through his body. He saw the body of Connors roll clear of the fallen table. He leveled the muzzle and squeezed the trigger until the gun was silent. He looked at the girl. She was sprawled on the floor, her face white.

He said to Lippe, very weakly: "She's just—knocked cold—fix her up."

He went over and looked down at Connors. The handler's eyes were half closed—already they had a stare in them.

Gus said in a whisper: "You can't fix *him* up—"

Lippe was muttering words Gus couldn't understand. He walked slowly past the fat man, went into the hallway. It took him time to get the lock turned. When he reached the street the air felt good. There was a bluish light down near the docks—he moved in that direction. His body felt like something that didn't belong to him. There was a moving coldness down his thighs. He walked a little like a drunken man.

When he reached the bluish light there was a lunch-wagon below it. It took him time to climb the three steps and get inside. A lean-faced man looked at him and grinned. Gus said weakly:

"Pack of—Camels—light me one—will you?"

The lean-faced man stared at him. Gus got his right hand inside a pocket, and tossed a half dollar on the counter. He said hoarsely:

"Make it—fast—"

There was a pounding in his ears that sounded a lot like the knockdown timekeeper's mallet, hitting the wood, in the Garden. The lunch-wagon proprietor was fumbling with a pack of cigarettes. It was cold inside the place.

Gus thought of Giant Pardo and said very softly:

"Don't look—at me—go to—a neutral corner—"

When the proprietor of the lunch-wagon heard Gus's body fall, he came around from behind the counter and swore. He put the lighted cigarette between his own lips. When he leaned over Gus's body he saw the red stain on the floor. Gus had been dead ten minutes when the first cop reached the place. It was a cold dawn, and they weren't easy to find.

The Parrot That Wouldn't Talk

Walter C. Brown

WALTER C. BROWN, a Pennsylvanian, quit his job as a bookkeeper to become partner in a bookshop, then acquired an extensive collection of criminological information, much of it unpublished. From these files, as well as a dedicated reading of mystery and detective fiction, he had sufficient material to make the decision to write mysteries himself.

His first short story, "The Squealer," was published in the pulp magazine *Clues* in 1929, the same year in which his first novel, *The Second Guess*, appeared. He went on to write two more mystery novels, *Laughing Death* (1932) and *Murder at Mocking House* (1933), as well as dozens of stories in the 1930s and 1940s for such pulps as *Argosy*, *Blue Book*, *Detective Tales*, and *Black Mask*, as well as such higher-paying slicks as *Liberty* and *The Saturday Evening Post*.

Several of his short stories were adapted for early television series, and his novella "Prelude to Murder," first published in the October 1945 issue of *Blue Book*, served as the basis for the highly suspenseful, if largely unknown, British motion picture *House in the Woods* (1957). It is the chilling story of a couple, played by Patricia Roc and Michael Gough, who seek solitude and rent an isolated house whose landlord, played by Ronald Howard (the son of Trevor Howard and once the star of a 1950s *Sherlock Holmes* television series), is an artist and very weird indeed. It was directed by Maxwell Munden, who also wrote the screenplay.

"The Parrot That Wouldn't Talk" was published in the January 1942 issue.

The Parrot That Wouldn't Talk

Walter C. Brown

The Feather Devil was perched on the window-sill of the vacant house.

A CHINATOWN NOVELETTE

Sah-jin O'Hara, Blue Coat Devil of the Chinatown Squad, had been handed some queer crime clues in his dealings with the slant-eyed Sons of Han, but never a plastered parrot that wouldn't talk—not even to utter the three little words that held the key to a fabulous fortune.

CHAPTER ONE
THE PURLOINED PARROT

THE PARROT IS KNOWN by many names, but call it *perico*, *papagei* or *perroquet*, it is still a remarkable bird. Bespectacled professors describe it as a zygodactyl of the order Psittaci; howl-

ing black savages of the Congo speak of it as The Talking Ghost—and down in Chinatown the slant-eyed Sons of Han call it The Feather Devil.

But mention the word "parrot" to Sergeant Dennis O'Hara of the Chinatown Squad and you will hear a shorter and stronger name for the species, for the Red-Hair Sah-jin, as the Yellow Quarter calls him, is not likely to forget the mystery of The Parrot That Wouldn't Talk.

"That's the kind of breaks you get in Chinatown," O'Hara said. "Everywhere else the parrot is famous for imitating the human voice—so I get stuck with one that wouldn't talk. We didn't want a whole speech, either—just three little words, but drunk or sober, that blasted Feather Devil kept its beak shut."

Then O'Hara grins at you. "Never heard of a drunk parrot, eh? Well, this one was plastered, all right—wobbling on its feet, and making noises like hiccoughs. Yes, sir, I've been handed some damn queer clues in my time, but that liquored parrot tops 'em all!"

It happened that the mysterious chain of events began one quiet evening as Yun Chee the tea merchant sat in his favorite bamboo chair, reading aloud from the poems of Li Po. Behind him, on a pedestal-stand near the open window, was a green parrot called Choy.

"Rawk-awk!" squawked the parrot, stirring restlessly.

"Silence!" Yun Chee commanded, frowning, then began Li Po's famous Moon Poem in a sing-song chant:

*"I fish for the Moon in the Yellow River,
I cast my net with cunning hand—"*

"Awk!" shrilled the parrot, and there was a swift sound like the rustling of feathers.

In rising anger Yun Chee twisted his head around—then his jaw dropped, and the wooden-bound volume of poems clattered to the floor, for a long arm had darted in through the open window, snaring the parrot in folds of black cloth. And before the startled merchant could spring to his feet, the pedestal was empty—the parrot gone!

"*Hai!* Thief! Thief!" Yun Chee yelled, dashing to the window in time to see a dark figure racing through the back garden. Snatching an antique Mongol dagger from the wall, Yun Chee dashed out to corner the brazen thief.

The marauder was halfway up a narrow ladder set against the high, spiked wall, when the merchant leaped forward and seized him by the legs, pulling him to the ground. As Yun Chee struck with his antique blade, his knife hand was seized in a grip of iron. There was a brief, sharp scuffle—a scream—a groaning fall.

Wei Lum, the merchant's servant, hearing his master's cries, came running through the back door as the black silhouette of the thief was poised atop the wall, hauling up his ladder, then making a headlong leap into the darkness.

"*Ai-yee!*" Wei Lum wailed, crouching down beside Yun Chee's prostrate body to strike a match. The spurt of yellow flame revealed the antique dagger which was buried to the hilt in Yun Chee's chest.

"Mask—thief—steal—Choy!" Yun Chee gasped, then gave a bubbling cough, shuddered, and subsided into limp silence.

"Poh-liss! Poh-liss!" Wei Lum screamed to the arousing neighbors, and dashing into the house, pounded out shivering crashes on a gong which hung in the hall.

Detective Driscoll of the Chinatown Squad came on the run from Mulberry Lane, but Yun Chee was already dead when he arrived. He was busy questioning the servant when Sergeant O'Hara reached the scene in a red prowl car.

"Yun Chee—stabbed to death," Driscoll reported. "This is gonna be a tough nut to crack, Sarge. The guy made a clean getaway. We've got the knife, but it belonged to Yun Chee himself, and worse luck, Wei Lum pawed it over, trying to pull it out of the wound. That kills our chance of getting decent prints."

"Hell!" was O'Hara's brief comment. He stood outside the window through which the parrot had been snatched, his glance taking in the details of the richly furnished room. A red-and-gold lacquered cabinet stood just inside the window, holding a jade figure of Kwan-Yin and a vase with a plum blossom design.

"Look at the stuff on this cabinet, Driscoll. Here's a Kwan-Yin in mutton-fat jade. And this vase is genuine Ming. A thousand dollars' worth of loot right under the thief's hand, and he steals a five-dollar parrot! Does that make sense?"

"Maybe he didn't know it was a Ming vase," Driscoll suggested.

"Could be," O'Hara conceded, "but show me a Chink who doesn't know mutton-fat jade when he sees it."

Driscoll rubbed his chin. "Look, Sarge, the parrot he stole wasn't even worth five dollars. For five bucks you can get a talking bird, and this one was just the squawky kind. Even so, it'll be enough to put a rope around that killer's neck— *if* he holds on to it! That's the catch. If the guy has ten cents' worth of brains, he'll wring the bird's neck and toss it into the first ash can."

"I don't think so, Driscoll. This looks like a planned job to me. I think this fellow wanted Yun Chee's parrot—and nothing else."

"But why?" Driscoll argued. "Why kill a man for a dumb, no-account bird like that Choy? There's the Ming vase—and the jade. Either one would buy a boat load of parrots."

"Well, screwy things happen in Chinatown," O'Hara replied, "but there's always a reason behind it, and I'm betting this is more than just a sneak-thief job. We'll see, Driscoll. As the Chinks say: Time holds the key to every lock."

"I'd say the parrot was the key to this one," Driscoll replied. "How's chances of tracing it?"

"No dice," O'Hara growled. "There are dozens of those damn green parrots in Chinatown. The Chinks buy 'em from sailors along the waterfront. Some are kept for pets, others make parrot stew. If we start a systematic search, the news will be all over the place inside of five minutes. Our man simply gets rid of the bird, and we blow our only chance."

But the Blue Coat Devils were not the only ones in Chinatown concerned over the deed of violence which had sent Yun Chee to join his honorable ancestors. The tea merchant had been a high official of the Tsin Tien Tong, which would suffer a Number One "loss of face" if his death went unsolved and unavenged.

Soon it was rumored that the Tsin Tien Tong offered a reward of five hundred Rice Face dollars for the capture of Yun Chee's murderer, and that the tong council had already voted upon the punishment to be visited upon the guilty man. He would not be delivered to the Rice Face Law—no, by Tao! He would be taken to a secret place to hear his doom. Death—death by the split bamboo!

"Aye, a life for a life!" the yellow men whispered. "The Scales of Justice must be evenly weighted."

"It's a race, Sarge," Driscoll said, reporting the rumors. "If that Tsin Tien crowd get their hands on the killer first, he's a dead pigeon."

"All right, then, it's a race," O'Hara replied. "But I'll give you odds that their five-hundred-dollar reward goes begging."

But while the two greatest powers in Chinatown pursued their grim manhunt in relentless rivalry, little Wei Lum, faithful servant of the murdered tea merchant, had his own ideas for tracking down the killer. Let the Blue Coat Devils hunt with death-dealing pistols, let the great tong bait its trap with silver. Wei Lum had a potent weapon of his own—music!

Every night the little servant went wandering through the crooked streets, pausing here and there in the shadows to play a Cantonese tune on his bamboo flute—a musical signal designed to catch the ear of Choy, the stolen parrot.

"In the house of Yun Chee," Wei Lum explained to O'Hara, "Choy always make a noise like whistling when I play the flute for the Master. *Wah!* Now I make music in the streets. If Choy hear my flute, he will whistle, wherever he is prisoner, and so I find him."

"That's a damn smart trick," O'Hara replied. "Keep at it, boy, but remember—if you're lucky enough to trace the parrot, don't try anything single-handed. This fellow's a killer. Just mark the house and come for me *chop-chop*."

So Wei Lum played his squeaky little tunes in Half Moon Street and Paradise Court and Mandarin Lane, in Pagoda Street and Peking Court and Long Sword Alley—and when he had finished he would search the night hush with ears alert for the faintest reply from the captive Choy.

Then one night Wei Lum came racing breathlessly into the precinct station, crying out for instant speech with the Red-Hair Sah-jin.

"I find stolen Choy!" he panted to O'Hara. "Tonight, when I make my music in Lantern Court, I hear him call out. Sah-jin, the Feather Devil is a prisoner in No. 14—in the house of Chang Pao!"

"Chang Pao!" O'Hara exclaimed. "You must be crazy!"

O'Hara's astonishment was twofold. In the first place, Chang Pao was quite wealthy—Chinatown's most famous silversmith until he had been forced into retirement by a paralytic stroke which had left him with a crippled hand.

And to make Wei Lum's accusation even

more fantastic, Chang Pao was at that very moment on his deathbed, speechless and completely paralyzed. O'Hara had the word of Doc Stanage, the precinct medico, for that.

"Chang Pao's had another stroke," Stanage had reported. "I stopped in to see him, but there's nothing I can do. It's just a question of time. He may linger this way for weeks, but the end is certain."

O'Hara placed these indisputable facts before Wei Lum, but the yellow man held stubbornly to his assertion that the stolen parrot was hidden away in No. 14 Lantern Court.

"Sah-jin, if there were a thousand Feather Devils in dark room, I will pick out the voice of Choy without fail!"

And Wei Lum's words rang with so much confidence that O'Hara was impressed. After all, there were two other persons in Chang Pao's house. There was his nephew, Chang Loo, who had been summoned from a distant city when the old silversmith's condition became worse— and there was his servant, Tai Gat, the limping *mafoo*.

But Tai Gat the *mafoo* was something of a Chinatown hero, noted for his unswerving devotion to his master. And as for young Chang Loo, a stranger to the quarter, was it conceivable that he would go about stealing worthless parrots on the very eve of inheriting a great fortune?

Nevertheless, Sergeant O'Hara reached for his hat. "O.K., Wei Lum, we'll go around to Chang's for a look-see."

In the darkness of Lantern Court, the silversmith's house at No. 14 had the frowning air of a fortress. Lights shining behind the drawn shades of the upper floor revealed the tracery of iron bars, while all the windows of the ground floor were covered by solid wooden shutters, for Chang Pao had developed a fear of thieves that amounted to a phobia.

O'Hara's brisk rapping was answered promptly by a grim-faced *mafoo* wearing a *shaam* of dark blue denim.

"*Hola*, Tai Gat," O'Hara greeted.

"*Ala wah*, Sah-jin," the *mafoo* replied, bowing gravely. He walked with a heavy limp, memento of his courageous battle against two armed thugs who had invaded his master's house some years before.

"Sah-jin, you come for see Master Chang?" Tai Gat inquired.

"Yes," O'Hara answered, "but first there's another little matter. Tai Gat, do you have a parrot here in the house?"

"Yiss," the *mafoo* replied, without the least trace of hesitation or surprise at the question. "Master keep Feather Devil long time."

"Well, I'd like to have a look at it," O'Hara said crisply. "This man—Wei Lum—is searching for a parrot that was stolen."

"Stolen!" Tai Gat cast a disdainful glance at Wei Lum. "*Tsai!* Is this a house of thieves? Wei Lum is *gila*—crazy!"

"You lie, *mafoo*!" Wei Lum retorted angrily, roused by the measured scorn in Tai Gat's voice and bearing. "The Feather Devil we seek is here—here in this very house! With my own ears I have heard it."

"Pipe down, Wei Lum!" O'Hara commanded. "Tai Gat's offered to show us the honorable Chang Pao's parrot."

"Words of wisdom, Sah-jin," Tai Gat declared. "One glance of the eye tells more than an hour's talk."

CHAPTER TWO
THE POH-LISS TAKE OVER

'Hara looked about him with interest as he followed the limping *mafoo* toward the stairs, for the house of Chang Pao was a corner of the Orient magically set down in the very heart of the White Devil's city, and he had not been inside No. 14 Lantern Court since the night, several years before, when Chang Pao's shrill voice had screamed, "Robbers! Robbers!" from an upper window.

Smashing his way in at the front door, O'Hara had found Tai Gat waging a desperate battle against two night robbers, and holding his own against them despite a badly hurt leg from a headlong tumble down the stairs, an injury which had left the faithful *mafoo* with his heavy-footed limp.

But the attempted robbery had left its mark on Chang Pao as well. Grown secretive and suspicious, the silversmith lived in a hermit-like seclusion, fortifying his house with barred and shuttered windows, lining his doors with sheet-iron strips, so that they swung open as slowly and ponderously as the gates of a prison.

Tai Gat's slippered feet were noiseless on the stairs, but O'Hara chanced to stumble, and at the sound a door opened suddenly above, and a young Chinese in a gaudy house-robe of yellow silk moved quickly to the upper railing.

"*Hai!* What name you? What you want?" he demanded, peering down at them with sharp-eyed suspicion.

O'Hara knew this must be Chang Loo, nephew and heir to the dying silversmith. But before he could reply, Tai Gat's voice cut in swiftly, naming the visitors.

"Poh-liss!" young Chang hissed, plainly startled. He straightened up stiffly, his right hand creeping into the folds of his yellow sleeve.

Tai Gat's voice went on in explanation. A Feather Devil had been stolen, and the Red-Hair Sah-jin merely wished to make a look-see at the Master's parrot.

The *mafoo*'s words seemed to banish young Chang's momentary tenseness, although the sharp arrogance remained in his voice.

"Feather Devils!" he echoed haughtily. "Shall we be plagued with such trifling matters in the hour when my venerable uncle stands on the threshold of the Shadow-world? Poh-liss— *tsai!*" Young Chang spat over his shoulder and made a quick sign with his fingers. "Bid them begone till a more seemly hour!"

O'Hara's jaw settled into square lines, not liking the arrogant tone of this silk-robed upstart who made the "finger curse" as he mentioned the name of police.

"That trifling matter, Chang, happens to be a murder—Yun Chee's murder. I want to see that parrot—and right now!"

For a few moments their glances met and held in a tug-of-war—O'Hara's eyes of frosty blue, Chang Loo's shoe-button eyes of cold jet, with reddened lids that checked with the sour smell of rice-wine about him.

Then Chang Loo stood aside, sullen and silent, but as the *mafoo* brushed past he seized hold of his robe and pushed him against the wall. "Brainless fool!" he snarled. "Must you open the door to all who knock?"

So saying, he turned on his heel and stalked back into his uncle's chamber, while Tai Gat led them to a small room on the top floor— a room hung with plum-colored draperies and fitted out as a prayer shrine. There was an altar with jade bowls and the Chang ancestral tablets, and a gilded wooden statue of Kwan-Yin, but O'Hara had eyes only for the green-feathered parrot perched on a shining steel hoop.

"*Hai!* It is Choy!" Wei Lum cried out, pushing forward, but the parrot gave no sign of recognition, merely staring at them with drooping, cynical eyes.

O'Hara caught the first dawning of doubt on Wei Lum's face as the yellow man scrutinized the green bird more closely—then saw the doubt deepen into reluctant conviction.

"I make mistake, Sah-jin," Wei Lum confessed. "This Feather Devil same for size and color, but it is not Choy."

"His name Shao," Tai Gat put in, and the green Feather Devil, cocking its head and crisping its claw, burst into sudden angry clamor with a raucous repetition of "Shao! Shao! Shao!"

"Shao—that means fire or flame," O'Hara remarked. "He should have some red feathers with a name like that. . . . Well, sorry to have troubled you, Tai Gat."

The *mafoo* made a polite bow. "You likee stop see Master Chang? Maybe you not see him again. Doctor Meng say Master go soon to join honorable ancestors."

On the way downstairs they stopped briefly at the room where the stricken silversmith lay silent and motionless on his *k'ang*, as though Yo Fei the Dread One had already tapped his shoulder.

Young Chang Loo stood at the window, smoking a cigarette. Doctor Meng the apothecary kept watch beside the *k'ang*, eyes fixed on Chang Pao's withered face. The gray-bearded *tuchum* of the Five Tongs Council was also present, and Sang Lee the scrivener, busy painting the prayers that would be burned the moment old Chang "mounted the Dragon."

They all bowed gravely at O'Hara's entrance, all but young Chang, who only turned his head far enough for a sullen, sidelong flicker.

O'Hara stood beside the *k'ang*, looking down at the unconscious silversmith. "Has there been any change?" he asked Meng.

The apothecary held a silvered mirror above Chang's nostrils and examined the result, peering through iron-rimmed spectacles which were without lenses. "Sah-jin, the Breath of Life grows weaker with every hour."

"I'm sorry," O'Hara said gently, for he regarded Chang Pao as an old friend. The Death Watch bowed gravely again as O'Hara turned toward the door, but out of the corner of his eye he saw young Chang scowl and make the same furtive "finger curse."

"Well, Wei Lum, we struck out on that clue," O'Hara remarked to the crestfallen yellow man when they were outside. "Are you sure you picked the right house?"

"Sah-jin, I play twice on the flute, and listen twice, to make sure it is Choy," Wei Lum declared.

O'Hara shook his head. "I suppose a couple of green parrots that look alike, sound alike, too. Don't give up your search, Wei Lum. Maybe you'll have better luck next time."

"*Kwei lung*—devil dragons!" Wei Lum muttered as he tucked the bamboo flute into his sleeve and padded off into the darkness of Lantern Court.

O'Hara glanced up at the lighted windows of Chang Pao's room. A distorted shadow slanted across the drawn shades—Chang Loo the lucky nephew, smoking his White Devil cigarettes, watching beady-eyed for the dawn of his Day of Riches.

And young Chang did not have long to wait, for the old silversmith died that night. Still unconscious, he breathed his last during the hour of the Tiger, which is between four and six a.m. by White Devil reckoning. O'Hara learned this from Doc Stanage, who had issued the death certificate.

O'Hara knew what routine steps would follow Chang Pao's demise. After prayers had been burned and the death candles lit, Chang's body would be placed in its ironwood coffin and conveyed to the Hall of Sorrows in the Plum Blossom Joss House.

hen the tong *tuchum*, with the proper witnesses, would seal the doors of Chang's house with paper strips bearing the tong insignia— seals which would not be broken until the silversmith's will had been read and his lawful heir placed in possession.

Later in the day O'Hara and Driscoll attended that brief ceremony in the silk-draped office of Lee Shu the Chinese banker. Lee opened his iron vault and brought out Chang's sealed will, which had been in his keeping for several years. It turned out to be a short, concise document, leaving his entire estate, without condition, to his nephew, Chang Loo.

So Chang Loo presented his credentials for formal inspection by Lee Shu and the tong council, and became master of No. 14 Lantern Court and its sealed riches.

"That guy was born with a horseshoe in each fist!" Driscoll remarked. "Chances are he never had one dollar to rub against another, and now look at him. I hear old Chang left a shelf-ful of ginger-jars filled up and running over with Rice Face cash. But I bet young Chang'll empty 'em quick enough. You can see he's just itchin' to step out high, wide and handsome."

O'Hara nodded. "Funny, how Wei Lum's tip on the parrot brought us to Chang's house. When I caught young Chang making the 'finger curse,' I thought maybe we had something."

"Listen, Sarge." Driscoll grinned. "If we started hauling in all the Chinks who hate cops, we'd run out of cell-space in half an hour."

"But there *was* a parrot in the house," O'Hara declared.

"So what?" Driscoll argued. "Wei Lum looked it over and told you it wasn't Choy. What more do you want?"

O'Hara made a restless gesture. "I don't know, Driscoll, but I have a sort of hunch that I've overlooked something—somewhere."

Then came the night when Sergeant O'Hara learned that stronger names than Feather Devil could be applied to a parrot. It was a night of lowering blue fog that turned the neon lights of Mulberry Lane into gaudy strings of smoldering jewels.

O'Hara, pursuing his usual rounds, paused at the gilded doorway of a tong house to put on the black slicker he had been carrying on his arm. The misty fog was changing rapidly to a steady, cold drizzle, and the few Celestials who were abroad drifted past like blurred shadows.

The iron bell of St. Mary's steeple tolled out ten solemn strokes—the hour of the Fox—as O'Hara came within sight of the glass lantern hanging beside the doorway to the Plum Blossom Joss House—a deep blue glow which floated in the smoky void like a sinister moon.

A globular shadow loomed up on O'Hara's left, bobbing along toward the brownstone steps of the joss house, and as the bulky figure passed under the peacock-blue lantern O'Hara recognized Mark Sin, Chinatown's Number One gambler.

He watched the slant-eyed master of gaming disappear through the Plum Blossom portals. Mark Sin's visits to the joss house were for one purpose only—to burn silver-paper prayers at the shrine of Liu Hai the Money God. Which meant there would be another "floating" fan-tan game tonight somewhere in Paradise Court.

"And just try to break it up!" O'Hara muttered, with the wry smile that came of long experience with the cunning ways of the Yellow Quarter.

O'Hara even knew who would be the principal players around Mark Sin's gaming table. There would be Wing Lung the silk merchant, Kim Yao the goldsmith, Meng Tai the apothecary, Long Jon of the Tea House—and yes, no doubt young Chang Loo, the two-handed spendthrift who was treading a silken path since he had fallen heir to the wealth of his uncle, Chang Pao.

"Beggar on horseback!" O'Hara growled, recalling the many stories about young Chang's unceasing round of carousing and drinking and reckless gaming. Chang Loo had not even made a pretense of mourning his dead uncle—no white sorrow-robes for him, no period of fasting and seclusion, no ancestor joss burning in the Plum Blossom.

Moving like a black shadow, O'Hara proceeded through Half Moon Street and into Lantern Court. In passing, he glanced at the shuttered windows of No. 14, standing dark and silent as a Ming tomb.

"I wonder what old Chang would say if he knew how his hard-earned money was being thrown around," O'Hara thought to himself. Well, when young Chang's follies had eaten up all the Rice Face dollars, he could replenish his purse by stripping the old house of its valuable antique furnishings and start all over again.

"If Chang Loo lives that long!" O'Hara thought. For the slant-eyed upstart was arrogant and quarrelsome in his cups, conducting himself with the haughty insolence of a red-button mandarin.

There was a whispered tale of a rash insult to a certain tongster—one of the dreaded Red Lamp men—a deed which might well have cost Chang Loo his shadow had not Tai Gat the limping *mafoo* come to his rescue. But instead of being grateful, young Chang had screamed drunken curses at his uncle's servant, and hurled a stone wine-bottle at his head.

"Guess I'd better give that blasted fool a talking-to, before he gets a knife between his ribs," O'Hara said to himself as he groped his way across Lantern Court. The slow rain was beginning to drip eerily from hidden eaves, and somewhere in the darkness an unseen musician was playing a moon-fiddle.

Presently O'Hara found the narrow opening to Mandarin Lane, and so came out upon Canton Street. He walked past the dark houses, peering up at an occasional lighted window. Then O'Hara felt cobblestones under his feet; and knew that the bleary yellow glow to his right was the lamp-post at the entrance to the three-sided Court called Manchu Place.

And O'Hara stopped dead in his tracks, for in the murky depths of Manchu Place a tiny light winked on and off, on and off—and his ears caught a whistled signal, low and toneless and continually repeated.

Following the sidewall with outstretched hand, O'Hara moved toward the mysteriously winking light. "Flashlight!" he decided, and tried to make out the vague, blurred figure directing the beam.

The winking light focused briefly on the shuttered window of a house, clicked on again, centered now on a doorway above five brownstone steps. The toneless whistle sounded again.

O'Hara, quietly moving his gun to the pocket of his slicker, crept nearer the winking beam, closing in at an oblique angle.

"What goes on here?" he demanded sharply. "Don't move, you! Stand there, and hold that light steady! I want a look at you!"

The beam steadied and seemed to freeze into rigidity as O'Hara stepped forward, but as he reached the brownstone steps he broke out with a muttered oath, for there was no one behind the light! At his challenge the quick-witted shadow had simply placed the flashlight on the top step and slipped away into the shrouding fog.

O'Hara snatched up the flash and swung the beam to and fro in a half circle, then clicked it off while he stood motionless, listening. His ears picked out the faint pad-pad of slippered feet—a whispering sound that fled and died.

"A flashlight in a fog," O'Hara muttered. "Now what in thunder would he be hunting for?"

As if in answer to his question, a muffled cry shrilled through the murky dark—the raucous "*Awk-awk!*" of a parrot!

O'Hara whirled toward the sound, and when the squawk was repeated, his flash beam picked out the parrot. The Feather Devil was perched on the windowsill of a vacant house, seemingly hypnotized by the glare of the electric eye turned upon it, for it made no effort to escape O'Hara's reaching hand.

"*Awk!*" said the parrot plaintively, and snuggled down in the crook of his arm. It was cold and wet and bedraggled, and one wing appeared to be injured. But it was green, this Feather Devil—all green—and a startling thought leaped into O'Hara's mind.

Could it be Choy, the parrot stolen from Yun Chee's house? Had it somehow managed to escape from its captor? And if this were so, the man with the flashlight might have been the masked killer of the tea merchant.

"And I let the guy run out on me!" O'Hara groaned. "Me, with a gun in my fist, and him not ten feet away! But at least I've got the parrot, and believe me, this Feather Devil gets a Number One going-over!"

Unconsciously O'Hara's hand had tightened on the bird, and he felt something soft under his fingers, something that made him quickly focus the flash beam. There was a tight little scroll of cloth wound around the parrot's leg!

Steadying the flashlight under his arm, O'Hara unwound the ragged strip of cloth, eyes glinting as he saw that it was covered with ragged columns of Chinese writing in a deep red tint.

"Blood!" O'Hara exclaimed. "It's written with blood!"

With the precious scroll tucked away in his pocket and the Feather Devil nestled inside his slicker, O'Hara hurried back to the precinct station. "Hey, Driscoll!" he called, sticking his head in at the Squad Room door. "Get Sang Lee the scrivener! And take it on the jump!"

O'Hara went into his office and put the green-feathered bird on the edge of his desk while he closed the door and pulled down the windows. "All right, birdie, let's have a good look at you. Sort of mussed up, eh? What's your name—Choy? . . . Come on, speak up. Choy?"

"Awk!" the parrot said, and made a clumsy swoop to the top of the desk lamp. It swayed there for a moment, preening its ruffled feathers, then slid off awkwardly to the desktop.

"Hey, keep your tail-feathers out of the inkwell!" O'Hara exclaimed. "What's the matter—got a lame foot? You're wobbling around like you were drunk—"

O'Hara broke off short on that word, and leaning over the bird, sniffed. There was an odor, a most unmistakable Oriental odor.

"*Samshu!*" O'Hara burst out. "By God, it *is* drunk! A drunken parrot! What in hell's going on here, anyway?"

CHAPTER THREE
A PLASTERED PARROT

 he parrot wobbled along the edge of the desk, swaying. Its beak opened and a gurgling sound like a hiccough issued from its throat. Then it rustled its feathers and trumpeted, "*Shao! Shao! Shao!*"

"What's that?" O'Hara stiffened alertly. "Say that again! Go on, speak up!" and he jostled the bird with his finger.

"*Shao! Shao! Shao!*" The raucous word rattled out like machine-gun fire. The angry parrot sidled away, hiccoughing.

O'Hara sat down, slowly, not taking his eyes from the bird. Not the murdered Yun Chee's Choy, after all. This was Shao—Shao, old Chang's parrot! How had it escaped from the silversmith's house in Lantern Court? And what desperate message needed writing in blood, to be sent out into the night with a drunken parrot as its fantastic messenger?

Unrolling the torn strip of cloth, O'Hara stared at the jagged red symbols as though he would tear out its meaning by sheer will power, but his limited knowledge of the "broken stick" writing was of no avail.

"Rawk!" The parrot made an awkward flight to the top of a filing cabinet as the phone whirred. O'Hara lifted the receiver. It was the switchboard man, telling him that Driscoll had returned with Sang Lee the scrivener.

"I'll be right out!" O'Hara replied, and hung up. The parrot was still perched, droopy-eyed, on the filing case as he carefully closed the office door behind him.

"*Hola*, Sah-jin," Sang Lee greeted him in the Squad Room.

"Can you read this?" O'Hara questioned, thrusting the cloth message into the scrivener's hands.

"It is Number One poor writing," Sang Lee commented, squinting at the scroll. Then his breath hissed and his eyes grew round as jade buttons. "Sah-jin, hearken!" he gasped, and began to read the scarlet text.

"My name is Chang Loo, nephew of Chang Pao, silversmith. I am a prisoner in the fifth house on narrow street within one hundred fifty paces of my uncle's house in Lantern Court. Large reward to finder if this message is delivered to Blue Coat Men."

"Chang Loo—a prisoner!" O'Hara gasped in a startled voice. "In a narrow street, 150 paces from No. 14! That must be Mandarin Lane. But why in hell doesn't he say Mandarin Lane?"

"Maybe he was taken there blindfolded," Driscoll suggested.

"If he was—how would he know it was the fifth house?" O'Hara replied. "But we're wasting valuable time. Get your hat and coat, Driscoll—and your gun. This is likely to turn out a shooting job."

"How about tools, Sarge?" Driscoll inquired.

"Bring a pinch-bar and a raiding ax," O'Hara directed, and hurried back to his office for his hat and slicker. But as he flung open the door, he stood rooted on the threshold, then let out a roar of angry surprise that brought Driscoll on the run.

"The parrot!" O'Hara fumed. "It's gone! Stolen again! I'll be damned!" He strode over to the open window, peering out between the wide bars. "This window was closed when I went out. That fellow must have trailed me from Manchu Place—"

O'Hara felt something crunch under his foot. He looked down, and found a number of melon seeds scattered on the floor by the window. "That's it!" he exclaimed. "This fellow opened the window and used melon seeds as bait to bring the parrot within reach of his hands. Then he pulled it out through the bars and ran—"

"And we'd better do some running of our own," Driscoll broke in. "Forget the damn parrot, Sarge. If that fellow gets to Mandarin Lane ahead of us, we're likely to find Chang Loo with his toes turned up!"

O'Hara commandeered one of the prowl cars and they sped to the Canton Street entrance to Mandarin Lane, picking up Detective Burke as they crossed Mulberry Lane. Leaving their car parked on Canton Street, the three men plunged into the darkness of Mandarin Lane.

"There's the fifth house!" O'Hara whispered, and they came to a halt, scanning their objective. It was not really a house, but a two-story structure which had originally been a stables, later a garage, and finally abandoned altogether, judg-

ing by its neglected appearance and the planks nailed across its doors.

"No light showing," O'Hara declared, stepping back to scan the grimy upper windows, black and staring as blind eyes. The original pulley bar of the hayloft still protruded between the dormer windows, like a hangman's gibbet. A separate door set in the sidewall led, apparently, to the upper floor of the building.

"O.K., Burke, stand guard here in the lane," O'Hara ordered. "Come on, Driscoll, we'll crash this side-door and—hello, it's not even locked! That's funny—"

Driscoll's flashlight lanced the darkness of a flight of narrow, dusty stairs, ending at another door. They went up cautiously, O'Hara's hand slowly turning the knob of the upper door, then flinging it wide as Driscoll sent his beam sweeping over a bare, atticlike room festooned with cobwebs, its windows covered with heavy sacking.

The moving beam picked out piles of rusty and dusty junk—then focused suddenly on a broken-down armchair to which a Chinese was bound hand and foot. The Oriental writhed and wriggled in his bonds, trying to call out through a cloth bag.

"Cut him loose, Driscoll," O'Hara ordered, and struck a match to light an oil lantern which stood on an upturned box.

"Blue Coat Men! Praise be to Tao!" the yellow man gasped as soon as the gag was removed.

O'Hara straightened up, staring at the young Oriental. "What name you?" he demanded. "You're not Chang Loo!"

Then it was the Oriental's turn to stare. "Who say I am not Chang Loo?" he challenged. "Take me to my uncle Chang Pao the silversmith—he tell you *chop-chop* that I am his brother's son!"

"Hey, what is this!" O'Hara exclaimed. "I've seen Chang Loo a dozen times—I looked at his papers, his *huchao*, his *chock-gee*, when Chang Pao's will was read—"

"Chang Pao is dead?" the yellow man broke in excitedly. "*Hai!* Now it is as plain as black writing on rice paper! Tajen, I am Chang Loo! This other one is a thief who has stole my name, my papers—and now he steals my dead uncle's wealth! Hearken, Tajen—"

And speaking in a staccato jabber that was half English and half Cantonese, the young Celestial poured forth as strange a tale of evil plotting as Sergeant O'Hara had ever heard in this devious quarter where the bizarre and the fantastic are a daily commonplace.

Chang Loo told how he had received a telegram advising him of his uncle's grave condition and had at once set out on his long journey to reach his dying uncle's bedside.

Arriving in the late evening, he had inquired his way to Lantern Court, but even as he set foot upon the steps of No. 14, a figure had loomed up behind him, jabbed a gun against his back, and growled a command to walk straight ahead and keep his tongue behind his teeth.

One hundred and fifty paces he had counted in the darkness, to this fifth house of the narrow street whose name he did not know. Still at gunpoint, he had been forced up the dark stairs to this dark attic, where he had been tied into the chair and then gagged, by a man who wore a black cloth mask over his face.

"You've been a prisoner in this room ever since?" O'Hara asked.

"Aye, Tajen," the young Chinese replied. The masked man had searched him thoroughly, taking away all his possessions, even a little jade luck piece with the seal of Wan-teh.

He added the other details of his strange captivity. Once a day the masked man appeared to give him food and water and a few minutes' exercise walking to and fro, but always with bound hands. The masked man never spoke, only raising his pistol in a gesture that threatened instant death if the prisoner tried to summon help.

O'Hara and Driscoll exchanged swift glances. Beyond all doubt this young Chinese was the true Chang Loo—he had names, dates, facts at his command; he described with minute accuracy the very papers which O'Hara had examined in Lee Shu's office, even to a small piece torn from the corner of his official *chock-gee*.

he other Chang Loo—the arrogant, wine-drinking, fan-tan-playing Chang Loo, was a daring impostor who had engineered a brazen and spectacular theft of the old silversmith's house and fortune!

"There's cool nerve for you!" O'Hara exclaimed. "But this phoney nephew must have had help to pull off a job as slick as that." He turned to the young Oriental. "This masked man—did he walk with a limp?"

"No, Tajen, no limp."

"Hell!" O'Hara said. "I was sure it was Tai Gat."

"Well, it could be a single-handed job, Sarge," Driscoll declared. "Chang here says he hasn't visited his uncle since he was a small boy, so it wouldn't be much of a trick to fool Tai Gat. How could he tell it was a phoney?"

"I think the mask man is *gila*—crazy!" Chang put in suddenly.

O'Hara turned quickly. "Why?"

"Because of the parrot, Tajen. Always he bring this green Feather Devil with him, hidden under a black cloth. He tie the bird's foot to the floor, then he give it liquor to drink and poke it with a stick until the bird scream with anger. All the time the mask man mutter curses, and one time he kick the bird and hurt its wing—"

"Sounds crazy to me," Driscoll declared, but O'Hara said nothing, his forehead knotted in thought.

"I think he is *gila*," Chang continued, "but it is Number One good luck for me. Tonight he bring the parrot with him, like always. He push it with stick, make it drunk. But while he is here there is big noise of bells and horns as the firewagons come close by the street—"

"That's right, Sarge," Driscoll confirmed. "There was a fire in the next block."

And young Chang gave the details of the sudden opportunity which had led to his rescue. The masked man, uneasy over all the commotion outside, slipped out to see if the fire threatened Mandarin Lane, leaving his prisoner bound to the chair.

But Chang had learned how to wriggle his arms free, although he could not release his feet, for the rope was knotted behind the chair. And since he had first seen the parrot he had worked out a plan for sending a message.

Coaxing the parrot within reach of his hands had been the hardest part, Chang declared. After that, everything had been easy. A feather from the parrot's wing gave him a quill pen, a scratch across his wrist drew blood for ink, a torn piece of cloth served as paper.

With the message hastily written and tied to the bird's leg, he had inched his chair over to a long-handled rake in the dusty rubbish. Perching the parrot on the rusty tines of the rake, he had lifted it up to a small air-vent under the roof.

"A push, Tajen, and the Feather Devil is on his way," Chang went on. "But I have just finish when the mask man returns. He make an angry shout and hit me. Then he tie my hands quick and run out, and I say a thousand prayers to Kwan-Yin that the Feather Devil will escape from him."

"That was a smart piece of work, Chang," O'Hara commended, "but you're lucky it didn't cost you your life."

"The fellow was too busy trying to catch the parrot," Driscoll suggested.

"Yes—the parrot," O'Hara said slowly. "We're always running up against a Feather Devil. Look, Driscoll, the man who murdered Yun Chee passed up a thousand dollars' worth of easy loot to steal a worthless parrot. Why? And Chang's masked man, with a fortune at stake, risks everything to recapture Shao. Again, why?"

"That's easy," Driscoll replied. "He wanted to destroy that message."

"All right, then, let's see how he went about it," O'Hara said. "He chased the parrot along

Mandarin Lane to Canton Street and then into Manchu Place, where I chased him away. O.K.?"

"O.K.," Driscoll said.

"I pick up the parrot *and* the message. That leaves the masked man with three choices of action: he can drop everything and take it on the lam, he can go back to Mandarin Lane and kill Chang Loo to silence him, or take him away to a different hideout. So what happens? He follows me back to the precinct and snatches Shao from my office. Why? What value has the parrot, after its message is in the hands of the police?"

"I don't know," Driscoll admitted, "unless the guy is *gila*, like Chang says."

O'Hara shook his head. "Well, we'll know more about that when we finish with No. 14 Lantern Court. Let's go!"

"We'll find nothing but an empty house," Driscoll predicted. "By this time that phoney nephew has packed up all the loose dough and skipped."

"And what about the parrot?" O'Hara queried. "Does the parrot go with the rest of the loot?"

"Oh, damn the parrot!" Driscoll snorted.

"Not so fast, Driscoll." O'Hara grinned. "There's a wild hunch floating around in my head, and if I'm right—there'll be a surprise waiting for us at No. 14 Lantern Court!"

Thus it came about that the real Chang Loo retraced the one hundred fifty paces which had deprived him of his rightful inheritance, with three Blue Coat Devils walking by his side, armed and ready to enforce his lawful claim to the riches of No. 14 Lantern Court.

Chang Pao's house was as dark and gloomy-looking as it had been earlier in the evening, although the lifting fog had taken away its ghostly aspect. O'Hara went up the brownstone steps and hammered a brisk tattoo on the door.

There was no response, and he pounded again, while Driscoll watched with a smile. "I told you it'd be an empty nest, Sarge."

Then Burke called out from the rear: "There's somebody inside, Sarge! I saw a face at the upstairs window!"

"O.K., then, we'll waste no more time," O'Hara said. Jabbing the pinchbar into the crack of the door, he gouged out an opening, then began to wrench. With a crackling of wood and a snapping of metal, the lock surrendered and the door creaked inward.

Gun in hand, O'Hara stalked into the hallway, where a silk-shaded light was burning. "Hey, Chang Loo! Tai Gat!" he shouted. "Come on down! Police!"

Then O'Hara scrambled for cover as Chang Loo's bright yellow robe moved in the darkness at the head of the stairs, and a long arm clutching a pistol reached snakily over the railings.

Flame spurted from the black muzzle, and the dark stairwell echoed and re-echoed with the explosive reports. The glass panes of the vestibule door fell with a tinkling crash—a bullet skittered wildly from the face of a bronze gong, adding to the roaring clamor.

"It's no use!" O'Hara shouted up the dark staircase. "We've got you cornered! The house is surrounded! I'm giving you ten seconds to throw down that gun—or we come up after you, shooting!"

A harsh laugh was the answer, and a bullet that tore a long furrow across the wall just missed Driscoll's head.

"O.K.—you asked for it!" O'Hara shouted as he sprang toward the stairs, with Driscoll right at his heels, both pumping bullets into the upper darkness to clear their path.

The yellow robe whisked from sight as they raced up the staircase. They pounded in hot pursuit up the next flight of steps, but as they gained the upper hall a heavy door boomed shut and a cross-bar rattled into place.

O'Hara hurled his weight against the door. "Damn! It's like iron—must be lined with sheet-metal."

Driscoll hammered on the armored door with his pistol butt, calling out. "Better give up, Chang! This is your last chance! You catch bullet *chop-chop*!"

For a few moments he kept his ear against the door, listening, then shook his head. "No answer, Sarge."

O'Hara nodded. "Bring the tools—we'll smash our way in. . . . Burke, cover the outside of the house. . . . Chang Loo, keep back there on the stairs. There may be more shooting."

Sergeant O'Hara was an experienced hand with a raiding ax, but it took him nearly twenty minutes of furious hacking before the metal-shod door yielded to his attack. With the final blows, Driscoll moved forward, finger tense on trigger, but when the shattered door sagged back there was no need for shooting.

The impostor who had masqueraded as Chang Loo lay dead on the floor of the room, a pistol clutched in his hand, his bright yellow robe splashed and stained from the pool of blood collected around his head.

"What a mess!" Driscoll breathed, kneeling down beside the body. "Put the muzzle in his mouth and pulled the trigger! Blew out the back of his head . . . Hey, Sarge, look! There's the parrot!"

The green Feather Devil was perched on the back of a chair, glaring at them with hostile intensity. "Rawk-awk!" it trumpeted, crisping its claws and ruffling its feathers.

"And look—the table!" Driscoll cried, pointing. "We were just in time! He was gettin' ready to take it on the lam, with what's left of the loot."

O'Hara looked at the preparations for flight—at the disorderly heap of crumpled bills turned out, apparently, from two ginger-jars which lay empty on the floor, at a small camphor-wood casket packed with choice jade carvings in mutton-fat and *fei-tsui* and ornaments of gold and silver set with precious stones.

"Well, this guy was no piker," Driscoll commented. "It was all or nothing, and he sure gave us a run for our money. You'd think a smart guy like him would've fixed himself for a fast getaway. This room's like a jail-cell—bars on the windows, iron on the door."

"They all make mistakes," O'Hara said. He went over to the windows and tapped his finger against the metal bars, then opened a closet and sounded the walls briefly. Frowning in thought, he stood looking down at the dead man. "Funny we didn't hear the shot."

"Through that iron door?" Driscoll scoffed. "Say, he could have kicked off with a cannon while you were banging away with the ax."

"Too bad we didn't get him alive," O'Hara remarked slowly. "There are a lot of questions I'd like to ask."

Driscoll was busy searching the dead man's clothing. "Look, Sarge, here are the identification papers he stole from Chang Loo, even the little jade luck piece. . . . Recognize it, Chang?"

"Yiss, yiss!" young Chang cried, darting forward to clutch his luck piece, while O'Hara examined the papers—the telegram which had summoned Chang Loo, his *chock-gee* and *hu-chao*.

"Hello—what's this!" O'Hara exclaimed, smoothing out a strip of red paper. "Chinese writing. Is this yours, Chang?"

Chang Loo ran his eye over the "broken stick" symbols, and his voice quivered with excitement as he said, "Not see this writing before, Tajen, but it is for me—a letter from my dead uncle Chang."

This writing, by the hand of Chang Pao, for the eyes of his nephew, Chang Loo.

Having great fear of thieves and night robbers, who have thrice broken into my house in search of plunder, I have hidden the greater of my wealth in a secret place, safe from all searching, even by eyes sharp as the needle. Trusting no man, I leave the key to this hiding place in the keeping of Shao, my Feather Devil. Hearken to the three words he will speak—from those three words make one word—and that one will guide you to the hidden treasure. Use thy wealth with wisdom, son of my brother, so that the house of Chang may ever be held in honor.

For a few moments there was absolute silence after Chang Loo's voice was still; then Driscoll burst out excitedly: "There's your parrot clue, Sarge! Now we know why this phoney Chang hung on to the parrot through thick and thin! He wanted to get at old Chang's hidden treasure, and he couldn't make the parrot talk! That's why he poked it with a stick and made it drunk with *samshu*—he wanted to make it speak those three words!"

"*Hoya!*" young Chang Loo exclaimed. "It is plain as the rising sun!"

"Yes, and it's also plain that he never did get those three words out of Shao," O'Hara put in. "He was still working on that parrot tonight, when Chang Loo sent out his message. So the treasure is still hidden where old Chang left it, and the parrot still has the secret!"

CHAPTER FOUR
TRIPLE FIRE

With a single motion they all turned to face the green Feather Devil, sidling along its perch, staring back at them with a sullen hostility, as if defying them to wrest its secret by fair means or foul.

"Come on, Feather Devil, speak up!" Driscoll coaxed, scratching its crest. "Give us those three little words!"

"Rawk-awk!" said the parrot, and drew blood from Driscoll's finger with a nip of its sharp beak.

"Nice birdie!" Driscoll said soothingly. "Give us those three little words—so I can wring that blasted neck of yours!"

"You've got a job on your hands," O'Hara said. "Shao's been worked on by experts."

While Driscoll went on trying to coax the precious words from the stubborn parrot, O'Hara heard Burke's voice shouting up to him excitedly from downstairs.

"Hey, Sarge! Here's Tai Gat!"

"Send him up!" O'Hara called back, and the limping *mafoo* came hurrying up the stairs, bursting with excited questions about the broken doors, the bullet-scarred halls, the Blue Coat Man's tale that the New Master was lying dead.

With grim brevity O'Hara pointed to the sprawled body lying there on the stained floor, and recounted what had taken place in crisp, terse sentences that left the *mafoo* gasping with astonishment.

"Chang Loo not real Chang Loo!" he stammered. "Can there be two moons in the sky? *Ai-yee!* It is a devil work past all belief! Sah-jin, I leave house after rice-time to burn prayers for Old Master at Plum Blossom Joss House. Young Master say he go to fan-tan game—now he is gone to ancestors. *Hoya!* The ways of the Lords of Destiny are hidden from the eyes of men."

O'Hara questioned Tai Gat about the arrival of the false Chang Loo. The *mafoo* replied that the impostor had simply rung the bell and presented the telegram as introduction. The silversmith had already lapsed into the coma which endured until the hour of his death, and Tai Gat declared that he had observed nothing to arouse suspicion about the stranger's identity.

Regarding Chang Pao's hidden treasure, Tai Gat professed complete ignorance. The Old Master had grown secretive and suspicious in his later years, and kept most of the rooms locked up, day and night. The *mafoo* was forbidden to enter his master's private quarters, unless summoned by the gong.

"Didn't you look after the parrot Shao?" O'Hara asked. "Feeding him, and so on?"

"No, Sah-jin," Tai Gat answered. "Shao live in Master's room until he fall sick. Then I move him to Kwan-Yin room so his noise not wake Master from sleep."

"Did you ever hear the parrot talk?" O'Hara questioned. "Did you ever hear him speak anything except his name?"

"Not listen, Sah-jin," Tai Gat replied. "Me not likee Feather Devil. Young ones good for eating, but old ones good for nothing but make noise."

"Well, you're wrong about Shao. Shao happens to be the most valuable parrot in the world." Abruptly, O'Hara turned to Driscoll, who was still trying to wheedle the magic words from the obstinate Feather Devil.

"Give it up, Driscoll," O'Hara said. "You're only wasting your time. You won't coax those three words out of him, not if you worked on it the rest of your life."

"Why, what do you mean, Sarge?"

"I mean that this parrot isn't Shao—not old Chang's bird at all! And it's not the parrot I picked up in Manchu Place, either!"

Driscoll straightened up, astonishment on his face. "But look, Sarge, how do you figure? Here, you can still smell the *samshu* on the bird, and here are the ink-stains on its feathers, from the inkwell on your desk."

"Yeah, take a good look at those stains," O'Hara replied crisply. "Those marks were made with black Chinese ink, thick as paint! Since when do I have Chinese ink on my desk?"

"Then—then there must be two parrots!" Driscoll exclaimed.

"Exactly! There's been a switch. This parrot is only a stand-in for the real Shao! But I haven't finished yet with the Chinese ink. Very interesting, that Chinese ink. It's going to tell us a lot of things, because the man who painted those marks on the phoney parrot spilled some on his own hand!"

O'Hara swung around suddenly, seized Tai Gat by the arm and twisted his hand into view, revealing a telltale smudge along the edge of the palm. "Now, Tai Gat, suppose you tell us how you got that stain on your hand!"

"Not know!" the *mafoo* declared with hissing breath, trying to jerk his hand away, but O'Hara only tightened his grip, pushing him against the wall.

"Where's that other parrot, Tai Gat? Where's

the real Shao? You know! You're the one who made the switch tonight!"

The *mafoo* glared at him, sullen as a cornered animal. "Tai Gat know nothing about Feather Devil," he insisted.

O'Hara straightened up, frosty-eyed. "So you spent the evening at the Joss House, burning prayers, eh? Well, we'll soon check up on that. The *bonze* will tell us if you were there, and how long you stayed. But I know you're lying, Tai Gat! You were in Mandarin Lane tonight—in the house where you kept Chang Loo prisoner! You were in Manchu Place, hunting for Shao with a flashlight! You followed me to the precinct to snatch back the parrot—then you came back here, back to this house, and *murdered* this fake Chang Loo!"

"Hey, Sarge!" Driscoll exclaimed in protest. "You're way off the course! This was suicide. Didn't we chase this guy up the stairs, didn't he shoot at us?"

"What we saw was a yellow robe," O'Hara replied, and leveled his finger at the dead impostor on the floor. "This man was dead before we set foot in Lantern Court. I could tell by the way his blood had soaked through the straw matting."

"I still think you're shootin' wild, Sarge," Driscoll said. "If this was murder, how did Tai Gat get out of this room? Look at it—door bolted, windows barred."

"I don't know how Tai Gat got out," O'Hara replied, "but I *know* he was inside. I can prove it. Look at this letter of Chang Pao's about the parrot. Here's that Chinese ink again—a fresh smudge, right across one corner. Tai Gat handled this letter within the past hour!"

"Not so!" the *mafoo* cried out. "It is a Number One lie!"

"I still don't see it, Sarge," Driscoll argued. "If you're right, why didn't Tai Gat keep this letter for himself, or else destroy it? It's the key to the whole thing."

"Wrong!" O'Hara corrected sharply. "The parrot is the real key. What's the letter worth if you haven't got Shao—the real Shao—to give you the three words?"

O'Hara eyed the *mafoo* in cold appraisal. "Your little game is all washed up, Tai Gat. You'll do no more hunting for Chang Pao's treasure, because you're going to jail for a long, long time. So you might as well hand over that other parrot. I know you've got it hidden somewhere in this house, and I'll find it, if I have to take the place apart brick by brick."

Tai Gat's tongue moved uneasily across his lips, his eyes darting here and there as if seeking an avenue of escape. But as O'Hara's hand gripped him in warning, his momentary panic passed; his slant-eyed face settled into the imperturbable mask of the Oriental.

"The Lords of Destiny frown upon me. *Wah!* I strive no more against the tide of evil fortune. Release your hands, Sah-jin, and I will deliver the true Shao into your keeping. He is hidden in the Kwan-Yin room."

"No more tricks!" O'Hara warned, alert for a treacherous move as he followed the limping *mafoo* into the little prayer-room. Tai Gat lifted the gilded statue of Kwan-Yin to the floor, and then pulled away the black cloth which covered its pedestal. And there, under the stand, prisoned in a square wire cage, sat Shao—the real Shao—bound to silence by an ingenious wire gag fastened over its beak!

Tai Gat took out the bird and perched it on his forefinger. "Shao not talk for me—not tell me the three words of wealth," the *mafoo* said softly, then his face contorted with sudden rage and his voice rose to a snarling screech. "Now I fix so he tell no one!"

And Tai Gat seized the parrot by the neck, twisted its head around with one vicious swirl and hurled the dead Feather Devil at O'Hara's head.

"*Wang pu tau!*" the *mafoo* snarled, wrenching free from O'Hara's clutching grasp and springing for the door, no longer the limping *mafoo*, but a frenzied killer darting toward escape with full-striding vigor, twisting away from Driscoll, hurling Chang Loo aside, slamming the door behind him to delay pursuit.

"The stairs!" O'Hara shouted, wrenching

open the door, gun in hand. But Tai Gat was not racing down the steps. The wily *mafoo* had darted into the room where the false Chang Loo lay dead and flung up the sash of the far window.

The two detectives reached the battered doorway in time to see Tai Gat lift one foot to the sill as the seemingly solid web of iron bars swung outward in their wooden frame, like a grilled gate.

Driscoll fired and missed, but Tai Gat turned at bay, snarling, reaching for a shelf that held an array of bottles and drinking-bowls. With the fury of a madman he hurled stone bottles and porcelain cups and pottery jugs in a crashing barrage that filled the air with flying splinters and the rising fumes of rice wine and white Chinese whiskey.

O'Hara stumbled backwards as a stone bottle caught him on the shoulder, while Driscoll crumpled and fell under the impact of a blue-glazed *samshu* jar, his second shot plowing wildly into the ceiling.

Tai Gat took advantage of the momentary confusion to scramble out over the sill, and by the time O'Hara reached the window, the *mafoo* had left the narrow outside ledge and was crawling up the steep slant of the shingled roof.

"Come back here, or I'll shoot!" O'Hara warned, leveling his .38.

Tai Gat turned his head, spitting curses as he glared down at the detective. Then his handhold slipped—

O'Hara leaned far out, snatching at the blue *shaam* as Tai Gat slid past, but the cloth tore away from his straining fingers. For one sickening moment the *mafoo* held fast to the rainspout, then the frail metal sagged and snapped off.

O'Hara's ears rang with the *mafoo*'s last wild cry—he heard the dull thump as the body landed on the hard brick pavement three stories below. He saw Burke come running from the house, his flashlight probing the darkness, but he knew that Tai Gat was dead even before Burke's terse shout reached up to him.

By that time Driscoll was stirring again, brushing aside the broken pieces of blue pottery.

"Are you all right?" O'Hara asked.

"I'm O.K., Sarge." Driscoll managed a crooked grin as he tenderly explored the lump on his head. "Hey, what about Tai Gat? Did he get away?"

"A permanent getaway," O'Hara replied grimly. "He slipped and fell from the roof. Not a bad little trick, this window with the phoney bars. Now you see how he made that other getaway, earlier tonight."

Driscoll shook his head. "White or yellow, Sarge, they don't come any slicker than Tai Gat. Everything phoney—phoney parrots, phoney nephews, phoney suicides—yes, even a phoney limp. And the guy hooked us at the end, too. There's Shao, dead as a doornail. That damn *mafoo*! Now we'll never get those three words!"

O'Hara turned to young Chang with a wide gesture that took in the cash and jades and jewelry spread out on the table. "Well, Chang, there's what's left of your inheritance. And of course, you'll have the house and the furnishings, so you won't exactly starve."

"*Kan hsieh*, Sah-jin," young Chang said, with a grateful bow. "What remains is wealth far beyond my simple needs."

"That's the spirit," O'Hara commended. "With the parrot dead, perhaps we'll never find the rest of your uncle's money."

"Yes," Driscoll agreed. "Parrot or no parrot, you can bet Tai Gat and his pal gave this house a Number One going-over—and no dice." He went over to the table and stood looking at the heaped-up valuables.

"The way I figure it, Sarge, they got the jitters when the parrot escaped with Chang's message and started packing up to take it on the lam. Then Tai Gat got the bright idea of bumping off his pal and letting the dead man take the rap."

"I think it goes even deeper than that," O'Hara put in. "I believe that this false nephew was only a stooge for Tai Gat's scheming. I doubt if he knew anything about the parrot, or the hidden treasure."

"But Chang Pao's letter!" Driscoll exclaimed. "We found it in his pocket!"

"Yes, but don't forget the smudge of China ink from Tai Gat's fingers," O'Hara replied. "I'll never be able to prove it now, but I'd bet Tai Gat planted that letter after the murder, to make the job look even more complete. He'd still have the inside track, so long as he had the real Shao under cover."

O'Hara opened out Chang Pao's fateful letter, and stood staring at it for a moment. "I'm convinced that Tai Gat engineered this whole job, from start to finish. Very likely he got hold of this letter when Chang Pao had his second stroke, and started the ball rolling by stealing Yun Chee's parrot as a stand-in for Shao.

"But the parrot wouldn't talk, and old Chang was obviously on his deathbed, so he cooked up his scheme to install a false heir while he went on searching for the hidden treasure. However, his stooge got out of control—drinking and gambling and quarreling—throwing away the money too fast to suit Tai Gat, so when the parrot got away from Mandarin Lane with the message, he saw a chance to eliminate his partner.

"His first job was to get Shao back in his possession. With that done, he scurried back to Lantern Court, fixed up the phoney parrot with China ink and *samshu*, and then disposed of his pal—by treachery, no doubt. He put on the yellow robe to fool us, fired a volley, then dashed in here, bolted the door, put the yellow robe back on the dead man, and made his getaway over the roofs. That's my line on what happened."

"It sounds O.K. to me, Sarge," Driscoll agreed. "That joss house alibi will turn out to be as phoney as Tai Gat's limp. . . . Phew! Smell the *samshu*, Sarge? I'm splashed all over from that damn jar. If I don't get these clothes off quick I'll get a drunk on just smellin' the stuff."

O'Hara pointed to the dripping stain on the wall where the blue jar had smashed. "You're lucky Tai Gat didn't aim a couple of inches lower, Driscoll, or you'd have been a gone goose. . . . Hey, what's this?"

O'Hara bent down and picked up a lustrous pink globule from the debris on the floor, and as he held it between thumb and forefinger his eyes lit with excitement.

"A pearl!" he exclaimed. "A big one—a beauty! And look, here's another one, and another!"

By that time Driscoll and young Chang had joined the hunt, eagerly turning over the jagged fragments of the *samshu* jar. They found more pearls, many more, some rolling free, others imbedded in a kind of waxy tallow which still clung to the broken jar.

"Pearls! A fortune in pearls!" O'Hara exclaimed, when they had finished their searching and young Chang Loo's hands held the gleaming heap of lustrous sea-gems. "Old Chang Pao dropped them into this *samshu* jar, then poured wax over them to seal them to the bottom. It's his hidden treasure."

"I'll say it was hidden!" Driscoll put in. "Why, even if you poured out the liquor and looked inside the jar, you wouldn't notice anything. Unless you smashed the jar, you'd never find 'em!"

And suddenly the solution to the strange riddle of the old silversmith's parrot flashed into O'Hara's mind. He turned excitedly to Chang Loo.

"Listen, Chang, the parrot's name was Shao, wasn't it? And Shao is the Chinese word for fire. But the parrot always squawked out its name *three* times—Shao! Shao! Shao! Get it? The three-word key to your uncle's hidden treasure wasn't three *different* words, as Tai Gat thought, but only *one* word, repeated three times—fire, fire, fire! Follow your uncle's directions, make one word of the three, and what do you have? Three times fire—triple fire."

"*Hai!*" young Chang exclaimed. "Triple fire—it is the name for *samshu*!"

"Exactly!" O'Hara said. "*Samshu* is a powerful liquor, distilled three times. It's as clear as crystal, once you get on the right track. Perhaps the parrot always squawked its name three times, and that's what gave your uncle the idea for hiding the pearls in a *samshu* bottle."

"Well, I'll be damned!" Driscoll exploded. "Think of that! Tai Gat prodding the parrot for its secret, and the bird screaming the answer at him all the time! And maybe the *samshu* he gave it was poured from this very jar!"

"Yes, it's strange the way things work out sometimes," O'Hara said thoughtfully. "You know, Driscoll, sometimes I almost believe those invisible Lords of Destiny the Chinks are always talking about do take a hand in things!"

Let the Dead Alone
Merle Constiner

(FRANCIS) MERLE CONSTINER (1902–1979) was born in Ohio and graduated from Vanderbilt University, then returned to Ohio, where he lived for the rest of his life. He wrote prolifically for the detective pulps, creating several series characters that were somewhat unusual for their venues because they were less hard-boiled than humorous.

Perhaps his best-known series features Wardlow Rock, known as "the Dean," an eccentric genius in the mold of Sherlock Holmes and Nero Wolfe. His "Watson" or "Archie Goodwin" is Benton (Ben) Matthews, who serves as both an assistant as well as the chronicler of the tales. There is even a Mrs. Hudson–like landlady, Mrs. Duffy, who runs the rooming house in which the detectives live. Not surprisingly, just as Inspector Lestrade calls on Holmes for help and Inspector Cramer visits Wolfe, Lieutenant Mallory consults the Dean when a case seems too complex or outré to be solved by the police department. There were nineteen stories published in *Dime Detective* between 1940 and 1945, collected in book form by editor Robert Weinberg in *The Compleat Adventures of the Dean* (2004). For *Black Mask*, he wrote a series of eleven humorous tales about Luther McGavock, a private detective who works for Atherton Browne, who runs a Memphis-based agency; most have rural settings. Constiner's only mystery novel was *Hearse of a Different Color* (1952), though he had numerous Western novels and pulp stories published.

"Let the Dead Alone," the first McGavock tale, was published in the July 1942 issue.

Let the Dead Alone

Merle Constiner

CHAPTER ONE
THE ROOFING NAIL

THE FIRST THING McGavock noticed when he entered the chief's office was that the old man was wearing a clean collar. "I see you've freshened up your neckwear," McGavock said. "Are you anticipating early burial?"

The old man glared at him with salty, inflamed eyes. "I've got on my traveling clothes. For the first time in twenty years I'm going to leave my desk and go out on a case. This thing is too important to me to sublet to any slipshod hired help. I'm handling it myself and I'm taking you along with me. We're leaving immediately. You can buy a toothbrush at a drugstore."

McGavock was small, sinewy, tough. His coarse black hair was cut in a short pompadour and there was a dusting of tweedy gray at his temples. He had a selfish, taunting quality about him that aroused instant animal antagonism in total strangers. He'd worked for every major

"I don't know a snowshoe rabbit from a horned owl," Luther McGavock admitted when asked if he was a hunting man. What he neglected to add was that he knew two-footed killers very well indeed—and had come to murder-ridden Bartonville for the express purpose of potting one on the wing or any other way that seemed handy, using the help of native beaters, if necessary.

McGavock, in close, connected three times—and the chubby man went backwards heels over breakfast.

agency in the country. A genius at getting results, he was a hard man to take.

McGavock flushed. "I work alone and you know it. I came here to Memphis and you gave me a berth. You like what I bring in but you don't want to know about my methods. I work on a roving license, one that you cooked up yourself, a contract that you can repudiate if things get too hot. What is this big-time job?"

The chief corrected him. "It's not big-time, it's just personal. A cousin of mine, a second cousin, had a little trouble with a friend of his—he wouldn't stay alive. Cousin Malcom lives at a place called Bartonville, a hill-town back by the Tennessee-Mississippi line. He just telephoned

me. He's in some sort of a hole. He says that blood is thicker than water and that he thinks I can handle the affair with greater delicacy than the local law enforcement. It seems to be an emergency. I thought we'd run over—"

McGavock snarled. "No soap! If I take it on, I'll do it alone." He rubbed a knuckle thoughtfully behind his ear. "When can I catch a train?"

"Trains don't stop there, Luther," the old man said mildly. He produced an envelope. "Here's a bus ticket. Good luck."

When the door swung shut behind McGavock, the chief turned to his secretary. A pleased cat-and-canary look came into the old man's watery eyes. He ripped off the new collar, tossed it in the wastebasket. "Ah!" He breathed happily. "That's better. . . . You know, Miss Ollinger, I was afraid for a minute that he was going to call my bluff. Luther McGavock is the best man that ever drew my pay. But he's dangerous, touchy. You have to handle him like a black panther—with an electric prod."

Bartonville was a little splash of houses and ramshackle business buildings in a nest of wooded, red clay hills. McGavock typed it the instant he stepped from the bus. It was lazy, quiet, intelligent—the sort of Deep South town he liked.

The Main Street sidewalks, raised two feet or so above the street, were hot in the sunlight. Hound dogs lay curled in the piercing heat and grizzled mules with riding saddles waited patiently at hitching posts for their masters. The few stragglers in view were mostly lean mountain men who returned his casual scrutiny with polite curiosity.

The town was evidently a county seat. Across the street was a barren court square with its customary park benches and old stone courthouse. The whole set-up, the rutted road, the mules, the court square, was typical, familiar. McGavock picked up his Gladstone and started down the sidewalk.

The one hotel, the Bradley House—a moldy, clapboard building with fly-specked windows— appeared deserted. McGavock walked into the musty lobby, waited a moment for his eyes to adjust themselves to the half-gloom.

A spiderish man in a Roman stripe silk shirt with pink rosetted sleeve garters put down a tin cup at the watercooler and sauntered behind a battered desk. He threw out a card with the practiced fingers of a tinhorn gambler. McGavock signed it.

"Luther McGavock," the clerk read. "Memphis. I'm Cal Bradley—Cal for Calhoun, suh, not Calvin. I own this hotel." He waited for enthusiastic congratulations, none were forthcoming. "What, may I ask, brings you to this garden spot?"

McGavock said: "I'm representing Boggs."

The man in the striped shirt blinked. "Boggs? You've got me there. What are boggs?"

"Boggs," McGavock announced scathingly, "are not things. Boggs is a man, a millionaire. Porthos R. Boggs—the Memphis celery king. He has more dough than he can spend. That's why he hires me—I help him burn it. They told him that Bartonville is good bird country. I'm here to look things over and buy a few hundred acres of land if I can find something that suits us."

Bradley asked slyly: "Are you a hunting man, suh?"

"Heck, no!" McGavock jeered. "I don't know a snowshoe rabbit from a horned owl. But neither does Boggs. Ha." He pointed to his bag, ordered curtly: "Take this up to the room. I'm going out to catch a little air."

or some reason or other, McGavock had expected to find his client living in a so-called Georgian showplace, one of those pillared mansions that always reminded him of a movie set. He was pleasantly surprised.

The squat, brick cottage was intimate, homelike. Its double-span cedar shingles were butted with bright green moss and the wind and rain of decades had buffed the old brick to a soft rose. The small, neat lawn was hedged with a spindrift of lilacs. Through a trellis of wisteria, he caught a glimpse of a cool flagstoned backporch.

An almost obliterated nameplate on the gate said: *Malcom Jarrell, M.D.* McGavock took the turfed path to the door, clanged the lever bellpull.

The door was opened by one of the queerest human specimens that McGavock had ever seen. A little pigeon-chested man in a seedy herringbone suit. He had a massive, shaggy head. From the bridge of his spectacles projected a short V of wire holding a second, squarish set of lenses: a

Bebe binocular of the sort used by dentists and naturalists. He unhooked the contraption from his goatlike ears, frowned.

"I'm Lute McGavock." The detective introduced himself. "I'm charwoman for the Atherton Browne Detective Agency. I hear you've got your lines fouled. I'm here to help you untangle them. You're Dr. Jarrell?"

The seedy man shook his elephantine head. "There isn't any Dr. Jarrell. That was my great-grandfather. But I'm the man you seek." He studied McGavock gravely. "So you're the person Atherton selected. Come in, sir."

Then, astoundingly, in direct contradiction to his words, he closed the door behind him and ushered McGavock—not into the house, but around it.

In a vine-hung nook, on the flagstoned back-porch, two wire-legged chairs were set by a kitchen table. On the table was a box of cubeb cigarettes, a partially eaten chocolate bar, and a wire cage containing a rat. The rodent was as big as a young pig, scaly-tailed, malevolent. "*Sigmodon hispidus*, the cotton rat," Jarrell remarked. "He doesn't like us, does he? I'm a naturalist, in a small way. I sit by the hour and study him."

McGavock said nastily: "You've got a stronger stomach than I have."

"I have a strong stomach," Malcom Jarrel answered quietly. "Or I couldn't tolerate you. You have an unfortunate personality, sir. There's something about you that makes me seethe. Something insolent. However, this is no time for character analysis. If Atherton foists you on me, I have to take what he sends. I'm just a poor country cousin and can't expect his most expensive talent. What about the garden mulch?"

"Says what?"

The big-headed man pointed out to the lawn. The setting sun, long sunk behind the crest of hills, dappled the yard in amber afterglow. Great sphinx moths, dusk feeders, were already shuttling among the delphiniums. McGavock had a feeling of unreality—as though he were a visitor in some eerie, goblin world. Unconsciously his gaze followed the line of Jarrell's heavy-jointed finger. In the rear of the grassy plot was a grape arbor; beside the grape arbor was a small pile of clean, fresh straw. "The garden mulch," Jarrell repeated. "It can't stay where it is. It's bleaching my lawn."

McGavock said tartly: "I'm no horticulturist. All the way down from Memphis and you—"

Jarrell smiled sadly. "There's a dead man under it."

The story was quickly told. The man was Lester Hodges—a recluse. He lived in a shack at the other end of town. Jarrell had been awakened the night before by a dragging sound outside his window; he'd slipped into a robe, gone out to investigate and had found the body of his old friend.

The naturalist had then covered the corpse with mulch straw and had ensconced himself on the back porch to wait for aid from Memphis. Sixteen hours on the deathwatch—no meals, no visitors. No break except when he'd phoned his cousin.

McGavock got to his feet, wandered out into the yard.

The detective laid aside the straw in fastidious handfuls, uncovered the body bit by bit—like a geologist exposing a rare fossil.

"His head," Jarrell said. "Look at the back of his head."

It wasn't pretty. Hodges was a birdlike man in his seventies, hard-bitten, wiry. A large roofing nail had been driven through his skull—into his brain. The metallic nail head, as large as a nickel, lay flat and firm against the old man's silvery hair.

"I can't understand it," Malcom Jarrell complained. "It's practically impossible! I can't drive a nail into a box and do it satisfactorily. Say the slayer crept up on him in his sleep, even then how could he do it? Imagine! Holding the nail in position with one hand and swinging the hammer with the other. Those roofing nails are like big tacks. It isn't feasible!"

"You're on the wrong track," McGavock contradicted him. "I think I know how it was done. A novel and a brutal weapon—but a simple and efficient one, too."

They hesitated by the gate. "I've a batch of important questions to ask you," McGavock said. "But they're personal and I've got you placed. You'd bat me around with evasions until I wouldn't know where I was. So—I'll circulate around town and collect a little lowdown on you—and you'll have to come in with me. Then maybe we can get someplace. I've handled clients like you before. In the meantime, I'm giving you advice and I want you to heed it. Go to the sheriff and tell him the whole yarn. Leave me out, of course, but tell him everything else. It'll be embarrassing but we'll have to do it if we want to flush our quarry."

Jarrell made a pretense at pondering. "Wouldn't it be a better idea," he said carefully, "to wait until nightfall and then to take Lester out into the hills and leave him by the road?"

McGavock was withering. "Who do you think it'll fool? Not the guy that unloaded him in your yard. Just try to dispose of that body and they'll have hemp around your neck so quick you'll think your ascot slipped!"

wilight was blending into night—it was that period that the natives called dusk-dark—when McGavock returned to the main drag. The air was sweltering. Somewhere, beyond the bridge, a revival meeting was getting under way. High-pitched voices lifted their rhythms to the summer sky. Storefronts blazed soft golden light. McGavock ambled through the jocular bustle of dallying citizens—family folk out for an evening stroll before bedtime, high school girls in their sweet-starched ginghams, village boys with pomaded hair and roving eyes. The detective located a hardware store, entered.

A clerk got up from the sidewalk bench in front of the store and followed him inside.

McGavock purchased a ten-cent compass.

The clerk was curious. "Buyin' a compass! I don't recollect seeing you in these parts. Are you aimin' to tramp the hills?"

"Skip it," McGavock said boorishly. "I'm not a revenuer. I see you have quart whiskey bottles as well as oak casks that can be converted to thump kegs. There's no copper on display but doubtless you've plenty hidden in the back room. Don't alarm yourself, I'm not in town to bloodhound any of your rural customers."

The clerk was abashed, befuddled. "You'll have to excuse me, Mr.—er—"

"Hodges." McGavock was expansive. "The name is Lester Hodges. At your service."

The clerk went bug-eyed. "Lester Hodges! Think of that. Listen, friend, we got a feller right here in this town by that very name."

McGavock reeled dramatically, grimaced with incredulity.

"Them's true words," the clerk insisted defensively. "Lester Hodges. Many a hour he's sat by that pot-bellied stove and whittled."

It came out like an appendix under a local anesthetic: where Hodges lived, his annual income—nil—and his likes and dislikes. "Why don't you look him up?" the clerk urged. "He might be kin."

"It's hardly likely," McGavock said dolefully. "All my kin were killed off in the battle between the *Monitor* and the *Merrimac*."

The shanty was in a hollow at the edge of town. It was built flush into a red clay bank. Above it, as a background, the ridge road passed it over a wobbly wooden trestle. A full moon was rising down the valley and the trestle with its crazy-angled supports looked like a gigantic tarantula against the sky. McGavock stood across the path and sized things up.

His calculations told him he had a good ten minutes on the sheriff. Yet a lighted lamp burned in the window of Lester Hodges' shack.

The detective climbed the rickety stairs to the narrow porch and knocked. There was no answer. He twisted the knob and stepped in. The room was empty.

The furnishings were scant—a dilapidated iron range, a pallet on the floor, a fire-blistered bureau. And that lonesome lamp flickering in the window.

The bureau drawers held the recluse's food stock: a sack of dried beans, a little cornmeal, a rancid ham hock. McGavock glanced about him angrily—it was a difficult layout to frisk. There was no place to conceal anything.

He found them in the cold ashes of the iron range, and when he found them he didn't know what to do with them. A few tiny firecrackers and a shank of fishing line, in a tobacco can.

He stared blankly at the tin, thrust it in the pocket of his sack coat.

The lamp bowl was almost full, it had just been lit.

The detective had got himself into a spot and knew it. The little one-room shanty had no back door. He'd realized the lamp was a trap but he'd planned on a back door. Someone out in the night was waiting for him. Someone who had a sense of engineering: the light was placed so that when he left he'd show up like a treed possum.

McGavock made a quick decision. He blew out the lamp, swung open the sagging door and stepped out onto the narrow porch. "O.K., Sheriff," he shouted. "Come on in. You want to take a look at this!"

A shadowed figure materialized in the blackness of the trestle timbers. There was the liquid glint of moonlight on a blue steel shotgun barrel. McGavock realized he was facing a desperate killer.

The phantom wavered. McGavock thought, He's trying to grapple with the new break, trying to play it so that he gets the most out of it—he wonders what I've discovered.

A husky, heavily disguised voice called back: "Take a look at what?"

McGavock dropped like a plummet, rolled tumbler-fashion down the red clay bank. The shotgun let loose with both barrels. There was a deafening, coughing blast and the shrieking of

splintered glass as the shanty window went into shard and dust.

A clump of sumac caught McGavock's fall. He got to his feet, listened a moment, heard nothing.

The detective made no attempt at quartering his attacker. He walked along a dry, brushy gulch, came out on a hillside and returned to the village through a weedy alley.

He drew up beneath the first streetlight, wiped his knees and elbows with his handkerchief, balled it up and lobbed it behind a picket fence. He was, he decided, fairly presentable.

The gent with the shotgun could wait.

One thing was certainly evident. Lester Hodges, the old recluse, hadn't met his death and been rolled in Jarrell's yard through some sort of grotesque accident. There was design behind this, cold-blooded merciless design. From now on anything might happen. The slayer was smart, cunning—and he knew he was being hunted.

The back street brought McGavock to the rear of the courthouse. He circled the building, selected a bench in the deserted court square, sat down and redigested a few conclusions. An inspection of his ten-cent compass showed that it had not been damaged. Main Street was nearly empty. This was a town that really closed like a mouse-trap at the stroke of nine.

One window alone remained lighted. A little office with an eight-foot front beside the undertaker's. A desk was pulled up close to the window, a man sat behind it in a swivel chair. He appeared to be looking through the pane, across the street, into the court square—directly at McGavock. The gold lettering on the door said: *Hal Maldron, Attorney.*

McGavock got up, crossed the street. Hardly had his instep touched the curb than the man leaned over his desk and rapped on the window.

It was a shrill commanding rap—a piercing, arrogant vibrato.

McGavock opened the door and strode in.

"If you want to speak to me," he exploded, "heist your pants off that sponge rubber cushion and address me like a gentleman. I don't go for window banging—"

Hal Maldron was a blubbery, grayish man with bad teeth and a pair of the smallest, cruelest eyes that McGavock ever looked into. He smirked at McGavock's rage. "Calm yourself, brother."

Maldron held up a hand, waved a huge horseshoe-nail ring. "It's this ring that does it, brother," he boasted. "It makes me the most hellacious lawyer in these hills. I'm sure-fire. I never lose a case. But why the ring, you ask? I'll tell you. Why chase around looking for clients, interviewing witnesses, suborning jurymen? No need for it. I just sit here in my swivel chair and let the world come to me. Across the street's the courthouse, yonder's the post office, next door's the undertaker's. What more could a lawyer ask? I'm plump in the middle of the county's bloodstream. Anyone with any kind of business has to pass my window sometime or other. Comes a prospect or a hostile witness, I just reach over and rap on the pane." A malignant look settled itself in his rubbery jowls. "And, believe me, they come when I call them!"

McGavock was speechless with fury.

"You got off the bus at seven fifty-eight," Maldron declared. "You registered at the Bradley House and then proceeded to Malcom Jarrell's, where he informed you that he was secreting a corpse. What you've been doing for the last half hour, I do not as yet know—but I'll find out. I summoned you in here to advise you that you are now working for me. There have been developments. Jarrell has given himself up to the police; he is at liberty, on bond. I'm representing him—"

McGavock managed to speak. "He's retained you?"

"That's beside the point. I said I was representing him. I'm being retained by another party, one who has his welfare at heart."

"Just who is this other party?"

Maldron showed his spotted canines. "That, too, is beside the point. I just wanted you to understand that there's been a shifting of conditions, a change of ownership, so to speak. You've been demoted. I'm head man. If you play with me, I'll keep you on the payroll. No cooperation and I'll send you scooting back to the city."

McGavock gave a low, strained laugh—a strangled sound, almost a whine. "I ought to kick your teeth in. Which wouldn't take much of a push." He held his breath, tried to control himself. "I'm not employed by Jarrell. I'm laboring for a guy named Atherton Browne. Try a tank-town frame on me and the boys will be in your hair like seventeen-year locusts. You'll learn a little about metropolitan detective agencies."

He was still boiling when he reached the hotel.

Cal Bradley, fussing behind the desk, was acting as his own night-clerk. The spidery little man seemed self-conscious, over-polite. "Mr. McGavock!" he greeted. "About to retire? A good night to sleep, suh. There's a breeze from the north." He laid the key on the blotter. "Number eleven, at the end of the hall. The best room in the house." Abruptly, as an afterthought, he reached inside his shirt, dragged out a rumpled, soiled envelope. "This was left on the desk—addressed to you. I didn't see who placed it there."

McGavock ripped open the flap. The note was written on hotel stationery: *Hodges can't use your help now. Let the dead alone. Get out of town.*

"It's written on your letterhead—and unsigned," McGavock snapped. "I suppose the entire town has access to your paper."

Bradley sighed. "That's true. Everyone filches from a hotel." He brightened. "Just think. You've only been in town a few hours and already admirers are sending you unsigned letters. You make friends quickly, suh."

When McGavock was halfway down the corridor, Bradley's strident voice rattled after him. "Another thing. It almost slipped my mind.

You've had a charming visitor—Laurel Bennett. She's dropped in three times within the last hour. Perhaps she wants to sell your employer, Mr. Boggs, the old Fern Springs resort?"

McGavock answered crossly: "I wouldn't know. I've never heard of her. If she comes again, I'm not seeing callers. I'm footsore and weary. I'm hibernating for the night."

CHAPTER TWO
THE HEAVY LOSER

Luther McGavock gazed at his room and flinched. It was about ten feet square. The wallpaper was water-stained in coffeelike splotches; the worn rug was as thin as a bait seine. There was an oval crayon enlargement above a washstand, a crockery bowl and pitcher—and a lumpy iron bed.

The single, grimy window looked directly onto the tin roof of an adjoining shed. Bradley's finest room was no bridal suite.

McGavock stuck the tobacco tin behind the crayon enlargement. He opened his Gladstone and took out a belly gun, a stubby thirty-eight cut back almost to the cylinder—and a pair of wire clippers. He shoved the pistol under his coat, turned back the mattress and with the wire clippers snipped off a foot of stiff wire from the bedsprings.

The detective took the wire to the door, threw a tight turn around the doorknob, pulled the ends down and threaded them through the eye of the key. He tested the apparatus; it was steady, strong. No outside manipulation could jiggle the bit in the lock; it was tamper-proof.

Cheap hotels with shaky door locks were no new experience to Luther McGavock.

He raised the window, laid the towel from the washstand over the sill. A landmark to help him identify the correct room on his return.

McGavock crawled through the window,

groped down the tin roof, lowered himself cat-like into the alley. The silence was oppressive, appalling. It was as though the village were quarantined. The detective glanced at the luminous dial of his wristwatch.

It seemed like two in the morning—yet it was scarcely nine-thirty.

Every small southern town has its leading family. The Bennetts assumed this position in Bartonville. McGavock had been aware of their prominence from the moment of his arrival. Everywhere he'd looked he'd seen the name: on the town's drugstore, the garage, the cotton gin. He could visualize the sort of home Laurel Bennett would be living in—a sleek white mansion with fluted columns and a veranda as big as a parade ground. She would, in other words, be occupying the house he had mistakenly allotted to Malcom Jarrell.

This time he was right. He found the place without much difficulty.

Pretentious, austere, it stood at the mouth of a short avenue of old magnolias. The porch light was on—McGavock was evidently expected.

Malcom Jarrell opened the door to his ring.

McGavock said dreamily: "I imagine a house, prowl around and locate it. I ring the bell and see you standing in the doorway. This case is dopier than a tael of opium. Who is this Laurel Bennett, what's your tie-in, and what does she want with me?"

The seedy naturalist tilted his monstrous head, stepped back, gestured the detective in. "We need your counsel. Mrs. Bennett is my godchild. She has a problem for you."

"A problem?" McGavock mocked him. "Now that's intriguing! A detective is like a doctor, anyone that comes along tries to panhandle a little free medicine. I'm up to my ears right now in a problem. Or haven't you heard? I'm trying to shoo the executioner away from you. It seems to me—"

Jarrell was crotchety. "Come now, you're not all that busy! This shouldn't take twenty minutes. Hear what Laurel has to say. I'm sure that Atherton won't object."

The lady of the mansion was just about seventeen years old.

A delicate figurine in black lace with a cameo at her throat, she leaned against the creamy marble mantelpiece and watched McGavock approach. Oil portraits hung high above her head. Antebellum ancestors: eagle-nosed gentlemen—firebrands—and haughty, whale-boned grande dames.

Laurel Bennett was slim, fragilely molded. Her glossy black hair was caught by a pearl bandeau. Her eyes were somber, brooding.

Seventeen years old, McGavock thought. He judged her age shrewdly by her lips. He tried to picture her in a middy blouse and Mary Jane pumps. It simply wouldn't work. The gal might be a child, McGavock decided, but she's not that kind of a child. She's wise, hard.

Her manner was impersonal, gracious. "I heard you talking to Mr. Jarrell in the hall," the girl began. "You seem reluctant to help me. You appear to believe that there will be no remuneration. Let me say that you are going to be paid and paid liberally. Present a reasonable statement to my attorney, Mr. Hal Maldron—"

"The window rapper? The guy with the eroded teeth?" McGavock was venomous. "So you're the party that had him bail my client. How do you people expect me to get anything done with all this meddling? Jarrell has popped off until—"

Malcom Jarrell said patiently: "You're balked. Completely confounded. So you're trying to put the blame for your incompetence on me."

McGavock barked at the girl: "What is this job you want me to do?"

"You're a man of experience," Laurel Bennett said throatily. "I think you'll be quick to sympathize. Gil, my husband, is middle-aged. Suddenly—for no reason that we can see—he has gone into an orgy of sowing wild oats. Not women, I mean, but drinking and gambling. It's mortifying, of course—most middle-aged husbands are proud to pay more attention to their young brides. If they're lucky enough to have a young bride, I mean. But it's not only embarrassing—it's critical. He's jeopardizing our security. He loses enormous sums. We have a joint account—he makes secret withdrawals. It has me half-mad. It can't go on!"

McGavock asked warily: "How do I come in?"

"He's out right now. At a place called Chunky's, a hell-hole down by the riverbank. I've been cruising around, I've seen his car there. I'll drive you up and leave you. I want you to get him out and bring him home."

"Is that supposed to cure him?"

"You could scare him on the way back," the girl suggested. "Tell him some terrible cases where men drank themselves into disgrace and their pitiful wives starved in the gutter and things like that."

"O.K.," McGavock agreed. "Let's go." He threw a parting remark at Malcom Jarrell. "Spend the night here. I'll see you in the morning. I want to ask you about your cotton rat."

Jarrell answered him amiably. "I'm an early riser. Any time after sun-up."

 hunky's Place was in the river bottom about five miles out on the old swamp trail. A desolate, poisonous five miles. Snake-infested sloughs, milky with muddy water, thrust fingerlike from the dense second growth along the roadside. The headlights of Laurel Bennett's car played on a ceaseless tangle of wild grape and willow and water oak. The air was brackish, dank—stagnant.

The girl was silent, intent on holding her swaying car to the boggy trail. McGavock sat beside her and whistled. It was a habit of concentration that he was unable to break. And he always whistled the same thing, the same way. The tune was "The Letter Edged in Black."

"Cal Bradley," he remarked, "thinks I'm a sap on the purchase for shooting land. He suggested that you might be anxious to sell me a pleasure resort, a place known as Fern Springs. Fern Springs is a new one on me and I thought I knew them all, from Florida Bay to Puget."

Laurel smiled stiffly. "It hasn't functioned since nineteen-ten. Maybe you don't know it, but the south is studded with old, abandoned resorts—tucked away in wild, unreachable places. Back at the turn of the century, in the red-spoked carriage days, it was fashionable to summer at some health springs. The fad passed but the old buildings remain. Almost any county south of the Mason-Dixon has a couple. Fern Springs belongs to me, it's back in the pine country. It's always belonged to my family and is not for sale. I'd sell my mother's wedding ring first."

McGavock said: "I'm not in the market for a wedding ring, but I'll keep your offer in mind."

She cursed him. He lay back on the cushions, closed his eyes and listened with real enjoyment.

Laurel Bennett braked her sports car at a bend in the road. "It's just around the corner. You'd better go the rest of the way on foot."

"How will I spot him?" McGavock asked.

"They'll all be drinking," she said bitterly. "But he'll be drunk. They'll all be gambling— but he'll be losing his shirt."

Abruptly, without warning, he reached forward and turned on the dash. Deftly, before she could prevent him, he laid the ten-cent compass on her knee. The needle was as steady as a rock.

The girl flushed angrily, knocked his hand aside. "If you want to take bearings," she spat, "take them from yourself!"

He gave a raucous, unpleasant laugh. "I'm not taking bearings. This is my electric eye. I'm just making sure that you're not preparing to put a two-inch roofing nail into the back of my skull when I step out." He restored the gadget to his pocket.

She caught him by the lapel as he slid through the door. "Watch yourself. They don't like strangers."

He bared his teeth. "Neither do I."

The building, the size of a domestic garage and covered with tar-paper, was a black ulcerous sore in the moonglow. Its windows were caulked to the frame with soggy, mildewed quilts. Not so much as a wavering cobweb of light showed. A moody scene, depraved and threatening. McGavock was familiar with these backwoods gambling dives. They were dynamite.

There were a few clay-caked jalopies in the clearing, and a powerful, gleaming coupe—Gil Bennett's.

McGavock knew better than to advance and knock. He slowed up at the fringe of the timber, called: "Hello. Hello, in there!" A ritual for strangers and one that had better be observed. The door opened.

A chubby, muscle-bound man with a receding chin stepped out. He was wearing a lemon yellow polo shirt stuck into new overalls and carried an army automatic casually at his side—as though it were a monkey wrench.

McGavock said: "I'm a friend of Cal Bradley's." He walked into the patch of light. "I'm a traveling man."

The chubby man chewed it over in his slow mind. "I guess you're all right," he decided. He led McGavock into the hut, closed the tar-paper door.

It was a low, vicious crowd. There were seven men in the room—three sprawled sullenly at a rough-sawed makeshift bar at the back; the remaining four were deadlocked in a game of stud under a hissing gasoline lamp.

Gil Bennett was in the poker game. He was easy to spot. Dressed in a quiet business suit, he was the only man present wearing neither leather boots nor denim. He was a decent-looking guy in his middle fifties. McGavock wondered what devious pressure had cast him into marriage with so young a wife and then perversely, had driven him to such a deadfall as this.

The detective rested his shoulders against a wall joist and watched the game. There were two bottles of red whiskey on the table and the liquor was kept in constant rotation. Bennett's play-mates lolled and simpered and put on a silly show of being skin-tight. The businessman appeared to be cold sober.

When Gil Bennett took the bottle to drink, he grasped the neck with his fist close to the bottle's mouth. The foxy pup, McGavock thought, he's *tonguing it*, cutting off his intake.

"I hate to break this up," the detective said cheerfully. "But Mr. Bennett's roast is burning. He has to hustle home."

There was an ominous silence in the little shack.

Gil Bennett asked: "Did my wife send you?"

McGavock nodded. "That she did."

The chubby houseman strolled over. "Out!" he ordered hoarsely. He tossed his knobby, dwarfed chin towards the door. "You're not wel-come here." He grabbed McGavock's wrist.

McGavock relaxed. He twisted his trapped wrist, caught the stocky man's forearm in a grip of steel—a double-lock. His opponent stiffened. McGavock stepped straight into him, thrusting his thigh behind the chubby man's knee. The chubby man went backwards heels over break-fast and McGavock, in close position, hit him three times at the hinge of his jaw. He was out before he struck the floor.

It was touch and go for a split second. Any-thing could have happened. Then everybody laughed. The show of brutality exhilarated them. A gambler with a Mexican leather-work holster peeping from his shiny blue serge suit got up from the table and shook McGavock's hand. A downy-faced youth at the bar hauled a mouth harp from his hat and began running off minors. There was an air of general festivity.

I n Bennett's coupe, on the way back to town, McGa-vock made an astounding discovery. His companion, in spite of all his bottle tonguing, was drunker than a shoat in a silo.

"How long have you been haunting that dump?" the detective asked genially.

Gil Bennett hiccoughed. "About two weeks. And, boy, have I had bad luck! All the time I lose! At first it wasn't so bad, seven-eight dollars. Now the jinx has really got me. I run as much as twenty bucks in the hole as regular as clock-work." He shook his head fuzzily. "I try to out-slick them but I can't seem to make any headway—"

"How much have you lost to date?"

"One hundred and eighty-three frog skins. Down the old sewer. That's plenty bucks. Wow!"

McGavock grinned to himself. The case was finally cracking; at last he was getting his teeth into it. "It's a heap of small change," he agreed. "But it's not what breaks up wealthy family life. Mrs. Bennett said your losses were enormous— that was the word she used. I thought it sounded fishy. I couldn't see how the town big shot, you, owner of the cotton gin, garage, et al., could find any real financial competition among the local bedrock sportsmen. Why then the secret with-drawals?"

Bennett chuckled. "You catch. This gam-bling business is a ruse. The Bennett Cotton Gin, the Bennett Drugstore—phooey! Every-thing I own is in partnership with my wife. And I don't mean matrimonial partnership—I mean business partnership. Hal Maldron looks after her end and the way they whipsaw me is nobody's business. Every time we get a little money ahead they put it into reserve pools and running expenses and stuff like that. I couldn't tell you within ten thousand dollars what my present capital is."

McGavock prodded him. "And?"

"I've got plans. They probably seem wacky to you but they're the best I can do. My wife and I have a joint bank account. That's my only access to cash. I make big withdrawals, as much as the traffic will stand. I send the money out of town to a city bank. I've got it deposited under a dif-ferent name. I can make a fresh start any time they give me the bum's rush. All I'm waiting for now is for Laurel and that leechy lawyer of hers to sock me with their divorce—"

"Divorce?" McGavock perked up.

"Sure. I bet they've got the papers all filled out." He went cagy. "What are you pumping me for? Where did you come from, anyway? By golly, you're a detective working for Hal and Laurel!"

"I'm a detective, all right," McGavock confirmed. "I might as well admit it. You're the only one who doesn't seem to know it. But I'm not working for Hal Maldron. I'm employed by a slave driver in Memphis. I'm here to find out who knocked off Lester Hodges—and, more important, how come?"

That sobered him. "Old Les Hodges has been murdered?" The idea seemed to give him some inner fear. "That's going to be a blow to Malcom."

"If so, he's standing up under it extremely well," McGavock remarked. "Why should it affect him?"

"They were bosom pals. The town's two nuts. Hodges illiterate, Jarrell overeducated." He said in a strained voice: "Laurel and Hal aren't mixed up in this, are they?"

"Not so far as I know," McGavock lied. "Why do you ask?"

Bennett pulled up in front of the court square, idled his engine. "Alcohol's treacherous. It makes me think I'm smarter than I am. Forget the whole thing. Thanks for your interest—and good-night."

McGavock produced his compass, handed it to his companion. "Listen to me and listen carefully. Are you sober enough to understand me? Good." He glared at the drunken man with a fond fierceness. "The slayer of Lester Hodges used a mean weapon. A magnetized hammer, like bill-posters use, only I imagine this was a big baby, like carpenters use. He carried the tack on the hammerhead, followed Hodges down a dark street. At the right moment he reared back and swung. That's the way it was done." The detective paused. "I bought this gadget for myself but I've decided to hand it over to you. If anyone approaches you with a bulky package, a bundle, something that might conceal a hammer, stall 'em while you make a few careless passes with

this compass. If there's a magnet in the vicinity, the compass needle will whip around and point it out."

Gil Bennett scoffed. "Why give it to me? I'm in no danger." He slammed the car door.

McGavock watched him from the street, saw him place the gadget tenderly in his breast pocket. The black coupe whammed off in a screeching of gears.

"He's afraid," McGavock said. "He thinks something is after him—and he doesn't know just what it is!"

McGavock had ordered Malcom Jarrell to spend the night with the Bennetts for a very definite reason. The detective wanted to give the little vine-covered brick cottage a thorough searching—and he wanted a free hand while doing it. One thing had bothered him all evening, the incident that had occurred when he had first visited his client. Jarrell had met him from the inside of the house, at the front door—yet he had closed the door behind him and led the detective not into the house, but around it.

McGavock had the impression at the time that he was being decoyed away from something, that the naturalist had been interrupted in something he wished to conceal.

It was pretty obvious that his client had been lying to him like a trooper ever since they had joined forces. According to Jarrell's story he hadn't left the back porch for sixteen hours, except to phone Memphis. The cubeb cigarettes and the half-eaten chocolate bar were evidence to the contrary. One doesn't keep a reserve of such tedium-breaking luxuries on one's back porch to be conveniently handy for just such an emergency. There had been other funny stuff, too. The naturalist's report had been as full of holes as a second-hand snood. He'd said he'd been awakened by a dragging sound outside his window—yet the corpse by the arbor was a good thirty yards from the house.

McGavock reconstructed it this way: Jarrell had probably seen the killer drag the body into his yard. Maybe he had recognized him, maybe not. In any event, the naturalist was reluctant to discuss it. It didn't look good.

The detective scowled. It wasn't the first time he'd had to plow through a client to get at the criminal.

uther McGavock swung open the squeaky gate, made a quick, cautious survey of the shrubbery. The white moon high overhead, now harsh and bright, struck the frothy lilac hedge to shimmering silver, laid ragged shadows of black velvet on the close-clipped lawn. It was indescribably beautiful—unearthly. McGavock thought, It's no wonder the big-headed naturalist is half cuckoo. I've never seen a place like this. It's actually narcotic. A human couldn't live in this dream world and retain his sense of values. It's a place for vampires and ghouls, creatures who flourish from the grave.

Lester Hodges had been taken to the funeral home, the mulch had been restacked in the stable lot. Only a few wisps of scattered straw by the arbor testified to the gruesome tragedy.

He inspected the rat in its cage on the porch. Its ruby eyes glared at the hooded flashlight in the detective's hand. "If you could talk," McGavock said thoughtfully, "we'd get this thing over in three minutes. You're the kingpin in this bloody mess." He fumbled about, discovered the key behind a flowerpot and entered Malcom Jarrell's kitchen.

He worked through the kitchen, the dining-room, the bedrooms. It took him twenty minutes to discover it: the hiding place in Malcom Jarrell's study. The detective lifted a Spanish tile in the hearth. Beneath it, in a narrow, boxlike space, lay a bulky brown envelope.

McGavock picked up a small hooked throw-rug from the floor, draped it over a student lamp on the desk, flicked on the light and examined his find.

The envelope contained a thick bundle of clippings, letters and papers held together by a rubber band. It contained something else, too— a little fuzzy, gray ball of hair about as big as a small marble. The detective's first unpleasant reaction was that he was looking at a wad of human hair, the hair of Lester Hodges.

But this hair was too fine, too dry.

Rat hair? Hardly likely. The fibers were much too long.

McGavock grinned. He realized what he held in his fingers, knew that this was evidence to hang a killer.

He wondered if Jarrell fully realized its significance. Probably yes. It all fitted in now. His call that evening on his client. Jarrell here in this cozy study, interrupted in his analysis of the furry object. It explained the Bebe binoculars and Jarrell's sidetracking him around the house.

McGavock slipped off the rubber band, fanned out the papers on the desktop and started through them systematically.

The first item was a yellowed newspaper clipping with a block headline. From the *Bartonville Clarion*, dated August 7, 1909:

NORTHERN GUEST VANISHES AT FERN SPRINGS
Devil's Elbow Claims Wealthy Manufacturer

A prosperously dressed individual giving his name as T. James Cortwright had, according to the article, registered at the Fern Springs resort on the night of the sixth. In a brief talk with Calhoun Bradley, the clerk, he had declared that he was from Cleveland, Ohio, and had inquired courteously if any of his fellow townsmen were, by chance, among the resort's guests. With regret Mr. Bradley informed him that the resort was patronized in the main by local gentry and expressed mild astonishment that even Mr. Cortwright had himself heard of its existence in such an out-of-the-way corner of the country. This remark had somehow angered the Clevelander. He had opened a wallet, paid for a month in advance, and had retired to his room.

Mr. Bradley had attempted to mollify him by informing him that the resort's season was at its height and that later in the evening there was to be a lawn party. Mr. Cortwright had made some unsociable remark and had left the desk.

The next morning a mountain man, snaking logs, had discovered the gentleman's hat and wallet a quarter of a mile from the hotel buildings. They lay at the edge of a patch of treacherous quicksand known as Devil's Elbow.

An examination of Mr. Cortwright's room showed that his bed had not been slept in. The management was attempting to inform Mr. Cortwright's family.

McGavock said to himself: "So Bradley was clerk. And the season was in full swing. Ten to one, Jarrell was there—and Maldron, and Bennett."

The next clipping, dated a week later, said:

CORTWRIGHT DEATH SUICIDE
Absconder Succumbs to Remorse

Here, the tale took a fantastic twist. Communication with the Cleveland police disclosed the stunning fact that T. James Cortwright was none other than Thompson J. Wainwright, a badly wanted absconding broker who had looted his firm of seventy thousand dollars in cold cash.

It seemed obvious to the Cleveland police and to the *Bartonville Clarion* that Wainwright had selected Fern Springs as a hideout and suddenly, for some unfathomable reason, had an uprising of conscience which induced him to take his life. What had become of the booty, no one could find out. The conclusion was that he must have spent it.

McGavock shook his head. Such goings-on!

How could a stranger, in the night, locate a patch of quicksand he couldn't possibly have known to exist? Why hadn't he taken his hat in with him? And just what kind of a conscience was it that Mr. Cortwright-Wainwright pos-

sessed? One that drove him to suicide yet refused to return his plunder to his victims. Horsefeathers!

There were three letters, each bearing a recent postmark and mailed a week apart. Each was addressed to Lester Hodges and each contained a blank sheet of paper clipped with a wire paper clip.

Bennett had said that Lester Hodges was unable to read. Someone had used the envelopes to send him money. Bills. And small bills probably—Lester Hodges changing a large banknote in Bartonville would have caused a sensation.

McGavock bundled the stuff back up, snapped on the rubber band and replaced things as he had found them—under the Spanish tile.

The light in the window of Hal Maldron's law office had been extinguished. The window-rapping attorney, like his fellow citizens, was home in bed—fighting mosquitoes in his old-fashioned nightgown, trying to get some sleep. McGavock palmed the brass knob and got out his key ring with its assortment of keys. The third one did it. He slipped in, left the door ajar behind him.

He knew just what he was going to do and how he was going to do it.

A wire basket on the lawyer's desk containing signed but unmailed correspondence gave the detective a specimen of Maldron's signature. It was bold, fancy, with loops and flourishes. The sort of signature a pompous man assumes cannot be forged.

The detective placed his hat over his flashlight, rummaged for a piece of scrap paper. He dipped the attorney's steel pen in the inkwell, got a generous nibful of gummy ink and wrote:

The bones of Thompson J. Wainright are
at Fern Springs. Seek and ye shall find!
                              Hal Maldron

McGavock wrote in large letters, lines wide-spaced. He filled his pen twice during the short inscription. The signature was a marvelous replica.

Quickly, McGavock slid the worn desk blotter out of its corner brackets. The underside, as he suspected, was new, unused. He blotted the message on the blotter's reverse—with the care of a master engraver.

The detective crumpled the paper, stuffed it in his hip pocket, refitted the blotter in the brackets in its original position—so that his handiwork was concealed.

Again on the street, the office door locked behind him, he gave a short, mirthless laugh. The entire operation had taken less than two minutes. He couldn't help thinking of Atherton Browne, wondering what the old man would say. It had been a busy evening with a rather heavy routine: three breaking and enterings, one assault and battery, one forgery.

It had been a busy evening and a profitable one, too.

McGavock had found out why Hodges had been murdered, had a good idea who the killer was. He understood now the double irony in the anonymous warning he had received: *Let the dead alone*. There was more than one corpse involved in this case. He was confronting a veteran, a two–time killer.

From the tunnel-black alley behind the Bradley House, he could see the white towel hanging from his open window. He caught the shed's low eave, drew himself up onto the tin roof.

His room was just as he had left it. The tobacco tin behind the crayon enlargement, the wire key lock on the doorknob. McGavock undressed, donned a violent purple suit of cossack-style pajamas, and was asleep by the time he hit the sheet.

CHAPTER THREE
THE HAMMER

The detective was just finishing a pungent, savory breakfast of chicken pie and eggs in the bare matting-floored hotel dining-room when Calhoun-not-Calvin Bradley materialized at his table. The puffy proprietor dragged out a chair and sat down. "You may be the owner of this flea-trap," McGavock said darkly into his coffee. "But the law books will tell you that I have a tenant's lease on this table. Scram!"

Bradley said artificially: "Did you have a sound night's sleep?"

"I did. In spite of that broken-down bed—"

"It's that bed," Bradley said smugly, "that I wanted to speak to you about. When you check out of here, you will notice an added debit of $6.80 on your bill. That is for mutilating my best bed—clipping the spring, suh, and twisting it through the key! I'm shocked—"

McGavock asked bleakly: "How do you know?"

"I saw it, suh. With my own eyes." The hotel man rolled his eyeballs reprovingly. "Shortly after you left the desk last night—to hibernate—I was under the impression that I heard you call me. I knocked on your door. No response. I rattled the panel. All was quiet. I became frantic. I've had guests with heart seizures. I raced around to the alley. With the aid of a ladder I reached your room from the outside. You were gone. I must say I was grieved to observe that you had—"

"Go 'way!" McGavock ordered. "You're constricting my digestive juices."

Bradley settled himself comfortably. "You're a deep one, full of dodges. It seemed a bit eccentric at the moment but this morning I think I understand. *Toujours l'amour.*" He squeezed a lewd wink from the corner of his eyelid. "Someone was telling me that they happened to notice you on the old swamp road with Laurel Bennett last night." He left the sentence up in the air, on a note of inquiry.

"You'd better take a reef in that limber tongue of yours," McGavock said quietly. "Or it will bring on an Act of God. You don't kid me a bit—I've been pumped by experts. You, and the whole population, know all about me by now. Who I am and what I'm here for. When the cat gets out of the bag in a village like this one—it divides and scatters. I met Mrs. Bennett by appointment—that was business. I went out along the swamp road and manhandled your friend Chunky—that was pleasure. I'm a detective and I'm here to find out who killed Lester Hodges."

Bradley tittered. "Who do you favor?"

"I favor you."

The hotel proprietor asked mockingly: "How do you make that out?"

McGavock folded his napkin in a neat cornucopia, got up. "The man that killed Wainwright killed Hodges. Lester Hodges' murder was bred in the homicide of that absconder back at Fern Springs thirty years ago."

Bradley said innocently: "Wainwright? I never heard of him." He went through a grotesque facial contortion, pretended to remember. "Oh. You mean the man that fell into the quicksand? I recall what you're speaking of now. A tragic incident. I was clerk at the time. I'd almost forgotten. Wainwright wasn't murdered." He lowered his voice confidentially. "The affair was very strange. I've thought about it a great deal. What became of the money? No one has ever answered that. Would you like to hear my personal hypothesis?"

"I would, indeed."

"It's this," Bradley announced brightly. "Wainwright didn't commit suicide. He just used Fern Springs as a blind to throw pursuers off his tracks. He signed up at the resort, paid weeks in advance, learned about Devil's Elbow—probably from the servants. That gave him an idea. He sneaked out of the back of the building, placed his hat and wallet on the edge of quicksands and left the neighborhood that very night. You see, he had a small cowhide satchel with him. It disappeared when he did. That proves my point. He hightailed and took his seventy thousand with him. Right today he's doubtless a pillar of society in some place like Johannesburg or Rio."

There was logic in the hotel man's statement—and McGavock had to admit it. "If that's your story," he rasped, "stick with it. It strikes me you're mighty clear on the details—considering it happened three decades ago."

Bradley simpered. "That's my story. And will remain my story—until a better one comes along."

Laurel Bennett, herself, was standing in the sunny foyer of the lobby waiting for McGavock. She was wearing jodhpurs and a baggy pearl-colored brushed wool sweater. A short, braided quirt was tucked into her armpit. The bright morning light was harsh, unkind to her. There were tiny crow's-feet at her temples, her lips were drawn, fagged. "I thought you'd never get up," she said. "I've been watching for you from across the street. Let's go somewhere and talk, someplace where we'll be alone. I'll meet you at the cemetery in ten minutes."

McGavock was ugly. "We'll do nothing of the kind. No clandestine conferences for me! If you have anything to unload, let's have it here and now."

"But this is too public—"

He prepared to brush past her. "O.K."

She clutched him desperately by the sleeve. "It's about the hammer! You have to listen. I've found the hammer!"

"I've lost no hammer."

"Don't taunt me. You know what I'm talking about. Gil came home with your compass last night and told us why you had given it to him. This morning, before anyone was up, I took it out in the toolhouse and found the hammer. It was in a big wooden chest with the rest of the tools. Its head was magnetized. It pulled the compass needle. I tried it out; it picked up nails."

McGavock said gravely: "Don't tell me you disposed of it!"

She raised her eyebrows innocently. "How did you know? That's exactly what I did. I took it out in the country and threw it in the river. I'll never tell anyone where. Wild horses couldn't drag it from me."

"It couldn't have been Gil's hammer?"

"Oh, no. It was a new one—I'd never seen it before." She smiled deprecatingly. "It was in Gil's tool chest but that doesn't prove anything, does it?"

McGavock guffawed. "Sister, you're a thing of beauty and a joy forever. You're more fun than a stampede at the circus. I wish I wasn't so busy; I'd like to give you more of my time. Cal Bradley tells me the town is pairing us off together, gossiping about our little trip to Chunky's last night. Answer me this: wasn't it you, yourself, that put out the story?"

Rage swept into her eyes.

"I think I'll leave," McGavock said hastily. "You're getting set to touch off a string of oaths." He left her standing there—frustrated and furious.

alcom Jarrell was seated on the side steps of the Bennett mansion in smoking jacket and carpet slippers. He had his four-lensed spectacles hooked on the bridge of his nose. He was feeding brown sugar to a procession of big, black ants. He'd bend down, watch for a second, and then scribble a note on a jumbled sheaf of papers. Hunched with his stubbled chin between his scrawny kneecaps, he reminded McGavock of some shabby sea monster.

"You'd better turn around," he said placidly as McGavock came into his vision. "And go straight back to town. The sheriff just phoned. He's mad enough to top the high cotton. He's waiting for you at Lawyer Maldron's." The naturalist smiled. "If I wasn't so occupied here, I'd trot along. It'd

be amusing to hear you bluster. You're going to have to do a bit of explaining—"

"It's you, my erudite friend of fur and feathers, it's you, suh, who have a bit of explaining to do." The detective bore down on him. "I want to know about that rat of yours. I want to know all about it."

"His name is Bertram," the naturalist said owlishly. "He's deficient in vitamins A, C and D—"

McGavock spat, "And don't take me for a sleigh ride. I'm talking about his hind leg. Just above the ankle, there's a raw place in the fur—a band of flesh where the skin's been rubbed off. What caused that?"

Jarrell nodded sagely. "I'm treating him for it. Bertram was caught in a trap. The mark of the trap's jaws—"

McGavock said happily: "Boy, you really think on your feet! That's a snappy answer. Now let's see what you have to say to this. As a matter of fact, there's no raw place on his leg at all! I know. I checked."

Malcom Jarrell's composure cracked. His florid cheeks went gravel-gray, sucked in, his eyes darted wildly—past McGavock's shoulder, past his hip, evading the detective's steady gaze.

The naturalist licked his lips. "I owe you an apology," he croaked. "I certainly misjudged you. I should have known that Atherton wouldn't send me a fool, that you must be smarter than you acted. Grant me this request: don't question me. Let sleeping dogs lie."

"No can do," McGavock said coldly. "I'm after a killer. Let's hear about Bertram, the whole story."

"You leave me no choice." Jarrell gritted his huge jaw. "I'm afraid you've guessed the worst of it. A few weeks ago a citizen of our town, someone Lester Hodges had known all his life, came to him with an extraordinary business proposition. Who this person was, Lester refused to tell me. The rat was involved in that business deal."

"Of course," McGavock declared. "That's been perfectly obvious from the start. You were keeping Hodges' rat for him. No naturalist would confine such a large animal in such a small cage. It's cruel. That was so Hodges could tie a string to its leg without the beast whipping around and fanging him."

"Exactly."

"What was this business deal?"

"This person employed Lester to search between the floors of an old, tumbledown health resort out in the pine country, Fern Springs. Hodges was half-mad—" Jarrell's voice was patronizing, amiable. McGavock remembered Bennett's statement: The two town nuts—Jarrell and Hodges. "Lester was half-mad," the naturalist repeated. "He tackled the problem with a system of his own. He tied fishing line onto the rodent's leg and used him some way in the search. I don't know how on earth he induced the animal to act."

"He was searching for obstructions under the floor," McGavock explained. "He placed the rat in an opening by the baseboard. Floor joists run parallel—under every floor there's a series of small tunnels. It was pretty clever. It saved him ripping up goodness knows how much floor space. It was the most plausible way to do it.

Malcom Jarrell frowned. "But how did he make the animal obey?"

"He scared him through with tiny firecrackers, a commodity obtainable at any Deep South country store. Hodges slipped his pet into the floor, popped off a firecracker—and judged by the length of slack in the line the progress his animal was making under the floor. Did the old man find what he was supposed to?"

"I don't know. I should say he was slain before he was successful. He'd come over in the evening and talk to me in a vague sort of way. I got the impression that he and his employer were satisfied with the way the business was going. His employer was paying him a steady salary of four dollars a week—sending him banknotes wrapped in blank paper. Lester was quite excited over his good fortune."

McGavock said: "You're being candid with me? You're telling me everything?"

Jarrell had his old poise back. "Oh, quite. You'll have to excuse me now. You have work to do." He resumed his scrutiny of the black ants. "And so have I."

As soon as McGavock laid eyes on the local law he knew that he was in for a catch-as-catch-can tussle.

The sheriff of Linden County was the direct antithesis of the old-style rural sharpshooter that pinned his rusty badge to his gallus elastic and toted a .38-in-a-.44 frame at a holster on his hip as big as an English riding saddle. The young man that lolled on the corner of Hal Maldron's desk was modest, friendly, self-effacing. He was dressed in well-cut blue-gray tweed. And his fingernails were a little over-manicured.

It was the fingernails that scared McGavock. This lad must have plenty on the ball. The hard-bitten mountain folk of Linden County wouldn't have elected him if he was as sappy as he seemed. The coon-hunting hillmen selected their sheriff like they selected their hound dogs—for brains and guts and stamina. McGavock had the strange feeling that he was in the presence of a hotshot, deliver-the-goods career man.

The young man smiled. "Howdy. I'm Steve Robley—the current and temporary head of our local crime and punishment bureau. It's mighty swell of you to look me up. I hope I'm not imposing?"

McGavock was stunned. "No," he said carefully. "It's a pleasure. Is Maldron, here, a deputy of yours?"

Hal Maldron lifted his fat lip, exposed his decayed teeth. "Yes," he announced, "I am."

"No," the sheriff said, "you're not. I'm sorry, Hal, but I'm going to have to revoke your authority for the duration of this brief but pleasant interview. We mustn't intimidate our new friend with a belligerent show of force." He got out a stubby briar pipe, loaded it, got it going. "I've gone over the hammer, Mr. McGavock. I can't find any prints."

McGavock remarked: "I left the hammer

under the body. As a proof to you that I wasn't down here to tamper with evidence." It was a bluff, a case of life or death. He surged with relief when the sheriff nodded.

"The very conclusion that I myself came to. I must say it gave me a bit of surprise—I'd always been under the impression that private detectives were not so cooperative."

"I've tried it that way," McGavock said. "It's the hard way. Now I cooperate." This boy really had a deadpan. He wondered if he was being maneuvered out on a limb. "Can I be of any service to you?"

"Yes," the sheriff said slowly. "You certainly can be. I'm stumped. What's it all about? Who'd want to murder harmless old Hodges?"

McGavock was impressed. "This is a long story. And a muddled one. I work for an agency in Memphis. For twenty years now we've been investigating a case for a brokerage firm in Cleveland. Back in nineteen-nine they had a guy abscond with seventy grand. He came down here to Fern Springs and vanished."

He had them entranced. They were swallowing it, every word. There could be no doubt of it.

Maldron said helplessly: "Why didn't you say so last night! I didn't apprehend that you had such powerful backing. You people have been working on a case in this vicinity for twenty years? I can hardly believe it!"

"We've been working on the case—but not in this community. It was the slaying of Lester Hodges that gave us the break we've been looking for."

Sheriff Robley was flustered. "I'll be perfectly honest with you, Mr. McGavock. A certain party—" Maldron looked miserable. "A certain party summoned me last night by an imperative phone call. He said that you were retained by a cousin of Mr. Jarrell's and that you came down here from Memphis for the sole purpose of obstructing justice. He said that he'd go into court and swear that you had consulted him last night about his client and had attempted to entice him into illegal conspiracy."

"These sure-fire lawyers," McGavock said

pleasantly. "No wonder they win cases. They butter their bread on both sides. Who's he representing—Jarrell or you? I may say at this time, that we in Memphis have had occasion to speculate a little about this Maldron. In fact, it wouldn't surprise us to learn that somehow he's directly involved. He knows something. He was at Fern Springs in that fatal August when Wainwright disappeared. He—"

Maldron glared. "And so were Bennett and Malcom and Bradley and half the town."

McGavock shook a finger dramatically. "Then, sir," he declaimed *basso profundo*, "then why, sir, did you write us that unusual note—the one about Wainwright's bones, seek at Fern Springs and ye shall find?"

The lawyer fidgeted. "Nonsense. You're out of your head."

Steve Robley looked suddenly intent. "Go on, Mr. McGavock."

"That's all," McGavock said. "Comes in this crank letter signed 'Hal Maldron' talking about a dead man's bones—"

The sheriff said softly: "The letter was typewritten, of course?"

"Not as I remember it. Written in big letters, in ink, as I recall it."

The young sheriff stepped to Maldron's desk, inspected the surface of the much-used blotter. He rubbed his chin, looked at the ceiling for a moment, turned the blotter over. The inked imprints stood out in heavy black scrawls. The sheriff took a pocket mirror from his comb-case, held it above the inscription.

" 'The bones of Thompson J. Wainwright are at Fern Springs,' " he read. " 'Seek and ye shall find!' Thank you, Mr. McGavock. You've been of great assistance. I'll not keep you any longer."

Alone, on the sun-splashed sidewalk, McGavock wiped a trembling hand across his forehead and said, "Whoo!" So the hammer was under the corpse all the time. He'd started his investigation by muffing the murder weapon. It had been a nerve-racking ten minutes. They had been waiting for him, all set to drive him out of town. He'd sidestepped it. For how long, he didn't know—but for the time being, anyhow. And time was what he needed.

"Six hours," McGavock decided. "Give me six hours more and I'll blow this thing seven ways to Christmas!"

Gil Bennett was in his office at the cotton gin. A little room not much larger than a chicken coop, its walls were plastered with commercial calendars—wild ducks in topsy-turvy flight, prize bulls, and turgid maidens in air-brushed bathing suits. Bennett sat on a rocker with a spliced leg by a cluttered roll-top desk. Laid out before him were a wine glass, an egg, a bottle of pepper sauce and a salt cellar. "Glad to see you," he said. "Hitch up and dismount."

The only other article of furniture in the room was a battered church pew along the wall. McGavock stretched himself out full-length, propped himself up on the arm, and grinned. "Do you think you'll live?" he asked.

Bennett's voice was hollow. "I doubt it." He broke the raw egg in the wine glass, dusted it with a sprinkle of salt and doused it liberally with pepper sauce. "A prairie oyster. Will you go along with me, sir?" McGavock shook his head. The businessman took it at a gulp. "You must break the yolk with your tongue as it goes down," he said. "Ugh!"

McGavock remarked sententiously: "The wages of sin." He laughed. "Get that wilted expression off your face. You're afraid I'm going to continue our conversation of last evening. I'm not. You were a guest at the Fern Springs resort back in nineteen-nine when a guy named Wainwright drifted in with a satchel of hot money—and evaporated. Do you happen to remember the attendant circumstances?"

"Very well, indeed." Bennett was grim.

"Swell. The place, I understand, is now owned by Mrs. Bennett, who inherited it. The episode occurred some years before Mrs. Bennett was born. Who did it belong to at the time?"

"To an invalid relative of hers down in Louisiana. She inherited it at his death. Mrs.

Bennett, by the way, comes from New Orleans. She's not actually a native of our country."

"I see," McGavock said. "If the resort had an absentee landlord, who ran the joint? Bradley?"

"Scarcely! Bradley was just a general utility man. Malcom Jarrell was the titled manager."

"I see. One thing more. Have you any personal theory as to what happened? I mean, were you satisfied at the time by the way the thing was explained?"

Bennett's answer was calm, detached. "There's always been bad friendship between Malcom Jarrell and myself. Everybody in town knows it—you should understand it before I express an opinion on so grave a point. My answer is no. I wasn't satisfied at the time and I'm less satisfied today. I think Wainwright was killed and his money was stolen."

McGavock was silent.

"It's this way," Bennett amplified. "We live in a small community here. We know each other—and our families have known each other—for a good many years. We can guess the income of our neighbors to a plugged nickel. Malcom Jarrell has a most scanty income—yet he has prospered."

McGavock retorted: "Isn't the same true of Cal Bradley?"

"In a way, yes. But Cal's case is a little different. He's a low, cunning trickster. Men like Cal Bradley are destined to prosper despite all laws of order and decency."

McGavock got to his feet, slapped his hat against his thigh. "I'd hate to go into court with that kind of a brief." His eyes narrowed. "You're holding back something, aren't you?" He dropped his hat on the floor, picked it up and cocked it on the crown of his head. "Don't let me shove you into anything."

Bennett answered wryly: "I won't. There's more to this mess than shows on the surface. Whenever you—"

He was interrupted mid-sentence by a timid knock on the door and the entry of a stalwart young hillman. The caller was dressed in a plaid cotton shirt; a three-inch brass-studded belt held up his faded denim trousers. He confronted them with wooden composure. "Which one of y'all might happen to be Mr. Bennett, the man that owned that ol' Fern Springs bat den?"

"Me," Bennett said. "And I still own it. Or rather Mrs. Bennett does. Why?"

"I'm Asie Tenniman. I'm yore south neighbor back there in the pine country. I shore hate to tell you, suh, but ain't nobuddy owns that building no more. It was farred down to ashes at daybreak this mornin'. I'm sorry I couldn't bring the word no sooner. Hit's eighteen miles by muleback an'—"

"Are you telling me," Bennett asked, "that our resort has been burned?"

"And I don't mean maybe. Some mighty mean folks live out there in the timber." The hillman added carelessly: "My woman claims she heard a boiler let loose jest about the time we seen the red."

"Shiners?"

The boy wouldn't commit himself. "I couldn't hardly say, suh. I'm jest a-telling y'all what I know. Good mornin', gentlemen."

And he was gone.

McGavock cut out: "Eighteen miles in and eighteen miles back—on a mule. And not a penny, not even a word of thanks."

"You don't understand these people," Gil Bennett observed quietly. "If I'd offered him money he'd have thrown it in my face. It's a favor and I'll remember it. Maybe sometime I'll have a chance to pay a doctor's bill or something for him. . . . What do you make of it?"

The detective fanned the air. "It's too much for me!"

CHAPTER FOUR
SEEK AND YE SHALL FIND

There was a telegram waiting for him on his return to the hotel. A pimple-faced kid with a muff of uncut hair skipped it across the register with an insolent flourish. He was wearing an oversize alpaca coat and black-ribboned nose glasses. "And who are you, my scrofulous adolescent?" McGavock inquired.

"I'm swing man to this joint. Mr. Bradley, he's takened him a day off. He's got a misery."

"Mr. Bradley's ill? You don't seem overcome with grief."

"Not me. It ain't no shingles off my smokehouse." He paused. "That's shore a nutty telegram in that there envelope. I chanct to hold 'er up to the light. I can't make no sense out'n—"

"You got a fine start, son." McGavock was warm in his encouragement. "Just keep on candling private correspondence and you've got a big future before you."

Behind the locked door of his room, McGavock slit the envelope, extracted the yellow flimsy. The message was signed Atherton Browne. It read:

EIGHT FOUR ONE COMMA TWO TWELVE FIVE COMMA ONE THREE ONE COMMA TWENTY ONE FOUR COMMA SIX ONE SEVEN COMMA ELEVEN NINE THREE YOU'RE NOT ON A VACATION.

McGavock glowered. He went to his Gladstone and got out his copy of *Dr. Trimble's Hygiene for Babies*, the Browne Agency keybook. Page eight, line four, word one gave him *what*. Page two, line twelve, word five was *if*. Laboriously, the detective leafed back and forth, broke down the code.

The deciphered message read: *What if anything are you accomplishing—you're not on a vacation.*

McGavock purpled. He grabbed the book till the veins stood out on his wrist. He drew back his arm to dash the volume against the wall, froze, grinned. He uncapped his fountain pen, settled down and filled out an answer.

It took him twenty minutes to get it the way he wanted it. The final draft said: *Page one seventeen, paragraph three, in toto.*

Paragraph three on page one hundred seventeen of *Dr. Trimble's Hygiene for Babies* said: *Keep your nasal passages clean!*

He left the wire with the kid at the desk with the injunction that he get it off immediately—and headed for the Bartonville garage. He wanted to rent a car and take a look at what was left of Fern Springs.

Sheriff Steve Robley was lounging beneath the shady marquee of the Magnolia Drugstore. He uncrossed his ankles, picked a short cigarette stub out of an ivory holder, put the holder in a little velvet-lined case. "Luther McGavock!" He saluted the detective. "The Man of Forty Faces."

McGavock came to a halt, squinted. "What's the rib, Sheriff?"

Robley gave him a quick, friendly grin. "You've really got this town on its ear. They've been comparing notes on you. I've had a dozen warnings about you. To Cal Bradley you're representing a mythical celery king named Boggs. Malcom Jarrell thinks he's your client. You tell Maldron and myself that you're representing some brokers in Cleveland. The clerk at Jones' hardware store tells me that you bought a compass from him and that you are not McGavock at all but a man named, singularly, Lester Hodges." The sheriff's lips quirked in a boyish smile but the skin about his eyes was tight. "Furthermore and furthermore. That 'seek the bones' message on Hal Maldron's desk blotter is just a little too good to be true. It makes me uneasy. I've put a call through to your agency in Memphis to check it but can't seem to get any satisfactory response. They must have the letter on file—if such a letter exists."

"Of course they have," McGavock declared. "That letter's going to clear up this case."

"That's my car yonder by the watering trough." The sheriff pointed lazily to a low, tan job bright with metalwork. "I was just pondering a trip out to the old resort. I'd like a little company. Think I could shanghai you into going along?"

McGavock frowned. "Don't pressure me. I got a schedule that's swamping me." He considered. "O.K.," he agreed. "If we can get back before suppertime."

The drive deep into the hills was rough and tiresome. Just out of town they struck the sloping red clay road and started their winding climb. Through a gap in the foliage, they could glimpse the village. It lay in the dank liquid-green of the bottoms, its buildings like tiny matchboxes. Main Street seemed one long, rambling shed. McGavock made out the red-painted cotton compress, court square and—in the distance—the rickety wooden trestle curving above the cut with its long, spindly supports. The trestle by Hodges' shanty where his attacker had opened on him with shotgun slugs . . . Great oaks closed about them and the picture was gone.

The high ridge caught the hot sun's rays, illuminating the tree shafts with preternatural clearness. The earth was brassy, scorched.

They turned from the pike, followed an indistinct trace of wagon ruts—and then, abruptly, it was cool, gray shadow. They were in the pine country.

Sheriff Robley stopped his car at a fork in the trail. "That's Devil's Elbow. Where Wainwright's hat and wallet were found. Shall we get out?"

McGavock glanced at the sink hole. It was a vile, grassy bog, saucer-shaped, bordered by dense hazel bushes and speckled with the sickly pastel blooms of wild orchids. "There's nothing here for us," he remarked. "Wainwright never saw this place."

"Perhaps you're right," Steve Robley agreed grudgingly. "It's the old hotel that holds the clues I'm after."

"Then you'll have to sift the ashes," McGavock gibed. "It's been torched."

The sheriff listened attentively while McGavock told him about Asie Tenniman's report. "So we drove out here for the trip! This is another of your tricks! What's behind it?"

McGavock said: "I've got a hunch. Play along with me—I think we can turn up something interesting."

he old resort, deep in a bowl of giant pines, was a shambles of flaming timbers. It was as if some giant hand had caught up the burning building, crushed it to splintered wreckage, and had dropped it, jackstraw fashion, to a blazing inferno. They could hear the vicious crackle and snap of the tinder-dry joists long before they turned into the little hollow.

The heat was searing, terrific.

"What are you thinking?" McGavock asked.

"I'm thinking the same thing you are," the young man answered calmly. "If this fire's been going on since daybreak I'll eat a box of .38s. The building's been exploded—and I should say within the last twenty minutes."

McGavock pointed to a blurred tire tread in the soft ground. "That's not a bear track. Our killer's been here, done his little chore—and gone."

The dapper sheriff was nettled. "We'll jusk ask a few questions of that hillman's wife, Mrs. Tenniman, who saw the building burn at daybreak. It looks like connivance."

"Mrs. Tenniman can wait." McGavock scowled, surveyed the surroundings with moody concentration. "Wainwright was killed in the hotel. There was a lawn party going on, a big fiesta out front. He signed up with Bradley and retired to his room. He'd been there a few minutes when somebody, another guest, knocked on his door, lured him into this guest's room and knocked him off. It's an old pattern, it's been done dozens of times before."

"It's very possible."

"I'm telling you that's what happened. The killer then went to Wainwright's room, got his cowhide satchel with the seventy grand and took it back with him to his room. Now listen to this, because the time's going to come when I want you to remember it: the murderer pilfered the satchel, pried up a couple of planks in the floor and hid it there."

"I don't see—"

"You will. It worked so well that time that he tried it later. And that's how we're going to catch him."

Steve Robley said suavely: "Well, we've got the body in our room, what are we going to do with it?"

"We're going to wait until about eleven thirty, when the lawn party's in full swing, and then we're going to lug it out a side door and dispose of it." McGavock added casually: "You don't happen to have a shovel on you?"

Steve Robley smiled. "Yes, I have. There's one in the car. I came prepared for almost any contingency. Don't look surprised." He walked away, returned with the two short-handled spades. "This is going to be pretty hopeless, isn't it? Where do we start?"

"We don't dig until we reason it out," McGavock declared. His words sounded silly to him. "Let's get the lay of the land, let's prowl."

The ferny springs, from which the resort had gotten its name, were halfway up the hillside. They lay in a grotto of fetid fronds—back beneath an overhang of black wet rock. There were seven of them and they drained into a silty pool where a rusty iron pipe carried their curative waters down the slope to an ornate pagoda-like bath-house.

McGavock leaned over the pool, peered into its scummy, yellowish depths. "And this stuff was supposed to be healthy! Yow!"

"He didn't toss the body in there," the sheriff said dryly. "That water was in constant use at the time. I don't see any bones. Do you?"

"No," McGavock answered. "But we will. Hold your horses."

At one side of the pool, far under the shelving overhang, a V trough had been cut in the limestone at the rim to check the overflow. A steady stream of water poured from this trough, struck a slab of shale and flattened out to a tiny brook which meandered down the bank in a little pebbled channel. McGavock began to whistle. He whistled "The Letter Edged in Black." He raised an impudent eyebrow at the young sheriff. "Just like Attila! I'll give you odds."

Robley showed wavering signs of temper. "Don't be cryptic. This thing is getting me down."

McGavock declared: "It has to be so. Our man's an engineer. Everything he does shows balanced planning."

He lifted the slab of shale from the brook, jammed it up against the drain trough in such a way that it diverted the overflow from the pool. A new runlet angled off down the hillside. Except for a few shallow puddles, the brookbed went dry.

"Get to work," McGavock ordered. "We dig in this dry channel." He cleaned a handful of tangled watercress from the ravine, thrust his spade blade into the gravelly earth.

"I'll start part-way down," the sheriff said, "and work up towards you." He disappeared down the slope in the brushy shrubbery.

Ten minutes later the sheriff's loud, clear voice called out excitedly: "By golly! Luther, I've found it!"

McGavock grinned at the young man's unconscious intimacy. "You've found what, Steven?"

"I've found the skull!" He sounded perplexed. "Wainwright must have been a midget. This looks like a child's skull."

"If you're not satisfied with your skull," McGavock yelled back, "come up and pick one from me. I've found three."

In a grisly hour they excavated the bones and skulls of six bodies. Two children and four adults. They laid the macabre relics on the marsh grass. Sheriff Robley was thunderstruck, nauseated. "A graveyard," he whispered hol-

lowly. "A ghastly funeral trench! What sort of charnel work went on here? I'll have half the town in my cells as soon as I return! It makes me dizzy. I can't seem to make heads or tails—"

"Charnel work is right," McGavock agreed gravely. "I was afraid of something like this." He looked old, cruel. "But I've got our boy in the bag. Meet me at Malcom Jarrell's tonight about eight and we'll go to town." He scraped the sandy loam from his shovel, started for the car. "Let's chat a bit with that south neighbor—Mr. Tenniman."

The ancient two-room cabin, with its log doorstep and its pack of yelping fox dogs, nestled at the turn of the trail. It was almost concealed by the waxy, swooping branches of aromatic pine. A wizened old woman, barefooted and smoking a juicy-looking pipe, sat in the runway. She pretended not to notice them as they approached.

The sheriff took off his hat. "Good evening, ma'am. Are you Mrs. Asie Tenniman?"

"I hain't her sister."

"I understand that at sun-up this morning you heard an explosion at the old hotel and that a few moments later you saw the sky redden as the building caught fire?"

The old woman chewed her pipe stem.

"I'm Steve Robley," the sheriff said placatingly. "Don't be afraid to talk to me. You probably knew my father. We mean you no harm. We understand—"

"You understand! You understand! Who-all's bin a-tellin' y'all these tales?"

The sheriff answered complacently: "Your husband, Asie."

The old woman said sweetly: "Now hain't that a marvel? If you was any sheriff at all you'd know your county. I'm a widow-woman. Asie's bin dead and gone three year now. The big-pox takened him."

There was a flustered silence.

McGavock put in his oar. "You tell us you're a widow. Those look to me like mighty fine fox hounds. Do you hunt foxes?"

The old dame went into a frenzy of rage. "Yes, by daddy! I hunt fox and I hunt deer and I hunt bear. And I got me a thirty-thirty inside that can roll you up like a cigarette paper. And if you fellers don't quit pesterin' me and git gone I'll shore haul 'er out!"

In the car, on the way back to town, the sheriff said: "The man that gave that false report to Bennett was an impostor. What did he look like?"

"He had a plaid cotton shirt and a flashy brass-studded belt. He was about eighteen years old. Do you make him?"

"I think I do. He's a character—and a bad one—from over in the Hostetter's Store neighborhood. How he got into the picture, I couldn't tell you. Maldron's defended him time and again—but that doesn't mean anything."

"Of course not."

There was an awkward interval.

The sheriff changed the subject. "Back there, before we started to dig, you said something about Attila. What did you mean?"

"Attila the Hun," McGavock explained. "That was the way his brother tribesmen buried him. They wanted to hide his body so they dammed a stream, buried him, and then turned the water back in its channel. I wonder how many anonymous killers have done it since!"

The sheriff parked behind the courthouse. "Promise me this," McGavock said earnestly as they separated. "Promise me you'll do nothing stringent until you hear what I have to say at Malcom Jarrell's tonight. Be there on the dot—and bring your buddy Hal Maldron."

The sheriff was hesitant. "It's mighty irregular—"

McGavock soothed him. "If it's the credit you're worrying about—don't! I don't want any headlines. All I want is this slayer."

That did the trick. Robley smiled. "I wasn't thinking of headlines but if you put it that way, it's mighty fine of you. I'll be seeing you."

he detective had an early supper at the Bradley House. Its lord and master was nowhere to be seen. But the boy in the alpaca coat was in a talkative mood. "A fellow was a-saying you're a detective," he observed. "You and Steve Robley been out all evening, ain't you? Fellow was a-saying y'all are teamed up to ketch you'uns a badman."

McGavock grabbed the boy's wrist, punched his hand in the inkwell, slapped it on a piece of paper. He gave the brat a terrible leer. "Fingerprints," he explained. "I'm not passing up anybody. I'll just send these up to Nashville and—" He paused, studied the paralyzed clerk thoughtfully. "Maybe you'd like to turn state's evidence?"

"But I don't know nothing about nothing."

"The heck you don't. Where's Cal Bradley?"

The adolescent licked his lips. "He's out in the country somewhere training a bitch pointer."

"Why didn't you say so in the first place? Why all the secrecy?"

"I swear I couldn't tell you. He threatened me not to. That's all I rightly know."

"If you see him before I do," McGavock ground out, "you tell him the sheriff said he's to show up at Malcom Jarrell's at eight."

He was dog tired. He rubbed his unshaven chin, knew that a bath and shave would freshen him, but decided to wait a little. In a far corner of the lobby—back in a sort of alcove—he could make out the outlines of a couple of comfortable-looking chairs in the half gloom. He sauntered over, sank down into cool, deep-cushioned leather and closed his eyes. He was half-asleep—thinking about that little ball of gray fur beneath the tile in Malcom Jarrell's hearth—when he heard footsteps advancing toward him.

Laurel Bennett burst out: "I have to see you. Thank goodness I've found you—" She was dressed as she had been that morning: baggy sweater and worn riding breeches. There was a disheveled, dramatic rumple to her hair.

"You haunt me," McGavock grated. "It's not right. You're a married woman. What now?"

"I have to confess," she said demurely. "I storied to you this morning. I didn't find any hammer. I just wanted to study your psychological reactions. When I was at college I wrote my thesis on—"

"Sure, sure." McGavock yawned. "Some other time, please!"

She ground her heel on the floor. "Where I come from," she stormed, "people pay me the proper respect."

"If they don't they get horse-whipped, eh?"

She went suddenly docile. Her somber eyes fastened themselves on him, intent and warm. "What makes you so attractive?"

McGavock kicked out a chair. "Sit down. What's all the bedlam about this time?"

"This. I've just been consulting with my attorney, Mr. Maldron. We want to retain you. Not through your agency, you understand, but on sort of a freelance job. We're so impressed with your energy and capability that—"

"That what?"

"Well, it's this way. I'm just a young girl. Gil came down to Louisiana and married me before I realized what was happening. Swept me off my feet and brought me back here with him. Now I'm beginning to regret it."

"How so?"

"My husband doesn't love me. He makes big withdrawals from our account and sends them to Paducah. He's keeping another woman up there. On my money!"

"Think of that!" McGavock snorted. "You overrun yourself, my child. Last night it was that Gil was gambling his dough away—now it's a new twist."

"You must believe me," she pleaded. "I'm sure I'm right. Hal, Mr. Maldron, says it's quite possible."

"How do I come in?"

"We want you to go up to Paducah right away and browse around. We want you to trace this woman down and get information on her. You can name your own salary!"

"It sounds highly attractive," McGavock decided. "But I'd like a couple of weeks to think it over." He ogled her. "I'll have to write my congressman." He called to her as she strode away. "Be at Jarrell's tonight at eight. The sheriff's orders—and bring your husband."

He sat there for perhaps five minutes, in a glow of pleasure at her anger, and then, on impulse, got to his feet and walked diagonally across the lobby—towards the rear. There was a door just beyond the desk which aroused his curiosity.

He turned the knob, pushed open the panel and stepped out into a small, enclosed court.

The little space, paved with brick and fenced on three sides with rotting eight-foot planks, appeared to be the hotel dump. Rusty bath tubs, broken crockery lay scattered in trashy litter. A wooden gate with a shoestring latch, inset in the fence by the alley, led down a short flight of stone stairs to an arch of brick. The entrance to an old cellar which lay behind the building's foundations.

McGavock descended the stone stairs, walked warily into the musty blackness. Just inside the arch, he stopped, got out his pencil flash. It was a "plunder room," a storage place for broken furniture.

He flicked his light in a swinging survey, across the great hand-hewn beams above his head, about the loamy, crumbling walls. Then, with the mathematical precision of a hawk circling for a field mouse, he crossed the floor with his beam, began a painstaking, clockwise examination of the cellar's cluttered contents.

He felt, knew, that he was in the presence of death.

His light indexed the hodgepodge: chests and highboys, cobwebbed and battered; rolls of rugs and matting disintegrating in the yeasty dampness.

From a frayed, red silk settee—in the heart of the untidy jumble—the corpse of Cal Bradley watched him with popping, lifeless eyes.

McGavock clicked his tongue, took a quick step forward. The hotel man's hair was a bloody spongy mass. "Our man likes hammers," McGavock thought. "And he's learning to get along without nails. This is a ball-peen job." He inspected the victim without the slightest twinge of sympathy.

Bradley had been dead for at least six hours. In death, the man's real nature showed itself. His puffy, spiderish face was grooved in lines of greed and malice. McGavock turned away in disgust.

On the earthen floor beside the settee was a granite washbowl full of gasoline. In the center of the bowl was a paving brick. On the brick, its base just awash with the gasoline, was a china teacup of gun powder. A new plumber's candle was thrust into the cup of powder.

The nape of McGavock's neck crawled. "He was coming back tonight to give it the works! When everyone was asleep. He's willing to burn down half the town. A fire here and all of Main Street goes like excelsior. And, according to his plan, I'm upstairs sawing wood."

The detective pocketed the candle, dismantled the apparatus. He dissipated the powder about the ground, carried the gasoline out into the court-yard and poured it on the paving bricks. "It's hardly likely he'll be back before dark—and I'll have him by then." McGavock frowned. "I hope."

The pimpled clerk was squatting behind the desk, his ear glued to the radio. A program was just signing off. ". . . How will Kent escape from the cannibals? Who is the mysterious little man with the blow-gun? Will Professor Lamphert discover the chemical which can unpetrify a human being? Listen tomorrow, same station, same hour."

"Exciting, eh?" McGavock made a comical arch of his eyebrows.

The kid nodded. McGavock said: "Give me my key and the house sponge. I'm going to my room and take a bath."

"We don't have no house sponge. You're supposed to use your wash cloth."

"Skip it."

McGavock's room had entertained a caller. All the bedclothes had been torn from the bed, thrown on the floor. The mattress had been ripped in vicious slashes, its cotton batting pulled out in handfuls. His Gladstone had been dumped on the carpet, there was a muddy foot-print on his purple sateen pajamas. The tobacco tin behind the crayon enlargement was gone.

The detective took in the chaos in cold, seething rage.

The final shock was waiting for him at the washstand.

Four black, lumpish objects lay on the flower-embroidered face towel. At first he thought they were potatoes. Like a kick in the stomach, it came to him what they were: rattlesnake heads. Meaty, evil-looking things, severed just back of the jaw.

"This cinches it," McGavock decided. "This is the lad that touched off Fern Springs. The footprint on the pajamas—that's where he got wet shoes. And that's where the rattlesnakes came from, too."

He slid a slip of paper from under the ugly things. A note, in the same script as that he had received the night before, and also on hotel sta-tionery, said: *These vermin got in my way. You see what happened to them. God be with you.*

McGavock considered. "He's scared. He's blown his top. He's mouthing threats. From now on we'd better watch our step—he's hysterical."

Fatigue disappeared with the first splash of cold water. He bathed to the waist, gave himself a brisk rubbing and selected the least crumpled of his shirts from the disorder on the floor. A shave, twice over, finished the job in short order.

He was all set to wrap this business up.

CHAPTER FIVE
MURDER SPA

 y the time McGavock hit the sidewalk the air was breathless—sultry. There was the electric threat of a summer storm about to break loose. In the south-west sky, above the hill-

crests, smoky thunderheads were gathering in a diaphanous haze. Even the hound dogs had vanished from the rutted road. The few mules left at hitching posts, their ears flat against their necks, stood stark and fearful in anticipation of the coming squall. McGavock didn't like it. Rain would bring an early nightfall and he was playing against darkness.

Lawyer Maldron lurked in the doorway of his office. The detective had the sensation that he'd been waiting there a long time for McGavock to pass.

He was a different lad from the one that McGavock had quarreled with last night. Somehow, in twenty-four hours, the attorney's cruel ego had withered almost to the vanishing point. "Good evening, sir." He was downright servile. "Could I speak with you a second?"

McGavock asked sarcastically: "What's the matter with the horseshoe-nail ring? Don't tell me you've given up window rapping?"

Maldron forced a cavernous laugh. "I don't rap for my friends, it's not polite." He threw a loop in his lower lip, screwed up his face. "That note on my blotter. You wrote it, didn't you? It was a joke?"

"I wrote it," McGavock said genially. "But it wasn't a joke."

Maldron was hugely pleased. "You admit it? Would you mind informing the sheriff? He's been after me—"

McGavock jeered. "Amnesia has come over me. I don't have the slightest idea what we're talking about." He asked sharply: "In the old days, back when Fern Springs was doing a rush business, how did the out-of-county guests get there? It's a long walk for gentlefolk."

Maldron was perplexed at the question. "They didn't walk, of course. Most of the guests were from right here in Bartonville. Those from out of the county came by train. There was a junction about eight miles from the resort. A surrey was sent out for them. Is that what you mean?"

"That's what I mean." McGavock turned up his coat collar. A sudden spray of raindrops, a premature warning of the storm on the way, whipped down the sidewalk in a swirl of tiny silver crowns.

The sheriff was not in his office at the courthouse. A turnkey greeted McGavock warmly. "Steve's done got Buck."

"Pardon?"

"I'm a-sayin' Stevie's done picked up Buck. He won't talk, though. Stevie says, should you drop in, for you to go back and make a try at him." He pointed a thumb over his shoulder. "He's at the end of the cell block."

McGavock said speculatively: "O.K. I'll see what I can do."

Buck was the phoney Asie Tenniman, the mountain boy with the plaid shirt and brass-studded belt. He was stretched full length on his bunk, reading a Sunday school paper. Every few minutes he'd take a glass jar of snuff from his pocket and rub a pinch of the powder into his gums. He looked at McGavock with glassy eyes, as though the detective were an unpleasant figment of his imagination. "You might's well leave me be. I hain't got nary a thing to say."

McGavock became chummy. "What you reading, Buck?"

"This-here paper was here when I come in. I'm a-whilin' away the time till Hal Maldron gits over to see me. You fellers'll be sorry then. I'm fixin' to sue y'all—"

The detective listened amiably. "But you haven't answered my question. What are you reading? It looks like a Sunday school paper."

The mountain boy said smugly: "That's what it is. It's a Bible paper. I'm reading a piece about how a lady preacher lived forty year amongst the Eskimos and spread the word of—"

McGavock took a little red leather book from his inside pocket. He leafed through it with great concentration, selected a page, tore it from the book and flipped it through the bars of the cell to the floor. "When you finish up the lady preacher you might start on that. It's a copy of the state arson laws."

"Arson laws?"

"That's right. You threw Bennett and me off

the trail while somebody rushed out and torched the old hotel. You're as guilty as the man that held the match. I've just been in consultation with Mrs. Bennett and she says it's the pen for the lot of you."

The mountain boy was thoughtful. "I'll make you a swap. I'll tell you what I know—if you'll promise to have Maldron scorch over and git me out of this."

"I'm not in a position to make such a trade. This is worse than arson—it's murder!"

The corridor and the cell block were growing dark. The boy looked out the small window at the smudgy clouds heaping themselves around the hilltops. "I think I been foxed," he said woodenly. "This-here was supposed to be a prank. I'm shootin' me a game of nine ball down to the Shamrock when Gussie says I'm wanted on the phone. It's a funny voice. It sounds like a woman tryin' to talk like a man—or maybe a man tryin' to talk like a woman, it's hard to place. Anyways, this voice says for me to go to Bennett and tell him about the fire—like I did. I was to go to Bennett's tonight at ten o'clock and Mrs. Bennett herself was to pay me ten bucks. I don't know anythin' about any murder and till the sheriff picked me up I didn't know that Fern Springs had really been burned. I'm a good boy. I'm deacon back in the settlement where I come from. I tithe, I eschew the ways of evil, like it sayeth—"

McGavock tossed him a crumpled package of cigarettes. "You don't know it but you're a lucky kid. Stay right where you are. The streets aren't safe for you tonight."

The first deep growls of thunder were bumbling across the opaque heavens as McGavock strode down the magnolia avenue of the Bennett mansion. The lawn shrubs were swaying to the pressure of the wind, showing the undersides of their leaves in silvery glitters. The great white mansion was a sulphur yellow beneath the racing storm clouds. Gil Bennett, in his singlet, wearing whipcord slacks and buckled sandals, was on the side lawn. His sparse hair, licked by the oncoming gale, lay plastered to his shiny pate. He was batting a wooden ball over the bent-grass sward, immersed in a solo game of croquet. He swung the mallet with a limp left hand; in his right he carried a jumbo sixteen-ounce mint julep. He waved to McGavock, beckoned him in.

"At it again, eh?" the detective observed dryly. He eyed the pint-sized goblet. "Tomorrow it gives prairie oysters. Where's Mrs. Bennett?"

"She's at Malcom's." He looked unhappy. "I'm supposed to join her there." He belched. "Ole Malcom, the man of nature, with his six eyes. That man gives me the creeps. I'm getting fortified." He walked to a wicker lawn chair, picked up a blazer jacket, slipped into it. "I thought you told me you weren't working for Hal and Laurel?"

"I'm not. They've been tempting me but I haven't succumbed. While I've got you alone I'd like to learn a little more about that divorce your wife is preparing to hang on you."

"You mean what I said last night? Forget it. It was just an alcoholic hallucination."

"That's what I thought at the time, it sounded like a drunken sympathy gag. Now, I'm not so sure. Do you want to come in on this with me or not? There's more at stake than meets the eye. There are wheels within wheels—if you get what I mean."

Bennett gave his head a blunt, decisive shake. "No thanks. You're a pal, and I appreciate it, but I'm a family man and I handle my own affairs."

"Your wife says you are sending money to Paducah. Where did she get that idea?"

"I gave it to her. She's been prying around, pumping me in a delicate offhand way about that money I've been withdrawing. I told her that I was footing the bills for a kid in finishing school up in Paducah. It wasn't very nice of me but she had me wacky with her nagging. Boy, did she show her claws!"

McGavock said: "That I can believe. Where are you sending this money, by the way?"

Bennett grinned. "Wouldn't you like to

know! I'm sending it to a big bank in a little town on the West Coast. More than that, I'm afraid I can't tell you. It's perfectly legal, you understand. It's my own money." He seemed uneasy. "Why the gathering at Malcom's? What's Old Spooky trying to pull?"

McGavock laughed. "Time will tell. It's not Jarrell's party—it's mine. The sheriff and I are going to saw this business off. It's the finale."

"Wheels within wheels is right!" Bennett studied his fingernails. "You've got your little scheme, Maldron's got his—and I've got mine. And ten to one, all our schemes, all our plans, are perfectly transparent to Malcom Jarrell. Well, as you say, time will tell. Let's go."

he storm hit them a half-block from Jarrell's cottage. It opened up with a deafening clap and a raging sluice of water. Lightning flayed the black sky. They broke into a lope and, sheltered by the arching maples, managed to make Jarrell's front porch.

Laurel let them in. She was wearing her jet lace semi-formal with the cameo at her throat. She seemed unnaturally stiff, apprehensive. Bennett brushed past her, towards the study. The girl stayed McGavock with an arresting hand. "I've discovered the most horrible thing," she whispered.

"Another hammer?"

She flared. "You're impossible!"

McGavock said quietly: "I can make a good guess as to what's disturbing you. You found the headless bodies of four rattlesnakes, didn't you? Well, dismiss them from your mind. They're a plant. I've got the heads, I knew the bodies would turn up somewhere."

"It's too repulsive! They're back in the kitchen—in Malcom's bread box."

"He's a naturalist, isn't he? Maybe he goes for gamy food. They're quite tasty if you pretend you're eating crab."

There was an atmosphere of subdued hostility in the study. The naturalist, his four-lensed spectacles hooked on his monstrous head, was busy sorting and mounting butterflies. He hardly seemed aware of the fact that he had company. Gil Bennett, his cheeks and ears flushed with open antagonism, lolled in the window bay. Behind him, the squall lashed the leaded panes in cracking gusts.

"Where's the sheriff?" McGavock asked.

"He'll be here later," Laurel said.

"That's just as good," McGavock commented. "Maybe we can thrash out a little domestic difficulty before he arrives. Are you planning to divorce your husband?"

Jarrell snapped an iridescent azure wing, fretted. "You have no idea how brittle these things are. I've ruined three since you people have been here. You distract me. Can't you go away and come back tomorrow?"

"No, you don't," Bennett said firmly. "Not in this downpour. Where's your southern hospitality, sir?" He addressed McGavock. "You've been here a day, now. What have you found out?"

"Plenty," McGavock answered. A bell in the hall clanged. Sheriff Robley, in a swanky gabardine raincoat, walked in on them. "Where's Bad-Tooth Maldron?" McGavock demanded.

"I don't know." The sheriff was annoyed. "I couldn't find him. I left messages for him all over town."

"There are a few things I'd like to run over," McGavock remarked. "Just to help us get organized. This case breaks itself into two installments: the old hotel murders, thirty years or so ago, and the present situation. You understand, this isn't what is generally known as a murder chain. It's just sort of a double outburst. The second, or contemporary, affair dovetails into the older business."

Sheriff Robley's calm eyes held him as he spoke. "I'm sure you're right, Luther. But it's the current mess that concerns me. Who killed Lester Hodges?"

McGavock ignored him. "Put it this way:

why was Hodges killed? Hodges was working for a rascal. The old eccentric was employed to search Fern Springs for the cowhide satchel in which Wainwright carried his seventy grand. This rascal had long suspected that the absconder had been knocked off. He reasoned that the satchel lay hidden beneath the flooring of one of the rooms. He'd been clerk at the time—"

Jarrell said petulantly: "Why the mysterious circumlocution? If Cal Bradley is the rascal you're talking about, why don't you say so!"

"Check. Names it is." McGavock watched the naturalist's nimble fingers in the lamplight. "Cal Bradley, as room clerk of the old inn, knew who had which room. Find the satchel under a certain floor and he'd know for certain who had slain Wainwright. He hired Lester Hodges to locate this satchel. Hodges did his searching by means of a rat."

"Did he," Bennett asked, "find the satchel?"

"No. But he made the killer nervous. This prowling, this attempting to uncover an old crime, got our murderer jumpy. He got him a magnetized hammer and a two-inch roofing nail and knocked off Lester Hodges. Is that clear?"

"It's clear enough," the sheriff agreed. "But it's highly speculative. Why isn't Cal Bradley here with us tonight? It appears he holds the key."

"He's absent through no choice of his own," McGavock retorted. "He's shuffled off this mortal coil. He's in the cellar of the Bradley House—stiffer than a briar root—"

There was a gasping silence. Laurel Bennett murmured: "We're doomed—all of us! There's an unholy hand at work among us. What have we done to merit such a fate?" She flung out her arms, crossed her hands piously over her heart.

McGavock barked angrily: "Won't you shut up! This is no time to mug for a spotlight." The storm outside dropped with a cleaver-like slash, there was only the low whine of the wind.

The girl cried dramatically: "Why isn't Hal here? Have they slain him, too?"

An oily voice from the doorway said: "Not me, Mrs. Bennett. Hal Maldron can take care of himself." The attorney barged his gelatinous body into the center of the assembly. "Sorry, Malcom, to pop in this way. Guess you didn't hear me ring. Got your message, Sheriff. Hustled right over. I was home peeling a bunion off my— But you folks aren't interested in that."

"You're all bunion, if you ask me," McGavock observed. "Quiet, please. Where was I? Oh, yes. Now let me tell you about Fern Springs. In its heyday it was a fashionable resort, no doubt very popular. It was more than that—it was a murder nest. I don't mean that the management was involved. I mean that somebody saw certain possibilities and summer after summer turned them to his bloody advantage. Jarrell, I'd like to ask you this question: who carted the guests to and from the railroad junction?"

The naturalist considered. "As I remember it we had a station wagon but we rarely used it. Usually the incumbent guests would take the out-of-county people to the railroad in their personal carriages. We were all one big family."

"Among you regulars," McGavock said, "there was a man who plied a terrible trade. He struck up friendships with wealthy guests. In weeks of intimacy he learned about his victims' contacts, learned who could be disposed of safely. Lonely men and women came to Fern Springs. Many of them would have no one to miss them. When their stay was up, he wheeled his buggy from the stables, gallantly offered to drive them to the junction." He paused.

"That, of course, was their last ride. He murdered them around the first bend—for their travel money. Men, women and children."

"It doesn't seem practical," Maldron argued. "Murder for a pittance."

"Pittance, says you. Wealthy vacationists went well-heeled in those days. I'll wager he cleared two thousand in a season."

"But Wainwright—" the sheriff put in.

"He broke his routine for Wainwright. And well he might! It netted him a fortune. He slew Wainwright the night he registered. He was afraid to wait, afraid that the absconder might slip from his clutches. Wainwright was his blunder. That's how I found out who he was."

"I knew who he was all along," Malcom Jarrell chirped up. "I saw him drag Hodges' corpse into my yard."

"You keep out of this," McGavock said. "When we need your comment, we'll ask for it. To continue the story. Hodges, working for Bradley, snooped around until he got himself eliminated. I appeared on the scene. Somehow, probably through Bradley's loose gossip, the killer learned a city detective was after him. He lay in wait for me at Hodges' shanty and threw a handful of number four shot at me, sent me a warning note at the Bradley house. I didn't scare. The next day he changed his tactics. He sent a hillboy named Buck around to Bennett's—when I was present—to say that Fern Springs had burned at dawn and then hightailed out to fire the building. Actually, there was no evidence in the old building, it had been long since removed, but he had heard about newfangled methods of detection and didn't know but what maybe a fluoroscope or something would turn up evidence."

"By the way," the sheriff remarked. "I've got Buck in the hoosegow. So far he won't talk—"

"He doesn't need to. He talked a little to me—and that is enough. Well, our killer by now is as busy as a squirrel in a hickory tree. He fires the old building, hunts out some rattlesnakes—those rocky ledges must teem with the vipers—zips back to town. He lures Bradley into the cellar, bashes in his head and sets a firetrap. He leaves the snake heads in my room with a final threatening note, scampers over here to Jarrell's and stashes the snake bodies in Malcom's bread box. He's really putting out steam—he's fighting for his life."

Maldron cleared his throat heavily. "It all comes back to me now. . . . How well do I recall that summer in nineteen nine. Every insignificant detail stands out crystal clear. Gil Bennett flouncing around among the ladies, taking them hither and yon in his yellow-spoked trap

and livery stable mare. Gil was shabby in those days—"

Jarrell said: "Hal, the time comes when I must speak the truth. You're my choice."

Bennett spoke quietly. "And you, Malcom, are mine."

he sheriff narrowed his eyes. McGavock looked cynical, happy.

"The thing that gives it away," Bennett explained, "is the rattlesnake theme. You'd know where to go to catch them and how to do it. You couldn't get Hal Maldron within ten yards of one. But there's much more to it than that. You were manager at the time of Wainwright's disappearance. You were no doubt right there at the desk when Cal Bradley signed him in. He looked prosperous, talked with a northern accent, and acted suspicious. You waited a bit, called him to your room and murdered him. Mr. McGavock says that Hodges used a rat in his prowling. Everyone in this town knows that you kept that rat for Hodges. I charge that Hodges was employed by you, that you murdered him on your own lawn and called in this city detective."

"Such a rigmarole!" Jarrell's massive head peered about the room. "I've no time to indulge in tomfoolery. Clear out, all of you, with your absurdities—"

McGavock said plaintively: "What about me? Doesn't anybody wish to hear my accusation?"

They stared at him.

"Maldron's correct. Gil Bennett's our man!"

"That's a serious charge," Steve Robley said gravely. "Is it official?"

"Of course I mean it to be official. He's a gory killer if you ever saw one."

Gil said whimsically: "Old pal, you've turned on me. And I bet you've built up a good case, too."

"Listen to it," McGavock whipped out. "And form your own opinion. It was you—old pal—and no one else, who planned and executed this entire massacre. You promoted your murder market at Fern Springs back in nineteen nine and buried your cadavers in the brookbed. You killed Wainwright, took his satchel to your room, looted it and hid it beneath the flooring. Cal Bradley suspected this. He employed the crackpot Hodges to ferret out the evidence. You killed Hodges—it would be simple for a man in the garage business to obtain a magnetized hammer—"

"But you gave me your compass to protect myself against this slayer—"

"You are a sly customer. I was fighting deceit with deceit. As I was saying, you killed Hodges and when I appeared on the scene attacked me. This morning when I visited you at the cotton gin, you saw me coming, grabbed a phone, called the Shamrock poolroom and asked for Buck. You disguised your voice to throw suspicion on your wife. Buck appeared, put across his little act and departed."

McGavock shook his head. "You made a mistake there, my friend. You may not pay a man for a thirty-mile trip on muleback but you at least *thank* him. It was a slip—I smelled a rat."

"I'd like to hear the rest of this tale." Sheriff Robley was modest.

"The rest of it you know. Buck stages his act and Gil, as soon as I leave, drives out and torches the place. While you and I are out there digging around, he's back in town beating in Bradley's skull. He'd planned to lay in wait for Buck when Buck showed up tonight at the Bennett mansion for his pay. With Buck gone, he figured he'd be safe." The detective smiled harshly at the businessman. "You know, Bennett, you plan well but you talk too much. You gave yourself away a dozen times. When you attempted to arouse my suspicions against Jarrell you said that he had prospered unnaturally. If anyone in this village has prospered unnaturally it's you, yourself—garage, drugstore, cotton gin. Last night in your car you invented a divorce that your wife was going to slap on you. This morning you realized that I could chase that down and expose it so you flew to Mrs. Bennett and got her excited about

an imaginary dream girl you were supporting in Paducah."

Bennett drawled: "It's pleasant listening to you orate—but do you have any proof?"

"Scads," McGavock answered. "Scads. Your gambling at Chunky's. A ruse to cover your withdrawals: *you were paying blackmail to Cal Bradley!*"

Bennett was completely relaxed. "The wildest sort of slander, sir."

McGavock spoke to Laurel. "That baggy pearl-gray sweater you've been wearing all day, is it yours?"

She tried to follow him, gave it up. "No. It's Gil's—but I like it. It's so roomy."

"Gil Bennett!" McGavock's voice was tight. "You were wearing that sweater when you dragged the body of Les Hodges into Jarrell's yard. Wisps of brushed-wool came off on the old man's corduroy. Jarrell saw the whole thing through his bedroom window but was doubtful as to your identity. He came out with a light and combed the gray hairs off before he covered the body with straw. He has that evidence beneath the tile there in the hearth—a little ball of wool. His testimony will hang you—"

Gil Bennett arose and turned his back on them. He stepped into the little bay window and began kicking out the leaded panes.

Hal Maldron seized him by the elbow, pulled him back. Bennett gave his torso a half twist, shot the lawyer through the shoulder and continued his glass smashing.

Sheriff Robley said calmly: "Bennett, you're not giving me any choice. I'm going to have to kill you."

Bennett dropped his pistol, advanced dazedly to the sheriff, who snapped on a pair of handcuffs.

"The satchel?" the sheriff asked.

"Bennett has it," McGavock announced. "Beneath the floor of his office. When I was in Bennett's office at the cotton gin I gave the floor special attention, dropped my hat, as a matter of fact, to give it a little closer inspection. The boards had been taken up and renailed. You'll find your satchel there."

Laurel Bennett burst out: "I'll never feel comfy in that old gray sweater again. And I loved it so!"

McGavock said sardonically: "But think, babe. You're married to a homicidal beast, a notorious public character. That means headlines, and reporters and three-column photos. I'll bet none of your bridesmaids back in Louisiana have done as well as that!"

The girl threw herself into his arms. "You can always see the bright side to everything!"

Knights of the Open Palm
Carroll John Daly

CARROLL JOHN DALY (1889–1958) was born in Yonkers, New York, and attended the American Academy of Dramatic Arts. His love for the theater led him to jobs as an usher, a projectionist, and an actor before he opened the first movie theater on the Atlantic City boardwalk.

Daly is remembered today as the writer who essentially invented the quintessential genre of American literature, the hard-boiled private-eye story. While there had been private detectives in literature before Daly, including Sherlock Holmes, and there had been dark, violent stories by such writers as Jack London and Joseph Conrad, it was not until *Black Mask* published "Three-Gun Terry," about the tough, wisecracking private investigator Terry Mack, in the issue of May 15, 1923, that the style and form coalesced. Daly's further contribution to the evolution of the genre came when he wrote his second story, this one featuring his best-known character, Race Williams, which he immediately followed with a another story about the same hard-boiled dick, thus creating the first series detective of his kind. While Williams tends to focus on his own massive ego and is preoccupied with guns and other forms of violence, he has a powerful sense of justice and fair play, undoubtedly serving as an inspiration for Mickey Spillane's Mike Hammer and, later, "Dirty" Harry Callahan.

"Knights of the Open Palm," the first appearance of Race Williams, was published in the issue of June 1, 1923.

Knights of the Open Palm

Carroll John Daly

Race Williams, who plays both ends against the middle, runs up against the hooded order and tackles a mystery which leads him into some fast and tragic action. His opinion of the Klan is not very high, but he tells about it in language which is rugged and dramatic, if not absolutely faultless.

RACE WILLIAMS, PRIVATE INVESTIGATOR, that's what the gilt letters spell across the door of my office. It don't mean nothing, but the police have been looking me over so much lately that I really need a place to receive them. You see I don't want them coming to my home; not that I'm over particular, but a fellow must draw the line somewheres.

As for my business; I'm what you might call the middleman—just a halfway house between the dicks and the crooks. Oh, there ain't no doubt that both the cops and the crooks take me for a gun, but I ain't—not rightly speaking. I do a little honest shooting once in a while—just in the way of business. But my conscience is clear;

I never bumped off a guy what didn't need it. And I can put it over the crooks every time— why, I know more about crooks than what they know about themselves. Yep, Race Williams, Private Investigator, that's me.

Most of my business I hunt up and the office ain't much good except as an air of respectability. But sometimes I get a call, one client speaking to another about me. And that's the lay of it this time.

I was in my office straightening out the mail, and enjoying some of the threatening letters what the boys who lack a sense of humor had sent me, when this Earnest Thompson blows in. And "blows" ain't no fancy way of putting it neither; this guy actually blows and it's near five minutes before he quits blowing and opens up.

"Are you afraid of the Ku Klux Klan?"

That's his first crack out of the box.

"I ain't afraid of nothing."

I tell him the truth and then, wanting to be absolutely on the level, I ask:

"Providing there's enough jack in it."

He trots out a sigh like my words had lifted a weight from his chest.

"You don't happen to belong to that—that order?"

I think he was going to call it something else—but from the twitching of his mouth I get the idea that he went in some fear of that same order.

"No," I says. "I don't belong to any order."

Of course I'm like all Americans—a born joiner. It just comes to us like children playing; we want to be in on everything that's secret and full of fancy names and trick grips. But it wouldn't work with me; it would be mighty bad in my line. I'd have to take an oath never to harm a brother—not that I wouldn't keep my oath, but think of the catch in it. I might just be drawing a bead on a lad when I'd spot his button; then I'd have to drop my gun. Of course that ain't so bad, but that same lad mightn't be wise that I was one of the crowd and—blooey—he'd blow my roof off. No, I like to play the game alone. And that's why I ain't never fallen for the lure of being a joiner.

Well, this lad must of had the idea that half the country belonged to the Ku Klux and that the other half went about in fear of them, for when he finds out that I don't belong he beams all over and pump-handles me a couple of hundred times. Then he comes out with the glad tidings that a gent I helped out of trouble had told him about me; with that he opens up with the bad news. His son had been took by the Ku Klux.

His boy, Willie Thompson, who is only seventeen, goes hunting around in the woods a bit outside of the town they live in. Clinton is the name of the burg and it's in the West, which is all

I'm at liberty to tell about it except that it's a county seat. Well, Willie stumbles across a bunch of the Klan and sees them tar and feather a woman—and what's more, he recognizes some of the Klan—this boy having an eye for big feet and an ear for low voices.

It appears that this woman had sold liquor to a member of the Klan who told her his poor old father was dying—you see, her husband run a drugstore. Now wasn't that just too sweet of the boys? Of course they checked up a lot of other things against her, too, and give her warning to leave town in twenty-four hours. Yep, they give her all those little courtesies what a lady should expect. But the real secret of the story goes that one of the lads of the Night Shirt Brigade was in love with the woman and wanted to get hunk because she couldn't see him a mile.

Now, that's Earnest Thompson's side of the story and not mine, but at all events the town of Clinton was pretty well stirred up and some of the Klan were actually in jail for as much as ten minutes. But when the trial came off this Willie Thompson had been kidnapped. The father worried, of course, but he thought the boy would be back when the trial was over. That was two weeks ago; the trial had blown up and the boy never heard from again.

Why, the whole thing seemed unbelievable. Think of it; here was this man with a good suspicion if not an actual knowledge of who had his son and he trots all the way to the city for me. Imagine if it had a been my boy—blooey—I'd a bumped that gang off one, two, three right down the line. But this lad was scared stiff; if he made a break to the authorities he got a threatening letter and—well, here he was.

But he made his offer a very alluring one: a good fat check, for this Thompson was a wealthy farmer. So I took the case and you should a seen his face light up.

"I didn't think that I could get anyone to defy the Klan." He takes me by the hand again. "I hope that you—that you won't give up when you find what you are up against."

Now that almost made me laugh.

"Don't you worry about me," I says. "And don't you worry about the boy. If he's alive and the Klan have him—why—I'll get him back to you in jig time; and no mistake about that."

Was I blowing a bit? Oh, I don't know. I'd said the same thing before and—well—I made good.

So the curtain goes up; he was to go back to Clinton that night and I was to follow in a day or two.

That night I trot down the avenue looking for some dope on this same Ku Klux Klan. I'd read a lot about it in the papers, but I didn't take much stock in it—mostly newspaper talk, it struck me.

It was in Mike Clancy's gin mill that I decided to get my information, for Mike belonged to every order under the sun.

But Mike shook his head:

"So you've fell for the lure, too?" he says sadly. "All the boys are crossing the river or going south to join the Klan—there's money in it and no mistake."

"Are you a member?" I ask him again.

"Not me." He shakes his head. "When it first hit the city I spoke to Sergeant Kelly about it. B-r-r-r-r! It ain't no order for an Irishman. Sure, it's the A.P.A. and worse. But if you must know about it, why, ask Dumb Rogers over there."

And he jerked his thumb toward a little dip what was sitting alone at a table in the corner.

And this same Rogers sure did give me an earful; that's how he got his name Dumb—he talked so much.

"The Klan?" he starts in. "I should say I did know about it. The boys is leaving the avenue by the carloads. You see they go south or west and join the Klan; then when there is a raid on and some lad is to be beat up, why the boys clean up a bit on the side. Suppose a jeweler is to leave town and don't and the Klan get after him—see the game—a ring or two is nothing to grab. And he dassen't say nothing—you write him a threatening letter or telephone him is better."

He paused a moment and looked at me.

"Don't tell me about the Klan—I know—I was a member and I was well on the road to making my fortune when they got on to me. They expelled me; threw me out like I wasn't no gentleman—that's what they done. And for why—just for going through a guy. Now, what do you think of that?" he demanded indignantly.

"That's tough, Rogers—tell me—how do you join?"

"Well, you got'a be white and an American and a Protestant—and you got'a have ten dollars—though if you've got the ten the rest of it can be straightened out. Yes, they got my ten, and what's more they got six-fifty for the old white robe—sixteen-fifty all together and they chucked me out—not so much as—"

But I interrupted him. I was after the passwords of the Klan and their greetings.

After a few more drinks he sure did open up; what with The Exalted Cyclops, Klaliff, Klokard, Kludd, Kligrapp, Klabee, Kladd, Klexter, Klolkann, Kloran and a host of others I didn't know where I stood and had to call a halt. But I got the grip out of him, which was a shake with the left hand. Then he give me the salute which I take careful note of. It was copped from the Confederate Army and is made by placing the right hand over the right eye and then turning the hand so that the palm is in front.

"But remember the one important thing." Dumb Rogers points a boney finger at me. "When you meet another Klansman you always say, 'AYAK,' meaning, 'Are you a Klansman?' If you ever hear a lad pull that on you—you answer, 'AKIA'—'A Klansman I am.' The rest of it is a lot of junk and most of the boys can't remember it—but them's the two principal things."

Then he showed me a cheap little celluloid button which he wore wrong end out in the lapel of his coat. When he turned it about I seen the letters KOTOP, which he explained meant "Knights of the Open Palm."

Do you get it—why it looked like they were stealing the waiter's stuff. That order certainly must have been started by a dish carrier. But I took a good look at the back of that button—you couldn't tell nothing from it, but I sure would keep my eyes open when I seen a lad sporting a decoration that way.

Three days later finds me in Clinton, a little burg of three or four thousand and the county seat. But don't get the idea that it was a one-horse town; even the farmers went about in flivvers and some of the people went about in real sporty cars. You'd never take it for a town that was in the grip of some half-baked organization.

The hotel, though, was the regular thing; I guess it had stood the same way for twenty-five years; it was called the Clinton House, which don't show much originality.

And with all my plans for my work being secret I wasn't there above half an hour when Earnest Thompson blows in. He was all excited; the Klan had come out in the paper that they had nothing to do with the disappearance of Willie Thompson and those who thought different had better hold their tongues. He showed me the clipping and sure enough it was a direct threat at the whole town.

But that wasn't why he come. Since seeing me he had received an anonymous letter hinting that his son knew something about a suspected Klan murder over at a town twenty miles away.

"I think he did, too," Thompson said. "I think that he kept it from me, but was going to give the information out at the trial. He didn't tell me all he knew because he feared for my safety." Of course that was news, but it wasn't good policy for him to drop right in on me. Why, if the Klan had half an eye out they'd know what was in the wind, and results proved that they did.

That very night Old Thompson was visited in his home by a number of white-robed figures and—well—we'll put it down to the fear that something might happen to his boy—but anyway he out with the whole story of how he had hired me to come down. He may have had some excuse; his nerves may have been shot to pieces, but this same Thompson sure lacked guts.

And the next day he lights out of town and calls me up. He tells me what happened and how he was forced to tell and then up and begs me to stay on the case. And what's more, he promises to double the check. What do you think? I stayed on, of course. I felt like bawling him out, but I didn't. The whole world might know why I was there and perhaps it wouldn't do this gang no harm to learn the sort of a man they had to deal with.

And that night the Klan honored me with a visit. Three of them there were and they must have put on their getup in the hall. Yep, all dolled up like the heavy chorus in a burlesque show they walked in on me.

Two of them stood one on either side of the door, rubbing their knees together, acting like they was a couple of businessmen what didn't like playing the fool. But the third lad was different—he was the real thing and no fake about him. He was big and powerful as he swung across the floor and faced me. He stood so a moment, glaring down at me through the slits in his white hood.

I just sat there in the chair looking him over and smoking; then I grinned. I couldn't help it. I could see the deadly threat coming.

"You are not a member of the Klan—the Great Invisible Empire?"

And he out with the last three words like he was announcing the batteries for the day's game at the Polo Grounds.

"No, I ain't," I tell him, pretending to wipe away a tear. "I wanted to join, but—well, you see I catch cold so easy. I got to stick to the pajamas."

But he never made a break, so I see I was wasting my time kidding that bird. So I made things easy for him.

"Don't try to figure it out," I says. "Come spill the sad news. Surely this ain't no pleasure call; out with the dirt!"

I don't know if he got it all or not, but he come out flat-footed and didn't make no more bones about it. And I'm giving him credit for a lad that talked like he meant business.

"You have caused the displeasure of the

Klan; we want no hired gunmen in Clinton," he said. "You have twenty-four hours to leave town—twenty-four."

"You couldn't make that twenty-five," I chirp. "You see, I want to attend your next meeting and sort of bust things up."

Oh, I just wanted to get him mad.

And it worked!

"You have heard me." I can almost see him glare through the slits. "And be careful of that tongue of yours, for I have a gun—a gun that I draw and shoot in one second."

And then he finished things up with a string of oaths that, if not original, were at least well chosen.

But he was speaking my language now—this gun business—and I just stood up and faced him.

"Listen, Dough-head." And I wasn't talking for pleasure now. "So you have a gun that shoots in one second, eh? Well, let me give you some advice. If that's the best you can do you had better keep that gun parked. I'm telling you flat that you'd be exactly one-half a second too late."

His hand half lowered to his side.

"If you don't believe me try it," I encouraged. "Your two friends there can carry you out."

Was I bluffing? Say, I was talking gospel and he knew it.

Then, when he didn't try nothing, I whipped out my gun and covered the three of them. And with that I make a grab and pull off the big lad's hood. I just wanted to get one look at his map and one look was enough—you could a picked him in a straw hat at Coney Island. He had a chin like one of the Smith Brothers or both of them— all whiskers and all hair and eyebrows.

"Listen, Feather-Face." I pound his ribs gentle like with the automatic. "You ain't dealing with no women nor a half-grown boy nor a distracted father now. You'll give me twenty-four hours, will you? Well, I'll give you twenty-four seconds to get out. And the next time you come around here I'll take that night shirt off you and shove it down your throat—whiskers and all."

I was mad now and meant it. This white-hooded frightener of women and children couldn't come none of that high-falutin game on me, and what's more I didn't like the names he had called me.

"You've had one look at my gun," I told them as they sneaked out. "The next time you have cause to see it you'll see it smoking; now—beat it!"

Which they done. Say, them boys had never had such a shock in their lives. I just sat down on the bed and roared.

The next morning I find a little slip under my door; it's from the hotel manager and it asks me to leave. So the Klan had opened up. Of course, I wasn't ready to go and I knew that they couldn't drive me out. You see, the town was about half and half; the authorities didn't side with the Klan nor they didn't come out against it; everybody was just sitting tight to see which way things was going to break. But if I was going to do a little gunning I'd need my night's sleep and if this manager was against me it would keep me pretty well on the jump. But I just shrug my shoulders and beat it downstairs, thinking things over.

I nod good morning to Jimmy O'Brien, the clerk. He's a real friendly lad and his handle tells me that he ain't no Klansman. There was no one else in the lobby, so I just wander to the doors and look out. And through them doors I catch a slant which is sure surprising even way off in that little Western town. Three men are coming down the street—single file—and there's about twenty-five feet between; right down the center of the main street they walk. Each has a gun swinging from his shoulder, but it don't hang over his back; it's swinging loose and mighty handy under the armpit—just a movement and it's ready to shoot.

The leader is a man which I place at over sixty; he's small but stocky—the other two must be in the thirties, big strapping giants of men.

I half turn as a figure comes to my side; it's Jimmy O'Brien. Of course I know that he's heard about my visitors last night. He was in the lobby when they beat it out.

"Who's the three desperadoes that take the middle of the road—more of the Klan?" I ask the clerk.

"No," says Jimmy. "That's Buck Jabine and his two sons. They are the only ones in town that openly defy the Klan. This Buck Jabine killed three men back in the old days—no, they ain't a family to fool with."

I could see that as they tramped up the street; they look business, all three of them.

"You see," Jimmy explained, "Buck talked against the Klan and then he began to get threatening letters. But he didn't leave town. He opened up with a warning that anyone found on his property after dark would be shot. This Buck shoots straight and quick—since that warning he ain't had no trouble—only letters. But they are coming here."

He breaks off suddenly.

The next minute they come in the door—one, two, three.

The old man takes one look around and then comes straight up to me.

"Stranger," he says, "I take it that you're Race Williams. Last night's doings got about a bit—shake—my name is Buck Jabine."

With that he sticks out his fin and the two sons do the same, though there ain't a yip out of them.

"I hear you ain't none too friendly with the boys, neither." I try to make things pleasant.

But he don't smile; he just looks at me. He's a chap what takes things seriously.

"Well." Buck just stroked his chin. "I just wanted to shake hands with you and tell you that I have a place out in the country—about two mile. Any time you want a place to sleep peaceful walk out—the house will be open to you day and night. I don't take no sides, mind you. Buck Jabine is only interested in his own family—he don't stand for no interference—but my house is open to you, wide open."

I thank him and then tell him about the manager's little note—just in the way of light con-versation, you know. I've made up my mind to stick at the hotel.

"When they put me out of a bum joint like this, they'll put me out in a cloud of smoke," I tell Buck.

"Humph!"

He strokes his chin again; then turns sudden and struts straight into the manager's office.

I try to get sociable with the sons, but don't make a go of it. I'm looking for dope on the Klan, but there is nothing doing. Oh, they're friendly enough, but don't go in for conversation. They don't even open up with a grin when I make wise cracks about night shirts and pajamas. They just stare at me. I could see that I'd have a right down sociable time over at their place.

"Yes" and "No" and a few "I don't reckons" is the best I gather, though once one of them opens up enough to ask me the time. So I guess the old man does the talking for the family; all together, it looks like a closed corporation.

And then Buck trots out of the office and the manager is right on his heels. My, but that manager is all smiles and tells me how it was all a mistake and begs me to stay on. And he means it, too, for behind that smile he looks real worried. Of course I ain't so stupid but that I know that this Buck Jabine has something to say about it and I sort of pity the manager. He's between Buck and the Klan and he ain't got much choice. Still, I think he was doing the right thing. He couldn't tell if the Klan would get him or not, but Buck—well, one look at Buck was enough; him and that family of his was all business.

"Ain't you worried about something happening to your house while you're away?" I ask Buck when he's leaving.

He just gives me the up and down for a minute and then he draws back his upper lip; I think it was meant for a smile, but I ain't sure. Then he chirps:

"There ain't no danger; Sarah's home and the boys' women. No, there ain't no danger."

With that they all file out and tramp down the center of the street—the same single file. So I see that this is sure one nice little family.

Now, this Klan ain't as secret as what I had thought. After Buck leaves, Jimmy, the clerk, up and gives me quite an earful. Sometimes them birds have even paraded right down Main Street and more than once they have taken out some citizen and tarred and feathered him. Then they'll bring the victim back and dump him out of a car right in the center of the Square by the fountain. See'n' they'll forget to put his clothes on again would seem like they lacked modesty.

When there were any deaths about the State due to the Klan's midnight playfulness, why, the Klan would come out in the paper denying it and announcing that they would expel any member who had a hand in it. Which is real generous of them, you'll admit; open-handed and fair-minded, to be sure. And then Jimmy outs with some real news: there's a Klan meeting that night. It's an open secret that they're taking in new members. So I see it ain't a falling organization but a growing one and I'd better work fast.

All day long that hotel is watched—there ain't no doubt about it. Three lads in the front and one out in the back. People what drop in dodge me like they would the plague and the general feeling is that I'm a marked man. Well, they may get me; the thing's possible; but if they do, the local undertaker is going to have more business than he's had in years.

Jimmy's a good scout and when he goes off duty about noontime he sneaks up and has a chat with me. So I take him into my confidence to a certain extent, and I believe if he didn't have a wife and kid he'd a been with me forty ways from the ace.

But he tells me where the Klan meeting place is and how people don't dare go near it. Then he tells me that he has a bicycle and after I bit I get his promise to hide it in a barn down the street behind the hotel; the fellow what owns the barn goes by the label of Dugan—enough said!

I watch out pretty carefully all evening and I don't see more than one chap watching the back of that house—so at nine o'clock I'm ready to pull off my little trick; I'm bent on joining in the festivities of the Klan.

There's a little partition off the back of the hotel and I get Jimmy to slip me in there unnoticed. Out in the dark of the tiny rear window I can see the solitary figure about ten yards away; it's a lonely little alley and no one else passes by. So I spring my game. I take my pillowcase, which I've made to look like a Klan hood, and, slipping it over my head, I light a candle and stand there in the open window; after a bit I give the Klan Salute—then I beckon the distant figure to me.

As I say, the whole Klan is a child's game, and that duck comes to me on the run; he most likely thinks that things are arranged for tarring and feathering me. As for me, well—I just club my gun and bat him over the head and he falls pretty—right in a nice dark spot.

Five minutes I wait and then, when there's nothing doing I step out the window and beat it down the alley. A few minutes later I'm on the bike, speeding out toward the open country and in the direction which Jimmy give me where lays what is known as the Klavern or meeting place.

All I need now is the regulation night shirt and I've laid plans to get that. Jimmy has seen the gang going to the meetings and knows the place that they stop their cars and put on the regalia. And what's more, he's told me about a lad whose business kept him late in town. It was this cluck that traveled alone in a Ford that I was looking for.

I guess I got to that spot a bit ahead of time. It was just around a bend in the road and very lonely. There was a nice place well back in the bushes where I parked my bike and waited. The night was dark, but I could see fairly well and in the course of twenty minutes about three cars pulled up and the occupants got all rigged out in their ghostly costumes. They'd just slip on the white robe and then crown themselves with the hood. If one party was decorating themselves there the next party would stop farther down the road.

After that I waited near an hour and then my man comes; all alone in a Ford he is and in some hurry. He don't even get out of the flivver, but tries to do the lightning change right in the car.

Say! I caught him with one arm in and one arm out of the shirt. Surprised! Why, he opened and closed his mouth just like a fish and a pretty far gone fish, too.

"None of your lip," I tell him when he started to spout about the terrible things that would happen to me. "You know me, kid."

I tickled his chin with my gat.

"I handled three of your breed last night. Come! Jump out of that night shirt or they'll bury you in it."

No laughter in my voice then—when I'm gunning I'm a bad man—none worse!

Enough! He showed good sense and handed over the whole outfit. It didn't take me more than a couple of minutes to bind him with the rope I had brought; then I tied him to a tree out of view of the road and, jumping into his car, I drove away.

A few hundred yards or more down the road I see the turn I'm looking for and a short drive down a rough lane and things are starting. A white-robed figure holds up his hand and stops me; of course in my robe he takes me for one of the clucks. I spot this lad for the Klexter, the outer guard.

"White and Supremacy," I say like a regular.

After that it's gravy; I go through my stuff which I got from Dumb Rogers. After a Salute he passes me and I turn into a field where there is near fifty cars parked.

Here I have to go through the speeches again with the Klarogo, the inner guard. But everything is rosy and pretty soon I pass down a narrow glade and into the Klavern itself. It was a fairly large open space surrounded by the thick woods—a good place to scatter if the cops come, I guess. There were near a hundred gathered about and when I slip in the show is already on.

"Imperial One, the men who seek admission to our legions stand prepared," a voice suddenly booms out, and with that all the robed figures gather about in a circle.

Then a lad with a cross all lit up breezes in and behind him march about eight lads—the candidates—looking for their ten dollars' worth.

And they got it; in wind at least. I never heard so much talking in my life.

The Head Goblin, a bird fixed up in white and scarlet, lets off steam about sending everybody to hell while the Klan took care of law and order. It was bum stuff, most of it, and if I'd a been one of the candidates I'd a hollered for my money back.

The members is not called brothers or anything like that; they are called citizens and the initiation is called being naturalized, and they take an oath which would knock you cock-eyed for length, bad English and rotten principles. And then the new citizens swear never to tell anything nor give any evidence against a Klansman unless he's committed rape, willful murder or treason. Hot dog! Burglars, counterfeiters, and check-raisers welcome—also arson might be appreciated—I don't know. But I sure do see why Dumb Rogers was sore and why all the crooks are joining.

Then the little buttons are given out with no extra charge but lots more wind; those buttons must have been worth all of ten for a cent—when I was a kid we use to pick better in a nickel's worth of popcorn.

But I don't get no real dope; not a mention of the boy nor a mention of me, which sure hurts my pride. Then I get the how of their pulling off the real dirt without being openly to blame. Committees is appointed, but they don't say what for. See the lay of it? If you have an enemy—why, get on a committee—it's hot stuff!

The real fellows who just enter the Klan because they are born joiners don't know half the time why they are beating up some helpless old man or weak woman. They just do it. Why—God alone knows. They forget their manhood and listen to all the wind about cleaning up the world and making it safe for the white race. And all for ten bucks. Oh, I'm a pretty tough egg—none tougher, I guess, but I felt as white as my robe in comparison with most of that gang.

And just when I'm wondering what good this whole show is going to do me, outside of improving my morals, I get a real shock. There's a commotion outside the circle and the outer guard rushes in and following him is—is my victim of the Ford.

Some excitement then and I can see my finish unless I duck and—and I ducked. In the excitement it was easy to slip back through the circle of white figures and into the thick foliage. I lay low there, where I can see what's going on. I'm not leaving yet—no—not me! I still got unfinished business. There sure will be a few dead Kleagles, to say nothing of a couple of Klodards and one thing and another, if this bunch get mussy with me.

You see, I suspect they'll unmask, looking for me, but no such thing. After they quiet down a bit the lad what thinks I wronged him starts around the circle, examining all the uniforms. He must have spilt soup or something on his, else how could he tell it? But he has no luck and after a little more talk they just bust up the meeting and beat it. The fear of Race Williams has been placed in their hearts. So I lay there a while, cussing my hard luck.

I'm wondering if they'll search the woods, but they don't. However, I shake my night shirt so as to be free and easy for gun-play; but these boys are not bent on committing suicide. About ten minutes pass and the chug of the motors has died away and I'm just about thinking of going back to town, when two white-robed figures suddenly enter the deserted glen. But they don't look around none, just lay off a bit. Then one of them, wanting a smoke, pulls off his hood and—and it's Feather-Face. Now, I got this bird sized up. Where he is, there is trouble.

Backing slowly out of the woods, I decided to sneak around and see if I can hear what they're saying. The moon is fairly bright, so I got to be mighty careful. And then, as I turn and go slowly through the trees, I hear the chug-chug of a motor. I peer through the trees and there by the roadside is a car—none of your flivvers this time, but a big touring car. The motor stops and a lad gets out and passes through the wood within ten feet of me. He ain't got no hood nor robe on, but I can't get a slant at his map.

I turn and follow him and as I reach the end of the clearing I hear him say to the others:

"Ed'll be here in ten minutes and then—"

"Sh!" cautions another voice.

But I don't wait to hear no more. I got ten minutes and I'm flying down the road to the place I left my bike. I ain't got time to duck in and out among the trees, but I don't meet no one, which ain't so much my luck as his.

And the bike's there and in less than ten minutes I'm about twenty feet behind that car, hidden in the bushes, ready to do a six-day race.

Five minutes later we all breeze off together—the four of them in the car and me following on the bike—none of us showing lights.

Now, the first part of that ride is not so bad, for they ain't bent on speed and the road is fairly level—but the moon goes behind a cloud and I got to hang close. On top of that we come to an upgrade and things are not so good. Then they turn up a steep and winding road and the bike ain't no good any more—at least, it's no good to me.

It looks like I'm stumped as I stand there panting and listening to the throb of the distant motor—and then the throb stops sudden—not just dies away. I look up the side of that hill and suddenly I see a light—it just flashes for a moment and is gone. Enough—I park the bike in the woods and start in to hoof it.

Twenty minutes later I'm at the top of a steep hill—on the other side of me is a cliff and below a roaring mountain stream. I can hear the water dashing by far below. And then out comes the moon and about fifty feet away I see a log cabin almost on the very edge of the steep cliff. A little ways from it I see the big car.

There ain't no one in sight and I just duck around that cabin, trying to look in; but there's nothing doing. Oh, I can catch the flicker of light from between some of the cracks in the logs, but can't see in. There is only one window and that is boarded up. I try the door softly, but it's locked tight; then I go round back with half an idea of climbing to the roof in the hope of finding a crack big enough to peer through.

And then when I get around the side I hear the door open—it creaks mighty loud. Only a second and footsteps are coming around to the back. Both guns ready, I back to cover behind the opposite corner of the cabin and wait. The moon is fine and I see two men plainly as they approach the edge of the cliff, forcing a lithe figure of a boy between them. His arms are bound, but his legs ain't, and he's pleading with them in a low voice.

"I won't never tell about the murder—I won't never say a word about who done it."

His feet are giving from under him and they help him along.

"You're right—you won't never tell."

One of the men give a gruff laugh.

"Here, you, Ed, give him the knife and get the job done," he says to his companion.

"Oh, push him over," Ed answers, and I seen his stomach ain't strong for such work, for his voice breaks a bit.

"Here—give me the knife."

The other has a sneer in his tones. The next instant I see a flash of steel in the air above the boy.

Crack!

Yep, it's my gun what speaks and that lad goes out like a light. The other lad draws a gun and looks around him, bewildered. But he don't see nothing; leastwise in this world he don't. I get him right through the head—there ain't no mistake where I land in that distance. He drops the wrong way—staggers a bit and I hear his body crashing down the cliff, tearing loose the rough stones as it goes.

Oh, I ain't a killer, but remember, there were four of them, that left two more to be accounted for yet; it wouldn't do to wound a lad and then have him pop up again when you least wanted to see him.

The boy just stands there—swinging back and forth on his weak legs—and I'm afraid he'll go over too.

"Lay down, you fool!" I says, and he drops like a log and lays still.

Then I wait. I know those gentlemen in the cabin must have heard the shots and be coming. Like a movie picture villain, a figure looms up from the side of the cabin; sneaking slowly along, the flash of nickel plainly visible in his hand. And like a movie villain he fades out of the picture. I got him.

"Number three," I says and wait; the party ain't over yet.

And then there's a step behind me; like a foot upon dried twigs.

Like a shot I turn and in the rays of the moon spot the evil, sneering map of Feather-Face. His gun spoke ahead of mine—I knew that from the red-hot burn that shot along my temple—just above the ear it seemed to hurt most.

Of course I fired—emptied both guns, I guess. But I didn't see nothing when I shot— there were dancing, blazing lights before my eyes and then darkness—a deadly black darkness followed by a sinking feeling. I had stuck on my feet while I shot, but now I knew I was slipping; every minute I expected to hear the gun bark— but didn't.

Then there was the chug-chug of a motor— the grinding of hurriedly shifting gears; my firing had scared Feather-Face off. With that thought I sagged to the ground—everything went black.

When I come to again I was in the cabin and several men were leaning over me. One of them was in uniform and I recognized him for the Chief of Police of Clinton.

I hear them talking a minute; how they had come across Willie Thompson staggering down the road and how they had come out to the cabin; and I gathered that Feather-Face had beat it— then curtains again.

I was all right—that is, to a certain extent— when I come to again. But I was in the coop, which was not so good. Yep, I opened my eyes in the jail at Clinton and a doctor was bending over me.

He had a real friendly face and his talk was good.

"You sure did for that gang," he said. "I hope you come out of it all right. Oh, not your head—

it must be as hard as rock—you're all right there. I mean this little killing. You have a good lawyer—none better—and the judge has no use for the Klan. Thompson has told him his story—and it's not a pretty one. Man, I tell you you have a first-class lawyer. I hear that it's fixed up to release you on bail—on a writ of habeas corpus, they call it."

"Then I'll get out all right," I said, relieved, for I had the idea that the Klan ran the town.

"Oh, the judge is with you, but the Klan—you see, there is a threat about town—death to the party that goes on your bail—and the trouble is that the people fear the Klan. They have a habit of making good on these little threats. Why, no one can visit you—the Klan's orders again—of course they wouldn't forbid you medical attention."

"Then no one will have the nerve to go my bail?"

I sure was some surprised.

"That remains to be seen." He shook his head, but there didn't seem to be much hope in his voice.

But he didn't tell me then that there also was a threat to storm the jail and there was much talk about asking for the State troops to be sent over.

And that's that. I didn't get much time to think; my mouthpiece sure did work fast, for by that afternoon I was hustled out of the jail by the Chief of Police and three or four other highly nervous gentlemen and rushed into court.

Some court; just one long, low-ceilinged room with great big windows on either side of it. It was warm and the windows were open and the bright sun shone in. But the faces about me—there was nothing bright and comforting about them; hostile, hard faces they were, and a murmur, a threatening murmur of disapproval, ran through the room as I was led before the judge's bench. The judge was hard too, but his face was honest and almost defiant as he looked over the crowded courtroom.

My lawyer was there and talking, but I didn't get much of what he said, but I guess the judge was hurrying things along; the people looked like

they might act up bad any minute. The District Attorney was objecting to everything—I wasn't surprised—I'd heard that he was mighty close in with the Klan.

Then the judge come out flat-footed and named the bail—not a large sum, neither; and he hammered on the bench as a low rumble of protest went up from the packed courtroom.

Then my lawyer says, slow and calm:

"Your honor, I have the bondsman here."

My, you could hear a pin drop when he said that, and half the court stood up and looked around where the lawyer had pointed toward the door at the rear.

There comes a sudden rattling of windows from both sides; I look first at one of the big windows and then the other. There, on the two opposite window sills, had appeared the huge, stalwart frames of the Jabine boys. Motionless as statues they stood with their rifles swung loose beneath their armpits.

"Buck Jabine!"

I hear the hoarse whisper go up from ten voices at once. And I look toward the back door of the courtroom.

Right through the swinging doors had come Buck Jabine, his head erect, his eyes looking neither to left nor right. Straight between that path of gaping, angry faces, he made his way until he reached the bench. Not a hand was raised to stop him—not a mouth voiced even anger. You see, everyone there knew Buck Jabine and the boys. Two minutes later and everything was Jake.

So it was that I left the courthouse a free man and joined the procession of the Jabines. I was third in that single-file line as we made our way up the Main Street and out into the open country toward the Jabine farm. Not a word did we speak—just hoofed it along. I wondered then if I made as forbidding an appearance as the family.

Thompson and his son were at the Jabine house and such a welcome you never did see. And the Jabines took it all without a smile—they were all business and no mistake.

Of course I got the lowdown on the whole affair from the Thompsons. Willie Thompson had made some discoveries about the murder at the town twenty miles away—it was Feather-Face and his three friends what had pulled it off in the name of the Klan. There was robbery behind it and Willie had come across that little cabin in the hills and seen them splitting some of the swag. Enough! They nailed him and was just waiting for things to blow over a bit before they bumped him off and let his body float away below the cliff.

After that things happened in town. The real story came out and I was never even brought before the Grand Jury. It appears that even with the truth most of the Grand Jury wanted to hold me at first—you see, they were thick with the Klan. Then things started.

Ten members of the Klan who were on the Grand Jury up and resigned from the Klan; they come out flat and told the judge how they felt and how they had joined the organization just like they would have joined any other fraternal organization. The end of it was that the judge discharged me without my ever showing up in court.

You see, it was better for me not to be seen about too much. The Klan was slipping and members were leaving it every day; and what's more, an Anti-Klan organization was forming, though Buck Jabine would have nothing to do with either one of them. Altogether things were bad in Clinton; both factions went around armed and defiant. The Klan had sure lost its grip.

But of Feather-Face nothing was heard; both sides sought him now, equally bent on vengeance. I could see that Feather-Face's position was not an enviable one—still, he kept clear of Clinton.

"There weren't no harm in the old order," Jabine opened up to me one evening. "My father was in the Klan back in the Sixties. But this modern Ku Klux Klan was a money-making graft bent on raising religious and racial hatred. Of course half the crime laid to their doors wasn't true, but it gave others the opportunity to masquerade under their name. You can't defy law and order and the rights of your fellow-man

without the criminal element sneaking in. Robbery, murder, private vengeance—that's all what could come of it. And it took you—you, a stranger, to show it all up in its proper light."

And from then until the day I left that was all Buck Jabine had to say on the subject.

The night that the Thompsons, father and son, came to the house in their little car to drive me to the station, Buck said:

"I have arranged for the train to stop at Haddon Junction, five miles down. You see"—he turned to Old Thompson—"the folks of Clinton were planning to give Race Williams, here, a little sendoff and it won't do. The Klan spirit is dead. Why bring it up again? There are enough left to make trouble if any popular demonstration is shown. The Klan is slipping—slipping fast and I say let it slip."

Well, I was agreeable, though I think Willie Thompson—who had become somewhat of a hero about town—was disappointed and felt badly about it. But the cash transaction was all that interested me. I had mailed the check which Thompson had given me along to my New York bank and—well—I didn't have no doubts on it—but I'd be glad to get home and do a little drawing on it.

So I shook hands with Buck and got a few grunts out of the Jabine boys. Then I said good-bye to the ladies—I didn't mention the ladies before, but it will be enough to say that they were sure some Amazons and would make a good showing in a free-for-all. And—well—I was off. Old Thompson and me in the front seat and Willie Thompson in the rear. It sure felt good to be on the go again with my twin gats parked nicely about me.

At nine-thirty we was only about a quarter of a mile from the station and ten minutes to catch the train, when we have trouble. Blooey! Both the rear tires go like a couple of cannon; so sudden did it come that I had half drawn my gun.

Then I watched the two of them stall around a minute. I could see the one light of the little station shining in the distance, so I decided to hoof it. These lads treated an automobile like a steamroller—only one spare tire and an inner tube on hand. They'd be a half-hour at least; what with scratching their heads and pulling up their pants.

I wouldn't listen to their protests about waiting over another night and I wouldn't let one of them come along to the station with me; they weren't fit to be separated—too slow-thinking birds they were. No, sir, I was booked for the city and going through.

So I swung out my suitcase and after a couple of handshakes started down the road. I hoofed it fast, but I got a-thinking while I walked; got a-thinking as I looked down and kicked some mighty dirty-looking pieces of glass and half a broken bottle from the road.

I could hear the train coming along and see her headlight flashing down the tracks as I reached the station. Now, there was no station master at this Haddon Junction and only one light on the north side of the station—the side the train was approaching from. So, bag in hand, I started to pass under that light and out onto the platform—then I stopped dead—that broken bottle had suddenly loomed up before me as big as life. I just ducked back and made my way cautiously around the other side of the station. Not really suspicious, you understand—only careful. And that's the secret of why I hope to die in bed.

Bang! Like that! I duck into a chap who is coming slowly from around the south end of the station. We hit with a crash and both step back a pace; he out on the platform toward the tracks.

Was he quick? Well, he never had no chance. Mind you, he had his gun in his hand, but he never used it. Just as clean as a whistle I had pulled and shot him straight between his blood-shot eyes. The train roared into the station as he fell and in the light of the headlight as it flashed by I got a look at his face. Oh, I knew it before, even in the dull light of the moon. Yep, you hit

it—it was Feather-Face. You recollect I once told him that he'd be half a second too late.

And then the brakeman swung out on the step; I climbed aboard; he swung his lantern and we were off.

"Thought I heard a shot," the brakeman said as he climbed up the steps behind me, where I struggled with the door.

You see, I couldn't tell what he had seen and I wanted to hear if he had any comments to make. I had half an idea that I had already done enough shooting to please the people of Clinton.

"Yep."

I turn and look the man over as the train gains headway.

"Yep, a dog snapped at me—a dirty dog—I killed him—with this."

With that I shoved my gun out under his chin sudden as I watched to see how he took it.

"Thought I saw a figure—a human figure."

He lays down his lantern and stretches his hand up toward the emergency strap.

Then in the dim light from his lantern I catch the glimpse of a tiny button beneath his coat—yep, his lapel is half twisted around and I take a chance that the letters on that button are KOTOP.

Looking him straight in the eyes, I suddenly raise my right hand and place it over my right eye, palm in—then I reverse the hand, giving him the Klan salute.

His hand lingers for a moment on the bell, but I see that his fingers loosen their grip.

"AYAK," he says.

"AKIA," I answer.

His hand drops from the bell and without another word he turns and enters the forward car. I stand so a moment; then with a grin I slip into the rear car. After all that is said against the Klan, I sure got to admit that there are times when it serves its purpose.

Waiting for Rusty
William Cole

WILLIAM COLE (1912–1992) was born in Manhattan and graduated from
Lehigh University. A freelance writer, he lived in New York City for the last
sixty years of his life. In addition to short stories, he contributed factual articles
on health, family relations, and other social issues to *Good Housekeeping, Family
Circle,* and *The Ladies' Home Journal.* He also wrote reports for the National
Institutes of Health and other federal agencies, as well as scripts for documentary films for the United States Information Service.

The short-short "Waiting for Rusty" was his only contribution to *Black
Mask.* Although very brief, it elicited more reader response than almost any
story ever to appear in the magazine. It was published in the October 1939 issue.

A BULLET FOR GUN MOLL NO. 1

Waiting for Rusty

William Cole

ONE OF THESE DAYS I'M GOING TO tell the sheriff. One of these days he's going to blow his mouth off once too often and I'm going to take him out there and show him. I may get on the wrong side of him but it'll be worth it. . . .

I'm just closing up my little roadside place for the night when they come in. Dotty and three guys. One of the men has a sawed-off shotgun and he stands by the window. Dotty and the others come up to the bar.

"Evenin', Professor," Dotty says, looking around. "You here alone?"

"Yeah," I says, when I'm able to talk. "Yeah, but—"

"Good," Dotty says. "Lock that back door and then start pourin' rye."

She's wearing a blue slicker turned up at the neck and no hat. Her light hair is a little fluffed from the wind. She looks about the same as I remember she did when she went to the high school at Milbrook, only now you can't look long at her eyes.

"Listen, miss," I says, "listen, you don't want to stay here. They're surrounding the whole county. I just got it over the radio."

"He's right," the man at the window says. "We gotta keep movin', Dot. We gotta keep movin'—and fast, or we'll wake up in the morgue."

"Get outside," Dotty tells him, "and keep your eyes open or you'll wake up there anyway."

She goes over and turns on the radio. The other two men keep walking around. They're all smoking cigarettes, one right after the other.

I know enough to do what I'm told.

There's nothing on the radio but some dance music. The two men look at each other; then the shorter one goes over to Dotty.

"I know how you feel, Dot," he says. "But they're right on our tail. We gotta—"

"I told you boys once," Dot says, "and I'm not tellin' you again. We wait here for Rusty."

"But supposin' he don't come?" the man says. He has a way of rubbing his wrist. "Supposin' . . . supposin' he can't make it? Supposin'—"

"Supposin' you dry up," Dotty says. "Rusty said he'll be here and when Rusty says something . . ."

The music breaks off and she whirls to listen to the press-radio flash. It's about the same as the last. The police have thrown a dragnet around the entire northern part of the State and are confident of capturing Rusty Nelson and his mob at any hour. Dotty don't think much of this but when she is called Rusty's girl and Gun Moll No. 1, she smiles and takes a bow.

"After the bank hold-up yesterday," the announcer says, "Rusty and Dotty split up, one car going north, the other northwest. The State Trooper who tried to stop Dotty at Preston this afternoon died on the way to the hospital."

"Too bad," Dotty says. "He had the nicest blue eyes."

A car goes by on the highway outside and they all stand still for a second. Then the music comes back loud and the men jump to tune it down low. The taller one is swearing under his breath.

"Canada ain't big enough," he says sarcastic-like. "We gotta meet here."

Dotty don't say anything.

In no time at all, they finish the bottle of rye. I open another.

"Maybe he couldn't get through," the shorter man says. "Maybe he tried to but couldn't."

There's another radio flash. The cops have traced Rusty to Gatesville.

This makes Dotty feel a lot better. She laughs. "He's near Gatesville," she says, "like we're near Siberia."

She gets feeling pretty good, thinking of Rusty. She don't mind the music now, the way the men do. She asks me if it comes from the Pavilion and I tell her yes.

"I was there once," she says. "I went there with Rusty. They were havin' a dance and he took me." The men aren't interested and she tells it to me. "I had to wear an old dress because that's all I had, but Rusty, he sees me and says, 'Gee, kid, where'd you get the new dress?' and we hop in his boiler and roll down there."

She has stopped walking around now and her eyes are all different.

"They have the whole place fixed up . . . those colored lights on a string and the tables under the trees and two bands on the platform. As soon as one stops, the other one starts. And there's a guy goes around in a white coat with those little sandwiches and you can take all you want."

There's the scream of a siren in the distance. The men take out guns.

"The girls all wear flowers," Dotty says. "And I don't have none. But Rusty says, 'You just wait here,' and soon he's back with a big bunch of flowers, all colors and kinds. Only I can't wear half of them, there's too many. And then we dance and drink punch until the cops come. And then we have to lam out of there; they say Rusty bust in the glass in the town florist shop."

The siren is much louder now. The man with the shotgun runs in.

"A patrol car just passed!" he says. "Come on, let's blow!"

Dotty don't seem to hear. "Get back out there," she tells him.

The man's face goes even whiter. He looks at Dotty and then at the others. "I say we move," he says. "Rusty or no Rusty. We'll be knocked off here sure."

The other men try to stop him but can't.

"And we don't even know that he'll show. He might've turned south, or kept west. All the time we're waitin' here he might even be—"

Dotty has put her back to the bar. She waves a gun at the man.

"Get away from that door," she says. She leans back on her elbows. "Drop that rattle and get over there. We don't want to have to step over you."

It takes the man a minute to get it. Then his knees begin to give. He opens his mouth a few times but nothing comes out.

Then there's that static on the radio and the announcer telling how Rusty was nabbed down in Talbot. Dotty stands there and listens, resting back on the bar.

"Not a single shot was fired," the announcer says. "The gangster was completely surprised by the raid. Alone in the hide-out with Nelson was a pretty dark-haired, unidentified girl."

Then there's that static and the music again.

Nobody looks at Dotty for a while. Then the man with the shotgun bolts for the door. No sooner he's opened it, he shuts it again. "There's a guy comin' up the road," he says. "He's got on a badge."

For what seems a long time, Dotty don't move. Then she reaches out and snaps off the radio. "Let him come," she says. "You guys get out in the car."

The men don't argue. They go out the back.

Dotty walks slowly to the door. When she speaks, her voice isn't flat any more.

"You know," she tells me, "it was funny about those flowers. They just wouldn't stay put. Every minute I'd fix them and the next minute they'd slip. One of the girls said the pin was too big."

She steps out on the porch, and I drop flat in back of the bar.

"Hello, copper," I hear her say. The rest is all noise. . . .

One of these days I'm going to show the sheriff. One of these days he's going to tell once too often how he got Dotty and I'm going to take him out on the porch and show him. . . .

Sure, she might have missed him, even Dotty might have missed him twice in a row. But she would never have put those two slugs in the ceiling. Not Dotty. Not unless she had reason to. Not unless she wanted to die.

Rainbow Diamonds
Ramon Decolta

RAMON DECOLTA was the pseudonym of Raoul Whitfield, who spent much of his early life in the Philippines, where his father was attached to the Territorial Government in Manila. His familiarity with the Philippines, and Filipinos, enabled him to make a significant breakthrough in the way Asians were portrayed in pulp fiction—and in Western literature in general. Although the Dr. Fu Manchu novels were extremely popular, they portrayed the "Devil Doctor" as a malignant force with no redeeming virtues until the late books in the series. Earl Derr Biggers represented Charlie Chan respectfully, but he had only a minor role in the first book about him, and then was often shown as a comic figure. But with Jo Gar, Whitfield created an important character without condescension in a series of twenty-six short stories, twenty-four of which appeared in *Black Mask* between February 1930 and July 1933; two lesser stories ran later in the 1930s in *Collier's*. It was only after the appearance of Whitfield's Jo Gar and the success he enjoyed in the pages of *Black Mask* that Hugh Wiley began to write about Mr. Wong (who became a popular movie character, played by Boris Karloff) and that John P. Marquand created Mr. Moto, famously portrayed in films by Peter Lorre. Gar is a private detective who works from a seedy little office but lives in a fancy gated house with a houseboy, Vincente. Eighteen of the *Black Mask* Jo Gar stories were collected in *Jo Gar's Casebook* (2002). The six connected stories that comprise *Rainbow Diamonds* have never before been published in book form. They ran in the February through August 1931 issues.

Diamonds of Dread

Ramon Decolta

Jo Gar, the Island detective, takes up a trail of justice and vengeance.

HE BROWN-FACED driver of the *carromatta* shrilled words at the skinny pony, tugged on the right rein. He stood up in front of his small seat and waved his left arm wildly. Jo Gar leaned forward and watched the approaching machine sway down the narrow street. It was a closed car, mud-stained. It swung from side to side, traveling at high speed. For a second its engine was pointed to the right of the *carromatta,* now crowded far to one side of the street. And then it careened straight towards the small vehicle.

The driver shrilled one word. His small, scantily clad body curved from the front seat. For a second Jo Gar had an unobstructed glance of the speeding car. He muttered a sharp "*Dios!*"—hunched his small figure forward and jumped.

His sandals had not touched the broken, nar-row pavement at the right side of the street when his ears heard the splintering of wood. A woman screamed, in a high, short note, down the street. There was another splintering sound—then the cry of the pony. Jo Gar's diminutive body struck the pavement; he went to his knees, lost balance and rolled over on his back. His pith helmet snapped from his head, thudded like a drum lightly struck, away from him.

He wasn't hurt, and got slowly to his feet. There was a great deal of excitement in the street. The pony had been dragged to the curb and lay on one side, tangled in the *carromatta* shafts. It was vainly trying to rise. The vehicle was a wreck. But the machine was still swaying on its way—a horn sounding steadily.

Near the Pasig the street curved sharply to the left. Even as Jo Gar stared after the machine, it swung far to the right. For a second he thought it would crash into the awninged Chinese shop at the curve. But it did not—it swung back into the middle of the street, was lost from sight. The sound of the horn died. Voices all about the Island detective were raised, pitched high. Chinese, Spaniards, Filipinos—the street was suddenly filled with them.

Jo Gar recovered his helmet, placed it on his head. The sun was still hot, though it was sinking over the bay. He moved towards the struggling pony, speaking sharply to the driver, who was shouting wildly after the vanished car. Together they freed the pony from the shafts and harness—it struggled to its feet and stood trembling, nostrils wide. The driver cursed steadily.

A brown, open car came down the street from the direction the other had come, horn screaming. Jo Gar narrowed his gray-blue eyes on the brown uniforms of Manila police—saw the face of Juan Arragon turned momentarily towards him. The Manila lieutenant of police shouted something—then the car was beyond. A wheel lifted wreckage of the *carromatta*, deposited by the crash car fifty yards distant, and sent it skimming towards the pavement. A voice behind Jo said excitedly:

"What the devil, Señor Gar! That was a close one for you—"

A man dressed in white duck was running down the street towards the wreckage of the *carromatta*. He wore no helmet. He shouted hoarsely, but slowed down as he neared the spot where the crowd had gathered. Jo Gar said in an unhurried tone:

"What is it, Grassner?"

The man in white duck was short, thick-set. He had the squarish face of a German. He widened blue eyes on the Island detective's narrowed ones.

"Delgado's!" he breathed heavily. "Robbery—there were three cars—different directions!"

Jo Gar said slowly: "Delgado's—yes. Of course. And three cars—"

The *carromatta* driver was standing near the

pony, cursing shrilly. Tears of rage ran down his brown cheeks. There was still much excitement. The Island detective said sharply to the driver:

"Please stop it! Your pony is not much hurt. You will be paid for the *carromatta*. That is enough!"

Grassner said thickly, breathing with difficulty:

"Herr Mattlien is dead. A bullet hit him."

Jo Gar frowned. He had little use for Herr Mattlien. But robbery had now become murder. He asked in a low, almost toneless voice:

"You saw—the robbery?"

Grassner blinked at him with his small, blue eyes. He shook his head. People were crowding around them.

"I was in the International Bank, around the corner," he said more calmly. "There were shots—and I ran out. Cars were moving away from Delgado's, and Mattlien was running towards them, a gun in his hand. There were more shots—he fell. I went to him—he was dead."

Jo Gar made a clicking sound. He shook his head, spoke to the *carromatta* driver.

"I am Señor Gar—come to my office later and I shall help you."

The driver said: "I am a very poor man—"

The Island detective nodded. "It is true," he agreed. "But you are also alive."

He moved along the street, towards the corner near the Escolta, occupied by Delgado's jewelry shop. A crowd was gathering; there were many police. A deadline had already been established, but Jo Gar was well-known; he went through the entrance, into the warm air stirred by the shop's ceiling fans.

Arnold Carlysle, the American chief of Manila police, had arrived and was listening to words from the short, black-mustached owner of the place. Liam Delgado's white hair was ruffled; he moved his hands nervously. Carlysle, listening, saw Jo Gar enter the shop. He beckoned to him.

Delgado was saying in his perfect English: "It was terrible! Ramon—my only son—dying as I came out from the vault—"

He turned away abruptly, covered his face with his long-fingered, brown hands. Carlysle spoke grimly to Jo:

"They used—American methods, Gar. Three cars—with license plates covered with dust. Four of the men came inside. Delgado's son resisted—they shot him down. Mattlien, the German guard at the International Bank—he was shot down, in the street. They escaped in all directions—but we'll get them, Gar!"

The Island detective nodded. He said in his toneless voice:

"One of the cars upset the *carromatta* in which I was approaching the Escolta. It was going towards the Pasig, and Juan Arragon was in close pursuit."

Carlysle nodded grimly. "We heard the shots—at the station," he said. "It was a daring robbery."

Delgado had dropped into a wicker chair, near a counter. Jo Gar said quietly:

"Three machines—a double murder. And robbery—how much did they get?"

Delgado said in a dull tone, softly: "The Von Loffler diamonds. All ten of them. Two hundred thousand dollars, at least. And some small stones—"

Jo Gar widened his gray-blue eyes. Carlysle went to the entrance of the store and gave orders in a steady, hard voice. There was the clang of an ambulance gong, in the distance.

The Island detective said: "The Von Loffler diamonds. But I thought they were in the bank vault—"

Delgado's tortured eyes met Jo's. He said in a broken voice:

"Von Loffler brought them here this morning. I was to set them into a comb for his wife."

Jo Gar narrowed his eyes and nodded his head slowly. Delgado got to his feet, hands suddenly clenched at his sides. He said in a terrible voice:

"They will pay—for this! By —— they will pay! My only son—"

Jo Gar spoke softly: "It is—very bad. You saw faces?"

The jewelry shop owner said: "They were masked—their whole faces. There were just the eye slits. Four of them were in here. They held guns, and the one who shot my son down was tall and well built. He was standing over Ramon—when I ran in—"

He turned away from the Island detective. Carlysle was coming into the shop again. There was a great deal of excitement outside, but inside there was almost silence. One white-clad clerk was walking back and forth behind a long display counter, muttering softly to himself.

Carlysle came close to Jo and spoke in the same grim tone.

"I have sent word to all the Constabulary stations. We shall pick up the cars in which they escaped."

Jo said: "Have there been reports of stolen cars lately?"

The Manila Police head frowned. "Two reports—one yesterday—one this morning."

The Island detective shrugged his narrow shoulders.

"I do not think it will help greatly to find the machines," he observed.

Carlysle said: "Juan Arragon was in close pursuit. There is a possible chance."

The Island detective nodded slowly. "Yes," he agreed. "A chance."

Liam Delgado faced them suddenly. His eyes were shot with red. He ran trembling fingers through his white hair. He said fiercely:

"There were four of them. I will have them—every one! I am wealthy—and I will use my wealth—"

There was the staccato cough of a motorcycle—a brown-uniformed figure rode to the curb before the shop. He dismounted, hurried inside. He was breathing heavily. He spoke rapidly in Filipino dialect to Carlysle. The head of the Manila police interrupted him sharply, telling him to speak more slowly. Jo Gar said quietly:

"He says Arragon's car skidded, beyond the bridge. There was a crash into iron railing—the driver was hurt and the car disabled. Pedestrians have told him that Juan stopped another car, and continued the pursuit. The bandit machine was far ahead, running along the right bank of the Pasig."

Carlysle groaned. "It will get away," he muttered. "The bandits were masked—the drivers of the three machines may not have been noticed—"

Jo Gar looked towards the back of Liam Delgado. The jewelry shop owner was standing near a counter, his body rigid. Jo said slowly:

"One leaves the Island only by boat."

Carlysle half closed his eyes. "There are many American visitors here—and English, too. Three boats sail in the next three days. Two of them are big vessels. It will be very difficult—"

He broke off. There was a little silence. Then the police head said slowly:

"But they have the diamonds—the Von Loffler stones. We can search thoroughly, at the docks."

Jo Gar touched the tips of his stubby, brown fingers to almost colorless lips. His almond-shaped eyes were slitted, three-quarters closed.

"We can do many wise things," he observed with a grimness strange in him. "But unfortunately, *others* can do wise things, also."

At seven o'clock Jo Gar paused before the Manila *Times* office and read the large-lettered bulletin before which a small crowd had gathered. It told him that none of the bandits had been captured, that they had got away with diamonds valued in excess of two hundred thousand dollars—the "famous Von Loffler ten," and that they had murdered Ramon Delgado and Herr Mattlien. It further stated that one escaping machine had crashed into a *carromatta* from which Señor Jo Gar and the driver had barely escaped with their lives. Also Lieutenant of Manila Police Juan Arragon, in pursuit of this crash car, was missing. He had hailed another car, with a Chinese driver, after the one in which he had been riding had skidded and crashed.

The machine, the Chinese and Juan Arragon—all had vanished along the right bank of the Pasig. The whole police force, aided by Island Constabulary, were hunting down the bandits. The *Times* offered a reward of five thousand dollars, and it was rumored that Liam Delgado would announce an offer of a large sum—for the bandits' capture. Two of the machines used in the robbery had been found, abandoned. They had each been stolen. They were being examined for fingerprints. It was the most daring crime in the history of Manila.

The Island detective smiled grimly, and then he thought of Juan Arragon and the smile went from his face. He was fond of Arragon—the lieutenant of police had often blundered in the past, but he had always tried. And the item that mentioned his disappearance was not pleasant to read.

Jo turned his back to the bulletin and waited for a *caleso* to pass—one with a strong-looking horse. He waited only a few minutes.

Across the bridge, on the far side of the black-watered Pasig, there were several police cars. Along the road over which Juan Arragon was supposed to have pursued the car that had struck the *carromatta* in which Jo had been riding there were Constabulary officers. On the left were moored *sampans* and various other type craft—on the right of the road there were hundreds of native huts, thatch-roofed and similar.

From the main road other roads angled off—many of them. Relaxed in the *caleso*, Jo Gar frowned at the roads. Three miles along the river road and the country suddenly became deserted. There were fewer crossroads—native shacks were scattered. The ground was rolling; there were curves. A half dozen times Jo stopped the *caleso* and made inquiry of natives, but always the answer was the same—nothing had been seen of the pursued car, or of the one in pursuit.

It was growing dark when Jo ordered the *caleso* driver to turn back. He breathed softly to himself:

"The bandits inside the shop were not recognized. No attention has been paid to the machine drivers; even I would not recognize the man who drove the car that crashed into us. Some say it was a Chinese who was driving the car that Juan commandeered, others say it was a Jap. No one seems to be sure of the type of car. It is always so."

He shook his head slowly. The *caleso* reached the Escolta, chief business street of Manila, and proceeded slowly towards the police station. Jo descended, paid the driver and climbed the stairs to the office of Carlysle. The American frowned into his eyes, shook his head slowly:

"Nothing—not a thing!" he breathed. "I don't like the way things look, Señor Gar. Arragon has dropped from sight. He was alone with that driver of the car he picked up. One of the police officers with him was stunned in the crash—and Juan ordered the other one to look after him. And he's dropped out of sight."

Jo said very slowly, wiping his brown forehead with a handkerchief, and narrowing his eyes on a slowly revolving ceiling fan:

"The killers are very desperate. That is natural. They have valuable diamonds, and they have murdered two persons. They would not hesitate—"

He broke off, shrugged. Carlysle swore beneath his breath and watched the Island detective. He said, after a little silence:

"Juan Arragon thought very well of you, Señor Gar. You showed him up many times, but he always was good-natured about it. If you—"

He broke off. Jo Gar smiled a little and said in his toneless voice:

"Herr Mattlien is dead. Ramon Delgado is dead. Ten extremely valuable diamonds are missing. The method of the robbery was very modern. I am interested, of course."

Carlysle said: "Good. Of course you are. The method was American, I'd say."

The Island detective shrugged. "Perhaps," he agreed. "But it does not mean that Americans were the bandits."

Carlysle said bitterly: "I hope not—for *their* sakes."

Jo Gar lighted one of his brown-paper cigarettes and said very slowly:

"I shall try to find Juan Arragon—but it is important that the vessels are watched. Very important."

Carlysle said: "I've got everything working— we're trying to find someone who can identify a driver of one of the three cars. The descriptions are all vague—guesswork."

Jo Gar turned his small body slightly. He said in a tone touched with grimness:

"I will return for a few minutes to my office, then I shall move about."

Carlysle's eyes were narrowed. He said with a touch of eagerness:

"You will let me know—as soon as you learn something?"

Jo moved towards the door of the office. He nodded his head a little.

"*If* I learn something—I will let you know," he said quietly, and went down the stairs to the street.

His small office was not far off the Escolta; the street was narrow and curving. There were few people on it; the shops were small and most of them had closed for the night. It was almost dark when he turned in at the entrance and climbed the narrow, creaking stairs. He climbed slowly, conserving his energy.

At the landing before his office he paused a few seconds, stood in the faint light from a small, hanging bulb. Then he went towards the door and reached for the knob. His office was seldom locked; he kept little of importance there.

When he opened the door there was a faint breeze from the window. He reached for the switch—and white light filled the room. For a second he stood motionless, his shoulders and head slightly forward. His eyes looked towards the wicker chair near the small table.

He recognized the uniform first. It was khaki in color. Next he recognized the figure. Juan Arragon's body was half turned away from him—head and shoulders rested on the table. The helmet was not in sight—Arragon was bareheaded. His dark hair glistened in the white light. There was a definite inertness about the position of the body.

Jo Gar said very steadily: "Juan—Juan Arragon!"

From the Pasig there was the shrill note of a river launch whistle. A driver called in a high-pitched voice in the street below.

Jo Gar sighed. Then he stepped into his office, closed the door. He went slowly to the side of Juan Arragon. He looked first at the head, with the half-opened eyes. Then he found the two bullet holes, not far from the heart. There was little blood.

There were books on the floor; they had fallen as though swept from the table with force. An ink bottle had crashed and broken. Near the right, outstretched fingers of the dead police lieutenant was a bit of white paper. A stubby pencil lay beyond it. There were scrawled words on the paper. Jo Gar leaned forward and read them. After a few seconds he reread them, aloud.

" 'Calle Padrone—house in palmetto thick—high porch—shutters—go at once—I am shot—French—' "

That was all. Jo Gar straightened and turned his back on his friend. He went to the window and looked down towards the street, unseeingly. He felt very badly. Juan Arragon was dead, shot to death. They had worked together on many crimes. Now that was finished. Often Juan had been wrong, but he had always been fair.

Jo Gar slowly lighted a cigarette. He drew a deep breath and moved his lips a little. He said:

"I will find them, of course. They have murdered him. And Ramon Delgado. And Mattlien. Because of diamonds—ten of them."

He stood motionless for several seconds. Then he shrugged, turned and went from the office. He did not look again at Juan Arragon. He walked, not too rapidly, the short distance to the police station.

arlysle said, looking with wide eyes at the body of Juan Arragon:

"God—they got him! But he scrawled the address of the hide-out. We'll get out there—"

Jo Gar shook his head slowly: "If you send men there—be very careful," he said tonelessly. "The address was meant for *me*."

Carlysle blinked. "Yes," he agreed, "but that doesn't make any difference—"

Jo Gar said softly: "You see the pencil—it is near the right-hand fingers. The writing—it is in English."

Carlysle frowned. "It's Arragon's writing," he breathed. "He could write English."

The Island detective nodded. "He wrote with his *left* hand," he said quietly. "If he were dying and wished to give me directions, I do not think he would write in English. And how did he get here?"

Carlysle stared at the dead police lieutenant. He muttered something the Island detective did not hear. Jo Gar said slowly:

"He was shot—and brought here. His handwriting was imitated. It is clever work. But they did not remember that Juan was left-handed. And I understand Filipino—he would have scrawled words to me in that language."

Carlysle said: "They wanted you—to go to Calle Padrone—to the house in the thicket—"

Jo Gar said very quietly: "I should be very careful how your men approach the house."

The American police head frowned. "They're afraid of you, Jo," he said grimly. "They planned this crime carefully. They know Juan has worked with you. They thought they'd get you—out of the way—"

He broke off. The muscles of the Island detective's mouth twitched. He said:

"It is possible."

Carlysle looked down at the scrawl. "They figured the shaky writing would get by—with you thinking Arragon was in bad shape when he wrote it. They didn't know—he was left-handed. And I'd forgotten—"

He checked himself. Jo Gar spoke very quietly:

"The killers know of Señor Gar," he said. "That is unfortunate."

Carlysle, his eyes still narrowed on the scrawl, spoke grimly.

"There is this word 'French,'" he said. "They wanted you to believe their nationality was French. That eliminates something—they're not French."

Jo Gar said nothing. He went to the window of his office and stood with his back to Carlysle and several of his men. The American police head gave orders. Then he spoke to the Island detective.

"The coroner will be here soon. I'm going to the Calle Padrone, with my men—"

Jo nodded. "I shall see you in a few hours," he said quietly, and added in a toneless voice: "I hope."

Carlysle frowned. "Delgado is offering a ten-thousand-dollar reward," he said. "I'm going to have the boat passengers carefully checked, the luggage searched."

He moved towards the door of the office. Jo Gar followed him. Carlysle said: "You going my way?"

The Island detective shook his head. His eyes were almost closed.

"I think it will be better for both of us," he said softly, "if I go alone."

Von Loffler sat across the table from Delgado and Jo Gar. He was a German who had lived many years in the Islands. His body was lean and he was not young. He looked at Delgado's white hair and said thickly:

"It is very bad. The diamonds are insured, of course. But in England. I sympathize with Señor Delgado, and I agree with him. You have done much good work in the Islands, Señor Gar. These bandits and killers must be caught."

Jo Gar said nothing. Delgado spoke in a firm, low voice.

"Señor Gar is more familiar with conditions here than other detectives might be. Lieutenant Arragon was his friend. I think we have much—the three of us—to work for, together. But Señor Gar—it is his business."

Von Loffler nodded. His face was grim. His blue eyes narrowed on Delgado's.

"Your son, Liam," he said. "Señor Gar's friend. And my diamonds." His eyes flickered to Jo's. "You will work for us, Señor?" he asked.

Jo Gar smiled with his thin, colorless lips pressed together. He parted them and said:

"Yes—but I feel it will be difficult. This was not an ordinary crime. It may mean that I must leave the Islands."

Delgado said firmly: "I want my son's killers—no matter where you must go."

Von Loffler nodded his head slowly. "It is right," he said. "You have the description of the stones—it is the best I can do."

The Island detective nodded. He said very quietly:

"Just the three of us must know what I am doing. Even the American, Carlysle—he must not know. I shall need funds. It may prove expensive."

Delgado shrugged. "That is simple," he said.

Jo Gar got to his feet. "When Carlysle took his men to the Calle Padrone address he found only a deserted shack. There was not a clue—nothing. But had *I* gone—"

He spread his stubby-fingered hands. Von Loffler said:

"It will be dangerous, Señor. But that is your business."

The Island detective looked expressionlessly at the room's ceiling.

"It is so," he agreed. "It is my business."

Carlysle was smiling when Jo Gar moved along the cell block of the old police station and reached his side. He spoke with enthusiasm.

"I sent for you—we've got one of them. It's just a matter of a few hours now, and we'll have the others."

Jo Gar made a clicking sound. He looked at the American head of police with widened eyes.

"That is very good," he said slowly. "But how—"

Carlysle cut in on his calm voice. "I didn't want you to waste time running around the city."

Jo lowered his lids slightly. The change in the manner of Carlysle was very evident. He was almost patronizing now. He had one of the bandits—he would shortly have the others. He had done it without Jo Gar's aid.

The Island detective was silent. Carlysle said with a narrow-lipped smile:

"Lieutenant Mallagin picked up the Chinese driver of the car Arragon commandeered, about an hour ago. Just after eleven. He was staggering along the Pasig road—on the other bank. He'd been badly beaten and was soaked. They had tried to drown him, but he regained consciousness and let his body float with the current. Then he crawled ashore. He recognized one of the bandits—a Filipino. We've traced the crime to Cantine, the half-breed that we turned loose from Billibid three months ago. He ran the hold-up."

Jo Gar said, in a slightly puzzled tone: "But you said you had one of them—"

Carlysle was excited; he made gestures with his hands.

"We'll have the one he recognized," he stated. "I meant we had found the Chinese driver."

Jo Gar said slowly: "That is—good."

Carlysle said: "I've got all the men out for the pick-up, and I didn't want you going off at an angle."

The Island detective half closed his eyes and spoke softly:

"And what became of the machine of this Chinese?" he asked.

Carlysle said: "He doesn't know. A bullet hit Arragon as they were gaining on the other car. He collapsed. The Chinese used brakes—but the other car had stopped, and he was rushed. They knocked him unconscious—the road was deserted; it was around a curve."

Jo Gar said slowly: "And you think Cantine was the leader—the half-breed?"

Carlysle made a grunting sound. "Sure of it," he snapped. "The Filipino that this Chinese identified was one that served a term at Billibid—he was one of Cantine's men. We'll have them all pretty quick."

The Island detective spoke in his toneless voice:

"That will be—very good."

The American head of police chuckled. "We won't have to worry about the boats that are sailing tomorrow," he said. "Didn't care much for that job, anyway. Passengers are easily insulted. It would have been difficult."

Jo Gar lighted a brown-paper cigarette and blew a thin stream of smoke above his head.

"I did not think this Cantine—possessed so much courage," he said slowly.

Carlysle grunted. "He learned something—and took a chance," he said. "He wasn't so smooth. There was too much killing."

The Island detective said: "May I talk—with the Chinese?"

Carlysle frowned a little. But he nodded his head.

"I'll go along with you," he replied.

Jo Gar smiled with his eyes. "I shall be honored," he said simply.

The Island detective rose from the small wicker chair and smiled at Carlysle. He narrowed his eyes on the brown, fat face of the Chinese.

"He is of good breed," he said slowly. "He speaks without becoming muddled, and clearly. You have been lucky."

Carlysle smiled expansively. The head of the Manila police was in a genial humor.

"Not lucky, but rather careful, Gar," he said.

Jo shrugged. "He staggered right into your hands," he pointed out. "I meant that it was fortunate he was not killed—shot or drowned."

Carlysle said nothing. He turned towards the door leading from the room in which Jo Gar had been questioning the Chinese. It opened as he faced it; Lieutenant Mallagin entered. He was breathing heavily, obviously excited.

He spoke in broken English. "I have captured—one of Cantine's men. He is hurt—very much. He fell from a *sampan* deck—but will not talk. The doctor—he say he may die quick—"

Carlysle frowned. Jo Gar was watching Mallagin with expressionless eyes. He glanced at the Chinese—the man's mouth was half opened; he was staring at the chunky-bodied Filipino.

The chief of police frowned. Mallagin said in a husky tone:

"I think it would be wise—to take this Chinese—to him—while he lives. He then might talk—"

Carlysle nodded. "Yes," he said decisively. We'll get him right there. Where is—this man?"

Mallagin said: "In the shop of Santoni, who deals in fruit—not far from the Spanish bridge. He is very bad."

Carlysle nodded. He looked towards the Chinese. He said sharply:

"You are going with us—you will identify a man who is hurt."

The fear that was in the eyes of the Chinese seemed to grow. He mumbled something that Jo Gar failed to understand; his hands were moving about strangely. The Island detective said:

"You think it is wise—"

The expression in the American's eyes checked him. He smiled slightly and bowed. Carlysle said slowly:

"I'm taking charge of this case myself. In the past Juan Arragon did much good, and much harm, poor devil!"

The Island detective said nothing. Carlysle spoke to Lieutenant Mallagin.

"We will use my private car. There will be the driver and myself, and the Chinese. Yourself, of course—and pick two men in whom you have confidence."

Mallagin nodded and turned away. Jo Gar said in a quiet voice:

"I should like to accompany you. Juan Arragon was my friend—"

There was a touch of coldness in Carlysle's voice.

"I'm sorry—there will not be enough room. But I shall keep you informed—"

The Island detective narrowed his almond-shaped eyes. He said softly:

"I might replace one of the two men you told Lieutenant Mallagin to choose."

Carlysle said steadily: "It is a police matter—and you are not of the police. Go ahead, Lieutenant—get your men."

Jo Gar bowed slightly. He said in a faintly amused voice:

"I would choose one who can make notes of what your injured man may say."

Carlysle frowned. "Of course," he said in a hard tone. "That is understood."

Mallagin looked stupidly at Carlysle. Jo Gar watched the Chinese with eyes that were almost closed. Carlyle glanced at the Island detective as he moved towards the door of the room. He said:

"I'm sorry, Gar—but this is a police case."

Jo smiled a little. "I am sure it is being handled very well," he said in a peculiar tone, and went through the doorway.

The black closed car of Carlyle pulled away from the police station, cut across the Escolta and headed towards the Pasig.

After a time they were close to the river on a street running to the Spanish bridge.

A half block behind, Jo Gar sat in a machine he had hired from Cormanda. His small body was not relaxed; in his right hand he gripped a Colt. Abruptly Cormanda jerked his head and said in a rising voice:

"Jo—they're slowing down—"

The Island detective leaned forward, caught a glimpse of two red lights, across the road. He said in a swift voice:

"They were not repairing—at dusk—"

The Carlysle machine had almost reached the two lights. It halted. Jo Gar said:

"Stop, Cormanda—"

The small, open car stopped. The chauffeur of the car ahead got to the street and looked back at the car in which Cormanda and Jo Gar sat. He gestured towards the two red lights. Jo Gar spoke softly to his own driver:

"Get down—Cormanda—it is not good—"

The first machine-gun started a staccato clatter from an alley on the right. Almost instantly there was the drum of a second one—from a shuttered window on the left. Metal started to make sound. The chauffeur ran a few feet and sprawled to the street. At that moment, the Chinese sprang from the car, doubled over and ran to a door nearest the car. He disappeared. The other occupants of the car were crouched, out of sight, below the metal sides.

Jo Gar slipped out the right side of the small car and bent his body forward. He ran back over the street, keeping his short arms close to his sides and his head low. Suddenly he turned and moved down a second alley. One machine-gun had stopped drumming, but the other was still beating sound against the quiet of the night.

In the darkness of the alley Jo Gar paused for a second. He breathed heavily as he got his head slightly exposed and looked towards the Carlysle machine:

"The Chinese—was lying—"

A door shot open—the figure of the Chinese was pitched into the alley. Almost instantly it jerked, half spun. Then the man dropped to the pavement. The second machine-gun started to clatter again.

Jo Gar muttered: "And yet—they murdered him!"

Cormanda was reversing the small car now. It whined back from the red lights and the drum of bullets. Jo Gar swung back into the alley, moved rapidly along it. At the far end he saw the Pasig water and the silhouette of a *sampan*.

The machine-gun fire died. No sound but the whine of the reversing car came from the street behind the Island detective. He thought: They got the diamonds, but they were forced to kill. Ramon Delgado, Mattlien—Juan Aragon. And now the Chinese, perhaps others. Why do they trap and kill? Is it because they must leave the Islands? He thought: It is because they are clever and must clear the way.

He reached the row of *sampans*, moored abreast. There was a narrow path between piled, rotted planks and empty fish baskets. It led towards the next alley. Jo Gar gripped his Colt firmly and moved along it. At intervals he stopped and listened. The street he had left was

very quiet. Only the river sounds reached his ears.

He had almost reached the next alley when he saw faint shadow. It was directly ahead—moving slowly.

A machine made sound in the distance; the engine getting into a roar—and dying gradually. A voice reached the ears of the Island detective; it sounded much like Carlysle's, raised hoarsely.

And then the shadow ahead of him became a figure. Jo Gar lifted his automatic and said very quietly:

"Raise your arms!"

The figure swung towards him—he caught a glimpse, in the wavering, reflected light from a *sampan*, of a brown, lean face and wide, staring eyes. The man drew his breath in sharply—his hands swung upward. But the left one went up first, and the right brushed the belt of his soiled duck trousers as it moved.

Jo Gar said sharply: "No!"

The reflected light caught the gleam of the blade. Jo Gar steadied the muzzle of his automatic and squeezed the trigger. He rocked back on his heels, curved his body to one side. The other man's right wrist made swift movement, even as his body jerked convulsively. The knife dug its blade point into the wood of a basket within six inches of Jo's left arm.

The man sank to his knees and pressed both hands against his belt, at the stomach. He groaned. Jo Gar stepped out from the piled baskets and jerked a small flashlight from his pocket. For a second he stood close to the man who had fallen, and listened for sound from the alley ahead. There was none. But in the distance voices were calling.

He flashed the beam on the one hunched near his feet, widened his almond-shaped eyes. Then he moved the beam to the knife that had been thrown. He breathed very slowly:

"Malay—"

He kneeled beside the groaning man, held the gun close to him. He said quietly, in the Malay tongue:

"Why was the Chinese murdered?"

The man widened his eyes and shook his head. Jo Gar smiled coldly and pressed the muzzle against the man's right side.

"If I shoot again—you will die," he said. "You were with others—what were their names?"

The Malay shook his head. He was muttering to himself. Jo Gar said:

"The Chinese told the police that a man named Cantine committed the great robbery and murder. He was lying—and yet he was murdered. Why?"

The Malay was getting his breath with difficulty now. There were footfalls in the alley from which he had come. Jo Gar lifted his head, and heard the voice of Lieutenant Mallagin, cautioning one of his men. The Island detective spoke softly:

"Quickly—the police come. I am not of them. Why was the Chinese killed?"

The eyes of the man hunched beside him were staring. He said weakly, in his own tongue:

"His family—was given money. He was to lie—and then to die. He was—very poor."

Jo Gar straightened a little and sighed. Then he lowered his head again.

"Who made—the arrangement?" he asked quietly.

The Malay shook his head. His body relaxed a little; he rolled over on his back. He said very weakly:

"It was—the one who walks badly—always in white—"

His lips closed; he shivered—cried out a little. There was a convulsive movement of his body, then it was still. From the alley Mallagin called:

"Who—is that?"

Jo Gar narrowed his eyes and rose. He was thinking: The one who walks badly—always in white. But he said in a steady voice:

"It is Señor Gar—I have shot one of them."

He heard the surprised exclamation from Lieutenant Mallagin. The Filipino came in close, stared down at the dead man. Carlysle, breathing heavily, was behind the lieutenant.

"The Chinese is dead—the chauffeur is dead," he said. "One of my men is wounded. Mallagin and I escaped. You followed us?"

Jo Gar nodded. He said quietly: "This one tried to knife me—I was forced to shoot. He did not die instantly."

Carlysle's eyes widened. He said eagerly: "He talked?"

Jo nodded. His voice was almost toneless. "Cantine did not commit the robbery or murders," he said. "The Chinese was paid to lie to you—and then to die."

Carlysle stared at Jo. "The driver—paid to lie and then—"

Jo Gar shook his head. "He was not the driver," he said slowly. "I spoke to him about machines—he knew very little. I was suspicious, and followed when you got word that one of Cantine's men had been hurt."

Carlysle breathed heavily. "You think it was a plan—to throw us off—" Jo Gar smiled a little. He glanced down at the dead man.

"If this man had not talked—you would have been after Cantine and his men"—he said quietly, a wrong scent.

Carlysle nodded his head very slowly. "He said nothing about who—"

Jo Gar shook his head slowly. "I have told you what he said," he replied, and closed his eyes.

When he opened them, Carlysle was looking down at the dead man and frowning.

"We shall have to watch the boats," he said grimly. "They have the diamonds—and they have killed many men." He looked narrowly at the Island detective. "They got away with their machine-guns—all but this man," he said. "You will help us, Señor Gar?"

Jo Gar smiled with his thin lips. His colorless eyes seemed to be looking beyond the American head of police. He shook his head very slowly.

"No," he said. "It is—a police matter."

Carlysle stiffened. "Juan Arragon was your friend," he reminded.

Jo Gar stopped smiling. "It is so," he agreed. "But I will not help you, Señor Carlysle."

The American turned away, muttering something that the Island detective did not hear. Lieutenant Mallagin moved after his chief. Jo Gar looked down at the figure of the Malay and breathed very softly:

" 'The one who walks badly—always in white.' "

He sighed, and his eyes half closed. He glanced towards the knife handle, protruding from the basket wood. River odors were in his nostrils—a pony whinnied in the distance. Jo Gar said very slowly, in a half whisper:

"For Juan Arragon—I will help—myself."

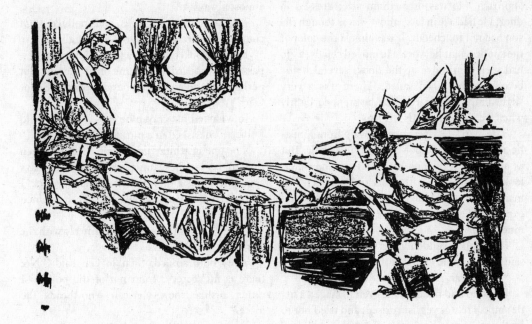

The Man in White

Ramon Decolta

An adventure of Jo Gar, the little Island detective, in search of murderers and their loot.

HE *CHEYO MARU* took red color from the setting sun; her boat deck was soaked in it. The sea was calm; even the white wings of the gulls that rose and dipped astern were tinted red. Manila and the Island of Cavite were no longer to be seen astern. There were few people in the deck chairs; the first dinner gong had already sounded.

Jo Gar relaxed his short body, kept his almond-shaped eyes almost closed. Now and then he lifted his brown-paper cigarette, inhaled. It was almost as though he slept between puffs, but that was not so.

When the Japanese steward came rapidly towards his chair, the Island detective lifted his head slightly. The steward had been well tipped, and had been asked only a simple task. He reached Jo Gar's chair now, bowed jerkily.

"He has left his cabin," he said. "The man in white—the one who limps. He is coming."

He spoke in his native tongue, which was the tongue in which Jo had spoken to him. When the Island detective jerked his head in a gesture of dismissal, the steward moved towards the stern of the liner and vanished from sight. Jo turned his head a little and watched the man in white approach. He was of medium size; dressed in duck. He had a lean face, and it was as though the sun had not touched it. It was almost the color of the spotless suit he wore. He moved slowly, as Jo had seen him move at the dock, several hours before the boat had sailed. There was a very slight limp; it appeared that he stepped lightly when weight was on his left leg.

The man's face was turned away from him as he approached the spot opposite Jo's chair. But as he neared it he took his eyes from the water, looked at Jo in a swift, searching glance. The man in white had blue eyes; they were small and expressionless. His lips were thin, and without much color.

He stopped suddenly, his eyes still on Jo. He said, a slow smile on his face:

"Señor Gar, isn't it?"

Jo sat up and nodded. He even managed a little smile. He was very surprised, and tried not to let the other man know this.

The one in white nodded his head and seemed very pleased. His voice was soft, almost careless.

"Leaving the Islands?" he asked.

Jo Gar smiled pleasantly. "I have relatives in Honolulu," he said. "Leaving the Islands—for more islands."

The one in white chuckled a little. He said in an easy tone:

"I am Ferraro. For a time I was connected with the Constabulary. I have heard of you."

Jo Gar bowed. Ferraro's English was good though not perfect. There was a clipping of words, a cutting short, despite his leisurely manner of talking.

Ferraro said: "You leave at a bad time. A terrible crime—Delgado's son, that watchman at the bank. And Juan Arragon. All dead."

He shook his head. Jo Gar said: "You were acquainted with Señor Arragon?"

Ferraro frowned. "No," he said. "But I had heard of him."

Jo Gar relaxed again, inhaled. The one in white looked at the sea, shrugging.

"The murderers will be caught, of course. And the Von Loffler diamonds found. It is almost always so."

Jo Gar closed his eyes and nodded. "Of course," he agreed. "It is so—almost always."

Ferraro looked at him again. "There are few passengers aboard, who came on at Manila. But perhaps you do not care to be addressed as Señor Gar?"

Jo widened his gray-blue eyes. "Why should I object?" he asked in a puzzled voice.

The one in white said: "Well, there has been this robbery—these murders. Only two days ago. There was a thorough search at the dock. I was asked many questions, myself. It seemed amusing."

Jo Gar said: "And you were formerly with the Constabulary?"

They both smiled; then Jo Gar said: "No, there is no secrecy. I am not of the police—I rather dislike the American who heads the force."

Ferraro said: "But Juan Arragon—he was one of your countrymen—a good friend—"

He paused, shrugged narrow shoulders. "At least, so I have heard," he said. "Having been in the Constabulary—"

Jo Gar nodded. "It is not so," he said quietly. "Juan Arragon was of the Manila police. He was always fighting me."

Ferraro said: "Oh, so that was it, Señor?"

The Island detective nodded very slowly. The man in white looked towards the water; then his eyes came back to Jo's again.

"I am dining alone," he said. "Will you join me?"

Jo thanked him and declined. "I do not think I shall dine tonight," he said. "My stomach pains me."

Ferraro expressed regret. He spoke a few words more and moved aft. His limp was barely noticeable, but it existed. Jo Gar reclined in his chair and remembered several things. Diamonds worth two hundred thousand dollars had been stolen from Delgado's jewelry store, on the Escolta, in Manila. Delgado's son had been murdered. A watchman had been murdered. And

Juan Arragon had been murdered, after he had vanished in pursuit of one of the fleeing machines. His body had been returned to Jo Gar's small office, with a forged note attached. And later in the night, while trailing a clue, the Island detective had been forced to shoot a Malay who had come at him with a knife. The Malay had talked. He had spoken of the leader of the diamond thieves as "the one who walks badly—always in white."

For Liam Delgado, whose son was dead— and Von Loffler, who wished to recover the ten diamonds, Jo Gar had left the Islands. He had left aboard the *Cheyo Maru* because another was leaving on the same boat—a man dressed in white, who limped when he moved.

Jo Gar shrugged his narrow shoulders. The sunset red was almost gone now. The Island detective thought:

When a man *is* a thief and a murderer he does not seek out one who hunts down thieves and murderers. And yet this Ferraro has approached me, has invited me to dine.

A little grimness came into the gray-blue eyes of the Island detective.

"Sometimes such a man is very confident," he half whispered. "And sometimes he has been of the police." He nodded his head a little and ceased to smile. "And sometimes," he murmured very softly, "a dying man lies." The Island detective sighed. "It is very difficult," he said softly. "Even my own thoughts contradict."

When Jo Gar turned his key in the lock of his cabin, stepped inside, he closed the door slowly behind him. He hummed a little Spanish tune, and his body was rigid. There were his two bags—and they were opened, the contents spilled about. The lock of his small trunk had been smashed; the tray lay crosswise. His clothes were scattered. The berth sheets had been ripped up—the cabin was almost a wreck.

Jo stood with his back to the door, stopped humming. He lighted one of his cigarettes, moved about the cabin carefully, using his eyes. He touched nothing. After a few minutes he pressed a button and waited for the Japanese steward. When the man came he was breathing heavily, and his black, round eyes were wide. They grew wider as he surveyed the cabin. The Island detective made a little gesture with his brown hands.

"You see," he said. "There has been a search."

The steward broke into his native tongue. He was very excited. He had just entered the cabin of Señor Ferraro, who was of the Philippine Constabulary. And it, too, had been entered. Luggage had been ransacked. An officer of the boat had been notified.

Jo Gar made a clicking sound and nodded his head slowly.

"A clumsy person—this thief," he said. "I have nothing of value here. I am a poor man. Yet see how he has thrown things about."

The steward shrilled words—apologetic words. He had been away from the section only a short time. He had come on deck to do as Señor Gar had asked—to tell him that Señor Ferraro had left his cabin. He had come quickly and had taken a shortcut to the spot in which Señor Gar's chair had been placed.

Jo Gar quieted the man. He narrowed his gray-blue eyes on the ransacked trunk, then turned abruptly. He said as he moved through the doorway to the narrow corridor:

"You do not think the cabin was entered— before you went above to tell me that Señor Ferraro had left his cabin?"

The steward was sure neither cabin had been entered before that time. Señor Ferraro's cabin was only fifty feet distant from Señor Gar's. And it was in the same condition.

Jo Gar said: "Perhaps there are others in similar state."

He went along the narrow corridor to a wider one. The steward followed. Two ship's officers, clad in white uniforms and gold braid, approached. The Chief Steward came from another direction. There was much swift talk— the Japanese who had charge of Jo's cabin led the way to the one occupied by Señor Ferraro.

It was an outside cabin, much similar to Jo's.

It was in the same sort of disorder. Jo looked in—the others went inside. The Third Officer said in English:

"And your cabin was entered, too, Señor?"

Jo nodded. "I was on deck," he said. "Señor Ferraro talked with me, about twenty minutes ago. Then he went to dine."

The Third Officer said: "You are friends?"

Jo shook his head. "Acquaintances," he corrected.

There was more talk. The Third Officer suggested that Señor Ferraro be notified, and while he was offering the suggestion the one with the limp came along the corridor. His blue eyes widened on the group. The Chief Steward said apologetically:

"Your cabin has been entered, Señor."

Ferraro looked at Jo Gar, went to the doorway of his cabin. His eyes moved over the opened bags, broken trunk locks. He drew in a deep breath and said slowly:

"But why? I am a poor man—"

Jo Gar chuckled a little. He said: "Those were my words, Señor. I, too, have been treated like this."

The one in white stared at Jo. Then he smiled a little with his thin lips. His face was bloodless; he had thin, yellowish hair.

His lips parted; he was about to speak, but he changed his mind. He went into the cabin and poked around among the clothes of a large bag. The officers were speaking with Jo when Ferraro uttered an exclamation.

"Ah—a woman!" he said.

Turning, he held out a white hand. In his palm lay the pin. It was perhaps two inches long. It had a setting so cheap that it could be immediately seen. There were a half dozen stones in the pin—but one was missing. They were glass—the glitter was false; they had not the appearance of even a clever imitation of diamonds.

The Third Officer took the pin and inspected it carefully. Jo Gar noted the cheapness of the metal—the flat backing. The pin clasp was bent—the whole thing a cheap job.

Ferraro stood close to the Third Officer. He said slowly, in his clipped-word manner:

"The sort of thing you buy on the Escolta for a few pesos. Cheap stuff—it fell while she was ransacking the place."

The Third Officer nodded. "You have not suffered a loss?" he asked.

Señor Ferraro shrugged. "I have nothing of importance—to lose," he stated.

He took the bar pin from the officer's fingers. He juggled it carelessly about in the palm of his right hand, without looking at it.

The Chief Steward addressed Jo Gar.

"And you, Señor Gar? You have not lost anything of importance?"

Jo Gar smiled at Ferraro. "I am much in the position of Señor Ferraro," he said quietly.

The Third Officer spoke in a peculiar tone.

"Neither of you gentlemen possess anything of great value—and yet each of you has been robbed."

Ferraro smiled a little, his blue eyes on the half-closed ones of the Island detective.

"It is very strange," he said softly.

Jo Gar spoke tonelessly. "It *seems* very strange," he agreed. "I shall return to my cabin and try to get things in order."

The Chief Steward said grimly: "We will make an investigation, of course. Perhaps the pin—"

Ferraro handed it to the Chief Steward. He looked at Jo.

"Señor Gar is quite skilled in these matters," he said slowly. "He is an interested person, in this case."

The Island detective smiled. "And *you* were formerly with the Island Constabulary," he reminded. "You see with what little esteem the intruder has regarded us."

The Third Officer said: "Perhaps it has been just a blundering affair—an attempt at quick robbery."

Jo Gar nodded his head, and kept his brown face serious.

"That is very possible," he agreed, and moved along the corridor towards his own cabin.

He was interrupted several times while he was adjusting things. It was not easy to think clearly, with so many people about. At ten o'clock the

Third Officer came into the cabin, shutting the door behind him. He said very quietly:

"In matters such as this we always are suspicious of the cabin steward. We have questioned him at length. He states that you have tipped him generously, and that you had him come to you, on deck this evening, and warn you that Señor Ferraro had left his cabin and was going above for a bit of air before dining."

The Third Officer paused. Jo Gar nodded, his brown face expressionless.

"It is so," he said. "You wish to know the reason?"

The officer spread his hands in a little gesture, half of apology, half of assent. Jo said:

"I am weary of discussing Island matters. I wished to be alone. With the cabin steward advising me in time, I hoped to avoid Señor Ferraro for a few days. Unfortunately, I was unable to rise from the deck chair in time. So we met."

The Third Officer frowned. Then he nodded his head, very slowly. He said:

"Thank you, Señor Gar."

Jo smiled pleasantly. He said in a careless voice:

"You are keeping that imitation thing—that bar pin?"

The officer shook his head. "There was no loss to Señor Ferraro," he said. "We shall make adjustment for any baggage damage. He asked me to leave the pin with him. He intends, I believe, to do some quiet investigating. He was with the Constabulary."

Jo Gar nodded pleasantly. "That is quite the wisest thing to do, I think," he said.

The Third Officer expressed regrets. The captain was disturbed. Such things seldom happened aboard the *Cheyo Maru*.

Jo Gar sighed. The Third Officer went from the cabin, turning at the door and smiling pleasantly. When he had gone Jo removed his palm beach suiting and got into clothes that were of dark silk. He waited a short time, went to the deck quickly, carrying a light blanket that bulked over his arm. His face held a tight smile as he approached the spot where his deck chair had been.

The night was warm and there was no moon. Most of the deck chairs had been collected and were being stacked together. Jo moved towards the deck steward, a tall Jap with eyes that were very black. He said:

"Please return my chair. I wish to rest a while on deck—I am sleepy and my cabin is stuffy."

The deck steward bowed. Jo showed him the spot, one that was fairly secluded, aft of the second stack. When the chair had been set up he relaxed in it. The deck steward smiled and moved away.

After a short time Jo turned his head to one side and appeared to doze. The deck steward passed him, treading very softly. He halted, and through slitted eyes the Island detective saw that he was staring at him. Then the steward moved hurriedly forward.

Jo Gar lay motionless in the chair. There was the steady vibration of the engines, and the faint sound of steam reaching the air. From some spot below music reached the boat deck. Jo said very quietly:

"How calm the sea is!"

His lips held an ironical smile. He breathed evenly, closed his almond-shaped eyes.

Five minutes later there were three shots. The first one was a muffled, Maxim-silenced pop-cough. The second was smothered but had more sound. The third was a sharp *crack* sound.

Jo Gar, his small body tense, stepped out from behind the ventilator—caught sight of a black figure moving aft. He bent his body low, ran along the deck, his automatic gripped tightly in his right-hand fingers. From some spot forward a voice called with the shrill of the Jap tongue a word that sounded like:

"Hai!"

The dark figure ahead had reached the steps of the port companionway. It seemed almost to dive down them. Jo Gar slowed his pace, approached the steps carefully. When he reached the bottom of them he heard shouts. Men were coming up from the deck below.

He tried to get past them, but a short, chunky

man caught him by the right arm and tried to get his gun away. Jo said sharply:

"Stop—a man came down here! I am after—him."

He was breathing heavily. The chunky one wore a white uniform. He said in bad English:

"I—ship police. I see no one—"

Other men were coming up. Several of them were in dinner clothes. Jo Gar watched the Third Officer come into the group. He shook off the grip of the ship policeman, said grimly:

"I was on deck. Three shots were fired. A figure in black ran towards this companionway. I followed."

A man in dinner clothes said: "I heard only two shots—from above."

The Third Officer was beside Jo. He spoke in a soft tone.

"You are dressed in black, also, Señor Gar."

Jo Gar nodded. "It is less conspicuous," he replied. "I was on deck—and wished to be inconspicuous."

The Third Officer said: "Why?"

Jo Gar raised his voice, but did not answer the question.

"And none of this group saw the man I was pursuing?" he asked.

None in the group had seen any person in black—but Jo. The Third Officer said:

"The shots were fired—at you?"

Jo Gar shook his head. "At my deck chair," he said quietly. "I was some distance away."

He read suspicion in the Third Officer's eyes. The one in dinner clothes, who had spoken before, said grimly:

"You say there were three shots—I heard only two."

Jo Gar shrugged. "The first was Maxim-silenced," he replied. "If you will come to the boat deck—"

He broke off, turning. He went up the steps of the companionway, closely followed by the Third Officer. The others trailed along behind. When they reached the boat deck there were several other people. Two stood near the spot in which the steward had placed Jo's chair.

The Third Officer used his flashlight; he muttered an exclamation as the beam fell across the chair. Jo Gar stood to one side, smiling a little. His eyes were on the brown mask that had rolled from the chair. He said:

"That is a mask that Sebastino, the Spaniard in Manila, made for me. It is a good likeness."

He moved forward, lifted it. The others crowded around him. The plaster had been broken in two places. There was a hole in the left cheek—another in the forehead. The Island detective said very softly:

"You see—the one in black was an excellent shot. The third bullet—"

He leaned over the chair and moved the cloth of the palm beach coat he had wrapped around the light blanket. There was a hole in the left lapel. He said in a toneless voice:

"There is where it struck. It was like this—"

He adjusted the trousers and coat, rested the face mask above the coat, laying it with the right cheek against the canvas of the deck chair. He said quietly:

"Switch off the light—and move back here."

The Third Officer switched off the flashlight. The group moved away from the chair, towards the vessel's port rail. They stood looking towards the mask and the palm beach material. In the faint light it resembled Jo Gar—sleeping in the deck chair. The mask was very life-like.

The Third Officer sucked in his breath

sharply. The man in dinner clothes, who had spoken before, swore.

He said grimly: "It was—attempted murder, all right!"

Jo Gar nodded. "And the one who attempted it has got away," he said. "Below that companionway—are there several avenues of escape?"

The Third Officer nodded slowly. "A corridor to the concert room. Another companionway, to the deck below. A narrow passageway to the radio room—"

Jo Gar said slowly: "That is enough."

The Third Officer made a clicking sound. "We shall talk with the captain—you and I, Señor Gar," he said.

Jo nodded. There was the sound of footfalls—of a man running. A Jap came into the group, clad in the uniform of a subordinate officer. He addressed the Third Officer.

"Deck Steward Kamogi, sir!" he breathed. "He lies up forward, near your cabin. He's—dead."

The Third Officer spoke in Japanese. "Dead?" he asked. "Shot?"

The subordinate shook his head. "It was—a knife, sir," he replied. "In the back!"

The Third Officer narrowed his eyes on the blue-gray ones of Jo Gar. He said very softly:

"The deck steward, Señor Gar."

The Island detective looked towards the face mask in the chair. He said in a voice that held a suggestion of grimness:

"He *would* have been the first person I would have questioned."

Captain Haroysan sat across the table from Jo Gar, his moon face crinkled, his black eyes narrowed on those of the Island detective.

"You knew your life was in danger—you changed your attire, arranged a trap—"

Jo Gar spread his brown, chubby hands.

"I *sensed* my life was in danger," he corrected. "It was the deck steward—"

The captain of the *Cheyo Maru* frowned. He spoke slowly, shaking his head.

"It is very bad. The vessel has never had anything like this—"

Jo Gar smiled a little. "I have been very frank with you, Captain," he said. "The one responsible for the theft of the Von Loffler diamonds is aboard your ship, I am sure of that. He knows that I am aboard. That does not please him. I think that he bribed the deck steward to tell him when I was sleeping. Then he wished to be safe. So the deck steward was knifed."

The captain frowned. "And *you* bribed the steward of your cabin, to be told when Señor Ferraro was approaching you, on deck."

Jo Gar nodded. "I wished to evade him," he said.

The captain shrugged. "I do not believe that," he replied.

The Island detective smiled. "Señor Ferraro's cabin was broken into—so was mine," he said. "That is puzzling."

Captain Haroysan said sharply: "You are changing the point of the discussion."

Jo Gar rose from his chair. "The Von Loffler diamonds are valued in excess of two hundred thousand dollars, Captain," he said. "Already, more than a half dozen men have been murdered, because of them. One of those men was Juan Arragon, my friend. Another was Señor Delgado's son. Both Von Loffler and Delgado have commissioned me to hunt down the thief and murderer. I had evidence that he was aboard your ship."

The Japanese stood up also. He said grimly:

"If it satisfies me—I will take charge of him."

Jo Gar sighed. "It is weak evidence," he said quietly. "A Malay involved in an attempt to kill the American head of the Manila police gave it to me. He was dying at the time. It is not strong enough to make an arrest."

The captain said: "And you want the diamonds, Señor Gar?"

Jo Gar nodded. "Of course," he agreed.

The captain shrugged. "A murderer is aboard the *Cheyo Maru*," he said. "In less than two weeks we shall be in Honolulu. But what is to happen—before we land—"

The Island detective said tonelessly:

"We will have the murderer of the deck steward. *Perhaps* we will have the Von Loffler diamonds."

Captain Haroysan made a guttural sound.

"I have radioed Manila—about you, Señor. And about Señor Ferraro."

Jo Gar said with a faint smile:

"And the information you received—it was good?"

Haroysan said with grim amusement: "It was even flattering. Señor Ferraro has seen honorable service with the Constabulary. You are much respected. And yet—"

The *Cheyo Maru* captain broke off abruptly. He shrugged. Jo Gar smiled sympathetically.

"And yet you are far from satisfied," he finished.

The captain said nothing. His eyes were narrow lines of blackness. Jo Gar bowed slightly.

"I can understand your feelings, Captain," he said softly. "I feel—much the same way."

n the fourth day out the sky clouded, and there was wind. It was wind that blew gently at first, but increased steadily in velocity. There were rumors of a typhoon; the *Cheyo Maru* rolled badly. Racks were on the tables, and things creaked and rattled in the cabins. At four in the afternoon, with the sea growing steadily rougher, Jo Gar moved cautiously towards the cabin of Señor Ferraro and rapped on the door.

Ferraro called out: "Who is it?" And Jo answered him. The door was opened almost immediately.

The Island detective smiled and said: "Does the roughness bother you, Señor?"

Ferraro's white face was a little twisted, but he managed a smile.

"I am not exactly a sailor," he said.

Jo stepped inside the cabin. Ferraro closed the door behind him. Jo said:

"For the last two days I have been moving around in second- and third-class quarters. I think you were doing something along the same lines, yes?"

Ferraro nodded. "I had no luck," he said.

Jo Gar smiled a little. "This morning I had a little," he said. "I came across this."

He placed a brown hand in a pocket of his palm beach suit and withdrew it again. In his palm was a pin. It was a bar pin, of cheap manufacture. It had four imitation diamonds in it—one hole was vacant. The glass was large in size, but not matched.

Ferraro stared at the pin. He took it in his fingers and inspected it. Then he looked towards the small table in his cabin. On an end of it was the pin he had found after his cabin had been ransacked. He went over and placed it beside the other.

"The same sort of junk!" he breathed. "It might mean something."

Jo Gar nodded. "It might, but I'm afraid not," he said. "There are always a lot of women traveling second and third class on these ships. Many of them like cheap jewelry. A lot of these women are the dregs of the Orient. Captain Haroysan has told me that often first-class cabins are robbed. Or rather, attempts are made to rob."

Ferraro said: "But in this case—it was your cabin—and mine. And an attempt was made on your life."

Jo Gar nodded. "Many attempts have been made—to murder me," he said. "I found this pin in an empty third-class cabin. It lay beneath a berth."

Ferraro said very steadily: "We were both in police matters. What if the person thought he could learn something, or she could learn something, by getting into our luggage?"

The Island detective nodded. "A possibility," he said. "I've thought of that, Señor Ferraro."

Ferraro looked down at the two cheap objects in his palm. He poked them over on their backs. Jo Gar said slowly:

"I don't think that cheap stuff means anything. However, it is good to be careful."

He smiled at Ferraro and lifted one of the pins in his fingers. He said:

"We each have one—now."

Ferraro's mouth muscles twitched. He started to say something quickly, but caught himself. Turning, he made a movement as though to toss the pin towards the table. The ship was rolling heavily: he was forced to brace himself. Jo Gar leaned against the door. Ferraro said, facing him, a smile on his face:

"Wait—this is the piece of junk *you* found, Señor Gar."

There was a half-careless tone to his voice, yet he spoke hurriedly. Jo Gar looked at the bar pin in his hand.

"Of course," he agreed. "I am sorry."

They exchanged pins, both smiling. Jo slipped his into a pocket. He said:

"I'm going to nap—it's getting steadily rougher. Sleeping helps."

Ferraro tossed the pin towards the table. It struck it, but rolled from the surface to the floor. The one in white made an instinctive motion towards it, checked himself. He yawned, faced Jo.

"I'll have a try at it," he said.

Jo smiled and went outside. It took him five minutes to get to the captain's quarters. In another ten minutes the cabin boy had been sent to Ferraro's cabin. The Third Officer and Jo Gar, five minutes later, watched the one with the pale face following the cabin boy towards the captain's quarters. He did not see them. They went swiftly to his cabin, and the Third Officer used the key. Inside, Jo Gar looked on the floor. The bar pin was not there. It lay on the small table, on its back, the cheap stones face downward.

Jo Gar picked it up and handed it to the Third Officer. They went silently from the cabin, locking the door behind them. The *Cheyo Maru* was rolling heavily.

The Third Officer said: "Getting a little rough, Señor."

The Island detective nodded. "I trust so," he said softly.

————

Fallibar, a diamond expert returning to the States, seated across from Jo Gar and Captain Haroysan, spoke quietly:

"The third stone is a fine diamond," he said. "The others in the pin are just glass. Even this real one has been painted, to give it false glitter. Painted on the back. And crudely mounted. But then, all of them are just stuck in holes of the metal."

There was silence. Fallibar studied the slip of paper Jo had given him. He nodded his head.

"It answers the description," he said slowly. "It's one of the Von Loffler stones. I've handled diamonds for thirty years, and I'd swear to that."

Jo Gar sighed. "And it was lost, while Señor Ferraro's cabin was being ransacked," he said slowly.

The Third Officer said in a hard voice:

"Two of us have gone through everything he has in there. The purser is still detaining him, telling him there is a mistake in his passage papers. But we're through—we have found nothing."

Captain Haroysan regarded Jo with narrowed, dark eyes.

"Señor Gar has traced this one diamond," he said. "I think it should be his affair."

Jo smiled. "That is good of you," he said. "I can think of only one way."

The captain of the *Cheyo Maru* said quietly:

"You will need assistance?"

The Island detective smiled with his thin lips pressed together. He ran brown fingers across the skin of his forehead, then shook his head.

"I do not think so," he said very softly. "It is difficult to tell."

Fallibar said grimly: "There has been a murder, and your life has been attempted—"

Jo Gar smiled at the diamond expert who was returning to the States. The *Cheyo Maru* rolled sluggishly in the seas kicked up by the tail end of the typhoon.

"I shall not need assistance," he said firmly. "If the captain will instruct the purser not to detain Señor Ferraro longer, I shall wait a little while, and then go to his cabin."

The Third Officer said: "But he will notice, perhaps, that the bar pin has vanished."

Jo Gar smiled with his almond-shaped eyes on the swaying walls of the Captain's office.

"I am very sure that he will," he agreed tonelessly.

When Jo Gar rapped lightly on the door of Ferraro's cabin it was almost six o'clock. The one in white called again:

"Who is it?"

Jo Gar said: "Señor Gar."

The door was opened and Jo went inside. He was smiling a little.

Señor Ferraro was dressed in white trousers and a white shirt. He wore slippers. He said in a rather sharp voice:

"I have been in the cabin only a few minutes. A mix-up in my passage papers, and the purser is very stupid. But when I returned here—that bar pin had disappeared."

Jo Gar stood with his back to the door and extended the palm of his right hand towards Ferraro. He said quietly:

"I have the honor—to return it."

Ferraro's face got hard. He took the pin, stared at it. He said, in a surprised tone:

"But now—there are *two* stones missing!"

His lips were twitching; he was breathing hard. Jo Gar nodded almost pleasantly. He put his right hand in a pocket of his palm beach coat.

"We removed one of them—one was already missing," he said.

Ferraro stared at the Island detective. He said nastily:

" 'We' removed one?"

Jo nodded again. "Mr. Fallibar aided me," he said. "He is a diamond expert—an acquaintance of the captain."

He watched the little jerk of Ferraro's body. The man in white was fighting for control. But he said in a hard, rising voice.

"But *why*—did you remove one?"

Jo Gar shrugged. "It was one of the Von Loffler stones," he replied. "I noticed a difference in the color, when you showed me the bar pin. I had

Mr. Fallibar inspect it. The stone we removed is one of the ten missing ones—and quite valuable."

Ferraro said hoarsely: "It's a mistake! How would that pin have been lost—in here—"

Jo Gar stopped smiling. He said patiently:

"It *wasn't* lost in here, Señor Ferraro."

He waited, watching the fear in Ferraro's eyes, watching the man's attempt at control. Then he said in an easy tone:

"A Malay that I shot in Manila was dying. He told me to find 'the one who walks badly—always in white.' I wanted to know who the leader was—of the ones that robbed Delgado's store. I came aboard this ship—when I learned *you* were coming aboard, Ferraro!"

Ferraro said hoarsely: "You're—mad, Gar! You think I—"

His voice broke. Jo Gar nodded and moved his right pocket material a little.

"I think the Malay made a mistake, Señor Ferraro," he said. "You were *not* the leader of the diamond thieves. But you had been with the Constabulary, and you could aid them. You were valuable, and for your services you received one diamond. A very valuable stone."

There was a sneer across Ferraro's face. Jo Gar said:

"You were not worried about me being aboard. Perhaps you were offered a bigger reward—for my death. You wanted to create a mystery, and to show me that you possessed nothing of value. You did not work alone. You thought that a safe way to carry your diamond was in the cheap pin. And you used it to attempt throwing me off the trail. But you wished to kill, also. You bribed the deck steward—and he told you I was asleep. You fired three shots at what you thought was Señor Gar, and you got away. You wore dark clothes—and threw them overboard. Then you were in white—a man in white."

Ferraro said hoarsely. "That is a lie! I did not—"

Jo Gar said: "It is not a lie. The dark coat did not get clear of the vessel. It caught over an open port, just above the waterline—"

Ferraro's voice was almost a scream. He cried:

"You lie—you lie!"

Jo Gar said grimly: "I think that the first shot knocked the mask to the deck—you knew you had failed. You were afraid—and you went forward and knifed the deck steward so that he could not talk—"

Ferraro made a swift movement of his right hand. Jo Gar squeezed the trigger of his automatic. The *Cheyo Maru* was rolling—the bullet struck the mirror above the wash basin. Ferraro's gun cracked—wood spurted from the door behind Gar.

The Island detective fired again. Ferraro's body jerked; his gun arm dropped. He slumped slowly to his knees, swayed for a minute, rolled to the left as the vessel tilted in the rough seas.

Jo Gar said slowly: "You were too sure—you were not suspected, Ferraro. Too certain."

The man in white turned his head a little. Jo Gar moved forward and got the gun away from him. He said in a steady voice:

"You tried to be careless—with that bar pin. But you showed it had value."

Ferraro groaned. "That—damned coat—" he breathed in a tearing voice.

Jo said: "I was bluffing, Ferraro—it didn't catch on the port. Who were the others? Who was the one who planned the diamond steal—"

Ferraro's face was splotched with red. Blood was on his lips. He said thickly:

"It was that—"

He was coughing, his face twisted. Jo bent over him. Ferraro's eyes were staring. He muttered thickly:

"The blind—Chinese—Honolulu—you can find—"

His muttering died. There was a convulsive shiver of his body. In the corridor there was the sound of foot-falls, voices. Jo Gar bent down, straightened again. He braced himself against the ship roll, opened the door. The Third Officer stared past him, at the body of Señor Ferraro.

He said: "He *was*—the one—you were searching for!"

Jo Gar shook his head. But he didn't speak. The words of the dying Malay had helped. He was wondering if the last words of Ferraro would help, too. And he was making certain that he would remember them.

The Blind Chinese

Ramon Decolta

Jo Gar, the little Island detective, finds strange things happen at the house of the blind Chinese.

T WAS JUST A LITTLE time after dusk. There was a crescent moon half-hidden by the jagged peak of the Pali; a cool breeze blew through the garden not far from the Royal Hawaiian Hotel. Jo Gar relaxed in the wicker chair in which his diminutive body rested. But his gray-blue eyes were alert; they watched the mild ones of Benfeld, the Honolulu representative of the Dutch Insurance Company. Benfeld sipped his cool drink and said with a slight English accent:

"Herr Von Loffler had cabled me. It was in code and therefore quite safe. We are interested, of course. My home company insured the diamonds. A terrible crime."

Jo nodded his head. "The murders were incidental," he said in his toneless voice. "The one who planned the robbery perhaps thought it could be accomplished without a killing. He was mistaken. Delgado's son was murdered in the jewelry store. There was the bank guard, who was killed outside. And then Juan Arragon, my friend, who was in pursuit. An attempt was made to murder the American chief of police. In Manila he is not too well liked. I was forced to shoot a Malay, and he spoke of a 'man in white—who walks badly.' I traced such a man aboard the *Cheyo Maru.*"

Benfeld said grimly: "And you were forced to shoot him to death. But you learned something."

Jo Gar widened his eyes slightly. He had only told the insurance representative certain things, not too much.

"Very little," he corrected.

Benfeld shrugged. He was a tall man, with a long face and blond hair.

"You recovered one of the diamonds," he said.

Jo Gar sighed a little. He smiled and straightened in his wicker. Palm trees swayed beyond the garden, and yet Honolulu was not like Manila. It was cooler, less tropical in a sense.

"Señor Ferraro was a fool," he said placidly. "The Malay who spoke of him might have thought he was the important one of the bandits. But he was not. Perhaps he talked with the Malay, who I think was one of the robbers. But Ferraro was given only one of the ten Von Loffler stones."

Benfeld relighted a thin cigar and nodded his long head very slowly.

"And you have said he tried to murder you, on the *Cheyo Maru*," he said.

The Island detective nodded. "In Manila—many people have tried to murder me," he said simply. "The stolen diamonds are worth more than two hundred thousand dollars. There was a diamond expert on the boat, by chance. He has valued the diamond I recovered from this Ferraro at in excess of twenty thousand dollars. It is one of the Von Loffler stones, of course. I think, had Ferraro succeeded in murdering me, he would have received another."

There was a flickering light in Benfeld's eyes. He said very softly:

"Who would have given it to him, Señor Gar?"

Jo Gar got a brown-paper cigarette from a pocket of his light-colored suit coat. He smiled with his almond-shaped eyes almost closed.

"Ferraro died during the fourth day out from Manila," he said very softly. "I spent the remaining days in attempting to associate him with some other person on the boat. It was a failure."

Benfeld frowned. Gray smoke curled upward from his thin lips. He was silent for several seconds.

"Then, as it stands, Señor Gar—" he said thoughtfully—"you have recovered one of the Von Loffler stones. You are thousands of miles from Manila. And you have completely lost the trail of the others."

Jo Gar closed his eyes. It was peculiar—the way Benfeld regarded the situation. It was almost as though the Dutch insurance representa-tive was pleased. He was certainly extremely inquisitive. He *had* received a cable from Von Loffler, there was no doubt about it. And Jo considered that the German owner of the nine miss-ing diamonds had been foolish, even though he had sent the message in code. But then, this man seated across from him represented the company that had insured the diamonds. That company would suffer a severe loss if they were not recov-ered.

He had not answered Benfeld's question—the long-faced one said quietly:

"Of course, I understand that your friend was murdered. Juan Arragon. And also that Señor Delgado wishes to bring to justice the person that murdered his son. And already you have recovered one diamond. But the trail—"

His voice died away; he frowned and shrugged. Jo Gar opened his eyes and smiled at the Dutchman.

"The trail is lost," he said simply. "There are nine diamonds still missing. They are worth almost two hundred thousand dollars."

Benfeld cleared his throat and said in a tone that was so careless Jo noticed it:

"If this Ferraro—had only spoken, before he died!"

Jo Gar inhaled smoke from his brown-paper cigarette. He lifted his glass with stubby, brown fingers. He sipped a little of the cool liquid.

"It would have helped—very much," he said simply.

He looked towards the swaying palm trees and remembered the words that Señor Ferraro had used. Benfeld did not know of those words, and he would not know of them. The man was getting at something.

The Dutchman shook his head and sighed heavily. He said:

"The company will investigate, of course. But it will be very difficult, I fear. And what are *your* plans, Señor Gar?"

Jo Gar shrugged. "The *Cheyo Maru* remains in port until noon tomorrow," he said. "She will be in San Francisco within six days. I shall make the voyage aboard her. Only a few passengers disembarked here—and I have made quite certain they are not involved."

Benfeld said slowly: "Of course, you have had much time to learn who was landing."

Again there was the peculiar tone of his voice. It was almost as though he were slightly amused. But the next second he was frowning, shaking his long head.

"The nine Von Loffler stones!" he murmured. "And diamonds are so simple—to hide away."

Jo Gar nodded and said wearily: "It will be good to sleep on shore tonight. Ship travel tires me. I think I shall retire, after a brief drive about."

He waited for the obvious offer. But it did not come. Benfeld lived in Honolulu; he had brought Jo to this garden from the small hotel in which he had taken a room. Yet he was not offering to drive him about for a short time.

Jo Gar waited in silence. Finally Benfeld said: "I was trying to think of some way—I have an engagement it will not be possible for me to break—"

The Island detective said protestingly: "Do not even consider it."

Benfeld said suddenly: "Of course, I have it! You will use my car. I shall get other conveyance. In the morning we shall meet again."

He smiled cheerfully. Jo Gar protested. But Benfeld would not listen to him.

"Better still—" he said, and his voice died away as he frowned thoughtfully. Then he said with a smile: "I have two cars. You will remain here, Señor Gar—and I will drive to my appointment. It is a monthly affair, an important one. I will then send my chauffeur to you, with the other car, the open one. I will drive my own, when I return home, which will be late. In the morning I will come to your hotel."

Jo Gar bowed a little. "You are very good," he said softly. "You are very kind."

Benfeld glanced at his wristwatch and rose to his feet. He called a Chinese waiter and insisted upon paying for the drinks. Jo Gar rose and they shook hands. Jo said:

"Of course you realize you must be discreet about this affair—"

Benfeld said sharply: "Of course, Señor Gar. I think you have done very well. I will have my chauffeur return here within twenty minutes, say. You will not be too chilled in an open car?"

The Island detective shook his head. "I would like an open machine," he replied. "It is very good of you."

Benfeld smiled. "You will be able to see more of the Island," he said. He bowed. "Until tomorrow, then."

Jo Gar bowed a little. "Until tomorrow," he agreed.

The Dutchman went slowly from the garden, towards the palm-studded street. He walked erectly, with his shoulders thrown back. He bowed to two men seated at a small table in the garden. Then he was lost from sight behind a high, tropical hedge. Jo Gar reseated himself and called the waiter.

"Iced claret," he ordered.

He slumped in the wicker and watched the crests of the palms sway in the breeze. It was true that he was many miles from Manila. But other things were not so true. Perhaps he had lost the trail of the remaining nine Von Loffler diamonds—perhaps not. The thing that Benfeld did not know was that Señor Ferraro had used a few words, lying on the floor of his cabin on the *Cheyo Maru*. Most men, when they felt death coming close, used words. And Ferraro had said: "The blind Chinese—Honolulu—you can find—"

That was all he had said. And in the city of Honolulu, with a tremendous Chinese population, there would be more than one Chinese who was blind. But that did not mean that the trail was lost.

The waiter brought the iced claret. Jo Gar sipped it and smoked another cigarette. He thought:

The Dutchman, he is well established here. He perhaps has a fine reputation. But why did he question me so? And he has not a poker face. He is not experienced in these things. There is much that he would like to know, yet he has an important engagement. And my boat is sailing at noon tomorrow.

Jo smiled a little, with his lips pressed together.

"And he feels I would enjoy riding in an open machine," he murmured softly.

Music from a stringed orchestra reached his ears. It was the soft, lazy music of the Hawaiians. The Manila detective nodded his head very slowly.

"There is a possibility"—he half whispered, looking down at his drink—"that he is correct. I shall very soon see."

Some twenty minutes later a waiter came to Jo Gar's table and said that his car was just beyond the garden. Jo thanked him and paid for the drink. He went slowly to the street in which the palms rose. The car was a short distance from the garden entrance. It was a small car, well polished. It seemed of an old make. The driver was a short Chinese. He wore a white coat that was several sizes too large for him, no hat. His trousers were not so clean as his coat. He smiled, showing broken yellow teeth, and bowed awkwardly.

"Señor Gar?" he asked.

Jo frowned. He thought first that Benfeld was a fool, using his name to a servant. And then he smiled with his eyes. He nodded.

"Yes," he said in English. "You are Señor Benfeld's chauffeur?"

He spoke slowly and clearly. The Chinese nodded his head. He said:

"It is so—I am—chauffeur."

Jo Gar nodded. He looked into the rear of the open car. The seat was clean, but the floor mat was not so clean. The top was back, and the sides of the car were low. It was not unlike many other cars Jo had noticed—cars that were hired out to tourists on the Island.

He stepped inside as the driver held the door open. He said:

"I do not care to go far from the heart of the city. Along the beach, and past the old Palace of the—"

He checked himself. The chauffeur was trying desperately to understand his English. He had spoken fast, but not too fast. And this man had spoken first in English.

Jo Gar sighed a little. He said very slowly:

"We will go—where you wish. You have been told—where to take me?"

The driver's face lighted. He jerked his head up and down, showing his broken teeth again.

"Me told—what do," he said cheerfully. "Me know—where go."

Jo smiled and nodded. The driver got into the front seat. When the car moved forward it jerked and made much noise. It reminded Jo of the car owned by himself, back in Manila. And the chauffeur was hardly the sort one might expect Benfeld to have.

The Island detective sat back in the seat. The streets were not too well lighted; as the car moved along the lights grew fewer, and there were not so many hotels. The foliage was thicker. There was a cross-roads ahead, and Jo was sufficiently familiar with Honolulu to know that the beach was to the right. But the driver turned the car jerkily to the left. The road grew narrower, and the houses far apart. There was the sweet odor of the foliage, and in the distance the slopes of mountains.

Jo Gar leaned forward and said above the clatter of the machine:

"I would prefer—the beach road—"

The driver jerked his head a little and nodded. He said in a shrill, raised tone:

"Me come—back along beach. He tell me—go by mountain road first—"

Jo Gar sat back in the seat and got his Colt from the holster under his left thigh. He smiled a little, but it was a grim smile. Once he turned in the rear seat, raised himself slightly and glanced behind. There were no lights of another car, but he was not reassured. The road on which they were driving was growing narrower. It was rough, and there were no shoulders.

Suddenly the headlights went out. They came on again almost instantly, then were extinguished. Jo's body was rigid; he could see that the driver was leaning forward slightly, back of the wheel. The lights flashed on. The car was moving slowly up a fairly steep grade. Foliage was thick on both sides of the road.

The Island detective leaned forward and called sharply:

"You have trouble—with the lights?"

The Chinese jerked his head around, nodded. His almond-shaped eyes held a hard expression; they seemed to glitter. His lips were drawn back. The car slowed down, halted. The Chinese used the emergency brake gratingly. He turned his head all the way and said shrilly:

"Him go bad. You wait—me fix."

He slid from the seat back of the wheel, got to the left side of the car. He went swiftly towards the headlights, which seemed to be showing dimly. Jo Gar was leaning forward in the seat, his gray-blue eyes narrowed.

He heard the other machine before he saw it. There was the roar of an engine—the car seemed to be speeding up the far side of the slope on which the car in which Jo was seated was resting. There were no lights, but the engine roar was increasing in sound.

The Chinese heard the roar, too. He stood near the lights, his small body rigid. He called shrilly:

"Me need—stick. Me get—him!"

His body swung around; he moved towards the right side of the road, the thick foliage. As he neared it there was a flare of light beyond the crest of the slope. Headlights of the approaching car had been suddenly switched on. But they slanted high, above the standing car and above the road.

The Chinese driver's body crashed through the foliage; his back was turned to Jo as he went into it. The island detective moved with surprising swiftness. In a flash he was out of the car. He ran, in darkness, his small body bent low, to the left side of the road, dived into the thick foliage. Branches and leaves struck against his outflung arms. He went to his knees, let his body drop flat. Back of him the road was suddenly yellow-white with the glare from headlights.

There was the increasing roar of the car

engine. And then the staccato beat of the guns. Metal made sound, and there was the shattering sound of glass. The air was filled with the clatter—Jo Gar could hear the bullets pounding into the body of the car.

The engine roar had diminished momentarily. Now it increased in volume. The clatter of the guns died away. There had certainly been more than one gun, and they had been machine-guns. Few bullets had missed the car in which he had been seated.

The engine roar became a hum as the car from which the bullets had been loosed sped back towards the heart of Honolulu. Jo Gar lay motionless, listening to the decreasing sound. His Colt was gripped in the fingers of his outflung right hand.

He moved about very quietly, pulling his body nearer the road and parting the foliage a little. He could see the machine now. There was light from the stars and crescent moon. The windshield was shattered, both headlights had been shot out. He could see bullet marks along the side facing him. The rear left tire was flat.

In the distance the engine of the departing car was making only a faint hum sound. Jo Gar smiled with his lips and kept narrowed eyes on the foliage ahead of the bullet-filled car, across the road. He half whispered:

"Machine-guns in Manila. And now here. Methods of the Western world, these are!"

There was faint sound from the foliage across the road. He saw the short figure of the Chinese chauffeur appear, crawling. The man glanced towards the car, then slowly straightened his body. For several seconds he stood motionlessly, looking towards the battered machine. Then his head turned; he glanced in each direction, along the road. He listened intently.

There was no sound of another car. The hum of the speeding one had died away. Jo Gar guessed that the spot was a deserted one, one from which the noise of the machine-guns would not reach habitation.

The Chinese chauffeur moved slowly into the rough-surfaced, dirt road. He stood for a few seconds in front of the car, then walked around it. He stood with his back to Jo as the Island detective rose and lifted his Colt a little. The Chinese moved closer to the car, getting up on his toes and peering towards the floor at the rear.

Jo Gar stepped from the foliage to the road-bed. There was crackling sound as he did so, and the driver's body swung around. His eyes went wide with fear as he stared at Jo. His breath made a whistling sound and he cried out shrilly in his native tongue.

Jo said quietly: "I was not—in the machine, you see."

He smiled a little. The Chinese was staring at the gun now. His lips were drawn back from his teeth; his face was a mask of fear. Jo said:

"I think—you must die—for what you have done."

He moved the gun up a little, and forward. The chauffeur started shrilling words in his native tongue. His body was shaking. Jo said:

"Stop it! You are not Benfeld's chauffeur. This is not Benfeld's car. It is a hired car. Perhaps your car. Will you answer my questions?"

The Chinese was staring at him. He jerked his head up and down.

The Island detective said slowly: "You will certainly die, if you do not answer me truthfully. Who were those in the machine that just passed? Those who used the guns?"

The Chinese shook his head. Jo Gar smiled with his almond-shaped eyes almost closed. He repeated the question in stilted Chinese, a tongue with which he had difficulty, in spite of his many years in Manila.

The driver said: "Me—not know!"

Jo Gar said, moving a little closer to the chauffeur:

"The Dutchman, Benfeld—he went to you and paid you money. Very good money. He told you that you were to act as his chauffeur. He furnished you with a new coat, though there was no time to make it fit. He told you where to drive me and how to signal with your headlights. He said you must then stop the car—and hide yourself. Is this not so?"

He had spoken very slowly and clearly. The chauffeur nodded his head. He said:

"He do not—tell me more."

Jo Gar nodded and smiled grimly. He was thinking that Benfeld had taken a big chance. And yet, he had almost succeeded. There had been only a few seconds' time between life and death—for Señor Gar.

The Island detective stopped smiling. He moved his gun hand a little.

"I think you must die," he said steadily. "You would have killed me—"

The Chinese shook his head and shrilled words. After a few seconds he spoke more slowly. He said that he did not know that the big guns were to fire into the car. He did not know what had been about to happen. He was a poor man, and Benfeld had offered him much money.

Jo Gar cut him off, after a little time.

"I will give you a chance," he said slowly. "There is a person I wish to see. He is Chinese. And he is—blind."

He saw instantly that the chauffeur knew of such a man. And he saw that the man was of importance. But the driver shook his head.

"There are—more than one—blind Chinese in—"

Jo Gar interrupted again. "There is *one* of some importance," he said. "Think carefully. Perhaps this one has a place where dishonest men go. Perhaps he is not a good person. Think well, for you are young to die."

He spoke very slowly, and with no smile on his face. He held his Colt low and slightly forward of his right side.

The Chinese driver stared at him wildly. But he did not speak. Jo Gar said:

"Very well—I shall find him alone. But first I must silence you, so that you do not again interfere with me."

The chauffeur threw out his hands. They were browned, and the fingers were jerking, twisting. He said:

"I know—him! I go—his place—"

Jo Gar lowered his Colt slightly. He nodded his head and smiled. His voice was almost tone-less when he spoke.

"You are wise—we shall go there together. We shall walk to a spot where perhaps we may obtain a ride. You will do as I say, and if you make one, slight mistake—"

He moved the Colt a little. The Chinese driver's facial muscles were twisting. He was breathing quickly. He said:

"Tan Ying—he is very bad. Even if he does—not see—"

Jo Gar nodded. "Many men are very bad," he philosophized quietly. "But after they are *dead*—how do we know what then happens?"

The driver half closed his staring eyes. He said in a shrill, shaken tone:

"If I take you to the place—they will kill me."

Jo Gar shrugged. "And if you do *not* take me—*I* will kill you," he said. "It is a difficult position."

The driver said: "I am a poor man—"

The Island detective nodded. "Then you have less to live for," he replied. "Let us start."

The hour was almost midnight when Jo Gar and the Chinese chauffeur moved through the teeming streets of the Honolulu Chinese quarter. There was the sound of discordant music—the shrill, reedy notes that came down from rooms beyond balconies. The section was well lighted in spots, very poorly lighted in others. Jo Gar kept his body close to that of the chauffeur, and his Colt within the right pocket of his light suit coat. At intervals he let the weapon press against the chauffeur's side.

They turned suddenly into a narrow alley that wound from the lighted street. There were few lights in the alley; the section was very quickly a poor one. The shops were squalid and dirty; no music came down from the rooms beyond the balconies.

The street curved more sharply at the far end. The Chinese at Jo's side said thickly:

"It is—there—"

He pointed towards a narrow entrance, an oblong cut in unpainted wood. Strips on which letters were scrawled in Chinese, hung on either side of the entrance. Streamers of painted beads hung from the bamboo pole at the top of the entrance; they obscured the store beyond.

Jo said softly: "You will go—first—"

The driver's face was twisted, but he forced a smile as his browned hands shoved aside the beads. They made a rattling sound; Jo followed into the shop. A kerosene light made odor and gave little flare. There was the usual musty, aged smell of such shops. Baskets were about, with nuts in them—and jars contained brightly colored candy. There were shelves with boxes marked with Chinese lettering.

No one was about, but at the rear of the store was another bead curtain. The Chinese driver glanced towards it. Jo Gar said in a half whisper:

"Do as you—were told."

The chauffeur raised his voice and called in a shrill voice:

"Tan Ying!"

A quavering voice replied, from the room beyond the second curtain. It said:

"Welcome, Dave Chang!"

Jo Gar smiled grimly. The Americanization of the Chinese never failed to amuse him. He touched Chang lightly and pointed towards the beads of the curtain.

The chauffeur said in Chinese: "You are alone, Tan Ying?"

Ying replied that he was alone. He asked that the driver would enter his humble abode. Chang moved towards the beaded curtain and Jo Gar followed him. He was very close to him as they passed through the beaded curtain into the rear room. Two kerosene lamps were burning, but there was a clutter of objects in the place. Buddha's figure was in a corner; the light from the nearer lamp struck the face from an angle, making the figure seem very life-like.

Tan Ying was an aged Chinese. He sat cross-legged, but there was some object against which his back rested. He was obese and fat faced. His eyes were open but sightless. They shone whitely as he stared towards Chang. It was almost as though he were inspecting the chauffeur.

Jo Gar stepped soundlessly to one side of the beaded curtain. He took his Colt from his right-hand pocket, held it low at his side. He breathed as quietly as possible. But it was not enough. Tan Ying said quietly, steadily:

"You are not alone, Dave Chang."

He spoke in his native tongue, and Chang sucked in his breath sharply. He twisted his head and looked at Jo. The Island detective smiled and nodded.

Chang said: "It is my Spanish friend, Mendez. He has arrived on the boat today."

The blind Chinese nodded his fat face. His face was expressionless, except that his sightless eyes gave it a strange intenseness. He said:

"Welcome, Señor Mendez!"

Jo Gar spoke in Spanish. "You are good to welcome me, Tan Ying."

The Chinese smiled; he was almost toothless. The wick in one of the kerosene lamps was low; it flickered now and then. There was a little silence. Then Jo Gar said to the chauffeur, in Chinese:

"Will you speak of the business?"

The chauffeur's body stiffened. He said very softly:

"You are expecting the Dutchman, Tan Ying?"

Tan Ying's fat body rocked a little from side to side. His lips tightened. He said:

"Why do you speak of him?"

Jo Gar said: "It is because I am to meet him—in Honolulu, Tan Ying. That is the reason."

The lips of the fat Chinese relaxed a little. A clock chimed, and Tan Ying listened to it. He said, after a little silence following the chimes:

"The Dutchman—he is already late."

Jo Gar sighed a little. He moved his body and turned so that when Benfeld came in he could easily cover him with his weapon. The driver was looking at him with tortured eyes; Chang was feeling fear.

The blind Chinese said suddenly, in very precise English:

"It has gone well, Dave Chang?"

Jo Gar felt his body stiffen. The driver nod-ded his head, and looked at Jo again. The Island detective nodded and smiled.

Chang said: "It has gone well, Tan Ying."

The blind Chinese smiled again. His body continued to rock from side to side. There was a small screen near the print-covered wall at Jo's back. It was perhaps four feet high, and as many long. It was within several feet of the wall. Jo Gar moved quietly to it, stood close to it. He raised his gun a little and nodded at Dave Chang.

The chauffeur hesitated. Jo Gar's face grew hard; he narrowed his gray-blue eyes. Chang said:

"Señor Mendez will be of use to the Dutch-man, Tan Ying."

The blind Chinese stopped swaying. He said in his native tongue:

"It may be so."

There was the sound of beads rattling, at the entrance of the shop. The blind Chinese stiff-ened, and Dave Chang half turned his body. Jo Gar raised his weapon, leveled it at the chauf-feur. Then he stepped behind the screen and bent downward. He got his right eye near a sec-tion crack. There was little light on the screen. From the outer room there was the sound of tap-ping. He counted a half dozen taps; they were soft and well spaced.

The blind Chinese raised his voice and said:

"It is the way of the Western lands—"

There was the sound of footfalls. The beads of the inner curtain rattled and Benfeld came into the room. He straightened, looked sharply about. He said in a hard tone, in English:

"You—Chang—what was it that happened?"

The blind Chinese said softly: "Dave Chang—he has told me it is well."

Benfeld said fiercely in English: "He lied! When we got back there, after ten minutes, there was no body in the car. You—Chang—"

The chauffeur said hoarsely, fear in his voice:

"I do not know—what happened! I did as I was told. I signaled with the lights, and when I saw the beam of your car—I ran to the foliage. When I returned, there was no sign of Señor Gar. I swear it."

Benfeld said grimly: "What did you do? Why didn't you stay near the car?"

Chang replied in a shrill tone: "I was frightened. One of the bullets from your machine—it almost struck me. I went into the foliage, wandered around. Then I remembered that we were to be here at twelve."

Benfeld drew a deep breath. He kept his right hand out of sight in the pocket of a light coat he was wearing. He had on a soft hat, pulled low over his face.

The blind Chinese was muttering to himself. He stopped it and said:

"Señor Mendez is here, you see."

There was a little silence. Jo Gar watched Benfeld stare about the room. There was a puzzled expression on the Dutchman's face.

The right pocket of his coat moved a little. There was fear in Chang's eyes, but he did not look towards the screen. Jo Gar's body was tense, but he waited. Benfeld said in English:

"What is this? What do you mean?"

The blind Chinese seemed to sense that something was wrong. His head did not move, but he spoke very softly and very calmly.

"Dave Chang—he brought with him Señor Mendez. I have spoken with him, but a few minutes ago. Chang said that he would be of use to you."

With his one eye back of the section crack, Jo Gar watched Benfeld move away from the chauffeur. He saw the glint of steel as the Dutchman's gun came out of his pocket. Chang was breathing rapidly; fear was gripping him. Benfeld's eyes went about the room in a swift glance. The low-wicked lamp sent light wavering over the walls.

Benfeld said: "By God, Chang—you've tricked us—"

The Chinese chauffeur said in a shrill voice:

"No—it is not so! I have not—"

Jo Gar raised his Colt and got the muzzle within a half inch of the section crack. Benfeld was in a line, but beyond the Chinese chauffeur. He had his long face lowered a little; his eyes were slitted on Chang's. He said:

"By God—you have. I've told you too much.

I've been a fool. But I've got you—in here. Gar had those diamonds on him. He got them from Ferraro. He lied to me. You took them from him—"

The blind Chinese said in his native tongue, his voice calm:

"Be careful—there is this Mendez—"

Benfeld's eyes went around the room again. He said savagely:

"There's no one else in here. If Chang said there was—he was lying to you, Ying. Or else he was—"

The chauffeur said in a shrill voice:

"I did not—steal the diamonds! That is not so—do not shoot—"

A knife was suddenly in the right hand of the seated Chinese. He held it out, his sightless eyes gazing straight ahead. He said calmly:

"Be careful—is not a knife better?"

Benfeld said in a low, hoarse voice: "I tell you— Señor Gar had the diamonds. He lied to me. Was I not informed that Ferraro was bringing them? Gar lied. Either he was trying to get away with them, or he wants them for himself. And you—"

The chauffeur said shrilly: "When I reached my car—he was not there—"

Jo Gar watched Benfeld, with thoughts running through his brain. Benfeld figured that *he* had the diamonds, had gotten them from Ferraro and had lied to him. But did that mean that Ferraro had had more than one stone? Did it mean that someone on the *Cheyo Maru* had received the others, after all? Had Ferraro lied to him, dying?

Benfeld was staring at Dave Chang. He said very quietly:

"Why did you say Mendez was here? Why did you tell Tan Ying that?"

Jo Gar held his breath. He expected Chang to break any second now, to fail under the strain. He was between two guns, and he knew it. Jo had already gotten information from him; he had spoken of Mendez, and Jo Gar had forced him to use the name. The chauffeur was in a tight spot, but surely he must realize that if Jo Gar were to go down under the lead from Benfeld's gun—he would have a better chance. He had talked, because Jo had forced him to talk. But with the Island detective dead—

Tan Ying said in the same passive voice:

"The knife—it is better."

The body of the blind Chinese was swaying again. Benfeld said in a harsh voice:

"Very well—throw it at my feet, Tan Ying."

The knife fell several feet from Benfeld, but the judgment of the blind man was not bad. Benfeld glanced down at it, but did not move.

"Why did you say that Mendez was here?" he asked again.

The blind Chinese said steadily:

"You do not hear me, Benfeld. I tell you someone—*was* here! I talked with him—"

The eyes of Benfeld were slitted on the screen now. Jo Gar held the muzzle of his gun steady. The chauffeur said weakly:

"It was Mendez—we met in the Street of the Lanterns. He was coming—"

Benfeld swore hoarsely. "Then where is he now?" he asked very slowly.

The Chinese driver made a little movement of his left hand. A browned finger pointed towards the screen. He said at the same instant:

"I do not know—he went out—"

The gun in the hand of Benfeld slanted a little. Jo Gar looked at it, squeezed the trigger of his Colt. When the gun jerked and the room filled with sound, he hurled his body to one side.

The bullet from Benfeld's gun struck the wood of the screen, and then the wall back of it. Jo Gar pulled himself to his feet and swung around. Benfeld was sinking to the floor—he half raised his weapon. The blind Chinese said in a high-pitched voice:

"Dog of a—"

Benfeld's gun crashed again. The aged Chinese screamed and pitched forward. The gun dropped from Benfeld's right hand. He said thickly:

"The dead—do not—talk—"

His right hand reached out and groped for the knife the blind Chinese had tossed near him. Jo Gar said sharply:

"No—"

But it was Dave Chang who suddenly moved forward, bent down. He was screaming shrill words that had little meaning. His right-hand fingers were almost on the hilt of the knife when Benfeld gripped him, pulled him down. With a sudden, last strength the Dutchman raised the knife and struck. Jo Gar fired again, as the Chinese chauffeur groaned and rolled on his back.

Benfeld sat up a little and stared at him. There was red on his lips.

"Dead men—do not—talk—" he repeated weakly.

He lowered his head into outstretched arms and shivered a little. Then his body was motionless.

Jo Gar went to him first. He was dead. The knife had struck into the chauffeur's throat. He was trying to mouth words, but they did not come. And Jo Gar knew that they would never come again. He turned towards the blind Chinese. But he knew before he touched him that the man was dead.

There was a babble of voices beyond the two curtains of painted beads. Jo Gar went swiftly into the outer room. He thought, for a second, of trying to get away, of merging into the crowd of Chinese.

But already the crowd was thick, and there would be police. He would be seen trying to get away, and there would be difficulties. It would be better to work *with* the police, to attempt explanation.

He lighted a brown-paper cigarette and leaned against the counter. Faces were beyond the beads that rattled from hands that swayed them. Benfeld had expected the diamonds to be brought to him. They had not come. He had thought that Jo possessed them. The blind Chinese had known things—and the driver of the car riddled with bullets had known something. Dying, Benfeld had silenced them both. Even at the end, he was protecting someone.

The Island detective moved his lips a little. He said questioningly: "Who is Mendez?"

When the first of the police entered the shop, Jo Gar had almost finished his brown-paper cigarette. The police officer was small and brown faced. He was breathing heavily. He said:

"What—is it?"

Jo Gar gestured towards the second beaded curtain, and the room beyond it. He said in a tone that was weary:

"It is—death."

The police officer said: "Robbery?"

Jo Gar smiled with his eyes looking towards the curtain, shrugged his narrow shoulders.

"Perhaps," he said simply. "But very surely—it is death."

Red Dawn

Ramon Decolta

Jo Gar, the little Island detective, waited with killers for the coming of the red dawn in Honolulu.

ARRINGTON REGARDED Jo Gar with frowning, dark eyes. He was tall, immaculately dressed, fresh-looking. He was the power and brains back of the native Hawaiian police force, and it was very evident that the Philippine Island detective's calm annoyed him.

"I strongly advise you to return to your ship, Señor Gar," he said slowly.

Jo Gar smiled with his thin, colorless lips. His almond-shaped eyes seemed sleepy, but were not sleepy. And Barrington sensed that. He stretched his long legs, rose from the wicker chair of his office. But he did not move about. He stared down at Jo.

"Ten extremely valuable diamonds—stolen in Manila," he said quietly. "You have got one back—but nine are missing. You were forced to kill the man from whom you recovered the one, on the *Cheyo Maru*. That was unfortunate."

Jo Gar nodded his head just a little. "Very unfortunate," he agreed. "But also—very necessary."

Barrington shrugged. "Perhaps you were too aggressive, Señor Gar," he suggested.

Jo Gar smiled a little more broadly. He shook his head very slowly.

"I am never aggressive, Señor Barrington," he returned very quietly. "Manila is a city of heat—heat breeds laziness."

The American made a peculiar, snorting sound. He turned towards his desk and glanced at the report of the Hawaiian police, made less than a half hour ago, at midnight.

"Benfeld, Tan Ying and Dave Chang—all dead. And you are not aggressive?"

Jo Gar shrugged almost casually. "Benfeld was the representative of the Dutch company that had insured the diamonds. For some reason he wished me to stop my search for them, and for the thieves who murdered to get them. He attempted to trap me. He used Chang for that purpose and Chang suffered. The blind Chinese, Tan Ying—I am not sure how he was involved. I think there was to have been a meeting at his place. More than one person was concerned in the Manila robbery and murders. Perhaps there was to be a meeting at Ying's place. But Benfeld thought I had been shot to death, on the road beyond the city. I upset his plans—and there was sudden death."

"Triple death," Barrington said steadily. "You are sure you learned nothing?"

Jo Gar rose from his straight-backed chair. He lied impassively.

"Nothing—that seems to lead me anywhere," he said. "It is like that Street of the Lanterns where Ying lived—much color and sound, and so difficult to see or hear beyond either color or sound."

Barrington half closed his dark eyes. He said very grimly:

"You are known to be in Honolulu, Señor Gar. It is known that you are after the Von Loffler diamonds, and that you seek the murderers of your friend Juan Arragon—and of that jeweler's son, Delgado. Already there has been death. And dawn is hours away. I should strongly advise—"

Jo Gar's lips made a clicking sound. "You have already suggested that I return to the *Cheyo Maru*," he said calmly. "It is kind of you to think of my protection. Perhaps I shall accept your advice."

Barrington continued to frown. "I hope so," he said. "We will do everything possible, here. You will be in San Francisco in six days—and I wish you luck."

Jo Gar smiled and bowed. They did not shake hands. The Philippine Island detective reached the street and kept his brown right-hand fingers in the right pocket of his light coat. A cool breeze swept from the direction of Pearl Harbor. The streets were almost deserted.

The Island detective smiled with his almond-shaped eyes almost closed, moved slowly in the direction of the docks. They were not far from the building in which Barrington had his office. And as he walked, with his eyes glancing sharply from the corners, Jo Gar sighed. His stubby fingers tightened on the grip of the automatic in his right coat pocket.

"Señor Barrington does not wish *more* death—in Honolulu," he murmured very softly. "He is anxious for my departure—he thinks of my health."

Jo's white teeth showed in a swift grin. It faded, and he reached with his left-hand fingers for one of his brown-paper cigarettes. The street became suddenly an alley; his eyes caught the slanting masts of ships, their rigging beside the docks. He was ten feet along the alley when he halted, struck the match. But even as the flare dulled his vision, he saw the shape that slid from the doorway less than twenty yards distant. He heard the swift intake of the short man's breath, saw the right arm go upward and back!

The Island detective moved his left hand away from his face, let his short body fall forward. As he went down his right hand shoved the material of his coat pocket ahead of him—started to squeeze the trigger.

But there was no hiss of a knife hurled through the air, and no crack sound from his automatic. He relaxed his grip, rocking on his knees, as he watched the figure of the man who had slid from the doorway bend forward. The man's head was held low—his body was almost doubled as he pitched downward. He choked terribly but weakly—there was a sharp crack as his head battered against the broken pavement of the alley.

Jo Gar swayed to his feet. He moved back into the darkness of a narrow doorway on the opposite side of the alley from that where the short one had fallen. He waited, his back flattened against a wooden door that did not give, holding his breath.

The man who had collapsed made no movement. His head had struck heavily, but Jo knew that he had been unconscious before he had fallen. And yet, when he had slid from the doorway across the alley, his movements had been swift and sure. He had sucked in his breath, drawn back an arm. And Jo was sure there had been a knife in his hand.

Minutes passed. There were the faint sounds of machines, in the direction towards the city center, away from the docks. A cool wind rustled some paper down the alley. It was quite dark, and Jo could not see beyond the body of the man. Once he had heard foot-falls in the distance, and the sound of high-pitched voices. The alley was on the edge of the Chinese quarter, perhaps in it.

His right forefinger pressed the steel of the automatic trigger—the material of his right pocket was held clear of his side. But he made no movement. Five minutes passed. Jo Gar shivered a little. He was sure that death had come to the one across the alley from some spot directly behind him—and that the person who had caused the death was waiting silently, for some other movement in the narrow alley.

He breathed slowly, carefully. His right wrist was aching from the tensity of his grip on the automatic, and his eyes moved only from the motionless figure on the pavement to the blackness of the low doorway behind the figure. The shacks along the alley appeared to be closed, deserted. But the entrances existed—and in the one almost opposite him was the human cause of another person's death. Unless—and there did not seem much chance of that—there had been an escape through the shack beyond the motionless, sprawled figure.

The Island detective listened to the shrill whistle of a small boat, beyond the docks. He relaxed his body a little, but suddenly it was tense again. He had heard, very distinctly, a faint chuckle. It had not come from the doorway in darkness, beyond the collapsed figure, but from some spot above him.

He raised his head slightly. The shacks were low—less than fifteen feet high. Clouds were over a crescent moon; the night had become dark. But he could see nothing on the roof of the shack opposite.

And then, very softly and quietly, the voice sounded. It was low and throaty—and very calm.

"Señor Gar—you are comfortable?"

Jo Gar did not move his body. There was a quality to the voice, an accent of grim amusement. He had a definite feeling that he was trapped—that the death of the man across the alley had been a part of the trap. He did not speak. The voice sounded again—from above, and to the left. The roof of a shack on his left and on his side of the alley held the speaker, he guessed.

"You will kindly disarm yourself—step into the alley, Señor Gar."

The Island detective raised his automatic higher, withdrew it from the right pocket. He moved only his right arm. The voice said, after a short pause:

"Do not be a fool, Señor Gar!"

The accent was clear. He had heard the same accent of precise English in Manila. It was Spanish—this man's native language. And the speaker was calm—very calm. He was sure of himself.

Seconds passed. Then the voice said, a little more loudly:

"*Sí*, but very low, and—now!"

Jo Gar heard the steely hiss of the knife. He drew his legs together. The left trouser material, just above his ankle, was jerked sharply. Wood made dull sound as the knife blade cut into the door at his left side. His body was rigid.

The voice somewhere above said with sharp amusement:

"Señor Gar—you are comfortable?"

The Island detective sighed. The cat played with the mouse, but more wisely than most cats. Jo Gar reached down, jerked the knife loose from wood and cloth. He tossed it into the alley. Straightening, he said as steadily as he could:

"What is it you wish, Señor Mendez?"

Again there was the chuckle. And then a short silence. Jo Gar was thinking: It is Mendez. Chang said, before dying in the shop: "It was Mendez. We met in the Street of the Lanterns.

He was coming—" That was what Chang had said. Mendez coming to meet someone, in Honolulu. Perhaps the one in white. The one Jo had been forced to shoot to death, on the *Cheyo Maru,* and from whom he had got the one Von Loffler diamond. But Mendez knew that Jo had killed, and he had trapped him now, and was toying with him, grimly amused.

The Island detective stood motionless, looking at the body across the alley. The voice from above came quietly:

"Kindly disarm yourself—step into the alley, Señor Gar."

Jo sighed again. He bent forward and tossed the automatic into the alley. There was a flashlight beam that picked it up, then faded. Jo stepped from the doorway, moved out a few feet. The voice said:

"Face towards the docks."

The tone was hard now, sharp. Jo did as directed. He stood for seconds, his eyes slitted, his body slightly relaxed. He expected death at any moment, from behind. But it did not come. There were sounds on the roofs of the shacks, sounds behind him. But he did not turn. And then the same, hard voice sounded, directly behind him.

"Go to the alley end, walk slowly. There will be a closed car. Enter it. I shall be near you, and I advise you to be wise."

The Island detective moved slowly forward. The alley narrowed, then widened. At the dock end there was a small, dirty machine. It was closed, and there was the fat, brown-yellow face of a Chinese faintly lighted by the instrument board light. The man did not turn his head, but a rear door of the machine opened as Jo neared it. The voice, now close behind, said:

"Step inside."

Jo got into the car. A figure made room for him. The seat had space for three, back of the driver. Jo dropped heavily beside the one already seated. The one who had spoken got in and sat on his right. The interior of the car was very dark, but Jo saw that the man's features were sharp, his face long.

He said to the driver, in an easy tone: "Yes—and do not go too fast."

It was as though everything had been carefully planned. Jo tightened his lips. He was sure that the one on his right was the man known as Mendez, and he was sure that Mendez was hard and extremely clever. He had been followed from the police station to the building in which Barrington had an office, and Mendez had waited. Perhaps something had gone wrong, and there had been a death in the alley, or perhaps nothing had gone wrong, and it had been part of the scheme of things.

The man on Jo's right said softly: "It will not take very long, I hope, Señor Gar."

Jo smiled a little. He nodded his head. "You are Señor Mendez?" he asked.

The man was tall and thin. He had long, slender-shaped hands and wore a dark coat. That much Jo could see as the car moved slowly along the street by the docks.

He said: "*Sí*—Señor Mendez. There have been words about me?"

The Island detective turned his head towards Mendez. He spoke very steadily.

"Chang spoke of you—and Tan Ying."

The grim quality returned to Mendez' voice again. He spoke very slowly.

"And both Ying and Chang are dead. That is too bad."

Jo Gar smiled, showing his white, even teeth. Then his lips pressed together.

"So many people die—for diamonds," he observed.

Mendez nodded. His face was turned towards the driver's back. The machine was running slowly out of town; it was not going towards the beach, but through the poorer section of Honolulu.

"It is so," Mendez agreed. "But you are a curious one, Señor Gar. Even so—why should *you* die—for diamonds?"

The Island detective said nothing. He tried to keep his body relaxed, but there was a threat in Mendez' words. It was a question that Mendez asked, and yet only half a question.

The machine was out of the town now; it was

running through the tropical growth, and there was suddenly a moon showing through the clouds.

Mendez made a gesture with his long right hand. He said almost cheerfully:

"It is pretty, Señor—these warm countries. They make one want to live."

The Island detective kept his eyes to the front. For almost five minutes the car moved at good speed over a road that was fairly smooth. Then it slowed, turned abruptly to the left. The road became narrower. It was of dirt now, and the country was rolling. The moon seemed strangely bright for its size—and the car passed through what appeared to be a pineapple plantation. The one on Jo's left let his body rock with the car motion, but he did not look at the Island detective.

Mendez made another gesture with his right hand.

"It is not unlike the Philippines," he said slowly. "You would like to return some day, Señor Gar?"

Again there was the mocking quality in his voice. Jo turned his head, and the two regarded one another. Mendez' skin was a light brown color; his eyes were dark. They were cruel eyes, and intelligent. The man's features were good, but his lips were very thin and the curve of his mouth was barely perceptible. He had a sensitive face—but it was also a brutal face.

Jo Gar said steadily: "Yes—I should like to return—some day."

Mendez nodded. "It will not be difficult for you," he returned. "You are not—a fool."

The car jerked suddenly off the road. It ran a short distance, scraping foliage, so narrow was the path it traveled. It stopped. The one on Jo's left leaned forward and looked at Mendez, but he did not speak. Mendez said:

"That is all—but stay."

The door on the left was opened. Mendez said pleasantly, as the one to whom he had spoken descended:

"We will leave the machine, Señor. I have a gun in my right hand. There is a small plantation house just beyond the car. Will you walk towards it?"

Jo Gar let his eyes widen a little on the dark eyes of the Spaniard. He said quietly:

"You can murder me here—just as well, Señor Mendez."

For a second he saw sardonic amusement creep into the thin-faced one's eyes. And then a puzzled expression showed. But he knew that Mendez was acting now.

"Murder you?" The Spaniard laughed in a chuckling way. "Why do you think of murder, Señor Gar?"

The Island detective smiled. "Does it seem so strange?" he replied. "After all—you are aware of the Von Loffler diamonds. For them there has been much murder."

Mendez nodded, his face suddenly serious. "That is so," he agreed. "But you were not satisfied."

Jo Gar's gray-blue eyes showed no expression. "Not satisfied?" he said very tonelessly.

Mendez frowned. "At the house we can talk more easily," he said. "Please descend."

Jo Gar shrugged. He got from the car, saw the thatch-roofed house through the thinned foliage, up a slope a short distance. There were windows, but no lights. The house was well protected from even the narrow path. The dirt road was a hundred yards or more distant, and the other road perhaps a half mile.

The Island detective moved slowly up a path that wound. He heard Mendez instruct the driver to turn the machine and take it down near the dirt road. As he walked slowly up the slope he heard the engine of the car changing speed. Twice the brakes made squealing sounds. There was no sign of the one who had been seated on his left.

He was certain of one thing—Mendez held death for him. Perhaps there was information that the Spaniard wanted first. Perhaps he would make promises. But in the end there would be death. He could read it in the dark eyes, feel it in the cold amusement of Mendez' voice. And it was in the mockery of the Spaniard's words, too.

Behind him he heard the Spaniard's footfalls, very close. He moved slowly, and he was thinking fast. There was a better chance outside, here on the path, than there would be within the thatch-roofed plantation house. If he could take Mendez by surprise—

The Spaniard said almost pleasantly: "It is the fine view that Señor Benfeld liked here. The dawn—it is all red. The sun rising from the water—"

He let his voice die. He was breathing a little heavily now. Jo Gar said, suddenly stopping and breathing as though with difficulty:

"Benfeld tried to kill me, Mendez. He was a representative of the insurance company handling the Von Loffler stones. He thought I would be off my guard, because of that. How much was he offered—for my death?"

Mendez said cheerfully: "Enough, Señor Gar. But he was a fool—and not careful enough. He knew that you were trained in hunting down people, yet he was careless."

Jo Gar moved slowly up the slope again. He was breathing very heavily, though he was not tired. Behind him he could hear Mendez. And he was sure that the Spaniard was not pretending. He slowed his pace just a little, spoke haltingly.

"I will make—a bargain with you—Señor Mendez. If you will let me—have the chance—"

He uttered the last word softly, easily. And then, like a cat, he let his body swing around— he leaped at the figure of the man behind and several feet below him on the path!

But even as his short body shot through the air—he knew that he had lost. He saw Mendez' body stiffen—the features of the long, sharp face were twisted into a mask of hate. The Spaniard's body swung to one side. His right hand went up and then came down. Something gleamed dully in it. The first time it struck Jo a glancing blow on the shoulder. But as his hands and knees hit the earth—it struck him again, in a second chopping motion. Pain streaked across the back of his head—the yellow light of the moon became a curtain of black. He lost consciousness.

 he room held little furniture, and what there was of it was bamboo. There was a table and two chairs, and between the windows a small bookcase. Mendez stood near the bookcase, his back to the wall of the house that was little more than a shack. The lamp on the table had a faulty wick, or the oil was bad. The light was faint and uneven. Shadows were on the walls. Mendez said in a conversational tone:

"You are lying, Gar. You have been lying for an hour. And there are few hours left to you. You were successful, in the Islands—but the Philippines are not like these islands. They are hotter—and the brain of that breed is stupid. You killed a man, on the *Cheyo Maru*. And that man had with him ten diamonds. They were worth more than two hundred thousand dollars. You tell me you found only one of them. You are lying."

Jo Gar slumped in one of the bamboo chairs. Pains stabbed across his head. The gun that Mendez used was a heavy one, and the Spaniard had struck him with a savage motion. There was blood on the Island detective's face, and on the fingers of his right hand. He was tired. Three times in the last hour Mendez had struck him. Once the one who had sat on his left in the car had struck him—he was a Chinese with a stupid, typical face. He sat in a chair and watched the Island detective now, his eyes expressionless. The driver of the car was not in the plantation shack.

Jo said thickly: "I have told you the truth, Mendez. From the one in white—the one the Malay spoke of before he died, in Manila—I got only one diamond. It was he who told me of the blind Chinese. That was why I went there."

Mendez' sharp face held a dull hatred now. It was clear that he did not believe the man who had tried to trick him on the sloping path that led to the plantation shack. Jo Gar knew that he had lost much, in that attempt. But he also knew that from the beginning Mendez had determined to kill.

The Spaniard said in a toneless voice: "You are a fool, Gar. For years you have been lucky. But that was with Chinks and Island half-breeds. I will tell you something—because now it will not matter. Either you are lying—or two others are lying. On the *Cheyo Maru* were three persons who might have had the Von Loffler stones. The man you murdered was one of them. But the diamonds were not separated. One person had the ten of them. That was agreed upon. And you got one from the man you killed. Which means that you are lying. You got them all."

Jo Gar shook his head. "Only one," he said steadily. "How do you know the truth of what you say?"

Mendez smiled. "*I* was one of the three persons—aboard the *Cheyo Maru*," he said steadily. "I did not travel first-class. I did not have the diamonds. The man you killed had them—all ten of them. And you have them now. You are a fool—because they will do you no good."

The Island detective pulled his short body up a little. He said very slowly:

"There was—the third man—"

He watched Mendez' eyes narrow. But the Spaniard shook his head.

"I said that either you lie, or two others lie," Mendez said grimly. "I am one of those two others, and I do not lie. And the other one—she is—"

His body stiffened; for a second rage showed in his eyes. And then suddenly, as though he remembered that it would not matter, he relaxed. He smiled grimly. Jo Gar widened his almost colorless eyes.

"A woman—" he said very slowly. "There was a woman who—"

His own voice died away. Mendez smiled coldly. He lighted a cigarette.

"It makes no difference to you," he said. "You have killed one of the three who might have had the diamonds. I tell you that I was one of the three, and I did not have them. A woman was the other. *You* say you have one of the stones. *I* say you have them all."

Jo Gar said thickly: "Then why did I go to the shop of the blind Chinese?"

Mendez continued to smile. "That is simple," he replied. "Benfeld, who had told us much about the diamonds because he was in Holland when they were insured, and because he needed money which we gave him, was desperate when told that if he did not help us he would be exposed. He attempted to have you murdered, but he worked crudely, and you were suspicious. You avoided our guns—but you knew that there was a blind Chinese in Honolulu who was important. You were curious. You had the diamonds, but you wanted the thieves, the killers. And you were lucky—until you left Barrington."

The Island detective shook his head. Mendez was about to bargain with him, to make an offer—a final offer. He knew that. But Mendez would not bargain honestly. He could not. There had been three persons on the *Cheyo Maru*—three who were important. And one had been a woman. One was Mendez. The other was dead. Jo Gar had recovered one diamond—nine were missing. Yet he believed Mendez in one thing—the Spaniard was convinced that the man he had killed had possessed all of the diamonds, and that the Island detective had them now.

Jo Gar said slowly: "I tell you the truth, Mendez. Ten diamonds were stolen in Manila. I have recovered only one of them. I do not think the man I killed had more than that one. I believe you—you have none of them. The woman has tricked you into thinking—"

The Spaniard moved across the room and struck him heavily over the face. He stepped back, rage in his eyes. The Island detective pressed his lips tightly together. Mendez backed across the room. He took his gun from a pocket, stared at Jo. His eyes flickered to those of the Chinese, and he suddenly became thoughtful.

Jo Gar's tongue touched his lips and tasted blood. His brain was working clearly, in spite of the blow. He had something to work on now. Benfeld had given information that had led to the thieves tracing the diamonds, learning where they were. Three had got away from Manila aboard the *Cheyo Maru*, and one was a woman. He had not thought about a woman.

He muttered very softly: "It is *she*—who has the other nine stones. In some way—she got them, leaving the man in white only one—"

His muttering stopped as he watched Mendez' eyes slit on his. The Spaniard was smiling with his thin, straight lips—but his eyes held a cold hatred. He looked at Jo Gar, but he spoke to the Chinese.

"You tell driver—no need him. You take rifle and go where I show. Driver go back to Honolulu—keep quiet or it be bad. You stay with rifle ready. You know what I tell—much gold for you. Good?"

The Chinese rose and grinned. He said in the same doggerel manner:

"Good."

He showed red gums as he grinned at Jo Gar. Then he went from the plantation shack, closing the door back of him. Mendez waited several minutes, and then glanced through one of the windows that faced the east. The shack was almost atop a rise—the moonlight seemed brighter now.

Mendez said tonelessly: "For you—it will be a—red dawn, Señor Gar. One way or the other. If you tell me the truth—you will watch the sun come up from the path and go back to town. If you refuse to do that—you will go out of this room—and the Chinese with the rifle—"

He broke off, shrugged. Jo Gar said wearily:

"I have told you—the truth."

The Spaniard walked to within a few feet of him, stared down at him.

"One of Tan Ying's men tried to knife you tonight, Gar," he said slowly. "That was hate. He did *not* knife you because he was knifed first. I used him—to help me. Two hundred thousand dollars is more money than I need. Half of that is sufficient—for me. The other half—that is for you."

Jo Gar stared at the Spaniard. "And—the woman?" he said slowly.

He watched Mendez' facial muscles twitch. But the thin-faced one showed his teeth in a smile.

"I will—see to her," he said slowly, softly.

Jo Gar shook his head. "You could not—run the risk of allowing me to go free, Mendez," he said steadily. "If I gave you five diamonds—you would kill me—very swiftly."

Eagerness showed in the Spaniard's dark eyes. He took a step nearer Jo.

"I swear to it—by the name of—"

His words died; rage replaced the eagerness in his eyes. Jo Gar was shaking his head slowly. The Island detective said:

"I have recovered—only one stone."

Mendez reached down and struck him across the left temple with his right fist. Jo pulled himself up from the chair, but was battered down again by a sharp blow. He slumped low, groaning. Mendez moved away from his chair.

There was the sound of a match striking, and a little later Jo smelled the odor of a cigarette. He rocked his head from side to side, but did not look up. Mendez said grimly, harshly:

"You will have—until dawn. And then you will go outside—walking. The Chinese is less than fifty yards distant, with the rifle. I will remain inside until the sound of the shots has died. The Chinese will go away—after he has seen you fall. It is all—very simple."

Jo Gar raised his head slightly. He wiped red from his face with the back of his right hand.

"That will not get you—the Von Loffler—diamonds," he breathed thickly.

Mendez pulled on his cigarette, leaned against a wall of the plantation shack and smiled.

"If you go to your death—that way—I will believe you," he said. "Then I will know where to look. But she has never—"

Jo Gar tried a grim smile. "She has never—lied before?" he muttered. "Women are often—like that. There must be—the first time. And white glass—worth thousands—is a reason for—lies."

Mendez pressed his lips tightly together. "You've tricked—too many men, Señor Gar," he breathed. "I hate you for that—and I do not believe you. You have the diamonds—ten of them."

Jo Gar raised his eyes. Suddenly his body stiffened. He said weakly:

"I do not think—they are worth it. But five—that is too many—to give. I will—give you—three—"

Mendez dropped his cigarette and crushed it with his shoe sole. He took rapid steps to Jo's side. His eyes were shining.

"You will give—five!" he snapped.

The Island detective stared at him stupidly. But he shook his head from side to side. Mendez swore and struck at him savagely. The Island detective let his head fall low; he closed his eyes. Mendez struck him again, then moved across the room.

"By dawn," he muttered hoarsely, "you will give me—the five!"

Jo Gar said weakly, his eyes expressionless:

"And what proof have I—that you will let me go away from here—safely?"

Mendez shrugged his shoulders. He was confident of winning. He felt that Jo was breaking down; it had been a long night. Ten diamonds—perfect and of large carat. Two hundred thousand dollars! The Island detective could read his thoughts. He was so sure of winning, so sure the man in the chair before him possessed the diamonds.

And Jo was thinking of a woman—of the third of the three who had held up the Delgado jewelry store in Manila, and one of those responsible for the death of his friend Juan Arragon. She would be one of many women aboard the *Cheyo Maru*, which would leave Honolulu for San Francisco at noon—but he knew that *he* would not be aboard the boat that had brought him from Manila.

Mendez would see to that. The Mendez who stood before him now, mocking and battering him. The Mendez who was convinced that he had the ten Von Loffler diamonds, and who had already told him too much.

"Red dawn"—the Spaniard had said. There had been a mockery in those words, too. His lips shaped themselves into a bitter smile as he remembered the advice that Barrington had given him—advice to return to the *Cheyo Maru*.

Mendez said very slowly: "Well—there is an end to this, Gar. I will give you five minutes. The sun is getting up. I have much to do. If you swear to me—"

Jo Gar got unsteadily to his feet. Mendez regarded him with a twisted smile. The Island detective was unarmed and very weak. And once before tonight he had failed to surprise the Spaniard. Mendez said grimly:

"Steady—you are not accustomed to being—knocked around—"

The Island detective said thickly: "I do not want to die, Mendez. I will tell you the truth. But *you* must swear to *me*—that I will go free."

Mendez' eyes showed eagerness again. But the next second they had narrowed, and held a hard expression.

"I swear to you—that you will go free—if you tell me where the diamonds are."

Jo Gar nodded his head. He knew that no matter what he said he would not go free. He raised his head and looked Mendez squarely in the eyes with his bloodshot ones.

"I *did* get them—from the one—on the boat," he said steadily, softly. "I have had them—with me—*on* me. But in the car—it seemed very bad. I was—afraid. I had them in one of my Manila cigarette packages, mixed with a few cigarettes—"

He paused, swayed a little. Mendez stepped in very close to him. His voice was shaking.

"In your—cigarette package!" he breathed fiercely. "You had them—"

Jo Gar nodded as Mendez' voice died. He said weakly, brokenly:

"The Chinese—on my left. He had a sack-like coat. I slipped the cigarette package—in a pocket—his right pocket."

Mendez swore sharply. He muttered angrily:

"The Chinese—"

His body swung away from Jo Gar instinctively. His fingers clutched at the knob of the door that opened on the path. And then, suddenly, he remembered. There was the rifle.

His body started to turn, but even as he threw up his arms in protection, Jo Gar swung outward and downward with the chair he had lifted from the floor. All his remaining strength was in the swing. Wood crackled as Mendez' arms were battered downward—the bamboo was not heavy, but Jo had found power for his final chance.

The Spaniard's arms swung loosely—his head fell sideways under the impact of the blow. He staggered back from the door, his eyes staring. And in a swift movement Jo Gar had the door opened.

Mendez struck at him weakly—the Island detective had little power in the blow that caught the Spaniard on the right shoulder, spinning him around. But it knocked Mendez off balance—he plunged towards the opened door. He was almost to his knees as his body angled beyond the plantation shack.

The first shot crashed. There was a second—

and then two more. Jo Gar stood motionless, listened to two more shots from the repeating rifle. Then there was silence, and later a crashing in the foliage below the shack.

After a long minute the Island detective went outside and made certain that Mendez was dead. Then he went back into the room. It was all red with the rising sun. He sat in a chair for a few minutes. He got a package of Manila cigarettes from a pocket and lighted one. He thought of the woman a man who was now dead had spoken about. Five minutes later when he stepped over the body of Mendez to leave the plantation shack he did not look down. But as he went down the path towards the road he muttered thickly:

"He did not lie—about two things. The Chinese was waiting—with his rifle. And the dawn was—very—red."

Blue Glass

Ramon Decolta

Jo Gar, the little Island detective, finds that bullets often come with diamonds—when the diamonds are stolen ones.

HEN THE CABIN PHONE made a buzzing sound, Jo Gar was dozing. A soft, warm breeze blew in through the port; the *Cheyo Maru* was some seven hours away from the Hawaiian Islands—and Honolulu. The diminutive detective sat up wearily and turned his bruised face towards the French phone. When he spoke his words were low and precise:

"Yes—this is Señor Gar."

The voice at the other end of the wire was flat, almost expressionless. It was low and a bit throaty.

"You would give much, Señor—to recover the other nine Von Loffler diamonds?"

The questioning note was very faint, but the words had an immediate effect on Jo Gar. His small body stiffened; he sucked in his breath sharply. There was silence at the other end of the line. Jo said, finally:

"Yes—much."

There was another silence. Then the voice sounded again, with no more expression.

"How much, Señor Gar?"

The Philippine Island detective narrowed his

gray-blue, slightly almond-shaped eyes. He said very quietly:

"I do not appreciate jokes. Many aboard this boat are naturally aware of my identity. Quite a few men have died because of the Von Loffler stones. If you are—"

"I am not joking." For the first time there was some tone in the other's voice. "I have information that will be of value to you."

Jo Gar said steadily: "Then pardon me. If you will allow me to talk with you in your cabin—"

For the second time there was an interruption. The other's words were sharp now—very sharp.

"I have asked you a question, Señor Gar. I am aware of many things concerning the Von Loffler stones. Ten were stolen from the jewelry shop in Manila. You have recovered one. Your friend Juan Arragon has been murdered. You have killed—and others have killed. You believe that the nine missing stones are aboard this vessel, and that a woman has them in her possession. Is it not so?"

The Island detective closed his eyes. "It is as you say," he said simply. His mind was working very fast; his head was clear enough.

The voice continued: "You very narrowly escaped death more than once—in Honolulu, Señor Gar. The missing stones are worth almost two hundred thousand dollars. I can tell you that the one who carried out the orders of Benfeld, and who was responsible for murders that included your friend Arragon—that person is aboard the *Cheyo Maru*."

There was a pause. The voice said: "Speak, please, Señor Gar."

Jo Gar smiled with a touch of grimness. "I am still in my cabin, Señor," he replied.

The other said: "That is wise. You will be wiser not to attempt tracing this call. It will prove useless."

The Island detective said: "Perhaps that is so."

There was a short silence. Then the other said in the same, flat voice:

"You would be well rewarded if you were to return to Manila with the missing stones, and the murderer, Señor Gar. There would be rest for you. That is why I ask the amount you would be willing to pay."

Jo Gar said slowly: "I am a poor man."

The other's voice became sharp again. "You have been fortunate, Señor Gar. In the States it will be different. And the diamonds will not be difficult to sell."

The Island detective's voice held a grim note. "They are very fine stones, and perfectly matched. By this time they are very well known. Perhaps they would be extremely difficult to sell."

Impatience was evident in the voice that came from the other end of the wire.

"You are not a fool—you know the stones will not be difficult to dispose of, Señor Gar. You know they will be smuggled through the customs officers. And in San Francisco you will lose the trail you were lucky enough to pick up. Even if you should blunder on—"

The voice died. Jo Gar said grimly: "All this being so, why do you call me?"

The voice said: "I do not care what becomes of the nine diamonds, or of a certain murderer. I need money. I call you to give you the chance, the big chance. You have traveled many miles, Señor Gar."

The Island detective spoke in a low voice. "How do I know that you will direct me to the right person?"

The voice held a hard note. "I do not expect you to trust me, señor. You may pay after you are convinced."

The Island detective was silent. The other said:

"The question is—how *much* will you pay?"

Jo Gar replied steadily: "There is a reward of ten thousand dollars offered by the owner of the Manila jewelry shop, whose son was killed. I imagine the insurance company would pay twenty thousand dollars for the return of the stones."

"No—that will not do." The other's voice was steady. "That is all in the future. I must have payment now. If I do not have it—the murderer and the diamonds will vanish when the *Cheyo Maru* arrives at San Francisco. That is all."

Jo Gar spoke gently into the French phone mouthpiece. His eyes were almost closed.

"I do not carry thousands of dollars about with me. I am a poor man."

The voice said calmly: "You are known to the captain of the boat. I am not asking much. Five thousand dollars, and one half of your reward, when you receive it, Señor Gar. And I am not to be betrayed."

Jo Gar widened his eyes and smiled. "You are only to betray," he said grimly.

The other's voice was very low and hard. "That is—quite so," he said. "You agree?"

The Island detective stopped smiling. "I agree," he said simply. "I will pay five thousand dollars to you, in the manner you direct, after the stones are recovered and the murderer is under arrest. I will give you half of my reward when it is paid. I am very tired. Your identity will not be known, only to me."

"No," the other said. "It will not be known to you. I will trust you. If you do not pay, I will kill you. That will be very simple, since you will not know against whom to guard."

Jo Gar said tonelessly: "Yes—very simple."

There was a short pause. The other's voice was very flat when it reached Jo's ear again.

"In Cabin C. 15 there was a woman named Jetmars. She has with her a little girl of about eight. She got aboard at Manila, and dresses in black most of the time. Possibly you have seen her."

The Island detective said steadily: "Yes—I have noticed her, and the little girl."

The voice said: "In her cabin or on her person, or on the person of the little girl—are the diamonds. When you have obtained them I will communicate again with you. I will know the time."

Jo Gar said. "And she is also a murderess?"

The voice replied flatly: "Yes."

There was a clicking sound, and when Jo spoke again there was no answer. He hung up the receiver, threw a light robe about him and hurried from the cabin. When he reached the small cabin that held the *Cheyo Maru* switchboard, he was breathing swiftly. A Chinese boy stared at him with dark, long eyes.

"I am Señor Gar," Jo said softly. "An important call just reached me in Cabin B. 10. I would like very much to know where it came from— what part of the boat."

The Chinese boy said easily: "I remember making the connection. It came from one of the three phones in the men's smoking room."

The Island detective smiled a little wearily.

"Thank you," he said, and moved back towards his cabin. Inside, he removed his robe, lighted a brown-paper cigarette and lay flat on his back, blowing thin streams of smoke towards the cabin ceiling. There was very little motion to the boat.

"Curious," Jo murmured. "A woman who dresses in black. A little girl. And the one who gives me the name tells me the woman is a killer and possesses the stones. He would share a large reward with me, and he will kill me if I refuse to pay his share. He is very careful—"

The Island detective sat up slowly as the phone made a buzzing sound again.

"Señor Gar," he said.

The flat voice came clearly. "I told you it would be useless to attempt tracing the call, Señor. You have made a bargain. If you do not stick to it—"

Jo Gar said grimly: "You will kill me?"

The other replied: "Yes."

The Island detective was silent for a few seconds. Then he said:

"In that case you will be able to collect the diamonds and the reward. You will not have to share anything."

There was a tight-lipped smile on his face as he spoke. But the one at the other end of the wire said sharply:

"It is simpler for you to do—than for me. That is why I made an offer."

Jo Gar inhaled smoke from his cigarette. "Look about the smoking room," he suggested.

"Is there a short man present—rather heavy? Smoking a cigar—very black?"

The man at the other end of the phone chuckled. It was a dry, rasping chuckle.

"Thinking that such a person might be present, I am not making *this* call from the smoking room," he said almost pleasantly. The switchboard boy will tell you I am calling from the sun deck, port side."

Jo Gar said: "Pardon—I shall make no further effort to learn your identity."

The other chuckled again. "Thank you, Señor," he mocked. "But even should you change your mind—it will be of no use. A pleasant trip—and good fortune."

Again there was the clicking sound. Jo Gar went away from the cabin phone, frowning.

"I think the gentleman is a liar," he muttered very softly, "but I can not afford to simply think. As for this being a pleasant trip—"

He squeezed the brown paper of the cigarette with stubby fingers, raised his narrow shoulders very slowly in a half shrug.

"He is too wise for that," he said with finality. "It will be extremely unpleasant—for *one* of us."

On the third day out the *Cheyo Maru* was rolling a bit; spray was breaking over the prow and there were not too many passengers on the decks. Jo Gar stood near the starboard rail, well aft, and watched the woman in black and the little girl who accompanied her. The woman was middle-aged, had a rather sharp, sunburned face. The child was not very pretty. She was stringing beads. The woman paid little attention to her, and none to the other passengers. Jo had been watching her closely for two days, and yet he had not appeared to be watching. And he had listened to many voices of men, hearing none like the one that had come over the phone. He had not expected that.

He was working under a handicap; he felt that he was being watched and he did not know the person who watched him. He had learned that the woman who wore black much of the time was

named Rosa Jetmars, that she had come aboard at Manila and that the child was her daughter. The purser volunteered the information that he understood Mrs. Jetmars was Spanish, had married an American in the Islands. Her husband had died very recently. His body was not aboard the vessel, but it was thought that his widow was going to the States and his family. That was all the Island detective had learned. It had little to do with the nine missing diamonds.

Someone near the rail called attention to a school of flying fish. It was a large one; the little girl jumped from her deck chair, started towards the rail. She tripped, fell awkwardly, crying out. Beads scattered and rolled across the deck. Jo Gar started forward, but an elderly man had already lifted the girl. Something blue rolled and struck against Jo's right shoe. The woman in black was bending over the girl. She seemed angry. She spoke in Spanish and very rapidly. Her back was turned to Jo.

He leaned down and picked up the bead. It was peculiarly cut, for a bead—touch told him that instantly. He glanced at it, his eyes narrowing. Several men were picking up other beads from the deck surface—much fuss was being made over the child. The woman in black had taken her back to her chair, was talking rapidly to her. Jo Gar slipped the bead in his pocket and stared at the vanishing school of flying fish.

When he glanced towards the woman in black again she was still talking to the child. Men were putting beads in the girl's lap. There was laughter now, and the woman in black did not seem so angry. After a few minutes Jo Gar went below, locked his cabin door and got the one Von Loffler diamond from its tiny pocket in the cork of one of his medicine bottles.

He compared it with the bead, which was blue. His lips parted and he said very softly:

"The cutting is—exactly the same!"

An hour later, in the captain's cabin, he had the diamond expert who had helped him earlier in the trip examine the bead. When the expert had finished his examination he said in a puzzled voice:

"It is exceptionally well cut—diamond cut. Nothing cheap about the cutting. A great deal of care has been taken—for a piece of blue glass."

Jo Gar said slowly: "There is no doubt but what it is glass?"

The expert smiled at him. "Not a bit—it is blue glass, cut as a fine diamond might be. A good-sized diamond. Like, say, one of the Von Loffler stones you—"

Jo Gar's frown stopped him. The captain raised his head and stared at Jo. But the Island detective simply reached for the bead, slipped it into a pocket of his light suiting. He reached for his packet of cigarettes.

The captain of the Japanese liner said in his stiff English:

"It is very curious, Señor Gar—"

The Island detective showed his white teeth in a lazy smile. He nodded his head very slowly.

"Very curious," he agreed cheerfully. "But many curious facts are not too important."

The captain said: "It will not be very long before we dock in San Francisco, Señor. It has been an exciting voyage for you, and not very successful. One diamond recovered—and nine still missing."

Jo Gar offered cigarettes, lighted one. The diamond expert spoke.

"But he has this bit of blue glass—it may be that it is important."

The Island detective smiled. "In what way?" he asked.

The two others looked at each other. The captain shrugged, smiled. The diamond expert muttered to himself. The captain said:

"Each of us has our profession—yours is a difficult one, Señor Gar."

The Island detective grinned. "Often I am given unexpected help," he said. "Perhaps it will be that way—before we land."

He went towards the door of the captain's cabin, still smiling. But when he had bowed to the two men and was outside, his smile faded. He went without too much haste to his cabin, and had been inside only a few minutes when the phone buzzed. The flat voice said:

"I have additional information for you, Señor. The diamonds are to be smuggled through the customs as the child's beads. Perhaps they will be dipped in ink, or painted blue."

Jo Gar said evenly: "Thank you. But the diamonds have no holes in them—how can they be strung?"

There was slight impatience in the other's tone.

"Perhaps there will be some beads cut somewhat like the diamonds, in a box the child has. Some will be strung, but others will not be strung. It is not likely the customs officers will examine each bead in the box."

Jo Gar was smiling grimly, but his voice was serious.

"That is so. It is a clever idea."

The other's voice said: "But do not work too fast, Señor. I do not think the child has the diamonds, at present."

The clicking sound followed. Jo hung up and looked out of the port, at the roughening water. He thought: Nor do *I* think the child has them at the present moment. The woman in black was not much concerned about the spilled beads, when the girl fell on the deck. If I were to get into the cabin occupied by the woman and child, find a box of beads—I would probably find no diamonds. And yet, if I wait until the customs inspection is made—

He turned away from the port, frowning. He breathed softly:

"This one who calls—he knows so much. And yet he would share much with me. He would lose a great deal of money by doing that. The whole reward would be his if he did not—"

He broke off, and his gray-blue eyes got very small and long. After a short time he inspected his Colt automatic, slipped it into a pocket of his light coat, stuffing a handkerchief over it. When he reached deck he walked slowly towards the bow, conscious, as usual, of the curious glances the passengers directed towards him.

He circled the deck twice; the second time he noted that the woman in black and the child had vacated their chairs. A middle-aged man approached, walking unsteadily as the boat rolled. He looked at Jo, but there was no expression in his blue eyes. He had flabby, pale skin and very thin lips. They were almost opposite each other when the boat rolled more sharply. The Island detective let his small body strike the left side of the thin-lipped one, knocking him off balance.

"Pardon," Jo said. "I'm very—sorry."

He stood close to the other man, watched anger show in the blue eyes. More than anger showed, he thought. It was as though the thin-lipped one hated him fiercely, and had hated him for more than seconds.

"It was very careless of me," Jo said.

The other man's lips parted. He started to speak, but did not. A faint smile showed in his eyes; slowly his face twisted with it. He jerked his head downward abruptly, in an awkward bow. He shrugged, moved away from the Island detective.

Jo Gar continued his walk around the deck. But he did not meet the thin-lipped one on the starboard side. He did not see him again in the next half hour, and when he did locate the man he was in the smoking room, seated at a small table and with his back turned to the entrance from the port side of the deck.

A steward strolled along and smiled amiably at Jo. He beckoned to him, handed him a dollar bill. He designated the chair occupied by the thin-lipped one.

"That gentleman I seem to know," he said. "I should like you to go to the far end of the smoking room, then turn and come back. You will be able to see him. I should like to know his name. You are the deck steward?"

The steward nodded. He went into the smoking room and Jo Gar went to the port rail. When the steward returned he was smiling cheerfully.

"I placed his chair for him," he said. "He is a Mr. Tracy. He came aboard at Honolulu."

Jo nodded. "Thank you," he said. "It is not the one with whom I am acquainted."

He did a few more turns on the deck, his face expressionless. Then he went below and talked to the purser. Mr. Eugene Tracy occupied Cabin C. 82. He had booked passage at the last moment and had been forced to take a cabin on the lower deck, though he had wanted better quarters.

Jo Gar went up above and saw that the thin-lipped one was still in the smoking room. He was reading a magazine, and was slumped low in a comfortable chair. The Island detective moved close to the chair, very quietly. No other person was near the two of them; Jo spoke sharply but low, his voice holding a faint questioning note.

"Mr. Tracy?"

His words were very clear, but the one in the chair did not move. Jo stepped directly in front of the chair and looked down at the magazine that hid the thin-lipped one's face.

"Mr. Tracy?" he said again.

The man in the chair lowered his magazine. He looked at the Island detective with his blue eyes wide and questioning. Jo stared at him stupidly, shook his head.

"I'm sorry—again," he stated. "It is another Mr. Tracy I'm looking for—and they pointed you out. Please pardon me."

The one in the chair smiled almost pleasantly. He nodded his head, raised his magazine. Jo said very quietly:

"Have you the time, by any chance?"

Anger edged into the eyes of the man in the chair. Then the forced smile showed again. He shook his head. Jo bowed and moved away. As he went towards his cabin there was a half smile on his browned face. He was thinking that the thin-lipped one was a very silent person.

 fter dinner Jo Gar watched the thin-lipped man take the same chair he had occupied hours before, in the smoking room. The Island detective went to his cabin and changed from his dinner clothes to a dark, lightweight suiting. He wore a dark-colored shirt and was knotting a black bow tie when there was a knock at the cabin door. At his call a tall, slender man entered, closing the door carefully behind him.

"The captain said you had something for me to do," he said cheerfully. "My name's Porter—I'm an American and traveling to Frisco from Honolulu through courtesy of the line. I do ship news for a San Diego paper, and this is sort of a vacation."

Jo Gar nodded. "It is very simple," he said. "In the smoking room at present there is a man named Tracy. I will go up with you and point him out. I would like you to stay as close to him as is possible, for the next few hours, and to remember what he does. That is all. I shall be glad to pay—"

Porter smiled, shaking his head. "Not necessary, Señor Gar," he interrupted. "I'm glad to help out. And I won't talk."

Jo Gar smiled back at the newspaper man. "You would be very foolish if you did," he said. "There wouldn't be anything to talk about."

They went on deck and after walking several times around it, Jo pointed out the thin-lipped man. There was a vacant chair near him; Porter said he would go in and use it. Jo nodded.

"Do not come to me and do not speak to me if we meet later. I will speak first to you."

The newspaper man went into the smoking room. Jo passed the woman in black and the child, on the way to his cabin. The boat was rolling quite a bit and the woman looked sick and tired. She wore no jewelry and she paid little attention to the child, who trailed along behind her.

When he reached the cabin his phone was making a buzz sound. Jo Gar closed the door behind him, locked it. He lifted the instrument, said slowly:

"This is Señor Gar."

The voice was flat and low. It said: "Mrs. Jetmars is having the child attract attention to itself. She is letting passengers see that the child has an interest in beads."

Jo Gar said nothing. The voice continued:

"I point this out to you, because perhaps you do not believe she has the diamonds for which you are searching."

The Island detective said with his almond-shaped eyes almost closed:

"Perhaps it would be wise for me to enter her cabin, with the ship's captain, while she is absent. A thorough search—"

"I do not think it would be wise," the voice cut in. "But that is up to you, of course."

There was the clicking sound. Jo hung up and went to the ship switchboard room again. When he had asked the question the operator smiled cheerfully.

"The call came from Cabin C. 80," he stated. "I have been paying attention to the calls since you first asked me—"

He had been looking at a small book as he was speaking. His voice died abruptly; he widened his dark eyes on Jo Gar's expressionless ones.

"Cabin C. 80 is vacant," he said stiffly. "It is one of the poorest cabins on the ship."

The Island detective nodded his head. "The doors of vacant cabins are not always locked, are they?" he asked.

The switchboard boy narrowed his eyes. "No, Señor Gar," he replied. "They are left half-opened, for ventilation."

Jo Gar moved towards the main saloon, frowning. Too many persons aboard the boat knew too much about him; even the Chinese boy at the switchboard was now addressing him by his name. He murmured to himself:

"It becomes—always more difficult."

In the smoking room the thin-lipped one was seated in the chair he had occupied before, still reading his magazine. The newspaper man was sprawled in a chair that faced the port-side entrance to the room. Jo Gar beckoned to him, watched him rise slowly, stroll towards the entrance. The Island detective walked slowly aft, and Porter followed in the same fashion. Behind a ventilator Jo halted and lighted a cigarette. Porter reached his side.

"Well?" The Island detective's voice was very low.

Peter grinned. "You didn't expect him to move around much in *that* length of time, did you?" he replied. "He only turned two pages of the magazine."

Jo said steadily: "He never left the chair?"

Porter grunted. "All he moved was his fingers," he replied.

Jo sighed heavily. Then he showed white teeth in a slow smile.

"You have been very kind—and I shall not need your help for the present, Señor Porter."

The newspaper man looked surprised. "He wasn't the right guy, maybe?"

The Island detective made the tip of his cigarette glow in the semidarkness.

"After I left you I went to my cabin. I received a phone call that I half expected. But I expected, also, that the gentleman you were watching would *make* the call."

Porter whistled softly. "He didn't," he said. "That's sure enough. He stuck right in his chair."

Jo Gar nodded. Porter said slowly: "I'm sorry it didn't work out the other way—the way you expected, Señor Gar."

The Island detective smiled with his lips tight against the paper of the cigarette. He stood with his short legs spread, swaying with the roll of the ship. He had picked the thin-lipped passenger as the one who had called him, using the flat, peculiar tone. He had listened to most of the others talk—those who had come aboard at Honolulu.

The others he had heard before; it had been a long trip from Manila. And the thin-lipped one had failed to answer quickly, naturally to the name of Tracy. He had not spoken to Jo—had not answered his question about the time. It was difficult to disguise a voice, and Jo felt that the thin-lipped one had not made the effort. Thus he had not spoken when addressed. And yet, there had been the phone call just received—and the thin-lipped one had not made it.

Jo frowned down at the cigarette glow. Then, suddenly, his small body straightened; he drew a deep breath. Porter was watching him closely.

"You got an idea—that time," he muttered.

The Island detective narrowed his eyes on Porter's.

He spoke very slowly and softly, and his eyes held little expression.

"That is so, Señor Porter—but it is so difficult to tell whether it is a *good* idea."

The newspaper man said grimly: "If it isn't—you'll probably find out quick enough."

Jo Gar smiled narrowly. "That is the trouble," he said simply.

The door of Cabin C. 82 was tightly closed, locked. Jo Gar took from his pocket the small, adjustable key, worked with it swiftly and expertly. It was after nine o'clock, but the thin-lipped man was still seated in his chair in the smoking room. The cabin steward for this section of the *Cheyo Maru* was on the opposite side of the boat; Jo had come to Cabin C. 82 slowly and carefully.

When the lock made a faint clicking sound he returned the master key to his pocket, moved the knob and slowly opened the door. He stepped inside quickly, shut the door without sound but did not lock it from the inside. The cabin was small and held the odor of cigarettes. There was little baggage about, but what there was bore the initials E. T. Jo Gar smiled a little, went towards cool-colored curtains that formed a protection for hung clothes. There was only a coat of gray material hanging behind the curtains.

"Señor Tracy is traveling very lightly," Jo observed in a half whisper.

He got his small body back of the curtains, arranging them so that he had a slitted view of the room, where they met. For several minutes he remained motionless. Then he stepped from behind the curtains and started the search. He worked very slowly and thoroughly, placing each object that he touched in the same spot from which he had raised it. Twice there was sound in the corridor, but neither time did he lock the cabin door. Instead, he got his diminutive body behind the curtains that faced the door from the opposite end of the cabin, waited.

He finished his search in a little over ten minutes, straightened and sighed. The phone made a buzzing sound, three times. Jo got his right-hand fingers over the grip of his Colt, moved behind the curtains and was motionless. Several minutes passed, and then there were footfalls in the narrow corridor beyond the cabin. A key turned in the lock—there was muttering. The door opened with a small crashing sound, but the thin-lipped one did not immediately enter. He stood in the doorway—his eyes going about the room. Through the very thin slit where the curtains met Jo Gar watched him.

His body relaxed suddenly; he entered the cabin, closed the door behind him, locked it. His eyes kept moving about. He lifted the smaller of the bags, opened it, looked inside. When he placed it on the floor again he was frowning. But the frown became a grin—a slow grin that twisted his thin lips.

"He's been in here," he said in a peculiar, flat voice. "A lot of good *that* did him!"

Jo Gar half closed his almond-shaped eyes. This *was* the one who had called him; he knew that now. He moved the muzzle of the Colt slightly, so that it was pointed towards the body of the thin-lipped one.

After he had drawn a small curtain across the port, the thin-lipped man placed a towel over the knob of the door, draping it so that it covered the keyhole. Then he seated himself at a small table beneath the center light, and faced the port. His left side was turned towards Jo. From a vest pocket he took a red-colored, large-sized fountain pen. His face was grim as he unscrewed an end of it. The table at which he sat had a green surface; the thin-lipped one spilled the diamonds across it very carefully. He chuckled, staring at them and poking them with a long, white finger.

Jo Gar straightened his cramped body a little. He drew the Colt from his pocket, extended it through the slit in the curtains. His eyes could count five diamonds—he thought there was another on the table surface but he could not see it.

"A hundred—thousand!" The thin-lipped one's voice was not so flat now. "And with Gar chasing the Jetmars woman—"

He chuckled again, huskily. Jo Gar said in a cold, hard voice:

"—you might easily have got the stones through the customs—"

The man at the table jerked his body straight.

His right-hand palm flattened over the diamonds; his white face turned towards the curtains. Jo parted them with his left hand, stepped away from them. His face was expressionless. He held the Colt very firmly.

"But you weren't so wise," Jo said calmly and softly. "You don't know how much I knew, how much I had been told. So you thought I might be watching you, rather than the woman in black. You didn't know that Mendez had told me a woman had the Von Loffler diamonds. You called me, after she had given you the diamonds, afraid of me. The two of you gave the child beads of blue glass, cut very much like the Von Loffler stones. You wanted me to *believe* what you had suggested—that the woman in black was smuggling the stones through the customs—so that *you* could get them through without trouble. But you played too strongly."

The thin-lipped man was staring at him, breathing slowly and heavily. His right palm was still flat over the diamonds; his left arm rested on the table. The ship rolled and his body swayed with it. Jo Gar said:

"You didn't disguise your voice—and you couldn't speak to me when I addressed you, for fear of detection. That worried you. You knew you were being watched by Porter, and you had a confederate call me while *you* were seated in the smoking room. You had worked well with him, but his voice was not exactly like yours. Even so, for a little time I thought that you were not the one who had called me. And then I realized what you had tried to do—to make me believe that very thing. And I knew that you *were* the one. So I came here—for the diamonds—nine of them."

There was a little silence. The thin-lipped man said in a harsh, strained tone:

"You got to Jetmars—you scared her and—she squealed."

The Island detective shook his head. "I haven't spoken a word to her," he said steadily. "You were too worried about yourself—and too greedy. You betrayed yourself."

The thin-lipped one took his palm away from the diamonds. Jo Gar said softly:

"Please keep both arms—on the table. How many stones—are there?"

The one at the table did not speak. Jo Gar moved the gun muzzle sharply.

"Many men have died because of the stones," he reminded. "One more thief—one murderer—it would not matter too much. How many stones—have you?"

The thin-lipped one said huskily, the peculiar flat note barely evident:

"Five—the woman has—the others. Three of them. *You* have one, Gar."

There was hatred in his voice as he used the Island detective's name. Jo said softly:

"I would not lie—where are the other three stones?"

The thin-lipped one said savagely: "I tell you—the woman in black—she has them. She would not give them all to me. She is the one who—"

The Island detective smiled coldly. His gray-blue eyes were almost closed.

"Raise your arms," he said slowly, "Keep them raised. If you do not—"

He made a swift—strangely swift movement for him, as the thin-lipped one obeyed. When he stepped away from the man at the table there were five diamonds in his left palm. They felt warm and very good. He said steadily:

"We will stay here until a certain diamond expert comes to the cabin, with the captain. When the stones have been inspected we will go to the woman in black. We will obtain the other three stones."

The lips of the man at the table were tightly pressed and thinner than ever. He parted them suddenly.

"It is she who—"

The phone buzzed. Jo Gar moved towards it, but did not take his eyes from the figure of the man in the chair. He spoke into the mouthpiece, as he slipped the diamonds into a pocket.

"Señor Gar—"

Porter's voice said: "Did the buzz catch you in time? He went from the smoking room pretty fast."

The Island detective kept his eyes on the thin-lipped one. He said:

"Yes—it reached me in time. I was prepared for Mr. Tracy. Will you please call the captain and tell him—"

His words died as the thin-lipped one hurled himself from the chair, slashing his right arm at the Colt. Jo squeezed the trigger of the gun as it was battered to one side. There was a crashing sound, and then the thin-lipped one's fingers were on his throat; his white face was close to Jo's.

He muttered hoarse, distorted words as his fingers tightened their grip. He was strong; the swinging arms of the detective failed to hurt him. Already Jo's breath was coming in short gasps; his efforts to get free of the man's grip were growing weaker.

His head was pulled close to the thin-lipped one's body; there was a mist in his eyes. Blackness was coming now; he was choking terribly. He felt his body swung to one side; his head was battered against the wall of the cabin. And then, once again, the room was filled with a crashing sound. The strangler's body jerked; he cried out hoarsely. His fingers went away from Jo's throat; he swung gropingly towards the cabin door. Jo stared towards it, his vision clearing. It was half opened.

Voices reached him faintly from the corridor; they grew louder. The thin-lipped one was down on his knees now; he sprawled at full length, his left-hand fingers pawing at the small of his back. Then, very suddenly, he was motionless.

Jo Gar stared towards the half-opened door. He breathed hoarsely, sucking in deep breaths of air:

"He would have killed me—and yet—he was murdered—the woman in black—"

He couldn't be sure, but he thought his eyes had seen dark color, just after the shot had crashed. And if the woman in black had thought that the thin-lipped one had said too much, if she had overheard, following him to his cabin—

Porter's voice was calling from the corridor:
"Señor Gar—Señor Gar!"

There were heavier footfalls now. Gar tapped

the pocket into which he had slipped the diamonds. He was sure they were real. Five of them, and there was the one he already had recovered. Six stones—with three still missing. And the one who could have told many things—he was dead.

The Island detective knew that, even before he bent over the man, calling hoarsely:

"Yes—Porter—it is—all right—"

Porter came into the room, pulling up short at the sight of the man on the floor.

"Heard the crash sound—over the phone—" he muttered.

Jo Gar straightened and smiled a little. "I was forced to shoot," he said more clearly. "But he got me by the throat—"

Ship's officers were inside the room now. The second officer stared at the figure on the floor, then at Jo.

"You shot him?" he breathed. "You had to shoot him, Señor—"

Jo Gar shook his head. Porter leaned down suddenly and lifted something from the floor near the doorway. The Island detective said:

"He had five of the Von Loffler diamonds—I've got them now. I tried to shoot him, but I failed. He was shot in the back, from the corridor."

The second officer drew in a sharp breath. "You saw who it—"

Jo Gar shook his head. "I saw nothing," he said very slowly. He was sure that he had seen black color—the color of a woman's dress. "He was choking me—"

The newspaperman extended a palm. "What's this?" he muttered. "Just picked it up near the doorway."

Jo looked at the bead in Porter's palm. He shook his head very slowly.

"It looks very much," he said huskily but with little tone, "like a bit of blue glass."

Diamonds of Death

Ramon Decolta

Jo Gar, the little Island detective, collects.

THE ROOM WAS IN A cheap hotel, a few blocks from Market Street. The room had two windows, one of which faced the Bay. Jo Gar, his small body sprawled on the narrow bed, shivered a little. San Francisco was cold; he thought of the warm winds of Manila and the difference of the bays. He sighed and said softly to himself:

"Four diamonds—if I had them I could return to the Islands. I do not belong away from them—"

The telephone bell on the wall jangled; Jo Gar stared towards the apparatus for several seconds, then rose slowly. He was dressed in a gray suit that did not fit him too well, and his graying hair was mussed. He unhooked the receiver and said:

"Yes."

A pleasant voice said: "Inspector Raines, of the customs office. I have information for you."

Jo Gar said: "That is good—please come up."

He hung up the receiver and stood for several seconds looking towards the door. One of his three bags had been opened, the other two he had not unlocked. The *Cheyo Maru*, bringing him from Honolulu, had arrived three hours ago, and there had been much for the Island detective to do. In the doing of it he had gained little. Perhaps, he thought, Inspector Raines had done better.

He took from one of his few remaining packages a brown-paper cigarette, lighted it. His gray-blue eyes held a faint smile as he inhaled. Down the hall beyond the room there was the slam of the elevator's door, and foot-falls. A man cleared his throat noisily. Jo Gar put his right hand in the pocket of his gray suit at his right side, went over and seated himself on the edge of the bed, facing the door. A knock sounded and the Philippine Island detective called flatly:

"Please—come in."

The door opened. A middle-aged man entered, dressed in a dark suit with a light coat thrown across his shoulders. The sleeves of the man's suit were not within the coat sleeves; it was worn as a cape. Raines had sharp features, pleasant blue eyes. His lips were thick; he was a big man. He said:

"Hello, Señor Gar."

Jo Gar rose and they shook hands. Raines' grip was loose and careless; he looked about the room, tossed a soft, gray hat on a chair. Jo Gar motioned towards the other chair in the room, and the inspector seated himself. He kept the coat slung across his shoulders.

Jo Gar said slowly, almost lazily:

"Something was found?"

The inspector frowned and shook his head. He took from his pocket a small card. His picture was at one corner of the card, which was quite soiled. There was the printing of the Customs Department, some insignia that Gar merely glanced at, a stamped seal—and the statement that Albert Raines was a member of the San Francisco customs office.

Raines said: "The chief thought I'd better show you that right away, as we hadn't seen each other."

The Island detective smiled. "Thank you," he replied, and handed the card back. "Something was found?"

Raines shook his head. "Not a thing," he said.

"We held her up for two hours, and we searched everything carefully. We even searched the child—the child's baggage. We gave her a pretty careful questioning. For that matter—everybody on the boat got about three times the attention we usually give. And we didn't turn up a stone."

Jo Gar sighed. Raines said grimly: "If the diamonds were on that boat—they got past us. And that means you're in a tough spot, yes?"

The Island detective said: "I think that is very much—what it means."

Raines said in a more cheerful tone: "Well, the chief said you recovered six of the stones, between Manila and San Francisco—that's not at all bad."

Jo Gar smiled gently: "I was—extremely fortunate," he said. "But the woman in black—I had hopes that the four diamonds—"

Raines said quickly: "So had we. When we got your coded wire telling us that you suspected her of the murder of the man you recovered five stones from, but that you couldn't prove a thing against her, we figured we might be able to help. We weren't. But we did as you requested—when she left the dock we had a man follow her."

The Island detective said: "Good—she went to a hotel?"

Raines shook his head. "Don't suppose you've ever been out around the Cliff House, Señor Gar. It's a spot out on a bunch of jagged rocks, about an hour from town. A sort of amusement park has grown up around it. Seals fool around in the rocks and the tourists go for it strong. The woman took a cab, and our man took another. She went to the amusement park near the Cliff House."

Jo Gar's gray-blue eyes widened slightly.

"She spent more than three weeks on the *Cheyo Maru*," he breathed slowly. "And when she landed and had been cleared after an exhaustive customs examination, she went to an amusement park. Strange."

Raines made a grunting sound. "Damn' strange," he said. "Took all the baggage, which included a trunk we'd gone very carefully through. And the child."

Jo Gar narrowed his eyes and looked beyond the inspector. He said quietly:

"In Manila we have an amusement park that is quite large. After entering the main gate there are many places one can go."

Raines nodded. "It's like that here. Only this park has several entrances, and you can drive through a section of it. The cab went in one entrance, stopped for a while near a merry-go-round—went out another. Then it went to a house and stopped. The luggage was taken inside, and the woman and child went in. Our man stayed around a short time, but nothing else happened."

The Island detective said: "You have the address?"

Raines nodded. He took from his pocket a small slip of paper, on which were scrawled some words, handed it to Jo Gar.

The Island detective read: " 'One hundred and forty-one West Pacific Avenue.' "

Raines nodded. "That's it—Cary said it was a frame house, set back a short distance from the road. The section isn't much built up out there."

Jo Gar nodded. "It is very good of you to bring me this information," he stated.

Raines made a swift gesture with both hands. "That's all right," he said. "Cary has another job just now, or he'd have come along to tell you about it. Looks queer to me."

The Island detective spoke slowly. "It is not *necessary* to drive through the amusement park, in order to reach this address?" he asked.

Raines said: "Hell, no—that's what seems funny. That woman was trying to hide where she was going. Maybe she figured she *might* be followed."

Jo Gar nodded. "I think you are right," he said.

Raines got to his feet, held out his right hand.

"Sorry the office couldn't get something on her at the pier," he apologized. "But you know where she is—and you know she acted funny getting there."

Jo Gar smiled and shook the inspector's hand. He sat down on the bed again as Raines took his hat. When Raines reached the door, he said:

"Luck on those other four." He grinned and went out. Going along the corridor he whistled. The elevator door slammed.

Jo Gar got to his feet with remarkable speed for him. He got his coat and hat, was out of the room quickly. He used the stairs instead of the elevator. When he reached the small lobby he saw Raines light a cigar, go outside and raise a hand. A cab pulled close to the curb. When it started away the Island detective hailed another parked some feet from the hotel entrance. He said to the driver:

"Follow that machine, please—but do not move too close to it. When it halts, halt some distance away."

The driver looked at Jo curiously but nodded his head. The two cabs moved from one street to another. There was a great deal of traffic, but Jo's driver was skillful. For perhaps ten minutes the two cabs moved through the city, apparently keeping in the heart of it. Finally the leading cab curved close to a building that had a large clock set in granite stone. It halted. Unfamiliar as Jo was with San Francisco, he recognized the building as a railroad station of considerable importance. There were many porters about, and cabs were everywhere.

As his own cab pulled close to the curb Jo watched Raines alight and pay his driver. The inspector hurried into the station, and when he was out of sight Jo paid up and left his cab. He pulled his hat low over his eyes, straightened his small body a little, went into the station. Almost instantly he saw Raines. The man was at a luggage checking counter; as Jo watched from a safe distance he saw Raines handed two large-sized valises. A porter picked them up; Raines gestured towards another clock inside the station and said something. The porter hurried away, followed by the inspector.

Jo Gar followed, being careful not to be seen. When Raines and his porter went through a train gate, the Island detective halted near it, a peculiar smile on his face. After a few minutes the colored porter came back through the gate. Jo beckoned to him.

"The gentleman whose luggage you just carried to the train—I think he was a friend of mine. You saw his ticket?"

The porter shook his head slowly: "He tol' me his car and seat number—didn't show no ticket," he replied.

Jo Gar frowned. "How did you know what train to take him to?" he asked slowly.

The porter grinned. "That's right," he said. "He wanted the Chicago train."

The Island detective drew a sharp breath. He handed the porter a quarter, walked slowly back into the station's waiting room.

"Mr. Raines had barely time to make his train," he breathed softly. "Yet he was very kind to me—and said nothing about leaving on such a journey."

He took a cab back to his hotel, found everything in his room in perfect order. He called the customs office and after considerable inquiry was told that Inspector Raines had left for his hotel some hour or so ago. He said:

"Yes, he has been here. I wondered if he had returned."

There was a pause, questions were asked at the other end, and he was informed that Raines was not expected to return for special night work, but that he would be on duty in the morning. Jo Gar thanked his informant and hung up the receiver.

He sat on the edge of the small bed and watched a light sign flash in the distance. A ferry boat was a glow of moving light, on the Bay waters. The air seemed very cold. Jo Gar decided that the real Inspector Raines had met with injuries, and that a certain person had impersonated him, had told him an untrue story about a certain woman in black—and had then departed from the city of San Francisco. He decided that he was expected to go to the house at One hundred and forty-one, West Pacific Avenue, that he was supposed to believe the woman had acted suspiciously in going there.

He said softly and slowly: "I have the six dia-monds—they have the four. I am in a strange city, and a card with a seal on it was expected to make a great impression. But one man's picture can replace another's—very easily—"

He rose and looked at his wristwatch. It was almost eight o'clock. He inspected his Colt automatic, slipped it back into a pocket of his coat. The phone bell rang, and when he lifted the receiver and gave his name he was told that the customs office was calling, and that Inspector Raines had been found unconscious in an alley not far from the piers. He was still unconscious and it was not certain that he would live. He had apparently been struck over the head with a blunt instrument. The customs office felt that Señor Gar should know why he had failed to arrive, and also that all passengers on the *Cheyo Maru* had been passed through the office. One had been followed as requested, but her cab had been lost in traffic. The office was very sorry.

Jo Gar said: "I am very sorry to hear of Inspector Raines' injuries. I will call at the office tomorrow. Thank you for calling."

He hung up the receiver, went to the window that faced the Bay and the distant, lighted ferry boat. His gray-blue eyes were smiling coldly. He thought: They did *not* expect Inspector Raines to be found so soon. They *did* expect me to go immediately to the address the impostor gave me. They might easily have escaped with the four diamonds, but they chose to lead me to them. They wish the six in my possession, being very greedy. But I am warned, directly and indirectly.

The Island detective turned away from the window and moved towards the room door. He breathed very softly:

"Just the same—I shall go directly to the address given me."

 o Gar left his cab a square from One hundred and forty-one West Pacific Avenue. He had picked the driver with care; the man was husky in build and young. He had a good chin and clear eyes, and he said his name was O'Halohan. Somewhere in the Islands Jo had read that the Irish were fighters.

He said now: "I am a detective—and I'm going inside of the house at One hundred and forty-one. Here is a ten-dollar bill. In about five minutes I want you to drive to the front of the house and blow your horn twice. After that just stay in your seat. Wait about ten minutes—then blow your horn again, twice. If I do not come to a window or the door, and call to you—go to the police and tell them I went into the house and was prevented from coming out. That is all—is it clear?"

The driver nodded. "I got a gun," he said. "And a permit to carry it. Suppose, after the second time I blow my horn, you don't show. Why not let me come in and *get* you out?"

The Island detective smiled narrowly. "You are young and strong, but neither of those qualities might be of too great value. Neither of us might come out."

The driver said: "If it looks that bad—what you goin' in alone for?"

Jo Gar continued to smile. He said patiently:

"I have an idea it will be better that way. You must follow my instructions."

The driver nodded. "You're doing the job," he muttered. "I'll be down there in five minutes, and make the horn racket. I'll give it to you again in ten. Then if you don't show I'll head for the police."

The Island detective nodded. "That is the way," he said. "Don't get out of the car."

The driver said: "Supposing I hear you yelling for help—I still stick inside?"

Jo said grimly: "You will not hear me calling for help, Mister O'Halohan. My visit is not at all complicated. After you blow your horn twice—

the second time, I will either give you instructions, or you will go for the police."

The driver said: "You win."

Jo Gar half closed his almond-shaped eyes. "It may be very important to me—that you do just as I have instructed. You are sure you understand?"

The driver nodded; his eyes met Jo Gar's squarely.

"It ain't anything tough," he stated.

Jo Gar spoke very quietly. "It is extremely simple."

He half turned away from the cab, and heard the driver say harshly:

"Yeah—if it works."

The Island detective moved along the broken pavement of the sidewalk, a thin smile on his browned face.

"It will be just as simple," he said in a low tone, a half whisper, "if it *doesn't* work. But much more final—for me."

Number One hundred and forty-one was a rambling one story house in not too good condition. There were no streetlights near it; tall trees rose on either side. The nearest house to it was almost a square distant; opposite was a lot filled with low brush. The section was quiet and pretty well deserted, but less than a half mile away there was the flare of colored lights in the sky. And at intervals Jo Gar could hear distant and faint staccato sounds—the noise of shooting gallery rifles.

He did not hesitate as he reached the front of the house. A yellowish light showed faintly beyond one of the side windows. The pavement that ran to a few steps was broken and not level.

Out of the corners of his gray-blue eyes, as he moved towards the steps, Jo saw that the lights of the cab had been dimmed—their color did not show on the street in front of the place. A cold wind made sound in the trees as he reached the steps, moved up them. His right hand was in the right pocket of his coat, gripping the butt of the automatic.

He stood for a few seconds, his eyes on the

number plate, which seemed new and had been placed in a position easily seen. The house was old, the section of San Francisco was not too good—but the number plate was in excellent condition.

The Island detective's lips curved just a little. But the smile that showed momentarily on his face was not a pleasant one. He had a definite feeling that this house marked the end of the trail. He thought of the ones who had died in Manila, when Delgada's jewelry store had been robbed—he thought of the men who had died since then. A vision of Juan Arragon's brown face flashed before his eyes.

He touched the index finger of his left hand to a button near the number plate, heard no sound within the house. One hand at his side, the other in his right pocket—he stood in the cold wind and waited. He had come to this house, but he had not been tricked. He was gambling—gambling his life, in a strange country, against his chances of recovering the four missing Von Loffler diamonds, against the final chance of facing the one who had planned the Manila crime.

He could not be positive of anything, but he sensed these things. This was to be the finish, one way or the other. He would return to Manila—or he would never leave this house alive. He felt it, and he was suddenly very calm. From somewhere within he heard foot-falls; there was the sound of a bolt being moved, the door opened very wide.

Jo Gar looked into the eyes of a man who had a smiling face. It was a thin, browned face, and the eyes were small and colorless. The man was dressed in a brown suit, almost the color of his skin. There was nothing striking about the one who had opened the door, unless it was the smallness of his colorless eyes.

The eyes looked beyond the Island detective, to the sidewalk and road. The man moved his head slightly and Jo Gar said:

"I am Señor Gar, a private detective who arrived only today in San Francisco. I arrived on the *Cheyo Maru*—and have come here in search of a woman who was on that boat. She had with her a child—"

He stopped and looked downward at the dull color of black that was the metal of the gun held by the man in the doorway. The man had made only a slight movement with his right hand; the gun's muzzle was less than three feet from Jo's body.

Jo Gar smiled into the smiling eyes of the one in the doorway.

"I have made a mistake?" he asked very quietly.

The one in the doorway shook his head. "On the contrary," he said in a voice that was very low and cold, "you have come to the correct place. I have been—expecting you."

He stepped to one side, and Jo Gar walked into a wide hall. The light was dim, and though there were electric bulbs about, it was furnished by a lamp whose wick was uneven. The place was very cold. It had the air of not having been lived in for a long time, and there was no evidence about showing that it would be lived in.

The thin-faced man said: "The first room on your right, please. Lift your hands slightly."

Jo Gar raised his hands slightly, went through a narrow doorway into a room that seemed even colder than the hall. The light in the room was better—there were two lamps. Blinds were drawn tightly. Beside a small table was a stool that might have been made for a piano.

The one with the gun said in the same, cold voice:

"Sit on the stool, Gar—put your hands on the table. Keep them there."

Hatred crept into his voice as he uttered the last three words. Jo Gar did as instructed. He said quietly:

"I knew that the man you sent to me at my hotel lied. I followed him to the station, and watched him leave the city. I returned to the hotel and the customs office informed me that one of their men, who was coming to me with information of no great importance, had been knocked unconscious. I knew then how the card presented me had been obtained, and that I was expected to believe a story that pointed to suspicious action by a woman I was interested in—and that I was expected to come to this address."

There was hatred showing in the small, colorless eyes of the thin-faced one. He stood almost ten feet away from Jo Gar, facing him.

"But you came, knowing all this."

Jo Gar smiled a little. "When you made that movement and held that gun on me—my fingers were on the trigger of my own gun. I could have shot you down—I did not."

There was a flicker of expression in the standing one's eyes. He said:

"You are very kind, Señor Gar."

Mockery and hatred were in his tone. Jo Gar said slowly:

"No—not kind. I have six diamonds that you would like. I think that you have four I would like. You wanted me here to bargain with me. You wanted me here so that you could trap me, then offer me my life for the six diamonds. You have worked that way, with your accomplices, since the robbery was effected."

The thin-faced one smiled and showed white, even teeth.

"You would risk your life and six diamonds—for the four you say I have?"

Jo Gar smiled gently. "My life is not too important," he said. "I have never regarded it that way. I came here because I knew the one responsible for many deaths would be here."

The thin-faced one said mockingly: "And you were not trapped? You simply wanted to see that person who you hated because of Arragon's death, and because of things done to you?"

The Island detective kept his hands motionless on the table surface. He shook his head.

"No," he replied. "Not exactly. I wanted to see that one taken by the police. And that is practically assured, now."

He watched the facial muscles of the thin-faced one jerk, saw his colorless eyes shift towards the blinds of the windows. His gun hand moved a little, in towards his body. Rage twisted his face, and then he smiled. It was a grotesque, mask-like smile. The brown skin was drawn tightly over the face bones and the lips were pressed together. Jo Gar said:

"I remember you, Raaker. You were in the insurance business in Manila until a few years ago. There was about to be a prosecution, and you left the Islands."

The thin-faced one said with hoarseness in his voice:

"And I have never forgotten you, Señor Gar. You tell me you have come here, not caring about your life—and that the police are outside. Well—I didn't bring you here to get your six diamonds, Gar—Von Loffler's diamonds. I brought you here because I hate you. I want to watch your body squirm on the floor, beside that stool."

Jo Gar said quietly: "That was how you knew about the Von Loffler diamonds—that Dutch Insurance Company. You stayed out of Manila, Raaker—you couldn't risk coming back. You hired men. Some of them tricked you—and each other. The robbery was successful, but you lost slowly. All the way back from Manila, Raaker, you lost. You used men and women, and they tried to kill me—too many times. They were killed—there were many deaths. Those were diamonds of death, Raaker—and you only got four of them. The woman in black brought them to you—I think she was the only one who was faithful."

Raaker was breathing heavily. He made a sudden movement with his left hand, plunging it into a pocket. When it came out four stones spilled to the surface of the small table. Three of them only rolled a few inches, but one struck against a finger of the Island detective's left hand. Raaker said fiercely:

"I hate you, Gar. You drove me from the Islands, with your evidence. I hated Von Loffler, too. He took all his properties away from me, because he learned that I was gambling, because he was afraid of the insurance. So I learned about the stones, where they were. And I planned the robbery. I stayed here—and got reports. I tried to direct. But you were on that boat—"

He broke off, shrugged. "You are going to die, Gar. So I can talk. The woman came to me with the diamonds. Four of them. And by the time she brought them to me here—she hated me. She had seen too much death. She's gone away, with her child—and you'll never find her, Gar. She killed a man on the *Cheyo Maru,* and that made her hate me all the more. She had to kill him, before he could talk—to you!"

Jo Gar said steadily: "I don't think—I *want* to find her, Raaker. I know now who planned the crime, who caused the deaths. And you are caught, Raaker—"

There was the sound of brakes beyond the room, the low beat of an idling engine. Two sharp blasts from a horn came into the room. Raaker jerked his head sharply, then turned his eyes towards Jo Gar again. The Island detective made no movement. He smiled with his lips pressed together. Raaker said:

"What's—that?"

His voice was hoarse. Jo Gar parted his lips. He said:

"A signal from the police—that the house is properly covered."

Raaker sucked in a deep breath. "I'll get more than one of them—as they come in!" he muttered.

Jo Gar shook his head. "I do not think you will, Raaker. They will not come in. It is easier to wait for *you*—to go *out.*"

Raaker smiled twistedly, but there was fear in his eyes.

"They'll come in, all right," he breathed. "I'll get you first—when they come. *You* won't see them come in, Gar."

Jo Gar smiled. "They will not come in," he said softly. "If I do not go out, within the next ten minutes, they will unload the sub-machine-guns and the smoke bombs. They will know I am dead—and that there is a killer in the house. The smoke bombs—and the tear gas bombs—*they* will come in."

Raaker said hoarsely. "——! How I hate you, you little half-breed—"

He jerked the gun slightly. The Island detective looked him in the eyes, still smiling.

"That is true," he said. "You *do* hate me—and there *is* the blood of the Spanish and the Filipino in my veins. But I am not a criminal—a thief and a killer."

Raaker turned his head slightly and listened

to the steady beat of the cab engine. Then his eyes came back to the small figure of Gar, went to the four glittering diamonds on the table. He said thickly:

"With the others—over two hundred thousand dollars—I would have been fixed—"

His voice broke. Jo Gar said quietly: "Yes, you could have had things easy, Raaker. If I had not taken the same boat that your accomplices took—if things had turned out differently in Honolulu—"

Raaker stared at him, his little eyes growing larger. He said slowly:

"Where are—the other six stones?"

Jo Gar smiled. "In the vaults of the customs office," he replied. "You did not think I would bring them here?"

Raaker's body swayed a little. The wind made noise in the trees beyond the house, and he stiffened. Jo Gar said in a voice that was hardly more than a whisper:

"If you had had even the courage of a certain type of criminal—and had gone to the Islands yourself, you might have had the diamonds now. If you had not used others—"

Raaker said fiercely: "Damn the diamonds—I've got *you*! They brought you here—"

Jo Gar half closed his almond-shaped eyes. "And they've brought the San Francisco police here," he said steadily. "They've brought tear gas and sub-machine-guns—and they're bringing death here, Raaker."

Raaker's eyes held rage again. He was losing control of himself. He made a swift motion with his left hand, shaking fingers pointing towards the four stones on the table.

"Look at them—damn you!" he gritted. "Look at the four you couldn't—reach! Look at them—"

Jo Gar looked into the eyes of Raaker. He shook his head.

"I've seen the *others*," he stated quietly. "I've seen many diamonds, Raaker."

Raaker laughed wildly. He backed towards a wall of the room.

"You'll never see diamonds again," he said in a fierce tone. "Never, Gar!"

He raised his gun arm slowly. From the cab outside there came the sharp sound of a horn, silence—and then another blast.

Jo Gar never took his eyes from the eyes of Raaker. He was smiling grimly.

He said very slowly: "Machine-gun bullets, Raaker. And choking, blinding gas. They'll be waiting for *you*—after you get through squeezing that trigger."

Raaker cried out in a shrill tone: "Damn you—Gar—that won't help *you* any—"

There was a sudden engine hum as the cab driver accelerated the motor. Yellow light flashed beyond the house, along the road. O'Halohan was going for the police, starting his cab. For a second Raaker twisted his head towards the sound and the light. He was thinking of machine-guns—and tear gas—

Jo Gar was on his feet in a flash. The table went forward, over. The Island detective leaped to the right as Raaker cried out hoarsely, and the first bullet from his gun crashed into the table wood.

The second bullet from the gun ripped the cloth of Gar's coat, and his right hand was coming up, with the Colt in it, when the cloth ripped.

He squeezed the trigger sharply but steadily. There was the third gun crash and Raaker screamed, took a step forward. His gun hand dropped; he went to his knees, stared at Gar for a second, swaying—then fell heavily to the floor.

Jo Gar went slowly to his side. He was dead—the bullet had caught him just above the heart. One diamond lay very close to his curved fingers; it was as though he were grasping for it, in death.

The other three Jo found after a five-minute search. Then he went from the room into the hall, and out of the house. The cab was out of sight; in the distance there was still colored light in the sky. The shooting gallery noise came at intervals. Jo Gar found a package in his pocket, lighted one of his brown-paper cigarettes.

He said very softly, to himself: "I have all—of the diamonds. Now I can go home, after the police come. I hope my friend Juan Arragon—knows."

He stood very motionless on the top step that led to the small porch, and waited for the police to come. And he thought, as he waited, of the Philippines—of Manila—and of his tiny office off the *Escolta*. It was good to forget other things, and to think of his returning.

The Ring on the Hand of Death

William Rollins Jr.

WILLIAM ROLLINS JR. (1897–1950) was born in Boston, Massachusetts, and served with the French Army during World War I (other references state that his experience was with the American Ambulance Service), after which he joined other expatriates in Paris, then settled in New York City to become a full-time freelance writer, mainly for magazines, both pulp and slick. His homosexuality was openly discussed by his friends, and Rollins wrote about the subject with sensitivity, though he never acknowledged his sexual orientation. A devoted Marxist, he believed communism was the only hope for democracy in America, though he never joined the party. He was a frequent contributor to *New Masses*, the Communist-supported journal, and his work, notably the proletarian novel *The Shadow Before* (1934), was much admired in left-wing circles, being praised by Lillian Hellman ("the finest and most stimulating book of this generation") and John Dos Passos, among others.

Rollins had begun his career as a mystery writer, frequently selling stories to *Black Mask* and other pulp magazines, as well as producing such novels as *Midnight Treasure* (1929), *The Wall of Men* (1938), and, after World War II, *The Ring and the Lamp* (1947); he wrote a single mystery, *Murder at Cypress Hall* (1933), under the pseudonym O'Connor Stacy.

"The Ring on the Hand of Death," one of twenty-one stories that Rollins wrote for *Black Mask*, was published in the April 1924 issue.

The Ring on the Hand of Death

William Rollins Jr.

A murder mystery which gathers speed as it goes along; with occasional scenes in Mr. Rollins' creepiest style.

I'M NOT MUCH. HORACE SPARTON always said so, and he ought to know; he was one of the two richest men in town. Old Man Carr was the other one. He used to say I would come to a no-good end, and *he* ought to know; he had a no-good beginning. But everybody forgot that, when he started raking in the iron-men. And then Old Wallace the Walrus says I'm the worst kid she ever had in high school, but that she couldn't expect much more, considering where I came from. But I've been making my own living somehow or other, ever since Mother died two years ago. And I've been able to work in

enough time to go to school, too. So I should worry!

Of course, I did worry whenever I met Irene Burnet. She didn't want to be seen with a bum like me. . . . Although she always said, "Hello, Jack," and smiled. And once when I was holding up a telegraph pole just as she was passing by, and I was staring at her without noticing I was doing it (she's that kind, awfully easy to look at), she dropped her eyes and started blushing. And then she smiled, just as if she didn't mind it at all!

And then one time, after I had finished fixing up Old Man Carr's front lawn to make it ready for the spring, and then wandered down the street and pulled myself up on the fence next to Burnet's place (it's a comfortable seat; that's why

I like it so much), I heard some people coming up the side street. And I heard her voice.

"He's a nice boy!" I heard her say, as if somebody else had just said he wasn't. "He's not only good-looking—I don't care so much about that—but he's honest and he works hard, and some day he's going to make a big man of himself!"

I was trying to think how I could get away before they saw me and wondering who this great person was that she was talking about, when they came around the corner—Irene and two other girls and three fellows. When she saw me, Irene suddenly stopped talking and blushed all over, and the girls started giggling, and the fellows burst out laughing, as if they'd all suddenly thought of a big joke, all at once. For a minute I couldn't help thinking— But I'm not going to tell you; you'll think I'm conceited.

And besides, that isn't why I started telling this incident. I just can't help thinking about myself, particularly if I'm thinking about Irene. That last sentence sounds funny, but I can't make it any clearer without getting all mixed up.

Well, just then Mr. Sparton (Horace Sparton, the district attorney) came walking down the path from the Burnets' little house. When he saw Irene and the others, he stopped short. Then he took off his hat.

"Good evening, Miss Burnet," he said. "I just called around to see your brother."

"But—why, I thought you knew he went up to Denver for a few days!"

"I did. But I hoped he would be back today. However, I'll call again in a day or two."

And he took off his hat again with a smile and walked on.

And then you ought to have seen that smile disappear when he saw me! He came up and stood right in front of me, his big jaw sticking out.

"Get down off of that fence!" he said.

Well, I got down, taking my time about it.

"Now! If I ever catch you spoiling the scenery of our beautiful town again, lazing around like that, you'll get no more work around my house! Do you understand?"

I thought a moment, and then said I did.

"The only reason I have you is to keep you out of the poorhouse," he muttered.

I knew better. I knew the only reason he had me was because I charged ten cents less than a full-grown man; but I wasn't going to lower myself arguing with him; and I let him go on, and then climbed back on the fence again. I had something I wanted to wonder about, and I can't think and walk at the same time; I always land up against a lamppost, or in front of a swearing autoist, and forget what I was wondering about.

I wanted to wonder why Horace Sparton had next to the prettiest and sweetest girl in town for a daughter. And then I wondered whether Miriam (that's she—or her) was going to marry Irene's older brother, Alfred. I would be tickled stiff if she did, for Al was about the nicest chap I knew, and that's what most of the girls around thought, too. But I knew Sparton was dead set against it, although he didn't say much; and the particular thing I wanted to wonder about was why he had been so sweet to Irene, when usually he wouldn't speak to her if he met her on the street.

You see, Al and Irene lived alone, and they were as poor as Croesus (or was it Diogenes? I get them twisted. One was an awful liar, I know). When Al came back from the war, he got admitted to the bar and has been waiting for trade ever since. That's what he was in Denver for: to get a job as a lawyer, or a judge, or something like that.

You see (that's the second time I've used that phrase. Wouldn't the Walrus be sore! But editors don't know so much as school teachers; if they did they'd get that job, you bet! Nothing to do but ask kids a lot of questions when they've got the book right before them! So that's all right). You see, Old Man Carr was Al's and Irene's father, but he was only their stepfather, which isn't so much.

Old Man Carr had a Past. (That's what everybody always says in New Paris when they're telling visitors about our prominent citizens and showing them the Opera and Slaughter and Court Houses and the cemetery and where the Soldiers' Monument is going to be.) He was put in jail for swindling, and his wife died for shame while he was there. They said she had a kid just before she died, but nobody knew what had happened to it. Then Carr went away, and when he came back next year, he had a new wife and two kids (the kids weren't his, of course. They were hers—Alfred and Irene Burnet). Then, just after Al came home from the war, his mother died and Old Man Carr kicked the kids out of the house; not because he was sore at them, but just because he wanted to save money. (He'd made a lot during the war.) Everybody said he'd leave them all his money when he died, but meanwhile it was pretty rough sledding; they hardly knew where their next meal was coming from. It came only when Al got some odd work to do, writing funny law things for dry papers.

Well, it was getting pretty dark, so I stopped wondering and got off the fence and went home. I live in a little shack at the edge of the town and do my own cooking, which is usually potatoes and eggs that aren't Strictly (excepting sometimes on dark nights), and things like that.

In the summer, I usually go to the woods, and sometimes at the end of the week in the winter and spring I go to a little cabin that—but you'll find out later. I can't stand big cities and New Paris is big and growing faster every day. She grew from 2,800 to 2,900 between 1910 and 1920, and when the local census was taken in 1922, she had jumped to over 8,000, and I can't stand that. If I get to wondering too hard on the main street it usually ends in a fight.

Well, I went home and rolled up my sleeves and put on my apron and set my potatoes on to boil, and that was the last I thought about the Burnets—I mean Alfred—for over a week.

The next time I saw him was late one night— or early in the morning, I don't know which. It was a warm night in early spring, and I had taken my potatoes up to the woods and boiled them there for a change. The sky was clear and starlit, and I was walking down the avenue, where all the big bugs live.

I was passing Old Man Carr's place, when I saw somebody stealing around the house. When he got to the path he started running.

I was near the bushes and I stood still. He came on, turning to look over his shoulder. Just as he got to the sidewalk, he turned suddenly to the right and bumped into me. I couldn't help squeaking; for it was Alfred!

You could have knocked me over with a steam-roller!

"Hey, Al!" I said. "What's the rush all about?"

He stood staring at me a minute. Something was wrong with his face. I think it was pale, but of course you can't tell when it's dark, even with stars. Finally he smiled, a little, quivering smile.

"Hello, Jackie boy!"

He always called me that. When I was a little kid he used to give me marbles and say:

"Here, Jackie boy! If you swallow them, I'll give you some more!"

But now he looked away and when he spoke he almost stuttered.

"You—you scared me!" he said with a little laugh. "What are you hiding in the bushes for?"

Well, up to now I'd been wondering what *he* was about, but suddenly I found I was on the defensive.

"Aw, I don't know," I muttered.

"Well, run along home to bed!" he said. "If a cop sees you, he'll think you're up to some mischief."

"All right, Al," I replied, relieved to find he wasn't going to ask any questions. I always feel I've done something wrong when people start asking questions, even if I haven't.

Al started off.

"Not that *I* think so!" he added over his shoulder.

"Thanks, Al! You're a good fellow!" I said. "So long!"

"So long!" And we each went in our own directions.

When I was on my way to school next morning, I saw a crowd standing in front of Old Man Carr's house. I went up to Jim Harley.

"What's up?" I asked.

Jim looked at me, with that air a fellow has who knows something you don't know.

"Why," he said, slowly, "don't you know?"

"If I did, I wouldn't waste my time talking to you!"

I knew I could get as fresh as I liked; he was just dying to tell me.

"Why . . . last night . . . some time or other . . . somebody murdered Old Man Carr."

Well, my heart just stood still. In a big city like New Paris, things like that are always happening. Only a few months before there was an auto accident and a lot of people were almost killed; one man was in the hospital over a week! But I never get used to those things.

"Gee!" I said. "Who did it?"

Jim shook his head.

"We don't know yet," he said, "but we're going to find out!"

Well, we stood and watched the house for a half hour; and then I remembered that the Walrus said she'd fire me out of school if I was late again, so I beat it.

I got there just in time and I waited until I got settled in my seat in the English class, and then I started wondering. Who could have murdered Old Man Carr? There were lots of times when I was working in his garden, and he was standing over me giving directions, that I thought about doing it pretty seriously; but then I remembered my twenty cents an hour and decided to wait until I got another job. I was still wondering about it when I realized that everybody in the room was looking at me and some were giggling.

"I'll give you just two seconds to get up and recite or to get up and leave this room forever, John Darrow!" the Walrus was saying.

I stood up.

"What do you want me to recite about?" I asked, meekly.

The Walrus put up a noble struggle with herself, but I thought she'd bust before she finally conquered.

"Recite today's poem," she replied in a weak voice, looking very pale.

I was willing to do that. I can always wonder about things when I'm reciting poetry, particularly if it's nice, inspiring poetry.

" 'O, wild west wind, thou breath of autumn's being!' " I commenced, starting at the same time to wonder who could possibly have killed Old Man Carr.

" 'O, lift me like a wave, a leaf, a—' Gorry!"

"A *what?*" the Walrus shrieked.

But I had dropped into my seat with a bang. I had just remembered whom I saw running away from Old Man Carr's house the night before. It just made me dizzy.

I must have looked pale, for the Walrus shut her mouth just as she was going to say something unfriendly, and all the kids stopped giggling.

One of the girls was standing up to recite the poem, when the door opened.

A policeman came in. The room was deadly silent while he walked to the Walrus' desk. They stood whispering for a minute. Then they turned and looked at me.

"John," said the Walrus; "you will go with the officer!"

I got up and walked to the door, trying to wonder whose patch I had been caught in. The cop took my arm, rather too firmly, for I wasn't trying to get away. We walked down the stairs and out the school door without saying anything. Then we walked down the street, while everybody turned to look at me. Gee, I felt cheap!

When we got to the Court House I was just about wilted, and the cop almost had to drag me up the steps. We went through the long, dark corridor until he stopped before a door and knocked at it. After a minute the key was turned and the door opened.

Then I knew it was all up, for there I saw young Judge Forest and I had been in his backyard the night before to see if I couldn't find a potato barrel or an apple barrel, for I was rather short of supplies. He was sitting there looking serious and there were several cops and people, and among them was Alfred Burnet!

Well, I thought that was pretty mean! Here I had thought right along that Al was a friend of mine, and now he was testifying against me, just because he saw me out late the night before! And after he had said that *he* didn't think I had done anything, too!

Well, they led me to a seat and I sat down hard. And then Judge Forest said:

"Good morning, Jack. How are you?"

And I answered him:

"Good morning, sir. How are you?"

I wanted to say, "How are your potatoes?" but I thought perhaps it would be better if I didn't.

Well, the Judge pulled his chair up and leaned over, just as if he were going to offer me a cigar, and then he said:

"Jack, I want to ask you a few questions."

"Yes, sir," I said, and looked at the window, and wondered how long it would be before I saw it from the outside.

They couldn't put me in the coop for over a month for just a couple of measly potatoes that I didn't get anyhow.

"Jack," said the Judge in a soft voice, "where were you last night?"

"I was in the woods," I told him.

"You were. . . . And what time did you come home?"

Well, I was scared, but I wanted to laugh at that. He was way off the track! I was in his back-yard *before* I went up to the woods. So I answered:

"Pretty late. About midnight, I reckon."

"You reckon? Aren't you sure? Didn't you look at your watch?"

"No, sir."

"You're sure you didn't look at your watch?"

"No—that is, no, sir."

I was a little rattled by the way he tried to catch me.

"Ah! You're just a little bit in doubt. . . . Now, Jack! Be careful! Are you *sure* you didn't look at your watch?"

"Yes, sir. . . . I haven't got any," I added, happening to think that might be a good argument.

Well, everybody laughed—except Al. He only smiled rather weakly. I thought he looked as if he was ashamed of himself when he had to face me. The Judge leaned closer to me and then he said, very softly:

"Well . . . we'll say about midnight. . . . And did you meet anybody on your way home?"

Well, Al was sitting there, looking at me, sort of white and determined, so I decided to be frank about it. Honesty pays—sometimes.

"Yes," I said.

And then there was a great silence and everybody—except Al—leaned over as if they would fall off of their chairs, and the Judge whispered:

"Who?"

And I said, with a loud, ringing, frank voice:

"Alfred Burnet!"

You could have heard a pin drop. Everybody who was facing Al turned away. The Judge never took his eyes from me.

"Where did you meet him?" he asked.

And then it suddenly flashed over me. I got dizzy and cold all over. All I could see was Al's white face and his big eyes looking at me. I'll never forget those eyes!

The Judge grabbed hold of my knee and pressed it, and his mouth became hard and cruel.

"Answer me, boy!" he commanded. "Where did you see Mr. Burnet?"

"I—I can't remember. . . ."

I'd heard that that was all right to say in courtrooms, but I reckon I made a mistake, for Pat Ryan, the biggest cop on the force, came up and grabbed my shoulder and the Judge pressed my leg until I thought it was going to break.

"I saw you at one o'clock turning down from the Avenue," said Pat. "I'll make you remember!" He shook my shoulder. "And I'll know if you're telling the truth!"

"Where did you see Mr. Burnet?"

"In front of—of his house."

Then the cop shook the upper part of me until I could hear my bones rattle, and the Judge almost squeezed the juice out of the lower part of me. And when they got tired Al said in a low voice:

"Tell the truth, Jackie boy."

"Where did you see Mr. Burnet?"

"I saw him in front of—in front of Ol—Mr. Carr's house."

"What was he doing?"

"He was . . . running."

"Away from the house?"

"Yes."

"Did he act as though he was frightened?"

The voice sounded miles away.

"Yes."

I could hear my own voice like a loud whisper.

There was a moment's silence. Then the Judge started asking me more questions that I couldn't see any sense in. And all the time I answered them, looking at Al's white face and staring eyes.

Finally the Judge stood up. He picked something from the table and held it behind his back.

"One question more," he said. "Did you ever see this before?"

And he pulled out his hand.

I was fairly sick. In his hand he held a German trench knife. It was one Al had brought home from the war. And it was covered with blood—new blood!

I nodded my head.

"Where did you see it?"

I looked at Al. He nodded his head slightly.

"In—in Al's house."

The Judge nodded to one of the policemen, who went to open the door.

"That will be all, Jack," said the Judge, smiling and holding out his hand. "Thank you very much. You are free to go. Only don't leave town before the trial. . . . Good-bye."

I stood up. I was almost bawling, but I wouldn't have let them see it for the world.

"There's one thing you didn't ask me!" I said, shouting to keep back the tears. "And that's whether I think Al murdered Old Man Carr or not!"

The Judge smiled.

"Well?" he said, picking up some papers.

"Well," I shouted; "I think there isn't a one of you who wouldn't do it a million times quicker than he would!"

And then I went out as quick as I could, without letting them think I was in a hurry.

I walked fast out of the town and then I just tore across the fields until I got to the woods. And then I sat down and cried like a girl.

Well, I got that off my chest and then I built a fire and lay down and started wondering. I wondered for a long while without getting anywhere, and then I reckon I must have fallen asleep, for it was almost dark when I turned over, shivering, and saw my fire was out. There were little flakes of snow coming down, although it was March.

I got up to go home, and then it occurred to me I might meet Irene, and I was scared stiff. So I decided to go to my cabin for the night. I've already spoken about that. It's a little cabin in the woods, about five miles from town. It really isn't mine, having been built by a young couple who live in Berlin, next town to New Paris. But they don't use it, except in the summer. I go out there a good deal in the winter, but I never bother them when they're around.

So I started down the little path, and it got darker and darker, because the trees were getting thicker and the night was coming on. And the snow fell very quiet, and my footsteps hardly made any noise because there was a carpet of thick, soggy leaves. And then, suddenly, after I had gone about three miles, I stopped short. For there ahead of me, I saw a girl, sitting on a stump, leaning over and trying to write something with a pencil on her knee. With a paper in between, of course.

Well, I advanced cautiously, for I've been in the Boy Scouts, and I've learned it's silly to expose yourself needlessly when you're in the woods. There's always apt to be a trap around when you see something awfully innocent-looking—like a young girl writing on a paper.

Then, all at once, I gave a shout, for I saw it was only Jane Brewster, the pretty girl who minds the babies at the Masons' and does odd chores at different houses in the afternoons.

Jane gave a little cry, and crumpled the paper up quick. I didn't blame her. It's a scary thing to have somebody yell at you like that when you're alone in the woods and it's almost dark. Besides, for all I knew, she might have belonged to the Girl Scouts one time.

But when I came up and she saw who I was,

she still looked pale and scared and hid the paper behind her.

"Hello, Jane!" I said, cheerfully.

She stared at me as I stood before her.

"What are you doing here?" she asked me, very hoarsely.

"Me? I'm on a vacation. Going to my winter mansion. But what are you doing here?"

Jane dropped her eyes.

"I'm going home," she said in a low voice.

"Going home!" I cried. "But your people live fifteen miles away from here! You can't get there tonight!"

But Jane didn't lift her eyes from the ground.

"I'm going home," she repeated doggedly.

Well, I was puzzled. I couldn't understand why Jane should be going back to her family suddenly this late in the day, when she could get a train the next morning. But that wasn't any of my business. All I cared about was the fact that I knew she would be lost in the woods when night came on for fair. So I said:

"I'll tell you, Jane. You can't ever get home this late. You come to my cabin! There are three beds there—and a screen to make a regular room for you. And you stay there for the night and start home first thing in the morning!"

Jane looked at me rather suspiciously; but I argued with her. Poor Jane! I wish she had told me to go to the devil and tried to get home as best she could in the dark woods! Still, if it hadn't been Jane, it would have been— But I've got to tell the story in order. The Walrus always said I get things tail end to, and I reckon she's right.

Well, Jane got up and followed me. We walked along the path in Indian file and without saying anything. Finally it got so dark I had to wave my arms about to keep from bumping into trees, and I told Jane to grab hold of my coat. And all the time I could feel the little flakes of snow touching my face.

At last we got to the cabin. I was used to it, but Jane seemed sort of scared when I opened the door for her after I climbed in the window. I reckon it *is* a pretty gloomy place.

But I lighted a lamp and built a fire in the pot-bellied stove. And then I got on my knees and felt under the bed, and brought out some potatoes and apples and a can of tomato soup I'd found in Jenkins' Grocery Store and which I'd kept for some big occasion like this. Then we cooked them and we had a big feast.

After supper I lighted my pipe and sat with my feet on the stove, while Jane washed the dishes. It was awful homelike. I wonder if Irene washes dishes good?

Then the first funny thing happened. When she finished washing the dishes and thought I wasn't looking, Jane tiptoed over to the coal scuttle that was used for ashes and dropped the paper she had been writing on into it and covered it with ashes. Then she came and sat opposite me. I was facing the stove. She was facing the window.

"This is a nice place," she said, folding her hands and looking around and smiling a weak little smile.

It *was* a nice place—a long cabin, with two cots at either end, under the windows, and a cot and a screen for when the owners had company, near the stove. Then there were a couple of tables: one with the lamp on it, that gave a mighty cheerful glow to the room.

"*I* like it," I replied. "It's a relief to get out here in the quiet, away from the excitement and noise in New Paris."

When I said "New Paris," the smile left her face, and that reminded me of what I was trying to forget. So I decided to talk about it. I like to have somebody to talk over my troubles with; I'm funny that way.

"Wasn't that a terrible murder!" I said, as an opener.

With that, Jane turned as pale as if somebody had sucked the blood right out of her. I decided that she was a sympathetic listener, so I kept on.

"Not that it wasn't a good thing to get Old Man Carr out of the way, but to think of their accusing Al Burnet—"

But Jane jumped up.

"What did you say?" she cried, looking down at me as if she was going to eat me.

"Haven't you heard?" I asked. "They've arrested poor Al!"

Jane dropped in her seat, and started staring at the button that wasn't on my coat.

"Anybody who'd think Al could murder his father, even if he was only his stepfather, is crazy!" I muttered.

Jane didn't say anything. She just stared, and her breath came hard.

"I'd rather think I did it myself," I went on.

I waited for Jane to answer, but she didn't. So I shut up and listened to the wood crackling in the stove. Suddenly Jane spoke and I jumped.

"Do you think they can—they can—"

But she couldn't finish it.

I knew what she meant, though.

"It looks pretty hard for him," I told her. "They made me testify I saw him outside late at night. And they found his German trench knife covered with blood there."

Jane had kept her eyes lowered all the time. Now she looked up and glanced around the room. She was trembling all over.

"Jack," she whispered; "can you keep a secret?"

"I reckon so," I answered.

"Can you keep it until it's a question of life or death—and then let me know two days before-hand?"

I looked at her in surprise.

"What are you driving at, Jane?" I demanded. But Jane was impatient.

"*Can* you?" she repeated.

"Of course I can!"

"Swear?"

"On the Bible." And I held my hand in the air and cussed.

She was still for a moment. Then she leaned forward and whispered:

"I know who killed Mr. Carr!"

I was dumbfounded.

"You *what*?" I cried.

Jane slapped her hand over my mouth.

"Sh!" she whispered. Then she drew her chair nearer. "I called at Mr. Carr's the other night after supper," she said, leaning way forward and staring at me wild-eyed. "He owed me some money, and I suddenly decided to ask him to pay me. Well, I went to his back door and rang, and after a while he came. He was mad when he saw who it was, and madder still when I told him what I wanted. He started to tell me to go away, but then he changed his mind and said he would pay me if I stayed and washed the kitchen floor.

"Well, it was late, but I needed the money, so I said I would. He went upstairs, and I took off my coat and put on my apron and got to work.

"I was about half done when the front door bell rang. I answered it. It was Mr. Burnet. He smiled and said, 'Hello,' and asked if Mr. Carr was in. I said he was, and he went upstairs, and I went back to work.

"Pretty soon I heard a lot of angry talk and shouting over my head. I had about finished my work then, but I wanted my money that night, so I decided to wait until Mr. Burnet left and then ask Mr. Carr for it. I sat down in that old rocking chair in the kitchen.

"I was pretty tired and I fell asleep. When I woke up, I looked at the clock. It was two-thirty.

"I thought it was funny Mr. Carr hadn't waked me up and sent me home, but I decided to creep out and come back next day. But just then I looked out and saw the light from his window reflected on the lawn. So I reckoned he was awake and thought I'd go up and get my money.

"I went out in the hall. It was dark and quiet. I walked up the carpeted stairs, very quiet, so as not to wake him, if he had fallen asleep.

"I got to the top of the stairs and saw the light in his room. I crept across the hall and when I got to the door, I peeked in. And there—"

Jane put her hand over her eyes as if she still saw it. I waited a minute, feeling the stillness of the little cabin creep over me. It made me uneasy.

"Go on, Jane," I said in a whisper.

She took her hand from her eyes and went on, trembling all over.

"And there I saw Mr. Carr, lying back in his easy chair, a dagger stuck in his heart!"

"I stood staring at him, so scared I couldn't even scream. And while I stood there, the door to his little alcove opened and there I saw— Ah!"

I jumped at her cry and looked up. She was staring before her as if she saw Death. I thought she was seeing the murderer in her imagination.

"Who did you see?" I whispered, on the edge of my chair.

She didn't seem to hear me.

"Who did you see?" I repeated.

She turned and looked at me as if she noticed me for the first time. Then in a loud, clear voice she cried:

"Alfred Burnet murdered Mr. Carr!"

I stared at her a minute. Then I dropped my head in my hands. So it was Al after all! My poor, beloved Al, Irene's brother!

I had a funny empty feeling. There wasn't anything more to do. There wasn't anything to wonder about. I raised my head slowly.

"Do you want to go to bed now?" I asked her.

She nodded. She didn't seem to have strength to speak. I dragged myself to one of the end beds and made it up with the blankets— there were no sheets. Then I put the screen around it and moved the table up outside of the screen so that she could reach around and lay her clothes there. It was too big to put inside.

"All right, Jane," I said, and she got up slowly and went behind the screen. I dropped again in my seat by the stove and started looking glumly at the coals.

But I reckon Jane got a little scared when she was in the dark back of the screen, for she started talking at a great streak.

"Do you think this snow is going to keep up all night?" she asked in a little, quavering voice.

I looked up and saw her pretty little hand reach around the screen and put her gingham dress on the table.

"I don't know," I muttered, "and I don't care much."

"Well, I do! You see, I want to get home as early . . ." And she went on talking and saying things that didn't interest me, just then when I was trying to wonder.

After a while she stopped, and I thought I'd put in a word, just to be polite.

"Don't you intend to come back to New Paris again?" I asked.

She didn't answer.

"Hah, Jane?" I asked again.

But still she didn't answer.

"She's gone to sleep, poor kid," I said to myself, and I took a little stick and started raking the coals to make the room a bit warmer.

Just then I heard her open the window.

"That's funny," I said to myself. "She's awake after all! . . . And she might have waited until I went to bed. It's as cold as blazes outside. . . . I suppose she's all upset. . . ." And I settled back, trying to figure out things.

I had seen Al leaving Carr's house after the murder. And that sure was his knife. And now Jane said he was the one that did it. But for all that, I couldn't believe it! I couldn't! . . . But if he didn't, who did?

I was sitting back in my chair until it almost tipped over, with my feet resting against the side of the stove. The lamp was burning lower, and the light was sort of contracting away from the corners of the room. The big, dark screen was spread out and made a regular wall, a few feet in front of me. The reflection of the light on that was getting dimmer and I could just see the edge of the blackness that was around Jane's bed.

Well, suddenly, while I was sitting there wondering, I saw Jane's hand reach out and feel around the edge of the table that touched the end of the screen.

That was funny. There she was quiet all the time, and yet she hadn't been asleep! I was just going to pipe up and ask her if I could get something for her, when I stopped, my heart in my mouth.

The hand that was feeling around was not Jane's hand!

The light was pretty low by now and everything was blurred, but I could see the hand feeling around and feeling around. I leaned way forward, as quiet as I could, and looked.

It was a man's hand! And on the finger you

point with, there was a ring with a long, funny-shaped bloodstone in it.

I could hear my heart pumping. I sat way over and kept just as still, straining my eyes!

But now it was so dark I could just make out the quiet, moving hand. Finally it touched Jane's underskirt. Its fingers closed on it and pulled it quietly off of the table. Then it disappeared.

I was scared stiff. I know sixteen's pretty old to be scared, but I admit it just the same. I watched that screen and listened. But the screen slowly disappeared in the darkness and all I heard was Jane moving over in bed.

That made me a little more comfortable.

"You're a big coward," I told myself. "That was just Jane's hand and you're such a scarecrow that anything'll get your goat."

But all the time something told me it wasn't and I knew I ought to get up and look.

I sat there, trying to get up nerve. I just sat tilted back, while everything got darker and darker and the open door of the stove made a light on the ceiling that grew brighter and brighter. And I heard a movement behind the screen as if Jane was restless: and then everything was still.

Finally I sat up with a plop.

"You go and look," I told myself, "or *I* won't ever speak to you again!"

So I got up.

The lamp was as good as out, but there was a candle in the cupboard. I got it and lighted it.

It didn't make the room any brighter. Just one little spot around me. However, I'd be able to see Jane.

I crossed the room on tiptoes, so as not to wake her. When I got to the screen, I hesitated. Then I stood off and peeked.

Jane was lying on her side, her back to me, and sleeping as peaceful as I could ask.

Gorry, you don't know how relieved I felt! I could have danced a jig! But instead of that I just tiptoed back to the bed in the center of the room and set the candle down and undressed. Then I got in bed and blew out the light and in two minutes I was fast asleep.

I sat up in bed with a bounce. I had been dreaming that Al Burnet had murdered me and they'd accused Old Man Carr of it and they wanted me to testify and I refused, feeling I'd had about enough to do with the affair. I was sitting up, because Judge Forest had pulled me that far out of my grave, and I wanted to get back in again.

Well, I sat there, looking at a lot of darkness, and trying to convince myself I was in bed and not in my coffin.

"You dumbbell!" I said to myself, "a corpse can't argue, and you're arguing as fast as your two-for-a-cent brain can work!"

Well, that sort of settled matters about the graveyard. . . . But still I wasn't quite satisfied. There was something wrong and I couldn't just think what it was.

I looked around, but I might just as well have kept my head still. It was as dark as a grave, and a lot more quiet . . . excepting I saw a bit of a bare, black tree trunk, and a piece of night sky on both sides of it.

Then I remembered I wasn't alone and I felt relieved; Jane was with me and—

—and I had seen a hand reach out from behind the screen, that wasn't Jane's hand!

I remembered that, and I got cold all over. . . . But I had seen Jane sleeping peacefully afterward. . . . And you could tell she was sleeping peaceful now . . . peaceful and quiet.

. . . A little too quiet.

I laid the blankets carefully back, so as not to make a noise. Then I crawled to the end of my bed that was pointed toward the screen.

I waited there, on my hands and knees, looking to where the screen ought to be. And I listened.

There wasn't a sound. I waited and listened, feeling something funny creep up from my stomach.

"Why, you nut!" I told myself. "Of course you can't hear her! You can't even hear your own breath!"

But then I decided that wasn't odd, because, after investigating, I discovered I hadn't been doing any breathing for some little time. So I grabbed the edge of the cot and leaned over until I almost fell into the darkness. Then I listened again.

But there wasn't any sound.

"Jane!" I called, softly.

She didn't answer.

"Jane!" I called again, louder; much too loud for a dark, empty cabin—for there was something empty about it. You can tell, somehow or other.

I got out of bed and felt around for my candle. Then I got a match and lighted it.

It was funny. Before I lighted it, the only light place was the patch behind the tree trunk. Then, suddenly, that was all swallowed up by the black windowpane, and now the room was lighted— not much lighted—just a flickering, shadowy light that hardly reached the corners and made the screen seem like a great, gloomy wall.

Then I walked up close (not too close), and peeked.

Well, it seemed all right. Jane was lying there, just as I left her. . . . She hadn't moved an inch . . . not an inch.

And then I saw something I hadn't noticed before: something white that was bunched near her mouth. (Her head was turned away, you see.) I took a step forward.

The bedclothes were off her, and she was lying right below the window, where the cold, icy wind blew in. I tip-toed over to cover her up. And then that feeling in my stomach jumped right up into my mouth.

I saw blood!

It covered her nightgown, right above her heart, and the sheet below was just soaked with it!

Well, I squeezed that candle until I almost squashed it, and I made myself go and look. I crept up between the screen and the bed and leaned over.

She was dead!

I touched her arm. It was cold and stiff. I pulled it gently and she fell over on her back. And as her head fell over, her white underskirt came with it, for it was stuffed in her mouth!

She had been dead for hours. Somebody had climbed in the window and scared her into keeping still. Then he had stuffed her petticoat into her mouth while she lay there frightened stiff. And then, suddenly, he had stabbed her. Right in the heart.

And it was the hand of the murderer I had seen feeling around in front of the screen!

I figured this out quick, while I stood before the bed, shivering from cold and fear. And then I turned and almost knocked over the screen and ran back to my own side of the room.

I got into my clothes as quick as I could. I didn't know who had murdered Jane, but I knew who could have stopped it if he hadn't been such a damn coward! That was the only thought I had in my brain as I got dressed—that, and the thought of getting out of the cabin as quick as I could. I'd notify the police in New Paris, or something, but anyhow, I'd *get out*!

I didn't know what time it was when I locked the door and climbed out of the center window, but when I dragged myself up the deserted street at the edge of town a couple of hours later, the sun hadn't risen.

I didn't have any thoughts in my head; just a funny jumble. So I went home and threw myself on my bed to wonder about it all. And then, before I knew it, I was fast asleep.

It was in the middle of the afternoon when I waked up. I lay wondering for about ten seconds. Then I jumped off my bed and ran out the door. I was going to tell the police about the murder of Jane.

I went down Main Street, wondering about poor Jane, until I had to stop doing that to wonder why I wasn't bumping into anybody like I generally do when I'm wondering on Main Street. I looked up and then I saw why: there wasn't anybody to bump into. Main Street was as deserted as it had been at dawn; and it was twice as dismal.

But I didn't have much time to wonder about that. I wanted to report Jane's death as quick as I could, and then gather some news about Al. So I headed for the Court House. And there I saw why Main Street was deserted.

The Court House was just chock-full of men and women, with little kids dripping out of all the windows. My heart started jazzing up, for I had a pretty good idea what the party was all about. I saw Jim Harley on the Court House steps and I wandered up to him.

"What's up?" I asked, sort of careless-like.

Jim stared at me, as if I was some new species off of Mars.

"What brook did you drown yourself in," he asked, "and you don't know they're trying Al Burnet?"

"I've been out to my country estate," I told him. "What are they trying him now for, two days after the murder?"

"They've got to. The crowd's been trying to get at him to lynch him all morning long, so Mr. Sparton's made them get a quick trial to save his life and hang him proper."

Well, I just felt myself turn white all over. Lynch Al Burnet! And this crowd of bums he'd always been so decent with, too! I had a lot of thoughts on the subject, and I expressed them in a loud voice to Jim and anyone else who might be around.

Jim listened, interested-like, until I got through. Then he turned and looked across the street.

"Do you think the branch of that there tree is very strong?" he asked me.

But I didn't answer him. Somebody had just got down from the window next to the steps, and I ran over to it and pulled myself up and looked inside.

The first thing I saw was old Judge Wharton who lives in Berlin, sitting up on the bench and looking important and frowning all over. Then I saw Horace Sparton, who is the district attorney, leaning over the table and glaring at somebody. I looked to see who he was glaring at.

It was Irene Burnet. She was standing in the witness box. I could just see the tip of her nice little nose beyond her curly, yellow hair, and a

bit of her cheek. But even that bit, I could see, was as white as marble, and her lips, that were quivering, were as pale as anything. She was holding on to the rail as tight as she could.

"What time did you say he got in?" I heard Sparton shout.

Irene's lips moved, but I couldn't hear anything.

"Louder, please, Miss Burnet!"

And then I heard, soft and awful weak:

"One o'clock."

Sparton smiled and then nodded to her. Irene left the stand, holding her head up, but looking like she was going to die.

"One more witness," Sparton said, "and then our case is finished."

And he turned and spoke to the clerk.

I was hunting for Al now, and I found him, sitting at the table. His face was almost as white as Irene's, but he was looking proud and handsome. He watched his sister sit down, looking as if he was awfully sorry for her. And then he turned toward where the people sat who were watching the show. And I saw who he was looking at.

It was Miriam Sparton, Horace's daughter. She looked terrible. You could see she believed Al was innocent and she was sore at her father for prosecuting him. And there was love in her eyes and she didn't care who knew it.

But she was the only one who had love in her eyes. The crowd around her were looking at Al as hard as she was, but there wasn't any love in their faces. All the hard-boiled guys in town were in front, and they were looking at Al just the way a cat looks into a mouse-trap if there's a mouse there. *I* couldn't have sat before them looking as indifferent as he did!

I saw this awfully quick, because soon I was thinking of other things. For after Sparton spoke to the clerk, the clerk turned and shouted:

"John Darrow!"

Well, I don't know whether it was quick thinking on my part, or whether I just fell off the window in surprise. Anyhow, in just about one jiffy, I was hiking down the pike as fast as I could go. *I* wasn't going to do any testifying against Al Burnet!

I beat it down the street and kept on going until the first thing I knew I was sitting on the fence next to the Burnets' place. It's so comfortable there and I can wonder easy. And I wondered along until suddenly I brought up with a bang.

"Well, you big, fat-headed fool!" I said to myself, among other things.

For I had just remembered the paper Jane had been writing on and hid in the ashes!

I'd been sure right along that the fellow who murdered Jane was the same one who murdered Old Man Carr, because, somehow or other, there was something fishy about the way Jane laid the blame on Al. I'd intended to tell the police all about it and what I suspicioned, but now I didn't dare to; they'd hold me for a witness against Al.

Now I'd thought of the paper, I felt a little happier. It might tell something interesting; and even if it didn't, it'd give me something to do. And if it did tell something, I could testify about it in the morning.

"I'll go out to the cabin now," I said. And as I said it, I couldn't help shuddering a little. It was already getting dark and I thought of that cabin, alone there in the woods—and what was in it.

However, I jumped down and started off. Before I went, though, I crept around the corner.

There was nobody at Burnet's house, and I ran up the path. They never lock the door, for they haven't got anything to steal, so I opened it and went inside.

I went into the living-room. Everything was sort of upside down. It made me feel rather bad, for Irene is usually awful particular, but you could tell she didn't care what happened now. The waste-paper basket was beside the big center table, and I picked a sheet of paper out of it that was almost clean. Then I wrote on it in big letters:

"Irene!

"Don't worry! Forces are working for you and Al!"

I started to sign "Jack" to it, but then I thought I wouldn't, and I put "A Friend." It sounds more important and mysterious.

Then I ran outside and started for the woods. Before I could reach them, though, I had to pass the foot of the Avenue. And who should I run into of all people, but Horace Sparton. He grabbed me by the shoulder.

"Here, boy!" he said. "Where were you this afternoon?"

Well, I was trying to think of about a million things at once, so I said the first thing that popped into my head.

"In church, sir," I answered meekly.

Then Old Sparton shook me.

"Don't try to be funny with me, boy!" he grunted. "You are supposed to be a witness for the state. We had to call off the trial because of you. . . . But I'll see that you're there tomorrow morning," he muttered between his teeth, and he started to march me off toward the lock-up.

I went along with him a ways, because I wanted to do some wondering, and it was easy to do it and walk with his hand on my collar. I didn't have to see where I was going. Finally, however, I craned my neck up and looked at him.

"Please, Mr. Sparton," I said, "won't you let me go?"

"No, I won't," he said; and he looked as if *that* was settled.

"Well, look, Mr. Sparton," I went on, "if you let me go now, I'll show up first thing in the morning! Honest I will! I swear on the Bible!"

"I don't care if you swear on the *Wall Street Journal*," he said. "You're coming along with me. And don't talk so much. You annoy me enough by just living."

"Well, look, Mr. Sparton! If you let me go, I'll find out the murderer for you!"

Well, then he swung around and stared down at me.

"What do you mean, the murderer?" he shouted. "We've got the murderer in the lock-up—unless they've already lynched him."

And then he looked at me sort of thoughtful and started shaking me, offhand like.

I waited until he got through. Then I decided the best thing to do was take him into my confidence.

"Well, look, Mr. Sparton," I began; "I know where I can get some dope on who murdered Old Man—Mr. Carr—a place in the woods where—"

And then I stopped. His eyes were glaring and his face kept coming lower and lower as if he was going to rub noses with me. Then he said, kind of hoarse:

"What kind of dope?"

"Well, look, Mr. Sparton, you just let me go and—"

But he had started shaking me again and the rest of my words came out funny; all twisted and different-sounding from the way they started out to be.

"You tell me all about it," he said, "and I'll tell the police and they can go out and investigate."

That made me just turn cold and sweat at the same time. If Sparton had let go of me then, I would have just dropped right through the sidewalk and come up in China or Ireland or some place. Because if any police had gone out to my cabin and seen Jane lying there, murdered, and known that I was there alone with her the night before—well, the boys would be tying two ropes to the same branch. And it didn't make me any more cheerful when Sparton squinted at me and said:

"It's mighty funny what you do by yourself all alone in the woods! I think the police had better go out and take a look at the place anyhow!"

I thought a while to think of some good reply to get him off of the track; and finally I said:

"Yes, sir."

"Well, come along!" he said, starting off.

And I said:

"Yes, sir," as I dragged along after him.

And then, suddenly, I threw up my arms and slipped out of my coat. It was a cold night, and he had thick gloves on, and hadn't been able to get a good grip on my body.

Sparton just had time enough to say:

"Well, I'll be—" as if he was displeased, when I turned the corner. In two minutes I passed the last house and the last street lamp in town and was looping across the dark meadow. Then I beat it into the wood.

It was as dark as blazes (only blazes is awfully light), and I had a job finding the path even with my pocket flashlight. I reckon it must have been after eight o'clock when I went flying over the stump where I found Jane sitting the day before; and when I reached the sharp corner in the path just this side of the cabin and started to go straight ahead, it was almost nine. I've got so I can tell time by the stars and things.

And then I slowed down. I wanted to go faster; I knew I ought to go faster; and the path was wide and clear—but I just couldn't make it. I don't know why, but my feet just dragged as if they were tied to a ball and chain.

And when I came in sight of that cabin, standing black and quiet underneath the trees at the end of the path, I just had to pinch myself in the back to make me go on.

The front window was just beside the path. I opened it and stuck my head in. I couldn't see anything. It was just all black.

And yet I couldn't help turning my head and looking to the left. It was black and silent like the rest. But I knew I was looking at the screen; and beyond that screen—

Well, I turned around and gave a last look at the outdoors, at the black, bare trunks and limbs, sticking up into the dark sky. There were five miles of thick woods between me and any other living human being.

I was thinking of that when I hoisted myself up to the window sill, and my arms sort of wobbled and I fell back again.

"Come on, you yellow baby!" I sneered at me.

Then I gave a big jump up and landed clear through on my nose.

I sat up in the dark, listening, while it got all quiet again. Then I stood up and felt around for the candle and lighted it.

Nothing had changed. The fire had gone out and my chair stood beside it. It was facing the screen as I left it. . . . And there was the screen, keeping Jane's body in her own part of the room.

I set the candle on the table and the wind blew it and made big, funny shadows on the ceiling. But I didn't want to close that window. I knew there wasn't anything but black woods all around. But that was better than being shut up alone with . . . Jane.

I stood a long while looking at that big staring screen. I started to go over to it, and then I decided I ought to eat my supper first. I reckon it was just an excuse, but I hadn't eaten anything since Jane and I had our supper the night before, and I suddenly found I was mighty hungry.

So I got the pail and unlocked the door and felt my way through the dark until I found the stream. Then I came back.

I'd left the door open, so's I could see, but I wished I hadn't. The path was oblique, so all the time I walked up it, I was just looking at that screen, standing there, and just a tiny bit of white—the bed.

Well, after I got in and closed the door, I sat down and carefully washed my potatoes. (I don't usually do that.) Then I started to pare them. (I don't do that, either.) I reckon I spent an hour doing that. . . . But all the time I was looking at the screen, that was so silent and big, and thinking of what was on the other side of it.

Then I got down and looked under the bed to see if there was something else to eat, although I knew there wasn't.

Finally I stood up and looked at the screen.

"Now, see here, crazy!" I said. "Dead people can't hurt you! You've got to go right over there and show Jane you're a man!"

I stood a second getting up nerve. Then, suddenly, I walked over to it and peeked.

She was lying just as I left her, with the wind coming through the window over her head and blowing her pretty hair.

And she was staring up at me, sort of reproachfully.

I felt terrible. First, I'd let her get killed without lifting a hand. And then I was so scared and addle-headed I'd run off and left her body lying there.

"I'm awfully sorry, Jane," I whispered. "I'll fix you nice, now, and then in the morning, after I testify, I'll tell them about you and we'll come up and bury you."

Then I pulled the bedclothes down and made her all straight. I folded her arms across her breast and covered her up again. I started to close her eyes, but I couldn't seem to get up nerve enough for that. Then I stood looking at her.

The candle was on the other side of the screen and she and I were in a shadow. Finally I leaned over the bed to put down the window. It was awfully black outside!

I just had my fingers on the window, when I heard a little noise.

I listened a minute. It was just the wind in the trees, I told myself. They were making that noise that cold branches make when the wind blows.

"Yes, that's all it is," I said to myself; "so don't get so scared."

And while I was saying it, I knew it was something else.

. . . It was footsteps, creeping along through the trees behind the cabin!

Well, I came from behind the screen and went to the middle of the room. And then I stood there, staring like a gawk and wondering what I ought to do. From the corners of my eyes I could see the gloomy room with the shadows moving back and forth as the candle flickered. And straight ahead of me I was looking at the middle window that I had left open.

. . . And while I looked there, a man passed in front of it, on his way to the door!

Well, I stood there, trying to think of something to do. Then I started to run and lock the door and shut the window. But I hadn't put one foot forward, when I saw the handle move.

Slowly the door opened and a man looked in!

He was a big woodsman with a fur cap and a thick black beard. He had on a mackinaw and heavy woolen gloves. And he had a knife in his belt.

He stood looking at me for a moment without saying a word. Then he stepped inside and shut the door.

"How d'y!" he said.

I made a little noise with my mouth. It was funny and dry. I reckon I must have been thirsty.

The man looked around. His eyes rested for a minute on the screen and I thought I'd drop. Finally he looked back at me.

"You live here?" he asked.

"Sometimes."

"Alone?" And his eyes squinted as he looked at me.

I wet my mouth with my tongue. Then I said:

"I got a friend staying with me."

The man sort of frowned.

"Where is he?" he asked.

"My friend's right around here." Which was true. Jane was right behind the bed.

The man looked around again. Then he looked back at me. And he sort of smiled.

"Well, will you give me some supper?" he asked. "I'm starved. . . . I'll pay you for it."

"Do you like potatoes?" I said.

"Pretty well."

"All right. Stick around." I was acting perky, but I wasn't feeling that way at all.

I had already built my fire, and put the potatoes in, and now they were boiling merrily. I got a fork and jabbed it into them to see if they were done.

While I was doing it, I heard the window close. I swung around.

The man was looking at me.

"It's coming up cold," he said. But a funny little smile flickered around the corner of his mouth. And then: "Is that window behind the screen closed?" he asked, taking a step forward.

"Yes, it is! It's shut tight!" I said, feeling sort of pale.

He hesitated a minute. Then he dropped into a chair by the table.

I fooled around, preparing supper and trying to get my nerve back. It seemed to have all dribbled out through my pores like sweat. It wasn't that I was a-scared of woodsmen. They're a pretty good sort, although they're hard-boiled eggs. But the dead body, lying just about three feet in back of him, and the general commotion of the last two days sort of made me wobbly. Besides, there was something about

that man's face that wasn't what you'd call just friendly.

But I got hold of myself at last and lugged the potatoes over to the table—and my heart just went plunk in my boots again.

The man had thrown off his coat and moved up to the table and was taking off his gloves; *and on the finger you point with was a long, funny-shaped bloodstone!*

I just sat and stared, and the pan with the potatoes dropped lower and lower until it touched my pants. Then I hopped up with a yell and the potatoes went flying. The man jumped up and leaned over the table.

"What do you mean, throwing those potatoes around like that!" he yelled.

I was down on my knees, trying to pick them up.

"It's a quick way to cool them off," I said, not to be funny, but because I couldn't think of anything better.

"I'll cool you off," he muttered.

But he sat down again and started pulling the peelings off with his sharp, gleaming knife.

Well, we ate there, awfully quiet, except for the funny noises we were making with our mouths. I say "we." *I* wasn't doing much eating. Every time I lifted my knife to my mouth I saw that black beard with the candle light on it; and behind that, in the shadow, the big screen.

Finally he'd eaten all he wanted, which I'd done before I started. Then he got up and stretched.

"What bed does your friend sleep in?" he asked.

"That one behind the screen," I told him.

I didn't know his game, but I knew he wanted to pretend he didn't know what was behind the screen. And *I* wasn't hankering after any showdown.

"Well," he said, "I'll take this middle bed and you can take the other end one."

Then, just as if we'd settled everything long ago, he pulled the table toward him and sat down on the bed.

"Better hurry up," he said. "I'm going to blow the candle out."

Well, I couldn't see anything else to do, so I went over to the other bed and sat on it. He took off his belt and laid it on the table, right within arm's reach. It was right under the candle and the light glinted on a bit of the blade that showed. It made my back feel itchy. He turned and looked at me a minute. He had tiny, gleaming eyes.

"Good-night," he said.

Then he blew out the candle and lay down, boots and all.

I lay in the dark, hearing him breathe. It was a sort of heavy breathing; you couldn't tell whether he was asleep or awake. Then I started wondering what to do.

I mustn't go to sleep! That was the first thing. I could just see that dagger sink down inside of me if I did. No, I mustn't go to sleep. Mustn't go to sleep . . . mustn't go . . .

Whether I'd been asleep an hour, or just a second, I didn't know. All I knew was that I was still alive when I woke up.

And I could hear that breathing, loud and regular, but you couldn't tell if he was asleep or awake. I lay, looking at darkness, and thinking.

I had to get out of there. But I had to get that paper first of all. I could have choked myself for not getting it before. The only thing to do was to get it quietly and then run for it.

And then I remembered a noise I heard while I was cooking the potatoes and I suddenly knew what it was. When my back was turned he had locked the door!

"Well," I said to myself, "the more you think, the harder it gets, so you better quit thinking and act!"

And with that I sat up in bed—and lay down again. That bed squeaked as if all the devils in hell were tied inside!

The man moved a little, but he kept breathing hard.

I lay a while longer, looking up and wondering why the noise my heart was making didn't wake him. Then I got up, oh, so quiet, and put my feet on the floor.

I stood up. Then I took a tiny little step and the boards didn't creak. And I took another one.

All the time I was staring as hard as I could in the direction of his bed. There was a little night-light that came through the window across the room to his bed, but at first I couldn't see anything. When I could make out something, I stopped short and so did my heart.

The man was sitting up in bed and looking right at me!

Well, I thought quick and walked on. I walked to the stove, right under his nose, and opened the door and stuck a log inside. Then I shut it and went back to bed.

I waited for him to lie down again. I turned over on my side, so's I could make out the outline of his body in the dark. . . . And I could just see him sitting there, not moving an inch, and staring at me. I knew he was staring at me, although I couldn't make out his eyes. And he couldn't see me at all, because I was in complete darkness.

Then his hand went out toward the table. It felt around, slowly and carefully, just as it did when he was behind the screen. It felt around . . . and then I saw, in the faint light, his knife gleaming as it rose from its sheath.

He put one foot on the floor. I couldn't see it, and I couldn't hear it, but I could make out his great body moving. He stood up; I could see his body rise.

All the time he looked in my direction, while I lay trembling all over and trying to remember how "Now I lay me" goes.

And then he turned and disappeared in the gloom.

Well, I decided there was something wrong. The next thing on the program was for him to come over and kill me, and I almost felt like calling to him and telling him he made a mistake.

But I listened and looked and I heard nothing and saw nothing. And then, suddenly, I knew what he was doing.

He was fishing through the body of the girl he had killed to take away all evidence!

And while I thought that, and was listening for some little sound, I heard something inside of me, an angel or a devil, shout:

"Now's your chance!"

Well, I would have flopped at the thought, if I hadn't already been in bed. But I listened and waited, and as nothing happened, I got braver and braver. And finally I sat up again.

There wasn't any sound in the whole cabin. It was just as if the man had been swallowed up, and I was left alone with the dead body.

I got up and tip-toed across the floor, stooping, and feeling for the coal scuttle. Finally I touched it softly. I took a look at the screen and then got down on my hands and knees.

I took the ashes and laid them on the floor. I took them one by one, so as not to make any noise, but I did it as quick as I could. It was awfully hard to keep them from slipping from my hand. The muscles just seemed to have stopped working.

I got lower and lower without finding the paper. Then I stopped.

Sometimes you can tell that somebody's around you without seeing or hearing them. Just a sixth sense, I reckon. I sat quiet. Then, slowly, I turned my head.

He was creeping toward me.

I could see him coming, but I couldn't hear a sound. He came closer and closer. When he got right above me, he stopped and looked down.

I looked up. I tried to say something, but I couldn't think of a word. I don't think my tongue would have worked if I did.

He just looked at me. Then he said:

"What are you doing up?"

"The wood's nearly gone. I'm hunting for good coals."

I don't know how I said it, but I did.

"All right. Go ahead and look. Don't mind me."

Well, I had to turn back and look. And all the time I felt him standing over me. I picked the coals over. . . . And I heard him take a step closer and heard his breath nearer and nearer.

He grabbed my neck. I gave a yelp and ducked low.

That saved my life, for my head hit the coal-scuttle and it fell over, knocking me sideways. . . . And I heard hard steel strike its tin side with an awful crack.

I was up in a second and running across the floor. I heard him swearing. I reckon he hurt his hand on the scuttle. I got to Jane's end and beat it behind the screen. I didn't have time to open that window, for everything was quiet now and I knew he was coming. So I stood behind the screen and waited . . . the dead body behind me, and him, creeping up, creeping up.

And I was waiting for him to jump around the corner, when I had a bright idea.

I knew he was right in front of the screen. I jumped on the edge of the bed and threw myself against the screen with all my might. He went over and the screen and me on top of him. And two jiffies later I had the window open and was outside.

I didn't stop running until I brought up against a tree. Then I went to sleep.

I had an awful head when I woke up. But I forgot all about that when I saw how high the sun was. I just got up and loped, swift as anything, for the village.

All the fellows had moved from in front of the drug store down to the front of the courthouse, so I knew things must be interesting. When they saw me they all turned and hollered.

"There he is!" they yelled.

I couldn't help glancing at the big limb Jim had pointed out the day before, but I kept going.

"What for did you make off you didn't know nothing about this trial yesterday?" Jim asked me when I hove up. "They've been looking all over the lot for you!"

Well, I didn't answer him, but I just pushed through into the courtroom. I reckon they had just started proceedings, for people had a sort of attitude of settling themselves and the clerk was droning a lot of stuff nobody was paying any attention to.

I kept pushing up front, and before anybody would let me pass he would have to stop me and tell me that everybody had been looking for me the day before. You could tell I was important. All the kids from school looked at me, jealous-like, and I could have had an awfully good time if I hadn't been having such a rotten one.

You see, I felt something else in the air. I couldn't quite tell what it was until I reached the bunch of hard guys in front. Then, as I started to push by one, he muttered:

"Save your breath, boy, save your breath. It's all settled long ago."

But just then the clerk saw me and shouted out:

"John Darrow!" so loud that the judge woke up.

Well, I shouted: "Present!" sort of getting it twisted with something else I couldn't remember, and I walked up to the witness box. Then they started asking me a lot of fool questions, such as whether I was born or not. But all the time I was answering them I was looking out of the corner of my eye at different people.

Al was sitting directly beneath me. He looked lots better than he did the day before; like a person who knows it's all over and is going to have a good time while it lasts. And he looked at me awfully friendly, almost as if he was sorry for me. And when he smiled he just as good as said:

"Don't you worry, Jackie boy! I'm doomed anyhow and nothing you can say will make any difference. Just go right ahead and tell the truth and we'll be as good friends as ever!"

I wanted to shout down to him that there was still a chance for him, but I decided I wouldn't.

And then I saw Irene, over in the mourner's bench, or whatever you call it. She didn't look friendly like Al. You could tell by her pretty white face that she thought I was betraying them. I couldn't look at her squarely.

The cop gave me a shove and I turned around to bat him in the eye. But he was pointing to the district attorney, and I'd suddenly realized I'd been wondering again and forgot to answer his questions.

Old Sparton was frowning at me.

"Don't hesitate, boy!" he was saying. "What time was it when you were walking up the Avenue?"

"One o'clock."

"One o'clock. . . . Two o'clock is probably nearer right. . . . And you saw somebody running away from something?"

"Yes, sir."

"Whose house was he running away from?"

"Old—Mr. Carr's."

"Mr. Carr's house . . . At two o'clock in the morning."

"One o'clock," I interrupted him.

He glared at me. Then he said, leaning way forward:

"And who was the man who was running away from Mr. Carr's house at two o'clock in the morning?"

I was aching and feeling sore and generally rotten. That always makes me obstinate. So I said:

"I won't answer until you say it right!"

There was a giggle in the courtroom and the Judge pounded his gavel. Sparton frowned at me until his eyes almost touched. But he said, finally:

"Well, at one o'clock, then."

I had to say it now. I tried to say it loud, as if it didn't mean anything. But it was hardly more than a whisper, a whisper in the big, quiet room:

"Alfred Burnet."

I could hear the big breath that everybody took. And I could feel Irene's eyes without looking at them. Then Sparton asked me a few more questions, and after I'd answered them, he turned around and smiled as if it was all over. And I could see the hard guys tensioning, as if they were getting ready to run in when the jury pronounced the verdict. I could see a bit of rope dangling behind some of them.

Sparton lifted the German trench knife, sort of careless-like.

"Do you recognize this knife?" he asked, as if it didn't much matter whether I did or not.

"Yes," I said.

"Whose is it?"

"Alfred Burnet's."

He turned around and faced the jury and shrugged his shoulders.

That was enough for me. I stepped to the edge of the stand and grabbed the rail, hard.

"But Al Burnet didn't do it, just the same!" I shouted at him.

You ought to have heard the silence in that

courtroom! I could just feel everybody's eyes coming out of their sockets. But I didn't look. I had a hard enough job holding on.

Old Sparton swung around and looked at me. He was too surprised to be mad.

"What are you talking about, boy? Nobody asked your opinion about that!"

"No, but I'm giving it just the same!" I shouted.

With that the Judge said something and the cop started to shove me out of the box. But I ducked, and when I came up I shouted, quick:

"I'll bet the same person killed Old Man Carr what killed Jane Brewster!"

"What?"

Judge Wharton jumped up and stared at me. All over the room there was a great commotion. Everybody looked at me as if I just dropped from Mars—except the kids at school. Gee, they were jealous! And I felt mighty cocky at having broken the news.

"What did you say?" the Judge shouted.

"Jane Brewster was murdered, sir," I said in a quiet sort of voice. "Somebody killed her in a cabin in the woods about five miles from here. Stuffed something in her mouth and stabbed her in the heart."

There was a gasp of horror all over the courtroom. Somebody started crying, a sort of smothered whimpering. It was little Ruthy Bingham, a girl who Jane had sort of mothered.

The Judge pulled himself together and looked very business-like, as if such things were mere trifles in a busy day.

"Officer Sullivan!" he ordered. "Find out from the witness the location of the cabin the moment he finishes testifying. The coroner and his men will go with you, examine the evidence and dispose of the body."

Everybody settled down, and I thought that that thrill was over, at least until the end of this trial, when I happened to look at Sparton's face.

It was as white as a sheet, and he was glaring at me so fierce that I was glad there was a cop around—for the first time in my life.

When the room got silent again, Sparton leaned forward.

"So little Jane Brewster has been murdered, has she?"

"Yes, sir," I said.

He took a step toward me and spoke, very quietly.

"And you know who murdered her, do you?"

"Why—" I hesitated.

He took another step toward me; and he was smiling, sort of knowing.

"And you know who murdered her, do you? You, and you alone?"

I'd forgotten all about that part of it for the moment. I'd been alone with her when she was murdered; and I didn't know who did it. I didn't feel quite so proud now of having broken the news.

Sparton kept coming nearer and nearer, and everybody in the room, including myself, held our breaths until we almost busted. Then Sparton spoke again, very, very low.

"And you know who murdered her," he said again. Then, suddenly, he raised his finger and pointed it at me. "Who murdered Jane Brewster?" he shouted.

I almost fainted away. I just held tight to the rail to keep myself up. But it wasn't because I was feeling guilty like you do when you're not and people think you are. It was because I was staring at Sparton's hand. For *on the finger he pointed with was a long, funny-shaped bloodstone!*

I stood staring at him. And he stared at me, while his dirty grin grew wider and wider. And I could feel everybody else in the room staring at both of us.

Then I leaned way forward, and in a voice that was hoarse and not much better than a whisper, I said:

"You did it!"

Well, everybody busted. And it was a good five minutes before order was re-established and the cops had got Sparton's hands off of me.

They held him away from me, while he kept saying:

"Prove it! prove it!" in a voice that sounded as though he was talking to the Angel of Death.

"By that ring on your finger!" I shouted back.

Then the Judge stood up.

"That's a serious accusation, young man!" he said. "And the whole affair is very irregular. If you can't offer some other proof than that, you had better descend and let us go on with the trial."

Well, I was stumped—for a second. And then I remembered the thing that had made me in such a sweat to testify: the paper Jane had written. My hand had landed on it the night before, just as the woodsman collared me, and I found it clutched in my fingers that morning when I woke up in the woods. While I was hurrying to town, I glanced at it, and read enough to realize that Jane had had some dope on the real murderer; but I had reached the courthouse before I'd found out who did it, and I had slipped it in my pants pocket and forgot about it.

I fished it out and handed it to the Judge.

"This is what Jane Brewster was writing night before last when I found her in the woods, Your Honor," I said. "She slipped it into the coal-scuttle and I only got it last night."

The Judge settled himself and commenced to read.

" 'This is the truth and nothing but the truth, so help me God,' " he read, " 'only you got to give me a two days' start before you show this to anybody, whoever you are. I'm going to hide this, and then if somebody else gets blamed for Mr. Carr's murder than the right person, I'll write somebody where this is hid and he can show it to the police.

" 'I saw Mr. Carr just after he was murdered. I went up to his room, and he was lying just as still, and while I was looking at him, the door opened, and who was standing there but Horace Sparton with a knife in his hand!' "

"She's a liar!"

The Judge stopped reading, and everything was dead still. Everybody looked at Horace Sparton. He was as white as a sheet, and he was standing up and clutching the back of his chair. The Judge glared at him a minute. Then he went on reading:

" 'Mr. Sparton was dressed like a woodsman and he had a black, false beard in his hand. I reckon it had slipped off and he was just putting it up to his face again. But when he saw me, he gave a yell, and I turned and ran.' "

So he had that costume on tap all the time for his dirty work! Sparton must have known that I was thinking of that, for, scared as he was, he turned and glanced at me. I was awfully sore at him, until I happened to look in back of him, and saw the hard-boiled eggs crowding up to the rail. The guy with the rope was rubbing his hands.

That made me a little sorry for him. But I was sorrier for his daughter, Miriam. She was having a pretty rough time of it! First her lover was accused of the murder, and they let up on him, only to prove it was her father. Everybody in town knew he wasn't a model father, but still, your old man is your old man!

Miriam was sitting with her head very low and her face very white, and Al was looking at her as if he wasn't awfully glad at what was happening. Lots of us felt sorry for her, while the Judge read on, until something he read made us all sit up and take notice and not feel so blooming sorry.

" 'I reckon I know why Mr. Sparton killed Mr. Carr,' " he read. " 'Mr. Carr got friendly and confidential with me one time and he told me a lot about himself. He told me he had a daughter once, which I had heard; but that after he was put in jail, his wife was so ashamed that she got sick and died. And before she died she made him promise to put their daughter somewhere where she wouldn't ever know he was her father. So he gave her to Mr. Sparton, when they were East together, just before Mrs. Sparton died, and he was giving him a lot of money to support her.

" 'And then he made out his will to Mr. Sparton, instead of to her. But when he found that Al Burnet and she were in love with each other, that tickled him, because he liked Al, although he was too stingy to give him anything. And he told me that the day they were engaged, he was going to change the will, leaving everything to Al. He said he had told Mr. Sparton, too.' "

Well, all over the courtroom there was a stir.

Miriam was staring at the Judge as if she couldn't believe her ears. And Sparton had sunk into his seat with his back to the Judge, as if he was too weak ever to stand up again.

But he jumped up with a yell, as if he had sat on a tack. For out of the corner of his eyes he had seen the rope which the guy was fixing in a knot. Sparton stared at it a minute, and then at the man, who was watching him with a smile, and then, slowly, he swayed and fell over onto the floor.

That was the signal. With a howl like a lot of wild beasts just let out of their cages, the whole bunch rushed in and made for Sparton. Somebody put the rope around his neck, while the others kept the cops off. Then they dragged him out of the courtroom.

Sparton had about five more minutes of consciousness. They could have taken him out and done the job without waking him up, but that wasn't their style. They wanted him to know what was happening and see how he took on.

The crowd stood around in a circle under the tree while he stood there and confessed it was all true.

"I got Burnet's trench knife out of his house when he was away in Denver," he said in a whisper, "because—because I wanted him to get the blame."

"Is that all you got to say?" said one of the bums, sticking his jaw into Sparton's face, real brave-like.

"That's all."

"Then all right, boys! Hoist her up!"

And that was enough for me. I turned around, and took my two legs, that were sort of wobbly, firmly in hand, so to speak, and sent them home.

It was six months before Al and Miriam were married. Everybody went to the wedding, for everybody knew now that Al was innocent. They believed him when he said he just went to his stepfather's house to borrow enough money to get his sister a square meal. And anyhow, they wouldn't have been awfully particular, even if they weren't sure, seeing as how Al was a rich man now.

Al and Miriam were married in the big Carr house where he and Irene were living. They invited me to go, but I couldn't. I didn't have anything to wear. My suit had long ago got so that if I'd worn it, there'd be a law against it, and I'd thrown it away and had been wearing my other suit regular since spring.

I walked by the house, which was all lighted up, although it was hardly dark. Then I went across the town and somehow found myself around the house where they used to live. Then I saw my old place on the fence doing nothing, so I climbed up on it. And I started wondering.

I was wondering what was the sense in living, and I was just winning the argument, when I heard a little noise.

I looked up and saw Irene standing there.

"What are you doing on the fence?" she asked.

"Just wondering."

It sounded silly, but I *was*. I was wondering now if it was too dark to see the color of a fellow's cheeks and I was hoping it was. Your cheeks just couldn't help acting funny if you saw a girl as pretty as Irene standing there.

"And we were wondering, too," she said. "We were wondering where you've been all afternoon."

"Why, you see," I said, and commenced fidgeting, so that I almost fell off the fence, "you see—you see, Irene, I just *couldn't* go into anybody else's house dressed like this!"

"Nobody asked you to go into anybody else's house," she said.

That made me feel terrible. I knew I'd received an invitation, but I decided they'd made a mistake and sent it to me instead of the right party. I tried to think of something to say, but nothing happened. I was just wishing the fence would bust and send me flying, when Irene spoke again.

"Nobody asked you to go to anybody else's house," she said again.

Then she reached up and gently took my hand. And in a very, very soft voice, she said:

"Come home, Jackie boy! Come home!"

That was a year ago. But Al's and Miriam's and Irene's home has been my home ever since. In another couple of years, though, when I start getting rich, there's going to be a secession from that home and another one started up with just two in it.

Two to begin with, Irene just said— But that's another story.

Body Snatcher

Theodore A. Tinsley

THEODORE A. TINSLEY (1894–1979) was a third-generation New Yorker who, after serving in World War I, began a prolific career writing for most of the major pulp magazines, including *Black Mask*, *Munsey's*, *Black Aces*, *Detective Book*, *All Detective*, *Action*, and several ghostwritten novels for *The Shadow* and *Crime Busters*, for which he created Carrie Cashin, the most successful female character in the pulps. A gorgeous and sexy private eye, she was the senior partner in the Cash and Carry Detective Agency in a series that ran for more than three dozen stories. She made her debut in the first issue of *Crime Busters* (November 1937); when the magazine changed its name to *Mystery Magazine* with the November 1939 issue, Carrie continued her adventures until nearly the end of the pulp; her last appearance was in the November 1942 issue. Tinsley's other successful series included Major John Tattersall, who formed Amusement Inc. to fight crime with equally stalwart companions, and Jerry Tracy, the likable, Walter Winchell–type gossip columnist for the Manhattan tabloid the *Daily Planet*. Three of the twenty-six Tracy stories that ran in *Black Mask* served as the basis for movies: *Alibi for Murder* (1936) starred William Gargan, Marguerite Churchill, and Gene Morgan, and was based on "Body Snatcher" (February 1936); *Manhattan Shakedown* (1937), with John Gallaudet and Rosalind Keith, was based on "Manhattan Whirligig" (April 1937). *Murder Is News* (1937) was based on an unidentified Tinsley story and also starred Gallaudet.

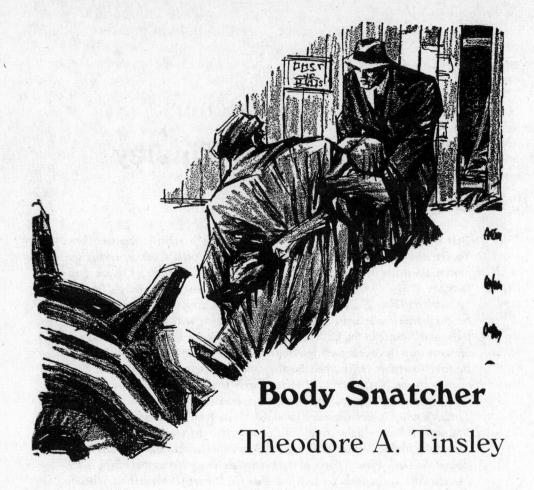

Body Snatcher

Theodore A. Tinsley

Jerry Tracy tries to switch a murder tag.

HE SHABBY SUBURBAN bus jolted to a teethjarring halt and the driver growled with patient boredom: "Locust Avenue!"

Jerry Tracy fell over a couple of legs and swung off the bus, conscious that his lips were wreathed in a faint, somewhat silly grin. If the boys at Times Square could see the *Daily Planet*'s famous little columnist out here in the sticks, could guess what was inside the two paper-wrapped parcels he was carrying, a jeering laugh would go up that would stop the hands on the Paramount clock! Wise guy Jerry, the lad with the case-hardened front—pulling a sentimental pilgrimage to a has-been, because no one else in roaring Manhattan would remember that today was her birthday.

Ordinarily, on a trip out of town, Jerry traveled in his very dodgy Lincoln, with Butch behind the wheel making delighted horn sounds like the *Normandie* going down the bay. But today the *Daily Planet*'s columnist had dived inconspicuously into the subway, ridden out to the end of the line and taken a bus the rest of the way. The big package under his left arm was a birthday cake with a pink, gooey trail on top from a baker's cornucopia that said: "Hey, hey,

Sweetie!" The flat, oblong package had come from a five-and-dime; fluted pink candles with tin shields to catch the grease and pins to stick 'em in the cake.

Sweetie Malloy had once been a name to adorn the most famous of the Victor Herbert operettas! Beauty, brains and a velvet soprano voice gone at last—turned out to a forgotten pasturage in a punk suburb. It angered Jerry to think that a woman like Sweetie Malloy should be permitted by fate to settle down in a one-horse, out-of-the-way dump like this.

Chilly raindrops spattered on Jerry's face. He stared at the gray sky and knew with a wry dismay that it was going to be one of those sullen all-night soakers. By the time he had rung Sweetie's bell, the dark pavement of the walk was a dull, glistening black.

The sight of Sweetie's face in the half-open door made Tracy's throat catch, as it always would at each new sight of her. The singer was gone but the woman remained. The pale yellow entry light fluffed her soft hair, was kind to the threads of gray. Time had padded the once taut line of her throat, had put wrinkles around the clear, amber eyes without disturbing their serenity or their fine courage.

"Jerry!" she gasped, with a quick, frightened inflection.

"How about letting a little guy in out of the rain?"

"Why—yes . . . Of course! Come—come in. . . ."

There was something in the manner with which she closed the door that put Tracy instantly on the alert, made him study the woman. She was scared to a sickish gray pallor. Stealth! That's what the careful click of the closing door had meant.

"Anything wrong, Sweetie?" he asked her, with a level stare.

"Wrong? Why, what a question! With you here?" Her voice steadied. "Everything is right, my friend. Come, let me take your coat and—and bundles. Gracious, what huge packages! Don't tell me they're for—for me?"

"Happy birthday," Tracy said gravely. "We'll open 'em later." He put his hands on both her shoulders as she turned tremulously. "Listen, keed. Do we have to put on an act—you and me? I'm not Ole Olesen or Jake Kazinsky. I'm Jerry Tracy. I came all the way out here tonight because—well, just because . . . I'm asking you as an old friend, is anything wrong?"

Rain, drumming at the closed window, made a softly sinister sound.

"Everything is very, very right, my friend!" Her laugh quivered. "As—as right as rain."

He let the subject drop for the moment. "The big package is a cake," he said. "Biggest damn' cake in the local cakery. Candles in the smaller bundle. Later on we're gonna let you inflate the lovely bosom—and Lord help you if you don't blow 'em all out with one big foooof! I thought that after dinner—"

"Dinner? Of—of course."

"Corned beef." Tracy grinned. "Same as it's always been, same as it always will be. Cooked à la Sweetie Malloy, with gobs of hot English mustard—"

"And—and chopped cabbage with plenty of salt and pepper, lots of b-butter—"

Her voice stopped quite suddenly. Her mouth twisted, began making queer, choking sounds. She turned away towards the couch. Tracy didn't move an inch from where he stood. The sound of her harsh weeping made his heart ache, but he let her alone, let her have the thing out by herself. After a while her fingers stopped bunching the covering on the couch's arm.

"Jerry, will you do something for me—if I beg you as an old friend?"

The look in her eyes made him wary at once. He didn't reply.

"I want you to leave this house immediately and go back to New York."

"No."

"You don't understand. For your own sake, Jerry, you've got to go! Just forget that you were here."

"No."

He winced at the sound of her tragic laugh.

"In that case, you will have to be convinced. You see, you're not the only one with a surprise this evening. I—I have one for you."

Her cold fingers touched his and held on. She walked silently towards the stairs, and Tracy with her. Upstairs in silence, past the bathroom, down a short, incredibly ugly hallway to a closed door which, being opened, disclosed a curtained bedroom where twin boudoir lamps burned softly atop a dresser.

Tracy stared at the room's quiet charm, doubly quiet by reason of the lash of the rain against the shade-drawn windows.

"So what?" he said in a puzzled voice. "Where's the surprise come in?"

"It's—on the other side of the bed."

"It better be a good one, because— Oh!"

He stopped short. His voice sounded like dried peas rattling in a tin pan. "How did this happen?"

"It—it happened."

"Who killed him?"

"I did."

Tracy said very softly: "I knew a guy once who used to lie the same way you do. The more he lied, the more truthful he looked. He never could fool me worth a damn."

erry Tracy bent downward above the sprawled body and surveyed it with narrowed eyes. The man had taken a small-calibered bullet almost exactly through the navel. The corpse was on his back, with his legs together, one arm trailing stiffly towards the dresser. The sleeve of the extended arm, Tracy noted, was quite rumpled. Black, silky hair, a little thin on top; a small black mustache that accented the curve of petulant lips. Eyelids shut tightly. Ears without lobes.

Tracy straightened. "You killed this fellow, Sweetie?"

"Yes."

"Right here?"

"Yes."

"Why?"

"For—for reasons I'd rather not discuss, Jerry."

"We'll skip the reasons. You killed him about a half hour ago, eh?"

"No," Sweetie Malloy said calmly. "I killed him early this afternoon."

Tracy's chuckle held no amusement. "Smart woman refuses to be tripped by cunning columnist." He shook his head. "It's no use lying, Sweetie. Too many other things to explain away. Corpse bled like a pig when he took the slug in the belly—but your rug's nice and clean. The gun on the rug could have done it—maybe did do it—but *not here*, Sweetie. And you should never try to bend an arm after *rigor mortis* has set in; it makes a lot too many wrinkles in the sleeve and sets the mind of a bright little guy galloping with the proper answers."

"Nevertheless, I killed him here in my bedroom," she said, stonily.

"What were you planning to do if I hadn't butted in?"

"I was going to call the police and confess."

"Mmmm . . . Going to, eh? Since this morning?"

Composure fled from her. "My God, Jerry—stop grinning at me like a—a hyena! Did you ever murder anyone—and—and try to decide what to do? Did you ever stare all day at a dead man and think—and think—till you almost went mad with terror and despair? And then, just when you had nerved yourself to take what you deserved—to have the doorbell ring and—and be tortured by a well-meaning friend who—"

Tracy strode grimly forward as her voice mounted shrilly. With deliberate brutality he shook the hysteria from her.

"Stop yelling. Do you want to get me into trouble, too?"

"No, no!" she gasped. "Please go—please, Jerry! I—I brought you up here to show you how dangerous, how suicidal it would be for you to remain until—"

"Save your breath. I won't budge an inch. Who you trying to shield?"

Sweetie didn't reply.

"Who's the lad on the floor?"

"A—a man named Phil Clement. He was a—lover of mine. If you're familiar with the movies we were—living in sin." The hard desperation went out of her voice suddenly. "Jerry, you must believe me! Phil Clement found out something that I couldn't bear to have exposed, and he—he tried to blackmail me."

"I happen to know," Tracy reminded her, "that the income you live on, Sweetie, wouldn't attract a grasshopper."

"For your own sake, leave before I call the police."

"I'm staying here until I find out the truth."

There was a telephone on the low night table and Sweetie sprang towards it. Jerry wrenched the receiver out of her hand before she could utter a word. He slammed it back on the prong and held the sobbing woman motionless for an instant. Something in the wild stare of her eyes gave him a sudden idea.

"If I promise to leave here in ten minutes, will you have one drink with me as a—a substitute for the birthday cake and the—the candles?"

Sweetie Malloy nodded haggardly.

"Where do you keep the liquor?"

"Downstairs. Kitchen. There's a bottle of Scotch in the little closet off the dinette."

She had sunk into a chair, her eyes closed. He closed the bedroom door softly, his mind grimly on the bathroom and the medicine cabinet. A sedative! There must be a sedative there! He was betting shrewdly on the habit that must have been a part of Sweetie Malloy at the height of her Broadway glamour. He had never known a celebrity yet who wasn't an insomniac. Jerry was one himself. Late hours and the constant whirl of excitement made a sedative as familiar as breakfast food. And where would it be but in the medicine cabinet?

He found a bottle of veronal on the lowest shelf. Soundlessly he tiptoed down the carpeted stairs, hurried to the kitchen. He made two stiff highballs. Into the glass with a slight nick at its edge he put a double dose of veronal. He placed both glasses on a tray and went back upstairs.

Sweetie Malloy reached out listlessly as he touched her shoulder and presented the tray. She took the glass without the nick.

"Whoa!" Tracy said humorously and plucked it from her fingers.

"What's the matter?"

"Ginger ale in the other one. Did you think I wouldn't remember?"

"Oh—thanks."

She took the one with the cracked rim and drank deeply. Finished it with a second long gulp. Tracy emptied his, too.

"Bum Scotch," she said faintly. "It's the best I can afford."

"That's all right, Sweetie."

She sat there holding the empty glass. Gradually the tense lines were smoothing out in her face. "You're the best friend I have in the world," she said dreamily. "I wouldn't drag you into a mess like this for a million dollars. On my birthday—that's funny, isn't it?"

"Pretty funny," Tracy agreed.

Rain drummed with insistent sound on the windowpanes. The overhang of the bedclothes hid the corpse from view. Tracy's lowered gaze watched the relaxing fingers on the empty glass. Sweetie clutched sluggishly as the glass dropped into her lap. It bounced off to the floor and she regarded it for an instant with a blurred grimace. Suddenly her eyes widened, knowledge brightening them.

"Jerry . . . What—what—"

"Take it easy, keed."

She swayed unsteadily to her feet, her eyes struggling to retain their fleeting look of tragic accusation.

"You've—you've doped—"

"Sure," Tracy said softly.

e caught her weight as she pitched forward. Holding her limp body in his extended arms, the *Daily Planet*'s wise little columnist stared down at one of the few really fine women he had known in his life. Sweetie Malloy harboring a blackmailing lover? Sweetie Malloy killing a man—for any reason whatsoever? The idea was preposterous, sheer lunacy.

Sweetie wasn't that kind. She had had no furtive lovers—and only one marriage. It wasn't her fault that Jack Malloy was a rotter and a total loss. He didn't even have dough! But she loved him, married him, stuck with him till the hour he died. She had saved enough from her own savings to purchase this cheap house in the suburbs and provide her with a meager income. Finished with the stage, forgotten by the blatant Broadway crowd, she had moved gallantly into obscurity. And this was the woman who was trying to assume the guilt for a sordid murder, who would have leaped into black, scandalous headlines but for Jerry's providential arrival in the rainy dusk.

He carried her sagging weight across to the bed and dropped her with a soft grunt. He had turned back towards the murdered man when he heard the peculiar sounds Sweetie Malloy was making. The high-necked dress was cutting into her throat, purpling her unconscious face. For an instant Tracy hunted unsuccessfully for hooks or buttons; then with a sibilant oath he whipped out his penknife and slashed the neck of the dress open.

The tiny gold links of a locket chain were rising and falling with her labored breathing. Tracy frowned, reluctant to pry into her personal possessions. But the thought of the corpse on the rug swept away his sympathetic instincts. He drew the locket gently upward from the white cleft of her bosom.

He snapped the flat case open and stared at the scrap of photograph inside.

Sweetie herself. Taken evidently when she was a child of about fourteen. Self-possessed, mature-looking, very lovely.

He was clicking the locket shut when a peculiar thought stayed his hand. The eyes—they weren't Sweetie's eyes. Even in the child's face, they were harder, clearer, devoid entirely of that shy reticence that had always been Sweetie Malloy's chief charm. He saw now that the hair-

dressing was too modern; the scrap of dress that showed in the photo was a fairly recent style that was not more than five or six years outmoded. Sweetie's own childhood belonged way back in the early nineties; it couldn't possibly be her. Then who was this clear-eyed, defiant little beauty? Tracy's memory told him he had seen this kid somewhere, was dimly familiar with the contour of the face, especially the reckless flame of the eyes. She'd be about twenty now. A grown woman.

He pried out the picture with the point of his penknife and his breath caught as he read the rounded, childish handwriting on the back of the photo: "To Mother from Lois."

Lois . . . He knew the face now! His imagination filled out the promise of beauty in the face, matured and hardened the lovely mouth, added a nude body misted to a milky radiance under the glow of diffused lights. . . . Señorita Lois; she used no other name. Poised in the perfumed darkness of the Club Español, dancing like a flitting white moonbeam behind the iridescent translucence of an enormous floating bubble.

Tracy closed the locket, replaced it gently around the neck of Sweetie Malloy. Poor, desperate, gray-haired Sweetie! Pleading guilty to murder, secretly conveying a dead body to her own home and bedroom—to save this same reckless-eyed child? It was only a guess, but to Tracy it seemed a guess perilously close to certainty.

A grim hatred for the charming Señorita Lois grew in Jerry's mind. Without Lois there was no need at all for Sweetie's desperate sacrifice. A childless Sweetie had no sane reason for attempting to frame herself to burn in the electric chair. But if she had a daughter . . . If her daughter had killed a man, had begged Sweetie in hysterical terror to save her—save her. . . .

Jerry's lean jaw hardened. All Lois had to do, apparently, was to lock her damned crimsoned lips and let her unsuspecting mother take the rap. Sweetie would never disclose the secret. Tracy himself, friend of years as he was, had never once dreamed that Sweetie's marriage with drunken Jack Malloy had produced this pampered and sinuous darling of the Club Español. A damned, cowardly murderess, if his hunch was correct. A gal whom Jerry Tracy was going to pay a grim visit before this tragic night was over.

He reexamined the corpse on the floor. Except for tailor marks the clothes were empty of clues. But Tracy was patient with his searching and his patience was rewarded by a stiff, oblong pressure in the lining of the man's coat. He found the hole in the inner pocket, ripped it wide with his forefinger, felt down through the lining and drew up the pasteboard. There were only two lines of print:

Phil Clement
Representing Señorita Lois

Rain still slogged viciously behind the drawn shades on the window. Tracy shuddered slightly at the sound; he knew what he had to do tonight before he called on Sweetie's unnatural and cowardly daughter. He'd get rid of the body, plant it somewhere else for the police to find. With the police short of all clues that might show where and under what circumstances the man had been murdered, Tracy himself would be free for at least one night to go to work on Lois, uncover the whole slimy truth. Sweetie would keep quiet as long as Lois' name remained a secret. Besides, if she stepped forward now and tried to reassume the guilt, it would drag Tracy himself into a criminal mess—and Sweetie, God bless her, wasn't built that way!

racy strode to the telephone on the night table and called his penthouse. To his disgust McNulty, his ancient Chinese butler, answered the call instead of Butch. In a steady voice Jerry assured the Chink that he was perfectly dry and in the best of health, that he wouldn't be home for dinner—and please put Butch on, like a first-class and intelligent Chinaman!

"You got him laincoat an' lubbers?"

"Sure, sure. I'm all right, keed. Honest!"

Then Butch's adenoidal bellow came over the wire. "Hello, Boss. Jeeze, what a night, huh?"

"Where's the Chink?"

"Gone back in the kitchen."

"Swell. I want you to phone my garage and get the car. The Chrysler, not the Lincoln. Don't tell the Chink where you're going."

"How kin I?" Butch asked in a puzzled voice, "When I dunno meself?"

Tracy gave him the address. "Drive out here right away. You can't miss the cottage. It's three from the corner of Locust. Pull into the drive and park at the back of the cottage. Keep your mug covered up as much as you can. I don't want anyone recognizing you on the drive through Manhattan."

"Oke."

"And tell Felix over at the garage to keep his trap shut about the Chrysler going out. If anyone asks later on, both my cars were there all night."

"Oke."

Tracy hung up with a nervous click. He prowled swiftly about the shaded bedroom, pocketed the gun from the rug, tidied the grim evidence of struggle that Sweetie had so pathetically counterfeited, made the room normal and neat except for the huddled corpse. Sweetie was still breathing with drugged regularity; she'd be asleep for hours yet.

The *Daily Planet*'s pint-sized columnist went downstairs to the kitchen and made himself a hasty sandwich with some Swiss and rye he found. He was as hungry as hell; and besides, it gave him something to do while he waited for Butch. Inaction always got on his nerves, made them raw and jumpy.

He had finished the sandwich and was hunting for a bottle of beer when the bell rang at the rear door.

Jerry Tracy stiffened. He knew that the prompt caller at the kitchen couldn't possibly be

Butch. Then who was it? And should he answer the ring or let the guy get tired and go away? Again the bell rang. The guy outside knew that the lights were on in the cottage, that someone was at home. Jerry would have to answer or arouse suspicion that something was wrong.

A plan formed instantly in his mind. He sprang noiselessly towards the gas range, turned on one of the burners. He grabbed an empty kettle from the table, filled it with water, stood it over the blue flame. Then he walked noisily towards the rear door, flung it open.

To his surprise the caller was a woman. Rain slanted against the columnist's bare head. He stared at the woman, trying to get a glimpse of her dripping face.

"Mrs. Malloy is quite ill," he said curtly. "What did you want?"

"Ill? I'm—I'm sorry."

Her beady eyes stared suspiciously, peered past him through the half-opened door. "I'm—I'm Mrs. Malloy's next-door neighbor. I came to borrow a cup of sugar. You see, we're having a little party and—"

Tracy leaned forward, glanced alternately to right and left. Both adjoining houses were dark from cellar to garret.

"I'm Doctor Rolfe," he told the woman with a cool smile. "We mustn't disturb Mrs. Malloy—but come in, by all means! And—er—get your cup of sugar."

His firm hand drew her unwillingly across the threshold. He took a good look at her in the light. She was fully dressed for the street: hat, coat, high-heeled shoes, gloves. Soaked with rain. Obviously out in the storm longer than it would take to run from an adjoining doorway. Pale angular face. Might be a Swede. Watching the suave stranger that she had not expected to run into with a puzzled, scared expression in her bovine eyes. That lump in the sagging pocket of her long coat was a gun bulge, or Jerry was crazy!

He lifted the lid of his kettle and peered professionally.

"Mrs. Malloy had a bad heart attack this afternoon. She's upstairs in bed, barely conscious. I'm heating hot water now for a—ahem—parallelogram treatment."

He smiled faintly.

"You no doubt know where she keeps the sugar. Help yourself."

The woman's eyes swept the cupboard helplessly. "I—I guess I won't bother, Doctor. Thank you; I—I won't stay."

"Shall I tell Mrs. Malloy who called?"

"No, no. Don't annoy her."

She backed towards the kitchen door, swung it open and ducked out into the drumming rain. The minute the door closed Tracy ran noiselessly into the front room. With his eye carefully glued to a corner of the shifted shade, he saw the woman hurrying from the driveway to the sidewalk. She melted into the darkness towards Locust Avenue. A liar and a faker. As bad an egg as Tracy had ever smelled. Who was she? Did she know about the corpse upstairs? Could she be—his jaw tightened—an emissary of Señorita Lois?

He went back to the kitchen and turned out the gas flame under the kettle. He heard the pulsing hum of a motorcar with a thrill of satisfaction. The car turned slowly into the driveway from the street. It braked behind the cottage and a moment later the bell rang briefly. It was Butch.

Tracy yanked the startled big fellow into the kitchen and snapped an eager question at him. "See any sign of a woman walking along Locust Avenue?"

"Naw." Butch snorted with derision. "On a night like this they ain't nobody walkin'. Street's as empty as a—a motorman's glove. I mean," he added hastily, with a silly grin, "a motorman without no hand."

"Did you see a car parked anywhere along Locust?"

"Oh, sure. About four blocks down. Parked without lights. You tol' me not to show me mug much, so I didn't give it no gander." He grinned. "Jeeze, let 'em park—I was young meself once!"

Jerry wiped the romantic grin off Butch's thick lips with a curt sentence or two.

"Huh?" Butch gasped. "Moider? Right here? An'—an' we're gonna snatch the body?"

"Right. And I don't want any mistakes."

Less than ten minutes after Butch had arrived, the body of Phil Clement was carried discreetly out the back door of the cottage and stowed away in the rumble of the Chrysler. He made a tight fit—but he fitted. The adjoining houses were still dark. Tracy smeared the license plates with a handful of wet earth. He was climbing in alongside of Butch when he suddenly remembered his two bundles—the birthday cake and the candles! Swearing grimly, he hurried back into the cottage and got them.

Butch swung the car through the driveway and out to the rain-pelted street.

As they turned into Locust Avenue, Jerry's eyes peered ahead through the slanting sliver of headlight-illuminated rain.

"Is that the parked car you saw?"

"Yeah."

"Slow down a trifle when we go by. Don't let 'em see your face. Cut in close and go right by 'em."

"Okey."

Butch ducked his head low over the wheel. Tracy, hunched beside him, gave the stalled car a lightning scrutiny from under the wet brim of his hat. Two of 'em—a man and a woman. The man's back was turned; all Tracy could see was a very sporty, extremely gray topcoat—almost a white-gray. The woman was the dame who had called at Sweetie Malloy's kitchen to borrow a cup of sugar.

Butch, who had glanced casually into the rear-vision mirror, gave a faint yelp. "Hey! They're follerin' us, Boss!"

"I know. Show 'em how fast you can go with a special engine job that cost me plenty of jack."

Butch crooned with delight. "Fast as I like?"

"Sure. Lose 'em."

Butch lost them in a straightaway mile of hair-raising speed along water-slippery concrete. He made doubly sure by two sneaking turns through the bumping darkness that brought the Chrysler to a parallel highway.

"We're going to Brooklyn," Tracy said. "We're going to dump the body in a vacant lot at the corner of Pike and Pacific."

The place registered instantly with Butch. "I getcha. The spot where the cops found Snipe Moretto last week." His smile bathed Tracy with fond admiration. "Jeeze, you sure got brains in that little nut o' yours. The cops'll think it's a gang killin'. They'll think Snipe Moretto's boys got hunk with the Peewee gang."

The flitting Chrysler roared smoothly through the Bronx, crossed into Manhattan, went all the way down to Canal and across the Manhattan bridge into Brooklyn. It was barely nine o'clock, but the steady torrential rain had swept the streets clear of all but a driblet of traffic. No signs of pedestrians at all.

At Pike and Pacific, Butch braked the car to a stop and got out with a hand-jack. Unmindful of the soaking rain he jacked up the rear axle and pretended to go to work on a tire. Tracy drifted unobtrusively to a gap in the rickety fence and peered into the vacant lot. He came back and rested one hand negligently on the closed rumble. An occasional automobile rocketed by, throwing water flying in a soggy splash.

"When I say ready—out with him!" Jerry whispered.

More cars. Tracy straightened nervously as the last one swerved out of sight around a corner. As far as he could see, the street was empty for the moment except for the sullen hiss of the October rain.

"Ready!"

Up went the lid of the rumble. Arms plunged and caught at the wedged-in corpse. In a moment Tracy and Butch had staggered across the deserted sidewalk and vanished through the gap in the fence. They were gone less than sixty seconds. Butch let down the jack and tossed it into the open rumble. Jerry closed the lid with a bang.

The Chrysler was in motion almost before the columnist could close his door. Butch's hands, he noticed, were shaking on the circumference of the wheel. His own were tremulous, too. The car took an erratic slide and straightened out.

"That's that, Boss."

"Yeah. That's that."

A vivid picture was still uppermost in both their minds: a dead man lying in a grotesque huddle in the rainy darkness of a vacant lot. Cold and inanimate, in a sordid welter of tin cans, mud and busted bed-springs . . . Tracy felt a little sick at the necessity of heaving even a dead man to a rest like that.

Jerry had a grim hunch that if he didn't make a quick job of this case, the gal who asked for a cup of sugar and the guy in the gray-white topcoat might do something damned nasty to a pint-sized columnist who had developed such an uncanny habit of minding other people's business—when they broke the law. Whoever they were, those two were in the thing up to their ears, along with the bubble dancer.

"Drop me off at Nevins Street," he told Butch in a low tone. "I'll grab the subway back. Remember to tell Felix that the car wasn't out of the garage tonight. Get rid of those two packages of mine somewhere. Be sure no one sees you do it. Better smash 'em both up and stick 'em in one of the garage trash cans."

He watched the crimson tail-light of the Chrysler vanish in the rain and descended frowningly into the Nevins Street station. He rode a Seventh Avenue express to Times Square, caught a cab, rode quietly with set jaw to the Club Español.

racy was soaked and soggy, a bit squishy at the heels, but the Español's doorman recognized him with a respectful grin.

"Bad night, Mr. Tracy." Jerry said, "Yeah," and made quick puddles towards the cloak room. Suddenly he stopped short in the center of the foyer. He was staring at a familiar white-gray topcoat. The coat was being handed across to Nita, the checkroom girl, by a thickset, muscular man of medium height, with bushy black hair and a neck almost as big as Butch's.

Tracy began backing quietly towards a convenient Spanish arch, but Nita's face had lifted and her pert red lips were smiling at the columnist.

"Hey, hey, Jerry *mío*! Lousy night, no?"

The muscular man whirled like a cat. His dark eyes focused on Tracy. Jerry advanced smilingly, fumbling casually for his cigarette case, taking in the guy's details with one slant-eyed flash. Didn't know the mug from Adam. The fleshy cheeks, blunt nose, shaggy black eyebrows made a brand-new tintype for Tracy's mental rogues' gallery. But the topcoat was an old friend!

The stranger grabbed the coat from Nita with a brusque snatch. "Forgot something," he muttered, and with his face averted from Tracy, barged through the lobby and butted out into the rain.

Tracy waited for ten hesitant seconds. The hard-boiled bubble dancer could wait, he decided. This was a guy to check on in a hurry.

There was no sign of him on the gleaming black lacquer of the rain-drenched sidewalk. A taxi was moving from the curb and Jerry said swiftly to the doorman: "A guy just came out. Did he take that cab?"

"Was he a sorta short, heavy mug in a light coat?"

"Yeah."

"He walked. Pretty fast, too. Went around the corner."

"Thanks."

Jerry caromed off a bobbing umbrella and made it to the corner without delay. His eyes narrowed with elation. That car parked at the curb down the street looked a hell of a lot like Light Coat's tin wheelbarrow. Might swish by and give it a look.

A hand clutched him as he passed a pitch-dark doorway. The clutch lifted Jerry off his feet, yanked him headlong into the narrow entry.

His fist swung instinctively and skidded off a wet ear. The force of his hasty blow threw him off balance but it saved him a fractured skull. A pistol butt hit Jerry's falling shoulder and laced it with numbing pain. Before it could hit again Jerry's left hand closed desperately on a thick ankle and toppled his antagonist.

Neither of them made a sound. The hiss of the rain on the black sidewalk and the scuffling of their entangled legs on the tiled pavement of the doorway was the only noise audible.

The clubbed gun swung backward for a bone-smashing blow.

Jerry butted his head against the man's nose. He bit his way through the hand that crushed his mouth and chin. The killer yelped shrilly and they rolled apart for an instant. Tracy staggered to his feet, slipped, went down jarringly on hands and knees. He managed to throw one arm upward and he took the savage gun smash on the wincing tendons of his forearm.

His assailant turned, chin and mouth crimson from his butted nose, and ran head-downward through the rain. He darted along the sidewalk and slammed headlong into his parked car. As the gears meshed Jerry leaped to the running-board, clutched at the wheel, tried to throw the automobile towards the sidewalk.

A straight-arm blow to the mouth tore him loose and sent him reeling backward. The pavement came up dizzily and socked the back of his skull with a force that bounced his teeth together. It took him a dazed minute to remember where he was and to sway dizzily upward from the cold puddle he was blotting with his aching back.

The car was in high, roaring towards Sixth Avenue. Its stop light flared crimson; the car skidded around the corner and vanished.

Tracy sat down on the uncomfortable spiked top of a hydrant and tried to pull himself together. His head still felt like an overstuffed chair. A man with a dripping umbrella came down from Seventh, stopped hesitantly.

"S'matter, buddy? Sick?"

"Nope. I'm all right."

Except for an arm that felt like boiled spaghetti and a lump on the back of his head where he had kissed the sidewalk, Jerry was beginning to feel normal. The man with the umbrella handed the columnist his hat and walked off. Didn't even look back.

"If I'd been jumped like this in Peoria," Tracy reflected grimly, "there'd have been six cops with notebooks, a hook and ladder company, and a thousand nosy gazabos. Get half killed in Manhattan and a lone guy with an umbrella hands you back your hat—and goes right on to the drug-store to buy his aspirin!"

The thought made him grin cheerfully. He went back to the Club Español with almost a jaunty stride.

He asked for an inconspicuous table and got it. Garcia, the swarthy and affable headwaiter, bubbled with friendliness for the *Daily Planet*'s expensive little hireling. Tracy had helped many a good show, had rescued many a lousy one, by a good-humored boost salted away in a pert paragraph.

Garcia rubbed swarthy hands together. "Señorita Lois goes on in about wan hour. You weel like her, I'm sure."

"I can't wait an hour. I want to see her now."

Garcia's chuckle seemed a bit strained. "Ah, no, no . . . Why not wait, have a few dreenks— see for yourself thees glorious dance she makes with thees glorious body, no?"

"You mean she doesn't *want* to talk to me?"

"Tonight she is a leetle bit upset."

"Sick, eh?" Tracy's tone was sharp.

"No, no. Worried, per'aps. Maybe a leetle temperament. Ha, ha! She snarl and she snap. She weel talk weeth no one."

"Tell her Jerry Tracy wants to see her."

Garcia shrugged, scowled, departed. When he returned his message was brief.

"She say—" He gulped. "She say how you lak to go to hell in a tin bucket?"

"I see. Got an envelope and a small hunk of paper?"

"But surely."

Tracy cupped the paper behind his left hand,

scrawled a brief sentence, sealed the envelope. "Take her this."

In three minutes Garcia was back. There was incredulity in his black eyes, a faint overlay of perspiration on his olive forehead.

"You are indeed a magician, *Señor* Tracy. She see you. Come weeth me."

Tracy threaded his way past crowded tables, paid no attention to the whispered buzz of comment his presence excited. He crossed a shining expanse of open floor, ducked under a curtain of heavy brocaded material and climbed a flight of wooden stairs to a closed door.

"Beat it," he told Garcia.

He opened the door without knocking, clicked it shut behind him.

"Hello, Toots."

is note was still in her hand. She had thrown a light robe over her shoulders but the thing gaped candidly and Tracy, in spite of the hard anger that gripped him, was forced to admit to himself that this kid was strictly the goods.

It was hard to say which was uppermost in her swimming dark eyes: rage, or a bright, over-mastering fear.

"Listen, you wise little newspaper heel! If you're trying one of your celebrated snoop acts, pulling a cheap bluff—"

"Shut up!" He was not an awful lot taller than the dancer, but he seemed to loom a foot higher as he tramped slowly towards her. "As far as I'm concerned, Toots, you're a two-bit strip act— and I'm doing you a favor to sneeze at you. I never fool and I never bluff. I asked you how you'd like to push a bubble around in a death cell. Think it over, *Miss Malloy*."

"You—damn you . . . Who said my name's Malloy?"

She sprang at him without warning, caught both his shoulders in a nail-digging frenzy. Her flimsy robe trailed but neither of them was aware

of anything but their locked double glare. Tracy kept his lips compressed, gave no indication whatever that the pointed nails of the dancer were hurting him like hell.

He flung her backward a step.

"If you don't talk—and talk plenty, Toots!— I'm gonna nail that kalsomined shape of yours to the cross. I'm calling you Malloy because you're Sweetie Malloy's daughter."

He heard the sharp hissing of her breath. There was a moment of utter silence in the room.

"Well? So what if I am?"

"I want to know why you're so damned scared tonight. Are you waiting to hear the newspaper extras that your mother has been pinched for murder?"

Her rouged face was as white as the notepaper that fluttered to the floor at her bare feet. "You're nuts. You're absolutely insane."

"Am I?" He stopped and placed the paper in his pocket. "If I'm insane, let out a scream and have me pinched for annoying you. I'd love to tell the cops why Sweetie Malloy *could not* have killed Phil Clement, your manager."

"Is Phil—dead?"

"You know damn' well he is. . . . You're the one that killed him. How about going straight back to your apartment and talking this over?" His glance was like the flick of a whip. "Well?"

"Let's go," she gasped.

She clutched at his hand, wrenched the door open. Barefooted, panting, she sprang down the wooden staircase, her left hand dragging the startled columnist. A chorus girl, ascending the narrow stairs, flattened herself against the banister as the almost nude dancer and the columnist swept on past her.

"Well, for Gawd's sake . . ."

"Hey, wait a minute!" Tracy growled. He pulled the fluttering robe tight, knotted the silken cord securely. "Where's your shoes? You can't go out barefooted, dope!"

There was almost an insane blaze in Lois' eyes. She jerked him forward, pattered through a darkened corridor, swung open a door. There-was a paved alley outside and a parked limousine.

"Yours?" Tracy snapped.

"Yes."

"Swell." He swung her up in his arms with a sudden heave and carried her through the rain. A sleepy chauffeur in a plum-colored uniform flung open the automobile's door, gaping stupidly.

Tracy bounced Lois in on the cushioned seat, crawled in beside her. "Tell this lad it's okey. Tell him home, James."

The chauffeur had recovered his scattered wits. He had the door open again, a wrench hefted menacingly in his gauntleted hand.

"It's—it's all right, Peter," Lois whispered fiercely. "I'm—I'm not feeling well. Drive us home."

"And toss that overcoat of yours back here!" Tracy snapped at him.

Lois Malloy jerked the speaking tube to her tremulous lips. "I won't need you any more tonight after we get there, Peter. You can put up the car and go home."

"Yes, Miss."

The apartment building was a swanky stone hive that went up and up through the rain like the side of a terra-cotta cliff. It had a canopy, a doorman, a rubber carpet to the curb and an umbrella ready to be snicked open for milady.

Tracy shoved all the hubbub away with a sweep of his arm. He grinned at the startled doorman. He was just beginning to realize that he was bareheaded and coatless himself. And the bubble dancer's appearance was enough to make any respectable doorman gulp.

Jerry carried Lois Malloy to the silver and onyx elevator. She wriggled loose and slid to her feet as the car ascended. Jerry didn't mind that a bit; it had been quite a trick to carry her with that numb left arm of his. Her eyes, he saw, were free of terror; they were colder now, wary, self-possessed.

"I haven't my key with me," she told the stolid elevator man. "Will you get a duplicate, please?"

"Yes, Miss."

She padded barefooted to her penthouse door and waited with Tracy while the elevator man descended.

"Maid out tonight?" Tracy suggested.

"Yes."

"What's her name?"

"Does it matter?"

"I think so."

"Her name's Selma."

"Selma what?"

She whirled at him suddenly. "How the hell do I know? Just plain Selma!"

The doorman appeared, inserted a key, opened the door, vanished. They went into a gorgeous living-room and Tracy said mildly: "Nice dump you've got."

Lois' bare feet made quick, meaty sounds on the floor. She jerked out a cabinet drawer, slammed viciously about with a gun in her hand.

"Listen, you! Stand right where you are. What do you know about my—my mother? And what do you know about Phil Clement?"

"I know why Clement was killed—and where," Tracy bluffed.

"Yes?" Her voice grated. "He was killed because my mother was dumb enough to take him on as a lover. And if you think you can drag me into her mess, you've got another think coming."

Tracy nodded a little. "I've seen and touched a lot of lice in New York," he said in a slow whisper, "but you're the first dame I've run into who tried to dodge a murder rap by jamming her own mother into the electric chair."

The gun in the dancer's hand was as steady as a rock. Her crimson lips jeered. "Sweetie Malloy gunned Clement in her own house. The body's on her own bedroom floor. She's surrendering to the cops—if she hasn't done so already."

"How do you know all this?"

"Because she phoned me and confessed."

"And you're letting her take the rap?"

"Why not? She killed the guy, didn't she?"

Jerry stared contemptuously until the hard eyes flickered and turned away. He said, quietly:

"Your mother was here in this penthouse today."

"What of it? I had some sewing stuff for her. She—she sews things for me."

"I see. Sews things for you. And won't tell the cops she's your mother. But you don't mind if she burns for murder. . . . God, you get better all the time."

"What you think about me doesn't worry me," Lois said sullenly.

"Is your maid coming back here tonight?"

"I don't know."

"Where does this Selma live?"

"I don't know."

"What does she look like?"

Lois' lovely lips curled contemptuously. "What does any Swede look like?"

"A Swede, eh? Thanks."

He leaned towards her, smiling, and with a sudden gesture wrenched the gun from her hand and shoved her into a chair. She landed with a force that made her bounce.

"I'm taking a quick look about this arty dump, just for the fun of it," Tracy growled.

He disappeared into another room. She could hear him moving about, but her rigid pose never changed. She was still sitting there, barefooted, creamy-bosomed where the coat gaped, when Tracy returned.

He snapped her eyes awake with a sharp question:

"Do you happen to know a guy who likes to wear very sporty gray topcoats?"

He could see the dancer freeze up inside.

"Well? Do you?" he repeated.

"Get out!"

"Sure," Tracy said unevenly. He threw her gun into her lap. "Do me a favor, Toots. Empty that thing into your rotten little skull. I'd do it myself if I had an exterminator's license."

"What's your angle on this thing, Tracy?"

He eyed her steadily. "I'm working for the lad in the gray topcoat."

Lois' breath sizzled briefly. "Do—do you know anything about architecture, Mr. Tracy?"

"Not a thing."

"This apartment is completely soundproof."

"So what?" he asked.

"So—this!" The gun he had tossed contemptuously into her lap streaked upward like a flash of light. Her finger pressed the trigger six times.

The six harmless clicks sounded almost like one. It was nearly twenty seconds before the knowledge that the gun was empty seeped into her rigid eyes.

Tracy gave her a scornful, sandpaper chuckle. "I emptied that toy while I was strolling through the apartment. Wanted to see what you'd do. Here—take 'em back! They stink in my pocket."

He threw the handful of loose cartridges at her. They bounded off her body, rolled helter-skelter across the rug. Lois didn't utter a sound. She was sitting there, watching him like a stone carving, when he slammed the apartment door.

He shivered a little while he waited for the elevator, blinked once or twice to get rid of the image of that baleful face.

The opening door of the elevator found him debonair and cheerful.

"Were any of you boys on duty this afternoon?" he asked on the way down.

"No, sir . . . That is, come to think of it—Roy was." This little bareheaded guy had eyes that seemed to dig right into a fella. "Roy was—was home sick one day this week, so he hadda take a double stretch to make up for it."

"I get it." The elevator stopped and the doors slid apart. "Which one is Roy? Call him over."

Roy was a tall, gangling youth with pale, good-natured eyes in a weak, taffy-colored face. The shrewd *Daily Planet* columnist tabbed his type instantly: a two-dollar racehorse sport, a policy ticket sucker, a sweepstake boob, an eager patron of small craps games. There were a dozen kids just like him in the *Daily Planet* building. A cinch for a bribe.

"Come here, son. I wanna talk to you."

He went with Roy down a short corridor off the lobby and halted in front of the service elevator. His fingers opened and left a crumpled ten-dollar bill in Roy's moist palm.

"All you've got to do is answer a couple of harmless questions."

Tracy's grin had never been more warmly appealing. His wink was a humorous, good-natured, man-to-man affair. Roy grinned back.

Once the kid had started, he spilled like a broken faucet. Tracy's respectful nods were subtle flattery to egg him on.

The señorita had gone out a little before two o'clock that same afternoon. Said she couldn't wait for the sewing woman, and to send her up for the stuff when she came. The old dame came a little after two. Went up. About a half hour later the service buzzer rang. The sewing woman and the maid met Roy in the kitchen doorway. They both looked scared and sorta funny, he thought. He didn't pay no particular attention; people were always looking funny in a big house like this.

"What did they want?" Tracy asked.

Well, they wanted a trunk up out of the storage room in the cellar. He brought it up. After a while—must have been around three o'clock then—he got another buzz. Went up. Took the sewing woman down and the trunk, too. Got it out to a cab and the old lady drove off with it.

"Did she say what was in it?"

"Yeah. She did. I didn't ask her, but she told me anyway. Old dresses of the señorita's. Felt as heavy as hell." He grinned weakly. "Maybe that was because the old sewing woman forgot to gimme a tip."

"Let's fix that right now." Tracy shot him another ten-spot. "What about the maid?"

Well, Roy thought, that was sorta funny, too. Selma, the maid, came down in the passenger elevator about twenty minutes later. With a heavy suitcase. Gave up her apartment key. Said she was called away suddenly and to give it to the señorita when she came back. The señorita got back around four or so, Roy thought. He gave her Selma's key and she looked pretty angry and pretty puzzled.

"Not scared?"

"No, sir. Just wonderin', sorta. She said okey and rode upstairs. And I guess that's all."

"Do you know Mr. Clement?"

"Oh, sure. Her manager, you mean?"

"Yes. Did he call on her any time today?"

"No, sir."

"How about a short, heavy-set man in a light gray topcoat?"

"Dunno him. There wasn't any visitors except the old sewing woman."

"Thanks, Roy. You've been a big help."

His pale eyes goggled. "You a detective, mister?"

Tracy grinned, leaned closer. "Say, ever hear of a guy named Jerry Tracy?"

"Jeeze, yes . . ."

Jerry tapped his chest briefly. "Me."

"No kiddin'. I—I always thought you was a much bigger guy. I'll be darned."

"Keep your eyes and ears open—and your mouth shut. Any time you run across a hot bit of dirt, gimme a ring at the *Planet* office."

"I sure will, Mister Tracy. Jeeze, thanks . . ."

Tracy went back to the lobby and out to the street. The rain had stopped but the gutter still raced with water. The doorman's shrill whistle brought a cab splashing east from the dark avenue.

Tracy murmured his own address, relaxed with a tired grunt—and immediately leaned forward again. "Change that! Take me to the Club Español."

No sense riding home like a shivering, bareheaded dope! His topcoat and hat were still in the checkroom; Nita would be wondering what the hell was wrong.

The Club Español was still wide-open. Nita grinned perkily at Tracy. "Hey, hey, *muchacho*! Where *you* been?"

He saw that she was looking at him with a peculiar stare.

"You sure gummed the works here tonight," she said tonelessly. "Garcia's still tearing his hair. I hear you pulled the señorita out in her B.V.D.s—and damned little of them. The customers raised Cain when they heard her late show was off. I dunno what Garcia told 'em." Nita grinned cynically. "Maybe he told 'em the señorita busted her bubble. Anyhow, there was a lot of arguing, one drunken brawl that was a honey; and half the customers scrammed out to the opposish down the avenoo. First time I ever saw Garcia cry. Tears like big round hunks of putty. I'm not foolin'."

"Yeah?" Tracy said inattentively and turned away. Nita's hand on his wrist pulled him around, restrained him.

"Remember when you first came in tonight, Jerry? There was a mug in a very light-gray topcoat. He scrammed the minute he saw you—and you ups and outs right after him. I wondered."

"Don't tell me you tabbed him!" Tracy's glare was so intent that she pulled back a little, her hand still on his.

"I didn't tab him the first time—but I did later."

"He came back here?"

"Yowsuh. I mean, *por supuesto, ciertamente,*" Nita kidded nervously. "Brought a dame along."

"A Swede?" Jerry whispered. "A big horse-faced number? Sorta pale and angular?"

"Right. She had on a street coat over a very punkerino and secondhandish evening rag. They both checked their coats. Didn't stay long; beat it the moment they heard the señorita wasn't gonna bounce through that 'Me and My Bubble' number."

"Did you dip their pockets, honey?"

"Sure did. Nothing in the dame's coat but a soiled handkerchief and a few hairpins. In the guy's pocket—this."

The slip of paper switched hands with deft invisibility. Tracy cupped it for an instant, read the penciled memo. Two lines: *Selma Borquist, 932 West 10th.*

Something in the way he crawled into his coat and popped the snap-brim hat askew on his rumpled hair brought a solicitous frown to Nita's dark eyes.

"You're not going down there tonight, for Gawd's sake?"

"I dunno yet."

"Listen, Jerry. You're dead on your feet right now. There's a lump on the back of your dome like a hen's egg, and that left arm of yours looks like it might hurt like hell. G'wan home to bed. The Swede'll keep till tomorrow."

"You're a sweet kid, Nita."

"It's the mother in me." She grinned, and wondered why the words should make Tracy look so suddenly queer, as though she had said the wrong thing.

"I feel all in," he admitted. "I think I'll head straight for home, a stiff drink and a swan dive into the hay. S'long. . . ."

He lurched out to the street and Nita, watching the tired drag of his feet, thought angrily: "He'll kill himself one of these days with his damned running around. About as big as a bag of popcorn—and more pep to him than a Mack truck . . . Crazy little runt . . ."

 hen Jerry awoke the sun was shining. He picked up his fresh copy of the *Daily Planet* and saw the expected headline on the front page. There was a photograph of the body, with a squat white arrow above it to help dumb tabloid readers pick it out from the tin cans and debris. No identification yet. Jerry, having carefully cut out all the labels from Clement's clothing, wasn't surprised. Twenty-four hours, he thought grimly. After that—Inspector Fitzgerald and the cops.

Butch was behind the wheel of the Lincoln when Jerry appeared on the sidewalk. Off like oiled lightning, down to Times Square.

Butch tossed his plaid cap at a peg and squatted in the outer office with a copy of *Variety* and the *Daily Planet* funnies. Jerry sat down at his desk and hooked the dictating machine closer with a tug of his patent-leather toe.

But before he dived into the column he

reached for the phone and called Garbo, the very snooty chief operator on the *Daily Planet* switchboard. He gave her Sweetie Malloy's suburban number.

"When you get it, say anything you like. I want to know how the woman sounds when she answers. Keep my line in. *Verstehen Sie?*"

"If you mean do I understand," Garbo said icily, "the answer is yes, Mr. Tracy, I do."

He hung on and listened with narrowed eyes to the brief two-way misunderstanding between Garbo and Sweetie Malloy. Garbo lingered a second after she broke the connection. "Satisfactory, Mr. Tracy?"

"Quite." He grinned. "Hey, Garbo—listen. Why don'tcha like me, keed? You mad because I call you Garbo?"

She sniffed audibly and clicked off. But Tracy was satisfied. The sleeping draught he had slipped Sweetie hadn't done her any harm. She sounded tired and listless—but she was out of the shadow of the electric chair, and there wasn't a way she could frame herself again. Call in the cops now, and they'd laugh at her!

He tackled the column with vim. At noon Butch appeared with a mound of Swiss cheese on rye and a pitcher of draught ale. Tracy took the stuff in his stride. When he got busy on an overdue column he was like the Twentieth Century singing along steel rails. At four-thirty a messenger arrived and took the cylinders away. Tracy stretched gratefully. He was done. McCurdy always edited the stuff and trimmed the edges. Nice guy, McCurdy. His youngest brat was named Jerry. On purpose.

Tracy went down to the sidewalk and thought things over, while a steady stream of pedestrians buzzed and bumped past him. Sam, his favorite hackman, was parked at the curb. He gave the *Daily Planet*'s columnist a wrinkled grin and gestured briefly towards his tin flag; but Jerry shook his head. The subway seemed a better bet for a well-known little guy on an anonymous mission. The small-calibered gun that he had picked up from the bedroom floor in Sweetie Malloy's suburban cottage was a sagging weight in his pocket.

The dump Jerry was hunting was west, between the gaunt Ninth Avenue El and the river. A mean, red-brick hovel, tucked away in a welter of dust and decay. An incredibly filthy fish store on one side, a secondhand plumbing shop on the other.

Tracy hesitated, rubbed his chin uneasily. "Whoa!" he thought. "You're galloping too fast, keed!" After all, he was a Broadway columnist, not a policeman. If he didn't tip the cops—and tip 'em right now—he might get his wise little nose so deep into trouble that it would take him eleven years to convince Headquarters that he was acting not to cover up crime but to expose it!

He stepped into a telephone booth in a cigar store near the corner and called Police Headquarters in a low voice. After a short wait he heard the welcome sound of Inspector Fitzgerald's deep voice.

"Fitz? Listen—"

"Jerry?" Fitz' heavy rumble exploded into a pleasant chuckle. "Haven't seen you in ages. Where have you been keeping yourself, you little bozo?"

"Don't talk!" Jerry snapped. "Listen!" He uttered a sentence or two with curt speed.

Fitz' voice changed instantly. "Right! I getcha." A smart cop, Fitz. Never wasted a second asking how or why. He knew Jerry Tracy well enough from past experience to wait until later for complete explanations. Jerry had a habit of handing him a crisis and a solution all in the same breath.

"You and Sergeant Killan get down here as soon as you can," Tracy said. "In the meantime I'm gonna have a try at the Swedish maid. She might beat it if I waited for you."

"Watch your step, Jerry!"

"You sound like a subway guard," Jerry kidded lightly; but there was a hard line to his lips as he hung up. He was aware that he had reached the point where a single misstep might lower his dapper little body into a graveyard for keeps. He had never thought much about the next world, but he knew he liked Broadway!

He went back to the red-brick tenement and

sauntered inconspicuously into the shabby, dirt-littered vestibule.

Jerry glanced at the scraps of paper stuck askew under a row of bell buttons. Most of the name-plates were empty. Borquist was under the last button. Top floor.

He climbed the stairs through pitch darkness, except for the faint flicker of light on the first and third landings. He could barely see the gun in his hand when he rang the bell, after a long, careful listen.

There was no answer to his ring. He waited for thirty seconds, then banged noisily on the wood with a clenched fist.

"Gas man! Gas man, lady!"

The door opened a mere crack, but Jerry was all set. He recognized the scared face of Selma. His foot blocked the door; his shoulder sent it flying open.

Selma backed into the frowsy living-room and Jerry closed the door and held the woman motionless with his gun.

"Up with the pretty arms, keed!"

"What—what's the idea?"

"I came to borrow a cup of sugar," he told her pleasantly.

There was no sound except the rickety roar of an El train slogging past in the growing darkness. Tracy forced the woman ahead of him. He searched every inch of the apartment—bedroom, kitchen, closets. There was no sign of any lurking boy friend. Smiling coldly, Jerry marched Lois Malloy's ex-maid back to the living-room. Selma's knees were knocking with fright.

"Why did you kill Phil Clement?"

"I didn't. I swear I didn't!"

"Who did?"

"Lois killed him. All I did, Mister, was to try and help that little devil of a dancer cover up. Her old lady butted in and gummed the works. She said she'd smear me with the murder if I didn't help her. So we packed the stiff in a trunk and the old dame took it out. That's all I did, I swear!"

"How much blackmail did you ask when you called up the dancer yesterday afternoon?"

No answer.

"Who suggested putting the bee on Lois? Your boy friend?"

"I—I got no boy friend."

"What's the use of lying to me?" Tracy snapped. "The guy was in the car with you out on Locust Avenue. You both beat it out there to stop Sweetie Malloy from crabbing your black-mail act. But you were late getting there—and I got there first. Good old Doctor Rolfe!"

"I dunno what you're talking about." She faltered.

"No?" Tracy's smile was knifelike. "I gave you a break by stealing the corpse myself. You tried to hijack me and get hold of the stiff again, but my Chrysler was too fast for that lousy can you were driving. So the boyfriend hunts me up at the Club Español and does his best to rub me out of the racket. He brought you back to the club later to proposition Lois for quick dough, but I foxed him again by kidnaping her in her cellophane panties. . . . For a virgin with no male acquaintances, you sure manage to get around, Selma."

Her bony face got suddenly triumphant.

"Drop that rod!" a voice rasped behind the columnist.

Tracy became very still. He let the gun fall to the floor.

"Take it easy, Emil!" Selma croaked, her eyes glassy with fear. "Don't shoot the guy in my flat, for God's sake!"

"Turn around, stupid," the voice ordered.

Tracy turned. Death was shining at him out of Emil's fishy eyes. Greed, ruthlessness, murder . . . No mistaking the gloating satisfaction in those eyes.

"You killed Phil Clement," Jerry breathed. "Not Selma. Not Lois. You."

"Sure I killed him. So what?"

"Shut up, you damn' fool!" Selma hissed.

Emil's chuckle was not pleasant. "This guy is so close to bein' dead that it don't matter much what I say. I killed Clement, and I'm gonna kill you. How d'yuh like that, Mr. Jerry Tracy? The smart guy! The wise little cluck from Broadway!

Too smart to look in the dumbwaiter shaft before shootin' off his rat mouth!"

Tracy forced himself to smile. "I guess you're a pretty smart guy at that, Emil," he said in a slow, persuasive voice.

"You're damned right I am."

"How did you work the murder job? You sure made a monkey out of me. Fooled me completely."

Emil kept the gun steadily aimed, but he smirked with pleased vanity.

"A cinch," he sneered. "Brains done it. Selma fixed up a fake love note that got Clement into the dancer's apartment. He fell for it like a sap. He was nuts about the señorita."

"Be careful, Emil," the maid said faintly. "This guy is smart. He's trying to pump you."

"This guy is gonna be dead in about two minutes." His grin widened. "All right, smart guy. I was in the apartment and fixed him and got out again. What more do you want?"

"Yeah—but why kill the guy?"

"Plenty reasons to do it, kid," Emil said cockily, "and if you want more, the stunt was for Selma to accuse this dizzy dancer of the murder the minute she saw the body in her bedroom and yell for the cops."

"But the old lady gummed that scheme," Tracy suggested tonelessly.

"Yeah. The old lady was too tough for Selma to handle. She stuck the body in a trunk and scrammed with it. Can you imagine that?"

"I can't imagine it," Tracy said faintly. He eyed the killer and allowed his tensed muscles to relax. A leap forward to wrest the gun from the watchful Emil would be sheer suicide. His own gun was on the floor. Sweat gathered in tiny beads on Tracy's pale forehead. He knew Fitz could never make it in time. He felt a sick horror at the pit of his stomach.

Emil's smile hardened. He gestured briefly towards his pale girlfriend. "C'mere, Selma."

She moved stiffly. She looked uneasy, frightened.

"Take this rod and—" His hand swung suddenly sidewise and the weapon crashed with horrible impact against Selma's skull. She crumpled to the floor without a sound.

"What's the idea of that?" Jerry whispered thickly.

"The idea, stupid, is to git rid of people I don't need no more. You first and then Selma. Nice?"

"You can't get away with it."

"No? Git moving! Through that hall. Into the kitchen . . . Right! Now git over by the window. Sit down on the sill."

The window sash was already raised. Tracy, obeying the menace of the leveled gun, sat down. He snaked his eyes outward and downward for an instant—and knew he was doomed. The window faced a narrow, five-story airshaft. There was a blank brick wall opposite. There were windows all the way down below the kitchen; but Tracy, remembering the empty name-plates in the vestibule, felt a sick shudder.

"Tough, ain't it?" Emil said. "We gotta wait for an El train to settle you—but Selma'll be easy. She'll go down like a bag of laundry." He grinned with ghastly humor. "You kin hold on to the window-sill if you like, while you're waitin'."

The dusk outside had deepened to chilly darkness. Away off in the darkness Jerry could hear a faint rumbling. It grew rapidly to the metallic clatter of a speeding El train.

"So long, stupid," Emil said.

As the roar of the passing train became a clamor that shook the ancient tenement, the killer's fingers tightened.

A woman screamed shrilly. A bullet whizzed past Emil and shattered the glass above Tracy's bent head.

A wave of hot, incredulous joy swept through the columnist's body as he recognized the face of the woman with the gun. He dived headlong from the sill as the startled murderer whirled. For an instant all three of them were inextricably tangled on the kitchen floor: Tracy, Emil—and Lois Malloy.

A kick from Emil sent Lois bouncing against

the wall in a moaning huddle. The man whirled to fire into Tracy's face, but the columnist's fist was already whizzing. It caught Emil on the Adam's apple and paralyzed his throat with pain. He dropped his gun, sprang frantically to recover it. Tracy's foot kicked it spinning towards the wall, where it rebounded towards Lois.

The dancer was hurt and badly rattled. Swaying there on her knees, she scooped up the gun with her left hand, but to Tracy's horror, instead of firing at the plunging Emil, she threw the weapon out the open window—and her own after it!

The two men tripped over her and went down in a flailing fury of fists and feet. Tracy fought like a silent, tight-lipped demon, his mind ablaze with a single thought: his own gun! Lying on the living-room floor where he had dropped it!

A smash on the jaw rocked him groggily, but he managed to dig his face desperately against Emil's neck and get the hold he wanted. He let Emil's own weight do the trick. A slight bend of the knees, the sudden instant of leverage he had learned on the gym mat from Artie McGovern himself—and the snarling murderer flew over Jerry's head and landed on the floor with a jarring impact.

Jerry dived out of the kitchen like a lean arrow, but Emil beat him to it.

Emil had ducked back, picked up Tracy's gun. He fired as Jerry appeared. A long sliver of wood jerked outward from the casing of the doorway. The panting columnist tripped over the unconscious body of Selma and fell in an awkward heap on his hands and knees. He was up in an instant, rigid with fear, his heart pounding inside his dry throat.

He saw Emil leering at him.

Emil was standing quite still, legs planted apart, barely five feet away. Tracy could see the black muzzle of the gun, the tautness of Emil's knuckles, the pressure of his bent forefinger on the trigger.

In that split second of eternity all fear whipped away from the mind of the doomed columnist. He thought with a kind of hypnotized clarity: "I'm gonna die. . . . He's gonna kill me. . . ." There was no horror in the thought; only a puzzled incredulity. Not someone else! Jerry Tracy!

The gun exploded. Tracy heard the racketing roar. He was still standing there, glassy-eyed— and unhurt! Maybe it didn't hurt when you got killed. . . . Then he realized that Emil's bullet had slanted astonishingly upward, not straight into his own stiffened flesh. There was a ragged hole in the plaster ceiling and Emil was falling limply forward. He landed on his face and lay there, full length on the floor.

Tracy could see the blood gushing sluggishly from Emil's back. A pair of legs seemed to be walking towards the columnist out of a dream. They were queer legs—blue serge pants that seemed to end in fuzzy nothingness at the hips— until a brisk palm slapped Tracy's face with stinging emphasis and brought him back to sanity.

He was gaping stupidly at Inspector Fitzgerald. There was a big blue gun in Fitz' paw and a faint haze of smoke at the muzzle.

"Hey—wake up!" Fitz barked. "You all right?"

"Yeah . . . I—I guess so."

"I shot him right through the kidney. Another second, Jerry, and you'd have been cold meat. Why didn't you duck when I yelled?"

"I didn't hear you."

Fitz grinned shakily. "Lord, I let out a yelp like a steamboat whistle! And you just stood there!"

"How—how did you get in?"

"Fire escape. Same way the girl did. We were right behind her, the sergeant and myself. Afraid she'd spoil the whole business. Killan tried to grab her, but she's as quick as an antelope. Up and in before we could do a thing. Damned glad it worked out that way. Otherwise you'd be deader than hell. I'm not kidding."

Tracy drew a long, shuddering breath. He still felt very woozy as he turned his head. Lois Malloy was in the living-room doorway, white-lipped, rigid. He saw her gazing fearfully at the body of Emil and the senseless huddle of Selma.

The sight of this slim, courageous girl brought reason back to the fuddled columnist. Lois had saved his life! She wasn't a rotten little coward! He'd been completely wrong about her from the very start!

He walked slowly towards her, laid a hand on her smooth arm.

"Beat it, babe," he told her gently. "You can't afford to show in this mess. Leave it for me to handle."

She shook her head. Her dark eyes never left his for an instant. They were deep, unsmiling, very lovely. "How about you, Jerry? You're in this thing yourself."

"I'm okey. Fitz knows about most of it already. Thank God it was Fitz' bullet that finished Emil. I'm in the clear. So are you, if you beat it right away—before a lot of reporters come smelling around like a pack of hungry hyenas."

"There's a fire escape in the rear," Inspector Fitzgerald suggested dryly. "If you both want to do a quick fade, it's all right with me. I can use all the credit this case is worth. I'll tell the newshounds I broke this case on an anonymous tip. . . . You've got about two minutes if you two want to dodge headlines."

"Thanks, Fitz," Tracy muttered. "You're a prince."

He seized the dancer's arm, hurried her to the rear of the apartment. The window was still open. He swung her slim weight up in his arms and helped her to the fire-escape platform. In the darkness there was nothing visible except the blank brick wall opposite and the shadowy dimness of a backyard far below.

They stood there for an instant in the darkness—a couple of clear-eyed square shooters. Human to the core, both of them.

"Why did you pretend to be such a rotten little tramp, Lois? You deliberately made me think you were out to frame your own mother."

She nodded ruefully. "The mule in me, Jerry. I was playing it close for a showdown; letting whoever was in it think it was running all their way. I was trying desperately for a lead, but I was almost ready to call a copper when you barged in. You made me damned mad for one thing. You called me dirt right off the bat. Remember? I won't take that from anyone.

"For another thing, what you did gave me more time. And I was hurt enough and stubborn enough to want to go on playing it my way without you. Of course I was wrong and rotten. I knew it all the time. Well, that's me."

Lois Malloy drew a deep breath.

"It was really Sweetie's own idea for me to live alone. She wanted me to prove myself—alone. She was always ready to step in, if I—I seemed to be failing."

"Failing?" Jerry whispered huskily. "I never want to meet anyone finer than you, Lois. You and Sweetie make a grand pair of thoroughbreds."

He swung her impulsively towards him. His voice was suddenly eager, boyish. "How would you like to drive out to the suburbs—right now? Is it a go? We'll pick up a birthday cake—"

"And some birthday candles—"

"And we'll give Sweetie the best damned—"

"Oh, Jerry . . . Come on—hurry!"

Murder on the Gayway
Dwight V. Babcock

DWIGHT V(INCENT) BABCOCK (1909–1979) was born in Ida Grove, Iowa, but lived in Southern California from childhood. Before becoming a full-time writer, Babcock worked as a banjo player, piano tuner, vice president of a grape juice company, and owner of a service station.

His first stories were sold to pulp magazines, including *Black Mask* when it was published by Joseph Shaw, who then became Babcock's agent. He wrote three novels, all of which were about Joe Kirby, as ordinary as his name, and Hannah Van Doren, who was anything but ordinary. A feature writer for crime magazines, she searches for stories, "the gorier the better, and with a sex angle if possible," and is known as "the Gorgeous Ghoul." She has the face of an angel but drinks "like a fish." The three novels about "Homicide Hannah" are *A Homicide for Hannah* (1941), *The Gorgeous Ghoul* (1941), and *Hannah Says Foul Play* (1946).

Having achieved only moderate success with his novels, Babcock turned to screenwriting and became a prolific author of motion pictures, including *Road to Alcatraz* (1945), *The Corpse Came C.O.D.* (1947), and several low-budget horror films, and an active TV writer, with scripts for scores of popular programs to his credit, including *The Lone Ranger*, *Dick Tracy*, *The Adventures of Kit Carson*, *The Roy Rogers Show*, *Racket Squad*, *The Adventures of Ellery Queen*, *Adventures of Superman*, and *Hawaii Five-0*.

"Murder on the Gayway" was published in the October 1939 issue.

Murder on the Gayway

Dwight V. Babcock

A knifer mingled in the crowd at Treasure Island's Nude Ranch. Guess who it was before Beek does!

MY DOGS WERE KILLING me when I reached the car. I'd have bet I walked a hundred miles, seeing the Fair in one day. I climbed into my coupé, unlaced my shoes, kicked them off and sat back wiggling my toes, sighing with the ecstasy of relief. After that I got a cigarette going and settled down to wait for Mac.

It was a little after midnight and there was a balmy summer breeze blowing in from the Golden Gate. My Zephyr was in the parking space at the north end of Treasure Island, and from where I sat in it I could see the lights of San Francisco across the water to my right and the lights of Berkeley and Oakland twinkling off to my left.

Most of Treasure Island was still lighted up too, and at night like that, with the buildings bathed in all the different colors, it looked like fairyland—though about all I could see of it from this dark end of the island was the tall spire of the Tower of the Sun. The exhibit halls had all closed at ten p.m., but the Gayway was still going strong, its lights and its noise reaching back here from a distance.

What was left of the crowd was on the Gayway. It didn't look as if there were many cars remaining on the lot, but that was because they had thinned out, were sprinkled far and wide

over the approximate hundred acres of parking grounds. Two men and a girl had come from the direction of the Gayway into the parking grounds, and having nothing better to do I watched them approach.

One of the men was so fat he waddled, and the girl was between him and the other guy. They each had hold of one of her arms and were walking her along as if she'd had one too many and wasn't able to navigate without help. It wasn't till they passed right in front of the Zephyr that I caught on there was more to it than that.

I heard the girl say in a fierce whisper, "Let me go!" and realized she was struggling against the grip the two had on her arms. I acted instinctively, leaned forward and switched on the headlights. Caught in the glare, the men's heads jerked up and around and their stride faltered.

"What's the matter?" I asked, sticking my head out the side window—and my nose into something that probably wasn't any of my business, a bad habit of mine.

"Nothing," the nearest one answered in an annoyed tone, and I recognized his face as the light hit it.

He wasn't the fat one, and his name was Art Vogelsang. I'd run into him off and on when I'd worked the police beat for the *Tribune* in past years. He'd been a runner for a crooked shyster then, until the lawyer got himself disbarred. Then he'd worked for a bail-bond broker who was later tried and convicted as a fence. Vogelsang had slipped out from under both times, and I didn't know what he was doing now. But I did know he was a smoothie, an opportunist who worked on the shady side of the law.

"Hold it," I said. "I've got a gun here. Are you sure everything's all right, miss?"

I didn't have a gun, but they stopped just

within the beam of light and the girl cried: "No—no, everything's not all right! These two men are forcing me to go with them!"

She was a tiny trick in a dark tailored suit, a rakish hat with a feather stuck in it at a jaunty angle. She had a round baby face and a turned-up nose. Her eyes were large and glistening in the headlight glare, but she seemed more angry than afraid. The fat man jerked her arm, growled in a deep bass:

"Shut up, you!" He squinted into the light. "She's drunk. She don't know what she's saying. Come on."

His eyes were almost hidden in his moon face and he had wet blubbery lips. He was built like a gigantic egg. I'd never seen him before that I remembered, and if I had I would have remembered anyone his size.

"Wait," I said. "I don't think the girl wants to go with you, fatty. Let go of her. Or would you rather I called some of the Exposition cops?"

Fatty looked at Vogelsang and Vogelsang's teeth made a white glitter as he smiled. He wore tweeds—a lean, sharp-faced blond man with expressionless blue eyes and a clipped mustache. His voice was oily as he said:

"This is all a mistake, brother. The little lady is slightly tipsy. We're going to see that she gets home safely."

"I'm *not* tight," the girl denied, and stamped one foot indignantly. "Let me go! I don't want to go with you. Please," she said, addressing her appeal to me, "make them let me go!"

"O.K.," I said, and got my teeth into the words. "Let the little lady go. I'll see that she gets home safely. She don't seem tight to me, and I'll take her word against yours anytime, Vogelsang, you cheap chiseler."

His mouth and eyes tightened down and he tried to see me through the light glare. "Who are you?"

"Never mind that," I bit out. "Let the girl go or I'm going to start squeezing lead and noise out of this heater and draw a swarm of cops around here."

He hesitated a moment, standing very tense

and still, then tossed his jaw at the fat man and they let go of the girl's arms. She moved away from them, straightening her jacket with a disdainful jerk of her shoulders.

"Let that be a lesson to you, you heels," she told them scornfully. "Picking on a lady!"

Vogelsang was still glaring in my direction, but I was pretty sure he couldn't see me. "You'll regret this, brother," he lipped tightly.

"So I'll regret it," I said cheerfully. "Scram, you and your fat stooge. Get in your car and highball out of here. If you're not off the Island in two minutes, I'll get some law on your tail. Molesting a girl—and she looks like a minor at that. Go on, beat it."

Vogelsang swung away without another word and, trailed by the waddling fat man, strode off toward a light sedan about twenty yards away. The girl moved around to the right side of my coupé and watched them as they got in their car. The sedan's motor came to life with a sputtering roar, its lights blinked on and it jerked forward, wheeled around and charged straight at the left side of my Zephyr. Headlight beams caught me in the face and I ducked back. The sedan veered off, went by the tail of the Zephyr in a rush that raised a miniature whirlwind, headed for the outlet along the west edge of the island which led across Yerba Buena to the Bay Bridge.

I watched it go, knowing Vogelsang and his fat partner had seen me and now knew who I was. And I had a feeling in my bones the guy hadn't been fooling when he'd told me I'd regret interfering.

Swearing at and to myself for the impulse that had made me stick my neck out again, I turned to the girl. She was standing by the open right-hand window and I flicked on the dome light so I could see her. She was pert and doll-faced with large doll-like eyes and hair the color of pine shavings. She looked about seventeen and spoke with the suggestion of a lisp.

"Thanks," she said, blinking long lashes at me and smiling shyly. "I—I don't know how to thank you, Mr. . . . ."

"Beeker," I told her. "Just call me Beek. So

what's your name and who are you and how did it happen those two lugs—"

"I don't know," she said, shaking her head in wide-eyed wonder. "I never saw them before in my life. I—I got separated from my—my friend in the crowd on the Gayway, and those men accosted me and drew me down a dark passageway and made me come out here. I don't know where they were taking me."

"Why didn't you scream?" I asked skeptically.

Her doll-like eyes got even wider. "But I couldn't! The fat one had a black-jack and he said he'd hit me with it if I let out a peep."

She was either very dumb, or putting on an act. I reluctantly pulled my shoes back on my aching feet, slid over to her side of the car and got out to stand beside her. "Maybe we'd better go report this at the Exposition Police Headquarters."

"No!" She said it quickly, almost too quickly, as though a swift stab of fear had forced it out of her. She sent a quick look swinging around the parking area. "I'll be all right now, I think."

"Well," I said, "at least I can help you find your friend. Who is he and where did you get separated from him?"

"In front of the Greenwich Village. I stopped to look at the dancing girls out in front and when I looked around Johnny was gone. He just seemed to have disappeared."

"Johnny who?" I asked patiently.

"Johnny Foster," she told me, gazing over toward the Gayway.

The name clicked. "Not the Johnny Foster who's heir to the Foster sugar millions?"

She looked at me, batting her eyelids. "I—I don't know. You see, I don't know him very well."

"Oh," I said. "And now, just to get the record more or less complete, suppose you tell me your name."

She hesitated before answering, glancing around again. "Daisy," she said then. "Daisy May Huggins. Who's that coming?"

Her hand had tightened on my arm and she was staring toward the dark back of the Gayway, at a figure who was coming toward us in a fast slouching shuffle.

"That looks like little Mac. Don't worry, he's a pal of mine." I looked down at her. "Daisy May Huggins," I said. "That's a pretty name."

She glanced up sharply, to see if I was kidding her, and I knew she wasn't as dumb as she was acting. I kept a straight face for her benefit, and then Mac was on us, croaking excitedly:

"Hey, Beek! I found her! I found her!"

"You found who?" I said.

He was a little guy with an oversize Adam's apple and a thin and crooked face. His moist eyes were usually sad as a setter's, but now they were lit up and glowing. He waved the newspaper he had clutched in one hand and his Adam's apple bobbled with excitement.

"The missing Ingraham babe," he said. "Take a swivel at this."

He snapped the paper open and thrust it into my hands. In the glow that fell out from the dome light I could see it was a bulldog edition of the *Morning Tribune*, and a head in midpage read:

HILDEGARDE INGRAHAM TRACED TO SAN FRANCISCO

I'd read the story before. Hildegarde Ingraham, daughter of a wealthy Chicago meatpacker, had disappeared from her home in the Windy City about ten days ago. At first a kidnaping had been suspected, but no ransom notes had been received, and the father had finally offered a reward for her return unharmed, or information as to her whereabouts.

Now, it had been ascertained—on good authority, according to the writeup—that a girl answering Hildegarde's description had left a trail that led to San Francisco after evidently just running away from home. There was no art with the story; due to an eccentricity of her parents and a fear of kidnapers, they had never allowed her photograph to be taken, either by reporters or in a studio. There was a description of the girl, a brunette of eighteen years.

I looked up and saw that Daisy May had drawn away a little and was watching me silently. I grinned at Mac.

"So what gives, pal?"

"So there's a reward. And I know where she is! She's one of the girls in the Nude Ranch. We can put the arm on her and cop off the reward."

His full name was Adelbert McGillicuddy and he was a former small-time crook with a record, on parole now and trying to go straight. Being sorry for him and not knowing what I was letting myself in for, I'd done him a favor in the past. In return he'd saved my life and attached himself to me like a porous plaster.

He was all right except when temptation was put in his path, and then he weakened very easily. I had a time watching him and keeping him fairly honest. He was a pest sometimes, but he meant well, and I couldn't get rid of him without hurting his feelings. Besides, I'd learned to really like the little twerp and I owed him something for saving my life, though that couldn't be worth a hell of a lot.

"So that's where you've been all this time—in the Nude Ranch," I said, and couldn't help laughing. "Nuts! What would a gal like this Ingraham kid be doing exhibiting herself in a place like that?"

"But she is!" Mac was very earnest, his crooked face screwed up into prunelike wrinkles, gesturing volubly with his hands. "Maybe she is one of these here now exhibitionists by nature. Or maybe she run out of dough and had to take this job. This twist is different than the rest. She's not bad, if I do say so myself, and she's got something the others ain't—class and stuff like that there. And she's young, a brunette, and with a mole on her left upper arm, just like that description in the paper. It's her, honest to Gawd, Beek. I know it!"

I sighed, shook my head. "Ever since we happened to be lucky enough to knock off that reward for recovering some letters for a gal, you seem to think we're in the dick business. Every time you read about a reward being offered for something, you start getting ants in your pants. You're driving me nuts. Drop wise, Mac. This girl isn't—"

"But, criminy, Beek." He looked hurt and his voice was wistful. "Five grand, this reward is! And I tell you honest that this is the girl. It wouldn't hurt none just to take a swivel at her, would it?"

"O.K.," I agreed, just to humor him. "We'll take a look. We've got to go back that way anyway and help Miss Huggins here find her escort. She got separated from him in the crowd."

"Oh!" He stared at her as if he hadn't realized she was there before. He doffed his hat and bobbed his head. "Pleased to meetcha, miss."

Daisy May smiled at him and I said, "Come on. We'll see if we can find Johnny and then take a look at this gal in the Nude Ranch."

The throng was thinning out along the Gayway and the blare and glitter were dying a slow death due to the lateness of the hour. We made one trip up and down its length to see if we could spot Daisy May's friend Johnny Foster, but it was no dice, so to satisfy Mac and get it over with we turned in at the Nude Ranch.

The Nude Ranch was a long, low building with a rustic, Spanish-type front. In the heart of the Gayway and its most popular attraction, the barkers out front were made up like copies of the Lone Ranger and didn't have to work very hard to lure customers inside at two bits a crack. The exhibit was coining money.

Daisy May seemed to want to stick close to us as long as we couldn't find Johnny, and now that we had her I didn't know what to do about it, so I shelled out six bits and we all went through the turnstile.

Inside, the building was divided into two sections by a glass screen that ran down the center. The audience, mostly of men, was on one side of the glass behind a railing, and the Nude Ranch girls were on the other side of the glass under lights in a simulated outdoor setting.

As you came in, you walked the length of the building along an aisle formed by the glass on your left and the railing on your right. Then you went around and stood behind the railing and could stay as long as you liked. I'd been in there an hour or so before and I'll swear I recognized some of the same faces lining the rail now, where the lights from the other side of the glass hit them.

The place was pretty well filled even if it was getting late, and we found a place at the rail near the far end, where McGillicuddy pointed out the girl he thought was the missing Hildegarde Ingraham, whispering hoarsely: "That's her!"

She was small and brunette and she was playing Ping-Pong at a table close to the glass screen. Other girls were playing horseshoes and badminton, practicing on an archery range, twirling lariats and taking turns riding a burro. They all wore bandannas knotted loosely around their necks, G-strings, boots, cartridge belts and holsters containing imitation six-shooters. Some wore sombreros and some didn't. Some were only passable, but most were built very nicely, the brunette with the large mole on her left arm included in the last category.

But she was different than the others in more ways than one, I had to admit that. In the first place, where all the other girls allowed their bandannas to hang down the back where they would be out of the way, she kept the triangle of the bandanna at the front, an inherent modesty apparently at work on her. She seemed to be acutely conscious of the many watching eyes while pointedly ignoring them.

She had an air of breeding about her, a way of carrying her head, and her face had a genteel intelligence that was out of place here. Her skin was like smooth ivory. Small-boned, almost dainty, she had a youthful, boyish figure, with slender hips and small budding breasts that the bandanna did not quite hide. It was a fact that she didn't look more than eighteen—the Ingraham girl's age.

"What'd I tell you, boss?" Mac breathed eagerly in my ear.

"It's screwy," I muttered, keeping my gaze on the girl as she and her partner batted the little white ball back and forth. "But could be. Could be."

We couldn't hear the girls on the other side of the glass when they spoke to each other, and they couldn't hear any of the conversation that went on among the customers. The glass screen was enough to deaden ordinary sounds.

I swung away at a sudden disturbance in the audience. Someone had grunted explosively above the murmuring voices, as though he'd been hit in the belly with a fist. A rough voice growled, "Hey, quit shoving!"

When I turned my head to look I realized that Daisy May wasn't with us any more, and I couldn't recall when she'd left us. There was a surging scuffle in the thickest part of the crowd up along the rail, but I couldn't see what it was all about at first because the only lights in the place were on the other side of the glass and they were like footlights, focused on the girls. The only illumination on the audience side was the back-glow and that didn't amount to much.

Someone said disgustedly, "Just another drunk."

The crowd parted, falling back away from a stocky, middle-sized man so that I could see him. He was almost chubby and he wore a gray fedora. He was staggering, lurching about with his hands pawing for support and his mouth working; but only senseless *glugging* sounds came from his throat.

He fell against a little guy with an ugly battered face and the little guy snarled, pushed him away viciously. The man tripped over his own feet, went down, with those in the way scrambling to get out from under.

"Migawd!" the one who'd shoved him squawked sharply. "The guy's all bloody!"

He was holding up the hand that he'd pushed the man with, staring bug-eyed at the glistening red stain across it that looked like a bright splash of fresh scarlet paint.

"Jeepers!" McGillicuddy croaked at my side, and just then overhead lights flared on.

The girls behind the glass had stopped their desultory game playing and were staring out at the audience for a change. Two of the barker guys in the Lone Ranger outfits were coming from the door, one shouting above the sudden babble:

"What's the matter? What goes on here?"

Slapping a quick look over the audience, which was pressing back in a ring away from the man on the floor, I still didn't see Daisy May. There were only a few women in the audience, and one of these screamed:

"He's been stabbed! Look!" Then she keeled over too and the guy with her caught her.

"Where's the girl that was with us?" I asked Mac, and he shook his head, his mouth hanging open loosely.

"I dunno. I ain't seen her since we came in here. Cripes, what's happened to that guy? Let's broom outa here!"

"Nix," I said and shoved forward, fighting my way through to the front part of the ring. The stocky man was on his back on the floor, one of the cowboys kneeling beside him. The other one was bellowing:

"Get back! Get back! Give this guy air."

"He needs a doctor more than anything else," I yelled, grabbing his arm. "Get one and some cops in here."

He looked at me, then nodded and shoved off. The man on the floor had the long bone handle of a clasp knife protruding downward from just under his wishbone. At its base, his vest was sodden with a slowly spreading stain of blood. The blade, at least six inches long judging from the handle, was slanted inward and up toward the heart, had been driven in that way by an underhand blow that had at first knocked the wind out of the man.

Now he lay with his head supported on the arm of the attendant, his chubby face beaded with sweat and convulsed with pain as he gasped for breath. He was a middle-aged, nondescript man with hair beginning to gray. He opened his eyes and stared upward, looking around almost desperately. His jaws opened and closed. He gasped something that sounded to me like, "Hilda-glug Ing—" and then the blood came, thick and frothy, pouring from his mouth.

It ended in a liquid rattling in his throat as he relaxed and died.

My insides turned over and I retched, swung away to keep from being sick. The hush that had fallen over the crowd was broken by one of the women with a shrill, hysterical scream. And there was a sudden stampede for the door, that was met and stopped by a couple of special cops in their fancy Fair uniforms.

But I was staring at the girls behind the glass then, wondering if the man had been trying to say, "Hildegarde Ingraham" as he died.

The girls were huddled together just opposite me, staring out. All but one—the brunette with the mole on her left upper arm. She stood aloof and alone, at one end of the Ping-Pong table, half leaning on it for support with one arm. Her patrician face was unnaturally white and strained, and her knees were bent a little as if they were about to give way and she might collapse.

The cops were forcing the audience back into the room, gradually restoring some semblance of order out of the chaos. Uneasy and murmuring, some frankly sick, the customers were being lined up between the railing and the glass. And all backs were turned to the glass now; the almost nude girls behind it had ceased to be the main attraction. I made sure again that little Daisy May wasn't among those present, worked my way to the side of the cowboy who had been on duty at the door.

"Did anyone go out of here," I asked him, "just before this happened?"

He was tall and pale and thin, all the sap knocked out of him by what he'd seen. He shook his head in a half-dazed way. "Judas Priest, I don't know. I came in here to see what was wrong, and anybody could have slipped out behind me then."

"That makes it just swell," I muttered, "for the killer."

A doctor came first and shook his head over the corpse, pronounced it dead. Then more Fair cops, and plain-clothes men stationed on the grounds. Finally the coroner and homicide squad from San Francisco.

From papers and identification in his pockets, the corpse was found to be one Rufus Moore, a Swinnerton operative from Chicago. Swinnerton Investigation Service has offices in every large city, is one of the largest private dick agencies in the world. But Rufus Moore had come all the way here from Chi, and I thought I knew why: The Swinnerton agency had been hired to trace Hildegarde Ingraham by her father in Chicago, and Moore had come here on her trail.

I didn't tell the cops that, though. For some reason I kept it to myself when we were all herded into a back room and taken aside singly for questioning. I knew white-haired Chauncey O'Toole, the inspector in charge, from my old days on the *Trib*, and so I got off pretty easy, furnishing McGillicuddy with a straight alibi.

The cops had found a blood-stained, plain linen handkerchief on the floor under Moore, and figured it had been used to hold the knife when the killer used it. So I was pretty sure there weren't any fingerprints on the knife handle, though they didn't say, and an expert was working on it. But a funny thing about the handkerchief—it was the small size used and carried by girls and women of all ages, and not by any of the kind of men I know.

No one of the audience could name the killer. It had been too dark for them to notice, and practically everyone had come in to get his money's worth, so was concentrating his attention on the Nude Ranch gals. The cops held the little guy with the ugly battered face who had pushed Moore and got blood on his hand, and three other known petty crooks who were in the audience, took names and addresses and let the rest of us go, one by one.

It was almost two a.m. when Mac and I got out of the place. The Nude Ranch had closed down, of course, but there was a mob hanging around out front, being kept back by a squad of the Exposition cops. None of the other attractions on the Gayway was getting any kind of a play. Word had got around about the killing, and practically everyone left on the Fair grounds had gathered here.

We were collared by a bunch of newshounds, my old pals of the fourth estate, who wanted to know who, what, where, why and how. I told them we didn't know from nothing but not to quote me and, fickle characters that they are, they left us to swoop down upon the next guy the dicks had let out of the place. I lit a cigarette and we were moving out of the limelight to become part of the crowd, when a voice said in my ear:

"I beg your pardon, but do you know if the police are keeping a girl inside—a blond girl?"

"Who!" I said, twisting my head to look at the man at my side.

His face was young and clean-cut and worried. He smiled apologetically. "I've been looking all over for her. We became separated earlier in the crowd and I can't find her anywhere. She isn't outside here now, so she must be inside. I saw you coming out and I thought maybe you could tell me if she's in there."

I lifted my brows at him, took the cigarette from my mouth and said slowly: "You mean as a customer, and not as one of the—uh, attractions?"

"Of course." He wasn't quite as tall as I was, but he was well built and you could tell he was wearing quality clothes. He looked like money, but there was nothing flashy about him. He had a good jaw, a cleft chin, crisp dark hair. "She's small and blond," he said, "and is wearing a dark suit, a hat with a feather in it." He used a gesture to illustrate the length of the feather.

"Her name wouldn't be Daisy May Huggins, would it?" I said.

He hesitated a moment before nodding his head and answering yes. There was an odd questioning gleam in his eyes.

"She isn't in there," I told him. "She was, but

she's not there now." Then I explained how I happened to know her name and told him about Vogelsang and his fat stooge trying to take her with them.

Mixed thoughts and emotions were chasing themselves all over the kid's good-looking face. "My God," he breathed. "Maybe they've got her again!"

"They could have come back," I admitted, realizing that one of them might have followed us into the Nude Ranch, and slipped out with the girl in the confusion just after Moore had been stabbed. I added, "You're Johnny Foster, aren't you?"

He looked at me in a blank, startled way; then his face got very expressionless. "No," he said shortly, turned on his heel and walked off, shouldering through the crowd.

He hadn't even bothered to thank me. He was too worried for that, and I was beginning to get an idea about Daisy May. On impulse, I fished out my car keys, shoved them at Mac, who had been standing silently beside me.

"Tail that guy, keed," I told him. "He's heading for the parking grounds, so that means he has a car. I'll ride a cab into town. Phone me at Ricopetti's as soon as he lights."

Mac looked puzzled when he grabbed the keys, but he didn't ask any questions. He said, "Right, boss. But you keep an eye out for that girl, huh?" Then he was gone, after the kid who had denied being Johnny Foster.

 was becoming more and more interested in the missing Hildegarde Ingraham and the possibility of knocking off a hunk of that five-grand reward. The Swinnerton dick getting knifed out and gasping what sounded to me like her name couldn't be just coincidence. And any part of the reward would come in very handy indeed in keeping the wolf from my door, as I did not have any particular prospects of a job and did not particularly relish the idea of work anyway since I'd got used to a life of ease and trailer tramping. Five thousand clackers was something worth gambling for, and what could I lose?

Right then I was really more worried about what had happened to Daisy May, but while on the spot I thought I ought to find out what I could about the dark-haired gal in the Nude Ranch that McGillicuddy had pointed out to me. The gals were still inside. The cops were questioning them too, to see if any of them had noticed anything in the audience at the time of the killing that might help them to tab the killer. They weren't off duty till two anyway, so I planned to hang around until they came out.

There was a back door and chances were they'd use that. I had to go up to the corner and around the building that held the Incubator Babies, and cut back along behind the row of buildings. It was darker back here and there wasn't as much of a crowd, only a scatter of the curious who were watching the building from the rear. I took up a position against the wall near the rear door, got another cigarette going and settled down to wait.

It wasn't long before the door opened and the gals started to drift out, mostly in pairs or groups chattering about the murder. There was a single bulb burning above the door, so when the one I was waiting for came out under it I spotted her without any trouble. She was alone and she was hatless and she was wearing a coat of dark sleek fur that matched her hair. That was something—a thirty-five-dollar-a-week nudist wearing a fur coat in mid-summer, a coat that looked like kolinsky, and you can't get kolinsky for peanuts.

She sent a quick searching glance from side to side as she passed under the light, then started to walk past me. I stepped up even with her and touched her arm.

"Pardon me, miss. May I speak with you a minute?"

She shied away from me like a frightened filly, her delicate face white and strained.

"Don't be afraid," I told her easily. "I'm

harmless. I'm not going to hurt you. All I want is to ask you a couple of questions."

She was pressed against the wall of the building, staring at me. "What—who are you?"

She spoke in a whisper and I kept my voice down too. "I'm curious," I said. "I saw you inside and you don't belong in a place like this. What are you doing here?"

"That," she said tensely, "happens to be my business."

"Maybe I can get you a better job," I lied. "Would you mind telling me your name?"

The fear had gone suddenly out of her and she straightened up away from the wall, tilting her chin. "I most certainly would."

Behind me a rough voice said, "Who is dis slug?"

I turned and looked at a hard-faced mug with a barrel chest who was fully six-feet-four and built like Slapsie Maxie Rosenbloom. The red knot of his necktie was on a level with my eyes and I had to look up to see his face, and even then his chin was in the way so I couldn't see most of it. His jaw stuck out like the prow of a battleship, and he had big black shaggy eyebrows that seemed to hang down over his eyes. He had been one of the customers in the Nude Ranch before and after the killing.

"I don't know," the girl told him. "I've never seen him before. I didn't see you when I came out and he stopped me and started talking to me, tried to find out my name."

"One of them kind of guys, huh," the gorilla growled. "What's da idea, slug, annoying a lady? I oughta hang one on you. Beat it, before I pop you one. On your way, on your way!"

He was pointing a thumb like a sausage over one shoulder, jiggling it. He was one of those the cops had questioned and let go, and I wasn't sure they hadn't made a mistake in letting him go, seeing as how he knew this girl. If she were actually Hildegarde Ingraham . . . I remembered he'd been standing close to the spot where Rufus Moore had fallen with the knife in him, and he'd been the one who'd told Moore to stop shoving, before the man had dropped.

"Don't scare me like that," I told him, getting ready to jump—the other way. "Who are you to order me around?"

I thought that might make him tell me who he was, but it didn't. And when he put his slab of jaw down on his big chest and started for me with his long arms swinging, I knew I'd met my Waterloo. I retreated and got out of his way. He didn't follow, just stopped and snorted, sneering at me. Then he swung back to the girl, said, "Come on, babe. Let's go."

She let him take her arm and they strode off, looking almost comical together like that, due to their difference in size. I let them go, as I didn't want to ask her any questions anyhow with the gorilla around to overhear. That would just be inviting mayhem, and I have a very well-developed instinct for self-preservation.

I'd been going at things the wrong way. If I'd been smart, I wouldn't have stopped the girl at all, but would have followed her home, where I could pick my time and see her alone. Another single girl had come out through the door and was walking past me.

"Hello," I said.

She looked at me blankly. She had a heart-shaped painted face and was wearing a miniature straw hat on top of glittering platinum hair. She had on a white sweater that clung to her full breasts, and a pleated skirt. I didn't remember her as one of the Nude Ranch girls, but maybe she looked different with her clothes off, and she suddenly smiled at me.

"Hello," she said. "Do I know you?"

She said it hopefully and I told her, "Sure, but we ought to get better acquainted." I was standing close to her. I nodded up in the direction where the gal in the fur coat and her gorilla boyfriend were walking away. "Who's that screwy girl that just came out—wearing a fur coat in weather like this?"

They were still in sight when the painted blonde took a slant at them, but she would have known who I meant anyway because of the fur coat. She sniffed. "That's Louise Madden. She just wears that coat to show off. She's only been working here a few days and she thinks she's better than the rest of us girls."

"Yeah?" I said. "And who's that missing link with her?"

"Oh, that's her brother. Or so she says."

"The hell it is," I said. "Well, thanks."

I tipped my hat and backed away and she looked startled, said disappointedly: "But I thought—"

"Some other time, baby," I promised, turned and walked away.

The gorilla drove the girl over the bridge into San Francisco in a small and ancient coupé. I followed in a cab. The coupé swung off the bridge approach and went out Mission two or three miles, turned into a district of old frame apartment buildings. There wasn't much traffic at that hour, but I took a chance on being spotted and had the driver take the cab into the side street after the coupé.

The side street was dark and deserted, except for the coupé, parked at the curb in mid-block with its lights burning. As we went by it, the lights blacked out and, looking back, I saw the gorilla and the girl getting out before a dark three-story apartment building. I told the driver to turn left at the next corner and stop, where I paid him off.

When he drove away, I went back to the corner, peered around. It was even more dark and silent and deserted than before. Somewhere down on Mission a truck was making a grinding racket, but the rest of the world seemed sound asleep. I stepped into the side street, moving along it on the opposite side from the coupé.

Nothing stirred in the deep shadow of the recessed apartment house doorway as I passed it. I didn't pause, but went on up to the corner, crossed over and came back. I had some idea of examining the cards on the mail boxes outside the door to see if two Maddens were listed—if the two did live together as brother and sister, or if I could count on the gorilla going away and leaving the girl alone.

But when I came even with the building, the coupé door swung open and the gorilla came out and up from the floorboards, where he'd been crouched, waiting for me; he and the girl had got back in the car when I was up around the corner. I just had time to swing around and set myself when he was on top of me. I didn't have a chance to duck or dodge. He got a big fistful of the front of my vest and jerked me toward him, growled:

"What's da idea, tailing us?"

I was suddenly mad, not at him but at myself for being so dumb and careless. They'd spotted me tailing them and had suckered me neatly into a trap. I pulled back one foot and aimed a kick at his shin. It connected and he said, "O-ow!" in a very surprised and hurt tone of voice, at the same time flinching back and giving ground. As he stepped back I let go with my right fist and buried it in his solar plexus.

Delivered right, a punch like that can bend a man double and paralyze him for a minute or so. I guess my delivery was wrong, because he only grunted and my fist bounced back as if his belly muscles were made of spring steel. He didn't even let go of me and give me a chance to hightail it away from there.

Instead, he muttered, "You ast for it, slug, now take it."

Then he hit me. His fist felt like a cannon-ball when it slammed into my jaw. It jarred me down to my toes and from the coupé I heard the girl cry out: "Buck, don't! Buck!"

And the sidewalk came up and kissed me. The last thing I remembered was the dim roar of the coupé's motor, which got fainter and fainter in the distance. I don't know how long the knockout lasted, but when I came out of it I was all alone and Buck and the girl were gone.

icopetti's is a hole-in-the-wall bar and restaurant on Columbus in the old Barbary Coast district. They know me there—too well. There was a phone message waiting there for me when I arrived—from Mac, telling me where to meet

him, which was at the corner of Kearney and Jackson, only two or three blocks away.

A bruise was blossoming on my jaw and it was sore as a boil. My head was also giving me merry hell. I needed a drink, but it was after two a.m. and the bar was closed. So I talked the night man, a pal of mine, into slipping a shot of brandy into the cup of coffee I ordered, and also got him to lend me his gun. I needed an equalizer in case I ran up against the gorilla again, as I didn't want to take another dose of the sample he'd given me.

When I left Ricopetti's I was feeling better, but I was still sore. I walked up to Kearney and over to Jackson through empty and lifeless streets, and Mac went, "*Hiss-hiss!*" at me from a dark doorway on the corner.

"What gives?" I asked as I joined him in the doorway. "Where is our boy friend you were supposed to be tailing?"

He jabbed a thumb out and down Jackson Street. "He's down there in that bail-bond office. That's his hoopie out in front of it. He drove straight here and went in about half an hour ago and I ain't seen him come out."

Jackson was a dark and narrow street here and the bail-bond broker's office was in mid-block at street level, inner light making a glowing square of its shaded first-floor window. Staring at it, trying to make out the letters stenciled on the glass, I stepped out of the doorway and thumbed back my hat.

"Whose office is it?" I asked.

"It's run by a fat tub of lard named Jonathan Kline," Mac told me. "He is not a big shot, but I would not be too surprised if he did a little fencing of stolen articles such as hot ice on the side."

"Oh-oh," I breathed, thinking of Vogelsang's fat stooge. I was pretty sure who Mr. Kline would turn out to be.

"Criminy, Beek!" Mac blurted suddenly. "What's the matter with your puss? You look like you'd happened to an accident."

Light from the corner street lamp had got under my hat brim. "I did," I admitted, palming my sore jaw. "You wouldn't happen to know a big gorilla by the name of Buck Madden, would you?"

Mac knew most of the small-time crooks and chiselers in town by sight, name or reputation anyway. He blinked, scowling thoughtfully. "That moniker sounds familiar." Then he snapped his fingers. "I think a bruiser by that name used to do some strong-arm work for Art Vogelsang, but I ain't heard of him for a long time. Why?"

There it was—Art Vogelsang again. Everything seemed to be tying up together. "The guy bopped me," I muttered, still smarting. "That Nude Ranch gal you think is Hildegarde Ingraham is supposed to be his sister—Louise Madden. I was tailing them and the so-and-so laid for me and then got away. We could find out for sure where they live by greasing someone at the Nude Ranch, but I had to try and play it smart and get my face pushed in for my trouble." I sighed.

"I don't know whether fooling around like this is going to get us anything or not; I don't know just how I happened to get sucked into it in the first place, but now that I'm in I'm going to stay, and find out what's what. I owe somebody something for this clout on the jaw. I've either got to get paid for taking it or else get hunk some other way."

Little Mac clucked sympathetically. "You and me should of stuck together, boss. Together we ought to be able to take the big heel, huh? Let's get him, huh? The big bully!"

"Not now," I said, grinning. "Later, maybe."

"But what're we gonna do here?"

"I've got a hunch," I explained. "Moore, that Swinnerton op who was knifed in the Nude Ranch, was on the trail of Hildegarde Ingraham, I think. It sounded to me like the last thing he tried to say was her name, only no one else seemed to get it. Art Vogelsang and his fat stooge were after Daisy May, and you know the kind of guy Vogelsang is. Also, Daisy May was in the Nude Ranch with us just before the killing, then disappeared. All that is either a hell of a lot of coincidence, or else Daisy May is Hildegarde Ingraham."

Mac's crooked thin face was screwed up in a scowl of concentration. "But Hildegarde is a brunette."

"She could have dyed her hair," I pointed

out. "Probably would have if she really wanted to avoid recognition. Anyway, why would a chiseler like Vogelsang be after a gal like Daisy May, unless there was some dough in it? And if I'm wrong we can always go back to the other gal; I'll admit she intrigues me, pal."

Mac was thinking it over, mumbling in his beard: "The dick said her name before he kicked off. . . ." He looked up brightly. "Maybe this Daisy May is Hildegarde and she knifed him, huh, because she didn't want to be caught? Maybe the dick was trying to name his killer!"

"Maybe," I said. "But whether she's a murderess or not, there's still a five-grand reward offered for her, and the thing for us to do now is to find her. At first she was with this kid you followed, who I think is Johnny Foster, and he was looking for her too. He came here, so—"

"So what?" Mac said, puzzled.

"So we're going to find out what. Something very squirrelly is going on, and there just might be a chance that we could pull that five-grand reward out of the fire yet."

"Five grand—boy!" He smacked his lips. "What do we do?"

"We pay a call on Mr. Jonathan Kline first and see what goes on. I think Mr. Kline is Vogelsang's fat pal, but I don't know just what we'll be walking into, so let's sort of take it easy. I'll go in first and you wait outside. If I get in a jam, I'll holler or something and you can get help if we need it."

I nodded back along Kearney past where the Zephyr was parked, toward Portsmouth Square and the gray pile of stone across from it that was the Hall of Justice. "The police station's only a couple of blocks away, but don't call a copper unless you have to. We don't want to have to split that reward with anyone, in case there is a chance of getting it. If we get too many cops in here, they'll ace us out entirely."

"I get it, boss," Mac said. "Are you heeled?"

"Yeah." I touched the short-barreled police special in my coat pocket that I'd got from my pal in Ricopetti's. "Wait here until after I'm inside."

"Take it easy, boss," little Mac warned pleadingly as I moved off into Jackson.

From the glow that filtered out through the shaded windows, I noticed that the kid's car was a low Packard convertible and carried Nevada plates. That wasn't odd, because Nevada is a taxpayer's haven and plenty of wealthy people maintain their residence there. I moved on and up to the office door, and had my right hand on the gun in my pocket. I put out my other for the door handle, and paused.

Thumping sounds were coming from inside, the scrape of furniture being pushed back, a splintering crash that sounded like a chair hitting the floor. On either side of me the window shades were tightly drawn. There was no crack or slit through which I might see.

Thumping sounds from within continued. I let my hand close on the door handle, thumbed down the latch. The door was unlocked and I pushed it open a little, so that I could see inside.

A railing bisected the room, and behind the railing were Art Vogelsang and the kid I'd tabbed as Johnny Foster, but they didn't notice me in the doorway. They were busy, completely wrapped up in each other, engaged in a slug fest that was a furious exchange of lefts and rights. They were viciously in earnest, going at it hammer and tongs, and the room was filled with grunting sounds and the thudding impacts of fists against flesh.

Battling back and forth, the kid's dark hair was hanging down in his eyes and his coat was ripped. Sweat and blood streaked Vogelsang's sharp face. The kid was boring into him like a buzz-saw, forcing the taller man to give ground. As I watched, the kid brought up his right in a pretty uppercut and Vogelsang's head jumped and he slammed back against a roll-top desk, started to slide down it to the floor.

The kid stood over him, panting, and behind the kid a bulky shape that I hadn't noticed there rose up from the floor—the fat man, Kline. I stepped inside, heeled the door shut behind me, said:

"Hold it!" The heater was out in my fist, but

either I spoke too late or Kline didn't hear me anyway.

He swung the metal wastebasket he'd brought with him up from the floor. It arced over his head, bonged on the back of the kid's skull. The kid staggered forward, went to his knees.

"Kline!" I bit out. "Drop it!"

He looked at me, his moon face dull, blubbery lower lip hanging slackly. Sweat glistened under the lights on the dome of his almost totally bald head. There was a threat of blood from one corner of his mouth, and his clothes were dusty from the floor. The kid had evidently got in at least one good punch on him before going to work on Vogelsang. He'd really been cleaning house.

Kline's eyes glinted, almost hidden in deep folds of flesh. He let the wastebasket drop from his hand to the floor, stood breathing harshly, his bulging torso expanding and contracting. The kid had only been knocked to his knees, catching himself there and holding his head in his hands. His coat sleeves had worked back along his arms and one shirt cuff was stained darkly with blood. His clothing was practically ruined, but he didn't seem to be marked up much physically.

Now he sobbed, "You ——!" and came up swinging, going for Kline. "Where is she?" he gritted.

"Hold it!" I said sharply, moving to the railing. "What goes on?"

He jerked his head around and stared at me as if he hadn't known I was there before. Behind the railing, a chair and a typewriter table had been knocked to the floor. Vogelsang had his back propped against the desk, was holding his jaw in one hand and looking up from the floor with dazed, glassy eyes. All three men were puffing, and the sound of their breathing was very loud.

"They've got the girl!" the kid blurted. "And they won't tell me where they've got her. They're holding her. They're keeping her against her will."

"What girl?" I said. "You wouldn't happen to mean Hildegarde Ingraham, by any chance?"

His head jerked in a nod. "Yes. They—they've kidnaped her."

"Then," I said slowly, "Daisy May is really Hildegarde."

An uncertain light flickered in his eyes, as if he realized he'd spoken out of turn, revealing a confidence, and now regretted it. Then he murmured resignedly, "Well, it's out now. Yes."

"Then these mutts must have kidnaped her right out of the Nude Ranch," I said.

"I don't know." His eyes were harried and he spoke heatedly. "But I know they've got her."

I pointed the heater at Kline. "Where is she, fat boy? Give."

His face was stupidly sullen and he didn't answer.

"Nuts!" Vogelsang said, and I looked down at him. The glassiness had gone out of his eyes, leaving them blue chips of hard sharpness. His thin, blood-streaked face was sneering. "We should tell you! So you can hijack her and collect that reward. You ——! You took her away from us once and now you're sticking your nose in again."

"The hell with the reward," the kid sobbed, quivering. His jaw was set in a rigid white line. "I don't care about the reward. I want to know where she is. You two aren't just after the reward. You're going to try to hold her for ransom or something, at least try to chisel more than the five thousand out of her father. Otherwise you wouldn't have hidden her somewhere."

Vogelsang looked up at him with his mouth tight and hard and unveiled hate showing in his cold eyes. Knowing him, I had a hunch the kid was right. Vogelsang would be up to something very crooked, something very tricky, though I didn't think he'd go so far as to take a chance on a kidnaping rap.

"Listen," I said. "A private dick was killed in the Nude Ranch at the Fair tonight. He was on Hildegarde's trail. You two mutts were there; you had to be, because you came back for the gal. Either you tell where she is now, or I'm going to call in some cops."

Kline's wet lips sagged at the corners. He

looked suddenly sick, gazed questioningly down at Vogelsang. Vogelsang flicked a quick glance at him and then his eyes got very thin and expressionless.

"We don't know anything about that!" he lipped resentfully. His voice had a thickness to it, as though it hurt him to move his jaw, but he suddenly changed his tone. "Now, be reasonable, for Pete's sake. We can all get a cut in this reward."

"I don't trust you, Vogelsang," I told him. "You're trying to ease out from under something. But I'll be reasonable. You tell us where you've got the girl, the kid and I will go get her, I'll collect the reward and we'll split it—unless it turns out that one of you two lovely personalities knifed that Swinnerton dick."

"Hell, we didn't have nothing to do with that," Kline said in his deep petulant voice. "What're you planning to do—frame us?"

"No," I told him. "But you had to be near there at the time—you had to follow us back to the Fair grounds to get the girl."

The fat man's grunt was a surly sound and his eyes receded into their pockets of flesh. Vogelsang was looking thoughtful, a cunning cast to his face.

"O.K.," he said reluctantly. "I don't like murder. We don't want to get mixed up in it, so we'll tell you. But you better play square with us and see that we get our cut after the reward is paid. You, one-third—we, two-thirds."

"How about the kid?" I asked.

"I don't give a damn about the reward," the kid gritted.

"Sure," Vogelsang said. "All he wants is the girl. He can have her."

"He can have her after she's returned to her father," I said. "But the split is fifty-fifty. I've got a pal working with me. Where is she?"

"She's out in the Sunset District," Vogelsang admitted cheerfully, as if we were pals now. "Staying with some friends of mine. It's the last house on Noriega Street where it runs into the sand dunes going west. We'll go with you."

"No, you don't," I told him. "You're staying here."

I moved through the gate in the railing, lifted my chin at the kid. "See if you can find something to use so we can tie these two mutts up."

"Hey, what's the idea?" Vogelsang muttered tightly, trying to get his feet under him so he could stand up.

I let the heater point his way. "Stay where you are. We just want to be sure you'll be safe and sound while we're gone. Your friends will be guarding the girl in that house, and I don't want you to phone and warn them before we get there. I'd have you phone them now and tell them we're coming and to turn her over to us, only I don't trust you; you might let something slip over the phone and they'd broom out with the girl before we could get there."

Kline had been standing, sullen and silent, his moon face set stupidly. For the moment, while speaking to Vogelsang, I'd looked away from him. That was a mistake. Maybe he got the signal from Vogelsang, but if he did I didn't see it. He moved with sudden abruptness. I sensed it, started to whirl.

The kid yelled, "Look out!"

And from where he was on his haunches on the floor, Vogelsang rocked backward, kicked out and up with one foot. His toe cracked into my right wrist, and at the same instant Kline's big fist jarred against the side of my neck. It knocked me sideways as the gun flew out of my hand.

The kid dived for it, but Vogelsang fell on it first, rolled, came up and caught the kid on the temple with the revolver. Turning, I took a swing at Kline's fat face, but was stumbling and off balance and missed. The kid had thudded limply to the floor. Vogelsang flicked the gun up at me and rapped:

"All right, wise boy! Freeze!"

There was an icy glitter in his eyes, and his face was sharp and dangerous-looking. I froze, but Kline didn't. His moon face was no longer dull and stupid, but alive with hate. He crowded close to me, bumped me with his huge paunch and swung his fist again. It was sort of a one-two punch—first the paunch, and then his fist. The first set me up in just the right position, and the second sent me to the floor. For a fat man, he was good. He may not have been fast, but he knew how to get all his weight behind a blow.

Bells were ringing and the room and everything in it was going round and round in blurred circles. I heard Vogelsang say, "Come on, let's get out of here," and their feet moved on the floor.

I wasn't completely out; some instinct urged me to be up and after them, but I couldn't move. The gate in the railing squeaked open and clicked shut. The front door opened. They were getting away!

And then a familiar voice croaked shrilly: "Hands up! Halt or I'll shoot! Get back inside and turn around before I blow you apart."

I knew that was Mac's voice and I think I tensed, expecting to hear the blast of the gun Vogelsang had taken from me. But instead there was a muttered curse, the shuffle of feet as they backed inside and turned. Mac's voice wavered and almost cracked as he ordered:

"Drop the roscoe, bo."

I heard it hit the floor; then there was a faint swish and a hollow thunk of impact, and another greater weight hit the floor like a dropped sack of potatoes.

"Hey!" Kline's deep voice protested. "What the—"

"Don't move!" Mac warned. "Let this be a lesson to you, fatty. Crime don't pay."

There was another smacking sound, like someone thumping a ripe watermelon. The floor shook as Kline dropped. Then little Mac was at my side, pulling me up, saying:

"Hey, Beek, what is it? What's the matter? Come on, snap out of it!"

I was sitting up, but I was still dizzy. Everything kept wavering in and out of focus. Little Mac was crouching over me, his funny crooked face twisted with worry.

"I can't take it," I told him, and my tongue was thick as an overstuffed frankfurter. "Fatso pushed me and I fell down."

"Tsk, tsk," he clucked sympathetically, and went on: "I gave those bimbos what for. I didn't know what they'd done to you, but when they tried to bust out of here alone, I knew something was wrong."

The room was settling down and things were clearing up. Even the ache in my jaw was getting more acute. "Thanks, pal," I said. "But how'd you stop them? I thought you never packed a rod."

"I don't," he answered piously, and looked down at the gun in his left hand. A black-jack dangled by its thong from his right wrist. "This here roscoe is the one Vogelsang had. But I just happened to have along my sleep inducer for pertection, and when Vogelsang stepped out the door I jabbed him in the ribs with the small end and he don't know the difference. Then when I get them back in here I just let them have it on account of I don't want them to find out how I have deceived them."

The black-jack—his sleep inducer—was small and harmless-looking, but Mac was very proficient in its use, as I'd learned from past experience. He was looking sideways at the kid.

"What's the matter with him?"

The kid was sitting up, looking around and blinking.

"Vogelsang clipped him with the gun," I said, "but it looks like he's all right now. How's it, fella?"

He pressed one palm against the swelling on his temple, squeezed his eyes shut, then opened them slowly. "What happened?"

I said, "Those two mutts took us, and then my little pal here took them. So that makes it even."

His eyes sharpened with comprehension. "Yeah? Well, what are we waiting for? Let's get out of here!"

He surged to his feet, reeled sideways and caught himself against the railing.

"Hey, wait a minute!" I said, but he didn't pay any attention.

He found the gate, was through it, making a bee-line for the street door. He tripped over one of the prone bodies on the floor, brought up against the door, jerked it open and was outside.

"Come on," I rapped at Mac, and lunged to my feet. But the floor tilted up at a crazy angle and I almost went straight over onto my kisser. Mac caught and steadied me, and after a moment the floor bent down to where it was supposed to be.

About then, from out in front we heard the starting roar of a motor. Gears clashed and tires spun on the pavement as a car—I knew it was the kid's car—shot away from the curb. I plowed forward. It was tough going for a while, but with Mac pushing I finally got through the gate in the railing and made it around Vogelsang and Kline, who were out cold on the floor.

The cool night air felt good on my face and in my lungs when we reached the street. Mac had switched off the inside lights and pulled the door closed behind us, and the street was just as empty and deserted as before—except for the taillights of the kid's car, which was scooting away up the hill toward Chinatown.

I knew where he was headed—to the house on Noriega Street where Vogelsang had said the girl was being held—and we had to get there before he could get away with the girl. The night air had cleared most of the dizziness out of my skull and we pounded up to the corner and around it to where Mac had left the Zephyr. I piled in behind the wheel, jabbed the starter button and gunned the motor to life, took out after the kid as Mac fell in beside me.

The other car was out of sight by now, but I knew the approximate location of Noriega Street; the Sunset District was clear across town toward the Pacific Ocean. I pointed the Zephyr's nose in that direction and toed down on the throttle.

bout half a mile south of Golden Gate Park and a mile east of the ocean, right in the center of the Sunset District, is a section of sand dunes where streets do not run through. Bleak and bare, it is a lonesome area at night, with only a few houses spotted here and there across the dunes.

The house we wanted was where Noriega Street dead-ended, running westward into this waste space of rolling sand. We spotted it as we passed the nearest other house, more than a block away and clustered about a corner street lamp as if for protection from the night. It stood by itself, inner light making glowing squares of its windows, a low stucco bungalow. There was a dark shape squatting out in front—the kid's car. We'd made good time, but he'd got here before us.

I braked the Zephyr to a stop behind the convertible, and jumped out. The kid was on the porch at the front door, his shoulder jammed against it, arguing with someone who was trying to close it in his face. Mac was right behind me when I skidded up onto the porch, and the short-barreled police special was out in my hand.

Looking back over his shoulder, the kid half sobbed: "He won't let me in!"

I saw he had one foot stuck in the door, and above and behind the white blob of his face I could see the outline of Buck Madden's gorilla head, silhouetted by the inner light. I was sure no one else had a head like that, and I wasn't particularly surprised to find him here.

"Stand back, Madden," I told him. "I've got a gun here and we're coming in."

"Oh, you again, huh?" he growled.

"Yeah, me." I let the police special glitter in the wedge of light that fell out through the opening. "Stand back."

He stood back and the kid rammed through the door and on inside. I followed more cautiously. The gorilla tried to jump me from the side as I came in. I was remembering the clout on the jaw he'd handed me before and was expecting something, and maybe that made me lean on the gun heavier than I might have as I laid it against the side of his skull. Anyway, he went down, falling loosely to the carpet.

"That makes us even, slug," I said, but he didn't answer. He didn't even move. He'd taken a quick trip to dreamland, stretched out peacefully on the rug.

There was a short, anguished cry in the room. I looked up. The small aristocratic-looking brunette from the Nude Ranch—Louise Madden—was standing in an arched doorway wearing a quilted black robe. Her eyes were wide and stricken with shocked horror. She cried in a strained voice:

"What have you done to him? Who are you? What do you want?"

"We want the girl you're holding here," I said.

"Oh!" Her eyes jerked as she recognized me, then she came running across the room and went to her knees at the gorilla's side, held his head up to her breast. She looked up at me again. "Take her. I didn't want Buck to keep her here anyway, but they made him. She's in the back bedroom and she hasn't been hurt."

We were in a small, low-ceilinged livingroom that was neat, but looked bare, it contained so few pieces of furniture. The kid was across the room at another doorway, had stopped there when this girl had appeared. Now he plunged through the doorway, toward the back of the house, and I nodded to Mac to follow him. Mac had come in behind me and closed the front door, and when he was gone after the kid, I asked the girl:

"*Who* made you keep her?"

Her delicate face was marred by a deep and bitter shadow of anxiety. "A man named Art Vogelsang, and Jonathan Kline. I've been trying to keep Buck going straight, but they have something on him and they try to use him when they can."

"Then he's really your brother," I said.

"Yes." She nodded with her face turned down toward his. She was jiggling his head, massaging the back of his neck. "Buck—Buck . . . !"

"Don't worry," I told her. "He'll be all right. You couldn't hurt a mass of muscle like him."

She was on the verge of tears as she glanced up, her fine mouth quivering. "I suppose he had it coming to him. I'm sorry he hit you when you were following us. Who is this girl you're after?"

I felt my eyebrows go up in surprise. "You don't know? She's that missing Hildegarde Ingraham. You know, the runaway daughter of the Chicago meat-packer. For a while I thought you might be her; that's why I was following you. That fur coat had me fooled, and you've got class, sister."

She let go of a bitter little laugh, shook her head hopelessly. "You surely don't think I'd be working at the kind of a job I have now if I were this Hildegarde Ingraham. The coat is just a relic of better days, the only thing I have to wear. The only reason we rent a place way out here is because it's cheap. I—I hope we don't get into any trouble over this. Buck has a record. He doesn't like to live on what I make, but he can't get an honest job. Nobody'll trust him."

"That's tough," I said, really feeling sorry for the kid. "But don't worry. And maybe we can work it so he'll get a split of the reward that's offered for finding this Ingraham babe."

She didn't look up or answer. Her shoulders moved convulsively and I knew she was crying silently. For some reason I felt like a heel. I was actually sorry I'd hit her brother, because when he'd clouted me he'd probably thought he'd been protecting his sister or something. Just then Mac and the kid came back with the other girl.

Her doll-face was blank, and her big doll-eyes looked a little bit more dazed than usual. But she didn't seem much the worse for wear. Somewhere along the route she had lost her hat with the feather in it, but she hadn't been mussed up any. Under the lights I noticed at the part in her hair there was a dark line where the unbleached hair had grown out a little in its natural color.

The kid had his arm about her protectingly, was wearing a resentful scowl. "They had her tied to the bed!" he complained.

The girl had looked over the room, blinking her large blank eyes, and now gazed up worshipfully at the kid's face. "Oh, Johnny!" she breathed ecstatically. "I knew you would come for me. You're wonderful!"

She was giving him the needle. It was pretty

sickening, but the kid went for it. His scowl smoothed out and he looked soulfully down into her eyes, said softly: "Come on, honey."

They started for the front door. Little Mac blinked and his Adam's apple raced up and down before he could get out a weak yelp of protest: "Hey!"

I stepped in front of the door. "Where do you think you're going?"

The kid stared indignantly at me. "Out," he said. "I'm going to take her away from here. She's had all she can stand."

I shook my head, smiling. "Oh, no, you're not."

His jaw crept forward and his brows came down. "Why not?" he asked belligerently.

"Because," I explained. "This little lady is worth money in our kick and it's share and share alike. We want to be sure we get ours. Besides that, there is a little matter of a murder to be cleared up. I want to find out where Hildegarde was when Rufus Moore was killed. The knife was held in a girl's handkerchief."

"Knife?" the girl said blankly, batting her eyelashes. "Who was killed?"

"A Swinnerton dick was killed in the Nude Ranch," I said. "I think he was on your trail at the time, and right after the murder I looked around and you'd disappeared. You'd been there just a minute before, because you came in with us. A clasp knife with a six-inch blade sounds like kind of an unusual weapon for a girl, but it's possible you could have used it. So suppose you just tell us where you were at the time."

The kid was glowering at me, and the girl was suddenly pale and weak and stammering, floundering for words. She said, "But—but I wasn't there! I went outside—before that. I didn't know anything about it. Those men took me. That fat one and the other one, the same ones that you made release me before."

I nodded. "They must have, because they brought you here, but it seems funny that they could come back and drag you away on a brightly lighted place like the Gayway. But maybe you wanted to go with them. Maybe you could use

the fact that they abducted you as an alibi later. It's very odd that you just *happened* to go outside at that time, after being so anxious to stay with us when we went in the Nude Ranch. Why?"

"I—I—" She shot a glance up at the kid's face, seemed numb with fear. The kid growled:

"Leave her alone, and let us out of here."

"In a minute," I told him. "I want to get a few things cleared up before you take this gal off and marry her. I want to be sure she knows who you are."

His eyes tightened and his face became very expressionless. The girl was batting her eyelashes at me again, looked as if she were gasping for breath.

"Where'd you meet this kid?" I asked her.

"In Reno." She gulped. "He drove me here, last week."

"And he told you he was Johnny Foster—*the* Johnny Foster, scion of the Foster sugar millions?"

She nodded dumbly, swallowing.

"Well, I don't believe it," I said. "I thought he was too, when I first saw him, but I stopped thinking so when it struck me as odd he knew just where to go after you when you disappeared—to Art Vogelsang and Jonathan Kline. He knew who they were, when I told him Vogelsang had been after you. He's had some connection with them before, and it seems funny a guy like Johnny Foster would have anything to do with a couple of chiselers of their stripe.

"I think your boy friend here is an imposter, a gigolo, one of those guys who hang around Reno posing as wealthy playboys and preying on divorcées with dough. The way I've got it figured, he was looking for a catch and thought he'd found one when he discovered who you were, so he decided instead of turning you in for the five-grand reward to run away with you and talk you into marrying him. That way, even if the marriage were later annulled by your father, he'd be in a position to chisel a handsome settlement.

"Somehow when he got to town here he let it slip to Kline and Vogelsang, who must be old pals of his, who you were. He must have been bragging about the catch he'd made, counting his chickens before they'd hatched. But his two former pals decided to double-cross him and go after you for the reward."

The girl was staring up at his face and trying to pull away from him, but he was holding her tightly and looking at me through slitted eyes. "You're wet!" he said through his teeth, and somehow it sounded vicious, like a threat.

Mac was looking on, goggle-eyed, with his mouth hanging open. Louise Madden was listening too, but giving most of her attention to her brother, who was beginning to stir his arms and legs and mumble senselessly.

"So I'm wet," I told the kid. Up to then I had been guessing, following a hunch. "But how about that blood on your right cuff?"

The kid was wearing a white shirt, and the starched cuffs extended about an inch below the sleeve of his torn jacket. The right cuff was stained with dark and crusted splatters of blood that I'd noticed before in Kline's office. The kid glanced at it, stared up and said:

"So what? I got that in the fight with Vogel-sang and Kline."

I shook my head. "Oh, no. Those stains were dried and dark, just as they are now, when I saw you in Kline's office. You'd got them before that. You got them when you stabbed Rufus Moore, that Swinnerton dick."

"What do you mean?" he snarled. "I wasn't in the Nude Ranch. I was outside."

"You could have slipped outside in the confusion right afterwards," I said. "When I mentioned the girl's handkerchief and the clasp knife, Miss Ingraham here suddenly seemed very scared." I switched my gaze to her. "Did you ever see a knife like that before, a clasp knife with a bone handle?"

She nodded fearfully, grimacing, choked out: "It was—his! I saw him in the Nude Ranch, left you and went over to where he was standing. I said, 'Johnny!' and he shushed me, then sent me outside to wait for him, told me he'd be right out. All the time he was talking he was looking

over his shoulder and pushing me toward the door. I went out, and those other two came up and walked me away so fast I didn't know what was happening."

"Shut up!" the kid sobbed, gripping her by the shoulders and shaking her. "Are you crazy? You don't know what you're saying. I wasn't there! What's the matter with you?"

"Not much you weren't there," I said slowly. "You even tried to frame Miss Ingraham by swiping her handkerchief and using it to hold the knife and wipe the fingerprints off the handle, but that still didn't stop his blood from getting on your cuff; the handkerchief was too small. You knew the Swinnerton dick was on your tail, knew he was after Hildegarde, and when she walked up to you, you knew the game was up unless you acted fast—a fortune was slipping out of your hands.

"So when he started to work his way toward you, you sent her outside, turned around and let him have it, covered by the gloom and the crowd who was all interested in the Nude Ranch gals. Probably the guy had been on your tail earlier in the evening at the Fair. You caught on he was following you, and deliberately lost the girl in the crowd and led him into the Nude Ranch, hoping to shake him there. But when she came in with us, that spoiled everything. You had to kill him. He must have been closing in for a show-down."

The kid's face was tight and white and murderous. He kept holding on to the girl's shoulders, glaring at me. "Nuts!" he bit out. "That pack of wild guesses doesn't prove a thing. What're you trying to do, frame me so you can get the girl and the reward?"

"I don't have to frame you," I told him. "The girl's testimony will send you to the gas chamber. The game's up, bright boy, so relax. Let go of her."

"Sure," Buck Madden growled, sitting up on the floor in the arms of his sister. "Sure. I seen dat guy in the Nude Ranch, just before dat private eye was stuck wit' da toad stabber. The eye was waltzing over to him and da guy just must of slipped him da shiv and then turned and ambled out."

"That just about ties it," I said. "Go call some cops."

Madden did a double-take. "Who, me?"

The kid let his shoulders slump in apparent defeat, then jerked Hildegarde over in front of him and shoved her, sent her lunging straight for me and the gun in my hand. I tried to duck out of the way and keep him under the gun, but she slammed into me, falling, her arms hooking around me for support, dragging my gun arm down.

The kid was right behind her, his face a tight grimace of desperation. I couldn't swing the gun and fire it without danger of hitting the girl. She was hanging on like a drowning swimmer, throwing me off balance so that I had to stagger sideways and brace myself to keep on my feet.

Seeing the spot I was in, the kid actually grinned, closed in fast and straight-armed the girl again between the shoulder blades. That did it. She sobbed and her feet got tangled up with mine. I started to go down and she carried me to the floor, lit on top of me. Mac was coming up behind the kid on tiptoe, the black-jack swinging from his wrist. But the kid was at the door, jerking it open.

I couldn't roll free from the girl, but I wrenched around and stuck out my foot, making a longer leg than I thought I had. I got my toe hooked in front of his instep, jerked it up and back, tripping him as he plunged out the door. He went onto the porch in a headlong dive. I scrambled around frantically, fighting to get untangled and on my feet. By the time I made it, Mac was at the door and on through. I followed him out.

The kid had picked himself up and made it to the bottom of the steps. Mac took off from the top step and landed on his back, carried the kid forward so they both spilled on the walk and rolled off, struggling. Mac had the black-jack, but otherwise was no match for the kid's strength, and the kid in jerking around had got hold of Mac's right wrist, was twisting it.

They rolled across the lawn, a squirming, fighting vortex of movement in which neither figure was distinguishable. It was comparatively dark out here anyway after the inner brightness. I jumped down off the porch, yelling:

"Hold it, Mac! I've got him covered."

Then I jerked the trigger and let a couple of shots fly over their heads and out into the sand dunes. A bellowing voice echoed the reports: "Hey! Quit it!"

I almost jumped out of my skin. Someone was out there in the dark, and I might have hit him. During the momentary distraction, Mac had stopped fighting, going stiff and rigid to give me a chance at the kid. But the kid didn't stick around. He left Mac like a shot and was bounding away like a jackrabbit, making for the dunes and the cover of darkness.

"Stop!" I yelped. "You damn fool, stop!"

 didn't want to shoot the guy even if he was a murderer, and besides, there was someone else out there in the dark whom I might hit if I missed the kid, and I wasn't such a good shot that I couldn't miss.

The kid was fading fast into the night and I lowered the heater. Then I heard a smack and a grunt, as if he'd run headlong into something solid. There was a brief threshing and a crunching thud of sound, then silence. Mac was on his knees and we waited, staring.

A figure loomed up out of the dark, a tall lean man in a gray topcoat and hat, walking toward us and dragging something behind him. He had hold of the back of the kid's collar with one hand, and the kid was a limp, dead weight. He dropped him on the grass, said:

"Here's your man. He ran smack into me in the dark. He tried to fight so I tapped him one and put him to sleep."

"That's good," I said. "He's a killer and he was getting away. Who are you?"

The automatic in his hand had a dull black

gleam. "The name is Daly. I'm a private investigator. You say this guy's a killer?"

"Yeah." A light had dawned. "You're a Swinnerton dick."

"How did you know?"

"I just guessed." I jerked my chin down at the kid. "It's lucky you stopped him. He's the guy you want. He used that shiv on Rufus Moore."

"Well, I'll be damned." The man's tone was hard. He turned and looked down at the still figure on the lawn. The kid was lying flat on his back with his face turned up to the stars, but right now he couldn't see them. His face looked relaxed and young and handsome. Staring down at him, the dick let his gun drop to his side and he swore with a brief and bitter harshness, muttered: "If I'd known that for sure I'd have really put the slug to the lousy ———. He must be Baby-face Blythe."

"Baby-face Blythe?" I said.

He looked at me. He had a lean, haggard face. He nodded. "Rufe said the girl was with someone and he thought the guy was Baby-face Blythe. He's wanted in Chi on a manslaughter charge. Or he was—until tonight. Now, California can have him for the murder of Rufe. He's Baby-face Blythe, all right, the dirty son!"

I knew then that most of what I'd guessed before must be right. Blythe had recognized Moore and had to kill him if he wanted to stay free, whether he could marry the girl and her fortune or not.

"How did you get here?" I asked.

Daly said, "I just came from Kline's office. Rufe and me were working together trying to locate Hildegarde Ingraham. He'd traced her here from Chicago, got a line on Blythe and was following him, hoping he'd lead him to the girl. Blythe spent some time with Kline and Art Vogelsang, and so when I heard Rufe had been knifed, I knew who'd done it and went to Kline's office, looking for him. I found Vogelsang and Kline out on the floor and I shook 'em into admitting that Blythe had been there. They were sore at him and gave me this address."

"When thieves fall out . . ." I breathed and

looked up at the porch. The light had come on and all the others had come out of the house, were standing there, staring. A car was coming fast along the street, its headlights rushing toward us. From the porch, the girl we'd just rescued said in a voice brittle with a touch of hysteria:

"So—he was a crook and a chiseler all the time! He tried to deceive me, the lousy heel." Her tone was scathing, contemptuous, in spite of its shrillness.

We turned to look at the car as its brakes squealed and it slewed to a stop before the house. Art Vogelsang dived out from behind the wheel, came dashing over, hammering words:

"Hey, don't forget we get cut in on that reward! Don't forget."

He was blustering, coming up to me and the Swinnerton dick, with fat Kline waddling along behind. I told him:

"You'll be damn lucky if you get off without being stuck with a kidnaping rap."

"Nuts to that." He gazed down coldly at the man on the lawn. "So you got him. We're going to testify against Blythe, so we'll be able to make a deal with the D.A.—don't worry about that. Where's the girl?"

I nodded toward the porch. "Right there."

Vogelsang started for her, and she shrank behind Louise and Buck Madden.

"Wait a minute," Daly's voice clipped out.

Vogelsang stopped and looked back.

"Who's that?" the dick asked, nodding toward the porch where the girl was trying to hide herself.

"That's Hildegarde Ingraham, the gal you're after," I said.

For the first time, Daly smiled—a brief ironic twist of his lips. He pulled a folded newspaper from his topcoat pocket, snapped it open and passed it to me. It was an early morning edition, off the presses less than an hour.

"Read that," he said, jabbing with one finger at a column on the front page.

By tilting the paper at just the right angle so that light from the porch hit it, I could make out the print. A head read:

MISSING HEIRESS FOUND IN RENO
Hildegarde Ingraham Marries Butcher Boy

I blinked and swallowed, feeling like a suddenly bursted balloon.

"What is it, Beek?" Mac croaked in my ear.

"We've been double-crossed, pal," I told him weakly. "We don't get any reward. This is the wrong gal."

"Give me that!" Vogelsang snapped, and grabbed the paper out of my hands.

"Well, starch my diapers!" Mac said in a dazed tone. "Pardon me, I think I'll go out and get measured for a straitjacket."

He wandered away across the grass, mumbling to himself. I marched to the porch and up the steps, reached for the doll-faced gal with the dyed blond hair, jerked her out into the open.

"You're not Hildegarde Ingraham—so who are you?"

"Me?" She blinked her eyes rapidly, looking up at me with an expression of injured innocence. "Why, I'm just Daisy May Huggins. Don't you remember, I told you? Miss Ingraham hired me in Reno to impersonate her and lead the detectives she thought were on her trail away. I met that heel Blythe and he let me think he was Johnny Foster, so I just sort of played him along for the good time that was in it, when all this happened. I—gee, I'm sorry."

"*You're* sorry!" I said, and felt my jaw. "To think I took a beating and risked my neck to rescue someone who turns out to be a ringer! So I get left holding the sack again. Somebody kick me. I'll bend over."

A big hand slapped me on the back, and Buck Madden growled with true sympathy: "Gee, mister, dat's tough. I'm sorry I busted ya one. I apologize."

"Forget it," I told him. "I made it even, didn't I—and you and your sister had it tough enough without all this."

The girl smiled at me tremulously, almost hopefully. Coming up to the porch, Daly, the Swinnerton dick, said:

"She had us fooled too. She led Rufe and me on a wild-goose chase"—his voice went harsh—"that got him killed. But anyway, you helped catch the killer and that's the way things break sometimes."

"Uh-huh," I breathed resignedly, and looked out across the lawn, trying to forget about the reward that I'd thought was in the bag.

Daly had handcuffed Blythe, who was still dead to the world. Vogelsang and fat Kline had slunk away, back to their car, and as I looked it started up, wheeled around in a U-turn and went away very slowly. Little Mac was sitting on the curb holding his head in his hands. I sighed.

I said, "O.K. I'll testify against Blythe. With the girl, that will be enough. But you've got to agree to keep the Maddens out of it. They've gone through enough."

Daly nodded. "If you say so. All I'm interested in is to see that Blythe gets the death penalty."

The sudden relief on Louise Madden's face and her smile of thanks were almost enough to pay me for what I'd been through. I began to feel better.

"Well, that's settled then," I said. "But I still wish somebody would kick me."

"I'd rather kiss you," she said.

The Key

Cleve F. Adams

CLEVE F(RANKLIN) ADAMS (1895–1949) was born in Chicago and had a variety of jobs, including copper miner, art director for films, life insurance executive, and detective, all of which helped provide background details for his fiction.

His first work appeared in such pulp magazines as *Detective Fiction Weekly* and *Double Detective*, but his major creation was private detective Rex McBride, who appeared in his first novel, *Sabotage* (1940), and subsequently in *And Sudden Death* (1940), *Decoy* (1941), *Up Jumped the Devil* (1943), *The Crooking Finger* (1944), as well as the posthumously published *Shady Lady* (1955). Unlike Philip Marlowe's ethos of a private detective being the equivalent of a knight, McBride borders on being a fascist, screaming that "an American Gestapo is what we goddamn well need" in a fit of extreme pique, and a racist, with ethnic slurs abounding in McBride's adventures. It is evident that Adams was neither, as he goes out of his way—oddly, it must be said—to make his own protagonist seem ridiculous and boorish.

Adams published three pseudonymous works as John Spain: *Dig Me a Grave* (1942), *Death Is Like That* (1943), and *The Evil Star* (1944), as well as a collaboration with Robert Leslie Bellem, *The Vice Czar Murders* (1941), as Franklin Charles.

"The Key" features the Los Angeles cop team of Lieutenant Canavan and Lieutenant Kleinschmidt; it was originally published in the July 1940 issue of *Black Mask*.

The Key

Cleve F. Adams

"I'd like to carve you into seven hundred small pieces,"
she said frankly.

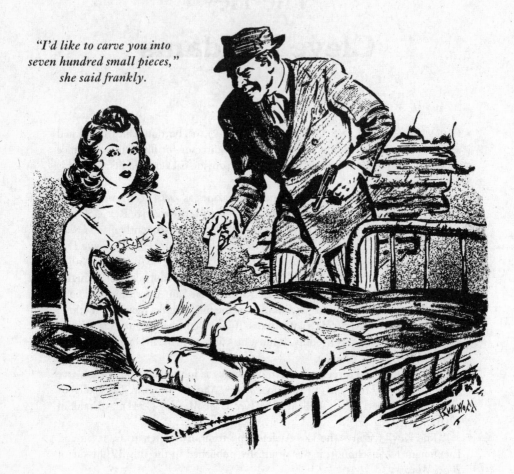

CHAPTER ONE
NIGHT-COURT GALAHAD

Lieutenant Canavan's trouble was dames—toward whom he behaved as a sort of cross between Walter Raleigh, Galahad and a bull in a china shop. It was a rare gal indeed who could appreciate his interesting efforts to be helpful when murder was on the loose.

HE DIDN'T LOOK LIKE the sort of girl they usually hauled into Night Court. There was nothing tawdry about her, nor defiant; and Canavan, always on the alert for the unusual, paused on

his way up the far aisle for a second look. The courtroom was packed, every seat filled and perhaps fifty or sixty spectators lapping over into the U-shaped aisle surrounding the rail. These last made a sort of human picket fence against the walls. Canavan, trying not to obstruct someone else's view, found himself wedged between George Kolinski and Terence O'Day.

Kolinski, known around town as Big George, was really big. Taller even than Canavan, and a hundred pounds heavier, he was a jovial, opulent picture of what the rackets could do for the man

at the top. Dewey, being three thousand miles away, hadn't gotten around to him yet.

Terry O'Day ran a daily column in the *Meteor* called "Night and O'Day." Night Court was only part of his beat. He was believed to have a speaking acquaintance with every crook, cop and play-boy in the whole city. He wore expensive clothes sloppily, as though he didn't give a damn what people thought—which he probably didn't—and his long, horsily waggish face was as apt to be seen in the Biltmore Salon as in Tony the Greek's Greasy Spoon. His stuff was brilliant and cynical and, on occasion, could tear the heart right out of you. A lock of thinning sandy hair usually straggled out from beneath a hat that was as familiar as the face under it.

Making room for Canavan he whispered: "Hi, flatfoot. You're a long way from headquarters."

Canavan nodded. "I had to bring a mug over here to keep his lawyer from finding him." He looked sidewise at Kolinski. "This time it isn't one of your boys."

Kolinski's fat face mirrored pleased surprise. "Thanks, pal. Thanks too much." A three-carat diamond twinkled merrily as he laid a pudgy finger alongside his nose. "Glad to know you're using Jefferson Heights as cold storage again."

Canavan kept watching the girl. She sat on the prisoners' bench together with two street-walkers, a giant scarred Negro and a kid in grimy overalls who looked as though he had been hauled off a freight train. An aged Mexican was being questioned by Justice Marie Tarbell. Canavan, on sudden impulse, left his place against the wall and leaned over the rail separating him from the clerk's table.

Justice Tarbell banged her gavel. "Lieutenant Canavan!"

Straightening, he waved at her. "Yes, ma'am?"

She glared at him. "This is a courtroom, not a thoroughfare. I wish you would remember that!"

The crowd tittered. Canavan, completely unembarrassed, begged the Court's pardon. He had all he wanted, anyway. His whispered colloquy with the clerk had given him the girl's name and the charge against her. She was accused of beating a dinner check at the Cathedral. Canavan's right eye, the one away from Judge Tarbell, drooped a little, and the clerk rearranged the charge slips so that the one concerning Miss Hope Carewe was on the bottom of the batch. Miss Carewe herself, unaware of the interest being taken in her, tried unobtrusively to put another inch between herself and one of the street-walkers. Against that drab back-drop,

perhaps because of it, she looked like a million dollars.

Canavan went back up the aisle and into the main lobby of the jail, and from one of the public booths called Luis Renaldo, who ran the Cathedral. "Luis? This is Bill Canavan. You filed a complaint against a gal named Hope Carewe."

Renaldo's voice was smooth as silk. "For eight bucks I'd file a complaint against my own grandmother."

"Maybe your grandmother," Canavan said. "Not against this gal, unless she wouldn't let you take it out in trade. Personally, I don't think she would."

Renaldo laughed softly. "Such a suspicious nature. So what, Lieutenant?"

"So I want you to call up and kill the charge. I'll take care of the eight bucks."

"Meaning she'd prefer you to me?"

Canavan cursed. "Listen, heel, this gal don't even know I'm alive. But for eight bucks I wouldn't have her spend the night in a tank full of tramps and worse. You get on the phone and kill that complaint."

"O.K." Renaldo sighed. "O.K., copper, but just the same I want the eight bucks. Tonight, not next payday, savvy?"

"You'll get it!" Canavan snarled. He suddenly felt like a fool. Pronging the receiver with a vicious swipe, he banged out of the booth and went down the tall steps to the street.

It was perhaps fifteen minutes later that the girl came through the swinging doors. Silhouetted against the light from within she seemed taller. She was wearing a street suit of some dark blue material, no topcoat. Beneath the matching hat with the little green feather her hair showed coppery gold, and Canavan guessed her eyes would have gold flecks in them too. The property clerk had given her back her bag.

Canavan stepped out of the shadows, lifting his hat. "Take you someplace, Miss Carewe?"

She descended the steps. Her eyes were, as he

had suspected, golden brown. They were also faintly contemptuous. "You're the man whom the judge reprimanded. Lieutenant Canavan, wasn't it?"

He admitted this without shame.

She said, still distantly aloof: "Aren't you presuming a little bit on the badge you carry?"

He had the grace to flush. "Maybe I am, at that." He put on his hat, turned away. Then, because he was a persistent sort of guy, he again faced her. "Listen, I can't exactly explain it, but when I saw you there in a place you'd no business to be—" He broke off as the full implication of her question hit him. "Hell's fire, if you think I make a business of rescuing ladies in distress—"

"Oh, so it was you who rescued me!"

"Well—"

She stood there a moment, considering him. "I can't quite make up my mind whether to be angry with you or grateful."

He gave her one of his very best smiles. "Couldn't you sort of compromise and just be friends? I'm not on the make. It's just that—well, a night in a Jefferson Heights tank is like the ill wind that blows nobody good. I knew a guy once that had to burn his clothes afterward."

"I see," she said. Then with the faintest of shrugs she came down the last step. "I think I shall avail myself of your kind offer. There's nothing like a police escort when you are thinking thoughts like mine." Her golden eyes had angry little glints in them. "Who knows? You may keep me from committing murder."

Canavan thought she was beautiful as hell, but he carefully refrained from saying this. Instead, he opened his car door for her, went around to the other side and climbed in under the wheel.

"Where to, lady?"

"The Hotel Wickersham," she said.

They rode in silence for a little while.

North Broadway was a magic lane of lights, weighted with the sounds and smells of Little Italy and, later on, with those of the new China-

town. Canavan, leisurely threading his way through ten-o'clock traffic, watched the girl's ungloved hands. They were good hands, indicative of character. Presently he said: "Care to tell me about it, Hope?"

At the use of her given name she shot him a swift glance. Then, apparently satisfied, she once more looked straight ahead. "I was to meet a man at the Cathedral, ordering dinner for both of us if he happened to be late." She shrugged. "He didn't show up at all and I had less than a dollar in my bag."

Canavan growled deep in his throat. "Didn't Renaldo proposition you?"

She shivered. "So you even know about that!"

"I know Luis Renaldo." Canavan swung the car west on Seventh Street. "Listen, Hope Carewe, I'm not trying to pry into your affairs—"

"Oh, aren't you?"

"All right," he said savagely, "then I am! Just the same, there's something about this business that smells. How come, if you stay at a place like the Wickersham, you haven't got eight bucks to square a dinner check? Who was the guy you were supposed to meet? Why didn't you contact him?"

"I couldn't," she said, answering the last question first. "I don't know who he is. As for the money, I left all I had in my room. They say it isn't there anymore."

"Who does?"

"The management."

Canavan took his eyes off the road long enough to stare at her. "You mean you've been robbed?"

She nodded. "That's what I mean. The hotel people seem to think it's all a figment of my imagination, that I never had any money."

"Well," Canavan said decisively, "we will certainly have to look into this."

He ran the car into the curb before the pretentious portal of the Wickersham. Getting out, the girl dropped her bag and the contents spewed all over the car floor. Canavan scooped up the miscellany and dumped it back in the bag. They entered the lobby.

There were quite a few people around, well-dressed, important-looking people. The Wickersham was that kind of hotel. Hope Carewe crossed directly to the desk. "See here, if there has been anything taken from my room I'm going to hold you responsible."

The clerk just looked at her. He was a tall, languid young man with the manner of a diplomatic attaché. His words, however, were not exactly diplomatic. "Valuables are supposed to be checked at the desk, Miss Carewe. If, as you claim, there really were any valuables."

She was outraged. "If I were a man I'd—"

Canavan leaned on the counter. "Look, punk, if the lady says she had some stuff in her room, then she had it."

The clerk examined him. "You sound like a policeman."

Canavan reached across and got a handful of coat lapels. "You said it, Lord Fauntleroy. I am a policeman."

A second man now made his appearance from behind a glass partition. This man was portly, dignified. He pointed a plump pink forefinger at Canavan's nose. "I take it that you are interested in Miss Carewe?"

Canavan pushed the finger aside. "And if I am?"

"Then perhaps you would like to pay her bill here."

"Meaning you're asking her to vacate?"

The portly man's mouth curved downward. "Exactly. We do not care for guests who have been in jail. Nor can I release her baggage until the account is cleared up." He coughed. "A matter of some eighteen dollars only. I am sure that—"

The girl's face was as white as paper. "Lieutenant Canavan, I think—"

"Shut up!" Canavan said. He fished a twenty-dollar bill from a pants pocket. "Change back, Shylock. And the key to Miss Carewe's room." He got both. Then, cursing under his breath, he

took the girl's arm and piloted her across acres and acres of carpet to the elevators. "A fine business!"

In the third-floor corridor she faced him. "See here, why are you doing all this for me?"

He glared at her. "What do you think?" He unlocked the door to 327 and they went in. Even to an untrained eye it would have been obvious that the room had been searched. Hope Carewe gave a little cry and ran to the dresser.

Something hard and heavy as an anvil clunked Canavan behind the ear. He went suddenly and definitely bye-bye.

CHAPTER TWO
A COUPLE OF GHOULS

anavan awoke to the realization that he had been tricked, and that there was a guy bending over him who could not possibly be anybody but the house dick. This man was small and neat and as inconspicuous as Mr. Average Citizen. Beyond him was the portly and pompous manager. Canavan propped himself on an elbow. "So who let you in?"

"I just sort of drifted in," the house dick said. His brown eyes were laughing. "Looks like you've been suckered into something, copper. Did the girl hit you?"

Canavan saw then that Hope Carewe was not among those present. Swift anger made him forget the aching lump behind his ear. He pushed himself to his feet. "Listen, what kind of a flophouse are you running around here?"

The manager's face purpled. "Are you insinuating that any of this is our fault?"

"You're damned right I am! This room has been prowled. Not only that, but the mugs that did it were still here when we walked in."

The house dick made disparaging noises. "Then you saw them?"

Canavan suddenly was aware that he was in a

swell spot to be ridiculed by every antiadministration newspaper in town. The knowledge did nothing to improve his temper. "Get out of here, both of you! And if you think all the signs about the hotel's liability will keep you from being sued you're crazy. I'll back up the girl's complaint myself!"

"By the way," the manager said, "just where is the young lady?" His tone implied that Hope Carewe was not a lady at all.

Canavan controlled himself with an effort. "I'll ask the questions, if you don't mind. This is police business now."

"Monkey business," the house dick said.

Canavan stabbed him with a hard forefinger. "Let's have your side of it. What do you know about the girl?"

The house dick shrugged. "She fooled us, all right. She looked like class, and"—he indicated the rifled luggage—"her bags were class. Registered from San Diego. Been here two days." He spread his hands. "Take it from our angle, Lieutenant. Renaldo, at the Cathedral, calls up and tells us she's trying to beat a dinner check. She claims there's money in her room to cover. So we come up and it looks like she's taken a powder on us, grabbing the best of her stuff and leaving the rest. There is no money."

Canavan took a deep breath. "The room was like this when you first saw it?"

"That's right."

Canavan had no choice but to believe it. The house dick's theory was plausible enough, when you came to think about it. The girl could have been taking a run-out on her bill. As a matter of fact, her story about meeting an unknown man at the Cathedral was pretty thin. The only thing was, she herself had certainly not been the one who conked Canavan. Still, she could have had an accomplice. But suppose she had? Where was the percentage? Canavan had paid her bill. He had aided her to get out of jail—

Quite suddenly he snapped his fingers. That was it! He had been instrumental in springing her, but instead of being free she found herself saddled with him. So she had just tolled him

along till the psychological moment and then— Swift hands rummaged his pockets. His wallet was gone!

The house dick grinned slyly. "So she rolled you too!"

Spots swam before Canavan's eyes. He had never been so furious in his life. To cover up he made a great business of pawing through the girl's effects. Silken underwear, stockings, handkerchiefs, everything bore the subtle perfume she used. He kept seeing her golden-brown hair, and her eyes, and her hands, the hands he had thought so indicative of character. He laughed harshly. "She get any phone calls, or make any?"

"There were a couple incoming," the house dick said. "Besides the one from Renaldo at the Cathedral. I can get you the numbers of any outgoing calls." He went to the phone.

The pompous manager plucked nervously at his lower lip, eyeing Canavan worriedly now. He was beginning to see that no matter what happened the hotel was due for a certain amount of notoriety. "See here, Lieutenant, we can forget this if you can." He appraised the girl's bags. "We might even refund your eighteen dollars."

"Keep it," Canavan said nastily. "I'm going to get this dame if it's the last thing I ever do."

The house dick replaced the phone. "Only one outgoing. Kester 5-6943. Want me to look it up?"

"No," Canavan said. He put on his hat, wincing as the sweatband bit into the lump at the back of his head. "No, thanks, I'll take care of it." He picked up the phone and called headquarters and filed a general alarm for Miss Hope Carewe. He was surprised to find that he could describe her so minutely, even down to the little feather in her hat.

Lieutenant Roy Kleinschmidt came on the wire. "Listen, we got a complaint from a undertaker. The old man says we should look into it." Kleinschmidt was Canavan's working-partner. "This guy was bopped on the head. Says somebody was trying to steal a corpse or something."

"The hell with that," Canavan said. "I'm busy trying to locate somebody I can make into a corpse." He thought a moment. "Look, Roy, send a couple of print men out to the Wickersham, will you? Tell 'em to see the house dick. I want every piece of baggage covered, just in case this dame has been mugged before."

"Well, sure, but—"

"And get me the address of this phone, will you?" Canavan repeated the number the house dick had given him. Waiting, he tapped his foot impatiently. He'd show her, by God. Kleinschmidt came back. The number was the Saints of Mercy Hospital. "But look, Bill, I still think we should ought to see this—now—undertaker. This Egbert Weems."

"You see him," Canavan said. "My regards to all the stiffs." He hung up, glared at the grinning house dick and the smugly pompous manager, went out and down to his car.

Ten minutes later Canavan walked into the lobby of the Saints of Mercy Hospital. He had cooled off sufficiently to be quite polite, yet strictly official with the nurse at the information desk. She was a red-head, and at another time Canavan might have been interested. Now she was just a white starched uniform among a lot of others. He showed his badge. "We are trying to check on a Miss Hope Carewe, who apparently called your number some time late this afternoon."

The red-head too, was quite official. "Do you know the reason for her calling us?"

"No," Canavan said frankly, "I don't. Perhaps your records—"

"I'll see." The red-head went away to confer with someone behind a glassed-in partition. Canavan watched people come and go through the tall doors. On a bench beside the elevators there was a little guy who looked as though he were about to become a father. He was sweating.

Presently the red-head came back. She had a file-card in her hand. "Miss Carewe must have been calling about her brother." She wrinkled her nose. "Odd, though. His name is given here as Carroll."

Canavan felt a pleasurable little tingle at the base of his scalp. He was getting warm. "Fine, that's just fine. I'll talk to her brother."

The nurse shook her head. "I'm afraid you can't do that, Lieutenant."

"Why not?"

"Because he's dead. He died at two oh five this afternoon."

Canavan said a very naughty word indeed and snatched the file-card. There it was, as plain as the nose on your face. Edward Carroll, admitted 1:18 p.m., Tuesday the 26th—that would be yesterday—operated on for ruptured gastric ulcers at 11:00 p.m. Died 2:05 p.m. Wednesday.

Canavan drew a deep breath. "O.K. I'll take a look at him anyway. And his things."

The red-head giggled. "You evidently didn't finish reading the card, Lieutenant. His sister paid his bill, his personal effects were released to her, and his body has been taken to a mortuary."

Canavan turned the file-card over. The mortician's name seemed somehow vaguely familiar. Then he got it. Egbert Weems was the undertaker Kleinschmidt had been talking about, the one who had been having trouble with his corpses. Canavan left rather hurriedly.

The Weems Mortuary was, even as the neon sign on the lawn stated, a place of beauty, though the chaste Old English rectory effect was slightly spoiled by an inordinate amount of mercury tubing. Under the blue lights even the grass looked faintly magenta. A tall stained-glass window did its best to maintain an air of dignity despite the encroachments of modern advertising. There was a police car at the curb.

Canavan, still breathing a trifle unevenly, as though he might have run all the way from the Saints of Mercy Hospital, got out and went up the walk and punched the night bell. The door was opened by Big George Kolinski, no less.

Canavan's jaw dropped. "Well, for crying out loud, what are you doing here?"

Big George's fat face was wreathed in smiles. "Hel—lo, Lieutenant! I see we can always count on the police—eventually."

Canavan glared at him. "What do you mean by that crack?"

Kolinski moved his well-tailored shoulders. "Mr. Weems reported the incident at least two hours ago. You boys are just beginning to take an interest."

"And what's that to you?"

Again that exasperating shrug. "Mr. Weems is one of our clients—the Morticians' Protective Association, you know."

"Another of your rackets?"

"A protective association," Kolinski said. "Naturally when the police department didn't function, Mr. Weems called us." The big diamond on his hand twinkled as he laid a fat finger alongside his nose. "Not me directly, you understand. I am merely a director of the association. But when I heard about it—well, the case was so unusual that I went down to headquarters to see why a taxpayer like Mr. Weems wasn't getting service. Lieutenant Kleinschmidt was just leaving, so I rode out with him."

Canavan almost choked. "It's getting so you can't even die without running into a racket. What do you do if the undertakers don't pay up—yodel at the funerals?" He pushed past Kolinski as Lieutenant Roy Kleinschmidt came through a door at the end of the short hall.

Kleinschmidt was big and blond and red-faced— a good cop, though without brilliance. He seemed relieved to see Canavan. "Look, Bill, this don't hardly make sense—" He paused as another man came through the door. "Mr. Weems, this is my— now—partner, Lieutenant Canavan."

Weems was a smallish, twittery man with a perpetually quivering nose. He had a bandage wrapped around his head. His harried eyes went from Canavan to Big George Kolinski. "I've paid my dues. I don't know why you should do this to me."

Kolinski's tremendous bulk seemed to solidify. "Look, punk, I told you before that we didn't do it. You think I'd be here if—"

"Shut up!" Canavan said sharply. He looked at Kleinschmidt. "You tell it, Roy."

Kleinschmidt coughed apologetically. "Well, of course, like Big George, here, says—"

"Never mind Kolinski!" Canavan yelled. "What happened? Was it—was it a guy named Edward Carroll?"

Kleinschmidt blinked stupidly. "How did you know that? It wasn't in the report."

Canavan could feel Kolinski's eyes on him, alert, questioning. He suddenly became quite calm. "Skip that for now." He looked at Egbert Weems. "Maybe you'd better tell me exactly what happened."

There really was not much to it. Weems was on duty, relieving his regular night man. A couple of guys had walked in and asked to see the body of Edward Carroll. Also his clothes and personal effects. Mr. Weems, becoming suspicious, had objected and been knocked on the head for his pains. Awakening some time later he had found his mortuary something of a mess, what with a couple of corpses dumped from their caskets and everything else topsy-turvy. He could find nothing missing, however, and it was probably this admission which accounted for the lack of hurry on the part of the police. His description of the two men was completely vague. It amounted to one tall man and one shorter man. Was there anything unusual about either? Not that Mr. Weems could remember. "I was naturally quite agitated," he explained. He breathed noisily and bent a jaundiced eye on Big George Kolinski. "Pure vandalism!"

Kolinski scowled. "Listen, punk, you try blaming this on the Association and you're liable to really run into something." He looked at Canavan. "You know who this guy Carroll is? He's Ed Stengel!"

Canavan took a deep breath. Stengel was, or had been, big-time. The police of half a dozen cities wanted him for twice as many very high-class jobs indeed. Kleinschmidt confirmed Kolinski's identification. "That's who, Bill."

"Let's have a look at him," Canavan said.

They all went through the door at the end of

the hall, into a room of smells and gleaming porcelain and a table that would have been suggestive even without the sheeted figure on it. A pair of bare feet, toes pointed ceilingward, protruded from beneath the sheet.

r. Weems, with that curiously hallowed air peculiar to morticians, uncovered the face, and Canavan stared down at it, trying to find some resemblance to that other face of which he was so conscious, Miss Hope Carewe's. This Stengel, alias Ed Carroll, had the same golden-brown hair and, in repose, the features had that same indefinable air of breeding. But there was a hardness, even in death, about the mouth and eyes. Of course, the man was older than the girl. Canavan placed him as around thirty-five.

Kleinschmidt said suddenly: "There was a girl made the arrangements with Weems, here! Claimed she was this guy's sister." He looked at Canavan with swift suspicion. "That explains it, by golly. Her name was the same as the one you— Hey, so that's how you knew who he was!" A slow, angry flush suffused his heavy face. "By God, Bill, you been holding out on me!"

Big George Kolinski pounced. "What was her name again, Weemsie? Carewe?" He smacked his thick lips. "That the girl you rescued from Night Court, Canavan?"

Canavan scowled. "What do you mean, I rescued her?"

Kolinski chuckled nastily. "I was there, remember? I happened to see her leaving in your car. And now it turns out that she is the sister, or the moll, of a guy so hot he was burning up." He rubbed his fat hands in pleasurable anticipation. "This is going to make swell reading in the papers, pal. Unless you can turn her up and offer a damned good reason for playing around with her." He stabbed a finger at Weems. "Take a good look at this guy. Could he be one of the mugs who knocked you over?"

Weems, startled, blinked his eyes at Canavan. "Well—"

"Don't say it!" Canavan yelled. "Don't even think it!" He balled his fists. "Listen, you fat baboon, why the hell would I be chasing a corpse?"

"Somebody is," Kolinski said significantly. "Or something the corpse had." He centered his attention on Roy Kleinschmidt. "Look at it this way, Lieutenant. Here we have a man who is notably big-time. Isn't it conceivable that he might be holding something worth heavy sugar? Obviously the girl knew about it, or suspected. She was in a hell of a hurry to get the body away from the hospital." He let his eyes slide up and down Canavan's length. "Then we have a supposedly honest copper practically hijacking the gal out of court. Why do you suppose he would do that?"

Kleinschmidt was still sore. "Where is the girl, Bill?"

"I don't know, I tell you! Why do you think I called in and had her description put on the air? Would I do that if I knew where she was?"

"You might," Kleinschmidt said. "You could have faked it to cover up her disappearance." His fist slid unobtrusively toward the gun in his holster clip. "Maybe you even killed her, Bill."

Canavan couldn't believe it at first. It was all too ridiculous. "You damned fool!" He sucked in his breath. "Listen, I happened to be passing through Night Court and I saw this gal. Obviously she didn't belong there, so I checked with the clerk and found she was charged with beating an eight-buck dinner check. Sure, I squared it! Any guy with half an eye would have done the same thing."

"Why?" Kleinschmidt said. Kleinschmidt was not a romantic man. "Why would they, Bill?"

Canavan resorted to heavy sarcasm. "Why, because I recognized her, of course. I knew she was Ed Stengel's sister, and that he had a double fistful of diamonds, so I planned to make her tell me where he was. Only she knocked me out first and got away. Nuts!"

"Maybe she didn't knock you out, Bill. Maybe you just made it look like she had." Kleinschmidt was definitely going for his gun now. "I hate to do this, Bill, but—"

Canavan hit him. He might not have done it if he'd stopped to think, but he was too mad to think. His fist connected with the Dutchman's chin, and even as the big guy went down Canavan snatched out his own gun and waved it at Kolinski and the stupefied Mr. Weems.

"Take it easy, you two lugs. And when Kleinschmidt wakes up tell him I said to use the few brains God gave him." He backed to the door. "And you, Kolinski, you'd better watch your step. When I get through with this little job I'm going to make it my business to tear your Morticians' Protective Association wide open."

He went out to his car. Neither Kolinski nor Mr. Weems made any attempt to stop him.

CHAPTER THREE
THE CORPSE IN THE FOLDING BED

The address given on the hospital card turned out to be one of those mediocre bungalow-courts just off Hollywood Boulevard where anything can happen. Broken-down character actors choose these places for some reason, and extra girls and bartenders and car-hops. There were half a dozen parties going on in as many different units. A man like Ed Carroll, alias Ed Stengel, could have found no better place to remain incognito.

Canavan went along the flagged walk till he came to 1217-A. There were no lights on inside, and he stood there in the shadows a moment, listening to the medley of sounds from adjacent units. Offhand, he couldn't have told you just what he expected to find here. It was just that the girl was indubitably bound up with the affairs of one Ed Stengel, and Bill Canavan was intent on

again meeting Miss Hope Carewe. This place, having been the temporary residence of Ed Carroll, might possibly offer a clue to the girl's present whereabouts.

He wondered if they really were brother and sister. The name Carroll lent a certain amount of credibility to this. The first syllable of both names was identical. Canavan frowned a little, remembering Big George Kolinski. Was Big George's interest merely what he had stated? Or was the business of the Morticians' Protective Association just a blind for a much deeper interest in Ed Carroll, alias Ed Stengel? Canavan was suddenly struck with Kolinski's own words. Obviously someone was looking for something, and rather seriously too. The search had encompassed not only Hope Carewe's hotel room, but also the corpse. Conceivably it would extend, or had already extended, to include this second-rate bungalow.

Canavan went up the three shallow steps and tried the door. It opened under his hand, and he went in quietly, closing it behind him before he turned on the lights. It was even as he had expected. The place had been combed thoroughly, and certainly not too carefully. Evidences of hurry were scattered all about. Canavan decided there was not much use in his doing the job all over again. Whatever was being sought for had either been found or was never there at all.

He went to the phone and called headquarters.

"Hey," the sergeant yelled, "we got a pickup order on you!"

Canavan cursed Kleinschmidt. "That heel!" He took a deep breath. "Listen, Donny, what did the boys find out about that girl?"

It appeared that the boys had found out nothing at all from the hotel room. There had been plenty of fingerprints, but none of these were on record at headquarters. "And anyway," the sergeant said gloomily, "I don't know where you got the idea she was hot. We checked with San Diego, where she registered from, and you know what?"

Canavan admitted that he didn't know what.

"Why, she's one of *the* Carewes. Her old man is worth around seventeen million bucks."

"The hell he is!"

"Well, he is." Lieutenant Canavan became suddenly conscious that the sergeant was prolonging the conversation unnecessarily. Obviously they were trying to locate Canavan by way of the phone he was using. He banged the receiver down and whirled as there was a creaking noise behind him. The folding-bed, apparently insecurely fastened, swung slowly down from its niche in the wall. Restraining springs allowed it to settle quite gently. There was a man on the bed. He was Luis Renaldo, who ran the Cathedral and to whom Canavan owed the sum of eight dollars. He was so dead that it hurt to look at him. Someone had cut his throat. The job had been done very thoroughly indeed and there was a lot of blood.

Canavan just stood there for a moment, fascinated by the sight. Not that he was morbid, but this happened to be the first dead man he had ever found folded up in a disappearing bed. Also there was the fact that he was more than intimately acquainted with the corpse, that he had spoken with him but an hour or so ago.

He wondered to whom he would now owe the eight dollars.

It was some little time before he attempted to rationalize Renaldo's being there at all, dead or otherwise. So far as Canavan knew, this latest dead man's contact with Miss Hope Carewe had been slight. It was beginning to be quite apparent, however, that any contact at all was the same as taking cyanide.

She was absolutely and positively poison.

Look what just a speaking acquaintance had got a guy named William Canavan. He had been conked, and robbed, and was now even a fugitive from his fellow cops. Indeed he was accused of violating the sanctity of the Weems Mortuary and the person of yet another corpse, though at least it seemed agreed by all that Ed Stengel, or Ed Carroll, had not been murdered. He had just died. Of stomach ulcers.

anavan, remembering suddenly that headquarters had probably traced his phone call, and that a prowl car was due any minute, had just decided that he had better get the hell out of there when the doorbell rang. It sounded loud enough to wake even Luis Renaldo. Canavan considered vanishing by the rear exit, but in case the bell-ringer was a cop he more than likely had his partner posted at the back door, and an attempted escape would make things look even worse than they were. Canavan compromised by folding Luis Renaldo and the bed back into the wall. He then opened the door. The caller was Terence O'Day, he of the horsily waggish face and caustic wit. He looked slightly drunk, but then he usually did. He did not seem surprised at finding Canavan here.

"Hello, handsome," he said.

Canavan stared. "Well!"

O'Day used his spread hand to push his disreputable hat farther back on his head. "Aren't you going to invite me in? I'm the Press, you know. The good old *Meteor*."

Canavan breathed gustily. "How did you find out about this place?"

O'Day grinned. "Everybody knows about this place, pal. Or almost everybody. And about you too," he added cheerfully. "You're getting quite famous, really you are, Bill, going around rescuing damsels in distress, and robbing corpses and one thing and another."

"I did not!" Canavan yelled.

"Well," O'Day said, "I'm only repeating what I heard. Kleinschmidt called in and my legman at headquarters passed the facts on to me. It was a simple matter to phone the hospital and get this address. Probably even Kleinschmidt has thought of it by this time."

Behind Canavan there was a tell-tale creaking. That damn bed was coming down again! Rather desperately he tried to close the door in O'Day's face, but he wasn't quick enough. O'Day put his foot against it. "Oh-oh, what have we here?"

Reluctantly Canavan stood aside. "Now look, don't go getting ideas. It wasn't me that killed him."

"Certainly not," O'Day said. He went over to the bed. "My, my, that prince of heels, Luis Renaldo!" He lifted a quizzical eyebrow at Canavan. "Didn't you owe him eight bucks?"

Canavan shook with impotent rage. "So you know that too!"

"Of course," O'Day said equably. His breath smelled of Sen-Sen. "When you escorted the little lady away from the bad, naughty jail I was just curious enough to find out how you did it."

"Someday," Canavan snarled, "your curiosity is going to get you a swift sock in the nose!" He mopped sweat from his upper lip, though the night was not cold. "Look, Terry, be a good egg and forget you ever saw me, will you? And let's get the hell out of here."

O'Day rocked back and forth on his heels. "Tell me about the little lady, pal. Is it true that she's Stengel's sister? Has her old man really got seventeen million dollars? Does she love you, or does she not?"

Canavan lifted a threatening fist. "All right, heel, you're asking for it!"

Behind him a harsh voice said: "Hold it, Lieutenant!"

Canavan whirled. There was a harness bull in the doorway, and the harness bull was holding his service gun as if he meant business. Out in back, someone was fumbling at the kitchen door. That indicated at least one other cop. The bull in the doorway caught sight of the corpse on the bed and he let out a yell and charged. Terence O'Day stuck out a foot and tripped him. Then, winking owlishly, he jerked a thumb at the open door. Canavan's lips formed a soundless thanks. He ran out.

From far down the street came the wail of a siren. That would probably be Kleinschmidt, and of all people Canavan did not want to meet the Dutchman. Especially with a murder victim at hand. He headed at top speed down the flagged walk, reached his car and had the righthand door open when two enormous shadows closed in on

him. Something that certainly was not a frankfurter rammed him in the right kidney.

"Be nice, copper."

Canavan was in no humor to be nice. With a sound like a maddened bull he pivoted and swung a devastating left at the nearest face. The face merely slid to one side and the momentum of the blow, missing, carried Canavan into a pair of outspread arms. "Sock him," the owner of the arms said. The second guy socked. Canavan had already been knocked cold once tonight. This second attack was just too much. Blackness as absolute as the bottom of a coal mine engulfed him.

CHAPTER FOUR
THE LETTER

He awoke with a sense of unreality, as does one who has been under an opiate for a long, long time. Blurred objects swam before his eyes, as though seen through layers and layers of gauze, or the opalescent depths of a gray-green sea. Once he had had a tooth extracted, a molar whose roots were wrapped around the jawbone, and the exodontist had given him several successive shots of novocaine. Canavan had passed out, awakening later with almost these same sensations. There was no pain, only the vague discomfort of incipient nausea. Voices were blurred too, and then the sharply insistent fumes of ammonia bit at his nostrils and the fog cleared away.

The guy with the ammonia flask said: "Jeeze, he looks green!" He was a small chunky man with eyes almost as naive as Kleinschmidt's. Canavan tried to hit him in the mouth but for some reason he couldn't get his hands up. Later he found that this was because they were tied to the chair he was sitting in.

Beyond this first guy there was a second, also small, though not so chunky. He had sallow skin and a habit of sucking air into his lungs through

the right-hand corner of his mouth. Canavan figured him for a reefer smoker, and this conclusion
was borne out by the faintly sickening odor of
burning weeds which saturated the atmosphere.
It smelled like the inside of an incinerator after
the gardener leaves.

The room belonged in a decrepit and abandoned farm house. The floor was of well-worn
pine, the walls covered with stained and moldy
wall-paper, with here and there a cleaner area
where once had hung a picture. Aside from
Canavan's chair, a cumbersome Morris, there
was only one article of furniture in the room.
This was a chipped iron bed with a stained and
lumpy mattress. On this unbeautiful couch lay
Miss Hope Carewe, wearing only shoes and
stockings and a slip. She was not there from
choice apparently. There was adhesive on her
mouth, and presumably there was more around
her wrists and ankles, though Canavan couldn't
be sure of this. Her eyes looked at Canavan with
horrified fascination.

In lieu of more authentic names Canavan
dubbed his jailers Tubby and Reefer. Tubby
smelled of the ammonia bottle. "Jeeze!"

Reefer's eyes narrowed. "Cut the clowning!
You gonna go back and find a phone or will I?"

Tubby licked his lips. "Let's ask the punk a
couple of questions first." He looked at Canavan.
"Where's the letter?"

"What letter?"

Tubby made a V of his first two fingers and
gouged Canavan's eyes. Canavan essayed a kick,
but here again he was thwarted. His legs were
also bound to the Morris chair. All he could do
was yell, and he did this quite effectively.
Nobody seemed to mind. Obviously there was
no possibility of a rescuer within earshot. Canavan ceased yelling. "Listen, lice, this is the first
I've heard about any letter."

Tubby winked at Reefer. "He says he don't
know about no letter."

"I heard him," Reefer said. "You don't have
to translate." He now addressed Canavan
directly for the first time. "Why don't you make
this easy on yourself, copper? You ought to
know we can't afford to let you circulate again,

but a good clean slug in the right place is a lot
nicer than some of the things we could think
up."

Canavan, strangely enough, was quite calm.
He could blow his top over some little inconse-
quential thing, but in an emergency he took the
breaks as they came. "I know what you guys can
do to me. The thought turns my stomach."

Tubby managed to look actually sympathetic.
"Then why don't you spill?"

"Because I can't, you fool! Believe me, I'd
give you all the letters in the Los Angeles post-
office if I had them. I'm a cop, not a hero."

"Sure," Reefer said, "sure." He stared meditatively at Miss Hope Carewe on the bed.
"Funny, she says she don't know about any letter either."

"Maybe there isn't any," Canavan said
brightly.

Tubby considered this. "Matter of fact, there
might not be, at that." He twirled the cylinder of
his gun. "Only if there ain't we're all going to a
hell of a lot of trouble for nothing." He looked at
Reefer. "We'd better get in touch with the boss."

"Kolinski?" Canavan said.

Both Reefer and Tubby ignored him.
Presently they held a whispered conversation
and finally, after flipping a coin, Reefer went out.
Somewhere there was the sound of a starting car.

Tubby sat on the edge of the bed beside Hope
Carewe, nursing his gun and a cigarette. The
utter silence was enough to set your teeth on
edge.

After a while Canavan said: "Look, you
didn't mind my yelling. Certainly the girl can't
yell any longer. Why don't you take that damn
tape off her mouth and let her breathe comfortably?"

"Why not?" Tubby said. He reached over
and worked a none-too-clean thumbnail under a
corner of the adhesive. Then, with a sort of
sadistic enjoyment, he ripped the strip free and
watched the tears start from her golden-brown
eyes. "How you like it, babe?"

"I'd like to carve you into seven hundred

small pieces," she said frankly. She tried to wipe her eyes on a bare shoulder, without much success because her hands were tied behind her. Giving up the attempt presently she regarded Canavan. "I seem to have caused you no end of trouble."

"And that's a fact," he agreed. "For a gal whose father owns seventeen million dollars you do get in the damndest jams."

Tubby became suddenly alert. "What's this about seventeen million dollars?"

"Didn't Kolinski tell you?" Canavan said.

Tubby looked positively sick. "Kolinski! That's twice you've— You mean to tell me Big George is . . . ?" He broke off to leer cunningly at Canavan. "Let's hear some more about this seventeen million bucks, copper."

Canavan, feigning a sincerity he did not feel, framed his next words carefully, like an artisan laying bricks. "It's no skin off my nose, monkey, but I hate to see even a punk like you suckered into anything. How much are you and your sidekick getting paid for all this?"

Tubby's pale eyes shifted. "A grand."

"There you are!" Canavan said triumphantly. "The boss gives you a cock-and-bull story about looking for a letter. Because why? Because if he told you this was a snatch job involving millions you'd want more dough!" He snorted. "Here you are, risking the G-heat and worse, and all for a lousy thousand bucks."

Tubby brooded on this for a moment. Then, muttering obscenities, he stood up. "Thanks, copper. Thanks too much." He went out, banging the door behind him.

Hope looked at Canavan. "You didn't believe a word of that."

"No," Canavan admitted.

e considered the possibility of escape, but there seemed little chance for it. His hands weren't even tied together. They were bound at the wrists, each to one of the rear legs of the Morris chair, and his arms were practically numb from being bowed over the broad arms of the chair. "No, I didn't believe it, but when in doubt it's always a good idea to get the other team fighting among themselves."

"You're a smart man, Canavan."

He made a bitter mouth. "Yeah, that's why I'm here." He glared at her. "Look, babe, I don't know how long this respite will last, but it would please me if I knew a little more than I do now. Is this Ed Carroll, this Ed Stengel, really your brother?"

A slow flush crept up around her eyes. "Yes, Canavan. His real name, as you may have guessed, is, or was, Edward Carewe."

"But when the cops checked back on you they found no record of a brother!"

"They will," she said, "if they check back far enough." She rolled a little on the bed to ease her cramped muscles. "Edward got into trouble when he was just a boy. He kept on getting into trouble. My father is a proud man. Finally he just erased Edward from the family album, and we didn't even speak of him any more."

"How old were you then?"

"Fifteen. Edward was eighteen."

"But you kept in touch with him?"

"I heard from him occasionally," she admitted. "Indirectly. I didn't know he was the much-wanted Ed Stengel. And then, on a shopping trip to Los Angeles, I ran into him. He was ill, and he told me he was going to the hospital for an operation." She caught her breath. "You know what happened after that."

"Damned if I do," Canavan said. "I know he died, but beyond that—"

"He was broke," Hope Carewe said. "I didn't have a great deal of money either, and I couldn't make up my mind to wire my father. Finally I decided to get him to an undertaker's at least."

"But he said nothing to you of a letter? What about his personal effects?"

"I got those," she said dully. "There was nothing. Some keys, the usual stuff a man carries in his pockets, a bag with a change of linen. Then, early in the evening, I had a phone call— the one asking me to go to the Cathedral. The man said I would learn something to my advantage—something to do with Edward. So thinking that possibly there might have been some money after all—"

Canavan took a deep breath. "So you ended up in Night Court!" He laughed a little wildly. "My God, that must have been a blow to somebody!"

She stared at him. He said: "Look, from what has happened since then it's perfectly obvious that the dinner date was just to get you out of your room while it was searched. But whatever it is they're looking for wasn't found. So they came after you and discovered you'd been pinched. After that—well, we've all been going around and around."

"And for what?"

"A letter," he said. He was quite sure by this time that there was a letter. "A lousy piece of paper that is dangerous as hell to somebody." His mind went back over the trail.

Big George Kolinski had been in Night Court. He, or his punks, could have trailed Canavan and the girl back to her hotel. Later he had turned up at the Weems Mortuary. All of these things together couldn't be called mere coincidence. First the girl had been caught, then Canavan, because it was thought that if Hope Carewe didn't have the letter, Canavan might. The murder of Luis Renaldo was a little more obscure, though it was possible that he too had scented something important in the furor created over the girl. It would not have been hard to trace back to the bungalow-court address of Ed Stengel. The record was there for all to see, and certainly the police department itself had made no attempt at secrecy.

 anavan stiffened at a sudden thought. Renaldo's killing was merely a protective measure. He had recognized, and been recognized by, someone else in that unit at the bunga-

low-court. So he had got his throat slit. Canavan said a very naughty word indeed. "Have you seen anyone else in this case but the two punks, Hope?"

Hope shook her head. "They were the ones who were in my room at the hotel." She added with a measure of pride: "It took both of them to handle me too. I fought like a wildcat and before we were through I'd lost all the buttons that kept my clothes on. One of them put his coat around me and they carted me off just as I am."

"Look, hon, these monkeys aren't going to stay away forever. Think you can hop, wiggle or roll over to me?"

At another time her efforts would have been ludicrous. Now they were just painful as hell. The sweat stood out on Canavan's brow as though he himself were going through all those contortions. Her wrists were strapped behind her and her ankles bound together. Every time she would attain her feet she would fall down again. It was heartbreaking. But finally, after what seemed like hours, she reached Canavan's side, stood up, teetered drunkenly a moment and fell across the arms of his chair. He attacked the adhesive on her wrists with his strong white teeth. Presently she was free and was busy freeing him.

He stood up, flexing his cramped muscles. Outside and below, as if this room might be on the second floor, there was the muted roar of a car motor and the creak of protesting springs. Probably Reefer coming back, Canavan thought. The single lamp at the end of a cobwebbed dropcord glowed yellowly. Naturally Canavan's gun was gone. He had expected that. But at least he was free, and for this he was properly grateful.

Two pairs of feet climbed the stairs beyond the door, and there was a whispered colloquy. Canavan motioned Hope to a spot behind the bed. Then, for want of a better weapon, he caught up the leather cushion from the Morris chair and waited, one hand on the snap-switch of the light-socket. It was odd that in that moment he should see humor in one old leather pillow against a couple of guns, but he did. He was actually grinning when Tubby opened the door.

There was just the fraction of a second that Tubby, paralyzed by surprise, forgot the gun in his hand. Canavan hurled the cushion and followed it with a plunging dive for the chunky man's knees. He didn't know that he was carrying the light bulb and the drop-cord with him until he hit. The bulb banged loudly, then a gun, and Tubby came down like a ton of lead on Canavan's back. Another gun banged, two or three times, and Tubby quit kicking suddenly. Canavan crawled out from under in time to see Reefer, backing away from what he had done to Tubby, lift his gun with a shaking hand.

"Stand still, you!" Canavan said, just as though he had a cannon in each fist. He was propped on his spread hands, with Tubby's body weighting his legs, as defenseless as a man could possibly be. But Reefer, who had just killed his own partner, was in no condition for careful analysis. He kept on backing away, nerveless fist trying to steady a shaking gun, and quite suddenly there was no floor under his feet. He went down the stairs, end over end, and the gun banged just once. Reefer only screamed once too; then there was a sound like a snapping stick, and silence.

Inside the room, Hope Carewe whimpered like a thoroughly frightened child.

Canavan got to his feet and examined Tubby. Reefer couldn't have done a more thorough job on purpose. All three slugs had entered Tubby's heart from the back. Cursing a little, Canavan went down the stairs. He felt no pride of accomplishment in finding that Reefer had suffered a broken neck. That was Reefer's own doing, not Canavan's. Swiftly he searched the hood's pockets, without result. Nor was he any more successful with Tubby. There was not a thing on either of the men to finger their employer.

Canavan stood up presently and draped his topcoat around the shivering girl.

"Come on, hon," he said. "Let's go bye-bye now."

She nodded a wordless acquiescence. They went down the stairs and out to a weed-grown yard. The car was Canavan's own.

CHAPTER FIVE
THE KEY

Canavan stood for a moment, considering the car and its implications. There was no other car in sight; consequently Reefer had used it a little while ago when he had gone out to find a telephone. Just as obviously, then, it was the one in which they had brought Canavan away from the Hollywood bungalow-court. With a little tightening of the lips he remembered the exact scene. Then, putting the girl in the car, he recalled something else, a ridiculous, everyday happening that was so common it had been forgotten in the press of events. "Look, hon, when you got out of the car in front of your hotel you dropped your bag, remember? You happen to mention that to anybody?"

She stared at him. "Why, no!"

He flicked on the dashlight and searched the floor. At the moment he couldn't have told her what he was looking for. It was just a hazy idea that in scooping up the bag's contents he might have missed something. Presently he slid the floor mat out from beneath the seat and a tiny object, bright and shiny, lay there winking up at him. It was a key—perhaps the key to the whole frantic chase. He held it up. "Yours?"

She shook her head. "It could be one of the three or four that Edward had. What is it?"

"Safety deposit box," he said shortly. "Only trouble is, we don't know which one. There isn't anything on the key but a number. It'll take hours, maybe days, to check up on it." He put the key in the fob pocket of his pants, looked at the gun he had taken from Tubby, finally put that in his pocket and climbed in.

Canavan started the motor and they bumped out over a rutted road to the main artery. Hope Carewe said: "Bill?"

"Yes?"

"Isn't it possible that whoever is behind all this will come out here?"

His mouth made a thin hard line. "Meaning we should stay here and wait?" He shook his head. "I'm not much good at waiting. Besides, we'll stop in Arcadia and send a couple of troopers back."

After a while he pulled up at an all-night café where a couple of white motorcycles bore evidence of the presence of coppers. He went in and used the telephone. Then, in passing, he mentioned almost casually that he thought he had heard shots over by one of the abandoned rock crushers. The cops made a hurried exit.

It was almost one o'clock when he parked beside the Club del Rey. "I want you to stick close to me, Hope. Close and a little behind. I wouldn't take you at all, only I'm afraid to leave you alone."

"Isn't this a job for the police?"

"I am the police," Canavan said. "Not that you'd think it, the way I've been pushed around tonight." He pushed in through double glass doors with the girl. On the right, through an arch, was the bar, and on either side of the main salon broad stairs climbed by gradual stages to the mezzanine.

The lights were romantically dim. Canavan, ignoring a beckoning headwaiter, pretended he had business in the men's lounge and went past the private dining-rooms to a blank white door. He was about to knock when the door opened suddenly and he was face to face with Big George Kolinski. "Hello, George," he said. His fist was wrapped around the gun in his pocket, but his face gave no sign that he was on edge.

Kolinski's eyes opened wide, sighting the girl behind Canavan. Then, ponderously polite, he stood aside. "Why, hello, Lieutenant! Come right in."

anavan went in sidewise, watchfully. He was not too surprised when a weasel-faced man in a snap-brim and midnight-blue Chesterfield stepped from behind the door. "Hello, Maury." Maury's right hand was buried in the side pocket of the Chesterfield.

He didn't say anything.

Kolinski closed the door behind Hope Carewe. "Well—Miss Carewe, isn't it?"

Hope admitted this. She was having trouble keeping behind Canavan and still avoiding Kolinski and Maury. Kolinski finally solved the problem himself by going over to his desk. He looked at Canavan out of sleepy-lidded eyes. "I take it you're not here alone?"

"Kleinschmidt ought to be along shortly," Canavan said. "He'll probably bring a platoon with him."

"I see." Kolinski did not seem worried. The big red-leather swivel chair creaked under his weight. "You must have fixed up a pretty good story, cop."

"I've got an idea," Canavan said. He watched Maury from the corner of his eye.

Kolinski sucked at his fat lips. "We feel pretty bad about Luis Renaldo, Canavan. Matter of fact, Maury is Renaldo's cousin. You think we ought to do something about it, Maury?"

Maury said: "It's a thought." The hand in the pocket of the Chesterfield began to shake.

Canavan said: "Here's another thought, Maury. Maybe it was Big George who killed Renaldo."

Maury was poised on the balls of his feet. "Don't be silly, copper. Renaldo worked for Big George. Kolinski owns nine-tenths of the Cathedral."

Canavan nodded as though he had half expected this. "In that case neither of you would be interested in what's in Ed Stengel's safety deposit box." He took out the key and tossed it on the desk. "Or would you?"

The hall door opened and Terence O'Day stood there. He had a gun in each fist and he breathed as though he had been running. "I'll take that, pal. Don't anybody move," he said.

Canavan shot from his jacket pocket, twice.

It was probably only accident he got O'Day in the legs. The tall thin man went down, arms flailing, both guns making a hell of a racket, and then Maury, risking half a dozen slugs, went over and kicked him in the chin. Lieutenant

Kleinschmidt barged in on the crest of the ear-splitting silence which followed. "Hell's fire, Bill, I didn't know things would move so fast!"

Canavan looked slightly sick at his stomach. "No," he said. "No, you wouldn't." He bent and picked up Terence O'Day and carried him over to the divan. The columnist's eyes fluttered open. His horse face was not waggish anymore, only very tired and disillusioned. His hat had fallen off and the lock of untidy sandy hair straggled down over his forehead.

"Sorry, Bill."

Canavan felt like hell. "I'm sorry too, Terry. It's just one of those things, I guess." His mouth drooped. "You couldn't have done anything with the key anyway. Not even the department could have. It'll take a long search, and court orders and a lot of red tape to find that box and get it open. And—"

Big George Kolinski bellowed, "Shut that damned door!" and came out of his chair like a lumbering elephant. "You, Canavan, what's this all about?"

Canavan shrugged tiredly. "By me, George. We'll have to wait till we find the box—unless Terry wants to talk." He looked down at O'Day's legs. "Maybe you'd better, keed."

O'Day was game. He asked for a cigarette and, getting it, propped himself on an elbow.

"First, tell me how you knew, Bill. You must have known. You were expecting me."

"Sort of," Canavan admitted. "I wasn't sure. Nobody could have been sure without knowing what you or somebody else was after. Matter of fact, I'd built up a pretty good circumstantial case against Kolinski. That's why I held the party here. I had to get his reactions first."

olinski grunted. Canavan looked at him. "All right, you were in Night Court. Also, you were at the Weems Mortuary, and you are in a position to tap the police department for information, and hire any number of hoods. Also,

with a finger in every pie you were the most likely guy to be in contact with a man like Ed Stengel. It didn't occur to me till later that a lot of these counts against you could likewise apply to Terry O'Day.

"He too was in Night Court. He too knew plenty of hoods and had an in with the cops. As a newsman he could have known even before you that Stengel, or Ed Carroll, had died in the hospital." Canavan took a breath. "But hell, I had no more reason to suspect him than you. Obviously Stengel had something of value, or inimical to the best interests of someone else. Because the girl had been in contact with him, and I with her, it was logical to cop us both off. Luis Renaldo just happened to be a chiseler who smelled something and started investigating on his own hook. He ran into a knife.

"Well, it was thinking back to this spot that finally brought Terence O'Day into it. He arrived at Stengel's place just a couple of minutes ahead of the cops. At the time, it looked as though he had helped me to escape. But later on it began to appear that he might have done this, knowing I would run smack into the arms of his two hoods."

Canavan stared down at O'Day.

"It was really the car that did it. When I got outside there were only three at the curb—yours, mine, and the cops'. The hoods used mine. Why? Because they had to leave yours and couldn't start the prowl car. But the point I got to thinking about was how did the hoods get there in the first place? Certainly not in my car, or with the cops, and probably not in a taxi, because they were expecting trouble. That left only your car, and that meant that you knew them."

O'Day exhaled a great cloud of smoke. "What happened to the hoods, Bill?"

Canavan almost told him. Then he decided that this was one more point he could use to sew up the case. "I got one of them cold. They're sweating Reefer now, and he's sore at you because I told him this was a million-dollar snatch and he was getting paid in pennies."

O'Day closed his eyes and a spasm of pain twisted his mouth. "That was smart, Bill. I always said you were smart, remember?" He wiped the back of a hand across his lips. "So you called Kleinschmidt and had him drop a hint to me that you might be at Kolinski's. He was to follow me if I fell for it."

Canavan shrugged irritably. "It was a showdown. My only hope was to—" He broke off, coloring. "I mean, aside from cracking Reefer—"

O'Day grinned. "So you killed them both! In other words, your only hope was to trap me into some kind of admission."

"I've still got the key," Canavan said.

"But you might not have had," O'Day said. "I figured I'd beat the cops here and clean up." He looked at a hand reddened with blood from his legs. "Well, nuts to it. I may as well give you the works. Stengel and I did a job together when we were just kids." His eyes crinkled in remembrance. "He was a smart guy too, Bill. He made me sign a joint confession. Oddly enough we became friends after that, but there was always that thing between us. After a while I decided to go straight. Ed kept on hitting the high spots." He smiled tiredly. "Funny, after all the chances he took that he should just die—of stomach ulcers." He looked faintly embarrassed as Hope uttered a little cry. "Sorry, sister."

Kleinschmidt snorted. "Sorry! What about Luis Renaldo? You sorry about him too?"

O'Day looked him straight in the eye. "Not a damned bit, copper. The guy caught me prowling Stengel's place and tried a squeeze play. He got what all chiselers ought to get."

There was a lot of noise out in the hall now. Apparently Kleinschmidt's platoon had really arrived. Maury and Big George Kolinski were in a close-mouthed huddle. Kolinski evidently trying to dissuade Maury from committing a neat job of murder.

Kleinschmidt glared at Canavan. "I'm not through with you, Bill. You knocked me cold in front of strangers."

"And I'm not through with Kolinski!" Canavan yelled. "I'm seeing what makes the Morticians' Protective Association tick. But for tonight—"

Miss Hope Carewe touched his arm. "Yes, Bill? For tonight—what?"

He put a big hand under her chin. "For tonight, hon, or at least for the rest of it, I'm going to try forgetting that your old man has got seventeen million dollars."

Miss Carewe said she would like to forget it too.

The Bloody Bokhara

William Campbell Gault

WILLIAM CAMPBELL GAULT (1910–1995) was born in Madison, Wisconsin, and attended the University of Wisconsin. He was the manager and part owner of a Milwaukee hotel before serving in the army for three years during World War II, after which he moved to Southern California to become a full-time writer.

Although one of the most highly regarded writers in the mystery genre, he was even more revered as the author of scores of sports books, many for children. His earliest stories sold to sports pulps, where he was highly successful before his first sale to a mystery pulp, *Clues*; "Marksman" appeared in the September 1940 issue. He wrote several hundred additional mystery stories before his first novel, *Don't Cry for Me* (1951), which won the Edgar Allan Poe Award. His most famous character is Brock "the Rock" Callahan, a former football player, who made his debut in *Ring Around Rosa* (1955); he also appears in *Day of the Ram* (1956), about the murder of a football player, and ten other novels. Gault used sports as a background for many of his stories and novels, including *The Canvas Coffin* (1953), about the boxing world. He also wrote novels under the pseudonyms Will Duke, Dial Forest, and Roney Scott.

"The Bloody Bokhara" is one of the few Gault books not set in California, using the antique rug business in Milwaukee as background; it was published in the November 1948 issue. Gault later expanded the plot and milieu into a novel, *The Bloody Bokhara* (1952).

The Bloody Bokhara

William Campbell Gault

Cut-rate carpets were Kaprelian's business, but when an Oriental prayer-rug turned up with a corpse wrapped in it, that was more than he'd bargained for.

IT HAD BEEN A slow winter. Cleaning and repairing had kept us going, but there isn't the money in cleaning that there used to be. Not if you've got any respect for rugs and if you clean them the real Armenian way.

It was spring and the door to the store was open. The shop was bright with color. In the window we had an eighteen-foot Sarouk, a lovely piece with a sheen like silk—a floral design on a deep rose background. Usually, when Papa is unhappy he can get a lift out of just admiring a rug like that. But not today.

"Why," he said, "did I ever get into this business?"

Ever since I'd known him, Papa had asked

I reached Selak just as he threw George Herro over the edge of the balcony.

himself that question. Even when business was good, he asked it. He didn't expect an answer.

I said: "The only thing wrong with this business is the people who are in it. It's your competitors who give you your gray hair, Papa."

"Competitors?" he said scornfully. "Competitors—huh! I've got no competitors. Contemporaries, I got."

"It's contemporaries," I corrected him.

He shook his head. "For them, I have nothing but contempt. They are my contemptoraries."

I started to laugh, and then an elderly couple walked into the store.

The frown on Papa's face was replaced by a smile as he rose and came forward to greet them.

"Good morning," Papa said. "A beautiful morning, Mr. Egan."

Years ago, the Egans had been good customers. Then they'd had their entire house carpeted wall to wall, in the fashion of the time.

Mr. Egan said: "Good morning, Mr. Kaprelian. I'm surprised that you remember me."

Papa's smile was beatific. "I never forget a friend," he said earnestly. To Papa, friend was synonymous with customer.

Mr. Egan looked faintly uncomfortable. "Our carpeting," he said, "is pretty badly worn, Mr. Kaprelian. We're thinking of having the house done over. Frankly, it's a choice between recarpeting and orientals. I wondered how prices were on orientals these days."

I knew Papa was wincing inside. But his face gave no indication of it. "Prices," he said, "have never been more favorable, Mr. Egan. Values have never been better." He called to me: "Levon, you will help me, please?"

To everybody I know, I'm Lee. To Papa, I'm still Levon. I went over to help him take down and spread some rugs.

I knew the pile he'd go to. Egan was shopping. Egan was buying on price and price alone. We had some very loosely woven Lilihans Papa had picked up as trade-ins. They'd been used less than a year: they were new, you might say.

Name alone means only the locality, you understand. There are good, bad and indifferent weavers in all localities. These Lilihans were not of the best, but they were good serviceable rugs.

The trouble is, they looked pretty bad against that Sarouk in the window. The memory of that was still in the Egans' mind, I could tell.

The price Papa quoted them made *me* wince. He wanted this sale. He wanted the Egans back.

Mr. Egan's eyebrows went up. He was interested. But Mrs. Egan was frowning. I thought of saying something to her, but I never interfere when Papa's selling.

"Beautiful, aren't they?" Papa asked.

Mr. Egan nodded. Mrs. Egan continued to frown. "I was wondering about the colors," she said doubtfully. "Our decorator tells me it's so hard to work a motif around an oriental rug."

Interior decorators . . . From the painter, the paper-hanger, the furniture and drapery dealer they get a cut. But not from the oriental dealers. No rake-off, no recommendation from them.

"These colors are not bold," Papa said. "They will blend with anything."

"Perhaps." She didn't look like she believed it. "The decorator also says we should not spend *all* our money on the floor."

All *their* money would buy three medium-sized banks. But maybe being careful like that is why they had it.

Papa looked grave. "Let me suggest something, Mrs. Egan. Let me bring some rugs up to your house, some rugs I will personally choose. Leave them there for a week or two. Then you can make your decision."

"That seems fair enough," Mr. Egan said.

But Mrs. Egan shook her head. "I want to look at some carpeting, first, this morning. If I don't find what I want, I'll be in again."

Papa started to say something, but Mr. Egan beat him to it. "Isn't your cousin over on Broad Street selling carpeting in addition to orientals, Mr. Kaprelian?"

"I believe he is," Papa said.

Sarkis had been selling domestic carpeting for seven years and Papa knew it well. Every Sunday, Papa and Sarkis ate chicken and pilaff together. Every Sunday, they played tavlu. The rest of the week they were busy cutting each other's throats.

Mr. Egan smiled. "Well, we'll be back. I'll see that she comes back, Mr. Kaprelian."

Papa smiled and nodded, his eyes sad.

He said nothing as I helped him pile the rugs back. For minutes after we'd finished, and he was back in his chair behind his desk, he said nothing.

Finally, he said: "Carpeting—" and shook his head.

"It covers the floor," I said. "It serves the same purpose."

He looked at me as though I'd uttered a sacrilege—which I had. "It covers the floor," he repeated. "It serves the same purpose."

I started to explain but he raised a hand. "We will pretend I am Rembrandt. We will pretend I have a fine, beautiful idea, and I get my brushes and my paint, and I work like a dog. I work weeks, maybe months—maybe longer, I don't know. When I finish, I have this beautiful picture, this work of art. The dealer says it is the best I have ever done. He puts it up, so people can look, so somebody can buy. The customers come in and admire it. It would look beautiful, they know, on their wall. Am I right?"

"Sure," I said, "but—"

He raised a hand to silence me. "No buts. It would be a credit to the wall. Now—do they say, 'Well, I want to look at some wallpaper first. I'll be back if I can't get the right wallpaper?' Don't they both cover the wall?"

"Rembrandt is dead, Papa." I said. "This is 1948."

"Both of these things I know. Have you some more things to say I *don't* know?"

"A Rembrandt is a work of art," I said.

"Oh. In the window, a Sarouk, a fine Sarouk. Maybe twenty-seven thousand knots to the square foot. Each knot is tied by hand. The finest wool is used, vegetable dye is used, care and cunning is used. This is not a work of art?"

"In a way," I admitted.

But Papa wasn't listening. He was rushing for the phone. "I forgot—" he said.

Now, he was calling Sarkis' number. Now, he had him on the wire.

"Sarkis, you're busy? No? Well, it's like this. One of my very best, one of my most loyal customers was in, a Mr. Egan and his wife. Old oriental customers. But the wife has some idea she would like to try carpeting and they were going to Acme, you understand, to look at some. But I told them you had a finer selection, Sarkis. I told them you had more reasonable prices. Together, we could make a dollar or two on these customers of mine. Right, Sarkis?"

A silence while Sarkis answered.

Then: "Oh, you know they have carpeting now? You sold them the carpeting they have now? They are your customers, Sarkis? Listen, my cousin, when you are still living in a mud house in Sivas, I was selling rugs to Mr. Egan. Good-bye." He hung up the phone angrily.

"Is that true what you told him, Papa?" I asked. "I thought you and Sarkis came to this country at the same time."

"I have been here some time when Sarkis arrived. A considerable time, Levon."

"How long?"

"Over a month." He went over to get his hat. "I am going to lunch." His face was stormy as he left.

I went into the back shop where Selak was washing rugs. Selak's a big boy, over two hundred pounds, with warm brown eyes and a timid smile. Selak's mind stopped growing when he was about nine, but he's kind and gentle. It's only his strength that scares you. He'd been with us for years.

"It's time to eat, Selak," I told him.

He nodded and smiled.

I wouldn't have to tell him it was time to start again, after lunch. Selak's old-fashioned; he likes to work.

I waited until he had unwrapped his lunch and started to eat before I went into the front shop again. That's when I saw the vision.

I knew it was a vision because no girl could be

that beautiful. No hair could be that golden, no eyes that blue. Nobody could wear simple green linen and still look like a queen. A slim, regal vision, standing right inside the doorway.

She was smiling. "I've been admiring that rug in the window."

"It's beautiful, isn't it?" I said. I hadn't moved since coming through the door. I just stood there, like some oaf, staring.

"It certainly is. It's a Sarouk, isn't it?"

I came forward, now. We lived on the same plane for the moment. "It's a Sarouk," I agreed.

"I'm not sure it would go with my furnishings, though," she said doubtfully. "The place is almost *too* modern, if you know what I mean."

"Perhaps a Bokhara, or a Fereghan, then," I suggested. "They work in very well with modern decoration."

"Perhaps—" she said. "I've got a Bokhara now. I mean a *real* one. There's so much confusion about Bokharas, isn't there? The *real* ones are called Khiva, sometimes, or Afghanistan. This was really made in Bokhara."

"You've been reading a book," I said.

Her laugh was music. "I have. For the past two weeks. You see, up until a year ago, I had no interest in orientals, at all. But a friend of mine died and left me these rugs. I kept them in storage until a month ago. But you're not interested in all this, are you?"

I wanted to tell her I was interested in anything she said. I said: "It's *very* interesting. It's possible you might have some very valuable rugs in the group."

Which was bad business, but I wasn't thinking about business.

"There's one," she said, "that could be valuable. It's an antique, I'm sure. I'd like you to have a look at it."

"I'd be glad to," I said.

"This afternoon?" she asked, and handed me a card.

There was no reason why my legs should feel weak at that. She wanted an appraisal. Whatever I'd read into those two simple words hadn't been intentional on her part, I was sure.

"This afternoon," I agreed. "Would two-thirty be all right?"

"Two-thirty would be fine," she said. The smile again, and she was gone.

At the curb, there was a Caddy convertible, and I watched her climb into that. I watched it until it disappeared up the street.

Papa would be unhappy, I knew. A girl with a Caddy convertible admiring the Sarouk and I hadn't sold her a thing. But I didn't care; I was looking forward to two-thirty.

When Papa came back and I told him about our visitor, he didn't look unhappy. He put his head on one side and studied me.

"You will stick to business, Levon. Maybe, it's because you look so much like Tryon Power?" He smiled slyly.

"It's *Tyrone*, not *Tryon*, Papa," I said patiently. "And there's no resemblance, none at all."

"Does the mirror lie? In the washroom there's a mirror. Why don't you look?"

"Don't kid me, Papa," I said. "She was driving a Caddy, a new one, a convertible."

He shrugged. "You might as well take the station wagon. Then you can take the Sarouk along. How can she tell it won't go with modern unless she tries? Take the Sarouk along, Levon. Selak will go with you, to carry it up."

"I don't think she wants the Sarouk," I answered.

"It's time for your lunch," he said. "We will talk of it after lunch."

I went out to lunch. I still had her card in my hand. The name was engraved *Claire Lynne*. The address was penciled on the card, and I recognized it; the Prospect Towers. That meant money.

And the fact that the address was already penciled on the card indicated that she'd planned the appraisal *before* she entered the shop. Which dimmed the day only a little.

I don't remember what I had for lunch. I don't even remember everything Papa told me before I left for the Prospect Towers. But I took the station wagon. I took Selak along, and the Sarouk.

CHAPTER TWO
CONSIGNMENT ON MURDER

The Prospect Towers was only about ten years old, a towering, modern apartment building of glass and white glazed brick.

The apartment of Claire Lynne was on the top floor, a studio apartment, a story and a half high. This would be the most expensive floor in the building with a terrace overlooking the bay.

It was modern, all right, but not obnoxiously so. Soft colors and bleached woods. The immense living room was carpeted; there were no orientals in here.

Claire Lynne was wearing black lounging slacks, and a white blouse. The blouse was low-necked, and I felt that weakness in the legs again.

"The Bokhara's in here," she said, "in the dining room."

I followed her across the carpeted expanse to the *L* at one end of the room. Here, separated from the living room by a low wall, at right angles to the living room, was the dining room. Here was the so-called Bokhara.

Finely spun wool, compactly woven. Octagons on a background of Turanian red. A beautiful, finely finished piece, with a sheen that comes only from wear.

"Well?" she said.

"A lovely rug, and fine for modern furniture," I answered. "Any dealer would call it a Royal Bokhara, because that's the name they go by, in the trade. It's from the Turcoman group. It's a Tekke. The real Bokhara is called Beshir in this country."

She didn't seem surprised. "That's what I was told," she agreed. "The man I got it from told me just what you have."

I bent down again. There was a stain running through the red, darkening it. "It should be cleaned," I said.

She didn't seem to be listening. "I think you're qualified," she said, "to look at another rug I have." She seemed thoughtful.

I rose and smiled at her. "This was a test,

Miss Lynne? You wanted to get my reaction to this one first?"

She smiled right back at me. "That's right. The other rugs are in here."

I followed her back into the living room and through that to the entrance hall. From there, she led me to a fairly large room that seemed to be an unfurnished guest room. There was a flat pile of rugs on the floor in here.

I went through them, one by one, identifying them as well as I could. There were some antiques and semi-antiques in this pile. There was a lot of money on the floor in here, all in wool.

When I'd finished, I said: "You said 'another.' That would mean one. Which one were you referring to, Miss Lynne?"

She opened the door to a closet. "In here."

I reached in and brought it out. I unfolded it, and stared.

I'd seen some fine pieces through the years, silk and wool and metallic. But this was far beyond any of those. This was the kind the old timers talked about—the inspired work of a master weaver, an antique prayer-rug.

It wasn't big, but it could easily be priceless.

She said: "Name it."

"An antique. A Persian, could have come from Kashan, but I wouldn't be sure. I wish my father could see this."

"That's why I had you come up," she answered. "You can show it to him. I want you to put it in your safe, if you would. You have a safe for your fine pieces, haven't you?"

I nodded. "For our silks. This—do you know what this is?"

"I think I do," she said. "You've heard of Maksoud of Kashan?"

I nodded. "He lived about four hundred years ago. The finest of the Persian weavers."

"That's right. His masterpiece is in the South Kensington Museum in London. It's called the Ardebil Carpet. His name is woven in the corner of the rug, in Arabic."

I nodded and looked down at the Arabic inscription on this rug. I looked up to meet her smile.

I said: "I understand he spent the better part of his life weaving that one in London. Thirty-three million knots. He wouldn't have much time for anything else."

"But if he had?"

I shook my head. I realized I'd been holding my breath and I expelled it, now.

"I think we ought to have a drink," she said, "don't you?"

"I could use it," I said.

We went back into the living room. I kept seeing that rug, I kept hearing the words, Maksoud of Kashan. And, for some reason, I kept remembering the blot on the dining room Bokhara.

I had Scotch with water. She drank rye. She sat on an armless love seat. I sat straight across from her, on its twin.

I couldn't quite understand her. I had the impression she'd been coached for her role this afternoon. Her information was too glib and detailed, too "bookish." We get customers like that once in a while, who spout information verbatim from one or the other books on the subject.

While I was thinking these thoughts, I was looking at her, and that was an unmixed pleasure.

"You clean rugs at your place, Mr. Kaprelian?"

"We do. I've a man waiting downstairs. I'll have him come and get that Bokhara."

She nodded.

"I brought the Sarouk along," I said, "but it would be too big for the dining room. I can have him put one of your other rugs down in there."

"Fine," she said, and studied her drink.

She was still looking thoughtful. She still hadn't said what was on her mind, I felt sure.

Finally, she said: "I'm not buying any rugs. I'm selling."

"The market's not too good," I said, "but of course, for rugs like those in that room . . ." I shrugged.

"The market's as good as the customers," she said. "I'd like you to sell those rugs for me on commission. I'll give you the leads."

"We'll be glad to try."

"I want *you* to sell them, not the firm. You see, the customers will be mainly women."

I frowned. "I don't follow you, Miss Lynne."

"Don't be modest," she said, and chuckled. "Oh, Lee, there's a mirror right down there at the end of the room. You can't be that blind. No one could be that naive."

I must have blushed like the village virgin, for my face was hot, my collar tight. In my discomfiture, the fact that she'd known my first name and used it didn't register right away.

I said: "We do some wholesale business, Miss Lynne. We have a few dealers who sell rugs that way. I don't think I'd want to be—"

"You've sold Henri Ducasse some rugs. Rather, you've given them to him on consignment, haven't you? And he's paid you after he sold them?"

Ducasse was a Frenchman who specialized in the widow trade. I nodded slowly.

"Do you realize the kind of money he was getting for *your* merchandise?"

"I've heard of a few deals."

"Well, Henri's aging. He's beginning to get that mummified look. He's not the man he was."

"And you think his shoes would fit me? You'd like me to become one of those—" I shook my head. "I don't know what to call him."

"Call him smart," she said quietly. "And call him rich. Because he's both of those."

What she was asking me wasn't exactly dishonest, though it might be considered unethical. I looked at her, and realized I'd be spending some time with her, if I accepted the offer.

I said: "I'll get the man up here to pick up the Bokhara."

"You haven't answered me, Lee."

"I want some time." I rose.

"Get the man up," she said. "Take the Bokhara along. Perhaps you'd better wrap up that prayer-rug inside of it. It's not the kind of piece to show just everybody, is it? It's too valuable to be advertising indiscriminately."

I went down and got Selak, and brought him up the back way. I helped him move the furniture in the dining room. Selak couldn't seem to get his eyes off Miss Lynne. When he first entered, he stared at her. All the time we were working, he continued to glance at her almost hungrily.

I brought the prayer-rug out, and laid it in the center of the so-called Bokhara.

Selak's attention wasn't divided any more. He knelt, to feel its velvet texture. In Armenian, he said: "One of the old ones. No rugs like this today. One of the old ones."

"One of the old ones," I agreed. "What kind, Selak?"

He started to answer, and then his eyes got crafty. I might be buying this rug. He wasn't going to build it up in front of the seller. He shrugged, but he couldn't take the admiration out of his eyes as he looked at it again.

"Kashan," he said.

Maksoud had lived in Kashan. It was like calling a Rembrandt an Amsterdam.

When he'd shouldered the rugs, and left, Claire said: "Why did he stare at me like that? He gave me the shivers."

"Selak admires two things," I told her. "Beauty and quality."

Her smile was mocking. "In that case, it would be my beauty."

"Now, *you're* being modest," I said. I wanted to reach out and pull her close. I wanted to do a lot of things that wouldn't be good business or good manners. "I'll let you know about—about the deal," I said.

She put a hand on my arm. "Come back tonight. There'll be somebody here I want you to meet."

"I've a date," I said.

"It'll be worth your while," she said. "After tonight, you can decide. I think you'll decide in my favor."

I could smell her perfume and her face was close as she looked up. I like to think there's no hay in my hair, but I felt like Selak at the moment.

"All right," I said. "About eight?"

"About eight."

The door closed and I was walking down the carpeted hall to the elevator. Her perfume was still with me, but it might have been only in my mind.

In the station wagon, Selak waited. "Keghetsig," he said, which is as close as I can come to the American spelling. In any event, it means beautiful.

"Beautiful," I agreed. "Both the rug and the girl."

He nodded.

I was no child, despite the way Papa treated me. I was no child, but I had a child's sense of guilt as we drove back to the store.

Papa was busy with a customer as we drove around in back to unload the rugs. Selak kept the Bokhara in the washroom; I brought the smaller rug into the store.

I opened the safe, and then decided to let Papa see the rug first. He would see it eventually, anyway; there was no reason to try to hide it from him. Nor was there any reason I should feel involved in whatever history it might have. It was just that damned unreasonable sense of guilt.

Selak came through from the back, carrying the Sarouk as the customer left.

"So she didn't want it?" Papa said.

I shook my head.

He started to say something, and then he saw the rug near the safe. He came over to stare at it. He knelt to study, to finger it, to turn it over. He was murmuring in Armenian too low for me to hear.

Then he looked up. "Levon, where did you get this?"

"She had it. The customer. She wants to keep it in our safe."

"It's been a long time since I've seen a rug like this, outside a museum, outside a private collection. Where did she get it, Levon?"

"I don't know," I said.

He was looking at me sharply. "Who is this woman? You think I wouldn't know if there was a rug like this in town? How long has she been here? Who is she?"

"You know as much as I do, Papa," I said. "Her name is Claire Lynne and she lives in the Prospect Towers." I told him about some of the other rugs I'd seen, the antiques and semi-antiques.

He shook his head, and looked down again at the rug. "Silk warp and weft. Wool pile. Kashan, antique. But these Arabian letters?"

"Why don't we ask Sarkis," I suggested. "Sarkis can read Arabic."

He nodded. "Sarkis can read Arabian. But I don't want him to know we have this rug. Levon, I don't want *anyone* to know we have this rug in the safe. The Marines we should have, to guard this rug."

Reverently, Papa put the rug away while I went over to get down a couple of books from the shelf above his desk.

In one I read: *The Ardebil Carpet was the life-time work of the greatest of all Persian weavers, Maksoud . . .*

In the other: *It is estimated that it took ten weavers more than three years to weave the famed "Ardebil Carpet," credit for which goes to Maksoud, the weave master, who supervised . . .*

Both books were considered authentic. There was no reason to think he hadn't woven the one now in our safe. There aren't more than three or four rugs in the world signed by their creator. If this one was genuine . . .

"Books," Papa said. "What are you going to learn about this business from books?" He tapped his head and breast. "Don't you know—*here* and *here*—when you see a masterpiece? Do you have to look everything up?"

"I was looking up the Ardebil Carpet," I said.

"Ardebil—from the mosque, you mean." He stared at me. "You think Maksoud?"

Selak came in from the washroom, then, looking troubled. I heard the word "Bokhara" and "blood" but the rest was too garbled for me.

Papa nodded, "A Bokhara will bleed. They must be washed carefully, Selak. Careful, you must be."

Some more I couldn't understand, and then Papa went back to the washroom with Selak.

It was quiet in the shop. Outside, on the street, people went by, traffic went by. But it seemed unusually quiet in the store.

When Papa came back in, his eyes were questioning. "A Bokhara will bleed, but not *blood* it won't bleed, Levon." He looked tired. "What has happened, today? This woman, this rug—" He extended his hands, palms up. "What are you hiding from me?"

"I'll know more after tonight," I said. "I'm going back there tonight."

His face was grave. "The dance is tonight. The Junior League of the A.G.B.U is having their spring dance tonight, Levon. You aren't going with Berjouhi?"

I shook my head. "Maybe I can get there, later. Sam will take Berjouhi, and I can meet them there, later, maybe."

Sam was Sarkis' boy. Sam was my rival. And Berjouhi? She's a lovely, quiet girl. I'd been going with her, more or less, for three years. If Papa had had his way, we'd be married, right now.

"You promised you would take her? You are going to break your promise to her?"

The only answer to that was to use his own weapon, the one he'd taught me. "Business *first*, Papa," I said.

He opened his mouth to answer, and then clicked his teeth. He sighed, and went over to look out the huge plate glass window, the one where it says, *N. Kaprelian and Son*, in big, gold letters.

We don't get a paper downtown. We get the home edition. That's why I didn't read about Henri Ducasse until just before supper.

Henri, who'd been described by Claire as smart and rich, was now something else. Henri Ducasse was dead.

He'd been found in a deserted garage stabbed to death. He hadn't, according to the authorities, been stabbed in the garage, as there was very little blood on the cement floor, and it was obvious he had bled a lot. He was identified as a connoisseur of rugs and tapestries—and a bon vivant.

My sister, Ann, was reading the society page across from me, and I asked her: "What's a bon vivant, Ann?"

"Oh, a lover of good living," she said. "A man who likes fine foods. Thinking of taking it up, Lee?"

"Not until business gets better," I answered. And then, at something in her voice, I looked up.

The paper was in her lap, and she was regarding me. "Papa says you're not going to the dance, tonight."

"He told you the truth."

"You've called Berjouhi?"

"From the store, before I left."

Ann shook her head, and her dark eyes were quizzical. "You get away with murder. I know *six* boys who'd like to take your place with Berjouhi. How do you do it?"

"With mirrors," I said, and went back to reading about Henri Ducasse.

At the supper table, Papa was unusually silent. He would look at me from time to time, and I had the impression he wanted to say something. But he didn't.

Ann and Mom got into a discussion about one of Ann's customers at the hat shop. They carried the conversation.

After supper, Papa said: "A game of tavlu, Leon?"

"O.K.," I said.

It's called backgammon in this country, but Papa and his cronies still called it tavlu. Also, they don't use a cup to throw the dice, a point I insisted on tonight.

"You think I would cheat, Levon?"

"No, of course not. But you get too many double sixes."

"That's the dice."

It was an old argument; there are more sixes than any other number, they claim, and play accordingly. They get them and it isn't due to manipulation. What those experiments at Duke are trying to prove now, they knew for ages, these old-timers.

As we set up the board, Papa said: "I've been thinking about that Bokhara. I sold that rug,

once. I'm trying to remember who I sold it to."

His memory was unbelievable, even for ordinary pieces.

"Maybe—Henri Ducasse?" I suggested. I kept my eyes on the board.

He shook his head. "Twenty years ago, or more, I sold that rug to somebody in this town. I can't remember." He tapped his forehead.

He played a sound game, making no mistakes, covered all the time, making all the traditional and routine moves. The only thing his game lacked was daring, and that's why I beat him three straight.

Which didn't prevent him from telling me: "You play a dangerous game, Levon. As you get older you will be more careful."

"I won," I said.

"You were lucky." He folded the board carefully, and put it in the bookcase. "You be careful tonight, Levon."

"I will," I promised, and went into my room to dress.

There wasn't any reason I couldn't wear the clothes I'd worn all day. No reason but that weakness in the legs. I wore my new gabardine suit and my best oxford shirt. I wore a tie of rich and simple dignity. I was, I realized, also wearing a smirk and I left that back in the bedroom, before going out into the living room.

Papa's gaze covered me over the top of his *Mirror-Spectator*. He said dryly: "You will remember the firm's reputation, Levon. You will make no promises for the firm before you talk to me." He went back to his reading.

I didn't answer him. He didn't expect an answer.

It was a warm night, a false summer night, and the moon was almost theatrical. The little convertible seemed to be humming to herself, as I cut over to Prospect.

The Prospect Towers were alive with light, the white brick reflected the moon's glow, the full-length windows of the top floor were like a battery of beacons against the sky.

Over at the Parkleigh Hotel, the party would

just be getting under way and I felt a moment's regret. I hadn't seen the gang all together for a long time.

Across the street, a broad, poorly dressed man stood under the shadow of a budding maple tree. For a moment, I stared that way, for it looked like Selak. But he made no move to leave the shadows, and I couldn't make out his face clearly from here. There'd be no reason for Selak to be up at this end of town, anyway.

As I waited outside of Claire's door, I could hear music inside. It was Aram Khachaturian's *Saber Dance,* a current juke box favorite. The timing was too pat; I felt like a fly waiting outside a spider's web. But perhaps I could turn into a bee, or perhaps this web wouldn't be as strong as its creator thought it.

Claire Lynne was wearing something misty in a pale green, something about as substantial-looking as a cloud. "You're on time," she said, her smile warm and friendly.

This didn't look like the start of an ordinary dealer-customer relationship.

We went in, and she asked: "Recognize the music?"

"Strauss, isn't it?" I answered.

She sighed. "And all the work I went to—" She chuckled. "No, it's not Strauss, Lee."

A man was sitting on one of the armless love seats, and he rose as we entered. A short, dark man with one of those unlined faces. He could have been forty or seventy. But I knew he wasn't forty.

It was George Herro, a Syrian we had frequently dealt with, another Henri Ducasse, another social salesman.

"Good evening, Lee," he said. "How's your father?"

He extended his hand, and I took it. I said: "He's worried about business as usual. And tonight, he's worried about me."

Claire went over to turn off the record player. Herro said: "About you? You're in trouble, Lee?"

"Not yet," I said. "But I'm young and innocent and don't know Khachaturian from Strauss. And here I am, in the major leagues."

Herro frowned. Claire laughed.

Herro said: "I don't—quite follow you, Lee."

"Yes, you do," I said. "And I want you to admit it before we go any further. If we're going to sell some rugs, we should understand each other, first."

Herro looked at Claire, and now they were both smiling. Herro said: "I underestimated you, Lee. Let's all sit down, shall we?"

We all sat down, neat and cozy.

Herro looked down at his hands, and up at me. "You've seen those rugs in the other rooms?"

I nodded.

"They need to be very carefully sold," he said. "They are not something to dump on the market."

"Any really fine rug needs to be carefully sold," I said.

His eyes were reflective. "That's right. In 1911, Lee, I sold an antique Kirman for thirty thousand dollars. Later, at an auction, the same rug was sold by its owner for seven hundred." He paused. "I sold an Ispahan for thirty-five thousand to the same customer. At the auction, it brought twelve hundred."

"I wasn't alive, then," I said, "but those were the golden years, at the beginning of the century. A lot of very wealthy men collected orientals as a hobby. Those were the collector's years."

"And those are collector's rugs."

"But this isn't 1911."

He stirred. "No. It isn't. A lot of bad management has come into the business since then. Throat and price cutting has come into the business, and dealers who try to compete with carpeting. This isn't the business it was—nor are those the kinds of rugs you'll find on the market today."

"Miss Lynne said something about customers—" I put in.

"That's what I'm coming to. There are still some of the discerning customers left. We know quite a few."

"Mostly women?"

He nodded, watching me, looking for a reaction.

"That's *your* field, George," I pointed out.

"It was." He smiled. "Before I became emotionally involved with a few of them."

"And these rugs—where'd they come from?"

"Most of them are from a St. Louis collection. I picked some of them up there. The rest are from town, here. They were bought through the years, by a man of breeding and taste and discernment. I don't have to tell you these aren't the kind you're buying today."

I looked at Claire Lynne. I said: "That's a different story than you told me when you came to the store today."

"I wasn't revealing my hand, at the time," she said. She looked at me levelly. "I thought it was a little early."

For a moment, nobody said anything. Then George Herro said quietly: "Well, Lee?"

I waited until my silence got through to them, and then asked: "What happened to Henri Ducasse?"

Neither of them flinched. Claire shrugged. Herro said: "I understand he was trying to sell a rug to a man named Dykstra. I understand the deal was almost completed when Dykstra discovered the rug wasn't as represented. This is just rumor one hears in the trade. I cannot vouch for it, personally."

"Dykstra—" I said. "We sold him some rugs a few years back. War profiteer, wasn't he?"

"Among other things. He was something of an expert on repeating weapons, I understand. And explosives, generally. Had a rather thriving, if illegal, trade in things of that sort." He smiled dimly. "Why do you ask about Henri Ducasse, Lee? What has he to do with this business?"

"I didn't know. That's why I asked. Claire mentioned him, today."

She said: "It was just a coincidence, Lee."

"All right," I said, "I'll work along with you." I didn't mention the Bokhara, then; I was saving that. "How about that rug you have in our safe? You've got a customer for that?"

Herro said: "We won't worry about that for a while. I've an idea we can get our price for that." He looked at the thin gold watch on his wrist.

"Well, I've an engagement at nine-thirty." His smile tried to read some intriguing meaning into the words, some romantic rendezvous. He rose. "I'll leave you two young people to amuse yourselves now."

Claire went to the door with him. I went over to the record player. She had all of the Gayne Suite there, and I put it on.

When she came back, I was sitting on one of the love seats.

"So?" she said.

"So, it's settled. You don't mind if I'm a little uneasy about it, though?"

She didn't answer that right away. She was bending over a decanter on the cocktail table between us. "Scotch, again, with water?"

"Fine." I averted my eyes, like a gentleman.

As she handed me my drink, she said: "Why are you uneasy?"

"For one thing—Ducasse, who was killed. Then—Herro. He's never been arrested, but he's had some close calls, I remember. And one other thing—that blot on the Bokhara. It was blood, Claire."

Poise, she had. Or innocence? I would settle for poise. Her eyes didn't waver; there was no visible tenseness in her.

She frowned. "Blood?"

"Blood. Enough of it to make me wonder how it got there."

"I can't tell you, Lee, because I don't know. It was that way when I got it. And I got it yesterday; George brought it up."

"You know where he got it?"

She nodded. "I know. But it would involve someone I don't want involved, Lee."

There seemed to be a lot of faith required from me in this business. I said: "All right. We'll forget about it—for now."

We didn't talk about rugs for the rest of the evening. We drank a little, and listened to some music. We went out onto the terrace, and there I obeyed that impulse I'd had at the door this afternoon. I pulled her into my arms and kissed her.

She seemed to enjoy it. She seemed to expect it.

When I got down to the car again, it was two-thirty. The broad man no longer stood under the maple tree. He was asleep in the seat of my car. It was Selak.

His mouth was open, and he was snoring heavily. I went around to the driver's side quietly and climbed in behind the wheel. I'd driven him more than halfway home before he woke up.

He shook himself and straightened in his seat, rubbing his eyes. I stole a glance at him. He seemed embarrassed and looked straight ahead. The clothes he wore were tight. But I knew they were his best.

I said: "I didn't expect to see you up at this end of town, Selak. Been to a show?"

Something that sounds like "Voch," which is "no."

By the tone of his voice, I realized he didn't relish any questioning. I said no more. He shared the silence.

When I stopped in front of his house, there was a light on. His sister, a thin, prematurely gray girl, was waiting on the porch, and she came down to the walk as the car stopped.

"Selak—where have you been?"

Then she saw me. "Oh, Lee—he was with you? Everything is all right?"

"Everything's all right," I assured her. "He was out with me."

"He's never been out this late, before," she said. "You were at the dance?"

"No. No, we were over to see a friend of mine."

Selak had left the car, was going up the steps to the porch. He hadn't said good-night. I didn't know if he was miffed or embarrassed. He'd probably been hit as hard as I was.

I said good-night to his sister, and turned the little convertible toward home. There was no reason I should sing, but I sang. There was no reason I should feel smug and sophisticated and adventurous. But all these things, I felt.

Papa's curiosity was greater than his temporary annoyance with Sarkis, evidently. For Sarkis was at the store when I got there the next morning, and Papa was getting the prayer-rug out of the safe.

Sarkis looked at it in awe, and some ejaculation escaped his throat. He knelt like a man in church.

"Maksoud of Kashan," he read, and, "the year is 940." He looked thoughtful. "That would not be our calendar. That would be about 1560 or '62." He looked at my father. "Where did you get this treasure?"

"It isn't mine," Papa said. "Can you believe it's genuine?"

Sarkis' broad face was grave. "It's an antique. But that rug from the mosque. It's an Ispahan, isn't it?"

"You could ask Levon," Papa answered. "He read the books."

"Not enough of them," I said. "In three books I got three dates for the Ardebil Carpet and no designation. What do you honestly think about it?"

He shook his head, and looked at it again. "What does it matter? There are none like it, today. A rug like this, if you owned it, you could ask anything, anything the customer could pay. There would be no other limits."

"Ethics, Sarkis," I chided him.

"Ethics?" Both of them looked at me blankly.

Then Sarkis said: "Across from me is a picture store. In the window, something you couldn't call a picture. Two weeks I've been seeing that picture every day and can't figure what it is. But the price card I can read—twenty-five hundred dollars. That's plain enough. Ethics?"

"All right, then, how much would you pay for that rug, Sarkis?"

"I'm a poor man," he answered. "My money is all in merchandise. I am a dealer, not a collector."

"You are a wolf, not a lamb, you mean?" I grinned at him.

He sighed, and looked at my father. "These young ones," he said.

Papa frowned at me. "You will remember Sarkis is my cousin."

Yesterday, Sarkis had been his contemporary. Today he was his cousin. Today they shared a reverence for craftsmanship.

I said no more. I concentrated on the Serapi I was repairing. I was only vaguely aware of the small, dark man on the walk outside, looking in through the open door.

Papa was saying: "And how did you make out with Mr. Egan, Sarkis?"

"All carpeting, the whole first floor," Sarkis answered. "And the rugs that man used to buy . . . But his wife, you know. His wife has the money, and it's carpeting for her." He shook his head sadly.

The small, dark man was in the doorway now, and I looked up. He was staring at the rug still on the floor in front of the safe. I don't know why I was suddenly nervous, but I was.

He had a thin face, this man, and a nose like a parrot's beak. He had the small, round eyes of a bird, too, eyes black as sin. He was wearing a black derby, which he removed, now, disclosing a completely bald head, glistening with perspiration.

"That rug, gentlemen—" he said. "It is for sale?" He reached into an inner pocket as he said this.

With one motion, Papa had tossed the rug into the safe and clanged the door shut. There had been something so malevolent about that gesture of his, Papa had reacted instinctively.

But the man had a handkerchief in his hand, now, and he was wiping the perspiration from his shining head. "It is for sale?" he repeated.

Papa shook his head. "It is not ours, sir. We are keeping it for a customer."

"I may see it? I believe I once owned it."

Papa shook his head stubbornly. "It is not ours to show."

The black eyes went from Papa to Sarkis, and back. "It is a secret? Or you do not trust me?"

Papa said: "It is a very valuable rug. It is not ours. I am sorry, sir."

Silence. The man looked at Sarkis, then at me, as though sizing up his adversaries before making an attack. Finally: "You gentlemen are

Christians?" The voice was faintly tinged with contempt.

We all nodded.

"You would not know, then, the value of that rug. In the mosque at Ardebil, it was woven by the slave Maksoud. To Allah it was dedicated, and to his Prophet, Mohammed. It was never intended for Christian use nor Christian admiration."

"We cannot help but admire it," Papa said. "We are not using it. If you will pardon me, sir, it is a busy morning. . . . If there is something else, I can show you—"

"There is nothing else you can show me. But you can tell me the name of the one who owns this rug?" A pause. "I can deal directly with him."

Sarkis said something to Papa in Armenian, and Papa's face was suddenly stone. Papa said: "You are—Turkish?" There was no "sir" this time. Papa had spent his youth under the Turks.

The man looked at Sarkis and Papa. If he felt any fear, he didn't show it. But he must have felt it; they were related to me, and still I felt the gooseflesh form on my arms and neck. The two men who stood there near the safe were no longer rug dealers in an American city. They were no longer rational.

"What does it matter?" the man said.

All of Sarkis' family had been massacred by the Turks. Papa's sister had been killed by the Turks. What does it matter? the man had asked.

"Answer me, damn you!" Papa's voice was hoarse; it was a voice I had never heard before. His face was white. "You come into my store in this free country. You speak of my religion with contempt. You interfere in my business. You—"

Now, the man was frightened as Papa stepped toward him.

I was up quickly standing between them. I had my hands on Papa's shoulders. "Please, Papa, no trouble—" I put an arm around him. "Your heart, Papa."

Sarkis said to the little man: "You had better go. You had better get the hell out of here quick."

The man surveyed us all. "I will be back," he said. "You will see me again." He turned abruptly and went out the door.

Papa expelled his breath and sat down on a pile of rugs, gasping. His eyes were reminiscent. His mind, I would guess, was back in Sivas, under the Turks.

Sarkis said: "I'm late, now. I must get back to the store. Be calm, Nishan. Do not think about the man."

Papa didn't answer. His face was still white; he seemed to be having some difficulty getting his breath.

I went to the washroom and got him a glass of water. Sarkis had left when I came back with it. Papa drank it slowly, his eyes watering.

"You're in America, now, Papa," I said quietly. "You must forget the old country and the people you hated."

He nodded and looked up at me. "I am in America. Levon, one thing you must always, always be thankful for. One thing you must thank God for, every night. You are an American."

"It's for me," I agreed. "How do you feel, now?"

"All right. Better." He wiped his eyes. "Levon, what kind of business is this you're in? What kind of people are these you're dealing with?"

"I don't know for sure," I told him. "I'm being careful. Don't worry about that. George Herro's in the deal, too."

"Oh." His glance traveled to my face. "George is getting old. You are going to be the new George Herro?"

"Not if I can help it. The rugs I'm going to sell are worth anything I can get, Papa. Nobody has to be ashamed of asking big money for rugs like those."

"But you will sell to women?"

"Some of them, I suppose."

"You've told Berjouhi this?"

"No," I said impatiently. "I'm not married to her, Papa. We're not even engaged."

"So? All right. But you haven't told me about everybody, Levon. You haven't told me about Mr. Egan."

I stared at him. "Egan? What about him?"

"I remembered this morning who I sold that Bokhara to, Levon. It was Mr. Egan. Twenty years ago I sold him that rug for his study."

I remembered Claire saying: "It would involve someone I don't want involved." I said: "I didn't know Mr. Egan was involved, Papa. And maybe he isn't. He might have sold that rug years ago."

Papa nodded. "Maybe. But I am going to ask around, Levon. Next time the Pinochle Club meets, I'm going to ask the dealers."

I thought of Herro saying: "They were bought through the years by a man of breeding and taste and discernment." Mr. Egan was a man who could fit that description. Mr. Egan had a wife who controlled the purse strings. But I couldn't see him as an accomplice to anything questionable.

A little later, Papa went out to deliver a rug and I was alone in the store. I phoned Claire.

I told her about the little man who'd been in.

"He's after it," she said, "and that's why he came to the store. He must have seen you take the other rug yesterday. He wants it pretty badly, Lee. He means to get it, one way or another. Our job is to see that he *pays* for it."

"It will be a pleasure," I said. "Anything lined up?"

"Yes. This afternoon. I've a customer I wanted you to show that Feraghan to."

"Good-looking customer?"

"She's lovely. She's well over sixty—or I wouldn't let you even talk to her, smarty. I'm changing the strategy, Lee. I think Herro will handle all the trade under sixty."

"We'll talk about that when I see you," I told her. "And I'll probably see you about one-thirty. Will that be all right?"

"I'll be waiting," she said.

When I turned from the phone, there was a man standing near the doorway just inside the store. He was a big man in a worn brown suit. He had a broad, pugnacious face and he didn't look like a customer.

"Mr. Kaprelian?" he asked.

I nodded. "Lee Kaprelian. My father is out, just now."

He displayed a shield in his wallet. "Sergeant Waldorf," he said, "out of Homicide, Mr. Kaprelian. I'm checking on an Henri Ducasse."

My breath was a little short. I said: "I read about him in the paper yesterday."

He nodded. "Knew him, did you?"

"He's handled some rugs for us. Or not exactly that. We've let him have some rugs on consignment and if he sold them, he'd pay us our price."

Waldorf seemed to be studying me. "Your price. But his price could be about anything, couldn't it?"

"So I've heard," I said. "This is a strange business, Sergeant."

"I'm beginning to find that out. And I've heard of buyer's strikes, too. But I can't quite see murder as a means of combating inflation, can you?"

"It would depend upon the customer," I said, and managed to smile. "Is that your theory, Sergeant?"

"No. But it's Vartanian's and Bogosian's and Herro's. They all told me about Dykstra. There seems to be a rug dealer's agreement that Ducasse tried to stick Dykstra and Dykstra bumped him."

I breathed easier. This was a routine check. I said: "I've heard that, too. I don't know much about Dykstra. My dad sold him a few pieces during the war, but I was in the army then, so I never met him."

He lighted a cigarette and watched the smoke for a moment. "And there's another gent walking through this case, too. Little guy in a derby hat. He's been hanging around all the dealers, but he didn't leave any name, with any of them. Seen him?"

"About a half an hour ago," I said. "But he didn't stay long. Papa found out he was a Turk. You almost had another homicide on your hands, Sergeant."

He smiled. "He doesn't like Turks, huh?"

"He came to this country to get away from them," I said. "He spent his boyhood in Armenia."

"What do you think he was after? This little gent with the black derby, I mean."

I hesitated. I said: "He was very much interested in a rug we have in the safe. He wanted to buy it."

Now, there was interest in the sergeant's eyes. He looked at me steadily. "Price?"

"No—it wasn't ours to sell. We're just holding it for a customer."

"Valuable rug?"

"Very."

"Who's the customer?"

Again, I hesitated. "I don't like to say, Sergeant. I don't like to involve our customers in this kind of investigation."

"He won't be involved," the sergeant said, "unless he should be."

For the third time, I hesitated. But I'd opened the door to this line of questioning; it was too late to shut it. I said: "It's a woman. A Miss Claire Lynne, who lives on the top floor of the Prospect Towers."

He put it down in a notebook he had. Then: "I suppose I'd better look at the rug. Not that it will mean anything to me. But I might have to identify it later."

I opened the safe and brought it out.

He studied it for seconds, some awe in his eyes. He nodded and I put it away.

"Anything else that might help, Mr. Kaprelian?"

I thought of the Bokhara. I said: "That's all, Sergeant."

"O.K. I think I'll check this Miss Lynne before I go up against Dykstra. I'll need all the ammunition I can get before I hit him." He looked at me closely a moment. "Thanks."

I nodded, saying nothing.

I watched him leave the store and climb into a car out at the curb. There was another detective behind the wheel of the car. When it pulled away, I went to the phone.

Claire answered almost immediately.

I said, "A detective was here, checking on Henri Ducasse. I told him about the rug, Claire."

A silence. Then in a low voice: "*Which* rug, Lee?"

"The one in the safe. He's on his way up to see you, now."

Something like relief in her voice. "O.K. I'm glad you called. Don't forget—one-thirty."

I went back to repairing the Serapi. *Which rug, Lee . . . It would involve someone I don't want involved, Lee. . . . I remembered who I sold that Bokhara to, Levon. It was Mr. Egan. . . . But his wife, you know. His wife has the money, and . . .*

Mr. Egan had been described as a man of breeding and taste and discernment, if Herro had been talking about him. Maybe, all the rugs were Mr. Egan's. That St. Louis story was too glib; one of the finest collections in the world was in St. Louis, and Herro would think of that town if he was looking for a fast answer.

The clock above the safe read twelve o'clock, and I went back into the rear shop.

"Time to eat, Selak," I said.

He didn't look at me today. He didn't smile as he had yesterday. He nodded, sulkily, and turned off the rotary-brush machine. I'd never expected to see Selak jealous of me.

When I went back into the store again, I heard the machine start. Evidently, he didn't have any appetite, today. Or maybe he didn't want to leave a rug half done and full of soap.

About twelve-thirty, Papa came in, and I told him about the deal I had for the afternoon.

He looked unhappy. "You're working on commission on this, Levon?"

"That's right. We'll split the commission, Papa."

He waved that away. "No. Not those kind of sales."

"It's an antique Fereghan," I said. "You think I should sell it cheap?"

He looked interested. "Green in the border?"

"All Fereghans have that. It's like velvet.

Yellow, rose, blue, purple, violet, red. And they all blend. It's an odd size, narrower than most."

He nodded. "Mr. Egan's?"

"Not that I know of."

"It sounds," Papa said, "like a rug he bought from Bogosian, years ago."

"Well, maybe it is, then. Maybe he sold it years ago."

"Maybe," Papa agreed. "I took some rugs over to Grace to be repaired."

Grace was Selak's sister, and she did our finer repairing. I didn't say anything.

Papa said: "She told me Selak was with you last night. You brought him home."

"That's right."

Papa put a hand on my arm. "I'm glad he was with you. I was worried about you, Levon."

"Don't worry about me," I said. "I'm a big boy now." I didn't feel any more like Judas than Judas must have felt. "I think I'll take Selak this afternoon if he's finished the cleaning. This is a high-class sale, and I don't want to be lugging the rug like some peddler."

"Sure," Papa said. "Take the station wagon, too."

I went back to the washing room, where Selak was running the big squeegee over the rug, taking out the surplus water. "Don't start another one, Selak," I said. "I'll need you after lunch."

He nodded, not looking at me.

When I came back from lunch, he was sitting in the station wagon. He'd changed from the sweatshirt he wears for washing to a semi-clean white shirt. His hair was plastered in a crooked part.

"Did you eat lunch?" I asked, as I climbed behind the wheel.

He nodded, looking straight ahead. I cut out of the alley, and over to the Avenue, up the Avenue to Prospect.

Using the station wagon, we didn't need to stick to the streets designated for trucks. And it looked better than a truck for this business.

The false summer weather still held. Most of the traffic along Prospect was toward the beach and the picnic grounds in the park. When I stopped in front of the Towers, I could see Claire up on the top-floor terrace. She waved, and I waved back.

I told Selak: "You can come along. I'm going to pick up a rug."

He was still staring up at Claire.

She met us at the elevator. She said: "I didn't expect you'd bring a chaperone."

"I thought I might need one. Have you made the appointment?"

She nodded. "For two o'clock. It's Mrs. Harlan Cooke. Do you know her?"

Mrs. Harlan Cooke was a woman of sixty who tried to look forty and looked eighty. "I've sold her a rug or two," I said.

We went into the apartment. Claire asked: "What do you think we could get for that Feraghan?" She paused. "George thought about six thousand—"

"Maybe. And maybe more. I'll get her reaction to the higher figure first."

She was looking uneasily at Selak. Selak's heart was in his eyes. I took him into the room that held the rugs and helped him pull the rug from the pile.

"Wait for me in the car," I said. "I'll be right down."

When he'd left, carrying the rug, Claire asked: "What's the matter with him? Why does he stare at me like that?"

"It's spring," I said. "It's been a long winter."

She studied me. "It's not spring for you, is it? You're all business, today."

"That's my training. The days for business, the nights for romance."

Annoyance was on her face. "There's something wrong, isn't there? You're different from—from last night."

"Maybe. Last night I hadn't met the Turk with the derby nor Sergeant Waldorf. Last night, I didn't know that was Mr. Egan's Bokhara."

She was quiet. She was chewing her lower lip vexedly and thoughtfully.

"I thought I was a partner," I said quietly, "not a stooge."

"Lee—" She looked up pleadingly. "You're not that. You know you're not." She took one of my hands in both of hers. "After you've seen Mrs. Cooke, come back. There isn't time to explain it all now, but I will when you come back."

"All right," I said. "But one thing before I go. How did you make out with Waldorf?"

"How should I make out with him? He was investigating Henri Ducasse's death, and I had nothing to do with that. As for the rug, I told him I'd had it for years. Which is a lie, but I didn't think it was any of his business."

"We'll talk about that, too, later," I said. "Good-bye for now."

She was looking up expectantly. I kissed her and my legs got rubbery again, and I had a hunger I knew pilaff wouldn't satiate.

"O.K.," I said, "it's spring. But I'll want the story just the same, Claire, when I come back. I'll want it straight."

"You'll get the whole story," she said.

CHAPTER THREE
SOUL FOR SALE

Mrs. Harlan Cooke lived in River Hills, the gold coast of this town of mine. She was a very careful woman with a dollar unless the dollar was to be spent for oriental rugs or male companionship. For these two, she would unlatch the roll. She was canny enough to try for both in the same deal. Henri Ducasse had been her boy, there.

A maid opened the door and led the way into a mammoth living room, expensively and ornately furnished.

Mrs. Harlan Cooke was waiting for us in here, posed graciously in a wing-back tapestry chair, smoking a cigarette through a long, ebony and gold holder.

The room was dim; the illusion was almost complete at this distance. But it needed distance. As I came closer, the make-up was too obvious, the sag in her thin figure too evident.

Ducasse, I was beginning to realize, had earned his money.

"Back from the wars?" she said in a high voice. "It's been a long time, Lee." She came forward to greet me.

"You haven't changed," I said. "Nor has this beautiful house. You've the most delicate and artistic taste in this town, Mrs. Cooke."

After that, the chiseling started.

It was a battle. The old girl knew how to dicker, and she held the upper hand, being the buyer. But when Selak spread out the Feraghan, I saw the expression in her eyes as she looked at it and I knew it was just a matter of time. She wanted that rug.

She got it, finally. For seventy-one hundred dollars, which was just four hundred under my opening price and eleven hundred higher than her opening offer.

As she wrote out the check, she said: "I'd expected Mr. Herro to bring the rug. He's still in town, isn't he?"

"I think so," I said. "He was last night. He certainly—admires your taste, Mrs. Cooke. He insisted there was only one customer in town who had the background to appreciate that Feraghan. I would have waited for him to come back this afternoon, but Miss Lynne had another customer who wanted the rug badly, and I wanted you to have the first chance at it." I smiled. "Regular customers first."

"Thank you, Lee," she said, and tried a smile herself. But the makeup threatened to crack, and she killed it half-born. "I wish you would tell Mr. Herro that I'm still in the market for any-thing worthwhile, though."

I felt faintly let down. Not that I believe what Papa says about Tyrone Power, but I didn't expect to run second to George Herro.

"I'll be sure and tell him," I said, and folded the check carefully.

She was frowning, as she walked with me to the door. There, she said; "By the way—who is this Miss Lynne? A friend of—Mr. Herro's?"

"A friend of *mine*," I said, and smiled reas-suringly.

"I see," she said archly. "Well, be sure and tell Geor— Mr. Herro I was asking about him."

This kind of business wasn't for me. My con-science was elastic enough to charge what the traffic will bear, but not enough to trade on an old woman's sentiment. Not that she wasn't a fraud. Not that she wasn't able to take care of herself—and her purse. It was just that I didn't believe a piece of your soul should go with every sale.

I dropped Selak off at the store on the way back.

When I got to the Towers, it was only three o'clock.

Claire said: "It didn't take you long."

I handed her the check. "It was a straight sale," I told her. "Mrs. Cooke's heart belongs to George Herro."

She nodded. "I know. But he's disciplining her. She bought a rug from Henri Ducasse a month ago."

I lighted a cigarette, saying nothing. I went over to stand near the door leading to the terrace. "I don't like this way of doing business, Claire," I said. "We wouldn't lose much if we were care-ful, selling them straight."

"Straight?" She cocked her head to one side. "There wasn't anything crooked about that sale, was there? I don't understand you, Lee."

"You understand me," I said, "and it isn't anything illegal, but I wasn't only selling her a rug; I was selling her a chance to see Herro. I don't like it. It's—messy." I paused. "And now, I'd like to hear the story, the true story, about those rugs."

"Sit down and relax," she said.

I sat down, but I couldn't relax.

"The rugs are Mr. Egan's, as you guessed. He's got a bill of sale for every one of them. He wants to sell out, and because he's known me a long time and trusted me, he's stored them here. He's the one who suggested George Herro. He's the one who suggested you." She paused. "Any-thing illegal in that?"

"Why doesn't he sell them from his house?"

Claire shrugged. "I don't know. He's willing

to sell them to us, to George and me, but neither of us had the money. So we give him a share, as each one is sold."

"His wife knows about it?"

Claire's face stiffened. "I don't—what are you driving at, Lee?"

"She has the money in that family," I said. "Mr. Egan buys some fine rugs with her money. To her, a rug is just a floor covering, and after a number of years must be replaced. After fifteen or twenty years, those rugs haven't lost a nickel of value. He was a very careful buyer. He has a big wad of money in a stack of rugs she considers worthless. Now, he sells out—and gets out?"

"You're guessing," she said. "It isn't fair to Mr. Egan guessing those kind of things about him."

"All right, I'm guessing. I'll find out, later, how well I'm guessing. And now the Turk?"

"Ismet?"

"I don't know his name."

"Ismet Bey," she said. "He ran a cult out in the town of cults, Los Angeles. It was part Mohammedan and part voodoo and part pseudo-science, I guess. He went out of town for a week on a trip with—one of his disciples, and the law stepped in. The disciple's papa had called them in. Ismet left town again when he heard the police were looking for him. His temple furnishings were sold at auction." She shrugged. "George was at the auction."

"That's where he picked up the rug?"

"That's his claim. I don't believe everything George says, though, do you?"

"Not always."

"Well, that's what I know. Your imagination will probably fill in a lot of things that aren't true, but that's my story."

I got up and went out to the terrace. I wanted to think about these things, without looking at her. I couldn't be rational while I was looking at her.

It was phoney enough. It was as phoney as a lead dollar or seemed that way to anybody who was sane. If I was going to get out, now would be the time.

From the doorway, she called: "Scotch, Lee?"

"No," I said. "I'll be running along. I'd like to get over and see Mrs. Egan this afternoon."

"Don't," she said. "It's his business, Lee. You've no right to go messing into his domestic life."

"O.K., I won't. That's answer enough for me. You can count me out of it—as of now."

She stood in the doorway like a statue, her face blank, her body motionless. "Now—what caused that decision?"

"An accumulation of bad angles," I said. "It wasn't any one incident. Let's just pretend we never met."

And then, because the weakness was on the way back, because she looked so startled and innocent there in the doorway, I got out fast.

I didn't look back when I reached the street. I had a hunch she'd be up there on the terrace.

At the store, Papa was in back talking to Selak, his voice high and excited.

When he came back to the front again, he said: "Selak wants to quit. But he won't tell me why." He shook his head.

"He's in love and jealous," I said. "Jealous of me, but you can tell him there's no reason to be."

"So—" Papa said. "So it wasn't all business?"

"It was mostly business, but bad business. I don't want to talk about it."

He shrugged and went over to check his books.

I felt noble and moral and miserable. The trouble was, it was still spring.

The afternoon dragged on. About five, Papa put his books away and said: "I think I'll go home. You can close up, Levon."

We closed at five-thirty. I nodded.

He paused in the doorway for a moment, and I could feel his eyes on me. Finally: "Levon—Berjouhi is beautiful, too."

"I know," I said. "I know. I'm all right. I'm no baby."

Papa sighed. "No . . . All right. I'll see you at supper."

He left and I went back to see Selak. But

Selak wasn't there. I went back into the store, just as Mr. Egan entered.

He's a good-looking gent, despite his years. He's close to sixty, I'd say, but he's the kind of thin, tall gent who can wear clothes. He never had enough troubles in his life to age him.

He seemed exceptionally uncomfortable, his face faintly flushed.

"Good-afternoon, Lee," he said. "Miss Lynne has asked me to explain some things to you."

"It's not necessary, Mr. Egan. You don't owe me any explanations."

"Perhaps not. But I'd like you to understand that—" He paused. "That my wife is fully aware I'm selling those rugs." Again, he paused. "You may phone her right now, if you wish."

"I'll repeat," I said, "that you don't have to explain anything to me, Mr. Egan. I'm out of it."

"That's why I'm explaining," he said. "I— don't want you out of it, Lee. I have too much faith in your sales ability. And too little faith in George Herro's integrity."

I didn't say anything for a moment. I was thinking of Claire.

Mr. Egan said, "This is very embarrassing for me. I'm not conditioned to—to begging, Lee."

It was embarrassing to me, too. Whenever I'd seen the word "gentleman" used, I'd always thought of Mr. Egan. He'd symbolized all the things an ignoramus like me thought of as a gentleman, a cultured person.

But I'd sold a lot of the carriage trade; I wasn't completely naive. I said flatly: "How about that Bokhara, Mr. Egan?"

He frowned. "It's mine, of course."

"I know that. But whose blood was on it?"

"Blood?" His surprise, I felt, was honest. "You're talking in riddles, Lee. I bought that rug from your father, more than twenty years ago. I—"

"Miss Lynne didn't tell you about the blood?"

He shook his head, saying nothing, staring at me.

"There was so much of it," I said, "so much,

it was suspicious. Maybe my imagination was too active. But you see, Henri Ducasse's death was in the papers that same day, and Claire— Miss Lynne—had talked of him. The whole set-up looked bad."

He wasn't listening. "Blood—" he said. "Dry, Lee?"

"Dried. So maybe it wasn't so important. Henri was just killed yesterday, I guess."

He shook his head. "Haven't you read the evening papers? Henri Ducasse was *found* yesterday. He was killed three or four days ago." His eyes were reminiscent. "Ducasse—" he said, and he was talking to himself. His face grew tight. "Lee, we'll talk about this later. Don't decide against us just yet."

He turned and was gone from the store.

It was nearly five-thirty, now. I locked the back door, and turned out the lights in the washing room. I checked the windows back there. In the store, I checked the safe also and set the alarm system.

All this I did automatically, thinking of Claire every second. Even Egan's sudden departure didn't interest me; there didn't seem to be any room in my mind for anything but Claire.

As for Selak, I felt sure he'd be back tomorrow. Grace would talk to him and straighten him out, if he told her he'd quit.

At five-thirty, I got the signal from the alarm system and left.

I went home by way of Prospect Avenue. It isn't the direct route, but I took it for the same perverted reason you'd prod a sore tooth with your tongue.

I didn't look up as I passed the Towers. It was an effort of will, but I managed it. That's how I happened to notice the derby going through the front door, and the narrow back of Ismet Bey.

It wasn't any of my business. I was well out of it. I was due home for supper, and after supper I intended to get drunk.

Only there was this parking space at the curb, beckoning almost, and I slid the convertible into it.

So he'd found the owner of Maksoud's rug.

Or, at least, the possessor. Had he come to make an offer? Or had he come to make a claim? There was danger in this ridiculous little man, I sensed; there was a threat to Claire.

When I reached Claire's door, I could hear their voices inside. I could hear the Turk saying: "It was my rug originally. I know how much it went for at the auction. I don't know what you paid for it, Miss Lynne, but I'm prepared to give you forty thousand dollars for it. In cash, of course."

Claire's voice: "I'll have to talk this over with Mr. Herro."

"It was Mr. Herro," Ismet Bey said, "who sent me to you, Miss Lynne." And now his voice was lower. "I mean to have that rug one way or another, Miss Lynne."

That's when I rang her bell.

She didn't smile when she saw me there. She said: "I can't think of any more you'd want to tell me, Lee."

"I saw Bey come in here." I took a breath. "I worried about you, Claire. I thought—"

"Come in," she said, without expression.

When I entered the living room, Ismet Bey rose and smiled. He bowed slightly. "The boy from the store." He nodded. "We'll make a deal, now?"

"First," Claire said, "I want you to tell Lee the history of your losing the rug, Mr. Bey." Her voice was brittle and she avoided my eyes. "Lee seems to think he's being hoodwinked."

He looked from me to her, and back to me. "Of course." The smile, again, and he seated himself. "As soon as we're all comfortable."

The story he told was substantially the same she'd told me about him. The only difference was that he put his own position in a more favorable light. His trip out of town had been a business trip, purely a business trip.

"That was in January," he told me. "At the auction in February, the rug was sold to settle some claims. I did not know who bought it. I heard only last week that it had come to this town. Today Mr. Herro contacted me and gave me this address and Miss Lynne's name."

"You want to buy it back? For how much, Mr. Bey?"

"For forty thousand dollars."

"You must want it badly."

"Who can value an altar? Who can appraise the symbol of a faith, Mr. Lee? If it were cotton and machine-made, it would still have value under those qualifications. But this—this could conceivably be the work of Maksoud. My disciples believe it is; I almost believe it is myself. There is no proof of this; there can be no proof. But there remains the faith."

"Forty thousand dollars' worth of faith?"

His face grew faintly harder. "We've mentioned the sum enough, I think. It will be cash and no record of the transaction need be made. It will be tax-free money. I am not a poor man, Mr. Lee, and it was the rug which helped to make me a rich one. The price I am suggesting is more than fair. It will be my only offer."

"It's the merchant blood in me," I said. "I like to haggle."

"I am not here for that purpose."

I looked at Claire. "You're the boss."

She looked at Ismet Bey, and I thought I saw uneasiness in her eyes. "It seems like a fair offer to me," she said quietly.

"It's a small rug," I said, "and even if Maksoud wove it, that's a lot of money, an awful lot of money."

"It is settled, then?"

"It's settled," Claire said. "Tomorrow morning, at ten o'clock, here. Bring the money. The rug will be here."

He nodded agreeably and rose.

I said: "Was it Mr. Herro who told you about the rug being in this town, Mr. Bey?"

He looked at me questioningly. Then he nodded.

"You've known him for quite a while?"

"For some time."

"He's—not a *disciple* of yours."

He shook his head. "No. No, I'm afraid faith is not one of Mr. Herro's virtues." He looked down at his derby. "Why do you ask, Mr. Lee?"

"Just curious," I said. "And the name is

Kaprelian, Mr. Bey, Lee Kaprelian. I'm the son of the man who owns that shop."

His smile was dim. "You were fortunate enough, it seems, not to have inherited his disposition. Good-evening, Mr. Kaprelian."

She went with him to the door. When she came back, her face was still grave. "Just a quiz kid, aren't you? I hope you have enough answers now."

Golly, she was beautiful as she stood there, looking down at me. To Papa, Berjouhi was beautiful, but no girl I was ever likely to meet could match Claire, I knew.

"I'm sorry," I said. "I came here, didn't I? I—worried about you. What did you expect, that I'd crawl? How truthful have you been through all this?"

"More questions," she said. "Allan had some, too, after you talked to him. He came up here screaming about the blood on that Bokhara."

Allan was Mr. Egan. I said: "Did you give him a satisfactory answer?"

She said tautly: "Yes. He trusts me."

"And Sergeant Waldorf trusts you?"

"He seemed satisfied."

"You're so beautiful," I said. "You're so damned beautiful. I wonder how your answers would sound if you weren't."

Her face was white; her blue eyes blazed. "We've nothing to say to each other, Lee. Nothing can be gained by this bickering." There was the glint of tears in her eyes. "Oh, why did you have to come back?"

"I don't know," I said. "But I had to, Claire."

And she was in my arms again. She was sobbing in my arms and I was soothing her as well as I could, feeling soft and rotten. But way under the softness, the hard core of my skepticism remained.

I called up Mom and told her I wouldn't be home for supper. I went out and got a couple of steaks and some rolls. Claire broiled the steaks and we ate out on the terrace.

Later, we sat out there and watched the stars, watched the lights of the traffic below, watched the lights of the downtown section grow. There were things about this business I was to regret.

There was nothing about the night I would ever regret or forget.

I like to think she'll never forget it either. Maybe just because for those hours I didn't ask any questions. Or maybe because she'd felt, at least for the moment, some of the emotion many must have felt for her.

It was around midnight when the phone rang, and she went to answer it. It was for me.

It was Papa. "Levon, Selak is with you?"

"No. I haven't seen him. He left the store before I did. I didn't see him leave."

"Grace called, Levon. She's worried. He didn't come home."

"I've no idea where he could be," I said.

A silence on the wire. Then: "Well, maybe it will be all right. Maybe he's with a friend somewhere." Another silence. "Berjouhi called, too."

"O.K., thanks. You'd better notify the police about Selak if he doesn't come home soon."

"That I'll do," he said, and hung up.

Claire said: "What's happened, Lee."

"Selak is missing," I told her.

"Selak?"

"Your silent admirer. That man who works for us. He left the store in a peeve this afternoon and he hasn't come home yet."

Her eyes were wide. "You don't think—" She looked around as though half-expecting to see him standing behind her. "I mean, the way he stared at me and—"

"Last night," I said, "he stood right down there across the street. When I left, he was sleeping in my car."

"He's—harmless, Lee?"

"He has been up to now. I suppose he still is."

We went out onto the terrace, but it wasn't comfortable out there any more. A wind had come to life from the north, and there was a chill to it.

In the living room Claire put a stack of records on the player and called to me: "Mix a drink, will you, Lee?"

I shook my head. "I have to go. I'm worried about Selak. I'll see you in the morning, when I bring the rug over."

"You're worried about that—that man? It's not your concern, Lee."

"Selak's always been my concern. It was my idea that my dad should hire him, and Grace, too."

She shook her head. "All right. It's been a grand evening. I suppose I shouldn't complain."

She came to the door with me and I kissed her. "Sleep tight," I said, "and dream of tomorrow."

She ruffled my hair. "Big day, tomorrow."

Big day, tomorrow. And a bad day, too, though I didn't know it at the time.

The downtown Western Union office was open all night, and it was from there I sent the wires. They were to some dealers I knew on the coast, and in them I inquired about Henri Ducasse.

The rain had started before I went into the telegraph office, and it was worse when I came out. The wind was cold; there was sleet mixed with the raindrops. Our false summer was over.

The wind howled down the Avenue, driving the rain before it. My little convertible was headed directly into it, and she shivered from time to time as the gusts hit.

It all shaped up. I'm no detective, but Ismet Bey had told me something that gave me a sequence. Tinker to Evers to Chance; was that the famous infield? Was that the triple trio, or was it double play?

When I turned into the driveway, the lights were on in the living room and on the porch. I could see Papa in the living room talking to someone. When I came up on the porch, I could see who it was. Sergeant Waldorf. He was working late; it was after one.

His eyes appraised me as I came into the living room.

"Anything about Selak?" I asked Papa.

He shook his head. "The sergeant thinks it has something to do with Henri Ducasse. And you didn't tell him about the rug, Levon, about the Bokhara."

Waldorf still hadn't said anything. I said: "How about Dykstra? Have you talked to him?"

"Dykstra's in the clear all the way," the sergeant said. "I've no idea where that rumor started."

Papa said: "I told him it was Mr. Egan's rug, Levon. He's been checking Mr. Egan."

I looked at the sergeant. He was still appraising me. I said: "You came here to see me, Sergeant?"

"More or less. Egan was in to see you just before you closed this evening, wasn't he?"

"That's right."

"What did he want?"

"That's a short question," I said, "but it would require a long answer. I'd have to give you some background first, Sergeant."

Somewhere a door slammed, and I could hear the wind roll the garbage can over.

"I've stayed up this long," Sergeant Waldorf said. "I may as well stay up a little longer and hear your story."

I told him about Egan, Herro and Bey. I told him some of the things about Claire. Papa sat there while I talked and missed none of it. The sergeant didn't interrupt me once.

"And his wife knows he's selling them?"

"He said she did. He said I could ask her."

"Does his wife know Miss Lynne has them?"

"I don't know if she does or not."

"Does she know they planned to leave town together?"

My heart stopped, I was sure. I couldn't get my breath for a second. "You're kidding, Sergeant."

"No, but she might be."

"Mr. Egan's a—he's old," I said. "It doesn't make sense."

"The older the wackier," he said. "I'm no spring chicken, myself, but I can't think of anybody I wouldn't leave, if *she* wanted me to." His voice was weary. He rose. "Well, I'll see this Mrs. Egan tomorrow." He looked at me quietly a moment. "You want to come out to the porch a second?"

Papa frowned, but I said: "Sure."

Out there, the sergeant smiled. I could hardly hear his voice, above the sound of the rain and the wind. "Anything you want to tell me privately? How bad you might be involved, I mean?"

I shook my head. "I gave it to you straight, Sergeant. You're positive Dykstra's in the clear?"

"Positive. Nobody I'd rather nail, but he's clean."

"All day," I said, "I've been worrying about this. All day I've been hoping against hope that it was Dykstra. I don't know the man, so that wasn't fair."

Sergeant Waldorf was looking out at the rain. He seemed to be miles away. He said: "She's a beauty, kid. I've never seen anyone like her. Years ago, I felt as you did tonight, and this babe didn't have half of what that Lynne girl's got." He turned to face me. "I'll try to keep it as clean as I can. You ought to get an answer to those wires in the morning, don't you think?"

I nodded.

He put a hand on my shoulder. "O.K. I'll see you in the morning. It's been a long day." Then he was trotting through the rain to the department car.

In the living room, Papa still sat in the chair he'd occupied through my recital. He looked at me sadly. He started to say something, then changed his mind. He rose.

"Time for bed, Levon," he said. "Another day, tomorrow."

Another day, big day, bad day . . . Outside, the wind grew stronger, and I wondered if Selak was out there somewhere in that wet, miserable night.

From upstairs, Mom called: "Is that you, Levon? Nishan, is Levon home?"

"Levon's home," Papa said. His voice was as sad as his face. I couldn't sleep that night. Didn't sleep. Laid down on the bed and thought about Claire. Sat up and watched the storm wear itself out, and thought about Claire.

I thought about Selak, too, but mostly about Claire.

At breakfast Ann and Mom had enough to talk about, so my silence and Papa's weren't so noticeable.

At eight-thirty, I was at the store. At nine, Sergeant Waldorf came in.

"You put in a long day, don't you, Sergeant?" I said.

"It's not usually this bad," he said. "I've just been over to Egan's. She knows, all right. He told her he expected to get at least five thousand dollars for that pile of rugs."

I shook my head.

"That seem reasonable to you?"

"There might be twenty rugs up there," I said. "I didn't count them, but that's a good guess, I'd say. I sold one of them yesterday. I sold it for *seventy-one hundred dollars*, Sergeant."

He whistled. He said: "Oh, oh." He shook his head. "So that's the angle. He gets a nice wad, clear, and he and Miss Lynne take off on the luxury trail. Or that's what he hopes, huh? She'd have the money, wouldn't she? And it might be good-bye, Mr. Egan."

"I don't know," I said.

"You look tired, kid. No sleep?"

"No."

He went over to the window. It was a gray day, outside. The rain had stopped, but the chill was still with us.

"You didn't get an answer to those wires, yet?"

"Not yet."

He turned. "I'm going out to get a cup of coffee. I'll be back before you leave with the rug."

There was one answer to my wires when he came back. It read:

Ducasse was out here in January and February. Made a few deals, but nothing sensational that I heard of. It's a bad town for orientals, as you know.

Jack.

Sergeant Waldorf looked at me when he'd finished reading it. "It still doesn't prove anything. I'll need more than that." He was looking thoughtful. "You take the rug up there and get your money from Bey. Find out what you can. I've an angle or two to check, yet."

He left then, and I went to the safe, got out the prayer-rug. Papa came in as I was looking at it.

"Selak came home at three o'clock," he told me. "Grace called. He left again around six. Where do you think he goes?"

I shrugged. I said: "I'm going to take this rug up to Miss Lynne. I'll be back before lunch."

He nodded, saying nothing. He went back to the washing room, as I went out with the Maksoud masterpiece.

There wasn't much traffic; the weather was keeping the shoppers at home. I made time getting to the Towers, even though I was earlier than I'd promised.

George Herro was there when Claire let me in. And so was Ismet Bey. We were all early.

The Turk's black eyes were gleaming as he looked at the rug. His face was enraptured.

"It's worth the money," I said.

He looked up at me. "Yes. About the money. I said cash, I know. This is the same." He handed me the check.

It was a cashier's check for forty thousand dollars, on the First National Bank. It was made out to George Herro.

"You've made it out to Mr. Herro," I said.

He nodded quickly and his bird eyes were shadowed. "That was all right with Miss Lynne."

I looked at George Herro. "And it would be all right with you, too, wouldn't it?"

His hard old eyes met mine. "Why shouldn't it be?"

"You can prove ownership?"

"For heaven's sakes, Lee," Claire said, "you're not going back to the questions again, are you?"

I didn't look at her. I continued to look at George Herro.

"What's on your mind, Lee," he asked.

"Murder," I said. "You didn't pick this rug up at the auction, George. The auction was in February. You were in Europe, then."

"Oh. Who did pick it up at auction?"

"Henri Ducasse," I said.

Ismet Bey was looking at George. Then he was looking at me: "Henri Ducasse? He is the man who was murdered?"

I nodded. "He knew rugs, too. He knew he had a good buy. But he didn't know the history of this one. You did as soon as he showed it to you, George. And you can read Arabic."

George Herro was very quiet in his chair. The hardness in his face had brought out his age and his cynicism.

I looked at Claire and tried to smile. "Baby, why don't you come clean? You're in fast company with George. I thought, at first, that the blood might have got on that Bokhara at Egan's house. But it was too much of a surprise to him. Ducasse was killed here, wasn't he, in your dining room?"

She was ready to crack up, again, just as she had last night. Her face was tight, her body rigid, as she stared at me.

Herro said: "Mr. Bey, I believe our transaction is completed. Thank you very much for the check. And good-bye."

The little Turk gave us all one last glance before nodding. He folded the rug carefully and walked out. Nobody went to the door with him.

"And now," George said, "I'll have the rest of your ridiculous story, Lee."

"It's all guesswork," I said. I paused. "The first deal," I said, "was between Claire and Egan. Egan wanted the rugs sold from here, so his wife wouldn't know what he was getting for them. You were called in, George, as the kind of salesman who could get the last dollar out of them. I'd say Ducasse heard about the deal and came here to chisel in on it. Henri was your biggest competitor, George, and he usually knew what you were doing. He brought the Maksoud piece along as an inducement, maybe, to let him in on the deal?"

Herro said nothing, nor did he move in his chair.

I looked at Claire. "That's right, isn't it?"

She nodded, still in that trance-like stage.

"For a rug like that one," I went on, "a man like you would go pretty far, George. As far as murder." And now I tried a lie. "We'll know if that was Ducasse's blood on the Bokhara. The police lab has a sample of the blood from the wash water, now."

That got to him. He stirred in his chair. He opened his mouth to say something, then closed it again.

I said: "You started the rumor about Dykstra among the dealers. You saw all the dealers from time to time, working on consignment as you do, and you started the rumor to throw Waldorf off the trail."

He said nothing.

"I don't know why Claire came down to the shop," I said, "but maybe it was at Egan's suggestion. Maybe she wanted an outside appraisal of those rugs, just to make sure you weren't holding out. And maybe they wanted a legitimate dealer in the business to give it some tone." I looked at her. "Was that it?"

I said: "You overestimate yourself, Claire. You're too young for a couple of old men like Egan and this one. You've been kidding yourself, Claire. You're too young and too soft."

She was crying. She said, "Lee, there was nothing between us. They were—" She put her face down into her hands.

"They were stooges, you thought," I finished for her. "Maybe Egan would be. But you don't know this Herro, baby. You don't know him like I do."

Herro's voice was an Arctic wind. "You don't know me well enough either, Lee. You didn't think I'd come to a deal like this unprepared, did you?"

He was still sitting in the chair. But now there was a gun in his hand. It was an automatic. It wasn't a big gun, but it was big enough to kill.

Claire looked up quickly and some ejaculation escaped her throat.

The gun was pointing at me. Herro said: "She won't talk as much as you hope for, Lee. She didn't see me kill him, but she knows I did. And that would get her some time in jail. She's too soft; you're right about that. Jail is rough on the soft ones." His smile was thin and cruel. "I'll take the check, now."

"Come and get it," I said.

"Don't fool with me, Lee. Bring it over."

Claire said: "Give it to him, Lee. You aren't involved in this. Don't get involved with him." Her voice was high.

In Herro's hand, the gun lifted. In Herro's eyes, I saw death. He would kill.

Then Claire was up, standing in front of me shielding me, facing the gun. "George, you'll get the check. Don't—"

That's when Selak walked in.

I'd left the door unlocked hoping Waldorf might break in on something incriminating. But I was glad to see anybody, including Selak.

He looked like a drowned grizzly bear. His face was black with beard, his rough hair matted, his dull eyes glaring. The gun, you see, was pointing at his Claire.

The sound that came from his big throat was nothing that could be called human, a rough, threatening grunt.

Herro turned to face him as I rose, to get away from behind Claire. Herro's gun was pointing at Selak, and Herro talked to him in broken Armenian.

Selak kept coming—and the gun jumped in Herro's hand.

Selak trembled as the slug hit him, but he kept coming. I was almost to Herro, now; I grabbed his wrist and twisted it as Selak closed.

The gun fell to the floor, but Selak's big arm sent me sprawling.

Then Selak had lifted George off his feet by the throat and one leg, and he lifted him high.

I heard Claire scream as Selak headed for the terrace doors, still carrying the struggling Herro high above his head.

I was up as Selak smashed through the doors, kicking them open. I was up and scrambling after him. . . .

I was out on the terrace and shouting at Selak as he stood there on the edge and now Herro was screaming.

I reached Selak, grabbed him blindly by the neck from behind—just as he tossed George Herro over the edge. . . .

Waldorf came five minutes later. I'd called

the ambulance by that time for Selak. Somebody had called the police.

I told Waldorf all about it, and Claire told him her part, not sparing herself. Selak died, in the hospital, while we were still talking.

When we'd finished, Waldorf said: "I'll do what I can, but you can count on five years, anyway, Miss Lynne."

Papa says I'm foolish. He says all young men have experiences of one kind or another, and the thing to do is to forget them. He says there's no sense in writing to her every week, up there, and going up, once a month. Papa says five years is a long time for a young man to wait, an awful long time.

As though I don't know it.

A Taste for Cognac
Brett Halliday

BRETT HALLIDAY WAS ONE of the pseudonyms of the prolific Davis Dresser (1904–1977). Born in Chicago, he spent his childhood in Texas, where he ran away from home at the age of fourteen to join the army until his true age was discovered when he was sixteen. He returned to school and received a civil engineering certificate but, when work was hard to come by during the Great Depression, began to write, turning out scores of mystery, Western, romance, adventure, and sex stories for the pulps. His first novel, *Mum's the Word for Murder* (1938), was published under the pseudonym Asa Baker, as was his second, *The Kissed Corpse* (1939). He also wrote as Matthew Blood, Peter Shelley, Anthony Scott, Hal Debrett, and many other pseudonyms.

It was with the character Michael Shayne, however, that Dresser found success. Based on a character he had met while working in Mexico on an oil tanker, the big redheaded private eye was one of the most popular detectives of the '40s, '50s, and '60s, with more than sixty novels, numerous short stories and novelettes, a magazine named for him, a radio series (starring Jeff Chandler), a television series (starring Richard Denning), and a dozen movies in the 1940s, the first seven of which starred Lloyd Nolan, while the final five saw Hugh Beaumont portraying a tough but humorous Shayne. One Shayne vehicle, *Time to Kill* (1942), was based on a Raymond Chandler novel, *The High Window,* with Philip Marlowe displaced by Shayne.

"A Taste for Cognac" was published in the November 1944 issue.

A Taste
for Cognac

Brett Halliday

CHAPTER ONE
MONNET '26

"You're horning in on things that don't concern you," the voice over the phone cautioned Mike Shayne. An unnecessary and futile warning, since the red-haired private shamus was always concerned with murder and lovely maidens in distress—particularly when his experienced nostrils sniffed a case of rare pre-war Monnet cognac as the payoff!

MICHAEL SHAYNE HESITATED inside the swinging doors, looked down the row of men at the bar and then strolled past the wooden booths lining the wall, glancing in each one as he went by.

Timothy Rourke wasn't at

the bar and he wasn't in any of the booths. Shayne frowned and turned impatiently toward the swinging doors.

A voice called, "Mr. Shayne?" when he reached the third booth from the end.

He stopped and looked down at the girl alone in the booth. She was about twenty, smartly dressed, with coppery hair parted in the middle and lying in smooth waves on either side of her head. She didn't wear any make-up and her small face had a pinched look. Her eyes were brown and shone with alert intelligence. Her left hand clasped a glass half-filled with dead beer as she smiled at Shayne.

The Miami detective took off his hat and stood flat-footed looking down at her. Lights above the bar behind him cast shadows on his gaunt cheeks. He lifted his left eyebrow and asked: "Do I know you?"

Shayne flung himself to the ground, jerking the car door open. Slim's and Pug's guns flashed in the sunlight as fire blazed from the back seat.

"You're going to." The girl tilted her head sideways and looked wistful. "I'll buy a drink."

"Why didn't you say so?" Shayne slid into the bench opposite her.

A waiter hurried over and the girl said, "Cognac," happily, watching Shayne for approval.

The detective said: "Make it into a sidecar, Joe." The waiter nodded and went away.

"But Tim said cognac was your password," the girl protested. "That you never drank anything else."

"Tim?" Shayne arched a bushy red brow.

"Tim Rourke. He thought you might tell me about some of your cases. I do feature stuff for a New York syndicate. Tim couldn't make it tonight. He's been promising to introduce me to you, so I came on to meet you here instead. I'm Myrna Hastings."

Shayne said bitterly: "When you order cognac these days you get lousy grape brandy. California '44. It's drinkable mixed into a sidecar. This damned war . . ."

"It's a shame your drinking habits have been upset by the war. Tragic, in fact." Myrna Hastings took a sip of her flat beer and made a little grimace.

Shayne lit a cigarette and tossed the pack on the table between them. Joe brought his sidecar and he watched Myrna take a dollar bill from her purse and lay it on the table. Shayne lifted the slender cocktail glass to his lips and said: "Thanks." He drank half of the mixture and his gray eyes became speculative. Holding it close to his nose, he inhaled deeply and a frown rumpled his forehead.

Joe was standing at the table when Shayne drained his glass. "I've changed my mind, Joe. Bring me a straight cognac—a double shot in a beer glass."

Joe grinned slyly and went away.

Sixty cents in change from Myrna's dollar bill lay on the table. She poked at the silver and asked dubiously: "Will that be enough for a double shot?"

"It'll be eighty cents," Shayne replied.

She smiled and took a quarter from her purse. "Tim says you've always avoided publicity, but it'll be a wonderful break for me if I can write up a few of your best cases."

The waiter brought a beer glass with two ounces of amber fluid in the bottom, took Myrna Hastings' eighty-five cents, and went away.

Shayne lifted the beer glass to his nose, closed his eyes and breathed deeply of the bouquet, then began to warm the glass with his hands.

"Tim thinks you should let yourself in on some publicity," the girl continued. "He thinks it's a shame you don't ever take the credit for solving so many tough cases."

Shayne looked at her for an instant, then slowly emptied his glass and set it down. He picked up his cigarettes and hat and said: "Thanks for the drinks. I never give out any stories. Tim Rourke knows that."

He got up and strode to the rear end of the bar. Joe sidled down to him and Shayne said: "I could use another shot of that stuff. And I'll pour my own."

Joe got a clean beer glass and set a tall bottle on the bar before Shayne. He glanced past the detective at the girl sitting alone in the booth, but didn't say anything.

The label on the bottle read, *MONTERREY GRAPE BRANDY—Guaranteed 14 months old.*

Shayne pulled out the cork and passed the open neck of the bottle back and forth under his nose. He asked Joe: "Got any more of this same brand?"

"Jeez, I dunno. I'll see, Mr. Shayne." He went away and returned presently with a sealed bottle bearing the same label.

Shayne broke the seal and pulled the cork. He grimaced as the smell of raw grape brandy assailed his nostrils. He said angrily: "This isn't the same stuff."

"Says so right on the bottle," Joe argued, and pointed to the label.

"I don't give a damn what the label says," Shayne growled. He reached for the first bottle and poured a drink into the empty beer mug. Keeping a firm grip on the bottle with his left hand he drank from the mug, rolling the liquor around his tongue. His gray eyes shone with dreamy contentment as he lingeringly swallowed the brandy, while a frown of curiosity and confusion formed between them.

"Any more of the bar bottles already opened?" he asked Joe.

"I don't think so. We don't open 'em but one at a time nowadays. I'll ask the barkeep." Plainly mystified by Shayne's request, Joe went to the front of the bar and held a whispered conference with a bald-headed man wearing a dirty apron that bulged over a pot-belly.

The bartender glanced back at Shayne, waddled toward him. He looked at the two bottles, and asked: "'Sa trouble here?"

Shayne shrugged his wide shoulders. "No trouble. Your bar bottle hasn't got the same stuff that's in the sealed one."

The hulking man looked troubled. "You know how 'tis these days. A label don't mean nothin' no more. We're lucky to stay open at all."

Shayne said: "I know it's tough trying to keep a supply."

"You're private, huh? Ain't I seen you 'round?"

Shayne said: "I'm private. This hasn't anything to do with the law."

The bartender regarded Shayne for a moment with murky, bulging eyes. "If you got a kick about the drink, it'll be on the house," he decided magnanimously.

"I'm not kicking," Shayne told him earnestly. "I'd like to buy what's left in this bottle." He indicated the partially empty one which he had moved out of the bartender's reach.

The man shook his head slowly. "No can do. Our license says we gotta sell it by the drink."

Shayne held the bottle up and squinted through it. "There's maybe twenty ounces left. It's worth ten bucks to me."

The big man continued to shake his head. "You can drink it here. Forty cents a shot."

"Maybe I could make a deal with the boss."

"Maybe." He waddled around the end of the bar and preceded Shayne to an unmarked door to the left of the ladies' room. Shayne saw Myrna Hastings still sitting in the booth watching him.

The bartender rapped lightly on the door, turned the knob and motioned Shayne inside.

enry Renaldo was seated at a desk facing the doorway. He was a big flabby man with a florid face. He wore a black derby tilted back on his bullet head, and an open gray vest revealed the sleeves and front of a shirt violently striped with reddish purple. He was eating a frayed black cigar that had spilled ashes down the front of his vest.

The bartender stood in the doorway behind Shayne and said heavily: "This shamus is kickin' about the service, boss. I figured you might wanna handle it."

Renaldo's black eyes took in the brandy bottle dangling from Shayne's fingers, and they became unguarded for a moment. He wet his lips, said, "O.K., Tiny," and the bartender went out.

Renaldo leaned over the desk to push out his right hand. "Long time no see, Mike."

Shayne disregarded the proffered hand. "I didn't know you were in this racket, Renaldo."

"Sure. I went legal when prohibition went out."

Shayne moved forward, set the bottle down with a little thump and said mildly: "This is a new angle on me."

"How's that?"

"Pre-war cognac under a cheap domestic label. Monnet, isn't it?"

"You must be nuts," Renaldo ejaculated.

"Either you or me," Shayne agreed. "Forty cents a throw when it'd easily bring a dollar a slug in the original bottle."

Henry Renaldo was beginning to breathe hard. "What's it to you, Shayne? Stooging for the Feds?"

Shayne shook his head. He lifted the bottle to his lips, let cognac gurgle down his throat and murmured reverently: "Monnet, Vintage of '26."

Henry Renaldo started and fear showed in his eyes. "How'd you . . ." He paused, taking the frayed cigar carefully from his lips. "Who sent you here?"

"I followed my nose."

Renaldo shook his head. He said huskily: "I don't know how you got onto it, but why jump me?" His voice rose passionately. "If I pass it out for cheap stuff, is that a crime?"

Shayne said: "You could make more selling it by the bottle to a guy like me."

Renaldo spread out his hands. "I gotta stay in business. I gotta have something to sell over the bar. If I can hang on till after the war . . ."

Comprehension showed on Shayne's face. "That's why you're refilling legal bottles."

"What other out is there?" Renaldo demanded. "Government inspectors checking my stock."

"All right, but let me in on it," Shayne urged. "A case or two for my private stock . . ."

"I only got a few bottles."

"But you know where there's more."

"Make your own deal," Renaldo said sullenly.

"Sure. All I want is the tip-off."

"Who sent you to me?"

"No one," Shayne insisted. "I dropped in for a drink. And got slugged with Monnet when I ordered cheap brandy."

"Nuts," sneered Renaldo. "You couldn't pull the year on that vintage stuff. I don't know what the gimmick is. . . ."

A rear door opened and two men came in hastily. They stopped in their tracks and stared at the detective seated on one corner of Renaldo's desk. One of them was short and squarish, with a swart face and a whiskered mole on his chin. He wore fawn-colored slacks and a canary-yellow sweater that was tight over bulging muscles.

His companion was tall and lean, with a pallid face and the humid eyes of a cokie. He was hatless and wore a tightly belted suit. He thinned his lips against sharp teeth and tilted his head to study Shayne.

Renaldo snarled: "You took long enough. How'd you make out, Blackie?"

"It wasn't no soap, boss. He ain't talkin'."

"Hell, you followed him out of here."

"Sure we did, boss," Blackie said earnestly. "Just like you said. To a little shack on the beach on Eighteenth. But he had company when he got there. There was this car parked in front, see? So Lennie an' me waited. Half an hour, maybe. Then a guy come out an' drove away, an' we goes in. But we're too late. He's croaked."

"Croaked?"

"So help me. Then we beats it straight back."

Renaldo said sourly to Shayne. "Looks like that fixes it for us both."

Shayne said: "Give me all of it."

"Can't hurt now," Renaldo muttered defensively. "This bird comes in with a suitcase this evening. It's loaded with twenty-four bottles of Monnet, 1926, like you know. It's pre-war, sealed with no revenue stamps. All he wants is a hundred, so what can I lose? I can't put it out there where an inspector will see it, but I can refill legal bottles and keep my customers happy. So I give him a C and try to pry loose where there's more but he swears that's all there is and beats it. So I send Blackie and Lennie to see can they make a deal. You heard the rest."

"Why yuh spillin' your guts to this shamus?" Lennie rasped suddenly. "Ain't he the law?"

"Shayne's private," Renaldo told him. "He was trying to horn in. . . ." He paused, his jaw dropping. "Maybe you know more about it than I do, Shayne."

"Maybe he does." Lennie's voice rose excitedly. "Looks to me like the mug that came out an' drove away, don't he, Blackie?"

Blackie said: "Sorta. We didn't get to see him good," he explained to Renaldo. "He was dressed like that—an' big."

All three of them looked at Shayne suspiciously. Renaldo said: "So that's how—" He jerked the cigar from his mouth and asked angrily: "What'd you get out of him before he kicked off? Maybe we can make a deal, huh? You're plenty on the spot with him dead."

Shayne said: "Nuts. I don't know anything."

"How'd you know about the Monnet?"

"I dropped in for a drink and knew it wasn't domestic stuff as soon as I tasted it."

"Maybe. But that didn't spell out Monnet, '26. Now my boy'll keep quiet if . . ."

Shayne slid off the desk. His gray eyes were very bright. He said dispassionately: "You're a fool, Renaldo. Your boys are feeding you a line. It's my hunch they messed things up and are afraid to admit it to you. So they make up a fairy tale about someone else getting there first, and you swallow it." He laughed indulgently. "Think it over and you'll see who's really on the spot." He turned toward the door.

Blackie got in front of him. He stood lightly on the balls of his feet and a blackjack swung from his right hand. Behind him, Lennie crouched forward with his gun hand bunched in his coat pocket. His pallid face was contorted and he panted: "Don't you listen to him, boss. Blackie an' me can both identify him."

Shayne turned and told Renaldo: "You'd better call them off. I've a friend waiting outside and if anything happens to me in here you'll have a lot of explaining to do."

"If I turn you over for murder . . ."

Shayne said: "Try it." He turned toward the door again, the open bottle of cognac clutched laxly in his left hand.

Blackie remained poised with the blackjack between him and the door. He appealed to Renaldo: "If it was him out there an' the old gink talked before he passed out . . ."

A sharp rapping on the door behind Blackie interrupted him. A grin pulled Shayne's lips away from his teeth. He said: "My friend is getting impatient."

Renaldo said: "Skip it, Blackie."

Shayne went past the dark, sweatered man to the door and opened it. Myrna Hastings stood outside. "If you think—" she began.

He took her arm firmly and pulled the door shut behind him. He slid the uncorked bottle into his coat pocket and started toward the front with her. She twisted to look back at the closed door, and said uncertainly: "Those men inside. Didn't one of them have a weapon?"

He said: "You're an angel and I was a louse to treat you as I did." They went out through the swinging doors and he stopped on the sidewalk. "Keep on being an angel and beat it. I have things to do."

Myrna looked up into his face and was frightened by what she saw there. "Something *is* wrong. I felt it when you acted so funny."

He shrugged and said: "Maybe this'll be a case you can write up." He went to his sedan parked at the curb and started to get in.

"Can't I go with you?" Myrna asked breathlessly. "I promise not to be in the way."

He took hold of both her elbows and turned her about. "This is murder, kid. I'll tell you about it tomorrow."

CHAPTER TWO
THE EMACIATED CORPSE

hayne drove out Biscayne Boulevard and turned right on Eighteenth Street. A slim crescent of a moon rode high in the cloudless sky overhead and the Miami night was humidly warm. He drove slowly to the end of the street and stopped his car against a low stone barrier overlooking the bayfront.

He turned off his motor and lights and sat for a moment gripping the steering wheel. Light glowed through two round, heavily glassed windows in a low, square stone structure at his left. It sat boldly on the very edge of the bluff overlooking the bay, and a neat shell-lined walk led up to the front door.

Shayne got out and went up the walk. The little house was built solidly of porous limestone and its only windows were round, metal-framed portholes that looked as though they might have been taken from a ship. The door had a heavy bronze knocker, and the hinges and lock were also of bronze.

Shayne tried the knob and the door opened inward easily. A square ship's lantern fitted with an electric bulb hung from a hand-hewn beam of cypress in a narrow, cypress-paneled hallway. An open door to the right showed the interior of a neat and tiny kitchen. Shayne went down the hall to another door opening off to the right. The room was dark and he fumbled along the wall until he found a light switch. It lighted two wrought-iron ship's lanterns similar to the one in the hall. Shayne stood in the doorway and tugged at his left earlobe and looked at the man lying huddled in the middle of the bare floor.

He was dead.

A big-framed man, his face was bony and emaciated. His eyes were wide open and glazed, bulging from deep sockets. He wore a double-breasted uniform of shiny blue serge with a double row of polished brass buttons down the front. His ankles were wired together, and wire had cut deeply into his wrists.

Shayne went in and knelt beside the body. Three fingernails had been torn from his right hand. These appeared to be the only marks of violence on his body, which was warm enough to indicate that death had occurred only half an hour or so before. Shayne judged that shock and pain had brought on a heart attack, causing death. He was about sixty and there was no padding of flesh on his bony frame.

Shayne rocked back on his heels and looked morosely around the room, which was bare of furniture except for a built-in padded settee along one wall. Bare and scrupulously clean, the room had the appearance of a cell.

Shayne wiped sweat from his face and went through the dead man's pockets. He found nothing but a newspaper clipping and the torn stub of a bus ticket. The ticket had been issued the previous day, round-trip from Miami to Homestead, a small town on the Florida Keys.

The clipping was a week old, from the Miami *Herald*. It was headed, PAROLE GRANTED.

Shayne started to read the item, then stiffened at the sound of a car stopping outside. He thrust the clipping and ticket stub in his pocket.

He heard footsteps coming up the walk and the voices of men outside. He got out a cigarette and lit it, blew out the match to look up with

lifted brows at the bulky figure of Detective Chief Will Gentry in the doorway.

Shayne said, "Dr. Livingston?" and Gentry snorted angrily. He was a big man with heavy features and a solid, forthright manner. He was an old friend of Shayne's and he said scathingly: "I thought I smelled something."

Shayne stepped aside and nodded toward the body on the floor. "He hasn't been dead long enough to stink."

Gentry strode forward and scowled down at the body. A tall, white-haired man hurried in behind the chief. He wore an immaculate white linen suit and his features were sharp and clean. He stopped at the sight of the body and said: "Oh my God, is he—"

Gentry grunted: "Yeah." He knelt by the dead man and asked Shayne in a tone of casual interest: "Why'd you pull out his fingernails?"

The tall man exclaimed in a choked voice: "Good heavens! Has he been tortured?"

"Who is he?" Shayne asked sharply.

"It's Captain Samuels," the white-haired man said. "I knew something must have happened to him, Chief, when he wasn't here to keep his appointment with me. If only I'd called you earlier . . ."

"What are you doing here?" Gentry's eyes bored into Shayne's.

"I was driving by and saw the lights. I don't know." Shayne shrugged. "As you said, something just seemed to smell wrong. I stopped to take a look and that's what I found."

"I suppose you can prove all that?" scoffed Gentry.

"Can you disprove it?"

"Maybe not, but you're holding out plenty. Damn it, Mike, this is murder. What do you know about it?"

"Nothing. I've told you how I drove by—"

Will Gentry raised his voice to call: "Jones. You and Rafferty bring in the cuffs."

A voice answered from the front door and feet tramped down the hall. At the same time there was the light click of heels outside and Myrna Hastings came in breathlessly from the rear end of the hall. "You don't need to cover up for me, Mike," she cried out. "Go ahead and tell them I asked you to stop here. Oh! It's Chief Gentry, isn't it?"

Gentry muttered: "I don't think—"

"Don't you remember me?" Myrna laughed. "Timothy Rourke introduced me to you in your office today. I do feature stuff for a New York syndicate. You see, I'm to blame for Mike stopping here tonight. I'd heard about Captain Samuels, about his shipwreck and all years ago, and I thought he might be material for an article. So I asked Mike to stop for a minute tonight and—well, that's how it was."

"Why didn't you tell me that?" Gentry growled at Shayne.

"I think he had some idea of protecting me," Myrna laughed merrily. "You see, I didn't tell him *why* I wanted to stop, and then when he found the dead man, well, I guess maybe Mike thought I knew something about it. Wasn't that it, darling?" She turned to Shayne.

"Something like that," he said stiffly.

"All right, Jones," Gentry said to one of the two dicks hovering in the doorway. "Put your bracelets away and go over the house."

"Now that you've got me cleared up," Shayne suggested, "why not tell me about it?"

"I don't know any more about it than you do," Gentry admitted. "Mr. Guildford called a while ago and asked me to come out here with him. Seems he had a hunch something had happened to Captain Samuels."

"I felt sure of it after I had time to think things over," the white-haired man said. "I had a definite appointment here with the captain for nine tonight and I waited almost half an hour for him."

Shayne said: "It's almost eleven now. Why did you wait so long before calling the police?"

"I had a flat tire just as I reached the boulevard driving away," Guildford explained. "I had it changed at the filling station there and was delayed. I called upon reaching home."

Shayne said: "Were the lights burning while you waited?"

"No. I'm quite sure they weren't. The house was dark and apparently empty."

"What was your appointment for?" Shayne pressed him.

Guildford hesitated. He glanced at Will Gentry. "I don't mind answering official questions, but what is this man's connection with the case? And the young lady?"

"None," Gentry said. "You can beat it, Mike, unless you feel like telling the truth."

"But we have told the truth," Myrna asserted, her eyes wide and childlike. "We were just—"

Shayne took her arm tightly. He said, "Come on," and led her out the door.

 either of them said anything until they were in Shayne's car headed back for the boulevard. Then Myrna leaned her head against his shoulder and asked in a small voice: "Are you terribly angry at me, Mike?"

"How did you get in that house?"

"You brought me. I hid in the trunk compartment of your car. Then I slipped in the house while you were searching the body. I was in the rear bedroom all the time, and when I heard you getting the third degree I knew you didn't want to tell the truth and I thought I'd better stick my oar in. Didn't I do all right?"

"How did you know the captain's name, about him being shipwrecked?"

Myrna chuckled. "I found an old log-book by his bed. I had my flashlight and there was a clipping in the book." She patted a large suede handbag in her lap. "I've got the book in here. It made a pretty good story if I did think of it on the spur of the moment—the one I told Inspector Gentry, I mean," she amended, and chuckled again.

"Why did you hide in the back of my car?" Shayne asked angrily.

"Because you were trying to get rid of me and I wanted to see the famous Shayne in action," she said. "But I must say you didn't do much detecting out there."

Shayne braked suddenly in front of an apartment building on the riverfront.

"I live here," he told her, and went toward a side entrance.

Myrna Hastings went with him. She said hopefully: "I'm dying to taste whatever is in that bottle you've got in your coat pocket."

She waited quietly behind Shayne in the hallway while he unlocked his apartment door. He went inside and switched on the lights and she followed him into a square living room with windows on the east side. There was a studio couch along one wall, and a door on the right opened into a kitchenette. Another door on the left led into the bath and bedroom.

Shayne tossed his hat on a wall hook and went into the kitchen without a word or glance for Myrna.

He soon came back from the kitchen with two four-ounce wine glasses and two tumblers filled with ice water. He walked past her, ranged the four glasses in a row on the table, and filled the wine glasses nearly to the brim with cognac. He pushed one of the tumblers toward Myrna, and set the smaller glass within easy reach of her hand, then pulled another chair to the table and sat down half-facing her.

It was very quiet in the apartment, very restful. Shayne sighed when he drained the last drop from his glass of Monnet. He frowned at the portion remaining in Myrna's glass. "Don't you appreciate good liquor?"

She smiled and told him: "It's so good I'm making it last."

Shane lit a cigarette and spun the match away into a corner, then got the purloined clipping and bus ticket stub from his pocket. He laid the stub on the table and read the short clipping aloud. It was an AP dispatch from Atlanta, Georgia.

It stated that John Grossman, suspected prohibition-era racketeer, sentenced to federal prison in 1930 on income tax charges from Miami, Florida, had been released that day on parole. Grossman announced his intention to take a long vacation at his fishing lodge on the Keys.

When Shayne finished reading the clipping aloud, he placed it beside the ticket stub and told Myrna: "Those two items were the only things I found in the dead man's pockets."

"You didn't tell the police about them?"

He shook his head in slow negation.

"Isn't that against the law? Concealing murder evidence? Who's John Grossman and why was the old sea captain interested in the clipping about his parole?"

Shayne said slowly: "I remember Grossman. He was one of our big-time bootleggers with a select clientele willing to pay plenty for high-class imported stuff. Like Monnet cognac. I don't know why the captain was interested in Grossman's release."

"What's it all about, Mike?" Myrna leaned forward eagerly. "It began back in the tavern with something funny about those drinks, didn't it? Why did you go back to the proprietor's office and come out with a bottle, and then drive straight out to the scene of the murder?"

Shayne said softly: "You've done me two good turns tonight—when you knocked on the door of Renaldo's office, and out at the captain's house when I didn't see how in hell I was going to explain my presence there without telling Gentry the truth." He hesitated, then admitted: "You deserve a break. You're in it now because you lied to Gentry and he'll probably discover you lied."

He began at the beginning and related what had happened in Renaldo's office. "You know what happened after I drove out to the house."

"And this is real pre-war cognac?" Myrna lifted her glass and her voice was incredulous.

"Monnet 1926," Shayne said flatly. "The captain sold Renaldo a case of it for a hundred dollars, and was tortured to death immediately afterward. Renaldo admits he had his men follow the captain to try and persuade him to tell them where they could get more, but they claim he was dead before they got to him."

"Do you believe them?"

Shayne shook his head. "It doesn't do to believe anything when murder is involved. Their story sounded all right, but that wire and those torn fingernails could very well be their idea of gentle persuasion. And if the captain did fool them by dying before they got the information, they'd hate to admit it to Renaldo and might have made up that story about his being murdered by an unknown visitor.

"And there's another angle. Maybe Blackie and Lennie are playing it smart and did get the information they wanted before the captain croaked. If they decided to use it themselves and cut Renaldo out . . ." He paused and shrugged expressively.

"What makes you and Renaldo so sure there's more cognac where that first case came from?"

"I imagine it was just a hopeful hunch on Renaldo's part. And I wasn't sure until I found this clipping indicating a connection between the captain and an ex-bootlegger."

"Would it be sufficient motive for murder? At a hundred dollars a case?"

Shayne made a derisive gesture. "A C-note for two dozen bottles of Monnet is peanuts today. That's what got Renaldo so excited. It shows the captain knew nothing about the present liquor shortage and market prices. It could retail for twenty or twenty-five dollars a bottle, properly handled today."

Myrna Hastings' eyes widened. "That would be about five hundred dollars a case!"

Shayne nodded morosely. "If Grossman had a pile of it cached away when he was sent up in '30," he mused, "that would explain why it stayed off the market all this time. But Grossman would know what the stuff is worth today." He shook his head angrily. "It still doesn't add up. And if the captain knew about the cache and had access to it all the time, why wait until a week after Grossman's parole to put it on the

market? Did you notice the condition of the captain's body?" he asked abruptly.

Myrna shuddered. "I'll never forget it."

"He looked," said Shayne harshly, "like an advanced case of malnutrition."

"Who was the white-haired man who brought the police?"

"Guildford. He's a lawyer here. Very respectable."

Myrna said hesitantly: "His story about waiting at the house half an hour for Captain Samuels to keep the appointment—do you think *he* could be the man the gangsters saw drive away from the house just before they went in and found the captain dead."

"Could be. If there was any such man. The timing is screwy and hard to figure out. Guildford claims his appointment was for nine and he waited half an hour. It was well past ten when the mugs got back to Renaldo's office. That leaves it open either way. Guildford could have waited until nine thirty and then driven away just before the captain returned with Blackie and Lennie trailing him. Or Guildford may have deliberately pushed the time up a little. Until we know why Guildford went there . . ." Shayne shrugged.

He poured himself another drink and demanded: "Where's that log-book you mentioned, and the clipping about the shipwreck?"

She reached for her handbag and unsnapped the heavy, gold clasp. She drew out an aged, brass-hinged, leather-bound book with SHIP'S LOG stamped on the front in gilt letters.

Shayne opened it and looked at the fly-leaf, inscribed, *Property of Captain Thomas Anthony Samuels. April 2, 1902.*

"The clipping is in the back," Myrna told him. "Lucky I saw it and made up a story that Chief Gentry would swallow."

Shayne said: "Don't kid yourself that he

swallowed it. He knows damned well it wasn't coincidence that put me at the scene of the murder." He turned the log-book upside down and shook out a yellowed and brittle newspaper clipping from the *Miami Daily News,* dated June 17, 1930. There was a picture of a big man in a nautical uniform with the caption, SAVED AT SEA.

Shayne read the news item swiftly. It gave a dramatic account of the sea rescue of Captain Samuels, owner, master, and sole survivor of the auxiliary launch *Mermaid,* lost in a tropical hurricane off the Florida coast three days before the captain was rescued by a fishing craft. He had heroically stayed afloat in a life-preserver for three days and nights.

"Where," asked Shayne, "was the book when you found it?"

"In a small recess in the rock wall at the head of his bed. The bedding was torn up as though the room had been hastily searched, and the bed was pulled away from the wall. That's how I saw it. Normally, the wooden headboard of the bed must have stood against the wall, hiding the recess."

Shayne began thoughtfully flipping the pages of the log-book. "This seems to be a complete account of Captain Samuels' voyages from—"

The ringing of his telephone interrupted him.

The voice of the clerk on the night-desk came over the wire: "The law's on its way up to your apartment, Mr. Shayne. You told me once I was to call you—"

Shayne said, "Thanks, Dick," and hung up. He whirled on Myrna and directed her tersely: "You'd better get out. Through the kitchen door and down the fire escape. Take your two glasses to the kitchen and close the door behind you. Key on a nail by the outside door."

Myrna jumped up. "What—"

"I don't know." Shayne heard the elevator stop down the hall on that floor. "Better if Gentry doesn't find you here. He's already suspicious. Go home and go to bed and be careful. Call me tomorrow."

CHAPTER THREE
BLACKJACK PERSUASION

hayne breathed a sigh of relief when she went without demur. Most women would have argued and asked questions. He opened a drawer and thrust log-book, clipping and ticket stub in it. A loud knock sounded on the outer door of his apartment and Will Gentry's voice called: "Shayne."

He darted a quick glance behind him and noted Myrna had closed the door as she went into the kitchen. He sauntered to the outer door and opened it, rubbed his chin with a show of surprise when he saw Chief Gentry and the tall figure of Mr. Guildford waiting in the hallway. He said, "It's a hell of a time to come visiting," and stepped aside to let them enter.

Will Gentry strode past him to the center table and stopped to look down on the bottle and two glasses suspiciously. He went to the bedroom door and opened it, stepped inside and turned on the light, then looked in the bathroom. Shayne grinned as Gentry doggedly opened the kitchen door and turned on that light.

The chief came back, shrugged his heavy shoulders and sat down heavily across the table from Shayne. "Where is she, Mike?"

"Who?"

"The Hastings girl."

"I told her she'd better go home and get some sleep. She was quite upset, you know. Seems she was rather fond of the old sea captain—though she'd known him only a couple of days," he added quickly.

"She isn't in her room. Hasn't been in all evening."

"How," asked Shayne, "did you know where to look?"

"I called Tim Rourke. He told me she was stopping at the Crestwood, but she's not in."

Shayne said: "You know how these New York dames are. Why come to me?"

"I hoped I'd find her here," Gentry admitted, "knowing how New York dames are, and knowing you."

Shayne said: "Sorry to disappoint you."

Mr. Guildford said: "May I?" He cleared his throat and looked at Gentry.

The chief nodded. "Go ahead."

"Knowing your reputation, Mr. Shayne," Guildford said flatly, "I suspect you withheld certain information tonight."

Shayne said: "That's illegal. Concealing murder evidence."

"To hell with that stuff," Gentry put in impatiently. "What did you and Miss Hastings find before we got there?"

"You know I wouldn't hold out on you, Will. Unless there were something in it for me. And who could possibly profit by the death of a poor old man like that? He looked to me as though he'd gone hungry for weeks."

"That's true," said Guildford helplessly. "I happen to know he was in dire straits. Our appointment tonight was to discuss a payment long overdue on his mortgaged house."

"But the poor guy was obviously tortured," Gentry broke in. "Death resulted from shock due to his poor physical condition. Torture generally means extortion."

"Which makes us wonder if he harbored some secret worth money to someone," Guildford explained. "We found none of his private papers but we did find evidence that the house had been burgled."

"So you think I did it?" Shayne fumed.

"Wait a minute, Mike," Gentry soothed him. "You see, we found that the bed had been pulled back and there was a sort of hiding place exposed. Mr. Guildford suggested you might have discovered the cache and taken the captain's papers away to examine privately."

Shayne snarled: "The hell he did! What's his interest in it?"

"As Captain Samuels' attorney and now his executor, I have a natural interest in the affair," Guildford snapped.

"Come off it, Mike," Gentry said wearily. "If you'll tell me what you were doing there I won't be so sure you're holding out."

"I told you. Miss Hastings did."

"That doesn't wash, Mike. Rourke told me she didn't hit town till this afternoon. How could she have met Samuels and learned about the shipwreck story?"

"Ask her?"

"I can't find her. I'm asking you. Did you get any stuff from the bedroom?"

"I wasn't in the bedroom."

"But Miss Hastings was," Guildford reminded him triumphantly. "And I suggest *she* found his papers and looked through them while we were in the other room with you and the body. And I further suggest that was how she learned about the shipwreck and her agile mind framed the excuse she gave us for your presence there."

Shayne stood up and balled his bony hands into fists. "I suggest that you get out of that chair so I can knock you back into it."

"Lay off, Mike. You've got to admit it's good reasoning."

Shayne swung on Gentry angrily. "I don't admit anything. Is a two-bit shyster running your department now?"

Guildford said: "I resent that, Mr. Shayne."

Shayne laughed harshly. "*You* resent it?"

Gentry said doggedly: "I'm running my department but I don't mind listening to advice. Are you willing to swear you and Miss Hastings just dropped in on the dead man by accident?"

Shayne said: "Put me on the witness stand if I'm going to be cross-questioned."

Gentry compressed his lips. He started to say something, then tightened his lips and got up. He and Guildford went out.

Shayne stood by the table until the door closed behind them. Then he strode to the telephone and asked for the Crestwood Hotel.

He frowned across the room and tugged at his left earlobe while he waited. When the hotel answered, he asked for Miss Myrna Hastings.

Without hesitation, the clerk said: "Miss Hastings is not in."

"How the hell do you know she isn't?" Shayne growled. "You haven't rung her room."

"But I saw her go out just a moment ago, sir," the clerk insisted.

Shayne told him: "You must be mistaken. I happen to know she just went to her room."

"That's quite true, sir. She came in and got her key not more than five minutes ago, but she came downstairs almost immediately with two gentlemen, and went out with them."

"Are you sure?"

"Positive, sir. I saw them cross the lobby from the elevator to the front door."

"Wait a minute," barked Shayne. "Did she go with them willingly?"

"Why, I certainly presumed so. She had her arms linked in theirs and I didn't notice anything wrong."

"Can you describe them?"

"No. I'm afraid I didn't notice—"

"Was one of them short and the other one tall?"

"Why, now that you mention it, I think so. Is something wrong? Do you think—"

Shayne hung up, went into his bedroom and got a short-barreled .38, which he dropped in his coat pocket. Then he went into the kitchen and tried the back door. Myrna had locked it behind her when she slipped out.

He turned out the kitchen light and strode across the living room, crammed his hat down on his bristly red hair and went out.

en minutes later Shayne parked in front of Henry Renaldo's tavern. He shouldered his way through the swinging doors and found half a dozen late tipplers still leaning on the bar. Joe was in the back with a mop bucket, turning chairs up over the tables, and the paunchy bartender was still on duty in front.

Shayne went up to the bar and said: "Give me a shot of cognac, Monnet."

The bartender shook his head. "We got grape brandy—"

Shayne said: "Monterrey will do."

The bartender set a bottle and glass in front of the detective, keeping his eyes secretively low-lidded. Shayne poured a drink and lifted it to his nose. He shook his head angrily and said: "This stuff is grape brandy."

"Sure. Says so right on the bottle." The bartender's tone was placating.

Shayne shoved the glass away from him. "I'll have a talk with Henry."

"The boss ain't in," the bartender told him hastily.

"How about his two ginzos?"

"I dunno."

Shayne turned and went along the bar to the back. Joe pulled the mop bucket out of his way and turned his head to stare wonderingly at the set look on Shayne's face.

He knocked on the door of Renaldo's office and then tried the door. It opened into darkness. He found the light switch and stood on the threshold looking about the empty office. He strode to the rear door through which the two gunsels had entered earlier, and found it barred on the inside. It opened out directly onto the alley.

He relocked it and went out of the office, back to the bar. The bartender was lounging against the cash register. He said, "I tol' you," and then backed away in alarm when Shayne bunched his hand in his coat pocket over the .38.

"Where," asked Shayne, "do Blackie and Lennie hang out?"

"I dunno. I swear to God I don't. I never seen 'em in here before tonight." He was frightened and he sounded truthful.

"Where will I find the boss?"

"Home, I guess."

"Where's home?"

The bartender hesitated. He pouched his lower lip between thumb and forefinger and said sullenly: "Mr. Renaldo don't like—"

Shayne said: "Give it to me."

The bartender wilted. He mumbled an address on West Sixtieth Street.

Shayne went out and got in his car. He started the motor and hesitated, with his big hands gripping the wheel. He got out and went back into the tavern. The bartender looked up with naked fear in his eyes and put down the telephone hastily.

Shayne said: "Don't do it, Fatty. If Renaldo's been tipped off when I get there, I'll come back and spill your guts all over the floor. The name is Shayne if you think I'm kidding."

He went out again and swung away from the curb. He drove north a dozen blocks and stopped in front of a sign on Miami Avenue that said, CHUNKY'S CHILI. It was crammed in between a pawnshop and a flophouse.

Shayne went in and said, "Hi, Chunky," to the big man picking his teeth behind the empty counter. The long, narrow room was empty save for the proprietor.

Chunky said, "Hi, Mike," without enthusiasm.

Shayne asked: "Any of the boys in back?"

"Guess so."

Shayne got out his wallet. He extracted the ten-dollar bill and folded it twice lengthwise. Chunky kept on picking his teeth. Shayne extended the bill toward him. "Blackie or Lennie in there?"

Chunky yawned. He took the bill and said, "Nope. Ain't seen either of 'em tonight."

"Working?"

"I wouldn't know. Gen'rally hang out back when they ain't."

Shayne nodded. He knew that. Chunky's chili joint was a front for a bookie establishment in the back that served as a sort of clubroom for the better-known members of Miami's underworld. He asked: "Seen John Grossman around since he was paroled?"

Chunky took the frayed toothpick from his mouth and squinted at it. "A guy's on parole, he don't hang out much with the old gang. Not if he's smart."

"Have you seen him around?" Shayne persisted.

Chunky put the toothpick back in his mouth and chewed on it placidly. Shayne grinned and got out his wallet again. Chunky watched him fold another bill twice lengthwise. He took it and suggested: "Might ask Pug or Slim. They usta work for John, some."

"Are they in back?"

Chunky shook his head. "Went out 'bout an hour ago."

Shayne said: "Tell them I'm passing out folding money." He went out and climbed into his car, drove north to Sixtieth and turned west.

Henry Renaldo's address was a modest one-story stucco house in the center of a block containing half a dozen such houses. It was the only one with lights showing through the front windows.

Shayne drove past it to the end of the block, swung around the corner and parked. He got out and walked back, went up the concrete walk lined with a trim hedge on both sides, and rang Renaldo's doorbell.

He got the gun out of his pocket while he waited.

He showed the weapon to Henry Renaldo when he opened the door. Renaldo was in his shirtsleeves with his vest hanging open. The cigar in his mouth looked like the same one he had been chewing on some hours previously. He blinked, wrinkled lids down over his eyes when he saw the gun in Shayne's hand, and backed away, lifting his hands, palms outward, and mumbling: "You don't need to point that at me."

Shayne followed him in and heeled the door shut. The living room was small and crowded with heavy overstuffed furniture. A gas log glowed in the small fireplace at one end. There was no one else in the room.

Shayne gestured with his gun and asked: "Where's Miss Hastings?"

Renaldo rolled up his wrinkled lids and looked at him stupidly. "Who?"

"The girl who left your place with me."

"I sure don't know anything about a girl," Renaldo told him earnestly. "Look here—"

Shayne's eyes were bright with a fierce light. He palmed the gun, took a step forward and hit Renaldo in the face. He staggered back with blood oozing from a cut lip.

Shayne said coldly: "Maybe that'll help your memory."

Renaldo took another backward step and sank down on the red divan. He got a handkerchief from his hip pocket and dabbed at his cut lip. He moaned: "Before God, Mike—"

Shayne rasped: "Where are your two gun-punks?"

"Blackie and Lennie?" Renaldo shook his head from side to side. "How should I know?"

"They grabbed Miss Hastings from her hotel half an hour ago."

"I don't know about that." Renaldo looked at the blood on his handkerchief and shuddered. "I haven't seen them for two hours."

"Didn't you have them tail me when I left your place?"

"What if I did? But I didn't tell them to grab any girl."

Shayne narrowed his eyes. It sounded like the truth. He said: "I'll search this dump anyhow."

Renaldo got up slowly. There was a certain dignity in his posture as he objected: "This is my house. If you haven't got a search warrant—"

Shayne said: "I'm not the police." He turned toward a passageway leading to the rear of the house.

Renaldo moved in front of him. He folded his arms stubbornly. "My wife and kid are asleep back there."

"We'll take care of him, boss," Lennie's voice rapped out behind Shayne.

Renaldo's eyelids twitched and his eyes showed frantic terror. "I told you to stay in the kitchen, Lennie."

"To hell with that. Drop the gat, shamus," he rasped.

Shayne dropped the gun on the rug. He turned slowly and saw Lennie hunched forward and moving toward him from an open door. Blackie sauntered through the door after him.

Lennie had a heavy automatic in his right hand and his eyes glittered. His face was twisted and tiny bubbles of saliva oozed out between his tight lips. He was coked to the gills and as dangerous as a maddened snake. He glided soundlessly across the rug, and the muzzle of his .45 was in line with Shayne's belly.

Renaldo said: "Wait, Lennie. We won't want any trouble here."

Lennie's hot eyes twitched toward the tavern proprietor. "He come here lookin' for trouble, didn't he? By the sweet Jesus—"

"Hold it, Len," Blackie said coolly from behind him. "Stay far enough back so's you can blast him if he starts anything." He moved around Lennie on the balls of his feet, one hand swinging his blackjack in a short, lazy arc.

Shayne jerked his head back and it struck him on the side of the neck just above the collarbone. It was a paralyzing blow and he hit the floor before he knew he was falling. He heard Renaldo cry out: "Watch it, Blackie. Keep him so he can talk. If he croaked the old man he's maybe got some info."

Blackie said: "Sure. He'll talk." He drew back his foot and kicked Shayne in the face.

The detective saw the kick coming but he couldn't move to avoid it. He closed his eyes and lay inert, pushing with his tongue at two loosened teeth.

Blackie put his heel on the side of his face and twisted it viciously with a downward thrust. It tore flesh from his cheekbone and the pain brought knots in his belly muscles. It also drove away the paralysis that had numbed him.

He sat up with blood streaming from his face and pulled his lips away from his teeth in a wolfish grin.

He asked thickly: "Didn't you bring your pliers along this time, Blackie? I've got ten fingernails to work on."

Blackie hit him viciously with the blackjack again.

Shayne toppled over and he heard Lennie laughing thinly somewhere off in the background.

Somebody got a pan of cold water and dumped it in his face. He lay quiescent and listened to Renaldo and Blackie arguing fiercely about him. Renaldo gave Blackie hell for knocking Shayne out so he couldn't possibly talk if he wanted to, and Blackie angrily reminded him of Shayne's reputation for toughness. Lennie put in an aggrieved voice now and then, begging for permission to finish him off.

It was all pretty foggy, but Shayne didn't hear any of them mention the girl. He gathered that they had followed him from the tavern to the little house on Eighteenth and had seen the police come. If they had followed him back to his hotel and tailed Myrna from her fire escape exit, it was evident that they were keeping that fact from Renaldo for reasons of their own.

"We gotta get him out of here," Renaldo said at last. "You boys've messed the hell out of this whole thing and the only way I see now is to finish him off."

"He pushed his face into it," Blackie muttered.

"Sure he did," Lennie said eagerly. "Don't worry about him none, boss."

"We'll take him out through the kitchen to our car." Blackie was placating now. They withdrew a short distance and began talking further together in low voices. Shayne kept his eyes closed and gathered together the remnants of his strength.

They came back after a time and he heard Lennie saying happily: "Once in the heart to make sure is the best way. We don't wanna muff this."

Shayne saw the glitter of a knife in Lennie's hand as he uncoiled and rose from the floor. He saw Blackie's mouth drop open just before he hit him in the belly with his shoulder. They went to the floor together and Shayne kept rolling toward the kitchen door. He stumbled through it just as Lennie's gun roared in the living room behind him.

CHAPTER FOUR
BOTTLED DEATH

ith a rush, Shayne jerked the back door open, staggered out into the night. He leaned against the side of the house and hoped Lennie or Blackie would follow him out. A light came on in the house next door and an irate voice bellowed: "What's going on over there? Was that a shot?"

Shayne tried to call back but his throat muscles were queerly knotted and he couldn't utter a sound.

He shambled down the alley to the street where he had left his car, and got in. He started the motor and drove away, made a circle back to Miami Avenue and drove to his apartment hotel. He didn't feel like tackling the side stairway, so he went in through the lobby toward the elevator.

The clerk hurried out from behind the desk when he saw the detective's condition. He exclaimed: "Good God, Mr. Shayne! What happened? . . . Here. Lean on me."

Shayne put his arm around the clerk's shoulders. He croaked: "It's O.K., Dick. More blood than anything else."

Dick helped him into the elevator and rode up to his room with him. Shayne was an old and privileged client in the apartment hotel and the clerk had seen him in bad shape before, but never quite in this condition. He took Shayne's keyring and unlocked the door, then stared around in amazement when he turned on the light.

"Good Lord!" he ejaculated. "Did the fight start here in your room, Mr. Shayne?"

Shayne looked around the room with bleary eyes that refused to focus on any object. Things seemed to be in a sort of jumble but he didn't see why the clerk was so excited. He pushed past him toward the center table and stared down stupidly at the drawer that was pulled all the way out. He knew he had left it closed—with the things he and Myrna had brought from Captain Samuels' house. His fingers closed around the neck of the brandy bottle still sitting where he had left it, and he used both hands getting it up to his mouth. A long pull at it relaxed his throat muscles and cleared the film away from his eyes. He looked around the disordered room and then at the clerk.

"Have I had any visitors since I went out, Dick?"

"Just that tall man with Chief Gentry—he came back right after you went out. He didn't stop at the desk, but went straight up. He came back almost immediately and went on out and I thought he'd come back hoping to catch you and found you'd already left."

Shayne took another slow drink of cognac. It brought the warmth of life back to him. "Was he up here long enough to do this?" He waved his hand around the room.

Dick wrinkled his forehead. "I don't think so, but I wouldn't say for sure. You know how it is. It's hard to judge time. It didn't seem as if he were up here more than a few minutes."

Shayne nodded. He said, "Thanks for coming up with me," in a tone of dismissal. He stood with the bottle in his hands until Dick went out and closed the door. Then he held it to his lips and drained it. He went out to the kitchen and set the empty bottle carefully on the sink beside the two glasses Myrna had put there on her way out. He tried the back door and found it unlocked.

He remembered it had been locked and Myrna Hastings had had the key when he went away a little while before.

He went into the bedroom and stripped off his clothes, turned water into the tub as hot as his hand could stand it. His face was pretty much of a mess, with both his lips puffed and bluish, lacerated flesh on his cheekbone clotted with blood, and streaks of dried blood running down his chin.

He grimaced at his reflection in the mirror, cautiously testing the two teeth loosened by contact with the toe of Blackie's shoe. They were wobbly but would probably grow back solid if left alone. All in all he was in pretty good shape, considering the way he'd been knocked around.

He got a soft washcloth steaming hot and held it gently against his face while he waited for the tub to fill, loosened the dried blood and cleaned it away carefully.

When he sank into the hot water to soak his long frame, he continued the ministrations with the washcloth. When he got out of the tub he swabbed his face freely with peroxide, then dusted it with antiseptic powder and plastered a bandage over the worst cut on his cheek. He vigorously toweled himself and put on clean clothes, then went to a wall cabinet in the living room and got out a bottle of Portuguese brandy guaranteed to be at least five years old.

During all this time he had methodically gone about the things he had to do, consciously refraining from thinking. He had a factual mind and he liked to use it in an orderly fashion.

He filled the wine glass on the table and got a fresh tumbler of ice water from the kitchen. He sank into a chair and lit a cigarette, letting it droop from an uninjured corner of his mouth, took a sip of brandy and began slowly and unhurriedly to go over the events of the evening, testing each incident as he came to it in the light of later occurrences.

It started with his entering Renaldo's saloon expecting to meet Timothy Rourke.

Myrna Hastings had been there instead. She accosted him, and he had only her word for it that she was what she claimed to be and had been sent to meet him by Rourke. Still, Gentry had phoned Rourke for her address, and at the captain's house she had mentioned that Rourke had introduced her to Will Gentry that afternoon.

Shayne went on from his meeting with Myrna. He carefully studied the scene in Renaldo's office, then jumped to Captain

Samuels' home on the bayfront. In secreting herself in the back of his car, slipping into the house without his knowledge, coming to his aid while Gentry questioned him, and finally in composedly stealing the log-book which she claimed to have found in a hiding place that another searcher had overlooked, had Myrna Hastings stepped out of character?

It was difficult to say. No one could guess what a young feature writer from New York was likely to do. She had left his apartment willingly enough and had gone directly to her room as he had told her to. Then she had been immediately escorted away from the hotel by two men vaguely described by the clerk as short and tall. Had she gone willingly, or been coerced? He had immediately suspected Blackie and Lennie of her abduction, but after the interview with them at Renaldo's house he was inclined to believe they might not be responsible. It didn't quite add up. Now that he was thinking along logical lines, he realized they would have to have trailed him back to his hotel and somehow learned of her departure via the fire escape in order to have followed her to the Crestwood. He saw it was necessary to determine whether the two men who had accompanied her out had been there waiting for her return or had followed her in and up to her room. If they had been waiting, it could not have been Blackie and Lennie—unless Myrna were involved in some way he knew nothing about. And that left the whole business of the missing murder clues up in the air. When she left the room they had been lying on the table. If she had come back to get them, she wouldn't have known to look in the drawer. She might have searched the rest of the room first. She didn't, in fact, know the table had a drawer.

He switched his thoughts from Myrna to Guildford. Had he told the truth about waiting for the captain to return? Or, granting that Blackie and Lennie had told Renaldo the truth about their venture, was Guildford the killer whom they had seen drive away after being closeted with the captain for half an hour? If Guildford were the killer, why had he drawn attention

to himself by calling Will Gentry? It would have been safer and more natural to say nothing about his visit and leave the body to be discovered by chance.

What about the paroled convict, John Grossman? This seemed to Shayne the crux of the affair. He was certainly mixed up in the possession of smuggled cognac somehow. Had Captain Samuels worked with or for him in prohibition days? Did both men have knowledge of a cache of illicit cognac undisposed of at the time of Grossman's arrest? If so, why had Captain Samuels waited fourteen years to put a case of it on the market—waited until he was weak from malnutrition? It seemed likely that the captain couldn't get his hands on it while Grossman was in prison, since the first case appeared soon after Grossman had supposedly returned to Miami.

But it seemed definitely unlikely that John Grossman was in on the deal with Renaldo. The ridiculous price accepted by the starving captain showed that it must have been his own idea. Grossman was smart enough to learn what the stuff was worth in today's market. It looked more as though the captain had put over a personal deal—one that for some reason he had been unable to put over while Grossman was in prison, one that Grossman might have resented even to the point of murder.

Shayne finished his glass of brandy and his musings at the same time. He needed more facts before he could do more than ask himself a bunch of unanswerable questions.

He heaved himself up from his chair and gritted his teeth against a wave of dizziness. The loose teeth pained sharply when he gritted them, and that dispelled the dizziness. He had lost his hat in the fracas at Renaldo's, so he went out bareheaded, thinking the cool night air would feel good on his head.

Dick frowned and shook his head despairingly when he crossed the lobby, but Shayne pushed his swollen lips into the semblance of a grin and waved a derisive hand at the clerk. He got in his car and drove to Second Avenue.

The Crestwood was a small, moderately priced hotel, and the clerk was a thin-chested 4-F who tried to conceal his hostile amazement when Shayne showed his battered face at the desk. He shook his head firmly and began: "I'm afraid . . ."

But Shayne reassured him by saying: "I don't want a room, bud." He showed his badge and went on: "About a guest of yours, Miss Hastings."

"Oh yes. Room 305. I'm afraid she isn't in. There's been—"

"I'm the guy who telephoned you about an hour ago. Can you describe the men she went out with?"

"I'm afraid I can't. You see, I didn't notice their faces."

"Could one of them have been holding a gun on her?" Shayne demanded harshly.

The clerk began to tremble. "I really don't know. I— Do you think something's happened to her?"

"Do you know if they came in after she got her key and went up, or whether they were up there waiting?"

"I really don't know. I didn't *see* them come in after she got her key but I'm afraid I can't swear whether they were upstairs waiting for her or not."

Shayne nodded and went over to the elevator. There was only one elevator in the hotel and it was manned by a young Negro boy who stood very stiff and straight but couldn't keep his eyes from rolling around toward Shayne's bruised face.

Shayne stopped outside the elevator and asked: "Do you know the girl in room 305?"

"Yassuh. I know the one you mean. Checked in jes' today."

"Do you remember her coming in late tonight and then going out again almost immediately?"

"Yassuh. That's what she did. Yassuh, I 'member."

Shayne got out his wallet. "Try to remember exactly what happened. Did you bring her down in the elevator with two men?"

The boy's eyes rolled covetously toward the five-dollar bill Shayne was extracting. "Yassuh. I sho did. Right after I'd done taken her *up*stairs."

"How long afterward?" Shayne prompted. "Did you make many trips in between?"

"Nosuh. Not none. I 'member how s'prised I was when I stopped at the third floor on the way down an' found her waitin' with them two gen'lemen 'cause I'd jes' dropped her off at three on my way up."

"Are you sure of that? You didn't take them up *after* you took her up?"

"Nosuh. How could I when I'd done taken 'em up prev'ous?"

"How much previous?"

"Ten minutes, I reckon."

"Did you notice anything peculiar about the way any of them acted when they came down together?"

"How d'yuh mean, peculiar?"

Shayne said: "I'm trying to find out whether she *wanted* to come down with them or whether they *made* her come."

The Negro boy chuckled. "I reckon she liked comin' all right. She was sho all hugged up to one of 'em. The skinny one, that was."

"Can you describe them?"

"Nosuh. Not much. One was skinny and t'other weren't. I reckon I didn't notice no more."

Shayne said: "You've earned this." The bill exchanged hands and he went out. He had learned something but he didn't care much for it.

His next stop was at the *Miami News* tower on Biscayne Boulevard. An afternoon paper, the early hours of the morning were the busiest ones for the staff, and Shayne found Tim Rourke in one corner of the smoke-hazed city room pounding out copy with one rubber-tipped forefinger.

The reporter looked up at Shayne with a startled oath and then laughed raucously and gleefully. "I'm not the beauty contest editor. You go down that hall—"

"And you," said Shayne bitterly, "can go to hell."

"Michael!" Rourke drawled the name disapprovingly. "Such language in a newspaper office. Did he get his littlum face scratched?"

"It's all your damned fault for sicking that female onto me."

"*My* fault? My God, don't tell me a female did *that* to you!"

"How well do you know Myrna Hastings?" Shayne demanded.

"Not as well as I'd like to. Or, is she that sort of girl? Maybe I don't want to—"

Shayne said wearily: "Cut it, Tim. I'm up to my neck in murder and God knows what-all. What do you know about the gal?"

"Not much." Rourke instantly sobered. "She brought a note from a friend of mine on the *Telegram*. I took her around and introduced her to a few places this afternoon. She found you at Renaldo's, huh?"

"She found me all right," Shayne said grimly.

"What's doing, Mike? I wondered when Will Gentry called me about her tonight, but—"

"Do you know if she's known in Miami?"

"I don't think so. Said it was her first trip."

"Has anyone else called you for her address, Tim?"

"Only Gentry. Is it a story, Mike?"

Shayne's gray eyes brooded across the room for a long moment. He and the reporter had been friends for a long time and he had given Rourke a lot of headlines in the past. He indicated the typewriter and asked: "Busy on something?"

"Nothing I can't give the go-by."

Shayne said: "I could use some help in your morgue."

Rourke led the way back to a large filing room guarded by an elderly woman rocking silently while she knitted. "I'm interested in John Grossman," Shayne told him.

"The bootleg king?" Rourke stopped between a double row of filing cases. "He's back in town on parole."

"When did he get back?"

"Three or four days ago. I tried to interview him but he had nothing to say for publication. All he wanted was to go down to his lodge on the Keys and soak up some Florida sunshine."

Shayne said: "I want to go back to his arrest by the Federals—June 1930."

"We've got a private file on him. It won't be hard to find it." Rourke checked a card index and went to a file at the back of the room. He brought back a bulging manila envelope and emptied it out in front of Shayne. He started pawing through it, muttering: "Here's the trial. It was a honey. With Leland and Parker representing him and not missing a legal trick. And here you are—June 17, 1930. Federal agents nabbed him at Homestead on his way in from the lodge." He spread out a large clipping.

"I remember it now." He chuckled. "They had the income tax case all set but had been holding off, hoping they could hang a real charge on him. They thought he used his lodge to receive contraband shipments from Cuba and they raided it several times but never found any evidence. This time they thought they had him for sure, with a red-hot tip that he was expecting a boatload of French stuff, and they kept a revenue cutter patrolling that section of coastline day and night for a week. Here's the story on that." He turned back to a clipping dated June 16, captioned, CUTTER SINKS BOOTLEG CARGO.

"I covered that story. I rode the cutter three nights and nothing happened, and after I was pulled off, on the night of the 15th, they encountered a motor craft creeping along without lights just off the inlet leading to Grossman's lodge. They tried to make a run for the open sea, and bingo! The revenue boat cut loose with everything she had. There was a heavy sea running, the aftermath of a hurricane that blew hell out of things the day before, and they never found a trace of the boat, cargo or crew. After that fiasco they gave up and decided they might as well take Grossman on the income tax charge."

"Wait a minute," Shayne said. "How bad was that hurricane?"

"Plenty bad. That's really the reason I missed the fun. The cutter had to run for anchorage on the 13th, and she couldn't put out again until the 15th on account of the storm."

"Then that strip of coast wasn't being patrolled the two nights before the sinking," Shayne mused.

"Nope. Except by the elements."

"Then that rum-runner might have been slipping out after discharging cargo, instead of being headed in."

Rourke frowned at the red-headed detective. "If the captain was crazy enough to try and hit that inlet while the hurricane was blowing everything to hell."

Shayne said gravely: "I think I know the captain who was crazy enough to do just that—and succeeded."

Rourke studied him quizzically. "You've got something up your sleeve."

Shayne nodded. "It adds up. Tim, I'm willing to bet there was a boatload of 1926 Monnet unloaded at Grossman's lodge while the hurricane was raging. And it's still there someplace. Grossman was arrested on the 17th, before he had a chance to get rid of any of it, and he left it there while he was doing time in Atlanta."

Timothy Rourke whistled shrilly. "It'd be worth as much now as it was during prohibition."

"More, with the country full of people earning more money than ever before in their lives."

"If your hunch is right . . ."

"It has to be right. How long do you think a man could stay alive floating around the ocean in a life-preserver?"

"Couple of days at the most."

"That's my hunch, too. From the 15th to the 17th might not be impossible. But the hurricane struck on the 13th and the 14th. Take a look at your front page for June 17 and you'll see what I mean."

Rourke hurriedly brought out the *News* for June 17. On the front page, next to the story of Grossman's arrest, was the story of the sensational rescue of Captain Samuels, which Shayne had already read in his apartment. Rourke put his finger on the picture and exclaimed: "I remember that now. I interviewed the captain and thought it miraculous he had stayed alive that long. Captain Thomas Anthony Samuels. Why, damn it, Mike, he's the old coot who was found murdered tonight."

Shayne nodded soberly. "After selling a case of Monnet for a hundred bucks earlier in the evening."

"He was the only survivor of his ship," Rourke recalled excitedly. "Then he and Grossman must have been the only ones who knew the stuff was out there."

"And now Grossman is the only one left," Shayne said flatly. "Keep this stuff under your hat, Tim. When it's ready to break it'll be your baby." He turned and hurried out.

CHAPTER FIVE
MURDER SETTING

 hayne didn't reach his apartment again until after three. He took a nightcap and went to bed, fell immediately into deep and dreamless sleep.

The ringing of his telephone awakened him. He started to yawn and pain clawed at his facial muscles. He got into a bathrobe and lurched to the telephone. It was a little after eight o'clock.

He lifted the receiver and said: "Shayne."

A thick voice replied: "This is John Grossman."

Shayne said: "I expected you to call sooner."

There was a brief silence as though his caller were taken aback by his reply. Then: "Well, I'm calling you now."

Shayne said: "That's quite evident."

"You're horning in on things that don't concern you."

"Cognac always concerns me."

"I'm wondering how much you found out from the captain before he died last night," Grossman went on.

Shayne said: "Nuts. You killed him and you know exactly how much talking he didn't do."

"You can't prove I was near his place last night," he was told gruffly.

"I think I can. If you just called up to play ring-around-the-rosy, we're both wasting our time."

"I've been wondering how much real information you've got."

"I knew that would worry you," Shayne said impatiently. "And since you know Samuels was dead before I reached him, the source of information you're worried about is the log-book. Let's talk straight."

"Why should I worry about the log-book? I've got it now."

"I know you have. But you don't know how much I read about the *Mermaid*'s last trip before you got it."

"The girl says you didn't read it any."

Shayne laughed harshly. "You'd like to believe her, wouldn't you?"

"All right." The voice became resigned. "Maybe you did read more than she says. How about a deal?"

"What kind of deal?"

"You're pretty crazy about Monnet, aren't you?"

"Plenty."

"How does five cases sound? Delivered to your apartment tonight."

Shayne said: "It sounds like a joke. And a poor one."

"You'll take it and keep your mouth shut if you're smart."

Shayne said disgustedly: "You're rolling me in the aisle." He hung up and padded across the room in his bare feet to the table where he poured out a good-morning slug of Portuguese brandy. The telephone began ringing again. He drank some of the brandy and grimaced, then lit a cigarette and went back to the phone, carrying

the glass. He lifted the receiver and asked curtly: "Got any more jokes?"

The same voice answered plaintively: "What do you want?"

Shayne asked: "Why should I deal with you at all? I've got everything I need with Samuels' description of where the stuff is hidden."

"What can you do with it?" the murderer argued.

"The Internal Revenue boys could use our dope."

"And cut yourself out? Not if I know you."

"All right," Shayne said irritably. "You have to cut me in and you know it. Fifty-fifty."

"Come out and we'll talk it over."

"Where?"

"My lodge on the Keys. First dirt road to the south after you pass Homestead, and the next to your right after two miles."

Shayne said: "I know where it is."

"I'll expect you about ten o'clock."

Shayne said: "Make it eleven. I've got to get some breakfast."

"Eleven it is." A click broke the connection.

He dressed swiftly, jammed a wide-brimmed Panama down over his face and went out. He hesitated a moment and then went back in. He flipped the pages of the telephone directory until he found the number of Renaldo's tavern, lifted the receiver and got a brisk, "Good morning," from a masculine voice at the switchboard downstairs. A frown knitted his forehead, and instead of asking for Renaldo's number, he said: "Do you have the time?"

He was told: "It is eight twenty-two."

In the lobby, Shayne went across to the desk and leaned one elbow on it. He simulated astonishment and asked the day clerk: "Where's Mabel today?"

The clerk glanced around at the brown-suited, middle-aged man alertly handling the switchboard and said: "Mabel was sick and the telephone company sent us a substitute."

Shayne went out, got in his car and drove to a drugstore on Flagler. He called Renaldo's number, and said briskly: "Mike Shayne."

"Mike?" Renaldo sounded relieved. "You're all right? God, I'm sorry about—"

Shayne laughed softly. "I'm O.K. Your boys could be a little more gentle but I feel I owe them something for last night. I've got a line on that stuff you were after."

"Yeah? Well, I don't know. . . ."

"I need some help to handle it," Shayne went on briskly. "I figure Blackie and Lennie are just the boys—after seeing them in action."

"I don't know," Renaldo said again, more doubtfully.

"This is business," Shayne said sharply. "Big business for you and me both. Have them meet me at your place about nine thirty."

He hung up and drove out to a filling station on the corner of Eighteenth and Biscayne. He said, "Ten gallons," to the youth who hurried out.

He strolled around to the back of his car and asked: "Were you on duty last night?"

"Until I closed up at ten. Just missed the excitement, I guess."

"You mean the murder?"

"Yeah. The old ship captain who lives down the street. And I was talking about the old coot just a little before that, too."

"Who with?"

"A lawyer fellow who'd been down to see him and got a flat just as he was coming back."

"What time was that?" asked Shayne.

"Pretty near ten. I closed up right after I finished with his tire. If that's all . . ." He took the bill Shayne offered him.

The detective swung away from the filling station and back south of the boulevard. He stopped on First Street east of Miami Avenue and went into the lobby of an office building mostly occupied by lawyers and insurance men. He stopped to scan the building directory, then stepped into an elevator and said: "Six."

He got off on the sixth floor and went down the corridor to a door chastely lettered, LEROY P. GUILDFORD—ATTORNEY-AT-LAW.

There was a small, neat reception room, and a tight-mouthed, middle-aged woman got up from a desk in the rear and came forward when Shayne entered. Her hair was pulled back from her face and tied in a tight knot at the back of her head. She wore rimless glasses and low-heeled shoes, and looked primly respectable and quite efficient.

She shook her head when the detective asked for Mr. Guildford. "He hasn't come in yet. He seldom gets down before ten."

Shayne said: "Perhaps you can tell me a few things. I'm from the police." He gave her a glimpse of his private badge.

She said: "From the police?" Her thin lips tightened. "I'm sure I don't know why you're here." Her gaze was fixed disapprovingly on his battered face.

He said easily: "It's about one of his clients who was murdered last night. Mr. Guildford gave us some help but there are a few details to be filled in."

"Oh, yes. You must mean poor Captain Samuels, of course. I know Mr. Guildford must feel terribly about it. Such an old client. So alone and helpless."

"Did you know him?"

"Only through seeing him here at the office. Mr. Guildford was trying to save his property but it seemed hopeless."

"In what particular capacity did he need a lawyer?"

"It wasn't much," she said vaguely. "He was one of Mr. Guildford's first clients when he opened up this office after resigning his position with the firm of Leland and Parker. There was something about the collection of insurance on a ship that had been lost at sea, and later Mr. Guildford handled the purchase of a property where Captain Samuels later built his little home."

"Do you know whether Guildford saw much of him lately?"

"Not a great deal. There was some difficulty about the mortgage and Mr. Guildford was trying to save him from foreclosure. He pitied the old man, you see, but there was little he could do."

"And this appointment last night. Do you know anything about that?"

"Oh, yes. I took the message early yesterday morning. Captain Samuels explicitly asked him to come at nine last night, promising to make a cash payment on the mortgage. I remember Mr. Guildford seemed so relieved when he received the message and he didn't seem to mind the unusual hour."

Shayne thanked her and told her she had been of great assistance. He started out, but turned back. "By the way, is Guildford generally in his office throughout the day?"

"Yes. Except when he's in court, of course."

"Was he in court last Tuesday?"

"Tuesday? I'm sure he wasn't."

"That's queer. I tried to phone him twice during the day and he was out both times."

She frowned uncertainly and then her face cleared. "Tuesday! Of course. How stupid of me. He was out all day with a client."

Shayne lifted his hat and went out. He drove north on Miami Avenue to Chunky's place and went in. A couple of men were seated halfway down the counter. Shayne took the stool by the cash register, and Chunky drifted up to him after a few moments. He leaned his elbows on the counter, carefully selected a toothpick from a bowl in front of Shayne and began picking at his teeth. He murmured: "Looks like someone prettied you up las' night."

Shayne grinned. "Some of the boys got playful. Look. I'm still hunting a line on John Grossman. Pug or Slim been in?"

Chunky shook his head. "Ain't seen 'em. Grossman usta have a fishin' place south of Homestead."

"Think he went there after he was paroled?"

"Good place to hole up," Chunky murmured. "I know he stayed in town just one night." He took out the toothpick and yawned.

Shayne got up and went out, leaving a dollar at the place where he had been sitting. There was a public telephone in the cheap hotel next door. He called Timothy Rourke's home number and waited patiently until the ringing awoke the reporter. He said: "There's about to be a Caesarian operation."

Rourke gurgled sleepily: "What the hell!"

"On that baby we were talking about in your morgue this morning."

"That you, Mike?"

"Doctor Shayne. Obstetrics specialist."

"Hey! Is it due to break?"

"It's coming to a head fast. Get dressed and hunt up Will Gentry if you want some headlines. Don't, for Christ's sake, tell him I tipped you, but stick to him like a leech." Shayne hung up and drove to Renaldo's saloon.

lackie jumped up nervously from his seat beside Renaldo's desk when Shayne pushed the door open. He sucked in his breath and stared with bulging eyes at the result of his work on the detective's face, while his hand instinctively went to his hip pocket.

Behind him, Lennie leaned against the wall with his hand in his coat pocket. Lennie's features were lax and his eyes were filmed like a dead man's. The left side of his pallid face twitched uncontrollably as Shayne looked at him.

Seated behind the desk, chewing savagely on a cigar, Henry Renaldo looked fearfully from the boys to Shayne. He said: "I don't know what you're up to, Mike. The boys didn't much like the idea. . . ."

Shayne closed the door and laughed heartily. He said: "Hell, there's no hard feelings. I'm still alive and kicking."

Blackie drew in another deep breath. He essayed a nervous smile. "We thought maybe you was sore."

Shayne said gently: "You got a pretty heavy foot, Blackie."

"Yeah." Blackie hung his head like a small boy being reprimanded. "But you come bustin' in with a gun an', jeez! What'd you expect?"

"That was my mistake," Shayne admitted. "I

always run into trouble when I pack a rod. That's why I'm clean now." He lifted his arms away from his sides. "Want to shake me down?"

"That's all right." Renaldo laughed with false heartiness. "No harm done, I guess. The boys'll forget it if you will."

"Whatcha want with us?" Lennie demanded thinly.

Shayne said bluntly: "I need help. I've run into something too big for me to handle, and after seeing you guys in action last night I think you're the ones I need."

"That's white of you," Blackie mumbled.

"I never hold a grudge if it'll cost me money," Shayne said briskly. "Here's the lay." He spoke directly to Renaldo. "I can put my hands on plenty of French cognac. Same as the case you bought last night. And this won't cost us a hundred a case. It won't cost us anything if we play it right."

Renaldo licked his lips. "So the old captain did talk before he died last night?"

"Not to me. I got onto it from another angle. Are you interested?"

"Why are you cutting us in?" Renaldo protested. "Sounds like some kind of come-on to me."

"I need help," Shayne said smoothly. "There's another mug in my way and he's got a couple of torpedos gunning for me. I need a couple of lads like Blackie and Lennie to handle that angle. And after that's cleared up, I still need somebody with the right connections like you, Renaldo. I haven't any set-up for handling sales. You know all the angles from way back. And since you put me onto it in the first place I thought you might as well have part of the gravy. Hell, there's plenty for all of us," he added generously. "A whole shipload of that same stuff."

"Sounds all right," Renaldo admitted cautiously.

"I'm the only one standing in this other guy's way," Shayne explained. "So he plans to put me on the spot. I've got a date to meet him out in the country this morning, and I know he'll have a couple of quick-trigger boys on hand to blast me

out of the picture." He turned to Blackie. "That's where you and Lennie come in. I'm not handing you anything on a platter. This is hot, and if you're scared of it say so and I'll find someone else."

Blackie grunted contemptuously. "Lennie an' me can take care of ourselves, I reckon."

"That's what I thought," Shayne grinned, "after last night. Both of you ironed?"

"Sure. When do we start?"

"Well, that's it," Shayne told Renaldo. "You sit tight until the shooting's over. If things work out right we'll do a four-way split and there should be plenty of grands to go around. I'm guessing at five hundred cases but there may be more," he ended casually.

Renaldo took out his cigar and wet his lips. "Sounds plenty good to me. You boys willing to go along?"

Both of them nodded.

Shayne said briskly: "We'd better get started. I'm due south of Homestead at eleven o'clock." He led the way out to his car and opened the back door. "Maybe both of you will feel better if you ride in back where you can keep an eye on me."

"We ain't worryin' none about you," Blackie assured him, but they both got in the back while Shayne settled himself under the wheel.

In the rear-view mirror he could see the pair conferring together earnestly in the back. Both sides of Lennie's face were getting the twitches and his hands trembled violently as he lit a cigarette. He took only a couple of drags on it, then screwed up his face in disgust and threw it out.

Shayne turned slightly and observed sympathetically to Blackie: "Your pal doesn't seem to feel so hot this morning."

"He's all right," Blackie muttered. "Sorta got the shakes is all."

Shayne said: "He'd better get over them before the shooting starts."

Lennie caught Blackie's arm and whispered something in his ear, and Blackie cleared his throat and admitted uneasily: "Tell you what. He could use somethin' to steady him all right. You know."

Shayne said: "Sure, I know. Any place around here he could pick up a bindle?"

"Sure thing," Lennie said, violently eager. "Couple of blocks ahead. If I had two bucks."

Shayne drove on two blocks and then pulled up to the curb. He passed four one-dollar bills back to Lennie and suggested: "Get two bindles, why don't you? One to pick you up now and the other for just before the fun starts."

Lennie grabbed the money and scrambled out of the car. He hurried up the street and darted into a stairway entrance.

Blackie laughed indulgently as he watched him disappear. "You hadn't oughta give him the price of two bindles," he reproved Shayne. "He'll be plenty high in an hour from now on one. Another one on top of it will pull him tight as a fiddle string. Like he was last night," he added darkly.

Shayne said: "I want him in shape to throw lead fast. Those boys who'll be waiting for me may not waste much time getting acquainted." He lit a cigarette and slouched back in the seat.

Lennie came trotting back in about five minutes. His pinched face was alive and eager, and his eyes glowed like hot coals. He slid in beside Blackie and breathed exultantly: "Le's get goin'. Jeez, is my trigger finger itchin'!"

Shayne drove swiftly south on Flagler past Coral Gables and on to the village of South Miami, then along the Key West highway through the rich truck-farming section with its acres of tomatoes and bean-fields stretching in every direction as far as the eye could see.

By the time they reached the sleepy village of Homestead with its quiet, tree-shadowed streets and its air of serene dignity, he began to feel as though he were the one who had sniffed a bindle instead of Lennie. There was a driving, demanding tension within him. It was always this way when he played a hunch through to the finish. He had planned the best he could and it was up to the gods now. He couldn't turn back. He

didn't want to, of course. The approach of personal danger keyed him up to a high pitch, and he exulted in the gamble he was taking. Things like this were what made life worth living to Michael Shayne.

He drove decorously through Homestead and looked at his watch. It was a quarter to eleven. He stopped at a filling station on the outskirts of the village where the first dirt road turned off the paved highway to the left. He told Blackie and Lennie, "I'll be just a minute," and swung out of the car to speak to a smiling old man in faded overalls and a wide straw hat.

"Does the bus stop here, Pop?"

"Sometimes it do. Yep. If there's passengers to get on or off. 'Tain't a reg'lar stop."

"How about yesterday? Any passengers stop here?"

"Yestidy? Yep. The old sailor feller got off here to go a-fishin'." The old man chuckled. "Right nice old feller, but seemed like he was turned around, sort of. Didn't know how far 'twas to the Keys. Had him a suitcase, too, full of fishin' tackle, I reckon. Him an' I made a deal to rent my tin Lizzie for the day and he drove off fishin' spry as you please. No luck though. Didn't have nary a fish when he come back."

Shayne thanked him and went back to his car. That was the last definite link. He didn't need it, but it was always good to have added confirmation. He wouldn't have bothered to stop if he hadn't had a few minutes to spare.

He got in and turned down the dirt road running straight and level between a wasteland covered with tall Australian pines on either side.

"This is it," he told the boys in the back seat calmly. "Couple of miles to where I'm supposed to meet these birds, but they might be hiding out along the road waiting for me. You'd both better get down in the back where you can't be seen."

"We won't be no good to you that way," Blackie protested, "if they're hid out along the road to pick you off."

"They'll just pick all three of us off if you guys are in sight, too," Shayne argued reasonably. "I don't think they'll try anything till we get there, and I want them to think I came alone so they'll be off guard. Get down and stay down until the shooting starts or until I yell or give you some signal. Then come out like a couple of fire-crackers."

The two gunsels got down in the back. Shayne drove along at a moderate pace, watching his speedometer. It was lonely and quiet on this desolate road leading to the coast. There were no habitations, and no other cars on the road. It was a perfect setting for murder.

CHAPTER SIX
LAST ROUND ON THE HOUSE

 narrower and less-used road turned off to the right at the end of exactly two miles. A wooden arrow that had once been painted white pointed west, and dingy black letters said, LODGE.

Shayne turned westward and slowed his car still more as it bumped along the uneven ruts. Sunlight lay hot and white on the narrow lane between tall pines, and the smell of the sea told him he was approaching close to one of the salt-water inlets.

The car panted over a little rise, and he saw the weathered rock walls of John Grossman's fishing lodge through the pines on the left. It was a low, sprawling structure, and a pair of ruts turned off abruptly to lead up to it.

Two men stepped into the middle of the lane to block his way when he was fifty feet from the building. This was so exactly what Shayne had expected that he cut his motor and braked to an easy stop with the front bumper almost against the men. He leaned out and asked, "This John Grossman's place?" then opened the door and stepped out quickly to show he was unarmed and to prevent them from coming to the side of the car, where they might look in the back.

One of the men was very tall and thin, with cadaverous features and deep hollows for eye sockets. He wore a beautifully tailored suit of silk pongee with a tan shirt and shoes and a light tan snap-brimmed felt hat. He had his arms folded across his thin chest with his right hand inside the lapel of his unbuttoned coat close to a bulge just below his left shoulder. His face was darkly sun-tanned and he showed white teeth in a saturnine smile as he stood in the middle of the road without moving.

His companion was a head shorter than Slim. He had a broad, pugnacious face with a flat nose spread over a lot of it. He was hatless and coat-less, wearing a shirt with loud yellow stripes, with elastic armbands making tucks in the full sleeves. He stood flat-footed with his hand openly gripping the butt of a revolver thrust down behind the waistband of his trousers.

Shayne stood beside the car and surveyed them coolly. He said: "I don't think we've met formally. I'm Shayne."

Pug said: "Yeah. We know. This here's Slim." He jerked the thumb of his left hand toward his tall companion.

Shayne said: "I thought this was a social call. Where's Grossman?"

"He sent us out to see you were clean before you come in." Slim's lips barely moved to utter the words. He sauntered around the front of the car toward Shayne, keeping his hand inside his coat. His deep-set eyes were cold and glittered like polished agate. His head was thrust forward on a long thin neck.

Shayne took two backward steps. He said: "I'm clean. I came out to talk business. This is a hell of a way to greet a guy."

Pug moved behind Slim. He was obviously the slower-witted and the less dangerous of the pair. He blinked in the bright sunlight and said: "Why don't we let 'im have it here?"

Slim said: "We do." His lips began to smile and Shayne knew he was a man who enjoyed watching his victims die.

Shayne pretended he didn't hear or didn't understand the byplay between the two killers. They had both moved to the side of the car now, and were circling slowly toward him.

He said: "I brought along some cold beer. It's here in the back." He reached for the handle of the rear door and turned it steadily until the latch was free. He flung himself to the ground, jerking the door wide open as he did so.

Slim's gun flashed in the sunlight at the same instant that fire blazed from the back seat. Slim staggered back and dropped to one knee, steadying his gun to return the fire.

Shayne lay flat on the ground and saw Pug spun around by the impact of a .45 slug in his thick shoulder. He stayed on his feet and his own gun rained bullets into the tonneau.

Slim fired twice before a bullet smashed the saturnine grin back into his mouth. He crumpled slowly forward onto the sunlighted pine needles and lay very still.

Pug went down at almost the same instant with a look of complete bewilderment on his broad face. He dropped his revolver and put both hands over his belly, lacing his stubby fingers together tightly. He sank to a sitting position with his legs doubled under him, and swayed there for a moment before toppling over on his side.

There was no more shooting. And there was no sound from the back of the car.

Shayne got up stiffly and began dusting the dirt off his clothes. He heard shouts and looked up to see excited men filtering through the trees and coming from behind the lodge to converge on the car. He went around to the right-hand side and opened the back door to peer inside.

Both Blackie and Lennie were quite dead. Blackie lay with his body sprawled half out on the running board, his gun hand trailing in the dirt. Blood was trickling through two holes in his yellow polo shirt. His mouth was open.

Lennie was crouched down on the floor behind him and there was a gaping hole where his right eye had been. His thin features were composed and he looked more at peace with the world than Shayne had ever seen him look before.

Will Gentry came puffing up behind Shayne, his red face suffused and perspiring. A tall, black-mustached man, wearing the clothes of a farmer and carrying a rifle, was close behind him. Other men were dressed like farmers, and Shayne recognized half a dozen of Gentry's plainclothes detectives among them. He saw Tim Rourke's grinning face and had time to give the reporter a quick nod of recognition before Gentry caught his arm and pulled him about angrily, demanding: "What the bloody blazes are you pulling off here, Mike?"

"I? Nothing." Shayne arched his red eyebrows sardonically at the chief of detectives. "Can I help it if some damned hoods choose this place to settle one of their feuds?" He stepped back and waved toward the rear of the car. "Couple of hitch-hikers I picked up. Why don't you ask them why they started shooting?"

"They're both dead," Gentry asserted angrily after a quick survey. "And the other two?" He started around the car.

"This one's still alive," Rourke called out cheerfully, kneeling beside Pug. "But I don't think he will be long."

Shayne sauntered around behind Gentry. Blood was seeping between Pug's fingers laced together in front of him, but his eyes were open and when Gentry shook him and demanded to know where Grossman was, he muttered thickly: "Inside. Cellar."

"You. Yancy and Marks," Gentry directed two of his men. "Stay here and get a statement from him. Find out what this shooting is about. Everything. The rest of you fan out and surround the house. Take it careful and be ready to shoot. The real criminal is in there."

Shayne took Gentry's place beside Pug as Gentry moved away to direct the placing of his men around the house. He leaned close to the dying man and asked: "Where's the girl, Pug? The girl. Where is she?"

"Inside."

Shayne got to his feet. Rourke got up beside him and grabbed his arm. "Sweet Jesus, Mike! I don't know what any of this is about, but it's *some* Caesarian."

Shayne pulled away from him and started stalking toward the fishing lodge. Rourke hurried after him, expostulating: "Hold it, Mike. Don't try to go in there. Didn't you hear the guy? Grossman's inside. Let Gentry and the sheriff chase him out in the open."

Shayne didn't pay any attention to him. Unarmed, he strode on toward the sprawling stone house, his face set and hard.

Gentry was spacing his men about to cover all exits. He saw Shayne's intention and called out gruffly: "Don't, Mike. No need for anybody to get hurt now. We'll smoke him out."

Shayne went on without hesitation. He mounted the wide stone steps, his heels pounding loud in the sudden stillness, and went on to a sagging screen door. He pulled it open and went in, blinking his eyes against the dimness.

The interior of the house had a stale, long-unused smell. It was cool and quiet inside the thick rock walls. A wide arched opening led into a big room on the right.

Shayne went in and saw Myrna Hastings sitting upright in a heavy chair fashioned of twisted mangrove roots. Her legs and arms were bound tightly to the chair and her mouth was sealed with adhesive tape. Her eyes rolled up at him wildly as he strode across the room, getting out his knife.

He slashed the cords binding her arms and legs, pulled her upright and put his left arm about her shoulders. "This is going to hurt," he warned. "Set your lips and mouth tightly."

She nodded and her eyes told him she understood. He ripped the adhesive loose in one jerk and put his other arm around her. She clung to him, crying softly.

He looked around the room and gave a grunt of satisfaction when he saw a square of water-soaked canvas on the floor with a pile of straw and bottles on top of it. An empty bottle lay on its side and another stood open.

Shayne drew her forward gently, instructing her: "Try to walk. Use your arms and legs and they'll limber up."

She said, through her tears: "I'm trying. I'm all right. I knew you'd come, Mike."

She drew away from him as he leaned down to pick up the open bottle. He studied the water-soaked label and his eyes glinted. It was Monnet cognac, vintage of 1926. The bottle was half-full. He drew in a long gulping breath of the bouquet, then put the bottle in Myrna's hands. "Take a good drink. Everything's all right now."

She obediently tilted the bottle to her lips. A flush came to her cheeks as she swallowed. Shayne laughed and took it away from her. "It's my turn." He drank from it and then led her over to a dusty rattan couch.

She sat down limply and he got out two cigarettes. He put one between her lips and the other in his mouth, thumb-nailed a match and lit them both.

She started violently when Gentry's voice bellowed at him from outside. "Shayne! What's happening in there?"

Shayne called back: "A lady and I are having a drink. Leave us alone." He laughed down at Myrna's bewildered face. "We're surrounded by a posse of detectives and deputy sheriffs. They're summoning their nerve to storm the place."

"What happened?" she asked tensely. "All that shooting. They were laying a trap for you, weren't they? I heard them talking before they went out. They were going to kill you because they thought you'd read the log-book. I told them you hadn't but they wouldn't believe me. I was so frightened when I heard the shooting. I was sure you'd walked right into the trap." She began to tremble violently.

Shayne patted her hand reassuringly. "I practically never walk into a trap."

They heard cautious shuffling footsteps on the porch outside, and Gentry's voice lowered to a rumble. "Mike. Where are you?"

"In here," Shayne called blithely. He put the bottle to his swollen lips and sucked on it greedily. He lowered it and grinned as Gentry tiptoed in with drawn gun, followed closely by the mustached sheriff with his rifle cocked and ready.

"You look," Shayne chuckled, "like the last two of the Mohicans."

Gentry straightened his bulky body and glared across the dim room at Shayne and the girl. "What the devil's going on? Who's that and how did she get here?"

Shayne said: "You met Miss Hastings last night, Will. Why don't you and Leatherstockings run along down to the cellar and look for Grossman? That's where Pug said he was."

Other men began to file cautiously into the hallway behind their leaders. Gentry turned to them and growled: "Find the cellar stairs. And take it careful. Grossman isn't the kind to be taken alive." He crossed the room heavily. "And you can start talking, Mike. What are you and this girl up to?"

"Nothing immoral—with so many people around."

Gentry stopped in front of him on wide-spread legs. "What kind of a run-around am I getting?"

Shayne said: "You're giving it to yourself, whatever it is. *I* didn't invite you out here."

"No. Thought you were pulling a fast one. Covering up for a murderer to get a rake-off on a bunch of smuggled liquor. By God, Shayne, you can't wiggle out of that one."

Shayne took a pull from the bottle. "It's mighty good liquor. Next time you send a stool to cover the switchboard on my hotel don't use a guy with d-i-c-k written all over him."

Gentry gulped back his anger. "I wondered who sent Tim Rourke to me with a tip there'd be fireworks. You can't deny you brought along a couple of gunsels to wipe out Grossman and his gang and keep the stuff for yourself. If I hadn't overheard the call and beat it out here you might have pulled it off."

Shayne laughed and sank down on the couch beside Myrna. "How much of the deal do you know?"

"Plenty. I always suspected Captain Samuels

was running stuff for Grossman when he lost his boat in '30. That's why Grossman killed him last night. Fighting over division of the liquor that was cached here when Grossman was sent up."

"You're fairly close," Shayne admitted. "When you find Grossman—"

"He'll talk," Gentry promised.

"Want to bet on it?" Shayne's eyes were very bright.

"I never bet with you. With your damned shenanigans . . . What's this girl got to do with it?" Gentry pointed a stern finger at Myrna. "One of Grossman's little friends?"

"She wanted to see a detective in action," Shayne replied.

Shayne set the bottle on the floor and sat up straighter when a detective trotted in and reported excitedly: "We've searched the cellar and the whole house, Chief. Not another soul here."

Gentry began to curse luridly. Shayne got up and interrupted him. "I don't think your men knew where to look in the cellar. Let's take a look."

He went out to the hallway and found Rourke coming up the cellar stairs with a flashlight in his hand.

"No soap," Rourke reported to Shayne. "He must have made his getaway when we left the house uncovered to see what the shooting was about."

"Your fault," Gentry said bitterly behind Shayne. "If we don't pick him up I'm slapping a charge of obstructing justice on you."

Shayne took the flashlight from Rourke. He led the way down into a small dank furnace room with a dirt floor. He flashed the light around, then walked over to a small rectangular area where the ground showed signs of having been recently disturbed. "Try digging here, but don't blame me if Grossman doesn't tell you the whole story when you find him."

"There?" Gentry gagged over the word. "You mean he's dead?"

"Unless he's a Yogi or some damned thing." Shayne shrugged and handed the flashlight back to Rourke. "Hell, he had to be dead, Will. Nothing else made any sense."

"You mean nothing *makes* sense," Gentry said perplexedly.

Shayne sighed and said: "I'll draw you pictures. One question first, though. Did Guildford make a phone call between the time you checked for Miss Hastings at the Crestwood last night and before you came to my place looking for her?"

"Guildford?" Gentry's tone mirrored his bewilderment. "The lawyer? What the hell has that got to do with it?"

"Did he?"

"Well, yes, I think he did, come to think of it. He called his home from the public booth in the Crestwood after we learned the girl wasn't in. I suggested that we see you and he didn't want his wife to worry if he got home later than she expected."

Shayne nodded. "He said he called his wife. But you didn't go in the booth with him and listen in on his conversation?"

"Of course not," Gentry sputtered.

Shayne took his time about lighting a cigarette, then continued. "If you had, you would have heard him calling Pug or Slim at Chunky's joint and telling them to hang around the Crestwood until Myrna Hastings came in—and then grab her. He was covering every angle," Shayne went on earnestly, "after he discovered that empty hiding place in the captain's bedroom. He knew the captain knew the location of the liquor cache after Samuels brought in a case and sold it for a hundred bucks to make a payment on the mortgage. And when the poor old guy died while he was torturing him, he must have been frantic for fear he'd never find the stuff."

"Are you talking about Mr. Guildford? The attorney?"

Shayne nodded. "Leroy P. Guildford. Once a junior member of the firm of Leland and Parker, which specialized in criminal practice and defended John Grossman in 1930. He must have

known of the existence of the liquor cache all the time, but it wasn't worth much until the recent liquor shortage, and Captain Samuels wouldn't play ball with him. After he killed Grossman, Samuels was his only chance to learn where the liquor was hidden."

"Are you saying Guildford killed Grossman?"

"Sure. Or had Pug and Slim do the job for him. He brought Grossman out here last Tuesday, then went to Samuels and told him what had happened, and suggested that with Grossman dead they might as well split the liquor."

"But Grossman talked to you over the phone just this morning," Gentry argued.

Shayne shook his head. "I knew that couldn't be Grossman. He *had* to be dead. The only other person it could be was Guildford, disguising his voice to lure me out here so he could get rid of the only two people who knew about the logbook and the liquor."

"Why," asked Gentry with forced calm, "did Grossman *have* to be dead?"

"Nothing else made sense." Shayne spread out his big hands. "Captain Samuels knew where the liquor was all the time and he was practically starving, yet he never touched it. Why? Because he was an honorable man and it didn't belong to him. Why, then, would he suddenly forget his scruples and sell a case? Because Grossman was dead and it no longer belonged to anybody."

Gentry said gruffly: "My head's going around. Maybe it's this air down here."

In the big room upstairs, Shayne knelt beside the bottles and straw. "Do you know where this came from, Myrna?"

"Certainly. Those men fished it up out of the lagoon this morning, all sewed up in canvas. They talked about it in front of me. I think they planned to kill me, so they didn't care what I heard."

"What did they say about it?" Shayne was shaking the bottles free of their straw casings and lining them up carefully on the floor.

"It's all in the bottom of the lagoon. A whole

boatload. Just where Captain Samuels and his crew dumped it overboard as he described in his log-book. That's why the authorities could never find any liquor here when they raided the place, the men said."

Shayne got up with a bottle dangling from each bony hand. He slipped them into the side pockets of his pants as Detective Yancy came hurrying in to tell Gentry excitedly: "We got the whole story from that man before he died. Grossman is dead, Chief. Buried in the cellar. And the real guy is—"

"I know," said Gentry wearily. "Get to a telephone and have Guildford rounded up right away. Leroy P.," he snapped.

"What are you doing?" he demanded, as he turned in time to see Shayne slide a third and fourth bottle into his hip pockets.

"Making hay while the sun shines." Shayne stooped stiffly to get two more bottles from the floor. "With you horning in I won't have any chance at all at that stuff underwater." He put two more bottles in his coat pocket and stooped for two more, looking wistfully at the remaining bottles on the floor. "This is the only fee I'll collect on this case."

Myrna laughed delightedly. "I can carry a few for you."

Gentry turned away and said gruffly: "There'd better be a couple of bottles left for evidence when the revenue men get here." He strode out and Shayne began stacking bottles in Myrna's arms.

"You owe me something," he told her, "for the turn I got when I went back to my apartment and found the back door unlocked and the place burgled. I thought you were mixed up in it and your feature writing story was just a blind."

She laughed as she swayed slightly under the weight of eight bottles. "I wondered if you'd suspect me after they found the key and I admitted that it was to the back door of your apartment. I'm afraid they thought I was an immoral girl. I hated to have them take it away from me," she ended gravely.

Shayne promised, "I'll give you another one," and they staggered out with as many bottles as both could carry.

Sauce for the Gander
Day Keene

DAY KEENE, BIRTH NAME Gunard Hjertstedt (1904–1969), was born on the south side of Chicago. As a young man he became active as an actor and play-wright in repertory theater with such friends as Melvyn Douglas and Barton McClain. When they decided to go to Hollywood, Keene instead opted to become a full-time writer, mainly for radio soap operas. He became the head writer for the wildly successful *Little Orphan Annie,* which premiered on NBC's Blue Network on April 6, 1931, and ran for nearly thirteen years, as well as the mystery series *Kitty Keene, Incorporated,* about a beautiful female private eye with a showgirl past; it began on the NBC Red Network on September 13, 1937, and ran for four years. Keene then abandoned radio to write mostly crime and mystery stories for the pulps, then for the newly popular world of paperback original novels, for which his dark, violent, and relentlessly fast-paced stories were perfectly suited, producing nearly fifty mysteries between 1949 and 1965. Among his best and most successful novels were his first, *Framed in Guilt* (1949), the recently reissued classic noir *Home Is the Sailor* (1952), *Joy House* (1954, filmed by MGM in 1964 and also released as *The Love Cage,* with Alain Delon, Jane Fonda, and Lola Albright), and *Chautauqua* (1960, written with Dwight Vincent, the pseudonym of mystery writer Dwight Babcock; it was filmed by MGM in 1969 and also released as *The Trouble with Girls,* starring Elvis Presley and Marlyn Mason).

"Sauce for the Gander," the first of only two Keene *Black Mask* stories, ran in May 1943.

Sauce for the Gander

Day Keene

He stepped silently through the window, the half-brick clutched in his hand.

What did the puny little schoolmaster, Rheumatic Romeo John Cansdale, hide behind the thick lenses of his horn-rimmed bifocals? What sinister plan to bludgeon his wife to death? *Careful, Cansdale! Take warning! Even a murder can be too perfect....*

FOR THIRTY-FIVE YEARS, six months, and seven days, ten of them mildly happy married years, John Benton Cansdale, A.B., M.S., respected chemistry instructor of the Laurell Park Senior High School, had lived a moral, upright, almost ascetic existence. That had been two years before *she* had come into his life.

It was during breakfast on the morning after his return from the annual teachers' convention in Detroit that he decided to kill his wife. It was strictly an economic move. Two years of playing hide-and-seek had proven conclusively to his modest savings that three cannot live as cheaply as two—especially when one of the three is demanding.

The decision sufficed for the moment. It would be a simple affair. Cansdale prided himself on being too intelligent a man to erect an elaborate structure for Homicide to tear down. Too many murderers had tried to be too clever.

When the proper moment had arrived he would simply hit her with a hammer, or whatever might prove handy.

It had been a broken lock on the kitchen window and the headline in the morning paper that had given him his inspiration. His wife had asked him fifteen times to have the lock repaired. He had promised that he would. The headline in the morning paper stated in bold type: *Killer Strikes Again.*

Cansdale read the details with morbid interest. For months a moronic killer had preyed upon the city, his victims always women. The police had sought for him in vain. No living person had ever seen him. The details of his crimes were revolting. Cansdale noted them with care. Passion was a strange and fearful thing. It warped and twisted a man from what he was into another being.

He thought of the week just past, smiled grimly as his blood began to pound. The week had been most satisfactory. There could be no chance of scandal. He had been too circumspect. He was in love, but not a fool. He had read of too many carelessly conducted triangles that imprudence had turned into wreck-tangles leading to the divorce courts and the chair.

He and Evelyn had been discreet. Both had their positions with the school board and their reputation to maintain. Still, they had managed. And once Mazie was out of the way—

"Mazie." He rolled the name on the tip of his tongue. It tasted bitter. Making full allowance for his youth, not to mention the ten-thousand-dollar dowry that she had brought him, most of which he had invested within the last two years in "little" things that Evelyn had wanted, Cansdale wondered why in the name of God he had ever married her.

She had no soul, no intellect, no fire. She had never read Balzac, Boccaccio, or Rabelais. He peered furtively around his paper at his wife. He was her superior in every way—still at times he had a feeling he bemused her.

She looked up as he peered at her. "More coffee, honey? Toast?"

Tiny, dark, languid, after twelve years of his superior association, she still spoke with the unaffected southern drawl of the hills where she was born.

Cansdale shuddered at the eager smile on her half-parted, too-full lips. He wanted it over with, wanted her dead.

"No," he told her curtly, "thanks. I'll just make my first class as it is." He folded his paper neatly and put it in his pocket so she wouldn't see the headline.

"I'll get your hat and coat," she offered.

He watched her leave the room, her slim hips swaying beneath the outrageously tight dressing-gown that she affected because she believed it made her look like some movie actress or other. Confession magazines, the movies, bridge, they were her life. She had been a pretty girl. In a way, she still possessed a certain charm at thirty.

"You'll be home early t'night, honey?" she asked as she helped him with his coat.

He wished that she wouldn't call him "honey." She called everybody "honey," from shopgirls to the milkman.

"No," he told her primly as he took his hat. "You know that I always work on my book on Friday nights."

The book had been an inspiration. He had thought of it just after the school convention at which he and Evelyn had met. It was to be a new text book on modern chemistry that of necessity entailed a lot of research. Each Wednesday and each Friday afternoon he went directly downtown after school, asked for and received several weighty volumes, then promptly proceeded to lose himself among the shabby homeless and earnest students who always crowded the great reading-rooms. Five minutes before the closing hour he would return the volumes. What neither his wife nor the librarian could know was that he had slipped quietly out of the library to spend the intervening hours in a more pleasant study of human chemistry as applied to anatomical research.

Mazie opened the hall door and raised her lips to be kissed. "It's just that I don't like to be alone," she told him.

Cansdale told her not to be a little fool. But he was pleased. Her fear of being alone had become a phobia that fitted perfectly into his plans. Her fear was well known to the neighbors. On the nights he was away from home she double-locked and barred both the front and the rear doors of their first floor apartment. On several occasions, when she had fallen asleep awaiting his return, he had been put to no little inconvenience trying to wake her up to let him in.

"Perhaps I won't work on the book next Wednesday night," he relented.

His wife seemed pleased. She smiled, almost shyly. "I *do* get so frightened here all alone."

Cansdale stooped to kiss her, paused to view his reflection in the hall glass. It wasn't bad, he decided. With his new-grown wisp of mustache he looked something like Ronald Colman might have looked if he had been a little man and wore horn-rimmed, thick-lensed, bifocal glasses. He tried to read murder in his eyes and failed. His decision didn't show. He, John Cansdale, had resolved to kill his wife and he looked no different than he looked on any other morning.

The adjoining hall door opened and Cansdale kissed his wife full on the lips with more feeling than he had shown in months. It would be the last time that he would ever have to kiss her.

Sergeant Mack, the detective sergeant who lived in the next apartment with his aged and widowed mother and who was just emerging from their door, apologized. "I'm sorry."

Mrs. Cansdale blushed. Cansdale smiled. "Not at all. We shouldn't have been kissing in the doorway."

He kissed Mrs. Cansdale again, closed the apartment door, and opened the outer hall door for the sergeant. He had never liked his neighbor. The policeman was as stupid as his wife, and of a type. He was uncouth, common, vulgar. Still, Cansdale accepted the chance meeting as an omen. He could envision the sergeant's testimony at the inquest. . . .

". . . yeah. Yeah. Sure. Perfectly happy as far as I know. Why, he was kissing and hugging her goodbye when I stepped out in the hall this morning."

The little teacher walked beside the big detective to their cars parked at the curb, pointing to the headline in his paper. "Terrible, isn't it," he demanded primly, "that such a fiend should be at large?" He snapped his fingers as in sudden recollection. "I must remind the janitor again to fix that lock on the kitchen window." He explained, his hand on his car door, "I worry so about Mrs. Cansdale when she's alone."

The big detective seemed embarrassed. "Yeah, yeah. Sure. I can imagine." He climbed into his car and swung out into traffic.

The little chemistry teacher smirked smugly. "The man is a moron," he thought. "He was afraid that I was going to ask him why the police haven't caught the killer."

The morning was warm with spring. It was pleasant to be alive. The weather forecast prophesied fair and rising temperature. The moon wouldn't rise until ten. It would be a lovely night for murder.

cuffing of feet, and the scratch of chalk on the school board, were the only sounds in the classroom as the students worked out the problems that Cansdale had given them, in order to work out his own.

Having a late-shift program, his last class would be over at five. Cansdale wrote the figure on a piece of paper after making certain that there was no other sheet beneath it and that the hard surface of the marble laboratory slab retained no impression.

At five thirty he could be in the Loop eating in the little one-armed restaurant near the main library on Wabash. By five forty-five he would have received and signed for his books at the library desk. By six he could be lost in the northbound, rush-hour traffic on the outer drive.

He made a neat time-table of the figures.

By six thirty, six forty-five at the latest, just when the evening dusk was blackest, he could be on his own back porch opening the window with the broken lock.

By seven his wife would be dead, her head battered in with some handy object and her nude body tossed on the bed to simulate an attack by the moronic killer. The absence of strange fingerprints wouldn't be a stumbling block. The killer always wore gloves. Both doors of his apartment would still be double-locked and barred if he left in the same manner as he entered.

He doubted if Mazie would scream when she saw him. She would be pleased. She could have no idea what he had come for. He continued with the writing of his schedule.

By seven thirty his car would be parked back on Wabash Avenue and he would be in the crowded library reading-room, perhaps exchanging his volume on chemistry for others, to call attention to himself. Shortly after the closing hour of nine he would return to his apartment to find both front and rear doors double-locked and barred. The police, perhaps the stupid fool next door, would help him batter down the door and find the body.

His alibi would be perfect. The thin-lipped, prim, old-maid librarian from whom he always got his books would swear he had been there between the hours of five thirty and nine. She had no reason to doubt it. But no suspicion would be attached to him. He was, in the public eye, a dutiful, loving husband. He had no known motive for wanting Mazie dead. He and Evelyn had been too circumspect. But for the convention week just past he had never seen her oftener than twice a week. They had never appeared in public together. In school they merely nodded and exchanged an innocuous morning note disguised as division business.

The little man's pulse began to pound as he allowed his thoughts to dwell on the charms of the blue-eyed, blond history teacher. She was a greedy little piece of baggage, combining intelligence with fire. But she was worth the sacrifice, if it could be called a sacrifice, that he was making. With Mazie's insurance, rings, and furs, there would be enough to satisfy even Evelyn's capricious tastes for quite some time.

Cansdale stroked his wisp of a mustache and smiled. Most murderers were fools. A lesser man with his knowledge of chemistry would undoubtedly have poisoned his wife and have wound up in the chair. The very manner of the murder he had planned would serve to divert suspicion from him.

Well pleased with his own intelligence the little man memorized the table of figures that he had drawn up, touched the paper to a Bunsen burner, watched it crumple into ash, then sat grinding it to pieces with a pestle.

Unknown to him, as he sat smirking, pleased with himself, one of his student seniors at the rear board wrote in tiny letters beside the table of elements that she was compiling: *Our romantic Romeo and his mental strip-tease Juliet must have phffttt. He isn't going to send her his morning sonnet disguised as "Where was Johnny Jones of your division as of last period? Worried!"*

The boy beside her sniggered, then wrote, as she erased her words: *Who do they think they're fooling? The whole school knows that he's carrying a torch.*

The girl added: *Chlorine—Cl—35,457—17,* to her list of elements, symbols, and atomic weights and numbers, then wrote beside them in small letters as before: *He's carrying a torch but she isn't. She's just taking him for whatever she can get. She was out at the Hi-Ho Club with the new football coach last night—and were they high and howling.*

Yeah? The boy underscored the word before erasing it.

Yeah, the girl answered him with chalk. *They—jiggers! The old dodo's coming out of his trance.*

John Cansdale took another sheet of paper, wrote:

"My dear Miss Parker:

In response to your inquiry concerning the progress of the pupil of whom you wrote me yesterday, can only report that matters are progressing satisfactorily and should come to a conclusion shortly. In fact . . ."

He changed his mind and touched the paper to the burner. Evelyn had thought that he was joking when he told her what he planned to do. It might be best if she knew nothing of the matter until the entire affair was over. Perhaps he would never tell her. It might be best to let her think, as the police would think, that it had been the killer who killed Mazie. He watched the hour hand of the clock creep around the dial. The day, it seemed, would never end.

he warmth of the day had disappeared with the setting of the sun. A cold wind blew off the lake. John Cansdale considered a drink as he parked his car against the Wabash Avenue curb and then decided against it. Drink muddled the mind and he must keep his clear. He checked back, as he had checked a dozen times, and could find no flaw in his plan. Still his throat was suddenly dry and his hands had begun to tremble. Perhaps murder wouldn't prove as simple as he thought.

"This is silly," he reproved himself. "In two more hours she will be dead and I'll be free."

He bought a paper from a boy before entering the lunchroom and read it thoroughly while toying with his poached egg, corn-beef hash, and toast. The one detail that might possibly invalidate his plan had not occurred. The police, as yet, had not apprehended the killer. Rumor was rife as to when and where he might strike again.

He forced himself to eat. He must above all else impress himself upon everyone connected with his alibi as normal. He must show no trace of nervousness or fear.

"Nice supper," he complimented the cashier when he had finished. He turned up the collar of his coat and pushed out through the swinging-door repeating: "Yes, sir. A very nice supper indeed."

"What the hell!"

The cashier started out from behind his cage, stopped as the manager of the lunchroom shook his head.

"But he didn't pay his check, sir," the cashier protested.

The manager shrugged. "Skip it. He'll pay next Wednesday night. He comes in here twice a week as regular as clock-work. He's probably worried or something tonight, you know, got something on his mind."

The cashier subsided, grumbling.

Out on the street John Cansdale scowled at his reflection in the window of a hat store. So far, so good. He was following his bi-weekly routine. Only tonight the hours that usually were filled with Evelyn in the snugness of her near north side apartment would rid him of his wife forever.

He thought of Mazie with disgust as he hurried up the great flat steps of the main library. The little fool was probably even now smearing her face with lotions, listening to the love-lorn programs on the radio, trying, in her common little mind, to figure out some way of winning back his love.

The thought gave him sadistic pleasure. She didn't know the meaning of love. They had never been physically, mentally, morally, or spiritually suited to each other. Still, he wondered why she smiled at him, at times, so very strangely.

The thought gave him pause as he checked through the library file cards for a certain book on the contributions of chemistry to human welfare. Women at times, some women, were very difficult to understand.

The librarian greeted him cordially. "Good evening, Mr. Cansdale. The book is coming nicely?"

"Nicely," he assured her, smiling. "In fact, it's almost finished."

His hat in his hand and the volume under his arm he turned away from the desk to scan the crowded reading-room, ostensibly looking for a place to sit.

"Crowded, very crowded tonight," he murmured as he moved away from the desk. There were, he estimated, perhaps five hundred persons in the several reading-rooms that comprised almost the entire top floor of the building. There were constant arrivals and departures. It was small wonder he was never missed. Miss Roby, the thin-lipped, prim, spinster librarian, would swear that he had been there since the time his card was stamped. He turned out into the corridor leading to the other reading-room and to the stairs.

Behind him, at the desk, Miss Roby adjusted her pince-nez as she stared after him, then turned to an assistant.

"I suppose," she said, "I should report him. I would if he wasn't a school employee. He always chooses a volume that isn't supposed to leave the library. But he always brings them back."

"But *where* does he go?" her assistant puzzled.

The librarian shrugged her thin shoulders. "Lord knows. He's supposed to be writing a book. I wonder. He's been coming in here at five forty-five, choosing a volume on chemistry, and then disappearing until nine for two years."

Her assistant laughed: "Meow."

"I wouldn't," Miss Roby sniffed, "be at all surprised."

In the corridor Cansdale waited until a good-sized group of youngsters had started down the marble stairs, and then joined them. The volume was under his coat. It was an unneeded precaution. The aged attendant in the foyer never even bothered to look up.

He remembered with a start as he unlocked his car that he hadn't phoned Evelyn and told her that he wouldn't call tonight. Perhaps it was just as well. She didn't need to know until it was all over. She might even try to dissuade him

because of the risk he ran. He stroked his thin wisp of a mustache and stepped on the starter button.

He ran no risk—or did he? His self-confidence oozed slightly as he swung his car down Randolph Street and waited at Michigan Boulevard for the green arrow. He must, above all else, drive carefully. Even a slight accident or a ticket could destroy his well-laid plans. The thought made him even more nervous as he recalled Robert Burns' immortal lines:

"The best laid schemes o' mice and men
* Gang aft a-gley;*
An' lea'e us nought but grief and pain,
* For promis'd joy."*

In his nervousness he killed his motor as the light changed and was bumped soundly by the cab behind him. He was glad it was a cab. Cab drivers took little notice of such matters. They were inferior, boisterous persons, always bumping someone. He joined the stream of traffic pouring north.

In the yellow cab in back of him an earnest youth, his first night behind the wheel, jotted the numbers 905—754 down carefully on the margin of his report sheet. The car ahead hadn't stopped. He doubted if there was any damage done, but when a man had been out of work for months, he couldn't be too careful. It might be just as well to report the incident when he checked in.

The Bridge, Chicago Avenue, Oak Street, and the juncture of the Outer and the Inner Drive. Cansdale chose the Inner Drive, his self-confidence returning. In another fifteen minutes, a half-hour at the most, it would be over and he would be returning to the Loop. Lincoln Park was dark and bleakly naked except for her necklaces of yellow gems strung in rows around her ample body.

The lights reminded him of Mazie's yellow diamonds. They would look well on Evelyn. But he must manage to show grief, perhaps even offer a reward for the killer. He would be safe enough in that. The thought amused him and he laughed, only to find the hoarse burst from his throat had frightened him. He realized that his hands and his body were shaking as with some inner palsy. The night was no longer cool. His collar had become too tight, his overcoat too heavy. Despite the cool wind blowing in the open window of the car he was perspiring freely.

"I'm acting the fool," he said aloud. "There's nothing at all to fear. I've been too circumspect. I've planned too well."

Cansdale wondered suddenly if he had planned well. He wished he had read a few of the trashy detective magazines that Mazie was always buying. There might, perhaps, have been a plot in one of them that would have suited his purpose better. But he couldn't imagine what it would be. The plot he had conceived was simplicity itself. No one would ever suspect a middle-aged, respectable high-school instructor of bludgeoning his wife to death.

He began to lash himself into a fury against Mazie to prepare himself for the actual deed. She stood in his way of complete happiness. She was stupid, insipid. But his mind could find no other flaws. She was as young, if not younger, than Evelyn. In her dark, southern way she was pretty. She had never denied him herself. Until he had met Evelyn they had been mildly happy. Even during the last two years she had been unsuspicious, undemanding. Her only other flaw, if it could be called a flaw, was the phobia she couldn't help, her dislike of being alone.

She would be, Cansdale thought, as he turned off of Sheridan Road onto the side street on which he lived, alone for a long time. He parked his car a full three blocks from his house and, turning up the collar of his coat so that it almost touched his hat-brim, slunk through the shadows of the alley paralleling the street on which he lived.

Only four persons saw him. One was the delicatessen owner's wife who caught a glimpse of his face in a lamp light as he crossed a street intersection. Another was the newsboy who happened to be late. A third was a neighbor empty-

ing garbage who had chanced to pause a moment for a breath of air in the blackness by the alley gate. The fourth was a man named Kelly who was unlocking the side-door of his garage. Of the four he was the only one who wondered at the time why Cansdale was walking down the alley.

"He shouldn't ought to short-cut through the alley," Kelly thought ungrammatically. "What with all the stickups now-a-days he's likely to get robbed."

ansdale saw none of them. His mind was intent on his business. He wanted it over with. The pounding of his heart was choking him. The actual act of murder was not as simple as it seemed. He paused at his own alley gate, almost tempted to go back.

"Well, of course, if you don't love me enough to give me the things that a man who loves a woman usually gives her—"

Evelyn's words hung suspended in the air just as she had left them.

"I can't. I won't give her up," the little teacher thought in panic. "I've a right to happiness."

He stared at the back windows of his apartment. Both the kitchen and the dining-room were dark. A light burned in the bedroom briefly, then it too winked out, leaving only a faint glow streaming out of the living-room into the hall.

Cansdale opened the gate and went in, groping in the darkness near the garbage can for the weapon he had decided he would use. The half brick was where he had thought that he had seen it. The inspiration had come to him during his last class. A half brick was the killer's favorite weapon.

The garbage can, balanced precariously upon three bricks instead of four, toppled over slowly and the tin lid clattered on the walk forcing open a basement window in the janitor's apartment.

"Scatt! Gott damn dogs! There should ought to be a law!"

Cansdale stood frozen where he was, half up the back steps to his porch until the clatter and profanity had ceased. Then the basement window closed and he began to breathe again. He wanted to retreat but didn't dare. The janitor might hear him. He continued to the porch.

He had never known the night to be so full of sounds and smells. The detective's mother in the next apartment was frying steak and onions against her son's return. The couple in the flat above were fighting. Through the closed windows of his own apartment he could hear their radio blaring out the news. Mazie always kept it tuned so high it was a wonder the neighbors didn't complain.

He remembered, tardily, that he had forgotten to put on his gloves. He laid the half brick on the window sill and did so, meanwhile listening to the news.

The foreign situation covered, the newscaster turned to the local pages, beginning with: ". . . While the police as yet have failed to apprehend the moronic killer who has preyed upon the housewives of Chicago for these last several months, the department is expending every effort to bring about his capture. Meanwhile housewives are warned not to open their doors to any suspicious strangers and to make certain that all first-floor windows, and windows leading off of fire escapes are locked. . . ."

Cansdale cautiously tried the window with the broken lock that led from the porch to the kitchen. It slid up easily. Now that the actual moment had arrived his self-confidence was oozing back and he sniffed contemptuously. Mazie was a fool. She had no right to be so stupid and live. She was afraid to be alone. A moronic killer was at large. Yet she lay on a sofa in the living room listening to a newscast with a perfect entrance open to the killer.

He straddled the open window cautiously, the half brick in his hand. In the faint light streaming down the hall he could see that the back door was locked and bolted. He stepped into the kitchen making no noise, leaving the window open behind him.

The newscaster had finished by now and there was a blare of transcribed music from the front room. And, as usual, Mazie had two stations on at once. Back of the *hi-de-hi-de-hi, ho-de-ho-de-ho* of a boogie-woogie program, some woman heroine of one of the soap-chip operas to which Mazie was addicted was telling someone she called "honey" in no uncertain terms how much she loved him.

The man's voice was gruff but eager and insistent. Sudden suspicion gleaming in his eyes, the little teacher paused in the center of the kitchen floor and listened closely. But either the program had signed off or the brass of the transcribed band had drowned it out. He smiled painfully with a guilty conscience.

"She hasn't fire, or soul, or brains enough," he thought. "I wish she had. I wouldn't have to kill her then."

The smile faded from his twisted lips as he thought of her insurance. He had to have the money. With the double indemnity clause, on which she herself had insisted, Mazie's death would pay him twenty thousand dollars. He and Evelyn could take sabbaticals on that. They could spend the year in travel, live in the best hotels. In California, perhaps, they would be married. Or perhaps in romantic Old Mexico or Hawaii. The police would never suspect the insurance money as a motive. He carried even more insurance in her name.

The half brick clutched tightly in his hand, he stole quietly past the open doors of the dining-room and the bedroom to the front of the apartment.

"She'll cry 'John' when she sees me," he thought, "and run to me. Then I'll hit her with the sharp edge of the brick and drag her into the bedroom just like the killer would do."

His gloved hand clutching the brick felt hot and sweaty. He must remember to leave the brick behind for the police to find. He stepped into the lighted front room. The radio was blaring cheerfully. The shades on the windows were drawn. A box of chocolates lay opened on a coffee table convenient to the sofa. Mazie's outrageously tight dressing-gown lay crumpled in a silken pool upon the floor. But Mazie wasn't there. The living-room was empty. From where he stood, Cansdale could see that the front door was locked and bolted.

He felt slightly cheated but relieved as he turned back towards the bedroom. This would make it even simpler. He could kill her while she slept. She would never even know that he had been there. She would die believing in him and loving him. On the several occasions he had returned to find her sleeping, and the doors bolted had resisted his key, he had had to pound on the door like a mad man to arouse her. Only Mazie could sleep with a radio blasting in her ear. Still, he supposed, she did get tired of reading trash and had to pass her time some way.

Halfway down the long hall to the bedroom, the program he had heard before began again. Only this time the man was speaking.

"Why don't you leave him?" he demanded. "I make enough to support you and my mother, too. Just one good break and I'll be a lieutenant and—"

The woman stopped him with a kiss, murmured with an unaffected passion. "It's not the money, honey. It's jes' I don't want to worry him now. He's so little an' funny-lookin', an' all he's got is me. But once his book is finished an' he's famous like he says he's goin' to be—"

Cansdale turned slowly towards the front room. The band was still playing, muted now. But the voices came from the bedroom.

An unreasoning fury should have seized him, but it didn't. The only emotion that he knew was fear, sudden and terrible. He had been so wrong. Perhaps he had been wrong in thinking that he could get away with murder. His eyes were suddenly open. The past two years rushed through his mind like the life of a drowning man. He remembered sly looks and glances that had failed to register at the time; smirks on the faces of his fellow teachers and his students. Even Miss Roby had looked strangely at him. He had forgotten to pay his supper check. There had been the matter of the cab. Perhaps someone had seen him enter. He hadn't been intelligent, he had been dumb. Step by step, rung by rung, he had allowed his blind infatuation to be the nails in the ladder he had built—a ladder leading to the chair.

No woman, not even Evelyn, was worth that. He wanted to be out in the night with the cold of the wind against his burning cheeks. Mazie was suddenly lovely. He wanted her as he had never wanted any woman. Perhaps it wasn't too late. She had loved him once. Perhaps she might again. She wasn't guilty. He was. If he hadn't neglected her, left her alone—

He tiptoed meekly down the hall towards the still open kitchen window. He would return at nine. He would never leave Mazie alone again. He would break with Evelyn in the morning. He would—

As he passed the opened door of the darkened bedroom a board squeaked beneath his feet. He tried to step more lightly, lost his balance, and the half brick scraped along the wall.

There was an answering scrape of springs from the bedroom as a man got suddenly to his feet. The little teacher turned instinctively. With his hat brim and his coat collar almost touching he formed a grotesque silhouette in the half light. The half brick raised above his head, in the hand flung out to keep his balance, looked like the squat barrel of an automatic.

"The killer! The moron!" Mazie's scream from the blackness of the bedroom was pure terror.

"No," Cansdale croaked, protesting from a throat so dry the single word rasped like a file. "I—"

He failed to finish the sentence. A blast of gun-fire lighted the room and the first of six soft-nosed .45 slugs pinned him to the far wall of the hallway. He hung there a moment pinned to the wall like a spitted butterfly, then crumpled slowly to the floor.

There had been not one but many flaws in his perfect murder. The worst of these, as Lieutenant Mack summed up the situation to his wife some twelve months later, had been: "So what can we do but keep our mouths shut? So what if he wasn't the killer. He was trading on his name. He intended to kill you. If I hadn't just 'happened' to be passing by, he'd a done it. The coroner's inquest proved that. No. I tell you, Mazie, all we can do is keep our mouths shut. This was just one of them there cases where—"

The newly promoted lieutenant paused to wipe the perspiration from his forehead and make a mental vow.

Still the same eager smile on half-parted, too-full lips. "One of those cases where what, honey?"

"Well," the former sergeant summed up the situation, "one of those cases where what was sauce for the goose turned out to be apple sauce for the gander."

A Little Different
W. T. Ballard

W(ILLIS) T(ODHUNTER) BALLARD (1903–1980) was born in Cleveland, Ohio, and, after college, briefly worked for his father's electronics magazine, then for a newspaper, followed by less than a year each at two movie studios. He had written sporadically for several pulps before creating Bill Lennox, a motion picture troubleshooter, for *Black Mask*, successfully using his work background at First National and Columbia to lend authenticity to his stories, which soon rivaled Dashiell Hammett, Carroll John Daly, and Erle Stanley Gardner in popularity.

Over the course of a half century, Ballard became one of the most prodigiously productive writers in America, his credits including ninety-five novels, more than a thousand short stories and novellas, and about fifty movie and television scripts. In addition to selling to the pulps, Ballard was published in the top slick magazines, including *The Saturday Evening Post, McCall's,* and *Esquire.* Lennox appeared in twenty-seven *Black Mask* stories between 1933 and 1942, five of which were collected in *Hollywood Troubleshooter* (1985), as well as four novels: *Say Yes to Murder* (1942), *Murder Can't Stop* (1946), *Dealing Out Death* (1948), and *Lights, Camera, Murder,* as John Shepherd (1960). He also wrote as Neil MacNeil and P. D. Ballard, and was one of many writers to produce novels under the house names Nick Carter and Robert Wallace.

"A Little Different," the first Bill Lennox story, was published in the September 1933 issue.

A Little Different

W. T. Ballard

Bill Lennox, studio trouble-shooter, finds real trouble
and the shooting not so good.

ILL LENNOX NODDED
to the gateman and climbed
on to the shine stand, just
inside the General gate. The
shine-boy grinned, his white
teeth flashing in his dark
face. "When is you all gwine
tuh star me, Mister Lennox?"

Bill said, absently: "Pretty soon, Sam. Lean
on that brush, will you; I'm in a hurry."

"I'se leaning." The boy ducked his head and
went to work briskly. A big beaming car came
through the gate. Bill could see the woman on
the rear seat, a dazzling blonde with dark eyebrows. He watched the car sourly until it halted
before the star's bungalow dressing-room. The
blonde descended, assisted by her maid, and disappeared. Lennox said something under his
breath, found a quarter, which he tossed to the
boy, and climbed from his seat.

Sol Spurck, head of General-Consolidated
Films, put his short fingers together and stared
at Lennox as the latter came into his office.
"Where was you yesterday?"

Lennox looked at him without visible emotion. "Out, Sol. Out doing your dirty work."

The short figure behind the big desk shifted

uncertainly. "I told you that you should watch out for that dumb cluck Wayborn. He's in a jam."

Lennox shoved his hands deep into his trouser pockets and sat down upon the corner of the desk. "What, again?"

Spurck seemed to explode. "Again—again! Always that guy—"

"Save it." Lennox's voice was very tired. "What's he done now?"

"Am I a mind reader—am I?" Spurck had come to his feet and was bouncing about the office. "What is it that I pay you for—what is it? Must I do everything—everything? I tell you that Wayborn's gone. Fifty thousand they want—fifty thousand for that—"

Lennox said: "Remember your arteries, Sol. Who wants fifty grand and for what?"

Spurck was wrenching open the drawer of his desk. He pulled forth a dirty scrap of paper and shoved it at Lennox. "Find him—find him quick. Are we half through shooting *Dangerous Love?* I ask you. Can we shoot without Wayborn? But fifty thousand for that *schlemiel.* I wouldn't pay fifty thousand for Gable yet, and they ask it for a ham like Wayborn."

Lennox said: "You wouldn't pay fifty grand for your grandmother," and stared at the piece of paper. On it were printed crude letters with a soft pencil. They said:

We've got Wayborn. You've got fifty grand. Let's trade. Go to the cops and we drop him into the ocean. More later.

Lennox looked at his boss. "Where'd this come from?"

Spurck threw up his hands, appealing to the ceiling. "He asks me riddles yet. Mein Gott! He asks me riddles."

Lennox said, roughly: "Cut it. Where'd this come from? Who's seen it?"

His voice seemed to quiet the little man. Spurck returned to his chair and lit an enormous cigar with care. "No one has seen it," he said in a surly tone. "I found it on the floor of my car this morning."

"How long has Wayborn been gone?"

Spurck shrugged. "Yesterday, he was here. Today, he is not. Find him? Yes—but fifty thousand—no. Ten maybe. Not one cent over ten."

Lennox said: "I suppose you know what this will mean? The picture is half in the can. If we don't find Wayborn, we shoot it over and Price is three days behind schedule now."

Spurck's eyes were narrow. "Why did you let me use Wayborn? That ham—what is it I pay you for?"

Lennox said: "Because I'm a fool"; he said it bitterly. "Because I stick around this mad house and keep things going. Some day, Sol, I'll quit this lousy outfit cold. I'll sit back and watch it go to the devil."

Spurck grinned. He'd heard the threat before, many times. "Find him, Bill." He reached across and patted Lennox's shoulder with a fat hand. "Find him, and I take you to Caliente. That's a promise yet."

2

Bill Lennox, trouble-shooter for General-Consolidated Studio, walked through the outer office. Trouble-shooter wasn't his title. In fact, one of the things which Lennox lacked was an official title. Those in Hollywood who didn't like him called him Spurck's watch-dog. Ex-reporter, ex–publicity man, he had drifted into his present place through his inability to say yes and his decided ability in saying no.

His searching blue eyes swept about the large waiting-room. A world-famous writer bowed, half fearfully. A director whose last three pictures had hit the box-office paused for a moment to speak to him. Bill grunted and went on. As he walked down the line towards the row of dressing-rooms he was thinking quickly. Wayborn was gone. They needed him for *Dangerous Love.* No one seemed to know anything about him.

Lennox paused before the door of the third bungalow and knocked. A trim maid opened the door. Her eyes were uncertain when she saw who it was. Bill said: "Tell Miss Meyer that I want to see her."

The maid's eyes got more uncertain. "I don't think—"

His voice rasped. "You aren't paid to think. Tell Meyer that I want to see her at once."

Elva Meyer's eyes were cold, hostile beneath her dark brows as he walked through the door. She was seated before her dressing-table, but there was as yet no greasepaint on her face. "Well?" Her voice was colder than her eyes.

He was staring at her blond hair. "I'm not so hot," he said, helping himself to a chair. "When did you see Wayborn last?"

The eyes flecked, glowed for an instant. "I told you some time ago that I was perfectly capable of looking after my affairs without your help."

"Yeah?" He'd found a loose cigarette in his pocket and was rolling it back and forth between his strong fingers so that the tobacco spilled out at both ends. "Well, sweetheart, it so happens that I'm not sticking my schnozzle into your playhouse at the moment. You and Wayborn were at the Grove last night; then you turned up at the Brown Derby about one—"

She pushed back her chair, noisily. "I'm not going to stand this any longer—your jealous spying is driving me insane. I'm going to Mr. Spurck."

He said, "Nerts! You'll get damn little sympathy from Sol today, honey. He left it at home, wrapped in moth-balls—but you're getting ideas under that peroxide-treated mat of yours. I'm not checking on you because I'm still interested. I'm washed up, baby, washed up. You're not the first chiseling tramp that forgot my first name after I boosted them into lights, and I don't suppose that you'll be the last. I always was a sucker for a pretty face with nice hips for a background; but this is strictly business. *Dangerous Love* should be in the can by the last of the week. It won't be unless Price can shoot."

She said: "I've been here all morning, waiting." She said it in the tone of one who does not like to wait.

Lennox grinned. For the first time in days he was enjoying himself. "You're good, baby." His voice mocked her. "You're plenty good. You should be. I found you, trained you, but you aren't good enough to play love scenes by yourself. Wayborn isn't around. He's been snatched."

She made her eyes wide. "Snatched?" she said, slowly. "You mean—"

His voice rasped with impatience. "Quit acting. You read the papers. You know what snatched means. They want fifty grand and they won't get it."

She sank back into her chair as if her legs suddenly refused to support her. "This is terrible. When did it happen?"

His eyes were sardonic. "That's what I'm asking you, sweetheart. You were with him last night. He hasn't been seen this morning."

Her eyes blazed and she made two small white hands into little fists. "You're lousy, Bill Lennox. You can't tie me into this." Her voice threatened to break. "Ralph took me home at one-thirty. I haven't seen him since."

His eyes searched her face. "I guess you're in the clear, kid." He sounded almost regretful. "Wayborn's boy says that he came in around two, but that he went out again, without his car."

She gained assurance at his words. "But what will Spurck do? He'll have to pay the fifty grand."

"Will he? You don't know Sol, sweetheart."

"But he can't junk the picture. Why, he's spent more than that on publicity."

Lennox shrugged. "We'll reshoot it if Wayborn doesn't turn up." He was on his feet; the girl came out of her chair.

"But he can't leave Ralph to—to—die. It isn't human."

Lennox's voice grated. "Want to pay the fifty grand yourself?"

She stared at him. "I pay the fifty thousand? Don't be absurd."

"There's your answer," he told her. "That's the way Sol feels, and Wayborn isn't Sol's boy-friend."

She said, angrily: "You're getting nasty again; but Sol will have to pay. I'll go to the papers, to the police."

"Do that," he suggested, "and you and me will be going to one swell funeral; that is—if they find the body."

3

Nancy Hobbs was eating in Al Levy's when Lennox came through the door. She nodded to the empty chair, and he sank into it. "Hello, Brat."

She smiled at him. "You look worried, Bill."

He ordered before he answered. "And you look swell. Why don't you go into pictures instead of writing about them?"

She said, "Because I know too much. You have to be dumb to get by, like Elva Meyer."

He scowled. "Seems I saw an interview in a fan magazine where you said that she was just a home girl—"

Nancy laughed, not nicely. "She is. Anybody's home girl. Look at the ones she's wrecked."

He said: "Lay off! I'm trying to think. I can't when you chatter."

She was silent with no sign of resentment. He broke a piece of bread savagely. "Wayborn's been snatched."

Her eyes were narrow. "What is it? A publicity gag?"

"I wish to——it was. The dumb cluck is gone; someone wants fifty grand."

Her eyes were still suspicious. "I don't trust you, Bill; not since you pulled that burning-yacht stunt."

He didn't grin. "I'm out of that racket, sweetheart. I've got to find Wayborn. The picture's half in the can and the big slob looks like a million. Sol is howling his head off."

She said: "Why don't you chuck it Bill—pull loose? You used to be a decent pal; now you're nothing but a two-timing mug. Get loose. Shove off to New York. Write that book. You've been writing it in your mind for ten years."

His mouth twisted with a shade of bitterness. "What would I use for money, sweet?"

She stared at him. "You're getting three fifty—"

He spread his hands. "It goes—I'm living on week-after-next now. Sol lets me draw ahead."

"Sweet of him. He knows that he can hold you as long as you're broke. Listen, Bill. I've got a few dollars that aren't working their heads off. I'll stake you. Get the Chief tomorrow and get the hell out of this town."

For a moment he was silent, then he patted the back of her hand. "It won't work, babe. I gotta find Wayborn. I gotta get that damn' picture into the can; after that, we'll talk about it."

She sighed, knowing that she had lost. "This Wayborn thing? It's on the level?"

He said: "So help me."

She sat there, playing with her fork, thinking. Finally she looked up at him. "Better see Red Girkin."

He stared at her. "Who's Girkin? What is this?"

She said, in a tired voice: "I'm helping, pal. Helping as I always do. Go on. See Girkin. He's got an apartment on Van Ness off Melrose." She gave him the number.

He said, roughly: "What do you know, babe?"

She shook her head. "Just a hunch. Go see him. Stall." She gathered her bag and gloves and rose. "You can pay my check, that is, if you have enough."

He said, absently: "My credit's good, but, Nance, what's the—"

"For a smart guy, you ask plenty of questions. You wouldn't believe me if I told you."

She was gone, leaving him staring after her. Lennox said something under his breath, then went on with his dinner. Afterward he took a taxi.

The cab dropped him at the corner of Melrose and he walked to the apartment house. A row of brass-bound mail-boxes stared at him from the tiled lobby wall. One of them, number five, had the name W. C. Girkin. There was another name, but Lennox did not notice it. He pushed the bell viciously. The door at the bottom of the carpeted stairs buzzed as the catch was released from above. Lennox pulled it open and started up the steps. At their head a man in a light, close-fitting suit waited.

The man said: "What the hell?"

Lennox stared at him and said: "Hello, Charley."

Charley took a thin hand out of his right coat pocket and wrapped the fingers around those of Lennox. "I'll be a so-and-so. How are you, pally? How'd you know that I was in this burg?"

Lennox started to say that he hadn't known, then stopped. "I know things." He grinned. "What's the matter? Cops in the big town get rough?"

The other shrugged. "Pal of mine had a doll out here. I drifted out with him. Jeeze. What a country!"

Lennox said: "Some of us like it. You ought to have blown in a year sooner. Could have used you in a gangster picture."

Charley said, "Me?" and made his eyes very wide. "You've got me wrong, pally. I'm just a businessman with ideas. But come on. Red will think they've put the finger on me." He turned and led the way towards the door of number five. The door was closed and he knocked, three knocks all together, another after a slight pause. The door came open and Charley said: "Okey, just a pal. Meet Red Girkin. This is Bill Lennox."

The red-headed man said hello without evident pleasure. He was big, with heavy shoulders and a rather short neck. He sat down on a chair before the small built-in desk and went on with his game of solitaire. Once he swore to himself and turned over a pile of cards to reach an ace. Charley said: "What are you doing in Suckerville?"

Lennox laughed. "That's one for the book. You'd make a swell gag man."

The other nodded slowly. "There's money in these hills, Pal. Like to cut you in."

The red-headed man at the desk said: "Shut up." He made it sound vicious.

Lennox looked at him with narrow eyes, then back at Charley. "Your friend doesn't like me."

The thin man grinned. "Don't mind him; it's just the bad booze. Lemme have your number. I might put you on to something swell."

4

ill Lennox said to Spurck, "I haven't found the slob yet, but I know who's got him."

Spurck was excited. He came out of his chair and bounced around the corner of the big desk. "You know—you know, and you don't go to the police yet?"

"Listen, Sol. Why don't you try thinking once in a while before you open that mouth of yours? I know who's got Wayborn, but I don't know why and I don't know where he is."

"Who's got him?"

"That's one thing that it isn't wise for you to know. These boys are tough, Sol. It don't mean a thing to them that you're the biggest shot in the industry. They'd as soon rub you out as look at you. In fact, they'd a little rather. You never won any beauty contests, you know."

Spurck sat down at his desk again. "What do we do, then?"

"We pay fifty grand."

"You're crazy!"

"Sure, I got that way, working for you. We pay the fifty grand, finish the picture, and then I try to get it back. If I don't, we spread the story all over the front page and charge the fifty grand to publicity. What the hell else can we do?"

Spurck swore. He raved. He almost cried, but Lennox paid no attention. "Take it and like it," he said. "You've spent more than that on New York flops and kept nothing but the title. Have you heard from the gang?"

The little man pulled out his desk drawer and found an envelope which he handed to Lennox. "They want I should bring the money down to Redondo, in a suitcase. I should bring it myself, and I should not bring the cops; no one but me and my chauffeur."

Lennox said: "Okey. Go to the bank and get the dough in small bills as they say. Don't be a sap and mark them. Then take a ride to Redondo tonight."

Spurck rolled his eyes. "It ain't that I'm afraid, you understand; but I don't like it, I'm telling you."

Lennox grinned. "I'm your chauffeur, Sol. I wouldn't miss this party for a lot."

At seven o'clock Lennox swung the Lincoln town car out of the driveway of Spurck's Beverly Hills home. Dressed in brown livery borrowed from the chauffeur, he was hardly recognizable as he cut across towards Inglewood and picked up Redondo Boulevard.

In the back seat Spurck, with a black bag clutched between his fat knees, was nervously watching the passing traffic. Lennox stepped the car up to sixty and watched the back road in the rear-view mirror. At Rosecrans Avenue a Chevrolet coupé swung in behind them and followed them through Manhattan and Hermosa. Lennox slowed down to twenty and the coupé slowed down also. As they reached Redondo city limits, the Chevrolet speeded up and ran them to the curb. Two men were in the coupé, hats drawn low over their eyes. Lennox saw that the one beside the driver carried a riot gun across his knees.

For a minute, the road was empty, no traffic coming either way. The man with the riot gun said: "Keep your hands on that wheel, mug."

Lennox obeyed, a thin smile twisting his lips for a moment. He knew that voice, knew it well. The man with the gun said to Spurck: "Toss the bag over, quick!"

With trembling fingers, Spurck obeyed. The driver of the coupé opened the bag, inspected the contents. "If these are marked, guy, it's curtains for you. Okey, Charley."

The man with the gun nodded. "Keep driving through Redondo and up through Palos Verdes till you come to where the road ends and another road goes off to the left and into Pedro.

Drive out in the field at the end of the road. You'll find your ham along the top of the cliff, tied up. We were set to push him over if you didn't show up." The coupé's motor speeded up and they jerked away, swinging left at the next street.

Spruck moaned: "Fifty thousand!" He sounded out of breath.

Lennox put the Lincoln in gear. They went through Redondo, climbed the hill beyond and skirted the ocean until they came to the road's end. Five minutes later, with the aid of a flashlight from the tool-box, Lennox found Wayborn. The actor was tied securely, lying flat on his back so close to the cliff's edge that had he made any effort to free his bonds, he might have rolled off. Aside from chafed wrists and stiff ankles, he appeared none the worse for his experience, nor was he even thankful. "You might have gotten here sooner," he told them, in a peevish voice. "I assure you that it was far from comfortable lying here, bound hand and foot."

Spurck exploded. For five minutes he called the actor everything that he could think of. Wayborn listened silently, then climbed into the car. Lennox grinned to himself as he turned the Lincoln towards town.

5

tan Braun, Spurck's nephew, walked back and forth across his uncle's office. He was slight, with black curly hair and long eyelashes. He looked like an actor and wasn't. He was production manager for the studio.

"It's strange," he said, "that Lennox advised you to pay that money. I wish that you'd have asked me about it." He pouted as a small boy pouts when his feelings have been hurt.

Spurck threw his hands wide. "Ask you? What good does asking you get me? Does it bring back Wayborn? Does it catch Price up with his schedule? It was you that wanted Wayborn—

that ham. It was you that held up the schedule three days, changing the story. Maybe you would have got him back and saved us fifty thousand—you—"

Braun said, harshly: "At least I'd have marked the money. You say Lennox wouldn't let you do that?"

Spurck's face became crafty. "Which shows what you know. Me, I got a list of them bills from the bank. Every number. A copy I have made which Lennox takes. If we had marked the bills, they might have killed Wayborn when the picture is only half shot, to say nothing of retakes. Such ideas you've got."

Braun's voice was stubborn. "You could have hired private detectives."

"A swell idea, when the barn door is closed and the horse is—"

"Anyhow," his nephew's voice rasped, "I've hired some. They're waiting outside now."

Abe Rollins and Dan Grogan came in. Grogan was big with a flat Irish face. Rollins was small, dark, with shifty eyes and too white teeth. He said: "Please tuh met yuh, Mr. Spurck. Braun's been telling us about your trouble. Don't worry, we'll turn these mugs up." He examined the two notes from the kidnapers. "I'd like to talk to Lennox," he said. Spurck hesitated, then pressed one of the buttons at the side of his desk.

Bill came through the door and nodded slightly to Braun. His blue eyes narrowed as they went over the two detectives; then he looked at Spurck. "What's eating you now, Sol?"

Spurck explained. As Lennox listened, his eyes got narrower. Then he looked at Rollins. "Okey. What do you want me to tell you?"

The man cleared his throat with importance. "Did you recognize either of the men in the Chevy?"

Lennox hesitated, then said: "No. Their faces were shadowed by their hats. I couldn't have recognized my grandmother."

"Yet you told Mr. Spurck that you knew who had Wayborn?"

Lennox said: "Yeah, I also told him that I'd try to get the fifty grand back, if he let me work it my way. I didn't figure that he'd run in a couple of lame brains to mess things up."

Rollins' face got red, Grogan shifted his feet. "Don't be too smart, fella," Rollins warned. "You're not in the clear on this thing, not by a damn' sight."

Lennox said: "Now isn't that just too swell? You'll be telling me next that I framed the whole play and got the fifty grand myself."

"That's not such a bad idea," Rollins snapped. "Maybe you did. As I remember it, you advised Mr. Spurck to pay the money."

"That's right, Bill, you did." Spurck sounded excited.

Lennox looked at him. "So you got me tagged as a kidnaper, too. Okey, Sol, get your own fifty grand back. I'm quitting, washed up." He swung towards the door. Rollins' voice stopped him.

"Not so fast, punk." The detective's hand was in his coat pocket, shoving the gun forward against the cloth.

Lennox shrugged. "You seem to be running the set." He turned back into the room.

Spurck said: "Just a few questions, Bill. Don't get sore."

Rollins said: "Isn't it true that you are always broke?"

"Ask Sol," Lennox advised. "He's my banker."

"And isn't it true that you told Mr. Spurck that you knew who had Wayborn?"

"What of it?"

"You may be asked to explain that statement at the D.A. office." Rollins' voice was threatening.

"Nerts!" Lennox found himself a cigarette and lit it.

"And isn't it also true that you offered to drive the car to Redondo? I should say that you insisted that you be allowed to drive; yet you made no effort to follow the kidnapers after the money had been passed?"

Lennox shrugged. "Go right ahead, bright boy. Wrap me up in cellophane and deliver me at San Quentin; but while you're talking, the mugs are spending Sol's dough." Spurck groaned, and Lennox laughed.

6

Nancy Hobbs said: "So you finally quit." She said it in the tone of one who hears about a miracle and does not believe.

Lennox nodded. "Can you feature that? After all I've put up with from that fat slob he accuses me of kidnaping. There's one of his funny-looking dicks outside this joint now. I'm getting important."

She said: "Now's your chance to get out of this town. No," as he started to speak. "I know you're broke, but I've still got a stake."

He was silent and she read refusal in his silence. "Too proud to borrow from a woman?" There was a jeer in her voice. "You've done worse."

He said: "It isn't that, Nance. You're a pal. I could borrow from you, but I can't scram with this hanging over my head. I'll get Sol's fifty grand back; then I'll take a powder; but I can't go until I do. I said that I'd find that dough and I will."

"Don't be a fool." Her voice was hoarse. "These boys play rough. If they get the idea that you're gumming their game, they'll plant you in a ditch."

He looked at her with narrow eyes. "What boys, Nance? You seem to know a lot about this play."

"I know plenty about this town that I don't print in fan magazines," she told him. "I get around."

"Words." His voice was harsh. "Why not pass out some names."

She said: "Girkin. I gave you that once."

"Where's he tie in? A cheap New York hood."

"He used to hang around the New York club where Elva Meyer undressed," she said, softly. "That wasn't her name then, but she's the same girl that you promoted into lights."

"Is this straight?"

"Did I ever give you a wrong steer, Bill?"

Lennox was silent for a moment; then he shrugged. "That's nothing to keep me awake nights. Girkin may be a big shot in New York, but he doesn't rate out here."

"Doesn't he? I saw him on the boulevard yesterday with French and they didn't act like strangers."

Lennox swore softly. "French of the El Romano Club, huh? Nice people."

The girl smiled with her mouth, but her eyes were serious. "Friend of yours, isn't he?"

Lennox shrugged absently. "So long." He rose. "I'll be seeing you in New York."

She rose also. "You're not losing me, Bill Lennox. I'm in this if you are." She followed him into the street. He grasped her thin wrist in strong fingers.

"Don't play the sap, sweetheart. It would be just that much tougher, having you along."

A cab cruised by. He let go of her wrist and jumped to the running-board. The next moment he was inside. "Go ahead fast," he told the startled driver. The cab lurched forward. Lennox peered through the back window. He saw Grogan cross the pavement and wave wildly to an approaching taxi. Lennox found a five in his pocket and passed it to the driver. "There's a guy following us. Lose him."

The driver grinned and turned sharply into Vine, right on Sunset, left at Highland, crashing a signal. Finally, at the corner of Arlington and Pico, he pulled to the curb. "Where to?"

Lennox said: "Take me to Melrose and Van Ness." The driver shrugged and turned towards Western.

Lennox got out at the corner and walked to the apartment house. He rang the bell of suite five, got no answer, tried nine and was answered by a buzz from the door. He jerked it open and started up the stairs. A woman's voice called: "What is it, please?"

Lennox said: "I pushed the wrong bell. Sorry." Her door slammed, and he paused before number five. He knocked without response, then tried the knob. The door was unlocked. He opened it cautiously and stepped into the small hall. For a moment he stood listening. There was no sound in the apartment. He closed the door softly and went along the hall to the living-room door. There he stopped and said something under his breath. The door was partly open. Through the crack he saw the figure of a man sprawled in the middle of the rug. His quick eyes went about the room; then he pushed the door wide and crossed to the body. The face, twisted with fear and pain, was that of Charley, and he was very dead.

7

ill Lennox found nothing in the apartment that interested him. There were no papers in the desk, nothing, in fact, except a soiled deck of cards. He went into the bedroom and looked through the closets. Two suits hung there, flashy garments of extreme cut, nothing more. He walked back to the living-room and stopped just inside the door. There was a man looking at the body, a man with a gun in his hand, who said: "Now isn't this swell?" The man was Grogan.

Lennox didn't say anything and the private dick laughed.

"Imagine finding you here." His voice held a note of gloating self-satisfaction. His gun came up so that it bore on the second button of Lennox's vest. "Get the paws in the air, nice boy."

Lennox obeyed, and Grogan picked up the phone. "Gimme Hollywood station, and make it snappy." His eyes never left Lennox's face, the gun did not move. "That you, Bert? Grogan of Rollins and Grogan. Yeah, listen. Is Lew there? Swell. Let me talk to him, will yuh? Hello, Lew, Grogan. Listen. There's a stiff in an apartment on Van Ness." He gave the number. "It's close to Melrose, apartment five. Yeah, I got the mug. He's standing against the wall with his hands in the air. Make it snappy." He hung up and

grinned at Lennox. "Nice weather we're having."

Lennox didn't say anything. He stood there with his hands in the air. They stood there seven minutes, then a siren moaned below, heavy feet made noise on the stairs, and three men in plainclothes came in. The leader nodded to Grogan and looked at Lennox, then at the huddled body on the floor.

He said: "What's going on here? Who's the stiff?"

Grogan shrugged. "I don't know who he is. I was trailing this bird. He came up here and I sneaked up after him. When I got here, he was searching the joint."

The city detective's eyes went to Lennox. "Well, what's the story?" His voice sounded bored, uninterested.

Lennox shrugged. "When I got here, Charley was on the floor with a knife in his guts. That's all I know."

Grogan pursed his lips and made a funny sound of disbelief. The homicide man said: "Charley who?"

"Bartelli."

"Where's he from?"

"New York."

Two other men came through the apartment door. One said: "What's going on here, Lew?"

The other looked at Lennox and said: "Hello, Bill." Lennox recognized Alder, of the *Post*.

The city detective said: "So you know this guy?"

Alder's eyes widened. "Sure, everybody knows him. He's Bill Lennox of General-Consolidated. What's it all about, Lew?"

The city man looked hard at Grogan. "Thought you said that you were trailing this dude?"

Grogan shifted his weight from one foot to the other. "I was, Sol Spurck's orders."

Both reporters looked interested. Lennox snapped: "Be careful, you fool."

The city detective looked at him. "When I want to hear you talk, I'll ask you. All right, Grogan. Go ahead with the story and don't skip anything."

Grogan said: "Well, yuh see, it's this way. Ralph Wayborn was snatched—"

"Snatched?"

"Yeah." He went on and told the whole story. The reporters looked at each other. "So I was trailing Lennox to find where he had the dough planted, and I walked in on this."

The city detective said: "So we've got a kidnaping charge on you along with a murder rap."

Lennox said, in a tired voice: "That man's been dead hours. If you birds would think before you open your mouths, you'd know that. Grogan here is my alibi. He can swear that I wasn't in this place five minutes before he walked in." Lennox smiled sweetly at the now silent private detective.

8

Nancy Hobbs said: "So you wouldn't listen to me and you get yourself into a worse jam." They were seated before the Hollywood Station in her car. "Will you go to New York now?"

"Such ideas you have, Brat. I'm going to get that fifty grand."

"You'll probably get a knife about where Charley got his."

"At least that would be a new experience. Who was it that said there is nothing new under the sun?"

She swore whole-heartedly and stepped on the starter. "Where do we go from here?"

"You don't go anywhere," he told her.

"I suppose I'm to hang around, ready to bail you out?" Her voice was sarcastic.

He grinned without mirth. "That's a thought," and unlatched the door at his side. "I'll be seeing you." He turned up the collar of his coat against the cold wind from the ocean and walked rapidly along. A block farther down he hailed a cab and climbed in.

"Know where the El Romano Club is?" The man didn't and Lennox gave him the address. Fog was beginning to roll in from the southwest. The street lamps looked fuzzy and the auto lamps glowed with funny rings. Lennox lit a cig-arette, snuggled his chin deeper into his coat collar, and stared at nothing.

The El Romano Club was located on the top of a storage building. The attendant looked at Lennox, nodded and motioned him to the elevator. They shot skyward, stepped out into a hallway with blank concrete walls. There were doors off this hall. Lennox knew that some of them opened into storage rooms. The door at the end seemed to open automatically as he stepped before it. He said: "Hello, chiseler," to the man that stood aside for him to enter.

The man grinned in what he thought was a pleasant manner. "Evening, Mr. Lennox. How are you?"

Bill said: "Pretty lousy, Bert. Big crowd tonight?"

The man shrugged expressive shoulders. "Fair. What can you expect with the studios on half-pay?"

Lennox nodded and tossed his hat and coat to the hat-check girl, "'lo, gorgeous."

She gave him a dimpled smile. "Hello, Bill. You look like the devil."

"Sure, that's because I've been working for him so long."

He went down the short, carpeted hall and into the main room. The room was large, high-ceilinged and comfortably filled. Three roulette wheels, set in line, occupied the center. In the far corner was a group of men and one woman about the crap table. Chuck-a-luck and the half-moon blackjack tables were ranged against the wall. Lennox crossed the room, conscious that people were turning to look at him. A blonde who a week ago would have rushed across the room to attract his attention presented a pair of too prominent shoulder blades for his inspection.

Lennox's lips thinned. "Just a friendly town," he thought. "When the knife falls, everyone helps you down into the gutter." He paused before the grilled window of the cashier's cage and, picking up a pad of blank checks, filled one in for five hundred.

The man behind the grille took it in his soft white fingers and pretended to study it. Lennox watched him with narrowed eyes. "Don't you read English?"

The cashier said: "You're sure that this is good, Mr. Lennox?"

Lennox said: "Hell, no; it isn't good, and you know it, but you've cashed a hundred like it. I've never failed to pick them up, have I?"

The man shrugged. "Sorry. My orders are not to cash any more checks."

"You mean any more of mine?"

Again the shrug, as he pushed the check towards Lennox. Someone behind him snickered. A voice said: "Did you hear that Sol was getting himself a new office boy?" Several people laughed.

Lennox apparently had not heard. He said: "Is French here?"

The cashier shrugged for the third time. Lennox picked up the check, folded it carefully and slipped it into his pocket as he crossed one corner of the room, went around the end of the metal bar and through a curtained doorway. Before him was a wide hallway with a door at the end. A young man with too black hair was seated on a chair in the bare hall, reading a confession magazine. He dropped the magazine and came to his feet with cat-like grace. "You can't come in here, you."

Lennox said softly: "I'm coming in, lousy. Out of the way."

For the space of a half-minute neither moved. The black-haired one's hand was in his pocket. He said, slowly, distinctly: "You don't rate around here any more, Lennox. Take a tip and get out."

Bill's smile was very thin. "That's where you have your cues mixed, handsome. I still rate, plenty. I'm seeing French, and he's going to like seeing me."

The other's voice was confidential. "Why don't you get wise? When you're through in this town, you're through. Go out easy, pal. I wouldn't like to throw you out."

Lennox hesitated, shrugged, and half turned. The other relaxed slightly. Suddenly Lennox's right shoulder sagged, his left came up, and his right fist crossed to the gunman's jaw. The black-haired one went down with a look of surprise and pain. Lennox caught him, eased him to the floor, knelt on his chest, pulled the gun from the side pocket and got another from the shoulder-harness. There hadn't been much noise.

"Now I'll give you a tip," he said, in a low, grim tone. "This town isn't healthy for you. Remember that killing at San Clemente? The D.A.'s office might hear something about that if you aren't out of the village before morning."

He straightened his coat, pocketed the two guns, and went on down the hall to the door. Looking back, he saw the gunman get slowly to his feet. Lennox stuck a hand into his pocket. The man looked at him once, then disappeared into the gambling room.

There were voices in the room beyond the door. One that Lennox knew said: "But, French. How was I to know they had a list of the numbers?"

"You fool! That's what you should have found out. A hell of a help you are. Why didn't you tell me sooner?"

"Because I couldn't get away sooner. My uncle kept me at the studio until late. He's half-crazy."

"Yeah." French's voice had a biting quality. "Now get out of here and don't let anyone see you go. I'll call you when I want you."

A door closed somewhere within the room, and Lennox retreated down the passage towards the gambling room. His eyes were narrow, but there was a thin, half-mocking smile about his lips. The voice he had heard belonged to Stan Braun, Sol Spurck's nephew.

He came back along the passage, taking pains to walk heavily.

"Hello, handsome," he said to the empty hall. He didn't shout, but his voice was loud enough to carry to the room beyond. "The boss in? Yeah, well, don't move, rat. This thing in my hand isn't an ornament."

He covered the remaining distance to the door in quick strides. It wasn't locked and he pushed it inward, only far enough to slip through. A man was just stepping around the flat-topped desk, a man with a young, cold face, and gray hair. He stopped when he saw Bill, his face showing no emotion, his eyes very narrow.

"Hello, Lennox! Didn't Toni tell you that you weren't wanted?"

Lennox's smile was almost child-like. "He did mention something like that, but I didn't believe him."

The gambler took a step backwards and sat down in the desk chair. "Maybe you'll believe me?" The direct, prominent eyes measured Lennox carefully.

Bill walked slowly towards the desk. He took his hand from his coat pocket, calling attention to the fact by doing so very slowly. "The cashier turned down my check. I got the idea that it was your orders."

The man at the desk shifted his weight slightly. "We've had plenty of trouble with your paper, Bill. That bank account of yours is like a sieve, a rubber one."

Lennox said: "You never howled about my paper before. It's always been covered."

The other shrugged expressively. "Spurck always took care of that. I hear that he isn't taking care of it any longer."

"Meaning?"

"Just that. You're off the gold standard as far as Spurck is concerned. Sorry, Bill. If ten will help you?" He drew a large roll from his pocket and hunted through the big bills slowly, insultingly.

Lennox grinned. "Thanks, French, but I'll eat tomorrow." He turned towards the door, then said, across his shoulder: "Don't mind if I hang around a while? I always did like raids."

The man at the desk laughed. "So you'll have me raided. Your mind's getting twisted. You've got yourself mixed with someone important. There isn't a cop in town that would dare touch this joint."

"Like that?" Lennox's voice sounded interested.

"Like that," French told him, blandly.

9

ennox went back into the main room. Toni, the slick-haired gunman, was not in sight. Lennox stopped before the bar and spun a half dollar on the polished surface. The white-coated bartender shoved across a scotch and soda, with a twisted bit of lemon peel in the bottom. Lennox tasted his drink; then, hooking his elbows on the edge of the bar, he considered his next move. The blonde, who had given him her back when he first came in, swept past with a black-haired youth in tow. She turned her head.

"Why, it's Mr. Lennox. My dear, I didn't recognize you."

He said, sourly: "It's your age, sweetheart. Age dulls the eyes."

Her face reddened beneath the rouge and she moved hastily away. Someone tugged at Bill's arm. He turned to see Frank Howe. He'd gotten Howe a job in the publicity department six months before. Howe was a little drunk, but it affected neither his speech nor actions.

"Listen, Bill." His voice was a hoarse whisper. "I heard that lousy cashier hand you the runaround. This is my lucky night. Beat the wheel, I did." His hand disappeared into his pants pocket and came out with a crumpled stack of bills. "Money's no use to me. Never had any, don't know how to handle it—hey, bartender, a drink. I'm burning up."

Lennox said: "Thanks, kid." He was genuinely touched. Out of a hundred people in the room that he had helped at one time or another, Howe was the only one who seemed to remember. "No can do. Get you in trouble with Spurck."

Howe said: "To hell with Spurck. To hell with the whole lousy industry. Swell job. You take some tramp from behind a lunch counter and build her up until she's writing autographs instead of orders."

He shoved the bills into Lennox's hand and went away from the bar, his drink forgotten.

Lennox watched him go. The bartender brought the glasses. Lennox drew a crumpled bill from the wad in his hand and started to hand it over. Then he stopped, stared for an instant at the number on the bill and put it into his pocket. He found some loose silver, paid for the drinks and drank both of them.

That done, he crossed the room and disappeared into the men's lounge. There was a shine stand in the wash-room. He crawled onto the stand and watched the kinky head bob as the boy applied the brush. After a moment, he drew a sheet of paper from his inside pocket and compared the numbers on the bills with those on his list. Five of them tallied. He put the five bills into his breast coat pocket, and shoved his white silk handkerchief on top of them, then thumbed through the rest of the roll.

As he counted them he whistled softly. There were four hundred dollars left. Certainly Howe had been lucky. Lennox knew him well enough to know that the ex-reporter seldom had four dollars at any one time. He paid the shine-boy and climbed from the stand. As he emerged into the main room a newspaperman with two girls walked past.

Lennox said: "Know Frank Howe?"

The man nodded.

"Didn't notice which table he was playing at a little while ago?"

The man nodded again. "Yeah, the center one. He was on thirteen and it came up. He let the money ride and she repeated."

Lennox said: "Thanks," and looked about.

A man came out of the passage which led to French's room. Play stopped at the first table while the man exchanged cases of money with the croupier. This was repeated at the other tables. Lennox frowned. He started forward, then stopped. For perhaps a minute, he stood, undecided, then moved towards the center table. He had the idea French was withdrawing the bills which bore numbers that were on Lennox's list.

As he stepped to the table, the rat-eyed croupier glanced at him sharply. Lennox appar-ently did not notice. He watched for several minutes, then bet twenty dollars on black. Red came up and he bet forty, only to be rewarded by double-O. He switched and played the middle group of numbers, won and let it ride. He won again, and shoved the whole pile onto black. Black appeared. He gathered up his winnings and moved towards the crap table.

The lone woman had the dice when he reached the table. He put twenty on the line and watched the green cubes dance across the cloth to turn up a five and six. He picked up his winnings and transferred them to no-pass. She threw snake-eyes.

French came through the curtained door at the end of the bar. He stood for a moment just inside the door, a striking figure, his shirtfront gleaming, his gray hair carefully brushed; then he walked across to the crap layout, just as Lennox picked up the dice.

"You're through, Bill."

Lennox turned slowly, deliberately to face him. The room was suddenly quiet. Everyone was watching, breathlessly. Lennox said: "Meaning?"

"Just that." French's voice held a flat quality which was almost metallic. "We don't want your play here. We don't even want you."

The dice rattled in Lennox's hand. He shoved the whole pile of currency onto the line and sent the green cubes dancing across the table with a twist of his wrist. They turned up six and one. Lennox's eyes met the croupier's. "Pay off, mister."

The man hesitated, his eyes went to French. The owner nodded imperceptibly and the man counted out bills beside those which Lennox had laid on the board. Bill gathered them up slowly, stripped two tens from the pile and tossed them to the croupier, then folded the rest and slipped them into his pocket.

"Okey, French. I thought that you were yellow." His voice carried across the silent room. "Now I know."

He walked calmly towards the door. No one said anything, no one moved. He got his hat from the check girl, slipped into his overcoat and tossed her a folded bill, then he rode down in the elevator. The elevator man said:

"Take it easy, Mr. Lennox." There was a gun in his hand.

Lennox grinned, "You, too, Mac?"

The man shrugged. "Orders." He stopped the car at the second floor and opened the door. Two men stepped in, one of them was Toni. He smiled when he saw Lennox. "If it isn't my little boy-friend." He ran quick hands over the other's coat and removed the guns. "Come on, mug. This is where you get off."

Lennox obeyed. They went along a poorly lighted passage and down a flight of stairs. Lennox said: "I never knew how French got rid of people he doesn't like."

Toni grinned. "There's lots of things you don't know. One of them is how to keep your mouth buttoned. In there." He pushed open a steel door and shoved Lennox into a curtained touring car. "Hey, Frank!" he called to the driver. Lennox turned his head a little and the gunman brought the barrel of his automatic crashing down on Lennox's skull. "That's for clipping me on the jaw," he muttered, as he shoved his way into the car.

10

Consciousness came back slowly. Lennox groaned, moved slightly, then lay still for several minutes, his eyes open, staring about the dark room. To the right, a window gave an oblong of lighter sky. Morning could not be far away. He raised a hand to the side of his aching head, felt the knob there, the hair, matted with dry blood. Sounds from another room reached him indistinctly. A cry, a thump as if a heavy object had been thrown against the wall, then the door opened. Instinctively, Lennox closed his eyes. Light showed against his lids.

French's voice said, from a distance. "Take the——in there and let him think it over."

Heavy feet made noise in the room. There was a groan, a hoarse laugh, and the door

slammed. The groans continued. Lennox opened his eyes. The room was again in darkness. Cautiously he swung his feet from the couch and sat for a moment, his head in his hands. Then he rose, swayed and looked about. There was a huddled shape in the chair beside the window. Lennox blinked at it and said, cautiously:

"Who're you?"

The groans ceased. The room was quiet except for the labored breathing from the chair. Lennox moved closer. His head was clearing.

"Come on!" His voice was louder than he intended. "Who *are* you?"

His hand fumbled in his pocket and found a box of matches. He struck one with fingers that shook. The match flared, and Lennox stared at the battered features of Red Girkin. He said: "My——!" and let the match drop to the floor. "They don't play nice, do they?"

Girkin swore heavily, tonelessly. "Let me alone."

Lennox's voice got sharp. "Your playmates will be back in a few minutes to give you another dose. What do you want?"

The gangster said: "Go to hell!" He said it indistinctly, as if his lip got in the way.

Lennox managed a laugh. "Boy, you love punishment. Come on! Who decorated Charley with the chiv?"

"Charley?" There was a new note in Girkin's voice. "What about Charley?"

"Only that he's dead."

"Say, who are you?"

"A pal of Charley's. Don't you remember? Bill Lennox. I was up at your place the other day."

The man in the chair said slowly: "Yeah, I remember, and Charley's dead. You sure?"

"I found him on the rug with the chiv in his side."

"That damned French."

"So it was French?"

"I'm not talking."

Lennox got mad. "Listen, sucker! Why don't you get next to yourself? Do you think that they've been pounding your pan because they love you? It's a wonder that you aren't in a ditch by now."

The man in the chair found a laugh somewhere and managed to turn it on. It was a poor effort. "They'll keep me until they find out what I did with the ten grand, the dirty—— They can beat me, but I don't talk."

Lennox tried a shot in the dark. "Still figuring that Meyer will help you?"

The gangster started to swear again. "That tramp! She got me into this; then she tied a can to me."

It seemed that the floodgates had opened. He talked and talked; finally he got to repeating himself. Lennox turned away and walked towards the window, his lips very thin, his eyes bright.

Suddenly the door opened, a light switch clicked, and Lennox swung about to see Toni. The gunman said, with surprise: "Look who's come to. Hey, chief! The boy scout's awake."

French's voice growled: "Bring him in."

Lennox took a quick step towards the window. Toni seized his shoulder, forcing him towards the door. With a shrug, Lennox relaxed. "Okey! You win."

Toni said: "We win every time, mug. Start walking."

French sat in a leather chair. His coat was off and the gray hair mussed. There were pouches under his eyes and he looked very tired.

"Well, Bill—"

Lennox said: "Not so hot. Your boy-friend here swings a mean gun."

French said: "Little boys who play outside their own yards get hurt sometimes. Why the hell can't you keep your nose clean?"

Lennox shrugged. "Mind if I sit down?" He moved towards a chair.

The gambler's voice cracked. "Stand still."

Lennox let his eyes widen slowly. "What is this?"

French said: "It's your show-down." He came out of his chair, and they faced each other. Toni shifted his feet, grinning loosely. "What did you tell Frank Howe?"

Lennox hid his start of surprise. "What did I tell Howe? When?"

The gambler growled: "Don't stall, Lennox. You and Howe talked it over last night at the bar. You gave him something and he went away fast. The boys didn't tell me about it until later. They haven't found him yet, but they will. Come on! What did you tell him?"

Lennox grinned. He was beginning to understand why he was still alive. French thought that he had told Howe something at the club, something about the money, perhaps. Lennox said: "I gave him some dough to take home for me, some dough to put in a safe place."

"You—" The gambler took a step forward, his hands clenching at his sides. "Where is he?"

"That's a little mystery you can solve for yourself." Lennox grinned carelessly, much more carelessly than he felt. There was a desk in the corner of the room. He stepped sidewise towards it. French said:

"Stand still, you."

Lennox nodded. "Okey, French, I wouldn't try anything with you." He took another step. "I'm in a jam; I know it. I've been around long enough to know when my number is coming up. What's it worth to you for me to get Howe on the phone and call him off? Does it buy me a ticket to New York?"

French said: "Yes," quickly. He said it too quickly. Lennox knew that New York meant a wash in San Fernando Valley, but—

"Okey! Gimme the phone."

French's eyes searched his. "Don't try any funny stuff," he warned.

"Would I try any funny stuff when Toni has his gun on me."

He crossed to the desk and, picking up the phone, called the first number that came into his head. As he waited, his hand toyed with a heavy glass inkwell hidden by his body from the other men. Toni still stood beside the door. He had his gun, but he let it hang carelessly at his side.

"That you, Howe?" Lennox demanded, as a sleepy voice asked what the hell he wanted. The voice protested that it wasn't Howe, that he had never heard of Howe, and that if he did now, it would be too soon. Lennox paid no attention.

"Listen, boy!" he said, making his voice sound serious. "That money I gave you, you know, those ——"

He picked up the inkwell and half turned so that he could see both French and Toni. "What'll I have him do with them?" he asked the gambler.

Toni's eyes switched from Lennox to his chief's face for an instant and in that instant, Lennox dropped the phone and threw the glass inkwell. He threw it underhanded, threw it with all the force that he had.

It caught the gunman just above the temple and he went over onto the rug without a sound. Lennox sprang at French. The gambler was tugging at his coat pocket. He had his gun half free as Lennox's fingers closed about his wrist. French tried to jerk free, couldn't and struck Lennox in the face with his free hand. Lennox grabbed his throat and tried to force the gambler's head back. French was too strong.

Slowly, ever so slowly, his hand came from the pocket, bringing his gun with it. Desperately, Lennox clung to the man. French hit him again, squarely on the nose. Tears started from Lennox's eyes; his fingers sank deeper into French's throat. The gambler swung about, carrying Lennox with him, and then across French's shoulder, Bill saw something which almost caused him to relax his grip.

The door into the other room had opened. Girkin, on hands and knees, was crawling towards the gun which lay on the carpet at Toni's side. Even as Lennox saw him, Girkin's hand reached the gun, closed over it, and he reeled to his feet, his eyes burning with hate, staring at French.

The gun came up slowly. Lennox cried out. He was never sure afterwards exactly what he said.

"French!" Girkin's voice cut across the room.

Lennox's fingers slipped from the gambler's throat. Girkin's gun flamed and French stiffened. Lennox threw himself sidewise, out of the line of fire. French paid no attention to him. It was as if the gambler had forgotten his existence. He turned slowly and, as he turned, Girkin fired again. French staggered, went to his knees.

His gun came up, and Lennox saw a hole suddenly appear between Girkin's eyes. The gunman pitched forward without a sound.

French stared at him, coughed twice, bent over on his hands, and then settled to the floor. For a minute there was silence in the room, then Lennox bent above Toni, and noted that he was still breathing, but unconscious.

Lennox rose, found a handkerchief, and dabbed at his bleeding nose; then he looked around the room. Behind the desk, a wall safe, its door half open, attracted him. He crossed to the safe and drew out bundles of currency. In all, there were thirty-five thousand dollars. He found a newspaper, wrapped up the money and moved towards the door. Everything was quiet. Evidently there was no one in the house. He wondered vaguely why the shots had not attracted attention.

Outside, it was broad daylight. The house, he saw, was set far up on one of the hillsides north of Beverly. He walked down the long, curving roadway without seeing anyone. He walked for a long time, his head aching dully, the sun growing warmer on his back. Finally he reached a drug-store and called a cab.

11

The shine-boy looked up as Lennox came through the General gate.

"Morning, Mr. Lennox."

"Hello, Sam." He went on across the lot towards the executive offices. Steps sounded on the concrete behind him. Nancy Hobbs' voice called.

"Oh, Bill!"

He turned and managed a grin. "How 'r' you, Nance?"

She said: "I've been hunting for you since I heard you were out of here, looking every— Your face! What's the matter? What happened?"

"I've been playing house with the boys." He grinned. "Come in while I see Sol, if you want some fun. Then you can drive me to the station."

She followed him towards Spurck's office. "So you're really going to pull out?"

"You said it. Just as soon as I see Sol."

"I'll wait out here," she said, stopping in the reception room. "And, Bill, don't let him talk you into anything."

He stopped also, and patted her shoulder. "Don't worry, sweet, I'm washed up." He went through into Spurck's office. Spurck's secretary was beside the big desk taking dictation. Spurck came to his feet.

"Bill?"

"Mr. Lennox to you," Bill told him. "Get Elva Meyer and that precious nephew of yours in here. I want to see them."

Spurck said, "But—your nose!"

"Never mind my nose. Get them."

Spurck swung on the secretary. "What is it you're standing there for? Get them—can't you? Must I do everything about this plant yet?"

"Yes, Mr. Spurck." The secretary bobbed, and disappeared.

Spurck said: "Where have you been? All night, I don't sleep, wondering."

Lennox clipped: "Save it until Braun gets here." He helped himself to a cigarette from the box on Spurck's desk and stood, rolling it between his fingers so that the tobacco spilled out a little at each end. The door opened and Elva Meyer came in. "You wanted—" She stopped when she saw Lennox.

Bill said: "Sit down."

"I—er—"

His voice snapped: "Sit down!"

She sank into a chair. Spurck looked at her, then at Lennox, started to speak, then changed his mind. Again the door came open and Braun entered the room. His face changed when he saw Lennox, losing its color; his lips grew almost pallid. "Hello, Bill?" he managed.

Lennox nodded. He crossed to the desk and tore the newspaper wrapping from the package. Money spilled out upon the desk. Spurck made a glad sound, deep in his throat. Braun and the girl exchanged quick, startled glances.

Lennox said: "There's thirty-five grand there, Sol. You'll have to take the rest out of Braun's salary."

Spurck, who had been fingering the money, looked up quickly. Braun made a strangled noise. "You can't—"

Lennox said: "Shut up! Listen, Sol! This relative of yours has been bucking the wheel. He dropped plenty to French. French had his paper for fifty grand and was threatening to come to you. Someone got the bright idea of snatching Wayborn and soaking you fifty grand to get him back. They figured that you'd call Braun in and let him handle it, but you didn't. You showed the letter to me." He stopped and lit the cigarette.

"Meyer here has been playing around with Braun when people weren't watching. He told her about his jam and the Wayborn idea and she put him in touch with Girkin. Girkin and Charley did the dirty work—"

"It's a lie!" Braun was on his feet.

Lennox said, coldly: "See this nose?" He

touched it with his finger. "The man that gave me that is dead. Shut up!"

Braun sank back in his chair with a sick look. Lennox went on:

"Girkin thought that Meyer was still his moll. He didn't know that he was washed up there. When he found out, he held up ten grand. I don't know where it is. Neither did French. They grabbed Girkin and tried to make him talk. They searched his apartment and stuck a chiv into Charley's ribs when he walked in on them. That's about all."

Braun said: "You can't prove it, you can't prove it."

Lennox looked at him. "For the first time in your life, you're right. French and Girkin are dead, but I don't have to prove it. Sol knows."

Spurck was looking at his nephew. "Loafer!" he shouted. "Loafer! Get out!" He waved his arms wildly. Braun tried to say something. Spurck moved around the desk towards him. Braun went out fast.

Lennox said: "That will be about all, Sol. I'm washed up here. It's New York and some rest for me."

Spurck said: "But listen once, will you? I—"

Nancy Hobbs had been waiting a long time. She looked at her watch again, just as the door opened and Lennox came out. She told him: "You'll have to hurry. There isn't much time."

He didn't meet her eyes. "I'm not going today, Nance."

"Bill!" She was facing him, her hands on his shoulders, forcing him to look at her. "You've let Spurck—"

He shrugged wearily. "Sol's got a new idea for a picture. All about an actress who has her leading man kidnaped to raise money for her boy-friend so that he won't have to go to the big-house. Sol says that it's the best idea in years. That it is 'superb, stupendous, colossal.' That's just the usual bunk talk, of course, but I think that I'll hang around and see how it turns out. A few weeks won't matter, and this picture may be a little different."

The Shrieking Skeleton
Charles M. Green

CHARLES M. GREEN was one of the pseudonyms of Erle Stanley Gardner. While most pulp writers struggled to earn a living, Gardner managed to leap into the big time very quickly. His first two fictional works were sold in 1921 to *Breezy Stories.* His third story, "The Shrieking Skeleton," was sold to *Black Mask* in 1923 under the pen name Charles M. Green. He continued to use this byline to sell stories and articles to such publications as *Life, Droll Stories, Mystery Magazine, Chicago Ledger, The Smart Set, Triple-X,* and, of course, *Black Mask,* for the next year.

Among the other Gardner pseudonyms are A. A. Fair, his most well-known, under which he wrote a long series of novels about Bertha Cool and Donald Lam; Carleton Kendrake, for a single novel, *The Clew of the Forgotten Murder* (1935), which has been frequently reprinted under Gardner's own name as *The Clue of the Forgotten Murder*; and Charles Kenny, also with a single novel, *This Is Murder* (1935), also reissued under Gardner's own name.

While Perry Mason is nearly a household name, Gardner created numerous other series characters for the pulps, including Ed Jenkins, known variously as "the Phantom Crook" and "the Gentleman Rogue"; Sidney Zoom, the master of disguise; Soo Hoo Duck, the "King of Chinatown"; Speed Dash, the "Human Fly"; Lester Leith, con man extraordinaire; Ken Corning, a lawyer in the Mason mold; Paul Pry, the brilliant grifter; and the Patent Leather Kid.

"The Shrieking Skeleton" was published in the issue of December 1923.

The Shrieking Skeleton

Charles M. Green

(A COMPLETE FAST-MOVING MYSTERY NOVELETTE)

When a man buys the body of his greatest enemy and makes a skeleton out of it, there are almost sure to be rare doings—not all of them easily explainable by human motives. You'll get a thrill when the skeleton and the detectives get to work.

I HAVE HEARD MUCH ABOUT THE POWER of money, but the greatest surprise of my life came when I learned that my friend Dr. Alfred Potter had purchased the body of his old-time enemy, Elbert Crothers, "for scientific purposes."

A long acquaintance with the numerous vagaries of my rich medical friend had so inured me to his eccentricities that I felt nothing from that quarter could surprise me. His long-standing antagonism to Elbert Crothers had furnished many spectacular quarrels, until Crothers had lost his fortune in one grand smash, after which I had heard but little of the feud.

I knew, it is true, that Dr. Potter employed detectives to keep him advised of the location and activities of his old enemy, who had become a common hobo; but I was at a loss to account for the motive which prompted the Doctor to obtain Crothers' body after the latter's death, or the means employed to secure such an unusual result.

The confidential note in which my friend gave me the information was typical of the man:

My dear Walter:

You will doubtless be somewhat surprised to learn that Elbert Crothers is dead. You will probably be more surprised to learn that I have obtained the body from the public institution where he passed away. (He was a penniless hobo at the time of his death, left no relatives, and would have been interred in the Potters' Field, or turned over to some university for dissection.)

I am in need of a skeleton for my residence, and it flatters my fancy to think that I can have the bones of the man who hated me more than anything or anybody on earth, hanging in my den.

I know you are in need of a vacation, and there are some legal formalities in connection with the matter upon which I desire your professional advice. If you can arrange to leave your law practice for a few weeks and come up for a visit, I will guarantee some pleasant golf, and you may have your fill of boating in the Santa Delbara Channel.

Sincerely yours,
Alfred Potter.

To say that I was puzzled to account for this latest eccentricity on the part of the wealthy doctor would be to put it mildly; but I was under sufficient obligations to him to make me feel anxious to comply with his request. A man much my senior, he had been responsible for putting me through law school, and had seen me started in the practice which was now bringing me in a very comfortable income. Each year he extended me an invitation to visit his Santa Delbara home for a week or two, and I eagerly looked forward to these trips.

Dr. Potter lived alone, except for his servants, in a magnificent house built on the hills nearly a mile from the city of Santa Delbara. He had long since retired from general practice, and devoted his attention to investigations along the line of scientific research. Of great wealth, and a recluse by nature, he was free to devote his entire time to experiments which were not only highly origi-

nal, but which, rumor had it, were sometimes a trifle weird in their nature.

In due course I arrived at Santa Delbara, and was met at the train by the Doctor's chauffeur, John Dawley, a young man whom I had met on my previous visits.

I had never fully approved of Dawley. He had seemed a trifle "fresh," and I greeted him with what I was convinced was formal dignity. It took more than a formal greeting to repress the young scamp, and he addressed me with that free and easy manner which was so distasteful.

"H'llo Guv'ner. See you're back with us again. The Boss'll be glad to see you, but it'll make a lot more work for me with no extra pay. That is, unless the tips is good. Ha, ha! Nothin' like askin' for what a feller wants these days."

I made some reply, and, ignoring the hint, entered the car. I never could understand why Dr. Potter, with his quiet refinement, keen mind and unfailing courtesy, permitted a man like John Dawley to remain in his employ. I remembered hearing some gossip about his being the relative of Dr. Potter's dead brother. Rumor said he was an illegitimate son of the dead brother, who had requested Dr. Potter to look after the boy.

Although I had eagerly looked forward to meeting my friend again, yet it was with grave misgivings that I approached the large, white mansion perched on the hill. Intuition told me Dr. Potter had something more in mind than the mere selection of a skeleton for his den, when he had arranged for the purchase of the body of his dead enemy.

I was met at the door by the Doctor's confidential manservant, "Kimi." I believe that originally Kimi's name was Kukui Shinahara, but the Doctor had always referred to him as "Kimi" (meaning "you" in the Japanese language), and "Kimi" he had become.

There is perhaps nothing more flattering on earth than the smile of a Japanese friend, it is so expansive and enthusiastic. Even when one doubts the absolute sincerity behind it, it is flattering.

In the case of Kimi I really numbered him as a friend following the custom of the Doctor, who treated Kimi with every consideration, and more as a friend than a servant. He had been with the Doctor for years, a trusted and loyal employee. He knew all of the Doctor's friends, and the manner in which he greeted them was a pretty good indication of just where they stood in the favor of his employer.

It was partly a knowledge of this custom on the part of the grinning servant which made me feel such pleasure at the sincerity of his greeting and the expansive smile with which he greeted me. He told me the "master" was awaiting me in the study, and I lost no time in following him to that portion of the house.

Dr. Potter really was glad to see me; of that I am positive, and subsequent developments proved it; but, to one who did not know his peculiar character, it would have been hard to believe, from anything in his greeting, that he had not seen me for nearly a year, or that he cared anything about me. His greeting was as casual and matter-of-fact as though I had just returned from an hour's absence.

Lest I give you a wrong impression of my friend, I must mention something of his wonderful control of his emotions, and his philosophy of life. A deep student of the "mystic," he believed both pleasure and pain were merely relative mental states, and had nothing whatever to do with the real facts of life. A rigorous schooling had taught him to absolutely control his emotions, and I doubt if I have ever heard him laugh; and certain I am that he has never given way to any expression or ejaculation of surprise or dismay in my presence.

Tall, thin, yet filled with a supple grace of movement, and with muscles like whipcords, in spite of his sixty years; by far the most striking thing about him was his face, calm, serene, immobile, almost expressionless, it furnished a setting for a pair of deep blue eyes from which seemed to emerge a species of violet ray, playing over one like a searchlight peering into the mind.

"Well, well, Pearce," he greeted in his crisp, well-modulated tone, "it is indeed a pleasure to see you once more, and a double pleasure to think that you responded so promptly to my note."

"And it's mighty good to see you!" I exclaimed, grasping him by the hand, with an eager enthusiasm I made no effort to control. "I should indeed be a sorry friend, to say nothing about being an ungrateful one, if I failed to accept an invitation to spend a week or two with you, when my presence might be of some benefit to you."

A flash of gratification momentarily played over his features. It was merely an emotional flicker which would have meant nothing in another man; but, in the case of Dr. Potter, it showed how deep and sincere was his pleasure and gratification, and was another indication of the fact that something was in the wind—a something which had not been so fully disclosed but which made him anxious to have me with him.

"Which brings us to the subject of my note," he rapped out in that direct, sometimes abrupt manner which was so characteristic of the man. "Run up to your room for a wash, for I know what a dusty trip you have had, and then rejoin me here for a chat over our cigars."

The study was in reality a private laboratory and workroom combined, and I knew that a conference held there would be upon strictly business subjects, and that the matter must be of something more than ordinary importance.

The room was perhaps thirty feet long by twenty wide, furnished with a few wicker chairs, deep and comfortable, yet severe in their lines; and by benches, shelves and bookcases. Here it was my friend spent by far the greater portion of his time, working, experimenting and studying.

The room was in the southeast corner of the house, and had only one door, that leading to a hallway on the west side. This door had a spring lock, and when experimenting or engaged in study, Dr. Potter would allow no one to enter on any pretext. It was his custom, on such occasions, to keep the latch on the door, so that it locked automatically when closed.

When I rejoined the Doctor in the study, no time was lost in getting promptly to the business in hand. Opening the door of a small closet on the south side of the room, he showed me, suspended on the inside of the door, a complete skeleton.

"Permit me," he remarked in the most serious tone, "to present my associate, and one-time enemy, Elbert Crothers.

"Crothers," turning to the skeleton, "This is Walter Pearce, an attorney of Los Angeles, of whom you have doubtless heard me speak."

I am as willing as the next man to face the vital facts of existence, and I realize only too well the lot of all mortal flesh, but there is something uncanny and creepy in a human skeleton dangling from the inside of a closet door, its sightless eyes staring hollowly into space, its lipless grin mocking the warm red corpuscles of one's blood, penetrating to and chilling the marrow of one's bones. This effect is enhanced when the skeleton is that of a man one has known, and the impression caused by the formal introduction was grim, unreal and hideous.

My flesh began to creep as the bleached bones that had once been the mortal abode of Elbert Crothers appeared to rattle and sway in acknowledgment of the introduction.

At first I thought Dr. Potter had some method of manipulating the door to make the skeleton gyrate in an uncanny shimmy of death; but a closer inspection showed that the joints had been so perfectly adjusted in articulation, and the skeleton hung with such a nice degree of accuracy, that the slightest motion of the door would cause the bones to sway backward and forward for several seconds.

I am not particularly nervous, and yet I know my face was a shade lighter than usual as I sank into my chair. The Doctor, on the other hand, positively seemed to enjoy the proximity of the skeleton, and stood by the door of the closet, his lean face expressionless as ever, the slender fingers of his right hand stroking the long bones of what had once been the powerful forearm of Elbert Crothers.

"Pearce," came the sudden inquiry, "have I title to this thing or not?"

The question took me somewhat off my guard.

"Just how do you mean?" I countered.

"Just this," resumed my host, concisely, "Elbert Crothers passed out in the County Hospital of a small Indiana town in which is located a medical university. Instead of burying the indigent casualties in a local Potters' Field, the custom is to turn the bodies, for a nominal consideration, over to the dissecting department of the university.

"This made things easier for me, although I should have had my way in any event; a little pull with the faculty of the university, a little money, and—presto!—the thing was done. Elbert Crothers, or all that was left of him, was delivered into my possession, to do with as I liked.

"Now in regard to title. Crothers, I understood at the time, left no direct relatives. Subsequent investigations show that he had a cousin who, it seems, is a spiritualist, or 'spiritist,' as he prefers to be called. In some way this cousin—Jorgensen is the name he goes by—has found out that I have the skeleton here."

The problem thus presented to me was one which is not often placed before an attorney in the course of a general practice, and I had to reason back to elementals before answering:

"As a general rule, a man, strange as it may seem, has no property in his dead body. It is really the property of the state. Custom and usage, in most jurisdictions, have decreed that a person may dispose of his remains, as far as indicating the manner of burial or cremation. The body itself is not an asset. It may not be attached, nor levied upon under an execution.

"In the present case if you have acted without regular permission from the proper authorities, and I take it that you have, there is a possibility that this man, Jorgensen, may make you some trouble; not particularly because of the relationship, but as an interested citizen who may start the proper judicial machinery of the state in operation to inquire how you came by the skeleton.

"What I can't understand is how you allowed him to find out that you had the body. Understand, I mean no criticism, but it seems strange that you allowed him to get the information."

My friend favored me with that twinkle of the eye, a mere relaxation of the muscles, which passes for a smile in his vocabulary of facial expressions.

"Thereby hangs a tale. Naturally, I acted with all secrecy, and you may imagine my feelings when I received this letter in the mail a few days after the body had been prepared into the skeleton which you see before you."

The paper passed over to me consisted of a single sheet on which was written, in a fine, Spencerian hand, presumably that of a clerical person, the following rather remarkable note:

Dr. Alfred Potter,
Santa Delbara, California.
  "Vengeance is mine," saith the Lord.
  I have been in communication with the spirit of my deceased cousin, Elbert Crothers, and am advised by him that you have secured his body from the hospital where he died; and that you have by acids, and other means, prepared a skeleton therefrom which now hangs in your office. That you have done this for the purpose of satisfying your private vanity, rather than for any reason of scientific research.
  On behalf of the departed spirit of Elbert Crothers, I hereby demand that you take this skeleton not later than the fifth of this month, and give to the same a decent burial, in accordance with established civilized custom.
  You will understand that, in writing this letter, I am merely acting on behalf of, and at the dictation of, Elbert Crothers. I have no personal feelings in the matter and make no threats. However, a knowledge of certain phases of life activity with which you are probably not familiar, leads me to warn you that this request from a departed spirit is not one to be lightly disregarded.
  You will hear from me no further in this connection; but, if you do not accede to the request, I do not doubt you will have ample reason to regret your decision.
    Very truly yours,
    J. E. Jorgensen.

I re-read the letter before speaking.

"Do you mean to tell me that you believe this rot? This is beyond question the work of a gang of blackmailers who have either traced the shipment of the body, or else have secured information from some member of your own household."

The Doctor spoke decidedly:

"There was no *earthly* way in which the writer of that letter could have traced the body to this house. When I tell you that I went to considerable trouble and expense to protect myself against developments of just this nature, and that even my own detectives did not and do not know who was their employer, or what was done with the body, you will understand that I am not speaking idly.

"My chauffeur, who might be considered open to suspicion by a stranger, unfortunately has not the advantage of breeding or education, but I have every reason to believe he is loyal, as he owes everything he has in the world to me. Kimi, I would trust anywhere, and he has been with me for years. The only other inmate of the house, Professor Gordon Kennedy, is a person whom you have not met, but one whose mind is entirely steeped in abstract scientific research. He is the typical absent-minded scientist, and has been employed as my assistant for the past few months.

"No, I have absolutely no doubt as to the honesty or discretion of the persons in this household or associated with me; but the real point is that they knew nothing of the receipt of the body nor the preparation of the skeleton; and when the skeleton was completed and I was ready to hang it on this door, I surreptitiously removed another skeleton I had been keeping in the study. It would take a skilled anatomist to detect the difference."

"Then how the devil could this cousin of Crothers have traced the skeleton here?" I puzzled.

"That is the problem which has given me some food for reflection. You are doubtless aware that scientific research has proven that most of the supposedly spiritistic phenomena are in reality based on mental telepathy. I believe that it is possible that this Jorgensen (the name is an assumed one, by the way) has learned of the location of the body, or skeleton, through some telepathic method. There remains the only other explanation mentioned in this letter."

I scrutinized the speaker narrowly, thinking at first he might be joking.

"Surely you are not seriously advocating spiritualism?"

The Doctor shrugged.

"Who knows?"

"If you really wish my candid opinion," he added, choosing his words carefully lest I misunderstand his meaning, "I have been greatly intrigued by some of the more recent claims of the spiritists; and some time ago I determined to investigate the matter for myself when a proper opportunity should arise. Upon learning of the death of Elbert Crothers I felt that if I could convey his body to my study in such a manner that no one could possibly know of it, I might lay the foundation for an instructive experiment.

"Crothers would use every ounce of any force which might be at his command on the other side to prevent my carrying out such a scheme. 'Haunt' me, I believe, is the popular word.

"Therefore, I substituted bodies in this Indiana town with all secrecy, sold the substituted body as that of Crothers to the dissecting department of the university, transported the real body by roundabout methods to Los Angeles, and from there drove it myself at night to the house here, after making absolutely certain that I was not followed.

"A few days after I had prepared the skeleton, which I did by secret and original methods, I received that letter in the mail. You will notice that the letter hints at the process which was used in preparing the skeleton from the body.

"Of course, I immediately left no stone unturned until I had located the writer of that letter. His true name is Phillips, he lives in San Francisco, and as he claims to be, is probably a cousin of Crothers."

The situation was getting too much for my conservative, legal type of mind, and I was about to bring to bear all my powers of logic to prove to my friend that he was the victim of some blackmailing gang, or otherwise mistaken in his premises, when—my blood froze in my veins!

Low and menacing, and from somewhere in the vicinity of the head of the skeleton, came a vindictive, ominous moan, long drawn out and indescribably weird. There was something in the nature of the sound which immediately convinced one that it could never have emanated from a human throat!

"For God's sake, what is that?" I shouted.

The Doctor did not answer for a moment. Apparently as calm and serene as ever, his head was cocked slightly to one side, in an effort to determine the exact location of the sound. It was nearly a minute before he spoke, and, when he did so, he might have been lecturing a classroom for all the emotion displayed.

"I was just about to mention those moans, and am very glad that you have had this opportunity to hear them. I cannot tell you what produces or causes the sound; but several times each twenty-four hours since I have had our friend Mr. Crothers hanging on that door, and usually while I am absolutely alone in the room, that moan or wail can be distinctly heard, lasting for a few seconds, and sounding much the same as you have just heard it."

I could feel the cold sweat breaking out on my forehead as I stared into the sightless caverns of the grinning skull.

"But," I stammered, "it seemed to come from the very mouth of the skeleton."

"That," was the rejoinder, "we shall soon discover. In anticipation of a repetition of the sound, I had constructed a coil containing a sound screen in a magnetic field, by which the direction of sound may be accurately determined. The method is not particularly new, and is an adaptation of the means used to ascertain the direction of a wireless sending station. When this moan started, I pressed the button you see here on the chair, which started the current flowing through the sound detector. There was no other sound in the room at the time, and, as I shut off the current immediately upon the cessation of the noise, we should have some results.

"If you will be so good as to take a look at that box in the corner, you will find an arrow suspended on the top of a needle. Sight along that arrow, and you will find the exact direction of the sound."

Dr. Potter indicated a box sitting in a corner of the study on the top of which was a little arrow, cunningly mounted on a swivel, on a thin steel rod. I had not taken three steps in that direction before I knew the answer.

"It is pointed directly toward the head of the skeleton!" I exclaimed.

"Exactly," came the dry comment of my host. "Now you will understand why I am giving to the matter of that letter more than a passing interest."

The events of the last few moments had left me shaken and excited. The unreality of the whole business, coupled with the tone of deadly menace in that moan, so apparently emanating from the dead bones gibbering at us from the closet door, had entirely upset my nerves.

"Let's get out of here," I gasped.

Without a word the Doctor arose, calmly closed the closet door, and escorted me to the floor above, where the luxuriously furnished living-room looked out over the blue waters of the Pacific. The room was directly over the studio beneath, and I was probably not over twenty feet away from the skeleton in a direct line; but there was something so serene in the tranquil sunlight pouring in the wide windows that I felt miles away from the gruesome thing in the room below.

Feeling ashamed of my emotion, I sank into a chair and stole a glance at my host. His face was as expressionless as ever. He was sitting, puffing reflectively on a cigar, exhaling the smoke in those short, crisp puffs which, experience has taught me, denote mental concentration in the habitual smoker.

A wave of emotion swept over me. I was probably the only confidant he had in the world, and he had done so much more for me than I could ever do for him that I felt humbled and meek.

"For heaven's sake, Alfred," I burst out with sudden feeling, "take that ghastly thing and give it a burial. Get rid of it. Get it out of the house tonight, now. Something seems to tell me that you are going to be exposed to danger unless that skeleton is taken away and taken away at once."

The face turned toward me was tranquil in its calm decision, and I knew the answer even before it came.

"If I did that, Walter, I should lose the best opportunity I will ever have to make an impartial investigation of modern spiritistic phenomena. This bids fair to be an unusual case, and I had much rather lose my life than back out of the solution of a problem of scientific interest."

I knew, indeed, that the scientist was speaking the simple truth, without boasting or bravado, merely making a plain statement of fact, and that any further argument would be worse than wasted.

I was on the point of making some reply, however, when I experienced that peculiar feeling which creeps over me when someone is standing close to me, and of whose presence I am otherwise unaware. The recent experience in the study had made me nervous, and I jumped from my chair, spinning around on my heel—to find Kimi standing at my elbow with the tea service.

This betrayal of my intense nervous state caused me considerable embarrassment, and the laugh with which I attempted to pass over the matter had a hysterical ring in it which chagrined me still further.

If anyone noticed this besides myself nothing was said about it. Kimi silently proceeded with the duties in hand, and the Doctor discussed a game of golf he had enjoyed the week before.

"You know," I remarked, as Kimi slipped out of the room, "there is something uncanny in the way Kimi moves in and out of a room without a sound. I remember commenting on the subject the last time I was here, and he has grown worse since. He glides around like a shadow."

My companion smiled.

"That is one of the things I have been trying to teach him. There is nothing more annoying to me than to be interrupted in the midst of some deep problem by the noise of a person crossing the room. I have been impressing on Kimi the necessity for absolute silence at all times when I am working. As you probably know, when I am locked in the study nothing is ever allowed to disturb me. In fact, I have the only key in existence for that door. I latch it when I go in and I am sure no one will interrupt me.

"Professor Kennedy, the assistant of whom I spoke, is sometimes with me, but when I am about to engage in private work, I do not allow even him in the room. As I said before, he is rather absent-minded. He is rather a character.

"Here he comes now, by the way. I am anxious to have you meet him, but you must not mind if he fails to acknowledge the introduction."

A rather short, heavy-set man entered the room. I judged him to be about forty-seven or -eight. His eyes were distorted by a huge pair of heavy, tortoise-shell spectacles containing lenses of unusual thickness. His features were heavy and his neck thick and muscular. I noticed a frown on his forehead as he approached Dr. Potter, absolutely ignoring my presence, and I am convinced he did not even know I was in the room.

"Look here, Doctor," he began in a thin, high-pitched voice, "I can't seem to get any proper results with my germ cultures. I had arranged an electric incubator, and now your confounded Japanese servant has juggled the thermostatic adjustment on me and the temperature has dropped twenty degrees."

It seemed such an oddity for so large a man to complain of what was doubtless so trivial a matter in such a querulous voice that I smiled covertly.

"Never mind that for the present, Professor Kennedy," said my host, and his slight accent on the title convinced me that his assistant was a stickler for that form of salutation, "I want you to meet my very dear friend and adviser Mr. Walter Pearce, the Los Angeles attorney of whom you have heard me speak."

If I had previously entertained any doubt as to the absent-minded abstraction of Professor Kennedy, it was removed right there. I was standing at his right, but he turned to his left, as if expecting to find me standing there; saw no one, turned to the right, and gave me his short, thick hand in a grasp of remarkable vigor, jerked out that he was pleased to know me, and returned immediately to the subject of his complaint.

"I don't know what's the matter; I can't seem to keep things in order in my laboratory. I'm afraid those cultures are ruined."

"Well, I will look into the matter later," soothed Dr. Potter. "At present I am taking Pearce out for a ride. If the cultures are ruined there is nothing for it but to start a new batch, and I suppose it will be possible to put a set-screw on the thermostatic control to prevent its being thrown out of adjustment again by any accidental jar."

"It wasn't any accidental jar that threw that incubator out of adjustment," squeaked the irate Professor, as he turned on his heel and, without a word to me, left the room with quick, nervous steps.

I smiled at Dr. Potter.

"Your assistant is certainly a peculiar combination. Where did you pick him up?"

I thought for a moment Dr. Potter was going to smile, the twinkle in his eye was pronounced, which was saying a good deal, for him.

"Yes," he replied, "he is certainly peculiar. He is a chemist of no mean ability, and as an electrical engineer, he is a wonder. There is nothing he cannot construct along the lines of electrical machinery. His periods of abstraction absolutely unfit him for a practical life, and prevent him from turning his knowledge to any financial benefit to himself. I pay him no fixed salary, but give him whatever money he requires from time to time, and he is really in the seventh heaven. Also, by the way, he is very jealous of his title of Professor, and be sure to address him by it when you have occasion to talk with him.

"I suggest that we take a drive for an hour or two in the fresh air. It will steady your nerves and give you an appetite for dinner."

I had no hesitancy about admitting that I would like an opportunity to recover my mental poise, and eagerly accepted the suggestion.

That afternoon was the most perfect I have ever seen in a climate which revels in perfection. The trip was simply wonderful, and my companion became unusually sociable. In view of later developments, I shall always look back upon that drive as the most delightful three hours I have ever spent with my friend.

There was only one thing which in any wise marred the pleasure of the trip, and that was the annoying habit of John Dawley, the chauffeur, of keeping his head partially turned in order to hear the conversation.

I finally suggested to my companion that the draught from the front of the car with the window open was slightly annoying, and he obligingly raised the plate-glass which separated the driver's compartment from the tonneau.

We spent three hours in the delightful, warm air, driving down to the white sand where the breakers washed almost to the wheels, and then in less than half an hour ascending the Pindola Grade, rising in a few miles more than four thousand feet above the blue Pacific.

Tucked away near the top of the grade, nestling in a little valley, surrounded by mountains, we found a ranch house, where we secured some excellent milk, and rested for a few minutes. I had been taking a short walk admiring the little valley and the stream of mountain water, purling and plashing down the canyon, while the Doctor chatted with the man who owned the place. Upon my return I found my host standing near the car, engaged in conversation with Dawley, who was talking rapidly and vehemently. Something in their postures indicated that the subject of conversation was not intended for my ears, and it was plain to be seen that Dawley was very much excited about something.

I therefore made some commonplace remark about the scenery while I was still several feet from the pair, and Dawley immediately broke away and busied himself about the car, the color of his face and the set of his jaw showing he was under a great emotional strain; but Dr. Potter was his usual self, quiet, courteous and patient.

Again I found occasion to speculate to myself what it was which could make a man of the refinement of the Doctor maintain such a young boor in his employ. There must be some bond, something which did not appear on the surface to account for the easy tolerance and courteous treatment he gave to one who was very apparently entitled to nothing except an immediate discharge.

It was after dark when we approached the house; but Kimi had the place blazing with lights, and it certainly presented a warm and cheerful aspect. Dinner was served shortly after we arrived, and I was pleased to find myself fully recovered from the shock of the afternoon.

A place was set at the table for Professor Kennedy, but we did not wait for him, and indeed he did not show up during the meal. Kimi had called him twice, and each time the Professor had promised to be right up, and each time had immediately forgotten all about it. Dr. Potter told me it was a frequent occurrence when the chemist was working on some problem for him to neglect to come to his meals, and to even resent the interruption when Kimi would bring his plate to him in the little laboratory he had fixed up.

During the evening my host announced that he had arranged an appointment with one of the best detectives from the office of the Sheriff of Los Angeles. This detective, he further announced, was to arrive on the evening train, and would stay several days, provided he appeared to understand the exact requirements of the situation.

As it was then only an hour before the train was due, it was apparent that arrangements had been made for the presence of the detective several hours previous, if not on some preceding day. It was typical of my friend that he had said nothing of this matter during our earlier conversations, and it was also an indication that there were developments of which I knew nothing which had made my friend feel the presence of a detective necessary.

He turned his keen gaze on my face as he said:

"Don't think for a minute I am turning this case over to a detective. I am merely taking precautions from a scientific standpoint to make sure that any phenomena I may observe and record, are not of a material and mundane origin.

"I am getting this detective for the same reason that I would perform a delicate physical experiment in a room isolated from sound waves and immune to thermal variations. I wish to eliminate all outside agencies which might form a disturbing element in my experiments."

I was on the point of replying, but the words never came.

I was sitting, facing the big window which opened from the dining-room on to the spacious front porch. At that hour of the night the window was dark and black; but, even as I looked, a white face, drawn and ghastly, pressed against the pane, the features sharply outlined against the black background, the eyes fastened on the back of my companion's head in a stare of such intensity that everything else within the vision of the apparition seemed excluded!

A moment the face showed startlingly clear against the plate-glass window, and then, silently and swiftly, it was withdrawn.

The calm tones of Dr. Potter brought me back to earth:

"From the expression on your face, Pearce," he observed, keenly and evenly, "I should say you had seen something or somebody peering in the window behind me. I noticed the shade had not been lowered when we drove up this evening."

"Have some of these olives. They are particularly good and grown and cured especially for me.

"Kimi, please lower the shades."

"My Heavens!" I shouted. "How can you sit there and talk in that calm manner! Within ten feet of your back, some prowler has just stared cold, deliberate murder at the back of your head—and you haven't even turned in your chair!"

"Come, come," soothed my host, as though he were talking to an excited child, "go on with your dinner. You are getting worked up over a trifle. I knew by the expression of your face that you had a brief glimpse of something at the window, and the natural supposition was that it was the face of some person. I also knew that the face had been withdrawn, and that it would, therefore, do me no good to turn around and look.

"Whoever it was, or what he wants will be disclosed in good time. Personally I do not care very much who or what it is unless it should in some manner interfere with my experiments. Hence the detective. Simply and purely, as I said before, to eliminate the possibility of outside agencies interfering in my research work.

"Speaking of the detective reminds me— By the way, Kimi, I wish you would take the car to the station, where you will meet a Mr. Arthur Dwire, of Los Angeles. He will be looking for you when the train pulls in, and will be staying here tonight, perhaps for several days."

Kimi, who had lowered the shades, signified his immediate departure, and silently withdrew from the room. As far as I was concerned, however, the meal was a failure. Time after time, I would start, peer over my shoulder, and fancy I had seen a shadow, or the outline of a face just beyond the closed shade. The shade over the window seemed to only partially hide a menace, lurking just within the shadow, and ready to strike. I felt that peculiar sensation which comes over me when someone is watching me.

I was unquestionably a very poor companion. My host, however, with that excellent tact and consideration which had endeared him to me so many times, continued as though nothing had happened, and acted just as though I was my natural self and holding up my end of both conversation and food.

I can't remember when I have ever been so frankly pleased and relieved to see anyone, as I was to see Mr. Arthur Dwire.

The detective was rather slender, and firmly knit, one of those alert, active men who radiate vigor and vitality. There was an efficiency and competency about him which made him seem capable of meeting and mastering any situation. Quick in his movements and very evidently possessing great agility and vitality, he upset my conception of the modern detective by proving a thorough gentleman, well read and a college graduate.

The speed and accuracy with which he grasped the situation were remarkable. Dr. Potter very briefly outlined the case, showed him the study and "introduced" him to the skeleton. The sight of that grinning skeleton swaying and rattling on the door revived my horror, and I never took my eyes off the hollow eye sockets of the gibbering skull, waiting with bated breath for a repetition of that awful wail, so menacing and blood-curdling.

However, nothing happened, and we returned the skeleton to the inside of the closet by the simple expedient of shutting the closet door, and returned to the living-room.

"Doctor," remarked Dwire, when our host had given a general summary of the events to date, "either someone is playing a prank on you, or you're entertaining a spook. Personally, I don't take much stock in ghosts, but that's neither here nor there. You've got all the scientific education, and if it's a ghost, you get him; if it's something else, that's my meat. The very first thing I want to do is to make a minute search of the house, especially that closet. We may find some interesting things."

It was with an approving twinkle of the eye the Doctor replied:

"Yes—search, by all means. Devote all day tomorrow to it if you wish. Tonight, however, I wish to try an experiment.

"You have grasped my idea exactly. It may be

that someday we will know a great deal more of the existence after death. In the meantime, I wish to satisfy myself there are no natural causes for the sounds we have heard before undertaking a serious investigation, based upon the theory there is something supernatural causing those noises.

"Now, then, what I first want to find out is whether those sounds are being made by some person concealed on the outside of the room. Inasmuch as the skeleton is hung on the south wall, it is barely possible someone might be directly in line with the skeleton on the outside of the house, making the noises.

"I usually hear them several times during the evening, when I am alone in the study, and tonight I am going to go down to the study as usual, and ask you two to keep a sharp watch from the porch above. You can easily see any person sneaking around the outside wall.

"I nearly always hear the sound when I have turned out the light for the night, or just before I turn it on when entering the room. It has occurred to me that darkness makes it easier for the noises to be produced, and tonight I will sit in the room without turning the lights on. There will be enough moonlight to enable me to distinguish the outlines of objects."

It may have been some premonition of impending evil, or it may have been the aftermath of the shocks to which I had been subjected that day, but I felt it would be tempting the fates for Dr. Potter to enter that room alone in the dark. I was about to voice my sentiments, when Professor Kennedy entered the room. As usual he walked directly to Dr. Potter, ignoring all other matters, and commenced to discuss some matter of research which was too deep for me to follow.

Dr. Potter, taking him gently by the arm, turned to Dwire.

"Professor Kennedy," he said formally, "may I have the pleasure of presenting my friend Mr. Arthur Dwire of Los Angeles? Mr. Dwire will be with us for the next few days.

"Dwire, permit me to present Professor Kennedy, my associate, who has kindly volunteered to spend the summer with me, and to assist in constructing laboratory equipment and carry on research work."

Dwire and Kennedy shook hands, the latter blinking away behind his heavy glasses, peering closely into the detective's face, taking much more interest in him than he had in me when I had made his acquaintance.

"You have known the Doctor long?" he inquired in his jerky, explosive manner.

The question was just a trifle awkward, as Dr. Potter had apparently wished to conceal from Kennedy the fact that Dwire was a detective, and in the house as such. I admired the skillful manner in which the detective turned the question.

"Not as long as you have, Professor, but long enough to have heard Dr. Potter speak of your work in glowing terms."

The Professor was plainly pleased.

"I have a little skill along my lines," he confessed. "The big trouble in this house is to keep my equipment in adjustment. Somebody always seems to investigate everything I construct, and manages to leave it out of adjustment. I can't help but feel that confounded Jap has his nose in about everything going on in the house."

Our host explained:

"I have the study on the lower floor on the south side of the house, and I have fixed up a laboratory in one of the northern rooms for Professor Kennedy; between us we have the house pretty well filled with apparatus, and I am afraid, Professor Kennedy, dealing as he does with electrical equipment, finds it difficult to maintain delicate adjustments in a house whose foundations were built for residential purposes, rather than those of scientific investigation. You see, it only takes a very slight jar on the floor of the house to cause a shock to be transmitted throughout the place, which is fatal to the microscopic adjustment of delicate instruments."

The chemist grunted.

"Your solution may be correct; but I think someone in this house who knows enough about electricity to understand the apparatus I am using is tampering with things.

"I will advise you here and now that in the future I want no servant in my room under any pretext. If I miss a meal, that's my own business. As for sweeping and dusting, I'll do it myself. I have just adjusted a lock and bolt on my laboratory door, and I want no Jap snooping around, or even knocking at the door. When I'm in, I'm in; and when I get ready to come out, I'll come out."

Having delivered this ultimatum, the Professor snapped around on his heel, nodded his head to us and left the room.

I turned to Dr. Potter and smiled:

"Evidently your assistant has some decided ideas of his own."

"It is really an insane prejudice," answered my friend. "He feels that Kimi is spying on him, and tampering with his delicate electrical apparatus. As a matter of fact, Kimi, while an excellent servant, has absolutely no curiosity, and, I am satisfied, has no ambition in life other than to attend to my wants."

"I notice that you did not intimate to Professor Kennedy what my real job is," Dwire broke in; "I therefore take it that you wish to keep my work a secret; but I was pretty sure that your Jap servant, who met me at the train, knew what I was here for. Are you taking special pains to keep the Professor in the dark?"

Dr. Potter looked troubled for a moment.

"I must admit the truth of what you say, but I don't want you to think I am suspecting Professor Kennedy of anything, nor do I want you to do so. As far as I know, he has no idea that there is anything unusual in the matter of the skeleton. The peculiar moaning noise I have described has never occurred while he has been in my study. He knows nothing about it."

Dwire smiled.

"I should say that the failure of the ghost to howl when Professor Kennedy was present was point number one."

Dr. Potter made no reply; seemingly this point had either been in his mind before, or else he was considering the significance of it.

"By the way," inquired the detective, "I presume it's in order to ask where you picked the Professor up, and what you know of him."

Dr. Potter answered readily enough:

"I know very little about him personally, and a great deal about him professionally. He is hardly the type one would expect to find as a professor of electricity and chemistry, but such is the case, and he is one of the leaders in those sciences.

"During the war I did some slight work along the line of developing new gases, and of controlling submarines by electricity. Professor Kennedy has some German blood in his veins; and, as it happened, was in Germany at the outbreak of the war. He was detained by the German government and forced to remain throughout the war, cooperating in the manufacture of war material, a work which was performed by him with reluctance, but which he was forced to do.

"Through the German secret service he, in some way, learned of my own modest activities in assisting the Allies along the same lines, and conceived the idea of making my personal acquaintance. Following the armistice he got in touch with me through a mutual friend, and has since been of the greatest assistance to me in connection with some of the electrical equipment I am making for my experiments. He has gradually become a fixture here, and has taken the position of assistant.

"However, all this discussion is keeping us from the real work at hand. Step out on the porch a moment and let me show you exactly what I wish you to do."

By leaning over the rail of the porch, we could see the entire south wall of the study, and the two windows opening to the south. As the porch had a projecting roof, and vines trailing up the pillars, our heads would not be outlined against the sky, and we could plainly see any person on the ground below, without standing much chance of being seen ourselves.

Dr. Potter looked around the porch, peered at the ground below, and then placed us near a pillar almost directly over the study window.

"Now if you two will just wait here, I will enter the study, carefully locking the door behind me. The entire outside wall will be under your observation; I will leave the window open so you can hear any sounds which may come from below, and can call to you if I desire. If you see any person approaching that study window, capture him at any cost. There may, perhaps, be more to this than appears on the surface."

"Alfred," I pleaded, "let me accompany you. Dwire can watch the wall all right, and I hate to think of you sitting alone in the dark with that thing."

"Nonsense," came the retort. "I sincerely and keenly appreciate your concern; but I rather expect there will be occasion for you to pursue a very material skeleton with flesh and blood on its bones, and there will be absolutely no one in the study except myself. I am merely the decoy. Keep a sharp watch on that window, and if anyone tries to get through it stop him, even if you have to shoot."

With no other parting than this, Dr. Potter abruptly took himself downstairs to the study, from the window of which we shortly saw his head protruding.

"That's fine," he said, in response to my inquiry as to our positions. "I will remain here with the lights out. There is enough reflected light in the room to see outlines, and you keep a sharp watch on the window and the ground. You will probably have to wait an hour or so until things quiet down."

With this whispered admonition he withdrew his head, leaving us straining our ears and eyes, and accustoming our vision to the semi-darkness of the night.

"Are there any servants, gardeners or other attendants likely to be about?" whispered the detective. "If I see anyone prowling around here I want to be sure of my ground, as I am likely to shoot first and ask questions afterward."

I answered in the same tone:

"No. Kimi has his own quarters, opening from the kitchen, does all the inside work, including the preparation of meals. The chauffeur lives in town, and goes home every night at five-thirty, Kimi doing any driving required after that. Professor Kennedy certainly is not a night prowler, and has given us his assurance that he will be locked in the laboratory at the north end of the house."

Dwire kept his eye glued to the ground and windows below, while I, mindful of the face I had seen at the window earlier in the evening, kept my attention about equally divided between the ground below and the porch on which we were sitting.

The moon was nearly half full, and barely visible through high fog clouds. The surroundings were enveloped in silence, penetrated at intervals by the whine of an automobile hurrying along the highway.

The influence of the calm night acted soothingly on my nerves, and I fell into a reverie, thinking of the courage of the scientist, and the stern control with which he mastered his emotions.

My thoughts were interrupted by a slight pressure on my arm. Almost at the same time I heard a faint noise, something in the nature of a rustle, apparently coming from the study itself. I strained my eyes into the darkness, and then, suddenly, without warning, the silence of the night was shattered by a cry from Dr. Potter such as I had never expected to hear.

"Quick, Pearce, Dwire! Here, quick!" he shrieked. "Good God—CROTHERS!!"

Then silence.

I knew the lay of the land better than Dwire, and was able to enter the study window ahead of him. After fumbling in the dark for a moment, I switched on the lights. I am satisfied that not more than ten or twelve seconds elapsed from the time of the first cry until the room was flooded with light.

Never will I forget the sight which met my eyes!

Sitting in a wicker chair, some ten feet from the south wall of the room, and facing the window, sat Dr. Potter; but, from the manner in which he was slumped over the arm of the chair, I knew the reason we had heard nothing more

from him after the first cry. A knife or other pointed instrument had penetrated his heart, and death must have been instantaneous.

Facing him, and some twelve feet distant, the skeleton of Elbert Crothers danced and swayed from its hanging on the closet door. Rattling and oscillating in an ever diminishing orbit, it looked just as though it had been walking around, and had suddenly climbed back on the door when it heard us enter the room!

The ribs scraped softly against the wood; the bones of the fingers quivered and rattled, and the fleshless face grinned into the dead countenance of my murdered friend!

I had just time to take in the situation when Kimi, with a bath robe around him, knocked at the study door, which Dr. Potter had latched with the spring lock when he entered the room. Kimi had heard the cry, even in his bedroom, and realized as well as I did that nothing within the realm of human experience could have forced his master to utter such a sound.

I opened the door for him and silently indicated the tragic sight. It took him a moment to realize that his beloved master was dead; and then, as his emotion overcame him, he bowed his head in silence, regardless for the moment of our presence.

At that instant, just as Dwire completed his examination of the body, and looked up to give his conclusions, a white, drawn face, the same I had seen earlier in the evening, peered for a moment against the dark background of the open window—and was gone.

Almost as quick as the face "registered" in my vision, Dwire had drawn his revolver and rushed to the casement. Unarmed as I was, I jumped through the window right at his heels.

The yard was deserted.

"You take that corner," directed Dwire in low, crisp tones, "and I'll take this."

It was not until after I had reached the corner of the house that I remembered I had no weapon, and should I overtake the mysterious prowler would probably be killed myself; but I had only to think of that still form in the chair to make me feel I would gladly chance my life just for the satisfaction of getting my hands on the murderer.

We made a thorough search of the yard, as well as we could in the darkness, but could see nothing, and again met at the back of the house following a ten-minute, fruitless search.

"Did you look in the garage?" whispered Dwire.

I confessed that I had not, and we started together toward the low building. Even as we did so, there came the whine of an electric starter, the roar of a motor, and Dr. Potter's car leaped from the building, skidded into the turn of the graveled driveway, and disappeared down the concrete highway at terrific speed, the whine of the tires on the smooth surface of the road sounding for several seconds after we had lost sight of the speeding car.

In the momentary flash of reflected light from the headlights of the automobile as it rounded the turn, I had recognized the form of Dawley, the chauffeur, crouched over the wheel.

"Hell!" exploded Dwire. "If we'd been five seconds earlier we could have stopped that bird. As it was, I could have taken a shot at him, but we can telephone the police at Santa Delbara and have him stopped before he has gone five miles. Come on, let's get to the phone."

We rushed back to the house, found the telephone in order, and were assured that two motorcycle officers would be sent out at once to apprehend the driver of the car. The sergeant who answered the telephone advised us Kimi had telephoned in a few minutes earlier advising of the murder of Dr. Potter and that a police car was even now on its way to the house.

We hung up the receiver and stepped downstairs to find Kimi. He was crouched before a door on the north side of the house, his ear to the keyhole, and an expression of diabolical hate distorting his dark face. When he heard us in the corridor, he straightened up and knocked at the door.

"Mista Ploffessa Kennedy," he advised us, "I tell him what happens."

It took three or four minutes of hard pounding, however, before we were able to rouse the Professor from his studies. Then he came to the door, unbolted it, jerked it open and immediately started to protest at being interrupted in his work. His querulous complaint was snapped out with a jerk of the head for each word.

Dwire quickly interrupted him.

"Dr. Potter has been murdered in his study. The police are on the way here, and it is advisable for you to prepare to meet them."

The Professor blinked his eyes rapidly for a moment or two; it seemed to take that long for him to get his mind down to earth and let the idea sink in.

"Murdered, murdered," he muttered. "Impossible! You talk like crazy men."

At this moment the shriek of a siren interrupted the conversation and the police car swept up the drive. We left the Professor still blinking and expostulating, and went to pilot the police through the house.

McDougal, the chief of police himself, had happened to be in the office when Kimi had telephoned, and had taken charge of the case in person. It seemed he was very familiar with the work and standing of Dwire, although he had never met the detective personally; and the two were soon plowing through a mass of detail, examining fingerprints, mapping the premises, and otherwise taking steps to preserve such clues as might exist. Once again I had occasion to be thankful for the presence of Dwire.

Not only was I greatly relieved to know that the best detective in Southern California was working on the case, but the fact that I had been with him at the time of the murder was certainly a means of saving me many embarrassing questions, and, perhaps, from having the finger of suspicion pointed at me.

Dwire frankly outlined all the facts at his command to McDougal, but I could see that the hard-headed Scotchman paid little or no attention to those facts which seemed to involve a supernatural agency. As far as he was concerned, the person who peered into that window was the person who committed the crime, and the rest of the case was all hokum.

The motorcycle officers had stopped Dawley, traveling at a rate of speed far in excess of the legal limit, and returned him to the house. He seemed white and shaken as he waited in the library, but refused to make any statement as to his business on the premises or the reason for his haste.

Professor Kennedy was summoned to the library, and McDougal, after a complete survey of the crime, held an informal examination. As I have mentioned, I was saved the ordeal of answering questions because of my having been with Dwire.

Professor Kennedy told one story, one story only, and he refused to elaborate on it, supply any further details, or to expand on what he had previously said when asked questions by the officers.

He said he had come to the house some three or four months before, was assisting Dr. Potter in research work, that he declined to state the nature of the work, that he had never noticed anything in the house which would arouse his suspicions, that he was at a complete loss to account for the murder, and that ever since he had left us that night in the living-room he had been locked in his laboratory at work and had heard no further sound until we pounded on his door to advise him of the crime.

During the time he was being questioned, he produced a pencil and paper, and from time to time would sketch diagrams. At these times his mind seemed entirely to wander from the matter in hand. McDougal became plainly exasperated, but the Professor did not even notice the impatience of his audience. He was plainly regarding the proceeding as an unwarranted interruption of his work.

Dawley, the chauffeur, proved rather more of a problem. He assumed an exasperating what-are-you-going-to-do-about-it attitude, and refused to make any statement as to his reasons for being on the place or taking the car.

On one subject he talked fluently. He claimed to be the child of a half brother of Dr. Potter, and as such felt that the Doctor owed him a living. He even went so far as to express the hope that the "old man" had remembered him in the will.

I do not think I have ever seen such a contemptible exhibition of selfishness and it was with difficulty that I managed to preserve my dignity and silence.

McDougal was in somewhat of a quandary. The facts pointed suspiciously toward Dawley, but they were hardly sufficient to warrant an arrest. The chief, after a conference with Dwire and myself, arranged to release Dawley but to keep him under surveillance.

A "drag net," as McDougal termed it, was thrown out after the spy I had twice seen looking in the window, and there the matter rested.

The next few days, as I look back on them, were more in the nature of a dream than a reality, the coroner's inquest and the attendant airing of the facts of the tragedy; the usual verdict of death at the hands of some person unknown, and the funeral at which the morbidly curious elbowed to one side the grieving friends who sought to pay their last sad respects to one who had advanced the cause of science and died a martyr.

And then came a new and surprising development. While I had known that Dr. Potter had no relatives, unless Dawley could be considered as such, I certainly had no intimation that I was to be the beneficiary under his will.

Although he had been a wealthy man, and what he had done for me had been little enough when compared with his means, it had been enough to leave me indebted to him for life, and I was astounded to learn, when summoned to the offices of his local attorneys in Santa Delbara, that the will left everything to me.

Here again I was faced with another strange fact. The will in my favor had been executed the day before my arrival, and with the will was a letter to me showing that my friend had recognized the gravity of the situation and felt something of the fatal menace of the mysterious force fighting against him.

The letter read:

My dear Pearce:

As I write this I know you have responded to my request to spend a few days with me and assist me in the matter of which I wrote you.

I have a premonition that the next few days will see us exposed to some considerable danger, from a force we do not entirely comprehend. If you ever have occasion to read these lines it will be because that force has brought about my death, and will be attempting to bring about yours.

As some compensation for your loyalty and for exposing you to this danger, I am leaving you my entire estate. I have no strings to tie to this gift, but I wish if possible you would continue with the investigation where we left off; that you continue Professor Kennedy with you until he has completed his vitamine experiments, and that you guard yourself at all times.

There is more to this matter than appears on the surface, and there are secrets of moment locked within that house.

Profit by my death and spare neither money nor energy in seeking a solution, for if you ever have occasion to read this you will be a marked man. Good-bye.

Your affectionate friend,
Alfred Potter.

I was greatly affected by the letter. The quiet dignity with which my friend had gone about settling his affairs in order to give me protection and compensation, his thoughtfulness of others, and the rare courage he had displayed moved me to tears.

Dwire, of course, continued on the case. He would have done so in any event, but I saw to it that lack of financial compensation was no hindrance. He was sending out numbers of telegrams, studying diagrams of the house and yard, and made one quick trip by motor to Los Angeles.

In the meantime I had taken a surreptitious trip to the study, once or twice, by daylight each time, rather expecting to hear the ghastly wail

from the skeleton, but ever since the murder we had not heard a sound from it, and for several days it remained mute. Dwire made a careful search of the closet where it hung and reported nothing suspicious in its construction or arrangement.

I had hardly seen Professor Kennedy. He rarely came to the table, and when he did, treated Dwire and myself as being so far beneath him intellectually as to have nothing in common with him. He would bolt his food in silence, blink owlishly at us, jerk back his chair, and leave the room with those short, quick steps which seemed so inconsistent in a man of his bulk.

At the repeated request of McDougal, I had continued John Dawley in my employ. The chief felt there was a great possibility he knew more of the murder than he was willing to admit, and wanted him where he could "keep an eye on him."

Then about a week after the tragedy Dwire announced a hurried trip to San Francisco. During his absence he arranged to have a loyal old Irish police officer who had assisted him on many cases quartered in the house with me.

"I'm glad," I assured him. "I wouldn't stay in the house for a minute without him. If it wasn't for the request Dr. Potter left in that letter that skeleton would have been buried a long time ago. I can't get it out of my head but what that grinning skeleton had something to do with the murder of my friend, and that we shall find somehow, somewhere, Elbert Crothers, alive or dead, has a finger in the pie."

Dwire merely smiled and made no comment. I felt that he had some more or less tangible clue.

So it happened that Kelley, the old patrolman, was quartered with me during Dwire's absence. At the suggestion of Dwire, who informed me Kelley was as superstitious as he was brave, I said nothing whatever about the connection of the skeleton with the murder. I was in the study with him once and he noticed the skeleton hanging from the closet door, but I made no explanation of how it came to be there.

The night Dwire returned Kimi met him at

the train and drove him to the house. He was just in time for dinner, and it was apparent that he was laboring under some considerable excitement. Once during the course of the meal he quietly remarked to me that he would have a solution of the mystery within the next forty-eight hours.

This announcement was made in a low voice, but Professor Kennedy, who sat at the end of the table, apparently engrossed in his own thoughts, snapped into immediate attention.

"What's that, Mr. Dwire," he exploded, peering through his heavy lenses at the detective. "What's that you say? A solution of the murder within the next forty-eight hours?"

Dwire gazed directly into the Professor's face. "Your hearing seems remarkably good tonight, Professor."

I fancied Dwire was slightly discourteous, but it also impressed me as strange that Professor Kennedy, who was habitually so absorbed in his thoughts as to make it necessary to speak two or three times to get his attention at the table, should have heard the low remark Dwire undoubtedly intended for my ears alone.

A few seconds later the Professor abruptly arose from the table and retired to his laboratory.

Kimi, who, I flattered myself, had always been devoted to me as a friend of the master's, had passed to me with the estate, and his quiet deference and efficiency was the one bright spot in the whole tragic chain of events.

That night he asked permission to spend the evening in town with friends, and I readily consented. Since the Doctor's death he had had very little opportunity to get out and I was glad to give him the chance for a little recreation, since both Kelley and Dwire were to spend the night with me.

Hardly had we retired to the library than Dwire pulled a photograph from his pocket, and asked me if I had ever seen the face before. The likeness was so perfect that I was startled. There could be no doubt of it. The face was that of the man I had seen looking in the window the night of the crime.

"I thought so," said Dwire. "That's a photo of the person who wrote to Dr. Potter demanding a burial of the skeleton, and signed himself 'J. B. Jorgensen.' However, unless I'm mistaken, he's not the man who committed the murder, but he can give us a lot of interesting information when we catch him—for catch him we will."

Hardly had the words left his mouth than, ringing and wailing through the house, rising and falling, louder than I had ever heard it before, came a ghastly wail, which I knew was coming from the grinning skeleton in the room below!

This time, however, it was not as it had been before, an isolated moan, but wail after wail shivered through the house, rising to the highest crescendo of fiendish menace, then dying away to the moan of a tormented soul. Never on earth could such a noise have been produced from a human throat, the volume of sound alone was such that no human being could have produced it, and the delicate nerves of one's body tingled with a psychic recognition of the unearthly quality of the sound.

Kelley, the rough police officer of hundreds of wild and dangerous experiences, turned white as a sheet and crossed himself repeatedly. As for myself, I know that the color left my face, and I could feel the cold chills chasing each other up and down my spine, while the roots of my hair tingled as the flesh crawled and crept on the top of my head.

Dwire alone seemed cool.

"So that's our friend again, howling for more blood, and I guess it's mine he's after this time."

"My Gawd!" shouted Kelley, "and do yez tell me 'twas a banshee that killed the Doctor?"

"Look here, fellows, and you, Kelley, get this," snapped Dwire. "Let's not get stampeded by some noise we can't understand. A noise is nothing to get afraid of.

"I'm going to show you men just how this crime was committed, and no fool noise is going to scare me out. The thing we've all been overlooking is that it was possible for someone to have sneaked in at that window in spite of the fact that Pearce and I were watching from the porch. Moonlight is a mighty deceptive thing, particularly when it's the light coming through a fog.

"Now I'm going to prove to you men that I'm right. The moon's full tonight, but the clouds are heavier, and, on the whole, it's just about the same light as we had the night of the murder. I'm going down into that room, sit in that same chair in exactly the same position the Doctor sat, and I want Kelley to keep a watch from the porch.

"Some time after ten minutes, and not later than half an hour—Pearce can, of course, choose his own time—he will sneak along the wall, just far enough away from the white surface not to be outlined against it, and I'll bet he can enter that window without Kelley seeing him.

"I will probably be able to 'spot' him as he enters the window, and I'll call out. In fact that's just what happened when Dr. Potter was killed. He saw someone entering the window, and called to us, thinking at first it must have been either Pearce or myself. Where we all made our mistake was in thinking it was impossible for such a person to have entered through the window without our seeing him. After the murder he could have simply left the study by the door which latched and locked automatically behind him.

"Come on out on the porch and I'll put you fellows in place."

As the detective finished speaking, there came again, in a lower key than before, but seemingly penetrating to every corner of the house, that wailing shriek. It is impossible to describe that weird and ominous ululation. I harked back to the stories I had heard of ghouls and banshees screaming for human blood. In spite of myself I felt my blood curdle, and I am willing to swear that the hair on the top of my head actually moved.

"My God, man!" I exploded to Dwire. "Are you crazy? I don't know what foolish theory you may have, but I'll bet all I have that if you enter that room alone tonight and sit in the dark with that skeleton, your life won't be worth a plugged nickel."

Outwardly Dwire was calm, but as he started to speak, I noticed that he gulped twice before the words came. His tongue was cleaving to the roof of his mouth!

"Come on out on the porch," he said, "and can that chatter about ghosts. You act like a bunch of school-kids!"

I might have resented the remark had it not been for what I had just seen. As it was, in spite of the awful feeling that some mysterious presence was shrieking and howling for my blood, I was forced to smile. Dwire was as scared as I was, but trying to "bluff it through."

I had expected that last shriek would have been the last straw as far as Kelley was concerned. He had heard nothing of the supernatural aspect of the case, but he was getting it in bunches right then, and I rather expected he would be ready to give up the fight right then and there; but when I looked at him I saw a surprising change had taken place.

Having convinced himself he was in for a battle with ghosts, Kelley had no thought of leaving us. I verily believe the lovable old Irishman never expected to see another sunrise, but he had pulled a silver dime from his pocket, bent it between his powerful teeth, and was engaged in cramming it down the barrel of his revolver.

"Yez may laugh all ye like, my boy," he remarked as he saw me looking at him; "but ye'll be battlin' fer yer life wit a banshee before the night's much older, and tiz a silver bullet that is a man's only hope in a time like that."

Dwire grabbed us by the arms and led us out on the porch; and, as he did so, a piercing shriek shattered the peaceful silence of the night. Now that we were on the porch, it became apparent that the sound was coming from the study below. The window had been left open, and that piercing, wailing, undulating yell rose to a veritable crescendo of triumph as we entered the darkness of the porch, and slowly died away in a long drawn moan of fiendish glee and unspeakable menace.

The manner of the detective underwent a rapid change. He started to whisper rapidly:

"Look here, fellows, my talk in the living-room was a blind. I'm going down in that study in the dark, and I'm pretty sure an attempt will be made to kill me within the next ten minutes, and the good Lord only knows what weird experience is in store for me—or I should say for us, for you will be with me.

"The same person or thing which murdered Dr. Potter will make an attempt on my life, and we must use our heads, and catch the murderer red handed. I believe that our talk in the living-room was overheard, and I took advantage of that fact to set a trap for the murderer. I'll go down the steps and into the study all right, but, instead of waiting here on the porch you'll go right on down and climb in the window as noiselessly as possible, and without a word to betray your presence will conceal yourselves as close to me as possible.

"Whatever is going to occur will take place within the next five or ten minutes, and you must remember that what took place the night Dr. Potter was in the study was sufficient to shatter even his iron nerve. Don't forget that he called the name of Crothers and don't forget the way that skeleton was shimmying on the door when we entered the room. I'm mentioning these things so you will be prepared for anything that may happen.

"Let's go."

With that, and without giving us a chance for any further argument, he passed through the French window just as Dr. Potter had done on the night of the murder and took his way to the dark study and the shrieking skeleton.

By common impulse Kelley and I shook hands, the silent tribute to a brave man. Then we sneaked quietly and rapidly for that chamber of horror.

We waited for a moment with drawn revolvers before the window (I had lost no time in purchasing a heavy revolver after the murder), while Dwire entered the room and seated himself in the wicker chair facing the skeleton. Then, without a word and with as little noise as possible, Kelley and I sneaked through the window and secreted ourselves in the dark behind the wicker chair occupied by the shadowy form of Dwire, who did not so much as turn to acknowledge our presence.

It could not have been over sixty seconds after the slamming of the study door announced the entrance of Dwire, before it became apparent that something was happening in the vicinity of the skeleton. The light was just dim enough to make it difficult to distinguish objects in the room, but bright enough to make the white bones of the skeleton readily visible as a white blur against the door on which they hung.

As we sat there in that dark room, straining our eyes toward the gruesome souvenir of the feud between Dr. Potter and Elbert Crothers, I reflected that the light must have been just about the same the night of the murder, and that I was now experiencing just about what had been the sensations of Dr. Potter as he sat there in that dark room and realized that those noises were caused by a stealthy, ominous rustling of the skeleton itself.

And then the skeleton *commenced to move!*

I felt the perspiration break out in cold, clammy beads as the bones, apparently of their own volition, silently and stealthily commenced writhing on the door of the closet.

Then the skeleton became a vague blur—*and disappeared*!

It was only with the greatest effort that I was able to control a desire to whisper, "It's gone."

Suddenly, and without warning, a glowing lambent fire broke out over the bones of that grizzly object, sharply outlining in a blotch of glowing light the dangling arms and legs, the hollow ribs and the grinning skull. Then I saw that the thing had climbed down from its place on the door, and was standing upright on the floor, supported by its own bony limbs.

I had hardly appreciated the full significance of this new development before the skeleton commenced to walk slowly toward us, emitting as it did so the wailing screech of a soul in torment. I could distinctly see the legs moving up and down, the articulation of the knee joints, and the swinging arms as the weird spectre walked toward us.

And then I saw something else! The hands were not empty! The bony fingers clutched a long knife, glinting and sparkling in the ghastly light given off by the dead bones of the approaching skeleton.

The voice of Dwire breaking the silence had a distinct quaver in it, and I confess I couldn't have spoken a word if my life had depended on it. As for Kelley, the brave old cop was crossing himself with one hand, but the gun which he held in the other was steady as a rock.

"Halt in the name of the law. You are under arrest," said Dwire.

The skeleton did halt for a moment, and then doubled on itself. The bones lost their support, and the joints collapsed, seeming unequal to the holding up of the weight.

At least that was the way it seemed to me at first, and then—suddenly I understood!

The skeleton had crouched for a spring!

I raised my revolver, but it was too late.

With a wild cry, the apparition sprang straight for Dwire, and, either because of the fact it was hard to judge perspective in the dim light, or because of some uncanny agility, it soared through the air like a bird, arms outspread, and the dagger pointing straight at Dwire's breast.

It all happened so suddenly, and the change from the slow, solemn tread to the flying leap was so abrupt, that it was too late for me to do anything by the time I had perceived the murderous intention of the horrible apparition.

Thank God that the others had more presence of mind, for, with a splitting roar, the revolver of Kelley blazed into the night; and, almost at the same instant, a spurt of flame from the automatic of Dwire leapt to meet the grinning skull.

Both bullets, fired at point-blank from heavy calibre revolvers, arrested the flying figure in midair, just as it was about to descend on Dwire, hurled it back and to the floor, where it fell with a human and solid thud.

By that time I had recovered my sluggish wits, and was racing for the switch, and flooded the room with lights.

Lying still on the floor, with a widening pool of blood spreading over the black robes which covered it, lay a very substantial figure. The skeleton of Elbert Crothers hung, swinging from the closet door.

Dwire, seemingly as cool as though performing an act of ordinary routine, raised the black robe from the still figure of Kimi, who had been instantly killed by a bullet in the forehead.

"I am sorry to have to prove to you that a trusted servant, and a professed friend, has been false," said Dwire, turning to me, "but I received evidence in San Francisco which pointed to Kimi as a spy in the employ of interests adverse both to Dr. Potter and our national government. I had made a secret search of his rooms before I left, and found data which gave me the first real clue, including the fact that, in his younger days, in Japan, the Doctor had deserted a native wife, who proved to be Kimi's sister.

"An examination of the cellar showed where he had constructed a cunningly arranged passage through the floor of the closet. You will find a phosphorescent skeleton painted upon the black robe which he wore. The rest was simple. He entered the closet through the trapdoor, moved the skeleton about a bit, stepped in front of it and with his back to the chair thereby concealing the phosphorescent skeleton painted on the robe he wore, and also concealing the bones for a moment, then by the simple expedient of turning around was able to present the spectacle of a glowing skeleton which had just stepped down from the closet door. His victim would ordinarily be paralyzed with shock, and it would be a simple matter to stab him before he could make a move.

"Kimi was an electrical engineer, which explains his interest in Professor Kennedy's apparatus, and will probably explain the mysterious sounds. He found Phillips, who wrote to us as Jorgensen, found out he was a spiritist, and through a corrupt medium led him to write the note he did, and to make a nocturnal visit to the house the night of the murder.

"Kimi had tried to steal the knowledge of a new and terrific war gas the Doctor had developed. Failing in that he resolved to murder him, both for his secret and to avenge his sister. When he learned that I was hot on the trail, he decided to work the scheme again and dispose of me, particularly after overhearing our talk in the living-room. You will find Professor Kennedy is the harmless scientist he appears to be, and that Dawley is just a fresh young hoodlum, who planned to take the Doctor's car to meet some lady friend."

A subsequent investigation proved Dwire correct in every detail. A modification of an electric automobile siren was found imbedded in the door of the closet directly behind the mouth of the skeleton, and a system of wires made it possible to work this siren from several parts of the house. The length of time the contact was maintained varied the volume and pitch of the noise.

Professor Kennedy, locked in his laboratory, and with his mind on his abstract, scientific problems, had worked through the evening, hearing neither the wails of the siren, nor the revolver shots.

The Santa Delbara police took charge of the situation and it was hushed up with as little publicity as possible, owing to the fact that a war secret was involved.

Since I have been in possession of the house, regardless of the elimination of the supernatural aspect of the case, I have had it completely remodeled, and you may be sure the skeleton of Elbert Crothers no longer hangs in the study. Spirits or not, I have never been able to rid my mind of the impression that my friend and benefactor in some way attracted to himself the events which led to his tragic death, by bringing the skeleton of his ancient enemy to hang on the door of his study closet.

Drop Dead Twice

Hank Searls

HENRY HUNT SEARLS JR. (1922–) received his B.S. from the U.S. Naval Academy at Annapolis, then attended the Stanford University Publishing Course. His background in the navy (he is now a retired lieutenant commander in the Navy Reserve), plus his avocation of yachting, provided authentic background to his many novels with military backgrounds, not to mention his novelizations of the movies *Jaws 2* (1978) and *Jaws: The Revenge* (1987). He had a long history of writing for the pulps, notably the series about San Francisco private eye Mike Blair, which appeared in *Dime Detective* in the 1940s and early 1950s; seven Blair adventures were collected in *The Adventures of Mike Blair* (1988). Searls has written of his inexperience when he began writing, learning his craft while earning a penny a word from the pulps, which served him well when he began to write full-length novels, frequently military thrillers, such as *The Crowded Sky* (1960), which was filmed the same year with Dana Andrews, Rhonda Fleming, Efrem Zimbalist Jr., and Anne Francis; *The Pilgrim Project* (1964), filmed by Robert Altman as *Countdown* (1968), starring James Caan, Joanna Moore, and Robert Duvall; *The Penetrators* (1965); and the TV movie *Overboard* (1978) with Angie Dickinson. Among Searls's other TV writing credits are episodes of *The Fugitive*, the miniseries *Wheels*, and the creation of *The New Breed*, which starred Leslie Nielsen.

"Drop Dead Twice" was published in the March 1950 issue.

"Not this time brother!" I said.

Drop Dead Twice

Hank Searls

When a lady dabbles in blackmail, she's begging for a shroud—and so is the private dick who goes calling on her corpse!

IT WAS A VERY NICE JOB—DEFINITELY professional. And final. The blonde lay across the hotel bed lengthwise, a gleam of golden flesh showing above her stocking, but otherwise perfectly presentable. A white linen handkerchief was clutched in her hand. She had been mugged—strangled—throttled. Whatever you wanted to call it, the killer had quite thoroughly known his business.

It was no place for me. The package in my pocket was suddenly heavy. I lit a cigarette and did some fast thinking. The more I thought the worse it looked. The desk clerk had taken my name, phoned the room. The blonde had apparently answered the phone and told him to send me up. One short elevator ride later I had walked through the open door, called her name, and gone into the bedroom.

And she was dead.

What do you do when you find a corpse? In the movies, you call the cops. The cops come and they want to know what you're doing there. You can't explain. So they stick you in the clink, and you stay, innocent as a new-born babe, until some smart dick solves the crime. Then they spring you and everybody lives happily ever after.

But suppose nobody solves the crime?

Maybe you burn. Maybe they adjust that last, uncomfortable necktie and spring the trapdoor. No, this is California. They put you in a quiet private room with a bottle of cyanide gas and tell you to breathe deep.

Not me.

I flicked the cigarette out the window and took a powder. . . .

Lippy Fargo adjusted his expensive bathrobe over his fat little belly and showed me into his apartment. He motioned to a chair in front of the big window and went to the bar.

"Whiskey, Pete?"

"A shot."

He waddled back with two glasses and plopped himself down opposite me.

"Did you give the stuff to her?"

I took the package out of my pocket and untied it. I removed four five-hundred-dollar bills and tossed the package to Lippy. I said: "The two grand is for services rendered. Cheap, considering."

Lippy counted the money absently. "Considering what?"

"Considering you tried to frame me."

Lippy's cherubic face turned red. "Suppose you quit talking in circles and tell me what happened."

"As if you didn't know."

"Look, Pete. I told you I'd give you five hundred bucks if you delivered the dough. You didn't deliver the dough and you kept two thousand. You better have a story worth two grand or else hand it over."

"You're damn lucky you're getting any of it back. If the cops had turned up there, you'd never have seen your money again."

"Cops? What cops?"

"The blonde was dead. Strangled."

Lippy looked up sharply. "Who did it?"

"You tell me. It just seems funny as hell that you sent me there, fat, dumb, and happy, and there was somebody waiting to kill her between the time the desk clerk called and gave her my name and the time I got up to the apart-

ment. It smells bad to me. How does it smell to you?"

Lippy shook his head. "So help me, Pete, I didn't have a thing to do with it."

"What were you paying off for?"

There was a long silence. "Sorry, Pete. That I can't tell you."

I got up and walked to the window. "You better tell me, and it better be good, because I'm calling the cops in about two minutes and telling them why I was there."

Lippy raised himself with a grunt. He took my arm. "Don't do that, Pete. We're friends. You know I can't afford to get mixed up in anything like that. I'm on parole."

I swung around. "What about me? Am I going to be the fall guy? Why was I there? 'Well, I'll tell you, Inspector, I was looking for my cuff link. I was passing the hotel and it fell off and rolled through the lobby and up the stairs.'" I paused. "What'll I tell them?"

Lippy walked back to his chair and collapsed wearily.

"I don't know, Pete. It'll kill my wife. Ever since I got out, I've been clean. You know that. Most of the people here don't even know I've served time. My kid's in college—it'll ruin her. When the papers get hold of it . . ." He rubbed his hand over his eyes. "I don't know. . . ."

I shook my head. "I'm sorry, Lippy. I don't know who did it. Maybe you don't either. But I've got to have a story when they pick me up, and it'll have to be the truth."

Lippy leaned forward intently. "You're smart, Pete. You can find out who did it. Name your own price. Just keep me out of it." His voice was desperate.

I looked out at the fog rolling into the bay. A foghorn moaned dismally. Lippy Fargo—reformed gambler. Worth sticking your neck out for? A good guy, a good friend, but . . . Finally I turned.

"OK. I'll take a crack at it. But I can't guarantee anything if the cops pick me up. And you'll have to come clean with me."

Lippy nodded. "OK, Pete. What do you want to know?"

"The pay-off. What was it for?"

Lippy took a deep breath. "Two years ago I was paroled. I wanted to get out of the gambling racket, and I was selling my clubs, one at a time. I went to Nevada to sell my Reno place—broke parole to do it. I was only there three days. I got in a game of stud with two other guys: Dude Wallon, a hood that used to work for me, and an Easterner named Wright.

"Dude was pretty drunk—he was just a gun-man anyway—and he claimed this guy Wright was hiding an ace. Wright gives him some lip, so Dude pulls a gun and kills him. Just like that. Then he looks in his coat for the ace. He looks up at me and grins. 'Wrong again,' he says. There was a girl in the room—Dude's girl. That was the blonde you saw."

I nodded. "So you couldn't report the murder without being caught violating your parole, and besides, Dude and the girl might have claimed you did it."

"That's right. Well, Dude got rid of the body, somehow, and headed for the East—and that's all there was to it. Until I read this in the paper the other day."

He walked to a desk and rummaged around. Then he handed me a clipping.

VICTIM OF GANG WARFARE

New York—May 10. The body of a man identified as John "Dude" Wallon was found floating in the East River today. Police believed that he was a victim of gang warfare.

"Well," Lippy continued, "the other day the blonde turns up. She's seen the clipping too, she says. She says that now Dude is dead it leaves only herself and me that know about Wright's murder, and she's awful broke, and could I spare twelve grand."

I whistled.

"I told her I'd think it over. I thought it over, and decided to pay. I figured she'd be back for more, but I had to protect my family, and what the hell—twelve grand. I didn't want to see her again myself, and you were the only guy I knew that I could trust with that kind of dough. That's the story, Pete."

I puffed at my cigarette. It sounded all right, but you never know.

"Can you think of anybody that might want to see the blonde murdered? Outside of you, that is?"

He shook his head. "No, not now."

I looked up. "What do you mean, *now?*"

"Well, when Dude worked for me he was quite a ladies' man. He dated this blonde you found dead, Sylvia Clinton, and a redhead named Flame Doreen that sang at the 411 Club, and I don't know how many others. The redhead didn't like the blonde, and vice versa. They had a fight once, right in my office. Dude stood there and laughed. But Dude's dead now, and there wouldn't have been any reason—"

I shook my head. "Were there any others?"

"Not that I know of. Of course, if she was using blackmail as a steady diet, anybody might have done it."

I drove back to my hotel to get my stuff before the cops moved in. I cased the lounge carefully—there was no one there but the desk clerk and a few of the girls who hung out in the lobby. I opened my door and switched on the light.

"Hold it, Butler," said a voice in the shadows. I looked down the barrel of a Police Special. A little old guy wearing horn-rimmed glasses stood behind the gun, and an overgrown kid in a police uniform stood behind the little guy. I stayed where I was.

"Search him, John," said the little guy. The cop ambled over and went through my stuff. "This is him, Inspector," he said, looking at my driver's license. "He's a private eye and a sheriff's deputy and—say!" He whistled. "Two thousand dollars." He handed me back my wallet.

"Does murder pay that well nowadays?" asked the little man. "Maybe I'm in the wrong racket."

"Look," I explained, "I was going to call you guys. I just wanted to check on something first."

"Sure," said the inspector. "Well, don't bother to call. The desk clerk found the girl."

"You're making a mistake. I didn't do it."

"Nobody ever does it, mac. I've been working in Homicide for twenty years and I never found anybody that did it."

"Listen," I said reasonably. "You think I'd have left my right name at the front desk if I'd gone up there to kill the girl?"

"In a word, yes. It's a very smart thing to do. It looks awfully good to a jury. That's why you'd do it, especially if you might get caught anyway. To make it look better, though, you should have reported the crime. Yes, I think you did it, whether you left your name or not."

"Well, you're wrong."

"OK, so I'm wrong. What were you doing up there?"

Well, now was the time. I thought of Lippy, sweating it out at home. I thought of his wife—not a bad old girl. I thought of his daughter in college. I knew I'd hate myself for turning soft, but what can you do?

"Just a friendly call," I said.

"OK, John, slip the cuffs on him."

"Now wait a minute," I said. "I can—"

The big cop moved over and clicked a handcuff onto my wrist, and that was that. A handcuff makes a very decisive sound. He put the other cuff on himself. I felt like tail-end Charlie on a chain gang.

"Take him down to the car. I'm going to look around."

The cop marched me to the elevator. We stood behind the elevator boy, saying nothing, as we started down to the lobby. The cop towered on my right, a real tribute to American breakfast food: tall, broad, healthy. I eyed him speculatively. I thought of spending the next six months in the city jail with the prospect of graduating to a quiet grave in the municipal cemetery, and

decided that it was worth trying. I never had much of a left, but if he had a glass jaw . . .

He did. I put everything I had into the blow, it went directly to the button, and he folded like a tired old man, almost pulling me down with him. The elevator boy turned, his face white.

"Mr. Butler, you shouldn't oughta have done that!"

"OK, sonny. Don't worry about it." I pulled the gun out of the cop's holster and the keys out of his pocket. I fumbled with the keys and tried two of them on the steel bracelet. The second one worked. "Let me out in the basement, and then let's see this elevator head for the top floor, and I mean the top floor."

I got out quickly, walked swiftly through the help's quarters, and out the side door into an alley. I ran down the alley and on to the main street. I signaled a taxi and told the driver to take me to the 411 Club. I sat back and wiped the sweat off my brow. My hand was shaking. We'd gone three blocks before I heard the siren start to wail. . . .

I sat at a table in the back of the 411 Club and ordered a shot of whiskey and a bottle of beer. The ten o'clock floor show was just coming on. I watched the girls swinging their legs, and listened to a refugee from a third-rate burlesque try to make like a comedian, and heard a washed-up tenor murder *Mother Macree*. Then the redhead walked from the shadows, leaned on the piano, and began to sing.

She had creamy white skin and shimmering long hair the color of burnished copper. And sea-green eyes, and a shape that couldn't have been natural but obviously was. She was wearing a low-cut white evening dress that rippled when she moved and she had a low, husky voice. When she sang, she sang to every man in the place. When she stopped singing, a long, male sigh escaped the room, and then applause. She sang again. I called the waiter.

"Is that Flame Doreen?"

"Yeah. Oh, brother!"

"Tell her I'd like to see her. A friend of Dude Wallon." I slipped him a five-dollar bill. He looked at it critically.

"OK, mac, but you're wasting your time. Strictly no soap."

"Tell her anyway." The waiter moved off toward the wings of the stage.

In a few minutes she appeared out of a side door, looked over the audience, and crossed the dance floor. She slid into the seat opposite mine and looked me over coolly.

"Yes?"

Now what? I tore my gaze away from the green eyes. "Drink?"

She hesitated. "All right. Whiskey and soda."

I ordered it and sat back.

"Miss Doreen, I'd like to find out what you know about Sylvia Clinton."

Her face froze. "Plenty. Who wants to know?"

I flashed my wallet with its sheriff's deputy badge, and put it back into my pocket. A shadow of fear crossed her face.

"What do you want to know?"

"When did you see her last?" I asked, watching her eyes.

She studied her drink. "The other day. I ran into her on the street."

"She's dead."

The fear lingered in her eyes. She lit a cigarette and took a deep drag. Coolly she said:

"I'm so sorry. It couldn't have happened to a nicer person."

"Murdered."

"That I can believe. Well, is there anything else?"

"Where were you this afternoon?"

She hesitated. "Shopping."

"What did you buy?"

"Clothes."

"Where?"

She flushed angrily, her eyes sending out emerald sparks.

"You don't think I killed her?"

"Maybe."

"Look Sherlock, why would I do it?"

"Jealousy."

"Don't be silly. On acount of Dude? That's all over with, and for your information, Dude is dead."

"How do you know?"

She paused. "Maybe I read it in the paper—maybe somebody told me—I don't know. Anyway, I heard that he was killed. Now if you're all through . . ."

Something was wrong. I didn't know what, but her story didn't ring true. There was nothing I could do. I stood up.

"OK, sister. But for *your* information, I don't believe you were shopping."

I paid the bill and left the club, my hat down over my face. I hailed a cab and gave him Lippy's address. . . .

Lippy was still up. He looked as if he'd had a tough night. His eyes were shadowed and his face was drawn. He let me in quickly.

He said, "Pete, thanks."

"Thanks for what?"

"Giving them the slip."

"How'd you find out about that?"

"The radio. They've broadcast your description. They have a dragnet out for you."

I sank wearily to the couch. "Oh, brother," I moaned. Lippy poured me a shot of whiskey. I gulped it and handed him back the glass.

"Well," I said finally, "I talked to the redhead. No soap."

Lippy shook his head. "She's the only one I can think of, Pete, and with Dude dead . . ."

I walked to the window. Lippy was right. With Dude dead, there was no reason for jealousy. That left Lippy. I began to wonder if I were getting the run-around. I turned.

"Listen, Lippy, I hope to hell you're playing ball with me, because if you're not, so help me, I'll—"

There was a crash of breaking glass and the roar of a gun. Automatically I hit the deck, grabbing for the lamp cord. I got a hand on it and pulled. The light went out. Silhouetted in the glare from the street I saw a shadow on the fire escape. I waited and then crawled to the window.

Cautiously I poked my head over the ledge. Two stories below I heard a movement. Someone dropped to the pavement and a dark shape flitted into an alley. In the apartment house across the street lights flicked on and people talked excitedly. I turned.

"You all right, Lippy?" I asked softly.

I heard Lippy grunt and the light clicked on. He was standing by the door, carefully inspecting a jagged hole in the stucco wall of the living room, a big hole with cracks radiating from it.

"Close," he said wearily, "but no cigar. Reminds me of the old days."

"Yeah." I lit a cigarette. "Who do you suppose has you on his list?"

Lippy shrugged. "Lots of people, I guess. Just the same, that doesn't happen every day. You suppose it's tied up some way with the blonde's murder?"

"I don't know. I do know I gotta get the hell out of here before the cops come to see who lit the firecracker."

The bedroom door opened and a tall, elderly lady with iron gray hair, still pretty, walked into the room in a negligee. Her face was a mask of fear.

"Lippy, are you all right? What happened?"

"It's OK, honey. Go back to bed. And don't worry. It's all over now."

I moved to the door.

"If you get any hot ideas, give me a ring at the Perry Hotel on Bush Street. I'll be registered under the name of Jones. Needless to say, don't mention I was here."

Lippy nodded. "Sorry I got you into this, Pete. I—"

I looked at the poor old guy standing there with his wife, scared and miserable.

"Forget it."

As I left the apartment I heard sirens screaming in the night. A streetcar was passing, almost empty, and I swung myself on. I got off on Bush Street and registered at the Perry Hotel. I went to my room and flopped on the bed.

I couldn't sleep. I lit a cigarette and watched a flashing neon sign play on the ceiling. On and off, on and off. The shadow of the fire escape began to look like a gallows. I swung my feet over the side of the bed.

The redhead had been lying. About what, I didn't know. But she had been lying, and she was the missing link. Lippy hadn't killed the blonde; the redhead probably hadn't either, but she knew who had. I looked at my watch. It was one a.m.

The 411 Club was still crowded. The last show was almost over and the redhead was singing. She saw me and faltered on a note. When the song was over and the applause had stopped, she walked swiftly through the cigarette smoke to my table.

"I thought you'd gone."

"I liked your performance so much in the first show that I decided I'd catch the second one."

"Yeah." She sat down again. I was surprised, and wary, but I ordered her a drink. She sipped it carefully, watching me with the clear, green eyes.

"I get off after the show," she said finally. "Sometimes this job bores me so much that I feel as if I *have* to go out afterwards."

Well, I'll be damned, I thought. *Little Red Riding Hood asking the wolf in.*

"Is that so?"

"I guess when you're off duty you like to go out too?"

"Sometimes."

She looked into my face suddenly. There was fear in her eyes, and an almost pathetic hope.

"Will you take me somewhere after the show?"

"Where?"

"Anywhere. Someplace for a drink. Anywhere we can have a good time."

I thought of the cops crowding the town, working overtime. Looking for me. The redhead was frightened of something, and I wanted to know what it was, but it was no time to start painting the town red.

"No," I said. "Not tonight. What's frightening you?"

She looked up and laughed. "Frightening me? Don't be silly. I might ask you the same thing. Or don't you like redheads?"

"I like redheads, when they come clean with me. Not when they hide things."

She laughed nervously. "Well, this makes the first time in a long while that I've asked for a date and been turned down." She stood up, smiling, but the fear was still in her eyes. "Drop in some day when you're not working on a case—then I can turn *you* down."

She was off to the dressing room and I was alone. I wondered what had frightened her. Conscience? Maybe she couldn't bear to be alone. And yet, the strangler had been a man—a woman wouldn't have had the strength. And the handkerchief in the blonde's hand—it had been not a woman's but a man's handkerchief.

The handkerchief. It had been clean, freshly ironed. Not a handkerchief that had come out of a hip pocket. A handkerchief that had come out of a breast pocket.

I ordered another drink.

Who wears a handkerchief in his breast pocket, nowadays? Flashy dressers. Dudes.

Dudes. Dude Wallon? But Wallon was dead. At least, the paper had said he was dead. But was he? Who had identified him? The blonde had gone East with him. Had she identified the body? A guy like that, permanently erased from the police files, can start all over again. He can take care of all the people who have anything on him and begin a whole new life. From scratch.

Two people who had something on Dude were the blonde and Lippy. The Reno murder. And where would Dude go if he came back West, if he returned from the grave? To a girl who had been in love with him—the redhead. He could hide away with her and take care of his old friends, one at a time. The blonde was gone, and somebody had taken a shot at Lippy. With Lippy dead the books would be closed and Dude could breathe freely.

Except for the redhead.

The redhead had been frightened. She hadn't wanted to go home. She'd been trying to tell me something all the time, thinking I was a cop. And I hadn't listened.

I shoved my chair away from the table and started for the stage. A waiter barred my way. He said, "No visitors backstage." I gave him a ten and he stepped aside.

I walked through the wings and down the corridor. I found a door with a star on it and the name *Flame Doreen* scrawled beneath it in chalk. I knocked. There was no answer. I opened the door and looked in. The room was a mess, but there was no one there.

I moved further down the hall and heard voices. I knocked on another door and opened it. There was a moment of silence. The room was filled with the girls from the chorus, in various stages of undress. A luscious young blonde looked at me blandly.

"Show's over, mister. Don't you knock?"

"I have to find out Miss Doreen's address."

The girls looked at me coldly. I pulled out my wallet and flashed the deputy's badge. The blonde shrugged.

"What's she done now? She lives at the Manchester Arms, on Wright Street."

"Thanks. And sorry." I walked swiftly out the back door and grabbed a taxi.

The Manchester Arms was a cheap apartment with all the trimmings. I asked the doorman for Miss Doreen's apartment and he winked at me sympathetically.

"It's 3A, brother, but you're a little late. There's a guy been up there all day, and he's still there."

"Personal friend of mine," I said, walking into the elevator.

I got off at the third floor and wandered down the hall, looking at the door numbers. When I came to 3A I stopped. Voices murmured inside. I put my ear to the door. I couldn't hear a word. I slipped the Police Special out of my pocket and lifted my hand to ring. Then I heard it—a low, desperate cry: "Dude—no!"

It was all I needed. I backed against the far

wall and launched myself against the door. It was a cheap lock; it snapped easily. I crashed the door open and went on through.

A big guy, handsome, with a bronzed, hard face and curly blond hair, was leaning over a chair. His face was turned my way, frozen in fear and surprise. His hand flashed toward his coat. As he straightened I glimpsed the redhead lying sprawled on the chair.

"Hold it," I said. He hesitated. I stepped toward him and relieved him of a gun from a shoulder holster. The girl on the chair moaned and her eyelids flickered.

"Not this time, brother," I said. "The legal limit on murder is one a day."

He spit out a curse. I didn't like the way he did it so I let him have it, backhanded across the mouth. "You don't make out as well with men as you do with women, do you, Dude?"

He watched me, his eyes glittering. The redhead sat up, holding her throat.

"I knew it," she whispered. "That's why I didn't want to come back. I knew it. . . ."

"Call the cops, honey," I said. "Tell 'em it's Butler. Quick, before I lose control of this gun."

I motioned toward Wallon with the gun. "I wish I had time to work you over, Wallon. I'm afraid the cops are gonna be kind of inhibited. But you're going to get the gas chamber anyway, so it doesn't matter."

"Try and prove something, buddy. Try it."

"Where's your handkerchief?" I asked. He looked at his breast pocket and turned white. I said: "You should have checked that before you left the blonde. I assume it has laundry marks on it—it shouldn't be very hard to prove."

There was a long silence and then footsteps down the hall. The gray-haired inspector stuck his head through the door. He saw me and whipped out his gun.

I said, "I'm working late, Inspector. Here's your man."

"Yeah? You're my man, brother. Put down that gun."

I nodded. "Watch him, Inspector. He's Dude Wallon." I tossed the gun on the floor.

The inspector's eyes bugged at the name. He hesitated.

I caught a swift movement from Dude. His hand flashed to his hip pocket and an automatic appeared from nowhere. He grabbed at the redhead and yanked her in front of him. "Outa my way," he whispered. "Outa my way."

The inspector's eyes glinted. Carefully he put away his gun. Wallon moved toward the door, shielding himself behind the girl. My heart sank. If he got away, he'd get me if he had to track me to the end of the world. And as for the redhead— it would be curtains for her.

Wallon's face relaxed into a grin. "So long, you," he said to me. "I'll be seein' you again." He stepped into the hall.

There was the roar of a forty-five down the hall and Wallon's face froze incredulously. Slowly he turned, and suddenly crumpled to the floor. Footsteps hurried down the corridor. It was the big cop I'd slugged in the elevator. He kneeled by the corpse and turned it over. He looked up, his face a mask of horror.

"This isn't Butler!"

"That's right, son," said the inspector. "But I wouldn't be surprised if it was just as good."

"Better," I said. "Much better."

I turned to the redhead. She was white-faced and shaking like a leaf.

"Now, honey," I said. "About that drink you wanted. I know a place. . . ."

The Sound of the Shot
Dale Clark

RONALD KAYSER (1905–1988), who wrote under the pseudonym Dale Clark, was born in a small town in the Midwest. At various times, he took jobs as a lumberyard worker, reporter, private detective, house-to-house salesman, editor, and creative writing teacher, but remained throughout his life a prolific writer.

In addition to more than a half dozen novels—*Focus on Murder* (1943), *The Narrow Cell* (1944), *The Red Rods* (1946), *Mambo to Murder* (1955), *A Run for the Money* (1956), *Death Wore Fins* (1959), and *Country Coffins* (1961)—Clark wrote more than four hundred stories for both the pulps and the more prestigious slick magazines such as *Collier's, Liberty,* and *This Week.*

Many of his stories are set in Southern California, where he spent most of his writing life. Although he inevitably created a wide range of characters, an unusually high percentage of them have an interest in contemporary technology. A forest ranger's station is jammed full of highly technical devices; Doc Judson, a detective-cum-criminalist, speaks frequently of the need for scientific methodology, though it is mainly limited to ballistics; the best-named of Clark's series characters, Highland Park Price (High Price), has amassed a collection of high-tech toys that seldom work because he is too cheap to buy new ones or reputable brands. In these comical private-eye yarns, High Price gouges his clients, frequently using blackmail.

"The Sound of the Shot" was published in the September 1946 issue.

The Sound of the Shot

Dale Clark

AN O'HANNA NOVELETTE

Crack! They all heard it, and half the crowd looked quickly back toward the hotel. The other half saw Gus Lambert stagger, spin half around and flop on his face.

CHAPTER ONE

PIN-UPS ON PARADE

Manager Endicott was in a spot—his Hollywood beauty contest had turned into a frame-up flesh show. Someone had brought in a murder package, all wrapped up in a special hand-loaded wildcat cartridge. The movie moguls were muttering, the beauties were bothered, and he was sure the paying guests were saying: "Oh yes, San Alpa—what a lovely place to come and get yourself murdered!"

HE WAS A STUNNING brunette swathed in a form-hugging beach coat, Eva Tarkey. Her eyes were sultry, incensed. She stormed, "I've been robbed! Somebody stole the top to my bathing suit! I'm being cheated out of my chance for the movie contract!"

The girl with her was a stunning redhead named Lola Lofting. She was just as angry. She said: "I was robbed worse. I came to get undressed, and somebody had stolen my entire swim-suit—and I'm the one who was practically a cinch to win the movie contract!"

Both girls were standing in the San Alpa resort hotel office, telling their troubles to Endicott, the thin-faced, graying manager of the million-dollar California mountain-top spa.

Endicott reared back in his swivel chair, and made motions like a man fighting bees. "I can't help it! I can't be responsible for lost swim-suits. You girls will have to argue that out with Mr. O'Hanna here—he's the head of the stolen goods department."

Mike O'Hanna was the house dick. He pointed this out. "I'm hired to be a hotel detective. This pin-up parade happens to be *your* pet baby."

This was true. Endicott had dreamed up the bathing beauty contest as a publicity stunt. He figured half the Sunday papers in the land would run rotogravure shots of the lucky lass who got crowned Queen of San Alpa. It would tie in nicely with the management's advertising campaign to extol the colossal San Alpa golf course, warmed salt-water plunges, and miles of scenic horseback and hiking trails. Eventually, it would lure flocks of well-heeled tourists into the de luxe fifteen-dollar-a-day-on-up hotel rooms.

Moreover, Endicott had foreseen this publicity stunt would cost hardly anything. San Alpa's clientele included lots of Hollywood film folks who came up for the week-ends, and Endicott had buttonholed Gus Lambert, the Mogul Films producer, and talked him into providing a thirteen-week contract for the winning girl. Endicott had argued astutely that a lot of free publicity in the newspapers and news-reels wouldn't hurt Mogul Films, either.

Gus Lambert had fallen for it, had even consented to act as judge of the beauty and talent on display. Endicott planned to have an afternoon promenade in swim-suits around the outdoor pool, and then in the evening the contestants could don low-cut gowns and go on as a special attraction instead of the usual Palomar Room floorshow. That way, the management would gain two entertainments for the paying guests.

As for the girls, naturally it wouldn't be necessary to hire them to try to win a crack at a movie career. Several dozen ambitious lovelies, Endicott had hoped, would be glad to pay their own expenses to San Alpa.

That's what he had hoped. What he actually got was several hundred of them. From early morning, girls had been unloading out of buses, or chugging up in jalopies, or arriving as hitch-hikers. It had been necessary to close off one of the big dining-rooms and convert it into an emergency dressing-room where two hundred contestants could primp, powder and change into their costumes.

But it hadn't been possible to lock them up in that room until the three p.m. parade started, of course. What happened was, they had parked their overnight cases or suitcases in the dressing-room and then turned themselves loose on the lobby, the grounds and the golf course. Quite a few of them had brought picnic lunches, littering the practically hand-manicured lawns with waxed paper and Dixie cups. Others had just trusted to luck, figuring some of the gold-plated, male paying guests would be glad to buy a girl a lunch.

Endicott had heard complaints about the lunch papers being wind-wafted over the golf course. He had listened to other complaints from the female paying guests—the idea of turning San Alpa over to a flock of painted hussies, common car-hops or worse, making eyes at decent women's husbands and fiancés and sons in the lobby! There had been complaints about chewing gum parked on the hotel furniture, too.

And now this—this stolen swim-suit business . . .

Endicott had taken about all he could take. He glared at O'Hanna, said: "O.K., it was my idea, but you don't have to rub it in! You'll have to attend to these minor details, Mike. This thing's due to start in fifteen minutes, and I have to see Gus Lambert, I have to—"

The redheaded Lola Lofting cut in: "Yeah, and what about me? What happens if my swimsuit isn't found in the next fifteen minutes?"

Endicott shrugged. "You'll have to drop out of the contest, that's all. You certainly can't take your place in the parade without a bathing suit on."

"That's what you think." Her voice was deadly.

Endicott was appalled. "Why, you wouldn't dare—you couldn't—Mike, you gotta stop her!"

Eva Tarkey tossed her brunet head. "Maybe she won't dare, but I'm telling you—there'll be no beauty contest today unless I'm in it."

O'Hanna's Irish-gray eyes hardened a trifle. In the swank, snooty elegance of San Alpa, an old-style hard-hatted lobby cop would have been as out of place as muskets in a modernized army. O'Hanna wore casual flannels like any paying guest, and could have passed as a vacationing playboy—until trouble started.

He said: "Let's drop the melodrama, you're not being screen-tested for a B picture yet. Suppose you just tell me what happened, and I'll go to work on it."

"How do we know what happened?" the redhead griped. "We left our stuff in the dressing-room, and when we came back it was gone—swiped, so we couldn't enter the contest."

The brunette's dark eyes gleamed. "And, big boy, I meant what I said. I paid bus fare all the way down from San Francisco, and either I'm in the parade—or the whole damn thing is coming to a quick, sudden stop."

This time he ignored the threat, used the opening instead. "You're from San Francisco, too?" O'Hanna asked the redhead.

Lola Lofting denied it. "No, I'm a Diego girl."

"You two'd never met before? So it probably wasn't a case of somebody trying to get even with the pair of you," O'Hanna mused. "Well, come on."

He led them down the side of the lobby, into the service hallway where foodstuffs from the kitchen streamed to the dining-rooms and the Palomar Bar. The Palomar was on the left, this dining-room to the right. O'Hanna raised knuckles to knock, but Eva Tarkey was in no mood to stand on ceremony. She went right ahead, shoved the door open, was greeted by alarmed squeals.

A soprano shrilled, "Oooh, a man!" and started a chorus of squeals, of frantic whisking of beach wraps and dressing gowns around tanned, trim figures.

Eva Tarkey said scornfully: "Can the comedy. I told you I'd call a cop, and it's going to go hard with whichever one of you tramps pulled this stunt."

"Which is your bag?" O'Hanna asked.

"Right here." She aimed a kick at a scuffed suitcase, one that looked as if it had been kicked around plenty.

"Unlock it."

"I lost the key years ago." She stooped, unstrapped the suitcase, hinged open the top. "It's a bra-top that matches this," holding up cream-tinted bathing briefs.

"And your bag?" O'Hanna turned to Lola Lofting.

"It's the next one, right here. I had it locked."

The redhead's was an overnight case, and O'Hanna ignored the need for a key. He tried, and all he needed was his thumbs to spring the lid free.

Straightening, he peered around the room. "Any of the rest of you missing anything?"

Nobody was. It seemed to be just these two bags, and they had been near the door, one unlocked and the other as good as unlocked. So it almost looked like sneak thievery, except, naturally, a sneak thief wouldn't have wanted a swim-suit and a half.

"Well"—O'Hanna shrugged—"come on, we'll see what we can do about it."

It would probably break Endicott's economical heart, but he marched the pair across the lobby, this time to the sport clothes shop—one of the classier Wilshire Boulevard establishments in Los Angeles found it profitable to run a branch shop here. O'Hanna hailed the manager: "Here, Baudry, fix 'em up and charge it to the house."

Baudry's eyes lit up behind their spectacles. "Yes? And what will it be?"

He heard what it would be, and his eyes dulled, his hands dropped. "Mr. O'Hanna, I'm sorry. I haven't a single swim-suit in stock. A Mr. Walther came in this morning and bought every last bathing suit from the shelves."

O'Hanna thought and said: "You girls wait here."

He headed to the lobby desk, asked: "Who the devil's this guy Walther?"

The desk clerk was owl-eyed. He exhaled. "She's beautiful, she's gorgeous, she's damned near almost divine, ain't she?" He hadn't seen O'Hanna, hadn't even heard the house dick's voice.

O'Hanna's Irish-gray glance shifted, followed the owl-eyed stare. Something blond had just stepped from the San Alpa elevator. For a moment she paused, almost as though she was going to dive into a pool. She was dressed for it, with just a golden cloud of diaphanous wrap that drifted away from her shoulders. The rest was vivid, scarlet swim-suit and a pearly complexion.

O'Hanna said: "Quit drooling, man!"

The clerk snapped out of it, colored. "That's Tra-La Brown, Mike, and I bet everybody drools when she walks up on the judge's stand today. If she doesn't win, there's something fishy about this contest, I'd say."

"There's plenty fishy about it already. Including a guy named Walther getting a corner on the swim-suit market."

The clerk seemed shocked to hear it. "You can't mean Jeremiah Walther? Why, he's a paragon of respectability."

"Where'll I find him?"

The clerk said in one of the chalets. A-10, San Alpa followed the California style and had private guest cottages scattered about the landscaped grounds. Jeremiah Walther had to be a paragon of high finance to afford A-10, since it rented for twice the room rate of the costliest suite in the main building. O'Hanna wondered, sometimes, how Endicott got away with it. After all, the chalets under their imitation Swiss roofs were only glorified tourist cabins.

He climbed the steps to this one, punched the bell. The man who answered was obviously that paragon of respectability, Jeremiah Walther. The old boy wore his white, silky whiskers in the mutton-chop fashion of the Gay Nineties. He was bald-headed down to a half-circle of white fuzz at ear level. He wore a hearing aid plugged into his left ear, eyeglasses with gold rims. A gold watch-chain sported its massive links across his black broadcloth vestfront.

He had hobbled to the door with the aid of a gold-headed cane. Leaning on the cane, he blinked waterily at O'Hanna, quavered his reply to the detective's question.

"Yes, young man, I bought those bathing dresses. I put them in the fireplace."

O'Hanna was fascinated. He wasn't old enough to remember, but he had an idea "bathing dresses" had gone out with bustles. He asked: "You mean you burned them?"

Jeremiah Walther aimed his cane at the front room fireplace. "That I did, and it wasn't much of a fire they made."

The sleuth went in, peered at close range. There remained a few smoldering rags, mostly where the Lastex-threaded fabrics had melted down.

He marveled: "I'll be damned if you didn't. Now would you please tell me why?"

With creaking-joint care, Jeremiah Walther lowered himself into a chair: "I had to protect my niece," he disclosed. "I'm Selena's only living male relative, so it was my bounden duty to act."

"Come again."

The white-whiskered man said: "Selena's a headstrong brat. She made up her mind she was going to participate in this contest today. I had to prevent it, naturally."

"Naturally?"

Jeremiah Walther bounced his cane on the floor for emphasis. "Young man, I'll have you understand our family tree has its roots 'way back in Pilgrim times. We're descended from God-fearing pioneers, sturdy whaling captains and even a few town councilmen. Our forefathers and foremothers would turn over in their graves at the thought of a Walther girl showing her unclad limbs in this noisome exhibition. It's down-right degrading to think of a civilized young lady strutting around in front of folks in a next-to-naked condition!"

O'Hanna mused: "Selena doesn't share your old-fashioned views?"

"No. The only way I could stop her was by destroying her bathing dress, and all the other bathing costumes she might have bought at the last minute." Abruptly, he tugged at his watch-chain, fished forth a family-heirloom style timepiece. "Speaking of the last minute, reminds me we better get a hurry on or we're liable to miss the parade. It's five minutes to starting time, and I'm a mighty slow-walking man."

The house dick stared. "You're going to degrade yourself by looking at such a shameful sight?"

Chuckles shook the white-whiskered man. "You're durned tootin' I am! Don't tell Selena I said this, but secretly I'm the black sheep of the family. I ran away from home at the age of eighteen to hunt for diamonds in darkest Africa. The family made up a fable I was a missionary, and that's what Selena thinks, but actually I've seen and done things that'd make your hair curl. I wouldn't miss these doings if it killed me to go."

He headed out the chalet door, hobbled down the steps, made off at a mile-an-hour clip. He was going to need all of the five minutes to reach the judging stand that had been built at one end of the outdoor pool, and from the size of the gathering crowd it looked as though he would be lucky to find a chair when he got there.

O'Hanna swung wide of the assemblage, circled a movie-news truck with a cameraman on its top. Gus Lambert, a pale dwarf with a giant Corona-Corona in his mouth, had already mounted the judge's throne. Manager Endicott was doing a mother hen act on the hotel driveway, trying to shoo two hundred swim-suited sirens into line. "And for heaven's sake, please, girls, quit chewing gum!" Endicott kept pleading frantically. Midway down the line, O'Hanna noticed Tra-La Brown peel the diaphanous golden wrap from her shoulders, hand it to a pinch-faced man with pince-nez who gave the wrap a shake, folded it neatly into an alligator leather bag at his feet.

O'Hanna had a cold, unhappy hunch about Tra-La Brown, and no time to ponder it. He made for the lobby sport clothes shop, found Baudry watching the proceedings through the shop front window.

"What became of the two girls I left here?" the house dick quizzed.

"They're gone, Mike. They left as soon as the line started forming."

It sent O'Hanna outside again. Eva Tarkey and Lola Lofting weren't in the line. He had not expected any such miracle, but he had to check, and by the time he had made sure, the parade had started around the pool to the judging stand.

O'Hanna thrust his way through the standing onlookers who had been unable to find chairs. He couldn't spot the brunette or the redhead anywhere in the audience, either. It worried him a little, remembering Eva Tarkey's threat. But if she really thought she could break up the contest, he reasoned, she'd have to reach the judging stand to do it.

He started that way. Polite applause was dying down as one contestant carrying a card marked *14* quit the stand. It became genuine applause as No. 15 came to pirouette before Gus Lambert's throne. No. 15 was platinum-haired, sun-tanned, and clad in what looked to O'Hanna dangerously like just a couple of bandanna handkerchiefs. Mixed with the handclapping, the sleuth caught a few whistles of male appreciation.

"The hell!" O'Hanna exclaimed, and leaped for the stand.

The redheaded Lola Lofting must have been hiding under the platform! He couldn't see any other way she could have instantly scrambled from complete invisibility into the center of the stage.

But there she was, waving her arms at the crowd, trying to drown the handclapping with her high-pitched soprano appeal: "Stop it! Hold everything, folks! I want to tell the world I'm getting a raw deal—"

Endicott was on the platform, plunging toward her. Gus Lambert got there first, with one wiry bound down from his throne. Lambert's was a foghorn voice that dated back to the era when he had directed silent epics via a megaphone.

He brayed, "Shuddup, you!" and grabbed at the redhead.

Crack! They all heard it, and half the crowd looked quickly back toward the hotel. The other half saw Gus Lambert stagger, spin half around, and flop on his face. They jumped up then, and they could see the red wet spot forming on the planks under his arm.

CHAPTER TWO
THE SOUND OF THE SHOT

here he stood, on the edge of the judging stand, O'Hanna could see it was an arm wound, and he swung to stare across the crowd. He didn't see a glimpse of a gun, or of anyone who looked in a hurry to leave. On the platform, things were happening fast. Gus Lambert's plump, male secretary was up there, and the Mogul news-reel cameraman, with the sound technician, beside the fallen producer.

"He's out cold!"

"He fainted, all right."

"Somebody call a doctor."

Endicott rushed the redhead over to O'Hanna. "I got this one, Mike. All you got to do is find that Tarkey girl. She threatened she'd break up the contest, remember?"

Lola wailed: "I don't know anything about this, honest! Why, that shot could've killed me—just as easy!"

O'Hanna asked: "Where's Eva?"

"I don't know that, either. I never saw her before today. You can't blame me if she was crazy enough to pull this stunt!"

A voice of a newcomer on the platform was authoritative, "Break it up, boys. We'll carry Mr. Lambert inside. Don't discuss this with anyone until Lambert himself decides what our line will be."

O'Hanna swung around, found himself confronting a pinched face with pince-nez panes bridging the narrow nose.

"You represent Mogul Films?" the house dick queried.

Pinched-face admitted it. "I'm Harry Farneye, in charge of casting."

"I'm Mike O'Hanna, in charge of crimes. Tell your crowd to let Lambert lie until our hotel staff doctor—yeah, here he comes now." Little Doc Raymond, the San Alpa house physician, was squirming his way up to the platform.

O'Hanna said: "Stick around, Farneye. I've got some questions you'd probably rather answer in strict privacy."

Something hard poked the house dick's leg. His Irish-gray glance dropped, irritably, and discovered the hard object was a cane. Jeremiah Walther was behind it. Walther quavered: "Young man, you tell Selena to come down from up there! Tell her she's shaming her own flesh and blood!"

O'Hanna followed the indignantly pointing cane, and it steered him to the other side of the platform and to the platinum-haired No. 15. "You're Selena Walther?"

"Yes. Why?"

O'Hanna confided. "I'm surprised. I understand your uncle burned your bathing dress to keep you out of this competition. Where'd you dig up this outfit?"

He had made exactly the right guess about her outfit. Selena Walther said: "It's just a little item I stirred from a few bandanna handkerchiefs. I know Uncle Jerry burned my swimsuit, and once and for all, I'm going to teach him he can't dictate my life to me! The fact that he's my long-lost uncle gives him absolutely no right to suddenly appear on the scene and start ordering me—"

O'Hanna wasn't listening to her. He had wheeled at the strained sound of little Doc Raymond's voice.

"The man is dead."

Endicott had heard it, too. He loosed his hold of the redhead, and strode over, with consternation spread across his thin features.

"You're crazy!" the manager protested. "He can't be dead! It's just a slight flesh wound in his arm."

Doc Raymond had slashed the sleeve away from the producer's arm. O'Hanna went to one knee beside the little medico and said: "It's a flesh wound, but it isn't slight. I saw a deer brought in that way last fall. It's one of those super-velocity jobs; the slug blows to powder when it hits, the shock kills whether it's a vital place or not. Right, Doc?"

"Technically, it's hydrostatic pressure," the physician confirmed. "The impact of such a projectile sets up a pressure wave away from the wound area. The blood literally recoils in the arteries so that it flows backward and halts the heart action."

Perspiration bathed manager Endicott's forehead. High-velocity ballistics and hydrostatic physics he savvied as little as he understood the principle of the atomic bomb, but he knew what murder meant to the hotel business. This wasn't a death that could be hushed up—it had happened in front of too many people. The newspapers weren't in the habit of hiding Hollywood celebrity slayings in their classified ad pages, either. . . .

Endicott breathed raspily. "Mike, quit standing here gawping at it. Go get that girl! The crazy little fool did this out of sheer, hell-cat spite!"

O'Hanna corrected: "If it was Eva Tarkey, she didn't do it out of off-the-cuff spite. This job was premeditated murder." His stare rested glumly on the frightsome mess the wildcat slug had made of Gus Lambert's arm. This killer was dealing with death by means of lead whipping along at upwards of four thousand foot seconds. It spelled a slayer who was really tooled for destruction!

Yet there might be a catch in it. O'Hanna dug for the catch: "Anybody here know of a gun crank in our midst?"

No cigar. Nothing but headshakes and blank looks all around.

Selena Walther, though, moistened her lips. "I can tell you one thing. That shot came from one of the hotel windows. I'm absolutely sure of it."

"Which window?" Endicott panted.

"I don't know, but I heard it come from that direction," the platinum-top insisted, pointing toward the hotel.

The cameraman chimed in. "She's right. I heard it behind me, too. That was from the hotel."

O'Hanna asked hopefully: "You got a picture on that film?"

"No, damn the luck! The camera wasn't rolling. I was waiting for Farneye to tip me the word."

He choked up, blushed.

O'Hanna turned to the pinch-faced casting man. "You can tip me the word. Suppose we drift on up to your room and chat."

Farneye kept a glacial silence as they moved through the crowd, into the lobby. In the elevator they were alone except for the operator, and he fixed a hostile, pince-nez-framed stare on the house dick. "You're wasting your time hounding me, O'Hanna. You ought to be checking all the rooms on this side, the front of the building."

"I ought to be hounding the hell out of everybody else, and let you cover up your tracks?"

O'Hanna rejected the plea, scowling. "How do I know? Maybe your little racket started the shooting."

They came out on the third-floor corridor. "My racket?" Farneye was testy-toned. "What's that?"

"Don't stall, chum. I'm hep to the fact that only one of those girls had a chance to win today. I mean your candidate—the blonde with the professional make-up and the press-agent name you cleverly concocted for her—Tra-La Brown."

Farneye said: "My God, don't blame me for her. Tra-La Brown was Gus Lambert's idea exclusively."

"Yeah?"

"Sure. He's been grooming Tra-La as a possible starlet. Your San Alpa beauty show came along at the opportune moment. By winning it, she could start her career on a wave of favorable publicity."

O'Hanna gibed: "You mean on the necks of two hundred simon-pure amateurs who never had a chance?"

"You're right. Of course, nobody but Tra-La had a look-in, with Gus doing the judging. But blame him, not me." The pinch-faced man pulled up at 318, fitted a key to the door, seemed surprised the door wasn't locked. He muttered, "That's funny," and stepped quickly inside.

The terrorized wail came shrilly: "Harry! Look out! He's got a gun!"

O'Hanna saw the gun, a moving mass of nickeled metal that seemed to leave a blur as it streaked. The blow was aimed at Farneye's head. O'Hanna couldn't stop it. The best he could do was pump out an arm, plant a hand between the casting man's shoulder blades. He planted it there so hard that Farneye went down on his face, skidded, plowed up a billow of rug in front of him.

The gun missed, finished down around the knees of the lad who had swung it. O'Hanna dived for the weapon, pinned the wrist, and got cuffed around the head by the other's free fist. He ignored it, closed his own free hand on the elbow above the pinned wrist. The two circled in a slow, straining dance, with O'Hanna pulling at the elbow, twisting on the captive wrist.

They waltzed around once, and then O'Hanna was behind the gunsel, was bending the gun-hand in a high, vicious hammerlock.

He heard the shrill, wailing voice again. This time it screamed: "Stop! You're breaking Benny's arm, you big brute!"

Benny was bent over double, the hammerlocked wrist shoved so near the nape of his neck that, as pain-wracked fingers let go, the gun fell over his shoulder in front of him instead of behind. He made one grab for it with the other hand—and O'Hanna's knee socked into the seat of his pants, sent him plowing on his face, raising another wave in the rug.

The sleuth picked up the gun—a nickeled, .32-caliber revolver that had apparently been fired and never cleaned, from the look of its fouled barrel.

Now the shrill voice said: "I tried to take it away from him myself, but he was too strong for me. . . ."

taring at Tra-La Brown, O'Hanna could see that she really looked as if there had been an earlier struggle over the gun. Her blond hair was mussed; the make-up from her lips and eyes made smears on her face now. The scarlet wisp of bathing beauty attire had taken a beating, too. She was trying to tug up the bra-top with one hand, trying to tug down the brief panty-skirt with the other.

O'Hanna said: "Everybody explain!"

Tra-La made her pretty lips into a pout. "You can count me out. This is absolutely all Benny's fault. He's jealous of me. That's why he's acting this way."

"Who's Benny? Your husband?"

"I'd die first!" the blonde scorned.

Harry Farneye had struggled to his feet. The pinch-faced man propped himself against a wall, tremblingly tried to fit the pince-nez back on his narrow nose. He didn't come very close, and anyway, one lens was missing. He said: "The punk's name is Benny Walsh, and what ails him is professional jealousy. He and Tra-La were in vaudeville up to a few weeks ago, and he's sore because she's going on up the ladder of success, and he definitely isn't."

"She was slinging hash in a Denver beanery until I gave her a job in my act, and now she's running out on me." The youth sat up, gave Tra-La the double-whammy with his hate-filled eyes.

The blonde came back at him. "And what was I doing when I walked out on you? I at least got my three squares a day when I was slinging hash. My God, you can't expect a girl to go on playing the haylofts when she's already passed a successful screen-test!"

Benny worked rust-colored eyebrows into a scowl. "I at least expect a dame to live up to her contract with the guy that learned her how to hoof!"

She screamed something at Benny, Benny yelled something before she was through, and Farneye drowned them both out. "Tra-La wasn't of legal age when she joined your act!"

O'Hanna waved the three of them to silence. "O.K., O.K., I get it," O'Hanna said. He peered at the young guy. "You found her in Denver, you took her on the stage, and she quit the act when she saw a chance to sign up with Mogul Films. So what did you figure you could do about it?"

Tra-La said: "He was going to louse up my chances today, damn him. He said I could either come back in his act, or he'd get up there and tell the crowd I was really a ringer."

"So—?"

She shrugged bare shoulders. "What could I do? I had to shut him up, didn't I? I brought him up here, and I thought I could give him the slip by going in the next room to change clothes."

Benny said sourly: "She's lying. She got me up here and pulled that gat on me!"

O'Hanna waggled the nickel-plated weapon. "Oh, this is yours, Tra-La?"

The blonde went wary. "Oh, it's just an old prop. It's to shoot blanks, see, in the act. What we had was one of those Apache numbers—you must've seen 'em? You know, I come on wearing one of those short French skirts and smoking a cigarette—and then Benny comes out. First he pretends to shoot the ciggy out of my mouth, then he knocks me down, then he picks me up, then he throws me down and walks over me, after that he throws me around by my heels. It's done to music, so he calls it a dance—"

"Five times a day, and six shows Saturday," O'Hanna finished it for her. "I was asking about the gun, remember?" The house dick broke out the cylinder, shook out the hulls. Darkly he queried: "You load in new police metal points, and it shoots out blanks? Bunk!"

Tra-La's eyes made circles of surprise. "I didn't know it was loaded!"

O'Hanna shook his head at the old classic line. "Coming from you, a screen-test ought to be good!" He half-turned at a sound of labored swallowing.

Harry Farneye was having throat trouble. "But, but," the pinch-faced man babbled pallidly, "you don't think Tra-La killed Gus Lambert?"

If she was acting now, the blonde maybe did have a career in pictures ahead of her. Her lovely features showed just the right shading of stunned incredulity. "Killed . . . what are you trying to give me?"

The casting man gave stiffly: "Lambert was shot dead a few minutes ago. They're trying to pin it on one of the girls in the contest. The shot was fired from inside the hotel, too."

The blond beauty seemed to soak Farneye's words in slowly, and then they spelled a different meaning to her. She turned to Benny. "You stinking little rat. You pulled that job. That's what I heard when I went in the next room here—"

Benny didn't let her finish. He was on his feet and he was yelling. "You mean that's what *I* heard when you went in the next room! How the hell could I shoot somebody? You had the gat, baby, I didn't!"

"You dumb hoofer, why'd I want to take a potshot at Lambert?" Tra-La raged. "He was the man that was going to make me a star!"

Farneye said: "She's right, O'Hanna. She wouldn't have killed the goose before it laid the golden egg. Benny may have been packing a gun of his own. He could have thrown it out the window after firing the shot."

The house dick's eyes lighted up with speculation. "I'll buy that. Anyway, I'll take an option on the idea. It's no sale unless we ultimately find the gun he threw away."

Benny seemed unworried. He sneered: "Jeez, you birds are dumb. The doll opens her big blue peepers, and says *daddy* when you squeeze her, and you think she's as sweet as she looks. That dame's dynamite. She'd cut your throat for a dime."

"Gus Lambert isn't worth a dime to me dead," the blonde countered.

"I don't say you tried to kill him. You aimed to wound the guy, I figure." The hoofer snapped his fingers. To O'Hanna, he said: "Hey, it plays perfect that way! Look what happened. I dragged her out of that pin-up parade. If she wasn't in it, one of those other girls had to be named the winner of a Mogul movie contract. She couldn't stop two hundred of them, but what she could do was wing the judge. The show couldn't go on if Lambert was wounded, and that's what she tried to do."

"I'll buy that, too." O'Hanna's grin was impartial; the wave of his hand included everybody. "We'll all hustle downstairs. Tra-La can tell one of our public stenographers all the reasons she thinks Benny fired the fatal shot. Benny can tell a different stenographer why he thinks Tra-La is a murderess. While you two are having fun, Farneye can be figuring out a statement on this frame-up flesh show that won't read too badly when it comes out in the newspapers."

Downstairs, he distributed them. He left the blonde to dictate one statement in the cashier's office, left Benny to dictate another in Endicott's office. Harry Farneye he led into his own, smaller office. The pinch-faced man was worry-gnawed.

"O'Hanna, what you're suggesting isn't a bit smart at all. A statement about that frame-up won't hurt Lambert, because he's dead, but it will backfire on you and injure your hotel's reputation."

O'Hanna said: "I agree. That wasn't what I really wanted of you. Look here."

He tugged open a desk drawer, ransacked around in it, came up with a vial labeled *naphth. sodium.* From another drawer, he lifted a San Alpha envelope. He swung out the cylinder of the revolver, laid the gun aside, opened a penknife blade. With care, the house dick uncorked the vial, trickled a spill of white powder onto the blade, balanced it cautiously there while he used the other hand to lift the gun, barrel pointing down.

"I've only got two hands. Hold the envelope down here and catch this." He tilted the knife blade, tried to run the white powder from the knife into the gun's breech. It didn't work too well, and he pursed his lips and blew at it. Most of it went down the barrel then, the rest settled in a miniature white cloud.

O'Hanna said: "O.K., seal the envelope. Write your name and the date across it." He was tugging open a third drawer, stowing the weapon away in there.

"What the hell is it supposed to prove?"

O'Hanna said: "It's a residue test. Tra-La claims that gun was used only for shooting blanks. Blank cartridge powder is pure guncotton mixed with an adhesive such as gum water. That's why it goes off with a bang, whereas ordinary smokeless powder would merely fizzle without being confined behind a bullet. Smokeless powders contain nitroglycerin, and this white stuff we poured through the barrel is a harmless little chemical which reacts with nitrous residues by slowly turning blue. In other words, what we're doing is finding out whether Tra-La's gun was used to shoot anything besides blank loads."

The pinch-faced man whisked out a handkerchief, mopped particles of clinging naphthionate of sodium from his fingers. "I see. You're one of those scientific Sherlocks."

"I'll tell you something, Farneye. I don't favor science at all. I'd really rather take my suspects down cellar and apply the rubber hose method."

"You don't mean it!"

"I can't get away with it." O'Hanna slammed and locked the desk drawers. "I can't even get away with searching those rooms for concealed firearms, as you suggested. If I did that, probably a hundred paying guests would resent being suspected and they'd check out. At the minimum room rate, I'd be costing the management fifteen hundred bucks. And that's just figuring this week-end. It makes no allowance for the fact that they'd never come back here again."

"It's a tough life you lead."

"You haven't heard the half of it. I've only got an hour before Sheriff Gleeson and the county coroner take this thing out of my hands. I'm racing against time with my feet hobbled. I'm desperate for a quick clue."

The house dick thrust his fingers through his hair, twice, irritably. "Furthermore, I'm not so damned sure this bathing beauty contest isn't sliced herring. Maybe somebody just grabbed a nice, confusing opportunity to take a shot at Gus Lambert. Tell me, he had enemies, surely?"

Farneye's thin lips grinned. "Every Hollywood producer has enemies, O'Hanna. But picture feuds aren't fought out with guns. There are so many more refined ways to knife a man in the ribs, and they're all on the safe side of the law." He toyed with the broken pince-nez. "I don't think it was that—any more than it was the note, for instance."

The sleuth went open-eyed. "What note?"

"It isn't important. Just some crank propped a crazy letter up against Lambert's door, so he'd find it when he came back from lunch."

O'Hanna asked: "Why doesn't somebody tell me these things? What became of it?"

"You'll probably find it in the wastebasket; that's where he threw it."

CHAPTER THREE
KILL RIDDLE

Lambert's was a fourth-floor suite, a de luxe layout on the building corner, with window exposures facing two views. The Mogul producer had had the big shot's habit of taking his office with him when he traveled and the suite's sitting room was littered with scripts, sketches, and such incidentals of the cinema industry. O'Hanna walked into a quiet little wake, where the news cameraman was tapping Gus Lambert's box of Corona-Coronas, the sound man was tapping Lambert's supply of Scotch, and the male secretary was talking long-distance on the phone. Obviously, none of the three were shedding any tears.

The note lay balled up at the wastebasket's bottom. O'Hanna smoothed it out, saw a sheet of the San Alpa stationery the management supplied in all the paying guests' rooms. *My dear Mr. Lambert,* the scrawled script began politely enough, but from there on the going got rough shod: *It's fiends in human form like you that are responsible for juvenile delinquency in this country! What is the use of parents trying to raise our younger generation to be respectable when men of your ilk put a public premium on immorality? Shame on you for luring young girls by dangling the bait of a movie career in front of them! Now, you either put a stop to this carnal exhibition, or I'll take steps myself.* This was signed, *I. M. Disgusted.* Then came a P.S.: *Think of the good effect you will have, standing up and denouncing the idea of girls winning fame and fortune by shedding off their clothes. They might catch cold and sue you, too.*

O'Hanna folded this away into his pocket, stepped over and tapped the secretary's shoulder. The secretary said: "Go away, I'm talking to the front office—"

"Talk them into sending us a print of Tra-La Brown's screen-test," the house detective requested.

He had no more than set foot out of the elevator into the congested lobby than Endicott rushed him. The manager was pallid. "Great Judas, Mike, where have you been? Haven't you located that Tarkey girl yet?" He came close, said thinly: "There's another one now—I told you she'd strike again."

"*Another bod*—"

"Hush, hush!" Endicott's head jerk was for the crowded lobby. "They don't know about it yet. It's outside—out in the bushes beside the golf course. One of the gardener's helpers found it while he was picking up that wastepaper on the grounds. Raymond's down there now."

O'Hanna headed out past the swimming pool again, this time swinging wide of the chalets. For the utmost in privacy, the chalets had been landscaped into the mountain slope, tucked into the natural cover of pines and black mountain oak. Then came the manzanita, head-high treelets of native shrub, a tangle of misshapen, red-barked boughs and branches. The groundskeeper stood by a gunnysack half stuffed with paper he had speared up on his spiked pole. He gestured with the pole as O'Hanna approached. "It looked to me like a paper napkin that had blowed in there, so I fished for it, and I started pulling out cloth—kay-ripes, with blood on it!"

O'Hanna thrust his way into the tangle, joined Doc Raymond over the No. 2 corpse. There had been a hasty effort at concealment, a shallow trench scraped among the manzanita roots, soil and decaying leaves scattered over the body.

"Strangled," the medico muttered, "and then beaten to hell and gone just to make sure."

O'Hanna peered at the battered features, at the beach-wrap the groundskeeper had speared and dragged from the body. His guts bucked, he tasted salt and acid in his throat. "Endicott can quit worrying about Eva Tarkey running amok," he said. "This is Eva."

Striding back through the black oak and pines, he found he could swallow the salty, retching taste—and he found it condensed into something else, a cold inner weight that was deadly, and not very logical. Gus Lambert's death hadn't affected O'Hanna like this. Lambert was a man, an elderly man to whom life had been immoderately kind. You could figure death had been kind, too, so instant he had probably never known what hit him. Eva Tarkey was only beginning to live her life, and her dying had been an anguish of choking horror. There was the feeling, too, that Gus Lambert had been a chess-master, and the girl had been merely a pawn on the board lured into this contest that hadn't been a contest at all, snatched off the board because she had got in the way of the killer's move.

He took the cold wrath up A-10's steps with him. Selena Walther had changed from the improvised bandanna swim-gear to form-fitting black. Her platinum hair fell down to her shoulders; her throat was roped with pearls. The black dress left her arms bare, was v'd down to the swell of her breasts in front, ended in a fish-tail train around her high, spiked heels. She said: "Don't look so startled. This is my costume for tonight. I'm taking no chances on Uncle Jerry repeating that little trick he pulled this morning."

O'Hanna was genuinely startled. "You expect the beauty contest to go on tonight in spite of all?"

"Why not? You know the old saying—the show must go on. Mogul Films can't welch on that offer of a movie contract. It was a legal offer, an inducement to two hundred girls to invest their time and money in this thing." She was as solemn as a Supreme Court decision. "If you've come here to try to talk me out of it, you're wasting your breath."

"I came here to see your uncle."

"Uncle Jerry has taken to his bed. The excitement proved more than his doddering constitution could bear."

"Then maybe you can tell me." The house dick delved into his pocket. "Did he write this?"

Selena Walther scrutinized the anonymous missive. "It sounds like his brain child, but unfortunately his handwriting looks more like drunken rabbit tracks than anything else. I'll show you a specimen." She crossed into one of the chalet's bedchambers, returned with a green oblong of canceled bank paper. "That's his signature on the back."

O'Hanna peered at the trembling *Jeremiah Walther* that wiggled lamely over the check. He turned it over, caught a quick peep at the face. The draft was for one thousand dollars, was signed *Selena Walther* and bore the notation, *Pension to date in full.*

The house dick hooped his eyebrows. "You're paying him an allowance? I don't get it. If you're supporting him, how come he can forbid you to enter a bathing beauty contest?"

"He's got me over a bicycle."

O'Hanna stared. "You mean, like over a barrel?"

"I mean a bicycle. My grandfather was a manufacturer of bicycles back during the nineties. Uncle Jerry ran away to Africa—he says to become a missionary, but I don't believe it. Neither did Grandfather. Grandfather wrote him a furious letter, called him a wastrel and a moron, and declared he was cutting Uncle Jerry out of his will. However, he did enclose fifty shares of the bicycle company stock. This was in 1895, the year Grandmother died, and the fifty shares were ones she had bequeathed to Uncle Jerry. Somehow, I suspect Grandmother never did get along too well with Grand—"

O'Hanna cut in. "Somehow, Grandma doesn't interest me. Let's get back to the bicycle business."

The girl said: "Grandfather became interested in gasoline motors. He took out a patent on a little novelty called the horseless carriage. You can guess the rest. The patent was an asset which made the bicycle company shares immensely valuable."

"Including Uncle Jerry's shares?"

"Exactly, but we all assumed Uncle Jerry was long since dead. You can imagine my surprise when he turned up fifty years later with Grandfather's old letter and that bundle of faded stock. At a conservative estimate, he has half a million in accumulated dividends due him." Selena Walther shook her platinum hairdo helplessly. "The hell of it is, we buried the family's financial genius in Grandfather's grave. My father mismanaged the company horribly. I inherited little more than a pile of debts. I'd be hopelessly bankrupt if Uncle Jerry took his claim to court. Originally, I told him the excess profits tax would eat up the value of his stock if he forced the company to liquidate immediately. So far, I've been able to stall him along with a pension check now and then. I'm afraid I can't get away with it much longer. He's a moron in financial affairs, just as Grandfather said, but even he must know the excess profits tax has been repealed. He'll hire a lawyer and take my last dime. Probably he'll pay me an allowance then—provided I wear long dresses, stop smoking, cut out the cosmetics, and wait on him hand and foot. His ideas haven't changed since fifty years ago, when men were men and women were washing machines."

"And you figure that's a fate worse than death," O'Hanna summed up. His eyes narrowed. "Why spill the deep, dark secret to me?"

Selena Walther said: "It all leads back to my insistence that this beauty contest go through on schedule. I've got to find a job of some kind when things explode. I'd like a job in the movies. I've got brains, a nice body, and a fair singing voice. I'm sure I can win this contest, get a contract, and make good. Then I can tell Uncle Jerry to sue and be damned."

"It's lucky you told me. I know just the guy for you to see." The house dick snared her arm. "His name's Harry Farneye, and we'll find him in suite 318."

arry Farneye was in 318, and he remembered Selena Walther. The pinch-faced man welcomed: "Oh, yes, you were on the platform when the shooting happened, weren't you," and guided the platinum-haired girl to an armchair.

Selena sat down, said, "Ouch!" and jumped, fast.

Farneye squinted through the one good lens of his pince-nez. "Good God, O'Hanna, look at this!"

The blued-steel hammer of a gun stuck up between the cushioned seat and the upholstered back of the chair.

O'Hanna came over, looked, asked: "Yours?"

"No, it isn't mine! I don't own a gun." Farneye's voice climbed. "O'Hanna, I was right! I told you Benny undoubtedly owned a gun! The damned little rat planted it here after he shot Lambert. I'll bet anything there's an empty shell—"

O'Hanna caught the casting man's dropping arm. "Don't touch. Fingerprints." He stepped across the room, plucked a decorative scarf from a desktop, covered his hand with that to fish up the weapon.

"Belgian," he said. "Shoots a .38 load." He sniffed at the gun's snout. "Shot recently, too." He wrapped up the gun, tucked it under his arm. He said: "But it isn't the murder I'm here about at all."

The pinch-faced man stared.

O'Hanna said: "It's about Miss Walther. It seems she's a hard-luck heiress. To be frank about it, she needs a job acting in the movies so she can support herself in the style she's accustomed to. I thought you wouldn't mind arranging for her to have a screen-test, giving her a headstart toward the career she craves."

Harry Farneye looked horrified. He said: "Good Lord, man, a movie career doesn't start with a screen-test. Anyway, the day is long past when stage-struck Cinderellas can break into pictures on their looks alone. Nowadays, it takes voice lessons, dramatic coaching, months and months of preliminary training. Miss Walther might go through all that at her own expense, and still not find a studio interested enough to spend the thousand dollars it costs before a camera can roll on a testing stage. I'd advise her to take up something practical, like stenography or—"

"That's what I thought when you gave me your spiel about Tra-La Brown," O'Hanna stemmed the other's flood.

The casting man tightened up. "Tra-La's different."

"Like hell she's different. She's a nice-looking blonde, I'll admit. But she's got a voice like a saw cutting pine-knots. Her theatrical experience consists of being manhandled to music by that cheap hoofer, Benny."

"You're discussing my business, snooper." Farneye was trying the quick-freeze method. "I think I'm the one who's qualified to judge Tra-La's talents."

O'Hanna said: "You're in the business, but I think you do a little wolfing on the side. Tra-La was dumb enough to devour that old line that you'd make a star of her. I don't doubt you gave her a screen-test—but that's as far as you could go without Lambert's O.K. Her test was nothing you'd dare show him, though. And she was demanding results. She was even toting around a .32, and it wasn't loaded with blanks. I say she packed that rod for you. I say you were going to wind up a wolf with lead poisoning mighty quick."

The quick-freeze was thawing, coming out in sweat on the pinch-faced man's forehead. "If that little tramp told you this, she lied!"

"You lied to her, Farneye. The contest hadn't been fixed so Lambert would let her win. For Gus Lambert, this show was strictly for publicity. Some girl would get thirteen weeks work as an extra, and Mogul Films would get a scrapbook full of favorable newspaper clippings. You simply gambled that only a handful of contestants would show up, and Tra-La would be an easy, walk-a-way winner."

"You can't prove that, O'Hanna."

The house dick grinned. "I can't prove that this Belgian gat is your gun, either, and you yourself parked it there!"

"I never saw it before in my life!"

"That'd better be true, Farneye, because naphthionate of sodium doesn't happen to be a test for smokeless powder. It's really a stop-thief powder," O'Hanna said happily. "I keep a supply on hand to discourage petty picking up of other folks' property. The stuff doesn't wash off, and the tiniest trace of it shows up under ultraviolet light. If you've naphthionate on your fingers, you're a trapped wolf."

Farneye threw his pince-nez and caution aside with an angered-bull headshake. He sprang at the house dick. He thought, possibly, O'Hanna could only use one hand, since the telltale gun was being treasured under the sleuth's right arm. If he thought so, he was right. O'Hanna licked him with one hand, with one punch, a left hook to the chin.

Selena Walther, wide-eyed and wordless up to this point, said now: "Was that contest fixed? If it was, I want to kick his teeth out."

O'Hanna said: "Nurse him back to health, then when he comes to, remind him you witnessed all of this. If you play it right, you might get that screen-test. But make him put the promise in writing."

Downstairs, Endicott was fretful. "Judas Particular Priest, Mike, the sheriff's due here any minute. You've found nothing—"

"I found this."

The manager snatched the Belgian gun. His thin features worked. "Thank God, it's been fired. That means—"

"It means nothing. Farneye followed a little hint of mine. He removed a slug from a cartridge; then probably he wrapped the gat in a towel and fired a virtually soundless shot. He's trying to cover up by framing Benny. Actually, what he's done is prove they're both innocent."

Endicott displayed outraged emotions. "Mike, that's wonderful. The possession of firearms makes them innocent, I suppose!"

"You suppose right," said O'Hanna. "They don't seem to know it, but a high-velocity load of the kind that killed Gus Lambert would make a mighty ruptured duck of any pistol."

He crossed the grounds, went back once more to chalet A-10. Without knocking, this time, he entered and tiptoed his way to the second rear bedchamber. Uncle Jeremiah Walther was peacefully bedded down, whiskers pointed ceilingward, chest lifting the coverlet in rhythmic rise and fall. O'Hanna stepped into the room, began opening bureau drawers.

Uncle Jerry sat up abruptly. "What the tarnation are you up to, young man?"

"I'm just looking for something to read." The house dick spread his hands, smiled. "To be frank about it, my job is often downright boring. Whole days pass when nobody commits a murder or steals a diamond necklace. Sometimes, just to kill time, I even read good books such as Mencken's classic on the American language. You ought to read that one yourself."

The white-whiskered man waved aside the covers, laboriously engineered his legs out of bed. He sat there, swathed from neck to ankle in an old-style striped-flannel nightshirt. "Cops have changed since my day," he complained. "You don't make sense to me."

O'Hanna said casually: "The language has changed, too. The word 'moron' is one Grandfather Walther couldn't possibly have penned in a letter dated 1895. It's a coined word, coined nearly ten years later. I'm forced to conclude that letter is a rank forgery."

Jeremiah Walther shrank inside his nightshirt as the sleuth swung to the bedside. O'Hanna scooped up the gold-rimmed spectacles from the bedside table, glanced through them, said: "These are window glass. I'll bet your beard is bleached, too. Everything about you is phony."

He stepped to the clothes closet, hauled out a pair of suitcases. Tossing them on the bed, he said: "Correct me if I'm wrong, but your name can't really be Jeremiah Walther. You're merely a shrewd operator who tumbled to the fact a member of the Walther family had disappeared fifty years ago. You boned up on the family genealogy, forged the letter to identify yourself, and forged some shares of stock. Confronted with a facsimile of her long-lost uncle Jerry, you figured Selena would make a quiet, out-of-court settlement."

The white-whiskered man gained his feet angrily. "If you're looking for any such letter, I have it in a bank box."

"The letter isn't really important to me. You'd never have dared submit it or the stock certificates to a showdown test." O'Hanna finished with one suitcase, found the next one locked. He paused, said: "You were bluffing, but so was Selena. You assumed she meant she'd actually have the company legally liquidated. That's why you tried to kill her."

"I tried to—!"

"Yeah. You tried to kill her. As the only other relative, you'd get the dough without any lawsuits. That's so clear that you had to try and make this mess look like the work of some lamebrained fanatic. It explains that phony note parked at Lambert's door, and the silly theft of a swim-suit and a bra-top from the girls' dressing-room. That was all build-up for killing Selena during the contest."

The other scorned: "Perfectly preposterous. You know I did my level best to keep Selena out of that show."

"Phooey. You knew she'd do her level best to get in it, regardless. She'd beg, borrow, or make herself a costume, and you counted on it. Then, after she'd been shot dead, you could say you didn't even know she'd be there on the stand."

The bearded man protested: "But Selena wasn't shot."

"She wasn't—because Gus Lambert jumped into your line of fire." O'Hanna drummed his fingers impatiently on the locked suitcase. "Do you want to give me a key, or shall I break this thing open?"

"You touch that and I'll sue the hotel—"

O'Hanna whipped out his penknife, sank the blade into the leather. He slashed, plunged two fingers into the opening, wrenched.

A gun lay tucked in there, diagonally, from corner to corner. To make it fit, the rifle barrel had been hack-sawed down to carbine length; the stock had been dismounted. Above the bolt action, a 'scope fitted the metal.

"A wildcat .25," O'Hanna said. "You carry it to plink butterflies, huh?"

"It's—it's a souvenir of my African hunting days."

"You're a liar. You ran back to the chalet, opened a window, and took a potshot intended for Selena. Squinting through the 'scope, you failed to see Gus Lambert and the Lofting girl." O'Hanna's Irish-gray stare grew bitter. He intoned harshly: "Now comes the really stinking part. Eva Tarkey had heard it said you'd cornered the local swim-suit supply. Tired of waiting, she came down here to demand one of them. The poor kid walked in just as you fired the shot. You strangled her, and later, you carried the body off into the bushes. It was risky, but not as risky as explaining a corpse in your chalet."

The other frowned. His voice was edgy. "There's only one answer to this rigmarole."

"Yeah, you're guilty as hell."

"Nonsense. The answer is, literally hundreds of people heard that shot. They'll all testify it came from the hotel." The white-whiskered man stepped over to the clothes closet door. "Now, if you'll kindly leave the room, I'll get dressed. I'm going to see Mr. Endicott and complain about your insulting behavior."

O'Hanna said: "You can get dressed, but you're going to see the sheriff. It happens that nobody in the path of a high-velocity bullet ever hears the gun go off. What they hear is something else, the bow-wave report of the slug traveling faster than sound. It isn't a whizz or a whine; it's a sharp crack of the slug splitting the air. It drowns the actual shot and causes an auditory illusion. The fact that everybody 'heard' the shot come from the hotel proves the gun was off at a different angle. A ballistics shark can measure the distance and figure the angle—"

The white-whiskered man whirled from the closet doorway, and he had the gold-headed cane in his fist. He had suddenly lost a third of his supposed seventy years, and he was cat-fast as he slammed the cane at O'Hanna's skull. The house dick ducked back, barely in time. There was plenty of muscle wrapped up inside that nightshirt, too. The cane head cracked down on the suitcase-bedded rifle, broke in pieces. The man tried to stab O'Hanna with the piece left in his hand. O'Hanna weaved away from that one, lashed out a punch. It was no one-handed tussle this time. The pair traded a dozen wallops before O'Hanna got in the finisher.

He stepped back, peered at the shattered cane. Now that the gold head lay in pieces, he could see telltale stains—Eva Tarkey's blood—that the killer hadn't been able to wash off when the thing was whole. Blood had seeped in under the gold fitting, discolored the wood. O'Hanna felt like gagging, and felt like beating the bleached white whiskers off the phony.

Flaming Angel

Frederick C. Davis

FREDERICK C(LYDE) DAVIS (1902–1977) was born in St. Joseph, Missouri, and graduated from Dartmouth College. The one word that is most conspicuously connected to his name as a pulp writer is *prolific*. In a career that covered more than forty years, he produced an astonishing one thousand short stories and fifty novels, under his own name and using several pseudonyms.

As Curtis Steele, he wrote the first twenty novels about James Christopher—Operator 5 (later Secret Service Operator 5), one of the great superheroes in pulp fiction. Virtually all novels in the series featured a massive invasion of America against pitifully small but brave forces led by Operator 5. The most popular stories under his own name featured Steve Thatcher, better known as the Moon Man—a policeman by day but a shady Robin Hood who wore a globe over his head to obscure his identity; fourteen of the stories were collected in *The Night Nemesis* (1984). As Stephen Ransome, he produced more than twenty semihard-boiled novels that many regard as his most accomplished work. A Ransome novel, *Hearses Don't Hurry* (1941), was filmed as *Who Is Hope Schuyler?* (1942), starring Joseph Allen, Mary Howard, and Ricardo Cortez. A Davis short story, "The Devil Is Yellow," was filmed as *Double Alibi* (1940), with Wayne Morris, Margaret Lindsay, William Gargan, and Roscoe Karns; another, "Meet the Executioner," was filmed as *Lady in the Death House* (1944), with Jean Parker and Lionel Atwill.

"Flaming Angel" was published in the March 1949 issue.

That was the first time we saw each other.

Flaming Angel

Frederick C. Davis

SUSPENSE-CHARGED NOVELETTE

Out of the burning flames of his ghastly crime came the searing realization that he would have to kill the same woman twice.

CHAPTER ONE
LAST GOOD-BY

THIS IS A DAY I WILL NEVER FORGET, Rhea, my darling, because on this day I cremated you. Do you remember, Rhea, sweet, the night you whispered to me in a serious moment while I held you in my arms in the dark,

"When I die, Johnny, please don't bury me. It makes me shiver to think of lying deep down in that heavy black earth, all alone through all eternity. Instead, let me rise off the earth in a glow of lovely dancing light. Make me what I've always yearned to become, Johnny—a shining, hot fire. Just a brief one, Johnny, but bright and beautiful before it goes out forever."

It was that way today, my sweet Rhea—just the way you wanted it.

We stood with our heads bowed in the crematory chapel—the nicest crematory in the city, Rhea, the one out on Rendezvous Road, which

secrets—but good-by, good-by forever, my sweet. We will miss you so much, so terribly much—both of us."

As I watched them rolling your casket into the great furnace, Rhea, I heard sobbing from your friends and neighbors who were present, and I saw tears glimmering in the eyes of our lovely daughter.

Bitter with deepest grief, our Darlene stood at my side, saying her own silent farewells to you, her mother. I could hardly look away from her and back to your coffin because Darlene,

direction you knew so well—and watched the attendants rolling your casket into the iron door of the great oven. I talked to you then, silently in my mind, just as I began to do the night you died and just as I am talking to you now.

I said, "Good-by, Rhea, my darling. You will never be really gone from me, never really gone. We will always be together in the keeping of our only eighteen, looked so very much like you, Rhea. It was almost as if you were not gone at all.

You would have been pleased to see how many attended your funeral, Rhea. Among the crowd in the chapel was one mourner you would have noticed especially. A man. A young man, very handsome—much handsomer than I ever was, Rhea, and very different also in his debonair manner, expensive suit and man-about-town reputation. Can you guess who? Of course, Bruce Dallas.

He was there to see the final flames consume you. I'm sure that most of the other mourners wondered why Bruce Dallas should turn up at the funeral services for Mrs. John Long. Most of them hadn't even heard that the late Mrs. Long knew him. They seemed so unlike each other—he the smooth-operator type; and she, apparently, just a homebody . . . the quiet little wife of a salesman of religious books.

He was looking a little worried, Rhea, and a little surly, too, almost as if it was not his own choice to be present. And he was not alone. The man with him was named Jennings, a police detective. Possibly Bruce Dallas had been forced by Jennings to attend the funeral services of Mrs. Long—but no one knew for what reason.

No one but me, Rhea.

The attendants gently closed the massive double door of the furnace—they shut you in, Rhea, while an organ played and a soloist softly sang your favorite hymn.

Then we began to hear, behind the melody, the rumble of the growing fires inside the thick refractory walls. You attained your long-cherished dream of burning.

For the mourners, and for Darlene and me as well, the services soon ended, although the muted thunder of the consuming flames continued to fulfill your wish.

Bruce Dallas, closely accompanied by the detective named Jennings, was one of the earliest to leave. As the others quietly dispersed, I could tell from their faces that they felt I had given you a very nice funeral—one done in a proper manner, showing the grief of a bereaved husband over the untimely loss of the wife he had loved.

I could also tell from their faces, Rhea—to my great gratification—that not one of these mourning friends and neighbors had the faintest suspicion that I had murdered you.

First inside the chapel, then outside on the marble steps, I went through the wearing process of saying good-by to all the mourners and thanking them for their friendly solicitude. Not dreaming that I had actually killed you, they saw me as the same upright and thoroughly proper man they had always known—a fairly successful salesman of religious books who had suffered a bitter loss and been left the lonely responsibility of his pretty eighteen-year-old daughter.

While I was still shaking hands with my well-wishing friends, Darlene came to me.

"The Fraziers want to drive me back home with them," she said, naming our nearest neighbors. "You won't mind, will you, Johnny?"

It startled me, Rhea. Not the fact that Darlene preferred to end this ordeal as soon as possible. The poor child was taking your death very hard. No, I was struck a small blow of dismay because Darlene had never before called me "Johnny." This was the first time she had ever called me anything other than Father.

This wasn't, of course, the place to rebuke her, particularly because she was so tired by the strain that she seemed hardly aware of what she was doing.

Somehow this grievous experience made her resemble you even more than before, Rhea. Her lovely oval face was pale, with vivid red touches on her cheeks; her full lips were parted a little, as if with an indefinable hunger, and there was a mist in her blue eyes—the same mist I used to see deep in your own lovely eyes, my sweet.

Only eighteen! You were so young-looking when you died that you might have passed for your daughter's older sister, and on this unforgettably sad occasion Darlene seemed more like you than ever before.

"You won't mind, will you, Johnny?" she had said.

Frowning slightly, I answered, "Of course, Darlene, run right along. I'll join you in a few minutes."

She went down to the Fraziers' car. When I had nodded my farewell to the last mourner, I turned back into the chapel. It was deserted now, except for the crematory director, who was prowling among the chairs looking for lost articles.

He discreetly tip-toed out, leaving me entirely alone. There was no hush in this chapel, no reverent silence. The dull roar of the hellish flames continued inside the great furnace.

I had come to say a final farewell to you, Rhea. A moment that might bring tears easily to another new widower's eyes, but it's possible that, instead, there was a hard shine in mine as I said to you silently, "Again good-by, Rhea, my good and faithful wife—as people think. You're finally being in fact the bright flame you always yearned to be. It will help you to keep our secrets together, my lovely. Good-by again. And may you go on burning longer than you expected—in hell."

*   *   *

Night was settling when I drove back along Rendezvous Road. I don't need to remind you, Rhea, darling, how that road looks when you're driving it after dark with something better and cozier than just your thoughts for company.

Turning then toward our little home on Laurel Street, I found myself retracing the same course that I had taken every day for years when coming home from the office. In this same car, alone like this, I came exactly this same way every day, with expectations far different from today's. In pleasantest anticipation, I used to know just what would happen.

I would leave the car in the garage and turn to the kitchen door for your greeting. You had your graceful, playful little way of popping out and piping, "Welcome home, Johnny!" Fresh and crisp in a bright flowered dress, you would throw your arms around my neck and kiss me full on the lips. You always seemed as happy to have me back home as if I'd been away for weeks rather than hours. Every time it was the same delightful routine. But today?

I was driving home in exactly the same way as always before, Rhea, but today you wouldn't greet me at the kitchen door with your lively, laughing embrace. Today you were back there in the crematory, a bright, hot flame in the furnace.

I missed you sorely as I turned the car into the driveway, Rhea. I almost wished I hadn't killed you—but only almost. You had destroyed all the goodness in yourself until only ugly sin was left. You deserved all the punishment I gave you, my little evil one. But before then my homecomings had been so pleasant—I felt a pang, thinking there would never be any more of them.

No more glad little greeting of "Welcome home, Johnny!" Your arms no more around me, your lips no more on mine. No more Rhea at all.

It had been such a trying day, seeing you cremated, my darling—I was utterly unprepared for the jolt that hit me next.

As I reached for the knob of the kitchen door it sprang open. Your voice—*your voice, Rhea!*—sang out in your old gay way, "Welcome home, Johnny!" Even more unnerving, Rhea, you actually appeared there before me—Rhea herself, alive, her eyes sparkling, her lips a happy smile. Rhea wearing her favorite flowered frock! *You, Rhea!*

Impossible? Yes, because you were back there in the crematory furnace, being devoured in the storming flames. Yet you were here with me, crying out my name. Calling to me as you always did.

A man doesn't easily admit having been unmanly, Rhea. It isn't easy for me to confess I fainted on the spot. But I did. Already overstrained, now suddenly overwhelmed, I simply dropped into a pit of blackness.

When the blackness swirled slowly out of my mind, I felt someone tugging at me. It was Darlene, asking breathlessly, "What happened, are you all right?" She helped me up to my knees, then into a chair at the kitchen table. I was still dizzy.

All I could say, when I found my voice, was, "Yes, what—what *did* happen, Darlene? Did you see?"

Darlene said, "I was in the living room, just sitting there, so tired, waiting for you to come home. Just as you came in the back door, you let out a hoarse kind of cry. I heard you fall. When I got to you, you were down on the floor in a dead faint. That's all I can tell you about it."

I looked hard at her—at her pretty face so much like yours, Rhea. She was still pale, except for the vivid spots on her cheeks. She was wearing the same black dress she had worn at the funeral—a simple dress snugly fitting a perfect figure. A figure the exact image of yours, Rhea.

I gazed at Darlene's image in the mirror, chilled through, and asked softly, "Darlene—are you sure that what you told me is what actually happened?"

She smiled a little and answered, "Aren't *you* sure? You couldn't be fooled by a thing like that—could you, Johnny?"

CHAPTER TWO
SHE-DEVIL'S DAUGHTER

After that I began watching Darlene closely, Rhea—with fear in my heart—the dread that had haunted me for years, that our lovely daughter had inherited the evilness of her mother.

You see, Rhea, I could not let myself be deluded into believing that you had supernaturally paid me a visit after death. I knew that could not be so. I was quite confident that you were destroyed as you deserved. Nor could I be such a fool as to imagine your ghost had begun to haunt me. So it came down to this, Rhea—either my senses had tricked me overwhelmingly—or I had reason to watch Darlene.

Watch Darlene! Isn't it odd, Rhea? Do you remember the time, right after we met, when it was my task to keep a watchful eye on you?

I find myself smiling at this romantic little reminiscence, Rhea. Our meeting *was* quite a romantic incident, you know. A meeting between a young book peddler and a young girl who was already losing her prettiness and her health, and her job as well, on a merry-go-round of sin—a kid skidding downhill fast. As you confessed yourself afterward, Rhea, you would have soon wound up in the gutter or in the river if I hadn't saved you from yourself.

That day I had gone down to the old Bijou Theatre. A squalid den, that place. A burlesque showhouse—catering to men's worst instincts.

When I went near that sinkhole, however, it was for reasons of business and high principle. Oddly, the burlesque people, especially the strippers, whom I usually saw in their dressing rooms between numbers, were ready buyers of the religious books I sold. Perhaps they never read the books but only bought them to salve their aching consciences. I liked to feel, though, that by going down into that vile valley of iniquity and leaving The Word among those misled people, I was doing good missionary work.

Just as I lifted my hand to the stage door, it opened. A girl was pushed out bodily, actually into my arms. Instinctively I held you. That was the first time we saw each other, Rhea—and your first glimpse of sweet salvation.

You huddled close to me, wearing almost nothing. You clung to me, Rhea, for the simple reason that you were almost unable to stand by yourself. You gave me a taunting smile. You were intoxicated—really staggering drunk. You had come to the theatre in that condition and had tried to get ready for the show, along with the other bare-skinned chorus "ponies." The stage manager, fed up because you had done it too often before, had chosen this moment to fire you out—straight into my arms.

Snarling after you, the stage manager said, "Don't bother holding her up, Reverend." They liked to call me that—"Reverend"—because I took my books seriously, and I really considered it a compliment. "Let the no-good little tramp fall on her face right now. It'll save time. She's hell-bent on wheels, and the sooner she hits bottom the less trouble she'll cause."

You clung to me, your lovely young body

starting to shake with sobs, your eyes full of teary pleading. In them I saw goodness, Rhea. Reeking with liquor though you were, I told myself there was womanly sweetness in you waiting only to be brought out. I knew then, at that moment, that I must do everything in my power to save you from the evil into which you had fallen.

So romantic, wasn't it, Rhea, the way I hustled you into my car, then brought you your clothes from that filthy dressing room, and how I stood on the sidewalk to guard you from ogling passersby while you dressed yourself as best you could? Then I brought you hot, black coffee and gently forced you to drink it. Next came a decent meal in a good restaurant.

You were actually past the verge of alcoholism already, Rhea. Your pretty face was already developing haggard lines and sags—but in you I saw goodness. At least I believed I saw it and knew I must devote myself wholeheartedly to your salvation. And best of all you really wanted to be saved.

"I've been a crazy-fool kid," you confessed. "All because of a guy I fell for too hard. Until I met him, I'd never taken a single drink. He taught me to like the stuff, and then I went overboard trying to keep up with him."

"That man should be jailed, except that jail is too good for him," I said. "What's his name?"

"Dallas," you said. "Bruce Dallas. There's no use trying to punish him, because I went along with him willingly enough. Anyway, he's left town now—went to Chicago where the pickings are richer. The worst part is the tough time I'm having, trying to get over him. Maybe I never will. I've drunk more and more just trying to get him burned out of me. I hate it—what drink does to me. Please tell me how I can quit."

"I'll do better than tell you," I said, putting my hand over yours. "I'm going to be right there at your side, leading you every step of the way along the path of rightness. That's the goal for both of us—to make you the good woman you can be."

_____

But it was not easy, Rhea, was it? We both struggled—you against the yearnings of temptation, I to give you the strength you needed to resist. There were little slips and relapses, but we both knew the long effort would win out. That was when I watched you, Rhea, to make sure you wouldn't weaken, even to the small extent of sneaking a single drink—because we both knew that that one taste, if you ever took it, would send you skidding straight toward hell again.

But we did it. My moral strength kept you good. Your health returned. You became sweeter and lovelier than ever. Indeed, Rhea, you were an angel on earth to me.

Our happiness was complete when we were married. When we moved into our little home on Laurel Street—the same home where you were later to meet such a sudden and tragic death—all the evil in your past was left far behind you. None of our friends and neighbors there dreamed you had once been an all-but-lost soul—a little alcoholic burlesque girl. You and I almost forgot it too in our simple blissfulness— you were so beautifully changed and purified, a model wife and mother.

It even made no difference at all, to judge from your visible reactions, when we later heard the news that Bruce Dallas had come back to this city, richer, smoother, an even hotter operator than before.

When Darlene was born, in the first year of our marriage, I had stopped watching over you for a possible relapse into sin. It had become unnecessary, your salvation was so complete. Now and then I would feel a twinge of fear that the seeds of evil might be lying dormant in you, and might come out in some moment of stress.

At times too I wondered whether certain tendencies to evil had passed from you to your daughter. . . .

Alone in our living room, I was casting about in my mind for an explanation of that incident at the kitchen door. Darlene had gone upstairs. I became aware of busy noises as she moved about. Puzzled, I went up the stairs and found her, not in her own room, Rhea, but in yours.

Darlene had gone into your room, Rhea, directly next to my own, with the connecting bath in between. She had seated herself at your vanity mirror and was quietly applying lacquer to her fingernails. She paused to gaze at me—looking so much like you, Rhea, that I felt my nerves squirming in my flesh.

"What are you doing, Darlene? Have you forgotten I've never permitted you to use paint on your nails? You're still too young."

She gazed at me with another of those new, quiet smiles. She had never smiled just that way before. Something in Darlene was changing. She seemed more knowing; she had grown a little bolder. There was an audacity, almost a challenging shine in her eyes as she answered:

"Perhaps you haven't noticed, Johnny, how much older I really am now."

She went on smiling and quietly applying the enamel to her nails, taking it from the bottle left on your vanity. She left me feeling strangely helpless. What could I do about it, Rhea? Darlene was quietly defying me and really there was no way I could force her to stop.

Moreover it was true, as she had just reminded me, that she *was*, somehow, suddenly grown up—too grown up.

"I really am older than you seem to realize, Johnny," she said softly.

In a shaken but stern attempt at discipline I retorted, "That's another thing, Darlene—your calling me Johnny. You never did that before this afternoon. Please don't do it any more. It doesn't show the proper respectful attitude which a daughter should feel toward her father."

"But I liked so much the way Mother called you Johnny," Darlene answered. "I thought that if I called you Johnny in the same nice way, it would help to make it seem that Mother isn't really gone."

"But she *is* gone," I said flatly. "She's gone never to come back. I will always love the memory of her, Darlene, and of course you are very dear to me, too, but in quite a different way. . . . That blue dress you have on is another thing—it's one of your mother's. You shouldn't have

touched it, at least not so soon. And what do you mean by coming into her room like this? It should be kept closed out of proper respect—"

"But, Johnny, I've always wanted this room," she broke in eagerly. "I love being amid Mother's things because they're all so very much like me and now they're all mine."

"Darlene!"

It struck me so deeply, Rhea, that my sense pinwheeled. Overstrained as my nerves were, I was hardly aware of leaving. Then I discovered that I was no longer in your room, Rhea, but in my own. I had a sleepless nightmare of a night. . . .

When I came home early the next evening, Rhea—after an interminable day at the office—I brought the engraved silver urn containing your ashes.

With the urn in my hands I turned from the garage toward the house, and paused, staring apprehensively at the kitchen door. Then I went to it slowly, watching at every step. Thank heavens that the incident of yesterday was not repeated. Entering that door, in fact, I found the kitchen deserted. But there were sounds overhead, indicating that Darlene was upstairs, and her voice carried down gayly,

"Welcome home, Johnny!"

Unable to answer, I carried the urn into the living room and placed it on the center of the mantel. Left there in plain sight, I hoped it would serve as a constant reminder to our daughter that Rhea would continue to be present in this house only as a handful of gray dust reposing inside that silver vessel.

But only the next day I came home, numbly tired again, to find that in one more detail Darlene had caused herself to resemble you even more closely. She had had her hair bleached a shade or two, to the shade yours had been.

It was adding up tension toward the cracking point, Rhea. Darlene had also developed your trick of sneaking a smoke now and then, in just the way you used to do it, believing I didn't know. Darlene was fully aware that I disapprove of women smoking, especially mere girls of her age—so she tried to hide her indulgence from me just as you used to hide it. But I could always smell the tobacco when I came into the house and I would find the butts stained with lip rouge, just like yours, in the trash basket.

This in itself was trivial, perhaps, except that Darlene had never before *liked* cigarettes. But now she was smoking in my absence, concealing it and undoubtedly becoming an addict.

Like mother, like daughter! Your evilness was your bequest to Darlene. Your sins were flowing in her blood, tainting it, cropping out of her now, more and more in hellish increase.

All these things were nerve-shattering. Darlene's new way of waiting for me just inside the kitchen door, smiling at me, was almost the worst trial to endure.

But then came the worst of all, Rhea—the dereliction proving once and for all that Darlene was going the evil way of her mother. It came so soon that it left me dazed and appalled—inherited evil completely claiming Darlene. Almost before I was aware of it, it came so slyly, she was plunging into your own secretly fatal sin.

CHAPTER THREE
THE NIGHT YOU DIED

I never told you in life, Rhea, just how I discovered your unforgivable secret. At the time I judged it best to use your own tactics of silence and craft. You didn't even suspect that I had learned—and perhaps you do not know even yet how I brought a righteous punishment down upon you.

The first sign of it, Rhea, was a strange new tenseness in you. Your cheerful, content manner was gone. You had become on edge, anxious. When I asked you what was bothering you, your answer was evasive. "I just seem to be a little nervous, Johnny, that's all—probably because the weather is so unsettled."

But after the weather changed, you stayed agitated. Coming home from work these afternoons, I found your customary greeting strained. The stench of tobacco was stronger in the house and more butts than usual were discarded in the trash basket. At night, too, you were restless—you tossed and squirmed in bed so endlessly that neither of us could sleep. That was when you suggested it might be better if you had a room of your own, so you moved into the second bedroom on the other side of the bath.

It did seem to help some, for soon your nervous tensions relaxed somewhat. In fact, you took on a new loveliness—there was a brighter flash in your eyes, a happier shine on your lips, and as you worked around the house you sang softly to yourself.

And I didn't suspect the reason, Rhea. Trusting my wife as a husband should, I didn't dream. . . .

The first inkling of it came, with bitter irony, as the result of my husbandly concern for you, Rhea.

That night in bed I was also restive. Usually I sleep the sound sleep of a man whose conscience is perfectly clear, but on this night something caused me to waken. My first thought was of you, Rhea. I rose, wanting to make sure you were all right, and without turning on any lights, stepped through the connecting bath into your room.

A light had been left burning inside your closet. Thinking you had overlooked it, I reached in to turn it out—and then I saw the bottle.

On the shelf, Rhea, just barely visible behind a hat-box—a liquor bottle. You were keeping it hidden there. Only a few ounces of whiskey remained in it.

I stood there too stunned to move, Rhea—staring at that bottle as if at the suddenly dead face of a loved one. In a soundless thunderclap of revelation, it told me that all my years of loving patience and guidance had gone in vain. You had secretly deceived me, Rhea. The sweet, good wife I had known was gone, for she had yielded again to sinful weakness.

Heartsick, I turned my unbelieving eyes to look at you, Rhea, and then an even more staggering blow rocked me.

Your bed was empty.

Just in the nick of time I choked off a cry of pain. Darlene was asleep just down the hall, and the Fraziers' open bedroom windows were no farther away than the width of the driveway. I could not bear to let them learn of my discovery.

The condition of your bed showed you had been lying there for a while, Rhea, but now you had left it. And the clock on your vanity said the time was 4:20 a.m.

In a stunned turmoil of conjectures—unwilling to believe this thing until I had made doubly sure—I quietly went down the stairs. It took me only a few moments to search the house. It was horribly true. You were gone. You had risen from your bed in the middle of the night, while your trusting husband slept, to sneak out of the house and away.

Where had you gone? How many times before tonight had you slipped out like this without my slightest knowledge? Did Darlene suspect, or the neighbors? I hoped to heaven they were as ignorant of it as I had been. I prayed that I could remain alone in my wretched wonder.

These questions would remain a torture in my mind even after they were answered. I resolved on the spot, in my heartsick dismay, that whatever the ugly truth about you might be, it must, at any cost, remain always concealed from our daughter and from our friends who thought so well of us.

Of one other thing I was instantly sure, Rhea. Whatever you were doing, I must stop you. You must be punished for your sins already committed, and I must not permit you to hurt me so ungratefully and so grievously with more of them.

First I must learn the dreadful truth. I went quietly back up the stairs. I left the bottle untouched on your closet shelf, the light burning just as you had left it. I closed the connecting door, leaving it as I had found it, and fell back into my own bed.

I lay there in acute wakefulness, listening and waiting.

Almost an hour later, just before dawn, I heard the sound of a car pausing in the street, then quietly rolling on. The faint sound of hurrying feet came down the dark, hedge-bordered alleyway behind the houses. You came into our home with such sly quietness that I could well understand why your secret prowlings had not disturbed me before.

All the while I lay still in my own room, letting you believe you were deceiving me again. Even when I heard you finally return to your bed, I kept my wretched silence—and planned.

The next night, Rhea, I was grimly ready to find the answers to the dark questions rankling in my mind.

At breakfast, to my secret amazement, you looked so fresh and unaffected. It showed your fine natural talent for sin, Rhea. As for me, I must confess finding it surprisingly easy to act as if nothing was wrong.

A shameful thing, Rhea, this mutual deception—but on my part it was justified.

Again when I came home that evening to receive your usual cheery greeting, the warmth of your kiss seemed an expression of your duplicity. I suspected liquor on your breath, too. But I pretended to notice nothing and was ready with a small deception of my own—one you had forced upon me.

"I came home by bus, honey, because I had a little clutch trouble with the car. Left it at the garage. Pick it up tomorrow."

That wasn't quite the fact, Rhea. Actually I had left the car parked down in the next block. I expected to have a special use for it during the night.

It wrung my heart to observe you during the evening, Rhea. Now I understood your nervousness. You were suffering pangs of guilt and remorse. You were tense with fear that I might somehow learn too much. Yet in your weakness you could no longer resist temptation.

Our double pretense went on through the evening until our usual time to retire to our separate rooms—and then the deceit became double-edged with a vengeance.

This time it was I who sneaked out of the house. Of course you didn't dream of such a move on my part, Rhea. While you lay awake or dozing in your room, giving me time to fall into my usual deep sleep, I slipped silently out of my room.

I managed it with great care and justified cunning, Rhea, and you never knew. You had no notion I had eased soundlessly out of the house and down the dark street to my waiting car.

Sitting behind the wheel, I pictured your covert actions. I could visualize you getting up very quietly. Perhaps before making a second move, you would fortify your evilness from the bottle hidden on the closet shelf. Then you might listen at my door, and, feeling sure I was sleeping as soundly as usual, you would sneak down the stairs and out the back door.

Then?

My intention tonight was to see for myself where my good and faithful wife went from there.

Sure enough, Rhea, you soon appeared. Having placed my car in the shadows of the maples to permit me to watch the mouth of the alleyway, I saw you hurry out. You turned to another car that was waiting there in the side street, a long convertible, gleaming new. I saw its door opened for you from inside. I watched you disappearing into it—and for moments of miserable suffering, I pictured you in the arms of the man you had met.

Finally the convertible lights gleamed on, its motor purred and it breezed into the boulevard.

You must not have noticed my car following you, or if you did you thought nothing of it. Many cars cruised that way, to the end of the boulevard, then along Rendezvous Road. I trailed you all the way, Rhea, until the shiny convertible pulled into a special parking space outside the Clover Club.

Yes, the Clover Club, that notorious road house. I saw you leave the car with the man who had met you—the man with whom you must have come to this noxious place night after night. I recognized his handsome face, Rhea—with a blinding flash of realization.

Bruce Dallas. The same man you had loved so eagerly and so evilly years ago. Now you had gone eagerly and evilly back to him. Abandoning all the sweetest things of your life, you had gone back.

How did it come about, Rhea? Where and when did your meeting with Bruce Dallas occur? Even now I don't know the details, my sweet. But my own feeling is that he happened to see you again somewhere—to see how sweet and good you were, and how amazingly like the young girl you had been—and then he sought you out.

From the darkness I watched you going into this garish resort which Bruce Dallas himself operated. I saw you both appear at a window upstairs, in one of those private dining rooms. I saw a drink in your hand and heard shrill laughter on your lips before the venetian blinds were closed, mercifully to shut the sight of you, up there with Dallas, from my stinging eyes.

Then I turned back, Rhea, laden with a great sickness of the heart, fired with a resolve that a just punishment must be meted out to you.

Before you sneaked back home again that same night, I did something, Rhea, which you may never have realized.

Thinking and planning in my silent, anguished resolve, I closely inspected the head of the stairway. Darlene was asleep in her room then, also unaware of what I was about. As you have excellent reason to know, Rhea, those stairs are very steep—I was always careful to caution you about going down them.

The post on the one side of the landing, and the molding on the wall on the opposite side, were ornately carved. I saw how it would be possible to brace a rod of some sort firmly across the top of the steps, a few inches above the edge of the landing, so that anyone moving onto the stairs would surely trip over it.

I tried it then and there, Rhea, using a tool of a completely innocuous sort. Bringing an umbrella up from the stand in the vestibule directly below, I found it was of exactly the right length to be placed in position. A slight bit of forcing kept it firmly in place. Black, it would be completey invisible in the dark.

I replaced the umbrella in its vase, undressed, got into bed and actually dozed off without waiting to hear you sneak back in. Because now my plan was complete. I could be confident that guilt would be punished. Tomorrow night I would set the trap of a just vengeance. . . .

I recall so clearly, Rhea, the night you died.

That evening, the normal course of incidents went along as it had on many other evenings. You didn't imagine I had learned of your deceit, and much less could you dream I had definitely arranged that you would pay for it within a few hours. Nor did you realize, Rhea, that you would never see Bruce Dallas again—that ·you had already held your last mortal rendezvous with him.

At her usual time, Darlene went upstairs. I heard her close her door—that door which could be counted on to stick shut for a few minutes when she tried to open it again. Soon I heard her bed bounce and knew she would be sound asleep within minutes.

These were your last living hours, Rhea.

You were reading a women's magazine, remember?—and waiting with secret impatience for me to go to bed.

I finished reading the paper, quite deliberately prolonging it a little. Finally I rose and said, "I'm turning in now, honey. Pretty sleepy. Good night."

You may have thought it a little strange that I placed my good-night kiss on your forehead this time, not on your lips. I could not bear to think of kissing the once-sweet lips which Bruce Dallas had defiled.

You said, "I'm tired, too, Johnny. Be up in a minute."

I climbed the stairs, entered my room, closed the hallway door, got ready for bed and lay down. All this was entirely routine, except that tonight I had no intention of sleeping. I waited until you came up to your room and went through the same process. Then, once you were settled down for a brief doze, I rose in silence.

I went down to the vestibule to get the umbrella, brought it up and wedged it across the edge of the landing, in just the right position, as I had tested it last night. Then I went back to bed and waited.

Waiting, scarcely breathing, I soon heard your furtive sounds. First a motion of your bed as you got up. Then a stealthy squeak from the cork of your hidden bottle. Then a few more moments while you got back into a dress. Next you were almost soundlessly leaving your room.

Then your scream, Rhea!

Next the thumping fall of your body to the very base of the stairs.

I saw a light come on in a bedroom window of the house next door. Your scream had been loud enough to waken our nearest neighbors. Seeing Marie Frazier putting her head out the window beside her bed to stare across, I made the clever move of turning on my bedroom light also and going directly to my own window to speak to her.

"What was that, Marie?" I asked quickly. "Something wrong over there?"

"It was a frightful scream, John," she said. "But it didn't come from here. It came from your own house. I thought it must be Rhea's voice."

"But it can't be Rhea," I answered. "She's sound asleep."

Through the windows Marie Frazier watched me hurrying first into your room, Rhea, then into the hall. Darlene had also been awakened by your shriek but she hadn't yet appeared from her room. As I had expected it to do, her door was sticking shut.

I hastened to the head of the stairs, dislodged the umbrella, ran down, then snapped on the lights.

You were lying huddled on the floor on your

back, your head oddly twisted over one shoulder. Your eyes were staring up into mine. You were not yet dead then, Rhea. Your neck was broken and you were paralyzed. The terrified light in your eyes seemed to show you knew what I had done—and why. I lifted you a little in my arms. At that moment Darlene succeeded in yanking open the door of her bedroom.

"Your mother's had an accident, Darlene!" I gasped out. "Call a doctor!"

Then you died, Rhea. You died and I felt an exultation.

CHAPTER FOUR
ANOTHER IS CLAIMED

Thinking back now, I can recognize that the disturbing change in Darlene showed itself the very first moment she learned her mother was dead.

I can bring back that moment very clearly, Rhea. Darlene had finished telephoning for the doctor. Hurrying back, she found me holding you in my arms.

I recall vividly that as she stood there she gazed wide-eyed not at her dead mother, but at me.

I made quite a convincing picture of a grief-stunned husband, I'm sure, Rhea, as I knelt there on the floor.

That was the way the Fraziers found me when they hurried in a few minutes later. I would not permit them to move you until after Dr. Kerwin arrived and pronounced you dead. I watched the good doctor solemnly filling out the death certificate—writing under the words *Cause of Death* his conclusion, *Accidental fall.*

The Fraziers and the other neighbors who came in all deplored the accident so sincerely, Rhea. "Such a terrible shame," they said.

But questions were buzzing in their minds—not about me, but about you, Rhea—questions none of them dared put into words. Finally Marie Frazier worked up the courage to ask, "How did it happen that Rhea was up and dressed, John?"

"But why shouldn't she be?" I said, sounding as if I hadn't the faintest idea what she was implying. "Naturally she had just gotten up to make breakfast for me."

"Poor John," Marie murmured. "You're so dazed you haven't even noticed what time it is. Only four o'clock in the morning now, and it happened about two hours ago."

I was the perfect picture of an unsuspecting husband, Rhea. Our friends privately wagged their heads. Not that they had any idea themselves of what an evil woman you really had been. But they did puzzle over the circumstances of that tragic little accident—never doubting that it *was* an accident—and marveled that I apparently could see nothing at all questionable about it.

It fell to the lot of the minister of our church, Matthew Parker, to break the disillusioning "news" to me.

"John—Darlene," he said gently. "I'm sure you must appreciate the fact that in a sudden death of this kind certain doubts inevitably arise and must be cleared away. For your own peace of mind, I feel I must explain the apparent cause for Rhea's fatal fall. When Marie Frazier and my wife were tidying up Rhea's room today they found—brace yourself, John—they found a bottle of whiskey hidden on a closet shelf."

I did not laugh in his solemn face, Rhea. Nor did I put up a pretense that this of course explained everything. Instead I simply stared at our old friend Matthew Parker and said flatly, "I don't believe it."

He insisted very gravely, "I'm afraid it's true, John. We can't help believing that Rhea had a secret addiction to alcohol. That accounts for her fall—she had over-imbibed. Probably she had dressed in order to sneak out for another bottle. I'm sincerely sorry, John, but at least this does clear up certain puzzling details."

"Rhea was too sweet, too good," I said. "I can't believe it of her. I can't."

"Bless your trusting heart, John," Matthew Parker said. "At least you may rest assured that the Fraziers and the Parkers won't breathe a word of this."

After he had gone I said to Darlene, "I'll never believe it. Never let it change your own feeling for your mother, Darlene."

She smiled at me. "Mother and I always understood each other."

That was the first of Darlene's disturbing cryptic remarks, Rhea—the first hint of evil forces rising in her as they had risen to claim you. But at that time I was more concerned with other dangers. For example—Jennings.

He came to the door soon after the minister had left, a small man with sharp, darting eyes and a notebook. I put on a disturbed and puzzled look when he announced he was from police headquarters.

"The homicide law requires us to look at every case of violent death, including accidents, Mr. Long," Jennings began. "So this is just routine. Except for one angle. How-come your wife was acquainted with Bruce Dallas?"

"Bruce Dallas?" I echoed. "Who's he?"

Jennings explained to me briefly.

I kept a puzzled frown on my face. "And what makes you imagine my wife was acquainted like that?"

Jennings said slowly, "I've heard a report on the grapevine that she was seen once or twice with him at a place called the Clover Club."

"It's incredible," I said. "This man—what's his name, Dallas?—may have been seen there with a woman resembling my wife, but it couldn't possibly have been Rhea."

He rose, apologizing for having bothered me. I smiled at his back as he left. He had come with a vague suspicion of murder—but the suspicion pointed at Bruce Dallas, not at me. That was his reason, of course, for later jockeying Dallas into your funeral service—to watch his reactions as the flames consumed you.

So then, Rhea, nothing was left but the ceremonies of cremating you, and after that the tragic little event would begin fading from all our minds.

It would have done so, Rhea, except for Darlene.

Every night when I came home from work, dreading the moment as profoundly as I had once welcomed it, you met me. It was becoming such a hair-trigger thing, Rhea, that I was fast reaching the point where I could no longer endure it.

But what could I do? Order Darlene out of the house?

No, I must stay and cope with it. I must come home every evening to hear your greeting— "Welcome home, Johnny!"—and to find a duplicate of you waiting for me in the kitchen.

It was getting to be more than my shaken nerves would stand. It was becoming a nightmare, Rhea. But then came even more—the worst thing of all—the proof that your heritage of evil was now claiming Darlene.

As before, the whole house was silent. For a while I lay listening in a silent torment of tension. Then, almost as in a dream, telling myself that somehow, somehow this insufferable situation must be ended, I rose, opened the door.

A light had been left burning in Darlene's closet. Stunned by the repetition of this incident, I reached in to turn it out—and then I saw the bottle.

Staring at that bottle, I realized it stood hidden at almost the same spot where you had hidden yours. Darlene had been sneaking drinks exactly as you had done, for only a few ounces of whiskey remained in it. Then I turned my stinging eyes to Darlene's bed.

Like your bed on that other night of terrifying discovery, it was empty.

CHAPTER FIVE
PAID IN FULL

The next evening was also much like another I had had with you, Rhea—casual and commonplace on the surface, while underneath a grim plan was being acted out.

Darlene and I sat together in the living room, both reading. I could sense the impatience in her and feel her covert glances. At the usual time and in my usual way I said, "I'm turning in now, Darlene. Good night."

She answered, "Good night, Johnny; I'll go up in a minute."

I could feel her senses quickening as I went up the stairs. I closed and locked my door and lay on the bed without undressing. Presently I heard Darlene's sounds on the stairs, then in the room next to mine. Quiet followed.

Then, just as it had occurred with you, Rhea, I heard a motion of Darlene's bed as she rose. Next a squeaking sound from the cork of her hidden bottle. A few more moments of quiet followed while she dressed. After that she left her room.

As soon as she was outside the house, I went into my own plan. Down the stairs and out the front door, I ran along the tree-shaded sidewalk toward the next corner.

I saw Darlene, halfway down the cross-street, hurrying out of the alley way. She ran to a car waiting nearby. A long convertible, Rhea—the same flashy car that had waited for you!

I went back into the house almost blindly—resolved that the evil of you, Rhea, as it was living again in the body of Darlene, must be destroyed once and for all.

I would have it exactly as before. The normal course of incidents would go along this evening just as it had on previous evenings. Darlene and I would be in the living room, reading. I would finally rise and say, "Pretty sleepy. Good night now. Better get some rest yourself."

Then I would go into my room.

Presently Darlene would come up to her room. She would lie down and doze. Making no noise at all, I would then silently go down to the vestibule for the umbrella. I would bring it up, wedge it in place just above the edge of the landing; then go noiselessly back to my bed.

I would wait to hear Darlene getting up. She would first sneak a drink, slip into a dress, then pad out in her stocking feet. I would follow the slight sound of her every step to the trap at the head of those steep stairs. Then—

At my first move, however, a small deviation occurred. When I finished reading the evening paper in the living room and said, "Well, I'm going up now, Darlene," she did not respond as I had expected.

Instead she said, "I feel sort of jittery for some reason, Johnny. I think I'll take a little walk, just down to the corner store and back."

I asked with concealed grimness, "Want me to come along?"

"Oh, no," she said quickly.

"All right, but hurry back, Darlene."

I told myself that the slight delay she was causing would not matter at all. I went up to my room to wait.

I lay in bed, fully dressed, waiting. It seemed to me that Darlene was taking too long a walk, and then, after I heard her coming back into the house, I felt she was remaining downstairs unusually long. But finally there were noises on the stairs. And presently an early-morning quiet pervaded the whole house.

I rose, making no sound, and went down the stairs. Coming back with the umbrella, I braced it firmly in the same place that had proved so effective with you, Rhea. Then I returned to my bed to wait for a just wrath to destroy the guilty.

Soon I heard furtive sounds in the hall. They rustled along the hallway to the top of the stairs.

Suddenly there was the thump of a foot catching under the barrier and a sharp, long scream from Darlene.

Next the thudding fall of a body to the very base of the stairs—followed by a terrible silence.

I sprang up from my bed. Again I saw lights appear in the bedroom windows of the house next door. Just as your scream had done, Rhea, Darlene's had wakened the Fraziers. This time I did not wait to speak to Marie. She had apparently seen me aroused from a sound sleep by the shriek, so now I let her watch me hurrying from my room in high alarm.

At the top of the stairs, seeing nothing else so far in the dark, I snatched the umbrella from its place. I ran down the flight hearing groans of mortal pain below. In the vestibule I put the umbrella in the stand with one hand and reached to the wall-switch with the other. The light brought a revelation that struck paralysis into my every fiber.

The victim of my trap lay huddled, helpless and bleeding at the base of the stairs.

But it was not Darlene, Rhea. It was Bruce Dallas.

What followed, Rhea, stays with me like a series of flashes from a nightmare.

Suddenly I found myself beating at Dallas with my fists, in a wild desire to destroy the last flicker of life in him. He lay limp and lifeless as I hit him, able neither to strike back or to feel the power of my blows. Then I looked up and saw Detective Jennings hurrying in the front door.

Darlene?

She was standing on the stair landing above, dressed as I had last seen her, held still by horror, both her hands pressed over her lips to stifle her cries.

In a moment of unfeeling selflessness, even of wonder, I watched her as she came slowly down the stairs. She moved past the dead body of Bruce Dallas—she seemed not to give me a glance—into the living room, gazing at the shining silver urn on the mantel, and her lips spoke.

I thought I heard her speaking to you, Rhea. She said, "Now both of them are paid, Mother, for what they did to you."

*   *   *

They didn't bring out the real truth at my trial, Rhea. They tried to prove that I had furiously quarreled with Bruce Dallas, and had deliberately thrown him down the stairs because I had caught him upstairs with Darlene.

Darlene testified—falsely, for your sake—that she'd known Dallas for some time, but hadn't told me about it—that it was she who had been seen dancing with him at the Clover Club,

and not you. She said that Dallas had had a flat tire down the street a ways that night and had come in and gone upstairs merely to wash his hands. That was when I had found him, had misunderstood and had flown into a rage.

We know better than this, Rhea, much better. I doubt that they could have convicted me on this story if Jennings, having suspiciously kept an eye on Dallas, hadn't been waiting outside the house for Dallas to come out again. And then, hearing the scream—

Darlene?

I hadn't dreamed how much Darlene had observed and planned. A deep one, that girl, Rhea, one needing to be watched. When she came here to the death house to visit me I accused her.

"You knew all along what had really happened to Rhea. Did you notice the umbrella was slightly bent? Did you find that the tip of it had left a scratch in the woodwork at the top of the stairs?"

She just gazed at me, Rhea, not smiling, not speaking. She was not so much like you anymore. She had stopped using your cosmetics and your perfume; her hair had returned to its own natural tint and her new clothes were her own.

No, she was not like Rhea at all now. And I could feel her thinking again as she sat there in silence gazing at me through the thick wire screen, *Now both of them are paid back, Mother, for what they did to you.*

She went away then, Rhea, and she has not come back since. I am sitting alone here in my cell, waiting for the sentence of death to be executed upon me within an hour, and I have stopped wondering whether Darlene will return to visit me for one last time. In my heart I know she will not come. I'm sure instead that tonight she is at home, alone there—except that she is with you.

Odds on Death

Don M. Mankiewicz

DON M(ARTIN) MANKIEWICZ (1922–) was born in Berlin, Germany, and moved to Los Angeles as a child. He attended Columbia University, studying law, but went into the army and did not graduate. When the first short story he wrote (in an hour, he claims) sold to *The New Yorker*, he decided to write full-time. Although he wrote numerous short stories and nonfiction for magazines, and three novels, all crime stories, he is best-known as a successful motion picture writer and, to a greater degree, television writer. *See How They Run* (1951) was his first novel. His second, *Trial* (1955), was filmed by MGM with Mankiewicz's screenplay; it started Glenn Ford and Dorothy McGuire. His final novel was *It Only Hurts a Minute* (1966). Among his screenwriting credits are *I Want to Live!* (1958), for which he was nominated for an Academy Award for Best Adapted Screenplay, *House of Numbers* (1957), based on a Jack Finney novel, *The Black Bird* (1975), *Sanctuary of Fear* (1979), *The Bait* (1973), based on a Dorothy Uhnak novel, and *The Badge or the Cross* (1970). Among the television series he created are *Ironside, Marcus Welby, M.D., Sarge, One Step Beyond, Lanigan's Rabbi* (based on the Harry Kemelman novels), and *Rosetti and Ryan*; he wrote numerous episodes for those and other programs, including *Hart to Hart, McMillan & Wife, MacGyver, Star Trek*, and Golden Age stalwarts such as *Studio One, Playhouse 90, Lux Video Theatre*, and *Schlitz Playhouse of Stars*.

"Odds on Death" was published in the November 1948 issue.

John started shaking the dice again and then he stopped.

Odds on Death

Don M. Mankiewicz

Nothing was left to chance on Rocco's gambling tables. But with the right odds, even a patsy can buck loaded dice and roll a natural.

NOW THAT YOU MENTION it, chum, it is kind of an odd decoration at that. Not the kind of thing you'd expect to find hanging on the wall back of a bar, particularly in a high-class place like this. Looks like a kid's cane to you, huh? I guess you've led a sheltered life, son. That's a dice stick. Every house-run crap game in the world has a stickman, and just about every stickman uses a curved stick like that to return the dice to the shooter between rolls. Most of them

are a little tricky, too, like that one there. They don't always return the same dice they pick up—if you get what I mean.

That stick was given to me by my old man. He'd carried it all over the world with him, like a good mechanic might carry a set of fine end-wrenches or a special pair of calipers that he liked. My dad was a pro, same as I was. He'd handled the sticks at dice tables in Caliente, Reno, Saratoga, Florida, Hot Springs, and even at some of the famous European gambling houses along the Riviera. He had a reputation for honesty that would get him a job with any gambling joint in the world. That may sound a little odd to you, Mac, but a guy who wants to work at a dice table had better be honest, even if his job is switching the dice back and forth so the house doesn't get hit. What I mean by that is, the boss has to know that his employees are all working for him; it'd be awfully easy for a stickman to get tied up with somebody from the outside and make a mistake on purpose with those dice sometime. Once, that is. Never twice.

I don't know why I should be telling you the story of my life like this, mister, but you asked about the stick, and I guess you'll stop me if I'm boring you. Well, when Dad got along in years to the point where it hurt him to stand up all night, he wasn't like most stickmen. He'd saved his money. And he quit. You know, like those fellows you read about in the insurance ads in the magazines, that go off to some cabin in the mountains and spend all their time fishing. Well, that's what my old man did; just quit and bought a shack out near Pikes Peak and there, except for a Christmas card every year, I haven't heard from him since. At the time he quit, we were both working as stickmen at Rocco's, up the street. You ever been there? Well, don't bother. If you ever feel like going there for an evening's pleasure, as the fellow says, just mail Rocco your money. That way you won't be pushed around and have to smell all the cigar smoke. And you got just as good a chance to win.

What I mean by that is, Rocco's joint is just as crooked as he is, which is the same as to say nothing is left to chance. I have an idea that was one of the things that got my old man to quit, Rocco's being such a crooked house, and him being too old to go traipsing around the country looking for a better job. When he quit, Dad gave me that stick and before he left for the mountains he gave me a quick course in how to operate it. There wasn't anything I couldn't do with that stick. The way it worked is this: a fellow would come in and start shooting. At the start of his roll he got a whole basket of Rocco's dice, every one of them honest, to pick from. Any two dice in the basket that he liked, those were the dice he used. Well, as long as he kept shooting for reasonable stakes, he'd keep those dice. Every time he'd shoot, I'd slide the dice back to him with the stick, and he'd roll them out again. The house would be taking its percentage out of the side bets, the guy would win-a-little-lose-a-little, and everybody would be happy, particularly Rocco and me.

That's the way things usually go at any crap table. The bets fairly even, no arguments, honest dice, pass, miss, pass, and the percentage gradually dragging all the money out of everybody's pockets.

But there are emergencies that do come up every now and then. Some guy will get hot and start letting his bets ride—which means he doubles his money with every pass he makes. When somebody starts doing that, that's when Rocco gets glad I've got my stick and know how to use it. You see, if a guy does let his money ride, and if he only gets fairly hot, let's say he makes eleven passes. Now, on that twelfth role he's shooting two thousand and some dollars *for every dollar he started with.* What we do when this happens is pretty simple, and, while it's not foolproof, it very rarely goes wrong.

We give the guy his perfectly honest dice that he's been shooting with all along for his first throw. If he comes out right there on one roll—if he sevens or elevens, that is—he's a winner and we've got to hope he tries again. He may crap out on that roll, too; that is, he may hit two, three, or twelve, and lose right there, but most likely he'll catch a point; that is, he'll roll four, five, six, eight, nine, or ten. And then he's got to make his point, roll it again before he rolls a seven, and the percentages say he's not likely to do it. That's why even an honest crap table (if there is such a thing) would make money. But percentage doesn't say he can't make or he won't do it, just that he's not likely to do it. That stick up on the wall there, Mac, that's what says he can't do it. To put it as simply as I can, that stick has a little slot in it, a kind of panel, and when I grab my end of the stick a little tighter than usual, that panel gets all loose and wobbly. When I push the dice with the stick they just wander in back of the panel and some other dice come flying out about a quarter inch further up the stick. Sure it's tough to make a stick like that, but it's tough to make a car, or a watch, or a hat that rabbits can hide in. It's hard to operate a stick like that and not get caught at it, too, and that's why Rocco was paying me a hundred and a quarter a week to push the dice back and forth on his table—and this was some years ago, when a hundred and a quarter was pretty good money. I won't bore you with a lot of details about those other dice, chum. They were made in Minneapolis, and to put it very, very simply, they couldn't come up anything but seven.

You get the picture now, don't you, friend? I mean here's this sucker, all set to try to make his eight or nine or whatever for a couple of thousand bucks, and here he is shaking these dice that can't come up anything but seven. Of course, real smart gamblers used to notice that nobody ever seemed to make a good score on the crap table, and most of the big-money boys stayed off it. But that didn't bother Rocco; there were plenty of guys in town that figured they could beat that table, and they used to contribute enough to pay my wages and leave the house with a handsome profit.

Every time a guy would miss out on his big roll, whether he did it because his luck was lousy or with some help from my old man's stick,

Rocco would look at him real sad and say: "Looks like you lose your dough, son. Two rolls, no coffee." "Two rolls, no coffee" always struck me as a pretty terrible pun, but guys who are winning in crap games all over the world think it's about the wittiest remark ever made.

The guy Rocco said, "Two rolls, no coffee," to oftenest was a fellow named Perino. "Patsy" Perino they used to call him. Rocco made that nickname up because he said Perino was the biggest Patsy that ever was, and the tag sort of stuck. As far as I know, nobody ever called Patsy by his right name; in fact, nobody seemed to know what his square name might be. But everybody used to just call him Patsy and it made him furious.

Patsy was convinced of two things in this world. First of all, he was convinced that he was the unluckiest gambler that ever drew breath, and I must say I can see where he got that idea, because he bucked Rocco's crap table every payday from 1933 to 1940 and I don't think he went away winner more than once. That once was close to Christmas, and I knew Patsy hadn't saved anything out of his pay up at the mill—which was about twenty bucks a week—and I figured he'd have to buy his girl a present, so I sort of let him win a hundred and forty bucks, figuring we'd get it back after the holidays. Rocco gave me hell for it and told me if it ever happened again it would come out of my pay, and, believe me, mister, it never happened again. The other thing Patsy believed was that some day his luck would turn and that when that happened he'd beat that crap table out of every cent he'd poured into it, and more, too.

Well, like I said, Patsy dropped every cent he could get his hands on into that crap game from 1933 to 1940, and when he stopped coming around, Rocco was worried about him. Not that Rocco gave a damn about Patsy, really. He just thought of Patsy as a kind of agent who had to work all week at a heavy machine and then bring his money to Rocco, and he was sore when Patsy didn't show up, same as a father might be if sonny boy failed to pony up the weekly check.

The upshot of it all was that he sent me up to Patsy's end of town to look around for him. It was along about November 1940 that I went wandering up to the bunch of little houses back of the mill where I figured Patsy must live. It's funny, but I'd never been up that way before; working late nights, I'd always had a room near Rocco's place, and when I wasn't working or sleeping I'd usually drop down here for a drink. Well, the first person I ran into was Patsy's girl. Real pretty she was, too, which is kind of surprising when you figure Patsy wasn't much of a catch, being just another guy who worked in the mill, and not even one of the steady ones who'd bring home a full envelope every Friday, but a born gambler who'd never have a nickel. But everybody's always known that Louise was Patsy's girl and that was that. I guess she started going with him in high school, before he'd really begun gambling, and when the dice bug bit him she figured she ought to stick with him, same as if he was sick or something, which, in a manner of speaking, he was.

Well, I gave Louise a big smile and an extra cheerful hello, and she just sort of froze up and went on up the street without a word. I followed her, and finally she went into a grocery store, and so did I. Once I'd told her that we were just curious about why Patsy hadn't been around to Rocco's in so long, that he didn't owe us any money or anything, she unfroze a little, and told me that Patsy was in the Army and that he wouldn't be back for a year; not, she was quick to add, that it was any of my business. Well, having nothing better to do, I walked her home, and when we got there, she asked me in, just out of politeness, I guess. Louise is about the politest girl there is. We talked of this and that, mostly about Patsy, and I could see that she didn't hold Patsy's failings against me, which was only right, after all. She told me about how Patsy had quit the dice time and time again, and how they were always figuring on getting married as soon as he'd saved up enough money, but how he'd

always break down as soon as he got his hands on his pay chit and go down to Rocco's and blow it in. Of course, like I said, it wasn't any of my fault, the whole thing, but listening to her tell it, I was almost ashamed of myself. I got Patsy's address from her, which was Camp Carson, Colorado, and wished her luck, and went back to Rocco's.

Well, Patsy turned out to be only the first of a lot of guys to go into the Army from our town, and eventually it got so the place was mainly populated by overage bankers, school-kids, and women. The guys who weren't drafted, it seems they all took off for the other towns chasing after the war-plants and the big money. Maybe for a lot of guys the war was a time for big money, but not for Rocco and me. We kept the house going as long as we could, even put in slot machines and let the women in, but it was no use. We started booking horses, and the horses stopped running. So what we wound up doing was the best we could, like the fellow says, and take my word for it, mister, it was no good. We liked to starve to death before the war was over.

Well, when it finally did end, the boys started coming back, and the dice started to roll again. Not just small-time stuff like before, real big-time, big money, games. The boys were all loaded from the shipyards and the airplane factories, and wages were way up at the mill, and what with one thing and another we raised the minimum bet at the crap table from half a buck to half a pound, and Rocco raised me from a hundred and a quarter to two-and-a-half. Things were really great; only one more thing we needed: Patsy. He didn't show up with the rest of the boys, and I was beginning to think that maybe he was as unhandy a soldier as he was a dice-shooter, and in that case he sure never would be back.

Then one night, after closing time at Rocco's, I was sitting right in here having a drink, not behind the bar like now, but over there at one of those little tables, when who should come strolling through the front door? That's right, chum, Patsy himself.

"Hiya, Patsy!" I said. I was really glad to see him—not just because of business, you know. He was like an old friend, even if I never knew him except as another guy to slide the dice to.

He looked at me kind of funny. "Name's John, Tony," he said. "Not Patsy. I learned a lot in the Army, Tony."

He came over and sat down and started to talk. He told me how he'd been overseas, in Italy with the ski troops, and how he'd seen a lot of killing and done a little himself. But he'd been careful. Real careful. "You know why I was so careful, Tony?" he asked me. I just looked at him. "I was careful, Tony, because I wanted to get back to this town. I wanted to go up to Rocco's and get hunk with that damn dice game of his. When you see him, Tony, you tell him I'm in town and I've got money and I'm coming up tomorrow night"—he glanced at his watch—"make that tonight, and give his dice game a real going-over."

Well, when he said that, I knew he hadn't learned as much in the Army as he thought. A man going duck hunting doesn't tell the ducks. It gives them a chance to get set.

Rocco and I got set, O.K. We checked over our board and our dice, and we went over to the bank and got a great big stack of crisp, fresh-looking hundreds, because in a big game it helps if the house has a lot of cash money to flash around.

When we opened for business that night, I could tell something was up. All the boys from the mill were there, and we figured Patsy had been telling them his big plans. Some of the lads came over to the dice table and started shooting, five bucks at a time, but you could tell they were just killing time. Rocco was walking around between the roulette wheel and the craps setup with an expression on his face like a cat that figures to eat a canary.

About ten o'clock Patsy walked in, and the whole crowd, as if it was a signal, moved over to the dice table. They were standing about four deep around it. The boy who was shooting made his point and picked his saw off the pass line. Then, instead of putting down some more money and shooting again, he set the dice down on the edge of the table. In any language in the world that means the shooter passes the dice.

"Whose dice?" I said.

Patsy shoved his way through the crowd just to the right of the boy who'd passed the dice and said: "I'll take 'em, Tony. O.K.?"

"Well, Patsy—" I began.

"John." He still didn't sound mad. Just firm.

"John," I said. "You're supposed to let the dice come around to you once, but unless there's some objection, they're yours."

Nobody objected. Patsy picked up the dice. Rocco came over and stood beside me to watch. There was an awful dead silence while Patsy rolled out. Every once in a while I'd say, "Pay the line," or, "Pay the field," but there weren't any other bettors. Just Patsy. He was betting twenty bucks at a time, and Rocco and I just stood there and watched him make five points in a row, which put him a hundred ahead and was a little unusual, but nothing shocking. He was shooting with perfectly honest dice, of course; any time a man shoots only twenty bobs in Rocco's he'll get honest dice, the way I told you. I was starting to relax a little when it happened.

Patsy slapped down another twenty bucks and rolled two fours. Then, while the dice—perfectly honest dice, you understand—were still lying there on the table, down at my end way out of his reach, he turned to Rocco.

"Lay the odds, Rocco?" he asked, very quietly, like you might ask someone the time of day. This meant he wanted to bet some more that he'd make his eight before he rolled a seven, and that he wanted Rocco to give him the odds, which are six to five he won't.

"For how much." Rocco sounded disinterested, and his voice let everybody know he'd handle any bet a punk like Patsy could make.

"A thousand," said Patsy.

"Laying twelve hundred to a thou," said Rocco, looking down at my stick.

I tightened my fist around the head of my stick and spun the dice back to Patsy. He didn't look at them, just picked them up in his right hand and shook them back and forth in his fist, holding them way over his head. He slipped his left hand into his pants pocket, hauled out his wallet, and tossed it on the table. "Tony," he said, "get a thousand out of there and put it on the pass line." I reached over, picked up the wallet, and glanced inside. There was a lot more than a thousand in there, at least a hundred C-notes, it looked like. I picked ten of them out and tossed them on the line. Rocco peeled twelve of his bills off the house stack and added them to the pile.

"Like to see what you're shooting for," Rocco said with that oily grin of his. I suddenly decided I didn't care much for Rocco. For a second, I wished I could get another chance at stick-handling those dice so I could give Patsy the honest ones back again.

Patsy started shaking the dice again, and then brought his hand towards the table. Everybody craned to get a better look. Then, before he turned the dice loose, he stopped again, and put his hand, dice and all, back over his head, like a football player about to toss a pass. He looked over at Rocco like he'd just had an idea.

"Hey, Rocco," he said, very casual, "how much money in that stack?"

"Come on, come on, fire your pistol!" Rocco came back, getting a little impatient. "You going to take all night for your lousy grand? There's enough down there to cover any bet you want to make, Patsy." He said "Patsy" like it was an insult, not like a nickname.

"Good," said Patsy. Then he looked at me. "Tony," he said, "would you please take ten thousand out of that wallet and put it on the 'come.'"

Like the fellow says, my life started to flash through my head a little bit at a time and I started to get dizzy. What Patsy was doing was, well, he was betting he'd come. "Come" in a crap game means to make your point starting when you make your bet. I guess you've never shot craps, mac, so I won't try and explain it to you; the important thing is, if you roll a seven, you've come, and you win. And Patsy was betting ten grand he'd win. And I'd just sticked him two dice that couldn't come up any way *but* seven!

I just stood there, and the guys from the mills started to mutter and chatter among themselves. "What's holding you back? You going to take all night for a lousy ten grand?" One of the mill guys gave a sort of nervous laugh. I looked at Rocco. He was just standing there with his mouth partways open, like he was seeing what was happening but he didn't quite believe it.

Well, what could I do? I tossed Patsy's ten grand over on the little kidney-shaped part of the layout marked "Come." I closed my eyes while he threw the dice, and when I opened them up again, all the mill guys were cheering, and Patsy was helping himself to ten grand out of Rocco's dough. When he had it all counted up and put away in his poke he turned to me and said: "I guess I lose my twenty, Tony. Two rolls, no coffee. Too bad."

Then he turned away and walked out of Rocco's place and you could tell he wasn't coming back. The twenty, of course, was still on the table, and, like I was dreaming, I picked it up and put it in what was left of Rocco's stack.

That wound up the crap shooting for that night, and I walked down here from Rocco's not seeing much where I was going or who I bumped into. It was all a kind of bad dream, like I said.

Well, I'd got a week's salary out of Rocco just the day before all this happened, and I had a kind of hunch it was going to be the last I'd ever get from him, so I sat down in here and drank most of it up. There was something in what Patsy'd done that didn't add up, something that was familiar, vaguely familiar to me, like I'd been through it all before.

About halfway through my ninth bourbon, or maybe my tenth, it came to me. A story my old man used to tell me, about a sucker who'd cleaned out a crap game he knew was crooked, just the same way Patsy did. It had happened to my old man years ago, in San Remo, Italy. I put down what was left of my drink and started some heavy thinking, or as heavy as you can think on eight-and-a-half, or maybe nine-and-a-half, bourbons. Then I remembered that Camp Carson, where the ski troops trained, is not really so very far from Pikes Peak. A guy like Patsy, on a pass, might easily have gone into some gambling joint in, say, Colorado Springs, and maybe . . .

Say, I hope I haven't been boring you, chum, but you know, bartenders are supposed to be a little gabby, and I've been a bartender ever since that night.

What's that, bub? What did Patsy do with his ten grand? Well. I don't know if I should tell you that. Your cigar's gone out, though. Here, have a light. Keep 'em. They're on the house. Courtesy of Patsy's Bar and Grill.

Those Catrini
Norvell Page

NORVELL (WOOTEN) PAGE (1904–1961) was raised in Richmond, Virginia, in a moderately wealthy family. He attended the College of William & Mary but at the age of eighteen was already working as a journalist, first for the *Cincinnati Post*, then the *Norfolk Virginian-Pilot*, before moving to New York to work for the *Herald Tribune*, the *Times*, and the *World Telegram*. His family had been ruined in the stock market crash of 1929, so he began to supplement his newspaper income by writing stories for the pulps, mainly mysteries for *Black Mask*, *Dime Mystery*, *Ten Detective Stories*, and others. In 1933, he began to write novels for the hero pulp *The Spider*, under the house name Grant Stockbridge. *The Spider* was created by Harry Steeger for his Popular Publications to compete with *The Shadow*. The first two issues of the magazine were written by R. T. M. Scott, then it was turned over to the twenty-seven-year-old Page, who gave the ruthless and fearless vigilante a mask and a disguise (as a fang-toothed hunchback named Richard Wentworth). The first issue appeared in October 1933; Page's first novel, *Wings of the Black Death*, ran in December. A series of horrific villains were hunted down and killed by Wentworth, who then branded his prey on the forehead with a seal of a spider. There were 118 *Spider* novels in all, as well as two movie serials starring Warren Hull, *The Spider's Web* (1938) and *The Spider Returns* (1941). At his most prolific, Page wrote more than one hundred thousand words a month, half for the *Spider* novels and the rest for a wide range of fiction.

"Those Catrini" was published in the February 1933 issue.

Those Catrini

Norvell Page

Jules Tremaine promises to be a notable addition to the Black Mask character group. Himself, his mission, are both a little mysterious. He walks boldly where one without courage would scarcely venture. He appears at odds with an established order of ruthless political power and of wealth drawn from such sordid source. At times he is as soft-spoken and sympathetic as a woman; at others, he is dynamite unleashed.

JULES TREMAINE STOOD erectly on the curb of Mulberry Street, facing a row of dirty red tenements, and plucked three preliminary chords from his black guitar. He began to sing *M'appari*.

Before and behind him carnival crowds pushed and gabbled. To each side stood a pushcart odorous with high stacks of clams. It was the festa of Santo Gennaro and the September night was soft. Women leaned from windows shouting at children who scrambled in the street under the arches of blue and red and yellow lights.

Jules threw back his head and his full voice soared. Before him a girl stopped. She was fifteen. Her breasts pressed roundly against the flamboyant pink of her dress. Her eyes were dark and liquid and they regarded the street singer somberly.

Jules sent the last note of the aria vaulting above the babble of the street, plucked an ultimate vibrant chord and bowed to her, a vital figure of a man just over five feet five and dapper in a modeled suit of dark gray. He swept off a black felt hat.

"Ah, *bella mia*," he said, laughter behind his eyes. "You have tonight the face of a very, very tired madonna."

The girl's lips parted slightly, showing white teeth.

"Every time I try to sit down the floorwalker gets nasty," she explained.

Jules clapped his hat back on his head and made a wringing motion with his two hands. His voice threatened. "If I ever get my hands on that floorwalker, I'll . . ."

His wide teeth flashed beneath the black of his small mustache. Angela's lips curved. She threw back her head so that her throat was a sweet white line and laughed three contralto bell notes.

"That is better," said Jules. "Now what is it that makes these dark shadows under your pretty eyes?"

The girl's smile diminished but still quivered at her mouth corners. She nodded her head gravely.

"I'm worried, Mr. Tremaine," she said.

Jules pursed his lips. When he did that the militant points of his mustache moved forward slightly. His blue eyes stared beyond the girl into the dingy bricks of a tenement front.

"I suppose it's that lazy Antonio again," he said, his syllables short.

Angela clasped her hands and watched her long, tapered fingers as she moved them slowly.

"What's your brother up to now?" Jules demanded.

The girl drew a deep breath so that her breasts strained against the sleazy silk. Her eyes remained stubbornly on her hands.

"He has not done anything, Mr. Tremaine," she protested. "It is those Catrini. They say they will do something because Tony drives his beer truck into their part of town. . . ."

Her words accelerated. She unclasped her hands and gestured with them. Her wide eyes, dark and frightened, met Tremaine's directly.

"—if Antonio works he must drive where his boss tells him. If he does not work we cannot eat. Ah, those Catrini . . ."

She raised her right hand with the thumb uppermost, the fingers spread, and clicked the nail of the thumb on her upper teeth with an outward gesture. For the moment her eyes were bright and narrow.

"I know those Catrini," said Jules softly.

The girl's body lost its tension and became supplicant. Her hands, palms upward, the slim, tapering fingers bent outward, pleaded with Tremaine. There was a pucker between the black, straight brows, between the dark, questioning eyes.

"What can I do?" she asked. "What can I do!"

Tremaine looked down at his guitar and plucked the G string, turned a white ivory peg, cocked his head to the side and touched the string again. He looked up at the girl.

"Go home, Angela," he said. "I will sing three more songs, then come to talk with you and Antonio."

Angela spun on her heel, whirling out the thin silk of her skirt. A boy with a laughing mouth showered confetti over her and she threw back her head and laughed and snatched at the colored snow with quick hands. Three white pieces of paper and a star-shaped pink one settled on her black hair. She turned and looked gravely into Tremaine's round blue eyes.

"I know you will make everything all right," she said. "I am so happy I could dance."

She spun completely around on her heel and walked with little skipping steps three doors down the street. She waved to Jules before she went into the darkness of the tenement.

hose Catrini! Jules Tremaine looked down at his guitar and his lips smiled with little mirth. His fingers touched the strings soundlessly, then twanged a chord and two more and he threw back his head and began to sing *La donna e mobile*. His fingers were lean and white. They had squared ends.

Behind him in a vacant lot across the street, a fireworks cannon made a muffled concussion. Children screamed and squirmed between the pushcarts, hurrying to get nearer. A whirling spark soared, hesitated and burst into a jagged splotch of yellow fire. Spider legs of light spanned out from it and at their ends bombs burst in dazzling streaks of white. The explosions tortured the ear drums.

Jules shrugged and stopped singing. He drew the black guitar down under his arm and up on his back so that it hung suspended from his shoulder by a crimson braided cord. He looked over the crowd and laden pushcarts and moved slowly down the street, a short man but with power in the square set of his shoulders, the erect poised arrogance of the head.

The pyrotechnic display faded momentarily; there was another muffled concussion, then clear and high a girl's scream tore the night. Jules whirled, staring up at the third-floor windows where Angela and her brother had rooms. A succession of deadened explosions that were not fireworks beat on the air, then every sound was drowned in the ripping burst of more bombs.

On the walk where Jules stood people no longer stared at the colored fire in the sky. They faced the door of the tenement where that scream had sounded. A handful of children gath-

ered silently. A fat man with wide red silk bands holding up too long sleeves waded through them. He entered the door. He staggered back, fell down the one step and sprawled supine. His feet jerked up and his heels thumped on the pavement.

Three men boiled out of the doorway. They had guns in their hands. Two raced down the street and separated. The third ran past Jules. He was a short and broad man. As he lifted and flung down his feet heavily Jules saw that the right shoulder was twisted so that it was at least three inches higher than the left. The man whirled about the corner.

Jules strode towards the door from which the three had come. The fat man who had been hurled to the street sat up and held his head in his hands. For five seconds he sat there, then reeled to his feet. His fat quivered with the speed of his flight. A boy bounded out of his way, staggering blindly towards Tremaine. Jules caught the boy with one arm and set him gently aside. He did not stop. His lips were pressed in a thin hard line, and a path opened before him among the thickening crowd. He entered the dark doorway.

Halfway to the second floor he was taking the steps two at a time. On the third floor he thrust through an open door and stopped and stood, his right hand gripping the end of the keyboard and holding in place the guitar on his back. The air was acrid with burned gunpowder. A single yellow light bulb dangled from the center of the ceiling by a twisted wire. It threw a glare on walls that had been scrubbed until they were streaked gray. Jules kept his eyes on them for a moment; then he looked down.

There were two bodies on the floor. One had crumpled near him, a knee drawn up towards its belly. That was Antonio. From under him a dark liquid pool spread. Angela lay over by a door beyond which the kitchen gleamed. She lay on her back, hurled close against the wall by the six-hundred-foot-pound impact of .45-calibre bullets. Her head was thrown back and her throat was a white sweet line and there was a blue hole between her wide, frightened eyes. Jules saw there were two pieces of confetti in her hair, one white and square, the other a pink star shape.

Jules' right hand was on the keyboard of his guitar. There was a snap as a white ivory peg broke and he stooped slowly and picked it up and looked at it. The peg was smooth and cold in his fingers and it had broken off just under the head. In the street a brassy whistle skirled. Jules dropped the peg in his pocket and the right corner of his mouth twisted so that a single sharp incisor showed. Heavy feet pounded on the stairs and mounted swiftly. Jules shook his head sharply, glanced once around the room, then plunged through the door. He saw the policeman at the head of the stairs, and ran for the dark back hall.

"Halt!" the policeman shouted. "I'll shoot!"

A pistol glinted in the dim light.

Jules moved slowly towards the policeman, his hands raised well above his head and the guitar bumping against his right side. His eyes were narrowed, watchful.

"I'm just a street singer," he said. "I heard the shooting and came to see if Angela and Antonio were all right. They were friends of mine, and—"

"Shut up!" the cop ordered.

His heavy fingers clamped on Jules' shoulder and whirled him about and he patted his hips and sides and under his arms.

"Threw your gun away, did you?" he said. "That won't do you no good."

Jules allowed himself to be shoved back into the room where Angela and Antonio lay.

"You louse!" the cop rasped. "You shot the girl, too!"

Lights blazed before Jules' eyes and blackness followed.

Tremaine had only partly recovered his senses when he was roughed into the patrol wagon. The rush of air as it sped with a softly whining siren back to the station-house largely restored him, but he staggered as he was booted into the white square office of the captain. The breath of his captor was harsh and fingers vised on his shoulder.

Jules measured the captain under heavy lids. The man was fat and his white hair was pomaded into a smooth pompadour. He ran a hand over it.

"Well, well, what have we here?" he asked, and his voice was fat and oily.

"O'Reilly caught him running away after them two was bumped," said the patrolman, his hand still on Jules' shoulder. "He'd throwed his gun away."

"Running away, eh?"

The captain was seated in a swivel-chair tilted back before his desk. He leaned forward and rubbed white, puffy hands up and down his thighs. Then his mouth opened in a little pink "O" of surprise; his small black eyes went flat.

"——!" he said. "It's Jules Tremaine!"

The captain straightened, stumbled to his feet and slid a chair out from the wall.

"Sit down, Mr. Tremaine," he said. "I'm sorry about this. O'Reilly didn't know you."

Jules heard the patrolman behind him gulp and the hand flinched away from his shoulder.

"Jeeze, Cap'n, did we pull a boner?" the man asked.

"Get out!" the captain yelled, and the door opened and closed quickly. The fat man in the dark blue suit looked at Tremaine and smoothed his pomaded hair and blinked.

"I'm sorry about this," he said.

Jules continued to stand. He balanced his guitar carefully on the chair, eased off his black felt hat and fingered the back of his head. He winced and his lips pressed hard together.

"I think you said O'Reilly was the cop's name?" he asked softly.

"He's just a dumb flatfoot," the captain spoke hurriedly. "He don't know no better. I'll take it out of him."

"Don't bother, Captain," said Jules gently. "Don't you bother at all."

He placed his hat on the chair beside his guitar and looked about the office slowly.

"I want to wash up a bit," he said.

The captain skipped his fat sides across the room, swung open a door with a flourish and revealed gleaming white tile. Jules doffed his coat and doused his face and head with cold water. The welt left by the cop's gun on his scalp stung. Jules cursed softly as he stroked his black hair to smoothness with a thin comb from his pocket. He pointed his mustache, shrugged into his coat and strolled back into the office. He adjusted his hat jauntily and slung the guitar over his shoulder.

The captain regarded him with troubled eyes. He opened his mouth and closed it again like a goldfish drinking air. He said: "You didn't see anything up there, did you, Mr. Tremaine?"

Jules revolved on his heel and looked up into the small black eyes. The captain shoved a puffy hand over his hair.

"I saw a boy and a girl had been murdered," he said, biting off the words. "Then O'Reilly slammed me over the head with his gun."

The captain frowned at his fingernails, though they were perfectly polished.

"You know how these young cops are," he murmured.

"Yes, I know," said Jules, and left.

A taxi weaved uptown with him and stopped at an address in the East Fifties where a dead-pan butler opened the door. Tremaine surrendered a gingerly removed hat but held on to the guitar, padding deliberately up the deep carpeted steps.

"That you, Jules?" a resonant voice boomed.

Jules retraced his way without answering, walked back through the dim, dusty-smelling hall and at its end entered a door to the right. The room was ten feet square and its walls were shelves of brown-backed law books. In its center was a desk, a reading lamp and a face that had the curious effect of floating disembodied in the air. Presently Jules could make out the spread shoulders of the man seated at the desk.

"Ah, it is you, Jules," came the resonant, slightly mocking voice.

Jules' face was expressionless as he studied the cadaverous countenance. A few strands of black hair had been oiled and laid carefully side by side across a bald dome-like forehead that lengthened the thin face extraordinarily.

"Who's the captain at the Houston Street station?" Jules asked.

The mouth corners of the man's face made creases like parentheses and strong white teeth showed momentarily.

"Going to use my influence at last?"

"No. The louse recognized me as a Tremaine. I was afraid I was beginning to look like you. My fears, I see, were groundless."

The creases about the mouth deepened; the head tilted back so that black smudges of shadow from the low desk lamp erased all the upper part of the face and made teeth gleam. The laughter was a faint roughened breathing, nearly soundless. When it stopped the face looked down again.

"My charming brother!" the man articulated. The creases smoothed themselves and the lips pursed. "The captain's name is Jimson."

The man stood and the shadows smudged his face again; the light revealed his length and the powerful sweep of his shoulders. Jules had to look up to meet his eyes. He smiled slightly and his mustache pointed forward a fraction of an inch. He bowed ceremoniously.

"My *dear* brother," he said, then swung about. The hall echoed the regular beat of his feet.

The room he entered was all gray and nearly barren. He laid his guitar face down on a couch bed and took a screwdriver from the top drawer of a Sheraton chest. He looked across at his guitar and smiled.

I t was after ten the next morning when Jules slid out of white silk pajamas and stepped into his shower. His stomach sucked in and the muscles of his chest and upper arms flexed and jumped under its cold pelting; then he dodged out from under and punished his tight lean body with a rough towel. As he bent forward his abdomen tensed into six ridges of muscle. He dusted himself with bath powder and hummed *M'appari*. He cut it short in the middle with a small tightening of mouth corners. A pulse throbbed in his throat.

A polite tap at the door caught Jules with his trousers just belted. He grunted: "Come in."

His brother, in striped morning trousers and cutaway, bowed himself in, clicked the door shut. Jules glanced at the domed forehead.

"I keep hoping those six hairs won't be exactly parallel." He sighed.

The mouth corner creases deepened in his brother's cadaverous face but the thin lips did not part. Blue eyes were sardonic. Jules drew on a linen shirt, thrust the tails into his dark gray trousers and plucked a heavy silk tie, gray, too, from a rack on the closet door. The taller man continued silent and Jules eventually toed about and faced him, his eyes half shut.

"Yes, my dear brother?" he queried.

"You aren't going back to Little Italy today, Jules?"

Jules brushed his left mustache with his right thumbnail. His still veiled eyes were amused. His voice was gentle.

"Surely, Andrew, you aren't at some thirty-and-six years of age beginning to worry about your younger brother?"

Andrew cursed in mild tones. He said with relish: "Some day you are going to get your well-muscled abdomen shot full of messy holes. Those Catrini—"

Jules lifted his right shoulder fractionally, moved deliberately to the closet. He tipped a vest off a hanger and drew it on. Buttoning it with lean, square-tipped fingers, he opened his eyes wide and focused their round blue gaze on his brother.

"Catrini?" he mouthed slowly. "Catrini? No, I don't believe I know anyone by that name."

Andrew smiled like a politician about to kiss a baby.

"I think I'll tell Captain Jimson I don't mind if you are picked up for those murders," he said, and added as an afterthought: "You louse."

Jules' lids drooped over his eyes again.

"Tell my dear friend Jimson," he said, "to have O'Reilly do the picking up, will you, Andrew?"

The eyes of the two brothers locked like slithering rapiers. The elder's tone was like May.

"Dear Jules! Don't tell me you're up to something?"

Jules laid the spread fingers of both hands on his chest, his eyebrows crawling up.

"I? My charming brother!" he exclaimed, shocked surprise vibrant in his words. "You can't mean your younger brother?"

Andrew's right hand, tense and straight as a knife, sliced across the air before him. He rasped a single monosyllabic obscenity and followed it with the word "you" and jerked open the door and slammed it shut behind him. Jules threw back his head and laughed with little sound. He shrugged into his coat, adjusting his black hat jauntily on his head, and turned towards his guitar. The door again swept open. Jules continued towards his guitar.

"Jules"—Andrew's voice was incisive—"you're probably as hard up for money as usual. I'll pay you to quit this stuff."

Jules lifted the guitar with both hands, then with one passed the red cord over his head, shoved his right arm through the loop. He turned slowly, eyes on his brother's lean, hollow-cheeked face, and said nothing.

Andrew thrust a bony hand into an inner pocket of his coat and drew out a black leather wallet with gold corner pieces. He fingered out five yellow-backed bills with 1000 in each corner and spread them out like a poker hand and held them towards Jules. "Lay off this comic opera stuff, will you? You're hunting trouble and I can't afford to have the name mixed up in anything so near election."

Jules eased the guitar under his right arm and up against his back, where he held it with a hand pressed against the end of the keyboard. The red cord was across his chest like an ambassador's riband. He bowed, his mouth corners depressed.

"My dear brother, you ask too much. Always I have long' to seeng een the streets. I make of eet my buseeness."

"Horsefeathers!" said Andrew. He put the money carefully back into the black wallet and restored that to his pocket. "You began this street singing to queer me with the party. You've always hated me. When you first started I figured you'd get tired of it. But you are a persistent louse. It may be that I shall have to take steps."

His face was wooden, but there were malevolent sparks in the depths of his eyes. Jules' face did not lose its mocking smile, but his eyes went flat and hard. He strode forward three paces until he stood within two feet of the taller brother, looking up into the cadaverous mask. A pulse throbbed in his throat.

"The truth is, Andrew," he said softly, "that I first sang in the streets for a lark. I was half tight and somebody made a bet. The wops were decent to me. They cheered when I sang. If it was sad, they wept. I like people like that, people who aren't afraid to have emotions. You and your politicians, friends and hirelings, can't figure that any man does a thing for the obvious reason. You always see intrigue.

"That's the truth of the matter, but if my street singing annoys you, I'm glad. I won't stop. Now get the hell out of my way."

A pall of white roses ornamented the weathered doorway of the tenement where Angela had lived. A baby of three stood and stared at it with grave eyes. As Jules walked slowly by he caught the faint sweetish odor of the flowers. Children scampered and cried. Tremaine stopped a half square away and stood on the curb with his back to Mulberry Street. His black hat sat at an angle. He touched his mustache with his thumbnail, considered a moment and struck a chord from his guitar that had curiously little resonance.

A fat man, his sleeves held up by red bands, sat on a chair on the walk. He heaved up and padded across to Jules.

"A man was here looking for you," he said.

Tremaine struck another slow chord.

"He say you come to Joe's place on Tenth Street he get you a job regular."

Jules showed his white teeth under the black militant points of his mustache. He said nothing, began to sing softly, plucking out a twanging bass accompaniment. He stopped and put his hand flat on the strings.

"What did this man look like?" he asked. "He was short and broad, eh? His right shoulder"— Jules hunched his own forward and upward three inches—"it rides like this, eh?"

The fat man blinked and regarded Jules' hunched shoulder and looked back to his round blue eyes.

"I give you the message," he said.

He eased back into his chair. Jules' head went back and he laughed almost soundlessly. The fat man sat and blinked at him. He looked up and down the street, then blinked again, put his hands on his knees, leaned far forward and levered himself to his feet. He picked up the chair and carried it into the tenement. Jules laughed again.

Militant chords leaped from the strident strings and he swung into the *Soldiers' Chorus*. A man in a rust-brown suit and with broad-toed black shoes and a derby jammed forward over his eyes halted before Tremaine. The street singer finished his song.

"What would you like me to sing?" he asked, his fingers walking over the strings.

The man growled in his throat. He was young and blond and weighed about two hundred and twenty pounds. His blue eyes glowered from a florid face.

"My name's O'Reilly," he said.

Jules bowed gracefully.

"I have heard the name before," he said, "but there seems to be some Freudian obstruction in my cerebration."

The young man frowned.

"Don't crack wise," he warned, "or I'll bang you over the head again."

"Ah, now I recall!" Happiness shone on Jules' face. "You are the gallant young policeman who last night apprehended me as I was calling on some recently demised friends. I am so glad to renew the acquaintance, Mr. O'Reilly."

The cop's scowl deepened. He grunted: "What was you telling the fat wop in the chair?"

Jules moved his right hand from left to right, palm upward, fingers spread, and shrugged his right shoulder.

"I tell him the day is lovely. I tell him it is too bad Angela and Antonio cannot see it. I tell him—" Jules shrugged delicately again, his hand completing the gesture. "I talk with him."

"Then why'd he go inside?"

"He, perhaps, do not like the song I sing."

"Huhn!"

O'Reilly stood with straddled legs, his head thrust forward. His hands swung at his sides, a slight rigidity in his arms.

"You bumped that girl because you couldn't get gay with her, then put the heat on the brother when he walked in on you."

Jules stopped smiling and his fingers stopped their soundless wandering over the strings.

"You fool!" he snapped. "I liked Angela. She was a nice kid, a clean hard-working little wop. The men who killed her were lice, and I'm going—"

"You're going to do what?"

Jules looked at O'Reilly from under half-lowered lids. He said softly: "It took you two minutes to get from the lot across the street to the door of the tenement where Angela was shot. I wonder why that was, Mr. O'Reilly?"

The policeman advanced his right foot a half pace, his left hand clenched into a fist. His eyes were bright and small.

"I've a good mind to run you in," he said, his words rasping.

"I wish you would," said Jules gently.

The florid color of the policeman's face deepened.

"I know your name is Tremaine," he said, "and I know you got off last night, but it won't work today. The captain said—"

Jules raised polite eyebrows as the man broke off. So there was another score against Andrew to be settled. Jules pursed his lips, the amusement in his eyes shaded by anger.

"Nevertheless," he said, "I wish you would run me in. There are a few other things I'd like to tell Captain Jimson, such as why it took you two minutes—"

"That's enough of that!" O'Reilly was tense, his voice hoarse. "If you know what's good for you, keep your mouth shut!"

Jules sighed deeply, with a theatrical lift and fall of his chest.

"I'm afraid, my dear O'Reilly, that it's too late to do that. I told the dear captain—"

"You told him what?"

"My dear fellow, you are so precipitate! This continual interruption grows irksome."

"You told him what?" O'Reilly's eyes were flat and menacing.

Jules returned the man's glare from under sleepy lids, his hands motionless on the guitar. The policeman's gaze flickered finally.

"That is much, much better, Mr. O'Reilly," said Jules softly. "As I was about to say, I told Jimson that I could identify the man who shot Angela and Antonio and that I would testify when they were arrested."

"You're lying," O'Reilly said hoarsely. "Jimson didn't tell me that!"

Jules shrugged, swung half about so that his left shoulder was towards the policeman, strolled up the street, plucking soft chords. O'Reilly's heavy stride kept pace with him.

"You're rough on a guy that's trying to do you a favor," he said, placatingly. "I came to tell you that Joe—he's got a place up on Tenth Street—says he's got a job for you."

"My dear fellow!" Jules exclaimed. "That is charming of you!"

He swept a lean forefinger across the five strings but the catgut gave forth a tinny sound as if the resonance of the wood were damped.

"But just why am I so honored, and why has not my good brother's suggestion that I be arrested not been carried out?"

O'Reilly walked stolidly along beside him.

"Jimson said you had an alibi. Said somebody saw you in the street at the same time they heard the shots. And the chief told me to tell you about the job."

Jules pursed his lips so that the black mustache thrust forward. A frown drew his brows together.

"You'll be glad to get the job, eh?" O'Reilly suggested.

"Perhaps," Jules said. "I do not know. If you see this Joe tell him he can find me here."

"He can find you here, eh?" O'Reilly was carefully casual.

Jules threw back his head; his mouth opened but only small laughing sounds emerged. He said: "Yes."

O'Reilly said, "Okey," and marched off.

Half an hour later, at the corner of Mulberry and Spring streets, Jules Tremaine was singing. For the moment the street was clear of festa crowds. Two children, the younger barely two with a meditative thumb thrust into his mouth, regarded him seriously. Something hard nudged into Jules' back. His eyes half closed and he moved a half pace forward and continued to sing. The nudge was repeated. He ended his song, swept his whole hand across the five strings, then turned slowly.

The man behind him was about his own height, but much broader. His eyes were black buttons under the edge of a gray fedora. His right shoulder was at least three inches higher than the left.

"Joe sent me around to see you about taking that job," he said.

His right hand was in his pocket. Apparently he had nudged Jules with whatever was in that pocket. Jules looked at it. He said: "But I do not think I want a job. I want to sing out of doors."

The left corner of the man's mouth lifted slightly, but he was not smiling.

"This job would be out of doors," he said.

Jules shrugged. "I do not know this Joe."

"Well, he knows you. Come on."

Jules began a protest he did not finish. The man stared into his eyes. His right hand was in his pocket and he thrust it forward a half inch. He said: "Come on."

Jules looked into the button eyes and at the man's pocket. Very carefully he maneuvered the guitar under his arm and up on his back, held it in place with his right hand pressed against the end of the keyboard. He cleared his throat. He said: "All right, I'll come."

The man jerked his head to the right and Jules walked that way, across Mulberry Street, the man moving stiffly at his left side, his hand still in his pocket. They walked one square east, then two north and turned to the left. Near the corner a large closed car was parked. The sedan looked very heavy. There were two men in it. When Jules was opposite the car, the back door swung open.

"Get in," said the man beside him.

Tremaine cast a furtive over-the-shoulder glance back down the street; then he looked the other way. A man in a rust-brown suit and a derby stood on the far corner. When Jules looked at him he walked slowly away, the heavy, studied tread of a policeman. Jules swallowed audibly.

"Get in," the man said again.

Jules removed his hand from the keyboard of his guitar and it swung around under his right arm. He held it with both hands and thrust it ahead of him and put his foot on the running-board. He looked about again with a panic-stricken face. The man in the rust-brown suit had disappeared. There was no one else in sight. Tremaine saw that the glass of the car door was thick and had a slightly yellowish tint. Bullet-proof glass. The man with the twisted shoulder jostled him and thrust something hard into his back.

Slowly Jules climbed in. The two men already in the car said nothing. The driver had a dead-white face in which were dry, feverish eyes. The man in the back was bony. Bunches of muscle knotted on his thin jaws. Jules sank down into the deep upholstery of the rear seat beside him and carefully placed his guitar between his knees. The man with the twisted shoulder got in and clicked the door shut. The car lunged forward. Still no one spoke. Jules watched the dingy buildings slide past as they jounced the length of the block, crossed Mulberry and swung right on Lafayette and picked up speed. Jules caught a flash of a street sign at a corner. It read *E. 10 St.*

When they sped past Twelfth Street, Jules spoke timidly: "I thought Joe's was on Tenth Street."

The man with the twisted shoulder snorted a laugh. He said: "It is."

The car swung around Union Square, beating a red light, and jockeyed through Broadway traffic.

"What's Joe's last name?" Jules asked.

The man's button eyes looked at him with no expression. "It won't do no harm to tell you. It's Catrini."

Jules screwed down in his seat. The car slewed to a stop on a red light, the brakes snubbing its nose down. The motor purred and a faint odor of exhaust gas crept into the tonneau.

"Couldn't we have a little more air?" Jules asked.

The man on his right leaned forward and cranked the door window tight shut. The left corner of his mouth lifted slightly. He put his right hand in his coat pocket. When the car sprang forward again he took it out with a snub-nosed revolver in it.

"I'm afraid you can't have any more air," he said.

He rested the gun across his left forearm so that the muzzle gaped at Jules' stomach, and he cringed away from it, raising his right hand so that the palm interposed between the revolver and his abdomen.

"Don't," he whispered. "It might go off!"

The man snorted another monosyllabic laugh. He said: "It might."

Traffic streaked past the windows and more buildings, flossier and expensive now. They swung east, then north, then swept up the ramp of Queensborough Bridge. The air sweetened, freshened by the water of the East River. It was filtering in from a ventilator in the car's roof.

Jules' eyes kept swinging back to the gun that was held carelessly cocked, the man's finger on the trigger. He pressed his body back in the deep softness of the cushion, shoving his feet against the floor. The snout still was leveled at his belly. He leaned forward, his hands clasped about the neck of his guitar. In this way he interposed his elbow between the gun and his body.

His left hand slid down the strings; his fingers inveigled themselves into the round sounding hole just below them. His lips trembled still. His sidelong glances at the gun were furtive and frightened but there was hardness at the back of his eyes. The car slid off the bridge, turned south, then east again. Jules saw that the continuous backward glide of buildings was interspersed now with trees. Traffic thinned. The car's speed picked up. Tremaine hunched forward over the guitar, fondling it. He swayed forward a little as the car slackened speed, but he was tensely braced when it swung around a corner and began to jounce over a rough road with long, heaving dives.

"Please uncock that gun," Jules quavered, glancing again at the black mouth of the snub-nosed revolver. "This bouncing might make it go off!"

The man with the twisted shoulder lounged back in the seat and said nothing. He allowed his eyes to slide about and looked at Jules out of their corners. Tremaine caught a flash of the chauffeur's white face in the small rear vision mirror above the windshield. He was grinning. The man beside Jules laughed outright, the knots of muscles on his jaws rippling.

The car swerved again and shoved its long snout up a narrow lane among trees. In fifty feet it was completely out of sight of the main road. The machine stopped and slowly turned around. The car was long. It took a lot of maneuvering. Jules' hands gripped the guitar until they ached. He could feel the bite of the strings across his fingers. When the car pointed back the way it had come, the driver, a sly grin on his white face, leaned back and opened the right rear door.

"What—what are you going to do?" Jules babbled. His legs were tense under him. He lifted the guitar slightly from the floor, his left hand sliding down to the sound opening. His lips trembled and his shoulders cringed.

The man with the twisted shoulder swung his head slowly about. The corner of his mouth lifted. He spoke gently, unpleasant laughter lurking in his voice. "We think we've got a flat tire. We want you to get out and look at it."

The chauffeur laughed aloud. Jules looked at him. The feverish eyes were mocking. He looked into the bony, grinning face of the man at his left. Neither of these two had a gun but both were looking at the gun in the hands of the man with the twisted shoulder. Jules looked at it, too.

"I don't think the tire's flat," he said, in a pleading tone. "I didn't hear anything like a flat tire."

The man leaned towards him slightly, his button eyes flat, and the gun pointed unwaveringly at his stomach.

"This is a good car," he said. "You wouldn't be able to hear anything like a flat tire."

Jules looked wide-eyed at the gun and opened his mouth and closed it again. He gulped and said: "All right."

He got to his feet, crouching with his head against the low roof. He did not turn his back to the man but kept his eyes on the gun and lifted the guitar so that he held it crossways in his hands, the big end to his left. His left hand

slipped the cord loose from its button at the base, then slid to the sound opening again and the first finger inserted itself in a ring there which could not be seen.

"All right," he said again

He struck down with the guitar. Its base bonged on the wrist of the hand that held the gun. It discharged and the bullet tugged at Jules' left trouser leg. In the same instant he leaped from the car and his right hand seized the inner handle of the door and slammed it shut as he whirled behind it.

Shouts and hoarse curses burst out in the car, slightly muffled by its heavy doors and the thick glass. Jules was sprinting on his toes at a diagonal from the back of the car, sprinting with his head back and his chest out. As he ran he counted slowly to himself: "Three—four—fi—"

Wind struck him from behind and hurled him face down on the earth. A twig jabbed his cheek and a muffled ripping concussion burst in his ears. For nearly five minutes Jules lay as he had fallen, the earth cold against his face; then slowly he thrust himself up from the ground, gravel biting his palms, his shoulders humped, his head sagging. He heaved to his knees, then reeled to his feet, steadied himself with one hand on a tree. He breathed deeply a half dozen times, shaking his head sharply; and then he stood erect and moved heavily around towards the car.

The sedan was not quite where he had left it. It seemed to have been lifted off the ground and dropped about four feet to the right. It listed to that side. The top was blown out and jagged ends of metal thrust spear points up into the air. One door sagged crazily and another was missing. The bullet-proof glass had vanished. Something red dripped on the right running-board, dripped and formed a sluggishly widening puddle. Jules' lips were pressed together in a thin hard line. Three men had been in that car. That left only O'Reilly to pay for Angela's death. And there was that score against dear brother Andrew. . . .

Jules looked down at his left hand. A steel

ring an inch across was on the forefinger and from that ring dangled a steel pin.

"Well, well," he said, and threw back his head and laughed with little sound. "That grenade must have ruined my guitar. I'll have to buy a new one."

Smoke in Your Eyes

Hugh B. Cave

HUGH B(ARNETT) CAVE (1910–2004) was born in Chester, England, but his family moved to Boston when World War I broke out. He attended Boston University for a short time, taking a job at a vanity publishing house before becoming a full-time writer at the age of twenty. At nineteen, he had sold his first short stories, "Island Ordeal" and "The Pool of Death," and went on to produce more than a thousand stories, mostly for the pulps (at one point, in the 1930s, his work appeared in more than fifty different magazines in a single year) but also with more than three hundred sales to national "slick" magazines such as *Colliers*, *Redbook*, *Good Housekeeping*, and *The Saturday Evening Post*. Although he wrote in virtually every genre, he is remembered most for his horror, supernatural, and science fiction. In addition to the numerous stories, he wrote forty novels, juveniles, and several volumes of nonfiction, including an authoritative study of voodoo. His best-selling novel, *Long Were the Nights* (1943), drew on his extensive reportage of World War II in the Pacific and featured the adventures of PT boats and those who captained them at Guadalcanal. He also wrote several nonfiction books chronicling World War II in the Pacific theater.

Cave was the recipient of numerous awards, including the Living Legend Award from the International Horror Guild, the Bram Stoker Lifetime Achievement Award from the Horror Writers Association, and the World Fantasy Life Achievement Award.

"Smoke in Your Eyes" was published in the December 1938 issue.

Smoke in Your Eyes

Hugh B. Cave

OHN SMITH GAZED with exaggerated tolerance at his fair companion. Of course it was not difficult to exercise patience with a young lady so scandalously lovely. He was, in fact, used to it.

"Ever so many men, Angel," he declared, "smoke long black cigarettes. Even I do at times."

"The heat, Mr. Edgerson, has made you lazy. Otherwise you'd jump at a thing like this."

Smith's other name was Philip Edgerson. He hated it because it brought to mind too many memories of birthdays, Christmases and people sick in bed. He was head of a greeting card company. Now he put down his cocktail and leaned back.

They were dining in Polinoff's, and it had not

The girl in a red cape pursues trouble and stumbles onto a plot where life means little.

been a good idea. Polinoff's on an August afternoon was far too hot, too stuffy, for the enjoyment of pig knuckles and spiced red cabbage.

"I'm thinking of abandoning Trouble, Incorporated, Angel."

"Said he, lying," she retorted.

"No, I mean it. Look, I've paid rent on that ninth-floor cell for eleven months now, and not a customer. Not a single client. A man's hobby, as I see it, should be more productive than that."

"It has been," Angelina said simply.

"Not financially."

"Mr. Philip Edgerson," she said, "makes quite enough money to support the hobby of John Smith. It's the heat, that's all."

"I suppose it is."

He reached out then and picked up the letter she had read to him. It was a neat little thing, written delicately in green ink on ten-cent-store paper which bore the gilt initials M.A.B. It read:

"Dear Miss Kaye,

"This is the third time I have tried to write to you, but on each previous occasion my courage has left me before I could finish. This time, however, I am determined to go through with it. You see, I am really desperate.

"Please do not be angry with me if this is a long letter. I know that you urge those who write to you to be brief, but I have so much to tell.

"I am nineteen years old, Miss Kaye, and was married just a little over a year ago to the dearest boy in all the world. Teddy was so loving then and so considerate. We saved money and planned for the future and were just as happy as two birds in a nest. And now all that is changed.

"I am not really sure when the trouble began. Now that I look back on it, I realize that Teddy acted queerly for days, even weeks, before he actually began staying out nights and leaving me alone. During that period he was awfully quiet and seemed always to be wrapped up in his thoughts. I thought he was worried about his job, and I tried to be tender with him, but he refused to confide in me. He even told me once that it was none of my business.

"Then, Miss Kaye, he began staying out late at night, sometimes until two or three o'clock in the morning, and I was sick with worry. When I spoke to him about it he told me to leave him alone and stop nagging him, but I wasn't nagging him; I was just frantic that our love would die and he would drift away from me.

"It went on this way for almost a month, Miss Kaye, and then he began bringing these men to the house. Three or four times a week they came, and they were nice enough, I suppose. At least they always said hello to me, but instead of sitting in the parlor like ordinary friends, they and Teddy would go upstairs to Teddy's den and close the door and stay up there until all hours. Sometimes there would be three of them, sometimes more.

"Well, Miss Kaye, I do not pretend to be any judge of character, but I am positive in my own heart that these men are not good for Teddy. They are not his kind. They are older, for one thing, and they seem very wise in the ways of the world. One of them, whom the others seem to look upon as a sort of leader, is a foreigner, at least twenty years older than my husband, and he smokes long black cigarettes continually, and the house reeks from it. And furthermore, if these men were proper companions for Teddy, he would introduce me to them, wouldn't he? But he hasn't. He just said, 'Boys, meet the wife.' Which hurt me terribly.

"Please, Miss Kaye, tell me what to do to win my husband away from these men. I am worried to desperation for fear I will lose him, and for fear he is getting mixed up in something that will bring trouble to us both.

"Anxiously yours,
"Margaret Arnold Burdick.

"P.S. If you print this letter in your column, please sign it 'Worried Wife,' because if you used my real name Teddy would be angry, I'm sure.

"M.A.B."

John Smith, president of Trouble, Inc., carefully folded the letter and passed it back. "Do you get many like that, Miss Kaye?"

She frowned at him. Her name was not Katherine Kaye any more than his was John Smith. Her name, when she was not opening letters from love-sick wives at her desk in the Star office, was Angelina Copeland. Angel to her friends.

"You think it's a rib, Philip?"

"As phony, Angel, as some of the sentiments I'm guilty of perpetrating."

"I don't. I think it's on the level. I'm going out there. After all, Philip, you've bored me to death for months about that fool professor who smoked black cigarettes and here we have a guy who—"

"You know the address?"

She took from her purse an envelope which matched the letter. "Spencer Street, 154. You *could* drive me out there," she said. "Otherwise I'll have to go by trolley."

Edgerson heaved an elaborate sigh. It was a hot, sticky afternoon. From nine to twelve he had faithfully perspired through his duties as president of the Edgerson Greeting Card Company, watching the clock and looking forward to a long, cool drive into the country with Angel, a dip in some shady lake, dinner and dancing at some quiet roadhouse far from the city's heat.

Now he was to be John Smith again. It was inevitable.

He disliked this silly Margaret Arnold Burdick intensely. He resented the fact that she had found it necessary to mention a large foreign person who incessantly smoked long black cigarettes. Because, after all, the thing was ridiculous. Dubitsky *was* dead. Dubitsky had been dead for at least four months. The Dubitsky whose strange death had intrigued him was gone forever. Margaret Burdick's foreigner would turn out to be a wrestler or a man selling carpets. Or a myth.

"I'll drive you," he said sourly, "but you'll regret it. Mark my words, Angel, you'll regret it."

t least half a dozen times since the birth of Trouble, Inc., Edgerson had been on the verge of closing the tiny office in the Mason Building and chucking the whole thing to the dogs. On each and every one of those occasions, Angelina had popped up with something "hot." It was she, not he, who kept his hobby, Trouble, Inc., going. He half suspected that the Trouble idea had been hers in the first place anyway.

When they reached Spencer Street on the outskirts of town, and found the house, he was relentlessly gleeful. He pointed to the sign in the window and said: "You see? I told you so."

The sign said, "For Rent."

Angel frowned at it. The frown was most becoming to her beauty. Edgerson gently patted her shoulders. "We still have time for the ride into the country, the swim, the—"

"Apply at 27 Brook Street," Angel said.

"What?"

"That's what it says. 'For rent. Apply 27 Brook.' That's the next street over, Philip."

He said nothing, merely groaned and put the car in gear. Angel was silent, too, until he stopped the machine in front of a small brown cottage on Brook Street. "The trouble with you, Mr. Smith," she said then, sweetly, "is that you give up too easily."

He followed her up the walk, between beds of marigolds. She rang the bell. In a moment the door was opened by a plump female in a flowered apron.

"How do you do?" Angel said in her nicest Sunday voice. "I'm Mrs. Smith. This is my husband."

The woman said, "How do you do?" wonderingly, and glanced at Edgerson and stared at Angel. Women usually stared at Angel. And envied her her slimness, her remarkable blond hair and her more than pretty face.

"We noticed a house over on Spencer Street, for rent," Angel said.

"Oh, yes."

"Is it occupied at present?"

"No." The woman shook her head. "We had a nice young couple living there, but they've moved out."

Edgerson, recovering from his shock at so casually being called "my husband," smiled slyly. He was John Smith now, and John Smith was at times a pretty fair detective. Angel, fishing for information about the nice young couple on Spencer Street, was going to encounter difficulties. The plump lady in the flowered apron was obviously not a talker.

"We've looked so long for a house," Angel said, "that I really don't know *what* I want. You know how it is, I'm sure. You go from one place to another and simply get all worn out."

The woman nodded sympathetically. There were chairs on the porch and she moved toward them. "Won't you sit down, Mrs. Smith?"

"Thank you," Angel breathed. "Thank you so much!"

"It's really a very nice house," the woman said. "My husband and I built it ourselves and lived in it four years. Then last year Mr. and Mrs. Burdick, the nice young couple I mentioned to you, moved in."

Angel looked thoughtfully at the tips of her fingers. "They didn't stay very long, did they?"

"No, they didn't. It wasn't because of the house, though. Mr. Burdick worked for the Glickman Company and lost his job. He had to go to another city to find work."

"Oh," Angel said. "That's too bad. And they'd only been married a year?"

"Only a year."

Angel widened her large brown eyes and looked soulfully at Edgerson. "You know, dear," she said, sadly shaking her head, "when you hear of the misfortunes that beset other married people, it makes you realize how terribly fortunate we've been." She turned the soulful eyes on the woman again. "Married only a year, and so in love with each other! I just know they were!"

"Well," the woman said dubiously, "well, yes, I guess they were."

"And are they coming back some day? To visit you?"

"Well, I don't know. Theodore, that's Mr. Burdick, said they were moving to some place near Boston. Margaret went last Wednesday to put things in order, and he went Saturday, with the furniture truck. They may come back, but of course I couldn't hold the house for them. Now if you'd like to look at it, Mrs. Smith . . ."

But Angel was looking at her "husband" again. "You know, darling, perhaps Mrs.—er—"

She glanced helplessly at the woman who said, "My name is Crandall."

"Perhaps Mrs. Crandall could recommend someone to move our furniture. Those last people we had were simply unbearable. I'll just never forgive them for ruining our twin beds."

Edgerson gulped.

"Could you recommend someone, Mrs. Crandall?" Angel cooed.

"Well, we like the Hartley people ourselves. If you're just moving a short distance, that is. The Burdicks used the McCullen Warehouse people."

"You saved her a lot of trouble," Edgerson thought. "She was going to ask you that in a minute. Twin beds! Of all things, twin beds!"

Angel stood up. "Would you like to look at the house now, dear, or come back tomorrow? It's quite late, and we did promise to meet the Burrs."

"Tomorrow," Edgerson said.

"Will that be all right with you, Mrs. Crandall?"

"Well, yes," Mrs. Crandall agreed.

"Then we'll see you tomorrow. . . . Come, darling. I really think we've accomplished something!"

In the car, Edgerson drew a slow deep breath and said, "You little hellion!"

She grinned. "It worked, didn't it?"

"It worked, but I've a mind to put you across those mythical twin beds and spank you."

Gnomes and pixies would have danced to her laughter. But then she was suddenly sober. "This thing sounds ugly to me, Philip."

"Why?"

"First, that letter. I received it Wednesday, the day she left. She must have written and mailed it Tuesday. Then, more important, why the sudden departure? If she'd known that they were leaving the city, she wouldn't have written the letter at all. I never answer letters personally. When people write to my lovelorn column they expect to see the replies in print."

Edgerson, silent for a moment, said, "Would it be all right with you, Angel, if I did a little detecting myself for a change? After all, I'm president of Trouble, Inc."

"You're not a very ambitious president."

"I might surprise you." He turned the car onto a main street. "The McCullen Warehouse is on Canal Street, isn't it?"

"Yes. Why?"

"We're going there. Between your nutty curiosity and my interest in any guy who smokes black cigs like Dubitsky did . . . I'll never believe that guy's really dead."

It was a huge red-brick building growing out of the damp, sticky smells of the waterfront. Smith went in alone and was gone a half-hour. Returning, he had a triumphant smirk on his angular face.

"They didn't move out of town," he said. "Their furniture is in storage, most of it. A studio couch, two easy chairs, a table and a large double bed—not twin beds, Angel—were trucked over to this address as soon as the van reached the warehouse." He passed her a slip of paper.

She peered at it. "Gayland Avenue. That's an apartment house district. Very snooty."

"You know," Smith said, putting the car in gear, "this is beginning to show signs of promise. Maybe your lovelorn wife was in trouble."

ayland Street was in a district of fancy dress shops, delicatessens and Pomeranians, and the figure on the slip of paper was the number of an imposing structure housing a nest of apartments. This time Angel refused to sit in the car while he investigated. She went with him up the gleaming steps into the hallway with its glittering brass mail-boxes, and she looked with him at the long list of names beside the long row of bells.

Bell number 17 had no name beside it, but Smith pushed it anyway. The studio couch, chairs, table and bed had been delivered to suite 17.

He pushed again and frowned. "They don't answer."

"I've been wondering something," Angel said.

"Yes? What?"

"If you were a young man fresh out of a job, Philip, would you feel able to afford an apartment in this neighborhood?"

Smith shrugged. "If we wondered at all the queer things people do, we'd wind up in a chuckle college."

"I'm serious, Philip."

"So am I. They don't answer."

Angel looked annoyed. She walked up two white steps and tried the door and it was locked. She said, "Damn!" and stood there glaring at it. All at once her eyes widened; she turned quickly, beckoned with an outstretched hand and said, "C'm'ere, quick!"

At her side, Smith peered through the thick clear glass of the door and saw a man backing out of an apartment at the end of the hall. A suitcase lay beside the open door and the man was lugging out another. He closed the door and picked up both pieces of luggage and plodded down the corridor with them, staggering a little because they were heavy and he was a small, thin-legged, bald little lad without much strength.

Plouffe, by gosh! Plouffe, of all private dicks.

The little dick kept his head down until he reached the door, and by that time Smith had faded back on one side, Angel on the other. Plouffe put down his burdens, opened the door, held it open with a foot and picked up the suitcases. He squirmed out and the door clicked shut behind him. Then he saw Smith.

He dropped the suitcases again and said, "Well, my, my! Look who is here!"

Smith looked at the luggage. It was expensive but old. It was initialed.

"So you're demoted to bellhop," Smith said.

"Huh?"

"You make a very handsome bellhop, don't you, Mr. Plouffe?" said Angel sweetly.

Nick Plouffe pulled a large moist handkerchief from his pocket and mopped his brow. He frowned, using his whole face, and said sourly: "At least I don't have to give myself no fancy name like Trouble, Incorporated, to get business."

"Of course you don't," Angel said.

"And I ain't a bellhop, see?"

"Of course you're not. You live here."

"Me? Live here? Say, are you nuts?"

"We're looking," Angel declared solemnly, "for my aunt Agatha. Apartment eighteen. We have a key to Aunt Agatha's apartment—she's in Bermuda, you know—but no key to the door you're leaning against. Could you let us in, maybe?"

Nick Plouffe blinked, registering suspicion. It was hard for him to register suspicion, or anything else, because his moist little face was small and V-shaped and not very elastic. He did his best, though, and then grumbled: "Well, all right."

He fumbled for a key and unlocked the door.

"Thank you so much," Angel cooed. "Come, John."

She and John Smith paced down the hall without a backward glance at the suspicious Plouffe, and Smith said dryly, "There, my dear, is a scraping from the lowest stratum of the private detecting profession. Dumb but dangerous. A mouse, but a mean mouse. I met up with him on another case and caught him pretending to be a G-man. He asked me to promise not to tell on him. Did you note the initials on the two suitcases?"

"I did. M.A.B. and T.L.B."

"The Burdicks."

"Or a monstrous coincidence, because Plouffe came out of this apartment," Angel declared, stopping beside a door, "and it happens to be suite 17."

Smith glanced back, then, to make certain Plouffe had departed. Satisfied, he knocked. After a moment's wait he knocked again.

"They don't answer."

"Perhaps we should tail Mr. Plouffe," Angel suggested. "Or is it too late?"

Smith leaned against the door of apartment 17 and scowled at her. Scowled fiercely, because he knew from past experience that Miss Angelina Copeland—she had once been his secretary and had since become both the bane and the beacon of his existence—would talk him out of it unless he were savagely stubborn. "It's too late," he said firmly, "for absolutely everything

except that drive into the country, that swim, and—"

"But tomorrow we start in again. Promise?"

"No!"

She rolled her eyes at the ceiling and tapped a toe on the tile floor. "No promise, no ride. It's for your own good, darling. If I didn't keep jabbing you, you'd turn into a Christmas card, and that would be such a waste of talent."

She took his arm. Smith sighed and went with her, muttering under his breath.

 iss Miggsby, who wore large rimless glasses, placed a sheaf of papers on Edgerson's desk and said, beaming: "We think, Mr. Edgerson, that these are simply delightful!" Miss Miggsby had been Edgerson's private secretary since the departure of Angel. She possessed some of Angel's brains, none of Angel's disturbing physical attraction, and was very, very easy on the nerves.

Edgerson gravely accepted the papers, glanced at them. The door of his private sanctum opened at that moment and he looked up. Looked up and groaned. He could tell by the grim little smile on Angelina's lips that something had happened.

Miss Miggsby fled. Angel, radiant in something ultra modern and startlingly yellow, came around the desk and looked over Edgerson's shoulder.

"Christmas?" she asked innocently. "Or just happy birthday to my ex-wife?"

He made sure that the door between Miss Miggsby's office and his own was closed before he answered. Then he said firmly, "Whatever you've found out, it's no go. I'm busy. I got in this morning with a prize hangover, thanks to your mania for daiquiris last night, and found enough work piled on my desk to keep three men busy for a week."

"Oh."

"Don't *you* ever work?"

"Uh-huh. I just finished my column. Look, Philip. I've discovered the whereabouts of Margaret Burdick."

"I'm not interested."

"You've got to be. It's terribly important." She cleared a space for herself on his desk and sat down, swinging a most attractive leg.

"First I went over to the Glickman Company where Mr. Burdick—Teddy, that is—used to work. I smiled my prettiest and found out that Teddy wasn't fired; he quit. He told them he had a better job offered to him in Boston. I deserve credit for that. The Glickman outfit is a big concern. They make chemicals and do a lot of work for the government. It took talent to go in there stone cold and come out with information."

"I'm still very busy," Edgerson muttered.

"So then," she continued, "I went over to that little dumpy hotel where your little Plouffe lives. The clerk told me he was in, so I slipped into a phone booth and called him and talked the way you'd expect Margaret Arnold Burdick to talk—after reading that letter she wrote me—and I told Plouffe to come right over because I needed him. And he fell for it."

Edgerson was not sufficiently surprised to show it.

"He fell for it," Angel declared, "and when he left the hotel I followed him. He didn't go far. He went to another grimy little hotel, the Lester, and that, Philip, is where Mrs. Burdick is hiding out."

"You saw her?"

"No, but—"

"What about her husband? Is he living there, too?"

"After all," she said, "I'm not the president of Trouble, Inc. I'm just an underpaid hireling. Don't expect too much."

"I can't see that you've done too much."

"But I haven't confessed all. Not yet. I've been to the morgue," she said.

That got him. His mouth sagged and he gaped at her.

"The newspaper morgue," she explained softly, "to check on Dubitsky. Do you know why I did that?"

He said nothing.

"Because," she went on, "I discovered over at the chemical company that young Mr. Burdick is a graduate of our nice big university here where Dubitsky taught. And when I found that out, I got to thinking about the foreigner who smoked the long black cigarettes, and so I went over to the university and did some snooping. Guess what I found."

"If you don't stop beating around the mulberry bush," Edgerson said, "I'll fire you!"

"Young Mr. Burdick was a student in some of Dubitsky's classes."

"You mean it?"

"It's the truth. He was an honor student. One of Dubitsky's pets."

"I'm not," Edgerson said, "as busy as I thought. Go ahead."

"You mean it?"

"Go right ahead. I've always been intrigued with Dubitsky. The Christmas ditties can wait."

"Well," she said, "I've brought you some of the newspaper accounts of Dubitsky's death."

"I don't need them. I know the details by heart."

"Do you? Lead on, Macduff."

"The great Dubitsky," Edgerson said, "left his bachelor apartment about six-thirty that night, intending to drive to a little camp he owned on Loon Cry Lake, sixty miles north of here. It was a miserable night, and he was alone. He stopped in Midville for gas, and the attendant warned him not to try the Loon Lake road because it was inundated and dangerous, and an electrical storm was coming up over the mountains.

"He went, and was caught in the storm. His car went over a cliff and caught fire, probably struck by lightning before it went over. The charred remains of Dubitsky were identified by a watch and a couple of rings."

"And I'll wager my next year's salary as non-paid vice president of Trouble, Inc.," said Angel calmly, "that you believe Professor Dubitsky is still very much alive. Now don't you, Mr. Smith?"

Edgerson scowled at a tiny image of Santa Claus which sat on his desk. It was a birthday gift from Miss Miggsby. "Now why," he insisted, "should a self-respecting professor of foreign languages, including the Malaysian, wish to plunge himself into oblivion?"

"What nationality is Dubitsky?"

"Darned if I know. German, Czech, Russian, Polish—he might be most anything."

"The point is," she said, "he's not American. He came to this country six or seven years ago, to take up his duties at the university. No one knows much about him, except that he's a mental giant. Put two and two together, Philip. Dubitsky. A mysterious accident. The Glickman Chemical Company. Young Burdick. It's positively sinister; that's what it is!"

"What," Edgerson said, "do you propose to do about it?"

"Have a talk with Burdick's wife. And you're coming with me. This, Mr. Smith, is the biggest thing that ever fell into the lap of our little organization, or I'm a monkey's uncle."

"I think a better move," Smith declared thoughtfully, "would be to call on Plouffe."

"Plouffe?"

"The girl might be a bit difficult. Plouffe, on the other hand, would hardly dare to be. I know too much about him. I might still talk about him impersonating himself as a G-man." He smiled, pushing himself out of his chair. "Trouble, Incorporated, is at work again," he said.

ick Plouffe, when not at his hotel, could generally be found between bottles of beer in his office or between martinis at the Andolf Tap. He was in his office this time, suffering from the heat. A cheap fan sent the hot air surging about the room and Plouffe's handkerchief was sodden from face-mopping.

He peered suspiciously at his visitors and said: "Well, my, my! Look who is here!"

"You're surprised," Smith said.

"I am pop-eyed!"

Smith shut off the fan and eyed the half-empty bottle of beer on the detective's desk. He sat down without awaiting an invitation. Angel followed suit. Nick Plouffe stood beside the desk, mopped his pleasant little face again and registered uneasiness.

"So what can I do for you?"

"You're not going to like this, Nick."

"I feel it in my bones."

"What we'd like to know, Nick," Smith said, "is how you got mixed up in this Burdick business."

Plouffe sat down. His tie was askew and his striped shirt was open down to the third button, revealing a moist undershirt and a few chest hairs. He said plaintively: "On a hot day like this you should come here to ask questions! What did I ever do to you?"

"Give, Nick."

"Give! Do I ask you to hand out professional secrets? Do I come barging into Trouble, Incorporated, and act like I was a partner?"

"You wouldn't want to be a partner," Angel said sweetly. "There's no money in it."

"Give," Smith said.

"So why should I?"

"Must we go through all that again? About how unhealthy our local jails are, and how bad the food is? Nick, you surprise me."

Nick Plouffe slumped lower in his chair. The desk hid most of him but his eyes were little gray bugs just visible over the rim.

"The Burdick girl is a client of mine," he mumbled.

"How come?"

"You would not be interested. So help me it would bore you, I swear it."

"I'll risk it. Go right ahead."

"Well, it is like this. It is very ordinary. The Burdick girl comes up here and says she sees the name of my agency in the phone book. Then she spills a sob story into my ears, and so help me, Mr. Smith, it is nothing that would interest you. It is like every other sob story you ever heard."

"I'll hear it again," Smith said.

"But it will bore you stiff!"

"The food," Angel chimed in gently, "is really atrocious, Mr. Plouffe. They feed you bread and mush three times a day, and sometimes the mush is maggoty. If it isn't, I'm sure Mr. Smith can arrange to have them inject a few maggots, just for your benefit."

Plouffe mopped his face. "She has a husband, see? And he stays out late at night, and sometimes he doesn't come home at all. She says to me, he is keeping bad company and will I look into it? So help me that's the whole story."

"The bell-hopping was just your own idea, eh?" Smith said.

"Huh?"

"If that's all there is to it, Plouffe, why'd you move her from a swank apartment house to a frowsy dump of a hotel?"

"She—she couldn't pay the rent them vultures was asking."

"Maggots, Plouffe, are apt to make you hellishly sick."

"Well," Plouffe muttered, avoiding Smith's steady gaze, "I had to get some dough out of this business somehow, didn't I?"

"Meaning what?"

"She pays me to tail her husband. There wouldn't be no dough in that even if I could locate the husband, which I can't. So I have to tell the dame something, don't I? Would you want me to let her down and have her get a wrong idea about the private detective business?"

"The light begins to dawn," Angel murmured.

Plouffe looked at her gratefully and forced a grin. "Sure. She wanted service, so I gave it to her. There wasn't no harm in that, was there? All I told her, I checked up on her husband and found out he was mixed up with some tough mobsters, and things looked pretty bad, and her own life could easily be in danger unless she put herself in my care for a few days until I got things straightened out."

"And she believed you?" Smith asked.

"Sure she believed me."

"And to make it more realistic, you moved her out of the apartment and obtained a room for her at the Lester."

"Yeah. Hell, if these dumb dames want adventure, Nick Plouffe sells it to 'em. Why not?"

Smith stood up. "I'm hiring you, Plouffe."

The gray little eyes grew to twice their normal size. "Huh?"

"You say you tried to locate Burdick and failed. Is that right?"

"Sure I tried."

"Hard?"

"I done all I could," Plouffe insisted. "I checked every lead the dame gave me."

"And you couldn't find him. Very well, Plouffe, he's missing. Something has happened to him. And if we're not careful, something may happen to the girl. Therefore, I'm hiring you to keep an eye on her."

"Listen," Plouffe said. "This don't make sense."

"It might, later. You're to watch the girl and keep in touch with me, report to me every move she makes. I'd do it myself, Plouffe, but I'm going to be busy. Very busy. So is Miss Copeland. And our staff at Trouble, Inc., is limited."

"Say, what's back of all this?"

"A certain crack someone once made," Angel replied quickly, flashing a smile, "about twin beds."

"Huh?"

"You wouldn't understand, Plouffe. Don't worry about it. Someday Mr. Smith is going to write a treatise on it. Then you'll know."

Smith turned to open the door. "You can get in touch with me, Plouffe, at Trouble, Inc. If I'm not there, Miss Copeland will be. And I'll expect your first report about an hour from now."

Outside, Angel said sweetly: "What I like about you, Mr. Smith, is your uncanny faculty for persuading people to work for you—for nothing. Including," she added, taking his arm, "me."

mith was busy the next day. Visiting the university, he spent two hours investigating the history of Professor Benedetto Dubitsky and another hour on the records of Mrs. Burdick's Teddy. To his work as president of Trouble, Inc., he applied the same tenacity which had made him president of a prosperous greeting card concern.

He then visited the Glickman Company's huge chemical plant and learned that Mr. Theodore Burdick, formerly employed there, had been hired in the first place because of flattering recommendations tendered by the university.

It dovetailed nicely. Just what it meant, Smith was not sure.

With Angel, in the tiny office of Trouble, Inc., he had a dinner which consisted of cold lobster and ginger ale, purchased at a delicatessen.

Angel was dressed, Smith thought, more like a devil. She had on a handsome evening dress that gleamed under a brilliant red opera cape. Its tiny hood was made to be drawn over her sleek hair.

"Why the fancy set up?" he asked.

"I thought you were going to buy me a dinner and dance. Instead I get this and a ride, I guess."

About that time Nick Plouffe, who had been calling every hour to make his report, phoned in again.

Nick Plouffe was excited. "Only two minutes ago," he wailed, "she give me the slip! I was watchin' the Lester, see? Like I been doin' right along. I'm standin' there earnin' the salary you don't promise me, and all of a sudden she comes out with a couple of guys, and they get into a car.

"This car is parked in front of the Lester ever since around eight o'clock, and there's a ticket on it. I myself see the cop put the ticket on it. So they get into it, Mrs. Burdick and these two guys, and I pile into a taxi and tail them. And I lose them. On account of the taxi driver is dumb as all get-out, I lose them. Up around Mitchell Street and the Avenue is where I last see them."

"You get the number of that car?" Smith snapped.

"Yeah, sure. C-3145."

"Where are you now?"

"In a drug store on Mitchell."

"Get into your cab," Smith ordered, "and come over here as fast as you can. You may be needed." He cradled the phone and gazed solemnly at Angel. "C-3145, Angel. Think you can find out to whom that car is registered?"

"I can try."

She called her newspaper and four minutes later reported: "The car belongs to Alvin McKenna, 92 Follett Street, vice president of the Glickman Company. Something?"

Smith, at his desk, wrote the name and address on a pad and stared at them, clicking the pencil along his teeth as a small boy would rattle a stick along a picket fence.

"McKenna—the Glickman Company—a ticket for parking," he mused. "And two men. Not one man, Angel, but two. Dammit, what's keeping Plouffe?"

There was a knock at the door. Angel opened it and Plouffe entered, out of breath.

"I got here quick like you told me, Mr. Smith."

"Now let's have it all, Plouffe. Slowly. Begin with the car. Did you see it pull up?"

"Sure I seen it."

"Two men in it?"

"Now that's funny," Plouffe said. "When the car drove up there was only one guy in it. I was standin' right there and I couldn't've made no mistake. The guy parks the car in a one-hour space and goes into the Lester."

"What kind of a car?"

"A Packard coupé."

"A man as wealthy as McKenna," Angel declared, "would have more than one car, Mr. Smith."

"I realize that. Now, Plouffe, how long was that car there?"

"More'n two hours."

"And when the two men came out, with Mrs. Burdick, there was a ticket on it?"

"That's right."

"One of those men was the driver?"

"Yep. One was the guy who parked it there."

"Did you get a good look at Mrs. Burdick? Did she look scared?"

"Without bein' no authority on women's looks, I would say she did. Definitely I would say she was at least uneasy."

Smith stared into space and drew meaningless circles and triangles on a desk calendar. The Smith brain was hard at work; you could tell by the roadmap of wrinkles that spread away from his eye-corners. He reached suddenly for the phone book, ran a finger down the long line of McKennas and impulsively snatched up the phone. Then slowly replaced it, shaking his head.

"If you want my opinion," Plouffe ventured timidly, "I'd say—"

"Quiet," snapped Angel. "He's thinking."

"Oh."

Smith seized the phone, dialed a number. Angel relaxed. "McKenna?" she asked softly. He nodded, waiting for the connection.

"I still think," Plouffe insisted, "that—"

"Quiet."

Smith registered impatience while waiting. He looked worried. Finally he slapped the phone down and stood up. "They don't answer," he said curtly. "Let's go."

"Out there?" Angel asked.

"Yes! Don't you see through it? McKenna's car—first one man, then two—and a deliberate ticket? It's plain as day!"

"Not to me it isn't," Plouffe complained.

Smith favored him with a scornful glance and went past him, grabbing at Angel's hand as he jerked open the door. Plouffe followed, not knowing what else to do.

"If you're thinking what I'm thinking you're thinking," Angel said on the way down the corridor, "I'll bet my year's pay that you're wrong. It's just your evil mind at work."

"You mean it's yours," Smith retorted. "Mine's way ahead of you. Come on, you two."

cKenna's house was a twenty-room affair with an acre of manicured lawn cut by a driveway and a colored fountain out front. Alvin McKenna, forty-nine, was a widower worth plenty.

The house was in darkness. The car crunched up the drive and stopped, and Smith jumped out. Before ringing the bell he tried the front door. It was locked. After ringing the bell he waited only a moment, then broad-jumped a flower-bed and hurried around the side. Every window he tried was locked.

He paused, baffled, and Angel caught up with him. "Sometimes," she said pleasantly, "you surprise me, Philip. So athletic!"

He ignored her. To Plouffe he snapped: "How do we get in here?"

"You want to get arrested?" Plouffe gasped.

"I want to get in!"

"Well, it could be done easy enough, but—"

"Do it!"

Plouffe looked around, shaking his head, and then sidled to a window. It wasn't easy but in a few minutes with a penknife he managed it. With a boost he was over the sill.

"I still don't like this," he complained.

Ignoring him, Smith leaned out and gave a hand to Angel. She climbed. Half-way over the sill she said, "Oh!" and when inside she looked down at her legs and said: "I'll send you a bill for that. My best stockings!" Then she said soberly: "What do you expect to find here, Mr. Smith?"

"I don't know. I'm just full of premonitions." He produced a flash-light, drilling the darkness with a thin sliver of illumination. "I hope," he said grimly, pacing forward, "I'm at least half wrong."

It was a bedroom. With Plouffe and Angel trailing, he went down a long hall to the front of the house, through two huge living-rooms, along another hall to a library. The house was a tomb.

Its owner was in the library.

Smith's light missed him at first. It played

over the walls, yellowing rows of books, a small wall safe, a few large portraits. There was no need to illuminate the floor until he began to pace forward. Then he almost stepped on the thing because it lay just a few feet from the threshold.

He looked down, holding the light on McKenna's face, and behind him Plouffe said explosively: "Hey!" Angel put a trembling hand on Smith's arm and was silent. McKenna gazed at the ceiling.

He was a big man, wearing an expensive blue dressing gown over white flannel trousers and a white sport shirt. The white sport shirt was now a Jap flag, with its red moon of blood.

Smith stared a moment, then bent over him. "Shot," he said softly. Then he straightened and focused the light on the wall to his left.

The tiny beam came to rest on the wall safe. Smith strode forward, looked at the safe, looked down at McKenna again.

"Have you a finger-print outfit at your office, Plouffe?"

Plouffe nodded solemnly.

"Take the car and go get it," Smith directed. "Come back as fast as you can and don't say a word about this to anyone."

"But the cops oughta know about it! We'll get in trouble!"

"They'll know in due time. You do as I say." Smith glared at him and he went out wagging his head, mumbling protests. Smith and Angel heard him fumbling along the hall in the dark.

"Who did it, Philip?"

"I don't know."

"But you know something, or you wouldn't have come here."

"I think I know who'll be blamed for doing it. That's all."

"Who?"

"Burdick."

She stood there in the dark, scowling at him. "But why?"

"It wasn't McKenna who visited the Lester Hotel tonight," Smith declared softly. "It could have been, of course, but it probably wasn't.

That's where you had me wrong when you tried to read my mind, Angel. This isn't any ten-cent clandestine love affair. Can't be. Too many angles."

"You think someone borrowed McKenna's car?"

"And deliberately got a ticket."

"Why?"

"Look. Burdick is missing. His wife goes to Plouffe for assistance. Guided by Plouffe, she takes a room at the Lester. Meanwhile this other thing—whatever it is—is moving on relentlessly to some kind of climax. Part of that climax is the planned murder of McKenna here. And McKenna's murderers are clever, clever enough to plan the alibi before the crime. They swipe McKenna's car, take it to the Lester, leave it parked where it's bound to catch a ticket. No one can deny now that McKenna's car was parked in front of Mrs. Burdick's hotel; the proof is down in black and white. You see? McKenna visits Mrs. Burdick at hotel with a bad reputation. McKenna is found dead. Angry young husband is arrested for murder."

"You're guessing."

"It's the best I do. We'll know more when Plouffe gets back."

She was silent a moment, and the silence of the big house crept in to take possession. Then she said, "Why the finger-print outfit, Philip?"

"Why is McKenna dead?" he countered.

"You mean the safe?"

"It's possible."

"A man as brainy as McKenna wouldn't keep any big amount of money in a house like this."

"Maybe not, Angel. But money isn't the only thing worth stealing. You're forgetting that McKenna was vice president of a chemical company."

Angel voiced a little snort. "You'll be telling me next that you're a G-man, tracking down scurrilous agents of a mysterious foreign power!"

"I'm not, really. I'm waiting for a street car."

Very shortly Plouffe returned, with a small black case wedged under his arm and a flashlight gripped in his left hand.

"You have any trouble?" Smith asked.

"Me? Oh, no."

"Get to work then. What I want to know is this: Has anyone recently opened that safe, and if so, who."

Plouffe opened his finger-print case and timidly stepped up to the safe. While he worked, Smith held the light for him, cupping it carefully to keep the glow from striking the room's only window.

Plouffe was good at this sort of thing. In a few moments he said definitely: "It's been opened all right. There's fresh oil from the hinges smeared down the side. Not long ago, either."

"I thought so."

"You see, Plouffe," Angel said sweetly, "Mr. Smith is really very smart. He sees all, knows all, tells nothing."

"This here," Plouffe declared, ignoring her and handing Smith a thin sheet of celluloid, "is a pretty fair thumbprint."

"Good. Can you get a print of McKenna's thumb?"

"I guess so."

"Be careful," Smith warned, "where you leave your own prints around here."

"You're damn right I'll be careful!"

Finished with the safe, Plouffe knelt beside the dead man. In a moment he rose, handed over a slip of paper. As an afterthought he stooped again and with a handkerchief carefully wiped a smudge of ink from the dead man's thumb.

"Looks the same to me," he said, "though I ain't no expert."

"So it was McKenna who opened the safe. Probably forced to and then killed so he could never identify the thief. We can go now, Angel. We've a job to do. A most important job, and one that may take a long time. We've got to find Mrs. Burdick. And her husband."

Angel twisted her lovely mouth into a scowl. "All we have to go on," she said, "is that car. The one Plouffe trailed."

Smith shook his head. "No go. It's probably right here in McKenna's garage by now."

"It is," Plouffe said. "I seen it when I come back. I was meaning to tell you."

"Then," said Angel, "we're stymied. Unless," she added, glancing suspiciously at Smith, "that brain of yours is working overtime again. Sometimes that brain amazes me."

Edgerson did some serious thinking as he drove away from the elaborate home of the slain McKenna. It was high time, he realized, to do some thinking. Up until now this affair had been little more than a pleasant diversion, a relief from the monotony of being president of a greeting card concern. A hobby, like amateur theatrics or peephole photography. Now it was murder.

He scowled at the windshield and mentally fitted together the pieces of the puzzle as he saw them. The pattern was a bit startling. "You know, Angel," he said, "the safest thing we could do right now would be to go straight to the police, tell them all we know and then go for a nice long ride into the country."

"Nonsense!" she said scornfully.

He sighed. "We'll do the next best thing. Plouffe, we'll leave it to you to phone the police and report McKenna's death. You can do it from a booth somewhere without leaving a trail."

"And what'll you two be doing?" Plouffe demanded.

"Pushing our noses deeper into affairs that don't concern us."

"Well," Plouffe said, "I don't like it."

"Neither do I."

Smith stopped the car at a restaurant. "There should be a phone inside," he said. "Use it, then go home. If we need you again, I'll call you."

"I still don't like it," Plouffe muttered, but he got out.

"And now," said Angel, when the car was under way again, "just what do we do?"

"What time is it?"

She looked at her watch. "Four-ten. Fine time of night to keep your best girl out."

"We drive to Warren Avenue now," Smith declared calmly, "and get out of bed a young man named Timothy Kenson. I don't believe you know Timmy."

"Who is he?"

"He works at the office. But for the past several hours he's been working at the Krashna Tobacco Store, downtown."

"Why?"

"You'll see," Smith said, "in due time."

She didn't like that. She glared at him. "He knows all, sees all, tells nothing." Smith ignored her and she adjusted her red cape about her angrily.

He drove in silence. The streets were deserted, and it was difficult to realize that on so calm and peaceful a night murder had been done. But Smith's mind, agile now, was ahead of the murder and groping for the motive.

He knew, or thought he knew, the elaborate steps leading up to McKenna's death, and the probable aftermath. But the motive still evaded him. Unless, of course, the answer lay at the Glickman Company.

He turned the car into Warren Avenue and stopped. "You wait here," he told Angel. Climbing the steps of a brown cottage, he put his thumb against the doorbell. In a moment a light winked on and the door opened. A young, red-haired man in wrinkled pajamas blinked at Smith and said, "Oh, it's you, Mr. Edgerson."

"Any luck, Timmy?"

"Sure thing. He came in late this afternoon. I been trying to get you ever since."

"A tall, dark man, Timmy? With a beard?"

"Nope. He was a little runt. Crummy-looking."

"Oh. You followed him?"

"Sure thing. He walked down the street a ways and got into a taxicab. So I did like you said. I jumped into another taxicab and told the driver to keep him in sight. He went into a house on Canal Street, down near the river. Wait a minute and I'll get you the number. I wrote it down."

He was back in a minute or two with a slip of paper which he thrust into Smith's hand. "Here it is, Mr. Edgerson. Number 23 Canal. Just a couple of doors down from the McCullen Warehouse, if you know where that is."

"Timmy," John Smith said, "you're a genius!"

"It was easy," Timmy said.

"It was masterful. Tomorrow you get a raise in pay."

Smith hurried back to the car, stuffing the slip of paper into his pocket. He said nothing to Angel, but the triumphant smirk on his face gave him away.

"You look," she said, "as if you just ate the goldfish. What's up? Where are we going now?"

"To the hideout of the dark foreigner who smokes long black cigarettes."

"What?"

"It was really quite simple. While you were holding down the fort I visited the only two tobacco stores in the city where a man can buy long black cigarettes. They're Cuban, you know. I discreetly asked questions. The man in the place on Fernald Street told me he used to carry them because he had a customer who came regularly, twice a week, for a large supply. The customer was Professor Dubitsky, and the fellow had sold no Cuban cigarettes since Dubitsky's death. But in the second store I had better luck, Angel. The man there informed me that he did carry them. He hadn't used to, he said, but about three months ago a customer placed a standing order with him, and the customer called twice a week to pick up his supply."

"The original Sherlock Holmes!" Angel gasped. "And all this time I thought you were just plain Philip Edgerson!"

"I got quite chummy with the man," Smith informed her, "and enlisted his aid. He agreed to let Timmy work for him. Timmy did so, and when the buyer of the Cuban cigarettes came in, Timmy followed him. That's all there was to it. Quite simple, you see."

"You mean Timmy followed Professor Dubitsky?"

"No. Dubitsky himself wouldn't come out in the open like that. But if we fail to find him at the address to which we're going, I'll be a most crestfallen sleuth."

She gave him a sidelong glance from beneath the red hood and then looked out the car window, noting the sinister section of town into which he was taking her.

"Are you armed, Philip?"

"I don't own a gun. You know that."

"Philip," she said in a manner of confession, "I have one. I borrowed it from my office."

He frowned. "Keep it," he said bluntly.

The car had entered the waterfront warehouse district, and at this time of night the streets were black, deserted, ominous. A short-lived downpour had beaten to life sour smells of fish and fruit, and the dampness held those unsavory odors in suspension. You smelled trouble. Danger.

Smith pulled the machine to the curb. "For you, Angel," he said firmly, "this is as far as the car goes. I may be a willing slave to my hobby, but I drag no hapless woman with me."

"It's not your hobby. It's ours."

"Nevertheless, you wait here—you and your silly popgun."

"That," she said, "is what you think."

"It's what I know," he said. Then, suddenly serious: "Look here, darling. We've not even the vaguest idea of what we're getting into. It may be as mean and dirty as the district it's in. I'd be scared stiff if you came along."

"So I'm to sit here and be scared stiff until you get back?"

"Or else," he threatened, "we go straight to the police. Although any self-respecting cop would arrest you in that devil's cape."

She was angry. He looked at her and saw that she was staring straight ahead, her lips tight-pressed, her chin rigid. He patted her knee and got out, walked away.

Just once, as he went past the warehouse a hundred yards or so distant, he turned his head to look back. The car's headlights owlishly stared at him. Uneasy about leaving Angel alone too long on a street so dark and unsavory, he quickened his step.

Number 23 was one of a row of tenements, all of which looked alike in the dark. A battered ash-can filled with refuse stood on the concrete stoop beside the door. The door opened when Smith pressed it.

He stepped over the threshold into a black, smelly hall. Stopped there, scowling, and realized that the house had three floors and he had no idea on which level to concentrate.

His flash-light winked, threading a narrow beam through the gloom of the lower hall. A baby carriage stood there. He went past it, past the door of the first-floor tenement, to the stairs. The building was a tomb, cold and damp and dark.

With the light cupped in his hand he climbed slowly, testing each ancient step before trusting it with his weight. The second-floor landing came level with his eyes and he stopped again. The light showed him a small and black cigarette stub lying by a door. He smiled a tight, twisted little smile and knew that the door was his destination.

He stepped beside it, scowled, and snapped out the light. There was no sound anywhere.

The fact that he was unarmed did not greatly worry him. It never had before. The day he began to carry a gun, he told himself, Trouble, Incorporated, would cease to be a hobby. Besides, he had no permit.

He tipped his hat back on his head and loosened his tie. He opened his coat, rubbed a hand over the floor and transferred the dirt thus collected to the front of his shirt, blackening it. For good measure he pulled off two buttons, to make the shirt sag.

He dirtied his face and rumpled his hair, and put on a pair of horn-rimmed spectacles, the lenses of which were clear glass.

Then he seized the doorknob and rattled it, and then he banged on the door and cursed it and began talking to himself.

Results were not long coming. A couch squeaked inside and a voice said sharply, "Who's there? Who's out there?"

"It'sh Percy," Smith slobbered. "Lemme in."

"Who? Who is it?"

"It'sh Percy! You lemme in or sho help me I'll busht the door down!"

A key turned in the lock and the door opened. It didn't open far. Just far enough to frame a short, thick-set man whose swarthy face was all scowl.

"Listen, buddy," the swarthy man said. "You're in the wrong place. Beat it."

"Who're you?"

"Never mind who I am. It's the middle of the night, see? And you're in the wrong alley. Scram!"

"Thish ish where I live," Smith snorted. "Don' you tell me I don' belong here. I know different."

The dark fellow was in no mood to argue with a drunk. He came a step closer, put his right hand flat against Smith's chest, and pushed. He slammed the door as Smith staggered away from it.

Smith smiled that tight little smile again and resumed his assault. If he made enough noise, the occupants of the tenement would do one of two things: either slug him or try to reason with him. He didn't think they would slug him. This was a hideout. They would want to avoid trouble.

And they most certainly would open the door if he hammered on it long enough.

It opened. The swarthy man said savagely, "Listen, buddy, will you for Gawd's sake go away and leave us get some sleep? Or do I have to get rough with you?"

Smith's eyes glowered at him out of a slack, stupid face. "You listen to me," he said. "My name'sh Percy Smith an' I live here. An' nobody'sh gonna keep me out!"

Behind the swarthy man an impatient voice said, "Let him in, Max."

"Oke, buddy." Max sighed. "Come on in."

"That'sh better," Smith said. "That'sh much better."

He walked in, weaving a little. Max closed the door.

"Now take a good look around, Percy," Max said, "and you'll see this ain't the place you thought it was. You're drunk and you're in the wrong house."

"Who saysh I am?"

"Look around. See for yourself."

Smith looked around. The room in which he stood was a living-room, furnished with table, chairs and a couch. The swarthy man, Max, had evidently been sleeping on the couch, in his clothes. His clothes were wrinkled and he wore no shoes.

The other man was bigger. He wore gray pajamas which hung loosely from his lank frame, revealing a generous expanse of hairy chest. His hair was in his eyes and he stood with his hands hipped, feet spread wide, just back of the table. A door behind him led to what appeared to be a bedroom.

"I—I guessh I was mistaken," Smith mumbled apologetically.

"Convinced, are you?"

"I musht've got mixed up somehow."

"Well, if you're convinced," Max said, "just scram like a nice guy and don't make any more noise'n you have to."

Smith stood where he was. "I—I don' feel sho good," he said.

"O.K., O.K.," the other man said tartly. "Beat it! Be sick outside!"

"I wanna shtay here. I wanna lie down somewheres. . . ."

The two men exchanged glances. The man named Max took his right hand out of his pocket, where it had rested since Smith's entrance. They stepped forward. "Sure," Max said. "We'll help you lay down, buddy. We wouldn't think of puttin' a nice guy like you out in the street at this time o' night. No-o-o. Would we, Vick?"

"Of course not," Vick said.

They took hold of Smith's arms. That was their mistake. He had been waiting for it. Waiting to get them both together, both in reach at the same time. Any other way would have been fatal, because undoubtedly both men were armed.

Smith's heel came down hard, piston-fast, on a shoeless foot that belonged to Max. At the same time he twisted, stabbed an arm out and caught the other man's wrist. He was suddenly not drunk any more, and before his adversaries were over their amazement, Smith had the situation in hand.

You didn't need a gun. All you needed was a slight knowledge of the fine art of Oriental wrestling, plus a fair to middling physique and a nickel's worth of nerve.

Max yelped, bent double at the waist as pain streaked up from his tortured foot. He bent into an upthrust knee that smacked his chin and snapped his teeth together. He staggered against the table, dazed, and had sense enough left to reach gropingly for the pocket where his gun lay. But he was too slow.

Smith had hold of Vick's wrist. He yanked Vick off balance, stooped, caught the arm above the wrist and pulled it. Not hard. Really not hard at all. But fast.

Vick's feet left the floor. He lost his breath in an explosive grunt as his big frame looped through space. His hundred and eighty pounds crashed into Max and Max was finished. Vick sprawled to the floor, stunned, and Max fell over him.

Smith waded in. What little fight remained in Vick was dissipated quickly by a hard, clean punch to the button. For his trouble, Smith had nothing to show except a few minor beads of moisture on his face and forehead.

He stepped back and surveyed the wreckage, highly elated. Luck, he realized, had been with him. He turned then and strode into the bedroom. It was empty.

Scowling, he walked through the bedroom into a kitchen. That was empty, too.

He went back to Vick and Max, sorry now that he had knocked them so thoroughly out. There were questions he wanted to ask. Questions concerning the whereabouts of Mr. and Mrs. Teddy Burdick.

He stared at them for a moment, undecided what to do; then, stooping, he went through their pockets. Both men were armed. He removed the weapons and placed them on the table, careful not to blur any finger-prints that might be on them. One of those guns, Smith was reasonably certain, had murdered McKenna.

In Vick's pocket he found a slip of paper. Penciled words, written in a stiff, marching hand, said: "Fix up the girl tomorrow night, provided the papers are in our possession by that time. The following night take care of the husband. Carefully now—suicide."

Smith read it twice, then pocketed it. An ugly fear took hold of him. Fear that he might have come too late. That the thing had already been done. He went into the kitchen, found an empty tin can and filled it with cold water. Returning, he knelt beside Vick and poured the water over his face.

Behind him a voice said quietly: "We will omit that, please. We will stand up and put our hands high and turn around very slowly."

It was a familiar voice. Quite a famous voice, in fact. Smith had heard it several times on the radio, had heard it also at university lectures. He knew, therefore, even before he obeyed the command, that at long last he had come face to face with the supposedly dead Dubitsky.

It was not a pleasant sensation. He turned, raised his hands, and stared glumly at Dubitsky's face. The hall door was open and the professor stood just inside it, tall and stoop-shouldered and grim. The automatic in his hand was small but deadly.

"Your name, please?" Dubitsky said curtly.

"It'sh Percy Smith, mishter." It was worth a try, anyway, Smith figured. "These two men shaid I didn' live here an' I had a dishcussion."

"We will omit that, also," Dubitsky snapped. "You were not drunk when you came from the kitchen!"

Smith sighed. "I'm not drunk now, either," he said, hunching his shoulders.

"Why are you here?"

"Vick's an old friend of mine."

"Explain, please."

"Sure. Back in the old days, Vick and I used to work together. So when I met him on the street a while ago, he invited me up here, just to talk over old times. Me and him and this other guy here, we got into an argument. That's all."

"You are lying," Dubitsky said.

"So help me, it's the truth!"

"Is it? Suppose, then, you tell me Vick's full name."

"Huh?"

"I thought so," Dubitsky said. "You are an agent of the government." He came a step closer, his eyes flashing. "Well, my meddling friend, you are too late. Most of the papers are already on their way to an agent of *my* government. Except for minor details, my work is finished. And you, my friend, will not interfere with those minor details, I assure you."

Smith did not answer. His gaze was on the door and he was frightened. His upraised hands trembled and perspiration gleamed on his face.

Dubitsky misunderstood. He smiled. "You have good reason to be afraid of me, my friend," he said.

Out in the hall, Miss Angelina Copeland placed on the floor the shoes she was carrying. They were her own shoes. She had removed them before ascending the stairs. She looked like Little Red Riding Hood, except Red didn't pack a gun. She measured the distance now between her outthrust hands and Dubitsky's broad back, and, still in a crouch, she set herself. Then she lunged.

The threshold creaked as she went over it, and Dubitsky whirled. He whirled too late. Angel threw herself at his knees and bucked him off balance. Smith closed in and caught him.

Smith's hands closed over Dubitsky's wrist and twisted. He hadn't used that particular twist before. It was dangerous. In the gymnasium where he worked out, it was outlawed. You could break a man's arm with it.

Smith put all he had into it, and the arm snapped. He stopped then and threw Dubitsky over his head, and when the professor crashed into the door frame something else snapped.

Dubitsky shuddered to the floor and lay in a sprawled, unlovely heap. Smith straightened, gasping for breath.

"Lord!" he said. "That was close! Angel, you were marvelous! Why didn't you shoot, though?"

"I was scared to," she declared, picking herself up and still clinging to the gun.

"I told you to keep out of here!"

"I know you did. So I drove the car up and parked it just across the street. You didn't expect me to stay in the bleachers when the ringside was vacant, did you? Then I saw Dubitsky walk in here, and my woman's intuition told me I'd be needed."

Dubitsky had not moved. Scowling a little, Smith knelt beside him.

"Is it bad?" Angel asked.

"Bad enough," he said, holding a hand over the professor's heart. "I suppose he'll live, though. They usually do." Then he turned to her. "Put that silly gun away."

"You'll be answering a flock of awfully embarrassing questions, darling, if he doesn't live," Angel said, letting the gun swing loose in her hand.

He stood up, glancing at Vick and Max. "Speaking of questions, I still want to ask a few." Vick, he saw, was coming to. The cold water had begun to take effect.

He put a hand on Vick's neck, groped for a moment with one finger and then pressed.

"Hey!" Vick choked.

"Nice, isn't it?" Smith said quietly. "Hurts a little." He pressed harder.

Vick jerked clear of the floor and fell flat again with a spongy thud. There was a nerve back there that was really sensitive.

"You're killin' me!"

"I will, too," Smith promised solemnly, "unless you cooperate. Tell me now—what have you done with the Burdicks."

"I never heard of no Burdicks."

Smith tickled the nerve. Not gently this time, but strenuously.

"They're upstairs!" Vick gasped. "For Gawd's sake, cut it out!"

"See if you can find some rope around here, Angel," Smith said. "If not, rip up a bedsheet. Now, Vick, it's my turn. I'll tell you what I know, or guess, and you can supply the rest."

"The place for that," Angel said, "is not here. Too much might happen. Let's take him with us. First thing you know, someone will walk in here with a machine gun, and then where will you be with your Chinese wrestling?"

"It worked, didn't it?"

"Yes, but even Steve Brodie didn't try it twice, darling. I'm going upstairs and collecting the Burdicks."

She walked out. Smith glared at Vick and said grimly, "One thing I do want to know. What's so all-fired important about those papers?"

"You go to hell," Vick snarled.

Smith found the nerve again. Vick shuddered to the tips of his fingers.

"It—it's a formula," he gasped. "It's some screwy formula for a new high explosive. That's all I know. I swear it!"

"I think," Smith said slowly, "I get it. At least, I begin to. Our friend Dubitsky was sent here by a foreign government. He took his time. He planned things carefully. Through him, Burdick and one or two other students obtained jobs at the Glickman Company. Through Burdick, the learned professor obtained information on the whereabouts of the formula. But things were hot. He decided to vanish. As Professor Dubitsky he did vanish. How right am I, Vick?"

"I wouldn't know," Vick mumbled. "Lay off of me, will you?"

"He found out," Smith said, "that the custodian of the secret was McKenna. With that to work on, he planned to rob McKenna's safe, and also, very cleverly, figured out an alibi because he knew he'd have to kill McKenna after he got him to open his safe. To cover up the murder Dubitsky planned that the police would discover after a while that McKenna was paying attention to Burdick's wife, and that Burdick himself, soon after McKenna's murder, had committed suicide. It would appear to be the usual sordid triangle, leaving Dubitsky and the real motive

thoroughly obscured. I like to reason these things out, Vick. It's half the fun."

Angel, appearing in the doorway, said impatiently: "Mr. and Mrs. Burdick are now in your car, Mr. Smith. Could you cut it short, perhaps?"

"One more thing, Vick."

"Huh?"

"Who murdered McKenna?"

"You go to hell!"

Smith caressed the nerve again.

"He did," Vick groaned. "So help me, I ain't lyin'. Dubitsky did it. After gettin' McKenna to open the safe with them papers in it Dubitsky had to kill him to keep him from ever identifying him."

Smith sighed. "It really doesn't matter who shot him, because I'm going to tie the three of you up, Vick, and as soon as I'm out of here I'm going to phone the police. You won't escape before they get here, Vick. Doing tricks with ropes is another of my little accomplishments, and you won't even wiggle when I'm through with you. So the police will come and find you, Vick, and find those two guns on the table; and if either of those guns fired the bullet that killed McKenna, the police will know it. Ballistics, you know."

"Here," Angel said, "are your ropes. Mr. and Mrs. Burdick were wrapped up in them, upstairs."

Smith went to work tying them up while Angel stood by with her gun trained on them. Finished, he stepped back and surveyed the results of his efforts, and grinned.

He took Angel's arm. "Let's go, darling," he said.

hat's right," Mrs. Burdick's Teddy said timidly. "I got the job through Dubitsky and then a couple of months later he died. And then he came to life again, and came to see me."

"And told you he was a Federal agent?"

"That's right, Mr. Smith. He told me he was a Federal agent, working to break down a spy ring. And I believed him. I guess I'd been reading too many stories."

They sat, the four of them, in the tiny office of Trouble, Inc. Teddy Burdick, Mrs. Burdick, Angel and Smith. Burdick was limp with gratitude. Mrs. Burdick was exactly like her letter—small, scared, not too gifted with brains.

"Dubitsky asked you then to help him. He told you the officials of the Glickman Company were under suspicion, and asked you to find out which of them had been entrusted with the safe-keeping of the formula. That it?" Smith asked.

"That's right. And when I did find out that Mr. McKenna kept it at home, he advised me to quit my job. He gave me a thousand dollars and told me to move to a small apartment somewhere and keep very quiet until the thing came to a head."

"What happened then?" Smith asked.

"Well, at the last minute, just when we were all set to move, he sent for me. He called me on the phone and told me to come to that address on Canal Street. When I got there, those two men, Vick and Max, jumped on me."

Smith leaned back in his chair, smiling. "You see it now, Angel?" he asked gently.

"There's one thing," Angel declared, "that still bothers me."

"Yes?"

"Look, now. Dubitsky planned this business very nicely, but right smack in the middle of it he 'died.' There must have been, at that time, a fear in his mind that he was being watched. In other words, government agents were closing in on him." She drew a deep breath and stared at the floor, marshaling her thoughts.

"Well," she continued, "he came to life again and went through with his plans. He got the formula. If Trouble, Incorporated, hadn't landed right ker-smack on the back of his neck, he and his buddies would have disposed of Mrs. Burdick, to keep her quiet, and then murdered Teddy, making it look like a suicide to give the police an answer to the McKenna kill and steer the investigation away from Dubitsky and his pals. You follow me?"

There was a knock on the door. Smith got up to answer it. "So far, yes," he said. "Go ahead."

He opened the door and Plouffe stood there.

"Well," Angel said, scowling, "what I want to know is why the G-men, after getting close enough to scare Dubitsky into temporary oblivion, didn't see through his phony death and ultimately get their hands on him."

Plouffe, blinking his gray eyes at her, said: "So help me, Miss Copeland, you're clairvoyant. Meet my friend here, Mr. Toomey."

He stepped aside and a man walked past him. "Mr. Toomey," Plouffe said, "is a G-man. It seems he's been keeping an eye on me ever since Mrs. Burdick came to me for advice."

"On all of you," Toomey said quietly. He was a tall, gray-haired man with a pleasant smile. "You see, Mr. Smith, we were just warming up to this case when you stepped into it."

Smith stood up, his face sheepish.

"What Dubitsky was after," Toomey said, "was the formula for a new explosive being manufactured for the government by the Glickman Company."

"And thanks to us," Smith admitted, "he got it."

"No. He never would have got it. What he took from McKenna was the original formula, long ago proved to be worthless. I doubt if Dubitsky even knew that the original has twice been revised, and that the only existing copy of the approved, final formula has never been out of government hands. What you did do, Mr. Smith, was save the lives of Mr. and Mrs. Burdick and save us a lot of work."

"Oh," said Smith.

"He's really very smart," Angel cooed.

"Thanks to you, Mr. Smith," Toomey said, "the dangerous Dubitsky and his two associates are in custody. I'm here simply to offer congratulations."

He thrust out his hand. Smith took it. Angel beamed.

"You know," Plouffe said, "he's really a pretty good guy. Maybe we should ought to tell him the truth, Toomey."

"Truth?" Smith said.

"You owe me some money," Plouffe declared, pacing forward to the desk behind which Smith stood. "I'll match you to see whether I get it or not."

He took a coin from his pocket and flipped it. Slightly bewildered, Smith did likewise.

"Heads," Smith said.

Plouffe thrust out his hand with the coin on the back of it. It wasn't a coin. Not exactly. It was a gold identification disc of the Federal Bureau of Investigation.

Smith gaped at it.

"A lot of things," Plouffe said softly, with a smile, "are not what they seem. Believe it or not, when I let you hire me I thought you were after that formula, too. I deliberately let you

believe I was impersonating an F.B.I. man so you'd feel you had something on me. That way I might get onto a lot of things. Sorry, pal." He turned to Toomey. "Well, Toomey," he said, "let's go. And you and your wife, Mr. Burdick, if you'll come along, too, and answer a few questions, you can go home afterward."

They went out. Smith looked solemnly at Angel. "I," he declared slowly, "will be damned."

She said, "Nothing surprises me anymore."

"I've another surprise for you," Smith told her, smiling.

"Really?"

"I'm going to pay you for all the work you've done."

"No! You don't mean it!"

"But I do." He put his arms around her.

"Like this," he said, and kissed her.

Blood, Sweat and Biers
Robert Reeves

ROBERT REEVES (1912–1945) was born in New York City and raised on the south shore of Long Island. He received an A.B. in history, english, and anthropology from New York University and worked as a driver of an armored post-office department truck, carpenter, cabinet maker, candy maker, reader for Fox Films, and in various jobs for Broadway theaters, including casting director, play doctor, stage manager, and assistant producer. He moved to Hollywood in the late 1930s, probably hoping to break into the movie business, as so many writers of the time did. In 1942, he joined the army, serving in the air corps, and was killed a month before the end of World War II, being buried with four other soldiers in a common grave, suggesting they died together in a single plane.

His career cut short, he is less remembered today than some of his contemporaries, having produced only three novels and eleven short stories, nine of which ran in *Black Mask* and two in *Dime Detective*. He wrote three stories about "Bookie" Barnes—not a gambling nickname but one earned because he went to college and, unusual for pulp characters, actually read books. But most of his work—all three novels and seven stories, were about Cellini Smith, a private eye, most of whose cases take place in Los Angeles. The first Smith adventure was the novel *Dead and Done For* (1939); the last the posthumous story "Alcoholics Calamitous" (September 1945).

"Blood, Sweat and Biers" was published in the January 1945 issue.

Blood, Sweat and Biers

Robert Reeves

A CELLINI SMITH NOVELETTE

The Bly-Wheaton fight lasted thirty-five seconds and ended in a one-punch knockout. Cellini Smith's job was to find out if the fight had been fixed, but his talents were soon diverted by more important matters—Murph, strong-arm man for gambler Jerry Lake, Bly's wrestler girl-friend, the Blond Bomber, "so round, so firm, so fully-packed," and a three-time killer who felt equally at home using a .38 automatic, an andiron, and sulphuric acid.

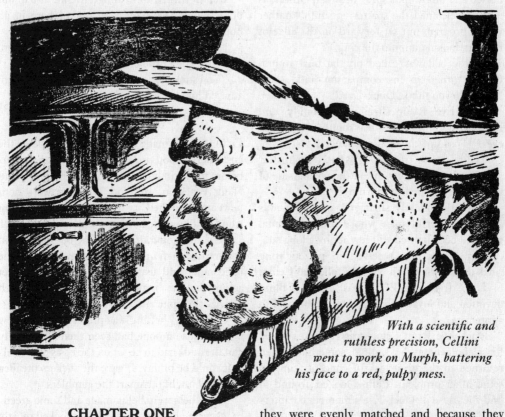

With a scientific and ruthless precision, Cellini went to work on Murph, battering his face to a red, pulpy mess.

CHAPTER ONE
RINGSIDE FOR MURDER

IT WAS A GOOD prelim. Two boys—one called Lopez, the other Sanchez—were trying to beat each other into a jelly, and with a marked degree of success.

It was a good fight because the boys were young, with strong biceps and backs, because they were evenly matched and because they didn't mind getting hurt for the customers. They stood flat-footed, in the center of the ring, hammering away blindly on the theory that one of those hard-thrown punches would sooner or later connect for a knockout.

A good scrap, thought Cellini Smith as he watched from his aisle seat in the second row, but a lousy boxing match.

The customers, too, thought that each of the boys was earning his fifty bucks for the night's work. Most of Hollywood's sporting crowd had shown up at the stadium. The ringside seats were filled with sports jackets, low-cut gowns and a sprinkling of uniforms.

Stately young starlets, hiding behind sun glasses, screamed delightedly as Sanchez or Lopez would go down for a couple of counts and bounce back. Some of the girls shielded their faces with a program as the soggy gloves connected and threw out a spray of sweat. Others, as if they welcomed the spattering, didn't bother with a program but sat forward on the edge of the seat, looking up into the ring.

As the bell was called on the final round, Cellini turned to his companion and asked: "What do you think, Duck-Eye?"

Duck-Eye Ryan shrugged gloomily and stared at nothing with those round, unblinking eyes. "Toss-up," he finally replied.

Cellini Smith frowned. "What's the matter with you? Did you get up on the wrong side of the whiskey bottle this morning?"

Duck-Eye merely shrugged again. He was a huge, powerful man whose limited mental gifts had been limited still further by a long succession of beatings received in prizefighting rings during his youth. He had followed Cellini to L.A., from the East Coast, with a blind devotion and loyalty that Cellini did not fail to appreciate.

Duck-Eye Ryan's ring-scarred face relaxed for a moment as he sighted something, then returned to the grim task of concentrating on some inner problem. Cellini looked around to find the cause of Duck-Eye's momentary interest.

Two women had just come down the aisle and taken ringside seats. The large, eagle-beaked one, who could have smoked a cigarette in the rain, looked as if she belonged on a broom. It was the other who must have caught Duck-Eye's attention. She had a full, hard, youthful body, a round, full-lipped, clear-skinned face. She was small, very blond and her beauty was inviting and accessible—a relief from that of the gilded starlets.

Someone behind Cellini clicked twice with

his tongue and murmured: "So round, so firm, so fully-packed."

The referee lifted two tired arms. The fight was a draw. The crowd roared approval, Sanchez and Lopez began hugging each other and the seconds started arguing the decision. The lights went on for a fifteen-minute intermission.

Cellini turned to his huge friend. "Snap out of it, Duck-Eye. You'll be out of here in an hour."

"It don't make no difference where I am, Cellini. I got a problem."

"You stick to the problem I gave you," Cellini advised him.

Cellini Smith made his way up the aisle as the customers stood up and stretched their legs before the main bout that featured Eddy Bly and Hank Wheaton. Bly and Wheaton were both newcomers to the City of the Angels and Cellini wondered how the betting was going.

It wasn't going too well. The betting section was located high up in the back rows, next to the bandstand, and usually showed a lot of quiet activity before a main bout. There wasn't much activity this time and Cellini found it strange.

Ordinarily, betting was pretty heavy on new boys because no one had seen them box locally and the odds had to be set on the basis of records that could be phony. It gave the suckers the idea that they might outsmart the gamblers.

A few bets were being made and some greenbacks were changing hands but it looked mostly like small fry. The big gamblers like Dan Turner or Jerry Lake sat back and waved away anyone who tried to place a bet. Cellini tried to catch Dan Turner's eye and the gambler suddenly became interested in the label on his cigar.

Cellini approached Jerry Lake and asked, "Who you betting on in the next one?"

"I'm not having any," was the reply.

"Why? Is it fixed?"

"I told you I'm not betting," Jerry Lake said. Then he added: "Any more."

"O.K., but what are the odds?" Cellini persisted. "Who's the favorite? Bly or Wheaton?"

The gambler hailed a passing candy butcher and bought a bottle of pop. Cellini let the matter drop. Once again he tried unsuccessfully to catch Dan Turner's eyes and then returned to his seat. Duck-Eye Ryan was still the picture of a man who had lost his best dope sheet.

"You shouldn't eat so much chocolate," Cellini said. "It'll always stuff you up."

"It ain't that, Cellini. It's my problem."

"All right. Let's have it."

"I need money."

Cellini extracted a five-dollar bill from his wallet and handed it to his companion. "Now relax and watch this next clambake. I've got to know if it's fixed."

Duck-Eye moodily wound the bill around his fingers and said: "This ain't enough, Cellini. I need a fortune of money. Two hundred bucks I need."

"What would you do with it?"

Duck-Eye sighed. "Cellini, I'm gonna be a father."

"Congratulations. I suppose you want all that dough for a Father's Day card."

"No, Cellini, it's—"

"All right, Duck-Eye. Let me use my imagination. We'll discuss it later. Right now try to concentrate on the next fight. Something smells about it."

From his pocket Cellini took a plain envelope that bore no return address. He extracted the typewritten note it contained and studied it once again: *Let me know if you think the main event isn't on the level.*

The envelope had been addressed to Cellini's office and also contained a crisp twenty and two tickets to the fight. That was all. But Cellini didn't have to guess its source. It had to be Dan Turner, the gambler. Turner trusted him, Turner had thrown jobs his way before. Turner had an occupational disinclination to sign his name to anything and, finally, only Turner was sufficiently tight-fisted to think that a twenty was adequate pay for a job like this.

elebrities took bows and the lights were dimmed. After a while, the two fighters came down the aisles and ducked through the ropes. They were lightweights, with Eddy Bly weighing one forty and giving Hank Wheaton two pounds.

Bly was from Fresno and Wheaton was a Seattle product. Both had excellent records, with a fair quota of knockouts, but they were records made against local, hometown talent. They had the long, loose arms of natural boxers and they looked ring-wise. The substantial blonde, who had come in just before intermission, yelled something to Eddy Bly and he waved a greeting.

Cellini said to Duck-Eye: "Pay attention, daddy."

Duck-Eye shuddered. The bell sounded for the first round and the stools were whisked from under the fighters. Wheaton rushed for the center of the ring and stopped short when he saw that Bly wasn't coming to meet him. For a long moment, Eddy Bly leaned against the ropes and measured his opponent. Then slowly, deliberately, he walked forward.

As they closed, Wheaton's left arm shot out and Eddy Bly took three jabs to the face in rapid succession. Bly did not step back, did not even bother to defend himself. He kept moving in and took a rapid one-two to the heart. The shoulders of the two men were now almost touching. Suddenly, Bly's right hand shot up. It moved no more than six inches but it was sure and powerful. Wheaton's mouthpiece flew into the air and he sagged to the floor.

The count was hardly more than a formality and people began leaving before it was finished. Bly helped Wheaton to his corner and watched anxiously till the fighter was fully revived.

"Well," asked Cellini Smith, "what do you think?"

"That sock was no fake," said Duck-Eye Ryan.

"I suppose not," Cellini conceded, but he was

worried. Perhaps Wheaton had left his chin hanging out on purpose. It wasn't easy to detect a fix in a fight, let alone in one that lasted only thirty-five seconds.

The stadium was nearly empty before Cellini finally moved. He said: "Come on. And stick close because there might be trouble."

"Where will I get the two hundred bucks?"

"Right now I'm trying to earn just twenty."

They left the building, walked down an alley to its left and reentered the stadium from the rear. A few fight fans were still in the corridor arguing the night's card.

Cellini decided that he'd let someone else take the chances for twenty dollars and said: "I've got another job for you, Duck-Eye."

"Sure, Cellini."

"I want you to hit somebody when I tell you to and to stop hitting him when I tell you to. Is that clear?"

"Sure." It never occurred to Duck-Eye to question or to doubt his friend.

They walked down the corridor and stopped by a dressing room. Through the half-open door they could see Hank Wheaton buttoning his shirt and they entered. There were three others in the room, watching as the scowling fighter dressed himself. Emphasizing his every word with a cigarette holder, Jerry Lake was talking to Wheaton in a high-pitched, angry voice. A handler, who had seconded the fighter, listened interestedly. The third member was the oversized, unhandsome woman who had escorted the small blonde into the stadium.

Jerry Lake cut himself short and whirled on the intruders. "What are you looking for now, Smith?"

"Don't let me interrupt. Go on with your conversation."

"Is he the guy I hit, Cellini?"

"No, Duck-Eye. I'll designate the right party when the time comes."

The gambler said: "What the hell's the matter with you, Smith? Has everybody gone crazy?"

"What else has gone crazy?" countered Cellini. "The way the fight turned out?"

Lake made no answer. Cellini nodded to Hank Wheaton. "That's the one, Duck-Eye. Try hitting him."

Duck-Eye lumbered forward. The blow he let loose could have flattened a case of K-rations. Hank Wheaton leaped to one side but could not entirely escape the huge fist and he staggered back, tripping over a bench.

Cellini had seen enough. "O.K., Duck-Eye. Let's go."

Duck-Eye said: "I'll kill him. I'll murder the guy. I'll—"

Cellini grabbed the back of his collar. "Stop making speeches. Wheaton's liable to realize he can take you."

Jerry Lake caught up with Cellini Smith and Duck-Eye Ryan in the corridor.

"What was the meaning of that, Smith?"

"I'm trying to earn an honest nickel, Lake. I wanted to find out just how good Hank Wheaton is."

"Did you?"

"Uh-huh. He's slow on the take. Duck-Eye couldn't touch any first-class man with a little speed. Besides, Duck-Eye threw his fist too high, but instead of ducking under it and moving in, Wheaton tried to jump to one side. That's not being bright."

"Go on," said the gambler.

"That's where it stops. I like this kind of thing to be give and take, and you don't give."

"Where do you get that idea?"

"You know damned well," said Cellini impatiently. "I asked you what you were betting on the fight and what the odds were, but you didn't seem interested. Then, a half hour later, I find you in Hank Wheaton's dressing room, reading him the riot act. If you know him that well, you'd know whether to take bets for or against him. What have you got to say to that?"

Jerry Lake had nothing to say to that. He turned on his heels and walked away.

Cellini said: "We'll try it again, Duck-Eye. And try to let me do the talking this time. You just take the beating."

"Sure, Cellini, sure."

There was no need to hunt for Eddy Bly's dressing room, for they could see him coming down the corridor with the small, tightly packed blond number hanging on his arm. The dark, set face was out of place for a fighter who had just won the main bout.

Cellini stepped in front of them. The blonde's eyes gave him a practiced glance. She didn't seem to like what she saw.

Bly said: "All right. I did a great job and I'm terrific. Thanks, and now get out of our way."

"That's not the idea," said Cellini. "My friend here claims he's tougher than you are. Try it again, Duck-Eye."

Cellini got out of the combat area. Automatically, Eddy Bly's arm came up and knocked Duck-Eye's first pass aside. The boxer leaned back against the corridor wall and then bounced forward with a fast, chopping blow. It was a smooth and efficient right that jarred Duck-Eye's huge form down to the patched toes of his socks.

Cellini called: "Cut." He took Duck-Eye's arm and they walked out, leaving the puzzled pair behind.

"I need two hundred bucks," Duck-Eye Ryan said.

"You won't make it with fighting."

They found Dan Turner tallying the night's bets in front of the stadium. When he saw Cellini he said: "You can drop that matter I wrote you about."

"Do you want all the money back?" asked Cellini with obvious sarcasm.

"No. Keep it."

"That's good, because I can tell you it wasn't fixed. Eddy Bly's a good boy. Wheaton doesn't belong in the same ring with him."

"It makes no difference," the gambler said. "I was betting on Bly and I would have been interested only if he lost. Thanks anyway." He nodded and walked away.

Cellini and Duck-Eye headed for the parking lot. They had gone not more than twenty yards when they heard a shot. It came from the direction of the stadium and a moment later they heard a woman's full-lunged scream. It sounded like the big, homely woman.

As Cellini raced back, he wondered why the blond number hadn't uttered a sound, hadn't even moved an eyelid, when Duck-Eye Ryan suddenly threw a punch at Eddy Bly.

CHAPTER TWO
COLD MEAT

ellini Smith, Duck-Eye Ryan behind him, pulled up short at the alley entrance to avoid colliding with a couple hurrying out. The two were Eddy Bly and his blond friend.

Cellini moved next to Duck-Eye to block their exit effectively and asked: "What's the rush?"

"Get out of our way!" Bly's fists were already in position to start swinging.

"Didn't you hear that shot? That was a gun, and that screaming sounded as if someone got in front of it."

"I don't give a damn what it sounded like," said Bly carefully. "Me and the lady are leaving. For the last time, get out of our way."

"You're good, Bly. But you're not good enough to stop the two of us."

There were others who had heard the scream behind Cellini now, trying to get into the back of the stadium.

Eddy Bly surveyed the crowd, shrugged and his arms dropped. "You know who I am and anyone knows where to find me if I'm wanted. I just don't feel like hanging around here."

"Get back in there, Bly. It's a bad time to leave. I'm a private dick and I pack a gun." Cellini didn't add that this was one of the times he had neglected to do so.

For the first time the blonde spoke. She thumbed a carmine fingernail at Cellini and observed: "I don't like that shtoonk." Then she said, "What the hell! Come on," and returned down the alley with Bly.

In the corridor, someone was shouting incoherently into the wall phone. They could make out the words: "Hurt . . . ambulance . . . police . . ."

Cellini shouldered his way through the crowd that overflowed Hank Wheaton's dressing room. The little blonde, who had preceded him, fought her way to the middle of the room with sharp jabs of her elbow. When she got there, she took in the scene at a glance and put her arm around the convulsing shoulders of her large, homely friend.

"Come, Prunella," she said calmly. "You can't help him now. You better sit down."

They moved aside, Cellini took Prunella's place and examined the cause of the commotion. Hank Wheaton had lost for the second time that night. There was no need for an ambulance, for the bullet had been neatly placed, entering behind the fighter's left ear. The body had been raised from the floor and put on a massage table and the onlookers gazed at it more in curiosity than in grief. Prunella's sobs, which punctuated the babble at clock-like intervals, provided the only tragic overtone.

In a knowing, triumphant voice, someone suddenly shouted: "Don't nobody touch anything till the cops get here."

The reminder of the police created a sudden, uncomfortable silence. Cellini knew that within another minute there would be a stampede for the doors. He flagged Duck-Eye and went out into the corridor.

"Have you got any friends around here?"

"Sure, Cellini. There's Sariola. He stopped me in the first round at an Elk smoker. And Rojo, there, fouled me below—"

"O.K. Get a few of them together and tell them to stop this gang from leaving. You take that exit and put someone at the other end. Have a couple of the others keep an eye on the windows."

"This is sure a load offa my mind, Cellini."

"What are you talking about?"

"You got a job now to work on this killing and you'll make the two hundred skins I need for—"

"We'll talk about it later, Duck-Eye. Get busy."

Cellini wondered why he bothered saving

suspects for Homicide. Ira Haenigson would probably answer a call like this and he held no love for Haenigson. It was the Homicide man who had talked up Cellini's drinking at the induction station until they took ulcer-revealing X-rays that barred him from the army.

Cellini returned to the dressing room. The window which fronted on the outside alley was broken. A round hole centered the pane and lines, where the glass had cracked, radiated from it. A couple of splinters of glass lay on the inside window sill. The shade was rolled to the top. From the alley, Wheaton had no doubt been a clear and well-lit target.

Cellini walked outside and headed up the alley. When he was nearly abreast of the late Hank Wheaton's dressing room, he found the object of his search. The gun, a flat .38 automatic, simply lay on the pavement where it had been dropped. The murderer had not even bothered to toss it over the brick wall that sided the alley.

"If the killer was in such a hurry to get rid of that, he's probably still inside there." The voice at Cellini's elbow belonged to Dan Turner.

"I suppose," Cellini replied. "But how did you get out here past the guards I posted?"

"That subnormal friend of yours, Duck-Eye Ryan, let me by. He said it was all right because you were working for me."

"And?"

"And I just wanted to make it clear that you're not." The gambler reached into his flannel jacket for a cigarette case. "You're not working for me, Smith, because I haven't the faintest interest in who killed Wheaton or why."

"So it's as hot as all that," commented Cellini.

The police cars, followed by the wailing ambulance, did not come too soon. Duck-Eye Ryan was having trouble. The men he had chosen to help guard the exits liked the implication that they were on the side of law and authority for a change and they didn't bother being tactful about it. Several men were banding together to rush the guards when Detective-Sergeant Ira

Haenigson strode in with his crew of men from the Homicide Division.

The police, Cellini had to admit, acted swiftly and competently. Within a few minutes, Haenigson had the broader details of the event and he had sifted out those who seemed to have a direct connection with the murder, dismissing the rest to an adjoining room.

A plainclothesman beckoned to Cellini and he entered Hank Wheaton's dressing room. Duck-Eye followed in his faithful fashion. The photographers seemed to be finished, but a couple of fingerprint experts were wandering around with hopeless looks in their eyes. Prunella and her blond friend were still there, as well as Eddy Bly. Jerry Lake was absent but Dan Turner leaned against the wall in his indolent manner and took in the proceedings.

Ira Haenigson waved affably. "It's good to see you, Smith."

"Why?"

The detective-sergeant rubbed his chin thoughtfully. "There must be some reason. I hope you're not still carrying a grudge against me on your notion that I kept you out of the Army. You're over twenty-six anyway, so you wouldn't have made it."

"What do you want?" asked Cellini.

"I want to thank you for posting guards and saving this gang till I got here."

"You're welcome. Shall I leave now?"

"I also want to know whose axe you're grinding."

"Duck-Eye Ryan," said Cellini, "is going to be a father and he needs money—but you wouldn't understand."

"Cut the doubletalk!" The Homicide man's voice became less affable. "Look, Smith, this isn't my birthday and I'd like to know why you went to that trouble for me."

"I like to turn the other cheek, Haenigson. Not the one on my face." Cellini reached into his pocket and pulled out the gun which he had rolled into a handkerchief. "I found this outside the window and picked it up in case someone else took a yen for it. I marked the spot where it was with a pencil."

"Better every minute. This may help a lot." Haenigson passed the automatic to one of his men.

"I doubt it," said Cellini. "This job looks like the work of a cool hand who probably knew it couldn't be traced."

The tall, eagle-beaked girl named Prunella had watched with fascination as the gun was being passed over. She suddenly screamed, "It's your job!" and leaped for Cellini. Her hands caught his left wrist unexpectedly but firmly, her right shoulder went under his left armpit and he found himself sailing through the air to end up against the wall.

The blonde yelled: "Good for you, Pruney!"

Duck-Eye Ryan leaped for Prunella and wound his arms around her. Ira Haenigson began to roar with laughter.

Duck-Eye asked: "Should I hit her?"

"No," said Cellini. He stood up unsteadily.

Prunella was suddenly composed and said to Duck-Eye in a lady-like fashion: "Take your paws off me, you big ape." Then she returned to her seat beside the blonde.

Haenigson's body still shook uncontrollably from laughter and Cellini snapped: "What the hell's so funny?"

The detective-sergeant blew his nose and wiped the tears from his eyes. He turned to Prunella. "That wasn't bad, madam, but would you mind telling me what it's all about?"

She pointed to Cellini. "That last week's garbage did it. He even had the gun."

"Let's start at the beginning. First, would you mind telling me exactly who you two girls are?"

"Do you want our professional names or our real ones?"

"Your professional names?" Haenigson arched an eyebrow.

Eddy Bly was quick to pick it up. "It's not what you think, copper."

"We're wrestlers," said Prunella hotly. She indicated the blonde. "She's known as the Blond Bomber but her real name's Juno Worden. I'm Prunella Wheaton, the—the"—she paused, then remembered the right phrase—"the wife of the deceased."

"Lady wrestlers," murmured Haenigson. "You've been thrown by a professional, Smith, so you don't have to feel so badly. Now, Mrs. Wheaton, do you mind explaining your accusation?"

"That guy had the gun, didn't he? And he was in here before, getting that big baboon to beat up on my husband."

"It was only a friendly experiment like," Duck-Eye explained. "We're working for Mr. Turner and—"

"Nobody's working for Mr. Turner now," provided Dan Turner.

Haenigson threw up his hands. "Shut up, everybody! You, Duck-Eye, get out and find your intellectual equal to explain things to. And don't take away his rattle!"

I ra Haenigson waited till the door had closed on Duck-Eye Ryan, then said: "Now, let's have it, Smith."

Cellini said: "Turner asked me to find out if tonight's bout between Wheaton and Bly was fixed. As you may know, it ended so quickly it was hard to tell, so I came back here and matched Duck-Eye against Wheaton and then Bly. I decided that Wheaton was no good, but Bly was, and I told Turner the brawl was on the level."

"What about it?" asked Haenigson of Turner.

"That's right," said the gambler. "I was taking a lot of bets and didn't want to be caught with the short end."

"What made you think it might be fixed?"

"Just some things I overheard. Nothing to do with the killing. Do you want me any longer?"

"Not right now, but stick around." Haenigson watched Turner leave. The police usually left Turner alone, as he had carefully built up a reputation for honest dealing. The unofficial policy was to allow Turner and others like him to operate, in the open and honestly, in preference to crooked underground activity that could not be watched.

"Is there anything you can add to your statement?" asked the detective-sergeant.

"Very little," Cellini replied. "Maybe you'd like to know that Jerry Lake was in here when I came in with Duck-Eye. Lake wasn't acting too friendly toward Wheaton."

"I would like to know that," Haenigson replied. He nodded to one of his men. "Get Jerry Lake."

When Lake came in, Haenigson asked: "What kind of an argument were you having with Wheaton?"

"I suppose Smith called it that," the gambler said, "but it wasn't an argument. Mrs. Wheaton was here all the time. I was just telling Hank he was asking for a knockout by leaving his chin stuck in the open the way he did."

"Did you lose much on the fight?"

The shrug that Jerry Lake gave tried to indicate that money meant little to him.

"What else, Smith?" asked Haenigson.

"When I went out," Cellini said, "Mrs. Wheaton and Lake were still in here. Eddy Bly and Miss Worden were in the corridor where Duck-Eye and I left them. I was out of the building when I heard the shot about a minute later."

"You didn't leave me anyplace," Juno Worden snapped. "Right after you left I went to the toil—the powder room, so I have an alibi."

"An excellent alibi," was Haenigson's gentlemanly observation to the Blond Bomber. "However, that leaves Eddy Bly in the corridor alone when the shot was fired."

"No, it doesn't," put in the fighter. "Jerry Lake was talking with me just at the time the gun went off, so I couldn't have gone into the alley to do the job—even if I wanted to."

"Did you?"

"Why should I? I took care of him in the ring. Besides, we were old friends."

Haenigson asked of the gambler: "Do you agree to all that?"

"Yes, I do," replied Lake.

"You'd be stupid not to," noted the Homicide man, "because if you claim you were talking with Bly at the right time, out in the corridor, it will not only alibi him, but also yourself."

"Do me and Miss Worden have to stick around here any more?" asked Eddy Bly.

"I suppose not. I'll probably want you again tomorrow."

"You better make it the afternoon. I'll be busy all morning."

"If I want you in the morning you won't be busy."

As Eddy Bly walked out with Juno Worden, he said, over his shoulder: "In the morning I'm burying my sister."

The detective-sergeant gazed speculatively at the closed door and asked: "Who knows anything about that?"

"I do," replied Jerry Lake. "Some hit-and-run driver knocked over his sister. She died this morning."

"When was she run down?" asked Cellini.

"Yesterday, on Wilshire."

"What difference would that make?" asked Haenigson.

"I was wondering how long she was in pain."

"You got a heart as big as all humanity, Smith. Now, suppose you beat it and don't start messing in this case, because as far as I can make out, you're not representing anybody. I'll be quite capable of managing everything."

Cellini said, "Bully for you," and left.

Duck-Eye Ryan was waiting in the corridor. "Cellini, what am I gonna do for that two hundred smackers?"

Cellini said: "I recommend you marry the girl and borrow the money from her."

"It'd be a hell of a life," Duck-Eye Ryan pronounced. "I'm going out to get drunk five bucks' worth."

CHAPTER THREE
CLIENT FOUND

ellini Smith looked at his watch. It was a few minutes after one in the morning, so there was still time before he had to show up for the two-to-eight shift at the aircraft plant in the Valley.

He could make out Dan Turner at the other end of the corridor and decided to try his luck again.

"How'd you get along?" asked the gambler.

"With Haenigson? Fine. We can't stand each other from way back. I don't think Jerry Lake or Eddy Bly approves of me, though."

"I would watch Lake if I were you."

"How about Bly?"

"I don't know much about him," the gambler said.

"I should think you did," Cellini persisted. "You knew enough about him to win a lot of money on his fight."

"I never said I won money on him. I just said I bet on him. Besides, it's none of your business, Smith."

"You're right there. How's your alibi for the killing?"

"I'm not worried."

Cellini gave it up. Turner wasn't using detectives today. He nodded to the gambler and went outside. On the street he paused to light a cigarette.

A figure stepped from the shadows and said: "Hold the match."

As Cellini extended his arm to light the other's cigarette he was wide open for the sudden, unexpected blow. The stranger's right fist caught him on the side of the jaw and sent him sprawling. He leaped up, then stopped short. Maybe it was a pipe that the stranger was pointing through the pocket of his jacket—or maybe it was a gun. It wasn't worth the chance to try and find out.

With an effort, Cellini controlled himself. He rubbed his jaw and looked at the other as if carefully memorizing every line and detail of the hard, shrewd face. Finally, he said: "What was that for?"

"I'm a meanie," replied the other. "I send caterpillars up telephone poles."

"Who are you?" asked Cellini. "I remember the smell but I don't seem to recognize the face."

"Now there's no cause for personalities," said the other. "You can call me Murph. All my friends do."

"I still want to know what this is all about?"

"Oh, it's kind of a message from Jerry Lake. He wants you should be more civil to him."

"What are you, his strong arm?"

"In a way," said Murph. "Lake's made me a sort of vice president in charge of complaints. It makes me feel like a white-collar worker. It—"

"Stop drooling. What does Lake want from me?"

"I don't know. Honest." Murph sounded hurt. "He just told me to take you down a couple of pegs. By the way, I never got that light. Just throw them matches, if you don't mind."

Murph caught the match book and struggled with one hand against his body until he had produced the light. "Thanks, Smith. I guess I'll toddle along. And don't try stopping me, because I can draw this rod real fast."

"It would never occur to me."

"Fine. No hard feelings, is there, Smith?"

"No, Murph, no hard feelings."

"It isn't like I had anything against you, personally, Smith. It's just like I was a surgeon with a job to do."

"I said, no hard feelings."

Cellini watched Murph disappear down the street. The night was cool but he could feel the beads of sweat on his brow. Being thrown at walls by a lady wrestler and hit by a gambler's bodyguard was a little too much to take in one night's work. Certainly too much for a twenty-dollar job with no prospect of more to come. Cellini looked at his watch. It was nearing one-thirty. Maybe, he thought, he'd have a chance to stick around this mess. For one thing, he was anxious to meet Murph again.

Cellini Smith did not reach his office till two the following afternoon. He sorted through his mail with bad humor. He had not had more than two hours of sleep and the events of the preceding night still stung him.

There was the sound of heavy footfalls in the outside hallway and three men entered. The sight of Ira Haenigson did little to make Cellini

feel better. The other two visitors were Boggs, Haenigson's beefy, young assistant, and Dan Turner. They found chairs and ranged themselves in front of the desk.

It was a long moment before the detective-sergeant spoke. "Smith, we haven't got much use for each other but I've had the feeling that each of us respected the other in a way."

Cellini frowned. When Haenigson talked in circles it usually meant trouble.

"That's why," the Homicide man went on, "I'm sorry I have to nail you on a thing like this. I know you, Smith, and I don't trust you too much but I've always felt that there were some things even you wouldn't do. Maybe I never liked the way you did things but you usually did them for the right reasons."

"You give me something to live for, Haenigson. Go on."

"This isn't funny, Smith. If you lose only your license you'll be lucky. Blackmail isn't a minor offense."

"Blackmail?" Cellini looked at each of the faces in front of him and his frown deepened.

Dan Turner said: "Ordinarily, I'd let a thing like this go by—especially with you, Smith—but the deal's too big. In the kind of a spot I'm in, I can't afford it."

"Wait a minute." Cellini enunciated each word carefully, as though he were speaking to children. "This is supposed to have something to do with blackmail. In the first place, what have Haenigson and the Homicide Department got to do with blackmail? In the second place, *what* blackmail?"

"Your letter happens to tie in with the murder of Hank Wheaton," replied the detective-sergeant.

"Now we're getting someplace. *What* letter?"

"Stop playing cat-and-mouse, Smith. Mr. Turner handed it over to me." Haenigson reached into his pocket and tossed a sheet on the desk blotter.

Cellini picked it. It was a piece of his own stationery and bore the preceding day's date. It read:

Dear Dan,

   Apparently, you don't fully appreciate the dangerous position you are in as a result of Hank Wheaton's murder. Your biggest mistake would be not to hire a private operative to watch over your interests. To put it mildly, the police would be very interested to know of your share in the killing.

   Naturally, when I recommend that you hire an operative, I'm thinking of myself but I'm also warning you as an old friend.

Underneath, in its broad, typical lettering, was Cellini Smith's signature. Cellini tossed the letter back.

"It was a little too thick for me to let it pass," said Dan Turner almost apologetically. "I couldn't afford to ignore it."

"That's the first time I've ever seen it," stated Cellini.

"That's your signature, isn't it, Smith?" asked Haenigson.

"I said I never saw it before."

"Your signature and your stationery," the detective-sergeant went on, "and Mr. Turner received it this morning in one of your envelopes. Now, what have you to say."

Cellini said: "Your slip is showing."

aenigson sighed. He nodded to Boggs. The young cop went over to the typewriter, inserted a sheet, typed a few words and then passed the paper over to his chief. Haenigson started comparing the type with that on the note to Turner. Finally, the Homicide man asked: "Have you got another typewriter, Smith?"

"No."

"Well, you didn't type this letter on your machine. That's obvious. Where did you?"

The knuckles on Cellini's hands whitened on the edge of the desk. "Listen carefully, you ani-mated septic tank, because I am repeating for the last time: *I did not write that letter.*"

"That's your signature, isn't it?"

"I don't give a damn what it is!" Cellini grabbed at the letter. The signature, he had to admit, did look like his. He held it up to the light of his desk lamp, and asked: "Do one of you Philo Vances sport a magnifying glass?"

Haenigson shook his head and Boggs said: "Never touch 'em."

"You use reading glasses, don't you, Haenigson? Let's have them."

"Sure, what's mine is yours." The detective-sergeant handed over a pair of spectacles.

Again, Cellini held up the letter to the light and examined the signature, using the lenses as a magnifier. A faint line, cutting into the surface of the paper, could be clearly discerned underneath the inked signature. Ira Haenigson, looking over Cellini's shoulder, whistled softly. "So somebody traced your name."

Cellini Smith leaned back and laughed mirthlessly. There was a moment of uncomfortable silence that was broken by the gambler.

"I'm sorry about all this trouble I made for you, Smith, but you must admit I had no other choice. Do we forget the whole thing?" Dan Turner extended a hand, which Cellini took.

"That goes for me, too," Ira Haenigson said. "When I nail you, Smith, I want it to be on something clean and wholesome like grand larceny—not a chiseling blackmail stunt."

"I'll bet," said Cellini dryly. "Only next time wait till you hear my side of a story before you start licking your chops. All right, we'll forget it but there's something else I want to know. Who faked my name and wrote that letter?"

Dan Turner nodded. "That's what I'd like to know, too. I don't care for its implications. Suppose you try your hand at finding the answers, Smith."

Cellini shook his head. "We can assume that the letter was written by someone closely connected with the killing or by the murderer himself. In that case he wants to involve me in this deal, so I'd be playing into his hands by taking the job."

"It's more likely that he wanted me to go gunning after you, figuring he'd rid himself of two birds with one letter. In any event, I'll give you five hundred dollars now to see how far you can get with this." Turner took out a wallet and counted bills onto the desk.

After a moment of hesitation, Cellini reached for the money. "Whoever sent that letter, Turner, must have known I'd be able to prove it was a fake."

With a casualness that fooled no one, Ira Haenigson said: "Maybe the signature was a fake and the rest of the letter wasn't."

"Meaning," asked the gambler, "that perhaps I did have a share in the killing?"

"That's right, Turner." It was no longer *Mr.* Turner. "Where did you say you were when the shot was fired?"

"In front of the stadium, looking for a cab."

The detective-sergeant tried to look mild and trusting and Cellini snapped: "Stop being clever, Haenigson. It's out of character. You have plenty of others to work on before Turner."

"What others?"

"Eddy Bly and that Blond Bomber of his, Juno Worden, were in a hurry to get away after the shot was fired."

"Bly had to go to his sister's funeral this morning and he didn't feel like staying around. Besides, he was in the corridor when the shot was fired, waiting for the girl to come out of the powder room, and he was talking to Jerry Lake at the time."

Cellini remembered Murph and said: "Lake might be lying."

"Why should he? He's only sticking his own neck out."

"Besides," Dan Turner added, "I happen to know that Jerry Lake was a friend of Hank Wheaton's, so he'd have every reason to help find the killer."

"Then Bly and Lake are in the clear," admitted Cellini, "if all that is so. But that doesn't clear

the girl. Instead of going to the powder room she might have gone around to the alley. And what about Wheaton's handler I saw hanging around there?"

"He's out, too," Haenigson replied. "He was in the middle of a crap game in the back."

"Then that would leave Wheaton's wife, Prunella, alone in the dressing room. The window's on street level and she could have climbed out into the alley, closed the window behind her, shot her husband and then reentered the room the same way and screamed."

"A woman as homely as all that," Haenigson remarked, "would hold on to any husband. Besides, what excuse could she give Wheaton for wanting to go climbing out of windows?"

"Any number of excuses. They probably didn't know why I had been in there with Duck-Eye, so she might have told Wheaton she was going out by way of the alley to follow me and find out."

The detective-sergeant stood up. "All of which leaves us where it finds us. Don't think that five hundred bucks and a client give you the right to pull any fast ones, Smith."

"I won't. What about the gun?"

"You were right there. No fingerprints and it doesn't seem likely that it can be traced." Haenigson lifted himself from the chair, said bitterly: "Nobody's giving me five hundred dollars to work on this case," and stalked out, followed by Boggs.

CHAPTER FOUR
ODDS AND NO ENDS

Hen the door had closed, Cellini Smith reached into a desk drawer and hauled out a bottle of some blended whiskey and two glasses. He poured, gave one of the glasses to Dan Turner and asked: "Was there any truth at all in that letter?"

"I didn't kill Hank Wheaton," said the gambler, "and even if I had, I expect you to play it my way. You're working for me now."

Cellini's grunt was noncommittal. "We'll try it another way. Could you have had any reason or desire to kill Wheaton?"

"Perhaps you didn't hear me, Smith. If you have wax in your ears, don't use a toothpick. The corner of a handkerchief—"

Cellini interrupted: "I'll patronize my corner druggist for such advice. You claim I'm working for you and you've paid for it, so act like it. I've got to get some kind of lead to work on and if you're not willing to cooperate, then—" Cellini caught himself. He had almost offered to return the five hundred.

"All right, Smith. I didn't kill Wheaton and I had nothing against him. Happy?"

"Frightfully. You said, last night, that you bet on Eddy Bly but didn't make any profit. How come?"

"A lot of Wheaton money suddenly showed up and I got scared. I covered my bets and played both sides."

"Where do you think the Wheaton money came from?"

"I'm not sure but I know why it came. Bly's sister was run over by a car and some of the boys must have figured that Bly would be too upset to know what he was doing in the ring."

Cellini poured refills. "But that had nothing to do with your thinking the fight was fixed. You wrote asking me that I check on that two days before the fight, and that was one day before the girl was run over."

"That'll be your headache, Smith. Some friends dropped a few hints and I promised to keep them to myself. It's a matter of keeping my word. I couldn't stay in this racket if I didn't."

"So be it. Do you know a goon called Murph who tags after Jerry Lake?"

"I've seen him around. Lake picked him up a couple of days ago. The idea of having a bodyguard probably builds up his ego."

"And what about this Blond Bomber?" pursued Cellini. "Do you think she might be married to Eddy Bly?"

"No, but she ought to be. She's married to a milquetoast called Forsythe Worden. He's well-named."

"There might be something there. I'd like to meet him."

"He'll probably be over at my house with his wife tomorrow," Turner said.

"I sleep late Sundays."

"This is a party and it'll keep going all afternoon. I throw them occasionally for the gang, to keep up with the latest gossip. If you want to come around, you'll find me in the phone book."

Cellini tried more questions and the answers became progressively less satisfactory. Dan Turner finished his drink and left. Cellini stayed at his desk, stabbing at the blotter with a letter opener. There was no place from which to start, no definite lead from which to work. That was the trouble. The only sure thing was that Duck-Eye could get his two hundred dollars now. He'd first have to know exactly how it would be spent—if he gave it to him.

After a while, Cellini locked the office and went down to his car. None of the bookie joints, gambling places or so-called poker clubs he visited seemed to know or care about who had won or lost on the Bly-Wheaton fight. The back numbers of newspapers, found in a library, revealed only that an eighteen-year-old girl named Jeanette Bly had been run over by a hit-and-run driver near the corner of Wilshire and La Brea. She had died a few hours later in the hospital.

It was nearing six when Cellini Smith entered the Main Street Gymnasium and not many of the boys were around. Someone was sweating over a rowing machine and Duck-Eye Ryan was earning a few cents by sparring with a fighter Cellini didn't recognize. Candido Pastor, one of the better welters, idly skipped rope in one corner. An old man, called Cyclops because of an eye lost in the bare-knuckles days, wandered about under the impression he was tidying the place.

Duck-Eye broke off when he sighted Cellini and hurried over. The big, grooved face wrinkled into a grin.

"I got big news, Cellini."

"What is it?"

"It was a mistake. You know. About what I told you."

"You mean you don't need the two hundred?"

"Uh-huh." The grin spread from one mangled ear to the other.

Cellini's mouth was open for a speech about flowers and bees and social conduct when he decided to postpone it until a more convenient time. Instead, he said: "Climb into your clothes. We're going to a wrestling match."

Duck-Eye lumbered off and Cellini wandered over to Candido Pastor. "Fighting soon, Candy?"

"How'ya, Smith? Next week." His words came brokenly, timed with the steady slap of the rope against the floor.

"What did you think of the Bly-Wheaton brawl last night?"

"Bly has a mean right but I'd like to see him go a few rounds against someone good."

"I thought it was supposed to be a fix, Candy."

The boxer's eyes swept the large loft-like room. The hopping feet didn't miss a beat. "You working on Wheaton's killing, Smith?"

"Something like that, Candy. What about the fix?"

"The fight game's funny," Candido Pastor observed. "You get a guy like Jerry Lake against you and you never get on a decent card again— no matter how good you are." He dropped the rope and moved over to a punching bag.

Cellini didn't feel like shouting to be heard over the rhythmic pounding of the leather and he accepted the not too subtle hint. Besides, he had gained an important item of information. He crossed the room to where the old man was hauling weights into a corner.

"Candy tells me you know about the fix that Jerry Lake made on last night's fight."

Cyclops snorted indignantly through his chew of tobacco. "Candy didn't tell you nothing like that, Mr. Smith."

"That's right. But you do know about the fix."

"Not at these prices, I don't," retorted the old man.

"At what prices do you think you can start remembering?"

The one eye measured Cellini as if trying to divine the contents of his wallet. "Ten bucks is a nice, even figure," he finally said, and added hastily: "Prices are high in everything."

Cellini took the tenner from his wallet but did not give it to Cyclops. "We'll see if it's worth it," he said.

The old man spat tobacco juice on the floor and spread it around with the sole of a shoe. "It's just a few things I picked up around here, Mr. Smith, and I ain't one to talk."

"I'm like Mr. Anthony. You can tell me anything. What gives with Lake?"

"Well, he wanted Wheaton to win."

"Why? Was he betting dough on him?"

"Not too much. I heard tell he was building him up."

"I don't get it. What has Lake got to do with that?"

"He owns Hank Wheaton. Not since Wheaton was killed, I guess, but he owned him before."

"So Jerry Lake was Hank Wheaton's manager," said Cellini softly. "You're doing fine, Cyclops. Now tell me why a smart boy like Lake would try to build up a second-rater like Wheaton."

"Wheaton's record fooled Lake," stated the old man, "so he got him down here from Seattle thinking he had something good."

"And when he found out otherwise," Cellini said, "he decided to fix the fight and save Wheaton's pretty record for a big killing later on."

"A big killing!" chortled Cyclops. "That's a good crack, Mr. Smith. He sure got himself a big killing."

"You ought to see me with my trained seals sometime. Now tell me about the fix, Cyclops."

"That there's kind of funny because I heard they would go fast for the first nine rounds and then Bly would dive in the tenth."

"What's funny about it?"

"It didn't happen, did it?"

"That's what I want to know. Why didn't it?"

"The kind of scum you get nowadays, Mr. Smith, it's even hard to arrange an honest fix." The old man started laughing. "A big killing! That was sure funny, Mr. Smith."

Cellini added another five to the ten and headed for the locker room and the comparatively brighter company of Duck-Eye Ryan.

The matches were already under way when Cellini Smith and Duck-Eye Ryan arrived at the arena. The place was only half-filled but the spectators made up for this deficiency by roaring their approval and providing a continuous stream of comments on the goings-on in the ring.

As Cellini and Duck-Eye leaned over the railing in back of the grandstand to watch, they found those goings-on very strange indeed. Four female wrestlers and a referee crowded the ring. The girls were apparently paired into two teams and they tossed each other around with a zest and gusto that somehow reminded Cellini of a jitterbug jamboree.

"Gee! Four of 'em!" was Duck-Eye's critical comment.

Despite the recent murder of her husband, Prunella Wheaton was meeting her professional obligations tonight. Her role was that of the villainess, for, to the delight of all, she confined her tactics to biting, kicking and gouging of eyes.

A red-head leaped across the ring and delivered a right-hand bar smash to Prunella's midsection. Prunella replied by grabbing a handful of hair and swinging her opponent against a ring

post. The red-head stood up and felt her hair. "You, you dirty thing, you," she sputtered, enraged over the ruin of an expensive permanent. The red-head jumped for Prunella and they tumbled to the mat. Prunella managed to get a choke hold on the other's neck.

The crowd yelled to the referee: "Choke, choke . . . Watch the ugly one, Sam."

Sam bent over to check the hold. Another girl jumped to the wrestler's aid, knocking Sam over, and then the fourth one came in on top of them. Sam crawled out of the tangle of arms and legs and pulled them apart. Prunella grabbed the red-head around the neck while her partner did the same with the fourth one. Then, in a moment of inspiration, they ran forward, bumping the two heads together. The match was over.

Cellini turned to find Murph next to him, leaning against the railing. Cellini produced a thin smile and used it by way of greeting.

Murph said: "Sure there's no hard feelings about last night?"

"No. Your boss here with you?"

"Sure. Lake and me are like two peas in a pod. Whatever a pod is. After this business is over I'll keep working with him."

The next match, between the Blond Bomber and a large girl called Maggie Scott, was announced. Juno Worden, straining against her purple one-piece suit like an overstuffed baloney, drew the usual quota of whistles. The two wrestlers received their instructions, slipped out of the referee's hold and began circling for an opening.

Cellini asked: "After what business is over?"

"After he don't need a bodyguard anymore. I guess I talk too much, don't I, Smith?"

The Blond Bomber was sitting on Maggie Scott's back, rowing back and forth on her right leg in a toe hold. It was a well-rehearsed act.

Murph yelled: "Stick a fishbowl in her hand!" He turned to Cellini. "Production for use. That's what she is. Lake, he's getting interested in that dish."

"I thought Juno was interested in Eddy Bly— not to speak of her husband."

"Nobody ever speaks of him. Lake just hangs around so he'll be handy when she gets tired of Bly. Like she got tired of Wheaton."

Cellini turned from the ring to Murph. "Tired of Wheaton? If that's true, why would Prunella and Juno be good friends?"

Murph shrugged. "Ask her."

"I will," said Cellini, and started to leave. Duck-Eye tore his eyes from the wrestlers and followed reluctantly.

Murph said: "If you don't mind, I'll tag along."

"I don't mind."

"That's good, because I'd come anyway. Lake likes me to keep him informed on what you do. I'm sure glad we let bygones be bygones, Smith." He eyed the mammoth Duck-Eye. "Especially with that guy tailing after you."

They were stopped by a watchman at the entrance leading to the back dressing rooms of the arena. Cellini Smith sent in a note and it was some minutes before Prunella Wheaton appeared. She wore a flowered print dress and hardly looked like a woman who had been widowed twenty-four hours earlier.

Cellini hunted for the proper words of flattery to bestow on a lady wrestler, and said: "That was quite a free-for-all you put on."

"I'm glad you liked it," replied Prunella coldly.

"He didn't say he liked it," Murph noted.

Prunella said, "Shut up," to Murph and, "What do you want?" to Cellini.

"I'm working on your husband's murder, Mrs. Wheaton, and I wonder if you happened to look out of the window just before or after the shot was fired through it."

"I didn't before and when the shot came I ran over to see how badly my husband was hurt. It was my first duty," she added primly.

Cellini decided he might as well ask it. "Do you happen to know of any enemies your husband might have had, any former girl-friends, for example?"

"He had no girl-friends."

Her eyes looked beyond Cellini and he turned around. Juno Worden and Maggie Scott had finished their match and they were coming toward them. A ring robe was draped around the Blond Bomber's shoulders and the powder on her skin was caked by sweat. She stopped by them and nodded pleasantly to Cellini. He wondered if Eddy Bly had told her to change her attitude toward him.

Prunella said: "This guy is trying to find out if Hank had any girl-friends. You tell him."

Juno looked shocked. "That's a hell of a thing to say so soon after the tragedy. Hank and Pruney were an ideal couple."

"Like you and your husband?" asked Cellini.

"Why, you louse!" Juno's body curved into the familiar crouch, ready to leap.

Cellini cautiously stepped to one side. Duck-Eye said: "I'll take care of it, Cellini. *Please* let me take care of it."

Prunella said, "Don't dirty your hands, Juno," and the two of them stalked toward the dressing room.

Murph began to laugh. Cellini regarded him sourly and said: "I could do with a drink. There's a bottle in my car."

"That's what I like to hear, Smith."

Cellini led the way out to the parking lot and to his car. The wrestling matches were still going on and, other than an attendant at the far end, the place was deserted.

"The time has come," said Cellini. He suddenly grabbed Murph's arm, twisted it behind his back and pressed him, with crushing force, over a fender. With his free hand, Cellini reached into a pocket, removed a gun and tossed it to Duck-Eye.

Then he said: "No hard feelings, are there?"

There was a dubious and unsure "No" from Murph.

"That's nice, because I want to see how good you are when you're not asking for a light."

"Good enough for you," said Murph, and suddenly lunged forward.

Cellini took the blow on his forearm and hit

out heavily at the other's heart. They circled cautiously in the restricted area, with Murph's left fist darting out in quick defensive jabs. Murph was fast on his feet and he seemed to know what he was doing.

Cellini side-stepped quickly and his left looped out and caught the other under the ear. Again and again, Cellini tried it until Murph's defense automatically moved higher. Abruptly, Cellini stepped in, feinted at the head, then shifted and delivered a smashing right deep into Murph's stomach. Murph stopped, stood unmoving and a tight-lipped groan escaped him. His arms dropped down and his head was unprotected, virtually inviting a knockout blow. But that was not Cellini's intention.

Cellini's arm lashed out and his knuckles struck down on the other's cheek as if he were splitting wood. Murph fell against the car, blood coming from a wide gash in the face. Then, with a scientific and ruthless precision, Cellini went to work. His blows came slower and more exactly, aimed now at the eyes, now the nose, now the teeth.

Cellini's left hand pressed Murph's chest, steadying him against the car door. The resistance was feeble and Cellini could calculate the probable effect of each blow as with a billiard shot. After a while, his arms began to feel a little tired. Now he was striking at a red, pulpy mess that bore little resemblance to flesh. It felt, to his fists, like the insides of a huge oyster.

Cellini stepped back to observe the artistry of his work and Murph slid to the ground. He said, "Now, there are really no hard feelings."

The car attendant suddenly showed up and began to yell. With his two hands, Duck-Eye Ryan gently lifted him by the waist and set him atop the radiator of an adjoining car. The attendant stopped yelling.

Cellini pushed Murph's inert figure out of the way with his feet. He was feeling hungry. He said: "Let's go out and see if we can find a good steak."

CHAPTER FIVE
DEATH OF THE PARTY

Dan Turner's house, in one of the Hollywood canyons, was large, rambling, Spanish-style. When Cellini Smith drove into the grounds, shortly after four on Sunday afternoon, he could see that the party had been under way for some time. A few guests were having a swimming race in the pool, apparently unaware that it contained no water. Others staggered about or lay asleep in some corner. The guests all seemed to represent a segment—and not the highest—of the sporting world. Duck-Eye Ryan, who had come on the promise of free drinks, wet his lips in happy anticipation.

They left the car, tried to get someone to answer the front door knocker, and finally entered. People were wandering about, drinking, and announcing their views on some phase of sport. Cellini could understand why Turner thought it wise to throw these clambakes every few weeks. Duck-Eye sighted a lonely bottle and made for it.

A small, brunette item yelled, "A man!" and threw her arms around Cellini's neck.

He tried, vainly, to free himself and she said: "I'm Toby but you're sober." She thrust a glass in his hand. "Try this. Good, huh?"

"That stuff could pull a nail out of a board," he replied, but he felt better.

Cellini quickly poured more liquid into his glass and drank it down. He asked: "Where's our host?"

"I thought it was you," replied Toby, her arm tightening around his neck.

He walked into the next room, the girl trailing after him. Prunella, a fixed, bleary smile on her unlovely face, waved at him from the depths of a club chair.

"I saw him first," snapped Toby. "He ain't in public domain."

"You can keep him, dearie. I just want to apologize about yesterday."

"What about it?" asked Cellini.

She emptied her glass before answering. "About me and Hank. It was a lie he had no girl-friends. Me and Hank were finished."

"Was Juno Worden one of his girls?"

"Maybe yes, maybe no. I never bothered to check. Hank said he'd never divorce me if I let him do what he wanted."

"I bet that's a lie," Toby snarled. "She's two-faced and I don't know which one I hate most."

Prunella struggled to get up and at Toby as Dan Turner and Eddy Bly came by. Bly took in the situation, shoved Prunella back and said: "Relax."

"Glad you came, Smith," said Turner. "How's your drink?"

"I wouldn't feed it to a robot."

"You'll get used to it after a while. Or at least you won't care after a while. How's the job coming?"

"I'm still trying to separate the lies from the half-truths. Everybody here or you expecting some more?"

"Everybody except Jerry Lake. He called a little while ago and said he'll be around later."

Eddy Bly said: "Smith, Mr. Turner says I had you tabbed all wrong. Why don't we make up?"

"Good enough." Cellini shook hands. "If you don't mind, we'll have a little talk later."

"Sure," replied Bly with well-restrained enthusiasm. "Any time you want." He nodded and moved off with Turner.

Toby said to Prunella: "Keep your chins up, dearie," and steered Cellini away.

Cellini refilled his glass from a large pitcher, tasted the stuff and gagged. Toby started laughing. "That's grape punch, you man."

"Why didn't you warn me?" He hunted over the sideboard and appropriated a nearly full bottle of bourbon. He raised it to his lips, and drank long and deeply. The party began to seem less dull, the guests much brighter.

A little man, wearing elevator shoes, who had observed Cellini admiringly, said: "I wish I could drink like that."

He was quite drunk and Cellini replied: "You have."

"Not like that. I'm not man enough. I'd choke. I got to mix it with all kinds of things so it shouldn't taste like liquor."

Cellini guessed that this was Forsythe Worden, the Blond Bomber's husband. He liked the wispy, mild-looking character and said: "It's all a matter of how your belly is lined. It has nothing to do with being a man."

Toby said: "Belly ain't a nice word, you wonderful thing. Use tummy. Like in soft under-tummy of Europe."

"You're just trying to make me feel good," said Forsythe Worden. "There are other things." He pointed. "Do you know my wife?"

Cellini looked to see Juno Worden entering with Candy Pastor, their arms hooked in friendly intimacy. She disengaged herself and came over.

"I see you met my loving husband, Smith." Juno giggled and appropriated the drink in her husband's hand.

The intonation of her words sounded ugly and mean and Cellini shivered slightly. "This one's my man," persisted Toby.

Juno said: "Forsythe, watch out what you tell Smith. He's a peeper and he's snooping around on Wheaton's killing."

Forsythe Worden was puzzled. "In that case don't you think we should try to help him?"

"You do as I say."

"He has something there, Juno," observed Cellini. "How about trying to be helpful for a change?"

"Forsythe is a milkhead," said the Blond Bomber. "I'm not trying to hide anything. I just don't want him to go around making up stuff about people."

"What people?"

"I mean generally. Anybody."

"She means nothing of the sort," stated Forsythe Worden. "She probably doesn't want me to tell you about Eddy Bly."

"Forsythe!" Juno's voice was sharp and threatening.

Eddy Bly joined the group. "What's going on here?" His face was flushed and he was drunker than before.

Juno indicated her husband and said: "He's making nasty cracks about you and me."

The fighter laughed. "Well, they're true, aren't they?"

He put his arms around her waist and started to kiss her. After a moment of struggle, she gave in and her arms coiled around his neck. It was a full half minute before they parted and she said: "Maybe they are true."

Forsythe Worden leaped to his feet, trembling. "Do you have to do it in front of everybody?"

Eddy Bly chuckled. "Keep your pants on, half-pint."

With a blind, unreasoning bravery, the little man rushed at the fighter. Eddy Bly barely moved as his right shot out and connected with Worden's jaw. Bly had not bothered to put any power behind the blow but it was enough to drop Forsythe Worden in an unconscious heap. Eddy Bly sighed. He went to the sideboard, got the pitcher of grape punch and poured it over Worden's face. The harassed Filipino houseboy took the pitcher and refilled it. Others in the room had barely given the scene a second glance. They were used to it.

Toby said to Cellini: "I'm tired of watching other people's scandals, you wonderful man. Let's make our own."

Cellini led her back to the first room, where Duck-Eye caressed his bottle in an easy chair. He picked up Toby and set her in Duck-Eye's lap. She sighed contentedly, curled up and immediately went to sleep.

Duck-Eye said: "Thanks a lot, Cellini. When should I return her?"

"Don't bother to. And don't get too drunk."

ellini found Eddy Bly on the back veranda and said: "Did you have to beat up that little guy that way?"

"No, I didn't," replied the fighter, "but I can't be blamed if I forget myself every once in a while. I've just lost a sister and a friend of mine is murdered and then that little mutt that Juno married starts yapping at my heels. I tell you it's too much, Smith."

"Maybe it's too much for him, too," said Cellini coldly. "Juno is his wife—not yours."

"That's just it. I wish she was mine."

"Won't he give her a divorce?"

"I never bothered to find out because it wouldn't make any difference. The trouble is Juno don't want a divorce. I think she likes the idea of being married to him because that way she has more freedom. I like her but I got to admit she's just a tramp." He stared gloomily at nothing.

There was a pause and after a while, Cellini said: "I've been trying to find out about the fix that was supposed to be arranged on your fight with Wheaton."

"What about it?"

"Everything. I'd like to know just what happened."

"Keep this between us, Smith, but after the fight was booked, Wheaton came to me with a proposition and I agreed to throw the fight."

"Why didn't you?"

"I got to know Wheaton better and we became friends and I found out he was a bum fighter, so I told them I wouldn't throw the fight because I didn't want it on my record that I was licked by third-class stuff like Wheaton. That's about all."

"Did Juno Worden go around with Hank Wheaton?"

"That's what I heard, Smith."

Forsythe Worden appeared and leveled a finger at the fighter. "You're just a bum. That's all you are. A bum."

Eddy Bly said: "I think I need a drink." He got up and left.

Cellini asked: "How's your jaw?"

Forsythe Worden sank into an ottoman and began to sob. It lasted for several minutes after which he blew his nose and said: "That's typical of me. I'm not a man. I only wear pants. That's all. But at least I'm not a bum, am I?"

"No," Cellini said, "you're not a bum. And I will tell you something else. You are a man."

Forsythe Worden gazed at Cellini gratefully but said: "We're both a little drunk and you're only trying to make me feel good."

"I don't give a damn how you feel, Worden. I just think you have guts—the real kind of guts, because you haven't got the body to back it up. The other kind, Bly's kind, is easy."

"Thanks. Thanks. Thanks a lot," repeated the little man.

Cellini said: "I also think you know the difference between right and wrong, and it makes me wonder why you ever married Juno."

"I suppose she's no good," Forsythe Worden admitted, "but a man doesn't stop wanting a woman because of that. And I want my wife. I wanted her when I married her and I still want her."

"I could understand that, but why did she marry you?"

"Because I was handy, and she was tired of the small town, and above all, I had money."

"Lots of it?" asked Cellini.

"Comparatively. About twenty thousand. Today I have nothing."

"What happened? Did Juno spend it?"

"Mostly. I lost the last eight thousand on Friday when I bet that Wheaton would beat Bly. Today I have nothing and Juno knows it. I've lost even that hold over her."

Cellini looked at the little man curiously. "Why did you bet dough like that? Did you think it was fixed or did you think Wheaton was better than Bly?"

"Neither one," Forsythe Worden replied. "I happened to be with Jeanette Bly when the accident happened."

"Who's Jeanette? Bly's sister?"

"Yes. A very sweet girl, and no matter what I think of Bly I have to admit he was crazy about her. That's why, after I did what I could for Jeanette, I went down and placed the bet on the fight. I figured Bly would be sure to lose, the way he cared for Jeanette, and I didn't see any harm in making money on it."

"Tell me about the accident," said Cellini.

"There's nothing to it. Jeanette stepped off the curb, near Desmond's, where I took her shopping, and a car knocked her over and didn't stop."

"Did you get a look at the driver?"

"Yes. A very quick look but I think I can recognize him if I ever see him again."

"You're sure you never saw him before?"

"Very sure," said Forsythe Worden.

From inside the house came the voice of the Blond Bomber calling her husband. Meekly, he said, "Yes, dear," and left.

Cellini went back into the house but couldn't find Prunella Wheaton. He mixed himself a triple shot of whiskey and very little soda and went out on the grounds. Prunella wasn't visible there either and he returned to the veranda. Through the window came the sound of angry voices. Cellini walked over to look. Eddy Bly was baiting Forsythe Worden again, as he suggestively stroked the Blond Bomber's neck and shoulders. Juno seemed to be having fun.

The little man screamed: "Can't you go away someplace? Why don't you leave me alone?"

Eddy Bly laughed loud and long. "Tell me what to do, crumb! You can't even hold a woman!"

Forsythe Worden jumped at the fighter. Cellini ran for the door but as he heard the sound of a fist against flesh and bone, he knew he was too late to save the little man from being knocked cold again. When he reached the room, Eddy Bly had already emptied the pitcher of grape punch over Worden's face again.

Bly pushed Juno away, almost as if in disgust, and mixed himself a drink. He saw Cellini and said: "I know, but I can't help it."

"Try that again and Worden's liable to kill you."

Forsythe Worden slowly began to stir. His hands went to his eyes and he rolled over on his stomach. He started moaning and Cellini walked over. There was a peculiar odor in the air.

Candy Pastor said: "He'll be right out of it, Smith."

As consciousness returned fully to Forsythe Worden the moans became louder and gradually turned into screams. Puzzled, Cellini knelt down to examine the little man.

Suddenly, Cellini exclaimed: "Holy mother of hell! Someone grab his legs!"

Candido Pastor came over quickly and did so. Cellini put his hands under the little man's armpits and they rushed him toward a bathroom. Over his shoulder, Cellini called: "Get a doctor!"

With little ceremony, Cellini shoved Worden into the shower stall and turned on the water full blast. Quickly, Cellini ripped away the little man's clothes and sponged water over his face. Now he knew what had happened.

"Get some sodium bicarbonate and make a solution," Cellini snapped. "Maybe it will help till the doctor gets here."

Candy Pastor hurried away. Others, hearing Worden's groans, crowded into the bathroom. Cellini said: "Someone hold his hands down so I can get at him."

The bicarbonate solution arrived and Cellini said to Pastor: "Wash his face with it and wherever the stuff got to him. I have to go down."

Cellini had stood under the shower while working over Worden and was completely and thoroughly drenched. He peeled off his coat, shirt and shoes and spread them on the floor. Then he returned to the room where the trouble had started. Turner, looking angry and baffled, was there talking with Eddy Bly.

"What the hell has happened?" demanded the gambler. "What's going on, Smith?"

"Nothing very pleasant," said Cellini. "Eddy Bly just poured a little grape juice and a pitcherful of what I think is sulphuric acid over Forsythe Worden's face."

CHAPTER SIX
SWANSONG

The boxer strode the room with a pardine lope, drawing deeply and nervously on a cigarette. For the fourth time, he said: "I can't understand it. It doesn't make sense."

"It makes plenty of sense," said Cellini Smith.

"That's right," Dan Turner agreed. "You had a nice little habit of socking Worden and pouring my punch over him to revive him and everyone knew you had that habit. So someone simply emptied a bottle of sulphuric acid into the pitcher of punch and waited for you to get around to having your fun with Worden."

"But why? Why?"

The gambler shrugged. "I paid five hundred dollars to Smith to find out why Wheaton was killed, why a letter was written to me in Smith's name. There are plenty of whys."

"I think we can get around to answering some of them," Cellini said, "but first, what do you know about this?" He held up a bottle. "I found this behind that potted plant there where some grape juice was emptied from the pitcher and replaced with acid from this bottle."

"That's my bottle," said Dan Turner.

"Really? And how come you have a bottle of sulphuric acid in your house?"

"I don't care for your tone of voice, Smith. Change it before I pitch you out of this house."

"Remind me to worry about all that later, Turner. At the moment, my main interest is to find out about the acid bath that was given Forsythe Worden—and I'm staying till I find out. If you have any plans about throwing me out, include Duck-Eye over there."

Duck-Eye Ryan stirred in a corner of the room to indicate his presence. Cellini poured himself another drink. His fingers shook, not from any nervousness but from a cold anger that knotted his insides.

"And Duck-Eye's heeled," Cellini continued. "With Murph's gun. By the way, what happened to Jerry Lake? He was supposed to come."

Turner shrugged. "I'm phoning for the cops."

"I've already done that," said Cellini. "Let's hear about that bottle."

"I do amateur photography as a hobby," the gambler replied. "I have a laboratory downstairs in the basement and I use the acid to tone the film."

"Who knows you have a lab?"

"Pretty near everybody, I guess."

A door opened and the doctor who had come to tend Worden stepped in. The men waited for him to speak.

"He'll be all right now," said the doctor. "Placing him under the shower, as you did, helped a lot. Of course, he'll be blind and scarred the rest of his life, but he'll live."

Turner said: "Thank you. Do you mind staying with him?"

"Not at all, though I've already given him a hypo to let him sleep for a while." The doctor left.

Dan Turner said: "I understand how you feel, Smith. I'd like to know myself who rigged up that punch with acid."

Before Cellini could reply, the door was thrown open and Murph stood on the threshold. It was a Murph with a taped face, puffed, slitted eyes, and swollen, partly open lips.

"Where's Lake?" he demanded. Then he saw Cellini and his hand made for a pocket.

"I wouldn't," snapped Cellini. "Duck-Eye has the drop."

"I sure have," Duck-Eye Ryan agreed amiably from the corner.

"That's O.K. Some other time." Murph spoke with difficulty and his broken teeth caused him to lisp.

Cellini walked over and removed a gun from Murph's pocket.

"Do what you want, Smith. I have plenty of time to take care of you." He turned to the others. "Where's Lake?"

Bly shrugged and Turner asked: "Where is he supposed to be?"

"He said he was coming right in." Murph's voice held a touch of hysteria. "I took the car around to park it and when I come back he wasn't there."

"He's probably out on the grounds some place," said Turner.

"I tell you he ain't. I looked."

"Perhaps he came into the house," Cellini suggested.

"I was here all the time," Bly said. "I would have seen him."

"Maybe he didn't get this far," said Cellini. "Let's look in the front rooms. Lake's whereabouts interest me, too."

They left and circled the front rooms and the main hallway. Their search ended in the telephone closet that was located underneath the stairway.

Crumpled underneath the telephone stand was Jerry Lake's corpse, his head an almost unrecognizable mass of splintered bone. The weapon, a heavy andiron, lay on the floor beside the body.

Detective-Sergeant Ira Haenigson said: "Now we may be able to get someplace." He had thrown open the doors separating the library and living room and had crowded everyone—servants and guests—inside.

Impressively, Haenigson announced: "There's a murderer among you. I've spent an hour listening to your stories and nothing connects. We may stay here all night but I'm going to find out exactly what happened this afternoon. I want to know where each one of you was when Jerry Lake was murdered and what each one of you was doing while sulphuric acid was being added to a pitcher of punch."

"What good will that do?" asked Cellini. "Everybody has been drinking all afternoon and most of them haven't the vaguest idea of what they did— let alone at exactly what time they did it."

"Maybe you know of a better way to get information than by asking questions, Smith."

"I don't need any more information. It's obvious that someone poured acid into that punch in an effort to blind Worden. Forsythe

Worden told me that he was present when Bly's sister was run over and that he'd be able to identify the driver if he ever saw him again. So obviously, the idea was to fix it so that he'd never be able to identify anything again."

"Go on," said Haenigson.

"It all began when Jerry Lake bought the contract of a Seattle fighter with a good record, and booked him to fight here against Bly. When Wheaton came down, Lake found out that he wasn't much good, so he tried to fix the fight with Bly. Lake was trying somehow to save his investment in Wheaton. Bly agreed to take a dive, but when he found out how bad Wheaton really was, he backed out."

"So that's where the sister comes in," murmured Haenigson.

"That's right. You caught it. Lake and Wheaton tried to put pressure on Bly to stick to his agreement and take the dive by threatening to hurt the sister. Bly wouldn't play ball and finally, the day before the fight, they went out to get Jeanette Bly."

"Who are *they*?" asked Haenigson.

"We can find out very simply. We'll bring down Worden and let him identify the person who drove that hit-and-run car. Fortunately his eyes weren't affected by the acid."

"I thought—" Haenigson began.

"That will be the fairest way to do it," interrupted Cellini quickly, "because the person who did that job will probably hang for it." Cellini called upstairs: "You can bring Worden down now."

Cellini turned back and waited as the seconds ticked off. In a little while everyone would realize it was a bluff, that Forsythe Worden would not be coming down, that he would never identify anybody.

Ten seconds of utter stillness had elapsed when suddenly Murph leaped to his feet and cried: "I didn't want to kill her! I swear I didn't! I just wanted to clip her lightly with the fender! Just to warn Bly! I swear that was all I wanted to do."

A stream of oaths came from Eddy Bly and he leaped at Murph. Bly's two hands closed around Murph's neck and slowly forced him to the floor. Murph's arms dropped and his face began to whiten. Boggs and Haenigson bore down on Bly but could not tear his hands away from the throat. Boggs produced a blackjack and brought it down sharply on the back of Bly's head. The fighter sagged to the ground. His hands, however, still clung to Murph's throat and could be pried off only finger by finger.

he Blond Bomber bent over Eddy Bly's unconscious form. "You didn't have to hit him so hard," she snapped.

"I'm sorry, madam," replied Haenigson, "but we have courts to try people and we don't like to have them choked first."

Most of the guests had already left and Turner said to Cellini: "That was good work."

"Yes," agreed Haenigson. "It was a neat way to get the killer to reveal himself."

"What killer are you talking about?" asked Cellini with irritation. "Murph accidentally killed Bly's sister when he just wanted to clip her slightly, but he certainly didn't kill Wheaton or Jerry Lake."

"That's so," considered Ira Haenigson. "I guess he wouldn't kill his own boss."

"There's only one possible answer," said Cellini. "After the girl was run over, Bly quizzed Forsythe Worden on what the driver of the car looked like and he figured out it must have been Murph, acting on orders from Lake and Wheaton. But Bly didn't let anyone know he had figured it out. He was crazy about his sister, so he got hold of a gun and decided to take care of matters himself. The one that Bly figured was most guilty was Hank Wheaton. He chopped him down quickly in the ring and later in the corridor he found his chance when Juno left him alone to go to the powder room. Maybe Bly suggested that her slip was showing or something like that to get her out of there. What was it, Juno?"

The Blond Bomber sat on the floor stroking Eddy Bly's hair. In a low voice she said: "He told me my nose was shiny and to go and fix it."

"Then it was nicely premeditated," Cellini

went on. "Bly simply went into one of the dressing rooms, climbed out of the window into the alley, shot Wheaton and returned to the corridor the same way without having to go out one of the stadium's exits."

The detective-sergeant held up a hand. "Wait a second, Smith. What you forget is that Lake said he was talking with Bly in the corridor when the shot was fired."

"If you remember, Haenigson, that was Bly's suggestion and Lake simply backed up Bly's alibi."

"Why should he back him up?"

"When Wheaton was murdered, Lake knew it was Bly's job because Wheaton had threatened Bly on the score of his sister. Lake knew Bly had murdered Hank Wheaton in revenge for the death of his sister, so he *had* to back up Bly's alibi. Lake could have sent Bly to the chair but, on the other hand, Bly would then have spilled about Lake and Wheaton having Murph run over his sister. So if Lake had refused to back up Bly's alibi it would have been a case of cutting his own throat to fit the collar."

"That makes sense," Haenigson admitted.

"And the rest of it is obvious. Lake chose to alibi Bly and to have Murph guard him night and day. It was a case of two killers knowing the other knew. Today, when Turner mentioned that Lake was coming over here, Bly decided he had to do something. He knew Lake would bring his bodyguard Murph, and that Worden would recognize Murph as the one who had run over his sister. That of course would bust the case wide open and nail him, Bly, on the murder of Wheaton.

"So Bly figured out a way that Forsythe Worden would never recognize anybody. It was his custom to empty a pitcherful on Worden after hitting him, so he thought it safe to fill it with acid. Everybody naturally thought it was a plant by someone trying to frame Bly. When I took Worden up to the showers, Jerry Lake arrived. He went to the telephone closet to make a call and Bly seized the opportunity to put him out of the way. That's about the whole thing."

Prunella Wheaton said: "Thanks, Smith. Hank and me were no longer really married but I'm glad you made it right with him."

"Sure, sure," said Haenigson impatiently. "But what about that letter with your name forged on it, Smith?"

"How should I know?" Cellini suddenly yelled. "I'm no mind-reader. Lake or Bly wrote it thinking they could louse up the case. What's the matter, Haenigson? Aren't you satisfied? Do you want me to go down to the precinct and write it all out for you? I suppose you think five hundred bucks is a lot of money. I take the lumps and the insults and you do all in your power to block me—and then you want to know about a letter." The veins stood out on Cellini's forehead as his fury mounted. "You know where you can stick that letter!" he shouted.

Without another word, Cellini stalked out. As he left, he smiled to himself. He had put on a good act, he thought.

Duck-Eye Ryan caught up with him on the driveway. "Gee, Cellini, you shouldn't get so mad. He just wanted to know about the letter."

"I couldn't tell him," said Cellini Smith, "that I typed the thing out in a telegraph office and then traced my own name because I wanted a job to pay for your wild oats."

The Black Bottle

Whitman Chambers

(ELWYN) WHITMAN CHAMBERS (1896–1968) was born in Stockton, California, and went on to become a prolific pulp story writer, mystery novelist, and screenwriter. Chambers is a member of the hard-boiled, wisecracking school of fiction, and his tone lacked sufficient originality to withstand the passage of time; he is seldom read today, though he is the stylistic equal of some writers whose works have sporadically been reprinted. It is his work as a screenwriter, and the mysteries that served as the source for still other films, for which Chambers will undoubtedly be best remembered. Among his chief works for motion pictures are *The Come On* (1956), based on his 1953 novel, which starred Anne Baxter as a manipulative woman who tries to convince a drifter (Sterling Hayden) to murder her husband. Chambers also wrote the screenplay for *Manhandled* (1949), another film noir starring Sterling Hayden, in which small-time hood Dan Duryea victimizes Dorothy Lamour; in 1960, Chambers wrote the novelization. Also his 1949 screenplay *Special Agent* features William Eythe as an agent for the railroads who goes after two brothers, played by George Reeves (later famous as TV's Superman) and Paul Valentine, who pull a huge payroll heist. His *The Campanile Murders* (1933) was filmed as *Murder on the Campus* (1933); *Murder for a Wanton* (1934) was filmed as *Sinner Take All* (1936); and *Once Too Often* (1938) was filmed as *Blonde Ice* (1948).

"The Black Bottle," his only *Black Mask* story, was published in the April 1936 issue.

The Black Bottle

Whitman Chambers

Three men, a girl, and—the black bottle.

IEUTENANT LARRY McMain came into the wardroom at nine. He dropped wearily into a chair, stretched his long legs with a sigh and sat watching Doc Lucas, who was practicing alone at the billiard table. There was no other person in the room.

It was one of those oppressively humid nights at the beginning of the rainy season, when a man's nerves are raw and there is no relief in sight from the maddening monotony of heat and dampness and deadly routine. It was a night when one thinks anything may happen, and yet knows that nothing will. Larry's face reflected the mood.

"Been dining out?" Doc Lucas asked, swabbing his shining bald head with a handkerchief.

"With the Murdocks . . . Everybody gone to the dance in Colón?"

"Yes." Doc Lucas squinted down his cue, chuckling. "You should be there, Larry. You're not going to let Tommy Glade beat your time with the little Southern girl, are you?"

McMain shrugged broad shoulders. "It's Tommy's last night in Panama. I hope he makes the most of it. He's going north on the S-96, with the Fourth Division, you know."

The pink-cheeked, round little doctor raised his cue and cocked a mild blue eye at the three balls. "Well, that's a break for you, isn't it?"

"I wouldn't say so. Not so long as Benson Clark is on deck."

"Benson Clark. He's the etymologist chap, isn't he? The one who's studying the San Blas Indians."

"He hasn't shown much interest in Indians lately," McMain said irritably. "He's dragging Billie Dean tonight."

"Tommy Glade won't think much of that."

"I don't think much of it myself," the lieutenant growled. "Clark's just a poser with money to spend, and why a girl like Billie Dean should fall for his line of—"

He broke off as a crash of thunder shook the thin walls of the bachelor quarters. Rain pattered briefly on the roof. The moan of the surf, pounding on the other side of the submarine base, came whispering into the room.

"I only hope," McMain muttered, "that Tommy Glade doesn't take it into his head to tangle with Clark. That kid is too damned quick-tempered."

"Yes," Doc agreed. "I heard him having it out with Pete Adams tonight."

"With *Pete!*" McMain sat erect, eying the pudgy little man at the billiard table. "Good Lord, why did he jump on that inoffensive old fellow?"

"Don't know, I'm sure. He had a hot argument with Pete in the pantry and then hustled off ashore."

McMain frowned. "Odd thing for him to do. He's quick on the trigger, all right, but I never knew him to quarrel with a servant. And speaking of servants, how about joining me in a drink?"

"An excellent idea." Doc Lucas racked his cue and waddled around the table. "I'll ring for Pete."

He touched the button on the wall and then came over and sat down beside McMain. Short and pot-bellied, the sixty-year-old medical officer was a sharp contrast to the tall vigorous submarine commander who sat beside him.

McMain leaned back in his chair and tried to relax. A long day in the sub's engine room had left him exhausted, his nerves on edge.

He thought of Billie Dean, cool, fresh and youthful, dancing the night away at the Strangers' Club.

He thought of Benson Clark, handsome, wealthy, dangerous enough to be enchanting to a kid like Billie Dean.

And he thought of Tommy Glade. It wasn't like Tommy to jump on poor Pete Adams, the old wardroom steward.

Again thunder rolled, banging across the sub base. McMain's head jerked.

"You're the last man in the world," Doc remarked very casually, "I'd expect to develop nerves."

McMain shrugged, grunted: "Until tonight I never knew the meaning of nerves. But tonight— Well, it's something I can't put a name to. A tension in the air. But where the devil is Pete?"

"I'll ring again."

Doc Lucas rose and stepped to the button. McMain glanced irritably towards the pantry, and felt his hair stand on end. He was out of his chair in a flash. He caught Doc's arm, whirled him around. He pointed to a shining dark stain on the bare floor next to the pantry door.

"Doc!" he gasped. "That's blood!"

The doctor took a slow deep breath and said calmly: "It certainly looks like blood, Larry."

McMain strode to the pantry and pushed the door. It jammed against something. He threw his shoulder against it and hurled it wide.

"Good Lord, Doc! Look!"

Old Pete Adams lay sprawled face downward on the floor of the little cubby. The negro's white uniform was soaked with blood, which had spread in a wide pool across the floor and under the wardroom door.

Doc Lucas, business-like and outwardly unmoved, bent down and turned the old man on his back. The eyes were wide open, the pupils rolled back until only the whites were visible. Set deeply in the black, contorted face, they were awesome and horrible. The throat had been slit from ear to ear by a long butcher knife which lay beside the body.

Doc Lucas slowly backed from the pantry and stood for a moment looking down at the lifeless old steward.

"I've seen him slice bread with that knife. It has an edge like a razor. Well, Larry"—the doctor's voice became brisker—"this is a matter for the commandant. Close the pantry, will you?"

McMain pulled the door shut and, turning, saw that Doc Lucas had sat down at the telephone stand.

"Wait a minute, Doc!" he blurted. "Look here! You mentioned an argument between Pete and Tommy Glade."

Doc Lucas nodded placidly.

"When was it?" McMain demanded.

"Oh, perhaps half an hour ago."

"What were they quarreling about?"

"I don't know. I was on the other side of the room here, practicing billiards."

McMain's dark eyes were bleak. "Doc, have you got the idea that Tommy Glade killed that poor devil?"

"It looks that way," the doctor calmly admitted.

McMain, glaring, took a step towards the round little man. "Doc, you're crazy!" he snapped. "Tommy Glade has been under my command for six years. I never knew a finer—"

"Now see here, Larry," Doc Lucas interrupted. "I haven't been out of this room for two hours. The last person to go into the pantry was Tommy Glade, and I tell you frankly he had blood in his eye. The last person to see Pete Adams alive was, so far as I know, Tommy Glade.

"Stop and think a minute. The lone window in the pantry is screened and perhaps you noticed that the screen hasn't been cut or tampered with. There is no other entrance but that door. Now! If Tommy Glade didn't kill old Pete—" Doc Lucas paused pointedly. . . . "Well?"

"Pete killed himself."

"Exactly. One or the other. Now I'll have to phone the commandant."

The doctor picked up the telephone. McMain stood indecisively for a moment. Then he turned and hurried into the passageway and down it to his own quarters. Feverishly throwing off his clothes, he took a quick shower. Within five minutes, dressed now in neat and freshly pressed linen cits, he was back in the wardroom.

"I'm going ashore," he said crisply.

The doctor shrugged. "Suit yourself. Personally, I think you ought to keep out of it. There is something, Larry, damned peculiar about this whole affair. I sensed it first tonight when we were talking about Tommy Glade, and this Benson Clark fellow and Billie Dean."

"Oh, yes? Why drag Billie into it? Or Clark, for that matter?"

Doc Lucas smiled gently. "Or Tommy. Well, call it a hunch."

McMain turned towards the outer door. Then he stopped and again faced the doctor. "What did you tell the Old Man?"

"I didn't get him. He's at some affair in Balboa. I notified the executive officer and he's on his way over here. We'll take care of the body."

"Chuck Dean is acting exec."

"I know. Billie's brother. What of it?"

"Look here!" McMain took a nervous step or two towards the doctor. "How about soft-pedaling this quarrel between Tommy Glade and Pete? Why spill it to Chuck? Why not wait till the skipper gets back? Better yet, wait till tomorrow. You can't do much tonight, anyway. And maybe after I've seen Tommy, we'll have some sort of a lead." McMain paused, breathless. "Well, how about it?"

Doc Lucas, his eyes half closed, asked slowly: "Are you taking the responsibility for investigating this murder?"

"Isn't it my duty, as senior line officer quartered in the wardroom?"

"I imagine it is," Doc Lucas said thoughtfully. "I imagine, in a case of this sort, a line officer ranks a staff officer."

"Do you want the job?" McMain asked flatly.

"I do not."

"Very well. Then leave it in my hands."

McMain strode out of the wardroom into the humid, oppressive night. Walking around the building to the officers' garage, where he kept his car, he regretted that he had been so downright short to Doc Lucas. He was too keyed up, however, to worry about it.

Where would this thing lead? Tommy Glade implicated in the murder of an obscure wardroom servant? That was nonsense!

Billie Dean involved? And Benson Clark? Absurd! The only possible connection was in his own mind, in associating Glade with Billie and Clark.

II

cMain parked his car in the driveway in front of the Strangers' Club and climbed the stairs to the hall on the second floor. A dance had just ended. He singled out Billie Dean and Benson Clark almost immediately. They were walking towards a table in the dimness of the far corner. Tommy Glade, the lieutenant reflected, would not be far away.

McMain strolled over to their table. There were three empty glasses on it. Three! Where was Tommy Glade?

"Good evening, Billie," he said. "How are you, Clark?"

Billie's eyes lighted as she smiled at him. "Hello, Larry. You're lookin' warm. Been dancin'?"

Her low-pitched, lazy Southern drawl was as calming and caressing as a cool breeze.

"No, I just got here."

Clark had risen, but he did not offer his hand. He was a tall, muscular man of thirty-five; he carried himself, he moved, with a studied grace and poise. His blond hair was brushed back from his high forehead in a nice wave. With his strong, cleft chin, his regular features, he was just a bit too handsome to be human.

"Good evening, McMain," he said crisply, and sat down again.

Where, the lieutenant asked himself, was Clark's usual, well-known courtesy? Even in the dim light McMain could see that the man's face was sharply drawn, his eyes restless. Had he, too, developed nerves on this hot and humid night? . . . Where was Tommy Glade?

"Are you with a party?" Billie asked.

"No. I'm on my own tonight."

Billie looked at Clark and the latter, with an almost imperceptible shrug, said gracelessly:

"Sit down and have a drink with us, McMain."

"Thanks, I will. Beer for me."

He sat down, feeling uncomfortable over the way he had forced himself on them. Clark gave an order to the waiter.

"Has Tommy Glade been around?" McMain asked casually.

"Tommy was here when we got up to dance," Billie said. "I reckon he's around some place. Down at the bar, perhaps."

McMain turned to Clark. "How are the Indian studies coming along?"

Clark stirred himself with an effort. "Not so well," he said, and blew a smoke ring towards the ceiling. "I've been pretty busy here in Colón."

McMain looked at Billie Dean and saw that her eyes, usually placid, were dancing with excitement.

"Are you holding something out on me, Billie?"

The girl asked breathlessly, "Haven't you heard the rumors about Mr. Clark?"

"Rumors about Mr. Clark?" McMain repeated. He had heard rumors, but they were hardly the kind to be discussed in mixed company.

Billie leaned across the table. "Mr. Clark isn't an etymologist at all," she whispered. "He doesn't really give a darn about those Indians he visits down there in his yawl. Actually, he's a Secret Service operative."

Clark's smile was patronizing. "According to rumor, my dear," he corrected.

"Isn't it thrilling?" Billie asked.

"Yes. Very thrilling." It didn't sound thrilling at all to McMain; it sounded impossible. "Where do you suppose Tommy Glade is keeping himself?"

"Are you ridin' herd on Tommy tonight?" Billie asked. "Because if you are, I reckon you'll have a job on your hands. He took two drinks with us and seemed quite tight."

"If he's tight, it will be the first time in the six years I've known him."

"What a model young man," Clark said dryly.

Billie Dean looked sharply at her escort; she frowned and the color rose in her cheeks.

The drinks arrived. They drank them in silence, under a pall of dissonance that was in sharp contrast to the gay chatter of the surrounding tables. The music started again and McMain stood up.

"Like to dance, Billie?"

He was conscious that Clark sat glaring at him as he swung the girl out onto the floor. They danced for a moment in silence.

"Larry!" the girl said abruptly.

McMain looked down at the shining black head nestled against his shoulder. "Yes?"

"What's wrong with Tommy tonight?"

McMain's heart skipped a beat. "Nothing that I know of. Why?"

"There's something wrong with him. I felt it."

"You said he was tight."

"That was just talk," Billie said. "He wasn't tight. He was—strange."

"How do you mean strange?"

"Well, it's hard to explain exactly. You know how he's always jokin' and kiddin'. Tonight he acted as though he carried all the troubles of the world on his shoulders."

"He's leaving for Boston tomorrow and he doesn't want to go."

"It isn't that. Tommy wouldn't whine over a transfer. It was something deeper." She leaned back and gazed up into his face with troubled gray eyes. "Larry, why are you lookin' for Tommy?"

"I can't tell you," McMain said stubbornly.

"Why cain't you tell me? Is—is it so serious?"

"It's damned serious, Billie."

"But what—"

They paused by common accord. There was a commotion down the hall, near the balcony which overlooked the bay. Everyone at that end of the floor had stopped dancing.

McMain saw Cal Clemens, one of the supply officers from the base, bearing down on him. Cal's face was dead white and he was shouting:

"Larry! Oh, Larry! Come here, will you?"

McMain's heart sank with a dread foreboding. "You'll have to excuse me, Billie," he said crisply. "Come! I'll take you back to your table."

He took her arm and started rapidly with her across the hall. "You stay with Clark. I'll be back."

He shoved her towards the table, turned and hurried over to Cal Clemens.

"What's wrong, Cal?"

"It's Tommy Glade." Cal's face was beaded with sweat.

"What about him?" McMain snapped.

"He's out there on the balcony," Cal said, "hanging over the rail."

"Good Lord!" McMain exclaimed in disgust. "Why all the fuss? Can't a man get drunk and—"

"He isn't drunk, Larry." Cal gulped. "He—he's *dead*!"

III

By the time McMain got out to the balcony, someone had lifted Tommy Glade off the railing and laid him on his back. McMain dropped to his knees, jerked a flashlight from the hand of a frightened waiter and shone the beam on Tommy's face.

The ensign's mouth was contorted. His plump cheeks were blue-black, his eyes staring and glazed. McMain scanned the circle of men who had gathered on the balcony, barked hoarsely:

"Who found him?"

"Hi did, sar," the waiter said, speaking with the unexpected British accent of the Barbados negro. "Hi see 'im 'anging there over the rail. First Hi think 'e's sick and Hi go over to give 'im a 'and. But he ain't sick, sar. 'E's dead."

McMain got to his feet. What an end for cheerful, happy-go-lucky Tommy Glade! Doubled over a railing on the balcony of the Strangers' Club, like any common drunk. Dying there. Dying alone and in agony.

Cal Clemens elbowed his way to McMain's side. "What do you think, Larry? Did he have a bad heart?"

"His heart was all right."

"But there doesn't seem to be a wound. Good Lord, man, what could have killed him?"

"Only an autopsy will determine that."

"You—you think—he killed himself?" Clemens asked.

"Not in a million years. Tommy Glade was murdered."

"Murdered! But—"

"Now see here, Cal! I'm going back to the base. This thing happened in Panama and the Colón police will have to take over. Call them, will you?"

"Okey, Larry."

McMain pushed through the hushed throng and made his way onto the dance floor. The music had stopped now and everyone was standing around, looking towards the balcony, talking in low tones. Clark and Billie Dean were not in the hall.

McMain ran down the stairs two at a time, leaped into his car and drove swiftly back to Coco Solo. At the entrance of the military reservation, where he pulled up at the sentry box, he asked:

"Did Lieutenant Dean's sister just go by in a car?"

"About two minutes ago, sir," the marine sentry told him.

"Who was with her?"

"There was a tall guy, some civilian, in the back seat and a native chauffeur driving. It was a black Cad touring car, sir."

McMain put his car in gear and drove on to the wardroom, shut off his motor and lights, and went inside.

Doc Lucas was gone. McMain glanced at the board beside the door and saw the doctor's peg had been shoved into the "sick bay" hole. Emergency call, probably, and every other doctor on the base ashore.

McMain walked over to the pantry and glanced inside. Pete Adams' body had been removed and the blood mopped up. He closed the door and walked down the corridor. Passing his own room, he went on to the end of the passage and paused before Tommy Glade's.

The key, he noted, was on the outside of the door. McMain turned the knob and stepped inside. The odor of some exotic perfume, so strong as to be almost stifling, smote his nostrils as he groped for the light switch, found it and snapped on the lights.

He heard a gasp before he saw the slim girl in the pale green dress. She was standing on the other side of the room, one hand at her breast, the other resting on a square black bottle which stood on the table in the corner. She was breathing fast and her gray eyes were frightened.

"What in hell!" McMain cried.

Billie dropped her gaze, but did not speak.

The lieutenant glanced around swiftly. Save for a heavy trunk which stood beside the bed, a few toilet articles on the chiffonier, the room was bare of Tommy's belongings.

McMain looked back at Billie. "For God's sake, girl, what's this all about? You rush away from the club the instant you hear Tommy's dead. You tear out here with Clark. And now I find you rifling Tommy's room. Are you, by any chance, a Secret Service operative, too?"

Her laugh was forced. "No, I'm just a member of the Ladies' Auxiliary." The attempt at humor was flat; humor was out of tune with the tragedy in her eyes.

McMain sighed and sat down on the edge of the bed. "Oh, hell!" he groaned. "Let's not try to be funny. What are you doing here, Billie?"

She came towards him, carrying the black

bottle in her right hand. Pausing at the foot of the bed, she pleaded:

"Won't you please not ask me that question? Won't you please let me go away from here and forget you ever saw me?"

"You know I can't do that," McMain said unhappily.

She met his eyes and then looked away. "And two weeks ago, that night drivin' home from the club, you told me you loved me."

"You're not being fair, Billie. Whether or not I love you doesn't enter this mess at all. Two men have been murdered tonight and—"

"Two!" the girl cried.

"We found Pete Adams in the pantry a while ago with his throat cut."

"Pete Adams!"

"Our old wardroom steward."

"Yes, I know." She stood there staring at him, her lips parted, her shining dark hair wind-blown and awry.

"What, precisely, do you know?" McMain asked gently.

"I know it all fits."

"*What* fits?"

"Don't you know?" Billie countered.

"I haven't the faintest idea. Can you tell me?" His voice was mild, patient. "Can you tell me why Pete's throat was cut? Can you tell me why that fine young officer was murdered? And how?"

"Tommy," she said, her voice trembling, "killed himself."

"How?"

"I—I think—he drank poison."

"Tommy Glade?" McMain shook his head. "No. Tommy Glade was a man. If he wanted to go out, he'd choose a man's way. He wouldn't drink poison at the Strangers' Club. He'd come here to his room and blow his brains out with a service .45."

"Don't! Don't!" Billie begged.

McMain tried a new tack. "Is that alleged Secret Service man waiting for you outside? Around the corner of the building where I didn't see him when I drove up?"

"Mr. Clark brought me over and then went back to town," Billie answered quickly—too quickly.

"And you had time, after he brought you home, to walk over here?" he asked skeptically. When he received no answer his eyes shifted to the square bottle. "What have you there?"

"A bottle of perfume."

"The perfume that's so rank in this room?"

"Yes."

"Then you opened it?"

"Yes."

McMain saw that the glass stopper was sealed with a heavy coating of wax. "Then how did you seal it up again? And why?"

She lifted the black bottle, staring in surprise at the wax around its neck.

McMain did not wait for an answer to his questions. His voice, now, was not so gentle. He was prodding himself, forcing himself to be hard. "Why did you open it in the first place? . . . Did you sprinkle it around the room? . . . If you did, *why?*"

The girl breathed heavily; her eyes were like a cornered animal's. She screamed suddenly:

"*Please!* Let me alone! I won't listen to you any longer. I won't answer your questions. I *won't!*"

Her eyes met his for a brief moment. Then, before he realized her intention, she had leaped towards him. Her open left hand, the whole weight of her body behind it, struck him in the face and bowled him over backwards on the bed.

By the time he gained his balance and got to his feet, the door was slamming behind her. He heard the lock snap home and then the patter of her footsteps running down the passageway.

A hurt, regretful smile twisted his lips. Then, with a quiet shrug, he switched off the lights and went to the window. He heard the outer door of the wardroom slam and a moment later the low purr of a powerful car.

Not until then did he release the screen and hop over the sill. Running around the building, he was just in time to see Clark's black touring car swing onto the concrete of the base's main street, heading towards Colón. McMain went back into the wardroom, picked up the telephone and called the sentry box at the gate.

"Lieutenant McMain speaking. That big Cad with Miss Dean is on its way up. Stop it. Close your gates and stop it if you have to use your rifle. Got that?"

"I got it, sir."

McMain put the telephone back on the stand. He was still smiling that twisted, regretful smile, but with his lips alone. His dark eyes were hard.

IV

cMain went out to his car and drove to the Deans' quarters. He found Chuck Dean, his wife and the Mayers in a bridge game. He greeted them, said briefly:

"Sorry to break up your game, but I'll have to see you for a few minutes, Chuck."

Chuck, a lanky, blond six-footer, rose from the table. He got his cap and followed McMain out of the house, down the stairs and to the small roadster.

"What's it all about, Larry? Pete Adams?"

"That's the beginning of it," McMain acknowledged, and briefly sketched the night's events.

"Good Lawd, I cain't understand it!" Chuck Dean said dazedly at last. "Billie has always been adventurous, reckless you might say, but getting involved in a thing like this— Why do you suppose she wanted that bottle of perfume? She must have got it for Clark. But why didn't he do his own dirty work?"

"He'd need her with him to get onto the base after nine o'clock."

"But after he was here, why didn't he drop her at home and go back to the wardroom himself? Why did he have to drag her into this?"

McMain said quietly: "Chuck, she was in it already."

"My sister?" Chuck raged. Then he caught

himself, asked more calmly: "You say this fellow is a Secret Service man?"

"Billie believes he is and he doesn't deny it. Personally, I think he started the rumor himself as a blind."

Chuck thought about that for a moment or two, while he nervously coiled and uncoiled his long legs. "And Tommy's room, you say, was rank with perfume?"

"Terrible. And yet the cork wasn't out of the bottle."

"Then where did the smell of perfume come from?"

"I didn't take time to investigate."

Chuck Dean sighed heavily. "Well, I reckon we better round up Billie and that Clark fella and see what they have to say."

"Right."

McMain drove through the silent base and down the road to the sentry box.

"Good Lawd!" Chuck Dean exclaimed. "Look at that gate!"

The double gate was a mass of twisted steel, folded outward. The marine guard came over, uncomfortably at attention.

"I'm sorry, Mr. McMain. I stopped 'em and told 'em they couldn't go through. They argued a little, and then the driver threw his car into gear and—blooey!—bang through the gate he went."

"You're a hell of a sentry!" McMain snorted. "Did you fire at the car?"

"No, sir. I was afraid I might hit Miss Dean. And I didn't like to take the chance, sir, just because of an elopement."

"Elopement!"

"Sure. Didn't you know, sir? They were eloping. Miss Dean and the big guy. He told me."

McMain viciously jerked his car into motion, shoved the gears into high, and shot down the road.

"Now what?" Chuck Dean asked.

"We have to find Clark's car."

McMain jammed the accelerator to the floorboard. The white ribbon of concrete, the black jungle on either side of the road, shot past at seventy miles an hour.

Suddenly Chuck Dean cried: "Hold her, Larry!"

McMain came down on his brake. "What was it?"

"Body, looked like. Back there beside the road."

"Not—"

"No. A man. Reckon you better come about, fella."

McMain cramped his wheel and swung the car around with its tires screaming. "Good God! This gets worse all the time. Where'd you see that body? Which side of the road?"

"My side comin' in. Your side now. Wait! There it is. See it?"

McMain drew up at the edge of the concrete. The body of a man, crumpled as though it had been hurled from an automobile, lay in the lush grass which bordered the highway. McMain and Dean piled out of the car and, in the glow of the headlights, turned the body over.

"Clark's chauffeur," McMain said laconically.

"You know him?"

"I've seen him around."

The man's face was bloody and caked with mud. He had been shot. The bullet had gone into his right temple at the height of the eye, passed through his head and come out at almost the same location on the left side.

"Must have died instantly, poor devil," McMain muttered. "Well, we'd better hit for town, report this to the police and get their help in finding Clark's car. Come on."

McMain had turned to the car when Dean caught him by the arm, almost jerking him off his feet.

"Good Lawd, Larry! He—he moved!"

"Nonsense. The man's dead as a mackerel."

"No! Wait!"

Dean dropped to his knees beside the chauffeur. He unbuttoned the man's coat with shaking fingers. Tearing the shirt open, he dropped his ear to the bared breast. He listened for a moment, and then sat up abruptly.

"By heaven, Larry. He's alive!"

"With a bullet through his brain?"

"I don't give a damn," Chuck stormed, "whether he has a bullet through his brain or not. The man's alive and his heart is strong. And we cain't leave the poor devil here to bleed to death."

"Then we'll have to take him to the sick bay at the base. I hate to waste time going back, but there's nothing else to do. Get hold of his feet."

The chauffeur was a slight man; they had no difficulty in lifting him into the car. Then, with Dean standing on the running-board holding the unconscious man erect, McMain drove back to the sub base and to the sick bay. There they found Doc Lucas, who, taking one look at the man, said crisply:

"It's a miracle, but not without precedent. Carry him into the operating room."

McMain and Dean carried him in and left him there. They were in too much of a hurry to make explanations and the doctor, for a time, was too busy to listen to them.

At police headquarters in Colón, a large and dingy room through which passed the cosmopolitan port's nightly stream of drunks and brawlers, they found the desk sergeant.

McMain introduced Chuck and himself. "Anything new on that death at the Strangers' Club?"

The harassed, sweating sergeant shrugged lean shoulders. "My men report, gentlemen, that the young officer took poison because a lady spurned him. A most unfortunate affair. I have ordered an autopsy performed. After that we shall hold an inquest. And then the body will be turned over to the naval authorities."

"And meanwhile whoever killed him has plenty of time to cover his tracks." McMain snorted.

"But the young officer killed himself," the sergeant insisted.

"Skip it," McMain retorted. "See here! I need your help in finding a Cad touring car. It's painted black and the radiator is probably caved in. Know anything about it?"

"Certainly. Such a car has been found, just as you describe. It was deserted. There was blood on the front seat. It is at the entrance of Pier 4."

McMain caught Dean by the arm and dashed into the street. "Clark keeps his yawl at Pier 4. There may be time yet to intercept them."

"His yawl!"

"The *Thelma.* The boat he uses to cruise the San Blas Islands. I should have thought of it before, but I never figured he was set for such a fast getaway."

They found the damaged car at the entrance of Pier 4. The *Thelma*, Clark's trim white fifty-footer, was gone.

"He must have had her all ready to shove off," McMain said helplessly.

"And that trip we made back to the sick bay gave him the time he needed to get away."

The two men turned and, heavy-footed, walked slowly back to the car. Misery and bewilderment had acted like a poison on McMain's brain. He had stopped thinking, but he couldn't stop the round of questions that kept turning over and over in his mind.

What was the meaning of all this insanity? Why had old Pete been murdered? Why had Tommy Glade been killed? What was in the black bottle? Why did Clark shoot his chauffeur? Where did Billie tie into the picture?

"It's a hell of a puzzle," he remarked finally, with a slow and regretful shake of his head. "And I'm afraid the end, Chuck, won't be pleasant. A woman, you know, doesn't go kiting around the country with a man, burglarizing rooms for him—unless—"

"Yes," Chuck prompted dully.

"Unless she *wants* to do those things," McMain finished with an effort. "When you consider the foray those two have been on, you've got to admit coercion was out of the question."

Chuck's lips were twisted; sad-eyed, he nodded in silence.

V

huck Dean and McMain drove back to the submarine base in the drenching rain.

"Clark's chauffeur may be able to tell us something," Larry remarked after a while, and added hopelessly: "If he ever regains consciousness."

"But not even he, prob'ly, will be able to tell us why Billie is messed up in it."

McMain slowed for the turn at the entrance of the military reservation. He began quietly: "If she's in love with Clark—"

"But she's not in love with Clark," Chuck declared.

"She's told you?" McMain asked.

"A dozen times. She doesn't love Clark. She didn't love Tommy Glade. She loves you! And if you hadn't been such a sap, you'd have known it and asked her to marry you months ago. . . . Oh, don't start makin' excuses. I understand your position. You were afraid she'd turn you down, and because of your silly pride, you wouldn't give her a chance."

McMain drew up before the sick bay and Dean ran inside. He came back in a moment, reporting that Doc Lucas had finished there and gone to the wardroom. They drove to the bachelor quarters and found Doc in his room getting ready for bed.

"Is that fellow going to live?" McMain asked without preamble.

Doc, a bit ludicrous in undershirt and shorts, nodded and said: "Without a doubt."

"With a bullet through his brain?"

"The bullet didn't touch the brain. It passed through the retrobulbar space, which is an area of fatty tissue behind the eyeballs. If a bullet goes through it, without touching the optic nerves, the patient usually suffers no permanent ill effects."

"Has this fellow regained consciousness yet?"

"More or less. He's still groggy."

"Can he talk?"

"He can, but I won't let you two men put him

through any third degree. He's lost a lot of blood and must have absolute rest. Who the devil is he, anyway?"

"Benson Clark's chauffeur," McMain replied.

"H-m." Doc Lucas regarded the two men with narrowed eyes. "What's happened?"

"Plenty. Tommy Glade killed himself—or was murdered—at the Strangers' Club."

Doc looked at Chuck Dean. "Not over—"

Chuck said unhappily: "I reckon Billie is mixed up in it. Tell him, Larry."

McMain sketched briefly the night's happenings.

"Strange about that perfume," the doctor mused when McMain had finished. "Tommy Glade bought one of those square black bottles this afternoon to take to his sister up North. And he happened to mention to me that old Pete Adams had given him a bottle of the same perfume to mail, when he got to New York, to Pete's daughter in Harlem."

McMain sat down on the edge of the bed and lit a cigarette. "I'm beginning to see a few things," he said thoughtfully. "You know, the good-hearted naval officer who smuggles dutiable goods into the States, in order to do some friend a favor, is pretty much of a damned fool . . . See here, Doc. This chauffeur's got to talk and he's got to talk quick."

"Tell you what I'll do," Doc offered. "I'll go over to the sick bay and ask him a few questions. I know the situation pretty well from what you've told me and I may be able to get something out of him."

"Good!" McMain said. "You don't have to endanger the man's life, but make him talk if you can. Chuck, let's see what we can find in Tommy Glade's quarters."

Tommy Glade's room still smelled of perfume.

"Where in the Lawd's name does it come from?" Chuck muttered. "If Billie took the bottle—"

McMain gave the room and its scanty furnishings a swift survey. Then he grunted and pointed to a large irregular stain on the bare floor beside the heavy trunk.

"Never noticed it when I was in here before. Doc told us there were two bottles. And that's where one of 'em went."

McMain strode briskly to the metal wastebasket beside the small bare desk and hauled out a crumpled roll of damp paper. He smelled it, made a face and said:

"Whew! Here's the wrapper. Tommy evidently broke the bottle."

He spread the paper on the desk and smoothed out the wrinkles. He turned it over and found an address. The ink had run badly but he and Dean could decipher a box number, a station number and "New York, N.Y."

"The bottle which Pete Adams gave Tommy," McMain asserted, "was wrapped in this paper. You note, Chuck, there is no 'U.S.A.' in the address. That means Pete expected Tommy to mail it after he got up North—without the formality of a customs examination. Mailing it in the States would have saved Pete four or five dollars' duty."

Chuck took off his cap and scratched his head. He looked tired and baffled and disheartened. "But where are the pieces of the bottle?"

McMain started through the chiffonier. From the back of the bottom drawer he dragged forth a small parcel wrapped carelessly in newspaper. He took it to the desk and opened it, revealing a double handful of broken black glass.

"The pieces of the bottle!" Dean exclaimed. "Now why did he save pieces of—"

"Good Lord! Look!" McMain gasped.

He pointed a shaking finger at a gleaming object that, plainly, was *not* glass.

"A diamond!" Chuck Dean said in a dazed whisper.

McMain cried: "Why, there's dozens of 'em!" He pawed through the pile of glass, spreading it over the newspaper. "And look at that. A ruby!"

"And that green one there! It's an emerald!"

For the space of half a minute the two officers pawed over the jumble of glass and precious stones.

"See here, Chuck," McMain said at last. "These stones represent a small fortune."

"Yes, I reckon they do. And Tommy Glade was supposed to smuggle 'em into the States. . . . Damn it, Larry. I cain't understand how a fine young man like Tommy Glade could have been messin' in a smugglin' plot."

McMain groaned. "Oh, you damned fool, don't be so dumb!" he raged. "Don't you get the picture? Tommy was the innocent go-between."

"We-e-ell," Chuck stammered. "I—I cain't see—"

McMain caught him by the shoulder, shook him angrily. "Tommy, I tell you, was not in on this plot. Pete Adams gave him the bottle of perfume and asked him, as a favor, to take it into the States for him."

"I get that part of it." Chuck Dean nodded morosely.

"And somebody," McMain rushed on, "has been using us to smuggle gems into the States. Pete Adams was their agent. Loyal, obliging old Pete, whom nobody would ever suspect and for whom everybody was willing to do a favor."

"And that *somebody* you just mentioned—"

"One guess, Chuck," McMain snarled.

"Benson Clark."

"It's a cinch! Look here!" McMain's voice was brusque. "Tommy in some way broke that bottle. He was always awkward. He was always stumbling around and knocking things over. There's his trunk. I know it's half full of books and weighs a ton. It would have been just like him, in the rush of packing and getting ready for the dance tonight, to tip it over on the package Pete gave him.

"In cleaning up the mess, he discovered the bottle contained more than perfume. What would he do about it? Knowing Tommy, what would you say he'd do?"

Chuck smiled wryly. "I reckon you could count on the poor devil doin' the wrong thing."

"Of course you could. Would he come to me, or to the Old Man? Not Tommy! He went to Pete Adams. He forced Pete to tell him where the bottle came from. And then Tommy, full of the romance of adventure, went out to do some sleuthing on his own hook. Thought it would be a grand idea to run down, single-handed, a gang of gem smugglers."

"And Clark got wind—" Dean began.

"More likely," McMain broke in, "Pete Adams warned Clark by telephone. And Clark was all set to handle Tommy when Tommy got to the dance. He slipped something in his drink. He murdered him."

Chuck Dean gave vent to his futile rage with a string of good Carolinian profanity. Then he asked: "But who, do you reckon, murdered Pete?"

"Pete wasn't murdered," McMain declared shortly. "Think a minute, Chuck. Pete was sixty years old and not too strong. Have you ever seen the inside of the Panama prison?"

Chuck slowly nodded. "I reckon I get it. Knowing Pete, it's easy enough to see how the poor fellow felt. He thought he was trapped. He didn't see any way out. He was an old man. So he cut his throat rather than face a term in prison."

There was a brief and pregnant silence. And then Chuck, avoiding McMain's eyes, said slowly:

"There's only one thing I cain't see."

McMain took a deep, sighing breath. "I know, Chuck. Where does Billie fit into the picture?"

VI

The wind now was steady and high, moaning dismally around the building. Rain pounded on the roof in a relentless deluge. Tommy's little room was like a steam bath and sweat dripped from McMain's face as he gathered up the gems and pieces of glass. He rolled them tightly in the newspaper and went out, with Dean, to the wardroom. There they met Doc Lucas coming back from the sick bay.

"Would he talk?" McMain asked quickly.

"Yes, he talked. What have you there, Larry?"

"A small fortune in unset gems."

Doc Lucas showed no surprise. "Cabrillo will be glad to hear you recovered them."

"Cabrillo? Who the devil's Cabrillo?"

"Clark's chauffeur. United States Department of Justice operative."

McMain blinked. "Department of *Justice!* Are you sure you don't mean——"

"I mean Department of Justice. There is more to this than a mere smuggling job. It seems that Benson Clark is the head of a gang of jewel thieves who have been working the coast-to-coast cruise ships operating through the canal. It was their custom to steal the jewels on the night before the ship reached Panama. On that night there is usually a masquerade or some other damned foolishness and the dowagers drag their jimcracks out of the purser's safe for the occasion."

"But how did the thieves get the jewels into Panama?" McMain asked.

"They were slipped to one of the crowd of bumboat men that surrounds every ship as soon as she drops anchor in the harbor. Then they were smuggled ashore. With the jewels once in Clark's hands, the stones were removed from their settings and concealed in bottles of perfume. The perfume was sent to a New York fence through old Pete Adams and the kindly co-operation of various naval officers going back to the States.

"Cabrillo tells me his department has broken up the gang that worked the ships and can pick up the New York fence whenever it pleases. Clark, he says, knew the jig was up, though he didn't know the fence was being shadowed. He was risking everything to get that one last shipment through."

"Yeah," Chuck Dean said, "but that doesn't explain——"

"Let's skip that, Chuck, for a while," McMain broke in. "Doc, how come this Cabrillo got himself shot?"

"Cabrillo realizes now that Clark has been onto him for some time. Tonight, after Cabrillo had driven through the gates with a gun at his back, Clark waited until they had gone a mile or so and then ordered him to stop. As he pulled up at the side of the road, Clark let him have it. By the grace of God, Cabrillo's head was turned sidewise and, with the odds a million to one against him, he came through alive."

"But why the devil," McMain queried, "didn't Cabrillo yell for help when he had Clark bottled up here on the base? There were three or four sentries within call while he waited outside the wardroom."

"Cabrillo was under orders to get his man with the gems in his possession. Clark evidently realized the situation, because as soon as Billie came out with the black bottle, he shoved a gun against Cabrillo's back. And from then on Cabrillo took orders."

Chuck Dean mused: "And that black bottle, after all, wasn't the one Clark wanted. Which, of course, is a lot of help to me in gettin' my sistah out of this mess, Doc! What does this Secret Service fella say about Billie?"

"He didn't say anything about Billie," Doc replied. "Incidentally, Cabrillo had me phone his chief, man by the name of Bridges, over in Balboa. The wheels of justice—of the Department of Justice, anyway—are already turning."

As a matter of fact, the Secret Service man was already on his way over, although McMain and Dean did not know this and spent half the night in impotent fretting.

At one o'clock that morning a plane roared in from Balboa. Ten minutes later the two officers were in the commandant's office, where they were tersely introduced to Thomas Bridges, chief operative in the Canal Zone for the Department of Justice. The Federal man was about forty, a slight, pink-cheeked little person with graying hair and hard, direct, ice-blue eyes.

The commandant said briefly: "I have gone over the situation with Bridges, McMain, and I want to compliment you on the excellent work you have done so far. From now on, however, you and Dean will take orders from him. The *Whipple* has steam up and you will go aboard her immediately. She will head east, towards the San Blas coast."

"We are almost certain," Bridges explained in his precise, mild voice, "that Clark has headed for the San Blas Islands. He knows that country and it offers his best chance for a getaway, either into Colombia or overland through Darien."

"Darien!" Chuck Dean exclaimed. "Surely that damnable cowa'd wouldn't drag a woman into Darien."

Bridges smiled gently. "That damnable coward, as you call him, is a bold and resourceful young man whose life is at stake." His smile faded as he added: "And I don't imagine the young woman will have to be dragged."

Chuck's fists clenched and his face went white as he glared at the little Federal operative. "You're not inferrin', are you, suh, that my sistah is a member of this ring of thieves?"

"I have found no evidence pointing to that conclusion," Bridges said, "until tonight."

Chuck's jaw set. "And I assure you, suh, that her actions tonight will be honorably explained in due time."

"I sincerely hope so, Lieutenant Dean." The Federal man's blue eyes were coolly skeptical.

The commandant said quickly: "By daylight the *Whipple* should be off Parvenir, the most westerly of the islands. I doubt if Clark's yawl, in this storm, can make half that run. You'll probably intercept him before he gets into the islands. Weather permitting, I shall send out all available planes in the morning. They will have no difficulty in picking up the yawl and they will keep in touch with you and direct you by radio. The rest will be up to you. That will be all."

"Very good, sir."

McMain saluted and walked out of the office in silence. He was vaguely aware that Bridges and Chuck Dean had fallen in beside him, but he did not speak.

What if the *Thelma* reached Parvenir and dodged into the islands before daylight? It was a run of only seventy miles and Clark, getting away about eleven, had seven hours of darkness. The *Thelma* should be fast with the wind on her beam and Clark would drive her.

He thought of the San Blas Archipelago, that amazing chain of more than four thousand islands and keys stretching along a hundred and fifty miles of coast, all the way from Parvenir to the Gulf of Darien. The *Whipple* drew too much water to navigate even the deepest of the narrow channels which wound through the group.

And behind that long necklace of green islands, protected by myriad uncharted coral reefs—was *Darien*!

Not a huge area, Darien. Perhaps fifty miles wide and three times as long. And yet, for its size, one of the wildest, most unexplored, most dangerous sections of the world. A land of high mountain and bottomless swamp, of heat and venomous insects and fever. Not many white men had gone into Darien and come out alive.

McMain thought of these things, and he thought of a girl in a pale green silk dress and high-heeled sandals, plodding through the swamps behind handsome Benson Clark.

VII

It was still dark at six o'clock the following morning when McMain climbed the ladder to the bridge of the *Whipple*. The destroyer, barely making steerage way, was rolling heavily to a beam sea. A fresh breeze from the northeast sang through the rigging and a steady deluge of rain thrummed the steel decks.

Holding to the hand rail, McMain groped his way forward and finally made out Ken Scott, the destroyer's captain, in the port wing.

"Morning, Larry," the commander greeted him cheerfully.

"Morning, Ken. What's your position?"

"We're about five miles due north of Parvenir. I don't dare run in any closer."

McMain peered over the weather cloth into the gray murk. Dawn was trying, with difficulty, to break. "Been here long?"

"Since five."

"No sight of the *Thelma* on the run down?"

"Lord, no! It was as thick as the inside of your hat all the way. Nice going for the yawl, though. Steady wind and just the kind of a sea she'd like."

"Think she beat us down?" McMain asked.

"No. We probably passed her along the way. Clark would cut the corners a lot closer than I could."

"He's probably standing in to Parvenir right now," McMain growled. "How's the barometer?"

"Falling slowly," Ken Scott said, "but very, very steadily."

McMain grunted. "A hell of a chance we've got!"

"One in a thousand. The Old Man won't send out any planes to help us, either."

"They wouldn't be of any use if he did. It's a tough situation, if you ask me, and damned little we can do about it."

McMain turned towards the ladder to the main deck; then he paused and asked over his shoulder: "How's your motor dory?"

"In good shape. Why?"

"I just wanted to know."

"Look here! You're not—"

"Good God, Ken!" McMain snapped. "We've got to do *something!*"

He went on down the ladder. It was virtually broad daylight now. And yet McMain, peering astern, could barely make out the after deck house, a hundred feet away. The rain came down in slanting sheets, steadily and relentlessly.

Below, in the small wardroom, he found Chuck Dean and Bridges, their chairs hooked to the table while a Filipino boy who looked sadly seasick served them breakfast. Chuck was haggard and hollow-eyed, but Bridges seemed cheerful.

"How are things outside?" he asked.

"Rotten. This storm has settled down for the day and Scott doesn't dare take his ship any further inshore. Clark will slip by us and get into the islands, if he isn't there already. And you know what that will mean. . . . Boy, bring me some coffee."

"No chance of this storm blowin' over?" Chuck Dean asked.

"The barometer's falling steadily."

The boy brought McMain's coffee. He drank it in three or four quick gulps, said abruptly: "See here! There's only one thing to do. We've got to take the motor dory and try to make Parvenir. We might intercept Clark there. But in case we miss him, in case he's slipped in among the islands ahead of us, we'll go after him. What do you say, Bridges?"

The Federal man smiled. "I say let's go."

They put a cask of water and a box of emergency rations in the twenty-one-foot motor dory. They stowed away a rifle and a belt of ammunition, and armed themselves with .45 Colts. They put in a chart and a boat compass, filled the gas tank.

Then Commander Scott made a lee and, with the dory's coxswain standing by to unhook the falls, the boat was dropped over the side. Bridges, McMain and Dean scrambled down the ladder and piled into the pitching dory.

Thirty minutes later the little island village of Parvenir loomed out of the rain almost dead ahead. Tall palms first, their fronds thrashing in the wind; then the white government house; finally the double row of thatched Indian dwellings.

Dean and Bridges came out from the hooded forward cockpit, and joined McMain, braced themselves and stood watching the village as the dory bore down on the white line of breakers which piled up on the shore.

"Well, what do you say, McMain?" Bridges asked.

"I say, if he isn't anchored in the lee of the island, he's ahead of us."

Bridges turned to the coxswain, who crouched in his oilskins in the after cockpit. "Head around the island, son," he ordered.

A few Indians, short men with broad shoulders, narrow hips and thin legs, came out of their huts and stolidly watched the dory go by. On the lee side of the island there was no sign of the yawl, nothing but a half dozen native *cayucos* pulled up on the beach.

"The next village is Carti," McMain said briefly. "And from there it's only a short way over to the mainland."

"How far away is Carti?"

"Ten miles across the Gulf of San Blas in an air line. Nearer fifteen or twenty by the channel."

"You think he'd head that way?"

"He's got to head that way. There's only the one channel until he gets further east, in the neighborhood of Nargana."

"Then Carti it is."

The coxswain, at McMain's order, cut his engine to half speed and they cruised along watching for the settlement. They made it out finally: a long line of native dwellings stretching along the beach and, anchored off shore, a gray and weathered submarine chaser which was used as a trading station.

"Pull over to the chaser, cox'n," McMain ordered.

As they drew alongside the ancient sub-chaser an old man came out of the cabin and stood staring at the dory. McMain threw him the painter. He caught it, expertly made it fast and shouted cheerily:

"Come aboard, friends."

"Haven't time," McMain replied. "We're looking for the *Thelma*. Has she been by here?"

"The *Thelma*, huh? What's Ben Clark been doin' besides marryin' a right nice little woman?"

Chuck Dean gulped, but McMain said quickly: "Clark is wanted in Colón for murder."

"Murder, huh?" The old trader never batted an eye. "Well, I ain't surprised. I never did like that young feller. He's too damned pretty."

"Hell!" Bridges spoke up. "Has Clark been along this way?"

"Huh? Sure he has. 'Bout an hour ago. Him and his wife stopped in and bought some supplies off me. Then he went ashore there and got a *cayuco*. He tied it astern of the yawl and headed east. He's prob'ly makin' for Cidra. That's a big island due east of here 'bout ten mile."

"Thank you and much obliged," McMain said. "Cast us off, will you?"

The old trader untied the painter, the coxswain kicked his clutch and the dory drew away.

"We'll have to get a dugout," McMain said.

"Why?" Bridges demanded.

"Because Clark means to head up a river and we can't follow him in this dory. It draws too much water. Cox'n, head in as close to the village as you can get."

"How do you mean to get a dugout?"

"I mean to take it!" McMain retorted.

He buckled on a .45 and, when the dory reached shallow water, leaped over the side and waded ashore. From the dozen or more *cayucos* drawn up on the beach, he selected one, saw there were paddles in it and laid hold of it.

The Indians crowded towards him, jabbering. He waved them back with his .45, hauled the dugout into the water, pulled it out to the dory and made it fast at the stern.

The dory drove on. No one mentioned Billie Dean. McMain tried not to think of her. It seemed so certain, now, that she was willingly, and knowingly, accompanying Clark. His one forlorn hope, that she was under compulsion, had been blasted by the trader's account of their visit.

Fifteen minutes after leaving Carti they made out a low line of dark green forest. A moment later Chuck Dean shouted:

"There's the yawl! My Lawd, he's scuttled her!"

Off to port, and not more than a hundred yards away, they saw the upper third of a mast sticking out of the water at a sharp angle.

"Water wasn't as deep as he thought it was," Bridges remarked. "H-m. Where's the nearest river? He wouldn't plan to go far on the open gulf in a dugout."

Chuck Dean smoothed out the chart with shaking fingers.

"Nearest river from here is the Carti, about half a mile farther to the east.

"That must be the one. Cut over to port, cox'n, and head along the shore. Well, boys, it won't be long now."

VIII

eading east they came shortly to an area of muddy water which told them they were at the mouth of the Carti. They found a break in the dense jungle which lined the shore and headed into it. The river here was a good two hundred yards wide and the current barely noticeable.

"Heah's where we'll pick up on him," Chuck Dean said tensely. "He can't make time in that *cayuco.*"

Half an hour later they ran, without warning, onto their first sandbar.

"All out but the cox'n!" McMain cried.

The three men leaped into the knee-deep water and hauled the dory astern until she was clear.

"Reckon we better take to the dugout?" Chuck Dean asked.

"Not yet," McMain returned. "Try it to port, cox'n. The channel seems to be that way."

During the next half hour, while the river grew steadily more narrow and shallow, they went aground three times. McMain finally gave up.

"We can't waste any more time with the dory. Cox'n, stay here till we come back."

The boy's jaw dropped. "How long might that be, sir?"

"It might be all winter," McMain snapped. "But it will probably be less than twenty-four hours. You have emergency rations. Put out a light tonight as soon as it's dark and keep your eye peeled for us."

As they stowed a box of rations and the rifle in the dugout, McMain said briefly: "We have eight hours of daylight left. Once it's dark, we can consider that he has slipped us for good."

They wasted no more time in talk. They got into the narrow dugout, took up their paddles and bent their backs to the task ahead. Within five minutes they had settled into a smooth rhythmic pace that shot them swiftly up the swollen river.

Within a half mile after leaving the dory the

three men were hauling their dugout over a short and rocky rapid. Above the rapid they found a quarter-mile stretch of river which ran deep and swift. It was all they could do to make headway against it.

And then Bridges, in the bow, raised his paddle and pointed to a sandbar in the middle of the river. They all saw the footprints there: the large prints of a man and the small prints of a woman. No one said anything.

But McMain hitched his .45 forward.

The three men toiled onward, doggedly, in silence, paddling the deep stretches, dragging the frail dugout through or around the rapids. They worked feverishly, rain and sweat streaming from their faces.

And then abruptly, unexpectedly, the chase was over. They rounded a bend, paddling in deep water. They saw Clark and Billie Dean standing beside their canoe at the foot of a rapid less than thirty feet away.

McMain's hand leaped to his Colt. Bridges reached for the rifle. But Benson Clark waved his empty hands and called, with a laugh:

"Put your guns away, gentlemen. I know when I'm licked."

McMain's hand did not leave his automatic. He sensed there was something wrong with the picture. It wasn't normal for a man in Clark's position to give in without a struggle. The Federal man must have felt the same way about the situation, for he kept his rifle ready and did not again pick up his paddle.

Only Chuck Dean, with a stricken, hurt look in his eyes, kept paddling towards the other *cayuco.* Benson Clark said:

"I see you don't believe me." He turned to Billie Dean, who, in a torn yellow slicker a dozen sizes too large for her, stood knee-deep in the water. "Billie, take the gun out of my holster and toss it in the river."

With a weary sigh, without looking at the approaching men, Billie pulled the revolver from the holster at Clark's hip and tossed it in the rushing water.

"You'd never have got us," Clark said cheerfully, "if I hadn't stove this damned *cayuco* on a rock."

They saw then that the dugout was half full of water and was afloat only by virtue of the buoyant wood of which it was made.

"Hold the boat steady, boys," Bridges ordered crisply.

He stepped out into the water. Producing a pair of handcuffs, he slipped them over Clark's wrists. He searched the prisoner with practiced hands. Then he jerked his head towards the dugout.

"In you go, Clark. Into the bow. You too, Miss Dean. Into the stern."

Then he grinned at McMain, as much as to say, "Well, that's that."

But McMain's hand remained on his gun. He felt no sense of triumph. For there was Billie Dean, haggard, bedraggled, ready to drop with weariness—her part in the drama still unexplained.

And he felt no sense of security. For there was Clark, tired but debonair, and *smiling*! Taking it all as a joke, though he knew he must go back to Colón and stand trial for murder.

It had been too easy. Much, much too easy.

IX

hey started down the river in the storm, five of them in a dugout built for three. Benson Clark, handcuffed, sat in the bow; Bridges behind him; then Chuck Dean and Billie, with McMain in the stern. They paddled in silence.

Billie, finally, turned and looked up at McMain. Her dark hair was wild and matted. Her gray eyes were tired, lifeless, her cheeks sunken. She spoke so quietly that McMain alone caught the words.

"Aren't you ever goin' to smile at me again?"

Her voice was husky and provocative, but McMain kept his eyes straight ahead. He didn't want to talk. He was too tired to talk. He felt empty and torn by strife.

"You haven't even so much as looked at me since you caught us," Billie pointed out. And then added querulously: "Cain't you even speak to me?"

At that moment Clark, though he could not have heard the conversation in the stern of the long dugout, turned and said:

"Look here, you people! You might as well get this straight right now. Billie Dean is in the clear on this job."

No one said anything. Clark wheeled further, glaring at Bridges.

"Steady, you damned fool!" the Federal man snapped. "Do you want to capsize us?"

Clark laughed hollowly. "I wouldn't mind," he retorted. "What've I got to lose? . . . Billie, tell them how you happen to be with me."

"Go ahead, Miss Dean," Bridges urged. "It'll help kill time. Besides which, I am very much interested."

"This gentleman is Mistah Bridges, Billie," Chuck Dean explained. "He's chief operative for the Department of Justice in Panama."

Sighing, the girl leaned back against McMain's knees.

"Clark told me at the dance last night that he was a Secret Service operative. He showed me credentials that certainly looked genuine and I had no reason for disbelievin' him."

"Didn't it strike you as odd that a Secret Service man would tell you his business?" Bridges asked skeptically.

"Odd?" Her voice was contained, slightly belligerent. "After all, when a man asks a woman to marry him, doesn't he usually tell her his occupation?"

"Sorry," Bridges said, without sounding at all sorry. "Hadn't realized he'd gone that far."

"Oh, shut up and let her tell her story," Clark growled wearily.

"Anyway," Billie Dean went on, "Clark had dropped a few hints about his mission in Panama, when we heard Tommy Glade was dead. Then he came right out and told me he was workin' on a big smugglin' plot and had all the evidence against Tommy, but hadn't arrested him because he wanted to get others too. Clark felt sure, he said, that Tommy must have taken poison when he found the law closin' in on him."

"He took poison, all right," Chuck Dean growled, "but he never knew it. Clark murdered that poor young fella."

"I realized that later," Billie replied. "But at the time—well, everything dovetailed and it seemed logical enough."

"But even if it all did seem logical," Chuck Dean said unhappily, "and even if you were convinced Clark was a Federal, why did you go out to the base and steal that bottle of perfume?"

"Because Clark convinced me that by getting the bottle of gems out of the way Tommy's name might be kept clean. I know Tommy's family, I know his two brothers in the service and"—she laughed humorlessly—"I'm a Southern girl."

Bridges' voice was no longer skeptical; it was merely tired as he said: "Southern chivalry can get a person into lots of trouble on occasion. Go on, Miss Dean."

"Well, Clark told me the situation as we drove out to the base. He told me that he, naturally, couldn't take those gems but he was willin' to stretch a point and let me do it. The government had to recover the gems, of course, but it would serve no purpose to dirty Tommy's name and disgrace his family now that he was dead."

"But Billie!" Chuck exclaimed. "When Larry McMain walked in on you there in Tommy's room, why didn't you tell him the situation? Why did you lie and evade?"

She said quietly: "I'll tell you, although a little later, when it was too late, I knew I'd made the mistake of my life. I know how much Larry thought of Tommy. He'd had him under his wing for six years. He was like a kid brother to him. He had a world of respect for him and high hopes for his career. And it was to spare Larry's feelings that I wouldn't tell him what I really thought then: that Tommy had been smugglin' gems. I took the risk of queerin' myself for life with him. Well, I took it. I was wrong, but—"

"Uh-huh," Bridges put in. "And perhaps it was all for the best anyway. We might never have caught him if it hadn't been for you, Miss Dean."

After a few moments Billie said quietly: "I didn't realize the true situation until Clark shot his chauffeur. Then it dawned on me like a flash just what I'd been doin', just what it was all about."

"And yet," her brother said in a stricken voice, "you went on with Clark. You let him take you aboard his boat. You fled into the jungle with him."

"Did you evah ride along with a gun proddin' you in the ribs?" the girl flashed.

"God knows," Clark said, still markedly cheerful, "I hated to drag her along at the point of a gun. But what could I do? I couldn't turn her loose. Not until we crossed Darien and I was in a position to make a clean break. Then I planned to turn her over to some friendly natives who'd get her back to Panama."

Chuck Dean growled something deep in his throat and jabbed his paddle viciously into the water. Billie patted his shoulder, turned and looked up at McMain.

"And now, darlin', do you suppose you could smile at me?" she asked softly. "Because you're goin' to marry me, you know, and it would be simply awful to go through life with a husband who never smiled. . . . You *are* goin' to marry me, aren't you? Because if—"

"Steady!" Bridges shouted. "There's white water ahead."

Benson Clark rose to his knees in the bow. "Look here, Bridges! I don't like the idea of heading into that rapid with my hands cuffed. I'm a lousy swimmer and this dugout is overloaded. If it capsized I'd go to the bottom like a rock."

"That'd be too damned bad," Chuck Dean jeered. "I'd feel right sorry if you got drowned."

Clark ignored the sally. "You men are all armed. I haven't a weapon of any kind. You certainly can't be afraid of me. If I'd wanted to fight, I'd have done it up the river. I gave in, without any resistance, because I figure I can beat this rap. For God's sake, Bridges, take off these cuffs."

A warning bell was ringing far in the back of McMain's mind, but Billie Dean was leaning back against his knees and McMain's heart was so full of happiness he barely heard it.

He did not protest when Bridges laid his paddle across the gunwale, took out a key and silently unlocked the handcuffs.

"Thanks," Clark said. "You're a right guy, Bridges, even if you are a dick." He faced forward again.

They ran the short rapid without difficulty and came out near the right bank of the river, which was fully a hundred yards wide. Here the water ran deep and black and swift.

Benson Clark looked over his shoulder. Something in his eyes caught McMain's attention, and the lieutenant's heart started suddenly to pound. He dug his paddle in the water, shot the frail craft shoreward with all his strength.

Clark, leering at the men behind him, cried:

"I may be a sucker, but not so much of a sucker as you damned fools think!"

He caught the gunwales with both hands. He threw all the weight on his left arm and jerked upward with his right. The *cayuco* tilted and went over.

McMain heard Billie Dean screaming as the warm black water closed above her head. He knew Billie was a poor swimmer and he realized, as the swirling currents tugged at him, that only a good swimmer could get out of this mess without help.

Fighting to the surface, he shook the water out of his eyes and took in the situation.

Bridges had struck out for the near shore, swimming awkwardly but adequately. Chuck Dean had caught hold of the overturned dugout with one hand and was holding his sister with the other. And Benson Clark, swimming a neat crawl, was churning the water to foam as he headed straight across the river towards the left bank.

"Can you handle Billie?" McMain cried.

"We're all right," Chuck Dean puffed. "Boy, get goin'!"

McMain got going. Clark, by that time, had a lead of fifty feet. The navy man cut it to forty in the swift swim across the river. He saw Clark gain the bank, slip in the muddy slime and fall. The man was up in an instant. Catching hold of a trailing branch, he hauled himself up to firm ground.

Then McMain's hands struck muddy bottom. He lurched erect in knee-deep water, steadied himself. Clark was leaping away into the jungle like a frightened deer.

It dawned upon McMain in a split second that Clark was escaping into the jungle on a trail he knew.

The man was thirty feet away, charging into the bush. McMain realized that in another second or two, he'd be out of sight. He clawed at his holster—and found it empty! His gun had slipped out when he was hurled into the river.

Splashing through the shallows, McMain caught a branch and swung himself up the slippery riverbank. He found the trail, a dark tunnel plunging straight into the thick forest.

McMain raced on, stumbling over protruding roots, catching his arms and head in trailing lianas, sinking at times almost knee-deep in mud. The sound of Clark's steps and his flounderings among the vines drew no closer.

The lieutenant lowered his head. With his arms close to his sides, his fists in front of his face to protect his eyes from the brush, he shot forward.

He did not know how far he went, nor how long. But at last when his breath came in sobbing gasps and his heart was beating like a riveting machine, he hurtled out of the bush into the dull gray light of a small clearing.

And there, not twenty paces away, was Benson Clark. The man stood in a half crouch, panting, waiting.

McMain dropped into a walk as he saw a knife gleaming in Clark's hand. And yet he did not stop. Fighting for breath, he moved relentlessly towards the fugitive.

"Go back, you damned fool!" Clark snarled. "Do you want me to have to kill you?"

McMain plodded forward. "I'll take a chance."

"You can't stop me," Clark snapped. "Nobody can stop me. If you want me to slit your throat first, come and get it."

The distance between the two men lessened until they were no more than three paces apart. Then Clark, nervous, screaming a curse that echoed through the forest, lunged at McMain.

As the lieutenant had hoped, and counted on, Clark misjudged his distance. McMain saw the knife coming. He knew what he must do and he had time to do it. Fancy footwork, in that jungle slime, was impossible. McMain threw his body to the left, falling on his hands with his right leg straight.

He felt a blow against his right calf and realized with a thrill, even before he heard the crash of Clark's body, that his tactics had been successful. He was on his feet in a flash, whirling to where Clark had fallen headlong.

He leaped on him, caught his outthrust right arm at the wrist. He whipped it backward and over, viciously. The knife fell out of the hand. And all at once, as Clark screamed in agony, the bone snapped and the arm went limp.

McMain caught up the knife and rose. Clark did not stir. Flat on his face in the mud, his right arm twisted grotesquely across his back, he lay motionless.

McMain waited a moment, getting his breath. Still Clark did not move.

"Fainted," the lieutenant muttered, and dropped to his knees. He tossed the knife into the jungle and reached out to roll Clark onto his back.

At that instant the man turned on McMain like a wounded jungle animal. He rolled onto his right side, oblivious of his broken arm. His left fist shot out with all the viciousness and inhuman power of desperation.

It caught McMain in the pit of the stomach; it struck him like a shot of high-voltage current. Flame danced before his eyes. Every muscle of his body was paralyzed. He knew he was on his back, his knees in the air. He knew he was helpless.

He saw Clark leap to his feet. He heard Clark curse. He knew what was coming but there was nothing he could do.

He saw Clark stand off a pace, like a place-kicker measuring the distance of the ball. He saw Clark's useless right arm hanging limp. He saw the insane gleam of desperation, and of murder, in his eyes. And he saw Clark's right foot go back, and then start towards his head.

Time slowed and all motion became slow motion. It seemed seconds that he lay there while Clark's foot grew steadily larger. Then, summoning all his will, he jerked his head sidewise. He saw the boot go past his face, still in slow motion.

All at once his nerves began to function. Time speeded up. He caught Clark's foot, while the man was off balance. He gripped it tight and rolled sidewise.

Clark's weight crashed on him. He felt the futile tattoo of Clark's left fist against his ribs. Still holding the foot, ignoring the other's blows, he lurched to his knees and finally worked himself to his feet.

He stood there, legs wide, Clark's ankle under his right arm.

"I can break this leg as easily as I broke your arm. . . . Well, how about it?"

"Break it, damn you!" Clark cried.

McMain gripped the toe and started to twist, while Clark kicked at him futilely with his other foot. Then McMain heard the crashing of branches, a moment later voices. He dropped Clark's leg and stood back.

"The jig's up, guy," he said quietly. "Why prolong the agony?"

Bridges and Chuck Dean came tumbling into the clearing.

"Got 'im, eh?" Chuck Dean cheered. "Nice goin', fella."

McMain grunted. "The next time you search

a man, Bridges, look in his shoes. He had a knife."

"Good Lord! Did he get you?"

"No, by the grace of God I got him." McMain turned wearily towards the river. "Where's Billie?"

"She's somewhere behind us. We got the *cayuco* righted and came after you."

Billie appeared at that moment, her yellow slicker hanging in ribbons, her hair awry, her face scratched and bleeding.

"Larry, are you all right?" she cried as she ran towards him.

"I guess I'll do now." He grinned and put his arm around her.

She didn't draw away. She snuggled closer. "Me too, Larry—if I can stay this way."

Arm in arm they walked back to the river, slipping between the branches and creepers, plowing through the mud. It would have been much easier if they had gone single file, sanely. Somehow they didn't seem to think of that.

The Corpse Didn't Kick
Milton K. Ozaki

MILTON K. OZAKI (1913–1989) was born in Racine, Wisconsin, and lived much of his life in Kenosha, setting many of his books in Stillwell, a faintly disguised version of that city. His other books were set in Chicago, where he also lived for many years. Born of a Japanese father and Caucasian mother, he is probably the first American mystery writer of Japanese heritage. He lost a leg in a childhood accident, yet worked as a journalist, tax accountant, and owner of a beauty parlor on Chicago's Gold Coast, though he claimed he mostly earned his living by playing bridge for money. His books were written in the smart-aleck school of private-eye or cop novel prevalent in the 1940s and 1950s. His first two books were set in Chicago and featured Professor Androcles Caldwell, head of the psychology department at North University, his young assistant, Bendy Brinks, and Lieutenant Percy Phelan of Homicide, who worked together in *The Cuckoo Clock* (1946), *A Friend in Need* (1947), and, a bit later, *The Dummy Murder Case* (1951). More than half of Ozaki's twenty-five novels were written under the pseudonym Robert O. Saber (a pun on his name, as *zaki* in Japanese can be translated as "saber"), several featuring private eye Carl Good. Fast-paced and frequently sexy, the novels were also often humorous, though not always intentionally, as his mixed metaphors and peculiar similes were the subject of several pages in Bill Pronzini's *Son of Gun in Cheek* (1987), an affectionate study of mystery fiction's worst writing.

"The Corpse Didn't Kick" was published in the November 1949 issue.

The Corpse Didn't Kick

Milton K. Ozaki

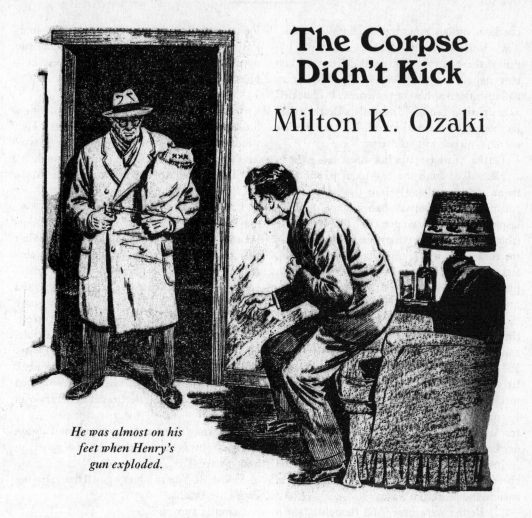

He was almost on his feet when Henry's gun exploded.

Slay-happy Henry put his wife in a triangle—to prove he was on the square.

HENRY EBBETT HAD SPENT WEEKS perfecting his plan. He had considered it from every possible angle, and there was absolutely no flaw in it. It was complicated, of course, but the reward was worth all the trouble and patience required. Everything fitted together beautifully—and the timing was perfect.

It was too bad he had to kill Joe Carson, but Joe was the keystone of the whole idea. There had to be a fall guy—or Henry hadn't a hope of getting away with the money. So Joe was the fall guy. It was as simple as that.

Henry soaped his hands carefully and rinsed them under the faucet. Removing his horn-rimmed glasses for a moment, he polished them thoughtfully, then replaced them on his small pudgy nose. They gave him an owlish look, but without them he would hardly have been able to see himself in the mirror over the washbasin.

"Contact lenses, that's what I'll get," he thought fleetingly. "In some other town, I'll get rid of these glasses and make a fresh start. A man can do anything with $20,000."

The thought of the money brought a smile to his lips. He had the money—all of it!—and no one would ever figure out where it had gone.

For weeks, he'd been purchasing traveler's

checks at various banks under a fictitious name. They were waiting for him in a distant city, mailed there in care of general delivery. When everything was settled here, he'd pick them up and cash them at his convenience. He chuckled as he dried his hands. "This will fix Bertha, too," he thought, "once and for all. No matter what she says, no one will believe her!"

Bertha, of course, was his wife. . . .

He walked from the bathroom to the bedroom, then went slowly into the living-room, pausing in the doorway like a stage designer inspecting a new arrangement. The lamp, the table, the chair—everything was perfect, even to the convenient ashtray, the bottle of bourbon, and the highball glass. Joe liked his bourbon with plain water. The glass and fixings were there, utterly devoid of fingerprints, waiting for him.

Impatient now that the critical moment was almost upon him, Henry walked to the window and looked down the deserted street. The cold had taken a sudden drop and the weather was freezing, but, fortunately, there hadn't been much snow. He wouldn't have to worry about footprints on the carpets, the back stairs, or the rear sidewalk. No one had seen him come in. No one knew he was here—except Joe Carson.

Inside the room, the steam radiator hissed cheerfully, spreading its warmth. Henry was anemic and he liked it warm.

"If Bertha were here," he thought, "she'd have the heat turned off and the window open." Involuntarily, he shivered at the idea. "As long as I pay the rent, I'm entitled to heat. This is the way I like it, and this is the way it's going to be—from now on."

As though in answer to his wish that Joe hurry up, a tall man in a heavy brown overcoat turned the corner and, his face lowered into the cold wind, made his way slowly toward the building. Henry nodded approvingly. Joe was on time. Everything was working out exactly as he had planned.

A moment later the downstairs door banged and Joe's heavy feet ascended the stairs. Henry's heart did an excited little dance as he waited for Joe to reach the landing. Then, moving soundlessly across the room, he unlocked the door and opened it. The smile he managed was perfect—pleasant, friendly, a little abstracted.

"Hi, Joe. Pretty cold, eh?"

"Sure is!" Joe came into the room, puffing a little and slapping his hands together. "That wind must have come straight from Alaska! You've got it nice and warm in here, though."

"Throw your coat on the couch, Joe. Make yourself at home."

Unconsciously, Henry kept his voice low, moving softly about the room in his old felt slippers so Mrs. Pettigrew, downstairs, wouldn't hear two pairs of feet above her. She undoubtedly was sitting out in front on her glass-enclosed porch, watching the goings and comings of her neighbors, but there was no sense taking chances. Henry liked things to be perfect.

Waving Joe toward the chair beside the table, Henry said: "Pour yourself a drink, Joe. I knew you'd be needing one, so I got the fixings ready."

"Thanks, Henry." Joe sighed and stretched his legs comfortably. "Bertha get to the train all right?"

"You know Bertha. Always ready and always on time. This is the first time she's been away in a coon's age."

"Uh-huh. You're a lucky guy, Henry, having a wife like Bertha."

"Don't I know it?"

Once again, Henry surveyed the room. No, everything was perfect. The stage was set for death. With a confident smile, he went quietly into the bedroom and put on his overcoat, muffler, and hat. He buttoned the coat, drew on a pair of light flannel gloves, then went to his dresser and, removing two guns from a drawer, slid them into his coat pocket—the revolver on the right, the automatic on the left. Bending carefully, he picked up a pair of black oxfords from the floor and tucked them under his arm.

When he walked into the living-room, Joe was smoking a cigarette and sipping a highball.

He raised one eyebrow in surprise as he saw Henry dressed to go out.

"Hey, going some place?" he asked. He set down his drink and started to get up, but Henry waved him back.

"Need a few things from the grocery," Henry explained briefly, "and I want to drop these shoes at the repair shop before it closes. Won't take a minute. Sit still and make like a guest, Joe."

"Glad to go for you, Henry, if—"

"Wouldn't think of it."

Henry wondered if Joe would notice he was wearing his felt slippers. Even if he did notice, of course, it wouldn't make any difference. But Joe wouldn't notice—and he didn't.

As smoothly as an actor going through a well-practiced role, Henry walked to the door, snapped his fingers to show he'd remembered something, and came back. With one gloved hand, he picked up the telephone and dialed Mrs. Pettigrew's number. The phone buzzed repeatedly, indicating that the phone was ringing. When it had buzzed four times, he set the receiver back onto its cradle. Mrs. Pettigrew would be on her way to answer it—and the phone was in the rear of her flat.

"No one home," Henry said cryptically. He shrugged and started for the door again.

This time he opened the door and went quietly downstairs. At the foot of the stairs, he sat down, removed the slippers and put on the oxfords. In a matter of seconds, he opened the front door, stepped onto the porch, and closed the door. He stamped his feet loudly on the boards of the porch, opened the door, banged it shut, shuffled his feet in the hallway. Hesitating only an instant, he rapped on Mrs. Pettigrew's door.

He heard her slow, dragging footsteps come from the rear of her flat. The slippers! With a whispered curse, he bent and snatched them from the hallway floor. With one swift jerk of his arm he tossed them up the stairs. What if he hadn't remembered them? What if Mrs. Pettigrew had seen them? He shivered at the thought, and, when old Mrs. Pettigrew opened her door,

he looked exactly like a man who'd tramped several blocks through freezing weather.

"Hello!" he said, smiling cheerily into the aged woman's face. "Cold, isn't it? Did my groceries arrive?"

"Oh, good afternoon, Mr. Ebbett. Winter's here, all right!" The old woman nodded her head and peered at him over her spectacles. "Thought you'd forgotten the groceries, Mr. Ebbett, when I saw that friend of yours come and go right up. Thought you'd come home without my noticing and—"

"Friend?" Henry's face as he stood in the cold, drafty hallway was a masterpiece of puzzlement. "You say one of my friends came—and is upstairs?"

"Sure is. The tall, thin one. Works the same place you do, I believe."

"Joe Carson?" Henry shook his head. "Didn't know he was coming." Bending quickly, he picked up the large bag of groceries sitting just inside the door. He grunted as he lifted the bag. The flour was heavier than he'd expected. "Well, thanks for taking care of these for me, Mrs. Pettigrew. I'll go right up. Perhaps Bertha returned, and—"

"No, she ain't been back," the old lady assured him. "I been watching for her."

"Oh." He mumbled a few words, then shook his head worriedly and started up the stairs like a weary little man whose wife had unaccountably left him and who now had to cook his own dinner. When he heard her door close, he sighed with relief.

At the top of the stairs, he shifted the weight of the bag onto his left arm and put his right hand into his coat pocket. A curious thrill trembled the length of his arm as his fingers closed about the hard steel of the revolver, and he stood there a moment, breathing heavily.

This was power. This was the moment he'd been waiting for. Death for Joe—but freedom and ease for him . . .

When he pushed the door open, Joe was sprawled comfortably in the chair with a half-finished cigarette drooping between his lips. He straightened sluggishly as Henry came into the room.

Henry said, "Take this bag a minute, will you, Joe?"

Joe was almost on his feet when the gun in Henry's hand exploded. A surprised expression crossed his face. The gun crashed again, and, without a sound, Joe collapsed.

Swiftly, Henry set the bag on a chair, crossed the room, got the automatic out of his pocket and pressed it into Joe's right hand. He grunted, straining mightily, as he forced Joe's body and arm up to the correct height.

With his finger over Joe's he pointed the automatic at the bag and pumped two bullets into it—and then, for good measure, another one into the wall, toward the bedroom doorway and at about the level of his own head. That done, he pushed Joe away, recovered his slippers from the hallway, and deliberately sent a lamp crashing to the floor.

Everything was crystal-clear in his mind. He moved swiftly and surely, setting the stage. First, the groceries. He lifted the bag, from which a trickle of flour was already coming, and let some of the flour stream onto his coat. Then he dropped the bag onto the floor.

The bag burst and a can of corn fell to the floor, to be followed an instant later by a bottle of catsup. The bullet hole in the flour sack tore wide and a white Niagara of flour cascaded onto the carpet. He overturned the chair on which the bag had rested.

Next, the bedroom—he made it in a single stride, jerked open the top drawer, rumpled its contents. He tossed the slippers under the bed. Was that all?

He scanned the room quickly. The ticket! Frantically, he got the envelope from his pocket, making certain that only his gloved hand touched it. Carefully, he slid it into Joe's breast pocket. As a final touch, he got one of the extra door keys from Bertha's dresser and laid it on the table beside Joe's highball glass.

The whole thing, from the first crash of the revolver to the final planting of the key, had taken merely seconds, yet already Mrs. Pettigrew was screaming in the hallway. "Mr. Ebbett! Mr. Ebbett!"

He'd done it!

Henry sucked his lungs full of air and walked to the telephone. He dialed a number and stood there, a slight smile on his round face as he waited for the connection to be made.

A metallic voice came over the wire: "Police headquarters."

Henry swallowed carefully and stared owlishly at the wall through his horn-rimmed glasses. Making his voice tremble, he said:

"Please come to 107 Pinegrove Avenue. I've shot a man. . . . He tried to kill me. . . ."

* * *

The police lieutenant was a heavy-set, dour-faced man in a rumpled blue serge suit. He eyed the body unhappily, almost as though he resented its presence, then looked at Henry. "Well, let's hear the story," he said heavily.

"He was here, waiting for me," Henry told him, remembering to shiver realistically. "I picked up a bag of groceries downstairs, then came right up. He was sorta crouched there in front of the chair, as though he'd heard me and was getting up, and as soon as I stepped into the room, he began shooting. I guess I reacted automatically, because as soon as I saw him with the gun in his hand, I dropped the groceries and ran for the bedroom. I got my gun out of the dresser drawer and I fired back at him—twice, I think." He shook his head dazedly. "I got him, thank God, before he got me!"

"Who is he?"

"His name is Joe Carson. He works the same place I do."

"Any idea why he wanted to kill you?"

"I'm not sure, but I think perhaps—well, I was sitting here, thinking, after I phoned police headquarters, and a lot of things I couldn't understand before began to make sense. My wife didn't come home last night, and now with Joe trying to kill me, it seems as if maybe—"

"Triangle, eh?"

Henry nodded weakly and bent his head. The lieutenant shook his head sympathetically and gestured to the other officers in the doorway.

"Well, get to work, boys," he said gruffly. "The usual photos, diagram, and so on. Keep a sharp eye out for prints." He walked over to the body, glanced shrewdly at Henry. "You touch anything?"

"No, sir." Henry's face became a picture of horror at the thought. "I called you, then sat down, right here in this chair, until you came. I was completely stunned, I guess, but the—well, you know."

A young man with a black bag strode in, his thin face flushed from hurrying. He nodded to the lieutenant and bent over the body.

"Dead," he said promptly. "One bullet passed between fourth and fifth ribs. Not long ago, either." As he got up, he loosened his heavy overcoat and added: "Lord, it's hot in here!"

The lieutenant grunted. "We called you ten minutes ago. Where do you docs hide during the day? You must have been holding a full house."

The coroner's physician smiled good-naturedly. "No game today, darn it. I was taking a shower and O'Brien wasn't available." He nodded toward the body. "It's okay for you to proceed. I'll have him picked up. Suppose you want the autopsy rushed through?"

"Yeah."

"Okay. Be seeing you." He picked up his bag, winked at one of the other officers, and went out. His feet clattered loudly as he descended the stairs.

"How are you coming?" the lieutenant asked, breaking the silence.

"Not bad, sir," one of the men replied. He paused to wipe his perspiring face. "A few more pictures, then I'll start in on the sketch. Would it be okay to turn off the radiator?"

"Leave everything as is," the lieutenant said shortly.

Walking slowly about the room, he peered at the bottle of bourbon, the highball glass, the ashtray, and the key on the table. Turning, he pushed his hands in his pockets and stared at the opposite wall. His eyes found the bullet hole and, evincing no surprise, he went over and examined it casually.

"Bullet in here," he announced. Swinging toward Henry, he said: "So you think he and your wife were trying to deal you out, eh?"

Henry wet his dry lips. "Yes, sir."

"Where do you work?"

"I'm a bookkeeper at the Safeway Loan Company."

"He a bookkeeper there, too?" The lieutenant nodded toward the body.

"No, he was a cashier."

The lieutenant shrugged and walked over to the bookcase in the corner. He scanned the titles, peered at the dust on top of the case, came back. As though he had all the time in the world, he stood and watched one of the officers pick the two guns up upon rods which he inserted down their barrels. "Might have a look in his pockets, Pete," he suggested mildly.

"Sure, Lieutenant." The officer deposited the guns in a cardboard box and carefully set the box on the couch. He knelt beside Joe's body then and slid his fingers into the pockets, expertly removing the contents.

"Coat, right pocket—nothing," he droned mechanically. "Left pocket—two theatre ticket stubs dated November 7th. Outside pocket—one clean white handkerchief, no initial. Inside pocket—a notebook, a bank book, an envelope, and—"

"Anything in the envelope?" the lieutenant asked.

Silence for a moment. "Yes, sir. There's a one-way ticket to Hot Springs, Arkansas."

The lieutenant's eyebrows flicked upward. He extended his hand. "Let's see." Frowning, he examined the ticket, then handed it back. "Be careful of that envelope," he warned. "There may be some prints on it."

"Yes, sir." The officer nodded and went back to his search. "Trousers, right pocket—a dollar and thirty cents in change. Left pocket—$46 in bills." With a soft grunt, he rolled the body over.

"Right, rear—a soiled white handkerchief and a key ring with six keys. Left, rear—a card case containing a few receipts for payments on a suit and several identification cards."

The lieutenant pursed his lips, nodded, and studied the neat piles of objects on the floor. He picked up the notebook, turned its pages carelessly, dropped it on the floor again.

"Make a list, Pete," he said.

He started pacing around the room again, stopped at the table, picked up the key which lay there. He walked to the door with it, pushed it into the keyhole, turned it. The lock snapped back. With a pleased expression on his face, he tossed the key to the officer named Pete.

"Be sure to label this. No prints, of course." More to himself than anyone in the room, he added: "They shouldn't be allowed to put that fancy engraving on keys." He looked at Henry suddenly. "Know anybody in Hot Springs?"

"No, sir."

"Your wife got friends or relatives there?"

"Well, I don't really know, sir. I don't think so. She did mention it once, but only to say that it'd be a nice place to go to for a vacation someday."

"Where was Carson from?"

"Some town in Wisconsin, I think."

Apparently satisfied, the lieutenant turned away. "How're you coming?" he asked. "Any prints?"

"Yeah, quite a few." The officer with the short curly brown hair stood up and wiped his forehead with a handkerchief. "There's a good set on the glass and the bottle."

"Hey, what do you know!" another officer exclaimed suddenly. "Look at this!" He held up a lead slug. "It was in the flour, Lieutenant! Why, if it hadn't been for that bag, it'd have killed him sure!"

Henry's eyes widened. "Good Lord!" he gasped. "Why, he—almost—!" He quivered so realistically that his glasses came very near to sliding off his nose.

"Very nice," the lieutenant commented. "In which arm were you carrying the bag?"

"My left. Like this." Henry bent his arm so the lieutenant could see how he'd carried the heavy bag of groceries.

The lieutenant nodded, studied the pile of spilled cans and flour, then announced: "I'm going down to talk to the old lady. Wait here until I get back." At the door, he added: "Give the bathroom and bedroom a going-over, too, boys."

He was gone fifteen minutes, during which time an ambulance arrived, two men climbed the stairs with a wicker basket, and the body of Joe Carson was removed, leaving only a chalked outline to show where his corpse had lain.

Henry sat hunched in his chair through all this, his eyes following the careful, methodical work of the officers as they took measurements, labeled and packed items in boxes, and dusted powder over various surfaces. From time to time the faintest suggestion of a smile touched his lips fleetingly as he saw them checking the details which he had anticipated. He had nothing to worry about. He'd read and studied dozens of detective stories and he knew what they were looking for. But let them look. He had thought of everything.

When the lieutenant returned, he glanced around the room and gestured impatiently. "Hurry it up, boys. I'm taking Mr. Ebbett to the station. When you finish, seal the door and report to my office."

Riding downtown in the squad car, the lieutenant explained: "It looks open-and-shut to me, Mr. Ebbett, but we have a certain routine we have to go through. I'm taking you to the station, where you'll be formally booked on a charge of murder. There'll be a coroner's inquest tomorrow morning, and then, following that, a hearing in Felony Court. If your story checks, you'll be released by the court. But first, of course, I have to get a detailed, signed statement from you."

Henry hadn't expected to be charged with murder. Somehow, he'd thought the police, knowing he was innocent, would simply take his statement and let him go.

But he didn't protest. He nodded quietly and looked sad, like a man utterly crushed by the fact that his wife had deserted him and that his best friend had plotted his murder.

At police headquarters, he was most cooperative. He gave the lieutenant a detailed statement, signed it, and let them take his fingerprints.

* * *

The coroner's inquest was called the following morning at nine o'clock, but, at Lieutenant Barr's request, it was adjourned for two days to permit the police time to locate Bertha Ebbett.

In the meantime, a score of detectives attached to the homicide detail began checking Henry Ebbett's statement. They found it to be surprisingly exact; in fact, in combing the city they learned details which Henry, though he had planned them, had not been able to mention.

They learned, for instance, that Joe Carson's accounts at the Safeway Loan Company were short. A hasty audit, made overnight by a crew of accountants, established that, over a period of months, a sum exceeding $20,000 had been cleverly embezzled. Many of the records were in the neat handwriting of Henry Ebbett, but that was to be expected. Ebbett was only a book-keeper. Joe Carson, on the other hand, had been a cashier and had had direct charge of the money.

What had happened to the money? The Safeway Loan Company, fortunately, was protected by insurance. Insurance investigators pored over the records and delved into Carson's habits, hobbies, and bank account, but there was nothing to suggest that Carson had ever possessed more than $450 at one time.

One of the investigators, a radical, thought of Ebbett and made a thorough inquiry regarding him. But Ebbett, it developed, was even more spotless than Carson. Ebbett didn't drink, didn't smoke, didn't gamble, and had never been known to pause to look at a well-turned ankle. His bank account was small, he possessed no jewelry, had indulged in no luxuries of any kind.

Obviously, Carson had stolen the money as well as poor Mr. Henry Ebbett's wife.

The investigators were helped to that conclusion by the discovery that a man resembling Carson had, a week earlier, purchased two tickets to Hot Springs, Arkansas. On learning this, Lieutenant Barr wired the Hot Springs, Arkansas, authorities to locate and hold Bertha Ebbett— age 26, height 5-8, weight 120, dark hair, brown eyes, regular features, probably registered at a local hotel.

That done, the lieutenant sighed, rubbed his brow, and sank back in his swivel chair. He raised his eyes wearily when the door of his office opened. "Well, Sergeant?"

"The ballistic reports are in, Lieutenant," his aide reported. "They check with Ebbett's statement. Carson's prints—and only his—were on the glass and liquor bottle. He evidently opened the door with the key we found, threw his hat and coat on the couch, and made himself at home. Ebbett can thank his lucky stars that he was carrying that sack of flour. They found a second slug in it, which accounts for all the empty cartridges."

"Okay. Anything else?"

"Well, Peterson checked those theatre ticket stubs we found in his pocket. They were to a neighborhood movie. The cashier recognized Carson's photo. Said he came there often, sometimes with a woman who wore a cheap silver fox jacket. There was that sort of a jacket in Ebbett's wife's closet."

"Uh-huh. Go on."

"That's about it. The revolver was Ebbett's. Bought it several years ago. The automatic was Carson's. His landlady saw it in his closet once when she was cleaning."

"How is Ebbett doing?"

"About the same. He keeps asking how long he's to be kept locked up."

"Asked for a lawyer yet?"

"No."

"Funny." The lieutenant rubbed his chin thoughtfully. "You'd think he'd be hollering habeas corpus, or something, at the top of his lungs."

"Huh! That guy, he's too tight! Says he can't

afford to waste money on a lawyer where there's no doubt of his innocence."

"Well, maybe he's right, at that." The lieutenant, in dismissal, swung his chair so he could gaze out the window. "Let me know if anything comes through from Hot Springs."

"Yes, sir." And the sergeant, knowing Lieutenant Barr's mood, closed the door gently.

An hour later the phone in Barr's office rang. The operator announced that a long-distance call from Hot Springs was waiting, charges to be reversed. Growling his acceptance, Barr waited expectantly.

When he put down the phone, his thick brows were knitted in a curious frown. In brief, he had been informed that Mrs. Bertha Ebbett had registered the previous morning at a local hotel under her own name, had paid in advance for a room, and, when told that her husband was being held for the murder of Joe Carson, had demanded permission to return home immediately. Barr had told the Hot Springs police to put her on a plane immediately and to wire him the exact time of the plane's departure. . . .

* * *

Later that afternoon, Lieutenant Barr phoned the coroner's office and advised the coroner that the witness he had been waiting for had been located and that the inquest could be resumed the following morning.

When Bertha Ebbett was shown into his office, Lieutenant Barr studied her with interest. She seemed slimmer and prettier than the girl whose photograph he had in a folder on his desk. Her pale face was attractive, though her eyes were faintly shadowed with gray. Her step was firm and brisk, and, when they shook hands across his desk, her grasp was cool but sincere.

"What is it about Henry?" she demanded anxiously. "I asked and asked, but all they'd tell me is that he's supposed to have killed Joe. It isn't true, is it?"

"Yes, it's true," Barr told her gravely, "but it

isn't as bad as it sounds. You needn't worry about Henry. He'll undoubtedly be released as soon as the coroner's inquest is completed."

"Henry really . . . killed Joe?"

"Yes." Barr studied her with his eyes, then said: "I need to know many things about this case, Mrs. Ebbett, which only you can tell me. I'm going to put my questions to you bluntly, without any fancy trimming, and I want you to answer them truthfully."

"Of course! If there's anything—"

"Is it true, Mrs. Ebbett, that you and Carson were friendly and that he was to meet you in Hot Springs as soon as—" He paused, stopped by the look of absolutely incredulity which flooded her face.

"What!"

"Is it true or not, Mrs. Ebbett?"

"Of *course* it isn't true!"

"Isn't it true that Mr. Carson was a frequent visitor at your home, even when your husband wasn't there, and that he often took you to the movies in the evening?"

"Why, yes—but not the way it sounds! The whole idea is fantastic!"

"Why is it fantastic, Mrs. Ebbett? According to your husband, you were unhappy and fought with him continually. Mr. Carson was more nearly your own age, unmarried, attractive, with many interests similar to yours."

"Henry told you that?"

"Yes."

She closed her eyes and sank back in her chair. Barr knew by the way her teeth sank into the red of her lips that she was shocked and fighting desperately for control. When she opened her eyes, her voice was a hoarse whisper: "Tell me . . . please tell me what happened!"

Barr hesitated, then reached for the folder on his desk. He removed a typed copy of Ebbett's statement. In a dry, expressionless voice, he read it to her.

"It's a lie!" she gasped, when he finished. "I don't understand what's happening. It's like a dream, a nightmare. But that"—she pointed at the typewritten sheets—"that's not true!" Her eyes stared into his, dark and hollow, like two great holes in a loaf of uncooked bread. "Henry couldn't have said anything like that!"

"He did say it, though," Barr assured her. "It's signed, sealed, and sworn to."

"But don't you see, I didn't run away from him! Henry knew I was going to Hot Springs. He gave me the money, bought the ticket!"

"Carson bought the tickets, Mrs. Ebbett. The ticket-seller at the station remembers him. He bought two one-way tickets to Hot Springs last week."

"But—" She shook her head helplessly. "Then he bought them because Henry asked him to. Joe often did little things like that for Henry, just as he took me to a movie, once in a while, when Henry had extra work to do at home. I tell you there was nothing to it."

"The second ticket was found in Carson's pocket," Barr said gently.

She didn't get the significance of his statement immediately; when she did, her hands clenched so fiercely that her knuckles stood out.

"Then Henry put it there!" she exclaimed. "When I left, the other ticket was in an envelope on Henry's dresser. That's why I engaged a double room. Henry was to have followed me in a couple of days."

"Did any of your friends know about that arrangement?"

"Joe Carson did."

"Anyone else?"

"I—don't know. I'm afraid not. Henry didn't want anyone at his office to know. You see, he asked for a vacation and was refused. But he was to receive a bonus this week, and, as soon as it was paid to him, he was going to quit his job and come to Hot Springs. I've had a bad cough for several months, and he was going to look for work there, so we could stay permanently."

"In that case, wouldn't it have been better for you to wait until he received his bonus before leaving? The two of you could have traveled together."

"Henry insisted that I go on ahead and look for an apartment. He said he'd pack our things

and arrange to have the furniture shipped. I didn't argue because, as I said, I haven't been well and it seemed like a sensible arrangement."

Lieutenant Barr shook his head slowly. "It may have seemed sensible to you, Mrs. Ebbett— but I doubt if the coroner's jury will believe it."

* * *

The coroner's jury convened the following morning and made short work of the case. Dr. Felix Adelman, the coroner's physician, testified to the approximate time of death, described the bullet wounds, and stated the results of the autopsy on Carson's body. Then Henry Ebbett's signed statement was read.

Experts testified that the bullets found in Carson's body were from a revolver admittedly owned by Ebbett, and that three bullets, fired from an automatic pistol registered in Carson's name and found in his hand, had been located in the apartment: two in the sack of flour which Ebbett had been carrying, and one in the wall adjoining the bedroom. Their angles of entrance and trajectory had been established and were in agreement with Ebbett's statement.

The experts further testified that Carson's— and only Carson's—fingerprints had been found on the highball glass, the bottle of liquor, and ashtray. A paraffin test revealed that Carson had actually fired the automatic. The envelope containing the railroad ticket had borne Carson's and Mrs. Ebbett's fingerprints—but not Henry Ebbett's. The ticket-seller identified a photograph of Carson and stated that Carson was the man who had purchased two one-way tickets to Hot Springs from him. A certified public accountant appeared in behalf of the Safeway Loan Company and testified that Carson had embezzled the sum of $21,125 from his employer. A locksmith identified the key found on the table as one made by him for Mrs. Ebbett. The ticket stubs were introduced as evidence, duly identified, and the theatre cashier repeated her story about Carson and Mrs. Ebbett.

Then old Mrs. Pettigrew was called. She stated that, on the day previous to the murder,

Mrs. Ebbett had left the house in the middle of the afternoon with two suitcases, and, when Mr. Ebbett returned home from work, he had been obviously shocked at discovering his wife was gone.

On the day of the murder, she had seen Carson enter the building at least fifteen minutes before Mr. Ebbett came in. Yes, Mr. Ebbett had knocked on her door and picked up a bag of groceries. He had gone directly upstairs. And had Mrs. Pettigrew heard the shots? Yes, indeed. Mr. Ebbett had hardly stepped into his apartment when the first shot rang out, to be followed quickly by four others. Mrs. Pettigrew had screamed, but, being a victim of arthritis, had been unable to go upstairs.

Henry Ebbett, called to clarify and amplify his statement, testified in a quiet, self-possessed tone in which his grief was evident.

His wife, Bertha Ebbett, on the other hand, testified that everything presented to the jury was a lie, was twisted, was utterly impossible. She admitted that she had attended movies with Carson, that she had been located by police in a Hot Springs hotel, where she had engaged a room, but she denied vehemently the implications which the admissions inferred. She also admitted that she had admired and liked Carson.

Throughout her testimony, Bertha Ebbett spoke in a low, reluctant tone, which the jury was quick to note. They took the indistinctness of her voice to be from shame. In fact, the general tone of her charges and testimony only made them the more certain of her embarrassment and guilt.

It took the jury hardly any time at all to reach a verdict: "Justifiable homicide, with a recommendation that Mrs. Bertha Ebbett be referred to the grand jury for possible indictment as accessory-before-the-fact to an attempted homicide."

Ten minutes after the jury's verdict was rendered, Lieutenant Barr and Sergeant Jablonsky entered a lunchroom across the street from police headquarters. They sat at the counter and ordered coffee.

"You taking Ebbett up to Felony Court this afternoon?" Jablonsky asked after a while.

"I suppose so," Barr admitted.

"You don't seem too happy about it."

Barr took a sip from his steaming cup, then set it down on the counter. He grimaced, as though the coffee had left a bad taste in his mouth. "Frankly, between you and me, I'm not."

"You think Ebbett could have framed it?"

"I don't know," Barr said heavily. "Ebbett is intelligent. Seems to me, if his wife had been playing around with Carson, he'd have known about it and been prepared. I'm not saying she didn't, because it's hard to tell a thing like that about a woman—but I'm not saying she did, either. She says she didn't, and she certainly was shocked when I suggested the setup to her, but the evidence is all the other way. But I will say this: Ebbett is nobody's fool. He wasn't as surprised as he said he was."

"But if Ebbett framed the murder, then he framed the embezzlement, too, and where's the dough?"

"Let the insurance investigators worry about that. I'm a homicide man, and I hate being outsmarted. If Ebbett is working a frame, I want to get him."

"Yeah."

"The thing is," Barr said slowly, "the whole darned thing seems to have gone off like clockwork. I've studied it from every angle, and it must have happened exactly like he said it did. That old woman having seen him coming home after Carson is the sticker. She saw him go up, then heard the shots fired. At that, I don't see how Carson missed plugging him. I'd have emptied my gun into Ebbett before he got to that bedroom."

"One shot would have been enough," the sergeant pointed out, "if it hadn't been for the sack of flour. Carson still had to make a getaway. Maybe he didn't want to fire any more than necessary."

"Maybe," Barr agreed.

"You don't think so?"

"I think Ebbett had to move darned fast, faster than a man surprised could ordinarily move. He had to see Carson, size up the situation, and get started for the bedroom almost before the first shot was fired. The evidence all says that that's what happened, but somehow it doesn't sound reasonable."

They sat there, sipping their coffee and looking out the lunchroom windows into the street. A car drove past, its radiator billowing steam.

"Really cold today again," Jablonsky commented. "Zero, at least."

"Uh-huh."

A man came in from the street and slammed the door. He wore a pair of rimless glasses on his sharp beak of a nose, and a red woolen muffler about his neck almost concealed his chin. He stopped just inside the door, stomped his cold feet, and began to grope in a pocket of his coat for a handkerchief.

Barr's cup hit the counter with a loud thud. "Good Lord!"

"Huh?" Jablonsky looked up.

"Get Ebbett and take him to that apartment of his," Barr ordered. "Don't tell him anything except that we want to check a few details before ordering his release. Take a couple of the boys with you."

Barr hesitated, then added grimly: "I'll take the other squad car and pick up his wife. I have an idea she'll enjoy being in on this!"

* * *

Bertha Ebbett stared stonily at her husband, but Henry refused to look at her. He sat in a chair near the telephone, his small eyes studying a wall through his thick horn-rimmed glasses. Lieutenant Barr appeared very much at ease. With his long legs stretched before him, he sat slumped in the chair Carson had occupied beside the table.

"This probably seems peculiar to you, Mr. Ebbett," Barr said conversationally, "but now that the coroner's jury has exonerated you, it's my responsibility to take you before the Felony Court for a hearing. That may only take a few minutes, but sometimes the judge asks for details and I like to have everything in apple-pie order before proceeding. Understand?"

"Of course, Lieutenant. If it's anything that isn't in my statement, I'll—"

"Just a detail, Mr. Ebbett. You said that, on the day of the shooting, you spent most of the afternoon calling at the railroad stations, airport, and bus depots, trying to trace your wife."

"Yes, sir, I did. I went—"

Barr waved one hand airily. "Yes, we checked on that, and you really did. But we forgot one thing. When you started back home, you came by streetcar and got off on the corner of Farwell and Elson. You walked from that corner to this building, a distance of three blocks."

"That's correct."

"How long did it take you to walk that distance?"

"Why—" For an instant, Henry's eyes flickered. "I don't know, exactly. Not more than a minute or two. Is that important?"

"It may be—and it may not," Barr said succinctly. "But I want to check on it, just to make sure. Jablonsky, suppose you take Mr. Ebbett to the corner of Farwell and Elson in the squad car and put him on the corner. Note the time he starts walking back, then drive slowly along beside him. You, Mr. Ebbett, I want to walk at about the same speed you did the other day. When you reach this building, knock on Mrs. Pettigrew's door, say a few words, and then come right upstairs. Maybe you'd better pretend you've got a bag of groceries in your arm, too."

"But, I don't understand," Henry said. "What possible bearing can that have on—"

"It's just a detail, like I told you," Barr informed him gruffly. "Remember, walk at about the same speed you did the other day."

For the first time, a worried frown creased Henry's forehead. But he went out with Sergeant Jablonsky, and a moment later those sitting in the small apartment heard the engine of the squad car roar into action.

Minutes ticked by, the silence broken only by the quiet hissing of the steam radiator in the corner. Barr sat with his head leaning comfortably against the back of his chair. Once Bertha Ebbett moved restlessly and glanced at the window. She got up and started toward it.

Without opening his eyes, Barr said: "Better leave the window alone, Mrs. Ebbett."

Her lips trembled, but she went back to her chair and sank into it with a helpless little sigh. More minutes passed; then they heard the sound of the downstairs door opening.

Henry's rap on Mrs. Pettigrew's door was loud and distinct. "Just wanted to tell you I was back, Mrs. Pettigrew," he was saying. "Thank you very much for speaking up for me at the inquest. . . ."

Then they heard Henry's feet on the tread. The apartment door began to swing open.

Barr leaned forward intently.

Bertha Ebbett stifled a scream. . . .

For as Henry came into the warm room, he stopped and stood utterly still before them, blinded by the vapor which immediately condensed on the lenses of his thick horn-rimmed glasses. . . .

Try the Girl
Raymond Chandler

RAYMOND (THORNTON) CHANDLER (1888–1959) was born in Chicago, then taken to England as a child and became a British citizen in 1907, but returned to America in 1912 and eventually regained his American citizenship in 1956. He worked in numerous jobs before selling his first short story to *Black Mask* in 1933 at the age of forty-five. Although he is regarded today as perhaps the greatest private-eye writer who ever lived, his pulp stories brought him little fame and not much financial benefit. The detectives in those stories bore different names (Carmady, Dalmas, Mallory, Malvern, and an unnamed protagonist), but they were essentially interchangeable with his most famous hero, Philip Marlowe. After he achieved success with the publication of his first novel, *The Big Sleep* (1939), the stories were collected in several volumes and the protagonists' names were all changed to Marlowe. Chandler produced only seven novels in his career, six of which were filmed (the seventh, *Playback*, is markedly inferior to the others). *Farewell, My Lovely* (filmed as *Murder My Sweet*, 1944) starred Dick Powell as Marlowe; it was followed by *The Big Sleep* (1946, with Humphrey Bogart), *Lady in the Lake* (1947, with Robert Montgomery), *The High Window* (1947, filmed as *The Brasher Doubloon*, with George Montgomery), *The Little Sister* (1969, filmed as *Marlowe*, with James Garner), and *The Long Goodbye* (1973, with Elliott Gould in a memorable masterstroke of miscasting).

"Try the Girl," Chandler's last *Black Mask* story, was published in January 1937.

Try the Girl

Raymond Chandler

THE BIG GUY WASN'T ANY OF MY business. He never was, then or later, least of all then.

I was over on Central, which is the Harlem of Los Angeles, on one of the "mixed" blocks, where there were still both white and colored establishments. I was looking for a little Greek barber named Tom Aleidis whose wife wanted him to come home and was willing to spend a little money to find him. It was a peaceful job. Tom Aleidis was not a crook.

I saw the big guy standing in front of Shamey's, an all-colored drink and dice second-floor, not too savory. He was looking up at the broken stencils in the electric sign, with a sort of rapt expression, like a hunky immigrant looking at the Statue of Liberty, like a man who had waited a long time and come a long way.

He wasn't just big. He was a giant. He looked seven feet high, and he wore the loudest clothes I ever saw on a really big man.

Pleated maroon pants, a rough grayish coat with white billiard balls for buttons, brown suede shoes with explosions in white kid on them, a brown shirt, a yellow tie, a large red carnation, and a front-door handkerchief the color of the Irish flag. It was neatly arranged in three points, under the red carnation. On Central Avenue, not the quietest-dressed street in the world, with that size and that make-up he looked about as unobtrusive as a tarantula on a slice of angel food.

He went over and swung back the doors into Shamey's. The doors didn't stop swinging before they exploded outward again. What sailed out and landed in the gutter and made a high, keening noise, like a wounded rat, was a slick-haired colored youth in a pinchback suit. A "brown," the color of coffee with rather thin cream in it. His face, I mean.

It still wasn't any of my business. I watched the colored boy creep away along the walls. Nothing more happened. So I made my mistake.

I moved along the sidewalk until I could push the swing door myself. Just enough to look in. Just too much.

A hand I could have sat in took hold of my shoulder and hurt and lifted me through the doors and up three steps.

A deep, soft voice said in my ear easily, "Smokes in here, pal. Can you tie that?"

I tried for a little elbow room to get to my sap. I wasn't wearing a gun. The little Greek barber business hadn't seemed to be that sort of job.

He took hold of my shoulder again.

"It's that kind of place," I said quickly.

"Don't say that, pal. Beulah used to work here. Little Beulah."

"Go on up and see for yourself."

He lifted me up three more steps.

"I'm feeling good," he said. "I wouldn't want anybody to bother me. Let's you and me go on up and maybe nibble a drink."

"They won't serve you," I said.

"I ain't seen Beulah in eight years, pal," he said softly, tearing my shoulder to pieces without noticing what he was doing. "She ain't even wrote in six. But she'll have a reason. She used to work here. Let's you and me go on up."

"All right," I said. "I'll go up with you. Just let me walk. Don't carry me. I'm fine. Carmady's the name. I'm all grown up. I go to the bathroom alone and everything. Just don't carry me."

"Little Beulah used to work here," he said softly. He wasn't listening to me.

We went on up. He let me walk.

A crap table was in the far corner beyond the bar, and scattered tables and a few customers were here and there. The whiny voices chanting around the crap table stopped instantly. Eyes looked at us in that dead, alien silence of another race.

A large Negro was leaning against the bar in shirt-sleeves with pink garters on his arms. An ex-pug who had been hit by everything but a concrete bridge. He pried himself loose from the bar edge and came towards us in a loose fighter's crouch.

He put a large brown hand against the big man's gaudy chest. It looked like a stud there.

"No white folks, brother. Jes' fo' the colored people. I'se sorry."

"Where's Beulah?" the big man asked in his deep, soft voice that went with his big white face and his depthless black eyes.

The Negro didn't quite laugh. "No Beulah, brother. No hooch, no gals, jes' the scram, brother. Jes' the scram."

"Kind of take your goddam mitt off me," the big man said.

The bouncer made a mistake, too. He hit him. I saw his shoulder drop, his body swing behind the punch. It was a good clean punch. The big man didn't even try to block it.

He shook his head and took hold of the bouncer by the throat. He was quick for his size. The bouncer tried to knee him. The big man turned him and bent him, took hold of the back of his belt. That broke. So the big man just put his huge hand flat against the bouncer's spine and threw him, clear across the narrow room. The bouncer hit the wall on the far side with a crash that must have been heard in Denver. Then he slid softly down the wall and lay there, motionless.

"Yeah," the big man said. "Let's you and me nibble one."

We went over to the bar. The barman swabbed the bar hurriedly. The customers, by ones and twos and threes, drifted out, silent across the bare floor, silent down the dim uncarpeted stairs. Their departing feet scarcely rustled.

"Whisky sour," the big man said.

We had whisky sours.

"You know where Beulah is?" the big man asked the barman impassively, licking his whisky sour down the side of the thick glass.

"Beulah, you says?" the barman whined. "I ain't seen her roun' heah lately. Not right lately, no, suh."

"How long you been here?"

"'Bout a yeah, Ah reckon. 'Bout a yeah. Yes, suh. 'Bout—"

"How long's this coop been a dinge box?"

"Says which?"

The big man made a fist down at his side, about the size of a bucket.

"Five years anyway," I put in. "This fellow wouldn't know anything about a white girl named Beulah."

The big man looked at me as if I had just hatched out. His whisky sour didn't seem to improve his temper.

"Who the hell asked you to stick your face in?"

I smiled. I made it a big, friendly smile. "I'm the fellow came in here with you. Remember?"

He grinned back, a flat, white grin. "Whisky sour," he told the barman. "Get them fleas outa your pants. Service."

The barman scuttled around, hating us with the whites of his eyes.

The place was empty now, except for the two of us and the barman, and the bouncer over against the far wall.

The bouncer groaned and stirred. He rolled over and began to crawl softly along the baseboard, like a fly with one wing. The big man paid no attention to him.

"There ain't nothing left of the joint," he complained. "They was a stage and a band and cute little rooms where you could have fun. Beulah did some warbling. A redhead. Awful cute. We was to of been married when they hung the frame on me."

We had two more whisky sours before us now. "What frame?" I asked.

"Where you figure I been them eight years I told you about?"

"In somebody's Stony Lonesome," I said.

"Right." He prodded his chest with a thumb like a baseball bat. "Steve Skalla. The Great Bend job in Kansas. Just me. Forty grand. They caught up with me right here. I was what that—hey!"

The bouncer had made a door at the back and fallen through it. A lock clicked.

"Where's that door lead to?" the big man demanded.

"Tha—tha's Mistah Montgom'ry's office, suh. He's the boss. He's got his office back—"

"He might know," the big man said. He wiped his mouth on the Irish flag handkerchief and arranged it carefully back in his pocket. "He better not crack wise neither. Two more whisky sours."

He crossed the room to the door behind the crap table. The lock gave him a little argument for a moment, then a piece of the panel dropped off and he went through, shut the door after him.

It was very silent in Shamey's now. I looked at the barman.

"This guy's tough," I said quickly. "And he's liable to go mean. You can see the idea. He's looking for an old sweetie who used to work here when it was a place for whites. Got any artillery back there?"

"I thought you was with him," the barman said suspiciously.

"Couldn't help myself. He dragged me up. I didn't feel like being thrown over any houses."

"Shuah. Ah got me a shotgun," the barman said, still suspicious.

He began to stoop behind the bar, then stayed in that position rolling his eyes.

There was a dull flat sound at the back of the place, behind the shut door. It might have been a slammed door. It might have been a gun. Just the one sound. No other followed it.

The barman and I waited too long, wondering what the sound was. Not liking to think what it could be.

The door at the back opened and the big man came through quickly, with a Colt army .45 automatic looking like a toy in his hand.

He looked the room over with one swift glance. His grin was taut. He looked like the man who could take forty grand singlehanded from the Great Bend Bank.

He came over to us in swift, almost soundless steps, for all his size.

"Rise up, nigger!"

The barman came up slowly, gray; his hands empty, high.

The big man felt me over, stepped away from us.

"Mr. Montgomery didn't know where Beulah was either," he said softly. "He tried to tell me—with this." He waggled the gun. "So long, punks. Don't forget your rubbers."

He was gone, down the stairs, very quickly, very quietly.

I jumped around the bar and took the sawed-off shotgun that lay there, on the shelf. Not to use on Steve Skalla. That was not my job. So the barman wouldn't use it on me. I went back across the room and through that door.

The bouncer lay on the floor of a hall with a knife in his hand. He was unconscious. I took the knife out of his hand and stepped over him through a door marked OFFICE.

Mr. Montgomery was in there, behind a small scarred desk, close to a partly boarded-up window. Just folded, like a handkerchief or a hinge.

A drawer was open at his right hand. The gun would have come from there. There was a smear of oil on the paper that lined it.

Not a smart idea, but he would never have a smarter one—not now.

Nothing happened while I waited for the police.

When they came both the barman and the bouncer were gone. I had locked myself in with Mr. Montgomery and the shotgun. Just in case.

Hiney got it. A lean-jawed, complaining, overslow detective lieutenant, with long yellow hands that he held on his knees while he talked to me in his cubicle at Headquarters. His shirt was darned under the points of his old-fashioned stiff collar. He looked poor and sour and honest.

This was an hour or so later. They knew all about Steve Skalla then, from their own records. They even had a ten-year-old photo that made him look as eyebrowless as a French roll. All they didn't know was where he was.

"Six foot six and a half," Hiney said. "Two hundred sixty-four pounds. A guy that size can't get far, not in them fancy duds. He couldn't buy anything else in a hurry. Whyn't you take him?"

I handed the photo back and laughed.

Hiney pointed one of his long yellow fingers at me bitterly. "Carmady, a tough shamus, huh? Six feet of man, and a jaw you could break rocks on. Whyn't you take him?"

"I'm getting a little gray at the temples," I said. "And I didn't have a gun. He had. I wasn't on a gun-toting job over there. Skalla just picked me up. I'm kind of cute sometimes."

Hiney glared at me.

"All right," I said. "Why argue? I've seen the guy. He could wear an elephant in his vest pocket. And I didn't know he'd killed anybody. You'll get him all right."

"Yeah," Hiney said. "Easy. But I just don't like to waste my time on these shine killings. No pix. No space. Not even three lines in the want-ad section. Heck, they was five smokes—five, mind you—carved Harlem sunsets all over each other over on East Eight-four one time. All dead. Cold meat. And the —— newshawks wouldn't even go out there."

"Pick him up nice," I said. "Or he'll knock off a brace of prowlies for you. Then you'll get space."

"And I wouldn't have the case then neither," Hiney jeered. "Well, the hell with him. I got him on the air. Ain't nothing else to do but just sit."

"Try the girl," I said. "Beulah. Skalla will. That's what he's after. That's what started it all. Try her."

"You try her," Hiney said. "I ain't been in a joy house in twenty years."

"I suppose I'd be right at home in one. How much will you pay?"

"Jeeze, guy, coppers don't hire private dicks. What with?" He rolled a cigarette out of a can of tobacco. It burned down one side like a forest fire. A man yelled angrily into a telephone in the next cubbyhole. Hiney made another cigarette with more care and licked it and lighted it. He clasped his bony hands on his bony knees again.

"Think of your publicity," I said. "I bet you twenty-five I find Beulah before you put Skalla under glass."

He thought it over. He seemed almost to count his bank balance on his cigarette puffs.

"Ten is top," he said. "And she's all mine—private."

I stared at him.

"I don't work for that kind of money," I said. "But if I can do it in one day—and you let me alone—I'll do it for nothing. Just to show you why you've been a lieutenant for twenty years."

He didn't like that crack much better than I liked his about the joy house. But we shook hands on it.

I got my old Chrysler roadster out of the official parking lot and drove back towards the Central Avenue district.

Shamey's was closed up, of course. An obvious plainclothes man sat in a car in front of it, reading a paper with one eye. I didn't know why. Nobody there knew anything about Skalla.

I parked around the corner and went into the diagonal lobby of a Negro hotel called the Hotel Sans Souci. Two rows of hard, empty chairs stared at each other across a strip of fiber carpet. Behind a desk a bald-headed man had his eyes shut and his hands clasped on the desk top. He dozed. He wore an ascot tie that had been tied about 1880, and the green stone in his stickpin was not quite as large as a trash barrel. His large, loose chin folded down on it gently, and his brown hands were soft, peaceful, and clean.

A metal embossed sign at his elbow said: *This Hotel Is Under the Protection of the International Consolidated Agencies, Inc.*

When he opened one eye I pointed to the sign and said: "H.P.D. man checking up. Any trouble here?"

H.P.D. means Hotel Protective Department, which is the part of a large agency that looks after check bouncers and people who move out by the back stairs, leaving second-hand suitcases full of bricks.

"Trouble, brother," he said, in a high, sonorous voice, "is something we is fresh out of." He lowered the voice four or five notches and added, "We don't take no checks."

I leaned on the counter across from his folded hands and started to spin a quarter on the bare, scarred wood.

"Heard what happened over at Shamey's this morning?"

"Brother, I forgit." Both his eyes were open now and he was watching the blur of light made by the spinning quarter.

"The boss got bumped off," I said. "Montgomery. Got his neck broken."

"May the Lawd receive his soul, brother." The voice went down again. "Cop?"

"Private—on a confidential lay. And I know a man who can keep one that way when I see one."

He looked me over, closed his eyes again. I kept spinning the quarter. He couldn't resist looking at it.

"Who done it?" he asked softly. "Who fixed Sam?"

"A tough guy out of the jailhouse got sore because it wasn't a white joint. It used to be. Remember?"

He didn't say anything. The coin fell over with a light whirr and lay still.

"Call your play," I said. "I'll read you a chapter of the Bible or buy you a drink. Either one."

"Brother," he said sonorously, "I kinda like to read my Bible in the seclusion of my family." Then he added swiftly, in his business voice, "Come around to this side of the desk."

I went around there and pulled a pint of bonded bourbon off my hip and handed it to him in the shelter of the desk. He poured two small glasses, quickly, sniffed his with a smooth, expert manner, and tucked it away.

"What you want to know?" he asked. "Ain't a crack in the sidewalk I don't know. Mebbe I ain't tellin' though. This liquor's been in the right company."

"Who ran Shamey's before it was a colored place?"

He stared at me, surprised. "The name of that pore sinner was Shamey, brother."

I groaned. "What have I been using for brains?"

"He's daid, brother, gathered to the Lawd. Died in nineteen and twenty-nine. A wood alcohol case, brother. And him in the business." He raised his voice to the sonorous level. "The same year the rich folks lost their goods and chattels, brother." The voice went down again. "I didn't lose me a nickel."

"I'll bet you didn't. Pour some more. He leave any folks—anybody that's still around?"

He poured another small drink, corked the bottle firmly. "Two is all—before lunch," he said. "I thank you, brother. Yo' method of approach is soothin' to a man's dignity." He cleared his throat. "Had a wife," he said. "Try the phone book."

He wouldn't take the bottle. I put it back on my hip. He shook hands with me, folded his on the desk once more and closed his eyes.

The incident, for him, was over.

There was only one Shamey in the phone book. Violet Lu Shamey, 1644 West Fifty-fourth Place. I spent a nickel in a booth.

After a long time a dopey voice said, "Uh-huh. Wh-what is it?"

"Are you the Mrs. Shamey whose husband once ran a place on Central Avenue—a place of entertainment?"

"Wha—what? My goodness sakes alive! My

husband's been gone these seven years. Who did you say you was?"

"Detective Carmady. I'll be right out. It's important."

"Wh—who did you say—"

It was a thick, heavy, clogged voice.

It was a dirty brown house with a dirty brown lawn in front of it. There was a large bare patch around a tough-looking palm tree. On the porch stood one lonely rocker.

The afternoon breeze made the unpruned shoots of last year's poinsettias tap-tap against the front wall. A line of stiff, yellowish, half-washed clothes jittered on a rusty wire in the side yard.

I drove on a little way and parked my roadster across the street, and walked back.

The bell didn't work, so I knocked. A woman opened the door blowing her nose. A long yellow face with weedy hair growing down the sides of it. Her body was shapeless in a flannel bathrobe long past all color and design. It was just something around her. Her toes were large and obvious in a pair of broken man's slippers.

I said, "Mrs. Shamey?"

"You the—?"

"Yeah. I just called you."

She gestured me in wearily. "I ain't had time to get cleaned up yet," she whined.

We sat down in a couple of dingy mission rockers and looked at each other across a living room in which everything was junk except a small new radio droning away behind its dimly lighted panel.

"All the company I got," she said. Then she tittered. "Bert ain't done nothing, has he? I don't get cops calling on me much."

"Bert?"

"Bert Shamey, mister. My husband."

She tittered again and flopped her feet up and down. In her titter was a loose alcoholic overtone. It seemed I was not to get away from it that day.

"A joke, mister," she said. "He's dead. I hope to Christ there's enough cheap blondes where he is. He never got enough of them here."

"I was thinking more about a redhead," I said.

"I guess he'd use one of those too." Her eyes, it seemed to me, were not so loose now. "I don't call to mind. Any special one?"

"Yeah. A girl named Beulah. I don't know her last name. She worked at the Club on Central. I'm trying to trace her for her folks. It's a colored place now and, of course, the people there never heard of her."

"I never went there," the woman yelled, with unexpected violence. "I wouldn't know."

"An entertainer," I said. "A singer. No chance you'd know her, eh?"

She blew her nose again, on one of the dirtiest handkerchiefs I ever saw. "I got a cold."

"You know what's good for it," I said.

She gave me a swift, raking glance. "I'm fresh out of that."

"I'm not."

"Gawd," she said. "You're no cop. No cop ever brought a drink."

I brought out my pint of bourbon and balanced it on my knee. It was almost full still. The clerk at the Hotel Sans Souci was no reservoir. The woman's seaweed-colored eyes jumped at the bottle. Her tongue coiled around her lips.

"Man, that's liquor," she sighed. "I don't care who you are. Hold it careful, mister."

She heaved up and waddled out of the room and came back with two thick, smeared glasses.

"No fixin's," she said. "Just what you brought." She held the glasses out.

I poured her a slug that would have made me float over a wall. A smaller one for me. She put hers down like an aspirin tablet and looked at the bottle. I poured her another. She took that over to her chair. Her eyes had turned two shades browner.

"This stuff dies painless with me," she said. "It never knows what hit it. What was we talkin' about?"

"A red-haired girl named Beulah. Used to work at the joint. Remember better now?"

"Yeah." She used her second drink. I went

over and stood the bottle on the table beside her. She used some out of that.

"Hold on to your chair and don't step on no snakes," she said. "I got me a idea."

She got up out of the chair, sneezed, almost lost her bathrobe, slapped it back against her stomach and stared at me coldly.

"No peekin'," she said, and wagged a finger at me and went out of the room again, hitting the side of the door casement on her way.

From the back of the house presently there were various types of crashes. A chair seemed to be kicked over. A bureau drawer was pulled out too far and smashed to the floor. There was fumbling and thudding and loud language. After a while, then, there was the slow click of a lock and what seemed to be the screech of a trunk top going up. More fumbling and banging things around. A tray landed on the floor, I thought. Then a chortle of satisfaction.

She came back into the room holding a package tied with faded pink tape. She threw it in my lap.

"Look 'em over, Lou. Photos. Newspaper stills. Not that them tramps ever got in no newspapers except by way of the police blotter. They're people from the joint. By God, they're all the —— left me. Them and his old clothes."

She sat down and reached for the whisky again.

I untied the tape and looked through a bunch of shiny photos of people in professional poses. Not all of them were women. The men had foxy faces and racetrack clothes or make-up. Hoofers and comics from the filling-station circuits. Not many of them ever got west of Main Street. The women had good legs and displayed them more than Will Hays would have liked. But their faces were as threadbare as a bookkeeper's coat. All but one.

She wore a Pierrot costume, at least from the waist up. Under the high conical white hat her fluffed-out hair might have been red. Her eyes had laughter in them. I won't say her face was unspoiled. I'm not that good at faces. But it wasn't like the others. It hadn't been kicked

around. Somebody had been nice to that face. Perhaps just a tough mug like Steve Skalla. But he had been nice. In the laughing eyes there was still hope.

I threw the others aside and carried this one over to the sprawled, glassy-eyed woman in the chair. I poked it under her nose.

"This one," I said. "Who is she? What happened to her?"

She stared at it fuzzily, then chuckled.

"Tha's Steve Skalla's girl, Lou. Heck, I forgot her name."

"Beulah," I said. "Beulah's her name."

She watched me under her tawny, mangled eyebrows. She wasn't so drunk.

"Yeah?" she said. "Yeah?"

"Who's Steve Skalla?" I rapped.

"Bouncer down at the joint, Lou." She giggled again. "He's in the pen."

"Oh no, he isn't," I said. "He's in town. He's out. I know him. He just got in."

Her face went to pieces like a clay pigeon. Instantly I knew who had turned Skalla up to the local law. I laughed. I couldn't miss. Because she knew. If she hadn't known, she wouldn't have bothered to be cagey about Beulah. She couldn't have forgotten Beulah. Nobody could.

Her eyes went far back into her head. We stared into each other's faces. Then her hand snatched at the photo.

I stepped back and tucked it away in an inside pocket.

"Have another drink," I said. I handed her the bottle.

She took it, lingered over it, gurgled it slowly down her throat, staring at the faded carpet.

"Yeah," she said whisperingly. "I turned him in but he never knew. Money in the bank he was. Money in the bank."

"Give me the girl," I said. "And Skalla knows nothing from me."

"She's here," the woman said. "She's in radio. I heard her once on KLBL. She's changed her name, though. I dunno."

I had another hunch. "You do know," I said. "You're bleeding her still. Shamey left you nothing. What do you live on? You're bleeding her because she pulled herself up in the world, from people like you and Skalla. That's it, isn't it?"

"Money in the bank," she croaked. "Hundred a month. Reg'lar as rent. Yeah."

The bottle was on the floor again. Suddenly, without being touched, it fell over on its side. Whisky gurgled out. She didn't move to get it.

"Where is she?" I pounded on. "What's her name?"

"I dunno, Lou. Part of the deal. Get the money in a cashier's check. I dunno. Honest."

"The hell you don't!" I snarled. "Skalla—"

She came to her feet in a surge and screamed at me, "Get out, you! Get out before I call a cop! Get out, you ——!"

"Okay, okay." I put a hand out soothingly. "Take it easy. I won't tell Skalla. Just take it easy."

She sat down again slowly and retrieved the almost empty bottle. After all I didn't have to have a scene now. I could find out other ways.

She didn't even look towards me as I went out. I went out into the crisp fall sunlight and got into my car. I was a nice boy, trying to get along. Yes, I was a swell guy. I liked knowing myself. I was the kind of guy who chiseled a sodden old wreck out of her life secrets to win a ten-dollar bet.

I drove down to the neighborhood drugstore and shut myself in its phone booth to call Hiney.

"Listen," I told him, "the widow of the man that ran Shamey's when Skalla worked there is still alive. Skalla might call to see her, if he thinks he dares."

I gave him the address. He said sourly, "We almost got him. A prowl car was talkin' to a Seventh Street conductor at the end of the line. He mentioned a guy that size and with them clothes. He got off at Third and Alexandria, the conductor says. What he'll do is break into some big house where the folks is away. So we got him bottled."

I told him that was fine.

KLBL was on the western fringe of that part of the city that melts into Beverly Hills. It was housed in a flat stucco building, quite unpretentious, and there was a service station in the form of a Dutch windmill on the corner of the lot. The call letters of the station revolved in neon letters on the sails of the windmill.

I went into a ground-floor reception room, one side of which was glass and showed an empty broadcasting studio with a stage and ranged chairs for an audience. A few people sat around the reception room trying to look magnetic, and the blond receptionist was spearing chocolates out of a large box with nails that were almost royal purple in color.

I waited half an hour and then got to see a Mr. Dave Marineau, studio manager. The station manager and the day-program manager were both too busy to see me. Marineau had a small sound-proofed office behind the organ. It was papered with signed photographs.

Marineau was a handsome tall man, somewhat in the Levantine style, with red lips a little too full, a tiny silky mustache, large limpid brown eyes, shiny black hair that might or might not have been marceled, and long, pale, nicotined fingers.

He read my card while I tried to find my Pierrot girl on his wall and didn't.

"A private detective, eh? What can we do for you?"

I took my Pierrot out and placed it down on his beautiful brown blotter. It was fun watching him stare at it. All sorts of minute things happened to his face, none of which he wanted known. The sum total of them was that he knew the face and that it meant something to him. He looked up at me with a bargaining expression.

"Not very recent," he said. "But nice. I don't know whether we could use it or not. Legs, aren't they?"

"It's at least eight years old," I said. "What would you use it for?"

"Publicity, of course. We get one in the radio column about every second month. We're a small station still."

"Why?"

"You mean you don't know who it is?"

"I know who she was," I said.

"Vivian Baring, of course, Star of our Jumbo Candy Bar program. Don't you know it? A tri-weekly serial, half an hour."

"Never heard of it," I said. "A radio serial is my idea of the square root of nothing."

He leaned back and lit a cigarette, although one was burning on the edge of his glass-lined tray.

"All right," he said sarcastically. "Stop being fulsome and get to business. What is it you want?"

"I'd like her address."

"I can't give you that, of course. And you won't find it in any phone book or directory. I'm sorry." He started to gather papers together and then saw the second cigarette and that made him feel like a sap. So he leaned back again.

"I'm in a spot," I said. "I have to find the girl. Quickly. And I don't want to look like a black-mailer."

He licked his very full and very red lips. Somehow I got the idea he was pleased at something.

He said softly, "You mean you know something that might hurt Miss Baring—and incidentally the program?"

"You can always replace a star in radio, can't you?"

He licked his lips some more. Then his mouth tried to get tough. "I seem to smell something nasty," he said.

"It's your mustache burning," I said.

It wasn't the best gag in the world, but it broke the ice. He laughed. Then he did wingovers with his hands. He leaned forward and got as confidential as a tipster.

"We're going at this wrong," he said. "Obviously. You're probably on the level—you look it—so let me make my play." He grabbed a leatherbound pad and scribbled on it, tore the leaf off and passed it across.

I read: *1737 North Flores Avenue.*

"That's her address," he said. "I won't give the phone number without her O.K. Now treat me like a gentleman. That is, if it concerns the station."

I tucked his paper into my pocket and thought it over. He had suckered me neatly, put me on my few remaining shreds of decency. I made my mistake.

"How's the program going?"

"We're promised network audition. It's simple, everyday stuff called 'A Street in Our Town,' but it's done beautifully. It'll wow the country some day. And soon." He wiped his hand across his fine white brow. "Incidentally, Miss Baring writes the scripts herself."

"Ah," I said. "Well, here's your dirt. She had a boyfriend in the big house. That is he used to be. She got to know him in a Central Avenue joint where she worked once. He's out and he's looking for her and he's killed a man. Now wait a minute—"

He hadn't turned as white as a sheet, because he didn't have the right skin. But he looked bad.

"Now wait a minute," I said. "It's nothing against the girl and you know it. She's okay. You can see that in her face. It might take a little counterpublicity, if it all came out. But that's nothing. Look how they gild some of those tramps in Hollywood."

"It costs money," he said. "We're a poor studio. And the network audition would be off." There was something faintly dishonest about his manner that puzzled me.

"Nuts," I said, leaning forward and pounding the desk. "The real thing is to protect her. This tough guy—Steve Skalla is his name—is in love with her. He kills people with his bare hands. He won't hurt her, but if she has a boyfriend or a husband—"

"She's not married," Marineau put in quickly, watching the rise and fall of my pounding hand.

"He might wring his neck for him. That would put it a little too close to her. Skalla doesn't know where she is. He's on the dodge, so it's harder for him to find out. The cops are your best bet, if you have enough drag to keep them from feeding it to the papers."

"Nix," he said. "Nix on the cops. You want the job, don't you?"

"When do you need her here again?"

"Tomorrow night. She's not on tonight."

"I'll hide her for you until then," I said. "If you want me to. That's as far as I'd go alone."

He grabbed my card again, read it, dropped it into a drawer.

"Get out there and dig her out," he snapped. "If she's not home, stick till she is. I'll get a conference upstairs and then we'll see. Hurry it!"

I stood up. "Want a retainer?" he snapped.

"That can wait."

He nodded, made some more wingovers with his hands and reached for his phone.

That number on Flores would be up near Sunset Towers, across town from where I was. Traffic was pretty thick, but I hadn't gone more than twelve blocks before I was aware that a blue coupé which had left the studio parking lot behind me was still behind me.

I jockeyed around in a believable manner, enough to feel sure it was following me. There was one man in it. Not Skalla. The head was a foot too low over the steering wheel.

I jockeyed more and faster and lost it. I didn't know who it was, and at the moment, I hadn't time to bother figuring it out.

I reached the Flores Avenue place and tucked my roadster into the curb.

Bronze gates opened into a nice bungalow court, and two rows of bungalows with steep roofs of molded shingles gave an effect a little like the thatched cottages in old English sporting prints. A very little.

The grass was almost too well kept. There was a wide walk and an oblong pool framed in colored tiles and stone benches along its sides. A nice place. The late sun made interesting shadows over its lawns, and except for the motor horns, the distant hum of traffic up on Sunset Boulevard wasn't unlike the drone of bees.

My number was the last bungalow on the left. Nobody answered the bell, which was set in the middle of the door so that you would wonder how the juice got to where it had to go. That was

cute too. I rang time after time, then I started back to the stone benches by the pool to sit down and wait.

A woman passed me walking fast, not in a hurry, but like a woman who always walks fast. She was a thin, sharp brunette in burnt-orange tweeds and a black hat that looked like a page-boy's hat. It looked like the devil with the burnt-orange tweeds. She had a nose that would be in things and tight lips and she swung a key container.

She went up to my door, unlocked it, went in. She didn't look like Beulah.

I went back and pushed the bell again. The door opened at once. The dark, sharp-faced woman gave me an up-and-down look and said: "Well?"

"Miss Baring? Miss Vivian Baring?"

"Who?" It was like a stab.

"Miss Vivian Baring—of KLBL," I said. "I was told—"

She flushed tightly and her lips almost bit her teeth. "If this is a gag, I don't care for it," she said. She started the door towards my nose.

I said hurriedly, "Mr. Marineau sent me."

That stopped the door closing. It opened again, very wide. The woman's mouth was as thin as a cigarette paper. Thinner.

"I," she said very distinctly, "happen to be Mr. Marineau's wife. This happens to be Mr. Marineau's residence. I wasn't aware that this—this—"

"Miss Vivian Baring," I said. But it wasn't uncertainty about the name that had stopped her. It was plain, cold fury.

"—that this Miss Baring," she went on, exactly as though I had not said a word, "had moved in here. Mr. Marineau must be feeling very amusing today."

"Listen, lady. This isn't—"

The slamming door almost made a wave in the pool down the walk. I looked at it for a moment, and then I looked at the other bungalows. If we had an audience, it was keeping out of sight. I rang the bell again.

The door jumped open this time. The

brunette was livid. "Get off my porch!" she yelled. "Get off before I have you thrown off!"

"Wait a minute," I growled. "This may be a gag for him, but it's no gag to the police."

That got her. Her whole expression got soft and interested.

"Police?" she cooed.

"Yeah. It's serious. It involves a murder. I've got to find this Miss Baring. Not that she, you understand—"

The brunette dragged me into the house and shut the door and leaned against it, panting.

"Tell me," she said breathlessly. "Tell me. Has that redheaded something got herself mixed up in a murder?" Suddenly her mouth snapped wide open and her eyes jumped at me.

I slapped a hand over her mouth. "Take it easy!" I pleaded. "It's not your Dave. Not Dave, lady."

"Oh." She got rid of my hand and let out a sigh and looked silly. "No, of course. Just for a moment . . . Well, *who* is it?"

"Nobody you know. I can't broadcast things like that, anyway. I want Miss Baring's address. Have you got it?"

I didn't know any reason why she would have. Or rather, I might be able to think of one, if I shook my brains hard enough.

"Yes," she said. "Yes, I have. Indeed, I have. Mister Smarty doesn't know that. Mister Smarty doesn't know as much as he thinks he knows, does Mister Smarty? He—"

"The address is all I can use right now," I growled. "And I'm in a bit of a hurry, Mrs. Marineau. Later on"—I gave her a meaning look—"I'm sure I'll want to talk to you."

"It's on Heather Street," she said. "I don't know the number. But I've been there. I've been *past* there. It's only a short street, with four or five houses, and only one of them on the downward side of the hill." She stopped, added, "I don't think the house has a number. Heather Street is at the top of Beachwood Drive."

"Has she a phone?"

"Of course, but a restricted number. She would have. They all do, those ——. If I knew it—"

"Yeah," I said. "You'd call her up and chew her ear off. Well, thank you very much, Mrs. Marineau. This is confidential, of course. I mean confidential."

"Oh, by all means!"

She wanted to talk longer but I pushed past her out of the house and went back down the flagged walk. I could feel her eyes on me all the way, so I didn't do any laughing.

The lad with the restless hands and the full red lips had had what he thought was a very cute idea. He had given me the first address that came into his head, his own. Probably he had expected his wife to be out. I didn't know. It looked awfully silly, however I thought about it—unless he was pressed for time.

Wondering why he should be pressed for time, I got careless. I didn't see the blue coupé double-parked almost at the gates until I also saw the man step from behind it.

He had a gun in his hand.

He was a big man, but not anything like Skalla's size. He made a sound with his lips and held his left palm out and something glittered in it. It might have been a piece of tin or a police badge.

Cars were parked along both sides of Flores. Half a dozen people should have been in sight. There wasn't one—except the big man with the gun and myself.

He came closer, making soothing noises with his mouth.

"Pinched," he said. "Get in my hack and drive it, like a nice lad." He had a soft, husky voice, like an overworked rooster trying to croon.

"You all alone?"

"Yeah, but I got the gun." He sighed. "Act nice and you're as safe as the bearded woman at a Legion convention. Safer."

He was circling slowly, carefully. I saw the metal thing now.

"That's a special badge," I said. "You've got no more right to pinch me than I have to pinch you."

"In the hack, bo. Be nice or your guts lie on

this here street. I got orders." He started to pat me gently. "Hell, you ain't even rodded."

"Skip it!" I growled. "Do you think you could take me if I was?"

I walked over to his blue coupé and slid under its wheel. The motor was running. He got in beside me and put his gun in my side and we went on down the hill.

"Take her west on Santa Monica," he husked. "Then up, say, Canyon Drive to Sunset. Where the bridle path is."

I took her west on Santa Monica, past the bottom of Holloway, then a row of junk yards and some stores. The street widened and became a boulevard past Doheny. I let the car out a little to feel it. He stopped me doing that. I swung north to Sunset and then west again. Lights were being lit in big houses up the slopes. The dusk was full of radio music.

I eased down and took a look at him before it got too dark. Even under the pulled-down hat on Flores I had seen the eyebrows, but I wanted to be sure. So I looked again. They were the eyebrows, all right.

They were almost as even, almost as smoothly black, and fully as wide as a half-inch strip of black plush pasted across his broad face above the eyes and nose. There was no break in the middle. His nose was large and coarse-grained and had hung out over too many beers.

"Bub McCord," I said. "Ex-copper. So you're in the snatch racket now. It's Folsom for you this time, baby."

"Aw, can it." He looked hurt and leaned back in the corner. Bub McCord, caught in a graft tangle, had done a three in Quentin. Next time he would go to the recidivist prison, which is Folsom in our state.

He leaned his gun on his left thigh and cuddled the door with his fat back. I let the car drift and he didn't seem to mind. It was between-times, after the homeward rush of the office man, before the evening crowd came out.

"This ain't no snatch," he complained. "We just don't want no trouble. You can't expect to go up against an organization like KLBL with a two-bit shakedown, and get no kickback. It ain't reasonable." He spat out of the window without turning his head. "Keep her rollin', bo."

"What shakedown?"

"You wouldn't know, would you? Just a wandering peeper with his head stuck in a knothole, huh? That's you. Innocent, as the guy says."

"So you work for Marineau. That's all I wanted to know. Of course I knew it already, after I back-alleyed you, and you showed up again."

"Neat work, bo—but keep her rollin'. Yeah, I had to phone in. Just caught him."

"Where do we go from here?"

"I take care of you till nine-thirty. After that we go to a place."

"What place?"

"It ain't nine-thirty. Hey, don't go to sleep in that there corner."

"Drive it yourself, if you don't like my work."

He pushed the gun at me hard. It hurt. I kicked the coupé out from under him and set him back in his corner, but he kept his gun in a good grip. Somebody called out archly on somebody's front lawn.

Then I saw a red light winking ahead, and a sedan just passing it, and through the rear window of the sedan two flat caps side by side.

"You'll get awfully tired of holding that gun," I told McCord. "You don't dare use it anyway. You're copper-soft. There's nothing so soft as a copper who's had his badge torn off. Just a big heel. Copper-soft."

We weren't near to the sedan, but I wanted his attention. I got it. He slammed me over the head and grabbed the wheel and yanked the brake on. We ground to a stop. I shook my head woozily. By the time I came out of it he was away from me again, in his corner.

"Next time," he said thinly, for all his huskiness, "I put you to sleep in the rumble. Just try it, bo. Just try it, Now roll—and keep the wisecracks down in your belly."

I drove ahead, between the hedge that bordered the bridle path and the wide parkway beyond the curbing. The cops in the sedan tooled on gently, drowsing, listening with half an ear to their radio, talking of this and that. I could almost hear them in my mind, the sort of thing they would be saying.

"Besides," McCord growled. "I don't need no gun to handle you. I never see the guy I couldn't handle without no gun."

"I saw one this morning," I said. I started to tell him about Steve Skalla.

Another red stoplight showed. The sedan ahead seemed loath to leave it. McCord lit a cigarette with his left hand, bending his head a little.

I kept telling him about Skalla and the bouncer at Shamey's.

Then I tramped on the throttle.

The little car shot ahead without a quiver. McCord started to swing his gun at me. I yanked the wheel hard to the right and yelled: "Hold tight! It's a crash!"

We hit the prowl car almost on the left rear fender. It waltzed around on one wheel, apparently, and loud language came out of it. It slewed, rubber screamed, metal made a grinding sound, the left taillight splintered and probably the gas tank bulged.

The little coupé sat back on its heels and quivered like a scared rabbit.

McCord could have cut me in half. His gun muzzle was inches from my ribs. But he wasn't a hard guy, really. He was just a broken cop who had done time and got himself a cheap job after it and was on an assignment he didn't understand.

He tore the right-hand door open, and jumped out of the car.

One of the cops was out by this time, on my side. I ducked down under the wheel. A flash beam burned across the top of my hat.

It didn't work. Steps came near and the flash jumped into my face.

"Come on out of that," a voice snarled. "What the hell you think this is—a racetrack?"

I got out sheepishly. McCord was crouched somewhere behind the coupé, out of sight.

"Lemme smell of your breath."

I let him smell my breath.

"Whisky," he said. "I thought so. Walk, baby. Walk." He prodded me with the flashlight.

I walked.

The other cop was trying to jerk his sedan loose from the coupé. He was swearing, but he was busy with his own troubles.

"You don't walk like no drunk," the cop said. "What's the matter? No brakes?" The other cop had got the bumpers free and was climbing back under his wheel.

I took my hat off and bent my head. "Just an argument," I said. "I got hit. It made me woozy for a minute."

McCord made a mistake. He started running when he heard that. He vaulted across the parkway, jumped the wall and crouched. His footsteps thudded on turf.

That was my cue. "Holdup!" I snapped at the cop who was questioning me. "I was afraid to tell you!"

"Jeeze, the howling—!" he yelled, and tore a gun out of his holster. "Why'n't you say so?" He jumped for the wall. "Circle the heap! We want that guy!" he yelled at the man in the sedan.

He was over the wall. Grunts. More feet pounding on the turf. A car stopped half a block away and a man started to get out of it but kept his foot on the running board. I could barely see him behind his dimmed headlights.

The cop in the prowl car charged at the hedge that bordered the bridle path, backed furiously, swung around and was off with screaming siren.

I jumped into McCord's coupé, and jerked the starter.

Distantly there was a shot, then two shots, then a yell. The siren died at a corner and picked up again.

I gave the coupé all it had and left the neighborhood. Far off, to the north, a lonely sound against the hills, a siren kept on wailing.

I ditched the coupé half a block from Wilshire and took a taxi in front of the Beverly Wilshire. I knew I could be traced. That wasn't important. The important thing was how soon.

From a cocktail bar in Hollywood I called Hiney. He was still on the job and still sour.

"Anything new on Skalla?"

"Listen," he said nastily, "was you over to talk to that Shamey woman? Where are you?"

"Certainly I was," I said. "I'm in Chicago."

"You better come on home. Why was you there?"

"I thought she might know Beulah, of course. She did. Want to raise that bet a little?"

"Can the comedy. She's dead."

"Skalla—" I started to say.

"That's the funny side," he grunted. "He was there. Some nosy old —— next door seen him. Only there ain't a mark on her. She died natural. I kind of got tied up here, so I didn't get over to see her."

"I know how busy you are," I said in what seemed to me a dead voice.

"Yeah. Well, hell, the doc don't even know what she died of. Not yet."

"Fear," I said. "She's the one that turned Skalla up eight years ago. Whisky may have helped a little."

"Is that so?" Hiney said. "Well, well. We got him now anyways. We make him at Girard, headed north in a rent hack. We got the county and state law in on it. If he drops over to the Ridge, we nab him at Castaic. She was the one turned him up, huh? I guess you better come in, Carmady."

"Not me," I said. "Beverly Hills wants me for a hit-and-run. I'm a criminal myself now."

I had a quick snack and some coffee before I took a taxi to Las Flores and Santa Monica and walked up to where I had left my roadster parked.

Nothing was happening around there except that some kid in the back of a car was strumming a ukelele.

I pointed my roadster towards Heather Street.

Heather Street was a gash in the side of a steep flat slope, at the top of Beachwood Drive. It curved around the shoulder enough so that even by daylight you couldn't have seen much

more than half a block of it at one time while you were on it.

The house I wanted was built downward, one of those clinging-vine effects, with a front door below the street level, a patio on the roof, a bedroom or two possibly in the basement, and a garage as easy to drive into as an olive bottle.

The garage was empty, but a big shiny sedan had its two right wheels off the road, on the shoulder of the bank. There were lights in the house.

I drove around the curb, parked, walked back along the smooth, hardly used cement and poked a fountain pen flash into the sedan. It was registered to one David Marineau, 1737 North Flores Avenue, Hollywood, California. That made me go back to my heap and get a gun out of a locked pocket.

I repassed the sedan, stepped down three rough stone steps and looked at the bell beside a narrow door topped by a lancet arch.

I didn't push it, I just looked at it. The door wasn't quite shut. A fairly wide crack of dim light edged around its panel. I pushed it an inch. Then I pushed it far enough to look in.

Then I listened. The silence of that house was what made me go in. It was one of those utterly dead silences that come after an explosion. Or perhaps I hadn't eaten enough dinner. Anyway I went in.

The long living room went clear to the back, which wasn't very far as it was a small house. At the back there were French doors and the metal railing of a balcony showed through the glass. The balcony would be very high above the slope of the hill, built as the house was.

There were nice lamps, nice chairs with deep sides, nice tables, a thick apricot-colored rug, two small cozy davenports, one facing and one right-angled to a fireplace with an ivory mantel and a miniature Winged Victory on that. A fire was laid behind the copper screen, but not lit.

The room had a hushed, warm smell. It looked like a room where people got made comfortable. There was a bottle of Vat 69 on a low table with glasses and a copper bucket, and tongs.

I fixed the door about as I had found it and just stood. Silence. Time passed. It passed in the dry whirr of an electric clock on a console radio, in the far-off hoot of an auto horn down on Beachwood half a mile below, in the distant hornet drone of a night-flying plane, in the metallic wheeze of a cricket under the house.

Then I wasn't alone any longer.

Mrs. Marineau slid into the room at the far end, by a door beside the French doors. She didn't make any more noise than a butterfly. She still wore the pillbox black hat and the burnt-orange tweeds, and they still looked like hell together. She had a small glove in her hand wrapped around the butt of a gun. I don't know why. I never did find that out.

She didn't see me at once and when she did it didn't mean anything much. She just lifted the gun a little and slid along the carpet towards me, her lip clutched back so far that I couldn't even see the teeth that clutched it.

But I had a gun out now myself. We looked at each other across our guns. Maybe she knew me. I hadn't any idea from her expression.

I said, "You got them, huh?"

She nodded a little. "Just him," she said.

"Put the gun down. You're all through with it."

She lowered it a little. She hadn't seemed to notice the Colt I was pushing through the air in her general direction. I lowered that too.

She said, "She wasn't here."

Her voice had a dry, impersonal sound, flat, without timbre.

"Miss Baring wasn't here?" I asked.

"No."

"Remember me?"

She took a better look at me but her face didn't light up with any pleasure.

"I'm the guy that was looking for Miss Baring," I said. "You told me where to come. Remember? Only Dave sent a loogan to put the arm on me and ride me around while he came up here himself and promoted something. I couldn't guess what."

The brunette said, "You're no cop. Dave said you were a fake."

I made a broad, hearty gesture and moved a little closer to her, unobtrusively. "Not a city cop," I admitted. "But a cop. And that was a long time ago. Things have happened since then. Haven't they?"

"Yes," she said. "Especially to Dave. Hee, hee."

It wasn't a laugh. It wasn't meant to be a laugh. It was just a little steam escaping through a safety valve.

"Hee, hee," I said. We looked at each other like a couple of nuts being Napoleon and Josephine.

The idea was to get close enough to grab her gun. I was still too far.

"Anybody here besides you?" I asked.

"Just Dave."

"I had an idea Dave was here." It wasn't clever, but it was good for another foot.

"Oh, Dave's here," she agreed. "Yes. You'd like to see him?"

"Well—if it isn't too much trouble."

"Hee, hee," she said. "No trouble at all. Like this."

She jerked the gun up and snapped the trigger at me. She did it without moving a muscle of her face.

The gun not going off puzzled her, in a sort of vague, week-before-last manner. Nothing immediate or important. I wasn't there any more. She lifted the gun up, still being very careful about the black kid glove wrapped about its butt, and peered into the muzzle. That didn't get her anywhere. She shook the gun. Then she was aware of me again. I hadn't moved. I didn't have to, now.

"I guess it's not loaded," she said.

"Maybe just all used up," I said. "Too bad. These little ones only hold seven. My shells won't fit, either. Let's see if I can do anything?"

She put the gun in my hand. Then she dusted her hands together. Her eyes didn't seem to have any pupils, or to be all pupils. I wasn't sure which.

The gun wasn't loaded. The magazine was quite empty. I sniffed the muzzle. The gun hadn't been fired since it was last cleaned.

That got me. Up to that point it had looked fairly simple, if I could get by without any more murder. But this threw it. I hadn't any idea what either of us was talking about now.

I dropped her pistol into my side pocket and put mine back on my hip and chewed my lip for a couple of minutes, to see what might turn up. Nothing did.

The sharp-faced Mrs. Marineau merely stood still and stared at a spot between my eyes, fuzzily, like a rather blotto tourist seeing a swell sunset on Mount Whitney.

"Well," I said at last, "let's kind of look through the house and see what's what."

"You mean Dave?"

"Yeah, we could take that in."

"He's in the bedroom." She tittered. "He's at home in bedrooms."

I touched her arm and turned her around. She turned obediently, like a small child.

"But this one will be the last one he'll be at home in," she said. "Hee, hee."

"Oh, yeah. Sure," I said.

My voice sounded to me like the voice of a midget.

Dave Marineau was dead all right—if there had been any doubt about it.

A white bowl lamp with raised figures shone beside a large bed in a green and silver bedroom. It was the only light in the room. It filtered a hushed kind of light down at his face. He hadn't been dead long enough to get the corpse look.

He lay sprawled casually on the bed, a little sideways, as though he had been standing in front of it when he was shot. One arm was flung out as loose as a strand of kelp and the other was under him. His open eyes were flat and shiny and almost seemed to hold a self-satisfied expression. His mouth was open a little and the lamplight glistened on the edges of his upper teeth.

I didn't see the wound at all at first. It was high up, on the right side of his head, in the temple, but back rather far, almost far enough to drive the petrosal bone through the brain. It was powder-burned, rimmed with dusky red, and a fine trickle spidered down from it and got browner as it got thinner against his cheek.

"Hell, that's a contact wound," I snapped at the woman. "A suicide wound."

She stood at the foot of the bed and stared at the wall above his head. If she was interested in anything besides the wall, she didn't show it.

I lifted his still limp right hand and sniffed at the place where the base of the thumb joins the palm. I smelled cordite, then I didn't smell cordite, then I didn't know whether I smelled cordite or not. It didn't matter, of course. A paraffin test would prove it one way or the other.

I put the hand down again, carefully, as though it were a fragile thing of great value. Then I plowed around on the bed, went down on the floor, got halfway under the bed, swore, got up again and rolled the dead man to one side enough to look under him. There was a bright, brassy shellcase but no gun.

It looked like murder again. I liked that better. He wasn't the suicide type.

"See any gun?" I asked her.

"No." Her face was as blank as a pie pan.

"Where's the Baring girl? What are you supposed to be doing here?"

She bit the end of her left little finger. "I'd better confess," she said. "I came here to kill them both."

"Go on," I said.

"Nobody was here. Of course, after I phoned him and he told me you were not a real cop and there was no murder and you were a blackmailer and just trying to scare me out of the address—" She stopped and sobbed once, hardly more than a sniff, and moved her line of sight to a corner of the ceiling.

Her words had a tumbled arrangement, but she spoke them like a drugstore Indian.

"I came here to kill both of them," she said. "I don't deny that."

"With an empty gun?"

"It wasn't empty two days ago. I looked. Dave must have emptied it. He must have been afraid."

"That listens," I said. "Go on."

"So I came here. That was the last insult—his sending you to me to get her *address*. That was more than I would—"

"The story," I said. "I know how you felt. I've read it in the love mags myself."

"Yes. Well, he said there was something about Miss Baring he had to see her about on account of the studio and it was nothing personal, never had been, never would be—"

"My Gawd," I said, "I know that too. I know what he'd feed you. We've got a dead man lying around here. We've got to do something, even if he was just your husband."

"You ——," she said.

"Yeah," I said. "That's better than the dopey talk. Go on."

"The door wasn't shut. I came in. That's all. Now, I'm going. And you're not going to stop me. You know where I live, you ——." She called me the same name again.

"We'll talk to some law first," I said. I went over and shut the door and turned the key on the inside of it and took it out. Then I went over to the French doors. The woman gave me looks, but I couldn't hear what her lips were calling me now.

French doors on the far side of the bed opened on the same balcony as the living room. The telephone was in a niche in the wall there, by the bed, where you could yawn and reach out for it in the morning and order a tray of diamond necklaces sent up to try on.

I sat down on the side of the bed and reached for the phone, and a muffled voice came to me through the glass and said: "Hold it, pal! Just hold it!"

Even muffled by the glass it was a deep, soft voice. I had heard it before. It was Skalla's voice.

I was in line with the lamp. The lamp was right behind me. I dived off the bed on to the floor, clawing at my hip.

A shot roared and glass sprinkled the back of my neck. I couldn't figure it. Skalla wasn't on the balcony. I had looked.

I rolled over and started to snake away along the floor away from the French doors, my only chance with the lamp where it was.

Mrs. Marineau did just the right thing—for the other side. She jerked a slipper off and started slamming me with the heel of it. I grabbed for her ankles and we wrestled around and she cut the top of my head to pieces.

I threw her over. It didn't last long. When I started to get up Skalla was in the room, laughing at me. The .45 still had a home in his fist. The French door and the locked screen outside looked as though a rogue elephant had passed that way.

"Okay," I said. "I give up."

"Who's the twist? She sure likes you, pal."

I got up on my feet. The woman was over in a corner somewhere. I didn't even look at her.

"Turn around, pal, while I give you the fan."

I hadn't worked my gun loose yet. He got that. I didn't say anything about the door key, but he took it. So he must have been watching from somewhere. He left me my car keys. He looked at the little empty gun and dropped it back in my pocket.

"Where'd you come from?" I asked.

"Easy. Clumb up the balcony and held on, looking through the grille at you. Cinch to an old circus man. How you been, pal?"

Blood from the top of my head was leaking down my face. I got a handkerchief out and mopped at it. I didn't answer him.

"Jeeze, you sure was funny on the bed grabbin' for the phone with the stiff at your back."

"I was a scream," I growled. "Take it easy. He's her husband."

He looked at her. "She's his woman?"

I nodded and wished I hadn't.

"That's tough. If I'd a known—but I couldn't help meself. The guy asked for it."

"You—" I started to say, staring at him. I heard a queer, strained whine behind me, from the woman.

"Who else, pal? Who else? Let's all go back in that livin' room. Seems to me they was a bottle of nice-looking hooch there. And you need some stuff on that head."

"You're crazy to stick around here," I growled. "There's a general pickup out for you. The only way out of this canyon is back down Beachwood or over the hills—on foot."

Skalla looked at me and said very quietly, "Nobody's phoned no law from here, pal."

Skalla watched me while I washed and put some tape on my head in the bathroom. Then we went back to the living room. Mrs. Marineau, curled up on one of the davenports, looked blankly at the unlit fire. She didn't say anything.

She hadn't run away because Skalla had her in sight all the time. She acted resigned, indifferent, as if she didn't care what happened now.

I poured three drinks from the Vat 69 bottle, handed one to the brunette. She held her hand out for the glass, half smiled at me, crumpled off the davenport to the floor with the smile still on her face.

I put the glass down, lifted her and put her back on the davenport with her head low. Skalla stared at her. She was out cold, as white as paper.

Skalla took his drink, sat down on the other davenport and put the .45 beside him. He drank his drink looking at the woman, with a queer expression on his big pale face.

"Tough," he said. "Tough. But the louse was cheatin' on her anyways. The hell with him." He reached for another drink, swallowed it, sat down near her on the other davenport right-angled to the one she lay on.

"So you're a dick," he said.

"How'd you guess?"

"Lu Shamey told me about a guy goin' there. He sounded like you. I been around and looked in your heap outside. I walk silent."

"Well—what now?" I asked.

He looked more enormous than ever in the room in his sports clothes. The clothes of a smart-aleck kid. I wondered how long it had taken him to get them together. They couldn't have been ready-made. He was much too big for that.

His feet were spread wide on the apricot rug, he looked down sadly at the white kid explosions on the suede. They were the worst-looking shoes I ever saw.

"What you doin' here?" he asked gruffly.

"Looking for Beulah. I thought she might need a little help. I had a bet with a city cop I'd find her before he found you. But I haven't found her yet."

"You ain't seen her, huh?"

I shook my head, slowly, very carefully.

He said softly, "Me neither, pal. I been around for hours. She ain't been home. Only the guy in the bedroom come here. How about the dinge manager up at Shamey's?"

"That's what the tag's for."

"Yeah. A guy like that. They would. Well, I gotta blow. I'd like to take the stiff, account of Beulah. Can't leave him around to scare her. But I guess it ain't any use now. The dinge kill queers that."

He looked at the woman at his elbow on the other little davenport. Her face was still greenish white, her eyes shut. There was a movement of her breast.

"Without her," he said, "I guess I'd clean up right and button you good." He touched the .45 at his side. "No hard feelings, of course, just for Beulah. But the way it is—heck, I can't knock the frail off."

"Too bad," I snarled, feeling my head.

He grinned. "I guess I'll take your heap. For a short ways. Throw them keys over."

I threw them over. He picked them up and laid them beside the big Colt. He leaned forward a little. Then he reached back into one of his patch pockets and brought out a small pearl-handled gun, about .25 caliber. He held it on the flat of his hand.

"This done it," he said. "I left a rent hack I had on the street below and come up the bank and around the house. I hear the bell ring. This guy is at the front door. I don't come up far enough for him to see me. Nobody answers. Well, what do you think? The guy's got a key. A key to Beulah's house!"

His huge face became one vast scowl. The woman on the davenport was breathing a little more deeply, and I thought I saw one of her eyelids twitch.

"What the hell," I said. "He could get that a dozen ways. He's a boss at KLBL where she works. He could get at her bag, take an impression. Hell, she didn't have to give it to him."

"That's right, pal." He beamed. "O' course, she didn't have to give it to the ———. Okay, he went in, and I made it fast after him. But he had the door shut. I opened it my way. After that it didn't shut so good, you might of noticed. He was in the middle of this here room, over there by a desk. He's been here before all right though"—the scowl came back again, although not quite so black—"because he slipped a hand into the desk drawer and come up with this." He danced the pearl-handled thing on his enormous palm.

Mrs. Marineau's face now had distinct lines of tensity.

"So I start for him. He lets one go. A miss. He's scared and runs into the bedroom. Me after. He lets go again. Another miss. You'll find them slugs in the wall somewheres."

"I'll make a point of it," I said.

"Yeah, then I got him. Well, hell, the guy's only a punk in a white muffler. If she's washed up with me, okay. I want it from her, see? Not from no greasy-faced piece of cheese like him. So I'm sore. But the guy's got guts at that."

He rubbed his chin. I doubted the last bit.

"I say: 'My woman lives here, pal. How come?' He says: 'Come back tomorrow. This here is my night.'"

Skalla spread his free left hand in a large gesture. "After that nature's got to take its course, ain't it? I pull his arms and legs off. Only while I'm doing it the damn little gat pops off and he's as limp as—as—" He glanced at the woman and didn't finish what he was going to say. "Yeah, he was dead."

One of the woman's eyelids flickered again. I said, "Then?"

"I scrammed. A guy does. But I come back. I got to thinkin' it's tough on Beulah, with that stiff on her bed. So I'll just go back and ferry him out to the desert and then crawl in a hole for a while. Then this frail comes along and spoils that part."

The woman must have been shamming for quite a long time. She must have been moving her legs and feet and turning her body a fraction of an inch at a time, to get in the right position, to get leverage against the back of the davenport.

The pearl-handled gun still lay on Skalla's flat hand when she moved. She shot off the davenport in a flat dive, gathering herself in the air like an acrobat. She brushed his knees and picked the gun off his hand as neatly as a chipmunk peels a nut.

He stood up and swore as she rolled against his legs. The big Colt was at his side, but he didn't touch it or reach for it. He stooped to take hold of the woman with his big hands empty.

She laughed just before she shot him.

She shot him four times, in the lower belly, then the hammer clicked. She threw the gun at his face and rolled away from him.

He stepped over her without touching her. His big pale face was quite empty for a moment, then it settled into stiff lines of torture, lines that seemed to have been there always.

He walked erectly along the rug towards the front door. I jumped for the big Colt and got it. To keep it from the woman. At the fourth step he took, blood showed on the yellowish nap of the rug. After that it showed at every step he took.

He reached the door and put his big hand flat against the wood and leaned there for a moment. Then he shook his head and turned back. His hand left a bloody smear on the door from where he had been holding his belly.

He sat down in the first chair he came to and leaned forward and held himself tightly with his hands. The blood came between his fingers slowly, like water from an overflowing basin.

"Them little slugs," he said, "hurt just like the big ones, down below anyways."

The dark woman walked towards him like a marionette. He watched her come unblinkingly, under his half-lowered, heavy lids.

When she got close enough she leaned over and spat in his face.

He didn't move. His eyes didn't change. I

jumped for her and threw her into a chair. I wasn't nice about it.

"Leave her alone," he grunted at me. "Maybe she loved the guy."

Nobody tried to stop me from telephoning this time.

Hours later I sat on a red stool at Lucca's, at Fifth and Western, and sipped a martini and wondered how it felt to be mixing them all day and never drink one.

I took another martini over and ordered a meal. I guess I ate it. It was late, past one, Skalla was in the prison ward of the General Hospital. Miss Baring hadn't showed up yet, but they knew she would, as soon as she heard Skalla was under glass, and no longer dangerous.

KLBL, who didn't know anything about it at first, had got a nice hush working. They were to have twenty-four clear hours to decide how to release the story.

Lucca's was almost as full as at noon. After a while an Italian brunette with a grand nose and eyes you wouldn't fool with came over and said: "I have a table for you now."

My imagination put Skalla across the table from me. His flat black eyes had something in them that was more than mere pain, something he wanted me to do. Part of the time he was trying to tell me what it was, and part of the time he was holding his belly in one piece and saying again: "Leave her alone. Maybe she loved the guy."

I left there and drove north to Franklin and over Franklin to Beachwood and up to Heather Street. It wasn't staked. They were that sure of her.

I drifted along the street below and looked up the scrubby slope spattered with moonlight and showing her house from behind as if it were three stories high. I could see the metal brackets that supported the porch. They looked high enough off the ground so that a man would need a balloon to reach them. But there was where he had gone up. Always the hard way with him.

He could have run away and had a fight for his money or even bought himself a place to live

up in. There were plenty of people in the business, and they wouldn't fool with Skalla. But he had come back instead to climb her balcony, like Romeo, and get his stomach full of slugs. From the wrong woman, as usual.

I drove around a white curve that looked like moonlight itself and parked and walked up the hill the rest of the way. I carried a flash, but I didn't need it to see there was nobody on the doorstep waiting for the milk. I didn't go in the front way. There might just happen to be some snooper with night glasses up on the hill.

I sneaked up the bank from behind, between the house and the empty garage. I found a window I could reach and made not much noise breaking it with a gun inside my hat. Nothing happened except that the crickets and tree frogs stopped for a moment.

I picked a way to the bedroom and prowled my flash around discreetly, after lowering the shades and pulling the drapes across them. The light dropped on a tumbled bed, on daubs of print powder, on cigarette butts on the window sills and heel marks in the nap of the carpet. There was a green and silver toilet set on the dressing table and three suitcases in the closet. There was a built-in bureau back in there with a lock that meant business. I had a chilled-steel screwdriver with me as well as the flash. I jimmied it.

The jewelry wasn't worth a thousand dollars. Perhaps not half. But it meant a lot to a girl in show business. I put it back where I got it.

The living room had shut windows and a queer, unpleasant, sadistic smell. The law enforcement had taken care of the Vat 69, to make it easier for the fingerprint men. I had to use my own. I got a chair that hadn't been bled on into a corner, wet my throat and waited in the darkness.

A shade flapped in the basement or somewhere. That made me wet my throat again. Somebody came out of a house half a dozen blocks away and whooped. A door banged. Silence. The tree frogs started again, then the crickets. Then the electric clock on the radio got louder than all the other sounds together.

Then I went to sleep.

When I woke up the moon had gone from the front windows and a car had stopped somewhere. Light, delicate, careful steps separated themselves from the night. They were outside the front door. A key fumbled in the lock.

In the opening door the dim sky showed a head without a hat. The slope of the hill was too dark to outline any more. The door clicked shut.

Steps rustled on the rug. I already had the lamp cord in my fingers. I yanked it and there was light.

The girl didn't make a sound, not a whisper of sound. She just pointed the gun at me.

I said, "Hello, Beulah."

She was worth waiting for.

Not too tall, not too short; that girl. She had the long legs that can walk and dance. Her hair even by the light of the one lamp was like a brush fire at night. Her face had laughter wrinkles at the corner of the eyes. Her mouth could laugh.

The features were shadowed and had that drawn look that makes some faces more beautiful because it makes them more delicate. I couldn't see her eyes. They might have been blue enough to make you jump, but I couldn't see.

The gun looked about a .32, but had the extreme right-angled grip of a Mauser.

After a while she said very softly, "Police, I suppose."

She had a nice voice, too. I still think of it, at times.

I said, "Let's sit down and talk. We're all alone here. Ever drink out of the bottle?"

She didn't answer. She looked down at the gun she was holding, half smiled, shook her head.

"You wouldn't make two mistakes," I said. "Not a girl as smart as you are."

She tucked the gun into the side pocket of a long ulster-like coat with a military collar.

"Who are you?"

"Just a shamus. Private detective to you. Carmady is the name. Need a lift?"

I held my bottle out. It hadn't grown to my hand yet. I still had to hold it.

"I don't drink. Who hired you?"

"KLBL. To protect you from Steve Skalla."

"So they know," she said. "So they know about him."

I digested that and said nothing.

"Who's been here?" she went on sharply. She was still standing in the middle of the room, with her hands in her coat pockets now, and no hat.

"Everybody but the plumber," I said. "He's a little late, as usual."

"You're one of *those* men." Her nose seemed to curl a little. "Drugstore comics."

"No," I said. "Not really. It's just a way I get talking to the people I have to talk to. Skalla came back again and ran into trouble and got shot up and arrested. He's in the hospital. Pretty bad."

She didn't move. "How bad?"

"He might live if he'd have surgery. Doubtful, even with that. Hopeless without. He has three in the intestines and one in the liver."

She moved at last and started to sit down. "Not in that chair," I said quickly. "Over here."

She came over and sat near me, on one of the davenports. Lights twisted in her eyes. I could see them now. Little twisting lights like Catherine wheels spinning brightly.

She said, "Why did he come back?"

"He thought he ought to tidy up. Remove the body and so on. A nice guy, Skalla."

"Do you think so?"

"Lady, if nobody else in the world thinks so, I do."

"I'll take that drink," she said.

I handed her the bottle. I grabbed it away in a hurry. "Gosh," I said. "You have to break in on this stuff."

She looked towards the side door that led to the bedroom back of me.

"Gone to the morgue," I said. "You can go in there."

She stood up at once and went out of the room. She came back almost at once.

"What have they got on Steve?" she asked. "If he recovers."

"He killed a nigger over on Central this morning. It was more or less self-defense on both sides. I don't know. Except for Marineau he might get a break."

"Marineau?" she said.

"Yeah. You knew he killed Marineau."

"Don't be silly," she said. "I killed Dave Marineau."

"Okay," I said. "But that's not the way Steve wants it."

She stared at me. "You mean Steve came back here deliberately to take the blame?"

"If he had to, I guess. I think he really meant to cart Marineau off to the desert and lose him. Only a woman showed up here—Mrs. Marineau."

"Yes," the girl said tonelessly. "She thinks I was his mistress. That greasy spoon."

"Were you?" I asked.

"Don't try that again," she said. "Even if I did work on Central Avenue once." She went out of the room again.

Sounds of a suitcase being yanked about came into the living room. I went in after her. She was packing pieces of cobweb and packing them as if she liked nice things nicely packed.

"You don't wear that stuff down in the tank," I told her, leaning in the door.

She ignored me some more. "I was going to make a break for Mexico," she said. "Then South America. I didn't mean to shoot him. He roughed me up and tried to blackmail me into something and I went and got the gun. Then we struggled again and it went off. Then I ran away."

"Just what Skalla said he did," I said. "Hell, couldn't you just have shot the —— on purpose?"

"Not for your benefit," she said. "Or any cop. Not when I did eight months in Dalhart, Texas, once for rolling a drunk. Not with that Marineau woman yelling her head off that I seduced him and then got sick of him."

"A lot she'll say," I grunted. "After I tell how she spat in Skalla's face when he had four slugs in him."

She shivered. Her face whitened. She went on taking the things out of the suitcase and putting them in again.

"Did you roll the drunk really?"

She looked up at me, then down. "Yes," she whispered.

I went over nearer to her. "Got any bruises or torn clothes to show?" I asked.

"No."

"Too bad," I said, and took hold of her.

Her eyes flamed at first and then turned to black stone, I tore her coat off, tore her up plenty, put hard fingers into her arms and neck and used my knuckles on her mouth. I let her go, panting. She reeled away from me, but didn't quite fall.

"We'll have to wait for the bruises to set and darken," I said. "Then we'll go downtown."

She began to laugh. Then she went over to the mirror and looked at herself. She began to cry.

"Get out of here while I change my clothes!" she yelled. "I'll give it a tumble. But if it makes any difference to Steve—I'm going to tell it right."

"Aw, shut up and change your clothes," I said.

I went out and banged the door.

I hadn't even kissed her. I could have done that, at least. She wouldn't have minded any more than the rest of the knocking about I gave her.

We rode the rest of the night, first in separate cars to hide hers in my garage, then in mine. We rode up the coast and had coffee and sandwiches at Malibu, then on up and over. We had breakfast at the bottom of the Ridge Route, just north of San Fernando.

Her face looked like a catcher's mitt after a tough season. She had a lower lip the size of a banana and you could have cooked steaks on the bruises on her arms and neck, they were so hot.

With the first strong daylight we went to the City Hall.

They didn't even think of holding her or

checking her up. They practically wrote the statement themselves. She signed it blank-eyed, thinking of something else. Then a man from KLBL and his wife came down to get her.

So I didn't get to ride her to a hotel. She didn't get to see Skalla either, not then. He was under morphine.

He died at two-thirty the same afternoon. She was holding one of his huge, limp fingers, but he didn't know her from the Queen of Siam.

Don't You Cry for Me
Norbert Davis

NORBERT DAVIS (1909–1949) was born in Morrison, Illinois, and moved with his family when he was a teenager to California, where he earned a law degree at Stanford University. By the time he had graduated, however, he had already established himself as a successful pulp writer and, having always desired the writer's life, never bothered to take the bar exam.

While he is most remembered today for his detective fiction (and rightly so), he also wrote other pulp fiction, including Westerns, romances, and adventure stories, as well as humor for the top slick magazines. He joined a group called the Fictioneers, Southern Californian fiction writers who met regularly to discuss writing and marketing tips; Raymond Chandler was an occasional participant. Davis's best-known characters are the private-eye team of Doan and Carstairs—the latter being a giant Great Dane, who, after closely reading their five cases, has proven to be the smarter half of the team. They appeared in two short stories—"Cry Murder" and "Holocaust House"—and three novels: *The Mouse in the Mountain* (1943), *Sally's in the Alley* (1943), and *Oh, Murderer Mine* (1946). The Doan and Carstairs stories are notable for being among the funniest of the "hard-boiled" genre of their time. Toward the end of his career, Davis abandoned the pulps, and then the slick magazines began to reject his stories. He split up with his wife, his agent died, and he was diagnosed with cancer. It was all too much, and at the age of forty he committed suicide.

"Don't You Cry for Me," one of Davis's thirteen *Black Mask* stories, was published in May 1942.

Collins flattened against the wall beside the door.

Don't You Cry for Me

Norbert Davis

The brawny piano-player had had his run-ins with the ghoulish Gestapo in the beer halls of Europe, but when he promised Myra Martin's mother to find the girl in the Mecca of the movie-struck, he ran afoul of a plot as fantastic as any Hitler pipe-dream.

J OHN COLLINS WAS playing the *Beale Street Blues* and playing it soft and sad because that was the way he felt. The notes dripped through the dingy dimness of the room like molasses and provided an appropriate accompaniment to his thoughts. He had a hangover.

He was short and squat and immensely wide. He looked a little bit like a frog—a friendly one. His hair was blond and as softly fuzzy as a baby's on top, and he had a scar on his right cheek.

The door-bell trilled faintly through the music. Collins stopped playing and sighed. He didn't really feel in the mood for company, but he got up and went across the rumpled living-room into the little entry-hall and opened the front door.

"Yes?" he said.

"You're Mr. John Collins, aren't you?"

The soft California dusk had gathered shadows against the front of the bungalow, and the woman was part of them, small and faintly rustling, dressed in black. Her voice was breathless and high, shaking slightly.

"Yes," said Collins.

"May I—see you for a moment?"

"Certainly. Come in."

Collins went back into the living-room and turned on the lamp with the pink shade. There were three empty highball glasses and an overflowing ashtray on the coffee table in front of the chesterfield, and he said: "The place is in a mess. Excuse it, please."

"You're—not married?"

"No," said Collins.

She sat erect and prim on the edge of the chesterfield just outside the throw of light from the pink lamp, and she was like a faded portrait painting against the cheap garishness of the room. She wore white silk gloves and a white scarf fastened with a cameo brooch and a black bonnet of a hat with a black half-veil. There were lines in her cheeks, and her hair glinted silvery-white. Collins caught the faintly old-fashioned odor of lilac toilet water through the smell of stale tobacco and old gin that hung in the room like a shroud.

"I'm Mrs. Della Martin," she said. "From Brill Falls, South Dakota."

"Oh?" said Collins blankly.

"I'm Myra Martin's mother."

"Is that so?" Collins asked, mentally running through the list of his feminine associates. He couldn't locate any Myras.

"She wrote me about you."

"That was nice of her," Collins said, wondering if it was.

"She said you were a detective."

"A what?" Collins inquired, startled.

"She said you knew how to locate people. She said you'd done a lot of that work in Prague and in Warsaw and in Berlin—finding people for their relatives over here. That is, before we declared war, of course."

"Oh, that was just amateur stuff," Collins said. "I happened to be playing in beer halls and cafes, and I did some investigation for friends in my spare time."

"Myra said it was very dangerous work."

Collins fingered the scar on his cheek. "I did have a run-in or two with the Gestapo. Nothing much."

"Would you—could you locate someone here in Hollywood? Will you find Myra for me, Mr. Collins?"

Collins stared at her. "What?"

Mrs. Martin twisted her slim gloved hands together. "Myra left Brill Falls a year ago to come to Hollywood to get into the motion pictures. She's very beautiful, and she's always been interested in theatricals. And then she won a Most-Beautiful-Back contest and got her name and picture in the papers, and several agencies and acting schools wrote her."

"Yes," said Collins. "Oh, yes."

"I have a little dressmaking shop, and I couldn't come with her, but I wanted her to have her chance. We saved the money for the trip, and she came alone. She was only going to stay two months if she didn't find some sort of picture work, but after the two months were up she said things looked so encouraging—"

Collins nodded slowly. "Yes."

"She stayed on and on, and I sent her what

money I could. Then six weeks ago, she wrote me that she had her big chance at last, but that it was all a big secret yet, and she couldn't tell me anything about it. She didn't write me any more, Mr. Collins."

"Six weeks—" Collins said.

"She had always written me twice a week before. And then—just nothing. I wrote and telegraphed, and the letters came back, and the telegrams couldn't be delivered because they couldn't find her. I—couldn't stand it, and so I sold my business and came here. I went to the Central Casting Office and the studios. They had Myra's name on their lists, but they hadn't heard anything of her for months. I went to the place where she had been living, and there was a horrible foreign man in a fez who owned the place, and he wouldn't tell me anything except that she had moved out six weeks before and hadn't left any address."

"Have you seen the police?" Collins asked.

"No," said Mrs. Martin.

"Why not?"

Mrs. Martin looked down at her hands. "Perhaps Myra doesn't want—to be found."

"Oh," said Collins.

"I don't want to bother Myra," Mrs. Martin said in a low strained voice. "If she doesn't want me . . . If I just knew she was safe and all right, if I just *knew* . . . Will you help me, Mr. Collins?"

"Yes," said Collins. "Of course. I'll try. I'll do all I can."

Mrs. Martin opened a shiny black purse. "I can pay you something now—"

"No," said Collins. "Never mind that. I have lots of money." He actually had five dollars and seventy-three cents, and the rent was two weeks overdue. "Where is this place that Myra had been living?"

"At 1271 Sales Street. It's a boarding house."

"Yes. And where are you staying?"

"At the Fortmount Hotel."

"All right, Mrs. Martin. You go back there and wait. Don't worry more than you can help. You'll hear from me soon."

"Thank you," she said. She got up, breathing a little unevenly. "Thank you very much. I didn't know where to turn. If I can just be sure Myra is all right, but I've had such a terrible empty feeling . . ."

"Yes," said Collins absently.

He showed her to the door and came back and sat down at the piano and stared at the worn keyboard. With one finger he began to plunk out a little tune to the words "Myra Martin." He couldn't remember the name at all, but then he met a great many people in a great many places, and he never paid very much attention to people's names.

He noticed suddenly that his one-finger tune was the first bar of a funeral march. He stopped playing it and shivered. It was cold in the apartment and dark in the corners where the light didn't reach. Mrs. Martin's drear, sad little story had left an ugly and chill echo behind it. It was nothing you could touch, nothing you could see, but it was there. It was black and twisted and wickedly mirthful, and John Collins didn't like even the thought of it.

He unearthed a half-empty bottle of gin from under the chesterfield, took a big swig, and then got his hat and went out of the bungalow.

ales Street was like quite a few others you can find in the back-washes of Hollywood if you care to look. It didn't have any tinsel or glitter or rackety-rax. It was dark and narrow and a little bit crooked, and the tree branches over it moved in the wind and threw sharply jagged shadows that danced dangerously back and forth across the bumpy sidewalk.

Number 1271 was a big brown house with a bulging bay-window and a discouraged sag in its roof. The front steps creaked under John Collins' feet, and the floor-boards of the porch moaned in protest as he crossed to the door and punched a bell under the feeble night light.

There was a discouraged jangle somewhere inside, and then slippers flip-flopped on bare boards, coming closer, and the door opened.

"Vell?"

Collins stepped back to take a good look. The man in the doorway was over six feet tall and as thin as a pencil. He stooped forward a little, as though the weight of his mustache was pulling him off-balance. It could have easily. It was a wonderful mustache. It ran as straight across his face as a ruler and turned up in sharp points at either end. Behind it, the rest of the man's face was dingy and nondescript. He was wearing a conical fez with a tassel on it, sharp-pointed red leather slippers, and a red sash.

"Going to a costume party?" Collins asked.

"Vet you vent?"

Collins said: "I've played in joints in Istanbul and Port Said and Cairo, but I've never heard a Turkish accent like that. Where'd you pick it up?"

"In books," said the man in an injured tone. "What's the matter with it?"

"Let's step inside," Collins suggested. He put a thick finger in the center of the man's chest and pushed him back into a narrow dimly lighted hall that smelled faintly of fried onions and cheap perfume. At the foot of the stairs there was a rickety little table that served as a desk, and there was a telephone on the wall above it.

"What's the matter with my accent?" asked the tall man again. "And say, who are you pushing, anyway?"

"I don't know," said Collins. "What do you call yourself these days?"

"Ali Singh Teke."

"Now, now," said Collins.

The tall man wiggled his mustache. "Well, all right. That's my picture name. That's the way I'm listed at Central Casting. My real name's Alfred Peters. I play Turkish parts in the movies. I got to keep in practice, don't I? What's the matter with my accent?"

"I couldn't begin to tell you. Where's Myra Martin?"

Something dark and sullenly secretive closed over Alfred Peters' face. "She ain't here no longer."

"I didn't ask you where she ain't. I want to know where she is. Give."

"She moved out without givin' no address."

"Did you throw her out?"

"What?" said Alfred Peters, startled. "Why, I never! It's a lie! Whoever told you that? Say, who are you, anyway?"

"Never mind. Let's talk about Myra Martin. She just walked out one morning and didn't come back, is that it?"

"Yes," said Alfred Peters.

"No."

Alfred Peters' mustache wiggled again. "Huh?"

"I said, no." Collins took his right hand out of his pocket and opened it to reveal the coin lying on his broad palm. "Know what that is?"

"Sure. It's a half-dollar."

Collins spun it on the bare scarred top of the desk. "Does it look all right to you?"

"Why, yes," said Alfred Peters, puzzled.

"Watch." Collins picked the half-dollar up and closed it in his fist. The big cords in his wrist bulged out thickly, and the blood drained from his knuckles until they looked like bulging white knobs. He opened his hand again and dropped the half-dollar back on the table. It didn't spin now. It rocked rapidly back and forth in the same spot, glittering. It was bent nearly double.

Alfred Peters stared at it in unbelieving fascination.

"Now," said Collins. "Let's start all over again. Where's Myra Martin?"

"Say, I never saw anybody do that—" Alfred Peters raised his eyes slowly to Collins' face. "I told you she didn't leave no address when she moved out. I don't know where she is. You doubtin' my word?"

Collins nodded slowly. "That's right."

Alfred Peters puffed himself up. "Where do you get comin' in my house . . ."

Collins picked up the bent half-dollar and flipped it up in the air and caught it again.

Alfred Peters swallowed. "You can't come in my house and get tough! You get out of here now, or—or—"

"What?" Collins asked.

"Well—well, you ain't got any right. . . . Anyway, I told you the truth. She didn't leave no forwardin' address. She just up and went. Only it wasn't in the mornin' like you said. It was at night. It was real late at night. She pounded on my door and woke me up and said good-bye."

"She was carrying her trunk on her shoulder at the time, I suppose?"

"No, she wasn't. She didn't have no trunk. Just a couple of big suitcases and an overnight bag."

"Did she have *those* on her shoulder?"

"No. I guess the fella carried 'em for her."

"Ah, yes," said Collins. "The fella. What was his name again?"

"I dunno. And I dunno what he looks like, neither! I never saw him! I don't know nothin' about him!"

Collins reached out and took hold of the spiked ends of Alfred Peters' mustache. "Find out something. And make it fast."

"You leggo— Ow! I don't want no trouble! I got a business here! I got to live—"

Collins' face was close to his. "Got to live? No, friend. Not necessarily."

"*Aaah!*" said Alfred Peters in a horrified gasp. "You wouldn't— Ow! Ow-ow! All right, all right! Leggo! I'll tell you—"

Collins stepped back. "Go ahead."

Alfred Peters tugged at his mustache tenderly. "You ain't got any right at all. . . . All right! I'm gonna tell you! It was just like I said. Now, wait! Only I heard a couple things when she was talkin' on the telephone. I wouldn't listen when any of my guests is talkin', but the telephone is right there by the desk—"

"Sure," said Collins.

"Well, it is. And she was always talkin', to this fella over it. She never spoke his name. She was always awful careful about that. At least, when I was around. But she sure put out a lot of love talk. She acted like she was dippy about this bird,

what I mean. And it was all of a sudden, too. She never made no calls or got any before, and then she was on the phone all the time."

"Did the guy come around to see her?"

"I think so, but I never saw him. Honest! She'd get all dressed up, and then she'd wait here in the hall until just two minutes to seven. Then she'd go out and walk over toward Sunset."

"And then?"

lfred Peters shrugged his skinny shoulders. "I dunno."

"Yes, you do. You followed her."

"Well, once," Alfred Peters admitted. "I was lookin' out for her own best interests. And what did I get for it? I got a slap in the face, that's what! She waited for me in a dark place down the street and stepped right out and slapped me in the face and told me to mind my own damned business."

"So you didn't. What did you try next?"

"Well, I got a pencil and a little pad there below the telephone for the convenience of my guests, and one time when she was talking she wrote a number down and tore off the page she wrote it on."

"But that didn't stop you, did it?"

"No," said Alfred Peters. "I took off the next page and blew some lead pencil scrapings across it, and then I could see the number she wrote."

"Which was?"

"Blakely 7-6222."

"Right on the tip of your tongue, eh?" Collins remarked. "Whose is it?"

Alfred Peters sighed mournfully. "I called it, and a fella answered and said: 'This is Derek Van Diesten's house.'"

"Who is he?"

Alfred Peters stared with his mouth open. "Don't you *know*? He's the big hot-shot Dutch director from Rotterdam. Hitler chased him out, and he come over here a year ago. He's one of the biggest guns in Hollywood. I sure figured on keepin' that under my hat. I figured on callin' him up someday and tellin' him who I was and all the experience in pictures I've had. Then I figured I'd say, just sort of casual, 'How's Myra?' "

"And then what?" Collins asked persistently.

Alfred Peters looked pained at such stupidity. "Why, he'd give me a job, of course. Lots of 'em."

"Why would he?"

"Well, he wouldn't want no scandal. Of course, I wouldn't tell anybody, but he wouldn't want to take no chances that I'd blab what happened."

"What did?"

"Huh!" said Alfred Peters. "It's easy for a smart guy to figure out, all right!" He looked around and then lowered his voice. "Why, Myra went away to live with him, that's what! She's livin' with him right now someplace under some other name! Sure! I know I'm right! You can't fool me!"

"You know," Collins said slowly, "I don't believe I'd call him up and say anything to him, if I were you."

"Why not?"

Collins took a long sudden step closer to him. "Because he might send somebody like me around to shut your big blabber mouth—permanently."

"*Aaah!*" Alfred Peters moaned, and his face was a queer greenish color. He made little noises in his throat, and his eyes bulged wider and wider, and then words mumbled out of his stiff lips. "Wait, wait, wait! I never—I didn't—I was jokin'! I wouldn't—I don't know nothin'! Honest, honest! I was just—*Aaah!*"

The telephone rang, and he jumped as though he had been stabbed through the heart.

"Answer it," Collins ordered. "If they want someone else, tell them the party isn't here. If they want you, tell them you're sick. You probably will be, pretty quick."

Alfred Peters fumbled the receiver off the hook with a shaking hand. "Huh-hello? . . . Wh-

what did you say? . . . A big, wide, ugly fella that plays the piano? I dunno who—"

Collins slapped him to one side and jerked the receiver out of his hand.

"Who is this?" he demanded.

"Hello." The voice was low and muffled and hard to understand. "Hello, John Collins. I'm a friend of yours. I just wanted to give you a word of warning. Don't look any further for Myra Martin."

"Why not?" Collins said.

"Because if you do, you might find her. I don't think you'd like it where she is. It's cold and rather damp and very dark. You'd better stick to piano playing. Good-bye, John Collins."

There was a soft click, and then the line hummed emptily. Collins slammed the receiver back on its hook, spun around and grabbed Alfred Peters by the front of his soiled shirt.

"Where's the nearest public telephone? Where is it? Quick!"

"Wh-why, over a block west on Sunset there's a little d-drugstore—"

Collins let go of him and ran out of the hall and across the front porch and vaulted over the rickety railing.

The drugstore was narrow and dingy and cluttered, heavy with the suggestive smell of patent medicines. The clerk was a little bald man in a blue smock, and he was hunched down with his chin resting on his hands, staring wearily at the smeared black headlines of the newspaper that was spread out on the prescription counter.

"What?" he said, looking up in a timidly surprised way. "Oh. Good evening, sir. I didn't hear you come in."

Collins indicated the telephone booth against the wall. "Did somebody just use that?"

"The telephone? Yes, sir. A man just put in a call."

"What did he look like?"

"Look like?" the clerk repeated vaguely. "Just—just sort of like anybody else, I think. I didn't pay much attention."

"How tall was he?"

"I don't know—about medium."

"Was he cross-eyed and did he have a green beard?" Collins asked patiently.

"Green beard? Oh, no. He didn't have any beard. He might have been cross-eyed, though. He was wearing dark glasses."

There was a sudden whip-like crack outside. In the same split-second a fat brown bottle on the shelf in back of the clerk burst like a bomb and threw shredded glass splinters in a glistening spray.

Collins dropped instantly into a crouch, below the level of the counter. In the street a motor blasted and then wound itself up into a high fading scream in second gear. The sound died away, and Collins straightened up slowly in time to see the clerk coming up in reluctant jerks on the other side of the counter. The clerk's face was as white as paper.

Collins smiled at him. "A friend of mine. Very amusing fellow. He plays practical jokes."

The clerk stared at the remains of the brown bottle and then turned his head slowly to look at the starred round hole in the drugstore's front window.

"Oh, no!" he said shakily. "No, sir! That wasn't any joke! That was a bullet—" He dodged around the counter and pelted for the front door, shouting: "Police! Help! Police!" in a thin falsetto wail.

Collins went quietly through the back room and out the door into an alley.

ollins arrived on Hollywood Boulevard a half-hour later after a series of zig-zagging detours through dark side streets and darker alleys. The Boulevard was crowded thickly with its usual pack of idly chattering, aimless strollers, and Collins drifted slowly along with them.

He was an expert at this. He had the trick of blending into a throng of people and becoming as hard to keep track of as an individual wave in the ocean.

After three blocks of sauntering and stopping to window-shop and sauntering again, he knew that he wasn't being followed, and he cut out of the crowd and entered another drugstore. This one was big and busy and brilliantly lighted. Collins located a row of phone booths and shut himself up in one of them.

A consultation with the directory informed him that Blakely was a Brentwood exchange, and he invested fifteen cents in a call to 7-6222. The telephone at the other end rang three times, and then the line clicked, and a precisely courteous voice said: "Yes?"

Collins reflected that they were no longer giving away information as freely as they had when Alfred Peters had called, and then he said casually: "I'd like to speak to Mr. Van Diesten, please. This is Mr. Fulham from Metro-Goldwyn-Mayer. It's urgent."

"Yes, sir!" said the precise voice. "Just one moment, sir! I'll call him at once!"

Collins waited, whistling softly to himself. There was another click on the line, and a hoarse baritone voice said: "Yes? Hello, hello? This is Van Diesten. Who is calling from Metro-Goldwyn-Mayer, please?"

"I'd like to speak to Myra Martin," Collins said.

"What? What is it?"

"I'd like to speak to Myra Martin."

The hoarse voice vibrated with anger. "You are not from Metro-Goldwyn-Mayer! I will report you!"

"I'd like to speak to Myra Martin, please."

"I do not know her! I do not know anybody by that name! You will stop calling and annoying me! You must be crazy!"

The receiver cracked in Collins' ear, and then the line was dead. Collins sat still for a moment, whistling softly and thoughtfully to himself. He was frowning a little, and he no longer looked friendly. He opened the door of the booth and went out of the drugstore and headed west on Hollywood Boulevard.

The Fortmount Hotel was tucked away on a side street off Vine. It had been all modern and shiny and Spanish once upon a time, but it was a little tired now. The shrubbery in the patio entrance was more ragged than luxuriant, and the lobby was as depressingly gloomy as a nightclub on Sunday morning. There were a few people sitting around and looking as though they wished they had somewhere else to go.

Collins crossed to the desk in the arched setback beside the elevators and spoke to the clerk.

"Will you call Mrs. Martin's room and tell her that John Collins is here?"

The clerk had shiny hair and a shiny round face. He put one pale hand up to his lips and coughed sharply. His eyes were blank with malicious little flickers of interest deep back in them.

"Did you hear me?" Collins asked impatiently.

"Yeah," said a voice in his ear. "So did we."

There were two of them—heavy-shouldered men with a solidly official weight behind their movements. They crowded close against Collins, pinning him against the desk, and one took him by each arm.

"Just take it easy," said the one who had first spoken. "This is a pinch, and you're it. Don't start a beef." He was taller than his companion, and he had a mangled cigar in the corner of his mouth. His eyes were the same color as the cigar.

The second one felt Collins' pockets with rapid patting hands. "He's clean." He had a sagging, surly face and black eyebrows that met in a bar above his eyes.

"Come along," said the tall one. "Nice and quiet now. Just like we're pals."

They still each had one of Collins' arms, and the three of them turned in unison, like a drill team, and started toward the elevator.

"Hey!" said a voice behind them. "Hey, wait a minute, guys!"

The detectives kept right on going with Collins between them, but the man darted around ahead of them and faced them excitedly, arms spread wide, as though he were trying to shoo some refractory chickens. He was thin and blond and a little hungry-looking. His eyes glinted eagerly behind horn-rimmed glasses.

"Hey, guy!" he said to Collins. "You! What's your name?"

"Scram," said the tall detective.

The little man waved his arms. "Aw, have a heart! Come on, let him tell me his name! Give me a break!"

"Beat it," said the tall detective.

The little man ignored him. "Listen, guy. I'm a reporter, see? Give me your name, and I'll—"

The surly detective stepped forward and put his meaty hand in the middle of the little man's face and shoved hard. "One side, louse!"

The little man went flapping backwards like a damp rag. He hit a chair and went over it with a clattering thud, and the last Collins saw as the detectives pushed him into the elevator were his two feet waving helplessly over the top of the tipped chair.

"That was mighty brave of you," said Collins conversationally. "I guess you're a couple of pretty hard guys."

"Shut up," said the tall detective.

The elevator was a self-operated one, and the door clanged shut as he pressed the button for the third floor. The elevator rose wearily and stopped with a sudden jump.

"Right down the hall," said the surly detective.

One on either side, still holding his arms, they marched Collins the length of the dingy hallway and stopped at the end door. The tall one rapped on it.

"Come on in," a voice ordered.

The surly one opened the door, and they boosted Collins through it and stopped him short just inside.

There was one man standing all by himself in the center of the room, scowling. "Well?"

he said. He was short, and he had a paunch and the beginnings of a double chin. He was wearing a green polo shirt and a yellow straw hat with a wide green-and-red band on it. Also, for contrast, he was wearing a brown sport jacket and brown checked slacks. His nose was flat, and his eyes were shot with reddish veins.

"This guy," said the tall detective. "He give the name of John Collins. He was askin' for the old lady."

"That true?" asked the man in the yellow hat.

Collins nodded. "Yes. Would you like me to show you something funny?"

"Sure," said the man in the yellow hat.

Collins suddenly spread both of his legs wide and then bent forward and brought his arms violently together in front of him. The two detectives couldn't have done it more neatly if they had rehearsed. They were jerked forward, off-balance, and they each tripped over a different one of Collins' legs. They hit the floor with a jar that jingled the chandelier.

"Yeah," said the man in the yellow hat, not at all startled. "That *was* funny. Grimes! Craig! Quit that! Get up off the floor and get the hell out of here! Go on out in the hall and wait there. You two clowns give me the pip."

The two detectives picked themselves up, red-faced and panting. They stumbled out of the room and closed the door very quickly and quietly behind them.

"Am I arrested?" Collins asked.

"Hell, no," said the man in the yellow hat, resuming his scowling survey of the room. "You wanta go home? All right. Good-bye."

"I think I'll stay."

"Suit yourself. My name is Tilwitz. I'm a lieutenant of detectives—Homicide."

"Has there been a murder?"

"How do I know?"

Collins said: "Well, are you going to talk to me, or are you going to stand there and sulk?"

"I got a headache," said Tilwitz glumly. "I got two headaches—both of them out there in the hall. What do you want to talk about, as if I cared?"

"About Mrs. Della Martin. Is this her room?"

"That's what they tell me, but people are liable to tell a cop almost anything."

"Where is she?"

Tilwitz sighed and went over to the bed and sat down on it. "You got a cigarette?" He took one out of the pack Collins extended and accepted a light. "I don't know where she is, but if you gave me a guess, I'd say she was dead."

"What happened?"

Tilwitz blew smoke in a long plume. "What kind of cigarettes are these? I don't like 'em. Well, about an hour ago the people on this floor heard a scream and then a shot. So they called up the clerk and told him he'd better scout around a bit. So he came up here with one of the bellboys and knocked on a few doors. Results: zero."

"Then what?" Collins asked.

"Crash of glass from inside this room. Thump-thump-thump—mysterious noises. So the clerk raps a while and calls a while and finally gets up nerve enough to unlock the door with the passkey."

"What did he find?"

Tilwitz pointed to the window. "That—upper pane broken." He pointed to the rug in front of the bathroom door. "That—bloodstain on the rug. That's all."

"Nothing else?" Collins said incredulously.

Tilwitz took the cigarette out of his mouth and looked at it distastefully. "These are awful. No. Nothing else. No body, no burglars, no Mrs. Martin—and no clothes."

"What?" Collins said.

Tilwitz nodded. "It's nuts, or I am. There wasn't—and isn't—one sign of Mrs. Martin in this room. She had a traveling bag and a suitcase when she came in. They're gone, and everything that was in 'em is gone. Barring a couple of dirty towels and sheets, this room is exactly the way it was when it was rented to her three days ago.

Nothing in the wastepaper basket. Nothing in the bureau drawers or closet. Just plain damned nothing."

"What do you think happened?"

"If I could think, I wouldn't be a detective. But it looks to me as if somebody doubled a rope around that radiator—it's out of line about six inches—and let the rope out the window—there's a scoured place on the sill—and lowered Mrs. Martin and all her baggage down into the alley. Whoever it was broke the window in the process of getting in or out or something."

"What are you going to do about it?" asked Collins.

"Do?" said Tilwitz sourly. "Not a damned thing, son. There's no law that says people have to keep their luggage in a hotel room and no law that says they can't use the window to go out of it. It's not a crime to have a nose bleed or even bust a window, if it's an accident. So there you are."

"You said you thought Mrs. Martin was dead."

"That was my unofficial opinion. Don't quote me. Have you got another cigarette?"

"I thought you said you didn't like them?"

"They're better than nothing," Tilwitz said. "Not much better—but some. Thanks. That was a nice little juggling act you pulled on Grimes and Craig. You're not supposed to be a detective unless you can read and write and count up to ten, but those two slipped through some way."

"Yes," said Collins absently.

"If I'm boring you, you can leave any time now. I'll have Grimes and Craig follow you, but that shouldn't cramp your style much. Just make faces at them if they should bother you too much. They'll run."

Collins looked up. "Did you know that Mrs. Martin had a daughter here in Hollywood?"

"Sure," Tilwitz answered. "She made a lot of inquiries and calls—talked about it to other people at the hotel."

"She asked me to find her daughter."

"Go ahead," Tilwitz invited. "Who's stopping you?"

"You're not going to do anything else about this?"

"Not now. I should run my legs off and have the old lady pop up and give me the bird and maybe sue me for invasion of her privacy. There's been no complaint filed by anybody—there's no concrete evidence that any crime has been committed. I haven't got any right to go prying around—even if I had the ambition."

"Do you mind if I do?"

"Me?" said Tilwitz blandly. "Mind? Hell, no. Fly right at it."

"I'll tell you if I find anything."

"Don't bother," Tilwitz advised. "Just keep it a deep dark secret."

"Do you want my address?"

"If I want you," said Tilwitz, "I'll find you."

Collins watched him thoughtfully. "No use giving your two stooges sore feet. I'm just going home now."

"What're you going to do when you get there?"

"Play the piano."

"That'll be nice. Play real pretty."

Collins smiled a little. "Good-bye."

Tilwitz nodded solemnly. "So long. I won't have the two dopes follow you. Tell 'em to come in here."

Collins went out into the hall. The two detectives were leaning against the wall, side by side, opposite the door. They glowered at Collins in grim silence.

Collins jerked his thumb over his shoulder. "Your master is calling."

"We won't forget that little stunt you pulled," the tall one promised. "We'll be seeing you again, baby. Don't think we won't."

Collins grinned. "Any time at all."

The shabby little man with the horn-rimmed glasses was waiting for him down in the lobby.

"Hey, guy," said the little man. "Wait a

minute—please. Look, I'm a reporter. Name's Rick Preston. I used to work for U.P., but I got boiled and got a couple of press dispatches mixed up, and they canned me. I can get back on again if I have a story to bring in with me. How about a break, guy?"

Collins shrugged. "I haven't got any story."

"There's one around here," Preston insisted. "I can smell 'em. What's Tilwitz doing upstairs?"

"Tilwitz is here because an old lady by the name of Mrs. Della Martin disappeared under rather mysterious circumstances."

"I know that," Rick Preston said. "What about the daughter she was looking for?"

"I don't know," said Collins.

"Aw, come on," said Preston. "Give me a break. What's your name?"

"John Collins. I can't give you a break, because I don't know anything to tell you. Mrs. Martin's daughter stopped writing, and Mrs. Martin was worried. She came around to see me because she'd heard I met a lot of people here and there. I told her I'd look for her daughter. I didn't find her."

"Daughter disappears," Preston muttered. "Then the old lady disappears. But, hell, there's nothing you can put your finger on!"

"No," said Collins. "Well, I'll give you a ring if I hear anything."

Collins came in the back door of his bungalow without making a sound. For a long time, he stood in the darkness of the cluttered kitchen, listening.

When he was sure there was no one but himself in the bungalow, he went on into the front room and closed the curtains and turned on the pink lamp.

Even now, very faintly, he could detect the odor of lilac toilet water that Mrs. Martin had brought with her, like a wistful old-fashioned memory of her own prim person. He sat down in front of the little piano and stayed there, hunched over, grave and motionless, frowning a little.

He had no illusions about his own position. He was involved in a train of events that coiled through the backstreets of Hollywood, touched the studios and the gaudy movie-rich mansions beyond them, and looped back to that ugly, empty little room in the Fortmount Hotel where Tilwitz sat and waited like a spider to see what would fall into his web. Tilwitz could be casual and disarmingly cynical, but he didn't deceive Collins any. Let something happen—anything to give him a start—and Tilwitz would pounce.

Collins began to play absently, and the tune tinkled through the room with a neat plaintive swing. There was something that prodded deep back in Collins' mind—something that had to do with secret cynical laughter and Mrs. Della Martin—something . . .

The telephone rang and jerked him back to reality. He got up and went across to the stand beside the door and lifted the instrument from its cradle.

"Yes?"

"Is this Mr. John Collins?" It was a feminine voice—low and throaty and theatrical—and unmistakably young.

"Yes," said Collins slowly.

"This is Myra Martin, Mr. Collins."

"What?" said Collins. "Who?"

"Myra Martin. I want to talk to you—tonight. Can you come to the old Regent Studios at once?"

"Are you—"

"Please come. Now."

The line hummed emptily, and Collins put the telephone back on its stand. He swept up his hat and started for the back of the house, and then he stopped suddenly and stared at the battered little piano. Now he remembered the tune he had been playing when the telephone rang.

It was "Oh, Susanna." And now he knew the meaning of the secret little doubt that had pried at his mind, and he knew why Mrs. Della Martin had disappeared and where, and he knew what had happened to Myra Martin and why.

Hollywood had gone away and left the Regent Studios. They were forlorn and alone in a residential area of small houses and small stores north of Santa Monica Boulevard. They dated back before sound—ancient history—and the tall stucco wall that surrounded them was crumbling and streaked with rain mold.

There was one small light, wan and dim, burning over the massive iron gates of the main entrance.

Collins shoved at one of the gates experimentally, and it moved back at once, slick and oiled and quiet.

The sets extended in long rows outward from the hub of the entrance, crumbling and sagging and tattered, holding within themselves the memories of epics long forgotten.

Collins picked one of the streets and walked along it, passing from London to Hong Kong to a Zulu village and back to Deadwood Gulch, Arizona, all in the length of a hundred paces, and then he stopped short and waited while a light flicked once brightly over to his left, flicked again, and then was gone.

Collins moved into the shadow of a tipsy balcony. He moved again, after a moment, slipping between rough-edged boards into the blackness back of the set. He moved without making any noise at all. The grass brushed clammily at his legs, and then he reached another street and drifted quietly across it in the shadow of a medieval tower.

The light flicked once more, very close now, glittering behind the doors of a building that was like an enormous white tombstone. Collins approached very slowly, watching his path for obstructions, and stopped before steps that had probably looked like marble once but were now boards scarcely covered with a rotted remnant of oil cloth.

The big double doors of the building were warped. They hadn't quite closed. Collins tested one of the board steps, finally rested his weight on it, and tested the next.

He reached the broad, dim stretch of the porch. He could hear the dull mumble of voices. He took two long quick steps and flattened against the wall beside the door.

". . . think I'm fooling?" said a voice that was thin and savagely tense.

"You are mad," answered Derek Van Diesten's hoarse, slightly accented baritone. "I think you must be insane."

"Yeah?" The light flicked. "Look over there."

"Ah!" said Van Diesten in a horrified gasp. "She is—she is—"

"She's dead," said the thin voice. "And they'll prove you killed her, and they'll hang you. I've fixed that. I've laid a trail—oh, a very careful one—that'll bring it home right to your door."

"You could not— They would not believe—"

"Oh, yes, they will. They'll find her—where do you think? In your car, and the car will be wrecked. You killed her, and you were fleeing somewhere to hide the body when you skidded and went off the road. You ran away. You won't be able to prove you didn't, because I'll leave you here all night. You'll have no alibi. And that won't be all. Oh, no. You see, I've prepared them for that find."

"Those telephone calls," Van Diesten said numbly. "Those calls to me about her . . ."

"Yes," said the thin voice. "Those were from people who think you were living with her."

"That is not true! I do not even know—"

"But they think you do, and they'll testify you do. I planted clues that point to you at her boarding house." The thin voice chuckled in an ugly way. "At a hotel, too. And other places, and with other people. Oh, they'll find you easy enough, and when they do you'll be finished."

Van Diesten's voice was shaky. "What— what do you want from me?"

"That's nice," the thin voice complimented. "I was afraid I was going to have to argue with you. I don't want anything much—nothing at all from you. I want you to get me a job at a thousand dollars a week at the Mar Grande Studios."

"I cannot—"

"Yes, you can. You work there, and you've got influence. I'll be a technical expert of some kind or other working in an advisory capacity. It won't cost you a cent, and you won't ever hear anything more about murder or Myra Martin."

There was no sound but Van Diesten's hoarse breathing, until Collins kicked his heel gently back against the wall. Instantly the light flicked out.

"What?" Van Diesten said in the darkness. "What is—"

"Shut up!" the thin voice snapped. "There's somebody outside! If you brought someone with you—"

"No, no!" Van Diesten denied. "I didn't—"

"Stand still! This gun's against your back, and it's cocked! If you move—if anybody comes near us—"

After a long time, Van Diesten said in a half-whisper: "There is nobody. . . ."

"Shut up. Don't move. . . . The door's open! *There's somebody in this room!*"

Collins dived at the sound. His shoulder smashed hard at the beefiness that was Van Diesten, and his fingers clawed and caught a thin wiry body beyond, and then the whole rickety structure swayed and groaned to the crash of their falling bodies.

He still had his grip on the wiry figure. The revolver blazed almost in his face, and the report was like a handclap against his ear drums. And then he got hold of the hand, felt the cramped rigidity of the fingers gripping the revolver butt, and twisted back and down.

The second report was a dull bump, muffled against cloth. The wiry body pulled back with crazed, insensate strength and then went limp and strangely heavy.

Collins said: "Van Diesten, are you all right?"

Van Diesten was choking for breath. "Yuh-yes."

"Find the light. Shine it down here."

————

The flashlight moved its beam down through the torn stretch of flooring. On the ground, crumpled in a limp pile, lay Rick Preston. His glasses were broken and glistening beside him, and his thin, hungry face was twisted into a frozen snarl. He still had the revolver clutched in his right hand, and his coatfront was sodden with blood.

"That one," said Van Diesten in numbed amazement. "That is the reporter that came only tonight to my home to ask me about this Myra Martin."

"He's dead," said Collins, climbing up on the floor again. "Where's the girl?"

The light moved away and circled across the floor toward the dark secretiveness of a corner. There was Myra Martin, at last. She was sitting up and smiling a little with her dead lips, and there was a red hole in her forehead and a trickle of blood that scarcely marred her still white prettiness.

"Poor little dummy," said Collins.

"What is it, please?" said Van Diesten. "This—all this—I do not understand."

Collins said slowly: "Myra Martin was a foolish little girl who wanted desperately to get into the movies. She couldn't in the ordinary way, because she didn't have enough talent or training, but of course she didn't believe that. She'd gotten quite a little fame out of some publicity she got from winning a beauty contest, and she thought the same thing might work out here. She was going to use you as a stooge."

"Me?" said Van Diesten. "But why?"

"You're a famous director. She disappeared, leaving a lot of clues that would, by inference, point to you. Then her mother appeared, searching for her. She inquired everywhere—drawing attention to herself with her pathetic little story about her lost daughter and her lost business. Then she, too, disappeared just as her daughter had."

"But why?" Van Diesten repeated blankly.

"To draw attention to Myra's disappearance. As soon as either of those disappearances were investigated at all, all the planted clues and hints would point right at you. There'd be inquiries made and publicity."

"And tonight?" Van Diesten asked.

"Tonight you were to have a mysterious interview with Myra. When questions were asked, you'd testify to that. Then Mrs. Martin would reappear, and you'd meet her. They'd bounce you back and forth between them, and you'd have to play along because you'd be more and more under suspicion of trying some dirty work. But right here, another party cut in. That was Rick Preston—very clever, very unscrupulous. He saw what Myra was up to—saw it quicker than I did. He wasn't interested in two-for-a-penny publicity. He wanted money and a lot of it, and he realized instantly that Myra's scheme was an ideal one for blackmailing you. If he changed that setup a little, you'd be right behind the eight-ball. You'd be accused of complicity in the disappearance of Myra and Mrs. Martin, and even if you could prove in court you had nothing to do with either, you'd be ruined in pictures. They won't take a scandal like that."

"No," said Van Diesten. "That was why I was so afraid. Why I came here when she called and told me to. And then, I am trying to become a citizen—for my two boys and my little girl as well as myself. If I was implicated in any crime, then they would not let me."

Collins nodded. "They figured on that. Mrs. Martin came to me, thinking I would go to the police after she disappeared. Myra was still after publicity. But Preston didn't want it—not through me. He tried to scare me off. He was already in touch with Myra. He found her at the Fortmount Hotel and got in with her by telling her he was a reporter. He played along with her until tonight, pretending to help her, and then he told her what he really meant to do—he wasn't going to get publicity for her. He was going to get money from you. She refused, and she made a scene. She was a little fool, and she didn't realize how dangerous . . . Preston didn't

think he could lose by killing her. She had planned her own disappearance too well, and it gave him another weapon to use against you—a real one, not a fake."

"But—but what is this publicity she was going to get?"

Collins said: "Myra was going to prove what a wonderful actress she was. Prove it by fooling an expert—you."

"How could she do that?"

"There is no Mrs. Della Martin. Myra and her mother are the same person. Myra played the part of her mother. That was her little scheme. If she could fool you—doing that—it would prove how clever she was."

"Same person . . ." Van Diesten repeated.

"Then, she planned, she would have suddenly faced you and proved to you that she had been playing two parts and playing them so well she had fooled you, and you'd have given her a job, in self-defense if for no other reason."

"How did—how did you know?"

"When she came to see me as Mrs. Della Martin, she didn't cry. She told a very sad story. She nearly made *me* cry. She should have at least shed a tear or two. But she couldn't. If she had, she'd have spoiled her make-up."

There was a long silence, and then Van Diesten fumbled uncertainly over words: "You did all this, and you do not even know me. . . ."

"Well, to tell the truth," Collins said, "I think I brought it on myself. The only way I can figure that Myra would know anything about me is that I must have gotten crocked at a party somewhere and talked too much about my experiences in Europe. She either heard me or someone she knew did. If I'd have kept my big mouth shut, I'd never have gotten in this in the first place."

"That does not make any difference. You have done so much, and I want to show you how I feel. . . ."

Collins chuckled. "Never mind. I don't even want a job. I've got a better one than you could give me coming up."

"Better?" Van Diesten said.

"Yes. The Army. I'm just sitting around and

loafing while I'm waiting to be inducted. You run along home now. I'll report this, and I won't even mention your name. There's a detective by the name of Tilwitz who is going to come steaming around here in a little while. He won't believe me no matter what I say, so I'll dream up something real fancy for him." Collins' voice sobered suddenly. "This is Myra's last chance, and I'm going to give her as big a part to play as I can."

T. McGuirk Steals a Diamond
Ray Cummings

RAY(MOND) (KING) CUMMINGS (1887–1957) was born in what is now Times Square and, in later years, made it a habit to eat at a restaurant built near the place of his birth, specifically asking for the table nearest the actual spot. His family was wealthy and he attended Princeton at a precocious sixteen years of age, but was removed after only a month to go to Puerto Rico, where his father and brothers had started a large orange plantation. He got a private tutor, but neither he nor the tutor was particularly interested in studying, instead enjoying the nightlife of the island. After brief stints working at oil wells in Wyoming and mines in British Columbia and Alaska, Cummings went to work for Thomas Alva Edison, mostly writing for and editing house organs and record album covers, before becoming a full-time fiction writer. His first story, "The Girl in the Golden Atom" (1919), became an instant classic of science fiction, helping to earn him the title "the founding father of pulp science fiction." He went on to produce more than seven hundred short stories, mostly science fiction and mystery, for the pulps, as well as numerous SF novels. In later years, the quality of his writing declined, so he collaborated with both his wife and his daughter. His imagination remained intact, and with them he wrote a series of "impossible crime" stories; a collection titled *Tales of the Scientific Crime Club* was published in 1979.

"T. McGuirk Steals a Diamond," the first of fourteen McGuirk tales written for *Black Mask,* was published in the December 1922 issue.

T. McGuirk Steals a Diamond

Ray Cummings

"I deman' to be let go!" said T. McGuirk, the quaint-est character in the underworld, when the pawn-broker's strong-arm man had searched him in vain for the missing diamond. You'll enjoy the doings of T. McGuirk because he has a system all his own.

T. McGUIRK LEANED FORWARD.

"What I'm sayin' is—I gotta steal a dia-mond!"

He half whispered the information, gazing about him apprehensively.

Lefty Lannigan's amusement was wholly undisguised.

"You got to—*what*?"

T. McGuirk's injured feelings showed in the flush that spread under his four-day stubble of beard. A hurt look came into his pale, watery eyes.

"What you laffin' at? I said I gotta steal a dia-mond. I need a diamond, wery bad."

The gunman surveyed his friend ironically.

"Oh you do? A real diamond? What for?"

T. McGuirk shook his head.

"That's my business," he stated with dignity. "I gotta girl an' I need a diamond. I ain't sayin' nothin' more."

"You don't need to," commented Mr. Lanni-gan.

"An' so I come to you," T. McGuirk added gravely, "to steer me into somebody where I can steal a diamond."

Mr. Lannigan pondered.

"You're not kiddin'? You're serious?"

"Wery serious," T. McGuirk stated suc-cinctly.

"Well, let's see. You're goin' to do the job alone?"

T. McGuirk nodded.

The gunman, after a moment of grave con-sideration, suggested Stone and Blackstone, leading Fifth Avenue jewelers.

"They got some real good diamonds," he declared. "You might try them."

But T. McGuirk shook his head vehemently.

"You ain't got no sense. I ain't lookin' for no job like that. Ain't you acquainted with no crook what's got a diamond to sell?"

Mr. Lannigan folded his arms, staring loftily down at T. McGuirk's wizened form.

"Want me to steer you into a pal of mine so you can lift a sparkler? You're a fine—"

"I thought you might have a enemy," T. McGuirk explained meekly. "A fence or some-thin' that maybe done you a dirty deal. If he's got a unset diamond to sell I'm a-goin' to steal it off'n him. See?"

An idea came to Lefty Lannigan—a most amusing idea, for he chuckled.

"I got just the man," he declared heartily.

He thumped T. McGuirk on the back so vig-orously that the little man's head seemed nearly to snap off.

"Just the man, Timothy. Ever heard of Ike Gluckstein?"

T. McGuirk had, vaguely. Gluckstein was a "fence" of unusually shady reputation even among those of the underworld with whom he did business.

T. McGuirk nodded. Mr. Lannigan went on:

"You try him. Go to his pawnshop—here, I'll write down the address—an' tell him you want to buy an unset sparkler. He's got some wonders. Mention my name an' he'll sit up an' take notice. He'll show you some, an' then—" Mr. Lannigan shrugged.

What would happen then obviously was past his understanding.

"Wery good idea," assented T. McGuirk. "Gimme the place where he is."

He pocketed the slip of paper with thanks.

"I'll see Mr. Gluckstein right at once, personally. Wery good idea."

A twinge of conscience overtook Mr. Lannigan. T. McGuirk was so trusting, and so obviously in earnest.

"You got a gun, Timothy?"

T. McGuirk shook his head emphatically.

"I'm a peaceable man. I don't never use no rewolvers."

He offered his hand, but still his friend hesitated.

"Hadn't we better talk it over, Timothy? I s'pose you got a plan? You know what you're doin'?"

"A plan? Sure I got a plan. I'm a-goin' to steal a diamond. I gotta have a diamond, right away."

Mr. Lannigan shrugged, discharging himself from further responsibility.

"Go to it then. But I warn you, Ike's a bad guy. You let him catch you tryin' to make away with a sparkler an' he'll wring your neck. If you pull anything queer make sure you get away with it."

T. McGuirk assented gratefully.

"Wery good idea, in-deed."

He shook hands and smiled his thanks.

Lefty Lannigan stood staring after him dubiously as he darted like a jackrabbit across the busy street, disappearing behind a passing stream of taxis.

* * *

The pawnshop of Isaac Gluckstein stood on an unobtrusive street of New York's Lower East Side. Mr. Gluckstein was closing up for the evening, preparing for his more serious and much more profitable business, most of which was transacted in a back room with access to an alley alongside the building, when T. McGuirk appeared through the front entrance. The pawnbroker paused in the act of opening his safe and surveyed his visitor. What he saw was some five feet three of rags and filth—an extraordinarily inoffensive-looking little man who stood just over the threshold and smiled ingratiatingly.

Mr. Gluckstein grunted with contempt and turned back to the safe; T. McGuirk padded forward with complete confidence.

"You got a diamond you wanta sell me, Mr. Gluckstein?"

The pawnbroker looked up again, staring.

T. McGuirk's smile widened, exposing an uneven row of tobacco-stained teeth.

"Lefty Lannigan sent me. He said you would sell me a diamond."

At this mention of the well-known gunman the pawnbroker seemed somewhat impressed.

"You say it, Lefty's a friend of yours?" he asked incredulously.

T. McGuirk nodded briefly.

"He sent you to me?"

Another nod.

"To buy a diamond?" Mr. Gluckstein's incredulity was melting.

Still another nod.

The pawnbroker smiled—quite as ingratiating a smile as T. McGuirk's.

"You could buy a diamond from me," he stated. "You've got the money, my friend?"

T. McGuirk frowned.

"I got plenty money. I ain't lookin' for no credit—cash, that's me."

Mr. Gluckstein rubbed his hands together—a slight, wholly instinctive gesture. Obviously he had heard of the adage that appearances are deceiving. He surveyed this cash customer with a new respect.

"You could buy from me a very fine diamond, my friend—and cheap." Mr. Gluckstein leaned forward confidentially and lowered his voice. "Lefty Lannigan did it to you a favor. He knows I got stones—at a price. You couldn't beat my prices, young man."

"Wery good," agreed T. McGuirk without enthusiasm. "Let's see some. About two carats—unset."

The pawnbroker stared again.

"An unset stone? I thought you wanted it a nice diamond ring—maybe for a lady. I got here many fine unredeemed pledges—"

T. McGuirk shook his head contemptuously.

"Me skirt's wery partic'lar. I gotta get a unset stone an' have it set special. Besides—"

T. McGuirk's eyes gleamed craftily. He raised himself on his toes to reach up nearer Mr. Gluckstein over the counter.

"Besides, I wants a real bargain. Lefty said you had some partic'lar sparklers—unset—an' I could buy one cheap an' no questions asked."

It was a stupendously complicated speech for T. McGuirk. He panted a little from the exertion of it.

Mr. Gluckstein pondered, then reached a sudden decision.

"Come with me," he said briefly. "Wait—I lock up the shop."

He locked the front door, pulled down the green shades and turned down the lights. Then he led his visitor through a door in the rear of the shop into a dim room adjoining. A man sitting there with his feet on a board table stood up as they entered. He was a huge man, thick-shouldered and barrel-chested, with a close-cropped, bullet head, blue jowls and a villainous countenance. T. McGuirk smiled at him naïvely.

"Meet Mr. Delancy," said the pawnbroker. "Pete, a friend of Lefty's. He wants to buy it a nice little unset diamond. His name is—"

"Me monicker's T. McGuirk," supplied the visitor promptly. "That's the name I goes by mostly."

Mr. Delancy acknowledged the introduction. A glance passed between him and the pawnbroker. Delancy nodded significantly and pushed his chair back to the wall. He seemed quite without further interest in the proceedings; as a matter of fact he was watching the visitor closely.

T. McGuirk sat down at the table, directly under the circle of illumination cast downward by the gas jet over his head. Mr. Gluckstein went to a small safe in a dark recess of the room, returning in a moment. In one hand he held a small square of black velvet, in the other an unset jewel. He laid the velvet on the table and placed the stone in its center.

"Such a diamond!" he murmured, half to himself. "Look how you could see it sparkle! Now *there* is a diamond—"

T. McGuirk looked calmly. He made no move to touch the stone.

"You got a glass?" he demanded. "Me eyes ain't so wery good."

The pawnbroker exchanged another glance with the saturnine Mr. Delancy. Then, reluctantly, he produced a magnifying glass from his pocket. T. McGuirk fitted it to his eye and with the air of a connoisseur bent forward to examine the diamond still lying untouched on its velvet background. After a moment he straightened. His glance was one of gentle reproof.

"I wanta buy a *real* diamond," he stated patiently. "Ain't you got a real diamond worth about four thousan' bucks?"

The calm naming of this amount softened the pawnbroker's disappointment at finding his customer could not be fooled.

"I got it absolutely what you want," he stated confidently. "Wait a minute—you could pick out the exact stone."

He removed his first offering; and returning, laid six unset diamonds on the square of velvet beneath T. McGuirk's critical eyes. There was no doubt of the genuineness of these stones; Mr. Delancy's immediate alertness was contributory evidence. He hitched his chair forward slightly, his eyes glued to the square of velvet with the six gems sparkling upon it. Quite evidently, though the visitor was not under suspicion, it was not part of Mr. Gluckstein's plan to have anything go amiss. The pawnbroker displayed his wares carelessly; but his confederate, from the shadows, watched T. McGuirk like a hawk.

"You couldn't find anything better at the price in America," declared Mr. Gluckstein emphatically. "Pick it out, the one your lady friend would like."

T. McGuirk sat with elbows on the table, staring at the six diamonds. He picked one up, gingerly, between thumb and forefinger. Mr. Delancy's gaze unwaveringly followed the stone as T. McGuirk raised it nearer his eyes.

"How much for this here one?"

He laid it back among the other five. Mr. Delancy breathed again and relaxed slightly.

"Four thousand dollars you could have it for," said the pawnbroker deprecatingly. "An' if it ain't worth six, s'elp me."

T. McGuirk's hands went suddenly into the side pockets of his ragged overcoat. Mr. Delancy leaned forward again. He saw quite plainly the six diamonds all lying on the black velvet. T. McGuirk's hands came back to the table. They held a tiny bag of tobacco, two matches and cigarette papers. Deftly he began rolling a cigarette.

"Four thousan'? Wery good. An' how much is this here one?" T. McGuirk touched another of the stones with the tip of his little finger. "Ain't this here a canary diamond?"

Mr. Gluckstein, at the question, passed around to his customer's left. For one brief instant he obstructed Mr. Delancy's view of the table. T. McGuirk was lighting his cigarette carefully, his hands cupping the flame.

And then, after an interval of two seconds, to Mr. Delancy's horrified gaze the square of black velvet presented only five diamonds! He counted them in a daze—five, not six as there should have been! Mr. Delancy sprang to his feet with an oath.

"Grab him, Ike! He's got one of the sparklers!"

Mr. Gluckstein's glance swung instantly to the velvet. He also could count only five diamonds. T. McGuirk had finished lighting his cigarette; he flicked away the match.

Quick as Mr. Delancy was to leap forward, the pawnbroker was quicker. He seized T. McGuirk by the collar unceremoniously, jerking him from his seat, shaking him as a terrier shakes a rat.

The cigarette tumbled from T. McGuirk's lips and fell unheeded to the floor; on the table, by the square of velvet with its five diamonds, lay his cigarette papers, a match, and the tiny bag of tobacco.

When Mr. Gluckstein's strength gave out from shaking his victim, he abruptly desisted. T. McGuirk's feet found the floor. He stood quivering, shrinking within his rags and mumbling vehemently.

Mr. Delancy's shock of surprise and alarm had now abated.

"Nothin' to get excited over, Ike. The little shrimp can't get away."

"I don't w-want to get away," T. McGuirk chattered. "What you doin' that to me for? How dare you do that to me for nothin'?"

"Shut up," ordered Mr. Delancy. "Ike, how many sparklers was there? Am I seein' things? I saw six."

"Six," verified Mr. Gluckstein briefly. "The Lady Vernon jewels we bought from Lefty."

Mr. Delancy nodded.

"Come on, you." This to T. McGuirk. "Hand it over or I'll break every bone in your damn little body."

"Not so loud, Pete."

Mr. Gluckstein had a very wholesome desire to avoid any uproar. He prided himself on the fact that never once had the police had occasion to invade his premises because of interior disturbance.

Mr. Delancy modified his tones.

"Come on, you—hand it over. You can't get away with that stuff here."

T. McGuirk suddenly began to snivel.

"H-hand w-what over?"

"The rock—the sparkler. There was six—now there's five."

"I ain't got no sparkler," declared T. McGuirk sullenly. "I ain't seen no sparkler 'cept them there what's on the table."

"You could search him, Pete," suggested Mr. Gluckstein hopefully.

He seemed a little confused, anxious to leave the initiative to his companion.

"Look out! Maybe he's got a gun!"

T. McGuirk's hand had gone to his pocket.

"I ain't," he asserted stoutly. "I'm a peaceable man—I don't never use no rewolwer."

His empty hands went up obediently at Mr. Delancy's command. Quite evidently he spoke the truth, for after a moment Mr. Delancy backed away again, surveying him from a distance.

"Search him good, Pete. You could find it. Right away we get excited—that ain't sensible."

After another peremptory but futile demand for the missing diamond, Mr. Delancy began searching the person of T. McGuirk. It was too slow a process.

"Take 'em off," he commanded.

T. McGuirk obediently stripped. When he was denuded of every vestige of apparel, Mr. Delancy and the pawnbroker avidly pawed over the pile of rags. Their search was fruitless. The missing diamond was not to be found.

"Where's his four thousan' bucks?" Mr. Delancy demanded.

He and the pawnbroker turned accusingly on their prisoner. T. McGuirk, shivering in his nudity, flushed with embarrassment.

"I ain't got no money with me," he explained. "Lefty's holdin' it. He was comin' here later to buy the diamond I picked out."

This remark, which T. McGuirk made quite on the spur of the moment, evidently gave Mr. Gluckstein considerable food for thought. His respect for Lefty Lannigan was great, his fear even greater. And he well remembered the gunman's ire at a little unpleasantness over these same Lady Vernon jewels. There was evidently more to this affair than Mr. Gluckstein had at first supposed. He was quite at a loss to explain it; but whatever it was, Lefty Lannigan must not be involved.

T. McGuirk, still shivering, remarked indignantly:

"Yous is wery, wery wrong, a-treatin' me this way. Gimme my clothes."

He began dressing, mumbling to himself.

"I'm a-gonna tell Lefty how yous is a-treatin' me over nothin'."

Mr. Delancy passed a hand over his blue chin reflectively. The situation was too complicated for him.

"You better put them other sparklers back," he cautioned, waving his hand at the five diamonds on the table. "We might lose another if we ain't careful."

The pawnbroker mechanically replaced them in the safe.

T. McGuirk was still dressing, some distance from the table, when Mr. Delancy suddenly thought of the little tobacco bag lying there. He examined it eagerly, but it yielded nothing but tobacco.

"Maybe the diamond got knocked on the floor," suggested T. McGuirk hopefully. "But I didn't see none, only them five."

The pawnbroker was already on his knees, searching about with a pocket flashlight. Mr. Delancy joined him. T. McGuirk, now completely dressed, sat down and watched the proceedings with interest.

For fifteen minutes the search went on. The room was ransacked thoroughly. Mr. Gluckstein verified his count of the diamonds in the safe. He searched his own pockets, and those of Mr. Delancy. The result was always the same. There had been six of Lady Vernon's diamonds brought in by Lefty Lannigan and purchased from him by Mr. Gluckstein—but now there were only five.

T. McGuirk sat meekly watching. On the floor near the table leg lay the cigarette he had rolled. He picked it up. But before he had time even to reach for a match, Mr. Delancy seized the cigarette with a cry of triumph.

"Here's where he put that sparkler, Ike! We're fools!"

The pawnbroker hastened to his side as he tore the little cylinder apart ruthlessly. There was nothing but tobacco within it.

T. McGuirk's glance was rebuking.

"I ain't seen no sparkler, I'm telling you. Yous is wery wrong, accusin' me this way."

The exasperated Mr. Delancy seized him by the collar; but this time T. McGuirk yelped shrilly.

"You take your hands off'n me. S'elp me, I'll yell for the cops. An' when I get 'em in here I'll tell 'em all about everything. I can't help it if yous is so careless with Lady Wernon's diamonds."

The pawnbroker shuddered. Mr. Delancy released his victim, and remarked hopelessly:

"Get him out of here, Ike, before I kill him. He'll land the bulls on us sure."

"I wanta go," T. McGuirk asserted. "Lefty's waitin' for me anyhow. I don't wanta buy no diamonds off'n you."

He cast about for his hat, but Mr. Gluckstein confronted him.

"If we let you go now you could shut your mouth about this? You could get out of here an' stay out an' right away forget you were ever in here?"

"Wery good idea," assented T. McGuirk readily. "I never seen no sparklers in here. I never heard of no Lady Wernon. Just lemme out. I deman' to be let go!"

Half a minute later, with a push from Mr. Delancy that propelled him headlong down the steps into the darkness of the alley, T. McGuirk made his exit.

* * *

Lefty Lannigan, with a curiosity that would not let him rest, chanced to be loitering at the corner waiting for his friend's appearance. T. McGuirk came shuffling along, still mumbling vehemently to himself.

"Hello, Timothy. You didn't get killed?"

T. McGuirk stopped.

"Did you get the diamond, Timothy?"

There was a shade of irony in Mr. Lannigan's tone.

"Sure I got it. Lady Wernon's—the biggest one. Wery easy job—wery easy, *in*-deed."

Mr. Lannigan stared, incredulous.

"How'd you get it? Show it up."

But T. McGuirk shook his head.

"Not here. Come on—let's eat."

In the semi-private alcove of a cheap Chinese restaurant off the Bowery, T. McGuirk faced his burly friend over the marble table.

"I was rollin' a cigarette—see?"

He suited the action to the word, rolling the little cylinder deftly and moistening it with his tongue. Then, with a bland smile, he removed a pivot tooth from his upper jaw. He held it out triumphantly. It was a realistically yellow false tooth with a gold top and a pivot sticking up. T. McGuirk turned it over in his palm. The back of the tooth was hollowed out and filled up with wax. And imbedded in the wax lay the missing diamond.

"You gets the sparkler on your tongue," T. McGuirk explained. "An' the tongue puts it in the tooth. It's wery easy—wery easy *in*-deed. All you needs for a job like that is system. System *an'* brains, *an'* no rewolver."

Wait for Me

Steve Fisher

STEPHEN (GOULD) FISHER (1912–1980) served in the U.S. Navy for four years from the age of sixteen, then settled in New York City to write full-time, becoming one of the most prolific and successful authors of his time, with hundreds of stories sold to both the pulps and the slicks, twenty novels, and more than one hundred scripts for motion pictures and television series.

His classic noir novel *I Wake Up Screaming* (1940) was his breakthrough when it was made into what is generally regarded as Hollywood's first film noir. The 1941 movie starred Victor Mature, Betty Grable, Carole Landis, and Laird Cregar; it was remade in 1953 as *Vicki*, with Jeanne Crain, Elliott Reid, Jean Peters, and Richard Boone. Fisher was the screenwriter for numerous mystery films in the 1940s, including the uncharacteristically dark final film in the popular Thin Man series, *Song of the Thin Man* (1947), *Johnny Angel* (1945, with George Raft, based on a Charles G. Booth novel, *Mr. Angel Comes Aboard*), *Lady in the Lake* (1947, based on Raymond Chandler's novel), *I Wouldn't Be in Your Shoes* (1948, based on a Cornell Woolrich story), *Berlin Correspondent* (1942, an anti-Nazi thriller), and *Dead Reckoning* (1947), a classic crime tale starring Humphrey Bogart and Lizabeth Scott. His early navy background lent authenticity to such war film screenplays as *Destination Tokyo* (1943, starring Cary Grant) and the aircraft carrier film *Flat Top* (1952); his other great war movie is *To the Shores of Tripoli* (1942).

"Wait for Me" was published in the May 1938 issue.

Wait for Me

Steve Fisher

A murdered spy evokes Death in Shanghai.

HER NAME WAS ANNA, AND SHE WAS beautiful, with golden blond hair that came to her shoulders and turned under at the ends, and a face like an angel, soft and aglow with color; gray-green eyes, and the slim traces of sunlight that were eyebrows.

She knelt there in the Shanghai street, and bowed her head, so that her hair fell a little forward, and like that, kneeling, there was both grace and divinity in her.

The sunset drifted across her red jacket and the shadow of her slim figure fell across the cobblestone street, causing even the fleeing Chinese to stop and turn and look, though they did not pause long. Now and again a white man stopped, and glanced at her, then went on when he recognized that she was Russian.

Anna leaned down and kissed the bleeding girl, kissed her cooling cheeks, and said softly:

"We will have no more sailors together, eh, Olga? Drink no more vodka." She smiled faintly, and shrugged, for Olga was gone, like yesterday's breath. Gone, Anna thought, quite fortunately and painlessly. A merciful stray bullet—and who to tell if Jap or Chinese?—had ended her troubles. But Anna, living, must go on.

She looked around, looked through the

streets for the man who had been following her, but she did not see him, and by now had forgotten the corpse of the girl.

She rose, and moved on, gracefully, her feet accustomed to the cobblestones, her face and eyes dry. She paused at each corner and looked up and down the street. Mostly she was looking for the man who had followed her from her apartment. She did not know who he was. He was wearing a coat with its collar turned up around his face, a white face with bleak, desperate eyes. He had called after her and she had run, losing herself in the fleeing crowd. She was terrified. Everything terrified her.

Since the evacuation order had come through to send all foreign white women to Hong Kong, and from there to their own countries, Anna felt that her time to die would come at any moment.

There was no escape for Russian exiles. There was nowhere they could run to get away from war. No passports would be issued to them; no country wanted them. Russian women were at the mercy of the mob, of the armies, of every band of men that came along. The evacuation order clearing white women had come two hours ago; in another sixteen hours huge transports would sail away with all those women, except the Russians. . . .

Ah, the Russians. Anna laughed into the clatter of the frightened street; and then she clenched her teeth and fled on, shadows and torch-light beating against her running figure. It was quieter in the International settlement. She did not slacken her pace, though she was breathing harder.

When she came to the hotel she swept inside the doors, and in that instant she saw the man who had been following her, the man whose coat collar was turned up. She saw him running past, and, not waiting to see if he would miss her, then stop and come back, she went to the desk.

"I wish to see Mrs. Turner."

The clerk bowed. "You may call her on the house phone, madam."

Anna moved nervously to the house phone and picked it up. When Rita Turner's silky voice came on the wire, Anna said: "I have a message from your husband. It is very important and most confidential."

Except in highly excitable moments Anna could speak English without an accent, for her finishing school had been a nightclub called the Navy Sport Palace, which was little more than third rate, and located on the Bund. There she had learned all the American and English and French slang; and she had learned other things too: how to darken her eyes, and redden her mouth, and wink her eye, and toss her head; how to drink without becoming drunk; how to muffle her sobs with laughter; the art of light love with a deep touch.

Rita Turner said nervously: "Please come up."

Anna moved gracefully into the elevator. She sighed as the doors slid quietly closed. Though she had been too young to remember Moscow, she thought it might be like this; the comfort and ease the White Russians had known; the old lost life about which she had heard her parents talk.

When she arrived on the fourth floor she walked down the heavily padded hall and stopped in front of the room number Rita Turner had given her. She knocked, and the door was immediately opened.

A tall, dark girl, her hair in a heavy roll on her neck, her skin pale, and her eyes bright and black and vivid, stood there, then stepped back. Anna walked in.

It was a beautiful apartment. A radio tuned to Hong Kong was playing "The Lady Is a Tramp"; from the window there was a magnificent scene of fire sweeping across the eastern section of Shanghai, and it was so vivid Anna almost thought she could hear the shrill despair of the screams beneath the flame.

The rug in the room was Oriental, the furniture quietly rich. Three bags lay open, light plane baggage, brown and smart and new. They were half packed. Women's clothes were strewn everywhere.

Anna turned slowly, as though she wished to take her time and enjoy this setting slowly without rush and hustle.

Rita Turner said, "What is the message, please? And who are you?" She was impatient.

Anna smiled with her teeth. "Your husband has been sent up the Yangtze?"

The dark-haired girl nodded.

"He will not return for three days?"

"That's right," answered Rita Turner, "but we're wasting time. What *is* the message?"

Anna flopped down on the divan and reached for a cigarette. She put it in her mouth and lit it.

"Your husband is an army officer," she went on, "and you have been ordered to evacuate? Is that not right?"

"Of course it's right."

Anna, only three puffs into the cigarette, snuffed it out. "I got the information from a man who sells such information to White Russians." She smiled again. "I will tell you that it cost me all I had been able to save during these meager years in Shanghai. Four hundred mex."

"Just what are you getting at?"

Anna rose. "It is easy, isn't it? The obvious thing. I kill you and transfer my picture to your passport. Then I can escape Shanghai." She raised one eyebrow. "Otherwise, I shall be left."

Rita Turner stared at her for a moment, then she dove for one of her bags. But a gun glittered in Anna's slim hand. Rita Turner saw the weapon and paused, terror draining her pale skin. Her eyes widened, and then she continued for the bag, stooping, fumbling with a large automatic, turning toward Anna.

The sound of Anna's shots did not penetrate the soundproof walls.

Rita Turner stood very still for a moment. Then the heavy gun slipped from between her slim fingers. Her lips twisted, as though she were about to laugh; and then blood welled from a hole just below her neck, and she crumpled, her figure like a question mark.

Anna looked down at her, neither pity nor compassion on her face, though it was the first person she had ever killed. Perhaps seeing so many dead and suffering had made her hard like this. She thought only: I will not be trapped here and die like the others. I will escape. I will have an evacuation order, and I will go aboard one of the big transports, and be taken to Hong Kong, and then to the United States. Freedom, peace! Murder has given me wings!

She was lucky, she thought, that the man who had sold her this information about an army wife whose husband was up the Yangtze River had not tricked her; for false information was sold for prices as great as the genuine. But then she had been "good" to her informant, plus the four hundred mex. He had known she would have to steal another woman's passport to escape the horror that was Shanghai. All he had done was supply the name of a woman—a woman who would surely be alone when Anna went to see her. . . .

Anna must change that passport now, put her picture in, and get the sailing orders. She must do a million and one things; she must go through all of Rita Turner's papers and learn everything about her.

Last of all, least of all, she had but to take the bags and get aboard the transport. Murder was easy!

 he had found some wine, and at midnight, Anna still sat in the room, feeling no glow but only half sick from the too sweet wine. She sat facing a desk full of papers, important documents with fancy seals, plans, blueprints, messages in French and German, even some in Chinese. Anna knew all about Rita Turner now. She knew what she hadn't known.

Rita Turner had been an international spy.

That meant only one thing: Anna, in taking over Rita Turner's name and identity, would have to pretend to be that same spy.

Anna's course had been clear, she had planned each last detail. She was to put the corpse in a steamer trunk and then send for the Chinese boys to come and get it with the other baggage; and later at sea she would put the corpse into a navy sea-bag and during the night drag it to the side of the ship and dump it over. There would be no trace of murder: only the living, breathing, the new Rita Turner.

But this new complication frightened and confused Anna. She knew no way in which to turn. If she fled the hotel and left the corpse here she still could not escape the city and murder would catch up with her. They would find her in Shanghai sooner or later, perhaps shivering in a hovel, and then for the murder they would put a gun to the back of her head and blow out her life.

She must make the transport with the corpse in the steamer trunk. But how? As a spy Rita Turner had definite orders to deliver some papers before her departure from the city, and even though Anna knew little about espionage she was aware that counter-spies checked on the activities of a spy; that people ordered to contact Rita Turner would be on the look-out for her. There was this alone, even if she didn't think about the risk of being captured as Rita, as the spy, and being punished in the ruthless manner of war.

To go straight to the boat was impossible. She must board it just before it sailed, and keep entirely to herself in case someone on board should know the real Rita Turner. Meanwhile there was the chance that she would be recognized as an impostor by other members of the espionage ring by which Rita Turner had been employed.

Anna poured herself a drink. She took it down, then she lighted a cigarette and got up and moved over to the window. She looked down at the street seething with torch-light.

She heard the music of the radio and she thought of her nightclub back on the Bund and wished that she was back in it—even what was left of it. There had been happiness there, a hard kind. Sailors saying: "Listen, babe, you're a tramp, but I'd die for you; a guy's gotta have someone to love, and when he loves he wants to make believe it's the real thing."

She remembered that now, those words, and other words; the quaint, tough, laughing Shanghai she had known before the invasion. But all of that had gone past her, and she was alone here with the body of a woman she had murdered—a woman who by dying had put her problems on Anna. The sailors were gone, and her girl friends were gone, even Olga, who was her closest.

Anna dropped the cigarette and rubbed her foot over it.

The telephone rang.

She stood and looked at it, petrified, feeling fear crawl up into her, making her sick. She held her hands out and watched them tremble; and the phone rang again. She moved toward it, only a foot, and it rang for the third time.

Then suddenly she leapt over and snatched up the instrument. She had dared herself, and now she had plunged.

"Hello?" She tried to remember the sound of Rita Turner's voice.

"Rita?"

"Yes."

It was a man's voice and went on now: "I know I shouldn't call at the hotel like this, but we had an appointment to—ah, go dancing. Have you forgotten? I've been waiting here quite a long time."

"I'm awfully sorry," said Anna. "Where have you been waiting?"

"*You* know where."

Anna laughed. "Oh yes, of course. I will be there at once."

"Will you? Nothing's gone wrong, has it? You weren't going to sail without your packet— ah, that packet of . . ." The voice trailed off.

Anna was quick on the up-take; her voice caught: "Oh, you mean that money you drew from the bank for me." She laughed gaily. "Oh yes, I get that tonight for—for—"

"Careful," said the man. "Ah—I'll be glad to get to meet you."

Anna took a chance: "How will I know you?"

"I'll be by the telephone booth," he said promptly. "It was prearranged." He sounded a trifle irritated. "Don't you remember anything? Frenchie's isn't so difficult to reach, I mean—"

"If anybody was listening in," said Anna, "they've had an earful by now." She had an earful herself. "I'll see you later," she finished.

"All right," the man replied.

She hung up and her blood tingled. Money. They were paying Rita Turner off before sailing. Money! Hers, to have and to spend. So easy! What had seemed a difficult situation was turning into a paying adventure. She had imagined espionage work was like this: Agents, strangers to one another, contacting each other. Nor was spying the highly clever profession she had been given to believe, for, fortunately for her, the man had even tipped his position over the phone: Frenchie's.

Anna had now but to send the baggage, with the corpse in the trunk, to the boat; and then contact this man and turn over Rita's papers to him—for money. After that, praise the great St. Peter, she would be free; possibly rich!

She gathered all of Rita's spy papers, put them down her dress. Then she looked down at the corpse of Rita Turner, which she had dragged to a corner, and now for the first time a shiver ran through her. She remembered that she had committed murder; she had never once forgotten, but now her conscience remembered, and she tried to laugh.

She remembered once a French sailor coming into the nightclub bragging that he had just stabbed a man. He had laughed; he had been so hard and carefree. Murder was really nothing. Not when there was a war going on, and people dying.

She was a fool to even think of it. She should laugh like the Frenchman. So she did laugh. She would kill twenty Rita Turners if she herself could escape with the living.

She set about to put the corpse in the trunk and to do hastily all the other things she had to do.

It was almost forty minutes before Anna could leave the hotel. A tenseness had come to her again. She had sent the baggage out without arousing suspicion because she had used Rita Turner's money to give the boys big tips so that the baggage would not have to go through the routine of being checked.

She knew that in this skelter of evacuation there would be no customs at the boat, for the boat was going first to Hong Kong. What she feared was trouble with the desk, though ordinarily there should be none. If anybody was curious, she had been visiting Rita Turner.

The elevator door swung open and she alighted on the main floor. It was crowded with people and she saw now that her escape, the escape from the hotel people, would be easy.

What she did not see at once was the man whose coat collar had been turned up—the man who had been following her. He was sitting in a leather chair in the lobby, waiting for her.

His coat collar was down now, and she could see his face clearly. It was white and looked very frightened. She stopped, straining to remember where she had known him. Surely, she had known him sometime in the past. Perhaps in the nightclub, but then she had known so many. . . . Why had he followed her?

He saw her, and rising, came toward her. Panic seized her. There could be no scene here. She must get to the street and away from him. She must talk to no one except the man who waited at the telephone booth in Frenchie's— perhaps with money, but certainly she must see him so that counter-spies would not trail the new Rita Turner from Shanghai.

The man followed her, however, and at the door he caught her arm, turning her half-way around. She looked again into his face, and for a moment his name, or his place in her past, was on the tip of her tongue; but it escaped her.

"Please," she said, "please, don't touch me."

"But listen, I—"

"Please!"

She jerked away from him, and in a moment she was in the street. He followed her out the door. She ran, and turned a corner. She could hear him chasing.

Her heart shoved against her side, and sharp pains from running came so that it was difficult for her to breathe. The man would kill her perhaps. No one meant any good in this mess. Her flight was instinctive. She heard him call out—then she was flinging herself out through the gates of the International settlement, climbing into a rickshaw.

"Frenchie's," she said.

There was no other conveyance, and when she looked back she saw the man standing there, waving at her to come back. Then, in the flare of a torch, she saw that he had begun running; he meant to follow the rickshaw. She heard him yell, "Wait for me! Wait!"

The wooden wheels of her cart clattered over the road, putting murder and the unknown man behind her. But she saw presently that the coolie was running like a fool with no sense of direction. She called at him to stop. Her voice grew frantic. The coolie kept running. She was terrified lest this be a trap of some kind, and yet common sense told her that it could not be that.

They turned up a street that was a tumult of noise and light, and then suddenly she saw that the crazed coolie was running right into the middle of a company of marching Japanese. She held on to the side and waited. The crash came. She saw a bayonet flash, and then she saw the blade sever the coolie's head so that it fell off, easily, like the loose knob on a door.

Then she was on the ground, struggling to escape. Desperate, like a rabbit, and somehow she squirmed away from them, shouting all the time: "I am English! I am English! You don't dare touch me! I'm English!"

She was running again, then telling herself she must keep her mind or be lost in this confusion.

She found herself on an open street, and somehow she had stopped and was looking up. She didn't know at first why she had done this; she didn't know until she heard the throbbing of giant plane engines, and saw the bright lights, and the wings that seemed to descend on her. She thought then that it was all over.

But it wasn't. It had just begun. A store, across from her, rose in a ball of streaked fire, and then Anna was crouching, holding her hands over her head, and the débris was coming down everywhere.

Just ahead of her she saw another bomb tear out the street and shower bricks everywhere. She could hear the bricks falling, one by one, like drops from a monster hail storm. And through all this, an ear-splitting roar of plane motors, and bursting bombs.

Anna could hear the steady, never-ending blend of screaming people . . . people dying . . . people lying all around her, some of them resignedly holding their arms in their laps.

She got up, and stumbled, kept trying to run. She saw a little baby sitting in a pool of blood, crying. She saw two little girls running and crying and dragging the corpse of an old Chinese woman.

She told herself she must keep sanity, she must keep going. Her murder—the murder she had committed—must not converge upon her. This couldn't be her punishment. Men died with guns in the backs of their necks, not from the débris of bombs, when they committed murder.

She must not die! What she must do was escape Shanghai. Escape war!

She ran into someone, suddenly. She looked up and saw the man who had followed her from the hotel. She didn't care now who he was. She threw herself into his arms; she pressed her shuddering body against his protecting one and waited for the noise and the death that was everywhere.

"We must escape. We must get away from here!" shouted the man.

"Frenchie's," she shouted back. "Frenchie's! We must go there."

"Kid," said the man, "I—"

"Don't talk. We must get to Frenchie's!"

"Anna!" he said. She looked up, terrified; so he knew her. Oh, good sweet God, that was funny, because she didn't know him from Adam.

"Don't talk," she said. "Frenchie's! Take me there." She was used to the easy companionship for men, and this did not seem strange, that she should make this request of him; he was here to use.

He started to talk to her again, but another

bomb exploded, and he picked her up and began running with her. She knew it was only a thousand-to-one chance that they would get through, get off this street alive.

But they did.

nna did not know how much longer it was, nor how many blocks they had come. She knew only that when the stranger who knew her set her down, it was in front of Frenchie's. He was sweating, and there wasn't much left of his suit. He was laughing, and half crying, and that way he looked much more familiar. He was saying:

"Babe, I love you like seven hundred dollars on Christmas day, and—"

"I must go in here," she said; "wait for me until I come out. I won't be long." She realized he could help her get to the transport; he was big and he was strong, and like so many men at many times, he loved her.

"Anything you say, babe, but you will come out?"

"Of course I will." She was a bit impatient. It did not occur to her to thank him for saving her life.

"You know why I'm here?"

"No," she said, "I don't know."

"Because I love you," he said.

She laughed, bitterly. "How very nice! But I must go in here now—"

"I'm A.W.O.L.," he went on, "and I'll get socked behind the eight ball for two months for this, but, geez, a guy—"

"So you're a sailor?"

"Of course," he said.

"Why didn't you tell me? Why are you wearing those clothes?"

He laughed. "How long do you think I'd last on the streets in uniform? They'd pick me up before I could move."

"And you risked all this to tell me you loved me?"

"Of course. You must have known how I've felt that time in—"

"I knew you at the Navy Sport Palace?"

"Sure. Aw, come on, baby, don't tell me you've forgotten. You're not that hard."

"Aren't I?" she thought; but what she said was: "Of course I didn't forget you, darling. Now wait for me. Wait here for me."

She turned and went inside, and the last she heard from him was when he leaned back against the building and began to whistle. She had heard the tune earlier this evening and it gave her a start. It was "The Lady Is a Tramp."

She looked a wreck and she knew it, but she was past caring. She moved from table to table, went to the back of Frenchie's where there was the bar. She stopped here and had a stiff drink. It made her feel better.

She heard soft muted music, and she saw people who were still trying to look gay. You'd never know there was a war; or that ten minutes ago bombs were raising merry hell, she thought. Human beings can play the damnedest games, and keep their nerve, or what looks like nerve from the ivory polish surface of their skin.

She went at last to the telephone booths. She spotted the contact man almost at once. He was tall and had iron-gray hair. He was wearing a white mess jacket, and highly polished black shoes. She could not distinguish his nationality; he looked cosmopolitan, smooth. He smiled when he saw her: one of her own kind of smiles—with his teeth.

"Ah, my dear," he said.

She looked arch. "Pardon me?" This was a come-on; there had to be some come-on, she thought. Marlene Dietrich had always had one in those films that played down by the Bund.

"But, my dear Rita," said the man, which gave the perfect rhythm to everything.

She nodded, and he went on: "Shall we go upstairs to the balcony?"

"All right."

"You have the papers?"

"Yes," she said.

She allowed him to escort her up a flight of

steps to a room over the main part of the club. It was rather dark, and the windows faced the street. He turned on a light, but it was only a colored Oriental lantern. His face seemed softer, somehow flushed in this illumination.

She lifted the packet of papers from her breast and handed them to him. He inspected them briefly in the half-light, and then he looked up smiling.

"Everything is here, I believe," he said.

"Then I can go? I can have some money, and then I can go—"

He bowed slightly, from the waist. "But of course."

It was then that she saw the small automatic in his hand. She turned to run from it. But another man was walking slowly up behind her.

"We've waited for this a long time, Rita," one of them said.

She saw now what it was. These men were agents from a government which opposed the one for which Rita Turner had been working. They had deliberately set a trap for her.

Bitterly in that flashing, horrible second, she remembered the entire telephone conversation. She had thought she was leading the man out; in reality he had been leading her; he had tipped her to Frenchie's to get her here. He had believed she was Rita, and he believed it now; the rest of these men believed it.

Rita must have been an elusive secret agent whose identity had never been entirely revealed, but the papers Anna had just handed the man with the iron-gray hair were sufficient to sign her death warrant.

This realization came to Anna quickly, suddenly, even as the men were closing in on her, and it did her ego no good to look back upon it and reflect that the real Rita Turner would never have fallen so blindly into an enemy trap. It was only she, Anna, the fool, playing a game she knew nothing about.

"It is too bad, Rita," she heard one of the men saying.

She knew it would do no good to protest that Rita Turner was already dead. They would merely laugh at her, deride her protestation. She saw from their expressions that Rita Turner must have been dangerous to them, for they meant now to kill Anna. They intended wasting no time or effort.

Anna saw a knife flash, and knew in a moment that it would pierce her throat. There was no way she could turn. There was nothing she could do. She hadn't time even to cry out, for all the good that would do her. . . .

For a moment there was only silence here in the half-light, and the men closed in so that they facaded up about her in a wall. And in this moment Anna was looking back at murder and wondering now what had finally happened to the Frenchman who had stabbed the man and laughed—for she knew now about crime and punishment, and that punishment wasn't something in storybooks so that little boys would go to Sunday school.

She knew, too, that there was no escape for murder, even in war. She knew that she had come to her last second on earth, and even in that there was too much time, to reflect, to listen to the echo of laughter down the long memory of years, to hear the screams of dying Chinese which would seem like a song now by comparison.

She saw again the baby sitting in a pool of blood, and a sailor, A.W.O.L. from his ship in a suit of clothes that were half torn off his back.

And she knew suddenly why the sailor downstairs had followed her. He had fallen in love with her at the club, poor fool, and he had ditched off from his ship to *come and marry her*; to come and marry her because he knew that she was a White Russian and she couldn't get out of Shanghai unless she was a Navy wife!

He had been sorry for her, and he had been willing to marry her so that she could be evacuated honestly as Anna on the big transport that was going to America by way of Hong Kong.

It was all clear now, in this final instant of life, that he had been following her to tell her, to marry her and take her away; and if she had remained at her apartment, if she had not gone to commit murder, this would have happened, and she now would be safe and free!

She remembered the sailor saying: "Babe, I love you like seven hundred dollars on Christmas day," and then she felt the point of the knife at her throat; and as she slid to the floor, the only sound that came through the silence was the familiar whistling of someone leaning in the front of the building outside whistling: "The Lady Is a Tramp."

Ask Me Another

Frank Gruber

FRANK GRUBER (1904–1969) was born in Elmer, Minnesota, and worked as a bellhop, ticket taker at a movie theater, writer and editor of trade journals, and creative writing teacher at a correspondence school before he became a full-time writer. He was still in his twenties when he sold his first story, beginning a career that produced more than four hundred stories, sixty novels, and more than two hundred film and television scripts, mainly in the mystery and Western fiction genres. Among his mystery novels are *The Silver Jackass* (1941, as Charles K. Boston), *The Last Doorbell* (1941, as John K. Vedder), *The Yellow Overcoat* (1942, as Stephen Acre), and, under his own name, more than thirty others, including *Simon Lash, Private Detective* (1941), about a bibliophile private eye, filmed by PRC as *Accomplice* in 1946, starring Richard Arlen as Lash. He also wrote more than a dozen novels featuring the amateur detective Johnny Fletcher and his partner, Sam Cragg, a pair of always broke con men who made their debut in *The French Key* (1940), which Gruber wrote in seven days yet which made most of the year's top-ten lists; it was filmed by Republic in 1946, with Albert Dekker as Fletcher and Mike Mazurki as Cragg. Perhaps his most beloved character, however, is Oliver Quade, the Human Encyclopedia, whose seemingly infinite knowledge of even the most arcane subjects helps him solve crimes in a long series of pulp stories. Ten of the tales were collected in *Brass Knuckles* (1966).

"Ask Me Another" was published in the June 1937 issue.

Ask Me Another

Frank Gruber

OLIVER QUADE WAS READING THE morning paper, his bare feet on the bed and his chair tilted back against the radiator. Charlie Boston was on the bed, wrapped to his chin in a blanket and reading a copy of *Exciting Confessions*.

It was just a usual, peaceful, after-breakfast interlude in the lives of Oliver Quade, the Human Encyclopedia, and Charlie Boston, his friend and assistant.

And then Life intruded itself upon the bit of Utopia. Life in the form of the manager of the Eagle Hotel. He beat a tattoo upon the thin panels of the door. Quade put down his newspaper and sighed.

"Charles, will you please open the door and let in the wolf?"

Charlie Boston unrolled himself from the blanket. He scowled at Quade. "You think it's the manager about the room rent?"

"Of course it is. Let him in before he breaks down the door."

It was the manager. In his right fist he held a ruled form on which were scrawled some unpleasant figures. "About your rent, Mr. Quade," he said severely. "We must have the money today!"

Quade looked at the manager of the Eagle Hotel, a puzzled expression on his face. "Rent? Money?"

"Of course," snapped the manager. "This is the third time this week I've asked for it."

A light came into Quade's eyes. He made a quick movement and his feet and the front legs of the chair hit the carpeted floor simultaneously.

"Charles!" he roared in a voice that shook the room and caused the hotel manager to cringe. "Did you forget to get that money from the bank and pay this little bill?"

Charlie Boston took up Quade's cue.

"Gosh, I'm awful sorry. On my way to the bank yesterday afternoon I ran into our old friend John Belmont of New York and he dragged me into the Palmer House Bar for a cocktail. By the time I could tear myself away, the bank was closed."

Quade raised his hands and let them fall hopelessly. "You see, Mr. Creighton, I just can't trust him to do anything. Now I've got to go out into the cold this morning and get it myself."

The hotel manager's eyes glinted. "Listen, you've stalled—" he began, but Quade suddenly stabbed out a hand toward him. "That reminds me, Mr. Creighton, I've a couple of complaints to make. We're not getting enough heat here and last night the damfool next door kept us awake half the night with his radio. I want you to see that he keeps quiet tonight. And do something about the heat. I can't stand drafty, cold rooms."

The manager let out a weary sigh. "All right, I'll look after it. But about that rent—"

"Yes, of course," cut in Quade, "and your maid left only two towels this morning. Please see that a couple more are sent up. Immediately!"

The manager closed the door behind him with a bang. Oliver Quade chuckled and lifted his newspaper again. But Charlie Boston wouldn't let him read.

"You got away with it, Ollie," he said, "but it's the last time. I know it. I'll bet we get locked out before tonight." He shook his head sadly. "You, Oliver Quade, with the greatest brain in captivity, are you going to walk the streets tonight in ten below zero weather?"

"Of course not, Charles," sighed Quade. "I was just about to tell you that we're going out to make some money today. Look, it's here in this paper. The Great Chicago Auditorium Poultry Show."

Boston's eyes lit up for a moment, but then dimmed again. "Can we raise three weeks' rent at a poultry show?"

Quade slipped his feet into his socks and shoes. "That remains to be seen. This paper mentions twenty thousand paid admissions. Among that many people there ought to be a few who are interested in higher learning. Well, are you ready?"

Boston went to the clothes closet and brought out their overcoats and a heavy suitcase. Boston was of middle height and burly. He could bend iron bars with his muscular hands. Quade was taller and leaner. His face was hawk-like, his nose a little too pointed and lengthy, but few ever noticed that. They saw only his piercing, sparkling eyes and felt his dominant personality.

The auditorium was almost two miles from their hotel, but lacking carfare, Quade and Boston walked. When they reached their destination, Quade cautioned Boston:

"Be sharp now, Charlie. Act like we belonged."

Quade opened the outer door and walked blithely past the ticket windows to the door leading into the auditorium proper. A uniformed man at the door held out his hand for the tickets.

"Hello," Quade said, heartily. "How're you today?"

"Uh, all right, I guess," replied the ticket-taker. "You boys got passes?"

"Oh, sure. We're just taking in some supplies for the breeders. Brr! It's cold today. Well, be seeing you." And with that he breezed past the ticket-taker.

"H'are ya, pal," Boston said, treading on Quade's heels.

The auditorium was a huge place but even so, it was almost completely filled with row upon row of wire exhibition coops, each coop containing a feathered fowl of some sort.

"What a lot of gumps!" Boston observed.

"Don't use that word around here," Quade cautioned. "These poultry folks take their chickens seriously. Refer to the chickens as 'fine birds' or 'elegant fowls' or something like that. . . . Damn these publicity men!"

"Huh?"

Quade waved a hand about the auditorium. "The paper said twenty thousand paid admissions. How many people do you see in here?"

Boston craned his head around. "If there's fifty I'm countin' some of 'em twice. How the hell can they pay the nut with such a small attendance?"

"The entry fees. There must be around two thousand chickens in here and the entry fee for each chicken is at least a dollar and a half. The prize money doesn't amount to much and I guess the paid admissions are velvet—if they get any, which I doubt."

"Twenty thousand, bah!" snorted Boston. "Well, do we go back?"

"Where? Our only chance was to stay in our room. I'll bet the manager changed the lock the minute we left it."

"So what?"

"So I get to work. For the dear old Eagle Hotel."

Quade ploughed through an aisle to the far end of the auditorium. Commercial exhibits were contained in booths all around the four sides of the huge room, but Quade found a small spot that had been overlooked and pushed a couple of chicken coops into the space.

Then he climbed up on the coops and began talking.

The Human Encyclopedia's voice was an

amazing one. People who heard it always marveled that such a tremendous voice could come from so lean a man. Speaking without noticeable effort, his voice rolled out across the chicken coops.

"I'm Oliver Quade, the Human Encyclopedia," he boomed. "I have the greatest brain in the entire country. I know the answers to all questions, what came first, the chicken or the egg, every historical date since the beginning of time, the population of every city in the country, how to eradicate mice in your poultry yards, how to mix feeds to make your chickens lay more eggs. Everything. Everything under the sun. On any subject: history, science, agriculture, and mathematics."

The scattered persons in the auditorium began to converge upon Quade's stand. Inside of two minutes three-fourths of the people in the building were gathered before Quade and the rest were on their way. He continued his preliminary build-up in his rich, powerful voice.

"Ask me a question, someone. Let me prove that I'm the Human Encyclopedia, the man who knows the answers to all questions. Try me out, someone, on any subject: history, science, mathematics, agriculture—anything at all!"

Quade stabbed out his lean forefinger at a middle-aged, sawed-off man wearing a tan smock. "You, sir, ask me a question?"

The man flushed at being singled out of the crowd. "Why, uh, I don't know of any . . . Yes, I do. What's the highest official egg record ever made by a hen?"

"That's the stuff," smiled Quade. He held out his hand dramatically. "That's a good question, but an easy one to answer. The highest record ever made by a hen in an American official egg-laying contest is three hundred and forty-two eggs. It was made in 1930 at the Athens, Georgia, Egg-Laying Contest, by a Single-Comb White Leghorn. Am I right, mister?"

The sawed-off man nodded grudgingly. "Yeah, but I don't see how you knew it. Most poultry folks don't even remember it."

"Oh, but you forget I told you I had the greatest brain in the country. I know the answer to all questions on any subject. Don't bother to ask me simple poultry questions. Try me on something hard. You—" He picked out a lean, dour looking man. "Ask me something hard."

The man bit his lip a moment, then said:

"All right, what state has the longest coastline?"

Quade grinned. "Ah, you're trying the tricky stuff. But you can't fool me. Most folks would say California or Florida. But the correct answer is Michigan. And to head off the rest of you on the trick geography questions let me say right away that Kentucky has the largest number of other states touching it and Minnesota has the farthest northern point of any state. Next question!"

A young fellow wearing pince-nez put his tongue into his cheek and asked, "Why and how does a cat purr?"

"Oh-oh!" Quade craned his neck to stare at the young fellow. "I see we have a student with us. Well, young man, you've asked a question so difficult that practically every university professor in this country would be stumped by it. But I'm not. It so happens that I read a recent paper by Professor E. L. Gibbs of the Harvard Medical School in which he gave the results of his experiments on four hundred cats to learn the answer to that very same question. The first part of the question is simple enough—the cat purrs when it is contented, but to explain the actual act of purring is a little more difficult. Contentment in a cat relaxes the infundibular nerve in the brain, which reacts upon the pituitary and bronchial organs and makes the purring sound issue from the cat's throat. . . . Try that one on your friends, sometime. Someone else try me on a question."

"I'd like to ask one," said a clear, feminine voice. Quade's eyes lit up. He had already noticed the girl, the only female in his audience. She was amazingly pretty, the type of a girl he would scarcely have expected to find at a poultry show. She was young, not more than twenty-one, and she had the finest chiseled features

Quade had ever seen. She was a blonde and the rakish green hat and green coat she wore, although inexpensive, looked exceedingly well on her.

"Yes, what is the question?" he asked, leaning forward a bit.

The girl's chin came up defiantly. "I just want to know why certain poultry judges allow dyed birds to be judged for prizes!"

A sudden rumble went up in the crowd and Quade saw the sawed-off man in the tan smock whirl and glare angrily at the girl.

"Oh-oh," Quade said. "You seem to have asked a delicate question. Well, I'll answer it just the same. Any judge who allows a dyed Rhode Island Red to stay in the class is either an ignorant fool—or a crook!"

"Damn you!" roared the little man, turning back to Quade. "You can't say that to me. I'll—I'll have you thrown out of here." He started pushing his way through the crowd, heading in the direction of the front office.

"If the shoe fits, put it on," Quade called after him. Then to the girl, "Who's he?"

"A judge here. Stone's his name."

"Well, let's get on with the show," Quade said to the crowd. "Next question?"

Quade had lost nothing by his bold answer to the girl's question. The audience warmed to him and the questions came fast and furious.

"Who was the eleventh president of the United States?"

"What is the Magna Charta?"

"Who was the 1896 Olympic 220-meter champion?"

"How do you cure scaly legs in chickens?"

"How far is Saturn from the Earth?"

Quade answered all the questions put to him, with lightning rapidity. But suddenly he called a dramatic halt. "That's all the questions, folks. Now let me show you how you can learn all the answers yourselves to every question that has just been asked—and ten thousand more."

He held out his hands and Charlie Boston tossed a thick book into them which he had taken from the suitcase they had brought with them. Quade began ruffling the pages.

"They're all in here. This, my friends, is the 'Compendium of Human Knowledge,' the greatest book of its kind ever published. Twelve hundred pages, crammed with facts, information every one of you should know. The knowledge of the ages, condensed, classified, abbreviated. A complete high-school education in one volume. Ten minutes a day and this book will make you the most learned person in your community!"

Quade lowered his voice to a confidential pitch. "Friends, I'm going to astonish you by telling you the most ridiculous thing you've ever heard: The price of this book. What do you think I'm asking for it? Twenty-five dollars? No, not even twenty . . . or fifteen. In fact, not even ten or five dollars. Just a mere, paltry, insignificant two dollars and ninety-five cents. But I'm only going to offer these books once at that price. Two-ninety-five, and here I come!"

Quade leaped down from his platform to attack his audience, supposedly built up to the buying pitch. But he was destined not to sell any books just then. Charlie Boston tugged at his coat sleeve.

"Look, Ollie!" he whispered hoarsely. "He got the cops!"

Quade raised himself to his toes to look over the chicken coops. He groaned. For the short man in the tan smock was coming up the center aisle leading a small procession of policemen.

Quade sighed. "Put the books back into the suitcase, Charlie." He leaned against a poultry coop and waited to submit quietly to the arrest.

But the policemen did not come toward him. Reaching the center aisle, the man in the tan smock wheeled to the left, away from Quade, and the police followed him.

Quade's audience saw the police. Two or three persons broke away and started toward the other side of the building. The movement started a stampede and in a moment Charlie Boston and Quade were left alone.

"Something seems to have happened over there," Quade observed. "Wonder what?"

"From the mob of cops I'd say a murder," Boston replied dryly.

The word "murder" was scarcely out of

Boston's mouth than it was hurled back at them from across the auditorium.

"It *is* a murder!" Quade gasped.

"This is no place for us, then," cried Boston. "Let's scram!"

He caught up the suitcase containing the books and started off. But Quade called him back. "That's no good. There's a cop at the door. We'll have to stick."

"Chickens!" howled Boston. "The minute you mentioned them at the hotel I had a hunch that something was going to happen. And I'll bet a plugged dime, which I haven't got, that we get mixed up in it."

"Maybe so, Charlie. But if I know cops there's going to be a lot of questioning and my hunch is that we'll be better off if we're not too upstage. Let's go over and find out what's what."

He started toward the other side of the auditorium. Boston followed, lugging the suitcase and grumbling.

All of the crowd was gathered in front of a huge, mahogany cabinet—a mammoth incubator. The door of the machine was standing open and two or three men were moving around inside.

Quade drew in his breath sharply when he saw the huddled body lying on the floor just inside the door of the incubator. Gently he began working his way through the crowd until he stood in front of the open incubator door.

The small group came out of the incubator and a beetle-browed man in a camel's hair overcoat and Homburg hat squared himself off before the girl in the green hat and coat. The man in the tan smock, his head coming scarcely up to the armpits of the big man, hopped around like a bantam rooster.

"I understand you had a quarrel with him yesterday," the big man said to the girl. "What about?"

The girl drew herself up to her full height. "Because his birds were dyed and the judge— the man behind you—refused to throw them out. That's why!"

The bantam sputtered. "She—why, that's a damn lie!"

The big detective turned abruptly, put a ham-like hand against the chest of the runt and shoved him back against the incubator with so much force that the little man gasped in pain.

"Listen, squirt," the detective said. "Nothing's been proved against this girl and until it is, she's a lady. Up here we don't call ladies liars."

He turned back to the girl and said with gruff kindness, "Now, miss, let's have the story."

"There's no story," declared the girl. "I did quarrel with him, just like I did with Judge Stone. But—but I haven't seen Mr. Tupper since yesterday evening. That's all I can tell you because it's all I know."

"Yesterday, huh." The detective looked around the circle. "Anybody see him here today?"

"Yes, of course," said a stocky man of about forty-five. "I was talking to him early this morning, before the place was opened to the public. There were a dozen or more of us around then."

"You're the boss of this shebang?"

"Not exactly. Our poultry association operates this show. I'm Leo Cassmer, the secretary, and I'm in charge of the exhibits, if that's what you mean."

"Yeah, that's what I mean," replied the detective. "You're the boss. You know the exhibitors then. All right, who was here early this morning when this Tupper fellow was around?"

Cassmer, the show secretary, rubbed his chin. "Why, there was myself, Judge Stone, Ralph Conway, the Wyandotte man, Judge Welheimer and several of the men who work around here."

"And Miss Martin—was she here?"

"She came in before the place was officially opened, but she wasn't around the last time I saw Tupper."

"Who're Welheimer and Conway?"

A tall, silver-haired man stepped out of the crowd. "Conway's my name."

"And the judge?" persisted the detective.

A long-nosed man with a protruding lower lip came grudgingly out of the crowd. "I'm Judge Welheimer."

"You a real judge or just a chicken judge?"

"Why, uh, just a poultry judge. Licensed by the National Poultry Association."

"And you don't hold any public office at all? You're not even a justice of the peace?"

The long-nosed chicken judge reddened. He shook his head.

The detective's eyes sparkled. "That's fine. All that talk about judges had me worried for a bit. But listen, you chicken judges and the rest of you. I'm Sergeant Dickinson of the Homicide Squad of this town. There's been a murder committed here and I'm investigating it. Which means I'm boss around here. Get me?"

Quade couldn't quite restrain a snicker. The sergeant's sharp ears heard it and he singled out Quade.

"And who the hell are you?"

"Oliver Quade, the Human Encyclopedia," Quade replied glibly. "I know the answers to all questions—"

Sergeant Dickinson's face twisted. "Ribbing me, ha? Step up here where I can get a good look at you."

Quade remained where he was. "There's a dead man in there. I don't like to get too close to dead people."

The sergeant took a half step toward Quade, but then stopped himself. He tried to smooth out his face, but it was still dark with anger.

"I'll get around to you in a minute, fella." He turned belligerently to the show secretary. "You, who found the body?"

Cassmer pointed to a pasty-faced young fellow of about thirty. The man grinned sickly.

"Yeah, I got in kinda late and started straightening things around. Then I saw that someone had stuck that long staple in the door latch. I didn't think much about it and opened the door and there—there he was lying on the floor. Deader'n a mackerel!"

"You work for this incubator company?" the sergeant asked.

The young fellow nodded. "I'm the regional sales manager. Charge of this exhibit. It's the finest incubator on the market. Used by the best breeders and hatcherymen."

"Can the sales talk," growled the detective.

"*I'm* not going to buy one. Let's go back on your story. What made you say this man was murdered?"

"What else could it be? He was dead and the door was locked on the outside."

"I know that. But couldn't he have died of heart failure? There's plenty of air in that thing, and besides there's a ventilator hole up there."

"He was murdered," said Quade.

Sergeant Dickinson whirled. "And how do *you* know?"

"By looking at the body. Anyone could tell it was murder."

"Oh yeah? Maybe you'll tell me *how* he was killed. There ain't a mark on his body."

"No marks of violence, because he wasn't killed that way. He was killed with a poison gas. Something containing cyanogen."

The sergeant clamped his jaws together. "Go on! Who killed him?"

Quade shook his head. "No, that's your job. I've given you enough to start with."

"You've been very helpful," said the sergeant. "So much so that I'm going to arrest you!"

Charlie Boston groaned into Quade's ears. "Won't you ever learn to keep your mouth shut?"

But Quade merely grinned insolently. "If you arrest me I'll sue you for false arrest."

"I'll take a chance on that," said the detective. "No one could know as much as you do and not have had something to do with the murder."

"You're being very stupid, Sergeant," Quade said. "These men told you they hadn't seen Tupper alive for several hours. He's been dead at least three. And I just came into this building fifteen minutes ago."

"He's right," declared Anne Martin. "I saw him come in. He and his friend. They went straight over to the other side of the building and started that sales talk."

"What sales talk?"

The little poultry judge hopped in again. "He's a damn pitchman. Pulls some phony question and answer stuff and insults people. Claims he's the smartest man in the world. Bah!"

"Bah to you!" said Quade.

"Cut it," cried Sergeant Dickinson. "I want to get the straight of this. You." He turned to Cassmer. "Did he really come in fifteen minutes ago?"

Cassmer shrugged. "I never saw him until a few minutes ago. But there's the ticket-taker. He'd know."

The ticket-taker, whose post had been taken over by a policeman, frowned. "Yeah, he came in just a little while ago. I got plenty reason to remember. Him and his pal crashed the gate. On *me*! First time anyone crashed the gate on me in eight years. But he was damn slick. He—"

"Never mind the details," sighed Sergeant Dickinson. "I can imagine he was slick about it. Well, mister, you didn't kill him. But tell me— how the hell do you know he was gassed with cy—cyanide?"

"Cyanogen. It's got prussic acid in it. All right, the body was found inside the incubator, the door locked on the outside. That means someone locked him inside the incubator. The person who killed him. Right so far?"

"I'm listening." There was a thoughtful look in the sergeant's eyes.

"There's broken glass inside the incubator. The killer heaved in a bottle containing the stuff and slammed the door shut and locked it. The man inside was killed inside of a minute."

"Wait a minute. The glass is there all right, but how d'you know it contained cyanogen? There's no smell in there."

"No, because the killer opened the ventilator hole and turned on the electric fans inside the incubator. All that can be done from the outside. The fans cleared out the fumes. Simple."

"Not so simple. You still haven't said how you know it was cyanogen."

"Because he's got all the symptoms. Look at the body—pupils dilated, eyes wide, froth on the mouth, face livid, body twisted and stiff. That means he had convulsions. Well, if those symptoms don't mean cyanogen, I don't know what it's all about."

"Mister," said the detective. "Who did you say you were?"

"Oliver Quade, the Human Encyclopedia. I know everything."

"You know, I'm beginning to believe you. Well, then, who did the killing?"

"That's against the union rules. I told you how the man was killed. Finding who did it is your job."

"All right, but tell me one thing more. If this cyanogen has prussic acid in it, it's a deadly poison. Folks can't usually buy it."

"City folks, you mean. Cyanogen is the base for several insecticides. I don't think this was pure cyanogen. I'm inclined to believe it was a diluted form, probably a gas used to kill rats on poultry farms. Any poultry raiser could buy that."

"Here comes the coroner's man," announced Detective Dickinson. "Now, we'll get a check on you, Mr. Quade."

Dr. Bogle, the coroner's physician, made a rapid, but thorough, examination of the body. His announcement coincided startlingly with Quade's diagnosis.

"Prussic acid or cyanide. He inhaled it. Died inside of five minutes. About three and a half hours ago."

Quade's face was twisted in a queer smile. He walked off from the group. Charlie Boston and Anne Martin, the girl, followed.

"Do you mind my saying that you just performed some remarkable work?" the girl said admiringly.

"No, I don't mind your saying so." Quade grinned. "I *was* rather colossal."

"He pulls those things out of a hat," groused Boston. "He's a very smart man. Only one thing he can't do."

"What's that?"

Boston started to reply, but Quade's fierce look silenced him. Quade coughed. "Well, look—a hot dog stand. Reminds me, it's about lunch time. Feel like a hot dog and orangeade, Anne?"

The girl smiled at his familiarity. "I don't mind. I'm rather hungry."

Boston sidled up to Quade. "Hey, you forgot!" he whispered. "You haven't got any money."

Quade said, "Three dogs and orangeades!"

A minute later they were munching hot dogs. Quade finished his orangeade and half-way through the sandwich suddenly snapped his fingers.

"That reminds me, I forgot something. Excuse me a moment. . . ." He started off suddenly toward the group around the incubator, ignoring Charlie Boston's startled protest.

Boston suddenly had no appetite. He chewed the food in his mouth as long as he could. The girl finished her sandwich and smiled at him.

"That went pretty good. Guess I'll have another. How about you?"

Boston almost choked. "Uh, no, I ain't hungry."

The girl ordered another hot dog and orangeade and finished them while Boston still fooled with the tail end of his first sandwich.

The concessionaire mopped up the counter all around Boston and Anne Martin and finally said, "That's eighty cents, mister!"

Boston put the last of the sandwich in his mouth and began going through his pockets. The girl watched him curiously. Boston went through his pockets a second time. "That's funny," he finally said. "I must have left my wallet in the hotel. Quade . . ."

"Let me pay for it," said the girl, snapping open her purse.

Boston's face was as red as a Harvard beet. Such things weren't embarrassing to Quade, but they were to Boston.

"There's Mr. Quade," said Anne Martin. "Shall we join him?"

Boston was glad to get away from the hot dog stand.

The investigation was still going on. Sergeant Dickinson was on his hands and knees inside the incubator. A policeman stood at the door of it and a couple more were going over the exterior.

Quade saluted them with a piece of wire. "They're looking for clues," he said.

The girl shivered. "I'd like it much better if they'd take away Exhibit A."

"Can't. Not until they take pictures. I hear the photographers and the fingerprint boys are

coming down. It's not really necessary either. Because I know who the murderer is."

The girl gasped: "Who?"

Quade did not reply. He looked at the piece of wire in his hands. It was evidently a spoke from a wire poultry coop, but it had been twisted into an elongated question mark. He tapped Dickinson's shoulder with the wire.

The sergeant looked up and scowled. "Huh?"

"Want this?" Quade asked.

"What the hell is it?"

"Just a piece of wire I picked up."

"What're you trying to do, rib me?"

Quade shrugged. "No, but I saw you on your hands and knees and thought you were looking for something. Thought this might be it."

Dickinson snorted. "What the hell, if you're not going to tell me who did the killing, let me alone."

"O.K." Quade flipped the piece of wire over a row of chicken coops. "Come," he said to Boston and Anne Martin. "Let's go look at the turkeys at the other end of the building."

Boston shuffled up beside Quade as the three walked through an aisle. "Who did it, Ollie?"

"Can't tell now, because I couldn't prove it. In a little while, perhaps."

Boston let out his pent-up breath. "If you ain't the damnedest guy ever!"

Anne Martin said, "You mean you're not going to tell Sergeant Dickinson?"

"Oh yes, but I'm going to wait a while. Maybe he'll tumble himself and I'd hate to deprive him of that pleasure . . . What time is it?"

"I don't know," Boston said. "I lost my watch in Kansas City. You remember that, don't you, Ollie?"

Quade winced. Boston had "lost" his watch in Uncle Ben's Three Gold Ball Shop. Quade's had gone to Uncle Moe in St. Louis.

"It's twelve-thirty," the girl said, looking at her wristwatch.

Quade nodded. "That's fine. The early afternoon editions of the papers will have accounts of the murder and a lot of morbid folk will flock around here later on. That means I can put on a good pitch and sell some of my books."

"I wanted to ask you about that," said Anne Martin. "You answered some really remarkable questions this morning. I don't for the life of me see how you do it."

"Forsaking modesty for the moment, I do it because I really know all the answers."

"All?"

"Uh-huh. You see, I've read an entire encyclopedia from cover to cover four times."

Anne looked at him in astonishment. "An entire encyclopedia?"

"Twenty-four volumes . . . Well, let's go back now. Charlie, keep your eyes open."

"Ah!" Charlie Boston said.

Dr. Bogle's men were just taking away the body of the murdered man. Sergeant Dickinson, a disgusted look on his face, had rounded up his men and was on the verge of leaving.

"Not going, Captain Dickinson?" Quade asked.

"What good will it do me to hang around?" snorted the sergeant. "Everyone and his brother has some phony alibi."

"But your clues, man?"

"What clues?"

Quade shook his head in exasperation. "I told you how the murder was committed, didn't I?"

"Yeah, sure, the guy locked the bloke in the incubator and tossed in the bottle of poison gas, then opened the ventilator and turned on the fans. But there were more than a dozen guys around and almost any one of them could have done it, without any of the others even noticing what he was doing."

"No, you're wrong. Only one person could have done it."

A hush suddenly fell upon the crowd. Charlie Boston, tensed and crouching, was breathing heavily. The police sergeant's face became bleak. Quade had demonstrated his remarkable deductive ability a while ago and Dickinson was willing to believe anything of him, now.

Quade stepped lazily to a poultry coop, took hold of a wire bar and with a sudden twist tore it off. Then he stepped to the side of the incubator.

"Look at this ventilator," he said. "Notice that I can reach it easily enough. So could you, Lieu-tenant. We're about the same height—five feet ten. But a man only five-two couldn't reach it even by standing on his toes. Do you follow me?"

"Go on," said Sergeant Dickinson.

Quade twisted the piece of wire into an elongated question mark. "To move a box or chair up here and climb up on it would be to attract attention," he went on, "so the killer used a piece of wire to open the ventilator. Like this!" Quade caught the hook in the ventilator and pulled it open easily.

"That's good enough for me!" said Sergeant Dickinson. "You practically forced that wire on me a while ago and I couldn't see it. Well—*Judge Stone, you're under arrest!*"

"He's a liar!" roared the bantam poultry judge. "He can't prove anything like that on me. He just tore that piece of wire from that coop!"

"That's right," said Quade. "You saw me pick up the original piece of wire and when I threw it away after trying to give it to the sergeant you got it and disposed of it."

"You didn't *see* me!"

"No, I purposely walked away to give you a chance to get rid of the wire. But I laid a trap for you. While I had that wire I smeared some ink on it to prove you handled it. Look at your hands, Judge Stone!"

Judge Stone raised both palms upward. His right thumb and fingers were smeared with a black stain.

Sergeant Dickinson started toward the little poultry judge. But the bantam uttered a cry of fright and darted away.

"Ha!" cried Charlie Boston, and lunged for him. He wrapped his thick arms around the little man and tried to hold on to him. But the judge was suddenly fighting for his life. He clawed at Boston's face and kicked his shins furiously. Boston howled and released his grip to defend himself with his fists.

The poultry judge promptly butted Boston in the stomach and darted under his flailing arms.

It was Anne Martin who stopped him. As the judge scrambled around Boston she stepped forward and thrust out her right foot. The little man tripped over it and plunged headlong to the concrete floor of the auditorium. Before he could get up Charlie Boston was on him. Sergeant Dickinson swooped down, a Police Positive in one hand and a pair of handcuffs in the other. The killer was secured.

Stone quit then. "Yes, I killed him, the damned lousy blackmailer. For years I judged his chickens at the shows and always gave him the edge. Then he double-crossed me, got me fired."

"What job?" asked Dickinson.

"My job as district manager for the Sibley Feed Company," replied Stone.

"Why'd he have you fired?" asked Quade. "Because you were short-weighing him on his feed? Is that it?"

"I gave him prizes his lousy chickens should never have had," snapped the killer. "What if I did short-weigh him twenty or thirty percent? I more than made up for it."

"Twenty or thirty percent," said Quade, "would amount to quite a bit of money in the course of a year. In his advertising in the poultry papers Tupper claimed he raised over eight thousand chickens a year."

"I don't need any more," said Sergeant Dickinson. "Well, Mr. Quade, you certainly delivered the goods."

"Not me, I only told you who the murderer was. If it hadn't been for Miss Martin he'd have got away."

Quade turned away. "Anne," he said, "Charlie and I are flat broke. But this afternoon a flock of rubbernecks are going to storm this place and I'm going to take quite a chunk of money from them. But in the meantime . . . That hot dog wasn't very filling and I wonder if you'd stake us to a lunch?"

Anne Martin's eyes twinkled. "Listen, Mr. Quade, if you asked me for every cent I've got I'd give it to you right away—because you'd get it from me anyway, if you really wanted it. You're the world's greatest salesman. You even sold Judge Stone into confessing."

Quade grinned. "Yes? How?"

She pointed at Quade's hands. "You handled that first wire hook with your bare hands. How come *your* hands didn't get black?"

Quade chuckled. "Smart girl. Even the sergeant didn't notice that. Well, I'll confess. I saw the smudge on Judge Stone's hands away back when I was putting on my pitch. He must have used a leaky fountain pen or something."

"Then you didn't put anything on it?"

"No. But *I* knew he was the murderer and *he* knew it . . . only he didn't know his hands were dirty. So . . ."

The girl drew a deep breath. "Oliver Quade, the lunches are on me."

"And the dinner and show tonight are on me," grinned Oliver Quade.

Dirty Work

Horace McCoy

HORACE MCCOY (1897–1955) was born in Pegram, Tennessee, and went to school in Nashville, dropping out at sixteen to get a job. After serving in the U.S. Army Air Corps during World War I, he became the sports editor of the *Dallas Journal*, a job he held from 1919 to 1930. He moved to Hollywood in 1931 to become an actor and to write motion picture screenplays. McCoy had been selling stories, mostly mysteries, to various pulps, the majority to *Black Mask*, between 1928 and 1932, after which he devoted himself full-time to film scripts and novels, most of which were filmed. His first book, a noir Depression-era existential novel, *They Shoot Horses, Don't They?* (1935), was inspired by his job as a bouncer at the Santa Monica Pier, where dance marathons were held; it was filmed by Sydney Pollack, with Gig Young, Jane Fonda, and Michael Sarrazin fourteen years after McCoy died of a heart attack. *No Pockets in a Shroud* (1937), about a corrupt American city and a crusading journalist, was published in England more than a decade before its U.S. appearance; it was filmed in France. The noir screenplay for *I Should Have Stayed Home* (1938) was never produced. *Kiss Tomorrow Goodbye* (1948) was filmed in 1950 with James Cagney as a near-psychotic criminal. *Scalpel* (1952) was mostly a medical story filmed as *Bad for Each Other* (1953), with Charlton Heston and Lizabeth Scott. *Corruption City* (1959) was a novelization of *The Turning Point* (1952), which starred William Holden and Edmond O'Brien.

"Dirty Work," the first Frost of the Texas Air Rangers story, was published in September 1929.

Dirty Work

Horace McCoy

*The Rangers
take to the air.*

 APTAIN JERRY FROST walked through the rotunda of the Texas State capitol, past the oils of Crockett and Houston and Hogg, and into the deep-toned offices of the Adjutant-General.

"What's on your mind, General?" he said, dropping himself into a chair and stretching his long legs.

"This Jamestown business." The Adjutant-General drummed on the desk with his incredibly long fingers. "It's quite a mess." Plainly he was just a little irritated.

Frost grinned. "Yes, sir. It's quite a mess." But the Adjutant-General didn't think it was so funny. He was quite serious.

"Jerry, for the life of me I can't understand why all police act so stupidly. This purely is a local case, but they can't handle it. They bump their heads against the wall and cry for the Rangers. I'm sometimes sorry we've got such a thing. Now the bigwigs are kicking." He held up a small packet. "Know what these are? Got any idea what they mean?"

Captain Frost confessed he hadn't.

"They're clippings from newspaper editorials in which the people who sit in the offices of the daily gazettes tell us how to run our great commonwealth. The robbery is up to us. I'm sorry, of course, you had to be ordered off leave. You know what that means, don't you?"

Jerry nodded. Did he know what that meant? Indeed! And since when had the Adjutant-General become so obtuse? He was tempted to laugh. Did he know what that meant? Hell, of course he knew. What did trips to this office usually mean? Dirty work—that's what. Dirty work.

He was not offended; he was too much of a soldier for that. It was that he just didn't have any illusions about the romance of criminal work. That was a lot of applesauce that looked good in print and nowhere else. He had spent two months in the Border Patrol on some tough work and had been promised a week's leave. He had got but two days of it. Two days on the Galveston beach, and when the messenger boy found him with that fatal telegram from the Adjutant-General he was waiting on a fair young person who would be due in ten minutes.

That annoyed him no end. He had earned a rest, why couldn't he get it? Now there was more dirty work to be done. That's all he had ever done, it seemed. God knows, there had been plenty of it in the old Lafayette Escadrille, where he won his wings, and that crazy hitch with the Kosciusko Squadron over in Poland hadn't been any pink tea. And those four years down in the Guatemalan banana country hadn't made a dilettante out of him.

Go into any Latin-American country and mention Captain Jerry Frost and nobody would have the slightest idea of whom you spoke. But mention El Beneficio to any *soldado* and he was all attention. In those countries where men still die for illusions and assume musical names, they tell you that El Beneficio was a bold, roistering Americano who could handle women and a machine-gun like nobody's business.

No, he was no stranger to dirty work.

"Well," the Adjutant-General interrupted his reveries, "you can take the pick of the staff. You can do anything you want to. Forty years ago a train robbery in Texas might have been ordinary, but this is 1929. This infernal publicity is bothering me. It's up to you and the men you name."

"I'd rather look around a bit first," Frost said, as he rose to go. "If I need anybody, I'll let you know."

"Good luck to you."

He accepted the hope with a nod of his head and walked out.

Captain Frost expected little information from the chief of police of Jamestown, and he was not disappointed. The chief pointed out that he and his men were after all merely humans, and that they were doing everything humans could do. That this had availed nothing was not his fault. Captain Frost could see that?

Very frankly, Captain Frost said he couldn't. "It beats me," he said. "Here it is, the high-powered twentieth century—a scientific age. And a gang of bandits sticks up a passenger train in orthodox Wild West manner and gets away clean with a fortune. Every copper in North Texas is caught flat-footed. I'd like to have the opportunity sometime to get in on top of a case instead of waiting two or three weeks. I sure would."

"Well," the chief observed pointedly, "maybe we can arrange that just for *you*. It's a funny thing, but criminals never invite us to their parties. However, they might make an exception for the Rangers."

"Never mind the wisecracks! Didn't anybody

in North Texas make any reports or anything after the robbery? It looks to me like a correspondence school sleuth could have done that."

"Ain't I been telling you they didn't? There wasn't nothing to report! My God, don't say that any more to me! It makes me sore all over. Every newspaper in this town has been plastering stories all over their front pages about it. It's got me goofy!

"Now, listen while I go over it again. Then you'll know as much as we do—or anybody else does. That train carried $300,000 in torn money that was going back to Washington. It left Jamestown, going east, at 8:45 and when it got to Reddy, about eight miles out, it was flagged down by a man on the track with a lantern. A moment later the engineer and fireman looked into the muzzle of a sub-machine-gun held by a masked robber.

"While this one kept the engineer and fireman covered, another went in the express car, blowed open the safe and got the coin. They slipped in on the messenger, tied him up, but when Cummings, the brakeman, ran through the door, they dropped him with a slug of lead in the forehead. Before anybody else knew what it was all about, the train started. It stopped a little farther on, but the bandits had disappeared.

"It happened right beside the highway but they had put red lights half a mile apart to stop the traffic. It's the general opinion that they are hiding out somewhere, but we've got the numbers of some of the bills and sooner or later we'll nab the men. Nobody can beat the law!"

It was the sort of a preachment Frost could expect from the chief. He was a man who had been in the chair for twenty years, and was slightly antiquated. One of the old school, as the newspaper boys liked to say.

"Now you know as much as we do."

"So that's all, eh?"

"All? Ain't it enough? It's been plenty to keep these newspapers in copy. It ought to be enough for you."

"Are you worried about what they think?"

The chief glared. "Ain't you?"

"Not particularly."

"Well, *I* am; you're damn well right I am. We

got an election coming off here next month and unless the right guy gets in, I go back to pounding a beat. Damn if these crooks can't pick fine moments to pull big jobs! So, you see how much I'm for you. Personally, I'll let you have my moral support and hope you have a lot of luck. *But I don't think you will!*"

omebody once wrote that clever crime detection is one-third luck, one-third hard work and one-third intuition. Great detectives rate luck and intuition as a stand-off, which is to say they reckon one as important as the other.

Jerry Frost was not a scientist, he was not a criminologist, he was not, in the technical sense of the word, a detective at all. But he had had a fair amount of luck thus far, he was perfectly willing to work hard, and he knew his intuition had stood him in good stead before.

And he was going to be able to use it this time. He realized that an hour after he had left the Jamestown chief of police.

He saw something that clicked in his mind—and would not be shaken. The very incredibility of the thing was what sold him.

He had dropped into the Secret Service offices of the government in the Federal Building, for, after all, it was their case. His conversation with the inspector had not been especially productive. But his eye caught a picture on the desk. It was a wrecked airplane, and he naturally was interested.

"This was a sweet one," he said. "Where'd it happen?"

"That," replied the inspector, "is an old one. It happened about a year ago. I was rummaging around my desk the other day and found it."

"Nasty spill."

"Yea, Charlie Cox got killed in it. You ought to remember that. The air-mail pilot. He crashed up in the Red River country. We lost a registered pouch in it."

"Oh," said Frost. "I do remember now. Never got anything on that case, did you?"

"Nope, never did. None of the bonds ever showed up."

"Ever have any ideas about it?"

"Well, not exactly. Charlie just crashed, that was all. Somebody came along and took the pouch. Anybody'd know the difference between registered mail and ordinary mail. We figured some farmer had got it, but we watched that country for a long time. None of the bonds ever showed up. Just another one of those mysteries."

It was at that moment that Jerry got his idea. But then it was too ridiculous. His intuition kept trying to tell him something, but he wouldn't listen. The voice was too faint. A little later the idea came bounding back again. And he couldn't lose it. The air-mail job. What made him think it was connected with the train robbery?

He wondered. Still, there had been innumerable baffling crimes solved by leads much more absurd than this. The air-mail job. Well, the idea was there to stay. He couldn't get rid of it.

He slept on it all night. Or tried to. Writing people and artists know how that is. You can't tear those things out of you. They weigh you down like an anvil. Sometimes you can't breathe comfortably. You think of it for hours and then very suddenly it comes, clear and clean, like big handwriting. All you have to do then is sit down and copy it.

Frost was like that. In the morning, it took definite form. It wasn't nebulous any longer. That air-mail job hadn't been an accident. It was premeditated. Everybody thought it was just one of those things that have to be a part of any new field of endeavor when man pits his brain and brawn against nature. But Jerry was willing to bet his life it had been premeditated.

Once, down south, when they were having a lot of fun with Salazar and Madero, a grizzled veteran had said, "Kid, when you get a hunch—*ride it!*" Well, that wasn't always so easy. The odds were big. No matter if you had a strong body, the odds were big. But Jerry Frost had a hunch. And he was going to ride it.

It all depended on one thing, and he went out to see about that. He wasn't the least bit surprised when he discovered the spot where the train had been held up was but a few hundred yards from Withers Field, the municipal airport. He had expected it.

He telephoned the Secret Service chief and the Jamestown chief and made the same request of both. It was for them to forget they had seen him.

Irrespective of the theories of the investigators, and their verdicts, Jerry was convinced the mail plane had been tampered with. To do that required cold nerve and daring that not every criminal possessed. Find the man who conceived that idea and you had the brains behind the train robbery. And he was a man who would need and who would have a sound knowledge of airplanes.

That afternoon he reported to the hangar of the Mid-West Air Transport Company at Withers Field with a letter of introduction to Captain Eads. An hour before Captain Eads had been telephoned that one Thomas Femrite, a name Jerry adopted for obvious reasons, was to be given employment as a mechanic and test pilot.

He knew, of course, that there was little chance of any of the bandits being at the Field now. But that flying field once had been the center of their operations. That wasn't much to work on, but it was something. It was considerably more than anybody else had decided.

"Captain Eads?" Jerry asked.

A man seated at the inside desk turned and looked. Before him in the door stood a man six feet tall and as brown as a nut. He had long arms, long legs and good eyes. He looked every inch a flyer. There is something about a new man who comes to a flying field that compels attention. You immediately size him up and wonder how much stuff he's got, and whether he's going to be a heel or a good fellow, and whether or not he can fly. Captain Eads decided this lad would do.

"Mr. Femrite, reporting for duty."

"Come in, Mr. Femrite. An old army man?"

"Yes, sir."

"I thought so. What outfit?"

"The Forty-seventh."

Captain Eads lifted his eyebrows. "Oh, yeah? Pretty good gang of crate-busters. The downtown office telephoned me about you. How many hours have you had?"

"Oh, six or seven thousand."

"Whoosh! That's plenty. Well, you've come to the right place if you're a seven-thousand-hour man. We need men who can assemble motors and who aren't afraid to fly those same motors. Know what I mean?"

"Yes, sir."

"All right. Red!"

An oily individual who escaped being a dwarf by a few inches shoved his auburn head through the door.

"Take Mr. Femrite around and make him acquainted. He's going to work for us."

Getting acquainted with the Mid-West crew was the work of but a few moments. Red was short, Jerry learned, for Fred Walker, and apart from him the only other veteran was Slimmer King. There were a couple of youngsters but they didn't count. They hadn't passed the prop-spinning stage.

Going over big was simple with Red and Slimmer. Jerry spoke their language. The kids were aloof, but after he had stunted one of the rickety Travelairs one afternoon, they warmed up and immediately made him a model.

Nor had his maneuvers hurt his prestige with the old-timers. Jerry had all but knocked the knob off St. Peter's gate. That particular day he went crazy. What he didn't do with that old bus hadn't been invented.

"Gee, you looked great!" Red beamed. "But I thought once or twice we oughta kissed you good-bye before you left the ground."

"Stop kidding, Red. I bet you can do things with a crate I've never thought of."

"Naw," Red confessed. "I ain't much of a stunter. I can get 'em up there and get 'em down and that lets me out. I wasn't born to kick no rudder bar. My head belongs in a motor."

After that, things came easier for Jerry. The ice had been broken. He came to know something of the other fellows on the Field. He was particularly attracted to the bunch in the No. 6 hangar. They were commercial men.

He sensed a sort of rivalry between the Mid-West fellows and the bunch in No. 6. There was no particular reason for it, but he did. Ostensibly, they just about had the commercial business at the field sewed up. The Mid-West wasn't in competition with them, yet they growled and glared every time Jerry got close. He spoke to Red about it.

"They're just a gang of five-dollar-a-lick boys," Red said. "Don't pay them any attention. They haul passengers, but personally, I wouldn't let one of 'em push me in a wheelbarrow. I just don't crave their company."

"There's no reason for them to be sore at me," Jerry said.

"That's their way. They're sore at everybody. The farther away from those guys you stay the better off you'll be."

But he had no intention of staying away. He was curious. So the next day, under the pretext of borrowing a porcelain, he invaded their hangar. He went up to the fellow who had been pointed out as Casey.

Casey gave him the porcelain. He was stocky and careless in his personal appearance, even for an airplane mechanic. "Where you come from, feller?"

"Oh, all over," said Jerry.

"I saw you yesterday doing some fancy flying. Looked like you'd wobbled a stick before."

"Yep—I've wobbled 'em before."

"You a new air-mail pilot?"

"Nope, just a mechanic."

"Well, there ain't many mechanics can fly like that."

"Oh, I dunno."

"A guy like you is wasting his time meddling with spark plugs and pushing a gasoline truck over a flying field. You'd ought to get in the big money. Commercial stuff."

"Sounds pretty good."

"It is good." Casey was positive. "Any guy what can bust clouds like you can is wasting his

time drawing two hundred bucks a month. Interested?"

"Maybe. Much obliged for the porcelain."

That night Captain Jerry Frost reported to the Adjutant-General by telephone. He reported that he had become established and that the outlook was promising and that something possibly would happen soon.

The Adjutant-General, still annoyed, retorted that something would happen soon—to the entire force. "They're still raising hell," he said bluntly. "Let me send you some help."

"Now, listen," said Jerry firmly. "Any outside interference will gum the whole works. You sit tight and stop worrying. And don't send anybody! Forget all about it."

The Adjutant-General grumblingly agreed, and then told himself he was glad Frost was on the job. If anybody could do it, Jerry could.

Jerry was convinced the gang in No. 6 hangar wasn't all everybody thought it was. He had been made an overture, and he expected another. To bring it about, he spent the next few days in direct defiance of all the laws of flying. He was either a plain damn fool or the sweetest pilot who ever brought a bus down on one tire. He almost tore the ships to pieces. All this time the gang in No. 6 looked on.

One night Casey and another man, of a distinct continental air, visited the Transport hangar.

"Meet Mr. Crouch," said Casey. "He's the boss of our outfit."

Jerry shook hands with him.

"I'm glad to know you," Crouch said. "I saw you the other day and I wanted to congratulate you. I've seen a lot of flying in my time, but I don't think I ever saw the equal of that."

The man spoke with a slight accent, and a high voice. It was an unusual tone. Something in Jerry's memory stirred. He looked into the face closely. Gray mustache. Black eyes, sharp and deep-set. A small mouth and thin lips.

He had seen that face somewhere before. But

where? The panorama of his life passed swiftly. It produced nothing.

"Thank you, sir," Jerry said. "I sometimes think I was born with my feet on a rudder bar."

"You were," Crouch agreed; "and that's just the point. You are the type of man commercial flying needs. Would you consider a change?"

"Well," said Jerry, "a fellow always needs—"

"Exactly. And you're worth just twice as much to us as you are to the air-mail people."

Jerry debated for a moment. He had no idea of refusing; he just didn't want to be too anxious.

"I'll take it."

"Good! When can you leave?"

"When do you want me?"

"Tomorrow. We're opening a hangar at Waco. You'll be on hand in the morning?"

"Yes, sir. I don't think they'll hold me."

"Of course they won't! If necessary, tell 'em to go to hell!"

Getting his release was simple. He merely got in touch with the home office, where the officials knew his mission and identity, and explained the situation. They in turn notified the Field. There was little comment. There seldom is. Young flying men are notorious nomads.

Waco was but an hour's hop from Jamestown, and as Jerry was eager to get there he left at once. During that hour he rolled his memory before him, seeking to pull from its kaleidoscope the face of the man called Crouch. That high voice rang in his ears above the drone of the motor; and gradually the years fell away.

Flying now, as he was flying then, the slender threads of memory were picked up more easily.

Once more he was in the air over Bapaume with the 47th. This was Richthofen's old stamping ground and the Boche knew it like birds. Jerry was flying a Camel at 8,000 feet. They were climbing in close formation. He looked ahead and to the right. There was Bapaume in all its raggedness, half-obscured in the mist. On his left were a couple of youngsters. They waved. They were going through the agony of their first patrol. He had gone through it two months before. But it hadn't wrecked him. He hadn't a

lot of imagination. He was sure of himself. But he knew it must be hell on the youngsters. He thought he'd better keep an eye on the eaglets.

There were clouds above—gray blanket clouds that came together in a solid roof, with only a gaping hole here and there to reveal the blue. Bad stuff. The squadron leader knew. He kept them climbing. Jerry glanced again at the youngsters. It bucked him up a bit to think about them. They were green. He squinted his eye and put up his thumb to have a look around the sun. They were up above now. He warmed his guns. The chatter reminded him that he was tired. So this was war. Well, they could have the damned war for all he cared. He was tired. He wished . . . And then he caught himself. A fellow couldn't do that. It wasn't decent. He was in it, no use wishing he was out. Then he saw he was straggling. Straggling was suicide. They were out in Richthofen's country. The Baron's men were devoted to stragglers. They ate 'em alive. He looked up. His intuition again.

His throat closed abruptly and his knees melted. An Albatross was coming down fast. His wing fabric was ruffling into lace and the wood of his camber ribs was splintering. He pulled up sharply and pressed his trigger. Both guns vomited. He was firing wildly. The Albatross slipped under him. Oh, for a fast bus! His Camel would do 100. An S.E. would do 135. A Spad would do 140. And an Albatross would beat that. A butterfly-winged Albatross. *Rat-tat-tat-tat-tat. Rat-tat-tat-tat-tat. Sping!* A shower of gasoline. His motor conked. He fell over in a dive. The Albatross followed him down. The Spandaus were rattling. He could hear them above the bite of the motor. A hundred red-hot needles hit him in the shoulder. Her dammed something warm back with his lips. Something warm and wet. The dirty, lousy swine! Fine stuff! What the hell? He was done . . . he was falling. The Spandaus rattled *fortissimo*. A drumlike roar, blackness swept, swirled over him. . . .

A high-ceilinged room. The penetrating smell of anesthetics. A face that bent over and shut out the depth of the room. An enormous face by contrast. He slowly made it out. He moved his body and winced. Bandaged. The face grinned. It spoke.

"Never," said a high, irritating voice, "break formation. How did I hit everything but your head?" The face came closer. The *Pour le Mérite* swung out on its ribbon. "Byfield, my name is. You're my personal prisoner. . . ."

Jerry tried to laugh. Instead he fainted. . . .

That had been eleven years ago. The vision passed and its present significance came upon him so suddenly he went into a *renversement* that almost popped his neck. Byfield! The German Ace! Crouch! By God! There was dirty work somewhere. His first vague hunch, even so soon, assumed the form of reality. There could be no doubt that he was on a trail that would lead somewhere.

Out of the mists loomed the Amicable Building, perennial landmark, sentinel of the Brazos, gaunt and lonely for want of companionship. Bearing to the left, he came over the field and settled down. He was trembling as if he had been out on his first patrol.

Byfield!

A luxurious cabin plane idled down and disgorged two men. One was Casey. The other was Crouch, *né* Byfield. It was all Jerry could do to keep his hands off the man's throat.

"You must have been in a hurry," said the high voice.

That voice! There was no doubt of it now. Von Byfield. Every step of the way now was fraught with danger. He half hoped Crouch wouldn't see it in his face.

"I was," he said finally.

"Well, there's a lot to do. We'll brush up and visit the newspapers."

They brushed, breakfasted, visited. Crouch planted all his ideas. But that was simple. He had them talking about it already. There were a dozen pilots coming in from New Mexico and Arizona to take part in the circus. A dozen men who, Jerry knew full well, were bums. And then he thought it was funny that he should be walking beside this man in such a placid way . . . the man who called himself Crouch, who had shot

him out of control and then followed him down. He had prayed to meet him a hundred times—and now he had. And he was helpless. Funny.

That afternoon the pilots dropped in. That afternoon they were not an impressive collection. Just as Jerry thought, they were tramps. He thought they were a tough-looking bunch of eggs to be pilots. Had it come to the point where there was as much evil in the air as on the ground? God forbid. The air was the last outpost of chivalry. Of romance. It was dead as hell everywhere else. And it wouldn't be long—

But his big shock came later in the afternoon.

e discovered a portion of the hangar falsely constructed. From the outside it seemed all right, but from the inside it seemed shorter than it should be. He opened a door and stepped into semi-darkness. A ghostly form confronted him. And another.

There is nothing quite so ghostly as to come across an airplane in a poorly lit hangar. Even if you are expecting it, you are half startled. There is something weird about it, even if you are an airman. It strikes at the roots.

Jerry recovered from his shock and opened the door wide.

The light revealed two planes. Two planes so lovely, so trim that his breath came in a swift intake of admiration. Two tiny planes that seemed unreal. Watch fob types. He moved closer. And stopped.

He saw they weren't so lovely. They were grim. Trench mortars looked like that. They looked like playthings—until they belched. Then they were hideous. On the cowling of each of the planes was mounted a machine-gun, its squat muzzle merging almost indistinguishably into the background.

He was amazed. He hadn't, in his wildest fancies, anticipated anything like this. He hadn't seen a plane like this since he had left the Polish front. Not even then. Those things were hayracks compared to this. Before him stood two of the highest products of scientific civilization.

"Good-looking, eh?"

The voice cracked through the hangar like a sputtering electric wire that has found a ground. For a moment Jerry was disconcerted. Only for a moment.

"I'd give a month's salary to fly one of them!" he breathed.

"Yes?" It was evident Crouch didn't know whether to be angered or amused. He decided on the latter course. "Maybe you will. They're patented. I'm trying to sell them to the government. I wouldn't like for *anybody* to know I had them."

Jerry caught the faintest hint of a threat in the words. Of course, it was a lie. It wasn't even a good lie. He knew that, and he knew that Crouch knew he knew. Crouch must have thought he was several different kinds of a prize fool to swallow that one. But he was just as anxious to repair the damage as his employer.

"Not a word. You can trust me."

When they went out, Crouch locked the door with a padlock. Jerry looked back over his shoulder and decided the compartment was well hidden. And he decided something else. To dally with this thing was to play with T.N.T. Crouch and his gang were dangerous. One man couldn't stand in their way. They had too much to protect.

But what had the air circus to do with it? Jerry felt that everybody knew more than he did. The flyers knotted into little clans and got their heads together. He stumbled around stupidly. It made him, for the first time since he had won his wings, terribly self-conscious.

He stopped Casey later in the day. "Say, I guess I stumbled onto a little family secret this morning."

"Yeah?"

"Yeah. I saw two of the sweetest little battle wagons—"

"Easy, feller." Casey turned on him and glowered. "Don't go around popping off your face. They're inventions. The old man's a nut. He's afraid somebody might steal his plans."

Jerry gestured disdainfully. "Don't make me laugh. I wasn't born yesterday. How come I don't rate some of the secrets."

"Listen, you! If there are any secrets, the old man'll let you in on them. In the meantime, keep your trap shut—*tight*!"

For the second time that day, Jerry was tempted to crown somebody. But that would have spoiled everything. He had been acting; he could continue.

"Now, now; ain't I one of the outfit? You pulled me away from a good job—for why? I don't even know what I'm supposed to do."

Casey melted somewhat. Maybe the kid was right. Maybe he ought to rate a few secrets.

"Well," he said, "I can't tell you nothing but this: if there hadn't been something big doing, the old man wouldn't have wanted you. He's a pretty good student of human nature—and he figured you'd been in a jam somewhere and wasn't too particular what you did as long as it was in an airplane. There's something about an airman that's written all over his face. He's like a schoolboy in love. He doesn't know it's there, and even if he did he couldn't do anything about it. You sit tight."

Jerry made up his mind to sit.

The air circus came off as scheduled. Good advertisement. It packed the field and roads for miles around. The spectacle of fifteen pilots in the air doing all manner of stunts was appealing anywhere—especially in Waco. They hadn't seen anything like it since the training days of the war.

Crouch's business acumen was sound. The trade rolled in. There were innumerable hops. Everybody wanted to fly. The young men visioned themselves not as Foncks and Guynemers and Bishops and Lukes, for they belonged to another age. It was Lindbergh now. The old people grinned as they came in contact with the onrushing age. Jerry caught a passenger to Austin one morning. He had gone on a rush call. He had an hour to wait.

He visited the capitol and found the Adjutant-General in another rage. This was getting to be the best thing the Adjutant-General did.

"What's the big idea?" he bellowed. "We're wasting time. I've had to fight with myself to keep my hands off. From your reports, we've got enough on those fellows to get a conviction now."

"From my reports—yes," Frost replied. "But my reports wouldn't convict them because I haven't got one single fact. It's pure hunch. But I'm going to nail them to the cross, and it won't be long. This is the toughest, nerviest outfit I've ever run across in my life. They'd stick up the National City Bank in New York with a little encouragement. But something's in the wind. I need help."

"Take anybody you want."

"It isn't that kind of help. Listen."

For five minutes he talked, all the while the Adjutant-General nodded and drummed on his desk top. Hardly had Frost left the office when the state official reached for the telephone and placed a call for the commandant at Kelly Field, the army base.

And thus, that night, one of the new A-3 battle planes, carrying six thousand rounds of ammunition and mounting six machine-guns, dropped out of the darkness at Withers Field and was quickly rushed into the hangar of the Mid-West Air Transport Company and covered with a tarpaulin.

Given that impetus, Jerry felt more confident. Nothing was likely to happen at Waco. If anything broke, it would be at Jamestown. And something was going to break—soon.

Riding his hunch, Jerry was sure Crouch and his gang had wrecked the air-mail plane a year before. They had held up the Rio Grande express. God knows what else they had done. Jerry felt it had been plenty.

He had fitted himself up a bunk in one corner of the hangar on a collapsible cot that was hidden away each morning. He didn't want to jeopardize the confidence Crouch might have in him.

A few nights later, as he lay there and stared into the darkness, and made up his mind to force the play within the next twenty-four hours, he heard the low drone of a motor. He rolled over and strained his ears. It was faint, then louder, then faint again. Then he heard another sound— a drone. There was enough noise to make him think it was a bombing raid.

Jerry looked at his watch. Four o'clock. Of course, it would be an hour like that. Something was up. Something was going to happen. He slipped into his pants and boots, knocked down his cot and shoved it under a fuselage and strapped on his guns. He went to the far corner of the corrugated hangar. There was an opening there wide enough for him to see. If there was anything to see. Right now it was black night.

Louder and louder the drones came. They were directly overhead now. Jerry wondered how Crouch expected to get away with anything like this. It amounted to pure suicide. And then it dawned that perhaps this was the very reason they had held that air circus. Adjacent residents might not be so curious if they heard motors at night. Or could Crouch have been that much of a psychologist?

Staring through the aperture, Jerry was momentarily blinded by a flash of light as the field was illuminated by two great searchlights. The motors throbbed, clawed furiously as they lost traction, and then whistled as the ships landed.

One was a cabin monoplane. The other was a tiny battle plane.

Then the lights went out. The entire operation consumed not more than two minutes.

Presently there were footsteps. Shuffling footsteps . . . and low voices. Out of the low conversation his ears picked strange words. Chinese!

Then: "Keep those Chinks quiet!"

Under cover of night, Crouch was running in Chinese.

Frost lay there for ten minutes, thinking. Crouch seemed to have his hand in everything. He heard echoes of automobiles on the highway, the grind of gears coming loud and clear through the stillness; then two men walked back. The office door opened, and a faint glow appeared through the cracks.

He got up and moved closer. He recognized the voices of Crouch and Casey.

"God, I'm glad that's over." This was Casey. "Two more trips and then we're Europe bound."

"Thompson's waiting in Mexico City."

"You wasn't sap enough to give him the dough, was you?"

Crouch laughed shortly. "Certainly not! Nobody knows where that money is—nobody but I."

"What do you mean?" Casey asked.

"Well, I moved it."

"You mean you moved our dough from that train job?" He was incredulous.

"Yes. Remember seeing some guys working on those old asphalt tennis courts behind our hangar at Withers Field?"

"Sure."

"Well, you thought they were repairing them, didn't you? So did everybody else. But they were just putting the asphalt over a little hiding place I'd previously fixed up."

"My God!" Casey ejaculated. "Suppose we wanna get away quick?"

"That's all right. We can smash that stuff in five minutes. And it was the safest place— believe me."

"Maybe it was wise. By the way, this wild man we got off the Mid-West ain't so certain everything's on the level. He cornered me and asked a lotta questions. I told him if there was anything to say, you'd say it. Might not be wise to stall him. He looks pretty sharp."

"I don't intend to. I'm going to talk to him today and he'll run in the next batch of Chinese. I figure he's got the nerve to help us pull a sweet one down South pretty soon."

"Course, you know what you're doing. But I don't see the point in hiring him. Never did."

"Perhaps there wasn't. But I collect good pilots just like other men collect stamps and books. I like to have them around. But you don't need to worry about this guy. He's been in a lot of jams before. You can look at him and tell that."

"I dunno—"

"Help me get that Moth in." They moved out on the field.

Captain Jerry Frost came alive. He had them nailed. His suspicions were confirmed. They had done the train job. And unless he missed his guess, those bonds from the air-mail plane were in that cache Crouch spoke of. He moved up in the dark until the two men got into the hangar with their plane. Then he started off on a dog-trot down the road.

At dawn the law forces of the sovereign State of Texas swung into action. They had long been waiting for this moment. The great, ponderous, clumsy law, with its thousands of tentacles, got going. The tide itself was not more relentless. It struck here sometimes, there sometimes, in a circle sometimes—but eventually it straightened out and began to roll. It was inevitable.

The Adjutant-General sat at his desk and manipulated the controls. He was the puppeteer.

Shortly after sunrise, two state planes were in the air. There were six men in each besides the pilot. Six tight-lipped, grim men, who would shoot their way into hell and back again to get their men.

The Rangers were moving up.

In the hangar at Waco, the telephone jangled. Casey answered it.

"Yeah, Casey . . . all right, Tommy . . . What's that? I can't hear you . . . wait a minute." He handed the receiver to Crouch. "The goof is excited. Get an earful."

Crouch took the instrument. "Hello, Tommy . . . Yes . . ." A long wait. Casey moved closer. Something had happened. One look at Crouch's face told him that. Finally: "Who told you? . . . Hell!" He slammed the receiver on the hook.

"We're fools!" He spat the words out. "One of the Mid-West fellows told Tommy this morning that this guy Femrite is a Texas Ranger. Come on!"

"Where?"

"That's the trouble with you damned Americans," Crouch cried. "You lose your head in a tight place. We're going to get that money. Maybe we can make it. He's waited this long without tipping his hand, maybe he'll wait a little longer."

"But what about the others?"

"This is no time to think of them. We can be in Mexico in five hours. Come on!"

They moved quickly to the hangar door, swung it open. They wheeled their tiny, speedy planes out into the starting line. They swung each other's props, the motors barked into life, and dust and pebbles swept into the backwash and puttered against the side of the hangars.

Crouch was first off. Casey followed. Tails whipped up and wheels bounced lightly on the uneven ground. They zoomed into the air in broad climbing turns. Casey saw Crouch was loading his guns.

They didn't know it then, but they were to be disappointed. Jerry already was at Withers Field, had been there when Ranger reinforcements arrived. And, of course, a perverse fate decreed they would start at the wrong end of the tennis court.

To see a half dozen apparently intelligent men digging into an asphalt tennis court in the early morning is not a sight calculated to be passed without stopping for a moment. Mechanics stopped, workmen stopped. There was a great textile mill near the field, and a crowd begets a larger crowd.

Jerry was trying to direct the traffic and the Rangers at the same time. Three young men in handcuffs, late of the No. 6 hangar, looked on in undisguised amusement.

Then a shout. Somebody had the pouch. Jerry grabbed it and, with a single movement, slit the side. A handful of currency was extracted. Torn currency.

"That's it!" he said. "That's it! Take those men and this pouch into the office. Those other fellows are coming here sooner or later. We'll make a reception out of it."

The news swept about the airport like wildfire. The textile mill was all agog. For the first time in many of their lives, they were sitting in the middle of a big event. "The train robbers have been found!" The doorman at the textile mill told the switchboard operator, and the switchboard operator told the secretary. The secretary thought the police ought to know so he telephoned them.

Eagle-eyed news hawks caught the message the moment the desk sergeant finished his yawn and copied it. They flashed their papers. Editors stirred their stumps, called circulation managers, engravers, operators and pressmen. Reporters on the city staff got going, the rewrite man lighted a fresh cigarette off the butt of an old one and rammed copy paper in his mill. He pulled the telephone close. And muttered: "I hope to Gawd this is as big as it looks!"

The word got about Jamestown. Sirens shrieked through the traffic carrying enough police to take Mont Sec. In thirty minutes, the highways leading to Withers Field were choked. Some of them knew what was going to happen, but most of them didn't. This was the Great American Public.

Speeding north for their plunder before seeking safety, neither Crouch nor Casey was aware of the plans being made for their welcome. Crouch, being of higher mentality, probably thought he had pushed his luck too far, but that was all.

He couldn't see Withers Field, he couldn't see Captain Jerry Frost beside the A-3 single-seater, positively the finest thing in battle planes. If Crouch's ships were lovely, there was no superlative for this. Jerry stood there, his eyes glued on the southern heavens, his propeller swinging idly.

He seemed just a little ridiculous to himself. He couldn't, for example, grasp that this was 1929. Imagine such a thing with so large a gallery? It was like an *opéra bouffe*. Still, he tingled. He almost, once, half admitted he liked it.

From out of the distance came a drone. Two planes were seen; they roared onward, still unaware of what awaited them. One dipped downward, the other, which was higher, began a long glide.

The cordon of police started forward.

"Wait a while," Jerry shouted. "Those ships have got guns on 'em! Take your time!"

But the police disregarded the command. They, too, had waited long. And neither were they self-conscious before the crowd.

Casey was in the first ship, and no sooner had his wheels touched the ground than he realized all was lost. He shot the throttle to his ship and the smoke belched from the exhaust. A policeman fired. The bullet whistled through the fuselage.

Then Casey either tried to zoom, or he lost his head. He later claimed he didn't know his finger was on the trigger. His guns barked through the propeller and two policemen pitched forward, twitched and lay still. A second later a shot got Casey and his plane dived into the ground.

Crouch had seen and heeded. He had gone into a climb—and he was going south.

Jerry throbbed and pinched. It was the old feeling. Something in him seemed to say, had always said: "Enjoy this, for it may be your last one." Not fear—and yet it might have been.

He swung his arm out for the chocks to be pulled. His motor whined and then caught with a roar. Something throbbed in his hands and feet and played along his nerves like tiny electrical impulses. He was talking to himself, and there was something terrible in it—prayer and hatred intermingled.

He opened his throttle and his propeller disappeared in a thin circle of light. Like a living thing his ship bounded forward. For a while he bounced along and then he went straight up like an elevator. He climbed 500 feet before it began to stall, then drifted his stick forward and presently flattened out at 140. His bus never even felt it. Tight. Solid. Maneuverable.

He warmed his guns with a burst of twenty. He rather hoped he wouldn't have to fight. Still, never could tell. Everything was different in the air. Once before, he had been in the same air with Crouch. He had remembered. Maybe there would be a fight after all.

He climbed to 7,500 and buckled on his straps. He had done that before, too. But this was something new. No straining the eyes to the right and to the left and above looking for black specks. No wondering if that was an L.V.G. two-seater—a decoy—with a half dozen Albatrosses lurking above. His man was just in front. Only one.

He crawled up on Crouch's tail and motioned for him to land. Crouch climbed to the left and got into fighting position. Jerry motioned again. His answer was a burst that raked through the A-3 ailerons.

"O.K.," Jerry bellowed. "Here we go!"

He half rolled to get on top, so did the other. Jerry touched the trigger and pulled up, dived again. Crouch Immelmanned and straightened out on Jerry's tail and another burst ripped through the fins. Jerry kicked it off into a slip and leveled out. Crouch was diving away. He was going to run for it. No doubt of that.

Jerry pushed his stick forward until the rush of air gagged him. The rattle of his guns came through the chatter of the motor. Crouch went into another Immelmann and Jerry dived by him. The German was a flyer. But he was not matching skill with the kid he had knocked down that day at Toul. This was another fellow.

Jerry pulled up and went into a climb. He banked sharply and started higher and higher. That was Crouch's mistake. His ship couldn't climb with the A-3. Jerry was so close now he could see the wheels on the other's undercarriage spinning.

Well, there he was. He had him. The trim white belly of Crouch's ship glinted along the tip of his guns. There he was. There was von Byfield, the great ace. *The* von Byfield. The one who had followed him down. He could still hear those Spandaus clacking as they raked his body in a steel flail.

Jerry touched his trigger. He could see holes tearing in the linen. He kept his guns open. There was a fan of flame. He noticed his altimeter: 14,000. Too high. And yet . . . He stalled and whipped out in a spin.

Crouch's ship hung momentarily like a leaf undecided whether to fall this way or that. Then it dipped its nose and wabbled. The glide became a dive; the dive went into a lazy, aimless spin, wings flopping, to the floor. The plane flattened, whipped out upside down, stalled, snapped out again in a final effort, and then again went downward in that grotesque way. Over and over. Over and over. Jerry watched it, fascinated. It was only a dot now, flashing in the sun as it keeled over. It was coming closer to the floor—closer, closer.

Then suddenly a tiny sheet of flame lashed out, a puff of dust. That was all.

Jerry sideslipped down, landed and taxied slowly in. He climbed out stiff-legged. He looked down and saw his pants were slightly torn. There was a gash in his leather coat. He looked into his cockpit. The floorboards were splintered. He looked up. The center section was riddled. The linen on his fins was ribboned.

Far down the field a group of police and civilians was rushing to the wrecked plane.

"Cigarette?"

Somebody gave him one.

"Match?"

Somebody else struck it. Frost thought those fingers were familiar. Long . . . white . . . He looked into the face. The Adjutant-General. He had his arms extended.

"Hurt, Jerry?"

"Nope. Tired." Quite matter-of-fact. The curious crowded around. The Adjutant-General very plainly was ill-at-ease. It had stirred him tremendously. He wanted to say something nice, but he couldn't. Men are like that. Especially men who are suddenly overcome with pride. They try to say flowery things, but the words clog up in their throats. They think them right down to the tip of their tongue, and then strange words come out.

It was like that now. The Adjutant-General said: "Well, take a rest. California, Florida. Any place."

"Nope, Galveston."

"Galveston?"

"Yep, Galveston. Unfinished business."

The Adjutant-General nodded. He didn't understand; he didn't want to understand. Captain Frost had come through. That was the code of the Rangers. It had been that way when the Conestogas squeaked their way through the Indian country, and it was that way in the day of science and aviation. When all else fails, when there is a knotty problem, when there's dirty work—the Rangers. Yesterday and today and tomorrow, to the ends of the earth—get him!

Merely Murder

Julius Long

JULIUS W. LONG (1907–1955) was born in Ohio, received a law degree, and was admitted to the Ohio bar, where he practiced. He was a collector of guns (at one time he owned the only Tokarev 7.62 ever offered for sale in *The American Rifleman*), and his extensive knowledge of firearms was often apparent in his articles for *Field & Stream* as well as in his crime and mystery stories.

Long wrote many different types of fiction for about thirty magazines, most importantly ghost and fantastic stories for the top magazine in the genre, *Weird Tales*, to which he was a regular contributor in the 1930s, and mystery stories for *Black Mask, Detective Story, Dime Detective, Dime Story, The Shadow*, and *Strange Detective Tales*. One of his *Black Mask* stories, "Carnie Kill," was selected for *Best Detective Stories of the Year* (1945). He wrote only one novel, *Keep the Coffins Coming* (1947), a murder mystery involving a beautiful woman, her millionaire father, a Communist leader, a German scientist, and several gorillas.

One of his short stories served as the basis for the motion picture *The Judge* (1949); it was released in Great Britain as *The Gamblers*. The story of a crooked lawyer who blackmails his client into killing his wife, it was directed by Elmer Clifton, produced by Anson Bond, with a screenplay by Samuel Newman, Clifton, and Bond, and starred Milburn Stone, Katherine DeMille, Paul Guilfoyle, and Stanley Waxman.

"Merely Murder" was published in the July 1944 issue.

Peterson's mother came out of the kitchen with a revolver in her hand. "I'm not going to let them take you away, son," she said.

Merely Murder

Julius Long

CHAPTER ONE
WARRANT FOR LIFE

I COULD TELL FROM Keever's stride when he came into the office that someone was in for trouble.

"Come in here, Ben. I've got a little job for you."

I looked sadly at Miss Spain, Keever's confidential secretary, and fol-lowed Keever into his inner sanctum. It was Monday morning, and the week was getting off to its usual lousy start. Being special investigator for Burton H. Keever, the dashing D.A., had never been a picnic, but now that a couple of sensational cases had inspired some loose talk of a governorship, he drove me like a slave.

There was a gleam in his eyes as he drew a document from his pocket and tossed it across his desk.

I picked up the document. It was a warrant.

A BEN CROCKETT NOVELETTE

"If I ever get my hands on the guy . . ." Peterson had mumbled. Well, he—or somebody—sure got his wish, because Shorty Waxman, the shifty little shyster, now looked like something only Homicide could love.

The man named was Sam Peterson. The charge was violation of the Habitual Criminal Act. The penalty, if Peterson was convicted, was life imprisonment. I eyed Keever.

"Holding out again, huh? When did you find out that Peterson had three more raps against him?"

It took four raps to rate a conviction under the Habitual Criminal Act, and the only thing against Peterson to my knowledge was his conviction of a little more than a year before. He had been tried then on two counts, breaking and entering and grand larceny. At the time he had been employed as a gardener at the Riverside

Road estate of Jimmie Harmon, son of the late great realty king James D. Harmon Sr. There had been one of those cute wall safes in Harmon's bedroom, and Peterson hadn't been able to resist the temptation.

"Peterson's an old hand at burglary," Keever confided. "Late Saturday afternoon I got a tip that he had a record out West. I wired the warden of a western penitentiary, and, sure enough, they had Peterson's prints. He'd been in twice for burglary and once for grand larceny. So I got a warrant for him the first thing this morning, and I want you to pick him up. No slip-up, understand?"

"Sure, no slip-up. You're sure the prints are Peterson's? We checked with Washington when Peterson was on trial before. They didn't have any."

"I know, I know. Seems Peterson had some drag with the trusty in charge of filing prints in that joint, and they were never sent in. It'll be quite a shock to Peterson when he finds out his past has caught up with him."

I took the warrant and went down to my car. I remembered Peterson's address, for I had checked up on him a few weeks ago when he had been let out on parole. He lived in a southside apartment with his mother. I could recall pleasanter jobs.

I hadn't had to ask Keever why he had wished it off on me. He could easily have used someone from the sheriff's office or the local police department, but by sending me, his personal flunky, he could reserve all the credit for his own office. I could see the headlines: KEEVER GETS CONFESSION!

Of course, Peterson would have no alternative if he really had done three stretches in that western can. And I had a sickening feeling that he had, all right, though the idea had given me quite a jolt. I would have sworn that Peterson had been on trial for his first offense when Keever had got him convicted a year ago. He wasn't quite thirty, clean-cut and clear-eyed. But you never can tell.

Peterson's mother answered the bell at their apartment.

"Why, it's Mr. Corbett! Won't you come in? But I suppose you want to talk to Sam again. He isn't here now. He's got a wonderful new job in a war plant!"

"I did want to see him. It's rather urgent. Will you tell me where he's working?"

She did. I think she worried a little about having a district attorney's investigator showing up to embarrass her son, but she appeared to have no greater worry. I decided that if Peterson did have a western record he had kept it from his mother.

My badge got me through the gates at the war plant and into the office of the head personnel man. I showed him the warrant.

"I was afraid of something like this!" he moaned. "Of course, we knew Peterson was on parole, but we need men so badly we can't be too particular. Well, I'll have him for you in a minute."

Peterson was slightly pale when he walked in. His pallor increased when he saw me. I showed him the warrant. He accepted it with trembling fingers and read the charge. His face lost all color.

So it was true—Peterson was a four-time loser. He handed back the warrant and said listlessly: "I guess my luck will never change."

"Then you are the guy?"

"What's the use of denying it? Prints don't lie." He turned to the personnel man. "I'm sorry, sir. I hope this doesn't make any trouble for you. I sure liked my job here. If there'd been jobs ten years ago, I wouldn't be in this jam now. I hope they give me a job in the pen—a job making stuff to smack the Japs the way I've been doing here."

I didn't handcuff him. He got his stuff, and we walked out to my car. He was beginning to recover from the shock of his arrest, and now his brow was furrowed in thought.

"Would you mind telling me how Keever got wise to those prints? I happen to know they were never sent to Washington."

"You'll think I'm kidding you, Peterson, but I really don't know. The first I heard about it was when Keever handed me the warrant this morning."

Peterson did think I was kidding.

"O.K., you don't have to tell me. I think I know. If I ever get my hands on the guy . . ."

He clammed up then. I drove away from the factory and turned downtown. Then Peterson said: "Will you do me a favor? I want to tell my mother about this before she hears it some other way. She doesn't know about my record. It's going to be terrible."

I drove two blocks without answering; then I made a U-turn in the middle of the street.

"Damn you, don't try anything!"

When we got to his place, he asked: "Will you let me break it to her alone?"

I gave him a sidelong look, and he shrugged. We went into his apartment. His mother came out of the kitchen with a worried look. She also held a revolver, and I could see that its hammer was cocked.

"What is it, son? I knew something was wrong, the way this man acted. I'm not going to let him take you away again!"

think Peterson was even more astonished than I was. But he recovered more quickly. In one leap he was across the room. He took the revolver from his mother's hand and covered me.

"I didn't ask for this break, Corbett, but I'm taking it. Don't try anything—so help me, I'll let you have it!"

"Relax. I'm no hero."

"You've got a gun. Hand it over—butt-first."

I minded like a little lamb. He took my thirty-eight and thrust it under his belt. Then he turned to his mother.

"I'll never see you again, Mom."

She stood there looking at him and trembling. He started for the door. It was touching. I could have kicked the dear old lady's teeth right down her throat. I didn't even dare to think of what Keever would have to say when I gave him the lowdown on this deal.

Peterson slammed the door behind him, and I heard him racing down the stairs. I faced his mother.

"Have you a phone?"

She didn't hear me. I didn't see any phone and decided there wouldn't be one. I went downstairs and into the street in time to see Peterson taking two dollars' worth of rubber off my tires as he rounded a corner. There was a drug store on the corner. I phoned the cops. Then I took a deep breath and called Keever.

Somehow I forgot to mention the part Peter-son's mother had played, and that didn't help my story. Keever emitted something that sounded like a death rattle; then he roared: "You blundering fool! You've made a laughingstock of my office! Get back here, and get back here fast!"

He hung up. That was all that kept me from telling him what he could do with his job. Of course, I could have called him back. I walked out of the booth instead. I knew deep down that this was one time when Keever had a legitimate beef. If I had been in his shoes, I'd have taken them off and thrown them at me.

It was well after eleven, so I hopped a street-car and got off at Mike's, my favorite eatery. The place was beginning to fill up. Not until I had squeezed into a wall bench did I discover that the man in the adjoining seat was Shorty Waxman.

"It's a small world."

Waxman looked up from his lunch.

"Oh, hello, Ben. What do you mean, it's a small world?"

"I just left one of your former clients—rather, he just left me, borrowing my car and my gun. Sam Peterson."

Waxman's face twitched.

"Oh, yes. I remember Peterson. What's he been up to?"

"Habitual Criminal Act. Keever just discovered that the Harmon job was his fourth. I went out to pick him up but had a bad case of butter-fingers."

Waxman suddenly looked as if he needed a blood transfusion. His round little eyes widened until they seemed about to pop from their sockets. He choked on his food.

"Let me out of here, Ben! I just remembered something I forgot to do. Excuse, please!"

He fairly fought his way over me before I could slide out of the seat. At the cashier's desk he threw down a bill and ran to the phone booths without waiting for his change. He was in a booth for about two minutes; then he raced out again and made his exit. I regarded the lunch he had left. It was virtually all there. I ordered and took my time eating. Waxman had left not only his lunch. He had left food for thought.

CHAPTER TWO
WHERE THERE'S A WILL THERE'S A SLAYING

It was one o'clock when I walked into the Criminal Courts Building, which housed Keever's office. I had intended to duck Keever until he cooled off, but curiosity gave me courage. I wanted to find out why news of Peterson's pick-up and escape had sent Waxman on the run. But I didn't get to Keever's office. Pop Martin, the elevator starter, stopped me the moment he spied me.

"Gee, Ben, am I glad to see you! Keever's had everybody on your trail. You're to meet him at the Mercury Tower—Waxman's office."

"Waxman? What's with Waxman?"

"Murder. Somebody got him half an hour ago!"

I used a cab. Half a block from the Mercury Tower I had the driver stop. I got out and crossed the street to a crummy-looking coupe on which a patrolman was placing a ticket. It was my coupe. It was in a parking meter stall, and the flag was up.

"Hold it, pal. That's my car."

The cop recognized me. He grinned gloatingly.

"It makes no difference to me that you're from the D.A.'s office, pal. I seen my duty, and I done it."

"Oh, you did? I suppose you reported finding my car. There's been a circular out on it for a couple of hours and—"

The ticket was snatched from under the windshield wiper and torn to bits. The cop almost burst into tears. "For the love of Mike, don't tell anyone about this! It'd break me!"

I regarded him thoughtfully. "I think I'll take your advice." I walked on to the Mercury Tower, took a kidding from a couple of patrolmen on guard at the door and paused to scan the list of tenants. My memory had been correct.

Jimmie Harmon's real estate office was in the same building, a couple of floors below Waxman's.

There was a mob of reporters outside Waxman's office.

"Give out," begged Lou Byrd of the *Globe*. Like the others, he was too desperate to rib me about my stolen car. "That bird-brained boss of yours won't give us a line, and this case is the hottest thing in years. A lawyer getting bumped is something that happens seldom."

"Too seldom," I said, and shrugged my way through them. Waxman's reception room was deserted save for a patrolman posted at the door, but his private office was so packed that there was hardly room for the corpse.

It was an all-out case. Dain Carrothers, Homicide's smartest cop, had a whole army at work. They milled over Waxman's body like a gang of females over a new baby. The body lay on its face in front of the safe, the door of which was closed. The arms were flung out, and there was an ugly slit in the back of the coat. There was no doubt about how the job had been accomplished—Shorty had been done in with a shiv.

"Well, thanks for coming around!"

I turned to face Keever. He spoke from across the room, where he was buttonholing an old guy in an elevator starter's gold braid. He beckoned me over.

"This is Corwin, the starter. He saw everybody who came into the building. You may be interested to know that he has identified this man as a visitor."

Keever exhibited a rogue's gallery set, complete with fingerprints and profile and full-face photos of Sam Peterson. I asked Corwin: "When was he here?"

"He came into the building at about a quarter to twelve. About fifteen minutes after that Mr. Waxman arrived. Then, about twenty minutes passed, and this man left the building."

Keever looked me up and down. His eyes were accusing slits. "I hope you're satisfied, Ben. When you let Peterson escape you cost a human life—the life of my colleague and a member of the bar!"

I laughed in Keever's face, and he reddened, for he knew why I laughed. During Waxman's lifetime, he had called him every kind of shyster that ever breathed, denouncing him on more than one occasion to the grievance committee of the Bar Association. But now that Shorty had passed out of this world, Keever would probably show up at the Bar Association meeting to read his eulogy. Among lawyers the only good lawyer is a dead one.

"Your theory of this case interests me," I told Keever. "What if Peterson did show up here? Wasn't it natural for him to come running to his lawyer? Waxman defended him before—he must have wanted to hire him again."

"Hire him, my eye! He didn't want to hire Waxman; he wanted revenge! He guessed that Waxman had spilled the beans about those three raps out West. He was positive it was Waxman, for his own lawyer was the only person he had told. That takes care of the motive angle. And when we nail Peterson, we'll take care of him!"

I remembered Peterson's threat with regard to the man who had turned him in. He had said: "If I ever get my hands on the guy . . ." And I had to admit that this time Keever's theory made sense. It was logical that Peterson had told his whole record to his lawyer, that Waxman would be the first and probably only man he would suspect. I nodded toward the corpse.

"Where's the shiv?"

"A fingerprint man's got it—took it over to the lab. It was a paper knife from Waxman's own desk. One of those things the patent lawyers send out."

"How about the safe? Was it opened?"

"It's locked, but that doesn't mean anything. Waxman could have had it open, and Peterson could have locked it after he knifed him."

"Haven't you checked the contents?"

"We're waiting for Waxman's secretary. She probably has the combination."

I looked at my watch. It was one-twenty. I looked at Keever. He rolled his eyes. A couple of minutes later, when Waxman's secretary sauntered in, I caught on. When they're built like that they rate two hours for lunch in any man's office.

Her name was Mickey O'Hara—she lived at 1109 West Crawford, and she immediately stole the show from everyone including Waxman. The entire Homicide detail promptly forgot the existence of a corpse as they began drooling over Miss O'Hara in the pretense of acting in the line of duty. But Keever, as usual, was equal to the occasion. He grabbed her by the elbow and took her into the library. I thought he needed help, so I trailed along.

She didn't know anything, including the combination of the safe. She had left for lunch at eleven-thirty and had missed Peterson.

"I just can't understand who could do such a thing to Mr. Waxman!" she cooed. "He was so nice—such a perfect gentleman."

She crossed her legs and exhibited hosiery that sells for half a secretary's salary. Appreciating the hosiery, Keever furrowed his brows in a shrewd manner and asked: "Then Waxman had no enemies?"

I laughed impolitely. "He was a lawyer, wasn't he?"

Keever reddened. "Ben, I've learned to overlook your not very subtle sarcasm. You are no doubt referring to the fact that lawyers, who of necessity handle the troubles of others, accumulate the enemies of others. But such enemies rarely murder. If they did there wouldn't be enough lawyers left to—to—"

"To fill an ambulance!" I cracked. Keever looked apologetically to Mickey O'Hara.

"You're sure then that Mr. Waxman hadn't received any threats of any kind?"

"Yes, Mr. Keever, I'm sure he hadn't."

It went on for about fifteen minutes, and I decided Keever was prolonging the interview only because he appreciated Miss O'Hara's hosiery. I liked it, too, but I still had a mild curiosity about who killed Waxman. I walked out of the library.

"You'll have to hire a locksmith," I told Carrothers. "The Petty girl doesn't know the combination."

"We may find it somewhere," Carrothers said hopefully.

I shook my head. "Five will get you ten that you don't." I went out.

he elevators were close by, but I used the stairway at the back of the building. I walked down two flights and found Jimmie Harmon's office. His secretary informed me that he was in but very, very busy.

"I'm the law," I said, showing my badge. "I think he'll see me."

He did. He came to the door and ushered me inside in a very cordial way. He even flattered me by remembering my name, though I had hardly more than met him at the time of Peterson's trial. He seemed a nice enough guy in spite of the million bucks he and his sister had inherited from James D. Harmon Sr., who had made his dough in the real estate business. This had been the old man's office. Jimmie pretended to be following in his father's footsteps, but he used the place mainly to recuperate from hangovers. As for selling real estate, he couldn't have sold a hideout to Hitler.

"I thought you'd like to know," I opened, "that I went out and picked up Peterson. He'll be on ice for a nice long time."

Harmon gave me a startled, then quizzical look.

"It's all right," I assured him. "Keever told me all about it."

Harmon looked a little hurt. "Damn it! I told Keever not to tell *anyone*."

I smiled. "But I'm his right-hand man. It was natural for him to tell me who'd tipped him to Peterson's record."

"I suppose it was." Harmon was studying me. "You didn't come here just to tell me you'd nailed Peterson."

"No, I didn't. I thought you'd like to know that Peterson got away. He's still at large."

Harmon got up and began to pace back and forth behind his desk.

"Thanks, Corbett. I appreciate your warning me. But I'm sure Peterson will never guess that I turned him in. Unless, of course, Keever's really started broadcasting it." He looked alarmed. "Do you think Keever's told anyone else besides you?"

"I'm sure he hasn't. Besides, it looks as if you're quite safe. There's a pretty generally accepted theory that Peterson put the blame on his lawyer. Anyway, Shorty Waxman's up in his office dead, and Peterson's been identified as a visitor. When they catch him a life stretch will be the least of his worries."

Harmon had stopped short.

"Waxman dead! Do you really think Peterson—"

"Maybe. By the way, do you have an alibi for this noon?"

"Me? Are you crazy? You can't—" Harmon glared. "But of course, you can! You cops can suspect anybody, for any reason, no matter how trivial. I suppose you think I might have murdered him merely because he tried to make a monkey out of me during Peterson's trial."

I had to laugh at the memory of it. Waxman hadn't merely tried to make a monkey out of Harmon—he couldn't have succeeded much better if he had had Harmon scratching for lice. Waxman had gone into the matter of this phony real estate layout, and a jury consisting of working folk had laughed their glee. But Waxman's jibes hadn't helped Peterson.

"I was just kidding about your alibi," I told Harmon, to cover up my laughter. "Of course we don't suspect you of bumping Waxman. You had no motive whatever. And the fact that your office is in the same building doesn't mean anything either. By the way, I'm curious about how you tumbled to Peterson's record. That's something Keever didn't tell me."

"That's because I didn't tell him," Harmon said sullenly. "I don't see that it makes any difference how I got the information, so long as it was right."

"Right. Well, I'll be getting along."

Harmon looked agitated as I left. I went back upstairs and found that even Keever had had enough of the eye-filling O'Hara and had sent her home.

"I don't know that there's anything to do," he was telling Carrothers, "until Peterson's picked up." He cast a side look in my direction. "If he'd never got away, this wouldn't have happened."

Pretending not to hear, I said: "I'm driving back to the office. Want to come with me?"

"Driving? You mean they've found your car?"

"No. I found it myself. Peterson didn't get very far."

"Where did he—"

"I'll tell you about it sometime. Are you coming with me?"

"No. I drove my own car."

The parking lot at the Criminal Courts Building was in back, and I entered by the back entrance. A figure startled me as it detached itself from a shadow.

"Hello, Mr. Corbett."

It was Peterson.

"Well, well. Fancy meeting you here."

"I'm giving myself up. I've been waiting to see you. I wanted you to be the one to turn me in. I hate it about that break. I hope you won't do anything to my mother. She didn't know what she was doing."

"Forget it. I forgot to tell Keever about her, anyway."

Peterson's eyes brightened.

"Thanks a million! When the radio news didn't mention her, I wondered if you'd left her out of it. But I didn't dare hope."

"Well, let's get going."

I walked down the gloomy corridor beside Peterson. I asked casually: "Did you have a nice talk with Waxman?"

Peterson started. "How did you know about that?"

"Well, you left my car right outside his office building."

"I did at that. I guess it doesn't make any difference whether you know about my seeing Waxman. I did see him. He told me to turn myself in."

"Oh, he did, did he? I suppose he told you he could beat the rap, that he'd take your case?"

"He told me to keep my mouth shut."

"It was pretty good advice. I'll have to warn you that anything you may say will be held against you."

"I don't get it."

"Waxman's dead."

Peterson stopped short. He was pale.

"Murdered?" I nodded. He started on again with exaggerated casualness: "Well, that makes me no difference. Nobody can hang that one on me."

This time I stopped. "Look here, Peterson, you're very inconsistent. A moment ago you indicated that Waxman was taking your case. It was plain from your manner that you had high hopes he would beat it for you, that Waxman was indeed your lifesaver. Now you're very indifferent about his murder. His murder means he wouldn't be in there to beat that habitual criminal charge for you. So either you're lying about Waxman helping you or you're lying about his death making no difference. Which is it?"

Peterson eyed me coolly. "I'm taking Waxman's advice. I'm keeping my mouth shut."

We were within ten feet of the elevator bank, and plenty of cops were coming in and out. They all knew about Peterson, but they never dreamed he could be the man talking with me. I took Peterson's arm and stopped him.

"You're not being very bright about this thing. I heard you make a threat about getting your hands on the guy who turned you in. It might interest you to know that the D.A. has a theory you did get your hands on the guy— Waxman."

Peterson made a wry face. "Then he's nuts; Waxman never turned me in."

"But he did know about your record?"

"Of course. I leveled with him. And he's always played straight with me." An idea came to Peterson. "Besides, why should he turn me in when he'd never been paid for defending me in that last case? I'd just started to pay him every week out of my wages. Going up for life would mean I'd never pay him another dime."

"So he took your case that other time without advance payment? That's not like Waxman. He always has to have it on the line."

"Well, he went to bat for me. I didn't have a dime, and he knew it. Even the money I'd stolen from Harmon's safe—he made me turn that over to him so he could turn it in. He did that. Every cent of it. And the other paper, too."

"What other paper? You weren't charged with stealing anything but the money."

"Oh, the other paper didn't amount to anything. Waxman said he'd give it back to Harmon personally. It was Harmon's will. I guess Waxman thought he wouldn't want it aired in public. It wasn't worth anything to anybody but Harmon, and he could easily have made a new one if he never got it back."

"That's very interesting. I'm sure even Keever didn't know about that angle. You didn't happen to read the will?"

Peterson looked a little shamefaced. "As a matter of fact I did. It was short. Harmon just left everything to Louise."

Louise was Harmon's sister. I regarded Peterson curiously. "Why in the world did you steal a will?"

"I didn't know it was a will. It was in an envelope, like the money. I just grabbed both envelopes and ran when I heard someone coming."

That sounded plausible. A servant had surprised Peterson at his thievery and he had fled in haste, but not effectively enough to prevent his identification.

"Well, if Waxman didn't turn you in, who did?"

"You're asking me!" Peterson's manner changed. He regarded me hostilely. "I don't like it a bit. You know damned well it wasn't Wax-man, yet you're trying to make out that I killed him for revenge."

"All right, granting that Waxman wasn't the one who turned you in, you had no way of knowing that. He would be the logical man for you to suspect. Right now you can't think of anyone else who could have turned you in!"

Peterson's face flushed. I was right. He couldn't think of anyone else. He muttered: "Damn you! You made me talk! From now on I'm keeping my mouth shut!"

And he did. Keever conducted a cross-examination that lasted till five in the afternoon. By that time he was trembling with anger. His face stayed red five minutes after Peterson had been taken away.

"The rat!" he growled. "He got Waxman all right! It couldn't have been anybody else. He killed Waxman because he thought Waxman squealed on him."

"You seem pretty sure. By the way, was it Waxman?"

"The rat!" Keever muttered. "Well, I'll break him down tomorrow if I have to grill him all day!"

CHAPTER THREE
PICTURES CAN LIE

So Keever was holding out on me, as usual. He meant to let me think that Waxman had turned in Peterson's record. He would probably let the jury think that, too, for it would point the finger of guilt more steadily at Peterson. Don't misunderstand Keever—he wasn't trying to railroad the youth. But years in the D.A.'s office had slightly warped his sense of ethics. He had fought so many legal battles with unscrupulous shysters like the late Shorty Waxman that he had himself picked up a few low punches.

He was morally certain that Peterson was guilty of Waxman's murder, and he meant to convict him by any means, fair or foul. But I couldn't quite accept the case as open and shut. There was something rank in Rotterdam, my nose told me, and I wanted to find out what it was. I lingered in the office long enough to phone Homicide and learn that there had been no prints on the knife that had stabbed Waxman. I hadn't hoped there would be. I got my car and headed out to Riverside Road.

Riverside Road is the swank highway that runs along the Silver River bank north of town. Everybody who is anybody has a big estate up there, and Old Man Harmon had been somebody. The Harmon place was one of the biggest. It was here that Jimmie Harmon and his sister, Louise, had lived since their father's death. No will had turned up, so the pair had inherited the place equally as heirs at law.

It was the wall safe in the wing occupied by Jimmie that Peterson had broken into. Peterson's job as gardener there had been full-time, but he had lived at his mother's apartment, commuting in an old flivver. Turning into the drive, I could easily see why it had been necessary to have a full-time man. The grounds were really magnificent. The house was something, too—not quite a mansion but almost large enough.

A maid answered my ring. I flashed my badge.

"I'm from the D.A.'s office. I want to see Miss Harmon."

A little gleam of satisfaction came into the maid's eyes. Evidently she enjoyed a hope that her mistress was in trouble. She let me in and went eagerly to report my visit. But I had to wait ten minutes before Louise Harmon showed up.

"I'm sorry. I was finishing dressing."

"That's all right. It was worth waiting for."

It was. This Harmon was a sloe-eyed brunette with a milky-white complexion that rocked you on your heels. It was plain she had devoted a lot of time to making the best of her natural assets—those last ten minutes had been well spent.

I introduced myself and said: "I'm just doing a little informal checking up. Please don't get excited about it. I only want to have your corroboration of your brother's statement that you were with him at the time of Shorty Waxman's murder."

Louise Harmon didn't look at all as if she intended to get excited. She looked at me as if trying to decide whether I had all my marbles.

"I don't understand. Why would my brother need an alibi for Waxman's murder? He certainly couldn't have had any reason to kill Waxman!"

I said lamely: "He couldn't have had any love for Waxman after the way Waxman treated him at Peterson's trial."

Louise Harmon now eyed me as if she had made up her mind about whether I had all my marbles. Her decision was plainly in the negative.

"Don't be absurd."

"Well, you haven't answered my question. Were you with Jimmie this noon?"

"No, and you know I wasn't. He never told you that I was."

"All right, if you weren't with Jimmie, will you tell me where you were then?"

Louise Harmon's eyes widened. For a split second they became angry; then they mocked me. "So I'm a suspect! Well, this is precious—little Louise has finally amounted to something! A murder suspect at last after twenty-two years of a drab, dreary existence! Are you going to take me down to headquarters for a third degree?"

"I hope not. It'll help if you just tell me where you were."

Her eyes gleamed with mock mystery.

"Everything's against me. I was in the Mercury Tower at noon! I can't deny it—the elevator starter would remember me. It's the curse of being so beautiful that every old man ogles you. Little did I dream—well, to go on with my confession, I dropped in to see Jimmie. He wasn't there. His office was deserted, and I waited maybe ten minutes in his reception room. Then I went out for lunch."

"So you don't have any alibi for ten minutes?"

Louise Harmon hung her head.

"No! It *was* careless of me, but then I didn't know that Shorty Waxman was being murdered!"

She laughed in my face. My face was very red. Then I heard a noise and turned. Keever had come into the room. I recalled Louise Harmon's ten-minute delay. So she had called my boss.

"What's going on here, Ben?" Keever's face was like a thundercloud.

Louise Harmon answered for me: "Oh, we're having a wonderful time! Isn't it marvelous— I'm getting the third degree as a suspect in the Waxman murder case!"

Keever slowly faced me. "Go outside, Ben. Wait for me. I'll be with you in a minute."

I went outside. I leaned dejectedly on a fender of my car and lighted a cigarette. I wasn't half finished with it when Keever appeared. He hadn't cooled off a bit.

"A fine spot you put me in! I had to apologize all over the place. Imagine treating Louise Harmon as a murder suspect!"

"I didn't. That was her idea. I was merely curious as to where her brother had been while Waxman was getting himself murdered. I found out one thing, at least. Harmon wasn't in his office—his sister just told me so."

Keever started to speak, then eyed me carefully. His anger subsided in favor of curiosity.

"Come on, Ben, give out. Why are you pointing your finger at Harmon?"

"Well, there was a will. It was in the safe Peterson robbed. Peterson says it was Harmon's will, and he gave everything to Louise. Somehow the will was never mentioned at the trial. Jimmie Harmon said nothing about it being stolen, and Peterson says he turned it over to Waxman. Supposing Waxman decided not to give Harmon the will. Maybe Harmon wanted it bad enough to kill him for it."

Keever looked at me with horror.

"I never dreamed it! I never dreamed that anyone could be so ignorant of the law! Evidently you think that Harmon had to get his old

will back and destroy it before he could make a new one! Why, all he would have to do to revoke the will would be to make a new one!"

"Well, I'm not a lawyer."

"And you're a hell of a detective! What's the idea of holding out this long about that will? Try to remember that you're working for me. Instead of running around in circles and trying to crack this case on your own, I want you to get Waxman's secretary, the O'Hara girl, and bring her to Waxman's office by eight. A locksmith's going to try to open that safe this evening, and Waxman's secretary should know something about the contents."

It was one detail I could accept without urging. I had been careful to jot down Mickey O'Hara's address, but I hadn't hoped to be able to use it so soon. Her place turned out to be the first floor of a duplex. When she came to the door and saw me she seemed a little disappointed.

"Oh, it's Mr. Corbett! I wasn't expecting you. Is your visit official?"

"Only if you want it to be. I'm to take you to Waxman's office, and I thought you might like to have dinner first."

I could see that she wasn't crazy about the idea, but she said: "Why, that would be lovely. I'll only take a minute."

Her place was furnished modestly enough. I dropped into a lounge chair and surveyed things casually. My gaze halted at a silver picture frame. It contained the smiling likeness of Jimmie Harmon. It was a good photo, but it had been mounted in such a way that the face bulged and looked a little bloated.

I averted my gaze from the photo as Mickey O'Hara appeared, but she gave the photo a sharp look, realizing I couldn't have missed it.

"So you and Jimmie are that way?" I ventured, when we had driven a block from the duplex. Mickey O'Hara gave a nervous little laugh.

"I consider Jimmie a very good friend, that's all. We used to bump into each other in the elevator and got to having lunch together. As for Jimmie being 'that way,' I don't have to tell you about his reputation as a bite-and-run wolf."

I let it go at that. I drove across town, out on

Broad and pulled up at the Arabian Grill. It's an expensive joint that I seldom patronize, for an obvious reason. But I had good cause for selecting it now.

"You'll have to run along and order for both of us while I go down the street and get a check cashed. They don't know me in there."

I waited till she had gone inside, then turned around and drove back to the duplex. Picking its lock took only a minute, and once inside I didn't bother to turn on the lights, for I knew where to go. I crossed the room to the silver picture frame and pried off its heavy cardboard back. The back and picture fell free to expose a folded paper between. I got out a pocket flash and scrutinized the paper.

It was the Harmon will. I read it through. It was a homemade job, all right, written by a guy who thought anyone can write his own will. I know better. I've whiled away quite a bit of time in Keever's office over a book on wills, and I know they're tricky things. A lot of people so hate to give a lawyer five dollars that they write their own wills, and after they're dead their crude mistakes cause long-winded lawsuits that result in the lawyers getting all of their estates.

I put out my flash, folded up the will and started for the door. Then I went out like a light. I knew when I came around that I'd taken a perfect rabbit punch. I got up off the floor and fell down again. The next time I stayed up, but I knew I was going to be sick. I went into the bathroom and got it over with. Then I went back into the room. The will was gone. I didn't waste time looking for it. My watch said eight-thirty. I went out to my car and drove to the Mercury Tower.

here was one of Carrothers' men at the door. He looked at me pityingly as he let me in.

"I'm sure glad I'm not in your shoes! Keever's layin' for you with a meat-axe!"

I couldn't think of a single cute thing to say. The night man took me to Waxman's floor. The first face I saw when I opened his office door was Sam Peterson's. He was flanked by two headquarters men, and Carrothers himself sat close by. But Peterson looked strangely at ease in contrast to the others in the room.

There was quite a gathering. Her silken knees crossed, Mickey O'Hara knifed me a look from a chair in a corner. Jimmie Harmon adjoined her. It was something of a shock to discover his sister seated on the opposite side of the room. Louise Harmon apparently had been in conversation with Keever, who stood beside her. His face got red the moment he saw me.

"So you've finally shown up!" he raged. "Pardon my curiosity, but would you mind telling me why it is that when I send you out to do even the simplest thing, you muff the job?"

"He was trying to cash a check," Mickey O'Hara said icily. "I hope you succeeded, brother, 'cause you owe me three dollars for the steak I ordered for you. Whether you have the chivalry to pay for the one I ate is purely speculative."

Somewhat grandly I paid up. But that didn't satisfy Keever.

"Well, what have you got to say for yourself?"

"Nothing. Anything I said would be used against me." I was busy trying to figure out Keever's angle in having Jimmie and Louise Harmon and Peterson here. What was up Keever's sleeve? "The safe," I said, "has it been opened yet?"

Keever shook his head.

"But it soon will be. We've got a good man in there." He indicated the inner office. "He's been at it since seven. He should be through any minute now."

Keever did have something up his sleeve, all right—plenty. Otherwise he wouldn't have left off riding me about my unexplained absence. I was glad to let it go at that, and for about ten minutes we all waited in uncomfortable silence. Most uncomfortable of all was Jimmie Harmon. He sat fidgeting, mopping his moistening temples from time to time. He started half out of his chair when the door suddenly opened, and a bald little guy stuck his face through.

"All set, Mr. Keever."

I knew the locksmith, Clyde Altman. He was a skilled man, trusted by the police, but Keever had seen to it that a headquarters man had been on the job while Altman had worked.

"Has anything been touched?" Keever questioned the man, as we filed into the inner room.

"Not a thing, sir. The strongbox door's been opened—that's the only thing that's been done to the inside."

We formed a semi-circle in front of the safe at a respectful distance. Keever, wasting no time with the stuff in the pigeonholes, removed the strongbox drawer at once. His eyes lighted as he saw the paper on top. He snatched it up, unfolded it and gave it a rapid inspection. There was triumph in his eyes as he turned mysteriously to Louise Harmon.

"Miss Harmon, will you please look at this signature?"

Keever exhibited the paper. The girl's eyes widened.

"Why—why, it's Dad's signature! What is this paper?"

"It's a will, Miss Harmon, your father's will. And now, Peterson, come over here and look carefully. Did you ever see this paper before?"

Peterson came forward and scanned the paper with growing astonishment.

"Yes, I saw it once. It's the will that I stole out of Jimmie Harmon's safe!"

"Exactly!" Keever's eyes flashed with triumph as they fixed their gaze upon Jimmie Harmon. The boy had lost all color. Satisfied, Keever turned to me. "You didn't realize it, Ben, but this afternoon you gave me the information that enabled me to crack this case. When you told me that Peterson had stolen a will and that it left the entire estate to Louise Harmon, you unwittingly supplied the key to the entire case.

"You see, it wasn't Jimmie Harmon's will that was stolen. Peterson thought so because it was in Jimmie's safe and because he was misled by the signature. As Miss Harmon has just stated, the signature was actually her father's— his name is the same as Jimmie's. It wasn't Jim-

mie who was leaving everything to his sister—it was James D. Harmon Sr. In his father's will, Jimmie was completely disinherited."

CHAPTER FOUR
THE REAL MCCOY

 eever's words seemed to echo in the still room. Suddenly he whirled again upon Jimmie Harmon.

"Do you dare deny it?" he barked.

The youth admitted hollowly: "It's Dad's will, all right. I found it after his death and hid it in my safe."

Louise Harmon gave a startled gasp.

"Jimmie! How could you do such a thing?"

Jimmie Harmon lost his hangdog look as anger reddened his face.

"Wipe that look of righteous indignation off your face! I wasn't doing anything you wouldn't have done! What you did was worse—you sold Dad the idea I was a spendthrift playboy who couldn't look out for himself. If only Dad would leave everything to you, you'd take care of me. Yes, you would! You'd have doled out a nickel at a time and made me crawl for it! When I hid that will, I was only protecting my rightful property!"

"And you were doing the same thing when you killed Shorty Waxman!"

Everybody subsided at Keever's accusation. Keever pressed home the advantage his shock had given.

"You killed Waxman because he had the will and because he had been blackmailing you! Though Peterson failed to understand the significance of the will, thinking it was your own, Waxman knew better. That's why he took Peterson's case, though Peterson didn't have any money to pay him. He knew he could collect plenty by threatening you with exposure. But he didn't know you'd get so desperate that you'd kill him! And you did kill him, didn't you?"

Keever had his long forefinger under Jimmie Harmon's nose now, and Harmon slapped it away with a sharpness that made Keever wince.

"Damn you, no! Sure, Waxman was blackmailing me. The dirty skunk started it even before Peterson's trial. He insisted that Peterson knew nothing about it, that only he knew the truth about the will. I paid and paid. I might have dropped the prosecution against Peterson if I hadn't been sore about the hell he had caused me. That's why I turned in his penitentiary record. Last Saturday afternoon I got half soused and spilled the beans to you. It wasn't very bright, but then I felt I had to take it out on somebody—I couldn't touch Waxman."

"But you did, Jimmie, this noon! You touched him deeply—with a knife! You killed him because his relentless blackmailing had made you desperate! You can't look me in the eye and deny it!"

Something inside Jimmie Harmon seemed to snap. Before Keever could dodge, Harmon had landed a solid punch on his jaw. Keever reeled and would have gone down if Carrothers hadn't caught him. Shaking with anger, he roared: "See? See, what he did—it all goes to show how he resorts to violence when cornered! I'm warning you, Harmon, that anything you say will be held against you!"

I took a deep breath.

"Might I say a word?"

Keever growled: "Well, Ben, what is it?"

I took another deep breath.

"I don't want to upset your little playhouse, but I think you ought to know that this will hasn't been locked in the safe since Waxman's murder. It was planted there. I happen to know because a couple of hours ago I saw it in Mickey O'Hara's apartment. It was hidden back of her photo of Jimmie Harmon. I'd just removed it when I got conked. I passed out cold—that explains why I didn't show up with Miss O'Hara as scheduled."

Keever's jaw hung open.

"Ben, are you sure about that? Are you sure this will was at Mickey O'Hara's apartment?"

"Positively. I read the whole will by my flashlight."

Keever looked lost. He turned slowly to face Mickey O'Hara.

"Is this true?"

Jimmie Harmon stepped forward, firmly grasping Mickey O'Hara's arm.

"Just a moment, Keever. Supposing Mickey did have the will and did conceal it the same as I did. I believe that the concealment of a will is a criminal offense. If she admitted that she had it, would she be laying herself open to a criminal charge?"

Keever nodded reluctantly. "That's right. Miss O'Hara, I'll have to warn you that your answer may be held against you."

Mickey O'Hara replied coolly and without hesitation: "This detective is right—the will was at my place, hidden in a picture frame. A short time after I met Jimmie he told me about the jam he was in and asked me to help him. I didn't have any trouble going through the files of the Peterson case—that's how I was able to find out about Peterson's criminal record and turn it over to Jimmie. It took me longer to find an occasion when the safe was unlocked and get into the strongbox. But I did find the opportunity, and I've had the will for a couple of weeks."

Jimmie Harmon's eyes widened as they stared.

"Why, Mickey—why didn't you tell me you had it?"

"Because I love you, you wolf! Your only interest in me was to get me to help you recover that will. Once I'd delivered it, you'd have dropped me like a hot potato. So long as I had the will, I had you."

"But, Mickey, I wouldn't have—"

"That doesn't change anything," Keever interrupted Harmon. "The fact that Miss O'Hara had the will doesn't alter the fact that you thought Waxman had it. Your motive remains as strong as ever."

I indulged in another deep breath.

"But that doesn't explain why Harmon would slug me to get the will and plant it in this safe where it was bound to be found! You've just heard him confess that he had concealed it and paid blackmail to prevent its exposure."

Keever had no comeback for that one. I pressed my advantage.

"The person who planted that will wanted it to be found, wanted it to be exposed. That person had the most to be gained from the will's exposure. It was that person that Waxman phoned this noon just before he left Mike's restaurant. He—"

"What phone call?" Keever demanded. "You said nothing about seeing Waxman at Mike's! Why are you always holding out on me?"

I shrugged.

"I didn't think it was important at the time. Now I realize what upset Waxman when I told him Peterson had been picked up on the Habitual Criminal Act. He guessed that Harmon had turned him in, and that showed him Harmon was getting too desperate to be blackmailed. It was time to make a deal with the one person who had most to benefit by the exposure of the will. So he called that person and made a noon appointment at his office.

"Waxman quickly made a deal with his visitor, selling the will for a cash price. But when he went to his safe and opened it, he found that the will was missing. It was never like Waxman to give up any money once he had his hands on it. He stalled. But the purchaser of the will suspected trickery, was angered into murderous fury. A paper knife was convenient. You can guess the rest.

"Later the murderer, aware of the romantic connection between Jimmie Harmon and Waxman's secretary, guessed that the girl might have got the will from Waxman's safe and might have it in her possession. So the murderer went to the girl's apartment, found that I had discovered the will, slugged me and took it from me. Then the murderer, who had memorized the combination of Waxman's safe, came here and planted the will where it would be found."

I paused. Keever had listened intently. Now he said: "But whoever planted that will had to have a key to the building and a key to Waxman's office."

I regarded Louise Harmon.

"Miss Harmon, do you have a key to this building?"

The girl was pale.

"Yes. Father gave me one several years ago. His office is now Jimmie's. I still have the key."

"And you admit that you visited the building this noon?"

"Of course. I told you that when you called this afternoon."

"But there was nobody here to corroborate your alibi?"

"No. I also told you that Jimmie wasn't here; nobody was here but me."

I turned to Keever.

"There you are. Getting a key to Waxman's office wouldn't be such a hard stunt for the murderer. It might have been taken from Waxman's pocket, or one might have been loose around Mickey O'Hara's place."

Keever had been staring incredulously at Louise Harmon. Slowly he turned to me.

"Then you think the murderer is Louise? She's the only one to gain from the exposure of the will."

"No, Burt, you're wrong. You glanced at the beginning of the will, the part that left everything to Louise outright. Read the last paragraph. It's a little vague, but the meaning is clear. Old Man Harmon knew how he wanted to leave his estate, all right. He meant that Louise should have it all but should pay out to Jimmie whatever he actually needed.

"But he didn't know how to say it. When he got through pecking out his homemade will on his typewriter, he had left everything to Louise but *in trust* for Jimmie! When Jimmie discovered the will after his father's death he didn't understand it any better than his father had, and he was afraid to go to a lawyer.

"So he hid the will in his safe. Peterson stole it, failed to realize that it was the old man's will and turned it over to Waxman, who understood it at a glance. Then Waxman contacted Jimmie and explained that the will really made him the sole beneficiary of his father's estate, that all Louise could ever get out of it was a nominal fee for administering the trust.

"Waxman had Jimmie over a barrel. Jimmie had concealed the existence of the will—he couldn't prove its existence now unless Waxman turned it over. Waxman held out for a price. Jimmie refused to meet it. They haggled for a year, Jimmie finally using Mickey O'Hara in an attempt to get his fingers on the precious paper. In a fit of meanness, he exposed Peterson's criminal record, and that scared Waxman. He knew that he was dealing with a desperate man. He phoned Jimmie, and they got together on a price. When they met in Waxman's office, and he couldn't produce the will, Jimmie blew his top and knifed Waxman to death."

Keever had been reading the last paragraph of the will as he listened. Now he stared at Jimmie Harmon.

"You really had it figured out, didn't you? By planting this will in the safe you made yourself seem the least likely suspect. Who would accuse you of doing the planting when you thought exposure of the will completely disinherited you?"

"Nobody," Jimmie Harmon answered promptly. "And nobody will ever believe I planted it there. For, in spite of your stooge's beautiful theory, it's nothing but a theory. You've got nothing against me but circumstantial evidence."

He calmly lighted a cigarette and blew the smoke into Keever's face. Mickey O'Hara had stood loyally by him until now, but she edged away. The revulsion she felt was shared by the rest of us, but we knew the truth was reflected in Keever's face. He and the rest of us knew that

Harmon's taunt was painfully true—we had nothing but a theory.

I faced Keever.

"I think it's time I should tell you that I've been holding out again. My theory didn't just come out of my head. I had something concrete to go on. When I got conked tonight I got a glimpse of the guy that conked me just before I passed out. It was Harmon. I guess there's something more than circumstantial about that."

Harmon whirled upon me. "You're a damned liar! You went out like a light!"

I grinned in his face. He started, saw that his slip was fatal. He wheeled, ran toward the door. Sam Peterson casually thrust out his foot. Harmon tripped and fell sprawling. The two headquarters men dragged Harmon ignominiously to his feet. He was blubbering as they took him out.

"So you held out on me again?" said Keever. "How am I going to cure you?"

"You don't have to. I didn't hold out this time. Harmon was right—I'm a damned liar. I passed out like a light."

Keever shook his head. He smiled at Louise Harmon, who looked stunned.

"Don't feel so badly about it. Your brother will get off with life—his murder of Waxman was only second degree because it was not premeditated but done in anger. As for the will, I must say that Waxman was really trying to make a sucker out of your brother. It isn't any will at all. Evidently your father didn't know he was supposed to have witnesses to his signature. Anyway, there are none, so you'll each get half of your father's estate, though Jimmie won't get much of a chance to spend his share unless he spends it on lawyers."

Louise Harmon didn't seem at all relieved. She looked first at Mickey O'Hara, who was quietly sobbing, then at Peterson. She turned to Keever.

"Must this man be prosecuted? Will he have to go to the penitentiary for life?"

Keever hesitated. Peterson spoke up.

"Thanks for your sympathy, Miss Harmon, but I don't need it. You see, I had quite a talk with Mr. Waxman before he was murdered. He told me something about my trial for the robbery of your brother's safe. I was tried both for breaking and entering and grand larceny, but when the jury returned a verdict of 'guilty as charged in the indictment,' they didn't specify which offense I was guilty of. Mr. Waxman said that though grand larceny is an offense listed in the Habitual Criminal Act, breaking and entering isn't. He says the jury's verdict would have to be strictly construed in my favor, so I'd be shown to be guilty only of breaking and entering, which isn't a crime in the eyes of the Habitual Criminal Act. Is that the McCoy, Mr. Keever?"

"That," said Keever, "is the McCoy."

Murder in One Syllable
John D. MacDonald

JOHN D(ANN) MACDONALD (1916–1986) was born in Sharon, Pennsyl-
vania, moved to Utica, New York, received a B.S. from Syracuse University,
then an M.B.A. from Harvard. He worked as a businessman without much success, then joined the army, serving from 1940 to 1946, achieving the rank of lieutenant colonel in the OSS. When he returned to the United States, he began to
write full-time, selling sports, adventure, fantasy, science fiction, and mystery
stories to pulp magazines and such slicks as *Liberty, Cosmopolitan,* and *Collier's.*
His 1949 move to Florida gave him access to the water and boating, which served
as the background for many of his novels, notably those about Travis McGee,
who lives on a houseboat named *The Busted Flush,* which he won in a poker
game. One of the great characters of mystery fiction, McGee is a combination
private detective and thief who makes his living by recovering stolen property
and, while living outside the law, victimizes only criminals. He is not a private
eye in the Raymond Chandler sense of being a knight, though he fills that role
more often than not as an avenger, coming to the aid of (invariably) beautiful
women who fall for the rugged outdoorsman. There are nineteen McGee novels, mostly paperback originals, beginning with *The Deep Blue Good-by* (1964).
His suspense novel *The Executioners* (1958) was filmed twice as *Cape Fear* (in
1962, with Gregory Peck, Robert Mitchum, and Polly Bergen, and in 1991, with
Nick Nolte, Robert De Niro, Jessica Lange, and Juliette Lewis).

"Murder in One Syllable" was published in the May 1949 issue.

Murder in One Syllable

John D. MacDonald

STARTLING MYSTERY-ACTION NOVELETTE

Bullets for breakfast were on the menu for thrill-hungry
Cynthia Darrold—when she picked up the right guy in the wrong tavern.

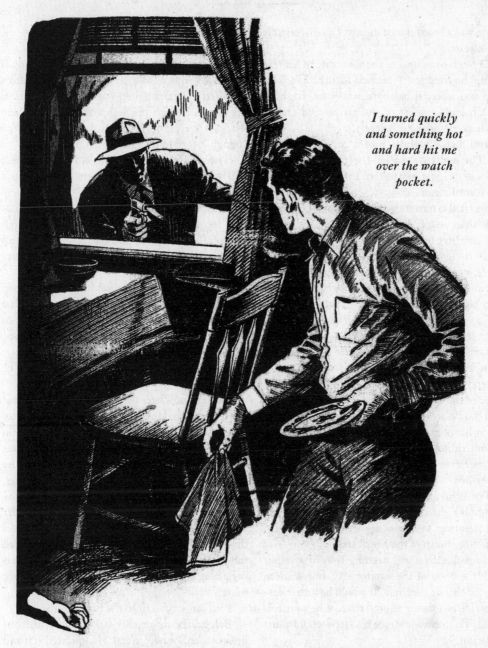

I turned quickly and something hot and hard hit me over the watch pocket.

CHAPTER ONE
PAUL JANUARY

IN CHILDHOOD THERE HAD BEEN A sentence, a trick sentence, to punctuate. That that is is that that is not is not that that is. "That that is, is." The sodden handkerchief, growing crusty furthest from the wound, was an actuality. It was wedged under his belt, just above the watch pocket of his gunmetal gabardine slacks.

Nor could the existence of a small bit of lead be denied, though its presence within him was more the result of circumstantial reasoning.

There was a hole for entrance, yet no discernable hole of exit.

Though conscious of the absurdity of his reasoning, he tried to tell himself that the handkerchief was where it belonged, crisp and fresh, in the left-hand pocket of his rayon cord jacket. Not tucked under his belt at all.

And that, of course, meant corollary reasoning. The bullet was still in the gun. Possibly the gun was still in a pawnshop. It had looked to be that sort of a gun.

And it also meant that the girl was somewhere other than on her back in the cerise and white kitchen where he had left her, with a bullet in her head.

He swallowed hard and wondered whether his nausea came from the memory of the girl, or from his own weakness.

The sun was very warm and it was remarkably difficult to walk, as though there was no hole in the taut belly muscles just over the watch pocket, no sticky handkerchief balled and wedged under the gray and white belt against the white mesh fabric of the shirt.

It was easier to think that the handkerchief was in his pocket, the bullet still in the gun, the girl out riding in a convertible, the wind in her hair, her eyes half shut, a warm and secret smile on her lips.

Try as he might, it was almost impossible to swing his right arm gracefully and naturally. He kept wanting to press the inside of his arm against the lump of the handkerchief.

He realized he was heading toward a rather shoddy section of the strange city, but wisdom dictated that he continue. It would be rather suspicious to be looking around to see if he were followed. To stop and retrace his steps would court suspicion.

A candy store was directly ahead of him. The buildings all reached to the edge of the rather narrow sidewalk. Two narrow-faced little children came whooping out of the candy store, sucking on ice cream sticks. They stopped dead and stared at him.

"Whacha walkin' like that for, mister?"

Apparently I am not walking properly. Straighten up, Paul, old man.

He gave them a peaceful smile, wondering if it looked more like a grimace. The effort required to straighten up was surprisingly great. He felt as though his flesh and bone had been doubled over, crimped or stapled in place, felt as though it tore him to straighten up.

The children solemnly sucked the ice cream and regarded him coldly. He went on and did not look back.

His feet had begun to feel as though they dangled inches above the hot pavement, as though by no effort could he stretch them down to an intimate contact with reality. He walked over and got into a parked cab.

As they neared the station he gave the driver a wise smile and said, "Look, old man, there's a woman waiting in there for me and I want to avoid her. Here's my check for two suitcases. Would you mind awfully?"

The driver winked at him. "I know how it is, mac."

Ten minutes later the taxi driver let him off at the bus station. He overtipped the man. The sun was getting low. His suitcases made long solid shadows on the dusty sidewalk. He knew it was going to be one of the most difficult things he had ever attempted. As he lifted the two bags, the sweat jumped out on his forehead and the world darkened around him. His shoulder struck the doorframe and he knew his mouth was drawn down in an absurd grimace. After he had sat on the hard bench for a few moments, his breathing quieted and he could see clearly once more.

Paul January went to the ticket counter.

Behind the ticketseller was a map of the bus lines marked heavily in red. He squinted at it and picked out a name.

"One-way to Rockwarren, please."

"That'll be two eighty-five, sir. Next bus leaves in twenty minutes out that side door over there."

Paul held himself very straight as he went back to his bench.

An old man sat beside him, lean jaw stubbled with white, shapeless gray cap, reddened eyes, roving in constant wariness. The old man jerked a pint bottle out of his side pocket, took long swallows, his seamed throat convulsing. He lowered the bottle, wiped his mouth on his hand, gagged and slid the bottle back in his pocket.

Paul January separated two dollars from the wadded bills in his pocket. "I'll give you two dollars for the rest of that bottle," he said.

The wary old eyes regarded him. "You look like you need it, friend."

He slid the bottle over, pocketed the two dollars. Paul January, ignoring the baleful eye of a matron on his right, tilted it up and finished it without once taking it from his lips.

The liquor hit his stomach, radiated warmth and strength in all directions.

The driver put the suitcases in the side compartment. Paul January went to the third seat behind the driver, inched in close to the window. He pulled his cocoanut straw hat low over his eyes. He was asleep by the time the bus started.

CHAPTER TWO
OLIVE MORGANTINE

She was a muscular and angular woman in her late fifties with teeth as white, as carefully tended and as artificial as the low white picket fence surrounding her tiny footage and white cottage. Though Henry Morgantine had died eighteen years before, Olive still talked about him in a manner which had sensitive guests on the verge of glancing quickly over their shoulders.

Her living room, a twelve-by-twelve cube, was jammed. In solitary and muscular splendor, Mrs. Olive Morgantine moved carefully among her possessions, dusting, oiling, polishing.

Her most startling variation from type was an addiction to very gay and quite youthful clothes, horridly embellished by whole areas of clattering, clanking costume jewelry.

During the past six months Olive Morgantine had been kept in a state of outrage. It was all due to the "development." She failed to see why the empty lot near her cottage, adjoining it, in fact, had been shrewdly split into two tiny lots, and a white house erected on each.

As if that were not enough, the couple who purchased the house nearest to hers had been of "a very low type, my dear. The things I could tell you!"

The facts were a silver thread running through her fabric of woe. A couple had bought the house next door. He was some sort of a salesman. She was a coarse-looking young woman, pretty in a rather vulgar way, blatant in her dress and her habits.

Olive Morgantine did not mind the shrill quarrels when the husband was home. Nor did she mind the lateness of their parties. She could have adjusted to those factors. The one thing she could not stand was the fact that Mrs. Darrold "stands out on that stupid little back porch and hurls, just hurls, mind you, all of the empty bottles and cans down to the foot of the yard. You have no idea what it is doing to the neighborhood. I suppose when their yard is full they'll start hurling them into my begonias!"

Cynthia Darrold's habits were just sufficiently regular to react on Mrs. Morgantine in the same way as the ancient torture of the slow dripping of water.

With her husband away, Cynthia Darrold apparently arose around eleven. She made her breakfast and loafed until late afternoon. At that time she would make herself some cocktails, quite a number, in fact, and later have a can of soup before going out.

Thus, every day, somewhere between four and six, a bottle or a can would be hurled out into the yard. No matter how Mrs. Morgantine tried to avoid hearing the noise, she would always hear it.

There was another factor in Cynthia Darrold's life that bothered Mrs. Morgantine a great deal. She was always asleep when Cynthia came home. And, rather too often, sometime during the following day, a strange young man, usually a different one, would walk from the Darrold house and disappear down the street headed toward the nearest bus stop.

Never did Cynthia stir herself to climb behind the wheel of the powerful red roadster and take the young man back to wherever he belonged.

It was four o'clock and Mrs. Morgantine was beginning to get her daily case of nerves over the routine of the tin can or the bottle. She stood well back from her windows and watched the Darrold house. At noon a tall young man had walked away from the Darrold house. He had been rather a good-looking young man, wearing gray slacks and one of those cotton sports coats. Of course, she could not say but what he had arrived just before she saw him leave, as she had been rather busy in her bedroom, sorting her jewelry.

Surely any minute now she would see signs of Cynthia's moving about in the kitchen. And then, indolent and sloppily dressed, Cynthia would shuffle out onto her porch, brace herself and throw a can or bottle down the yard.

Mrs. Morgantine made herself some tea, drank it, paced restlessly about, looked at her watch. A little after five. And still no crash and clatter in the back yard. Yes, the red car was still parked beside the house.

Five-thirty . . . quarter to six . . . six . . . five after six.

Mrs. Morgantine stood up. She had been sitting by her beautifully polished dining room table, drumming on it with businesslike fingernails.

Mrs. Darrold had never been this late.

She went to the phone. "Information, please. Do you have a phone listed for a Mr. Gaylord Darrold on Hillside Drive? Thank you very much."

She dialed the number they had given her. She cocked her head on one side and listened. Yes, she could hear the distant ringing of the Darrold phone. She counted the rings. After it rang twenty-four times, she hung up, began to tap on her front teeth with the back of her thumbnail.

Cynthia Darrold surely could not be sleeping that soundly!

Mrs. Morgantine paced back and forth through the little house. She made her decision. Of course, if Cynthia came to the door, it would be a very neighborly thing to have done, and might mean that the Darrold woman would be in her hair until she could successfully freeze her out again.

Mrs. Morgantine emptied a small sugar bowl back into the big sugar tin. She put a wide, shallow smile on her knobbed face, walked briskly down to her garden gate, stepped delicately over the maze of cans and bottles and climbed the warped steps to the Darrold back door. The buzzer inside was startlingly loud.

After giving the buzzer seven long rings, she thumped heartily on the door with a capable fist. No answer. She half turned, then, lips compressed, snatched the doorknob and turned it. The door opened readily.

She tiptoed into the back hall. A big refrigerator hummed. A distant clock ticked. Sunlight fell in a fading pattern on the rather grubby linoleum.

Holding her breath and clutching the sugar bowl, Mrs. Morgantine tiptoed her way into the kitchen.

The blue sugar bowl slipped from her fingers and smashed on the floor. The first three screams were high and thin. She stood staring down at the dead woman and screamed again and again until her voice itself was almost gone and had become a hoarse bellow.

It was then that she realized that with the as yet unoccupied house on one side and with her own empty house on the other, and with no houses across the street, screaming was a singularly empty procedure.

She moved sideways to the sink, turned on the cold water, cupped her hand and liberally spattered her face. It felt very good.

Mrs. Morgantine's appetite for the mystery story was almost insatiable. She began to think in terms of "murder weapon" and "motive" and "suspects" and "scene of the crime."

She found the weapon, a disappointingly inoffensive-appearing automatic, on the far side of the kitchen, almost under the kitchen table. She knew enough not to touch it. She regretted touching the faucet.

She backed out of the kitchen, scurried down the steps and began to run down toward her garden gate.

She was standing impatiently in front of the Darrold house when the white police sedan appeared five minutes later. She gave them no chance to ask questions. As she followed them up to the front door of the Darrold house, both policeman had begun to walk with their knees bent, as men who brace themselves against a storm.

CHAPTER THREE
DORIS LOGAN

She wrinkled her nose at the ripe stink of alcohol as she took her seat beside the sleeping man. She half stood, lurching as the bus started, but there were no other vacant seats. Well, if he kept sleeping, he'd be no trouble.

She wondered vaguely why she was always getting entangled with amorous drunks. Doris Logan was remarkably devoid of pride or pretense. When she thought of herself, which was seldom, she thought of a girl who was too tall, with a mouth that was too wide, hair of a strange red color, eyes that were an odd greeny-pale. She did not know that it all added up to a striking attractiveness.

She thought of herself as a husky and capable nurse. Which she was. Though vaguely conscious of missing some important and integral part of life, she found that men bored her, almost without exception. A kiss was a remarkably unsanitary gyration.

But, on the bus trip, she had no time to think of vague matters. Her problems were more specific. For three years she had been the surgical assistant to a very fine doctor. She had followed him in so many operations that she could anticipate his every move.

A week before, the doctor she worked for explained that the hospital administration was requesting him to return to the system whereby he took on internes as surgical assistants, thus complicating his own operations, but furthering their education.

He gave her a month off with pay, and she had spent one week at a rented cabin at Lake Morris near Rockwarren. She had thought of offering her services to another surgeon whom she knew, and had left her car at the bus station in Rockwarren, had taken the bus down to the city. She found that the other surgeon had the same problem.

After the three years of acting as surgical assistant, she doubted whether she could force herself to return to a nursing routine.

So Doris Logan was worrying about her future. Unless she could find the means and the opportunity to go to medical school, further progress in the field was denied her. In fact, they wanted her to retrogress. To an individual of her spirit, this was very irksome indeed. She thought of her mind as one of the little white mice she had seen once in a laboratory maze. It ran back and forth, bewildered, its pink nose twitching. The bus was getting well out into the country. The sun had gone below the horizon and the after-work traffic had lessened. Neon was flashing up in front of the juke spots on the highway, and some gas stations were already floodlighted. The driver clicked on the inside lights in the bus.

Her seat companion stirred restlessly and his hat rolled off his head, blundered down into her lap. She picked it up with distaste, glanced at him, half stood and put it on the overhead rack.

She looked at him for a time. Silly man to get so drunk. Yet rather a nice-looking man. Sensitivity in that face. And intelligence. The eyes were set well in the face, and the mouth, though slack in sleep, had a certain firmness and character. She suddenly felt a warmth that surprised her.

Doris, my girl, if you start feeling mushy about drunks in buses, you are really in a sad, bad way.

There were spots of color in the man's cheek. His breathing was a shade too rapid. Professional interest immediately swallowed personal interest. She watched him narrowly.

If she took his wrist to find the pulse, he might awaken. She moved her head to where she could watch a pulse in his throat. Her watch, of course, had a sweep second hand. She counted.

One hundred and twelve! Not good at all. Ever so lightly, she touched the back of her hand to his dry forehead. It was alarmingly hot.

The slight pressure disturbed him. His right arm moved up and the inside of the forearm pressed against his side just at his waistline.

His hand slowly slid back to the seat. She looked at the place where he had pressed. There seemed to be a slight bulge there. She wondered what it was. She carefully grasped the edge of the rayon cord jacket, lifted it until she could see his gray and white belt. She caught her underlip between her teeth. Even under weak artificial light in a moving bus, she could tell dried blood when she saw it.

It led to a very direct line of reasoning. The man was hurt. There were doctors in the city. He was leaving the city. Thus the wound would be either a knife wound or a bullet wound. She wondered which. She did not doubt for one moment the correctness of her reasoning.

She remembered a ticket stub inside the gray hatband. She stood up and glanced at it. Rockwarren. At Rockwarren she would turn him over to the police. He would probably be wanted.

But ten miles from Rockwarren, he moaned. He opened his eyes and looked at her with the glaze of partial delirium. She saw his teeth shut hard, saw him slowly pull himself together.

He sat up and said weakly, "Could you tell me how far it is to Rockwarren?"

She liked his voice and she liked his eyes. "Another fifteen minutes." She leaned toward him and said, in that trained voice that doesn't carry as far as a whisper, "How far do you expect to walk with that wound?"

His hand lifted to his side, then slowly dropped. Surprisingly, he smiled. "You got me, pal," he said.

"Can you make it about fifty yards?"

"By myself, yes. But not carrying two suitcases."

He sank into the seat of the small coupe with a heartfelt sigh. She got behind the wheel and drove back to the bus station. He waited and she came out in a moment carrying his bags. In the center of the small village she went into a drugstore.

When she came out she saw that he was either asleep or had fainted. She got behind the wheel, stowed her package in back, considered a moment, and then lowered him so that his head rested in her lap. She threw his hat in back.

Five miles from Rockwarren she turned off the county road onto a dirt track with grass growing high in the middle. It brushed the underside of the car. Her lights made a bright tunnel through the darkness of the woods. The road went down a steep pitch.

She steadied him with her right hand on his shoulder. At the foot of the incline she turned sharply left, her lights brushing across a split-log cabin.

Beyond the cabin was the lakeshore. She left him in the car, went up onto the porch, went into the spare bedroom and turned on the lights. Deftly she made up the bed with her extra sheets.

She could not rouse him when she returned to the car.

With her hands in his armpits, she dragged him out, his heels hitting the ground. She rested when she got him to the steps. She rested again when she got him to the top of the steps. After dragging him across the small living room and into the bedroom, she made one final effort and managed to get him up onto the bed.

She saw that the dragging had opened the

wound again, if indeed it had ever been entirely closed. She boiled the probe and scalpel on the kitchen stove, put the sulpha powder, gauze and adhesive on the nightstand.

In five minutes she knew that she would not have to drive back to the village for the doctor as she had planned. The slug had hit at an angle, had followed all the way around his side, not far under the skin, and had lodged within an inch of his backbone. She felt the lump with her fingers.

Deftly she made the short incision, popped the ugly-looking chunk of lead out by pressing delicately with her thumbs on either side of it. She washed both wounds, packed them with the sulpha powder, bandaged them expertly.

His fever was just under a hundred and two. She gave him sulpha tablets which, in his unconscious state, he choked on. She then injected penicillin into him, covered him up, clicked out the bright light and left the room. At the doorway she paused, intending to go back and take his wallet and look for identification.

But she couldn't do it. She could not bring herself to snoop among his papers.

After she had quietly closed his door, she realized how tired she was. She went out onto the screened porch and looked at the moon pattern across the water. She tried to bring her mind back to the problem of her future. But somehow she could not work up a sufficient amount of interest. She smoked two cigarettes and, when she began to yawn, she went to her bedroom. Then she realized that he might wake up and leave. With a determined stride she went back to his room, collected both suitcases, took them back to her room and shot the bolt.

CHAPTER FOUR
GAYLORD DARROLD

He sat on the kitchen table and could not keep his eyes off the heavily chalked outline on the floor. The outline of Cynthia. There were two men in the kitchen with him. The big, dull-looking one who leaned against the sink was a Lieutenant Krobey. He had a flat tanned face and blue eyes that looked like marbles freshly spray-painted in watery blue.

The other one was a fat and asthmatic man with a cherub face, a shining bald skull and a deep, somehow sickening, dimple in his forehead. His name was Sergeant Love. He had been an exceedingly doleful and lugubrious man until one day a hopped-up seventeen-year-old had shot Sergeant Love square in the forehead with a twenty-two pistol. The tiny slug had gone an inch deep into the gray tissue of Sergeant Love's frontal lobe and had turned him into a jolly and optimistic man who told his wife every day of her life that he was living on borrowed time.

"Give it to me slow again," Krobey said.

"Our marriage had turned into something pretty dull some time ago. She lived her life. I lived mine. When I was home she cooked for me and kept my clothes in shape. When I was away I didn't care what she did, just so long as she didn't spend too much money."

"You buy her the car?"

"She had some money of her own."

"You got any idea who she might have quarreled with?"

"No," Gaylord Darrold said.

The gleaming young man from the district attorney's office came back into the kitchen. He gave each of the three men an identical nod. Mr. Gaylord Darrold had arrived home at ten-fifteen in the morning, exactly sixteen hours after the discovery of the body of his wife by Mrs. Morgantine.

The burnished young man from the district attorney's office was named Haggard. De Wolfe Haggard. He had been in and out of the kitchen five times.

Gaylord Darrold was the sort of lean-headed man, the type who, in his twenties, is called "wise," in his thirties is called "sophisticated," in his forties is called "dissipated" and in his fifties is called "well preserved." Darrold was edging from sophistication into dissipation.

He glanced mildly at Haggard, brushed some invisible lint off his sharply creased trousers.

Krobey said heavily, "I just want leads. People kill people and we like to know who." Krobey seemed intent on making sense.

The phone rang. Gaylord Darrold slid easily from the table, walked into the hall and took the call. He turned and handed the phone to Krobey.

Krobey grunted into the phone a few times and then hung up. He said to Sergeant Love, "That's the Rockwarren lead. A guy answering the description that old lady give us took the bus about six last night to Rockwarren. But we can't track him from there. Anybody we can't track is a good bet."

"You think he's got a hole in him?" Love asked.

Krobey shrugged. "No screens on the house. That window over there was open. A slug goes out the window, we never find it if it's angled up a little. If he has a hole in him, it isn't important."

De Wolfe Haggard struck a pose in the middle of the kitchen. He rested his chin on his fist and glared at the floor.

"This is my reconstruction, gentlemen," he said soberly. "Mrs. Darrold went out the night before last. She struck up an acquaintanceship with this Mr. X. He carried a gun. Lieutenant Krobey has explained to us that since it is rather an old gun, a Browning patent manufactured in Belgium, we will probably never trace it. The young man came here with Mrs. Darrold. She had been dead five hours when she was found. That puts the time at one o'clock.

"For some reason they quarreled. He wrapped the gun in that towel, and fired twice at her. The towel muffled the sound of the shots. He missed her once and the bullet went out that window. She was running from him in terror. The second shot struck her in the back of the head. He wiped the gun on the towel, tossed both the gun and the towel on the floor. Then he calmly walked out. Mrs. Morgantine saw him. It matches with the time of death. All we need to do, gentlemen, is inquire around at those places where it is likely that Mrs. Darrold and Mr. X may have met."

He looked around the kitchen, said to Gaylord Darrold, "Where did they go?"

"They left some time ago."

"Oh." For a moment De Wolfe Haggard looked very young and very vulnerable. He swallowed hard, and in what was obviously a gesture to gain face, marched two paces closer to Darrold, leveled a finger at him and said, "This alibi of yours will stand up, you believe?"

Gaylord Darrold selected a cigarette from a battered leather case. He lit it, flicked the match away. The match bounced off the polished toe of Haggard's right shoe.

Darrold said flatly, "Don't raise your voice at me, junior. And don't pick words like alibi to use on me. Somebody killed my wife. You've been boring me off and on all afternoon. Now why don't you go finger a brief or something and let the cops work on this. They know how."

The burnished young man coughed, touched his fingertips to a dark blue Windsor knot and fled from the kitchen.

Darrold stared at the chalked outline on the floor. His eyes narrowed and he sucked the smoke far down into his lungs.

The phone rang again. Love came from the front of the house to answer it. He listened for a long time, said, "Okay, Joe," and hung up.

He walked out into the kitchen and smiled at Darrold. "Okay, so you're clear, Mister Darrold. We got you located at Barnston, fifty miles east of here, at noon yesterday, and that Mr. Walker, the bookkeeper guy, reported that he put you on the Empire City at just five minutes of twelve, headed east. That train makes its first stop two hours later, at two in the afternoon, a hundred and seventy miles east of here. And I guess nobody jumps off that Empire City, hey?"

"Hardly."

"Then in Richfield, a hundred and seventy miles away, you called on customers, checked in at the Richfield House after dinner; left your room early this morning, checked out, picked up your car from the Wilson Brothers Garage and drove back here."

Darrold smiled tightly. "You people really follow it up, don't you?"

"Brother, we have to. With characters like De Wolfe Haggard running around, we can't have any holes in our cases."

"Probably a good thing from my point of view."

"Sure, figure what happens if we catch the guy and some jury lets him go. You don't want any suspicion on you. It's better we check it all the way."

"Thanks," Darrold said dryly. He yawned. "Look, Sergeant. All this has been pretty rough. I'm sort of shot. Okay with you people if I take a nap?"

"Go ahead. We'll know where you are if we want you."

"If there's any way I can help . . ."

Sergeant Love clapped him on the shoulder. "Turn in, fella. You do look sort of shot."

CHAPTER FIVE
PAUL JANUARY

It was a bit like waking up on the morning of final exams, knowing that there was a horrible day ahead, without being able to remember the reason. At first he thought it was a hangover, but aside from a dull roaring in his ears and a tiny pulse somewhere behind his forehead, he felt fine.

The mattress had obviously been stuffed with old tire irons and petrified bits of cabbage. It rustled and jabbed him when he moved. He wondered why he had taken a bed with such a foul mattress.

The ceiling was of tired-looking plywood.

Suddenly the picture flashed into his mind of a girl on a kitchen floor.

He was wide awake in a fraction of a second. Awake, tense and afraid. The window was unbarred. Clean sheets. He touched his side, felt the comforting firmness of a professional bandage. There was a new area of pain also. He rolled up onto his side, explored the new place, found a second bandage.

An orifice of exit, no doubt. The slug was no longer with him.

He frowned. There was a girl on a bus. Quite a nice girl, in fact. A small car. Headlights.

He stood up with determination, wavered for balance, managed to remain standing. Something clattered. A kitchen sound.

Three steps took him to the bedroom door. He opened it. Same girl. Her back was to him. Red slacks and a halter.

She spun around. "You shouldn't be up!"

"I feel fine. Just fine."

She came over to him, took his arm and led him to a deep wicker chair. He sank gratefully into it.

He smiled up at her and said, "In words of one syllable, lady. Please."

"Certainly. I sat next to you on the bus. I'm a nurse. My name is Doris Logan. I rent this cottage. The noise out there is Lake Morris slapping the dock. I saw you were hurt. I brought you here, extracted one small bullet which you will find over there on the mantel, and gave you some items to knock off the infection which had started. I don't know why I did it. Who did you kill? How would you like your eggs?"

"My name is Paul January and I didn't kill anybody and scrambled soft, please."

She went back to the stove, cut down the flame under the percolator and began making housewife motions over the eggs.

Once she turned and said, "Of course, you'd say that anyway."

He thought it over. "Yes, I guess I would. Not the killer type, though. I even hate to watch bugs after they get a jolt of DDT."

In a few moments she pushed the table over to his chair, brought over his plate and cup, sat opposite him.

"I still don't know why I did it," she said softly.

He bent busily over the eggs. This was indeed a remarkable young woman. She seemed to have a little transparent sheet over her emotions.

"They'll be coming after you, you know," she said. "That is, unless you were a good deal cleverer in getting to the bus than you were after you were on it."

"They won't be coming after me," he said with decision.

"Oh, then you were clever?"

"Not at all. They won't come after me, because I will go to them, Miss Logan. I don't know why I ran in the first place. Shock, I guess. The whole thing is still pretty foggy in my mind. I just wanted to get away from there. Anywhere. Just away."

"Away from where?"

"Suppose I think over the whole thing while I drink the coffee and then tell you later."

They sat on the screened porch. It was a placid morning, slightly overcast. The lake had a steel-gray sheen. The morning held, for Paul January, a peculiar and haunting unreality. No other camp was visible from the porch. On the far side of the lake silent pines cast deep aqua shadows.

He liked the way she did not press him for explanations, but was content to sit quietly and wait for him to tell her in his own good time.

"This makes me sound like seven kinds of fool," he said. "And probably I am. I had just arrived in the city. I had never been there before. I checked my luggage in the station rather than cart it around with me while looking for a place to stay. I'm an unsuccessful architect—one of those visionary guys who build marble palaces and forget the plumbing. My idea was to hit the new Planning Commission for a job. I've got a letter to the chairman of the commission.

"I arrived in the late afternoon, and after trying three hotels and getting nowhere, I went into a sort of steakhouse place to eat. I had a couple of drinks. It was a paneled place, with an orange glow to the lights and a lot of glitter on the backbar and oversized prices on the drinks and food. But I was too lazy to look for another spot.

"Sitting at the bar was a woman. This probably sounds completely screwy to you, but I never did find out all of her name. Just Cynthia. Long black hair curled in at the ends and when she bent her head over the bar a long strand of it

would swing around in front and she'd push it back with an impatient gesture. Maybe you can guess how a man alone will watch a woman who is alone. It's sort of a speculative procedure. But the milquetoast type, such as myself, never gets past the speculation stage.

"She had rather coarse lines about her face. Heavy lips, wide across the cheekbones, snub nose, dense black eyebrows. She sat at the bar and from my table I could see her face reflected in the backbar. She had what I call princess eyes. It's a silly term. They were nice eyes. Straight and true and sensitive. I played a mental game of trying to figure her out.

"I felt vaguely disturbed when the man moved in on her. Conservative pinstripe, immaculate hands and an air of extreme extroversion. I guessed at once that he'd call all waiters 'Charlie' and make a practice of sending food back to the kitchen.

"When he nuzzled up beside the girl and began to make small talk, I got a look at her eyes. All they seemed to hold was an incalculable weariness and resignation. My chops came and I kept an eye on them as I ate.

"The man made the mistake of being too big a shot in the drink department. He bought too many rounds. With more conservatism, she might have remained agreeable. But the liquor broke through the crust of self-disgust, and suddenly she began to snarl at him. I saw the anger on his face. He grabbed her arm and she shook him off. He sulked like a little boy. His fingers had made red spots on her arm.

"She chased him away, but he had a certain grim look that spelled trouble. I had finished eating, and I should have gone off to look for a room, but some hunch made me stay. She should have eaten, but instead she had more to drink. When she walked out, I paid my check and followed her.

"She walked an invisible tightrope to the door and went out onto the street. The man appeared out of the shadows and they argued. I could only hear the tone of voice. Then he put his hands on her shoulders and tried to wrestle her toward a waiting cab. I turned hero and shoved in on him.

"He was too easy. I stabbed him in the middle with my fingertips and backhanded him across the mouth when he bent over. Cynthia crowed with laughter. He blundered into the cab and was whirled away. Cynthia wavered toward a red roadster. She was too far gone to drive. I got behind the wheel and she directed me to a small white house on Hillside Street.

"Halfway to the back door, she collapsed. I got her inside, found the lights, made coffee for her. The house was deserted. After she had the coffee, she locked herself in the bathroom and took a long shower. Then she joined me in the kitchen and we drank coffee and talked. It was a strange talk. We covered psychological and philosophical concepts that were way over our heads. We were impersonal with each other, if you can believe that."

"I can believe it," Doris Logan said quietly.

"In the small hours of the morning she went to bed. I slept on a couch in the front room, with her permission. It was all very platonic. In the morning she was going to drive me down to the center of the city and I would find a hotel, clean up and make my appointment.

"She was worn out, I guess. She slept very late and I didn't want to disturb her. I was up about nine and I debated leaving quietly. I guess I should have. But, I liked Cynthia, and I wanted to say goodby to her properly.

"It must have been close to noon when she got up. She came out in a coral housecoat, and she looked years younger than she had the night before. We kidded around about the rejuvenating aspects of turning over a new leaf. I asked her while we were eating breakfast whether she would find a job. She said that she had enough money to keep herself for some time, and that most of all she wanted to go to some quiet place.

"After we ate, I helped her carry the few dishes to the kitchen sink and she washed them. I was on the far side of the kitchen.

"There was a sound, and I thought that she had pushed a book off the kitchen shelf and that

it had fallen flat on the linoleum. It was that sort of sound. I looked over at her and she was bending over the sink, her face almost touching the faucets. I thought that very strange. There was a funny smell of fireworks in the air.

"As I watched her, her knees bent and she slid down, falling over onto her back. My mind was working slowly, but when I saw her face and her eyes, I knew she was dead. There was a faint sound off to my right. I turned quickly and something hot and small and hard hit me just over the watch pocket. I staggered back and my heel caught in a throw rug and I fell heavily. Something clattered on the floor.

"The thing which had hit me gave me cramps. Gasping, I got to my feet. I was bleeding. I looked at the small ugly hole in myself and balled my handkerchief and wedged it under my belt against the hole. The thing which had clattered was a gun. It was nearly under the kitchen table. I walked to the window. The curtains blew in the breeze. There was no one outside.

"I draw a blank for the next few moments. I was walking toward the city. I can remember funny little snatches. Kids sucking on ice cream. An old guy with a pint bottle. Telling a lie to a cabdriver. I bought a bus ticket to some place called Rockwarren. Now I know that I was silly to run. If you'll drive me into town . . ."

Doris Logan's wide and generous mouth had a set look about it. "Wait a minute, Paul. This is an illogical world which feels itself to be supremely logical. Let's play cop for a little while. Man goes home with Cynthia. Cynthia dies. Man leaves. Just for a moment let us assume that there are no prints on the gun, that the gun is not traceable. Also assume that whoever killed the fair Cynthia has a very solid alibi. The newspapers will try you before the court does. It won't be pretty. And the average person would find it a bit hard to think of you and Cynthia having a good old-fashioned bull session, all very palsy."

Paul January felt all the comfort drain out of the morning. He listened to his own story from the viewpoint of a policeman—and found it thin indeed. Thin and more than a bit ridiculous. He saw for the first time that even had he remained at Cynthia's house and phoned the police, he would have come in for more than a trace of suspicion. And having run away made it far, far worse.

He glanced at Doris. Her capable hands were resting on the arms of the porch chair, but they were not relaxed. The knuckles were white.

She got up suddenly and went into the cabin. "Right back," she said.

He waited. The morning was quiet. He heard a gasp of pain from inside the cabin. He stood up and went in.

Doris Logan stood by the kitchen sink, her face pale. Blood ran down her arm from a deep gash just above her elbow.

"What happened!" he cried.

She managed to smile. "It was a shade deeper than I wanted to cut," she said. "Stop jittering for a minute and help me. Pick up that gauze pad by the corner and put it lengthwise along the cut. Fine. Now tear off an adhesive strip three inches long. Right across here. Now another. Three ought to hold it."

With the cut bandaged, she cleaned the blood from her forearm.

Before he could ask her, she said, "Look here, Paul. I left the bus station and went to a drugstore. I bought a few things. If they traced you to the bus, they might connect the two of us. And that means I need a reason for the purchases I made. Infected arm. See?" She grinned and held out the bandaged arm.

He took her by the shoulders and shook her gently. Her odd red hair fell across her eyes and she blew it out of the way with a protruding underlip.

"Fine!" he said. "The boss takes charge. You decide that I'm going to keep right on running. Wouldn't it have been nice to let me know?"

Anger faded as he grew conscious of the warmth of her bare shoulders under his hands. He was suddenly impressed with her unusual loveliness. He pulled her close and kissed her.

He released her, feeling extremely shy. She did not meet his glance. Awkwardness was between them, like the faltering lines in a poor play.

She broke the tension by saying, "Pretty rigorous stuff for the walking wounded, Mr. J."

He reached for her again. She put her hands against his chest and pushed. Firmly. "Don't let my self-mutilation go for nothing. We are going to make you a woodsy nest. You and your suitcases. Off in the brush. And then I am going into town and find out the current status."

CHAPTER SIX
DE WOLFE HAGGARD

When he thought of himself, which was frequently and with delight, he became the lean, suave and sober district attorney who not only shows the humble police the error of their ways, but concocts a courtroom boomerang that fells the mighty. The big trouble was that the police, notably that vulgar Lieutenant Krobey, insisted on treating him as though he were a frail substitute trying to make the first team.

Whenever De Wolfe thought of Krobey, he flexed his muscles and imagined a series of violent gestures ending in Krobey falling backward across a table to lie huddled and silent on the floor. It was too bad that there was no way to prove Krobey guilty of a crime. Also it was too bad that Krobey was so—muscular.

Take the way Krobey had acted with that beautiful Doris Logan. Anyone could see that she was not, of all things, a liar. What if someone had seen her talking to the suspect on the bus? Was Doris Logan the type to make a cheap pickup the way Cynthia Darrold did? Of course not!

It was infuriatingly stupid the way Krobey had made her repeat her story over and over again. When De Wolfe shut his eyes he could still see her intent face.

"Yes, Lieutenant, I spoke to him on the bus. He asked me how long it would take to get to Rockwarren. He was quite drunk. No, his face was shadowed. I really couldn't tell you what he looked like. He was young and I think his face was plump and his hair was blond."

"But Mrs. Morgantine said the man had a lean face and dark hair."

Doris Logan had smiled. "Possibly we are talking about two different people."

"How about the person who swears they saw the young man getting into your car, Miss Logan?"

"I can't explain that. But the gas station man told you that when I passed his station I was alone in the car. The young man tried to follow me in the darkness when I went back to get into my car. And then he disappeared. I don't know where he went."

"How about those purchases you made?"

"I wanted to treat my own infected arm, Lieutenant. Is there a law against that? After all, Lieutenant! You people searched my camp and found no trace of any man being there. This whole inquisition is getting a bit ridiculous, isn't it? The murder was committed the day before yesterday. The murderer must be a thousand miles away by now. And you waste good police time asking me silly questions. I've told you all I know."

De Wolfe scowled as he thought of how Krobey had reacted. The stupid man should have at least apologized. Instead he had smiled placidly at Miss Logan and had said, "We'll be talking some more. If we want you, we'll send a sedan up to the camp and bring you back."

"I may stay in town for a few days. You have my apartment address."

De Wolfe Haggard picked up a fresh yellow pencil, tested the needle point with a pink thumb. He sat at his desk in the outer office and stared at the blank sheet of white paper in front of him. The blank sheet became a movie screen. A drama was being enacted.

De Wolfe Haggard, district attorney, stood in the crowded courtroom and pointed to the defendant who had taken the stand. The defendant was Doris Logan. De Wolfe Haggard, with voice of booming bronze, pointed a dramatic fin-ger at the defendant and said, "Would you believe this fair and innocent creature to be capable of the foulness imputed to her by my learned . . ."

No, that wasn't right. He would have to be the prosecutor. . . .

He glanced toward the doorway. He shook his head to remove the mirage standing in the doorway in a green dress. The mirage stayed, came walking toward him.

He got up so eagerly that he tipped his chair over. He picked it up, moved another chair eagerly into position and said, "Do sit down, Miss Logan. I can't tell you how sorry I am about the . . . indignity of the questions you were asked."

Doris Logan sat and gave him a warm smile. "I knew you felt that way, Mr. Haggard. It's so nice to feel that someone is on your side. That—that horrible attitude of suspicion."

"I know. I know," he said soothingly. "How can I help you?"

"I may seem to you, Mr. Haggard, like a very foolish girl. It's the first time in my life I've ever been mixed up in this sort of thing. I don't believe I've ever had my picture in the papers before. As a nurse, the notoriety isn't good for me. Surely you realize that."

De Wolfe nodded sagely.

"I wondered if there is any way I could help the authorities. If I could take an active interest, then possibly that horrid Lieutenant Krobey wouldn't . . ."

Her voice trailed off. De Wolfe stared at the yellow pencil. He felt very alive and very reckless. He lowered his voice. "Actually, Miss Logan, I should discourage you. But you seem to be a person of high intelligence. Suppose you assist me in this case."

"How exciting!" Doris said.

"If we could meet outside the office we can go over my case notes on this whole affair. Say about four? The cocktail lounge at the Hotel Rogers?"

She stood up, held out a cool hand. "Thank you so much, Mr. Haggard. I'll be there."

"Could you call me De Wolfe?"

"And you must call me Doris." She held his hand tightly. "After all, we *are* working together, aren't we?"

As soon as the outer door had closed behind her, De Wolfe Haggard walked twice around his desk, smacking his fist into his palm and saying jubilantly, "Oh boy, oh boy, oh boy . . ."

He felt the sere and aged eye of the chief female clerk upon him. He gave her a frosty and metallic look and sat down. He stared at the sheet of white paper and slowly another courtroom scene began to materialize. Krobey was the accused. Doris Logan was a juror. He leaned over the jurybox railing and talked directly to her. Her lips were parted and her warm admiring eyes were on him. . . .

She sat at his side, so close to him that, if he moved another inch, their shoulders would touch. He moved a half inch. When the drinks were before them, he took out his notebook and placed it on the table. Together they leaned over it.

"You see," he said proudly, "one of my methods is to put the name of each person concerned at the top of a sheet and put under that name all the facts we have. Here are five names of men who have been seen with Mrs. Darrold. The police have cleared each one of them. Mr. Darrold has been cleared also. Thus our Mr. X is obviously the man."

"How do you go about 'clearing' someone? Take Mr. Darrold, for example."

"Wait a moment. I can barely read my own writing. Ah yes: The home offices of the company he works for are in Barnston, fifty miles or so east of here. A Mr. Daniel Walker, bookkeeper at the home office, put Mr. Darrold on the Empire City headed east from Barnston at noon the day of the murder. Mr. Darrold could not possibly have returned here to kill his wife in the time allowed."

"And I suppose they checked at the other end of his trip?"

"Oh, yes. Mr. Darrold was in Richfield that same evening, all right. No doubt about it."

CHAPTER SEVEN
MAYLA BARAN

Really, she thought, Dan is getting to be a horrid bore. She lay on her side on the wide windowseat, her head cradled on her arm, a glass on the floor just under her hand. The windowseat was padded in white leather, with red cording. Mayla liked white and red. She was a small girl with very white skin. She had a petulant mouth, eyes set into her head at a roguish tip-tilt, hair the color of the heaviest cream.

She had a predatory quickness of movement, thin, greedy little fingers, and a trick of slowly widening her eyes whenever she looked at a man. Her tiny body was superbly fashioned, and she never sat, walked, stood or reclined without a definite attempt to display its most pleasing lines.

Yes, Dan was becoming definitely a bore. She watched him as he paced. He walked from the white fireplace over to the far red couch and back again. There was a disgusting stubble of beard on his jaw, and discolored pouches under his eyes. The hair, which usually was carefully combed to cover the maximum area of a balding head, was in disarray, and a lank lock fell almost to his cheekbone.

"For heaven's sake, sit down!" she snapped, in her high, childish voice.

"Shut up, Angel," he growled.

She pouted. There was one good way to take Dan's mind off his troubles. She said, "Today I'm going to order the terrace furniture."

He whirled on her. "Angel! What furniture? How much?"

"About three hundred dollars. That terrace stuff is battered, Dan. Horribly battered."

He stood over her. His eyes were strange. He frightened her a little, as in the old days before she had found that he would obey a gesture or a whistle, like a well-trained dog.

"Angel," he said. "Remember what I asked you last night?"

"That silly idea of yours?"

"It's not so silly. Let's sell all this stuff. Let's get out of here. Let's get out of this stinking town of Barnston and go places. Mexico, maybe. Guatemala."

She narrowed her tilted eyes and her mouth turned hard. "Not the way you want it, brother. Not in the tourist court class. I'm not a hamburger and soda-pop gal. Don't you know that by now?"

"I—I can raise some fast money."

"Out of your savings account?"

"Sure. Sure. Out of my savings."

She looked him over, head to heels. She felt as though inside her head there was a little machine of shining gears, oiled efficiency, bathed in white light. Dan was absorbed into the little machine and came out neatly added up into plus and minus factors. As she had suspected for over a month, the minus factors outweighed the plus. Today was kiss-off day.

She swung her tiny feet off the windowseat, sat up and yawned in his face. She stood up and pushed by him, walking slowly across the room.

"You'll do it?" he asked eagerly.

She smiled at him. "I'm about to pack. But just your things, not mine."

His mouth sagged open. "Huh?" he said stupidly.

"You bore me, Dan. Sure, a trip is in order. For you. You can go anywhere you want to go."

The reaction was as expected. He caught her in two strides, turned her around, his fingers biting into her shoulders, his eyes wild. "You don't mean it! I bought you all this stuff. You can't mean it, Angel! I love you. I took the money out of my—savings."

Kiss-off day. She yawned in his face. "Danny boy, you never had a savings account in your life. I'll pack you up and you run far and fast or I'll call the cops."

For a moment she thought the little machine in her mind had given her the wrong balance. His right hand slipped off her shoulder and chill, damp fingers closed on her throat. She stood very straight, looking up into his eyes. His fingers almost closed her throat, turning her voice into a tiny rasp as she said, "You can't even kill, Danny."

When his hand slipped away from her throat, she doubled a small white fist and struck him in the mouth. She left him standing there and went into the bedroom.

She hummed softly to herself as she packed his things. When she came out, struggling under the load in the suitcase, he was sitting on the windowseat, his face in his hands. She dropped the suitcase over by the door, handed him his jacket.

"Rise and shine," she said.

He didn't move. Humming again, she walked to the phone, dialed a number, leaned against the wall, holding the phone, watching him.

He lifted a tortured face and looked at her with frightened eyes. She cooed into the phone, "Joe, darling! That's right. Honey, there's a stupid man here annoying me and I can't get rid of him. Um-hmmm. He wouldn't give you much of a battle, Joe. About five minutes? Hold the line a moment."

She cupped her hand over the mouthpiece. Dan stood up. He held his jacket over his arm. With no expression on his face he walked to the door, picked up the suitcase and left. He slammed the door behind him.

She listened to the phone. Somebody was saying, "Hey, lady! Who is this Joe? You got maybe the wrong number. Lady! You still on there?"

She hung up, banging the phone down onto the cradle with unnecessary force.

She walked slowly into the bedroom, delaying the pleasure. In the second drawer of the bureau, far in the back, was the savings account book, her bank's name stamped in gold on the cover. She stretched out on the bed on her back, her silky hair a pool under her head. She looked and marveled at the neat, precise, miraculous little numbers the tellers had written into her book. Rustle of bills. Slap of the date stamp against the book. Scratch of pen. "Thank you, Miss Baran."

And Dan thought he had been so clever about the money. The pout was always useful. "But,

Dan, honey, see how sheer these are? They cost four dollars." Actually they had cost a dollar eighty-three. Two seventeen for the little leather box which, when it held enough, was emptied for the bank deposit.

"Danny boy, this dress is an original. Two hundred and seventy-five. Yes, I know it's cotton, but look at the lines, Dan. Look at the lines!" The dress cost twenty-nine ninety-eight.

And thus the neat little figures added up to a respectable total. It was funny to think of the term "respectable" and then remember how Dan had obtained the money.

It was time to back out. His nerves were shot. Much worse during the past four days. Unaccountably worse. He'd crack, and if a girl had booted him out before he cracked, then that girl wouldn't be implicated in what might turn out to be a most unwholesome mess.

She tucked the little book tenderly away.

Within minutes the hot water was steaming the inside of the glass door to the coral and ivory shower stall. The water drummed on her small body, on her firm flesh.

She stood, her face uplifted, and in that moment she could have posed for a calendar presentation of an angel. There was a dedication about her, a look of silvery, hallowed beauty.

It was kiss-off day for Mayla Baran . . . Angel, to her friends. . . . At the moment Mayla stepped out of her shower, Paul January crushed a mosquito against his cheek and suddenly tensed as he heard the crashing in the brush.

The moon of early evening had drifted under a cloud. He listened and the furtive noise stopped, continued with more caution. Paul frowned. Police would be carrying lights. He wondered if it were someone lost near the lakeshore.

The sudden silence was ominous. He listened, heard the night noises of the insects, the baying of a distant dog, the rustle and chuff of a faraway train, hooting its sorrow at the stars.

"Paul?" The voice was close, strained, cautious and very dear.

He spoke and then she was beside him. He could not see her. With his arms around her he could feel her tremble, the convulsive gasps of her breathing, the race and hammer of her heart.

"Oh, Paul," she said softly. "They—they have been following me. A man named Krobey made them follow me. But I got away. I took the other road. The car is parked across the lake. I didn't dare come here through Rockwarren. My darling, you've got to come back with me. It's dangerous for you here. The newspapers have given it such a big play. Some policeman might find you here and shoot you before you could . . ."

"Before I could strangle him?"

"Come on with me. Bring the blanket. I know where you can stay in the city. It will be safer there. And I have a lot to tell you on the way."

"Do we walk across the water?"

"Silly! I took a boat. I—I borrowed it."

"Aha! Thief consorts with murderer. Now I can blackmail you, my proud beauty."

"It's really a safe place. Can I carry the little suitcase? It's the home of the doctor I worked for. His wife and children are away for a few weeks. He trusts me. He didn't ask any questions. He has a vacant room you can use."

Together they blundered down to the lakeshore, had a moment of panic before they found the rowboat. She sat in the stern and he rowed, favoring his bandaged side. Halfway across the lake the moon came out from under the large cloud. Her face shone in the moonlight. Her lips were parted. She smiled at him and said, "This is silly. I've got so much to tell you. But you'll have to stop looking at me or I won't be able to say it right. Listen, Paul . . ."

CHAPTER EIGHT
DORIS LOGAN

She stood in the upper hall of the desolate rooming house until she was weary of standing. There was an old newspaper on a radiator. She unfolded it, placed it on the floor and sat, her feet on the top stair, her chin on her hands. The gnarled little man who smelled of stale sweat and who called himself the superintendent had been very talkative, never once looking at her face.

"Yeah, he's been living here two years. Year ago he sort of moved out but kept the room. Slept here every once in a while. Got his mail here. Come in drunk last night, case you're interested. Slept most of the day. Didn't go to work, far as I could see. He took off late this afternoon. Guess you missed him by an hour or better. I guess he'll be back alright tonight, but I couldn't guarantee nothing."

She felt like a woman in a scene from a cheap melodrama. And she had dressed for the part. A dress of the wrong color, too tight a fit, a foolish buy of several months ago. Earrings longer than she liked. Too much lipstick, smeared heavily to give her mouth a square look, a ripe hardness.

Early in the evening there had been much traffic, many pedestrians. But the night had grown more still. Far down the street a juke blasted the cool night air. The heavy rhythm came through, pretending to be a faster heartbeat.

She leaned against the railing post and near her right foot was a neat array of the four cigarettes she had butted against the dry-rotted wood.

The screen door slammed and she straightened. The man moved slowly toward the stairs, walking with the wooden method of the very drunk. He was partially bald, the skin of his scalp glowing under the hanging bulb with a sick pallor.

He kept his eyes on the stairs. She was directly in his way. She didn't move. At last he saw her feet, stopped and stood very still. Slowly he lifted his eyes to her face, full of an unbearable expectation.

The look faded into dullness. "Thought it was her," he muttered.

"Dan Walker?" she asked.

He walked carefully around her, went to the door on which she had knocked, reaching for his key. It fell onto the floor. She bent and picked it up.

He looked at her as though seeing her for the first time. "I'm Walker." He said his own name with an odd mixture of contempt and disgust.

Unlocking the door for him, she pushed it open. The room was dark. It smelled sour and dusty.

With the lights on, it became one of those impersonal rooms such as are seen in fourth-rate hotels. A bed, chair, table, bureau, rug, radiator and window. The sheets on the unmade bed were gray and twisted.

She shut the door behind her. He turned and stared at her, puzzled. "What do you want?" he demanded.

Before she could answer he said, "You're another of them."

He reached clumsily for her. She evaded him easily. Blundering against the door, he turned around, scowled and said, "Who the hell are you, anyway? How did you get in my room? Did I bring you here?"

"Darrold sent me."

Once again he froze the way he had on the stairs. She couldn't read his face. He sat on the bed. "Go on," he said huskily. He seemed suddenly to be more sober.

"He couldn't come, himself. You know how it is, Mr. Walker. He has to stick around and answer questions, and besides, it would look funny if he came here."

"Go on."

"Mr. Darrold asked me to come over to see you and tell you that you'd better stick to your story."

"What story?"

"About putting him on the train. He says it's important."

Walker laughed. It was a yelp without humor. "He thinks it's important. What do you know? Darrold, the man of distinction. Wouldn't that hand you a laugh, though?"

"Why should I laugh?"

Walker stood up, walked to the bureau, steadied himself against it and looked at his face in the mirror. He took a comb from the top of the bureau and carefully combed his hair to cover his baldness.

To his reflection in the mirror he said, "I don't like it and you can tell Darrold that I don't like it. Where the hell does he get off bringing in women on the deal? How much did he tell you?"

It was the critical point. Doris Logan managed a smirk. "How much did he tell me about you? You and the money?"

Dan Walker cursed. He took a bottle from the top drawer of the bureau, drank deeply, corked it and replaced it. Turning on Doris, he said, "It isn't half as important as Darrold thinks it is. You understand that? Not half as important. It was important yesterday. Right up until the minute Angel . . ."

He sat down on the bed again and cried. There was no dignity in his tears. Small-boy tears, with contorted mouth, gasping sobs and squinted eyes.

He looked at her through the tears, and suddenly stopped crying. "I've seen you," he said. "I've seen you before!"

"Sure. Right out there on the stairs."

"Some other place."

"Was I with Darrold?"

"No, you weren't with Darrold." He imitated her tone of voice.

What was the name he had said? She wondered if she should take a chance. "I think I saw you with Angel," she said.

"Never again. Never any more." Once more he began to cry.

She sat down. When he looked at her, she shrugged and said, "Friend Darrold gets all the breaks. He'll go free, and from what he told me, I wouldn't be surprised if he hooked up with Angel."

It couldn't have been more effective if she had stabbed him with a hot poker. He jumped up, his eyes wide. "What did he say?"

"It wasn't important."

His fingers hurt her shoulder. "Tell me!"

With her head tilted to one side she said,

"Oh, he just said that Angel had more brains than she needed to see through a punk like you."

Walker paced the room, with much better coordination. "Oh, he did, did he? A punk like me, hey?"

It was the moment to test the guess that she and Paul January had made. She said casually, "Of course, if a man happened to be in a little jam, and if he could put the finger on a man who was in a much bigger jam, it might go a lot easier with him."

The anger went out of him. He sat on the bed for a moment, then with blank face walked to the door, opened it and went down the hall. She heard another door slam. Suddenly she had a horrid suspicion. She ran after him, her heels skidding on the bare hall floor.

He had stretched out in the tub to do it. And he hadn't done it very well. She had time to find the gaping artery, pinch it shut between finger and thumb. She sat on her heels, holding his life fast, and began to scream with all the force of her young lungs.

CHAPTER NINE
GAYLORD DARROLD

The hammering at the front door and the ringing of the bell awakened him. He waited for a time to see if they would go away. They didn't. He sat on the edge of the bed, nodded politely to the empty bed beside his and said, "Good morning, Cynthia, my dear."

After he had scuffed into slippers, belted the robe around him, he padded down the stairs. He pulled the front door wide open, smiled at them and said, "Quite a committee for so early in the morning!"

"It's a little after eleven," Lieutenant Krobey said. With Krobey was the burnished De Wolfe Haggard, the jovial little Sergeant Love, a tall and lovely redhead and a quiet-looking young man.

"This here is the murderer, Mr. Darrold," Krobey said. Darrold saw that the young man was manacled to Sergeant Love.

Darrold felt an enormous tension within him relax. A spring suddenly broken. He cursed deep in his throat and jumped at the quiet young man. He felt the jolt from his knuckles all the way up to his shoulder. The young man sagged and Love supported him.

Krobey grabbed Darrold and said, "Hey! None of that, now. We know how you feel, but none of that. Just settle down. We want to re-enact the murder. This killer is named Paul January. This young lady will play the part of your wife. First we want Mrs. Morgantine to get a look at this guy. Then, if you want, you can watch our little play."

Mrs. Morgantine, shrill, positive and exultant, had been hurried off. The group adjourned to the kitchen.

The kitchen was exactly as it had been the day of the murder. In fact, a few traces of the chalk outline on the linoleum remained.

Sergeant Love unlocked January's wrist. "No breaks, fella, or we shoot," Love said severely.

January rubbed his wrist and then fingered the lump on his jaw. Darrold thought that January had a proper hangdog look.

Krobey took charge. "Okay, Miss Logan. You stand over there. Where was she, January?"

"Closer to the sink."

"Like this?" Doris asked.

"That's fine," January said, swallowing hard. Darrold leaned against the far wall.

"I was right here," January said, "and Mrs. Darrold was over by the sink."

There was the sudden, surprising crash of a shot. Doris Logan sagged over the sink, toppled back onto the floor. Darrold watched her, intensely amazed. He was confused. He turned and stared out the open window.

He stared and stared. Then he looked back at Krobey and Love. They were both moving toward him.

"Hey!" he said weakly. A patrolman in uniform appeared in the doorway to the kitchen.

"Them blanks are loud, hey?" the patrolman said.

"Are you men crazy?" Darrold demanded.

"Like foxes," Krobey said. "All you got to do is tell us why you looked out that window, Darrold."

"Well, I . . . well, nobody had a gun and . . . well, it seemed the logical . . ."

"But, Mr. Darrold," Krobey said sweetly, "you didn't look around at us to see if we had fired a gun. You looked from the girl to the window. Why?"

Darrold's lips felt like dry pork fat as he stretched them in a smile. "Don't be absurd," he said in a thin voice. "There's your man!"

But January wasn't where he pointed. He looked. January was over by the sink. He had helped the redhead to her feet. And hadn't let go of her.

"Could it be you fired through that window and killed your wife, Darrold?" Krobey asked.

"Do you have to lean over me and breathe in my face?"

Darrold had moved back until he touched the wall and still Krobey's face was inches from his. "Damn it!" Darrold yelled. "January is your man. They quarreled. Cynthia shot him and . . ."

Krobey underlined it for him by asking, "Who said anything about January being shot, Darrold?"

Out of the fear that enveloped him, Darrold made one last effort. "Nonsense, Krobey! When she was killed I was on a train a long way from here. You people proved that."

"Oh, you mean Dan Walker, the bookkeeper? Yeah, his books were checked this morning. You were pretty clever to find the way he was rigging the books. And then, to make him play ball with you, you told him you'd squeal on him unless he swore he put you on the Empire City."

Darrold looked from one face to the other. Suddenly it felt good to be leaning against the wall. "Unwritten law," he said. "Deserved to die. Sure, I killed her. I borrowed Walker's car, drove over here, parked on the high road, came down through the brush to the new house next door. The window was always open. I killed her.

When he started toward the window, I had to give him one. I drove back to Barnston and took a later train, made a few of my appointments in Richfield, stayed overnight and drove back here the next morning."

"Unwritten law? What unwritten law, Darrold?" Krobey asked.

"She drove me crazy," Darrold said, his mind racing for escape.

"And so you killed her?"

"Yes. I bought the gun nine months ago."

Love snapped the handcuff onto Darrold's wrist, yanking heartily.

As Love walked out with Darrold trudging along behind him, Krobey looked at January and the redhead.

Krobey said, "That Walker guy cut his throat and died last night without opening his mouth to confess."

Krobey watched them for a moment, sighed heavily and walked over to the open window, put his elbows on the sill and looked out.

Three Apes from the East

H. H. Stinson

H(ERBERT) H. STINSON (1896–1969) lived in California, where he worked as a journalist and police reporter. While working as a newspaperman, he also wrote fiction for the pulps, selling a Western to *Top Notch* in 1928. He also wrote plays, including *Ace Is Trumped*, a one-act published in *Hollywood Plays* (1930). His career as a pulp writer lasted about two decades, with contributions to most of the major magazines of the era, including *Argosy*, *Dime Detective*, *Dime Mystery*, *Detective Fiction Weekly*, and *Black Mask*. His best-known series character, Ken O'Hara, appeared in fourteen *Black Mask* stories, beginning with "Give the Man Rope" in the April 1933 issue. Joseph T. Shaw, when he compiled *The Hard-Boiled Omnibus* (1946), his important anthology of *Black Mask* stories, selected this story for inclusion, but his editor at Simon & Schuster thought it weaker than the other stories and dropped it, along with several others. The tales about O'Hara, a gritty, two-fisted reporter for the *Los Angeles Tribune*, featured an authentic newspaper background based on Stinson's own career. He also wrote a series about another tough detective, Pete Rousseau, for *Dime Detective* in the post–World War II years. In all, Stinson wrote more than sixty mysteries for the pulps, as well as other genre stories for both the pulps and such slicks as *Liberty*. Only one Stinson novel made it into book form: *Fingerprints* (1925), which was published under the pseudonym Hunter (his mother's maiden name) Stinson.

"Three Apes from the East" was published in the March 1938 issue.

Three Apes from the East

H. H. Stinson

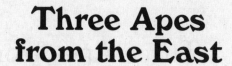

"Speak no evil, see no evil, hear no evil"—but a killer forgets to do no evil.

 IM HARPER, LOS Angeles manager for International, likes to keep his office as unadorned as a gun turret, his desk as bare as the Mojave desert. He doesn't believe in doodads, mementoes, bric-a-brac. So I was surprised to see what he had in front of him when he called me in late in the afternoon.

A third of the desk top was occupied by three apes in brass. Everyone knows the three monkeys I mean—one has his paws over his mouth, the second has them over his eyes and the third is holding his ears. I guess every family in the country has acquired one of the things some time or

other and the gag that goes with the knick-knack is: "Speak no evil, see no evil, hear no evil."

"That," I said, "is a swell mascot for a detective agency."

The boss said without a smile, "The way our office has been producing lately, you and two other ops must have sat for it."

Somebody in a chair off to the side of the boss' office giggled. I looked over and it was Sue Jordan, small and blond and as dumb-looking in her very lovely way as ever. Behind that ga-ga beauty-winner's map, though, is a combination of plenty gray matter, no nerves and a heart that could double, most of the time, for the business section of an electric icebox. Sue is the ace-in-skirts op of International and they shoot her around the map wherever necessary. She admits she's good and usually proves it.

I said, "Hi, mug. I thought you were annoying the boys in the Chicago office."

"I was, Kerry," she cooed, "but they decided you boys out here needed the help of an expert, and here I am."

"Cut the so-called comedy, you two," Harper growled. His eyes jetted away from me toward the good-looking lad beside Sue.

The lad was in his thirties, as sleek as an oiled seal. There was a dark sharpness to his eyes, a leanness about his olive-skinned face. He had on snappy clothes, just saved from being too snappy by their sober color.

Tim Harper said, "Mr. Kirkwood, this is Mr. Thorne, one of our better operatives in his serious moments. Between Thorne and Miss Jordan, I believe we can wind up your case."

Kirkwood looked at me with an impersonal and very country-club stare but didn't bother to say hello. I got the idea without much trouble

that, so far as he was concerned, I ranked a lot below guys like caddies and locker-room attendants. He probably spoke to them. It was either that or else he was putting on the swank front to cover up a bad case of the jitters. Some lads are like that.

Apparently they had talked the case pretty well out before I was called in. Kirkwood said curtly to the boss: "You understand that you're to use only the threat of publicity but that the papers must not get a whisper of it. If you think you're apt to bungle it . . ."

The boss starched his voice a little, said, "International knows how to handle a case, Mr. Kirkwood. There isn't a press agent in the organization."

"Very well," Kirkwood said in his down-the-nose manner. "And Miss—er, Jordan is to report to me what has happened immediately afterward."

He spared the boss half a nod as a good-by, didn't include Sue or me and beat it.

I said, "He'll have to take four hot showers to get himself clean after associating with us."

"I think he's too handsome for words," Sue purred.

"Not for some words," I said.

Tim Harper rumbled, "You don't have to fall in love with him. All you have to do is work for him. So get going—or are both of you waiting for wheelchairs?"

"Am I supposed to guess what this is all about, boss?"

"Sue can tell you. Beat it—and take this triple atrocity with you."

I gathered he meant the three apes so I picked them up. They weighed about six pounds. I said, "What'll I do with 'em?"

"Think something up."

In the outer office, I told Sue: "I know I don't catch on very quick but to date this all seems very screwy to me."

"Never mind, darling," she said. "Just leave the brain work to me."

When I put the three apes down on a desk, they tumbled over and the credit line underneath said, "Made in Japan." I said, "That reminds me. I've got an aunt in Japan."

"The Japanese branch of the family?"

"Have your fun. This is Aunt Frieda and she's on one of those world tours. She sends me a carved elephant from every place she hits. The score now is sixteen and I never did like elephants. What's this all about?"

"I'm so hungry, Kerry. I could talk better if you'd take me to dinner."

"Sure," I said. "And we'll make it Dutch."

Over wienerschnitzel at the Bauerhoff, Sue told me. It seemed Kirkwood was married to the daughter of an old dame, named Helen K. Woodring. I knew about her vaguely: a widow with money, more or less social position, and a yen for chasing around with guys half her age. The daughter was blind, Sue told me.

"A break for her," I said. "She doesn't have to look at that smooth slug she's married to."

"Perhaps some of us girls like 'em smooth, you old rough diamond, you," said Sue, surrounding wienerschnitzel in her stride. "Anyway, she married this Paul Kirkwood about five years ago. He came out from the east and nobody knew much about him except that he could make a golf course sit up and beg. He's a broker now but I gather he still golfs better than he brokes."

"Even if he was open champ, I still wouldn't like him."

"He's probably all right, I think. But the point is that the Woodring lady has the protégé complex, provided the protégés are young and good-looking. Two years ago she was backing a candidate for Clark Gable's niche; next it was a young second Caruso and now it's the founder of a cult, the cult of Man's Triumph Over Evil."

"It'll be a flop. The name's too long for headlines."

"I gather it hasn't cost her much in the shape of money yet," Sue said, inspecting her beer stein carefully on the theory, maybe, that there was a trap-door in the bottom and she'd find more beer under that. "But I suppose Kirkwood is afraid the cult will operate too heavily on her purse and he's beating trouble to the punch. Anyway, he hired us to find out about this grand lama of the three apes."

"That's where the monkeys came from?"

"They're the symbol of the cult. I bought the monstrosity when I joined up, so I brought it to the office as evidence for my expense account. How about more Pilsener, Kerry?"

"You can have all you can pay for, sweet-heart."

We had more and Sue drew the rest of the picture. A lady op had been indicated so Harper had requisitioned Sue and she had dropped out to the cult headquarters in a big, old house on top of Mount Washington where you could see all over the city. The grand lama operated under the name of Doctor Sivaja but his real name was Eddie Levy and he was a disbarred lawyer from St. Louis who had done a rap in Atlanta for abusing the mails. Sue had got his prints by dropping her vanity case practically between his ankles so he had to pick it up and the F.B.I. had done the rest.

That evening we were to see him, put the cards under his nose and tell him we'd wise the newspapers to his real identity if he didn't fold his turban, steal away in the night and lay off gullible old gals like Mrs. Woodring. Only it had to be all bluff because we couldn't wise the papers and maybe let Mrs. Woodring in for a lot of kidding publicity.

"But I have a hunch," Sue said. "I've a hunch it won't be as easy as that."

"Nuts," I said. "No guy on the make can stand up under the threat of publicity."

"You haven't seen him, Kerry. He's different than the usual faker. He acts as though he really had something."

"So the great Jordan is beaten before she starts."

Sue gave me her poor-chap-you're-so-dumb smile. "No, little man. I merely said it wouldn't be quite as easy as you, in your naïve fashion, expect. I know something about psychology."

Sue can get under my skin more easily than any other dame in the world. I said, "You and your psychology. Five bucks says he'll be travel-ing inside of forty-eight hours."

"You've made a bet." Sue grinned.

The waiter brought two checks like I'd told him. I picked mine up and Sue took hers, began to fumble in her purse. Her face got apologetic.

She said, "Kerry, you can't guess what I've done."

"Yes, I can. You've left all your money in your other pants. O.K., give me the check."

Walking out beside me, she cooed: "Thank you, Kerry, for the lovely dinner."

"Thank you," I said, "for the lovely buggy ride."

Doctor Sivaja—or Eddie Levy—was a dark-faced, young-looking bird, who wore a black turban and conventional tuxedo. He did a nice, quiet, convincing talk that was half religion, half modern psychology. He talked from a dais in what had been the living-room of the old house while a circle of about thirty women and five men, who looked sheepish, as though their wives had dragged them there, listened piously. The symbol of the three apes was everywhere—worked into the hangings, the decorations, the up-holstery of the furniture.

After the talk the doc did a little bow and dis-appeared through black curtains at one side of the room. The audience came out of its trance and began to straggle from the room.

"He draws a nice house," I told Sue. "The woman in gray is president of a woman's club, the one behind her knocks out two grand a week writing movies and I think the dame with the long nose and jaw is a socialite from the polo set."

"Are you sure of her," Sue wanted to know, "or are you just making that guess because she looks like a horse?"

"Where was la Woodring tonight?"

"Kirkwood promised to keep her home tonight."

We were the only ones left in the room when a girl who looked like Jane College from Bryn Vassar—flat-heeled shoes, horn-rimmed specs and black hair as straight as violin strings—put an eye on us.

Sue said under her breath: "Miss Frake, the

doctor's secretary." To the girl as she came over to us, Sue explained that we'd like to consult with the doctor.

Jane College looked doubtful but finally said she'd see and went through the black curtains. She came back in a minute, said: "Doctor Sivaja will see you, but only for a few minutes. He is very tired tonight."

We followed her through the curtains and after a moment came into a long room, a book-lined room. Sivaja—or Eddie Levy—sat in a big chair at a big desk the length of the room away from us. The three apes were everywhere in this room, too, including a big figure on the desk. It was a nice room, a quiet room, and the only thing out of place was a big packing case, opened, at one side.

The doc said, sort of gently, "Thank you, Miss Frake."

Jane College went out and the doc said, "Sit down, Miss Jordan. And you, too, Mister—ah—"

"The name, Eddie," I said, "is Thorne. Kerry Thorne."

I'd expected my approach to get a rise out of him. It didn't—much. He looked sort of interested, not at all upset. He said, pleasantly enough: "I noticed you in the audience, and I had you spotted for a private dick. When I put that together with Miss Jordan's vanity-case stunt to get my prints the other night, I was sure of it. Sit down and get your errand off your mind."

I had to admit he'd thrown the first punch and for a moment it had me backing up. We sat down and I looked at Sue. She was looking at me. The doc smiled.

He said, "Maybe I can help you get started. You're being paid by Paul Kirkwood. Is that correct, Miss Jordan?"

Sue nodded.

"And you've found out that my real name is Levy and that I'm an ex-convict. That's correct, also?"

I said, "You know the answers, Eddie."

He seemed not so indifferent as he was unworried. He said, "And what comes after that?"

Sue pulled out the sympathetic stop in her voice. She said, "Perhaps we're doing you an injustice, Doctor. Or should I say Mr. Levy? I have a feeling that you're not up to any particular mischief, that possibly your meetings are doing these people some good. But by faking your identity, you've put yourself in a spot. Mr. Kirkwood means to expose you unless you agree to leave the city and not communicate with Mrs. Woodring any longer."

The guy didn't say anything for a little while. He wasn't looking at me at all and the eyes he kept on Sue weren't panicky, weren't even unfriendly. His right hand kept tossing a small replica of the three apes into the air, catching it as it came down again.

Finally he said, dryly: "Thanks for the vote of confidence, Miss Jordan. Just tell Mr. Kirkwood for me that I'm not worried. In the first place, I have reasons to believe he won't expose me. In the second place, if he does, it can't really harm me."

For the first time some feeling showed on his dark face. He put down the figure of the three apes, spread his hands and said, "Has it occurred to the pair of you that I may be quite sincere in my philosophy of Man's Triumph Over Evil? I'm quite frank in saying that in the past I've been an evil man. I'll even admit that in the beginning I founded my school of thought with something evil—the lust for money—in my mind. But I discovered I had stumbled onto the truth, and in convincing others I have convinced myself. If I don't relish having my pupils know that I am an ex-convict, it is only because it will handicap me in importing my philosophy to them, not because of any fear for myself. For I know that if I refuse to recognize the existence of evil, then no evil can really harm me. Do I make myself clear?" He really sounded as though he meant what he said.

Sue said gravely, "Doctor, I believe you're sincere. But Mr. Kirkwood is just as determined as you are sincere. Why can't a compromise be worked out? I'm sure he'd be satisfied if you merely went on a nice vacation—six months or so. By the time you got back, his mother-in-law would have another enthusiasm and everyone would be happy."

The doc shook his head. "That's quite ridiculous, Miss Jordan. After all, while Mrs. Woodring is a charming woman and one of the most prominent members of my little circle, she is only one of quite a number to whom I am bringing my message. I have no intention of giving up my work and Mr. Kirkwood had better think carefully before he exposes me. You can tell him for me that even a good man isn't entirely helpless against an evil man and that he who speaks evil often brings evil upon himself."

I said, "Listen, Eddie, we're using a lot of dollar words here. Can you put that in ordinary English?"

He smiled. "Kirkwood will understand. And I'm like the first of my three little monkeys here: I'd rather speak no evil."

"I still think you're shadow-boxing," I said.

He bowed as though he didn't care what I thought. The conference seemed to be over and I tracked Sue through the curtains, feeling clumsy-footed compared to his quiet sureness. Jane College met us outside the study, flat-heeled ahead of us to the front door.

Under her breath, Sue said, "At least I win five bucks."

"It was an act," I said. "Wait forty-eight hours and see."

We were half-way through the front door when things started to go *boom-boom* back in the study. There was one shot before I could get around, another while I was turning and a third by the time I got my feet going. Sue was behind me and I had a vague impression that Jane College was under way in our wake.

I got through the black curtains and the picture smacked me in the face. The doc was on his knees by the desk, clawing at the top, trying to pull himself up. He didn't have a chance of making it and while I was still a dozen feet away, he caved and went down in a heap. His clawing hand pulled objects off the desk onto him, among them the large figure of the apes. The phone was already on the floor, receiver off. The three small monkeys, the ones he'd been playing with a few minutes before, lay on the rug beside the phone.

He coughed, retched and the brightness of blood jumped across his chin. And he died while I was easing him into a less tortured position. No wounds showed in front and I figured he'd been shot in the back, while he was sitting at the desk.

Beside me, Sue said, "The poor guy!"

"Anyway," I said, getting up, "he was right on one angle. He'll speak no evil from now on, not even about the guy that gunned him."

Behind us, Jane College was tuning up with hysterics. She had her hands over her eyes and her mouth open, making lots of noise. I thought what a swell thing it would be if she weren't around, for more reasons than one, and I got ideas. Between her screams, I tried to find out from her if there was another phone in the house. She paid no attention until I grabbed her shoulders, shook her.

"Is there another phone in the house, another outside wire?" I said.

"W-what?"

I said it over and she told me, still looking half-witted from fright, that there was a phone upstairs in the doctor's bedroom.

"Then get on it and call the cops," I said. "We can't use this one. We can't touch anything in here until the cops arrive."

She looked as though she finally understood and I let go of her. She streaked out through the curtains.

I gave Sue a shove, said, "Out there with her. Keep her away from this room as long as you can."

Sue didn't argue. She went. I snapped on more lights, cased the room with my eyes in a hurry. Down the room a door was open, a door that hadn't been open before. I looked through the doorway, saw the room was a small, bare one, furnished only with a big chair, a couple of straight-backed chairs, as though the doc had used it as a sort of confessional for folks who didn't like talking in a big room. The thing that interested me was that the room opened to a patio and the patio door swung gently in the night wind. The picture was clear. Somebody— perhaps they'd been in this small room while we were talking—had opened the door to the study, shot the doc through the back and beat it through the patio.

As I say, that was interesting, but what I had on my mind were letters, papers, anything that could hook up Mrs. Woodring with the doc. After all, International was being paid to keep her clear. I went through the doc's big desk fast and found nothing I wanted. One of the pictures on the wall looked a little cockeyed and on a hunch I lifted it away. Behind it was a wall safe and I began to believe in luck. The outer door was ajar and keys dangled in the inside door.

Inside I found cash, a sheaf of A-1 bonds and a thick package of letters held together with a rubber band. I got the rubber band off and leafed through the letters. He'd had 'em from socialites, top-flight picture people, even from big-shot business guys. I found five on the stationery of Helen K. Woodring, slid those in my pocket and stuck the others back in the safe. I knew the newspapers would have a lot of fun with those letters and their senders but la Woodring was my only lookout.

When I had the picture back in place, I eased up a little. There might be other stuff around that would tie in the Woodring dame but I'd have needed hours to prowl the entire layout and I had to gamble on the letters being all there was. Just out of curiosity I got down on my knees and put my ear to the phone receiver. If the doc had merely unhooked the receiver by knocking the phone off the desk, I'd have got the dial tone. I didn't. That meant he had been starting to dial a number when he was shot.

While I was down on my knees, the small replica of the monkeys caught my eye. Light shone on the flat, solid bottom of the figures, showed me scratches that looked like letters. I picked the thing up, held it closer to the light.

The scratches were letters and numbers reading: HI-M-N-3-7-S13. Underneath that in raised letters was the mold mark: MADE IN JAPAN. I didn't have time to think about whether the letters and numbers might mean something or nothing because just then I began hearing siren noise. But, on the chance they might connect with Mrs. Woodring, I popped the three monkeys into my pocket.

I was looking wise and doing nothing when two cops came busting into the study like a rash. Jane College was looking a lot more collected than before but as though she could still have the weeps if someone would give her the right signal. Sue was her usual composed self.

A big, red-nosed cop, in the lead, saw the body and started on us. "What's happened here? Who're you people? What're you doing here?"

I recognized the second cop, said, "Hello, Haggarty."

"Hi, Thorne," said Haggarty. He was a thin, mouse-haired guy with uneven, yellow teeth and I'd met him a couple of times out fishing on the live-bait boats. He looked at the doc's body, said, "Suicide or murder?"

"Murder," I said.

"Better call Homicide, Oscar," said Haggarty. His partner went out in tow of Jane College and Haggarty said, without bothering to fuss with the body, "What's it all about, Thorne?"

I gave him a few fragments, not mentioning the letters and the apes that I had in my pocket.

"Umm," Haggarty said. "Well, we'll wait until the Homicide boys arrive. No sense in a dumb flatfoot doing any detecting and getting stuck for a week in court. Done any fishing lately, Thorne?"

Haggarty and I cut up a lot of bait and made a tentative date to go after yellowtail in a couple of weeks. While we were doing it, Oscar came back and started to prowl the room, heavy-footed.

He wound up at the packing case and I saw him fish around in it. He said, "Jeez, a zoo."

We all took a look inside and the case was full of small figures of the three monkeys, matching the one I had in my pocket. Apparently that had come out of the case because there was one missing from the top layer. I did some quick counting of the top layer and some estimating. There must have been at least six gross of the things in the case.

"Jeez," said Oscar, "what would a guy be wanting with all them monkeys? He musta been up to monkey business."

It was a pretty weak effort but nobody topped it so we let it lie.

It wasn't long before Captain Fisher of the Homicide squad, fat and gimlet-eyed and sloppy in a blue suit that hadn't been pressed for a week, arrived with two dicks named Ahearn and Kirk.

The minute Fisher saw me, he said, "Why'd you do it, Thorne?"

I grinned. "Who's been informing on me, skipper?"

"Nobody. You've just got a naturally guilty look. What're you doing around here?"

That was something that had been on my mind from the moment I knew the situation called for cops. I couldn't say that Sue and I had been putting the pressure on the doc in order to get him out of Mrs. Woodring's pocketbook; the papers would get it and have a holiday with it.

I said, "The dead man was the founder of a new religion, a cult. And the little lady here, Miss Jordan, was one of his followers. She wanted me to meet him and hear one of his lectures. You know how I am about the ladies, skipper, so I humored her even though I did think it was screwy."

Sue gave me a sweet glance and managed to look ga-ga, although I knew she wanted to tie me up by the thumbs. She said in a coy, wounded fashion, "Why, Kerry, I thought you were really sincere."

Fisher looked as though he believed the act but I wasn't too sure of it. He's a long ways from being dumb. But all he said was, "I see. And what happened?"

I gave him the bare physical facts, how we'd talked to the doc and been at the front door with the secretary when the blasting began. Fisher scouted around a little, looked into the small room, came back. He said, "That door was closed when you were in here first?"

I said it had been.

"All right," Fisher said. "You and Miss Jordan and the other lady wait out in the next room. I'll want to talk to all of you later."

Out in the lecture room I stalled until Jane College had picked a chair near the dais and then I ambled Sue down to the other end of the room. Oscar, the red-nosed cop, stood in the doorway and kept an important eye on us.

"So I'm cult-screwy, am I?" said Sue. She had her voice low so Oscar couldn't hear what she said, but not low enough to seem suspicious. "You'll pay for that crack, Kerry. And, also, how about paying off on that bet?"

"Me pay off? Listen, I bet the doc would be out of town inside of forty-eight hours. He is, isn't he?"

"So you're going to quibble. I'll remember that. Did you find anything in there while I was phoning the cops?"

"You phoned?"

"Miss Frake was too occupied with her jitters to do it. Did you find anything?"

"Some of Woodring's letters."

She smiled. "And three apes on the floor?"

I said, "Damn clever, these Jordans."

"I saw the thing on the floor before I went to the phone. It was gone when I got back."

"It probably didn't have any bearing," I said, "but I didn't know. The way I looked at it, the doc might have been more stirred up about being exposed than he seemed on the surface. We know he pulled that crack about Kirkwood regretting it and I know he'd started to dial a phone number when somebody let him have it. That call might have been about Kirkwood, and the chicken tracks on the figure of the apes might have counted in some fashion. A lot of 'mights' but I grabbed the apes on the strength of them."

"What chicken tracks?"

I told Sue about the numbers and figures that had been scratched on the bottom of the monkeys. She made me repeat them slowly. I said, "You got any inkling?"

"None. Who do you think killed him?"

"I'm not thinking. That's the Homicide Squad's headache. We'll turn these letters over to Kirkwood and then we're out of the case."

"How about the apes you have in your pocket?"

"On those we'll wait. If it seems the cops should have them, the cops'll get them. Where were you to reach Kirkwood tonight?"

"At Mrs. Woodring's home."

"Oke. As soon as Fisher turns us loose, we'll go out there and turn over the letters."

She looked at me sort of queerly, said, "Suppose we pretend. Suppose we pretend Kirkwood had a lot to do with this killing. It will look swell for International to be playing on his side against the cops."

I chewed over that one. "What makes you think he might have?"

"Nothing. But possibilities are possibilities. We'll have to watch our step, Kerry."

There was some kind of a disturbance at the front door and then Haggarty came through the lecture room, towing a tall, young, blond guy. The blond saw me and nodded, said, "Hello, Thorne."

For a moment I didn't place him. Then I did. I said hello and Haggarty took him on into the study.

"Who?" said Sue.

"His name is Fred Manners. He's a kid who angled himself a private license some time ago. I ran into him on the fringes of a case a year ago and then never saw him again until now. I thought he'd probably faded into something that was more his speed."

A few minutes later one of the dicks came to the curtains and beckoned to Jane College. She went to the study with him and we waited. We waited some more and then we kept on waiting. It was pretty close to an hour before Fisher came out of the study. He didn't look unhappy when he sat down beside me.

I said, "Don't tell me, skipper, that you've already got it all untangled."

"Not exactly," he said, "but we've got a pretty nice lead. Did you know this guy, Sivaja, was really an ex-con named Eddie Levy?"

"What?" I said. Then I looked reproachfully at Sue. "A nice spot you led me into, Miss Jordan—associating with ex-cons."

Sue choked but she managed to mutter something about she hadn't known and she was sorry.

"Yeah," said Fisher. "An ex-con. We got that out of this secretary gal and the private dick that showed up a while ago. It seems this guy went up for mail fraud from St. Louis after taking some old Dutchman there for his life's savings. The kraut never got over it and he located this Eddie Levy here six months back and took a shot at him. Levy kept it quiet but he hired this shamus, Manners, as a body-guard. The Dutchman hasn't shown around here since then but he's written Levy a lot of threatening letters. We found those in a wall safe in the study. So tonight Manners takes the night off and it looks to me like the kraut took the opportunity to get square. Anyway, we're putting out a teletype on him."

"Here's luck," I said. "And now how's about letting Miss Jordan and me go places and get some drinks? I need two or three or seven."

"Sure," Fisher agreed. "I can reach you at the agency. And what's your address, Miss Jordan?"

Sue gave him the name of her hotel and we got under way.

A s I pulled my roadster around the corner from the side street into North Figueroa, I said, "When we get out to the Woodring place, Sue, we will go—"

"Not 'we,' Kerry."

"What do you mean?"

"I mean you can handle it from here. Why should I lose sleep?"

"Oh," I said. "Lone wolfess stuff."

She said sweetly, "Why, Kerry, I don't know what you're talking about."

"Listen, babe, I know all about you and the way you like to show us pants-wearing ops up. You think you've figured out a hot angle on this and you want to work it all by yourself and grab all the credit."

"I'm hurt, Kerry."

"Yeah," I jeered. "Nothing short of a solid crack in the jaw would hurt you. But if you want to make it a contest, we'll make it that way."

"Make what a contest?"

"I don't know but you probably do." I'd been watching the lights of a car in my mirror. When the car behind jogged through the radiance of a streetlight, I saw it was a squad car. I said, "Some cops are tailing us. I guess Fisher didn't believe everything I told him. Now my feelings are hurt."

I took the next dark cross street, unlatched the door on my side and told Sue to get ready to slide under the wheel. Around another corner, I made the street and let the impetus of my jump carry me across the curb and into some shrubbery. The roadster slowed for an instant and then spurted. The police car tagged along, and as soon as it was out of sight I walked back to Figueroa, found a drug-store and got on the phone.

I had Sue Jordan on my mind nearly as much as the phone call I was going to make. She had an angle on the fire. I felt pretty sure of that and I wasn't too pleased. She's a nice gal but she has a way of wandering off by herself and "stumbling" onto some hot lead in a case, thereby making the guy who's working with her look and feel like a first-class jackass. Not that she ever hogs the credit with the bosses; but no guy likes to feel he's a jackass.

It took a while but finally a low British voice at the other end of the wire admitted that I was connected with the home of Mrs. Woodring. I told the voice I wanted to speak to Kirkwood.

"That," said the voice, "will be impossible. Mr. Kirkwood cannot come to the phone at the moment. What is it about, sir?"

I asked who was talking.

"This is Osgood, Mrs. Woodring's butler."

"O.K., Osgood," I said. "Just tell Mr. Kirkwood a detective by the name of Thorne has something he'll be interested in and that this same guy named Thorne will be ringing the front doorbell in about twenty minutes."

Another phone call landed me a cab. . . .

The Woodring place was no less than an estate. It stood in an acre of lawns and semi-tropical shrubs out on West Washington, the whole of it surrounded by a high, balustraded wall that had cost as much dough as the average guy's entire home. There were bronze gates in the wall but they weren't closed and between them a graveled drive headed up toward a huge, white blur of house.

A block past the place, I paid the cab off and walked back to the gates. West Washington was fresh out of pedestrians at that hour but a streetcar clanked along noisily three blocks away and automobiles whirred by at wide intervals, going fast and sucking at the macadam with drawn-out, whining sounds.

Inside the gates I got off the gravel, walked on the grass. Streetlights were cut off by the wall, trees and distance, and it was dark, almost completely black. That, I guess, was the only thing that saved me from stopping a nice hunk of lead.

A clump of bushes half-way to the house swayed a little just as I came abreast of them, although there wasn't any breeze. I hadn't been expecting any rough stuff and if I ducked my head and shifted my feet fast, it was due entirely to the involuntary nerve reflexes of being damn good and scared. The clump of bushes snapped a flat, jarring explosion at me, along with a burst of blue and orange flame. The clanking streetcar was going by at that exact moment, so the shot didn't seem very loud. But it seemed plenty in earnest.

My feet, doing a rhumba as I tried to get around to face the clump of bushes and drag out my gun at the same time, tangled with the head of a lawn-sprinkler system. I went into the air, spread-eagled, and made a one-point landing on my chin. At least, I think it was my chin because I was picking blue grass out of my teeth for two days afterward.

My face was still nestling in the center of a divot when I began to remember things again. I remembered groggily for a moment and then very clearly and I didn't know whether to be sore at myself or get a laugh out of it.

"At least," I mumbled as I got my feet under me, "I'm probably the first shamus in the history of International that could knock himself out with one dive to the chin."

But when I started to pat my pockets, there wasn't anything to laugh about. Everything I'd had on me had been lifted—wallet, watch, keys, gun, a pocketful of change. And the Woodring letters and the three brass apes.

It was pretty. And to make things complete, I took three steps in the darkness and put my hoof down on top of my new hat, for which I'd laid out seven bucks just the day before. I swore for a while but there wasn't any satisfaction in it.

"Go on up to the house and take your medicine," I told myself, "you long-eared dope."

I got the wreck of my hat on and headed for the house. It turned into something definite as I got nearer, a big and very white affair of Norman architecture with a long stretch of two stories of blank windows.

Faint light inched through venetian blinds at a lower window and I leaned on the bell-push. After a minute or so, a light went on over the door. The door opened three inches on a chain and a long, white nose and eyes that had all the genial expression of marbles looked out at me.

A mouth under the long nose said, "Yes? Are you the detective person? The detective person who phoned?"

"You weren't expecting any detective persons who didn't phone, were you?"

Osgood couldn't seem to think offhand of the answer to that one but he didn't take the chain off the door.

I said, "Yes, Osgood, I am the detective chappie, the one that phoned. And I'm here to see Mr. Kirkwood. How about it?"

He finally collected himself enough to get the door unchained and I went in. When I got in, I took a good look at Osgood and he squirmed around a bit under it. In fact, he seemed to be in somewhat of a dither about something. He looked a lot like a fish but a husky fish with good shoulders and big hands that had plenty of bone and muscle to them. He wore a woolly bathrobe but trousers showed below the bathrobe and he had shoes on, not slippers. The shoes were damp around the soles, the toes.

"Lot of dew on the grass tonight, Osgood," I said.

"Dew? I don't understand, I'm sure," he said. But his eyes couldn't help darting down toward his shoes and then back at me.

"Yeah," I said. "Or did you get your shoes wet running around on these Chinese rugs?"

He licked his lips and tried to go English butler on me. He said, "I went outside a short while ago, it so happens, sir. I thought I had heard a shot somewhere on the grounds and I made a brief investigation." His eyes fastened themselves on my skinned-up face, my wreck of a hat. "I found nothing but it occurs to me that perhaps you might know quite a lot about it."

"Maybe I do," I said. "How about Mr. Kirkwood?"

"Please wait in there."

He showed me a small reception room off the hall and left me there with a reluctant look on his face, as though he didn't quite trust me not to walk off with the bric-a-brac.

The room was furnished with Louie-or-something furniture, all very elegant, and the one thing out of place was a big, bronze figure of the three apes on a small table. They made me remember the yarn I was going to have to tell Kirkwood and I felt like asking them to move over and make room for a fourth and the biggest monkey of all.

But it wasn't Kirkwood that showed up. It was two women. One of them I knew must be Mrs. Woodring and the other, the younger one, her daughter. The Woodring dame gave me the impression of a dowager queen, aching to go on the loose. Her hair was brassy yellow and, even at this hour, put up in curls and ringlets and waves. Her negligee was a generation too young for her and gave the world a load of a not-so-small bosom. She had wrinkles in her cheeks and a roll of fat between her shoulders and eyes that had a yen in them. She looked like October playing at being April and it made you sorry for her and disgusted with her at the same time.

The daughter, Mrs. Kirkwood, was another order. She had a tall, lithe body and blue eyes that would have been beautiful if they hadn't had the blank, expressionless look of the blind. Her face was pale and strong and stopped just short of being pretty. She came into the room, holding on to her mother's arm, but she had so much more to her that she almost gave the impression of leading the older woman.

Mrs. Woodring's voice sounded scared and patronizing and coy, all at the same time. She said, "You wished to see me, young man?"

I said, "No, ma'am. I want to see Mr. Kirkwood."

She arched her bosom a little farther out of the negligee. "Young man, this is my home. You can tell me whatever you have—"

The girl said in a low voice, "Mother, please. Paul will take care of this."

"Nonsense, Anne," la Woodring said. "There are a lot of very queer things going on around here this evening and—"

The girl protested again, "Mother, please—"

"I say there is something mysterious going on. Why was Paul so insistent that I stay home tonight? Why is this young man here at this hour? I insist on knowing what it's about."

But she didn't have a chance to shoot any questions at me because just then the draperies at the door parted and Kirkwood was there. He was immaculate and sleek and casual on the surface but he was breathing a little fast, as though he had just stopped being in a hurry as he got to the door of the room.

He slapped a look of pure venom at me and then shifted gears with his face so fast that by the time Mrs. Woodring had her eyes around to him, he was wearing a smile for her that damn near had a caress in it.

She looked back at him the same way, and I thought it just as well that Anne Kirkwood was blind.

La Woodring said, "Paul, what is it that's going on tonight? You're all acting so queerly and what's this man here for?"

"Now, Mother," Kirkwood said, "don't you bother your head about this man. Osgood should have told me at once that he was here instead of disturbing you."

"But, Paul—"

Kirkwood kept on smiling, patted the old lady on the shoulder. The way he did it was sensuous. The old dame beamed horribly.

He said, "You're just imagining things, Mother. This man is here to give me a report on a business investigation. Now you and Anne trot along upstairs and I'll join you there as soon as I've finished with him."

Mrs. Woodring didn't argue. She said, "Very well, Paul, dear," as meek as oatmeal, and the two women turned to go. It was pretty apparent that Kirkwood called the shots around that household and no wonder he didn't want Sivaja chiseling in on his territory.

When the women were gone, Kirkwood turned on me and there wasn't any smile in his eyes. He said savagely, "You fool, I told you and that woman detective merely to get in touch with me. The last thing I wanted was for you to show up here. I'll see that your agency hears about this in the morning."

I let it pass. I said, "Have you heard about Sivaja?"

He didn't say anything right away. His eyes bored at me and then he said, more quietly, "What should I have heard?"

"He's dead," I said. "Murdered."

Kirkwood didn't look shocked but he did

look surprised. I couldn't tell whether the surprise was real or not and I wished I hadn't led up to it quite in that way, that I had socked him with the information without any preliminaries. Then, maybe, I could have told whether he was actually surprised or putting on an act.

He found a cigarette and lit it very carefully, his face dark and taut with thought. Finally he said, "That changes things. Or, rather, it accomplishes what I wanted accomplished, although in a different way. Have your agency send its bill to my office."

"You're not interested in who killed him or why?"

"There's no reason why I should be, is there?"

"When I've finished," I told him, "you can figure that out for yourself." I gave him the scenario from the moment we'd walked into Sivaja's study until the time I'd picked my chin out of the blue grass, minus all my belongings, including the letters and the three brass apes.

As I wound up, Kirkwood was looking faintly worried and also pretty sore and not a little contemptuous. He said nastily, "You call yourself a private detective and come to me with a story like that?"

"That's my story," I said, "and I'm stuck with it. The point is, are those letters important enough to you so that you want 'em back?"

Kirkwood said, still nasty, "After a performance like this, you think you should get them back?"

"They won't shoot a guy for trying," he said, "except sometimes. Now if it was the letters that someone was after in particular, it spells blackmail. With Sivaja dead, have you any idea who would have blackmail notions in connection with Mrs. Woodring?"

Kirkwood said he didn't. But he looked thoughtful.

I said, "How about the butler?"

"Osgood? That's ridiculous. He's been with Mrs. Woodring for ten years. If that's a sample of your thinking—"

"Maybe it isn't as lousy thinking as it seems,"

I said. I was getting a little fed up with his down-the-nose attitude. "It so happens that outside of Miss Jordan, Osgood was the only person I'd informed that I was going to show up here when I did. And it's sort of plain that whoever took the pot shot at me was waiting for me and that he knew who he was waiting for. Also, Ossie has been prowling around outside just this evening. Of course, he might have passed the word to someone else after I'd talked to him on the phone."

Kirkwood said, "Ridiculous," again but he wasn't so sure of it this time.

I stood up, said, "Whoever got the letters, you want them back. That's the main idea."

"And how do you propose to get them back?"

"Whoever has them will want money for them. In order to get money, they have to ask for it. Just as soon as you or Mrs. Woodring receive any communication about them, let me know. We'll go on from that point."

Kirkwood agreed to let me know but I wasn't too certain whether he meant it or was just "yessing" me to get me on my way. He let me out without benefit of butler and I started a six-block hike to Western and Washington, where I figured I could find a cab.

I tried to do a bit of thinking while I hiked but, after all, a guy has to have a few facts to build his guesses on. I didn't even feel too sure of my guess about Osgood. If he had been with the Woodring dame for ten years, he must have had plenty of chances in that time to blackmail her if he was that kind of a guy. Maybe, at that, it hadn't been the letters that were wanted when someone let fly the slug at me; maybe it had been the three apes.

Those apes were certainly running through the whole thing, even to the extent of finding counterparts among the people involved. Sivaja had bragged that he spoke no evil and he undoubtedly wouldn't speak any from now on. And Anne Kirkwood, poor woman, didn't have to hold her hands over her eyes like the second ape because those blind eyes couldn't see evil right in front of them.

That was stretching the comparison a little, because very probably neither Kirkwood nor la Woodring were what you could call evil. My guess was that Kirkwood was a gigolo who had married himself into a dough-heavy family; and Mrs. Woodring's tired coyness was sickening rather than nasty. But, even so, I wouldn't have wanted either of them before my eyes long at a time.

As for the third ape, the one that couldn't hear any evil, I felt as though I could match that one, myself. If I'd been holding my fingers in my ears all night, I couldn't have known any less about what was really going on. That wouldn't have bothered me too much if I hadn't been working with Sue Jordan. I knew that sooner or later I'd probably find out what it was all about but when I got to that point, I had a hunch, I'd probably discover Sue sitting there and waiting for me.

At Western I found a Yellow and gave the hacker my address. When we got to the apartment where I park my extra shirt, I said, "Listen, cap, I haven't got any money on me."

The hacker stuck a steamboat-jawed face through the door at me and growled, "You're the second ginzo that's pulled that one on me tonight. What do I look like, Santa Claus?"

"No," I said, "although a beard would improve you. But what I'm trying to tell you is that if you'll come upstairs with me, I'll find some dough."

He looked happier and we went inside the lobby. It was dark except for a floor lamp in a corner. Somebody sitting in a chair in another corner got up and started for me. My hand began to go for my gun before I realized I didn't have any gun and then I started backward, getting tangled up with the cabdriver.

The guy coming toward me said, "Hello, Thorne. I've been waiting to see you."

He came farther into the light and I saw it was Fred Manners. I said, "For cat's sake, don't do things to me like that. How do you know I haven't got a weak ticker? Have you got a buck?"

"Huh?" Manners said. He had a friendly, kiddish-looking face and it was puzzled.

"What I said was, have you got a buck?"

He still seemed as though he was trying to add things up and make sense but he said, "Oh, sure," and fished a dollar bill out of his pocket. I passed the bill to the cabdriver.

Up in my apartment I found some Teacher's Highland after knocking over a couple of Aunt Frieda's elephants that I'd parked wherever I could find room. I cussed the elephants, picked them up and poured a couple of drinks. After I had them poured, Manners said he didn't use it, so I slid mine down and held the other one ready to follow when reinforcements were needed.

He scratched one pale eyebrow and grinned uncertainly. He said, "I'll bet you wonder why I showed up here at this hour."

"If you could find anyone to lay the bet with, you'd win."

"Well, it's this way. This little thing tonight does me out of my job as the doc's body-guard."

"I'm sorry," I said. "But that doesn't make me the WPA."

"Sure, I know. I just thought—well, I've had some experience and I thought maybe International might have something."

I said, "It's a lot too late for kidding. Or do you really expect me to believe you stayed up all night just so you could make out an employment application? What's on your mind?"

"That's really it," he said. He spread his knees, put a hand on each knee and looked at me straight. "At least, that's mostly it. I knew that in order to get a job with International, you have to have something more than just a wild desire to please. Well, I've got something more and it's too hot to let lie around forever. Your agency would like to solve tonight's killing, wouldn't it?"

"Not particularly," I said. "That's the police department's worry. What made you think we'd be interested?"

He laughed at me, said, "Now you're trying some kidding. After all, you're working for Kirkwood, aren't you?"

"What would you know about that?"

"Pal-enty, Thorne, pal-enty. Do you want to hear what I've got to tell?"

"Sure," I said. "I like to hear anything. Go ahead."

He shook his head. "I've always wanted a job with a top agency. If this is good—and it will be—do I connect with International?"

I was watching his face and there was youthful confidence plastered all over it; he knew he had something hot. I said, "Tim Harper does the hiring. All I can do is put in a good word for you."

"Fair enough. I've heard your word carries weight there. So here it is. Maybe I'd better start about six months back when the doctor hired me."

"I've been wondering how you happened to hook up with him."

He told me, "Through Gerda."

When I looked blank, he said, "Gerda Frake, who was secretary for Levy. She's my fiancée. I met her when we were both working for the Hunter Medical Lab. That was before I decided I'd have more fun starving as a private dick than as a stock clerk. The lab let her out and she got this job with Levy. So when this Dutchman from St. Louis tried to kill Levy, Gerda recommended me as a body-guard."

"What about this Dutchman?" I said.

"Do you mean, did he kill Levy? It's possible. He certainly hated Levy's guts. It's a funny thing, too—Levy wanted to pay back everything the guy had lost but we couldn't locate him. You see, Levy was really on the level about this Doctor Sivaja stuff of his. He'd got so he believed the 'no evil' stuff he was dishing out and he was trying to live up to it. However, I sort of doubt this Dutchman did it. From all I've heard, he was one of these guys that has to shoot off his mouth for five minutes before he does something and Levy, so the cops say, was knocked off fast and quiet."

"Go ahead. You're just getting a good start."

"That's right," he said. His eyes were pale gray under the pale eyebrows and very sharp but not hard. "Have you given a thought to Paul Kirkwood as a possibility?"

"No," I said, sounding surprised. "Why should I?"

"Because he's a swell possibility. Maybe you work for him but I'll lay odds I know more about him than you do. It so happens he started to put pressure on Levy three months ago to leave the Woodring dame alone. Levy wasn't a sap, even though he had fallen for his own line, and he put me to work checking on Kirkwood.

"It took me a while but I finally got a line and, to cut it short, I found out Kirkwood wasn't any lily, himself. He left New York six years ago just one train ahead of an indictment for embezzlement from a stock firm he was working for. About a year after he married the blind Woodring girl, the indictment was quashed. I suppose he settled up with dough he'd found in the family treasury."

"Did Kirkwood know that Levy had this information?"

"No. Levy wasn't going to use it unless Kirkwood forced him to. Like I told you, Levy was really trying to be a good boy."

"Then," I said, "it doesn't add up. Kirkwood wouldn't have any reason to do it."

"Maybe I ought to say that Kirkwood didn't know anything about it until just before the meeting tonight. Levy was tipped off during the day from St. Louis that somebody was checking his record there. He figured Kirkwood must be behind it and he phoned Kirkwood about six o'clock and asked him to come over after the meeting. I didn't hear the conversation but I'm betting Kirkwood got a hint that he wasn't sitting so pretty, himself."

That reminded me that when I'd called the Woodring house, the butler had told me I couldn't talk to Kirkwood. And that when he had come into the reception room later, I'd had the feeling he'd just arrived from some place.

Manners went on: "However, that's just

background. I don't think Kirkwood pulled it because I've got two much better candidates. How do you think Levy got himself set up in this cult racket? It took dough."

"I wouldn't know. Maybe he had some."

"He didn't have two nickels to bounce together when he got out of Atlanta. All he had was a swell idea and a couple of pals that were willing to stake him while he put the idea over. Levy never broke down and told me all this, I just picked it up a little here and a little there, and put it together. The idea was that a lot of rich screwballs, particularly women, fall for cult stuff and will let their hair down in private to the high yogi. Levy was supposed to get the dirt, pass it on to his pals and they'd put the squeeze on the saps."

For the first time I felt as though I was getting warm on the case. I said, "Who were these pals?"

"Two cons that Levy met at Atlanta. One is Skip Morris, a racket guy who went up from Chicago for income tax stuff, and the other is Harry Lake, a hot number from New York. I don't know what he was in the can for. As a matter of fact, I never saw the pair except once when I body-guarded Levy over to the Roosevelt and he talked to them there. But I know they were the reason the last couple of months why Levy kept me on."

"How do they fit into last night's caper?" I said, killing my Teacher's. I thought I could guess that but I was willing to let him tell me. I figured also that I knew just about where the Woodring letters had gone, although I couldn't dope out how anyone had managed to be waiting for me outside the old gal's house.

"Levy's idea was a swell idea," Manners said, "except that Levy went holy on these guys. He got plenty of dirt on a lot of suckers but he wouldn't pass it on to Lake and Morris. He paid them back the dough they'd staked him to but they still figured he was double-crossing them. They as much as told him last week they were going to give him the business." He grimaced, wagged his head a little. "And last night they didn't do anything else."

"Why didn't you tell the cops all this?"

"That's easy. I don't want a job on the cops, I want a job with International."

"Yeah," I said. "Incidentally, you didn't happen to knock Levy off, yourself, did you?"

For a moment Manners looked startled. He said, "You serious?"

"No," I said. "That was just to keep conversation going."

"Oh." He dripped sarcasm and I couldn't blame him. "Well, on that basis, sure. I polished him off so Gerda could lose her job at forty a week and I could lose mine at seventy-five bucks. You see, I figured I'd blackmail Kirkwood, so the first thing I did was blab all I knew to the dick that was working for him. It was kind of hard for me because I put in the whole evening lifting beer at the Lotsatime Café until fifteen minutes or so before I got back to the house. But I managed to shoot him from the café, using mirrors."

"Oh, well," I said. "I was just keeping the record clear. If I wanted to locate Morris and Lake, what kind of guys would I look for and where would I look?"

He described the pair, said, "I don't know where they hang out but maybe I can find out for you. Now how about that job?"

I told him I'd put in a word with Tim Harper and he got up to go. I was amused at this kid craving to be a dick.

At the door, I said, "There's one thing I've been wondering about. Levy had a packing case full of the three apes. What was he doing, starting a curio shop?"

Manners grinned. "Levy was as nutty about his cult as any of his suckers. He was going to pass the monkeys out the way Rockefeller did dimes. It might have been a good publicity stunt, at that."

That sounded nutty to me but no nuttier than the rest of the case so I forgot the apes. What I wanted was the letters and I had a notion that if I could locate Skip Morris and Harry Lake, I'd be locating the letters. When I got the letters, I'd toss the mugs to the cops and ease out of the picture.

So I phoned a little redhead who works the cocktail bars on Figueroa and on West Seventh.

She said she knew Skip Morris but she didn't know the other guy. "If I can find out where Morris lives," she said, "I'll call you, Kerry."

I said that would make her fifty bucks better off. . . .

When the phone rang, I'd been asleep for two hours. The redhead said in my ear, "Try the York apartments, Kerry," and hung up without saying anything more.

t ten the next morning I got Harper on the phone at the office. He sounded grouchy and what I had to tell him didn't make him feel any better and he let me know about it. I said, "Well, maybe things won't come out so badly. I'm going out to the York apartments and prowl around. Incidentally, have you heard anything from Sue?"

"No," Harper said. "And if she hasn't anything better to tell me than you have, I hope I don't hear from her."

The York apartments were four stories of dingy red brick out on Santa Monica Boulevard. There were brass plates on the hallway wall that held the cards of tenants. None of the cards showed me the names of Morris and Lake; not that I had expected it. I pressed the button under the card that said, "Manager."

A woman in a purple wrapper came to the head of the stairs. She was about fifty and very thick through the body and she had a lumpy face, a whiskey-veined nose and blue eyes as hard as agates. When I got up to her I had a card out. The card said that I was Jasper Q. Pahl of the Western Collection Agency.

I gave her the card and said, "Good morning, madam. I'm looking for a man named Morris and another man named Lake."

She backed her thick body away from me and into the open door of an apartment just off the stairway. She looked at the card and back at me and said, "Nobody here by that name."

She started to shut the door and I stopped it with my foot. I said, "They wouldn't be using those names. They skipped with a mortgaged car and it'd be worth ten bucks to locate them."

The pressure came off the door and the woman said, "What do they look like?"

"Morris is tall and about forty with a black mustache and black hair. He's sort of bald on top." I remembered Manners' description.

I hadn't heard feet coming up the stairs until I'd gone on with: "Lake is smaller. His nose has a hump where it was broken and he has one gold tooth."

The woman said hurriedly, "I told you there wasn't anybody named Lake or Morris in this building," and backed away and slammed the door quickly.

Behind me, about the level of my knees, a man's voice said, "You looking for a fellow named Lake, buddy?"

I turned around and a tall mug, who had a black mustache and black hair where it showed below a gray Homburg, was just taking the last step upward to the hallway. He was also just taking his hand out from beneath his coat and it was holding a blue-black automatic.

The tall man, who was undoubtedly Morris, said, "Come on, buddy. I'll take you to this guy named Lake."

When I didn't find anything to say, he grinned and said chidingly, "Hell, can't you even say thanks?"

We went up two more flights of stairs to the top floor, where there were only two doors along the hallway. Morris knocked on one of them with his left hand while he held the gun on me with his right. He had to knock again before the door opened and a man in his shirt-sleeves looked out at us. The shirt-sleeved man had very square, muscular shoulders and ropy forearms. He had small eyes like shiny licorice drops and the eyes twinkled at me. His nose had a hump and he had a gold tooth.

Morris said, "This guy wants to see you, Harry."

Lake said in a husky baritone, "Bring him in, Skip. We got quite a party now."

We went in single-file, with me between Morris and Lake, into a big living-room. There were two men already in the room. One of them, who was Fred Manners, sat in the exact middle of a big divan. His mouth was bloody and one of his pale eyebrows was torn. He was holding his hands tightly across his stomach and moaning and he didn't look up when we came in.

The other man was Paul Kirkwood. His skin was malaria yellow and he looked scared and a little sick to the stomach. He jerked his head like a startled horse when he saw me and his mouth opened and closed a couple of times but didn't say anything.

Morris said, "Where did Blondy come from?"

"Don't you remember him?" Lake said. "He's the guy Levy had body-guarding him. When I was coming back here with Kirkwood, I saw the guy just getting out of his car in front, so I brought him upstairs to find out why he was gum-shoeing around."

"Has he told you?" Morris asked, interested.

"He talks but he don't make sense." Lake walked over to the kid with a swing to his walk like a boxer, straightened him up with a light left to his face and then sank his right four inches into Manners' belly. Manners' retching noise was loud in the room and he doubled over again, holding his stomach muscles.

Lake walked back to me and twinkled his shiny eyes at me. He said, "From that nosy look you got, brother, you look like a dick to me."

"You ought to know," I said. "You don't have to put on an act for me."

Lake whipped the right at me without telegraphing it. It smacked me high on the cheek and shoved me off balance. I hit the wall and bounced back with my fists coming up. Morris wiggled his gun at me and I put my fists down.

"I'll learn you," Lake said, "to give me funny answers."

Skip Morris said soberly, "We're not getting any place this way, Harry. Let these guys alone

and we'll get our business with Kirkwood over and get going."

"We've got penty of time," Lake said. "It always gives me the creeps when guys follow me around and I don't know just who they are or why. I'll work on 'em awhile."

Morris shook his head. "You're nothing but a damn sadist, Harry. You like to beat guys up."

"Yeah," Lake said. "And this blond kid is perfect for it—not too soft, not too hard."

He stalked Manners again but even the light tap of Lake's left didn't straighten him up this time. Lake licked his lips and then he reached down and got a fistful of Manners' vest and hauled him upright. The kid fell forward and sideways and Lake pulled him erect again, the ropy muscles in his forearm standing out. He let him go and instantly threw his right from the level of his shoulder. The fist hit Manners' jaw with the sharp impact of a whip being snapped.

Manners' knees didn't even buckle. He went over backward, straight and stiff like a piece of wood. There was a table in the way and the back of his head hit the carved edge of it, making a dull, mushy sound. The table fell over, throwing its legs and its top around Manners' body on three sides like a fence.

Manners didn't move. Not a muscle twitched and if there was any motion in his chest, I couldn't see it. His mouth sagged wide open and saliva drooled from it; his eyes were wide open, too, but only the whites showed.

Morris made an angry, bitter sound in his throat. He said, "You damned fool, you've killed him. You've fixed us up fine." But he wasn't upset enough to take his rod off me.

Lake stooped and felt Manners' wrist. After a few seconds, he dropped it and stood looking down at him. He said sheepishly, "Hell, how could I guess the guy was a softy?"

Skip Morris began to storm at him and Lake's eyes got cold and small. They didn't twinkle anymore. He said in a soft, nasty way, "Shut up. I'm thinking."

I noticed that Morris shut up. He kept the gun pointing my way but his eyes were half on me, half on Lake, and they were worried. After a little Lake turned around and went out of the living-room. He came back right away and he had a wet bath towel in his hands, wringing water out of it as he walked. The drops fell on the carpet, making a damp trail.

"What's the idea?" Morris demanded. His voice was anxious.

"Don't you worry what I'm going to do," Lake said. He got a gun out from under his armpit and began wrapping it in the wet towel. "There's only one guy here that would do any talking about what just happened, Skip."

He looked at me and then at Kirkwood. He said, "You wouldn't do any talking, would you, handsome?"

The malaria yellow of Kirkwood's face was turning to green. He didn't try to speak, merely let his head waggle from side to side. Then he turned around and went wooden-kneed toward a window. He stood there with his back to us.

"See?" Lake said. "Handsome won't talk. He doesn't even want to see things." He had the gun wrapped in the wet towel now and he looked at me. There were orange lights behind the shiny blackness of his eyes and he looked as though he was enjoying something hugely. Nerves crawled in my stomach and my mouth was suddenly dry and my tongue was stiff. He said, "I'll bet you won't talk either, shamus."

The towel-shrouded gun was beginning to come up when out of the corner of my eye, I saw movement on the floor by the overturned table. I said loudly, hurriedly, "For cripes sake, hold it! The kid isn't dead."

Manners was moving his hands, his legs with little jerks as though he were receiving a series of electric shocks. His chest moved convulsively and a long sigh hissed through his mashed lips. Lake started to unwrap the gun, looking disappointed about something.

He said reflectively, "I don't know; maybe the guy might die yet."

He got the gun unwrapped, wiped off dampness from its barrel and put it away in his shoulder holster.

igured damask draperies divided the living-room from the small foyer through which we had come and the draperies moved a bit now. Skip Morris and Lake weren't looking that way so they didn't see Sue Jordan step into sight between the hangings. She had her pearl-handled .32 in her hand and if she had worn wings, she couldn't have looked any more like an angel.

She waited until Lake had brought his hand away empty from the shoulder holster and then she said, "That's much better."

Lake and Morris began to jerk around and Sue's voice was like a whip-lash. "Don't move, gentlemen."

Lake froze but Skip Morris got his head around over his shoulder and stared at Sue and her gun with amazed fascination.

She said, "Take their guns, Kerry."

I did just that in a hurry, saying, "If you had a uniform, Sue, you could double for the Marines at this moment."

She grinned. "I talked to the boss on the phone right after you'd told him you were coming out here. These two playboys fitted right in with what I was looking for, so I beat it out here, too. And when the manager downstairs found out I was looking for you, she got the shakes and finally told me you were up here. I talked her out of a key and here I am."

On the floor Manners was breathing a lot better.

I said, "Can you hold these guys a minute or two, Sue?"

She looked scornful. "Do you think I'm a sissy?"

I got water from the bathroom, slopped some in Manners' face. He opened his eyes. I looked at Kirkwood for the first time in minutes. He'd turned around from the window and was watching me with his eyes sunk deep in his head.

There was a bedroom off the living-room. I started through the room like a northeast gale but I didn't have to go far. The Woodring letters and my gun were in a suit-case under the bed. I stuck the gun in my pocket and, with the other two guns loading me down, I felt like an armory. I went back into the living-room and handed the letters to Kirkwood.

I said, "How much were they asking for them?"

He put the letters in his pocket without looking at them, said dully, "Thanks, but they— This isn't all; there's something else they know."

I got it. "You wouldn't be meaning something like a New York indictment?"

He didn't answer but he didn't have to. I looked at Morris and Harry Lake. I said, "Where did you guys get that information?"

Lake's licorice-drop eyes sparkled hatred at me. He snarled, "You dicks aren't the only guys that find out things."

"Keep your mouth shut," Morris said swiftly. "They haven't got a damn thing on us if you'll just keep that big mouth shut."

"Just like that," I said. "I suppose I didn't have some letters and a gun swiped from me last night and I suppose I didn't just find 'em here?"

Morris' eyes were opaque and crafty. He said stubbornly, "I don't know anything about any letters or any gun."

"You'll remember about them," I said, "when we turn you over to the cops and lay everything in their laps."

There was a little laugh. It was Sue. She said, "You're not really that dumb, are you, Kerry? International is being paid to keep Kirkwood and Mrs. Woodring out of a scandal, not shove them in. We'd be earning our money in a big way, telling the cops about letters and indictments and so on."

She was right. I said, "Yeah," and scowled at Lake and Skip Morris. "But," I said, "murder is murder, after all. We can't turn these guys loose."

"We don't have to," Sue said quietly. "All that's necessary is to show that they had another reason and a lot better one than blackmail to have killed Levy. The blackmail was just pin money."

Maybe I sounded skeptical. "And I suppose you can show that?"

"I think so. Unless I'm very wrong. We'll know soon, as soon as it will take to get all our friends here out to Doctor Sivaja's—or Levy's—cult place."

Kirkwood was looking very unhappy. He said, "But, Miss Jordan, I'd better not. If this gets into the papers—"

"I think you'd better," Sue said firmly. "Just in case. And don't worry, there'll be no reporters there."

Manners had been on his feet for a couple of minutes. He was leaning against a shiny walnut radio cabinet, looking pretty shaky. Now he stood away from the radio and took three steps in the direction of Harry Lake. His right moved fast and slammed Lake in the face. The punch didn't seem to have been thrown very hard but there was a sound of bone snapping and cartilage smashing and Lake went down as though he had been tapped with a mallet. His broken nose was broken all over again and covered half his face.

Manners slipped brass knuckles off his right hand and dropped them in his pocket. He grinned with his battered face and said, "That makes me feel a lot better."

Kirkwood had a big, expensive car downstairs and we all piled into it. Skip Morris and Harry Lake didn't make any fuss about coming with us but maybe that was because Manners and I were holding guns on them.

Kirkwood slid through traffic at fifty as though he was anxious to get the whole thing over with. I was busy clearing up some angles that had had me winging. Kirkwood admitted he hadn't been at Mrs. Woodring's place when I called; he'd gone over to see Sivaja but he hadn't got there until after the murder, he said, and all the police cars had scared him away. Lake had phoned early that morning, given him a blackmail hint and set a meet for a certain corner. That's how he'd got lured to the York apartment. He admitted he hadn't tried to get me the way he'd agreed; he'd been willing to pay off and forget it all and I couldn't blame him too much for that.

Manners had put out some feelers and had located the York apartment spot the way I had.

"And we both stuck out our chins," he said. "Lake came along with Kirkwood and caught me just getting out of my car in front. He made me right away as Levy's body-guard and the fireworks started." He shook his head, remembering some of those fireworks. "Say, how about that job now?"

I told him I hadn't had a chance to speak to Tim Harper.

Morris and Lake sneered at us largely but they were carefully not having any of the conversation.

And neither was Sue. Whatever she had up her sleeve, she was keeping there. Personally, I didn't think she had very much; the blackmail angle still looked plenty good to me.

In daylight the House of No Evil looked like just what it was: a tired, old-fashioned place that had started out life in good society forty years before and had dropped out of the parade long ago. We went in, Manners and I keeping a peeled eye on Skip Morris and Harry Lake. They were meek as lambs.

Inside the lecture room Cap Fisher was sitting on a chair only half big enough for him, talking to Jane College or Gerda Frake, Manners had said her name was when he told me he was engaged to her.

A Homicide dick, named Malloy, was lounging with his hands in his pockets and there was another guy there that I didn't know.

Jane College looked around and saw Manners and her face went white and anxious. She jumped up, said, "Freddie, what's happened? Oh, what have they done to you?"

The way she looked at him, it was easy to tell they sort of liked each other.

Manners grinned, said, "I'm O.K., Gerda. I just slipped and skinned my face on a knuckle."

"I'm a little late," Sue said. "I'm sorry, Captain."

Fisher said, "It's O.K. Us Homicide men aren't supposed to get any sleep. Anyway, I wanted to go over some things here with Miss Frake." He smiled, said, "I think I've got your drift, Miss Jordan. It sort of puzzled me when you phoned last night and said not to lose track of that packing case full of monkeys but when this lad"—he gestured at the guy I didn't know—"showed up this morning, I began to figure things out. What made you think of it?"

"It was just a hunch," Sue said. "I couldn't imagine why Sivaja—or Levy—would want six gross of the little figures. Then on the bottom of one of the figures was scratched a sort of a cipher, HI-M-N-3-7-S13."

She didn't say what had become of that particular figure and, fortunately, Fisher was too interested in what was coming to ask.

Sue continued, "I kept wondering and finally it occurred to me that maybe Sivaja hadn't wanted the monkeys but he had wanted something the monkeys brought in with them from Japan—narcotics."

Fisher said admiringly, "You're a smart girl."

"Thanks," said Sue. "This morning I called the Customs at the harbor and found Sivaja had received two other similar shipments in the last few months, one of them aboard the *Hideyoshi Maru* from Nagasaki. That cleared up the letters HI, M and N, scratched on the one figure, and the clerk at the Customs said the rest was probably a date, Jap fashion. They date their year, it seems, from the coronation of the living Emperor, which made it read March 7 of Showa Thirteen, or March 7 of this year. And the clerk said the *Hideyoshi Maru* would be sailing from Nagasaki for Los Angeles about that date. Which indicates another shipment of apes is due to arrive here on that voyage of the *Hideyoshi Maru*."

The guy I didn't know said, "I want to congratulate you, Miss Jordan, on an exceedingly clever piece of work. I sawed one of the figures open and found it contained approximately three ounces of heroin. If all the rest of the figures contain the same amount, it will be one of the largest seizures made by the Government Narcotic Bureau on this coast in a long time. Your agency has a nice amount of money coming by way of reward."

He showed a mutilated figure of the three apes and a little bottle full of snowy powder. A chunk had been sawed out of the ape that had its hands over its ears and there were traces of powder inside.

Captain Fisher said, "Swell, but where do I come in? I still got a murder on my hands."

"We even thought of that, Captain," Sue said. "We rounded up some lovely suspects for you. Introduce them, Kerry."

"Huh?" I said, looking up from the three apes. "Oh, yeah, skipper, meet Skip Morris and Harry Lake, ex-cons and pals of Doc Sivaja. They set him up in this racket here so I guess they can tell you plenty you want to know."

"Well, well," said the skipper, putting a hard and happy eye on the two of them. "They're the sort of lads I like to meet."

Harry Lake snarled through his busted nose but Morris was smooth, nonchalant. He said quietly, "We don't know a thing about this, Captain. We've got nothing to worry about."

"There's one thing you won't have to worry about, boys," the skipper told them, heavily humorous. "And that's the dope-smuggling charge. After we run you through the gas chamber for murder, the Feds won't be interested in you any longer."

Skip Morris still looked unworried. He had a very nice front. He said, "You'll need a bit of proof, won't you, before you can convict even two ex-cons of murder?"

Fisher looked at Sue, at me. He said, "How about it? You got any proof these guys pulled the killing?"

"Well," I said, "all I know is they'd threatened to get him because he'd used their dough to set up the cult racket and then double-crossed them by believing his own stuff and turning holy on them. My guess is he'd turned so holy he was even going to tip off the law on the dope smuggling and they had to shut his mouth."

"Yeah, yeah," said the skipper, "but that's guesses. Can't you give me a tighter case than that against them?"

Sue grinned. She said, "Am I to understand, Captain, that you want International to do all the Homicide Squad's work?"

Fisher reddened but he managed a grin, too. "I guess we can find out a few things ourselves from these boys."

He turned on Morris and Lake as though he meant to reach down their throats and drag the truth up.

I listened for a little and looked at the three apes in my hand for a while and thought I had never run into a screwier case. Three apes that could speak or see or hear no evil—and look what they'd accomplished along that line. I looked at them and again saw Levy lying dead on the floor of his study; I felt a slug of lead fanning my face in the darkness outside the Woodring home; I saw a blind girl and her man-crazy mother and her money-mad husband; I saw young Manners on the floor with his face battered to a pulp. The three apes had worked out swell for everybody—three apes that could speak no evil, could see no evil, could hear no evil. It was all very screwy.

But presently I began to wonder if it really had been so screwy. I got up, caught Sue's eyes and said, "Come here, sweetheart."

I walked her down the length of the room away from the rest of them.

"Listen," I said under my breath as we walked slowly toward the hall, "you were pretty smart. You figured this whole thing out all by your little self. Jordan the Magnificent!"

"Don't be sore," Sue said. "I knew you could handle Kirkwood's case without even drawing a deep breath. When I realized I probably had a big narcotic reward for International by the tail, I had to stay with it. I'd have tipped you off, Kerry, before it was all wound up. Honest!"

"Skip it," I said. "I'm not sore. But I've got to have my fun. I'll give you ten to five I can pull one out of the hat right now that you never even thought of."

Sue said, "You've made a bet."

We had come to the archway between the lecture room and the hall. I said, "O.K. Stand right where you are. Don't turn around."

She didn't turn but I did. Facing her, I could see the group down at the other end of the lecture room. I could see Kirkwood watching us out of the corner of his eye and Gerda Frake talking to Manners and Cap Fisher shaking his fist in Skip Morris' face and the Homicide dick helping him and the Narcotic man watching us in a bored fashion.

I merely wagged my chin and twisted my lips around at Sue for about thirty seconds and Sue said, "You make beautiful faces, Kerry, but so what?"

"Wait and see," I muttered, and dodged past her and walked down the room fast. I got halfway down the room before the break came.

Gerda Frake said something to Fred Manners and then she screamed on a high, sustained note that rippled my spine. Manners spun like an open-field runner, caromed off the Narcotic man and knocked him down. The Narcotic man fell into Gerda Frake, who was running toward the study doorway, and she fell flat on her face.

Manners was already in the doorway. I have to give the kid credit; he could still have made his getaway alone because everyone but myself was paralyzed with surprise. But he wasn't going to leave Jane College.

He stopped in the doorway, his gun out and swinging, and he shouted, "Gerda," and waited.

I made the mistake of continuing to come at him and his gun blasted in the room, the bullet shaving hair off my head just above my left ear. I ducked and the room boomed to another shot and when I looked up, Manners was just beginning to fall forward. He fell on his face beside Jane College but by the time I got there, he had squirmed over on his back.

Fisher stuck his gun, still smoking, back into his holster and looked down at Manners. He said in an amazed voice: "For cripes sake!"

The skipper's slug had slammed through Manners' belly. I could see a little blood oozing

out, staining his shirt front. I said, "I'm sorry, Manners."

"Yeah," Manners said, making heavy weather of it. "I'm sorry too, Thorne. Now—now I—don't get that International job. And, hell, I wanted to be a shamus—with a good—agency. But no job—now, eh?"

 ne hour later a deputy jailer let me out of the prison ward at the receiving hospital. On the street I caught a cab and lit a cigarette as the cab started rolling. The cigarette didn't taste good but that was because I didn't feel so good. I never did like seeing guys die.

When I got to the office, I walked to Tim Harper's office, stuck my head in. Tim was there, looking not so sour now, and Sue was there, too.

She said, "Well?"

"As well as you could expect," I said. "Manners died but they got a yarn out of him before he kicked off." I sat down and put my feet on Harper's desk. He was too interested to bawl me out about it. "Manners was the guy who thought up the gag of getting heroin in by ordering the apes, supposedly for the cult, and loading them with dope. Sivaja found out about it when he overheard Manners making a phone call from the house a couple of days ago about the shipment that was due.

"Sivaja beat Manners to the shipment at the Customs and told him he was going to turn him in to the Narcotic folks. So Manners had to shut his mouth. He told us plenty more, too. He was the guy that took a shot at me outside Mrs. Woodring's house. He wanted to get the figure of the apes away from me and he took everything else off me to cover up that it was just the apes he wanted. He told us how he knew I had the figure and that I was heading for the Woodring place."

"I've guessed that all by my little self, now," Sue said. "Gerda Frake is deaf. She reads lips and I remember that she was in the room with us after the murder when we were talking about the letters and the figure of the apes."

"Exactly," I said. "She told Manners and he beat me to the Woodring place. Then, having the letters and knowing about Morris and Lake, he thought up a fast one. His smuggling game was washed up and he really did have a yen to be an op for a good agency, so he figured he'd plant the letters and my gun in their place, tip me off and cinch a job with us. Also, as he doped it out, if the cops had them to play with, it would divert suspicion from him. So he beat it to their place, watched them leave, got in and planted the stuff. Lake caught him outside by his car but made the mistake of thinking Manners had just climbed out of the car instead of being about to get in. But that made the planted letters and gun just as good as though Lake hadn't caught Manners. And he was willing to take a beating to let it stay that way."

"You didn't have this under your hat all the time," said Sue.

I admitted I hadn't. "I pulled it out of the air just about thirty seconds before I walked you down that room. I wasn't satisfied with the thing as we had it. Morris and Lake were taking it too easy, there were too many loose ends. Why were they wasting time on a shakedown when they should have been worrying about a hundred grand worth of heroin? While I was wondering about that, I kept looking at the three apes who couldn't speak evil or see evil or hear evil. And suddenly the thing popped out of the blue. We'd had a guy that wouldn't speak evil, a girl who couldn't see evil. So why couldn't we have somebody who couldn't hear evil—a deaf person?

"Some deaf folks can read lips so well that you'd never suspect they were deaf. If that hunch was on the level, I knew I had something. Kirkwood and the Woodring household certainly wouldn't be in on the dope setup but they were the only ones, outside of you, that I'd told about heading for there.

"Then I began to figure who had seen me talking to you about it and that pointed the fin-

ger right at the Frake girl. I started remembering things. She and Manners had worked for a medical laboratory and that put them on the fringes of the drug racket. And Manners had as an alibi only his claim that he was at the Lotsatime Café when the shooting took place and in a crowded joint like that, who's to say just what minute a guy leaves?"

Nobody answered me. I went on:

"Also I recalled how the Frake girl hadn't seemed to hear me when I told her to call the cops, not until I shook her out of her hysterics and made her look at me. Even then she had finagled it so you did the calling because she probably can't hear well on the phone. So I decided to pull my little gag on them and it worked!"

Sue said, "You certainly made the nastiest faces. What were you saying?"

"I didn't say anything but I made my lips work as though I was saying: 'We've let this thing go far enough. I'm going to put the finger on Manners and the girl and get cuffs on them before they know what it's all about.' I knew she was watching me, and I figured if my hunch was right, she couldn't help slipping Manners a warning and he'd be so startled that he'd do something to give himself away. You know the rest."

Sue got a five-dollar bill out of her purse and handed it to me. She said, "Gee, Kerry, but you're wonderful."

"Thanks, sweetheart," I said. "You're wonderful, too."

Tim Harper had been listening, not saying anything. He growled at us now but he did it with a twist to his mouth. He said, "Wonderful, my eye. All the detective work you both did on this could be put on the end of a sharp needle. Scram and make out your reports."

Sue and I got to the outside office and the office boy lugged a big package toward me and slammed it on a desk. Mailed in the Orient by my aunt.

Sue said, "Ah, another elephant from Aunt Frieda."

"If it is," I said, starting to unwrap the thing,

"I'll go nuts. I've already got Aunt Frieda's elephants strung around my apartment like a circus parade. So help me, I'll go nuts."

I got the thing unwrapped and reached in and pulled out three big brass monkeys, holding mouth, eyes, ears.

Sue laughed and laughed. She said, "You lucky, lucky boy! It isn't an elephant, after all. In case you don't know what it is, it's three apes from the East."

"Pardon me," I said, "while I go nuts anyway."

"I'll help you," Sue offered.

Death Stops Payment
D. L. Champion

D('ARCY) L(YNDON) CHAMPION (1902–1968) was borne in Melbourne, Australia, and fought with the British Army in World War II before emigrating to the United States. His first published work was a serialization under the pseudonym G. Wayman Jones, a house name, of *Alias Dr. Death* in the February to October 1932 issues of *Thrilling Detective*; it was published in book form later in the same year. In 1933, he created the character of Richard Curtis Van Loan, better known as the Phantom Detective, under another house name, Robert Wallace. He wrote most of the early episodes of the Phantom Detective, the second hero pulp to come out after the Shadow. It ran for 170 issues between 1933 and 1953, the third-longest-running hero pulp, ranking just behind the Shadow and Doc Savage. Under his own name and as Jack D'Arcy, he created several other memorable characters. Mariano Mercado is a hypochondriac detective who appeared in eight novelettes between 1944 and 1948 in *Dime Detective*. Inspector Allhof, a former New York City policeman who lost his legs while leading a botched raid, is retained by the NYPD because of his brilliance and in spite of his arrogance. Allhof appeared in twenty-nine stories from 1938 to 1945, mainly in *Dime Detective*; twelve of the tales were collected in *Footprints on a Brain: The Inspector Allhof Stories* (2001). Perhaps his most popular series featured Rex Sackler, known as the "Parsimonious Prince of Penny Pinchers." The hilarious series began in *Dime Detective*, then moved to *Black Mask*.

"Death Stops Payment," Champion's first *Black Mask* story, was published in the July 1940 issue.

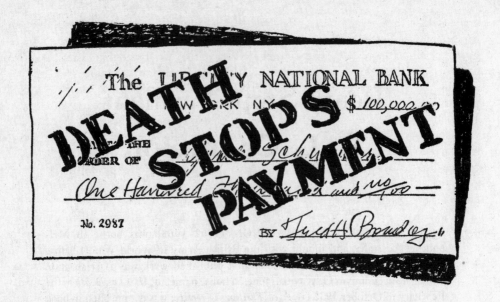

Death Stops Payment

D. L. Champion

Anything to make a couple of grand—or even a plugged nickel. That was Rex Sackler's code of life—and death.
For he was equally quick to euchre lucre from the living or cash out of a corpse.

CHAPTER ONE

AFTER ALL—WHAT'S MONEY?

I ARRIVED AT THE office at ten minutes past nine and received a surly good-morning from Sackler. He glowered at a story of the national debt in the *Tribune* and I sat down, lit a cigarette and grinned at him. His dyspeptic mood was no stunning surprise to me.

This was Wednesday—pay day. And Rex Sackler parting with money was as gay and lighthearted as Romeo taking his leave of Juliet.

I took the cigarette from my mouth and coughed politely. He lifted his head from the paper and stared at me with his dark sullen eyes. With nice delicacy, I scratched the palm of my left hand with the index finger of my right. Sackler folded the *Tribune* with great deliberation and sighed the sigh of a sorely tried man.

"Joey," he said, "you're a money grubber. A beaten slave of Mammon. Your job, to you, is a matter of dollars. Service, you know nothing of. Loyalty is beyond your limited ken. The noble pleasure of sheer altruism is something your material mind cannot grasp."

That, coming from Rex Sackler, was uproarious. He had quit the police department because of his theory that a man of his talents could make a fortune as a private detective. To the regret of several people, he had been right. Not only was he competent but he could smell a nickel before it had left the mint. He possessed all the business instincts of a Scotsman, an Armenian trader and a bank vault. He made money hand over fist. He disgorged it with the reluctance of a slot machine.

I put out my cigarette and stood up. "I'm strictly a strong-arm guy," I told him. "However, I *can* grasp the simple fact that you owe me some sixty-five slugs for last week's wages. Do I collect?"

Sackler shook his head and this time his sigh came from the soles of his feet. He put his hand inside his breast pocket and withdrew his wallet as if it had an anchor attached. He counted out some bills with the meticulous care of a near-sighted croupier and laid them on the desk.

I put the money in my pocket. I said, very politely: "Now just what plans have you formulated for taking this away from me?"

He looked at me reproachfully. "Joey," he said, "your misconstruction of my motives is incredible. Merely because I sometimes gamble with you for pastime, you appear to believe I really care about winning. Crass, Joey. And gauche. After all, what's money?"

I picked that cue up fast. "Money," I said, "is what you've got socked in every Postal Savings account in the city because you think banks are a wild gamble. Money is what you'd sell your grandmother to the Arab slave-dealers for. Money is what you reluctantly pay me every week, then devise schemes for winning back. Money—"

He wasn't listening to me. He had taken a pair of dice from his pocket and was caressing them in his hand. There was a little click as he spun them over the desk blotter. I watched them come to rest, revealing a pair of deuces. Then I suddenly caught myself and walked to the window.

"Oh, no," I said. "You can put those right back in your pocket. You're not getting a nickel out of me this week, even if you offer a dime for it."

I stood at the window showing him my back and contemplating the thrumming Madison Avenue traffic. I still heard the gentle click of the dice behind me and the gambling corpuscles in my veins throbbed nervously. Resolutely, I stared through the glass.

I turned only when I heard the door of the outer office slam. Sackler lifted his head like a hyena scenting prey. He adjusted his cuffs and cleared his throat, preparatory to the onslaught on the client's pocketbook. Inspector Wolley of the Headquarters Squad strode into the room.

Sackler's phoney smile of welcome faded. He reached for the dice again and said ungraciously: "Oh, it's you."

"It sure is," said Wolley with loud affability. "And how's business, Rex? How's every little thing with the sharpest shamus in town?"

That speech coming from Wolley was far, far phonier than Sackler's smile had been. As a general rule Wolley and Sackler go along like Martin Dies and a liberal thought. Sackler believed Wolley a pompous incompetent, which he was; while Wolley's heart dripped envy every time he compared Sackler's income with his own.

"Rex," said Wolley, "I'd like to ask you a question. To settle a little discussion we were having downtown. Exactly why did you quit the department to go in business on your own hook?"

Sackler took a package of ten-cent cigarettes from his pocket and lighted one. Carefully, he replaced the burnt match in its book. When he answered he did not speak the truth.

"Public service," he said virtuously. "With my talent it stands to reason I can accomplish more civic good than under the orders of a block-headed police commissioner."

"Exactly," boomed Wolley. "That's just what I said. Now how about lending us a hand on the Capek case?"

Sackler blinked at him. I leaned forward in my chair and said maliciously: "Free, Inspector?"

"Well," said Wolley as if he were the Chamber of Commerce and I was looking over the factory site, "we're all working for the public good together. After all, what's money?"

 his magnificent indifference to money on the part of all hands was beginning to overwhelm me. But in spite of all this idealistic chatter, I knew damned well Sackler wouldn't stir out of his chair to solve a tabloid cross-word puzzle until someone slapped a large bill on the desktop.

He was staring unpleasantly at Wolley. He resented the trap into which the inspector had led him. He took a deep breath and proceeded to squirm out of it.

"Wolley," he said with a fine air of regret, "I'd like to help you. But it wouldn't be fair to my other clients. You see, if they pay high rates for my services it isn't right for me to work for nothing. It would offend them."

Wolley grunted skeptically. "Well," he said slowly, "I sort of thought of that myself. So I got together with some of the boys and raised a little purse for you."

Sackler's eyes gleamed. "A purse? How much?"

"A couple of hundred."

Sackler looked insulted. The gleam went from his eyes faster than it had come in. I knew quite well he wasn't going to let that two hundred get away from him. But he was going to indulge in some very fancy haggling first.

"That's not much money, Wolley," he said. "Make it five."

"My God," said Wolley. "Ten coppers put together don't make as much money as you do in a year, Rex. Besides, we're gambling with you. We'll give you the two hundred free and clear. We ask no guarantees. Even if someone else breaks the Capek case you can keep the dough."

That didn't sound so bad. This Capek case was no cinch. Capek was a very odd character. With all the dough he'd piled up I suppose he had a right to be. He'd come to this country, a ragged immigrant boy, about fifty years ago. He'd rolled up his sleeves and gone to work—hard and successfully. Today, he controlled a dozen corporations and half a dozen banks. He was a strong, square-jawed character who possessed a great deal of pride and no friends. Hardly any acquaintances, save for a young guy named Rawson, who had once been his secretary and was now his partner.

Capek had been missing for about two weeks. His household on Long Island and the police suspected kidnaping, although no ransom demand had yet been received. Anyway, it made a good newspaper story and the whole police department was going nuts looking for Capek.

As Wolley's unprecedented visit attested, they hadn't had much success.

Sackler was looking at Wolley and there was a shrewd glitter in his eye. I knew quite well what he was thinking. As Sackler's fees went, two hundred bucks was no fortune. But this was an opportunity to get it for nothing. I knew, moreover, that he was going to accept the deal ultimately, but first he was going to break his neck to have Wolley raise the ante.

"Three hundred," he said, "and it's a deal."

Wolley drummed angrily on the desk with his fingers. He got very little more than three hundred a month. Sackler yawned elaborately and picked up the dice again.

The telephone jangled suddenly. I picked it up. It was for Wolley. I handed him the phone and he talked rapidly into the receiver, listened for a moment and hung up. He turned to Sackler, a wide grin on his face, and all the false affability had vanished from his voice as he spoke.

"Wise guy," he jeered. "Just a shrewd business genius. Well, you just haggled yourself out of two hundred bucks, my friend. They've found Capek."

Sackler dropped the dice and jerked his head up angrily.

"Where?"

"In the caretaker's lodge on his own estate. And dead. Apparently a suicide." But Wolley wasn't interested in Capek anymore. He reverted to the subject nearest his heart. "But you—you could have had two hundred bucks just for sitting at your desk until that phone call came in. You wouldn't have had to move a muscle of a brain cell."

He walked to the doorway, grinning triumphantly, and added: "And it's breaking your chiseling marble heart."

The door slammed behind him and he was gone.

hether or not there were any cracks in Sackler's cardiac region, I didn't know. But I was very happy about it all. It wasn't every day I was granted the privilege of seeing Sackler lose money.

He looked up suddenly, saw my grin and rolled the dice again. Double six came up.

"What do you say, Joey? Just one roll. For a buck."

I hesitated. Sackler had been rolling craps with a fair degree of regularity this morning. Besides, if the law of averages hadn't been suspended, I was due. I took a dollar from my pocket and laid it on the desk.

"Just once," I said. "One fast roll. That's all. Win, lose or draw."

"Sure, Joey. Just one."

Twenty minutes later when the outer door slammed for the second time that day, I was out precisely thirty-three bucks. Sackler snatched up the dice as our caller entered the room.

He was tall, well built, about thirty-five and exceedingly well dressed. He gave out a strong aroma of ready cash and Sackler came to point like a bird dog. I sat down sulkily at my desk and wondered why the hell I'd ever got in that crap game. In four years I'd never won a dime from Rex Sackler at anything.

The stranger nodded his head and said briskly: "Mr. Sackler?"

Sackler admitted his identity.

"I'm Rawson. Harold Rawson."

Sackler's face lit up. Wolley's two hundred was water under the dam now.

"Rawson," he said quickly. "Karl Capek's partner?"

"Not anymore," said Rawson briefly.

"Ah," said Sackler like a doctor at the death bed, "that suicide. Very unfortunate. Very—"

"It wasn't suicide," snapped Rawson.

Sackler's eyes opened wide. It was neither surprise nor shock, I knew. It was wholehearted satisfaction that here, indeed, was a fee.

"You're sure of that?"

"Positive," said Rawson. "I have information which precludes all suicidal possibilities."

"Ah," said Sackler again, "and you want me to find out—"

"I want you to find out who killed him."

Sackler rubbed his hands together and gazed dreamily at his client.

"The fee," he murmured, "will be twenty-five hundred dollars. In advance. Make the check out to cash, please."

Rawson sat down. He took a fountain pen and a check book from his pocket. He said, "Quite satisfactory," and proceeded to write. Sackler watched him happily. Then Rawson spoke again.

"I'm a little short of cash, Sackler. Been out of town on business. Just got back to find this awful tragedy. Can you let me have fifty in cash if I make the check out for that much additional?"

"Of course," said Sackler, always willing to exchange fifty for twenty-five hundred. "Glad to oblige."

He counted out five tens and picked up the check. "Now," he said, "first, what is this information you have that makes you so sure Capek was murdered?"

Rawson stood up. There was a hard coldness in his eyes. "I shall tell you that tonight," he said. "Can you be at the Capek mansion tonight, at nine o'clock?"

"Yes."

"All right," said Rawson. He turned and walked to the door. He paused on the threshold and for a moment his brusque businesslike air dropped from him.

"Karl Capek was a great man," he said, and there was a peculiar huskiness to his voice. "He was my best, my only friend. And by God, I will avenge him!"

He swung around on his heel and marched into the corridor.

Sackler held the check in his hand as if it were a diamond he'd just picked up in the gutter, which it more or less was.

I stood over by the window bathed in envy. Here Sackler had just had twenty-five hundred dollars dropped into his avaricious lap while I was out thirty-three bucks of last week's salary. If there was any justice in the world it never seemed to get around to this office.

"Joey, my lad," said Sackler, "run over to the bank with this check. Get it cashed right away."

That was Sackler all over. Whenever he got a check he rushed it over to the bank, cashed it and sank it in one of his Postal Savings accounts. Nothing short of the revolution was going to get a nickel out of him.

I sighed, put on my hat and coat, and went out into the street.

I returned half an hour later. I was grinning happily from ear to ear. There was a soothing, gloating sensation in my heart that almost made me forget about my thirty-three bucks. Sackler looked up as I approached his desk.

"Ah," he said, "get to the bank all right?"

"And had a very pleasant trip," I told him. "Here."

I groped in my pocket and laid Rawson's check down on the desk before him. He looked at it, then looked at me.

"Well," he said testily, "where's the cash?"

I smiled at him sweetly. "There isn't any cash."

"What the devil are you talking about, Joey? What do you mean there—"

"There isn't enough cash anyway. Insufficient funds."

He looked for all the world as if someone had slugged him over the head with a mallet.

"My God, Joey, you don't mean—"

"I mean that Harold Rawson, who's probably worth several hundred thousand times as much dough as you are, has given you a bum check. Moreover, you've been taken for fifty bucks in cash. I might add, I think it very, very funny."

"My God," said Sackler in an anguished tone, "twenty-five hundred and fifty bucks. I've been taken for twenty-five hundred and fifty bucks. I'm a ruined man. I—"

"Do we still keep that appointment at Capek's joint?" I asked him.

"You're damn right we do," he said explosively. "I'm going to see that Rawson. He can't do this to me. Good heavens, twenty-five hundred and fifty bucks is one hell of a lot of dough, Joey."

"You're actually out only fifty," I pointed out. "That's all you gave him in cash."

He paid no attention to me. He buried his face in his hands and muttered over and over again: "Twenty-five hundred and fifty bucks, my God!"

In my book he was still out only fifty but in his present distrait condition all the arithmetic in the world wasn't going to convince him.

CHAPTER TWO
YOU CAN'T GET CASH FROM A CORPSE

t was a raw blustery night as we drove through Long Island on the Grand Central Parkway. Sackler had recovered somewhat from his fiscal grief. He had arrived at the conclusion that it was a ghastly and horrible mistake, but nevertheless, a mistake. Considering Rawson's position, his wealth, the fact that he was Karl Capek's partner, I was reluctantly inclined to agree with him.

But I wasn't so optimistic about my thirty-three bucks as Sackler was about his twenty-five hundred and fifty. All afternoon, I'd been racking my brains for some cinch bet which would

enable me to win it back, without success. Now, as I heard Sackler humming gayly at my side in the car, I tried another tack.

"Hey," I said, "I'll make a deal with you."

Sackler kept on humming.

"If Rawson makes good for you on that check, how about giving me back that dough I lost at dice?"

The melody died on his lips. "Why, Joey," he said reproachfully, "they're two entirely different things. Yours was a gambling debt. I couldn't insult you by offering to return it."

I sighed and said: "No, I hardly thought you could."

We made the rest of the trip in silence. Some twenty miles out I turned through an elaborate pair of wrought-iron gates and drove through the heavily wooded estate of Karl Capek. The wind blew cold from the Sound and the sky was starless. It was a cold cheerless night that fitted in well with my own mood.

I brought the car to a halt underneath a high Colonial portico. A moment later Sackler pressed the doorbell. After another moment the door was opened by a liveried butler.

The first thing I heard was Wolley's familiar voice. We found him in the living-room, a glass of brandy in his hand, a cigar in his mouth, holding forth on his police adventures to a politely bored audience. We were introduced all around and informed that Rawson hadn't arrived yet, although he was expected soon.

Without delay we went into our usual routine. Sackler demanded he be assigned a room in which to mastermind. I whipped out my notebook and proceeded to do the rounds, picking up bits of information I thought might be useful. Since Sackler was actually starting to work before he had negotiated about the check, I became more certain that he wasn't really worried much about it.

I snooped around the house for a good hour. I questioned Wolley, the servants and everybody else. I went out into the windy night and personally examined the caretaker's lodge where they'd found Capek's body.

came back cold as hell, commandeered a pint of brandy from the butler's pantry and went up to the second-floor study which had been assigned to Sackler. I took out my notebook and sat down.

Sackler was having one hell of a time with a humidor of cigars he had found. His pocket was stuffed and he was rolling one around lusciously in his mouth. Since they were free the taste, I presume, was much improved.

"All right," he said. "What have we got?"

"Not Rawson," I told him. "He phoned a little while ago. He'll be another half-hour. Business held him up."

"What else?"

"First, those guys downstairs. That watery-eyed young blond guy is a relative of Capek's. Name of Crosher. Only living relative as far as anyone knows. He's been here for a month. He's broke and was trying to get some dough from the old guy. Came from Chi. Never seen his cousin before. In fact, he only just found out he *was* Capek's cousin. He's in direct line for the estate."

I thought maybe I had something there. But as I glanced quickly at Sackler he seemed more interested in his cigar.

"Next, the Union League Club stuffed shirt in the wing collar is Granville S. Colby, of whom you may have heard."

"Often," said Sackler. "Lawyer. Old family. Blue-blood stock. Stiff-necked. Don't like him."

"Then there's that guy Benjamin. He's the skinny one with the thin face. Another lawyer. Colby's assistant. They've both been here for a little over a month. Colby's supposed to be resting. Doctor's orders. But he was handling some legal stuff for Capek and Rawson. Was doing it out here."

Sackler looked up. "Notice anything funny about that Benjamin?"

"Yeah. Face seems familiar. Can't quite place it. Maybe I've seen him somewhere around in court. Why?"

"Keep talking," said Sackler. "What about Capek?"

"There's a caretaker's lodge out there in the forest," I told him. "They don't use it anymore. It was all boarded up. That's where they found Capek. A revolver was in his hand and his brains were on the floor. There was a portable typewriter there with a suicide note in it. Capek's fingerprints were on the keys. The doc said he's been dead three days."

"He was missing two weeks," said Sackler. "What was he doing the rest of the time? Contemplating suicide?"

"You think you're kidding," I told him, "but you're dead on. That's exactly what he said in the suicide note."

For the first time, Sackler appeared interested. "What's exactly what he said in the note?"

"I got it from Wolley. He didn't have a copy of it with him. Gave it to me from memory. Something about being tired of life, retiring to the lodge alone to think things over. Deciding finally to die. Wolley seems to think it's on the level. Thinks Rawson's crazy for asking him to come out here tonight."

"Don't bother me with Wolley's opinions. Anything else?"

"Well, there was the faucets."

"The faucets? What about the faucets?"

"The ones in the lodge. They were smashed. There was a stove lid on the floor. I guess that's what had been used. There was one faucet over the kitchen sink, another in a washroom just off the kitchen."

Sackler frowned. "And they were smashed?"

"They'd been battered about a hell of a lot. But that might have happened a long while ago."

Thoughtfully, he crushed his cigar out in a silver ash tray. I took a cigarette from behind my ear and lit it. A moment later Sackler sniffed and said: "That's a fancy brand for you, isn't it? What is it, Egyptian?"

"Right," I told him. "And from the exalted case of Granville S. Colby."

Sackler grunted. "Must cost a lot of dough."

"The way he smokes them it does. He's a

chain smoker. Lights one from the butt of the last."

Sackler stood up. "Well," he said, "since there's nothing more to do until Rawson gets here, I guess I'll go downstairs and bum one from him. Come along, Joey."

I followed him down the winding staircase. In the living-room Wolley was still holding forth to Crosher and Benjamin. They didn't appear very interested. Colby's eardrums must have revolted already. Sackler and I found him alone in the library on the other side of the foyer, with a half-smoked Egyptian cigarette in his hand.

Sackler, who wouldn't hesitate to ask the President for a match, put the bite on Colby for a smoke. Colby patted his pockets, looked up and said coldly: "My cigarette case is in my overcoat pocket. It's hanging in the hall closet."

I took that to mean why in hell didn't Sackler buy his own butts but that spendthrift said casually, "Don't get up. I'll find it," and walked out into the hall.

I followed along aimlessly; then I turned into the living-room just in time to catch Wolley's recital of the time he raided the murderer's nest single-handed. Just then there came the sound of a wounded banshee and the cook ran into the living-room, her mouth wide open and her larynx vibrating like an off-key harp.

Sackler and Colby came racing into the room. We got the cook into a chair and poured a slug of brandy into her. At that she became coherent enough to shriek: "The garage! Mr. Rawson! For heaven's sake—"

There was more to it than that but we didn't wait to hear. I was in the lead with Sackler and Wolley on my heels. We rushed out into the bitter night, across the sweeping back lawn to the garage. The door was open and the light was turned on. There was a car inside, its headlights aglow.

At the wheel slumped Rawson. There was a gun in his hand and an ugly hole in his head. He was as dead as hope in Poland. Wolley, Sackler and I did some routine looking around and found nothing.

Behind us, young Crosher said: "My God, this is awful. There's a murderer in this house."

"Maybe," said Colby's deep bass, "it wasn't murder."

Wolley seized on that. "My idea, too," he said, his voice thickened by the brandy he'd been drinking. "Rawson worshiped Capek. Brooded about his death. Killed himself."

"The only virtue in that theory," said Sackler, "is its convenience. Everybody commits suicide so the coppers can go home. Otherwise it stinks."

Wolley turned on him angrily. "Maybe you got a theory, wise guy."

"Maybe," said Sackler. "Has anyone been outside the house tonight?"

"I have," I reminded him.

"I don't suspect you, Joey," he said magnanimously. "Anyone else?"

Individually, everyone denied having left the house since dinnertime. We trooped back to the Capek mansion. Wolley went to the telephone to call headquarters. Colby used his best courtroom persuasion on the cook, assuring her it would be quite safe for her to sleep in her quarters above the garage. Sackler, registering heavy thought, retired again to the second-floor study. I trailed along behind him.

Sackler sat down at the desk and rested his head in his hands. There was utter despair on his face. It was hardly customary for Sackler to take violent death so seriously and I commented upon it.

He looked up at me. "Joey," he said, and his voice was drenched in gloom, "don't you see what this does to my check? It may never be good now."

I hadn't thought of that, but now that I did I brightened considerably. It would be an edifying spectacle to see Rex Sackler solve a case free.

He looked up again and now there was an odd light in his eyes. He slapped his fist on the desk.

"Joey," he said, "I think I've got something. Go and see that Benjamin guy. Ask him what a writ of replevin is."

That didn't sound very sensible to me. But I went downstairs and did it. I came back and reported: "He says he's a little rusty on it but he believes it's something like a habeas corpus."

"Good," said Sackler. "I thought so."

I needled him by deliberately misunderstanding. "You mean you think it's like habeas corpus, too?"

"No, you idiot. I mean that guy's not a law clerk at all. He's Benny Bagel. I've been trying to place him all night. But now I'm certain."

"Bagel?" I said. "Benny Bagel? Sounds vaguely familiar, but it still doesn't click."

"Forger," said Sackler, and there was a little tremor of excitement in his tone. "Indicted twice. Never convicted. I've seen his picture in the tabloids. Considered the best guy in the field."

"What's he doing here as Colby's law clerk?"

"It'll take me all night to figure that," said Sackler. "But at last I'm beginning to see the light. Hey, get me the phone number of that bank Rawson's check was drawn on. I want to call them early in the morning. Tell Wolley he better stay over tonight, too. Then get the hell out of my sight and let me think."

I let him think for the rest of the night. In the morning, Wolley, sticking stubbornly to his double suicide theory, was anxious to get back to town. Sackler insisted he stay. I saw little of either Sackler or Colby before lunch. When neither of them appeared then I went up to the study to find Sackler still sitting at the desk.

"Well," I said, "what have you got?"

He drew a deep breath. "Plenty," he said. "Do you realize, Joey, that Capek never made a will, never owned a driving license, that Rawson held his complete power-of-attorney in every deal?"

"So," I said, "what? Maybe Rawson killed him, then got the horrors about it and killed himself."

Sackler snorted. "That sounds like a Wolley theory," he said. "You get to the phone, Joey. Call Postal Union. Tell them to send me their most trusted messenger. And tell him to hurry. Then tell Wolley I'll be right down to solve his case for him."

"Free?" I asked maliciously. But to my surprise even the mention of his lost dough didn't get a rise out of him. He smiled benignly.

"By the way," I said as I went to the door, "where's Colby? I thought he was with you."

"Somewhere around," said Sackler vaguely. "Hurry with that messenger, will you?"

CHAPTER THREE
MADMAN'S MILLIONS

It was two thirty in the afternoon and Wolley was getting impatient. He paced the broad living-room floor, scowling at Sackler, who sat at his ease before the fire and smoked a cigar he'd cadged from Crosher. Crosher stood by the window twining his fingers about each other like nervous snakes.

Benny Bagel, the forger law clerk, avidly conned a stack of old-fashioned stereopticon views. At last Wolley stopped his pacing. He came to a guardsman's halt in front of Sackler and spoke his vehement piece.

"Damn it, Sackler. Last night you said you'd have something this morning. This morning's gone. So's half the afternoon. Capek was a suicide. Quite obviously he was something of a wack and he killed himself. Can you improve on that theory?"

"Infinitely," said Sackler.

"Well, go ahead."

"I'm waiting for my messenger boy," said Sackler. "I can't do a thing until he arrives."

"My God," said Wolley, "what the hell can a

messenger boy have to do with the death of Karl Capek?"

"Nothing," said Sackler. "But he may have a great deal to do with the solution."

The doorbell jangled then. Benny turned to answer it but Sackler stayed him with a gesture. He strode out into the foyer and admitted a Postal Union boy. He spoke to him earnestly for a moment and in a tone so low I couldn't hear him.

I admit I tried.

There was an expression of relief on his face when he returned to the living-room. He drew a Windsor chair up to a table and sat facing us all.

"Now," he said with a businesslike air, "how do you figure this Capek case, Wolley?"

Wolley glared at him. If he'd told him how he figured the Capek case once, he'd told him a dozen times. Now he lifted his voice and told it again—loud.

"Capek was an eccentric. A nut, as I figure it. His typewritten note gave that away. He went out to that unused lodge to think things over. After a few days of brooding, he killed himself. It's obvious, isn't it?"

"No," said Sackler. "And what about Rawson?"

"Rawson was devoted to the old guy. Capek gave him everything he had. He was so broken up at Capek's death that he killed himself, too."

"That," remarked Sackler to me, "is typical modern police work. When you can't solve a killing you call it suicide in a loud authoritative voice, then go back to a nice warm station-house and finish reading the comic papers."

There was confidence in his manner. As a matter of fact he seemed so assured I began to think he'd cooked up some way to save his twenty-five hundred dollars.

"All right," said Wolley, annoyed. "I've told you. Now you tell me. What did happen to Capek?"

"What was the first official police theory?" asked Sackler. "Two weeks ago when Capek was first reported missing?"

"Kidnaping. But we exploded that."

"Ah," said Sackler gently, "did you? This may be incredible to you, Inspector, but you were right the first time."

"Hooey," said Wolley. "Who the hell would kidnap a guy and hold him prisoner on his own estate?"

"A very bright guy indeed," said Sackler. "The coppers never looked for him there, did they?"

"There were no ransom notes, were there? What the hell sort of a kidnaping would it be without any ransom notes?"

"An extremely unusual one," said Sackler.

I watched Sackler closely. This talking in circles wasn't like him at all. When he had a case broken he usually threw it in everyone's face abruptly and without waste of words. But now his eyes kept straying to the big clock on the mantelpiece and his manner was that of a man who is just trying to use up time.

 looked around the room. Our old pal Benny now stood a graven image by the fireplace. Crosher had turned his back to the window and stared at Sackler. I reflected that had I killed Capek and Rawson, I would have made a point of appearing less apprehensive than Crosher.

Wolley's face was ruddier than usual. Sackler invariably irritated him and today's circumlocution was angering him even more than was customary.

"Sackler," he said, "will you stop horsing around? If you've any evidence, present it."

"All right," said Sackler. "Let's begin with the kidnaping premise. There's a guy, a certain guy who knows Capek. He's in a jam—a financial jam. He needs dough badly. So he takes Capek down to that boarded-up lodge and demands a juicy check. Capek won't give it to him. So he kills him."

That was too much even for me. Wolley was just two points this side of apoplexy.

"That's the screwiest thing I ever heard," he yelled. "What good is Capek to him dead if he needs dough?"

"None whatever," said Sackler, "but the killer didn't know that at the time." He paused for a long moment; then he glanced over at the fireplace and added: "Did he, Benny?"

Benny Bagel almost fell over the fire tools. His face was suddenly pale. His eyes opened wide and his jaw dropped so quickly I expected it to bounce off his chest. Wolley noted his expression and some of his doubt left him.

"What's he got to do with it?"

Sackler turned to Crosher, who viewed the proceedings blankly.

"You see," he said, "there's your police department for you. Benny's a forger. He's served two raps and is considered by his pals the top man in the business. Right, Benny?"

Benny had recovered somewhat by now. "I'm afraid you're making a mistake," he said politely. "I've been in law or law school all my life. You're confusing me with some criminal."

"Of course," said Wolley hopefully. "Of course."

"Sure," said Sackler. "Did you see him register when I threw it in his face? He's Benny Bagel. You've got his fingerprints downtown, Wolley. You've got his Bertillons and everything else. In a very short while you're going to have him in person."

Wolley looked from Benny, who appeared very uncomfortable, to Sackler, who didn't.

"What's it all about?" he asked. "Are you saying this guy killed him?"

"Accessory," said Sackler. "After and during the fact of murder."

"Well, for the love of God," roared Wolley, "who did the actual killing?"

Sackler looked at the clock again before answering. It was two minutes to three.

"First," said Sackler, "let me tell you why and how."

"For heaven's sake," snapped Wolley, "tell me something."

"This certain guy I mentioned a little while ago—let's call him Smith. Well, he was in trouble. So he took Capek out to that caretaker's lodge and proceeded to put the bite on him. He demanded that Capek write a letter asking for a hell of a lot of ransom. A note which would be delivered to Rawson, who, being quite fond of the old guy, would undoubtedly pay. Colby was named as the intermediary."

"Colby," said Wolley suddenly. "Where the devil is he?"

"Don't bother about him," said Sackler. "We don't need him until later."

Benny Bagel screwed up his brow and shot a puzzled glance at Sackler. Wolley banged the table impatiently with his fist and said: "All right. Get on with it."

"Well," went on Sackler, "Capek wouldn't sign. This guy Smith got pretty sore about it. He knew Capek was a pretty stubborn guy. Torture, ordinary physical torture, was rather out of this Smith's line. So he hit on what he thought was a brilliant idea. He thought of a torture which was bloodless, horrible and very effective."

By this time Sackler had me as bewildered as anyone in the room. Usually, I could follow his reasoning at least halfway. But for a guy who apparently had nothing to work on he was delivering one hell of a lot of detail.

"So," said Wolley, "what was this unusual torture?"

"Water," said Sackler, "or rather, lack of it."

Benny Bagel uttered a little sigh and sat down. I said: "Now how can you figure a thing like that?"

"It's not too hard, Joey. First those smashed faucets. If they'd been smashed in rage or blind fury, it's quite probable that something else, the furniture, the light bulbs, would also have been wrecked. But it was only the water faucets. Smashed by a man who is dying of thirst, who turns on the tap to get nothing but emptiness for perhaps the hundredth time. Then he did go nuts. He took the stove lid and crashed it down on the taps."

I thought that over and conceded to myself there might be something in it. Wolley scratched his graying head in silence. Crosher opened his mouth for the first time.

"It's impossible," he said. "What about the medical examiner? He would have noticed dehydration. If Cousin Karl had been on the verge of death from thirst, the medical examiner couldn't have failed to notice it."

"Right," said Wolley emphatically. "Absolutely right. You're screwy, Rex."

"You all forget," said Sackler, "that Capek was in that lodge for fourteen days. He had been dead three when he was found. Suppose he'd been deprived of water for a week. That's enough to drive a man mad. But after he was mad there was no point in dealing with him. This Smith decided to kill him then. But he waited some four days before he did so. During those four days he gave Capek water and food. He did that so that the medical examiner wouldn't know just what had happened."

"If this Smith guy was so smart," I said, "couldn't he figure Capek might go nuts from lack of water?"

Sackler shook his head. "No. He thought Capek would give in to his demands before then. Besides, when Capek proved adamant, Smith got himself another idea. He figured out how to get the money even after Capek was dead."

Wolley shook his head and shrugged his shoulders. "Rex," he said, "it won't do. First, Capek had one hell of a lot of money. It seems reasonable to me that he'd be quite willing to surrender any amount of it to save his life, particularly if he was going mad for water."

"Besides," said Crosher, "how could he obtain a signed ransom note if Cousin Karl was dead?"

"I'll answer the second question first," said Sackler. "That's where Benny Bagel came in. Faced with Capek's point-blank refusal, our friend Smith cooked up a second idea. He

decided, since Capek was going nuts, he'd have to kill him anyway. So he brought in Benny here."

"Why?" said Wolley.

"My God," said Sackler wearily, "are you that stupid? I told you Benny is a forger. The best in the business. Benny was going to sign Capek's name to the note."

"All right, then," snapped Wolley. "So why didn't he?"

"Because," said Sackler slowly, "they couldn't find anything to copy."

"Couldn't find what to copy?" shouted Wolley impatiently. "Rex, what the devil are you talking about?"

"To forge a signature, you must have an original to copy from. It's a prime rule of the profession, isn't it, Benny?"

"Listen," said Benny Bagel in a low hoarse voice, "I want to see a lawyer. Where's Colby?"

"Well, why couldn't they find a signature of Capek's to copy from? There must be plenty of them around the house somewhere," Wolley stated.

"That," said Sackler, "is where you're wrong. There's not a single signature of Karl Capek in existence."

Wolley and Crosher gaped at him. But at this point something lit up in my brain.

"You mean he couldn't write?"

"I'm glad someone got it at last," said Sackler. "Capek couldn't write. He was a proud man, a strong character and a man whose success had made him ashamed of his lack of education. Capek couldn't write and there was only one person in all the world who shared his secret. That was Rawson."

olley was half convinced. His brow was corrugated, his eyes shaded with deep thought. "How can you arrive at that conclusion, Rex?"

"Consider the circumstances. Capek never held a driver's license. He never made a will. All his business, even his income-tax returns, was handled through Rawson's power-of-attorney. In Capek's desk I found a hundred documents, all in the same handwriting. That handwriting was Rawson's. Consider again. Capek had no friends, no acquaintances, save Rawson. We know he came here from Middle Europe as a lad of seven. We know he never went to school. We know, further, that he was generous with his money. He'd made munificent endowments and donations, yet he wouldn't spend any of it to save his life."

"You mean," I said, "that he died rather than admit he couldn't write?".

"That's my theory," said Sackler. "Of all the statements I'm making this afternoon, that one will always have to remain a theory. But nothing else fits. It's quite logical. It was Capek's secret. No one knew it. He intended no one ever should. He wouldn't admit it to Smith until thirst had driven him mad, probably too mad to know what the hell was going on. So Smith called in his forger and killed him."

"Then," I said, "he killed his own scheme because he couldn't find any signature of Capek's to copy."

"True," said Sackler, "but he did salvage a little from the wreck, didn't he, Benny?"

Benny stared at Sackler in horror but he didn't answer.

"Seeing all was lost," continued Sackler, "our pal Smith embarked on a new plan. After Capek's body and phony suicide note which Smith had typed with the dead man's fingers, Smith was told by Rawson that Capek couldn't write. Told today, in fact. That fact, once known, was dangerous. So Smith planned to murder Rawson, too. The afternoon before he killed him, he had Benny here forge his name to a check for a hundred thousand dollars. That cleaned out Rawson's bank account."

I might have known that Sackler would find out why he hadn't got his twenty-five hundred and fifty bucks. Undoubtedly, he'd checked on that before anything else.

"Wait a minute," croaked Benny Bagel, "you can't prove that."

Sackler smiled at him benignly. "The hell I can't," he said. "I called the bank. The last check that was presented was for something in excess of a hundred grand. That check is down at Wolley's fingerprint bureau right now."

"So what?" said Benny. "There'll be a dozen sets of prints on it by now."

"True," said Sackler. "One of those sets will be yours, and what is equally important, none of them will be Rawson's. Even you can't forge a check with gloves on, Benny. And it'll be conclusive proof of forgery if Rawson—the supposed maker of the check—hasn't left his own fingerprint on it."

"Well," said Wolley grudgingly, "at last we've got some evidence instead of theory."

Crosher coughed nervously. "Who is this Smith?" he said suddenly. "Why have you deliberately concealed the name of the killer? Who is it?"

Wolley spun around on his heel. He had been so engaged in trying to figure how Sackler could be wrong, he'd completely overlooked the minor fact of the killer's identity.

"Of course," he snapped. "Who did it? Who's the mastermind? Who was working with Benny, here?"

Sackler suddenly looked acutely uncomfortable. He stared at the clock. I followed his gaze and noted it was exactly twelve minutes past three.

"Well," said Wolley again. "Who is it? Is this whole thing a fairy story or do you know who it was?"

Sackler appeared more upset than he had a moment ago. In inverse ratio, Benny seemed to perk up a bit.

"Well," said Sackler with obvious reluctance, "maybe it was Crosher, here. It's quite possible that—"

Crosher's mouth twisted suddenly. His eyes shone like pale blue ice. He took a step forward toward Sackler and his voice trembled as he spoke.

"Damn you!" he screamed. "Are you accusing me of killing my own flesh and blood? Are you saying that—"

"Pay no attention to him," said Benny, and there was relief in his tone. "He knows nothing. It's all wild guesswork. He can't check anything he says. He—"

The doorbell sounded imperiously. Sackler took a deep breath. He lifted his head to heaven and said fervently: "Thank God! Joey, open the door!"

CHAPTER FOUR
BLOOD FROM A TURNIP

 I went out, opened the door and returned with the Postal Union boy Sackler had sent out three-quarters of an hour before. I led him into the living-room. He stood before Sackler, thrust his hand into his hip pocket and pulled out a thick roll of bills.

The boy began to count aloud. I was seized with a sudden cold suspicion that Sackler had somehow contrived to get his twenty-five hundred bucks after all. I remembered, abruptly and without satisfaction, that I still hadn't retrieved my thirty-three.

Wolley gaped at the mounting money on the desk. Envy, frank and hostile, was in his gaze.

"Great God," he said, "is this a murder case or a private business deal?"

Sackler didn't answer him. He was gazing at the stack of bills with an ethereal light in his eyes. The Postal Union lad laid a final fifty on top of the pile, announced: "Twenty-five hundred and fifty. That's right, isn't it?"

That, as I knew too well, was absolutely right. To the penny. Sackler took a worn leather change purse from his pocket and handed the boy a dime. He was impervious to the look of scorn he received in exchange. The messenger left the room and Sackler stood up, stowing the bills away in his pocket like a hophead who has just come upon a mountain of cocaine.

He walked into the foyer and called back over his shoulder: "Hey, Joey."

I went along, not having the slightest idea what he wanted. I could almost feel Wolley's outraged glare on my back.

"Joey," said Sackler in a whisper, "within the next three minutes sneak out of the room on some pretext. Go upstairs to the attic. The third door on the right at the head of the stairway. There's a transom there. Half open. Throw this over it into the room."

He handed me a sealed envelope. There was something small, hard and heavy inside it. I put it in my pocket without asking questions. By the time I returned to the living-room, I began to have vague visions of getting back my thirty-three bucks.

"Do you mind telling me," said Wolley, restraining his wrath with a noticeable effort, "what the hell is going on here? Damn it, Rex, in the name of the law, I demand to know who your murderer is. You're obstructing justice."

Sackler nodded frantically to me. I murmured something about going to the bathroom and slid out of the room. I raced upstairs to the attic. I stood for a moment before the door Sackler had designated, listening. Then I tossed the envelope over the transom. I heard the metallic click as it hit the floor within; then heard a sigh and a shuffling footstep. I scooted back down the stairs.

When I got back to the living-room, Wolley was pounding the table savagely. His voice roared against the tapestried walls and reverberated back again. He threatened Sackler with decades of imprisonment for obstructing justice. He accused him of being an accessory after the fact of murder for withholding evidence. Sackler sat there in uncomfortable silence till he saw me. Then he brightened.

"All right, Joey?" he shouted above the noise of Wolley's voice.

I nodded my head. "Shut up, Inspector," said Sackler. "I'll give you your killer."

Wolley shut up for a moment, breathless. He inhaled quickly and said: "Who is it?"

"Colby," said Sackler. "Granville S. Colby. Embezzler of his clients' trust funds. Murderer.

Kidnaper and a consorter with a forger. There's your man."

"Colby!" yelled Wolley. "Where is he? He was here this morning. Search the house. My God, perhaps he got away. Perhaps he—"

The shot sounded through the house like a fragment of thunder. Benny sat up in his chair. Wolley froze where he stood and Crosher looked more afraid than ever. Sackler stood up. He pointed at the clock.

"The time," he yelled. "Note the time. I want witnesses. It's exactly three twenty-eight. Look!"

We all looked at the clock.

"Come on," yelled Wolley. "Let's investigate that shot. It was upstairs."

I caught Sackler's eye. "It seemed to me to come from the attic," I said.

Wolley grabbed Benny before he raced up the stairs. He was taking no chances on losing one of his prisoners. The rest of us followed him to the attic.

There was a smell of cordite coming over the transom through which I had thrown Sackler's envelope. Wolley tried the door. It had a mortised lock which had been secured. He handed Benny over to me, and smashed his broad shoulder against the door. At the second thrust, the lock gave.

The five of us catapulted into the room. "My God," said Wolley. "I bet you were right, Rex. Look at that!"

I didn't have to look. I knew quite well what was there on the floor. It was Colby. Colby with a revolver in his hand, a bullet in his brain. A trickle of blood stained the dusty boards at our feet. Crumpled and lying across the room was the envelope I had brought upstairs a moment before.

Wolley looked at the body closely, then turned around and examined the door.

"Say," he said. "There's no key here. If he locked himself in here where's the key? Say, don't tell me this isn't a suicide either."

Rex Sackler heaved a profound sigh.

"This one's a suicide," he said. "I personally guarantee it."

Wolley went pounding down the stairs again to the telephone. Crosher, Sackler and I followed leisurely. I was holding on to Benny's arm and I could feel him trembling. We arrived on the ground floor as Wolley completed his call to headquarters.

"Rex," he said, "there's still some things I don't understand. First about Rawson. Are you sure Colby killed him, too?"

"That's the first thing I was sure of," said Sackler. "That's what started my whole train of thought. Once I decided Colby had killed Rawson, it was easy to figure the rest."

"But how, Rex? How?"

Wolley was almost respectful now.

"Colby was a chain smoker. Do you remember? He'd light one butt from the end of the other. Last night when I asked him for a cigarette he patted his coat pockets and told me his case was in his overcoat. It was. I got it out myself."

"So?"

"Yet Colby swore he wasn't out of the house last night. A chain smoker like that doesn't keep butts in his overcoat so he's got to go out to the hall closet every time he wants a smoke. But if he went outside, he would put them *in* his overcoat. That's just what Colby did. He undoubtedly lit a cigarette after he killed Rawson and he hadn't finished smoking it when I borrowed one from him."

"Borrowed," I said. "Very funny."

But Sackler was so pleased with himself he didn't even glare at me. However, I didn't much care. Sackler's play was over. I still had a little something up my sleeve.

"Well," asked Wolley, "why the hell didn't he get Benny out of here when the job was done?"

"He didn't know Rawson had called me in. He didn't expect the police to question the suicide theory. But the servants may have mentioned Benny and it'd look funny if he wasn't on the spot, since he'd been staying here for three weeks as Colby's clerk. You see how simple they made it? Living here in Capek's house, holding him a prisoner on his own estate, who'd ever suspect them?"

"And the dough?" said Wolley. "What about the dough that boy brought you?"

"Oh, that," said Sackler, as if he'd never given it a second thought. "Just a little personal matter."

I drove the coupe for a good five miles before I opened up. Then I said, very casually: "It'd be a good idea if you got rid of that key before we got back to town. Wolley might start thinking and figure out the whole deal."

Sackler raised his eyebrows. "Deal?" he said. "Key?"

"Key," I said. "Deal. Maybe I'm not quite as dumb as you think I am."

He looked at me for a long time. Then he put his hand in his pocket and took out a key. He said: "I imagine it's safe to throw this out the window here."

I said that I guessed it was. He flung it into the ditch.

I drove another five miles. Then I said: "There's a couple of minor items I'd like to discuss with you."

He nodded a trifle grimly. "I was afraid of that, Joey."

"First," I said, "I'd like a bonus."

"A bonus, Joey? How much?"

"Thirty-three bucks," I told him. "Cash money."

For once he was very quiet at the mention of money. Finally he said, in the tone of a man suffering great physical pain: "I think that can be arranged, Joey."

"Good," I said. "Then there's the matter of a ten-dollar-a-week raise."

Now he looked like a man with the black cholera. "Joey," he exclaimed. "That's over five hundred a year. That's a lot of money, my boy."

"It's only one-fifth of twenty-five hundred," I told him.

There was another long silence. Then, "Suppose, Joey, I didn't see my way clear to letting you have it?"

I made a clucking sound with my tongue and shook my head sadly.

"It's my conscience," I told him. "My damnable conscience. It's driving me to perform my civic duty. To tell Headquarters how you told Colby what you'd figured before you told Wolley. How you explained to Colby how you'd figured he must be in a bad financial jam in order to have murdered Capek. How you pointed out that his peculations were bound to come out when you had him pinched for murder."

"Yes, Joey," said Sackler weakly. "Anything else?"

"Why, yes," I said. "It occurs to me that you offered him an easy out. Instead of being pilloried in the press, instead of bearing the sneers of his upper-crust friends, you offered to let him commit suicide. For a consideration."

"A consideration, Joey?"

"Twenty-five hundred and fifty dollars," I said. "Of course, you couldn't let him kill himself before the check was cashed. It wouldn't have been legal. That's why you called our attention to the time when we heard the shot that killed Colby. Your check was in the bank by then."

I looked at him and observed with vast satisfaction that for the first time in our joint careers I had him on the run.

"To ensure his not dying before you cashed the check you locked him in the attic and gave him a gun with no ammunition. Moreover, you referred to him as Smith so that Wolley wouldn't arrest Colby, at once, thus wrecking your deal. Then when you had the dough in your pocket you sent me up with a bullet, all as per private and strictly extralegal agreement with Colby."

"Joey," he said, "you figured all that out yourself?"

"I did, indeed," I said. "And my reward will be five hundred and twenty dollars spread over the coming year, plus thirty-three bucks in cash—now."

He sighed heavily. He thrust his hand into his pocket and took out some bills. He handed them over to me, then delivered a speech which, coming from Rex Sackler, has always seemed a classic to me.

"Joey," he said reproachfully, "sometimes I think there is nothing you wouldn't do for money."

The Color of Honor
Richard Connell

RICHARD (EDWARD) CONNELL (1893–1949) was born in Dutchess
County, New York, and went to Harvard, where he edited the *Daily Crimson* and
the *Harvard Lampoon*. He took a job as a reporter for the *New York American*,
then became an advertising copywriter. After serving in World War I, he became
a full-time freelance writer, moving to Hollywood in 1925 to work in the film
industry, writing stories for several films as well as a large number of short stories for the pulps and the top American slick magazines.

His most famous story, and one of the most anthologized stories ever written,
was "The Most Dangerous Game," the now-familiar tale of a man, Sanger
Rainsford, who falls off a ship traveling up the Amazon River and saves himself
by swimming to an island, where he is greeted by General Zaroff. Ensconced in
a luxurious mansion, Zaroff is a dedicated hunter whose passion for the sport has
driven him to pursue the ultimate game—man—and Rainsford is the prey. The
story has been filmed numerous times, sometimes credited, as with *The Most
Dangerous Game* (1932, RKO, starring Joel McCrea and Fay Wray), *A Game of
Death* (1945, RKO, with John Loder), and *Run for the Sun* (1956, United Artists,
with Richard Widmark and Jane Greer). Films based on other Connell stories
include *F-Man* (1936, Paramount, with Jack Haley) and *Brother Orchid* (1940,
Warner Brothers, with Edward G. Robinson, Ann Sothern, and Humphrey
Bogart).

"The Color of Honor" was published in the June 1923 issue.

The Color of Honor
Richard Connell

This Southern Klan story—by one of America's best-known writers—needs no
comment from us, except this: a number of people have told us Courtnay would
not have acted as he did in this story. What are your ideas about it?

WHEN CATER COURTNAY WAS ELEVEN
years old his father whipped him with a black-
snake whip until he could hardly stand because
the boy, in some juvenile game with some lads
from a nearby plantation, had cheated. Afterward the father talked to his son in the paneled
library of the old house.

"You see your great-uncle, Carroll Courtnay,
up there?" said the father, pointing to a picture,
done in oil, of a darkly handsome man in a grey
uniform.

The boy nodded; he was very white but not
once through it all had he sobbed.

"General Lee trusted him," went on the
father.

"He trusted him, son, because he knew the
stuff the Courtnays are made of. At Shiloh your
great-uncle could have saved himself from death
by one little act of dishonor—most men
wouldn't have thought it dishonorable at all—

but, of course, he didn't. He remembered that he
was a Courtnay, and Courtnays do not cheat, or
lie, or do any dishonorable action. They stand by
their word, and by their kind. You are a Courtnay, son—the last of the name, when I am
gone—and while the breath of life is in you you
must not forget the proud name you bear."

The boy nodded again.

"Now, shake hands with me, Cater," said the
father. "I hope I didn't hurt you much."

The boy held out his hand to his father. His
father never again had any occasion to whip him
for cheating.

When Cater Courtnay was nearing thirty,
and was still unmarried, his father died and from
him Cater inherited many broad acres of rich
cotton land, and the great pillared house in its
grove of live oaks. He was a serious young man,
tall, sun-bronzed, almost saturnine of aspect,
and he took seriously his duties as overlord of the

estate, with almost feudal powers over the men and women who lived on it and worked for him.

One night in the early autumn he sat in the library talking with a guest, a man from the North, whom he had known in college.

"But I tell you, Godwin, you can never understand," said Cater Courtnay, his voice low, intense.

Godwin puffed at his pipe before he answered.

"Men are men," he said finally.

Courtnay shook his head impatiently.

"There are white men," he said, "and there are black men."

"But," returned Godwin, "they are both men. Color doesn't count. Underneath there's no difference."

"You're wrong, Godwin. A Northerner just can't understand; but there are differences, real differences—"

"For example?"

"Did you ever see a nigger who was a gentleman?"

Godwin laughed.

"There are precious few white gentlemen," he said.

"Granted. But there are some—"

"Yes, of course—"

"Well, what are the marks of a gentleman?"

"Honor, first, I suppose—" said Godwin.

"Precisely. Honor. But a nigger with honor? That's ridiculous, Godwin."

"Is it?"

"It is. I know. I've handled niggers for years, thousands of them; I've over two hundred on my place right now. I know them as you could never know them, Godwin, and I tell you it's not only their skins that are black—they're black all through—"

"But they've had no chance," Godwin replied, "down here. That's why I suggested to John Greel that he start a school here."

Courtnay's tanned face showed that the subject of Greel had been discussed and that it was an unpleasant one.

"Godwin," said Courtnay, "you're an old friend of mine, and I'm going to take the liberty of speaking very frankly to you. Down here we feel capable of managing our own affairs. We don't want Greel and we don't want his school."

Godwin shrugged his shoulders.

"It's too late to prevent Greel coming," he said, "even if I agreed with you that the negro is invincibly ignorant and that schooling will do him no good. Greel's mind is made up and you know what a determined fellow he is."

"How should I?"

"He was in college in your time."

"What of it? I don't make a point of associating with niggers, Godwin."

"Well, you've seen the plucky way he played football," said Godwin, with a laugh.

"Let him stay up North. There's work enough for him up there." Courtnay's voice had a menace in it. "I tell you, Godwin, Greel's not wanted here and you would be doing him a service to tell him so. The men around here haven't much patience with these fancy, educated Northern niggers."

Godwin made no reply; for a time he smoked.

"You won't help the school then, Courtnay?"

"I will not."

Godwin stood up.

"It's getting near my train time," he said. "I'd better be starting."

"Sorry you have to go, Godwin. I don't get much civilized society these days. Lots of old families down here, but pretty well gone to seed. Mammy Stella, my housekeeper, would call them 'reeefine but oneducate.' "

"Really?"

"Yes; you've no idea how they resist any new methods in farming; and of course the niggers are impossible; they will do things the way their grandfathers did them—"

"You've tried to teach the negroes then?"

"Have I tried? Till my head nearly burst."

"They seem to work hard—I noticed that in the fields today—"

"Oh, I get a lot of work out of them. They're a little afraid of me. They know I'll stand no nonsense from them. Also, they know I'll treat them squarely. You've no idea, Godwin, what children they are: I have to feed them, clothe them, nurse them and bury them. But it isn't gratitude that makes them work—it's fear."

"Fear?"

"Yes; even their motives are dark."

"They need education; now, Greel's school—"

Courtnay held up his hand; his face tightened into stern lines.

"Please! Let's not discuss that anymore. I won't stand for Greel and his school; that's final. There's the car outside. I'll ride down to the station with you."

II

Ten white men sat around the long mahogany table in the library of Cater Courtnay's house, and from their faces and their manner it was clear that business of a most serious nature had brought them together. They were men whose faces had long known the sun, prosperous-appearing men, who among them owned most of the good farming land in the county.

Sam Hull, big-faced, untidy, in a wrinkled suit, was speaking.

"Yes, sirs," he was saying, an overtone of hate in his voice, "right now is the time to call a halt. Learn 'em a lesson they won't forget in a hurry; they got one coming to them. I reckon you all have noticed how they been getting out of hand of late."

The men about the table nodded and growled. Cater Courtnay at the head of the table said:

"Yes, yes, I guess we all have. Go on, Sam."

"But this last thing—that's the limit with me."

"You mean that voting business, Sam?" asked one of the men.

The big-faced planter nodded.

"What were the facts, Sam? I was down to Mobile when it happened."

"Well," said Hull, "last week on registration day over at Live Oak Corners, little Ned Harris, the election clerk, was dozing in the polling place, when in come two niggers, that big boy Ike, that works for Cassius Pryor, and Courtnay's boy Matt. Ned Harris sings out, 'What in hell do you want here?' and do you know what Matt says?"

The narrator paused before he answered his own question.

"Matt says, 'Mr. Harris, please, sir, we all would like to vote, if you please.' At first Ned Harris thought they was fooling, and he says, 'You want to what?' 'We want to vote,' says Ike and Matt, together, like they had rehearsed. Well, you know what a hair-trigger temper Ned Harris has. 'You get out of here and get damn quick,' he says. And do you know what Ike says?"

The listeners did not know but expressed a keen interest in knowing.

"Ike says, 'Mr. Harris, sir, in the Constitution of the United States it says we all can vote and—and—we want our constitutional rights.' Well, with that Ned Harris jumps up to knock him down; but Ned ain't very strong and the blow only staggers Ike, and then do you know what Ike does?"

The speaker looked round the ring of attentive eyes before continuing:

"He pushes Ned Harris back into his seat, and says, 'Mr. Harris, sir, you don't respect the Constitution,' and then he and Matt walks out."

"Where are those two niggers now?" demanded one of the men, sharply.

"Matt's lit out," Cater Courtnay informed him.

"What about the other one—Ike?"

"Oh, after what Cassius Pryor did to him I guess he won't be overanxious about his constitutional rights again."

They all laughed. The man who had been in Mobile threw out a question.

"How come these niggers are so glib about their constitutional rights? Those boys can't read, can they?"

Courtnay stood up.

"Gentlemen," he said, "Telfair, here, has put his finger on the sore spot of the whole business.

Who put these niggers up to acting this way? Ike and Matt and the rest of them haven't the brains or the nerve; someone is behind them, telling them what to say. I reckon all of us know who I mean."

There were growls of, "Greel. That skunk Greel."

"I always figure, gentlemen," went on Courtnay, "that the way to stop a thing is to stop it at its source—"

"In other words," interjected Sam Hull, "get Greel."

"Precisely."

They looked at each other; there was no dissension.

"I had Greel come to see me last week," said Courtnay. "He's a smart, educated nigger, not at all like the hands down here. He's full of a lot of wind about racial equality—"

He saw that his words were goading them; he went on:

"No. I didn't hit him. That's not the way to handle his kind. I just gave him a strong hint that if he valued his skin he'd better take his school up North, where it would be appreciated."

"Getting mighty polite, ain't you, Courtnay?" one of the men suggested.

"Oh, I didn't mince words. I told him point blank that if he didn't shut up his damn school and get out of the county, some night something highly unpleasant would happen to him. That was a week ago—"

"He's still here—" said one planter.

"And the school's still running," said another.

"And the niggers are having their heads pumped full of nonsense—" put in a third.

"Dangerous nonsense for us," said a fourth.

"That's why we're meeting here tonight, gentlemen," said Cater Courtnay. "We're the responsible white men of the community. What are we going to do? Greel has had his warning; he has ignored it; he told me a week ago he was going to stick—his duty to his people or some such rot—and he has stuck."

"We must teach him a lesson," Sam Hull declared, his voice rasping. "We must teach them all a lesson—"

"You don't mean—" The man who interrupted did not finish his sentence; he was a small bird-faced man who appeared, habitually, never to finish anything—his tie was not tied, his buttons not buttoned. . . .

"You know what we mean, Wood," said Courtnay. "Are you with us?"

"Yes, yes, of course. But, good God, Courtnay, is there no other way? You know how such things set the papers up North snarling at us. We can't afford—" His voice trailed off, leaving the end of the sentence ragged, for Courtnay's austere eye was on him, and there was contempt in it.

"Duty is duty," said Courtnay, "no matter how unpleasant it is. None of us likes to do what we're going to have to do. But if the whites are going to keep their place, the blacks have to be kept in theirs."

"I know, I know," the little unfinished man twisted out the words, "but this isn't right, it's—

"It's—"

Courtnay cut in.

"We can't be soft, Wood. We'll try not to hurt the man."

"That is," put in Sam Hull, "if he listens to reason."

"But," Wood said, "you know Greel's not like the others—he's got guts—he'll fight back—he may—"

"Suppose he does fight back—" said Courtnay. "We can fight a bit ourselves, eh, gentlemen?"

Their laughter was hard.

"Well, when shall it be?" asked Sam Hull.

"Why not tonight?" Cater Courtnay said this.

"Tonight?"

"Yes; let's get it over with. It's got to be done."

"Good. Tonight."

"Yes, tonight."

"But I didn't come—prepared," said Sam Hull.

"Nor I."

"Mine's home, too."

"Gentlemen," said Courtnay, "it's only nine. You'll have time to go to your homes and get what you require. Remember, we want to do this thing in an orderly, business-like manner."

"Shall we wear hoods?" asked one.

Courtnay considered.

"Yes," he said, "that's a good idea. The niggers still have a superstitious dread of the old Klan; pillow cases with holes will do—"

"When we get Greel," suggested Sam Hull, "we can stage a little parade through the cabins. Might as well put the fear of God into them right, while we're about it."

"He'll fight, I warn you," the unfinished man, Wood, quavered. "He'll shoot—"

They did not wait for him to finish.

"Then there'll be one less fancy nigger in the world," said Sam Hull.

"We'll meet at eleven sharp," Courtnay said; he spoke as an accepted leader. "Under the oak at the cross-roads. Each man will bring a gun, a hood and a whip. No one is to speak a word till we order Greel to come out. He sleeps in that little shack about a half mile from the cross-roads near the old Claymore creek bridge. Let's set our watches now. Eleven sharp, remember. Any man who isn't there will be left behind."

"He'll put up a fight, I tell you."

Wood's voice shaded off into a near-whimper.

"Take no chances with him," directed Courtnay. "If he doesn't give up at once, well—" He finished with a gesture of his tan hand.

They understood; into the darkness moved the men; their tread was determined.

III

When they had gone, Cater Courtnay poured himself a leisurely drink from the carafe on the venerable sideboard. There was no hurry; his house was not far from the cross-roads where they were to meet. He sat down in an easy chair and examined his pistol minutely; it was loaded, oiled, ready. Idly his glance roved along the row of paintings on the walls, men in uniform, mostly, with the lean, serious faces of the Courtnay breed. A thought struck him. He rang a bell, and presently an ancient negress, her eyebrows like tufts of cotton, her manner the respectfully familiar manner of the old and trusted retainer, came into the room.

"Mammy Stella?"

"Yes, Mr. Cater—"

"Isn't there up in the attic somewhere an old trunk that belonged to my grandfather, Colonel Courtnay?"

He did not notice that her hands took a sudden grip on the edges of her apron.

"I disremember," she said.

"Oh, come now, Mammy Stella. You were up there only the other day. Wasn't there an old trunk of my grandfather's?"

"Mebbe so."

"You packed it, didn't you?"

"I reckon so."

"Do you remember what you put in it?"

"Not 'zactly. It was more than forty years ago."

"Well, what did you put in it?"

"Nothing but a lot of old clothes, Mr. Cater."

"Ah, that's what I'm after. Do you remember putting in a sort of white garment, like a big night-shirt, with a hood on it?"

He saw from her eyes and the look that came to her face that she remembered.

"Will you get it for me, Mammy Stella?"

The old woman had begun to tremble.

"Mr. Cater," she said, "ask me to do anything, but don't ask me to do that—I'm scared—it's up there in the dark."

"Scared? Nonsense."

"Before the Lord, I am, Mr. Cater. I know that robe, Mr. Cater. It's the old Klan robe. I—I'm scared of it."

"Just an old piece of cloth! Nonsense, Mammy Stella. Why should it scare you?"

"They come one night—to our cabin—I was a little girl then—and they took my brother—I'll never forget—"

"Oh, well, I suppose I can get it myself."

He rose.

"Mr. Cater—"

"What?"

"You ain't plannin'—to use it?"

"Never mind what I'm planning, Mammy Stella. Run along now."

"For God's sake, Mr. Cater, don't—don't—"

"Don't what?"

He regarded the old woman tolerantly; she had been his nurse.

"Don't be cruel—because he's a black man."

"I've no intention of being cruel," he said stiffly.

"But—" she ventured. "Greel—he's a good man—"

"He's poisoning the niggers' minds; we can't permit that."

Courtnay spoke partly to her, but mostly to himself.

"But must you go, Mr. Cater? Can't you leave it to the others—"

His voice was not unkind as he said:

"Mammy Stella, you know better than that, after sixty-five years in the Courtnay family. You know when Courtnays have a duty to perform they don't leave it to other folks. Now run along to bed. I'm going up in the attic."

He stepped toward the door, but the old woman held him back, her wrinkled hands on his arm.

"Don't go, Mr. Cater," she begged. "It's haunted—up there—I tell you—"

"Haunted? The old trunk?"

"It's locked," she cried. "You can't open it."

"I'll break it open."

"You mustn't—oh, Mr. Cater, you mustn't."

"I mustn't? Why not?"

"It's haunted, I tell you." She was clinging to his arm.

He tried, quite gently, to free himself.

"White folks don't believe in haunts, Mammy Stella," he said, with a short laugh. "Let go my arm; let go, do you hear?"

"Oh, don't go up there—your father never let you—" Her voice was desperate.

"I'm a man now," he said, smilingly. "I'm not afraid of the dark—"

"He'll get you, if you go up. He'll get you if you go up."

"Who'll get me?"

"The devil in the trunk," she cried.

"I eat devils," laughed Courtnay.

He took her by the wrists and made her loosen her grip. Then he bounded up the stairs, still laughing.

It was dark in the beamed, stoop-shouldered attic, and in the corners under the eaves was the dust of years. With lighted candle, Cater Courtnay peered about. He had not been up there since he was a boy; then he had gone up once, and had been strictly forbidden by his father to go again.

In the circle of light he saw piles of old trunks and boxes, discarded pieces of furniture, garments, wrapped in muslin, hanging from hooks like so many dead murderers, the odds and ends of a hundred years. Impatiently he pushed the boxes right and left, his eyes searching. He bent over a leathern chest—no, that was not the one. A sound made him start; it was only the creaking of a blind.

"Nerves a bit jumpy," he muttered. "The old fool and her talk of haunts! Funny it should affect me."

He started again, at another sound, but checked himself, with an oath; it was the sputtering of his candle. He continued a brisk search. Then, as he bent to examine a corner, he wheeled about, his hand plucking at his hip-pocket—he had sensed something moving in the attic. He laughed aloud. It was his own shadow, grotesque, misshapen in the candle's wavering flame. His laugh echoed; to his own ears it sounded unreal, smothered.

"A ghost's laugh," he said to himself, and he didn't like the way his voice cracked.

He pushed aside a pile of boxes; then he found what he was seeking—a very old, flat, brass-bound chest, marred by time, its lock rusty, and his grandfather's initials on it, in faded paint.

———

He could not understand why his heart was beating with fast, irregular beats; why his brow felt damp; why the words of a superstitious old black woman should just then be dancing in his brain. He bent over the chest with a determined frown, and with a snatched-up poker pried at the rusty lock. A violent twist, and the lock shot open like a hound showing its fangs. He jumped back from it, cursed his nerves, bent over the chest again.

In the old chest there was nothing to alarm him; there was nothing in it but a pile of old clothes, the folded grey uniform of a colonel, the crushed wide felt hat, the black boots. He took them out, one by one, with careful pride. Then came his grandfather's frock coat with silk facings, his grey pantaloons with straps under the insteps, his white, frilled shirts.

At last, at the very bottom, Courtnay found it—a robe of some coarse cotton stuff, white once, but yellowed by time; to it was attached a hood, with eye holes, and on the breast was a cross, rusty red, like an old bloodstain.

His fingers, unbidden, recoiled from it. He forced them to pick it up, and his hands, usually so steady, were trembling, and he shuddered as he laid it aside.

Courtnay glanced into the chest to see if he had entirely emptied it. The candle, as if to aid him, sent up a spurt of flame, strange flame that seemed greenish in the silent gloom of the room, and Courtnay saw that in the bottom of the chest was a raised place, a swollen place, like the lump after a blow.

He examined it. He saw that the leather lining had been slit, and something flat thrust under it, and the lining stitched together again. His finger-nails tore at the stitching; he was breathing through his mouth, jerkily; he fumbled for the poker, grasped it.

The stout seams resisted at first, then gave up and the slit gaped open like a fresh wound. He pulled out what had been hidden there. It was an envelope, worn and smelling of the must of years. He ripped it open and, by the candle's light, read the long communication in the handwriting of his grandfather.

Then he screamed, the cut-short scream of a man stabbed through the lungs. He staggered. The candle was overturned and utter blackness filled the attic.

"Lord God, have pity on me! Oh, Lord, oh, Lord—"

He was sobbing, moaning in a delirium of fear.

"Lord, have pity. Lord, have pity. Lord, have pity."

He was on his knees and the words came from him in the terror-spurred, yet rhythmic, chant of the revival meeting. He struggled to his feet, wildly, as a fallen horse does, and plunged through the darkness for the door; his head struck a beam and the shock steadied him for an instant. He made the door and half leaped, half fell down the stairs.

Mammy Stella was still in the library when Cater Courtnay stumbled in, the paper from the envelope still grasped in his hand. She was kneeling there, praying aloud as she swayed her body back and forth—

"Don't let him find the devil! Don't let him find the devil!"

He heard. He shook her, his fingers digging into her shoulders.

"It isn't true," he cried. "Tell me it isn't true."

The old woman moaned. A hot, blind wave of fury swept over him.

"You knew all the time. Why didn't you tell me? Why didn't you tell me?"

She raised her eyes to his; she faltered at first; then she spoke clearly:

"Because, Mr. Cater, I know what it is to be a nigger," she said.

A spasm of pain twisted his face at the word. He sank into a chair; he sat staring dully at the paper in his hand, still held in a grip like the rigid grip of a corpse. He knew now why he had felt that nameless fear in the attic.

He did not see the old woman as, with a cat-like movement, she stole to his side; before he could stop her she had snatched the papers from his hand, and had cast them into the fire that blazed in the fireplace. He leaped up, bewildered. She thrust her body between him and the blazing papers.

"Now," she said, and her lips parted in a toothless smile, "no one need ever know."

He stared at her as if he did not understand. Then, thickly, he said:

"No—one?"

"No one but me—and you."

He leaned against the library table; he shook his head, then half muttered:

"But *I* know. But *I* know."

The old negress was about to speak, but he stopped her.

"Please go, Mammy Stella. I want to be left—alone."

She left him standing there, and he might have been dead so motionless was his body, so fixed his black eyes.

How long he stood there, his stunned brain trying to take hold of what had happened to him, Courtnay did not know. The knell-like stroke of a clock on the mantel broke in upon him, and galvanized him into action, at first dulled and aimless, then, as he got a better grip on himself, into action more coherently directed. For the stroke of the clock pricked him into the consciousness that it was ten-thirty—and at eleven he had a duty to perform. He was due at the cross-roads; if he did not arrive they would start without him; later they would say he had weakened, had shirked. Time pressed.

Mechanically his hand felt at his hip-pocket to reassure him that his pistol was there; the hand that touched the cold metal leaped back as if it were glowing hot. The pistol was there, and ready. Ready? For what? To shoot a nigger. He drove his teeth into his lips.

The ticking of the clock seemed inordinately loud and insistent. Twenty-five minutes to eleven. They would be beginning to gather under the live oak at the cross-roads, relentless men, silent in their white hoods.

Even as they gathered, half a mile from the place of their assembling, Greel would be asleep in the little shack where he tried to teach the alphabet to men of his own color. He would be tired after his day's work, reflected Courtnay, worn out in mind and body, for it must be a heart-breaking job. The hooded men would steal upon the cabin, surround it, order him to come out, and then . . .

Courtnay remembered Greel and the interview they had had. There was a deep gentleness and patience about the schoolmaster, but when Courtnay had ordered him, peremptorily, to close the school and go, there had been a light in Greel's eye and he had held his head high as he had refused. Greel would fight. . . .

Courtnay wished the clock would not tick so loudly. Twenty minutes to eleven. He had barely time to reach the cross-roads. But he did not start; he stood there in the library and his eyes were fastened on the paintings that hung there . . . his father, his great-uncle Carroll, his grandfather . . . honorable men. . . .

Tick, tick, tick. They would be starting on their grim errand soon. They looked to him—to a Courtnay—to lead them. And still he stood staring into the eyes of his great-uncle Carroll who had died at Shiloh. *Tick, tick, tick.* Cater Courtnay straightened; in the hearth's dying light he seemed very tall and erect. Then, all action now, he went from the library and the house, and with long, swift strides hurried through the heavy blackness of the night.

IV

It was just eleven. In the village the drowsy church clock announced the hour. Breathless, Cater Courtnay darted up to the door of Greel's cabin. There was no light; he rapped with tense fists.

"Who's there?"

The voice of the colored schoolmaster was firm, alert.

"I—Cater Courtnay—a friend—"

The door opened an inch.

"What do you want?"

"Quick!" Courtnay whispered. "Let me in. They're coming to get you."

The door opened wide enough to admit a man. By the embers on the hearth Courtnay saw that Greel was fully dressed, and that he held a pistol in his hand.

"You knew they were coming then?"

"Every night," said Greel, "I wait like this."

Courtnay's words were swift, incisive.

"We must act quickly. They'll be here in five minutes. They'll murder you like a dog."

"I'll fight—"

"No use. They're nine to one."

Greel shrugged his shoulders; he kept his pistol leveled at Courtnay's heart.

"You can't talk me into giving up, Mr. Courtnay," he said. "Go back and tell them they'll never take me alive."

"Don't be a fool, Greel. You'd be no good dead. You've work to do—I didn't come to betray you—I came to help you escape—"

"Too late," said Greel.

"No. You've got a chance. Go now. Run down the path by Claymore creek; cross the footbridge; you can catch the midnight train as it goes through Bayardville—"

"No use; I'm too tired to run fast; they'd find the cabin empty; they'd follow and catch me; I'll stay."

"They won't follow you—"

"Why?"

"Because they won't find the cabin empty."

Greel looked at Courtnay sharply.

"You mean—"

"Yes."

"But why?"

Courtnay drew himself up.

"My grandfather—damn him—had a mulatto slave—damn him—damn him to Hell—my father had her blood in him—we're black—damn him to Hell. But you've got to hurry."

Greel looked out of the cabin door; a faint moon, just come out, showed far down the ribbon of road something white moving toward them.

"Go, Greel," Courtnay whispered fiercely.

"But why should you do this?"

"Because I choose to. Now run."

Greel moved toward the door.

"I don't understand—" he said. "But I'm going to go. But before I go, there's one thing I want to do—"

"Quick. What?"

"Shake hands with you."

In the almost dark room the hand of Cater Courtnay and the negro schoolmaster met for an instant; then Greel slipped out into the night and disappeared in the tangle of weeds and underbrush through which the creek path ran.

Greel was across the footbridge when he heard through the night's silence a hard, high voice call out:

"Greel! Greel!"

Then he heard another voice, but not his own, call back:

"Yes? What do you want?"

The hard, high voice answered:

"We want you. Come out, Greel."

No reply. Greel sped on through the night.

"Come out, Greel, do you hear?"

No reply. Other voices took up the cry.

"Come out, Greel. Come out, you black skunk. Come out, or we'll come and get you out."

Then as he ran, Greel heard a terrible voice that seemed to fill the whole night, cry:

"Come get me, if you can, you white devils. I'll show you how a nigger can die!"

He heard the staccato bark of shots.

Greel had come to a bend in the path; he was panting, but he felt he was safe now; he could see the lights of Bayardville not far off; he stopped to catch his breath. He looked back toward where he had come from. Against the brooding sky he saw the bloody orange-red of flames.

Middleman for Murder
Bruno Fischer

BRUNO FISCHER (1908–1992) was born in Berlin, Germany, and emigrated to the United States at the age of five, his family settling in New York City. He was educated at the Rand School of Social Sciences, which had been established by the Socialist Party in 1906 and closed in 1956 during Joseph McCarthy's anticommunist reign. Fischer became a sportswriter for the *Long Island Daily Press* (1929), then worked for the Socialist newsletter *Labor Voice* (1931–1932) before becoming the editor of the *Socialist Call* (1934–1936), the official weekly magazine of the Socialist Party. He went on to run for the New York State Senate on the Socialist Party ticket and retained his dedication to Jewish causes and socialism until the end of his life, spending his final summers at a socialist cooperative in Putnam County, New York.

As was true of most of the pulp writers whose names remain even slightly familiar more than a half century after the last pulp died, Fischer was a prodigiously prolific writer for numerous pulps, though many of them were not the first tier, with only a few sales to *Black Mask* and *The Shadow*, but numerous stories sold to *Dime Mystery, 10-Story Detective*, and *Strange Detective Mysteries*. In addition to his hundreds of stories, both under his own name and as Russell Gray, he wrote more than two dozen novels, several of which featured his brainy detective Ben Helm, said to have been modeled after Norman Thomas, the three-time Socialist presidential candidate.

"Middleman for Murder" was published in the November 1947 issue.

Middleman for Murder

Bruno Fischer

I grabbed a book-end and socked him before he could yell.

Poor Perry Pike! My old pal sure looked seedy—his hat battered, shoes scuffed, suit shabby. All Perry had was seventy grand in cold cash—too cold to touch!

PERRY PIKE WASN'T GLAD TO SEE me. He was wearing his hat and topcoat when he answered my knock, and he just stood there and scowled. He had a good face for scowling. It was pinched at the cheeks and his thin mouth turned down easily when he was displeased about something.

"Now this," I said, "is a fine welcome home."

"Home?" Perry said, and gulped. "You're back for good?"

"That depends on business prospects." Over his shoulder I looked into the living room. There wasn't anything in sight to make him bar my way, though from where I stood I couldn't see into the bedroom.

"You going to keep standing in the door?" I demanded.

"Oh," he said, and stepped back so that I could get into the apartment.

The place looked pretty good after eight months of west coast rooming houses. A decent-sized living room, an adequate bedroom, a tiled bathroom, a kitchen you could practically turn around in. The furniture was mostly bleached oak except for the daybed and the brown leather chair.

A couple of years ago I'd bought that furniture after I'd picked up some change by selling half a dozen letters to a married banker which he'd written to a woman who wasn't his wife.

The lady didn't give me the letters. I sort of borrowed them without her knowing it, and prevented her from using them dishonestly by returning them to the author for only five grand. A couple of days later I dropped the money in a crap game at Lou's, less what I'd paid for the furniture I'd bought meanwhile. If I hadn't made that purchase, I would have dropped that part of the money too, so I always figured I'd got the furniture for free.

"Where are you going to stay?" Perry Pike asked gloomily.

"Here in my apartment," I told him.

I put down my bag and looked in the other rooms. Nobody else was in the apartment, hiding or otherwise. I returned to the living room.

Perry was sitting on the daybed, with his hands dangling forlornly between his bony knees. "Maybe you'll be more comfortable in a hotel," he suggested.

"Listen, pal," I said, getting sore. "We rented this apartment together. The furniture is mine. I've come home, and I'm staying here even if I could afford a flophouse, which I can't at the moment."

"Broke, eh?"

"Flatter than the treasury of a European country," I said. "Last month I hiked a couple of checks, but on the way home to New York I dropped the dough in a crap game."

"You and your crap games," Perry said disgustedly. He lifted his head. "You're not hot, Willie?"

"Me hot!" I laughed. "The California bulls are looking for a small, dark foreigner around sixty years old."

I was a big guy. I was blond. I could trace my family back to the Revolution. I hadn't seen thirty-five yet.

"I'm kind of broke myself," Perry said unhappily.

Well, I was home, so I decided to make myself at home. I took off my coat and went to the closet to hang it up. I'd glanced in there a few minutes ago to see why Perry Pike wasn't giving me a rousing reception, but now as I searched for a hanger I had a good look at what hung there. The hanger rod was crowded with a couple of overcoats, a couple of topcoats beside the one Perry was wearing and seven suits. There were four hats on the shelf. Everything was expensive and his size.

I turned to him in surprise. "What'd you do, rob a bank?"

He got pale around the mouth. "Those clothes?" he said. "A fella gave them to me."

Perry Pike could lie as smoothly as a diplomat, but he'd lost his touch. Or maybe he hadn't had time to prepare a convincing story. But that wasn't all of it. The topcoat he was wearing wasn't fit for a rummage sale. His hat was battered. His shoes were scuffed and needed new soles. His suit had been old a couple of years ago.

Yet there in the closet were all those new suits and coats and hats.

"How's about telling Papa?" I said.

He shoved his arms deeper between his knees. "Tell what?"

The best cops in New York hadn't been able to make him talk on the two or three occasions they'd tried, so what chance had I? I went into the bathroom to wash up.

When I came out, Perry was still sitting dejectedly on the daybed in his hat and coat.

"Don't let me keep you from going anywhere," I said.

He seemed to wake up. "I'm not going anywhere," he said, and stood up, removed his hat and coat and sat down.

I sat in the brown leather chair and looked at him.

After a while Perry said: "There's no food in the house. Aren't you going out to eat?"

"You going with me?"

"I'm not hungry."

"Neither am I," I said, though I was. "Think I'll hit the hay."

Perry jumped up. "You take the bedroom. I'll sleep here on the daybed."

He was too generous. "The way I barged in on you," I said graciously, "I wouldn't think of taking the bed."

He didn't argue. I opened the daybed, fetched sheets and blankets, got into pajamas, stretched out. It was only nine p.m., the beginning of the evening, but Perry didn't leave the apartment, though he'd been all set to a few minutes ago. He hung around the living room for a while and then went into the bedroom.

Time passed. A radio next door was turned on to the Giants game, and I lay listening to it. After the game, soft music came through the wall.

It wasn't until an hour or two later that I heard Perry snore. I slipped out of the daybed.

Enough light came in from the street lamp five floors below the window to show me what I was doing. There wasn't anything in the mattress or among the springs. The frame of the daybed was upholstered. I moved my fingers over the material.

When I straightened up to go to the other end of the daybed, my head turned, and Perry Pike in faded blue pajamas was standing in the bedroom doorway.

For a moment we just looked at each other. Then I said with a very small laugh: "I was hunting for bugs."

"There aren't any," Perry said woodenly.

"That's good." I climbed back into the bed. "Good-night, pal," I said.

Without a word he returned to the bedroom. A couple of minutes later I was fast asleep.

I awoke with the sun in my eyes. The moment I stirred Perry Pike came into the room. By the looks of him he hadn't slept a wink all night.

"Fine morning," I said heartily.

"Yeah," he said glumly, and sat down in his pajamas.

He sat while I shaved, showered, dressed.

"Anything in the kitchen to make breakfast?" I asked him, though I knew the answer. I'd looked and found a bulging refrigerator.

"Not a thing," he said. "I've been having all my meals out."

"So dress and let's go down for breakfast."

He wriggled his bare toes. "I'm not hungry. I guess I'm not feeling so good."

It would have been fun keeping up the torment, but I was getting almost as impatient as he was. I put on my hat, said, "I'll be back in an hour," and went.

I went as far as the self-service elevator. When it came up to my floor, I sent it down without me; then I returned up the hall, walking on my rubber heels. I listened through the door. In the apartment there was a heavy, scraping, dragging sound, like furniture being moved—the daybed, no doubt. Then a minute of silence, then a thinly harsh sound, not at all loud.

After listening to that for a while, I decided that a floorboard was being ripped up. But I couldn't quite believe it. I couldn't see a hiding place under a tongue-and-groove hardwood varnished floor in a modern apartment.

Silence returned to the apartment. I waited a full minute by my watch. He had, of course, locked the door, but I still had my key. I unlocked the door and entered.

He had moved the daybed to the middle of the room. Where it had been, he sat on the floor, a skinny little man in faded blue pajamas.

"So it wasn't the daybed, Perry," I said cheerfully. "It was behind the daybed."

His eyes blinked and his lips quivered. I half-expected him to burst into tears. He didn't say anything.

I walked over to where he sat on the floor and squatted beside him. It hadn't been one of the floorboards I had heard him pry up; it was the eight-inch molding that ran along the base of the wall. The screwdriver he had used was still in his hand. There was an empty space behind the molding; probably he'd gouged it out of the plaster himself. I could see small rectangular bundles wrapped in newspaper in the hole. He had taken three of them out.

"I knew it," Perry said bitterly. "I fooled the coppers, but the minute you walked into the apartment I knew I wouldn't be able to fool you."

"The way you acted, one would've got you ten it was in the daybed," I told him.

"But you'd look and look till you found it," he said, trying to break the screwdriver in two with his bare hands. "The coppers had a look, but living here in the apartment you would've done better, so I knew I had to get the stuff out of here quick." He sighed. "You were always smarter than me, Willie."

"Sure," I agreed.

I unwrapped one of the bundles. The shape had told me what was in it, but when I saw that I was right, I was too experienced to give way to ecstasy.

"Queer money?" I asked him.

"See for yourself."

I picked off the top bill—a fifty. I looked at it in the light, I crumpled it, I felt it. Beyond doubt Uncle Sam's mint had manufactured it.

I shuffled through the rest of the money in that pile. The bills were in larger denominations, but not so large that you couldn't cash them at a bank without arousing suspicion. I made a quick count. Six thousand bucks, about.

"How many bundles in all?" I asked him.

"Ten."

I whistled. "Sixty grand!"

"Seventy grand," Perry said miserably. "But the dough's no good."

"Hot, eh?" I said. "The banks have the numbers. The coppers will nab you as soon as you start passing them. That it, Perry?"

He shook his head. "This is strictly legitimate dough. No serial numbers on file. Only I can't spend it."

"Why not?"

Perry stood up and went to the daybed and sat down. "I know you, Willie," he said. "You'll ask questions all over town and find out what the coppers think they have on me and figure out the answers, so I might as well tell you myself."

I settled myself on the floor, with my back to the hole in the base of the wall. It looked like merely an accident that I was between Perry Pike and the seventy grand.

"A guy named Norval Avery was in the white goods business," Perry said. "He was a legitimate character, manufacturing white shirts and men's underwear. Had a small shop off Seventh Avenue and maybe half a dozen workers. Lived in Queens with the missus and two kids in one of those attached brick houses where you can walk blocks and blocks and not tell one house from another. He wasn't poor and he wasn't in the dough—till the war came and the OPA and the white goods shortage."

"You're telling me," I commented. "I used to pay twelve bucks for a white shirt worth no more than two."

Perry nodded. "And a large slice of the difference went into Norval Avery's own pocket. So there was Norval Avery suddenly rich out of the black market, living high, sending his wife and kids to Florida every winter all winter long, buying everything he'd always hankered for. Of course he paid for everything in cash on account of all that black market dough he got was in cash. Then the war ended and a year later white goods started coming back into the stores and business went back to normal or worse, and Norval Avery found himself with better than one hundred grand in cash."

"Very nice," I said.

"Think so?" Perry said. "Wait and see. Of course this Norval Avery didn't pay income tax on this black market dough. Even if he'd wanted to, he couldn't on account of his tax would be so high, the OPA would start asking him how come he made so much in just a small shop. But he also had the Treasury boys to worry about. And Norval Avery was a guy who worried plenty. Like when he had all that cash in a bank safety deposit box and then read in the papers that maybe Congress would pass a law to open all safety deposit boxes for a look, he grabbed the dough out and then didn't know what to do with it."

"Spend it," I suggested.

"Sure, he spent it here and there, but not too much. Like when he visited his missus and kids in Florida and started plunging at the racetracks and then heard how Treasury agents were hanging around the tracks to get a line on heavy bettors who hadn't paid heavy income taxes. So after that he was scared to buy even a two-dollar ticket. Then, just before the OPA was kicked out by Congress, they nabbed some guys who were in the white goods black market and they sang plenty. One of the lads they sang about was Norval Avery. And so the OPA boys asked him this and that, such as how come he was richer than he should be. But they didn't know the half of it on account of all the transactions had been in cash and they hadn't any idea about the pile of it he had socked away. But they couldn't do anything to him. That got the Treasury boys on his tail, and even after the OPA was no more, Norval Avery had the unpaid income tax to worry about. All they had to do was know about all that cash and they'd have him good."

"Cute," I said. "That's what happens with legitimate lads having illegitimate dough. Now if I had it . . ."

"Yeah?" Perry ran the back of a hand over his mouth. "So there he was with all that cash and scared to spend more than a few bucks of it now and then. Scared to invest it, buy a house, play the horses with it. And he had another headache—where to hide it. Once he buried it in his backyard, but he started thinking that one of the neighbors might've seen him, so next night he dug it up again. He hid it in his mattress, and then thought he was cooked when the cleaning woman cleaned the room and made the bed. He hid it in the cellar, but next week a plumber came to repair something down there, and he was sure the plumber would find it. He nearly died waiting for him to leave. Every couple of days he hid it somewhere else."

"But he didn't hide it where you couldn't get it," I observed.

Perry Pike was silent for a long minute. We both listened to the music coming through the wall. The radio in the apartment next door hadn't been turned off for a moment since last night.

"Last month I was playing poker in Norval Avery's house," Perry went on. "It wasn't the first time. The way I figured it, he had an idea

that if he went in for heavy poker, he could say he'd won the dough. Only the trouble was he was a hunch player, and he never won even once. This night I'm talking about he played like he didn't care if he took a pot or not, like he was just going through the motions of playing on account of a week before he'd made the date for that game. I wasn't doing so good myself, but that's got nothing to do with the story. After a while it so happened that I left the game for a few minutes to go upstairs to the bathroom. I happened to look into a room that was fixed up like a study, and I happened to go in."

"To see if anything valuable wasn't nailed down," I said.

Perry didn't care for the interruption. He scowled darkly at me. "There was a letter face down on the desk," he told me. "I turned it over and saw it was addressed to the Bureau of Internal Revenue, so I read it. He'd written them the story I've just told you, a confession, and at the end he said he was going nuts worrying over that dough and was ready to pay the tax and fines and hoped they wouldn't start criminal action against him on account of he was telling all. After I read the letter, I went back to the poker game."

"How'd you find it?" I asked.

"The dough?" He practically smiled. "You're not the only smart cookie, Willie. After the game broke up, I hung around the house. Norval Avery's missus and kids were in Florida and he was alone in the house. I waited an hour after all the lights went out and then slipped into the house. The first place I looked was the right place. There was one of those artificial fireplaces, but with real bricks in it, and I knew that sooner or later he'd hide the dough there because sooner or later anybody would. And sure enough there was a loose brick. When I pulled it out there was the dough. While I was counting it, the light went on and I looked around and Norval Avery was in the room."

I ran my tongue over my lips. I had a pretty good idea what was coming.

"What could I do?" Perry complained shrilly. "I grabbed a book-end from a table and socked him with it before he could yell. It wasn't such a hard sock, but the book-end was iron or something, and he . . ." Perry stopped.

"So you killed him," I said softly.

"I just wanted to keep him quiet for a few minutes."

"Murder," I said softly.

"I guess so." He wiped his nose on the sleeve of his pajamas. "Well, I was almost out of the house with the dough when I remembered that letter upstairs he'd written to the Bureau of Internal Revenue. So I went back for the letter and took it with me."

I stood up and stuck my hands in my pockets and leaned against the wall. "I can finish it," I said. "When the body was found, the coppers pulled in everybody who was at that poker game for questioning. But they had to let them all go, including you, because they couldn't prove anything, especially no motive."

"That's what you think," Perry said. "That letter to the Bureau of Internal Revenue was a copy he'd made for his own lawyer. The other copy he'd mailed out that afternoon. So then they knew that Norval Avery had had more than seventy grand in cash in the house and that it was gone. Then they had the motive for his being knocked off."

My toes nudged one of the bundles on the floor. "I see," I said. "When you got your hands on that dough, you couldn't wait. You started splurging. You went out and bought yourself a lot of clothes. The coppers were shadowing all the suspects to see which one had become suddenly rich. You were the lad."

Perry nodded unhappily. "They piled on me. Wanted to know where I'd got the dough for all those clothes and why I'd bought so many suits at a time. I said I'd picked up a little in poker, a little on the ponies. You see, I hadn't spent enough yet for them to prove it wasn't so. They got a warrant and searched this apartment, but they didn't rip off the molding. But they're still watching me. Every time I buy a pack of ciga-

rettes I got a feeling somebody's watching how much I'm spending."

"Poor Perry," I said sympathetically. "The local coppers aren't bad enough. You got the Federals sniffing at you, too, because tax wasn't paid on that dough."

"That's just about it." His arms hung dejectedly between his knees. "Now I know what Norval Avery went through with all that dough begging to be spent and him scared to spend it. As soon as I start spending heavy, the coppers will be sure enough to pull me in for murder and go to work on me. I'm not such a brave guy, Willie. I'm not sure I can stand up to their third degree. And the Federals will bring in their lie detectors, and I hear that intelligent, sensitive guys like me are pushovers for those machines. So like Norval Avery I'm being driven nuts by that dough which is no use to me."

"You don't have to hang around New York," I pointed out.

"The Federals are all over the country," Perry said bitterly. "They never let up on dough they haven't collected tax on. And if they catch up with me on that, they'll turn me over to the New York coppers to burn me. Maybe I can jump to South America, but they'll be watching me if I try to take the dough onto a boat. Anyway, New York is the one place where I'd enjoy spending it. Only I can't."

"Which is," I said, "where I come in."

"That's right," Perry said. "You're always talking about your brain. It'll be worth ten per cent—seven grand—if you figure out how I can remain in New York and spend the dough and not have the coppers down on my neck."

"My brain," I told him reflectively, "tells me that you're going to give me the whole seventy grand."

His head snapped up. "You're nuts!"

"No, you won't give it to me," I corrected myself. "What I'll have to do is gather up these ten bundles and walk out of here. I don't think you'll go yelling to the coppers that I relieved you of seventy grand."

Perry Pike looked at me and shivered. He was

a little guy and I was a big guy. I could take him with one hand.

He stood up. I watched him, but all he did was go as far as the bleached oak desk and lean against it. He looked sick. I felt a little sorry for him. He wasn't a bad sort of lad.

But there was work to be done. I stooped and came up with a bundle of money in each hand—and looked into the muzzle of a compact .38 automatic pistol.

The gun was in Perry's hand. "I think you'll leave that dough where it is, Willie," he said hoarsely.

I stared at him in surprise. Perry wasn't a firearms lad any more than I was. I wasn't even sure that he knew how to use one. His hand wasn't steady, but he was close enough to hit anything he shot at and too far away for me to take him.

"Perry," I said pleasantly, "there's no point getting sore at your closest pal. Didn't you just trust me enough to confide in me?"

"Yeah, I confided in you," he said grimly, "on account of you would've gone to the library and dug into newspapers and read how last month a guy named Norval Avery was knocked off in Queens and seventy grand missing, and you'd have added it up to me. Now beat it."

"Perry," I said, "let's sit down and talk. For a fifty-fifty split—"

"Beat it," he said.

I didn't care for the look in his eyes or the way the gun was pointed right at my heart. I beat it.

I sat in a restaurant eating breakfast and wondering where Perry Pike would stash the dough next. New York was the hardest place in the world to hide anything which had bulk. Especially if you wanted it where you could get your hands on it now and then, you were limited to the tiny area in which you lived hemmed in by dozens or hundreds of other people.

No wonder Norval Avery had given up, and Perry was in the first stages of going nuts with worrying. The fact that he'd got himself a gun proved it.

I gave him about an hour to cool off before I returned to the apartment. For a lad who lived by his brains, I'd been in too much of a hurry to grab off the whole seventy grand. Now I'd have to work at getting Perry's confidence back, at convincing him that I was his one pal in a cold and hostile world.

When I let myself into the apartment, I saw that Perry had straightened up the living room. The molding was on the wall and the daybed pushed back to where it belonged.

"Perry?" I called.

No answer. I started to feel sick. He'd beat it after all with the dough which had practically been mine, and I'd never again see him or, what was more to the point, it.

I glanced into the kitchen, then into the bathroom, then opened the bedroom door.

I saw something and heard something at the same time. What I saw was Perry lying motionless on the floor between the bed and the dresser. What I heard was a small sound at the side of the door. I was turning toward the sound when the ceiling fell on me.

My knees buckled. A cloud whipped over my eyes, and through it I saw something move. It didn't have form or substance, but in a vague way I knew that it was a human being and that he'd just conked me over the head with a blunt object.

My shoulder hit the floor. The cloud thinned a little and I could see legs. Legs wearing pants, and they were moving toward me. Dully the thought ran through my aching head that he was going to hit me again, and this time he'd make sure to bash my skull in.

I didn't want my skull bashed in. I waved a hand at the legs. Above me there was a panicky yelp. The legs vanished from my line of vision. I heard them run out of the bedroom, across the living room. I heard the hall door open and slam.

I lay back on the floor and closed my eyes. The door slammed again. He's coming back to finish me, I thought, and twisted on my hip toward the door. I could see part of the living room; nobody was in there. I didn't hear anybody.

I pushed myself up to my feet and wobbled out of the bedroom. Nobody was in the apartment except Perry and myself. I must have dreamed hearing that door slam twice.

I returned to the bedroom. Perry Pike hadn't moved. He would never move under his own power. There was too much blood on his shirt and on the floor. And his eyes were open, staring up at me without seeing me.

A knife had done it to him. An ordinary steak knife. The handle was still sticking out of one of the half dozen wounds in his chest.

I felt very bad. I'd known a lot worse lads than Perry. While we hadn't trusted each other in the matter of seventy grand, who would have? He'd still been a good pal.

My eyes moved about the room. A weekend bag stood on the dresser. I opened it and found ten rectangular bundles. Seventy grand.

Where Perry had intended to go with the dough nobody would ever know. He had dressed and then put it in the bag and then somebody had come into the apartment. Somebody whose nerves had made him strike again and again with the knife and then run in panic when I'd waved my hands at him.

Sure, somebody. Why wouldn't the cops be convinced that I was that somebody? Motive, opportunity, everything pointed to me. Willie, I thought, you're in a spot. Start thinking.

I didn't touch the money. I went into the bathroom and soaked my head. Then I sat in a living room chair which didn't face the bedroom and lit a cigarette. Through the wall the radio which was never turned off sent soft music. It was too soft. It sounded to me like a funeral dirge—to my own funeral.

Seventy grand in a bag in the bedroom.

I could beat it with the dough. Then when the body was found, the police would check and find that last night I'd come back to live in the apartment with Perry. They were already pretty sure that he was in possession of Norval Avery's seventy grand. Added up, my disappearance would

mean that I'd knocked Perry off for the dough. Result: I'd be seventy grand richer, but I would have as good as confessed to a murder I hadn't done. I'd be a fugitive for life. My fingerprints were on record, and any time I was picked up for anything anywhere, I'd be shipped back to New York to burn in the chair.

There had to be a better way.

Say I walked out of here with the dough and hid it somewhere. Just where I'd hide it I didn't know yet, but I could work that out later. Then tonight I'd come back here and pretend I'd just found Perry murdered and I'd call the coppers myself.

So what? They'd still wonder what had happened to the seventy grand. And they'd come to the same answer: I'd knocked Perry off for it.

Only they wouldn't be able to prove it. They'd take me to headquarters and sweat me, but eventually they'd have to let me go because merely knowing was not legal evidence. And I'd be free with seventy grand in small bills.

And then? Then wherever I went, the coppers and the Federal agents would be sniffing at my tail, and if I was found with that money anywhere it would be all the evidence they'd need. Like Norval Avery and Perry Pike, I'd get heart failure every time I spent an extra nickel.

Whatever you do, Willie, I told myself, you're not going to be any too comfortable. Make with the brains.

The music coming from the radio next door cut out and a man started to enthuse about furniture polish. Instead of thinking, I sat listening to that voice and idly wondering about two doors slamming.

Two doors, I said to myself suddenly. Not one door, but first one and then another.

I stood up and hunted for Perry's gun. It was on the dresser behind the bag. I checked the clip. Fully loaded.

I looked at the bag and sighed. I looked down at Perry and said aloud: "I'll see what I can do for you, pal, and incidentally for myself." Then I went out to the hall.

Softly I turned the doorknob of the apartment next door. It was locked, of course. It so happened that a couple of years ago I'd borrowed the building superintendent's passkey without him knowing it. I'd had a duplicate made and then put the original where the superintendent would find it and think he'd dropped it.

I used that passkey now. I turned it in the lock and kicked the door open and plunged through behind Perry's gun.

I heard and then saw the radio—a small table model against the wall. The lad who liked to listen to the radio day and night wasn't in the living room, but I heard him in the bedroom.

"Who's there?" he yelped frantically.

I rushed into the bedroom. The man cowering against the bed was somebody I'd never seen before; he must have moved in recently. He was tall and thin. He needed a shave and had bloodshot eyes, possibly from listening to the radio instead of sleeping. His shirt and pants were on the floor. He'd taken them off because there was blood on them—blood that had spurted out of Perry's wounds.

"Uh-huh," I said. "A door slamming twice. My door slamming when you ran out of my apartment, and your door slamming when you ran into yours."

He straightened his scrawny, half-naked body a bit. "I don't know what you're talking about," he said.

"I'll draw you a picture," I said. "These walls are thin as paper. If I could hear the radio turned down very low in your apartment, you could hear us talking in my apartment. You heard Perry tell me the tale of the seventy grand. You waited till you heard me leave; then you grabbed up a knife and went next door and knocked. Perry figured you were a delivery boy or something like that and opened the door. When you didn't seem to have any special business, Perry got leery and dashed into the bedroom for his gun. You went after him and stopped him with your knife."

"You're crazy," he said in a thin, small voice.

"What's that on your pants and shirt—red paint?"

He looked down at his bloody shirt and pants and then up at my gun, and, except that he was breathing, he looked about as dead as Perry.

"You must be an honest citizen," I said. "No experience in crime and murder. You had to kill Perry because he knew your face, but you were too frantic and got blood all over yourself. After you conked me, I was more or less helpless, but when I waved a hand at you, you fled like a scared rabbit." I shook my head disapprovingly. "Very sloppy work, mister. I bet that steak knife in Perry's chest matches others just like it in your kitchen. The coppers ought to return their pay for solving this one."

What I'd said about the steak knives must have been true because he broke completely. He buried his face in his hands and rocked from side to side.

"I was such a fool!" he moaned. "But seventy thousand dollars—"

I nodded. "I know just how it is, mister."

His hands flopped away from his face. A remote hope came into his eyes. "Listen," he said tightly. "The money's still there. You take it and let me go."

I smiled. "Wouldn't you like that? Because the lad who has the seventy grand will be burned as the killer." I stroked the barrel of the gun and added reflectively: "For my part, that bag could be full of rattlesnakes instead of currency of the realm and it would be the same thing."

He didn't say anything.

I looked at him for a moment and then asked: "What's your name, mister?"

"Thomas K. Allenby," he muttered.

"Think of that," I said, and I backed into the living room and, keeping him covered with the gun, reached for the phone. . . .

It was an experience having coppers shake my hand.

"That solves two murders at one shot," Detective-Lieutenant Goldblatt told me. "Finding that seventy grand on Perry Pike proves that he was the one knocked off Norval Avery in Queens last month, and you handed us Pike's murder all wrapped up and sealed. That was an honest and courageous thing you did, Mr. Turner."

Nuts, I thought. But I didn't say it out loud. I smiled with becoming modesty. I shook hands with cops and posed for newspaper cameramen. Then I went to a restaurant to catch up on my eating. It wasn't much of a dinner because my financial status couldn't afford better.

But the bean soup and corned beef hash tasted better than I'd eaten in even the best of jails. And when I washed it down with coffee and lit a cigarette, I felt pretty good.

Willie, I told myself, you've got your freedom and your health, which is a lot more than Norval Avery and Perry Pike and Thomas K. Allenby have. Willie, I said to myself, who the hell wants seventy grand anyway?

The Man Who Chose the Devil
Richard Deming

RICHARD DEMING (1915–1983) was born in Des Moines, Iowa, and received his B.A. from Washington University, St. Louis, and his M.A. from the University of Iowa. Soon after, he served as a captain in the army during World War II, then worked for the American Red Cross in Dunkirk, New York, from 1945 to 1950, after which he became a full-time freelance writer.

It was an understood verity of the pulp-writing community that practitioners had to be prolific in order to survive financially, and Deming was one of the most prolific of the later toilers of the craft. He came to the field as it was dying and moved to the new markets for such professionals, including the digest magazines, such as *Alfred Hitchcock's Mystery Magazine* and *Manhunt*, and paperback originals, of which he wrote more than sixty under his own name, as Max Franklin, and as a ghostwriter for Ellery Queen's Tim Corrigan series. He wrote novelizations of popular crime shows of the 1950s, 1960s, and 1970s, including *Starsky and Hutch* and *Charlie's Angels* under the Franklin byline and, as Deming, *Dragnet* and *The Mod Squad*. His short-fiction output exceeded two hundred titles, and he provided stories for several television series, including *Alfred Hitchcock Presents, Mickey Spillane's Mike Hammer, Suspicion*, and the *Gruen Guild Playhouse*. His novel *The Careful Man* (1962) was filmed as *Arrivederci, Baby!* (1966, written, produced, and directed by Ken Hughes, starring Tony Curtis).

"The Man Who Chose the Devil" was published in the May 1948 issue.

'Twas mighty odd for my satanic fat friend Longstreet to be
swearing oaths on a sacred locket—oaths which would surely
send him straight to hell. But perhaps that was the idea.

The Man Who Chose the Devil

Richard Deming

WHEN I THOUGHT ABOUT IT AFTERWARD, it seemed the fat man must have been puzzled that I paid no attention to his standing on my foot. But I was actually unaware of it until I tried to slide off the bar stool and found one foot pinned to the floor.

Of course, he didn't realize there was no feeling in my right limb, that instead of flesh it was an intricate contrivance of cork and aluminum strapped to a stump below my knee. The government paid me $180.00 a month for not having

Leaning across the rail, he planted his fist squarely on the sergeant's nose.

a right leg. They were also going to buy me a brand-new car—when they got around to it.

Just before I tried to leave my stool, I caught a glimpse of Anton Strowlski in the bar mirror. The dapper gunman approached with one hand negligently carried in the pocket of his tailored suitcoat. Since I had never rubbed against Anton, I knew he wasn't looking for me, but I automatically grow observant when gunmen, even friendly gunmen, get behind me with their hands in their pockets.

Anton's expression was casual, his eyes on no one in particular. But something in the face of the fat man standing next to me, as it was reflected in the bar mirror, caused me to shift my glance from the gunman to him. The fat man's face was expressionless, but his eyes unwinkingly followed the image of Anton Strowlski.

It was then I decided to move from my stool. Not that I expected anything to happen in as public a place as the Jefferson Lounge, but some inbred caution prompted me to want a large section of the Jefferson's air-conditioned atmosphere wedged between myself and the fat man. And I found myself stuck to the floor.

The fat man stood half-faced away from me, his left elbow propped on the bar and his left foot solidly crushing the full weight of his two hundred forty pounds on my right shoe. With one eye still on Anton, I tapped his arm.

The gesture caught Anton's attention and he flashed me a quick glance, nodded in recognition and made an abrupt right wheel toward the far end of the bar.

Without moving his body, the fat man turned at me a florid face which would have meant a fortune to a burlesque comedian. High-domed, round-cheeked and pug-nosed, and with bright, heavy-lidded eyes over which satanic eyebrows arched upward at the ends, instead of down, it was the face of a rollicking satyr.

I pointed at the floor. "If you don't mind, I'll take my foot with me."

His lips drew back over dazzling mail-order teeth, and a chuckle worked its way up from his gargantuan paunch, coming out baritone and

amused. Without moving his foot, he turned his back.

I began to get sore, but not enough to slug him. The Jefferson Lounge frowns on commotion. It even frowns if you drop your money on the bar instead of laying it down noiselessly. It features organ music and quietness, apparently ashamed of being a saloon and trying to disguise the truth under a church-like atmosphere. I tapped my fat drinking mate again.

"Your foot is on mine," I explained clearly.

"I know." He turned his back again.

"Move it," I said to his back, without raising my voice.

His big head swiveled at me for the third time. Satanic brows quirked upward and his ready-made incisors sparkled again.

"You move it."

His bright eyes glinted mischievously, completely lacking the contentiousness of a stew picking a fight. I saw he was dead sober, yet for some reason, which I vaguely linked with the presence of Anton Strowlski, was deliberately trying to start a scene. So I gave him one.

Sliding my stool to the left, I let the side of my chest drop across it, grasping the seat with both hands for support. Rapidly crossing my left leg over my right until the sole of my foot rested against the inside of his far knee, I pushed.

His right leg buckled, throwing him off balance, and he grabbed at the bar with both hands. At the same time he involuntarily moved the foot imprisoning mine a step backward. Snapping erect, I smashed the heel of my released right foot into the underside of his left knee. He sat down with a crash that shook the room and stopped the organist in the middle of a bar.

With surprising agility for a fat man, he bounced to his feet and swung a roundhouse at my head. In a brawl, I watch a man's eyes. His showed no anger, only an increased mischievous joy. My knees bent and his fist whistled a foot over my hair.

He was easy. One short jab in that soft stomach jackknifed him forward with his jaw conveniently out-thrust. When he hit the floor this time, he stayed there and slept.

I looked up from his sprawled body just in time to see Anton Strowlski let the street door swing closed behind him.

You simply did not brawl in the Jefferson Lounge. Fatso was hardly asleep before a cop had me by either arm. I think management keeps cops under the bar, along with ice-cubes and lemons.

When they finally got Fatso awake, they put us both in a prowl car. The Jefferson's manager stood at the curb wringing his hands and looking horrified.

"No charges, Officer," he kept saying. "Just take them away."

The older of the two cops said testily: "All right. All right," and the manager moved away.

The Jefferson Lounge is situated in one corner of the elaborate Jefferson Hotel. As the Lounge manager passed back into the dispensary, I noticed Anton Strowlski a few yards up the street under the hotel marquee. With his back against the brick wall near the main entrance, he watched us broodingly. I recognized our driver, a stocky, middle-aged cop, without being able to recall his name. I know most men on the force, at least by sight. The other cop was young and unfamiliar, probably a rookie.

The driver twisted in his seat to look us over. Fatso was shaking his head and working his jaw back and forth with one hand.

"You're Manny Moon, aren't you?" the driver said to me.

"Yeah."

"Who are you?" he asked my sparring partner.

"Willard Longstreet." The fat man turned to me. "Manville Moon, are you? The private dick?"

I nodded shortly.

"What you hit me with?"

"With great enjoyment, you big ape."

He grinned his satyr grin and mischievous brightness returned to his eyes. He fixed them on the driver.

"What are your plans, cop?"

The policeman frowned. "They were to let you go, if you promise to behave. But I don't like 'cop.' "

"I want Moon booked for assault and battery," Longstreet said calmly. "Drive along."

"Why you . . . !" I started to say, then stopped and relaxed. "Go along," I told the driver.

Shrugging, the cop faced forward and started the motor. I glanced over at Anton once more, saw him frown at us worriedly, and on a spur-of-the-moment impulse decided to make the party complete.

"Hold it!" I told the driver.

Gears clashed as the driver, starting to release the clutch, suddenly braked and slipped back into neutral. Locking the emergency, he peered at me in the rear-view mirror.

"Now what?"

I said: "The guy standing under the hotel marquee is Anton Strowlski. Know him?"

Both cops glanced that way and both shook their heads.

"Chicago boy. Even money you'll find a gun if you shake him down."

Anton, noting our eyes on him, began to move away slowly. Swinging open his door, the younger cop bounced from the car.

"You!" he called.

Pretending not to hear, Anton increased his pace. The cop legged after him, drawing his service revolver as he ran.

"Halt, or I'll shoot!"

The command improved Anton's hearing and he stopped dead in his tracks and turned. The cop gestured toward the building with his gun and Anton, familiar with the routine through much previous experience, faced the wall with his hands elevated about to shoulder height.

Deftly running his free hand over the gunman's body, the policeman relieved him of a dainty, snub-nosed automatic. He found it in the same pocket Anton's hand had occupied when I first glimpsed him in the mirror.

Reholstering his revolver, the cop let Anton precede him back to the car. Without a word the gunman took his place in the rear seat between Longstreet and me.

As we made our second start, I said: "Who you working for these days, Strowlski?"

Eyes brittle as broken glass swung to my face. He ignored my question. "You finger me, Moon?"

"Mister Moon," I said.

His lips quirked upward, lacking mirth. "I've heard that gag about you. I don't mister nobody."

Without moving my body or changing expression, I drove my right elbow into his chin. His smirk was absorbed by a vacuous look and he slumped heavily against the shoulder of Longstreet, who flashed me a startled glance and pushed the gunman away. Anton's head slumped forward, hiding his vacant expression, and his body, wedged between us, remained erect.

Neither of the cops suspected anything wrong. Traffic sounds had drowned the slap of my elbow against Anton's jaw, and the younger cop, periodically turning to look us over, apparently assumed the gunman's bowed head was the result of bashfulness.

Anton was still resting when we arrived at the station. I got out one side of the car, Longstreet got out the other and Anton rolled slowly forward on his face.

Before either cop could open his mouth I said: "What's the matter with him?" threw a suspicious look at Longstreet and asked, "You do something to him in the car?"

Longstreet's outraged expression faded into one of amusement. "He was all right a minute ago."

"Looks like he fainted," said the younger cop.

The middle-aged cop glanced at Longstreet suspiciously, then said to his colleague: "Well, drag him out and slap him awake."

Without waiting to see his instructions car-ried out, he waved us ahead of him and followed us up the steps grunting audibly.

CHAPTER TWO
MURDER BY MAGIC

Sergeant Danny Blake was working the desk at headquarters. When he saw me, he flashed his gold front tooth and asked hopefully: "What's the charge? Homicide?"

"Assault and battery," said our chauffeur. He pointed his thumb first at Longstreet and then at me. "On him, by him."

"The old man will be disappointed," Blake said, enjoying himself. "Only assault and battery."

I said: "Fill out your forms, clown, or it will be homicide. Only someone else will have to enter the charge."

Throwing open his log book, Blake entered my name and other identifying information, put down Longstreet as complainant, then, pen poised, looked inquiringly up at the arresting officer.

"Jefferson Lounge," the policeman said. "About a half hour ago." He glanced up at the clock on the wall. "That'd make it 2:30 p.m. It was about 50-50, according to the manager. They both swung, only Moon connected."

Blake looked at me. "You filing counter-charges?"

Ever since we left the Jefferson, I had been thinking that over. I turned toward Longstreet and caught the same mischievous laughter deep in his eyes. I didn't understand him. I didn't understand anything, except that up till now I seemed to be reacting exactly as he wanted. I decided to change that.

"No counter-charge," I said, and the lights went out of Longstreet's eyes as though someone had thrown a switch.

He watched me thoughtfully as I posted $250.00 bond, which left my checking account at five figures: a one, a two, a six, a decimal point and two zeros.

"It'll help my civil suit if you're convicted in

police court," he remarked pleasantly. "I'm going to sue you, of course."

"Do that." I took my receipt and turned to leave.

"Wait a minute," Longstreet called.

I looked back at him, waiting.

"I withdraw all charges," he said to Blake.

Sergeant Blake's face reddened and he rose to his feet. "Lissen . . ." he started to say, but that was as far as he got.

"Don't raise your voice at me!" Longstreet interrupted. And, leaning across the rail, he planted his fist squarely in the sergeant's nose.

Two things happened rapidly. Sergeant Blake sat on the floor, and the cop who brought us in twisted Longstreet's arm up behind his back until the fat man stood on his toes.

"Lock him up!" Blake roared, using his desk to pull himself erect. Blood trickled across his mouth from each nostril.

Still cramping Longstreet's arm behind his back, our cop dogtrotted him toward the corridor leading to the pokey. As they passed through the door, the fat man twisted his head over his shoulder to grin at me. The familiar mischievous laughter was back in his eyes.

"He had a devil of a time getting arrested," I said to Blake.

But the sergeant was too busy holding a handkerchief to his nose to care what I said or did. I picked my check off his desk, dropped the receipt and left.

As I went down the steps, Anton Strowlski, partially supported by the rookie cop, groggily stumbled up. The look he threw me tried to be venomous, but it came out more punchy than baneful.

I returned it with a grin.

The phone blared me out of a sound sleep at four in the morning. I let it ring while I strapped on my leg and slipped into a robe, being in no rush to end the wait of anyone who phoned at that hour.

"Moon," I said, when I finally got to the phone.

"About time," a familiar voice rapped in my ear.

It was Inspector Warren Day, Chief of Homicide, who for years had been trying to decide whether he hated my guts or loved me like a brother.

"Go to bed," I said.

"Get your clothes on. Hannegan is on his way over to pick you up."

"Yeah? What's the charge?"

"No charge. Want to see you."

I was silent for a minute. Then I said: "You've seen me lots of times. Go home and sober up."

Day's voice sank to its normal growl. "Listen, Moon. I'm in no mood for your sass. You come with Hannegan, or I'll send him back with a warrant. You're a material witness in a murder."

"Nuts. I haven't seen a murder since the last time I unraveled one you'd fouled up."

"Get your clothes on," Day repeated, and hung up.

I brushed my teeth, felt the rubble on my cheeks and wondered if a shave would bring me awake. Deciding against it, I jolted myself alive with a shot of rye instead. I was dressed when Lieutenant Hannegan arrived.

His expression was wary when he came in, a result of past experience with my resistance to Inspector Day's arbitrary orders.

"You ready?" he asked uneasily.

"All set."

He looked relieved and a little surprised. I followed him outside to the squad car, and asked no questions until he got it in motion.

Then I asked: "What's the deal?"

"Corpse named Carmichael. And the guy who did it, couldn't have."

"Come again?"

"The guy who did it was in jail when it happened. That's where you come in. Fellow named Longstreet."

"Oh," I said softly. "A faint light glimmers."

Inspector Warren Day paced back and forth in his office, chewing his eternal dead cigar and periodically ducking his skinny bald head to peer at one or another of us over his glasses.

Willard Longstreet sat on a straight-backed chair in the center of the room, his fat seat protruding beyond both edges. His clothes hung in perspiration-soaked wrinkles and his round face sagged with fatigue from hours of answering questions. But a faint mocking light still glimmered in the back of his eyes.

Hannegan sat alongside Day's desk, and I relaxed in a chair tilted against the wall.

"You can't get away with it," Day snarled at Longstreet for the twenty-seventh time. "At 3:30 p.m. you had a phone argument with Carmichael. Your joint secretary recognized your voice. At 5:00 p.m. you phoned again and told Carmichael you'd be there in ten minutes. Your secretary swears it was your voice. When she left for home, Carmichael was in his office waiting for you. At 5:30 a shot was heard and the medics confirm that as the time of death. Your gun was found on the office floor too far away for it to be suicide. Your prints, and nobody else's, are on it. You got plenty of motive. You did it. How?"

"Anyone could have stolen my gun," Longstreet said patiently, also for the twenty-seventh time. "I live in a hotel and passkeys are easy to get. Besides, I was in a locked cell from 3:00 p.m. on."

"Locked cell! Locked cell!" Day screeched. "Shut up about locked cells! You got out and back in some way." He turned on Hannegan. "Get him out of my sight! Chain him to the wall. And post a guard in sight of him, so he doesn't get out and murder the whole police department. He's got Houdini beat!"

Hannegan got to his feet and motioned the prisoner erect. Longstreet rose slowly, his shoulders drooping with tiredness.

"Would you like to earn ten thousand dollars, Moon?" he asked me casually.

"Mister Moon," I said.

"Mr. Moon, then," he said agreeably. "Would you like to earn ten thousand?"

"Depends on the method."

A mischievous twinkle pushed past the fatigue in his eyes. "Break this case. I don't think the cops can."

I looked him over thoughtfully. "If I prove you did it, where do I collect? From your estate?"

He shook his head. "I didn't do it."

I said: "I'll drop down to your cell later on."

When Hannegan and Longstreet were gone, Warren Day threw himself into his desk chair, traded his cigar butt for one just like it in his ashtray, carefully dusted it off and stuck it in his mouth.

"What do you think, Manny?" he asked dispiritedly.

"I think four in the morning is a hell of a time to wake me up when the murder was discovered ten hours earlier."

"How'd I know you'd been brought in with Longstreet? A different man was on the desk at six, and I didn't hear about you till just before I called." He ran a hand over the place his hair had been. "What you think about all this?"

I said: "You're sitting on dynamite."

"I know I am."

"Wait till the papers learn you've charged a guy with committing a murder that happened while he was locked in one of your escape-proof cells."

"He's not charged with murder. We're holding him for assaulting a cop."

"What's bond?"

"Five hundred."

"Five hundred!" I said. "Longstreet only cost me two-fifty. Cops aren't worth twice as much as people."

Day wiggled his thin nose and studied his cigar. "He hasn't inquired about bond. Seems in no hurry to get out."

"But he can, whenever he wants. Then what do you do? Charge him with murder?"

The inspector rubbed the side of his nose. "I'd get laughed out of town. Jeepers creepers, Manny, you got any ideas at all about this?"

I felt sorry for him. Normally he would cut off his head before he would ask my opinion about the weather. But he was stopped so cold by this that he hadn't even cursed me once. And it was the first time in our eight-year acquaintance that we had met without trading profanity and a few mild threats.

I said: "Only what I told you. I'm as sure as I sit here that Longstreet deliberately got himself arrested. That was his sole purpose in picking a scrap at the Jefferson. And when he couldn't needle me into filing counter-charges, he slugged Blake. You have to conclude he was building an alibi. Why else would he try to get in jail?"

"No reason else," he agreed reluctantly. He looked at his watch. "Six forty-five. Nearly ten hours I questioned that guy."

"Learn anything at all?"

He shook his head. "Only that he's got a motive. The best there is. Money."

Reswapping his cigar butt for the one he had originally, he struck a match, then shook it out without lighting up and dropped the dead stick on the floor. "Ninety percent of the stock in Rex Amusement Corporation was owned by three guys. Willard Longstreet, George Carmichael and Marden Swope. Ostensibly Swope is president, but actually they were equal partners. They had some kind of a business contract leaving their stock to the surviving partners. So Longstreet inherits half Carmichael's interest in the business. On top of that Carmichael carried a fifty-thousand-dollar insurance policy with Willard Longstreet as beneficiary."

"How much of a business is it?"

"Tremendous, according to Longstreet. They handle coin machines, juke boxes, cigarette vendors, pinball games and one-armed bandits."

I raised my eyebrows. "One-armed bandits, eh? Illegal, aren't they?"

"Not for private clubs. There're a hundred and fifty private clubs in town, according to Longstreet. About a hundred own their own machines, and Rex Amusement Corporation supplies the others for forty percent of the take. The clubs average about twelve machines and take in about fifteen hundred a month each. I did some arithmetic and the company's share comes out to over a quarter million dollars a year. On top of that they service the machines owned by clubs for fifty dollars a month per club. Just that part brings in sixty thousand dollars a year, and two men can handle the servicing. And all this is only one phase of the business."

He stopped and stared bitterly at his dead cigar, probably thinking about an inspector's salary. "No wonder Longstreet can say ten thousand dollars like you or I would say ten cents."

I rose. "You through with me?"

"Yeah. Go on home to bed."

At the corridor fountain I mouthed a swig of water to clear the fuzz from my tongue before going back to Longstreet's cell. There, in the center of the hall, I found a uniformed cop seated on a chair facing the cell door.

The sun had risen, and light streaming through a small, barred window set high in the wall showed me Longstreet stretched flat on a drop-down bunk, his right wrist and right ankle cuffed to the wall as Warren Day had ordered.

"Allowed to go in there?" I asked the cop.

"Sorry," he said. "Lieutenant Hannegan's orders."

"Can I talk to him?"

The cop scratched his head. "The lieutenant didn't say anything about talking through the bars."

Longstreet turned his head in my direction. "That you, Moon?"

"Mister Moon."

"O.K. . . . Mr. Moon. Why the formality?"

"I like to keep murderers in their place."

His tufted eyebrows rose. "That doesn't include me."

"We'll still keep it 'Mister.' I'll apologize if you turn out innocent."

He pursed his lips in an expression of grudging acceptance. "Taking my proposition, Mr. Moon?"

"Maybe. What is it?"

"Simple enough. Solve Carmichael's murder within twenty-four hours and I'll pay ten thousand dollars."

"Why twenty-four hours?"

"I want it solved before I leave here."

I considered this answer from all sides without growing any wiser. My prospective client was a man hard to understand and, I suspected, not anxious to be understood.

"Why don't you leave now?" I asked. "All you have to do is post bond."

Gazing up at me blandly, he handed me one of the screwiest answers I have ever gotten from a client. "Want to catch up on my sleep."

For a moment I watched him speculatively, forming new questions in my mind. But having a hunch that even a thousand well-phrased questions would get nothing more from him about why he stayed in jail, I changed tack.

I said: "Suppose I take the case and you turn out to be the murderer?"

"Would I hire you if I were?" he asked. "I could get out of here in ten minutes by posting bond. And with my alibi I could bust Warren Day right out of a job if he booked me for murder. He knows it, too."

I thought this over and saw the logic of it. "All right. I'll go along. But I can't work in the dark. I want better answers than you gave the inspector."

He glanced at the guard. "Not with a cop listening in."

I turned to the cop, who was silently taking down everything we said in shorthand.

"Oh, a spy!" I said. "Run down the hall where you can watch without hearing. I want a confidential talk with my client."

His head moved back and forth sidewise. "The lieutenant said keep my eyes on him."

"Gonna make me get a lawyer?"

"Yep."

"I'll be back in a minute," I told Longstreet.

Warren Day was still in his office, morosely puffing on an actually lighted cigar.

"Thought you went home," he said.

"Been talking to Longstreet. He's willing to tell me things if you move the big-eared cop from in front of his cell."

"Yeah?" His eyes narrowed. "You take his ten-thousand-dollar proposition?"

"Depends on what he has to say," I evaded.

"If I move the guard, will you tell me what he spills?"

I shrugged. "That's up to him. He has the right of confidence as my client, if I listen to him."

Day shook his head. "No sale. Go home and go to bed."

I took out my check book. "You said five hundred, didn't you?"

The Inspector's nose, which was the barometer of his blood pressure, whitened at the tip, indicating that he was irked. When the whole organ paled, it meant he was boiling.

"You post bond," he said, "and I'll charge him with murder!"

Spreading the check book on his desk, I reached for his desk pen. He slapped aside my hand.

"Put it up, damn you! I'll give you five minutes."

He slammed back his chair and made for the door. By the time we reached Longstreet's cell, the inspector's nose was dead white.

"You!" Day growled at the guard. "Post yourself at the end of the hall and keep your eye on this excuse for a private detective. He gets five minutes. If he passes anything through the bars, shoot him. Kill him and I'll make you a sergeant."

He wheeled and marched back to his den.

"You certainly get your way around here," Longstreet said admiringly. "How'd you swing that?"

"Stow the blarney," I said. "We've got five minutes. Spill it fast."

With his free hand he fumbled at his shirt front and drew out a locket on a chain.

"See this?"

I nodded.

"A girl gave me this when I was seventeen. Twenty-seven years ago. It's the only thing in the world I got any sentiment about."

"Your wife?"

"I'm a bachelor." He paused to peer down at

the locket as it lay on his chest. "This locket got me a local reputation. Ask my partners . . . or the one who's left, Marden Swope. Ask our secretary, Marie Kincaid. Ask anybody knows me well. They'll all tell you when I swear on this locket, it's God's own truth. I'd cut off my nose before I'd tell a lie on this locket."

"All right," I said. "Get to the point."

He put his hand over the locket. "On the memory of her who gave it to me, I swear I didn't kill Carmichael."

"I'm deeply impressed," I said. "We have three minutes left."

"Ask anything you want." He pushed the locket back in his shirt.

"Leave it out," I suggested.

His brows went up. "You'll get the truth. I don't necessarily lie when I'm not holding the locket."

I glanced at my watch. "Why was Anton Strowlski after you?"

"Anton who?"

"The rod man brought in with us," I said impatiently. "The only reason you started that brawl was because you saw Anton in the mirror and wanted cops on the scene fast."

He shook his head. "Never saw him before."

I looked through the bars at him in vexation, and he gazed back at me blandly. "Why'd you deliberately get yourself thrown in jail?" I asked finally.

He blew out his lips, there was a sound of released suction, and he used a thumb to push his plate back in place. "What makes you think I did that?"

Apparently my bothering to have the cop moved to the end of the hall had been wasted effort. I said: "If you won't answer questions, I can't help much."

He raised tufted eyebrows. "Believe me, if I could tell you a single thing about Carmichael's murder, I would. But I can't. If the answer was in me, would I pay you to dig it out?"

From the corner of my eye I saw the guard start toward us. Longstreet looked up at me without a sign of mischievousness in his suddenly serious face.

"Believe me, Mr. Moon, my being in jail has nothing to do with Carmichael's murder. You still with me?"

"Time's up," the guard broke in behind me.

I said: "I'll play along for a while," and left him to catch up on his sleep.

When I reached the front desk, Sergeant Danny Blake was just coming on duty. His nose looked like a blue turnip.

"How's the nose?" I asked.

He grunted something unintelligible.

I said: "What happened to the guy brought in with us? Anton Strowlski."

Danny thumbed through his log book. "Released on bond at 7:30. I was off then. Go off at 5:00."

CHAPTER THREE
THE GOLDEN LOCKET

The night before I had gotten to bed at one in the morning and been routed out at four. I felt like falling in bed for a week, but clues have a habit of disappearing unless you follow a murder trail while it is still hot. From the desk sergeant's directory I learned the Rex Amusement Corporation was in the Bland Building, and took a cab there.

The corporation was on the first floor. It had its own entrance, separate from that to the offices on higher floors. The entrance was centered in a long loading ramp for trucks, presumably used for loading and unloading various types of coin machines. An empty, driverless truck was backed against one end of the ramp.

I found the door unlocked and walked into a huge storage room filled with hundreds of coin devices. Juke boxes, cigarette vendors, pinball games and slot machines stood in orderly rows, arranged so each type was easily accessible. At the far end of the warehouse I saw a door labeled OFFICE.

Pushing open this door, I found myself in a large, but simply furnished reception room containing only an office switchboard, a typing desk, two file cabinets and a few odd chairs. Centering one wall of the room was a glass-paned door bearing the title M. SWOPE, PRESIDENT. Two similar doors, respectively labeled G. W. CARMICHAEL, CUSTOMER SERVICE and W. H. LONGSTREET, SALES MANAGER, opened in the opposite wall. The wall directly across from the reception room entrance was full of windows.

A sleek, brown-eyed blonde with nice accessories was beating the typewriter. She gave me a cool smile which meant: "State your business, please. I'm very busy."

I came right to the point by flashing the identity card which states I am a private dick and am bonded to twenty thousand dollars.

"We don't need a private detective," she said. "The police are doing fine."

I said: "Maybe you don't, but you've got one. One of your bosses hired me."

She raised carefully molded eyebrows. "Mr. Swope?"

"Longstreet." I took the chair she hadn't offered and stretched out my legs. "What's your name?"

She thought me over before she finally decided to answer. "Marie Kincaid."

"You the whole office force?"

"All that works in. We have ten service men and a crew of salesmen."

"Where are they all?"

"We don't open till eight." She raised her eyes to the wall clock and I followed suit. It was ten till.

I asked: "You been here long?"

"About five minutes."

"I mean have you worked here long?"

"Four years."

"Know about a locket Longstreet wears?"

She glanced at me quickly, then laughed a tinkly, indulgent laugh. "The swearing locket? That's what we call it behind his back. He's a nut on the subject."

"Is he serious about it, or is it just a gag?"

"Oh, he's serious. I wouldn't believe his oath on a Bible, but anything he swears to on the locket is pure truth."

I got to my feet. "I'll take a look at the room. It been cleaned up?"

"Not yet," she said.

Opening the door which bore Carmichael's name, I went in and looked around. Except for a spot of dried blood on the carpet beneath the desk, there was little to see. I wandered around looking at the floor, the desk top, the window sills and the bookcase without finding any cigarette butts of queer oriental brand, any Egyptian scarabs or any of the other highly informative clues detectives are always running into.

Marie Kincaid came to the door and looked in at me.

"Know where they found the gun?" I asked.

She pointed to the floor near her feet. "Right there."

"How'd you know?"

She raised her nose. "I saw it. The police brought me over here from home before anything had been moved."

I estimated the distance from the desk to the gun as about twelve feet, which ruled out suicide, as Inspector Day had said.

"Let's go over the story you told the cops," I said. "I understand Longstreet phoned here twice yesterday."

"That's right."

"When did the calls come?"

"The first was at 3:30, for Mr. Carmichael. I plugged him in and they had a terrible argument."

"You listen in?"

Her nose went up again. "I did not! Mr. Carmichael's door was open."

"What was the argument about?"

"I don't know. But Mr. Carmichael swore something awful."

"Where was Swope at the time?"

"In his office." She pointed at his door across the reception room.

"Hmm. How about the second call?"

She said: "That came just at five. I had my hat on ready to leave when the phone rang. It was Mr. Longstreet again, for Mr. Carmichael. I plugged Mr. Carmichael in and, through the open door, heard him say: 'All right. Wait ten minutes and come on over. I'll be here.'"

"Then what?"

"I went home. An hour later the police came after me."

I asked: "How do you account for Longstreet being able to phone when he was locked in a cell from three o'clock on?"

Her nose went up a third time. "I don't. You're the detective. You account for it."

"How do you know it was Longstreet phoning?"

"She said it was."

"What?"

"She said it was."

"Who?"

"The switchboard operator. She said: 'Mr. Longstreet calling Mr. Carmichael.'"

I thought this over while I wandered around the room some more. Finally I said: "You told the cops you recognized his voice."

"I thought I heard it in the background," she said quickly.

I shook my head. "You told the cops Longstreet himself phoned. You didn't mention any woman."

"The woman wasn't phoning," she defended. "She was just a switchboard operator somewhere."

"Where?"

"How would I know? Wherever Mr. Longstreet phoned from."

I said: "Did you actually hear Longstreet's voice at all?"

"Well"—she hesitated—"I thought I heard it in the background asking the operator to hurry up."

I asked bluntly: "Who paid you to change your story?"

Color warmed the coolness of her cheeks and her brown eyes threw flame at me. "Just what do you mean by that?"

"I read your sworn statement. You told the cops you definitely recognized Longstreet's voice, and when your questioner remarked that imitation is easy, you said: 'After four years, an imitation wouldn't fool me.'"

"It was the way the police asked questions," she insisted. "They put words in your mouth. I *am* sure it was Mr. Longstreet phoning. I'd be

sure even without the voice, because when I plugged in Mr. Carmichael, I told him Mr. Longstreet was phoning." She ended triumphantly: "If it had been anyone else, Mr. Carmichael would have bawled me out afterward!"

I switched to another subject. "What kind of guy was Carmichael?"

She examined me so appraisingly before answering, I expected some sort of startling disclosure.

But all she said was: "All right. If you like wolves."

"Married?" I asked.

"No. Bachelor."

"What'd he look like?"

Her brow puckered thoughtfully. "Tall and lanky. Slightly stooped. Gray hair. Nothing very individual, except the wolf gleam in his eye."

"How old was he?"

"Forty, forty-five. Somewhere in there."

"Have any enemies?"

She shook her head. "None I know of."

"Any arguments recently?"

"Only the one over the phone with Mr. Longstreet." Some inner thought brought her up short. "Except . . ." She shook her head in self-impatience. "That wouldn't count."

"What wouldn't?"

"Nothing. It's nothing to do with the murder."

I let my eyes harden over. "Listen, sister. If you know something, loosen up fast."

"It's nothing," she insisted. "It would only start gossip."

I said: "I don't spread gossip. Let's have it."

Reluctantly, she said: "It's Mrs. Swope. I think she and Carmichael were carrying on." She paused, then rushed on, apparently wanting to unload it fast once she had started. "The other night I forgot my purse and came back for it after closing. They were in Mr. Carmichael's office and didn't hear me come in. I heard him say: 'It's got to stop, Isobel. Suppose Marden found out?' Mrs. Swope said, 'Suppose he does? I really think he'd be glad.' Then after a while Mr. Carmichael said: 'I won't be party to breaking up a home. Especially that of my own partner. It's got to stop.' I heard Mrs. Swope begin to cry, and she said: 'You're tired of me, that's all.' I left then and didn't hear any more."

I said thoughtfully: "The spurned-mistress motive, eh? Worth checking." Then I had an inspiration. "That switchboard operator you mentioned. Remember her voice?"

The secretary looked doubtful. "You mean could I identify it?"

"I mean do you remember it? How it sounded? Whether you'd ever heard it before?"

Her head moved back and forth slowly. "You don't remember switchboard operators' voices. It was just a voice."

"Could it have been Mrs. Swope?"

Her eyes went wide. "Mrs. Swope! Why ever would she pretend to be a switchboard operator?"

"Maybe she had a code arrangement with Carmichael," I said. "With her husband in the same office, she'd hardly phone and give her own name."

She looked doubtful. "But suppose Mr. Longstreet had been here when she called? She'd have felt kind of silly."

"Who knew Longstreet was gone?" I asked.

She looked less doubtful. "Everyone. He'd been talking about going up to his summer camp for weeks. Mrs. Swope would have known that he left at noon yesterday." She looked down at the tiny watch on her wrist. "Eight o'clock. Time I got back to work."

She turned and went back to her desk. I moved back into the reception room just as the outer door opened and Marty O'Brien came in. Marty had been a muscle man back in the days of the now defunct extortion ring, but I hadn't seen him around in recent years. Probably he had been in jail.

He said: "Hi, Marie. Boss in yet?" And then he saw me.

He didn't say anything. Just looked.

"Hello, Marty," I said.

He nodded.

Marie said: "You're the first one here," and went on with her typing.

Marty threw me another deadpan look and drifted out again.

"That one of your salesmen?" I asked Marie. She said: "Our best."

The door opened again and a smooth-cheeked, middle-aged man entered. In a sleek, pointed-nose and thin-lipped sort of way he was handsome. He wore expensive clothes and rimless eyeglasses with an air of needing both.

His face was all set in a big smile for Marie, but it faded when he saw she had company.

"Good morning, Mr. Swope," Marie said in a prim, secretarial voice.

Swope doled her out an adulterated version of the original smile and gave me an inquiring glance.

"Manville Moon," I said, showing him my license card. "Retained by Longstreet."

His brows knit. "I see."

He failed to offer his hand, but stood chewing his lip while he thought me over. Finally he seemed to come to a decision.

"Come in," he said, and preceded me to his office.

When we were seated and he had offered me a cigar, which I politely refused after noting the brand, he leaned back and crossed hands over his stomach.

"I've told the police everything I know about this terrible affair," he said. "But of course I'll be glad to give any further help I can."

"Fine. Will you just run over what you told the police?"

He raised his shoulders and let them fall again. "It wasn't much, I'm afraid. I knew nothing about the two phone calls until Marie told of them when the police were here. I left at four-thirty yesterday, and didn't know anything had happened until a policeman came to my home about six."

"Know what Carmichael and Longstreet could have been arguing about over the phone? That is, if it was Longstreet."

He shook his head. "They always got along. We all did. Why, we grew up together, the three of us. We were playmates in grammar school." A reminiscent smile spread across his face. "We even chased the same girl. In high school Mrs. Swope went with all three of us before she finally settled on me."

"Could your wife have been the cause of the argument?"

He frowned. "Of course not! They sometimes joked about both remaining bachelors because of Mrs. Swope, but purely in fun. She hadn't gone with either of them for five years before our marriage. And we've been married twenty-two years."

I said: "Do you think it actually was Longstreet who phoned yesterday?"

He looked uncomfortable. "Marie is sure of it. And I can think of no reason she would lie."

"How do you account for his being able to phone at three-thirty and again at five, when he was locked in a cell from three on?"

He shrugged. "I make no attempt to account for it. The police are paid to unravel such questions." His fingers drummed on the desk top. "I don't understand how he got in jail in the first place. When he left at noon yesterday, he was intending to drive up for a week at his camp on the river. He'd planned it for weeks, and I know he intended to start at one o'clock. By two-thirty he should have been there, so what was he doing in a bar in town?"

Suddenly an expression of amazed inspiration crossed his face. "I just thought of a possible explanation!"

"Yeah?"

"I haven't been down to the jail yet. How do we know the man in jail is Longstreet?"

That jolted me. Thinking back, I couldn't remember anyone identifying Longstreet, and no one who knew him had looked over the prisoner.

I said: "About two-forty pounds, grizzled hair, false teeth, hairy eyebrows that curve upward like horns, and an expression like a kid getting ready to heave a snowball at a high hat."

The enthusiasm faded from Swope's face. "That's Willard to a T."

"It's still a straw," I said. "How about dropping down and looking him over?"

He glanced at his watch. "Can't this morning. Be glad to this afternoon. Is that all you want of me?" He glanced at his watch again.

"Not quite. Assuming Longstreet did commit the murder, what motive could he have?"

His lips curled in a faint smile. "We have a business contract leaving our stock to the surviving partners. Half of Carmichael's interest in this business is motive enough. And in addition, Longstreet is primary beneficiary to a fifty-thousand-dollar insurance policy on Carmichael."

"How'd Carmichael happen to carry a policy like that?" I asked.

"We all did. If I died, the money went to Carmichael, with Longstreet as secondary beneficiary. Longstreet's policy named me, with Carmichael as secondary beneficiary. I was secondary on Carmichael's policy. It's not an unusual business arrangement. Quite common in partnerships."

I said: "How did the murderer get in and out of here without being seen? Don't you have a watchman?"

"No. We have adequate locks, a burglar alarm system and are protected by Burns."

"About Carmichael," I said. "What kind of guy was he?"

He frowned down at his hand, which beat a swift march on the desk top. "George was a good businessman and an excellent partner." The sentence ended on a slightly raised note, as though an unspoken phrase beginning with "but" should have been attached to it.

I said: "But what?"

He glanced at me, startled. "What are you? A mind reader?"

"Just a guesser. What was wrong?"

His expression was reluctant, as one unwilling to speak ill of the dead. "I suppose it was more virtue than fault. He was too strait-laced."

After Marie Kincaid's evaluation of Carmichael as a wolf, the answer amused me. Fleetingly a quotation passed through my mind. Something like: "Women and men see friends through different eyes."

I said: "About women?"

"No. He was human enough, I suppose. Perhaps strait-laced isn't the right word. Unforgiving would be better. He gave absolute loyalty to his friends and demanded the same of them."

"Hardly sounds like a fault."

"Perhaps not," he admitted. "Except he carried it too far. As an example, we used to retain a lawyer named Howard Tattersall. He's an excellent lawyer and has saved the firm considerable money in lawsuits. He also happens to be a minor stockholder in the company, owns about five per cent of the common stock. About a month ago we were preparing to offer a few new shares for sale on the open market to help finance opening a branch in another city. Tattersall, of course, had advance information and a few hours before our release, he dumped his entire holdings on the market. The sudden dumping of such a large block caused a temporary drop in price, and before it could recover, Tattersall rebought his own stock plus part of the new issue without it costing him a cent. His total gain was about twenty thousand dollars, and George was furious. He insisted that Tattersall be kicked off the payroll immediately."

I said: "I think I'd agree with him about that."

Swope shook his head impatiently. "You misunderstand. What I gave was merely the bare outline of the transaction, and actually there were several ramifications. One was that a speculating broker took a flyer and bore the brunt of the loss. It didn't cost our firm a cent. But George remained adamant, so we switched lawyers, thereby losing the best corporate legal advice in town." He studied his tapping fingers glumly, still vexed by his late partner's stubbornness.

"Was Tattersall sore?" I asked.

He looked up again. "Naturally. We're a fat account."

I kept my tone casual. "Sore enough to do anything about it?"

"Do anything?" He frowned. "You mean like shoot Carmichael?"

"Yeah?"

For a minute he brooded over the question, not liking it too much. "I haven't the slightest idea," he said finally. "My only relations with Tattersall were business ones and I don't know what kind of person he is otherwise."

CHAPTER FOUR
GANG-UP

Then the door began to open slowly, as though the person on the other side were hesitant to disturb us. Swope watched it expectantly; then his expression soured to a frown as the door finally swung fully open. Our interruptor was a short woman, this side of forty-five and beginning to spread. Probably she had once been beautiful, but corsets and cosmetics no longer could hide middle age. She wore expensive clothes that looked altogether much too young for her.

Swope said: "Didn't Miss Kincaid say I was busy, Isobel?"

I guessed that this was Mrs. Swope, and didn't miss that while Swope familiarly referred to the secretary as "Marie" in conversation, she was "Miss Kincaid" to his wife.

Isobel said: "I'm sorry. I have to see you. Will you be long?" Her tone was a curious mixture of embarrassed apology and determination.

Swope looked at his watch. "We're nearly finished. You may as well stay, now you're here." He performed belated introductions. "This is Mr. Moon, Isobel. Mr. Moon, my wife."

I asked her how she did and offered the chair I had left when she entered.

She said: "No. Keep it," and took another in the corner.

I said: "I was just leaving, Mrs. Swope." Then to her husband: "One more question and I won't bother you any more. Are you familiar with a locket Longstreet has?"

The color drained from Mrs. Swope's face, leaving it stark white behind its oversupply of rouge.

Swope said: "I've seen it. Why?"

"Know the story connected with it?"

He knit his brows thoughtfully. "Some silly sentimental thing, as I remember. Left to him by his mother or someone. He takes oaths on it. I always thought he was a little hipped on the subject. What about it?"

"Nothing. Just curious."

I was watching Mrs. Swope. Her color began to come back, but she was still obviously shaken. With a sudden flash of inspiration I combined Longstreet's mention of the locket as a gift from a girl when he was seventeen, with Swope's casual reference to his wife's high school romances, coming out with the interesting answer that Mrs. Swope could be the locket's donor.

I said: "I've got to go. Glad to have met you, Mrs. Swope."

She dipped her head in my direction without meeting my eyes.

Three men had come into the reception room while I was closeted with Swope. Two I recognized as compatriots of Marty O'Brien in bygone extortion ring days, but could not recall their names. The third was Tiny Sartt, a flat-headed, bow-legged killer with a criminal record longer than MacArthur's war record.

I said: "Hello, Tiny. You a star salesman here, too?"

His constantly darting eyes touched my face and moved away. "Hello, Moon."

"Hello, what?"

"Mister Moon," he corrected. His eyes darted back at me and down again.

I said to Marie: "What's the name of the outfit over you?"

"Riverside Seed Company."

"How do you get there?"

"You have to go outside and use the main building entrance."

A visit to the Riverside Seed Company got me nothing that I hadn't already learned from Warren Day. The Rex Amusement Corporation closed at five, but the seed company stayed open an hour later. At about five-thirty the whole office force had been startled by what my informant described as a "terrific blam," and one of the clerks said: "That's a shot!"

Nearly everyone in the office, about twelve people, had gone to investigate. They found the entrance to the place downstairs unlocked, entered in a group and found the body. No one had seen the murderer leave.

The Drake Hotel is as expensive as the Jefferson, but in a quieter, more snobbish way. While not exclusively an apartment hotel, it caters to permanent residents and makes no effort to attract the tourist trade through decorative cocktail lounges and elaborate dance floors. The only entertainment facility offered its guests is a small, clean dining room which closes at eight nightly.

At the desk I asked for Howard Tattersall's room number.

"Suite four-seventeen," the room clerk said. "I'll ring to see if he's in."

I said: "Never mind. He's expecting me."

The elevator surged upward like the smooth stroke of a piston and eased to a cushioned halt. Silent doors parted in the middle, disappearing into the walls, and when I stepped out into the deeply carpeted hall, they slid soundlessly together again.

The silence was almost reverent. As I started down the hall the leather straps of my false leg squeaked and I felt guiltily self-conscious—as though violating the sanctity of a cathedral.

The man who answered my knock at the door of suite four-seventeen was of medium height and beginning to put on weight. Dark hair, parted in the middle, was brushed straight back from a wide, short forehead. Heavy black brows surmounted a strong nose and hard but wide lips clamped around a short briar. He wore a lounging robe.

"Mr. Tattersall?" I asked.

He nodded.

"I'm Manville Moon. Your office told me I'd find you home today."

Removing his pipe from his mouth with his right hand, which conveniently prevented him from offering a handshake, he said: "If it's business, I'm sorry, but this is my day off."

"It's business about a murder," I said. "May I come in?"

"Are you police?" he asked sharply.

"Private." I watched his face for a minute, saw no invitation there, and said: "I'm coming in."

He stepped back, swung the door wide and let me go past him into the room. It was a large room, much better furnished than my walkup parlor. Doors on either side of it leading to other rooms made it at least a three-unit apartment. I wondered how many hundred more a month he paid than I did for my three-room flat.

I tried an easy chair, liked it and settled back with a cigar in my mouth. The lawyer remained standing, frowning down at me while I applied flame to the cigar end.

"You've heard of George Carmichael's death," I said finally, making it a statement instead of a question.

"On the radio," he said shortly. "I don't get a morning paper."

"Used to work for him, didn't you?"

He looked displeased and faintly insulted. "I was retained by his firm as legal counsel. They weren't my only account."

"Why'd they drop you?"

"I don't see that it's any of your business," he said testily. "Mind telling me what you want?"

"Not at all. Know Willard Longstreet?"

"Of course. One of the company directors. Sales manager, I believe he calls himself. He also happens to be a neighbor of mine. Lives down the hall."

"Yes, I know. Longstreet retained me to solve the crime. You wouldn't have heard it on the radio, but he's the prime suspect. Matter of fact, he's in jail."

His eyes showed mild surprise, but no particular concern. "So?"

"His gun was found at the murder scene. Longstreet claims it was kidnapped from his room."

"So?"

"So you and Carmichael had a falling-out. So you live within crawling distance of Longstreet's door. So where were you yesterday about five-thirty in the afternoon?"

His eyes narrowed. "Pardon me a moment."

Abruptly he did an about-face and passed through one of the doors into another room. I heard the click of a phone being raised, got out of my chair quietly and circled toward the door. As I reached it and got my ear near the jamb, I heard him say, "Right away," and drop the phone back in its cradle.

Circling back to my chair, I settled in it again and was drawing slowly on my cigar when he reentered the room. I looked up and got a surprise.

A sardonic smile lifting the edges of his wide mouth, he leaned in the doorway and accurately pointed an army automatic at my cigar.

I removed the cigar, but the muzzle failed to follow it, which led me to believe my head was the actual target. I waited for him to speak, but he seemed perfectly content to continue leaning and pointing.

"What am I supposed to do?" I asked finally. "Raise my arms, bark like a dog, or just go home?"

"Just sit," he said. "And keep your mouth shut."

So for twenty minutes I sat and kept my mouth shut. When my cigar became a stub, I set it carefully on the ash stand next to my chair, moving my hand slowly because I could see the automatic's hammer was back and the safety off. At the end of twenty minutes a key turned in the outer door's lock.

Anton Strowlski came through the door, nodded to Tattersall and turned his brittle eyes on me.

"*Mister* Moon, isn't it?" he asked with heavy sarcasm, deeply underlining the "Mister."

I didn't feel called on to reply.

"Stand up," he said.

I rose slowly, turned my back and raised my arms without waiting for the order. Anton's hand snaked under my armpit from behind, removed my P-38, then carefully patted my pockets.

"Turn around," he commanded.

Facing my host again, I dropped my arms. Anton drew a short, dainty automatic from his side pocket, a twin of the one he had lost to the police, removed his smart snap-brim hat and dropped it over the gun.

"Only a .32," he said pleasantly. "But I use dum-dums. It makes a hole like a saucer." The mock-pleasantness left his voice and his lips drew thin. "We're going out now, and if you make a move I don't like, you get it."

He waved me toward the door, then followed, keeping a pace distance between us. Tattersall stayed home, presumably not caring to participate in murder on his day off, but just before the door shut behind us he said: "It's been very pleasant, Mr. Moon. Do come again."

I said: "If I can't make it, drop in on me. I'll be in the river." It wasn't good, but it was the best I could do with that hat-covered little gun aimed at my back.

Our trip down was uneventful. Just two well-dressed men, one of the modern school who wears his hat in elevators, the other with his politely draped over his fist. It stayed there even after we left the elevator, clear across the lobby, down the steps and into the waiting Buick coach at the curb.

Anton and I shared the roomy back seat. Our bullet-headed chauffeur was a stranger. Getting in, I caught a quick glimpse of his knuckle-bent profile and knew I had never seen him before. As we pulled away, I started to memorize the back of his head, on the remote chance that I'd ever get an opportunity to look for it.

It was an interesting head. The neck was a weal of creased muscle that bulged out beyond the flattened rear of his skull, and the ears were mere blobs of broken gristle bunched into shapelessness.

Without instruction he wheeled the car through traffic toward the south edge of town. He kept the speed moderate until we reached the river road, then opened up and we rolled along at highway speed.

Anton spoke only once during the trip, when we reached a long, straight stretch and bullet-head pressed his foot to the floor.

"Cut the horses," Anton said curtly.

Our speed immediately dropped to a sedate fifty-five.

A few miles later we slowed and turned onto a dirt road. We passed a farmhouse, went on about two miles without seeing another and the road began to grow rougher. Now entirely away from public view, Anton uncovered his gun and put his hat back on his head. I glanced down at the gun and got my second shocking surprise of the day. Only this one was pleasant.

They say that every criminal eventually makes some stupid mistake which ends his career. Anton Strowlski had just made his and it exceeded the criminal's prerogative of stupidity. His neat and deadly little automatic had the safety tightly on.

Selfishly I kept the secret to myself. My right hand slashed sidewise and the hard edge of my palm caught him directly between the eyes. I had learned that blow with the Rangers, and twice used it on German sentries. It worked just as effectively on Polish-American gunmen. I felt the bone crunch and he was dead before his automatic dropped to the seat between us.

Quietly easing him back in the far corner, I picked up the gun, flipped off the safety catch and settled back to enjoy the rest of the ride.

The road grew rougher and rougher, finally becoming nothing but two weed-choked ruts. Bullet-head halted the car alongside a dense growth of bushes.

"This O.K.?" he asked, peering out at the tangled cluster of undergrowth.

"Just fine," I said.

Startled, he spun in his seat and gaped at me and my lifeless seat-mate. Then his hand dove toward a shoulder holster. I let him bring his gun as far as the top of the front seat.

Anton had told the truth. It made a hole like a saucer.

The doorman at the Drake Hotel gave me a more courteous greeting than I deserved after parking a Buick containing two dead men at his curb. The elevator operator remembered my previous visit too, and shot to the fourth floor without waiting for instructions.

I had recovered my P-38 from one of Anton's pockets and found his key to four-seventeen in another. Approaching Tattersall's door with the former in my right hand and the latter in my left, I unlocked the door, kicked it open and charged in.

My dramatics were unnecessary. Howard Tattersall sat in the same chair I had occupied while enjoying my cigar. But he wasn't smoking, because a bullet had left too little of his mouth to hold a cigar.

He slumped sidewise with one arm hanging over the edge of the chair so that fingertips just touched the floor. The other hand lay in his lap, gripping the Army automatic.

Kneeling next to the body, I sniffed the gun muzzle. It had been fired.

Rising, I entered the room from which Tattersall had phoned and found the telephone standing on a desk by the window. I dialed Homicide and asked for Inspector Day.

"Moon," I said, when he finally came to the phone. "I'm at suite four-seventeen in the Drake Hotel. Dead lawyer here named Tattersall."

Day asked: "Murder?"

"Can't say. Either suicide or framed to look like it. Unless you want an unscientific opinion."

"Give it," the inspector said.

"Murder, then. No evidence. Just a hunch."

Day was silent for a minute; then he said: "I'll send Hannegan. Got to take a nap before I drop dead."

As though bringing up an afterthought, I said casually: "There are also two bodies in a Buick parked in front of the hotel. License 207-309."

"What!" Day yelped. "What you got there? A massacre?"

"Just a rough party." I gave him a quick sketch of what had happened.

When I finished the résumé he asked: "Think Tattersall bumped Carmichael?"

"Possibly."

"Wish you hadn't eliminated all the witnesses," he complained. "Complicates things."

"If they were still alive, I wouldn't be."

"That's not a bad idea either," he growled, and hung up.

Glancing at my watch, I was surprised to discover it was only a quarter of eleven.

Beginning to feel the effect of only three hours' sleep, I found a sidestreet barroom and took on a rye and water. I was the only customer at that time of day, and as I dawdled over my second drink, the bartender dropped a coin in the record machine to play a Phil Harris number. When it played out, I picked a nickel from my change on the bar and started over to play another. Then I noticed a pinball game against the wall. Right next to it stood a cigarette vendor.

I changed my mind and went back to my stool. Three coin machines in this small, neighborhood bar had started a train of thought. I began visualizing various stores I had been in recently, trying to remember whether or not they were equipped with coin machines. The drugstore near my flat had one pinball game. The confectionery next to it had one. I thought of two filling stations and a barbershop where I had noticed them, and suddenly the tremendous size of the business registered on me. I could not think of a single tavern, restaurant, drugstore, grocery, filling station or barbershop I had been in during recent months which was not equipped with one or more coin devices. I motioned to the barkeep.

"You own this place?" I asked.

"Yeah," he admitted.

"Where you rent your coin machines?"

He rubbed his chin. "Why?"

"Because I want to know."

"You a cop?"

"No."

"What are you?"

I said: "I'm the guy just asked you a question. Get up an answer before I kick your teeth in."

He widened his eyes at me, sucked in his breath and said: "Fellow named Sartt."

"Tiny?"

"That's the guy."

I said: "Next time he's in, tell him to take 'em out. My company's taking over this territory."

The bartender paled. "Listen, mister. I can't tell Sartt that. I'd end up in the gutter."

"You'll end up in the gutter if you don't."

He ran a hand over his forehead. "Geez, mister. I'm just trying to make a living. I don't want any damn machines in here at all. But I want trouble less than I don't want machines. If you guys start squeezing me between you, I lose no matter which way I jump. Why don't you talk to Sartt, and I'll take whichever machines the both of you say."

I grinned at him. "Relax and have a drink. I was just fishing for information. Now I've got it."

Some of his color came back, but now he looked worried. "You are a cop, ain't you?"

I shook my head. "Just a guy who doesn't like Tiny Sartt. Forget it. You won't get in trouble."

I had the final segment of the puzzle.

CHAPTER FIVE
CLOSE-IN

I went home and shaved, ate a quick breakfast and took a cab to police headquarters. I found Warren Day asleep on the cot in his office. I shook him awake.

"Go away," he said.

"Get up. I've got your case solved for you."

He sat up and rubbed his eyes, groped over to the desk and found his glasses. "What time is it?"

"About noon."

Sinking into his chair, he took a pint bottle from a bottom drawer, swished a slug around in his mouth, swallowed and started to put it back.

I said: "Do I drink alone when you come to my house?"

Grumpily he reopened the drawer, examined the bottle's liquor level over the top of his glasses and handed it to me. He watched suspiciously as I raised it to my lips and said: "O.K. That's

enough," before I even downed the first swallow. I handed it back after the second.

"If you're going to get me up at four in the morning to break your cases," I said, "you've got to keep me awake."

He fumbled a dead cigar from his ashtray, dusted it off and popped it in his mouth. "O.K. Spill your story."

"Not yet. I've got it figured out, but we have to prove it. I've no urge to be sued."

"Oh," he said. "You got a theory."

"Sure. What have you got?"

"Nothing," he admitted. "I'm listening."

"This is what I want. You have Marden Swope, Mrs. Swope and Marie Kincaid picked up separately and brought here. Keep them apart and I'll talk to them one at a time."

He eyed me fixedly over his glasses. "What do I pick them up on?"

I waved that aside impatiently. "That's your problem. If you're leary of warrants, lure them down. Tell 'em the jail's on fire and you need a bucket brigade. Tell them anything." Then I remembered something. "Swope was coming in anyway, to identify Longstreet. He suggested your prisoner might be someone else."

Day snapped erect. "He what!"

"Don't get excited. Just a screwy idea he had. It's Longstreet, all right."

He leaned back in his chair again. "And when all these people get here?"

"I'll talk to them."

He scratched his head. "Knowing how you like to grandstand, I don't suppose you'd outline your case first?"

"Don't suppose I would."

"O.K.," he said wearily. "What can I lose? I haven't got a case anyway."

He picked up his phone, gave the necessary orders and we sat back to wait.

Inspector Day sent out for sandwiches and coffee after pointedly informing me that my share of the bill would be thirty-five cents, and collecting it before he ordered. We had just finished our uninspiring lunch when Hannegan stuck his head in the door.

"They're all here," he said.

"Separate?" I asked.

"None of them even know the others are here."

"Send in Mrs. Swope," I ordered.

Hannegan looked at Day, his eyebrows raised.

"I'm just a figurehead around here," the inspector said bitterly. "Don't pay any attention to me."

The lieutenant shrugged, started to smile and wiped it off fast when Day roared: "Get a move on!"

"Yes sir," he said, and backed out hurriedly.

"See what happens when I let you give orders?" Day asked aggrievedly. "Discipline shot to hell!" He rubbed his bald spot and mumbled: "Impertinent pup."

"He didn't say a word," I said in Hannegan's defense.

The inspector snapped, "I know what he was thinking!"

A knock sounded. Day growled, "Come in," and Hannegan opened the door nervously.

He stepped aside to let in Mrs. Swope, then asked the space between Day and me if we wanted him to remain. It was impossible to determine which of us he was addressing.

I nodded imperceptibly and Day said: "You can stay if you keep your mouth shut."

Mrs. Swope waited uncertainly, kneading her hands together and looking frightened. I introduced her to the inspector and asked her to have a chair. She looked around hesitantly, finally deciding on the one farthest from Warren Day's desk. I walked over and looked down at her.

"Ever hear of truth serum, Mrs. Swope?" I asked.

She looked puzzled, then nodded doubtfully.

"We gave it to Longstreet, and his locket couldn't help. He told us all about it."

I might have told her that the world would end in five minutes. She turned paper white and clutched at her throat. "No," she whispered. "No."

"Don't hold it against him, Mrs. Swope. He meant to keep his oath, but you can't fight truth

serum. He had to tell." I made my voice sympathetic.

She asked in a dead voice: "Everything?"

I played the hunch on which my whole case was based, holding my breath as I played it, because if I were wrong, Mrs. Swope would know my whole attack was bluff.

I said: "Even that you were the girl who gave him the locket twenty-seven years ago."

It worked. The shock of it, superimposed on the shock of Longstreet breaking his oath, nearly heaped her on the floor in a faint. She managed to retain consciousness, but all resistance was knocked out of her. The hopeless eyes she turned up at me were utterly convinced I knew everything.

"What do you want of me?" she asked.

"We just want you to clear up a point or two. How you learned of the plot, for example."

She was too far gone for suspicion, but she said in dull surprise: "Didn't Willard tell that?"

"We didn't ask him," I said easily. "It's not an important point. We know you warned him, after making him swear on the locket he'd never tell. We know why you warned him. . . . That you couldn't bear to see an old sweetheart framed, even though your husband was the framer. . . ."

"Framed?" she asked wonderingly. "I didn't know it was a frame-up when I told Willard."

"I was merely using a figure of speech," I rapidly backtracked. "You see, we know enough of the story so that we have already arrested your husband. He's beyond all possible help, so you have nothing to lose by telling us how you learned the plot."

Her head drooped and she gazed helplessly down at her hands. "I overheard them in Marden's office."

"Overheard who?"

"Marden and Miss Kincaid. It was a week ago. I dropped in to see Marden, and Miss Kincaid was in his office. The door was open a crack and I stopped to listen. I don't know why, because I'm not a suspicious woman. After listening, I thought it best Marden not suspect I had heard, so I left without going in."

"What did you hear?"

"I heard Miss Kincaid say: 'Suppose at the last minute Longstreet changes his mind about going to the camp?' Marden said: 'I thought of that. Anton will tail him when he leaves the office at noon. If he looks like changing his mind, Anton has orders to stick a gun in his ribs and make sure he's at camp by four at the latest.' "

I suddenly understood a lot of things which had not previously been clear. "How'd you know what they were talking about?" I asked.

"I didn't," Mrs. Swope said dully. "If I'd had any idea . . ." Her voice faded away for a minute, then went on: "I'd have spoken to Marden. I'd . . ." She looked up at me helplessly. "I don't know what I'd have done. I didn't know what it all meant, and I kept brooding about it until I was nearly sick, and it got closer and closer to the time, and finally the actual morning arrived without my doing anything about it, and I couldn't stand it any more so I went to the office and told Willard just before he left at noon."

She began to cry, making no sound, but with her shoulders jiggling up and down in jerky rhythm as tears slid across her face.

I said to Hannegan: "Got all that?"

He looked up from the notebook in which he had been unobtrusively writing during the entire interview. "Yeah. Got it all."

"Have someone type it up in the form of a statement for Mrs. Swope to sign. And while it's being typed, bring in Marden Swope. Get Longstreet from his cell too."

He said: "Check," rose from his chair and escorted Mrs. Swope from the room.

As the door closed behind them, Warren Day burst out: "What in hell's going on? All that nonsense about truth serum!"

I grinned at him. "Worked, didn't it?"

"Is Marden Swope the killer?" he demanded.

"I doubt it," I said, enjoying myself. "Can't tell yet."

He peered at me sourly over his glasses. "Damn grandstander," he muttered.

A knock sounded and Day said: "Come in."

It was Marden Swope, followed by Hannegan.

I said to Swope: "You've met Inspector Day, haven't you?"

"Yes. Yesterday."

Day grunted something unintelligible, then said begrudgingly: "Have a chair."

Another knock sounded and Day said: "Come in."

It was Willard Longstreet, flanked by two bluecoats. He looked the group over without speaking, then moved over and took a chair next to me. Apparently he had gotten some sleep, for he looked rested. But his clothes were in terrible shape and he needed a shave.

In a self-conscious voice Marden Swope said: "Hello, Willard."

Longstreet nodded at his partner gravely, no sign of humor in his eyes.

"Swope suggested you might be an impostor," I told Longstreet. "We brought him down to identify you."

A mischievous twinkle replaced the serious expression in Longstreet's eyes. "What made you think that, Marden?"

Marden Swope said embarrassedly: "It's Willard, all right, Mr. Moon."

"What made you think I wasn't?" Longstreet asked.

Swope remained silent, so I said: "He couldn't understand how you got in jail. Weren't you supposed to be up at your camp yesterday?"

"Planned to be. Changed my mind."

"Why?"

Longstreet eyed me quizzically. "No law against it, is there?"

"None I know of. Especially since you had a good idea of what awaited you at the camp."

Swope asked: "You through with me now?"

"Not quite," I said. I turned back to Longstreet. "I have the case solved."

There was a sharp click as Longstreet's upper plate dropped and was snapped back in place by his tongue. Swope licked his lips and watched me curiously.

"Funny thing about this case," I said to Warren Day. "Longstreet hired me to find out something he already knew. That probably sounds silly, and it was in a way. But Longstreet couldn't figure any other way to handle the impossible situation he found himself in."

I paused to let tension build up in the room. The only reason I occasionally grandstand is because Day hates me for it. He was glaring at me now.

"Another peculiar thing about the case," I went on, "was that all of the evidence was false. So to solve the case, you had to ignore the evidence and depend on pure reason. That's why the police fell down."

Glancing sidewise at Day, I noted his nose now shone pure white against the inflamed background of his face.

I said: "The first premise I worked on was that Longstreet here couldn't possibly have committed the murder. The police should have decided that at once also, but they preferred to play around with weird theories about his pulling a Houdini jail break and then breaking back in again. My second premise was that Longstreet deliberately got himself jailed.

"Combining these two facts, you immediately get some inevitable conclusions. First, Longstreet knew someone was after him, and the forces involved were too much for him to fight. So he chose jail as the only safe place to be. Second, he had been framed for Carmichael's murder. Luckily for Longstreet, his being in jail not only made him temporarily safe, but gave him an iron-clad alibi and upset the framer's applecart.

"The third inescapable conclusion is that the testimony of Marie Kincaid was a lie from beginning to end. There never were any phone calls. Her story was prepared in advance of the crime. If I hadn't, out of pure cussedness, pointed out a gunman named Anton Strowlski to a cop, which prevented him from phoning Marie and telling

her the plot had gone sour, she never would have told the story she did. And after finally learning too late that Longstreet had been safely in jail all the time, she tried to wriggle out of her sworn statement by inventing another story which never happened.

"And the last obvious conclusion is that from the moment Longstreet learned Carmichael had been murdered, he was able to figure out exactly what had happened."

Marden Swope was gazing at me in wide-eyed amazement. Longstreet's face, directed at his partner, contained an expression of unholy glee. Warren Day had half risen, and glared at Longstreet.

"If you knew the answer all along," he rapped, "why'd you keep quiet?"

"That's the silly part of the whole affair," I answered for Longstreet. "He has a sacred locket he takes oaths on. *Before* Mrs. Swope warned him he was on the spot, she made him swear on the locket that he'd never repeat a word. That left him in the peculiar position of being framed for a murder and unable to say anything in his own defense. He was literally between the devil and the deep blue sea. So he hired me to expose what he already knew."

Day said: "He chose the devil," guffawed ferociously and suddenly stopped when no one else smiled.

Ignoring the inspector, I went on: "In a desperate effort to keep his oath, he gave me twenty-four hours to solve the case. If I hadn't made it, I suspect he would have talked anyway. Keeping the oath was worth ten thousand dollars to him, but I doubt that he wanted to gamble his life on it." I looked at Longstreet. "Right?"

He merely grinned without answering.

Swope, suddenly coming to life, rose from his chair. "What was that about my wife?" he demanded.

I said: "Shut up and sit down."

He looked at me whitely, his eyes narrowed to slits. Hannegan crossed the room, put his hand on Swope's chest and pushed him back in his chair.

Warren Day snarled at me: "If you're through grandstanding now, spill the works. Is this guy the killer?"

I took him out of his misery. "No. It was a good old-fashioned gang killing. Swope ordered it and Marie Kincaid was an accessory. If Longstreet had received the warning earlier, he'd probably have skipped town. But when he got it, Anton Strowlski was already on his tail. And when he couldn't shake Anton, he got himself arrested.

"What gave me the first steer was that even after his alibi was established, Longstreet insisted on staying in jail until the case was solved. The only reason I could see for that was that he was afraid of something, and I learned what he was afraid of by a visit to the Rex Amusement Corporation and a conversation with a bartender. The corporation's salesmen are the finest bunch of professional extortionists and killers you ever saw. They've spread coin machines all over town by delivering them and telling proprietors to keep them. You can pass that to the rackets squad.

"So it was all of them Longstreet was afraid of. He'd been put on the spot in typical gangster fashion. Swope here was tired of splitting three ways, so he had Carmichael killed and framed Longstreet. Howard Tattersall, who had access to Longstreet's room, obtained the gun, probably on Swope's promise that he'd be made a partner. But Swope wasn't splitting with anyone. After Tattersall served his purpose, he conveniently committed suicide.

"Swope picked a time he knew Longstreet would be at his river camp alone and without an alibi. Undoubtedly one of Swope's killers was waiting at the camp to arrange Longstreet's suicide in remorse for having slain his partner.

"Marie was merely a tool. She's probably Swope's mistress."

Swope said: "I want a lawyer."

Paying no attention to him, Warren Day said: "So after all this circus, we still don't know the name of the actual killer. I'm going to find out right now!"

It turned out to be Tiny Sartt. The state rewarded him with a free trip to another world. Swope got life, Marie five years, Longstreet my apology and permission to call me "Moon," and I got ten thousand dollars for eleven hours' work, which is nine thousand, nine hundred and seventy-five more than my standard day rate.

Beer-Bottle Polka

C. M. Kornbluth

C(YRIL) M(ICHAEL) KORNBLUTH (1923–1958) was born in New York City and attended the University of Chicago, graduating after his service in World War II, where he received a Bronze Star for his action at the Battle of the Bulge. Although not known as a writer of mystery fiction, he is regarded as a giant in the world of science fiction in spite of his death of a heart attack at the age of only thirty-four. He was a member of the Futurians, an organization of left-wing, occasionally communist, activist figures of the SF fan community, many of whom went on to become successful writers and editors, including Isaac Asimov, Damon Knight, Frederik Pohl, and Donald A. Wollheim.

Kornbluth began writing science fiction at the age of fifteen, selling his first work before his eighteenth birthday. His most famous short story, "The Little Black Bag," in which a doctor who has become an alcoholic derelict finds a bag containing advanced medical technology from the future which he uses to benefit mankind, was filmed by the BBC for its *Out of the Unknown* television series in 1969, and in the following year by Rod Serling for *Night Gallery*. Kornbluth used numerous pseudonyms in his career, mostly for short stories; many of his novels were coauthored with Judith Merril (*Outpost Mars*, 1952, and *Gunner Cade*, 1952) and Frederik Pohl (*The Space Merchants*, 1952, and *Search the Sky*, 1954), and many stories were completed after his death.

"Beer-Bottle Polka," one of his two *Black Mask* stories, ran in the September 1946 issue.

Beer-Bottle Polka
C. M. Kornbluth

**Y PHONE RANG.**
"T. Skeat, private investigations, Skeat speaking," I said.
"This is Angonides, Skeat. I'm at 3609 Columbus Avenue. Get down here right away."
"What about?"

"I said, get down here right away. It's a killing." He hung up. I locked the office, put on an overcoat and caught the first taxi I could get.

It was a crummy address, in the heart of the brownstone-furnished-room neighborhood. There were cops in front of the place. They sent me up to the third floor.

Detective Lieutenant Angonides was waiting

He hit me just under my bottom rib, on the left side. It was a pile-driver.

A private eye is supposed to be in the know. That was where the blow came to Tim Skeat's pride—he was *supposed* to be, but that was all. A carved-up corpse, a punk with a gun, and a mob at his heels for a secret he didn't have—tough-guy Skeat took and gave a lot of punishment before the ugly picture began to make sense. And he was almost sorry when it did.

for me in the corridor. He handed me a dirty bit of paste-board.

"This your business card?" he asked.

I looked it over. "Of course it is. How's it figure?"

"We found it in the hatband of the guy in there. Go on in." The big Greek gave me a push that I didn't like.

The little hall bedroom was full of people. An M.E. was mumbling to himself as he filled out his forms. Two photographers were yapping to each other about film grain. A fingerprint man was swearing at a uniform cop who had sat in his powder.

One of the people in the room wasn't making any noise. He was lying naked on the bed. He was tied down with clothesline.

Somebody had tied him down, gagged him with paper toweling and slowly, nastily and completely had shredded him with the broken base of a beer-bottle. Blood soaked the dirty, rumpled blanket and pillow; blood stained the floor. It looked black and unreal under the photographers' lights.

"Do you know him?" asked Angonides.

"Can you wipe the blood off his face?"

He looked at the photographers and they nodded. He wiped, standing at arm's length.

"I know him," I said.

"Name?" asked Angonides, taking out his note-book.

"I don't know that. He's just a nut who stumbled into my office last Tuesday. He said he had a secret to sell me for five hundred. I told him what he could do with his secret and he stumbled out again. That's all."

The big Greek closed his note-book with a snap and shoved it into his pocket. He began to bully me in a tired sort of way: "What the hell are you trying to tell me, Skeat? You got a client and didn't even take his name?"

"I don't take the brush-man's name when he calls. This guy wasn't even a brush-man. He was just a nut."

"How about the card he had?"

"My cards are all over the city. That doesn't mean a damned thing and you know it."

"Maybe I do," he said, and his head swiveled around to the stiff. He picked up the beer-bottle and hefted it.

The slashes on the body were none of them very deep and not one was in a vital place. He had died of shock and blood-loss. Some of the cuts were in exquisitely painful places—the inside thigh, soles of the feet and others—but I couldn't guess whether those were part of the random pattern or intentional.

"The killer changed hands at least once," said Angonides. "And he worked from both sides of the bed." He studied the cuts, his brows wrinkled.

"What the hell," I said, "you'll trace him by his papers and then you'll get his buddies and one of them'll be the killer."

"He didn't have any papers except your card," said the detective. "He was a skip."

"How do you know?"

"He tried to lose himself. Five laundry-marks on his clothes, different one each week. Different restaurant every day. This is the third rooming-house we've traced him to. His trail's so completely doubled back on and loused up that he's been dropped from the books."

"Then you'll get a flimsy from some M.P.B. in Idaho or Maine and you'll be on his tail."

"If he's a fugitive from justice. If he's just on the lam from a mob—well, this means the mob caught up with him."

The M.E. mumbled to himself and the photographers yapped at each other about photometers. The fingerprint man whistled "Annie Laurie" as he packed his kit. I felt sick. The blood on the stiff and the blanket and the pillow and floor stank hotly.

"Come down to Center Street with us," said Angonides.

"That a request?"

"Yes," he said, slowly and unwillingly. "You're the one and only lead, Skeat. If you're holding something out we're going to get it, one way or another."

"Don't muscle me, George. You'll be sorry if you do."

"I've got to be sure," he said, staring at me.

We rode down to Center Street in a squad car. In one of the old-fashioned paneled offices I filled out an affirmation repeating my story. Then Angonides and his boys politely and coldly ushered me into a basement room.

"This the place?" I asked, looking around. The walls were stone, the ceiling was low and ominous. There were no windows. In one corner stood a big, heavy chair screwed to the floor with angle-irons. There weren't straps nailed to it; that wouldn't have looked good.

One of the boys held me by each arm and Angonides went to a wall switch. The ceiling light clicked out and a photo-flood in a kid's magic lantern went on. The detective lieutenant lowered it so it glared into my eyes. I closed them and the light went right through.

"You'll never get away with this, George," I said.

"Maybe not, but I'm going to try."

"In the funny papers I'd get to sit down," I said, wiping my eyes.

"This isn't the funny papers," said Angonides flatly.

I took out a pack of cigarettes and somebody's hand held my wrist while another hand took the pack out of my fingers.

"You don't smoke when you're being sweated," said Angonides from the darkness. "Didn't you know that?" I heard a match explode on somebody's finger-nail and smelled the sulfur, then the reek of a cheap cigar. The smoke drifted into the cylinder of light.

I brought my watch up to my eyes. "Another day shot to hell," I said. "How long do you keep this up, George?"

"How long do you, Skeat?" he asked.

"I'll tell it again," I said. "Turn off the damned light."

"Nope."

"Then I'll tell it anyway. The character came into my office on Tuesday—" I finished the story. "Now turn off your damned light." My eyes were streaming. When I wiped them they just got sorer.

"Nope. Not good enough." He whispered something in the darkness and the two boys holding my arms held them tighter. Angonides' face came between me and the light. He had a curious, thoughtful look—a couple of short, vertical wrinkles between the eyes. He was slowly wrapping a towel around his right hand.

"George, for God's sake!" I yelled at him, sweating.

"Tell it again," he said, drawing the towel tight and smooth, not leaving a wrinkle in it, tucking the end under.

I told it again, almost babbling.

He hit me just under my bottom rib, on the left side. It was a pile-driver. It jarred my guts and shot up and down my backbone like chain lightning.

He pounded me again. And again. And again. He wasn't standing like a boxer but like a big-league batter, very square and steady. His right hand pumped forward and back at his hip level. There was silence in the room except for my breathing and his.

He stopped and said: "I can keep this up all night, Skeat. Can you?"

I tried to talk and found that I couldn't. But I didn't have anything to say that he hadn't heard. So I nodded my head to say, Yes, I can keep this up all night, you brainy detective lieutenant.

He sighed and began again. He pounded me slowly and methodically and with all the steam he had, six times, twelve times, eighteen times, always in the same place, as if he were trying to chop down a tree with his fists. The tissues of the spot just under my bottom rib began to whimper, then to shriek at every blow. Finally the spot felt soft and ice-cold and hurt just as much between blows as when he landed.

Eighteen. Twenty. Twenty-five. He stopped.

"It's seven-thirty, Skeat. How about some dinner?" he asked flatly. "You're tying up some good men in this crummy basement. Open up and let's all go home."

I retched and shook my head for "no."

Angonides felt the spot he'd been pounding and then wordlessly fired his fist into a new part of my hide, six inches to the right. He took his stance again and pounded, I don't know how long. My body felt swollen and waves of pain swept over it. Between the waves the light seemed to dim. Then I slipped and began to speed down the longest, slickest, steepest toboggan slide in the world. The photo-flood bulb in the kid's magic lantern went out.

The detective was shaking me. I tasted cheap whiskey on my tongue and felt it burn my lips. When my eyes opened things were blurred, but I saw Angonides' big, serious face staring into mine.

"Skeat," he said, "you won't get anywhere if you try to put through a complaint. You understand that?"

"So what?" I asked thickly. "What happened?"

"You got tired and went to sleep. But you didn't talk. The hell with you."

"You shouldn't have muscled me, George," I said. He left his face blank. His boys silently led me out.

I found myself on the sidewalk outside 32 Center, rocky as a drunk at the end of a three-week bender. I walked to a subway trying not to swing my shoulders. They hurt. I hurt from the waist up—and down.

At the Russian Baths on Second Avenue I bought a cot for the night and went into the steam room. I sat on the top tier where it's thickest and hottest. My skin became pink all over and then two pinker blotches appeared just under my bottom ribs. That was all. Angonides knew his stuff.

I told the rubber to take it easy. He was a big, gray man with knowing hands and an Eastern Europe accent. He touched the two faint bruises once and asked: "Mugs or cops?"

"Prunes," I said. "That happens whenever I eat too many prunes."

He grinned and shut up. A little later he began to talk about the Cossacks of the tsar and what they used to do to nihilists and liberals.

I asked him if the Cossacks ever used to shred liberals with beer-bottles. He left off the massaging and showed me page three of the *Mirror*: "SUSPECT HELD IN BOTTLE DEATH." The story said a little less than nothing. My name wasn't mentioned, though I suppose I was the suspect.

"Never heard of it." I yawned. I was so sleepy he had to lead me to the cot.

"'Night, mister," he said. "Lay off them prunes."

The next morning I woke with ice-picks under my ribs, but in pretty good shape, considering. I had a barbershop shave and some coffee and wheat-cakes in a cafeteria. I went uptown to my office. It was only nine-thirty, but I had a visitor already in the little waiting-room I keep unlocked for the drop-in trade.

He was young and trained-looking. He was dressed in gray and had hot, dark eyes that wrinkled at the corners.

"'Morning," I said. "I'm Tim Skeat. Is there anything—" I was unlocking the office door when I saw that he had a little gun out.

I locked my office door again and put the key in my inside breast pocket. "What's the caper?" I asked.

He jerked the gun toward the office door. It was a short-barrel .32 revolver. He held it right, with his thumb horizontal along the frame.

One word came from his lips, in a gray, chilly monotone: "Open."

"Not for you, punk."

The cold monotone said again: "Open or I'll shoot your guts out." But his hand didn't tighten on the gun.

"Nope. You aren't coked up, so you won't shoot. If you want the keys, come and get them. Only I don't think you're man enough."

He didn't waste words; he took two steps

toward me, like a boxer—exactly like a boxer. He shuffled forward his left foot and didn't bring the right up until it was planted. His left hand was out, the gun was in his right hand at waist level. If I grabbed for it his body would be in the way of my grab. If he fired my body would be in the way of his bullet.

He dipped the left hand into my jacket. His hot, dark eyes didn't leave my left shoulder. That was the hand I'd have to grab with, and my shoulder would telegraph the grab.

His hand closed around the key-ring in the pocket.

"Your safety's on," I said, looking down.

His eyes flicked down.

My left hand went out, the thumb slipping under the hammer, the fingers clamping on the cylinder. The cylinder twitched but didn't turn as he jerked the trigger and the hammer slammed my thumb-nail. As he yanked his hand out of my jacket pocket the ulnar surface of my right landed in his wind-pipe and then crunched on his right wrist. He dropped the gun and squared off like a manly little Golden Glover.

I back-handed him with my right and he jabbed me nicely in the nose. I apologized hastily to the Marquess of Queensbury and caught his wrist as his hand bounced back to the guard. The Ito Soji doesn't often work unless you practice daily, but this time it didn't let me down. He went spinning through the air and fetched the office partition an awful smack.

Moe Baumgart, the insurance agent next door, yelled: "Skeat, for God's *sake!*"

"Sorry, Moe!" I bellowed back through the partition. I rolled back Junior's eyelid. He was faking. I picked him up by the collar, pocketed his gun and opened my office door. Suddenly he was writhing like a crazy wildcat in my grip, clawing for my eyes, my throat, my hair. I threw my right arm around his throat from behind in a stranglehold and coldly put the pressure on, and then I held it.

His eyes popped and he made faint, gargling noises. His face went blue. I let him drop and booted him through the door. I locked it and went to the phone.

"I want a young, intelligent policeman," I said to the operator. "Room 917, Greenleaf Building, Broadway at Fifty-first Street. There's no great hurry about it."

She repeated the address and thanked me, I don't know why.

"Get into a chair," I said to the kid. He glared at me from the floor. I picked him up and dumped him into the client's seat. He wasn't going to talk, he was saying over and over to himself. I grinned at him.

"They'll trace you through the A.A.U. welterweight division," I said.

His eyes widened for a moment; then he looked away from me. He wasn't going to talk.

He didn't have to.

"Lots of form," I said. "Lots of form and no guts."

"The hell with you," he said. The movie-gangster chill was gone from his voice.

"They shouldn't have sent you," I said. "They should have sent a man."

He grinned wolfishly. I was glad I had the gun.

"Being a detective is hard on the stomach," I said. "Every time I meet a punk like you it makes me want to throw up. And you don't know how many punks like you there are, in the new suits with the new guns they don't know how to use. 'Your safety's on, Junior—take your safety off before you shoot the man!' And you *fell* for it!"

He grinned his animal grin again and said slowly: "Someday I'm going to meet you again, buddy—" The words trailed off.

"Merry hell you will. You're headed up the river right now. And when you get out you won't be able to fight those good, clean amateur fights for thirty-dollar suits and fifty-dollar watches. The mob won't even hire you back after the way you fluffed this job."

"The hell I won't meet you, buddy." He grinned tightly. "And the hell I won't get hired."

He was beginning to talk, and then the law had to pound on the door.

"*Hey!*" yelled the law. Bang, bang, bang on the door with the nightstick. "You want a cop in here?"

I unlocked the door. "Hello, Benelli. I asked for a young, intelligent policeman and they send you. What's the force coming to?"

Benelli grinned. "Is that the emergency?" He indicated Junior and hung his nightstick on his badge.

"Yep. Assault with a deadly weapon. Maybe assault with intent to kill. Here's his gun."

Benelli pocketed it and flipped a chain come-along on the kid's wrist. He twisted it once and the kid shot out of the chair with a yelp.

"Comfortable?" asked Benelli solicitously. He twisted it again and the kid bit his lip.

"Don't be brutal," I said.

He didn't grin. "I know these punks, Timmy. I don't like them worth a damn. Let's all go to the precinct."

I looked at my watch. The kid started and his eyes twitched to my desk. I looked at him and he stared out the window. He wouldn't meet my eye.

Half a hunch is better than none.

"It's nine-thirty," I said to Benelli. "I have a big-deal phone-call coming up. I'll be there at eleven."

Benelli took him away.

I sat by the phone and smoked a chain of cigarettes until ten sharp. The phone rang.

I picked up the speaker and said, in the kid's movie-gangster rasp: "It's O.K."

"Did you cool him?" asked a woman's voice excitedly.

"Between the eyes," I hissed.

"Maxie'll be there in five minutes."

"O.K.," I rasped, sweating.

"Morgan's tonight?"

"Uh, sure."

"See ya." She hung up and I scrambled for my safe to get out the .38 before mysterious Maxie arrived. I locked the door again. It would be locked.

At ten-five there was a knock.

"Maxie?" I hissed.

"That's me," said a pale, thin voice.

I opened the door and Maxie came in. His jaw dropped when he saw himself covered by all that caliber.

"I'm O.K., kid," he said, surprised. "I'm here for the box."

He didn't know me!

"Where's the, er, stiff?" he asked nervously.

"There—" I waved the gun at the lavatory door and put it away. Maxie could be handled without a gun—he wasn't much of a man except for his hands. They were big, muscular and manicured. I found out why in a moment. He made a bee-line for my office safe and squatted before it.

I didn't understand half the things he did— maybe some of it was mumbo-jumbo. Every crook dramatizes himself. But in three minutes the door swung open.

He practically dove in, ignoring me. I keep a little cash in my safe, a small set of burglar tools, my gun and cartridges, and all my case reports. Maxie set the cash aside, whistled over the tools, ignored the bullets and spread the reports on the floor.

While he pawed them I took time out to wonder what the hell was going on, but I couldn't seem to get anywhere.

Maxie gave up the reports, puzzled. "Have I got it straight, kid?" he asked. "The guy's name was Anson Charles English and he hired Skeat last Tuesday. He could've used a phony name, but Skeat didn't open any files on Tuesday at all."

"Who was that dame on the phone?" I asked. "Who is Anson Charles English? Why was Skeat supposed to be killed? Where is Morgan's?" I took out the pistol again. His jaw dropped again.

"I'm Skeat," I said. "Your gunsel didn't keep his left up. You look silly with your mouth open."

He closed it and gulped faintly.

I said: "You look silly with it closed, too."

"I won't talk to you," he said.

"I'll bet you want to see your lawyer."

He looked at the door.

"It's locked," I said.

He went over and tried it.

"See?" I told him. "Just you and me."

"I want to see my lawyer." He gulped.

"No law here, Maxie. I'm getting sick of cops. They punch you around and then they say the hell with you. You get your suspect talking and they bust in and take him to the precinct. Here's one I learned from a cop." I belted him just below the bottom rib on the left side.

He quacked like a duck and his face went gray. He was a little man.

I pounded him in the same spot until his face was like putty and his breath crowed from his throat.

"Lay off—*agh!*" he said.

"Sure," I said. "Lay off. Where's the stiff. Oh, the stiff's in there. Guy named Skeat. Lay off, Skeat. See what I mean?"

"*A-a-agh!*" He retched as my fist sunk in again.

By ten-thirty I was sweating from both armpits. Don't let anybody tell you it isn't hard work to bounce even a little man like a handball.

By ten-forty he was talking. I slammed him whenever he stopped, and he'd begin again like a turned-on radio.

He said Morgan's was a gambling house in the Village.

He said English was a petty blackmailer who'd put the screws on Morgan for something. He said also that English was the corpse which had been shredded with the beer-bottle.

"Where the hell do I figure?" I asked.

He said a *Mirror* reporter had told somebody that I was a key-figure in the case and it had got to Morgan.

"Who's the dame?"

He said she was just Morgan's steno.

"What did English have on Morgan?"

Maxie shivered. "Mister, I don't know. I'm very damned glad I don't know. What English knew got him killed. You were supposed to have got the story from English, so you were sup-posed to be killed. I got sent here to see if you had the story on paper and if you did, to burn it.

"If I found a file on English in your safe I would have burned it without looking inside, as soon as I read his name on the folder. I'm—I'm glad I don't know any more than I do about it."

He couldn't walk, or thought he couldn't. I hoisted him and booted him into the corridor. He got up and made it to the elevator.

Moe Baumgart came out of his office next door and coldly asked whether I'd been holding a three-ring circus all morning. I apologized nicely and went in again to lock up.

I went to the precinct to file charges against the kid.

The part I hated was that there wasn't any money in it for me. Maybe keeping alive's more important than money. If it is, why does anybody get into the detective business? But I had something to do with it. They were sure as hell going to shoot my tail off unless I got the drop on them. I could call the cops and tell them the whole story, but what *was* the story?

A punk who wouldn't talk. A phone-call that only I knew anything about. A little peterman who could sue me for assault and collect. Another gambling house. A nasty kind of murder still unsolved.

The cops would laugh.

But I wasn't laughing.

I was going to see Mr. Morgan and tell him that I didn't know him from Adam.

How was I going to find Mr. Morgan without getting chopped down? Ah-hah, that's the catch. Maybe I *was* going to get chopped down. Wouldn't that be funny as hell? To be killed so I wouldn't spill a secret I didn't know?

I went out and rented a dress suit.

"Got a wedding job?" Sol asked, and I said yes. After the deposit was paid I got the quakes.

I felt somehow that the ten dollars changing hands had committed me. There was no turning back now.

In my hotel room I tried on the dress suit and it looked lousy. I pressed it myself, and it didn't fit any better but it lost that off-the-shelf look. I filled the pockets with a set of cheap, flashy accessories—cigarette case, lighter, wallet, pen, memo pad, silk handkerchief. They were all monogrammed C. McC.

In my top left bureau drawer I keep a tiny Belgian .25 automatic. It's a slim, dainty woman's gun, no bigger than a pack of cigarettes and not as thick. I hefted it for a long minute and pondered. I slipped it into the little pocket half-way down the left tail of the dress-coat. It didn't bulge. The tail swung a little too heavily when I tried the jacket on and walked. That was all.

I got into the gray suit again and took the subway for Washington Square. That's Greenwich Village, where the suckers go, and I felt like the biggest sucker who ever drew breath.

Morgan's was a brownstone front three stories high, with curtained windows. I walked past it a couple of times—it looked like three stories of absolutely nothing.

By six I was back at my hotel. The manager got three hundred dollars of my money from the safe and I stowed it in the C. McC. wallet. It was probably going to be gone before the evening was over. I might not be alive to miss it.

I shaved myself clean again and took off my sideburns. From that top bureau drawer on the left I took a sissy-looking pair of horn-rim glasses and put them on. I parted my hair and plastered it down. Usually I comb it back with water and the hell with dandruff. I polished a pair of dancing-pumps—old-fashioned, but they and the hair would take more than an inch from my height.

By eight I was dressed and staring dubiously at myself in the mirror. Nuts. I put on a chesterfield and the rented opera hat and called the desk for a taxi.

The taxi took me to a clip-joint nightclub six doors from Morgan's. The place was the last water-hole, and some gambling parties were sure to stop there. The rest was up to me.

The clip-joint loved me. Only half a dozen parties were in dinner-jackets, and my tailcoat was almost too good to be true. The captain scraped and gave me a ringside table. I ordered a club sandwich, to the dismay of the waiter, and a side-car.

By the time I'd finished that side-car and another the nine-o'clock floor show had begun. There was a soapy little emcee who told three fairy jokes and then brought on the unrivaled, unparalleled, lavish and magnificent chorus of five retired scrubwomen. They listlessly hipped their way through a Hawaiian number and then the emcee was back.

He told three fairy jokes and brought on that brilliant tip-top tapper, favorite of Broadway, star of stage, screen and radio, Joe Nobody. Joe pretended to work up a sweat doing a steal of Bill Robinson's staircase dance, milked a little applause by keeping up a double-shuffle for a full minute, and pranced off to the thunderous clapping of the waiters, bus-boys and the hat-check girl.

The emcee dashed on again. While he was telling three fairy jokes I ordered another side-car and looked over a party of six who'd just come in. They were in evening clothes and looked like money. They got a good table, three away from me, and ordered bonded whiskey highballs. They drank them, ordered more and stayed through the scrubwomen's high-hat-cane-1931-Broadway-rhythm-hotcha number. They tittered hysterically at the emcee's three fairy jokes that followed. They drank up and left in the middle of a blue-lit fan dance by the lumpiest of the scrubwomen.

Two men came in, one of them badly plastered. They were both dressed, but had a cheap look about them. They had a couple at the bar, then decided to sit for a while. They got the table next to mine. The sober one ordered coffee for the drunk one and a highball for himself. The drunk babbled that he din' wan' coffee and the manager began to flutter nervously in the vicinity.

The emcee was on again. When the coffee arrived the drunk threw it on the floor and bellowed: "I don' *wan'* any coffee!"

The emcee thought he would make like Eddie Davis and quell the heckler with a witty, biting gag.

"Ya know, buddy," he said, pointing, "theh's on'y two kines a animals 'at make a noise like 'at. One's a—"

The drunk realized he was being talked about, took two steps onto the floor and bashed the emcee in the mouth.

"I sai' I din' *wan'* any coffee!" he challenged the whole clip-joint and its customers.

Waiters began to flow toward him. The drunk's friend and I each took an elbow and led him off the floor. The drunk started to apologize to the manager, who grinned and said: "That was a nice poke you gave him. The damned loudmouth needed it. I got to throw you out now. One check?"

"Sure," I said. "Let me have it." We got our coats and went out together. "Where to?"

The drunk said: "Le's go Morgan's. I gotta blackjack sys'em works ev' time. Le's go Morgan's."

"You know Morgan's?" asked the other one.

I shrugged. "They don't know me."

"I'll get ya in. They took enough from me by now ta let a friend of mine in."

We got into the anteroom just by knocking. There was a little doubt about me there. A cauliflowered bruiser in a beautiful dinner-jacket politely refused to let me in until Hellman, wounded in the pride, swore he'd known me for seven years and that I was Square Joe from Rightville. That did it. That more than did it. The bruiser wrote me out a card—just like speakeasy days!—and I was a member. We went on in.

The whole first floor had been opened; all partitioning walls were down. There was a big chandelier with hundred-watters in it. There were plenty of hundred-watters in wall brackets. It was bright—hard on women customers and their complexions, hard on the dirty walls, but you could see what went on when the dice bounced and the cards flipped.

There were three blackjack tables, a chuck-a-luck layout, two wheels and a battery of big slot-machines.

"Craps and poker on the second floor," said Hellman.

"I gotta blackjack sys'em works ev' time," said his friend, starting for the tables. Hellman hurried after him and I let him hurry.

There were about thirty women there and about twenty men. I could tell the two house men circulating gently around the room. They were big and looked darkly southern. They were watching the dealers and stickmen as closely as they watched the customers.

I left my coat and hat at the check stand, which was operated by the big bruiser who doubled as receptionist. He tripled as cashier, too, slapping down a stack of silver dollars on the counter.

"Twenty for a starter, Mr. McCowan?" he suggested.

"Forty," I said. He doubled the stack and took my two bills. The cartwheels made an awful bulge in my pocket. After ten minutes at the roulette wheel the bulge wasn't there anymore. I bought forty again and ran them up to forty-two in an hour at the chuck-a-luck cage.

I started upstairs to the crap games. A bulky, dark man drifted from nowhere to murmur: "Sorry, sir, no silver used on the second floor. Please change your money if you wish to go up."

Upstairs not even a stab had been made at decorating. There were three poker tables, three craps layouts and shoulder-high screens between them. There was a twin-tube fluorescent fixture hanging over each stand.

A dark little man standing at the head of the stairs said: "Sir?"

"Craps," I said. "High table."

I watched the roll until I got the gun, then shot twenty and made it with a four-three.

I let it ride and rolled a five, a nine, another nine, a six and a five.

I took off thirty, rolled and crapped out with a two. The gun moved left, my fifty said he wouldn't. He didn't. I took off fifty, bet wrong again and collected again. I bet a hundred right on the next gunner and lost, fifty wrong on the next and won.

I got the gun and shot the hundred. I eighted the hard way and made it with a six-two on the second roll. I shot the two hundred and rolled six-five.

Shoot the four, something told me.

"Shoot the four," I said.

The stickman didn't flick the dice at me.

"I thought this was the high table!"

"Let him shoot the four," said a little, dark man who had joined us.

"Yes, Mr. Morgan," said the stickman. The dice rolled into my cupped hand.

"Nice place you have, Mr. Morgan," I said, cackling the dice.

"We like it," said Morgan. Only his name wasn't Morgan, or hadn't been long. Morgan's a Welsh name, and Welshmen aren't olive-skinned little men with small hands and white teeth. Welshmen don't use perfume either.

There was something about Mr. Morgan, something just outside my reach—

"*Four* hundred!" I breathed, and rolled. It was a four-three again. Everybody at the table sighed.

Morgan—what *was* there about that guy?—counted out four C-notes and said: "Good for you, Mr. McCowan. Try again?"

"Shoot twenty," I said. I rolled a six, a three, a nine and sevened out.

Somebody else came up from the first floor and started to the third. It was Maxie, the little peterman. I turned my back, but he recognized me. The house man at the head of the stairs saw that something was up, though Maxie had started climbing again, looking innocent and virtuous. He started after him and I heard them talk in an undertone, his voice gentle and Maxie's nervous. I slipped down the stairs, left unguarded. I heard a buzzer somewhere.

When I turned at the landing I saw the two house men of the first floor and another I hadn't spotted standing there at the foot of the stairs.

I stopped. The second-floor man came down the steps and frisked me lightly. He took out the flashy cigarette case, looked in it and put it back.

"Will you come upstairs, sir?" he asked.

"You bet I will," I said.

We went up to the third floor. I was politely ushered through a door that clicked behind me. It was a nice little waiting room with three chairs. Maxie was sitting in one of them as if it were the hot seat.

"How's the gut?" I asked him politely. It was a very courteous place.

He stared at me. "What did you come here for?"

"Why didn't you blow town after you bungled the job?"

"I was going to bluff. After Morgan paid me I was going to blow."

"Looks like you're going to get paid," I said.

I pointed to a door where one of the house men was silently standing. He beckoned to Maxie. Maxie went with him. There was a look of doom on his face.

The door opened again after a couple of minutes. The man beckoned to me. I went with him.

I wondered what my face looked like then.

I wondered what it would look like in a couple of hours.

The man took me through a corridor to the back of the house. He knocked on a door and opened it. I went through and he followed me.

There was a table, four chairs, a couple of pictures. Morgan was sitting behind the table.

"Sit down, Skeat," he said. "Maxie told me you were here. I want to know what happened."

I flipped the tails of my coat into my lap. "You have a secret, Mr. Morgan."

"That's right," he agreed, smiling. I stared at

the smile until he relaxed and waited. What *was* there about this little guy?

I went on: "A grifter named English found out what it was. He tried to peddle it to me. I didn't want it, but you didn't know that. You had English killed and you sent a boy to kill me. After I was killed Maxie was supposed to show up, open my safe and destroy the secret if I had it in writing. But I got the drop on your boy and I beat hell out of Maxie until I got the story."

"Does Maxie know my—secret?" he asked, his face growing wintry.

"No. He's scared of it. I'm scared of it too. I didn't know it and I didn't want to know it. I came here to look over your layout, maybe say hello and tell you I didn't know what you're covering up."

Something clicked.

I said slowly and carefully: "Only now that I take a good, long look at you, I do know what you're covering up."

"You're crazy to tell me that, Skeat. It means you die."

I grinned, sweating. "Send your men away or I'll yell what I know so loud they'll all hear it. Can you kill them all?"

Morgan waved at the house man in a tired way. "Leave him to me," he said. "I don't want anybody else on this floor for a half hour."

The man left silently.

Morgan leaned earnestly over the table and nodded at me. "It must sound crazy to you," he said.

"People over here don't kill for that," I said.

"I'm from over there. . . ." His eyes clouded and he nodded his little nod. "You don't know what it's like," he said. "All you crazy-rich Americans—the garbage you throw away after dinner would feed two of our families all day.

"It is because we have so little—a handful of stony soil, a few saucepans, a leaking little hut and the rags we wear. We have nothing, Skeat, nothing except our families to love and protect.

"My brother and I were orphaned when we were six and eight. Our father died with the bends—he was a sponge-diver. Very hard life.

Our mother died because she could not live any longer. An uncle in America sent for us and raised us. We went two different ways. I've been crooked as hell since I was sixteen. He's been straight as a die all his life.

"Years ago I realized that I was doing my brother terrible harm by being what I was, so I changed my name. English found out my true name, so he died. Now nobody knows except you, who recognized my brother's features in mine.

"If my true name were known my brother's career would be at an end. He would drift back into obscurity and heartbreak. That is why you must die—because over there we are so poor and have nothing to love but our families."

He reached in the drawer of the table. I reached in the left tail pocket of my dress-coat. The little Belgian .25 automatic flicked out as Morgan lifted a big revolver.

I fired at his hand a split-second before he could drag back the ponderous action of the .44. My tiny bullet burned him and his hand wavered as he fired. My second shot landed in his chest. So did my third, fourth and fifth. My ears rang with the roar of his big gun. My shoulder felt cold as ice, then began to tingle.

"Skeat," I said drunkenly, "you're shot." I swayed to my feet and clawed my way to the table and the phone that stood on it.

I called a man and told him something. "And bring a doctor," I added.

In the movies there's a trick called "iris out." It's what you see when blackness creeps over the screen until there's just a little circle of light left in the center and then the light winks out. That's what happened to me then.

The little circle of light appeared again. It expanded and was the chest of somebody in hospital white. There was a low, heart-sick wailing somewhere, and lots of people.

The man in white said: "He's coming to."

"Did you phone that tip in?" asked somebody.

"Hell, yes," I said. I could still hear the wailing.

"Good guy! We made a beautiful haul."

My shoulder smelled of alcohol and had a bulky dressing on it. I looked around.

There was Angonides crouched by the corpse of his brother, wailing: "*O Demetrios! O, delph' Demetrios!*"

"He shouldn't have muscled me," I said sleepily. "But we're all square now."

I felt very tired and contented.

Borrowed Crime
Cornell Woolrich

CORNELL (GEORGE HOPLEY) WOOLRICH (1903–1968) was born in New York City, grew up in South America and New York, and was educated at Columbia University, to which he left his literary estate. A sad and lonely man who desperately dedicated his books to his typewriter and to his hotel room, Woolrich was almost certainly a closeted homosexual (his marriage was terminated in short order) and an alcoholic, so antisocial and reclusive that he refused to leave his hotel room when his leg became infected, ultimately resulting in its amputation. Perhaps not surprisingly, then, the majority of his work has an overwhelming darkness, and few of his characters, whether good or evil, have much hope for happiness—or even justice. No twentieth-century author equaled Woolrich's ability to create suspense, and Hollywood producers recognized it early on. Few writers have had as many films based on their work as Woolrich, beginning with *Convicted* (1938), based on "Angel Face," starring Rita Hayworth, and continuing with *Street of Chance* (1942), on *The Black Curtain*, with Burgess Meredith and Claire Trevor; *The Leopard Man* (1943), on *Black Alibi*, with Dennis O'Keefe and Jean Brooks; *Phantom Lady* (1944), on the novel, with Ella Raines and Alan Curtis; *The Mark of the Whistler* (1944), on "Chance," with Richard Dix and Janis Carter; *Deadline at Dawn* (1946), on the novel, with Susan Hayward; *Rear Window* (1954), on "It Had to Be Murder," with Grace Kelly and James Stewart; and fifteen others.

"Borrowed Crime" was published in the July 1939 issue.

Borrowed Crime

Cornell Woolrich

THE DOCTOR LOWERED HIS STETHOSCOPE with an irritable gesture. "No improvement at all," he snapped. "He's losing ground, if anything, staying here!"

The kid's ribs were sticking out like a fish's backbone. The doctor turned to him and spoke more gently than he had to the man and woman. "Put on your shirt, sonny; don't catch cold." He eyed the row of medicine bottles ranged above the bed, swept his arm at them impatiently. "Throw them out; they're not doing the boy a bit of good! I gave you my diagnosis over two months ago. He's got to be taken out West, where the air's dry and the sun's hot. I can't do anything for him; you're just wasting your time and mine by sending for me."

The woman had begun to cry soundlessly into her apron, with the terrible resignation of the poor. The doctor banged his instrument case shut, stalked ill-humoredly out of the room.

Swanson slouched dejectedly after him. "But, Doc, I ain't got—" He faltered.

The doctor stopped short in the outer doorway, looked around at him short-temperedly. "I know," he said, "you haven't got the money! That's the hell of it. It'll take a thousand dollars."

The boy had started to cough again in the room they'd just come from. The woman closed the door, but it came through anyway.

It seemed to infuriate the doctor even more. Maybe he was a conscientious man, hated the feeling of helplessness a case like this gave him.

"Hear that?" he exclaimed. "You better find some way of getting that kid out of here, or you won't have to hear it very much longer!"

Swanson kept staring at him helplessly. "If there was only some way . . ."

The doctor looked him squarely in the eye. "If it was my child, I'd find a way; you bet your bottom dollar!" he said wrathfully. "Go out and hit somebody over the head for it! Hold up a bank! I don't care where you get it, but see that you get it!"

He went stomping down the tenement stairs outside, swearing audibly all the way down. His bad temper didn't mislead Swanson any; he knew he was a sympathetic, honest man.

He closed the door and went in again, hanging his head. The kid had stopped coughing now—until the next time. His wife came out of the room, carrying a cloth half-hidden so he wouldn't see it. He knew those cloths, knew what color they were apt to show if you unfolded them.

He sat down at the table in the shabby room, held his head in both hands, staring down at nothing; at the soiled oilcloth and the newspaper resting on it. He had no chance of borrowing; money was only loaned to those who already had something, who could offer security. Even a loan-shark wouldn't have considered him a worthwhile risk—he had no job that could be milked later on.

Even the doctor's sinister suggestion, although it had only been angry rhetoric, was beyond his scope. Bank robbery was an organized business nowadays; what chance had a solitary, unarmed amateur against all their guards and tear bombs and alarm systems? And you didn't find a thousand dollars on the first man you held up on the streets these days.

The paper had been there under his eyes the whole time. It was no use looking at the Help Wanteds any more. He'd tried too long and hard, broken his heart, smashed his head against the stone wall of conditions as they were. Besides, even if by a miracle he could land something tomorrow, what hope had he of getting anything that would pay a thousand dollars even in a year's time? He flung it tormentedly away from him, with its black scarehead: *No Clue Yet in Ranger Slaying.*

Some murder case or other. What was it to him? Let the whole world murder and be murdered; he only cared about his kid and Helen. The front page furled over with the fling he had given the paper, and bared the page beneath, and after a while he became conscious of a dollar sign peering up at him from it. Next to it there was a one, and then a comma, and then three naughts. Funny, he must have been thinking so hard of one thousand dollars that he thought he was seeing it staring up at him from the printed page.

He drew the paper back toward him again. It was in a little box down at the foot, in heavier type than the rest. "Reward," it said, and then underneath: "The *Daily Reflector*, in a spirit of co-operation with the police, is prepared to pay the sum of $1,000 to anyone furnishing information leading to the identification and capture of the murderer of Robert J. Ranger. Members of police force not eligible. Information must be legitimate. No telephone calls. Apply City Desk, *Daily Reflector*, 205 East, etc, etc."

He turned back to the first page. He took a deep breath, pulled his chair up closer, and started to read his way through from the beginning, shading his eyes from the naked light overhead with one hand across them.

When he'd finished, he got up, went into the kitchen, and brought the previous night's paper back with him. They kept their back-number papers to start the fire with. He read that one exhaustively too. There was a photograph in it, of someone he had never seen before. "Robert J. Ranger," it said under it. He studied it carefully, then he closed his eyes a minute, as though he were etching it into his memory.

When he'd finally finished his recapitulation, there were three back numbers of the paper littered about the table before him, and he had obtained a composite and sketchy outline of what the whole thing was about:

A prosperous investment broker named Robert J. Ranger had been found murdered by hammer blows in the living-room of his home, in the smart suburb of Northchester, the previous Wednesday—that is to say, four days before. There were signs of a terrific struggle, and it was obvious that the man had sold his life dearly. A priceless blue porcelain Ming vase standing near the door was shattered, tables and chairs were overturned, the carpet was furrowed into corrugated ridges by the two pairs of feet that had scuffled back and forth over it.

It was fairly obvious to the police (they declared in print) that it had been committed by an intruder, someone unknown to Ranger. A nominal sum of money that had been on his person was missing, but a far larger sum within easy access had been overlooked. The intruder had apparently become terror-stricken at the sight of his own crime and fled the house without pursuing his search any further.

Ranger had had an engagement to go to dinner and the theater with his wife, had already bought the tickets (*Stars in Your Eyes*, Row C), and then at the last minute had been prevented from going by a vicious headache. Not wishing to disappoint Mrs. Ranger, he had arranged to have his business partner, Allen Cochrane, escort her in his place, had phoned him to meet her at a restaurant in town.

Mrs. Ranger had left shortly after dark, and distinctly remembered that the door of her car had been opened for her, unasked, by a seedy-looking individual of the type who performs that service for a pittance. It was highly probable, she thought (also in print) that this was the man who had later forced his way into the house under the mistaken impression that no one was home—Ranger had put all the lights out and lain down in the dark to ease his head—and murdered her husband when discovered ransacking it.

Unfortunately, Mrs. Ranger was unable to furnish a very exact description of this man. The fact that she was wearing most of her jewelry, and his accosting her by her car like that, made her nervous, had caused her to start the car quickly and drive off without looking closely at him.

Swanson read this passage through twice, tracing his finger under it.

At any rate, the crime did not occur for some time after her departure. She had telephoned from the Majestic Theater at 8:25, just before the curtain went up, to find out how her husband was, and he had spoken to her himself and said he felt much better. Then when she returned at midnight . . .

Swanson stopped reading.

"Helen!" he said. "Helen!"

She came to the door and looked out at him hopelessly.

"Get the kid ready," he said. "Start packing your own things, too. You're taking him with you to Tucson—right tonight."

"But how are you ever going to clear yourself again, once you get into their clutches?" she said, when he'd finally beaten down her objections. "It isn't just a case of spending a little time in jail for contempt of court or taking money under false pretenses. I mean, you'll be in so deep by that time that you'll never be able to explain your way out of it. They'll go ahead and convict you, and—and maybe even execute you for it, Jerry. It's too risky. Don't do it, don't do it!"

"That's where you come in. You're my living alibi. *You* know I wasn't anywhere near Northchester last Wednesday night, that I was sitting here in the flat with you and the kid the

whole time. Now here's what you do: You take the boy out there and board him with someone. Then you sit tight and wait until you hear from me. When I need you I'll send you a wire. Leave the kid out there—he's got to have his chance—and you come on back and do your stuff."

"But I'm your wife; suppose they won't believe me?"

"Well, if worse comes to worst, I still have the doc to fall back on. He was up here, too, last Wednesday, treating the kid. He knows I wasn't out murdering anyone. After all, look at it this way, Helen: All that connects me with the crime is my own say-so. That is, *one* person's word. On the other hand I have *two* people's words to clear me, in a pinch. One against two, those are fair enough odds. What more could anyone ask?

"Another thing, the real murderer may be turned up long before they're ready to try me, and I won't even have to have any help getting out of it. The kid has to have his break. I'm willing to do a short jail stretch to see that he gets it, and that's all that's involved. So put out the lights and let's get started."

He kissed them both good-by on the streetcar riding downtown, the kid bundled up in a blanket, his wife with a heavy suit-case beside her. "Now you wait there in the bus terminal until I send the money over to you. As soon as it reaches you, buy your tickets and take the next bus out; don't stick around."

He swung down and the streetcar went rumbling past. He walked east until he came to a chunky-looking office building, rode up on an express elevator, stepped off it and went into a reception room. "I want to see the city editor," he told the girl at the switchboard.

"Another." She sighed wearily. "All right, sit down over there with the rest of them." She pointed to where three or four nondescript-looking people were ranged uncomfortably along the wall on hard wooden chairs.

A blown-glass door in the three-quarters partition that walled the reception room opened and a woman came out, forcibly escorted by an office boy. "I did so see him, I tell ye!" she declared indignantly over her shoulder. "I saw him plain as day! I was on me way to get a pail of beer and—"

A male voice came booming out after her above the clatter of typewriters: "Well, go back and get another pail; then you'll see him twice!"

The office boy said, "He ain't wasting his time on any more of you false alarms, so give them chairs a breath of fresh air!"

The sitters got up and drifted sheepishly out, with an air of "We didn't think we'd get away with it, but no harm in trying anyway."

Swanson got up, too, but he went the other way, toward the inner door. "Take me in with you," he said. "I'm no fake."

The office boy looked at him for a minute; there must have been something convincing about his taut manner. He hitched his head, led him across a great open barn of a place, subdivided by innumerable wooden rails and buzzing with typewriters, into a cubicle at the opposite end with *City Editor* blacked on the door.

A disheveled-looking man was sitting in there, hair awry, coat off, elastics holding up his shirt sleeves. He swung his arm wearily. "Get out. Every crack-pot in town—" But Swanson's silent tenseness got to him too. "Well, what d'you think you know?" he said impatiently. "You seen him? You know who he is?"

"I wouldn't be here if I didn't," was the tight-lipped answer.

"Well, d'you know *where* he is?" He wanted to save his paper a thousand bucks if he could. It had been his idea, after all.

Swanson tapped a fingernail on the desk. "I know where he is at this very minute."

The editor jack-knifed his hands closed, then open again, in a grasping gesture. "Well, let me have it quick! If it's any good we can still make the midnight final with it!"

"Wait a minute. Just when, and in what form, do I get the thousand?"

"Our check will be mailed to you just as soon as we've verified the information—and if it has resulted in the arrest of this guy."

Swanson narrowed his eyes. "I thought that was coming. Trying to welsh out of it, eh? Nope, I want it in cash, I want it right here and now while I'm in the office with you, I want a bonded messenger standing outside the door to deliver it to a certain place, and I also want your word that where it was delivered won't be revealed to the police afterwards."

"I can't do that. How do I know your information is valid? Our terms are the guy has to be apprehended first be—"

"You'll know how valid it is as soon as you hear it. You don't have to worry about verifying it, it's self-verifying. The whole works is bound up in it automatically, whereabouts, identity, and apprehension. Now take it or leave it. Because I can go across the street to the *Daily Views* office and get as much or more for it."

The disheveled one got even more disheveled than before, if possible, at this last threat. He did a good deal of hectic telephoning, to the managing editor at his home, to the treasurer, to the press room in the basement.

Fifteen minutes later twenty fifty-dollar bills lay on his desk in a manila envelope, a messenger's form was silhouetted outside the glass of the door, and the typewriters were breathlessly holding their fire all over the place as though esoterically aware something momentous was in the air.

"This better be good." The editor heaved an exhausted sigh. "O.K., O.K., now spill it! Where is this Ranger murderer at the present time?"

"He's standing right across your desk looking square at you," said Swanson calmly.

"Wha-at? Y-y-you mean *you?*" The editor jolted his chair back, partly in surprise, partly in sudden precautionary retreat.

"I'm turning myself over to you. Here I am. Now come on with your money."

The editor dazedly picked up the manila envelope, partly extended it toward him. But he held on to a corner of it tightly without letting go. "Where you been hiding out since then?"

"Movie shows from morning to midnight, the subways from midnight to morning. If I gotta read another cough-drop ad I'll go wacky!"

"Well, just a minute, I gotta be sure; what was on the left side of the living-room doorway up at the Ranger place, as you went in?"

"A big blue vase; I knocked it over and busted it in the scrap."

"What'd you do with the hammer?"

"I slanted it against the curb about a block away from their place. Then I jumped on it and snapped the handle off short with my foot. I shoved the wooden part down a sewer opening; it must be floating outside the harbor by now. I carried the hammer head around in my clothing for a while, wrapped in a piece of paper so—you know, it wouldn't leave any stains. I finally got rid of that in a refuse can on one of the subway platforms. Don't ask me which one. I've got a headful of arithmetic from watching them tick past the last few days."

"I guess you're the ticket, all right," the editor said ruefully. "But why did you do it?"

"For dough. What else? Didn't get much, though." Swanson jerked the envelope out of his reluctant grasp. "Call the messenger in here. Is he bonded?"

"Don't worry about him, he's O.K."

Swanson sealed the gummed flap of the envelope. He drew the messenger aside out of earshot, said in a low voice: "Take this down to the Transcontinental Bus Terminal. There'll be a woman in the waiting-room, with a kid wrapped up in a blanket. Give it to her. That's all. Don't talk to her; come right back."

The messenger hurried out. The editor looked after him longingly. "Your moll—er, sweetheart, that who's getting it? Gee, that would make a swell human-interest angle."

"The agreement was that's to be kept from the police and out of the paper," Swanson said harshly. "I haven't got any girl; I'm a lone wolf. I'll tell you as a man, but not as an editor, just so you won't think there's any mystery about it. It's—it's a conscience fund, to try to make amends before I take my medicine. I told him to give it to the first needy-looking mother and child he came across at a certain place. Now go ahead, bring on your cops, I'm ready."

"Whoa!" The editor semaphored alarmedly, both arms in air. "We want an exclusive on this first, we can't keep you to ourselves forever." He grabbed up a phone, barked into it: "Rip out your first page down there! Get ready for an extra. I'm sending you down a slue of pictures!" He jumped over to the door, bawled out: "Rewrite man! Pix! Tearjerker! All of you! Everybody in here! I've got the Ranger murderer with me in my office!"

The small office was suddenly gorged with people, jostling, staring over one another's shoulders, banked solidly around Swanson, who was passively seated now in a chair. They were all talking at once to him, elbowing one another aside, jockeying to get next to him.

"Quiet, everybody! What is your name, we haven't even got that yet."

"Jerome Swanson."

"All right, let's get going. The presses are waiting. Stand back and give him air. Let's have it, Swanson."

Swanson's eyes sought the ceiling, which was the only clear space there was in the cubicle, in search of fluency. "Last Wednesday night, about six p.m. in the evening . . ." he began, and a sudden reverent hush fell on the yapping pack.

Policemen came in with a fine authoritative surge at about two in the morning, streaming across the newspaper office like a tide that has been held back past its time. Two plainclothesmen in the lead pounced on a haggard unshaven reporter by mistake, first of all.

"No, no, no!" wailed the city editor. "That's one of my feature writers. Him—over there."

They desisted and came on at Swanson, but not without a backward look of suspicion at their first objective. Swanson was the only calm person in the place, still sitting there on the chair, smoking quietly, one ankle hoisted to the opposite knee.

"So this is the guy, eh?"

They all said it in turn, with slight variations. A manacle clicked and fastened itself around his wrist. He looked down at it fascinatedly, changed the impeded cigarette he was holding over to his other hand.

He was jerked to his feet by the man on the other end of the manacle, with a proprietary "Come on, baby!" They formed themselves into a phalanx around him, one on each side, one leading the way, one behind him.

The *Reflector* staff followed them in a body as far as the elevator bank. He looked around, and a scrub woman had climbed up on one of the desks to look over everybody's heads at him. His last impression was of the long lines of luminous white bowls in the ceiling converging toward a distant point.

They took him far down below the lighted theatrical and night-life district to a gloomy, castellated silhouette on a dark, lifeless street, and in through various shabby rooms and along bleak corridors, where the few denizens to be met with were all uniformed. The surreptitious excitement among them in his wake was only less than up at the newspaper office; policemen turned to stare after him, sergeants at desks leaned out across them to get a better look as he went by.

The momentum of the arrest finally came to a stop in some sort of a back room, with windows that hadn't been washed in years and a green-shaded light throwing the upper half of it into dismal shadow. The handcuff was detached, and he was deposited on a chair under the circle of light like a package that has been brought in.

Finally the disconnected activities crystallized once more, and he found himself again at their center. A high official, hastily summoned from bed and non-uniformed, came in and seated himself before him, but outside the radius of light. Other figures, some new, some already familiar, ranged themselves about. The atmosphere became charged with impending drama, gathered to a head, and finally dissolved into a downpour of questions.

His complete lack of reticence, his willingness—even overanxiety—to answer them all to the best of his ability, threw them off-key time and again. That is to say, they would gather themselves up to batter into denial, contradiction, and then flounder when nothing met them in opposition.

His rehearsal in the newspaper office stood him in good stead, but even so he got into a number of uncomfortably tight places. Such as when one of them asked him, although in a minor key immediately after a far more leading question, "But if you spent all that time riding the subways, how is it your clothes ain't more rumpled than they are?"

Helen had always worked hard to keep this one suit of his in as good shape as she could. He got good and frightened for a minute, held his breath while the whole structure he'd laboriously built threatened to come toppling down around his ears.

"Well, you see, I didn't lie down and sleep in the cars, I was afraid I'd attract the guards' attention if I did; I rode them sitting up. It was the movie houses where I slept, and they've got upholstered seats, not as hard on the clothes."

"Why'd you kill him?"

"I went in to rob him. He caught me at it, put up a battle. I had to. And all for a few lousy bucks!"

All in all, he was glad when it was over, as glad as a man attempting to prove his innocence instead of his guilt would have been. A police stenographer came in and they ran through the whole thing again, with his help. When he went astray once or twice, they put it down to fatigue. Then there was a wait while it was being typed. It was brought in and read back to him, and a few final polishing touches were added, in which he again cooperated. Finally he was brought forward to sign it.

They took him out now and stood him up before one of the desks, and he had to give his name and address. He took the precaution of not giving the one he and Helen had been living at until tonight. He gave the one they'd been dispossessed from three months before. "My last address," he qualified it; let them think he'd been homeless since then.

That seemed to conclude the formalities for the time being, and he was taken into an adjoining building, which communicated with the first but where the floors were at a different level, and led into a cell, where he was asked if he would like a sandwich and a cup of coffee.

So many things had happened all night long that he hadn't had time to notice until now whether he was hungry or not, but he remembered that Helen and he had had one of their usual scanty suppers, and it was now nearly his usual breakfast time, so he assented gladly.

They were brought in to him, and they were excellent; the coffee was a much better quality than they could afford at the flat. They also provided him with a whole pack of cigarettes, without the usual obligation he felt under to ration himself on them for days on end. And the bunk, when he stretched out on it, was definitely no harder than that broken-down iron bedstead of theirs at home.

The bus must be way out by now, way out beyond recall, he thought contentedly. He fell effortlessly into a deep tranquil sleep.

"What're they going to do to me now?" he asked, riding out to the re-enactment several hours later with four officials in the car around him, a second car following, and an escort of two motorcycle policemen.

"Make you do it over in front of the cameras, so you can't welsh out of it afterwards," one of his escorts said in answer to his whispered question.

When they finally arrived there, he was given terse instructions to do exactly as he had done Wednesday night, retrace his steps and repeat his movements. One of the detectives was to substitute for the vanished Ranger.

Suddenly, as the ice-green lights flared up around him, he knew stage fright in its worst form. This was going to be far worse than the questioning last night at Headquarters had been; that, by comparison, had been confined to generalities; this permitted no slightest deviation.

One of them passed him a hammer which had abruptly materialized from nowhere, but he accepted it unhesitatingly instead of shrinking away from it, and that, he could see, left them non-plussed once more. He thrust it absently into his inner coat-pocket, head-downward, as though it were no more than a fountain pen. He had to keep up the pretense a while longer, he reasoned. Suppose the messenger boy was followed; suppose they got his wife back before she settled the boy out there. . . . The screen test commenced. He "felt" his way along, step by step, mentally consulting the newspaper texts he had absorbed, like a cheating Latin student with a pony concealed behind his Caesar.

The encounter with the synthetic Ranger was not particularly abhorrent to him; he certainly felt no qualms about it. It was mostly a matter of jockeying him into position so that he would fall in the right place. The papers had been accommodatingly explicit about this, even publishing diagrams marked with large X's to keep their readers geographically informed.

He saw them shake their heads slightly at his cold-blooded lack of emotion. Unfortunately, he swung the hammer in an entirely wrong arc, having no past experience in homicidal attacks, and when this was pointed out to him he nearly blew up altogether.

"He must have turned the other way, I guess, to get away from me," he said after a bad moment. "Everything gets blurred when you're seeing red."

The crime safely on celluloid, as if to prove unarguably to everyone's satisfaction that there had actually been one, he was whisked back down again downtown.

In the afternoon he was taken over to the adjoining building again and made to confront a personable blond young woman seated in the midst of detectives and officials in one of the rooms over there.

They looked at one another. There was, for a fleeting moment, an equally detached, impersonal curiosity on both sides. Then she quickly took refuge in a balled-up handkerchief at hand.

"Is this the man you saw outside your house the night of the murder?"

"Yes, that's the man. I positively identify him."

She took a deep breath into her handkerchief, as though nerving herself for something she felt obliged to do but would have preferred not to. Then she jumped suddenly from her chair, ran out at him.

"Why did you do it? Why did you take my husband from me?" she screamed tinnily. She made flailing motions toward his unprotected face; she was quickly restrained, drawn back by the men around her. But something had been faulty about the timing of the scene. She had had ample time to get in at least one good raking claw down his cheeks, and she hadn't; she had just held her magenta-lacquered nails poised in clawing position, as if waiting for them to be restrained.

"She's not sore at me," Swanson said to himself with sudden deep-seated inner conviction; "she's glad he's gone. She's play-acting just as much as—I am."

And more than that, he even had a fleeting impression that she was afraid of him. Like someone is when you both know something that no one else does, and one of you is afraid the other will give it away.

She was led out with her head stiffly averted, as though she couldn't get away quickly enough. Well, the whole thing was too involved and deep for his mental processes to be able to cope with.

The next day he had a visitor in his cell. He was a rather awe-inspiring man, with a short, neat graying beard and spectacles on a black cord.

"I'm Markovitz," he said bluntly. "I've been appointed by the state to defend you." He rested a paternal hand on Swanson's bony shoulder. "You should not have taken a life; you know that, don't you? But I am going to do the best I can for you. We must be practical. In a case like this we must use whatever weapons are put into

our hands." He removed his glasses, polished them, pointed toward the hypnotized Swanson.

"Insanity, of course," he stated bluntly.

His client sprang to his feet, stood there white to the gills, shaking from head to foot in a sudden ungovernable horror. Like many ignorant people, he had dreadful formalized visions of strait jackets, straw pallets, and clinking chains, in connection with mental derangement of any sort. "Oh, don't do that to me!" he wailed. "Don't! Don't put me in one of those places, I'll never get out alive again! I *will* go insane!"

"You committed murder," the lawyer reminded him coldly. He stood up. "I'll petition to have you examined by alienists, as the first step toward entering a plea of insanity for you." He left abruptly, all smiling encouragement.

As soon as he was gone, Swanson began to rattle the bars desperately, to call the guard back again. The latter, when he finally came, was surprised to see this erstwhile phlegmatic, untroubled prisoner suddenly turned into a white-faced, panic-stricken hysteric.

"Malloy," he panted. "Oh, for the love of heaven, get me a piece of paper and a pencil right away, will you? I've got to send a wire!"

And when the guard had acceded to his request, this is what he handed back to him through the cell grate:

Mrs. Helen Swanson,
c/o General Delivery,
Tucson, Arizona.
  Come back right away, I'm in for bad trouble.

                                   Jerry.

"Send this right off for me, will you, Malloy?" he pleaded.

"What's the matter, what's come over you all of a sudden?" asked the guard, trying to calm him down. "Here, want to read the paper? Here's today's paper." He thrust it through the bars at him, turned to go and get permission to file the message. He had hardly reached the end of the corridor when a deep groan sounded in the cell he had just left. He turned and went trotting back again.

Swanson was sitting where he had left him, white as chalk and shaking uncontrollably from head to foot. The paper that he had just opened across his knees had fallen to the floor and he was staring with glazed, horrified eyes at the blank cell wall opposite him.

The guard, alarmed, unlocked the grate and let himself in to find out what was the matter with him. He picked up the paper and read: "Seven Dead in Arizona Bus Crash." And under that a list of casualties!

Identified Dead

———————————

Swanson, Mrs. Helen, of New York

———————————

The boy had escaped injury; his name was among the survivors. Swanson was on his feet, pawing pathetically at the guard's uniform. "Lemme out of here! What am I doing in here now? My kid's alone in the world. I've got to get out of here! I didn't do it, I tell you, I didn't do it. *I didn't do it!*"

"Did you want to see me, Swanson?" the dick named Butler asked gruffly, as he entered the cell.

"Any one of you fellows, I don't care which one. They told me you were the most human of the lot; that's why I asked for you."

"Most human, eh?" The detective grunted. "What was I supposed to be, chromium-plated? I feel a favor coming up." He grunted again.

"If your kid was dying by inches under your eyes, if your wife was starving, and you were broke and had no job, and you read in a paper that you could get a thousand bucks just by telling them you killed someone, what would you do?"

"A man can't answer that truthfully until he's

been in that same fix," Butler told him gravely. "And I haven't, so I can't say. Are you trying to tell me that's why you're in here?"

"Trying is right."

The dick fanned his hand scornfully between their faces. "The attempt is unsuccessful."

"I figured it would be," Swanson said desolately, biting the tips of both thumbs at once. "But that isn't why I asked to see you. I've got to have a chance to talk to Mrs. Ranger again."

"What do you want from her?"

"Mister, I know what I know. I don't ask you or anyone else to believe me. Mrs. Ranger is mistaken about my coming up to her outside her house when she was leaving for the theater that night. She may have been excited, high-sterical; just because she saw me handcuffed in front of her, she thought it was me. In fairness to me, won't you let her give it another try? She may be ashamed, in front of all of you, to admit she was wrong the first time. Won't you let me see her alone, without any of you guys around? Won't you give me that one chance? It's my only one. That's all I'm asking; I won't ask another thing."

Butler got up and went toward the cell door to be let out, left Swanson hanging on his delayed answer. He didn't give it to him until after he was already outside in the corridor. "See what I can do for you." Which meant yes.

Mrs. Ranger came into the room with one of the other dicks, not Butler. At sight of Swanson, she turned to her escort displeased. "I didn't know I'd have to face this—this criminal again. It's very painful for me. I was under the impression I was simply wanted down here to—" Then as she saw the guard with Swanson about to withdraw: "You're not going to leave me *alone* in here with him, are you? Why, this man's dangerous; he's liable to—"

"There'll be somebody within call, Mrs. Ranger, just a few steps down the hall. He's asked to be permitted to speak to you alone. It may be to your interest to hear what he has to say."

"I still don't like the idea at all," she complained querulously. The dick and Swanson's guard strolled out of the room without seeming to hear her, softly closed the door after them.

She sat down as far across the room from him as she could get. "Well, what is it you want of me, murderer?" she said brittlely, lighting a cigarette. "Make it snappy."

"Mrs. Ranger." Swanson faltered. "*Please* take another look at me. Look *closely*. Look good. Look at my height when I'm standing straight like this. Look at the shape of my face. Look at the distance between my eyes. I know there are plenty of people that look like somebody else, but can't you *see* I'm not that man that came up to your car outside your house that night? You *know* I'm not."

"Do I?" she said mockingly.

"This is just between us—"

"Is it?"

"We're alone now by ourselves, there isn't anyone in here with us."

She pronounced each word with the slow clarity of a death sentence. "*You are the man I saw!*"

"But I know I couldn't be, because I wasn't there where you say you saw me that night. Don't you see you must be mistaken?" In his despair he groped for any argument that might possibly convince her, blurted out the first thing that came to his mind. "There's a doctor somewhere in this town will tell you—" He stopped suddenly, checked himself.

"Will tell me what?" She held her cigarette poised half-way to her lips.

He finished it, as long as he'd gone that far. "Will tell you I couldn't have been there at the time, because he was up at my flat, my wife's and my flat, that Wednesday night working over our kid, from nine until nearly midnight, and I was up there with him the whole time. He'll tell you more, he put the idea into my head—"

She was staring at him with fixed intensity, but that wasn't unnatural. "He put the idea into your head of going out and killing my husband?"

"No, no. He first put the idea into my head of getting the money in any way I could, by hook or crook. But he'll remember that he was up there, he must keep a record of his calls."

"A likely story!" she sneered, but her eyes, hard, glittering, calculating, kept roving the room, along its baseboards and its ceiling joints.

"It's true, I tell you!" Swanson burst out helplessly. "Meredith is his name, Dr. Bradley Meredith. Please! You call him up for me. You ask him! He'll tell you I wasn't out that night. Then you can tell the cops you were mistaken. Please call him!"

Again she stared at him inscrutably. "Dr. Bradley Meredith," she repeated mechanically. Then she let the cigarette fall out of her hand, put the tip of her shoe over it, stood up. She adjusted the silver fox piece over her shoulder. "I will do no such thing! I still say I saw you, and"—very low, almost inaudibly as she moved toward the door—"it's *my* word against yours."

Then suddenly anger seemed to strike at her, as though held in leash until now. As though she had not thought it worthwhile to waste it on just one onlooker, desired a larger audience. She flung the door open and stormed indignantly out. Her raised voice filled the corridor with angry remonstrance.

"I won't be subjected to such an experience again! It's outrageous and inconsiderate! I wouldn't have agreed to come down here in the first place if I'd known that was what was wanted of me! It's an imposition!"

Butler clicked off the dictaphone in the adjoining room, straightened up, with a lopsided mouth. "The lady doth protest too much, methinks," he murmured pensively. "She only got sore after she was outside in the hall where she could be heard."

He picked up a phone on the desk, said to the Headquarters operator: "Get me the office address of a Dr. Meredith, Bradley Meredith." It rang back shortly and he jotted something down, said, "Thanks." He started to pick it up a second time, then thought better of it, put on his hat instead and went out of the room.

He had to travel a considerable distance uptown to reach his destination. The doctor's office turned out to be his home too. He wasn't, judging by the appearance of the McKinley-era apartment building it was located in, prospering. That, reflected Butler, pushing the bell of the ground-floor rear flat, was nothing against a man these days.

A young housewife opened the door after a wait of several minutes; Meredith couldn't even afford an office assistant, evidently.

"Dr. Bradley Meredith?"

"You just missed him!" she said regretfully. "He was called away, stepped out only a minute or two before you got here. It was an emergency call, but I don't believe he'll be gone long. Would you care to come in and wait?" She motioned him into a forlorn little waiting-room, snapped on a bleak light that didn't dress it up much. "Did you have an appointment?" she asked. "The doctor's without an assistant right now and—er, sometimes things get a little mixed up."

"I'm not a patient," he said, to ease her embarrassment. He didn't tell her he was from Headquarters either, in order not to frighten her unnecessarily. "But as long as I'm here, I wonder if you could tell me whether he had a patient by the name of Jerome Swanson? I want to make sure I've come to the right man."

"I'll look among the unpaid bills; that's the quickest way of finding out. Most of them are un—" She didn't finish it, but she didn't have to.

There must have been an awful lot of unpaid bills to wade through; it took her a good five or ten minutes to riffle through them. Finally she came out again, said, "Yes, there's a Jerome Swanson down among his patients. I can't find any record of his calls, though." She sniffed the air suspiciously. "Oh, the doctor's supper!" she wailed. "Excuse me!" and ran down a long inner hall to the back.

Butler shook his head pityingly. This Meredith couldn't be anything but a square-shooter, to let his patients get away with their bills the way he seemed to. He killed time thumbing through a number of 1935 magazines strewn about the waiting-room. Fifteen minutes went by. Half an hour. Not once did the phone ring, nor the doorbell.

The little housewife ventured back again finally, anxiously twisting her apron. "Didn't he come back yet? I can't understand it. He told me he'd be back in five or ten minutes at the most. These are supposed to be his office hours, and I know he wouldn't stay out at this time of the day if he could possibly avoid it."

Butler was beginning to have an uneasy feeling himself, that he couldn't understand and at the same time couldn't quite shake off. "Was the call from one of his usual patients?" he asked her.

"I don't believe so, or he would have mentioned the name to me. He simply said it was some woman whose child had swallowed something; it simply needed to be stood on its head and spanked. He took the call himself; I was in the back."

"Where was he to go? Take a look, will you, and see if he jotted it down on his pad."

She came back with it in her hand. "The pad's blank. He must have torn off the top leaf and stuffed it in his pocket, to make sure of not forgetting the address."

The uneasy feeling was deepening in Butler minute by minute. "Let me have that pad a minute just as it is. Can you get me a pinch of coal dust or soot of some kind from your kitchen, any dark substance?"

She came hurrying back with a little held in the hollow of a torn scrap of paper. He took it from her, sifted it over the top of the pad, then breathed on that very lightly, barely enough to clear it off again. It remained seamed in the identations left by the doctor's pencil point pressing down on the leaf above. A gray tracery, faint but not too indistinguishable to be read, was the result.

"Karpus," he said, squinting closely at it, "270 Hanson Road. That's a little far out, isn't it, for an emergency call to an unknown doctor? Does he use a car when he goes out on calls?"

"Yes. It's not much of one, but it gets him there."

"Then all the more reason why he should have been back by now. Let me have its license number." He got to his feet and started for the door. "I'm going out there myself and see what's what. If I miss him and he comes back while I'm gone, have him wait here for me. But—" He felt like saying, "But something tells me he won't come back," but he didn't; she was badly enough frightened already without that.

He flagged a cab, said: "Get me out to 270 Hanson Road, and get me there fast; this is police business!"

They drew a motorcycle cop presently, by the rate at which they were bulleting along, but Butler changed him into an escort by a flash of his badge and a shout of explanation from the cab window.

It was way out, in a half-built-up, weed-grown sector. "Somebody's handed you a bum steer, guv'nor," said the driver, tapering off uncertainly and pointing.

Butler had already seen the vacancy sign tacked up on the door-frame, himself, and noted the decrepit condition of the place. "Yeah, it was a bum steer, all right," he said, "but it wasn't me it was handed to."

The cop had circled and come back. "That place is vacant," he called out unnecessarily, from the opposite side of the dirt-surfaced street.

Butler got out and started through the ankle-high weeds toward the door. "I only wish it was," he hollered back. "Put in a call for me from the nearest box. Then scout around until you dig up a second-hand car; here's the license number. It ought to be around here somewhere not very far away."

He climbed the two creaky wooden steps of the frame place, tried the door. The knob promptly came off in his hand, and he was able to get the rest of it out of the way with one good, swift kick.

There was a man's huddled body lying just a couple of yards away from where he was standing, just far in enough to let the door swing past.

Butler just nodded his head as he crouched down by him, turned him over on his back. The blood hadn't altogether coagulated yet from the three bullet wounds he counted, it had been so recently done. His instrument case was a little further on, where it had fallen from his hand.

He noticed an ordinary watchman's oil lamp, that had probably been appropriated from some street excavation, hanging from a nail on the wall. He tested the chimney with his knuckles, and the glass was still faintly warm, as though that, too, had only recently been in use. He went outside and inspected the vacancy sign. It wasn't nailed down fast, just punched on over a nail in the door-frame.

"So that's how it was worked," he murmured. "Took the sign down temporarily and let him see a glimmer of light coming from inside. Probably the woman who put in the call met him outside on the street somewhere and steered him in, to distract his attention. He needed patients too bad, poor devil, to turn down anything that came his way. Someone must have been waiting for him right behind the door, didn't even let him get down two steps inside the house. Took his car and ditched it somewhere afterwards."

He went inside again, stood looking down the beam of his light at what had been Dr. Bradley Meredith. "Somebody hasn't been so clever about this," he said aloud. "Planting conviction where there wasn't even suspicion before."

He was shown into Swanson's cell at the unholy hour of three that same night, or the following morning rather. Swanson was a huddled cylinder, asleep under a gray blanket on the iron cot that was let down broadside from the wall like a slab on chains. "I'll call you back when I'm ready to go," he said, to get rid of the guard.

The reclosing of the cell gate partly roused the sleeper. He stirred; then as he made out the detective's outline against the dim corridor-light outside the bars, he shot upright on his shelf. "Who is it?" he gasped frightenedly.

"Me," said the dick. "I want to talk to you. Keep your voice down. Here's something to smoke. Now, are you awake?"

Swanson swung his legs down to the floor, crouched low over his own knees. "Yeah, I guess so."

"If you're not, here's something that ought to do it. Your friend, Doc Meredith, was murdered early last evening."

Swanson jolted ruler-straight, then buckled over again, held his head. "Oh, now I *am* hooked!" he groaned. "First my wife, now the doctor. They were the only two who could have proved— Now there's no one who'll believe me! I'll never get out of it now; I'm finished!"

"All right, quit wailing through your adenoids," Butler told him impatiently. "You're a lot better off than you were while Meredith was still alive."

Swanson blinked at him stupidly in the cell twilight. "How do you mean, how could I be?"

"What his murder has managed to do is start me to thinking there may be something to your story after all. It looks too much as though someone didn't *want* anyone to be able to clear you, now that you're conveniently under indictment and the wheels have something to feed on. What happened to Meredith may just be a coincidence. The fact remains that he was lured out on a fake call, that robbery wasn't the motive, and that he had no personal enemies of his own; the way he never pressed his patients to pay their bills is the best guarantee of that.

"Add to this the fact that his name was never spoken by you until this afternoon, to my knowledge; that it was mentioned to only one person— Ranger's widow—and that his murder followed within a few hours, and the coincidence becomes a little too wobbly for my liking.

"You stuck your neck out," the dick went on, "and you're not going to be allowed to pull it in again, even if a second or third murder has to be piled on top of the original one. That's one line of reasoning we could take—just to see where it gets us." He stopped, thought it over. "Yeah, that's our play: A second or *third* murder. Given the same circumstances, if it comes through again, it's our pay-off."

He took a quick turn around the cell. "That's what I looked you up at this ungodly hour for.

Isn't there someone else who could go to bat for you like Meredith could have if he had stayed alive enough?"

"No, no one," said Swanson mournfully. "Only the doc was up there that Wednesday night with us, and he's dead now."

Butler didn't seem to be listening. "How about a guy named—" He stroked his chin thoughtfully as he went along. "Lindquist, let's say."

"But I don't know anyone named Lindquist; I never did!" exclaimed Swanson in surprise.

"Oh, yes, you do!" he purred with slow emphasis. "Now get this and see that you hang onto it tight; it's your only chance to keep from being railroaded into the hot seat or a bughouse.

"Your last possible remaining alibi is a guy named Lindquist, a doctor like the other one was. Dr. Carl Lindquist, we'll call him. He also happens to be an old friend of yours as well; Swedish ancestry like you, and all that.

"Now Meredith called him in that Wednesday night of the murder in consultation, at you and your wife's urgent request, because you wanted a second opinion on your boy. You're sure he'll remember the date, be able to vouch for you. He hasn't come forward until now because, you understand, he moved his practice out to St. Paul soon afterwards, probably hasn't heard about the case. Does all his reading in Swedish-language papers. You're sure a wire from you will bring him back again, though.

"Now you tell all this to one of the other men in the department; any of 'em, it don't matter which. I'll arrange it so that you're given a chance to do your pleading in that same office in the next building where you were the last time.

"Plead to be allowed to send this wire for help. Here's what this Dr. Lindquist looks like: He's an elderly guy, sort of a country fogey, doesn't know his way around so good. Got a big corporation and dresses sloppy in clothes that fit him like a tent. Wears thick-lensed glasses and a little white goatee on the end of his chin. Be sure to tell whichever dick you're talking to all that, whether he asks you or not.

"Now, have you got all that? I hope you have

for your own sake, because you won't be seeing me around much from now on."

"Would you mind waiting in here a few moments?" the detective who had ushered her in asked Mrs. Ranger politely. "They'll be ready for you in the D.A.'s office in just a minute or two." He drew out a chair for her.

She sat down in it with a poor grace. "You know, this is really becoming a nuisance. I don't mind cooperating all I can, but this is the third time I've been sent for by you people."

"I'm sorry, Mrs. Ranger," the detective said deferentially. "I'm sure this is the last time you'll be troubled, before the case goes to court." He moved toward the door. "You don't mind if I ask you not to touch that little lever there on the table in front of you while you're in here—it's a dictaphone leading into the next room, where suspects are sometimes interviewed. I'm not supposed to bring anyone in here, but seeing it's you, Mrs. Ranger . . ."

She smiled faintly, mollified. He closed the door discreetly after him and she could hear his heavy tread recede down the corridor outside.

She reached out and snapped the lever defiantly, as if to say: "Just for that, I will!" A faint buzzing, like a fly trapped in a bottle, sounded. She picked up the head-set and gingerly brought it around to the back of her head, careful not to disturb her modish hat.

A gruff voice said in her ears: "What do you want now, Swanson? You have been beefin' all week long to be let in here to talk to me. All right, out with it."

Mrs. Ranger changed her original intention of immediately discarding the head-set; brought it in closer around the base of her skull.

"There is still one person who can tell you I was in my own flat that Wednesday night Ranger was killed. Please let me get in touch with him, that's all I ask you!"

"Yeah? Who is he?"

"He's an old friend of my wife and mine, an old Swedish doctor named Carl Lindquist. He was up there that night; we asked Dr. Meredith

to call him in in consultation, just to make sure there was no mistake about the kid's condition. We've known Lindquist so long, we knew if *he* told us, it must be true."

"Yeah? Well, then, why didn't he show up before now and speak up for you, if he's such a good friend of yours?"

"He went to St. Paul right after that; he probably hasn't heard about it out there. He only reads Swedish newspapers, anyway. He's slow and kind of old-fashioned, you know; dresses sloppy in baggy clothes; can't see so good any more, wears thick glasses; and he's got a little white billy-goat beard stuck on the point of his chin. But I know that if he hears I'm in trouble he'll take the first train east and do all he can to square me. *He'll* tell you; *he'll* be able to tell you that I was home minding my business that night. He even stayed on with us, after Doc Meredith left, talking over ways in which I might be able to raise the money to help my youngster."

"All right, all right, can the sob stuff. So what do you want us to do?"

"Just let me send him a wire; that's all I ask."

The heavy tread was returning along the corridor once more. Mrs. Ranger deftly replaced the head-set on the table before her, pushed the lever down.

The door opened and the detective who had originally shown her in said, "They're ready for you at the D.A.'s office now, Mrs. Ranger. Sorry you had to wait like this."

"That's all right," she said vaguely, as though she were thinking of something else entirely.

"Hundred and Twanny-fif' Strit!" the conductor whined dolefully down the aisle of the lounge car from the vestibule entrance. The nearsighted old doctor with the white goatee and thick-lensed spectacles glanced up indifferently as the Twentieth Century began to slow up, flush with the upper stories of the below-track-level Park Avenue tenements that marked its next-to-last stop—125th Street. Then he resumed peering at the St. Paul Swedish newspaper he had been occupied with ever since he had got aboard—

one stop before, at Harmon-on-the-Hudson, where inbound trains halt to change from coal-burning to electricity-driven locomotives.

The train came to a full halt. It seemed to linger a little longer than usual at this penultimate stop. Then a darky porter from one of the Pullmans appeared in the vestibule, pointed to the old doctor reading the Swedish newspaper. A well-dressed heavy-set man in his late thirties pushed past him with a muttered "Thanks a lot," came on down the aisle, stopped opposite the reader's seat. He had to tap him on the shoulder to attract his attention.

"Are you Dr. Carl Lindquist, of St. Paul, Minnesota?"

The old fossil peered at him over the tops of his glasses. "Yuss. Vhy, who are you?"

The intruder tactfully lowered his voice so that it would not reach the others in the car. "I'm from Police Headquarters. I was sent to meet you at the train, ask you to get off here with me, instead of riding on down to Grand Central."

The old Swedish doctor looked innocently apprehensive. "I am not under arrest, no?"

The detective laughed outright at this. "No, no, nothing like that. The D.A. would like to question you privately, that's all. I'm just delegated as sort of an escort to take you to him. By leaving the train here, there won't be any unwelcome publicity to your arrival, no nosy newspapermen to buck. I have an official car waiting for us downstairs. Better get your things, if you don't mind; they're holding up the train for us."

"All right, I yust as soon," Lindquist said willingly. "I ache all over from riding on this train so long, anyway." He struggled to his feet, pulled down a ponderous, battered-looking case from the rack overhead. The detective obligingly took it from him, started down the aisle with it, swaying from its weight. Lindquist waddled flat-footedly after him.

As he passed the Pullman porter who had pointed him out to the official envoy, he slipped something into his hand, as though this service had been prearranged between them. He alighted on the station platform beside his escort.

"Now, no offense," the Headquarters man said, "but have you got some proof of your identity on you; can you show me some credentials, before we go any further? Your name and description tally, but still I don't want to show up with the wrong man; it might cost me my job."

The doctor fumbled about his balloon-like clothes. "I ain't got much," he said, pursing his lips. "Just a couple of unpaid bills, maybe. Vait, here's the telegram from my friend, vhat brought me back here." He stripped it out of the envelope, passed it to him.

The detective unfolded it, read:

"DR. CARL LINDQUIST

ST. PAUL, MINN.
"PLEASE COME QUICKLY AM IN JAIL ACCUSED OF MURDER AND YOUR EVIDENCE CAN CLEAR ME.
JEROME SWANSON."

He nodded approvingly. "That's fine; that's all that's necessary." He led the way down the station stairs to street-level, still carrying the doctor's bag for him. The official car he had mentioned was standing several blocks away, inconspicuously parked under one of the granite arches of the elevated structure that carried the railroad.

There was no official sticker or designation on its windshield, but this too might have been a precautionary measure to avoid attracting the newspaper publicity that the D.A. seemed to detest so. In any case, the shaggy old doctor was hardly the type who could be expected to notice a thing like that, unfamiliar as he was with the metropolitan police system.

There was no one else waiting in it; the detective evidently intended to do his own driving. He shoved his protégé's bag in the back and got in under the wheel. "Sit in front with me, Doc," he suggested friendly. "Keep me company getting there; we've got quite a ride ahead of us."

They started off. The detective made little

attempt at conversation, in spite of what he had said about wanting to be kept company; the doctor made even less.

"Have a hard trip?" he asked his charge after a while.

"It cost so much," lamented the doctor. "And I ain't doing so well out there, neider. If it wasn't that Swanson is an old friend of mine . . ." He wagged his head. "Nothing but trouble that poor fellow's had. How did he get mixed oop in such a t'ing?"

"Sorry," said the detective pleasantly but firmly. "I'm under orders not to discuss the case with you beforehand, until you've been questioned." He switched back to their former topic, which seemed to interest him more. "So you're not so well off, eh, Doc?" he suggested understandingly.

"Who iss?" sighed Lindquist, folding his hands mournfully across his vibrating middle.

"Ever think of going back to the old country, to try your hand at building up a practice there?" the detective went on, apparently at random.

The pupils behind the doctor's bulgy lenses flicked sidewise toward him, then back to center again. Then he showed postponed enthusiasm. Like Mrs. Ranger's anger at the time of her interview with Swanson, the timing was a little slow. But then, maybe his mental processes weren't so quick on the trigger.

"Yah!" he agreed vehemently. "Now you talking! But you know vhat it cost to make the trip over there? Vhere vould I get the money?"

"I guess it does come high," said the man at the wheel, and the discussion was allowed to languish for the time being.

They drew up finally before what, for a District Attorney's residence, was a singularly isolated and poorly kept little bungalow, on a remote, wooded Northchester lane far from all the main highways and any neighboring habitation. To make it even more uninviting it was rapidly growing dusk.

"In here?" said Lindquist, as the dick threw the car door open.

"Yeah, get out," was the taut answer. The detective's hand slithered from the wheel down toward his own hip joint, as if he expected opposition, but Lindquist was evidently a trustful sort; he struggled acquiescently out without further ado. The detective followed him, again carrying his bag, and they went up toward the entrance together.

The detective opened the door, motioned him through, closed it after them. He set the bag down, led him down the hall toward a room at the back. "Just wait in here," he said tersely.

"He issn't here yet?" asked Lindquist.

"No, he'll be here in a few minutes." He closed the door on him, left him in there alone.

Lindquist moved toward the closed door with surprising agility and stealth for anyone so bulky; tried the knob. It was locked. That didn't seem to disturb him particularly. He touched his hip bone, then crouched, put one eye to the keyhole, tilting his glasses out of the way. The key blocked the hole effectively.

He straightened, put his ear to the door-seam instead. Voices came through, from one of the other rooms near-by. One was a woman's, sharply recriminatory. "What'd you bring him here for? Now you'll only have to take him out with you again, do it somewhere else!"

"I'm going to try it another way first," he heard the man who had met him at the train say. "I think I can fix it without having to do what we did last time."

Lindquist was seated in a large wing-chair at the far side of the room, patiently steepling his fingers together, when the lock clicked and the door reopened. The detective came back in alone, closed it behind him.

"He didn't come yet?" asked the doctor ruefully.

"Forget about him," said the dick curtly. "Now, Dr. Lindquist, just what form is this evidence in that your friend Swanson is so confident will clear him? Documentary, or just verbal?"

"Vell, partly one, partly the other. I got my little book here, in which I keep my calls written, with his name and the date and the hour. But mostly it should be enough I tell them I vas vith him the whole time that night; I ain't never told a lie in my life—"

"Lemme see the written stuff," said the dick. Lindquist placidly fumbled, brought out a dog-eared memorandum book.

The detective glanced at it, raised his eyes craftily. "This won't do him much good; it could have been written afterwards. It's not worth a damn. On the other hand, it could be worth a good deal—to you."

"So?" said the doctor stupidly.

"How would you like to go back to Sweden, all expenses paid, and *stay* there?"

"Very mooch," Lindquist admitted stolidly. "Who vould pay the expenses?"

"I would." The other man took out a wallet, shuffled bills out of it, dealt them rapidly on the table before them like playing cards. "Two thousand bucks. Enough to set you up for life in Swensky money."

Lindquist took it very matter-of-factly; nothing seemed able to surprise him. "Thank you very much." He nodded. "So soon I see the D.A., find out vether I can do anything for this poor fellow Swanson, I take the next boat to Stockholm, you bet."

A single note of harsh mirthless laughter rasped in the other man's throat. "No, you take the next boat to Stockholm-you-bet, right away, without going near the D.A. or Swanson or anyone else—that's what the whole proposition is. You also leave this little appointment book of yours with me, and keep your mouth closed over on the other side."

Lindquist seemed to ponder the matter, took his time about answering. "But then if I don't go and tell them vhat I know, Swanson might get the chair, and he's an old friend of mine." He looked up finally. "No, I can't do it that vay," he said imperturbably. "If I got to do vithout going back to Sweden, all right I got to, but I couldn't turn my back on an innocent man."

"Is that your final answer?"

"Yuss. I only give one answer, never two, to anyt'ing."

"I told you so!" a voice said stridently from the doorway. A woman came slowly forward into the room. She was blond and might have been pretty ordinarily, but her face wasn't pretty just then. "Now you see? You'll have to!"

"I'm going to, don't worry," he said softly out of the corner of his mouth. "Just take it easy, will you? This place is in my name."

He addressed Lindquist. "All right, Doc. Let's forget the whole thing. Come on, get your bag; I'll drive you back to town again, drop you off at a hotel. You better come too, Rose."

Lindquist, whom nothing seemed to surprise, went with them out into the hall, picked up his heavy bag, and carried it out to the doorstep. The woman came out on one side of him, her two hands thrust into a small barrel-muff now, the man on the other.

"You sit in front, next to me, like before," the detective said dryly.

"I put my bag in the back, yah?" the doctor said, and waddled over with it. He heaved it in, set it on the floor, fingered its latches and straps carefully as if to make sure it was securely fastened. Then he climbed in next to the detective. The woman got into the back from the opposite side of the car.

They started off, but instead of turning and going back the way they had come previously, they continued on up-country in the same direction as before.

"This is far enough, Allen," the woman remarked finally. "No use taking all night!"

Reeling and scraping to a stop, the car turned off abruptly into an opening between the trees, climbing over half-hidden roots and spewing up dead leaves. The man at the wheel braked with a grim sound of finality, and there was a moment's breathless silence after the car's racket.

Lindquist's voice broke it, in calm interrogation. "Vhy are you stopping here? Vhat are you going to do here?"

"Get out, you cold-blooded Swede, you'll find out. I don't want my car all messed up when I shoot you full of holes!"

Nothing seemed able to get a rise out of the

doctor. "But vhy are you going to shoot me? I never saw you before until you met my train this afternoon."

"Just to make sure you don't horn into that Swanson case!"

The doctor was evidently the type of man who becomes garrulous during crises. "But vhy don't you vant me to help Swanson? What have you got against him?"

The man next to him had unleashed a gun. "Because he's the guy that's taking the rap for us, and we wanna make sure he takes it!"

"Oh, so that's what you did to Dr. Meredith, too?" The doctor's voice suddenly lost its Swedish accent.

"So you know that, do you?" The man's face contorted violently. "Well, we'll see that it doesn't go any further!"

"Will you get him out and finish him?" the woman screeched wildly, standing up in back of them.

She swung the small pistol she had been carrying in her muff, backhand, brought it down butt-first toward his skull. But out of the corner of his eye he had seen the blow coming. He swerved his head aside and the reversed butt chopped down past his shoulder.

He caught the butt with both hands, dragged it forward, twisted it around, her hand still pinned to it, into the other man's face.

"Now just drop that gun, Cochrane, or I'll blow your pretty Greek nose off. If there's going to be any shooting in this car, I'll do it!"

The woman had the more courage of the two, the courage of despair. Dragged half across the top of the front seat, unable to extricate her own hand from the gun because of the intended victim's stranglehold on it, she urged breathlessly: "Shoot him, Allen! Don't be afraid of getting hurt! He's some kind of a dick! Don't you see it's either him or us?"

Butler, alias Dr. Lindquist, who could see Cochrane nerving himself to pull the trigger even in the face of the bore pointed straight at his own face, fired first, tilting it a little to avoid killing him if possible. It tore a long crease up Cochrane's scalp. The heavier weapon he was

holding thundered out by reflex finger-action, harmlessly puncturing one of the air bladders Butler wore under his balloonish Lindquist clothes.

Cochrane fell over backwards across the front seat, with his head hanging down over the rim of the door, baying with the pain of the burning track across the top of his skull.

Butler, who was momentarily in danger of losing his eyesight from Mrs. Ranger's flailing left hand, swung a pulled but powerful fist straight under her jaw, as the easiest solution, and knocked her limp and passive across the back seat.

"You're too damned vivacious for a recently bereaved widow!" the detective grunted.

He detached the thick-lensed glasses, which were hanging from one ear by now, blew out his breath, leaned across the back of the seat, and switched off a little unobtrusive lever protruding from his bag.

"It's got about everything on it I need now," he remarked to the writhing Cochrane. "They won't care to listen to how loud you can howl just from a little nick in your dome."

He straightened him up by the shoulder. "So you were his friend—his business partner! I suppose you dipped into his money in the firm's assets, played his wife, and then took the easiest way out of both predicaments. Came out and met her a block or two away from the house that night, instead of waiting for her in town; slipped inside and gave it to him.

"Then the two of you calmly went in to the theater and pretended to phone him to see how he was. Well, that'll all come out at the end of a garden hose. Now, hold your little handy up and pull your cuff back out of the way; I've got something for you."

"Is the paper going to bring charges for—for defrauding them?" Swa apprehensively when he had been the central figure of an impendin to merely a second-string witness

"Probably not," Butler assure what I know about papers, the s at large forgets the little transaction the better they'll like it. And the only reason all of us down here at Headquarters don't take turns giving you a good swift kick in the pants is because in a way you really helped to break this case for us.

"If you hadn't plumped yourself down in the middle of it and made them show their hands a couple of times more, it might still be unsolved. Y'better take my advice and don't try anything like that again. Go out to your motherless kid in Arizona; he needs you. Leave crimes alone that don't belong to you. There's enough going around that have lost their rightful owners as it is."

"I'll go," Swanson said.

PERMISSIONS ACKNOWLEDGMENTS

"Come and Get It" by Erle Stanley Gardner from *Black Mask Magazine*, April 1927. Copyright © 1927 by Erle Stanley Gardner, copyright renewed 1954. Reprinted by permission of the Estate of Erle Stanley Gardner and Queen Literary Agency.

"Cry Silence" by Fredric Brown from *Black Mask Magazine*, November 1948. Copyright © 1948 by Fredric Brown. Renewed. Reprinted by permission of the author's estate and Barry Malzberg.

"Arson Plus" by Dashiell Hammett writing as Peter Collinson from *Black Mask Magazine*, October 1923. Copyright © 1923, copyright renewed 1951 by Dashiell Hammett. Reprinted by permission of the Dashiell Hammett Literary Property Trust, administered by the Joy Harris Literary Agency, Inc.

"Fall Guy" by George Harmon Coxe from *Black Mask Magazine*, June 1936. Copyright © 1936 by George Harmon Coxe. All rights reserved. Reprinted by permission of Brandt & Hochman Literary Agents, Inc.

"Doors in the Dark" by Frederick Nebel from *Black Mask Magazine*, February 1933. Copyright © 1933 by Pro-Distributors Publishing Company, Inc., copyright renewed 1961 by Popular Publications, Inc. Reprinted by special arrangement with Keith Alan Deutsch (keithdeutsch@comcast.net; www.blackmaskmagazine.com) proprietor and conservator of the respective copyrights, and successor-in-interest to Popular Publications, Inc.

"Luck" by Lester Dent. This previously unpublished piece is an earlier draft of the selection "Sail" from *Black Mask Magazine*, October 1936. Copyright © 2010 by the Estate of Norma Dent. Reprinted by permission of Will Murray, Agent for the Estate of Norma Dent.

The Maltese Falcon by Dashiell Hammett from *Black Mask Magazine*, September-December 1929, January 1930. From the novel *The Maltese Falcon*. Copyright © 1929, 1930 by Alfred A. Knopf, a division of Random House, Inc., copyright renewed 1957, 1958 by Dashiell Hammett. Reprinted by arrangement with Alfred A. Knopf, a division of Random House, Inc.

"Ten Carats of Lead" by Stewart Sterling from *Black Mask Magazine*, August 1940. Copyright © 1940, copyright renewed 1968 by Popular Publications, Inc. Reprinted by special arrangement with Keith Alan Deutsch (keithdeutsch@comcast.net; www.blackmaskmagazine.com)

proprietor and conservator of the respective copyrights, and successor-in-interest to Popular Publications, Inc.

"Murder *Is* Bad Luck" by Wyatt Blassingame from *Black Mask Magazine*, March 1940. Copyright © 1940 by Pro-Distributors Publishing Company, Inc., copyright renewed 1968 by Popular Publications, Inc. Reprinted by special arrangement with Keith Alan Deutsch (keithdeutsch@comcast.net; www.blackmaskmagazine.com) proprietor and conservator of the respective copyrights, and successor-in-interest to Popular Publications, Inc.

"Her Dagger Before Me" by Talmadge Powell from *Black Mask Magazine*, July 1949. Copyright © 1949, copyright renewed 1977 by Popular Publications, Inc. Reprinted by special arrangement with Keith Alan Deutsch (keithdeutsch@comcast.net; www.blackmaskmagazine.com) proprietor and conservator of the respective copyrights, and successor-in-interest to Popular Publications, Inc.

"One Shot" by Charles G. Booth from *Black Mask Magazine*, June 1925. Copyright © 1925 by Pro-Distributors Publishing Company, Inc., copyright renewed 1953 by Popular Publications, Inc. Reprinted by special arrangement with Keith Alan Deutsch (keithdeutsch@comcast.net; www.blackmaskmagazine.com) proprietor and conservator of the respective copyrights, and successor-in-interest to Popular Publications, Inc.

"The Dancing Rats" by Richard Sale from *Black Mask Magazine*, June 1942. Copyright © 1942, copyright renewed 1970 by Popular Publications, Inc. Reprinted by special arrangement with Keith Alan Deutsch (keithdeutsch@comcast.net; www.blackmaskmagazine.com) proprietor and conservator of the respective copyrights, and successor-in-interest to Popular Publications, Inc.

"Bracelets" by Katherine Brocklebank from *Black Mask Magazine*, December 1928. Copyright © 1928 by Pro-Distributors Publishing Company, Inc., copyright renewed 1956 by Popular Publications, Inc. Reprinted by special arrangement with Keith Alan Deutsch (keithdeutsch@comcast.net; www.blackmaskmagazine.com) proprietor and conservator of the respective copyrights, and successor-in-interest to Popular Publications, Inc.

"Diamonds Mean Death" by Thomas Walsh from *Black Mask Magazine*, March 1936. Copyright © 1936 by Pro-Distributors Publishing Company, Inc., copyright renewed 1964 by Popular Publications, Inc. Reprinted by special arrangement with Keith Alan Deutsch (keithdeutsch@

"Wait for Me" by Steve Fisher from *Black Mask Magazine*, May 1938. Copyright © 1938 by Pro-Distributors Publishing Company, Inc., copyright renewed 1966 by Popular Publications, Inc. Reprinted by special arrangement with Keith Alan Deutsch (keithdeutsch@comcast.net; www.blackmaskmagazine.com) proprietor and conservator of the respective copyrights, and successor-in-interest to Popular Publications, Inc.

"Ask Me Another" by Frank Gruber from *Black Mask Magazine*, June 1937. Copyright © 1937 by Pro-Distributors Publishing Company, Inc., copyright renewed 1965 by Popular Publications, Inc. Reprinted by special arrangement with Keith Alan Deutsch (keithdeutsch@comcast.net; www.blackmaskmagazine.com) proprietor and conservator of the respective copyrights, and successor-in-interest to Popular Publications, Inc.

"Dirty Work" by Horace McCoy from *Black Mask Magazine*, September 1929. Copyright © 1929, copyright renewed 1957 by Popular Publications, Inc. Reprinted by special arrangement with Keith Alan Deutsch (keithdeutsch@comcast.net; www.blackmaskmagazine.com) proprietor and conservator of the respective copyrights, and successor-in-interest to Popular Publications, Inc.

"Merely Murder" by Julius Long from *Black Mask Magazine*, July 1944. Copyright © 1944, copyright renewed 1972 by Popular Publications, Inc. Reprinted by special arrangement with Keith Alan Deutsch (keithdeutsch@comcast.net; www.blackmaskmagazine.com) proprietor and conservator of the respective copyrights, and successor-in-interest to Popular Publications, Inc.

"Murder in One Syllable" by John D. MacDonald from *Black Mask Magazine*, May 1949. Copyright © 1949, copyright renewed 1976 by Maynard MacDonald. Reprinted by arrangement with Maynard MacDonald.

"Three Apes from the East" by H. H. Stinson from *Black Mask Magazine*, March 1938. Copyright © 1938 by Pro-Distributors Publishing Company, Inc., copyright renewed 1966 by Popular Publications, Inc. Reprinted by special arrangement with Keith Alan Deutsch (keithdeutsch@comcast.net; www.blackmaskmagazine.com) proprietor and conservator of the respective copyrights, and successor-in-interest to Popular Publications, Inc.

"Death Stops Payment" by D. L. Champion from *Black Mask Magazine*, July 1940. Copyright © 1940, copyright renewed 1968 by Popular Publications, Inc. Reprinted by special arrangement with Keith Alan Deutsch (keithdeutsch@comcast.net; www.blackmaskmagazine.com) proprietor and conservator of the respective copyrights, and successor-in-interest to Popular Publications, Inc.

"The Color of Honor" by Richard Connell from *Black Mask Magazine*, June 1923. Copyright © 1923 by Pro-Distributors Publishing Company, Inc., copyright renewed 1951 by Popular Publications, Inc. Reprinted by special arrangement with Keith Alan Deutsch (keithdeutsch@comcast.net; www.blackmaskmagazine.com) proprietor and conservator of the respective copyrights, and successor-in-interest to Popular Publications, Inc.

"Middleman for Murder" by Bruno Fischer from *Black Mask Magazine*, November 1947. Copyright © 1947, copyright renewed 1975 by Popular Publications, Inc. Reprinted by special arrangement with Keith Alan Deutsch (keithdeutsch@comcast.net; www.blackmaskmagazine.com) proprietor and conservator of the respective copyrights, and successor-in-interest to Popular Publications, Inc.

"The Man Who Chose the Devil" by Richard Deming from *Black Mask Magazine*, May 1948. Copyright © 1948, copyright renewed 1976 by Popular Publications, Inc. Reprinted by special arrangement with Keith Alan Deutsch (keithdeutsch@comcast.net; www.blackmaskmagazine.com) proprietor and conservator of the respective copyrights, and successor-in-interest to Popular Publications, Inc.

"Beer-Bottle Polka" by C. M. Kornbluth from *Black Mask Magazine*, September 1946. Copyright © 1946 copyright renewed 1974 by Popular Publications, Inc. Reprinted by special arrangement with Keith Alan Deutsch (keithdeutsch@comcast.net; www.blackmaskmagazine.com) proprietor and conservator of the respective copyrights, and successor-in-interest to Popular Publications, Inc.

"Borrowed Crime" by Cornell Woolrich from *Black Mask Magazine*, January 1938. Copyright © 1938 by Cornell Woolrich; copyright renewed. Reprinted by permission of J. P. Morgan Chase Bank, N.A., as Trustee for THE CLAIRE WOOLRICH MEMORIAL SCHOLARSHIP FUND under the will of Cornell Woolrich R671100, dated March 6, 1961.